THE INTREPID SAGA

BOOKS 1-3

(Including Book 1 of the Orion War: Destiny Lost)

M. D. COOPER

Cover Ship Illustration by Tom Edwards
Cover Design by M. D. Cooper

Edited by Erin Marion, Brenda Tippin Deliantoni, Krissy Smith, Amy DuBoff

THE WORLD OF AEON 14

For the seasoned science fiction reader, there will be little here which they have not seen in another story; be it planetary rings, nano technology, AI, or mind-to-mind communication.

However, for those who may not know what a HUD is, understand the properties of deuterium, or be able to name the stars within the Sirius system, I encourage you to visit www.aeon14.com to read the primer, glossary, and timelines.

To get the latest news and access to free novellas and short stories, sign up on the Aeon 14 mailing list: http://www.aeon14.com/signup.

OUTSYSTEM

The Intrepid Saga – Book 1

M. D. COOPER

DEDICATION

This book is dedicated to my children, born and unborn, who will inhabit the future far longer than I. May your future never be utopian, but always struggling toward perfection. May it never be idealistic, but always founded on ideals.

ACKNOWLEDGEMENTS

There is only one acknowledgement that matters, and that is to my wife, Jill. Without her, this world would remain only imagined and never written.

But once her inspiration spurred me on, it took a host of people to help get Outsystem to where you see it today. Most notably: Greta van der Rol for being the first person not related to me who thought my writing was a good read; MV Merchant for reading everything providing excellent feedback; and Erin Marion for being a tireless editor and giving way more attention to minute detail than I even knew was possible.

If you have read any amount of science fiction, you will see certain authors' influence in this book. Foremost are: Larry Niven whose Ringworld series changed the way I thought about science fiction; Tanya Huff for writing one of the best damn female military characters in any book anywhere; Elizabeth Moon for showing that a book taking place almost entirely on one ship can be awesome; and Anne McCaffery for writing Dragon Quest and opening the world of science fiction and fantasy to me.

ACCEPTANCE

STELLAR DATE: 3226929 / 12.07.4122 (Adjusted Gregorian)
LOCATION: Edge of the Grey Sea, Pluto
REGION: Jovian Combine, Sol Space Federation

A young sapling exploded beside Tanis and she dove for cover, scampering away as splinters flew in every direction. She slipped into a depression, flattening herself as much as possible, hoping it was enough to stay out of sight. Another shot hit a rock nearby and liquid fragments of stone rained down, beading off her armor.

<*Does anyone have a location on that shooter?*> Tanis sent the question over the Link.

Both Sorensen and Reynolds signaled negative.

Angela was covering tactical coordination and placed several pointers on the team member's HUDs.

<*It could be any of these. The plasma bolts are firing at over ten kilometers per second and they have their muzzle flash masked.*>

<*Sorensen, get behind that knoll to your left. See if you can deploy nanoprobes to get Angela triangulation data,*> Tanis directed.

<*Aye, sir.*>

<*Reynolds, hold the center, I'm going right into that stream bed.*>

Several more shots impacted the ground around the team's position. Reynolds slipped his rifle up over his cover and fired two electron beams before pulling back and rolling to a new location. He continued to draw as much attention as possible while Tanis and Sorensen worked toward their new positions.

Tanis made it to the stream bed without drawing any fire and her retinal HUD indicated Sorensen was in position and had deployed his nanoprobes.

<*Better view?*> Tanis asked Angela.

<*Resolving…I just need a few more incoming beams to triangulate their source.*>

The enemy obliged, returning fire at Reynolds' previous location.

<*Got em!*> Angela highlighted a position on each team member's HUD and Tanis set a countdown. The soldiers set their rifles to a magnetic proton beam, and when the timer hit zero, they all fired on the enemy position.

There was a moment of silence, the rippling of the water flowing past her body seemed to grow in volume; then the desired explosion flared up and streams of plasma sprayed in every direction.

Tanis's visor darkened to shield her eyes. When the tint faded, she saw a hundred-meter swath of young forest on fire.

<*You sure do know how to shake things up, Major.*> Sorensen's rasp sounded in her mind.

<*All other teams have made their objectives,*> Angela said. <*The main strike force is on its way in.*>

Tanis rose out of the water, unlocked her helmet and tucked it under her arm. Above her, the roar of orbital drop craft and the accompanying streams of fire turned the night sky into a spectacular show—arcs of color and plasma painted across the backdrop of Jupiter's dark bands.

It had been some time since she had been in a primary assault force, the last five years had been filled with out-of-the-way assignments, such as this one.

Strangely, the familiar yearning to be in on the larger action just wasn't there. For that matter, the exultation she should have been feeling in securing her target wasn't there either

<You're just anxious for the GSS's response.> Angela sounded a bit nervous as well.

Over the nine years since Toro, Angela had become closer than a sister or a best friend; it was almost as though Angela was simply another side to her. Tanis knew that wasn't entirely true—the AI residing in her head was a distinct individual, even though at times it didn't feel that way.

<And you've never been vetted this thoroughly before. This gen-ship is being rather particular.> Tanis slipped a smirk into her mental tone, then felt momentarily guilty. *<But you'll do fine. You're not the one with the soiled record.>*

<That doesn't matter. The GSS will have access to the truth. They'll know you aren't the monster the media made you out to be.>

<Let's hope so.>

Tanis met up with Sorensen and Reynolds several minutes later. Sorensen was covered in mud and Reynolds was grinning like a Cheshire cat.

"You shoulda seen it, Major. He came striding up, all cocky as shit, and then caught his boot on this tiny twig—couldna been bigger than my pinky. Gun goes flyin', arms are wavin', and the big man just topples over like a felled tree."

Sorensen wasn't smiling. "Goddamn planet. Why'd they have to make it rain so much here? Place is an effing mudball."

Reynolds slapped him on the back. "That's progress, lad. Besides, you know the Jovians, once they got a few worlds orbit'n Jupiter they just had to try'n collect the whole set!"

"What does that have to do with how much it rains?" Sorensen grunted and Reynolds merely shrugged his response.

Tanis smiled at the two men and drew some comfort from their camaraderie as the team walked back to the pickup point. It was bittersweet, though, after the massacre on Toro she never felt like the enlisted troops looked at her quite the same way. It sapped some of the satisfaction from moments like this.

Later, after her team had arrived at the TSF's northern continent HQ, she passed her electronic authentication tokens to the TSS *Midway* orbiting above and checked her personal messages over the Link.

There it was; the message from the GSS. She stared at the glowing icon for several minutes before finally mustering the courage to open it. She could feel Angela in the back of her mind, as intent on the contents as Tanis.

Major Tanis Richards

References and qualifications accepted. Final, in-person interview scheduled for 3227134.75000 (local time) Enfield Building, Jerhattan, Earth.

GSS Colony Operations

"This is it, Angela." Tanis kept her voice soft, afraid that the emotion in it would be picked up by some officers nearby. "We finally made it."

WELCOME TO MARS

STELLAR DATE: 3227162 / 07.28.4123 (Adjusted Gregorian)
LOCATION: *Steel Dawn III*, En-Route to Mars
REGION: InnerSol Stellar Space, Sol Space Federation

Tanis entered the forward observation lounge on the *Steel Dawn III.* The windows were crowded with passengers, weary after the two-week voyage from Earth, catching their first glimpses of Mars.

Her HUD identified the passengers and she saw that most were fellow colonists, destined for the *Intrepid* and ultimately the world of New Eden. Near one of the windows on the starboard side stood Patty and Eric, who she had spent some time with during the voyage.

Threading the crowd, Tanis walked to the window and stood beside the pair. Eric looked up at her and smiled a greeting. Patty nodded and pointed toward the planet.

"You can just make out the ring now."

Tanis peered out the window and cycled her vision to a higher magnification.

"So you can."

The Mars 1 ring was a large orbital habitat which wrapped around the world like a glistening silver halo. It was over one hundred and eighty thousand kilometers in circumference, and sixteen hundred kilometers wide. It rotated at over twenty-two thousand kilometers per hour above the blue-green planet. On the world below, the Borealis Ocean filled the viewport, and the large Mariner Valley lakes slowly slipped past the day/night terminator.

Built in the twenty-fifth century, the ring was a marvel of human engineering and provided the energy management to terraform and power Mars. The Mars 1 ring was the gateway to the stars. Without it, modern terraforming techniques would never have been invented.

"Home sweet home," Eric said.

"Not exactly." Patty pointed to her left. "You can see the Mars Outer Shipyard coming around the ring over there. That's where the *Intrepid* is being completed. We'll be staying on the station or the ship, I imagine."

The Mars Outer Shipyard was a thousand-kilometer arc which was tethered to Mars's second artificial ring, the Mars Central Elevator Exchange, known by the locals as the MCEE. That outer ring linked to Mars 1, and from there massive elevators provided access to the planet below.

Though it was not the largest planetary superstructure, Tanis always found it to be one of the most beautiful. The Marsians had opted to build it with materials that glistened in the sunlight. With all of the orbital stations and outlying habitats tethered to the MCEE it sometimes appeared as though the planet had been caught in a celestial cobweb.

"I can't make it out," Eric said after peering out the window for a minute. "You two keep forgetting I have these organic eyes. Not special hopped-up mod jobs like yours."

Patty laughed. "Well, I don't know how hopped up mine are; the major has the super eyes."

"Your tax dollars hard at work," Tanis smiled.

"So how long till we arrive?" Eric asked.

Eric had only a rudimentary Link to the shipnet. While he could look it up himself, Patty and Tanis already had the information overlaid on their retinal HUDs.

"Just over an hour," Tanis said.

"Doesn't look like it should take that long." Eric leaned forward, still trying to make out the shipyards.

An announcement over both the shipnet and audible systems interrupted their discussion.

"All passengers, this is your captain speaking. We are beginning our final descent into the Mars Outer Shipyards, which the locals call the MOS." The captain pronounced the word 'moss'. "In thirty minutes there will be two 0*g* maneuvers separated by a hard 15*g* burn. We apologize for that hard burn, but Marsian traffic control has busy inbound lanes today and we need to clear the space as quickly as possible.

"During these maneuvers we require you to be in your cabin and strapped down to your bunk, for your safety.

"Mars Outer Shipyard is a class 1A environmental space with 0.8*g* centripetal gravity and a standard temperature of nineteen degrees Celsius. Be sure to have your customs forms filled out and debark only after the announcement is given to do so.

"Thank you for flying Dawn Transport. To all of you colonists, good luck, and to everyone else, we hope to see you again."

"Well, I guess I'll see you ladies after we finish docking," Eric said.

"You will indeed," Patty said. "We'll meet tonight for drinks at that restaurant I mentioned."

"You going to come, Tanis?" Eric asked.

"I'll see. I have to report in and get my assignment by 0800 station time, but if I'm not busy I'll be there." The military life brought her comfort, but the last few weeks on the *Dawn* had given her a taste of what a more relaxed life could be like. It made the offer tempting.

With final farewells the three left the lounge with the other passengers and proceeded to their cabins.

One of the privileges of rank was that Tanis had a room to herself. She made certain all of her belongings were secure, and lay down on her bunk. She didn't bother to strap down, but did hold on to the rails along its sides. The ship shuddered several times as it shed all of its velocity relative to Mars. The process took several minutes, following which the vessel rotated and the engines fired again.

The cabin systems displayed a holo count-down and also flashed a warning that the air would jell to help ease the discomfort of the upcoming maneuver. The cabin systems knew her body could hold up the strain, so the nano-injectors didn't deliver the frame firming nano bots into her body, but it was quite likely Eric was undergoing the rather uncomfortable procedure at the moment.

The captain wasn't lying; the 15*g* burn was hard. Tanis's body weight increased to over a ton and she was pressed deep into the acceleration cushioning of her bunk as the ship matched the twenty-two kilometers per second orbit of the Mars Outer Shipyards. Once that velocity was reached, the fusion engines powered down, eliminating the gravity their thrust had created. In the resulting 0*g*, Tanis let go of the rails and allowed herself to slowly rise above her bunk as the air thinned out once more.

She could feel the telltale vibrations of thrusters firing as they eased the *Dawn* into its external berth on the planet side of the MOS. Once the ship was in place and latched onto the station, the thrusters slowly phased out until the physical coupling supplied the ship's angular momentum. During that process the ship gradually fell under the centripetal force of the shipyard and achieved the station-standard 0.8*g*.

Tanis let the increasing gravity pull her back down to the bunk. It was an experience she always enjoyed; a ritual that had persisted since her first stellar flight with her father some sixty years earlier.

An announcement came over the shipnet indicating a successful docking. The passengers were reminded to remain in their cabins until the debarkation signal was given.

Shortly afterward, the low thud of the passenger and cargo umbilicals linking the *Dawn* to the station could be felt through the ship. Fresh air from the MOS filtered through the vents. Tanis could practically taste the difference after the stale stuff the *Dawn* had been recycling over the last few days.

The debarkation signal came over the shipnet and a glowing green icon flashed on the door's holo display, indicating that passengers could leave their cabins. Tanis took her time giving the sparse space a final check, making certain nothing was left behind. It would give the corridors a chance to clear out. No point in rushing into a crowd of people.

The sounds of other passengers outside her cabin had ceased and Tanis had just stepped into the corridor when another tremor shook the ship. It was followed by the roar of an explosion flooding the hall, forcing Tanis to grasp the doorframe to maintain her footing. A moment of stillness followed and then alarms began to blare. Tanis set her auditory systems to filter them out, only to have the telltale whack of pulse rifles and the chip of beam weapons fill the silence.

In a single swift motion she dropped her duffle and pulled her pulse pistol from its holster. She couldn't imagine who the hell would use beam weapons on a ship. One shot in the wrong place and it would disrupt the electrostatic shields and cause explosive decompression.

The sound of high-pitched whines and supersonic booms joined the other weapons fire. *Even better*, Tanis thought, *some idiot was using a railgun!*

<*Some idiot has a death wish,*> Angela commented.

<*Except they're wishing for* our *deaths,*> Tanis replied as she bent to a knee and pulled her lightwand from the duffle.

Angela was attempting to query the shipnet to determine what was going on. <*It's at the dock. Someone blew two of the umbilicals and started firing on passengers as they debarked.*>

<*That's going to be a massacre! Have they boarded the ship?*> Tanis asked.

<*Hard to say, the sensors are jammed in that sector, I'm guessing someone is hiding something...so yes.*>

<*Your guesses are usually right.*>

Angela's reply was smug. <*Of course they are.*>

<*Can you raise the captain?*>

<*Shipnet is sporadic, looks like it's under some viral attack.*>

<*An all-out assault? This is more than some robbery.*>

<*Your guess is as good as mine,*> Angela responded.

Tanis took a deep breath and altered her thinking patterns for combat. Any concern and worry left her as the calm born from being in more firefights than she could remember took over. Controlled and cool, no emotion. Feelings got you killed.

<*I've reached the ship's AI on an auxiliary band. We'll handle the net battle, you find whoever's turning this ship into a screen door.*>

<*A screen door?*> Tanis didn't get the analogy.

<*Full of holes.*> Angela replied.

<*Did I ever mention humor is not your strong suit?*>

Starting down the corridor toward the remaining umbilical, Tanis listened for the sounds of weapons fire. Most were distant, but the odd snap sounded nearby. She was nearing the fore end of the hall when the deck plate shook with another explosion, this one further aft, closer to the engines.

<*Are they—?*> she asked her AI.

<*It would seem so. If they blow the* Dawn's *engines they'll make a pretty big boom. There's a D2 fueling station about a half klick away. That would go up for sure and it could take out the* Intrepid.> Angela's thoughts were clipped. Tanis could tell the net fight against the viral attack must be consuming much of her attention.

<*So you're saying we can't let that happen.*>

<*I think that goes without saying.*>

Tanis ignored the jibe. <*Have you been able to make contact with anyone? We need to get the word out.*>

<*Still just the ship's AI, who is barely able to form a sentence right now. I've got to concentrate on this attack. You stop them from blowing the engines.*>

The engines were in the other direction and Tanis pulled up the ship's layout on her HUD, determining the best route aft. If she cut through the galley she could get to the engineering section via service areas and avoid the section closer to the boarding hatch and destroyed umbilicals.

Tanis turned, moving back down the corridor. After a hundred meters, it ended in a three-way intersection. She eased around the corner, checking for hostiles, when the deck shuddered beneath her feet. Her footing slipped and her head jerked out into the intersection, fully exposed.

"Hey! Stop!" The call came from her left.

Tanis berated herself for not deploying nanoprobes to scout ahead. Normally Angela covered that, but with her AI battling the virus that was trying to take control of the ship it was up to Tanis to manage the nanoprobes.

She spared a glance at the man who had called out before pulling her head back. He stood just over twenty meters away, raising his rifle to fire.

"Whatever happened to letting me halt?" Tanis muttered as she pulled back out of sight. She pressed herself against the bulkhead as two bursts of energy lanced through the space where her head had been moments before. Two black patches of melted plas steamed across the corridor from her, making certain she knew just how close the brush with death had been.

The shots were followed by a string of curses and the pounding of heavy boots. A quick listen told her he was running at full speed. When he had to be within three meters of the junction she crouched and launched herself across the intersection, firing her pulse pistol at him.

He wore light body armor and though the shots stunned him, he shrugged off the effect in moments and let loose his own series of blasts. Tanis scampered back across the intersection and resumed her place against the wall. She waited, hearing his heavy breathing just around the bend; neither person wanting to make the first move.

"Get out here, you bitch. I'll make it quick."

Tanis looked at the conduits above her and as quietly as possible leapt up and wrapped her arms around one. "I think it's your turn to stick your head into the line of fire."

He cursed her again and when she didn't respond; the nose of his rifle edged around the corner firing wildly. Tanis had pulled her feet up, and though the shots missed her, she let out a pained scream.

With a laugh her attacker strode into view, eyes downturned, looking for her body. Tanis dropped her legs around his head and clamped her knees as hard as she could. The man reached up and wrapped cybernetically enhanced hands around her thighs. She gritted her teeth against the pain, but didn't let go, twisting as hard as she could in an attempt to break his neck.

It refused to snap, most likely modified in some way. Tanis resorted to plan B and drove her lightwand through his right eye, trying to angle up into his brain.

The man bellowed in agony and let go of Tanis as he collapsed to the floor. She landed lightly a pace away from him as he pulled the lightwand out and clamped both hands over his ruined eye.

"Yagh… You bitch!" He screamed, trying to get up. Tanis calmly set her pulse pistol to stun and fired several shots point blank at his chest.

<Gonna cauterize that?> Angela asked about the man's eye as he collapsed to the deck.

<I was going to, but all the bitch comments got to me. Get some nano ready to wipe the DNA security on his rifle.>

<Sorry, nano's all you right now, remember?>

<Force of habit.> Tanis launched the bots and set them to remove the security features from the unconscious man's rifle so that she could use it. Without clearing the DNA lock, grabbing the rifle would have caused it to electrocute her, or possibly explode, depending on its configuration.

The weapon was an Amhurst MK CXI; not the latest TSF military hardware, but still not a weapon that should be in anyone's hands other than the space force. In addition to energy beams it could fire a focused pulse and she set it to that. No point in holing the ship more than these goons already had. Weapon secure, Tanis ran down the hall, keenly aware that taking out the thug had wasted precious time.

The kitchens were empty; the cooks had left their realm spotless and glistening before heading to the docks for their shore leave. Tanis slipped through the vacant area and into the service corridor that ran aft toward the engineering section.

She heard voices at the end of the hall and cycled her vision through various modes. The metal construction of the ship blocked infrared, but the free radical overlay showed a smudge of radiation moving toward engineering.

They were going to detonate a nuke on the ship, certainly an effective way to destroy the ship and a good part of the MOS with it.

<How's access to station comm?>

<MOS has a general alert out on wideband; that's all I can get right now.>

Tanis reached the end of the hall and pushed the hatch open half an inch. She prepared several nanoprobes and felt the restructuring plate on her arm tingle as they left her body and flew into the next room.

VA and sensor readings from the probes lined her vision as they surveyed the room. It read clear and Tanis ducked into it and crouched behind a row of backup oxygen tanks.

<Not really the safest place to hide.>

<Only if they're stupid enough to shoot at an oxygen tank. They won't be able to arm their nuke if they blow themselves up by starting an O2 fire.>

<You assume they're smart.>

<They'd have to be to insert a virus that takes you this long to overcome.>

<Good point.>

Two men entered the room at the far end and Tanis flattened herself against a tank to avoid detection. Her probes circled, giving her a clear view of their positions. She waited until both men were facing away from her and then leaned out, shooting each in the lower back with the pulse beam. They crumpled and Tanis crept over to them, keeping an eye on the hatch they had come through. Angela deployed several nano to disable the fallen rifles.

<You back up to snuff?> Tanis asked.

<All set. I've helped the AI somewhat. She has access to some of her systems again. There are four men and your nuke in the main engineering bay. Through that hatch over there.>

The opening flashed in Tanis's sight and a map of the ship appeared over her vision. A short corridor lay beyond the exit and beyond that another hatch opened into the main engineering bay. The bay was long and narrow; two of the intruders were at the far end and another two were positioned at either side of the entrance she had to go through.

"Let's do this," Tanis said to herself. She picked up a second rifle, opened the hatch soundlessly and crept down the corridor to the bay's entrance. It wasn't sealed tightly and her probes slipped through the cracks. As the readout had shown, there was a man on either side of the hatch, weapons charged and positioned to nail anything that came through.

Tanis pulled the hatch inward and stood behind it. Who knew, maybe they'd fall for something simple. Visual input from her probes showed one man stepping through the entrance, his eyes darting suspiciously.

Tanis raised a boot and kicked hard, slamming the hatch into the man's head. He fell backwards, clutching his nose as blood poured down his face. The second man was distracted by his falling comrade and Tanis used the opportunity to step into the clear and let loose with both pulse rifles. The man crumpled to the deck as she delivered another blast to his bleeding partner.

With both of them taken care of, she sent her nano over the various machines dedicated to moving and powering the ship. Luckily, the engineering bay was far from silent and the two figures at the other end hadn't noticed the commotion. Either that or they were simply concentrating on their little pet nuke.

<Got nano ready for that thing?> Tanis asked

<Already released. What do you take me for, a yearling?>

<Gotta ask so it's on the logs—you know that.>

<And I have to complain, it's in the AI regs,> Angela added a mental snort to her missive.

Tanis darted down the length of the bay, leaping over equipment and ducking under conduit. Her movements were silent and she went unnoticed. Ten meters from the pair she swung around a set of cooling conduits and stepped into view.

"I strongly recommend you step away from the device." A twinge of panic was in the back of her mind, shouting *run away from the nuke!* She schooled her face not to show it—dozens of enemies were one thing; a nuke was something else.

The two figures straightened; a man and a woman. The man had long hair that fell well past his shoulders, held away from his face by a thin band around his head. A scowl creased his angular features. The rest of his form was hidden by a long dark coat. The woman moved into view and Tanis cursed softly under her breath; she was wearing a shimmersuit. As Tanis approached it shifted from a glossy black color to completely translucent, rendering the woman's body invisible.

"I think you made a wrong turn." The man scowled. "If you run now, you can get off the ship before it blows."

"I don't think I can allow that to happen," Tanis replied.

The woman didn't say a word; with her body invisible she was just a disconcerting floating head, which disappeared too as the shimmersuit's material flowed up over her face.

"Think you can do that faster than I can twitch my trigger finger?" Tanis asked. "I'm MICI; we don't arrest—we just shoot." After a moment's pause, the material flowed back down the woman's face.

"Military Intelligence and Counterinsurgency?" the man asked.

Usually having MICI show up meant you had a leak; he had to be considering that possibility, a doubt Tanis was more than happy to plant.

"Then this will really hurt," he continued.

Tanis's vision turned white and pain erupted behind her eyes.

<Gah, remote pulser, how'd we miss it?>

<Focused on the nuke, I think,> Angela replied. *<Pulser is disabled. Your retina will reset in one second.>*

She felt a throb behind her eyelids and, as Angela predicted, in one second she could see again. The woman had vanished and the man was standing with the nuclear bomb between them.

He hadn't pulled out a weapon, and simply wore a wicked smile. "Thanks for the treat. There's little I enjoy more than watching Kris work."

Tanis scanned the room for the woman while keeping her weapons trained on the man. *<How are you doing with the nuke?>* she asked Angela.

<Questions, questions—I'm working on it. It's good stuff, not the usual pinball machines most terrorists have.>

<What's a pinball machine?> Tanis asked.

<Never mind, you've got bigger issues. I can't detect that Kris woman.>

<What do you mean you can't detect her?> Tanis asked as she flipped through various vision modes. There was nothing on infrared, UV, or even air disturbance detection. *<Damn… She's actually invisible!>*

<I said that.>

A fist impacted Tanis's face and she staggered backwards, kicking out at where the attacker should have been. Nothing.

Tanis took a deep breath and brought her fists up in a defensive position. The room was loud and she set her hearing to filter out the ambient sounds, trying to listen for the whistle of the woman's limbs.

Another series of blows struck Tanis and she stumbled, tripping over some equipment. *<I can't hear a thing.>*

<She must be dampening with remote emitters.>

Tanis tried to move unpredictably while Angela hunted down the devices. Her arm tingled as thousands of nano left her body and filled the air in the bay. In moments the microscopic machines located the sources of the dampening waves and converged. The unseen robotic war was short, and punctuated by flashes of light as the enemy nano was destroyed.

Tanis's sensors were suddenly able to detect air turbulence again and fed an image to her visual overlay. *<Good work—I can catch a glimpse of her now when she moves fast.>*

<You're welcome. Now don't get killed. I'm in here too and those punches weren't soft.>

<Thanks for the vote of confidence.> Tanis saw a foot flying toward her head just in time. Reaching across it, she twisted around and grabbed the leg under her arm while swinging an elbow back. She felt it connect with the side of the woman's head and heard a satisfying grunt.

The woman's shimmersuit was slick; Tanis was unable to maintain her grip and her opponent slipped away. She blocked a punch and then they were apart, Tanis circling slowly, moving as quietly as she could.

The man swore, having realized while he watched the fight Angela's nanocloud was disarming the nuke. He bent over the console, trying to undo Angela's work.

"Just kill her already, Kris. We're running out of time. She must have AI that's hacking the nuke."

Kris didn't respond, but Tanis heard the telltale sound of a foot pivoting on the deck. With a quick flick of her wrist, Tanis let fly her lightwand, satisfied when her opponent screamed.

In front of Tanis, part of the shimmersuit flickered, turning black, and then red around the area the wand had struck. From the height, and bits of exposed teeth, it was safe to say it was Kris's jaw.

"Bet you wish you'd surrendered now." Tanis reached out and ripped the lightwand free.

The woman staggered back, but didn't make a sound. She must have pain suppressors.

Wordlessly, Kris pulled two thin blades from what Tanis guessed were her forearms. With most of the shimmersuit still functional, they appeared to float in midair.

The blades began a deadly dance and Tanis blocked with her pulse rifle, narrowly avoiding losing an arm in the first flurry of blows. The man was still cursing as he bent over the nuke, trying to do battle with Angela's nano—though it was likely his AI was doing most of the fighting.

Tanis blocked an overhand blow from Kris and followed up by driving the butt of her weapon into the woman's chest. Kris fell back and the shimmersuit failed, reverting to a glossy black.

"So much for your unfair advantage." Tanis pointed the pulse rifle at the woman's head. "Now drop the blades and put your hands behind your head."

The woman snorted, a sound that didn't work well with part of her face sliced open, and raised her right hand. As a static shield sprung out of her forearm Angela fed an intercepted Link communication to Tanis:

<*Trent, are you going to get that thing set or not?*>

<*Her nano is blocking me, but I've almost gotten past it.*> The man replied.

<*Is that true?*> Tanis asked Angela.

<*Unfortunately, yes. He's got a small army over there and they're chasing my bots away. Any chance you can go and hit him so I can land a big dose and disrupt his personal systems?*>

<*Consider it done.*> Tanis gave Kris an evil smile. "Sorry, I have to go kick your friend's ass." She fired several rapid pulses at the woman. Even with the shield, the impact bowled Kris over.

Tanis dashed over to the man and held one rifle on him, while firing several shots in Kris's direction with the other.

"I'm going to have to ask you to step away from the nuke, Mister."

He didn't even look up, frantically working the manual interface, using every possible edge to stay ahead of Angela.

"Fine, have it your way," Tanis muttered before smashing a fist into his face. The blow forced him to his knees and Angela signaled approval.

<*Excellent. I'll shut down his Link; that'll isolate his nano and I'll secure the nuke.*>

<*Good, then I just have this psychobit—*> Tanis's thought was cut off as one of her nano-cams alerted her to an incoming projectile. She ducked just in time to avoid a thrown blade aimed at her head. Tanis turned to see Kris racing toward her, shield down, swinging her other blade wildly. She stepped sideways to put the nuke between them and fired a few more shots.

<*Incoming,*> Angela warned. <*They've got some reinforcements.*>

<*They do? What about* our *reinforcements? Doesn't the MOS have security?*>

<*They're coming too; they just won't be here in time.*>

At the far end of the engineering bay, two men stepped through the hatch and leveled large caliber slug throwers at Tanis.

<*Sweet lord, where did they get those things?*>

<*Stay behind the nuke. Its casing can withstand those things.*>

<*Logical, yes; comforting, no.*>

Kris helped Trent to his feet and they backed out of the engineering bay as the hail of bullets pinned Tanis down.

"It was nice meeting you." The man called out. "You may have disrupted our little event today, but I'll make sure you get a front row seat for the encore."

The pair slipped past the two heavy weaponers, who turned and followed them out. Overwhelming silence filled the bay. <*You did disable the nuke, right?*>

<*Yes, mother, the nuclear bomb is safely deactivated.*>

<*Thanks, Ang.*>

Tanis stood and looked at the damage caused to the *Steel Dawn III*'s engine bay. "Why do I get the feeling this was the easy part?"

THE NEW BOSS

STELLAR DATE: 3227162 / 07.28.4123 (Adjusted Gregorian)
LOCATION: Mars Outer Shipyards (MOS)
REGION: Mars Protectorate, Sol Space Federation

"Well, I can see you get right to work."

Tanis looked up from her cup of coffee to see two men entering the sector chief's office where she was finishing up her report with Chief Ian. She spotted four stars on the collar of the man who had spoken and rose before snapping off a salute. "Thank you, sir."

He returned the salute. "I'm Admiral Sanderson and this is Captain Andrews of the *Intrepid*."

"Impressive work, Major Richards," the captain said.

"Thank you, sir," Tanis replied. "It was a pretty easy decision. Stop them or get blown up."

"I'm sure there was more to it than that." Captain Andrews gave her a warm smile. The admiral was smiling too, but it was more of a grim, got-a-job-to-do sort of smile. He cast an unreadable look at Captain Andrews as they both sat.

Tanis took a moment to examine the two men as they all got comfortable. Each was older than her; a quick records check showed Admiral Sanderson as having just passed his three-hundred and fiftieth birthday. She already knew of Captain Andrews; he was an old spacer, born over a thousand years earlier. Much of his life had been spent in stasis making the run between Sol and Alpha Centauri. Because he was recently returned from an interstellar journey, none of the images of him were recent, and she was surprised to see visible aging.

<*I like him. Seems to be a good choice of a man to run this ship,*> Angela commented.

<*Yeah, but why is his hair silver?*> Tanis asked. <*I don't see any medical conditions in his record.*>

<*Haven't you ever watched old vids?*> her AI asked. Angela always liked to flaunt that she knew more about ancient cultures than Tanis.

<*Do you mean his hair naturally went grey with age?*>

<*It still happens sometimes.*>

<*Why wouldn't he get that fixed?*>

<*How would I know, you're the human.*>

"I didn't expect you two to come down here." Chief Ian of MSF pulled Tanis out of her private conversation as he addressed the captain and admiral. "Though I can't say I'm surprised either."

"Someone tries to detonate a nuke three klicks from where my girl's tied up, you'd better expect I'd come down here." Captain Andrews' expression brooked no argument.

"Will Stevens be joining us?" Admiral Sanderson asked.

Tanis looked up the reference and found that Stevens was the MOS stationmaster. Her TSF security clearances brought up additional data pertaining to several complaints the stationmaster had filed against the *Intrepid* for incoming shipments causing disruptions on the station.

Tanis suddenly realized she hadn't checked on Patty or Eric. Emergency Response Status would have ID'd the dead, so Tanis accessed their net. The list scrolled over her HUD and she felt her heart drop as their names slid past. She made a note. There should be a memorial for the dead, and she would contact their relatives.

<*They didn't serve under you—you don't need to do that.*> Angela's tone was soft and comforting. Tanis resisted the urge to retort, knowing the AI was just trying to be supportive in her own way.

<*In a way they did. I have to take responsibility for the lives of people around me.*>

<*That's why you're so burnt out and looking to leave.*>

<*Perhaps, but it's still a part of who I am.*>

She returned her attention to the conversation around her to hear Chief Ian explaining the stationmaster's whereabouts. Apparently he was down on Mars for a meeting with the Marsian government.

"And getting a strip torn off him, no doubt." Captain Andrews glowered. "It's what he gets for letting a goddamn nuke get smuggled onto his station."

"Now, Captain, we don't know that nuke didn't come in on the *Steel Dawn III,*" Chief Ian countered.

"If I may..." Tanis waited for a nod from Admiral Sanderson before continuing. "There were no abnormal emissions on our trip from Earth to indicate the nuke was with us during transit. It could have been stowed behind some sort of shielding on the ship, but frankly I don't know where that could be. Every shielded location is heavily monitored. Also, on my way out I saw scuff marks on the bulkheads that indicated the nuke came from the dock."

"Still, you can't be sure." The chief's jaw was set at a stubborn angle.

"She's right." A man with commander's bars stood in the doorway. "Sir." He addressed Admiral Sanderson. "You asked me to keep you advised of what we found. It turns out the device was brought on board MOS a week ago on a small transport. It was stored in a nearby holding facility until today when it was moved to this sector as it was marked for the *Dawn*'s return trip to Earth."

"Thank you, Commander," Sanderson said. "Will you join us? This is Major Richards; she will be heading up your security unit going forward."

"Yes, sir." Commander Evans nodded to the admiral, and gave Tanis a long look as he sat down. It was either a look of guarded relief or territorial disgruntlement.

Tanis kept surprise from showing on her face. She looked the commander up and saw he was Joseph Evans, a TSF pilot added to the colony roster several months ago. Initially his duties consisted of piloting assembly craft, but according to the records several acts of sabotage resulted in his transfer to ship's security. As the ranking TSF officer, the admiral placed him in command. Knowing that a flyboy ran security gave Tanis new insight into why her interview had seemed so perfunctory. These folks were desperate and apparently needed someone with her skills.

The knowledge raised more questions. Why didn't an operation like this have the cream of the crop available to run security, and why hadn't she heard of sabotage on a GSS ship?

"We're damn lucky you were on that ship, Major," Captain Andrews said. "My report indicates that the blast would have taken out over ten percent of the shipyard, and while it wouldn't have completely destroyed the *Intrepid,* it certainly would have set the launch date back. Way back."

"That's not something we can tolerate," Sanderson growled. "That damn *Dakota* down at the MIS is beating its milestones every month. If we have many more setbacks we're going to have to prove ourselves to get the colony assignment."

Tanis knew the *Dakota* was proceeding well, but she hadn't realized it stood a real chance of moving up its completion date. Looking up the data, Tanis realized if the other GSS ship maintained its accelerated timetable and the *Intrepid* kept slipping, New Eden's assignment would be referred to an advisory board and could be assigned to the other ship.

"It's getting bad. Those radicals are getting bolder every week," Chief Ian said.

Tanis shook her head. "Those were no radicals on that ship; they were too well armed and equipped. I expect that will be confirmed when they are interrogated, sirs."

"Are you sure?" The admiral's eyes narrowed. "All of our information points toward this being the work of small cells of anti-colonization groups."

"As certain as I can be at this point," Tanis replied. "They were far too well equipped, as I said. Consider that they took the dockside; then the ship. Within minutes they disabled the AI and were hauling a nuke on board. They would have detonated it too if Angela hadn't already had the training on disabling devices of that design. All of this was accomplished in a matter of minutes.

"I've worked against anti-colonist, anti-expansion groups before. They are determined, but they aren't that well set up. The folks we were up against had serious credit and decent talent behind them."

"If you say so." The admiral shrugged. "If the evidence bears that out, you will report it to me. In your capacity as head of the *Intrepid*'s security, I will be your commanding officer; however, since you are a colonist and are on Captain Andrew's boat, you will also be under his direction."

<*Great,*> Tanis complained to Angela. <*A mixed chain of command.*>

Ignoring his ship being referred to as a boat, Captain Andrews spoke to Tanis. "Did you notice anything else of interest?"

"Well, for starters, that nuke was military grade, and their nano was up to spec as well. Angela had considerable difficulty handling them and disabling the weapon. Also, their personal armaments were military grade."

"I wasn't made aware of that," the admiral interrupted.

Tanis looked at Commander Evans. She didn't want to show him up in front of the admiral and captain, but pussyfooting around really wasn't an option. "TSF doesn't use them, but they're a recent spec for Jovian and Scattered World space forces. One of the operatives, a woman named Kris, also had one of the best shimmersuits I've ever seen. It incorporated sound-cancelling emitters Angela had to take out before we could even hear her move."

Commander Evans whistled, and the captain nodded in agreement. "That does sound like better stuff than you'd expect some radicals to have."

Admiral Sanderson shook his head. "Let's hope not. I prefer radicals; they're not nearly as messy. If what you say is true, this could be coming from a government or a major corporation." He leaned forward, looking at each person in turn. "I don't have to tell you that it is imperative we keep the media from this. If they start posting stories about the *Intrepid* being under attack by unknown, well-funded terrorists, we'll have the folks down on the *Dakota* all over the GSS for preliminary hearings."

His gaze lingered on the chief for more than a moment and Tanis glanced up to see the man fidgeting.

"Yes, sir," he said. Tanis was impressed with how the admiral's cold gaze could elicit compliance even from people outside his chain of command. Or in the chief's case, not even in the same military.

"I've caught wind of some issues with the schedule and security. How many breaches have there been?" Tanis asked.

Captain Andrews laughed. "This one's not afraid to ask questions."

Admiral Sanderson sighed as he leaned back in his chair. "I know. It's both the best and worst part of being an MICI officer."

Captain Andrews answered. "There have been several dozen. None like today, but cumulatively they are affecting the schedule. I think we've beaten that horse to death, so I won't belabor the point. You know what's at stake."

"I understand, sir," Tanis said.

"Good. Commander Evans will brief you on his progress on the *Dawn* so far and then show you to the *Intrepid*. You've got a lot to catch up on and I want security very tight tomorrow night at the ball," Admiral Sanderson instructed.

"Ball?" Tanis shot the admiral a querying look.

Captain Andrews gave another rich, warm laugh. Tanis wondered if she was the butt of some joke, but his smile appeared genuine and she found herself liking the man despite his odd choice of hair color.

"Joseph will fill you in on that—I'm sure he'll be overjoyed at not having to oversee the event." Captain Andrews smiled. "You'll find that despite our tight schedule we are still required to hobnob with all the deep wallets that keep this sort of thing afloat."

Sanderson didn't let a lip twitch. He rose, as did Tanis and Commander Evans. He snapped off a salute, which they both returned, and left the chief's office. Captain Andrews stood after the admiral left and clasped Commander Evans on the shoulder before he followed the admiral into the hall.

Chief Ian breathed a deep sigh once they left the room.

"If my report is satisfactory…" Tanis said to the chief.

He didn't even glance at it as he nodded and waved them out of his office. Once in the corridor outside his office, Commander Evans chuckled. "He's got a stash of vodka in his desk he likes to dip into at times like this; it's far more important than your report."

Tanis's brow furrowed. "People are smuggling nukes onto his station and he's getting sloshed? No wonder folks can slip anything under his nose."

The commander shot her a glance. "Hey, there are still a lot of hardworking people doing their best to keep things safe. Keep in mind that the security team on the *Intrepid* is a mix of GSS, TSF, MOS security, MSF, and our own internal security. We have to step carefully." He paused and took a deep breath. "Sir."

<Relax, Major. You're ruffling your new underling.>

Tanis calmed herself and gave Commander Evans an understanding look. "Those are a lot of toes you're dancing around. I see why you may have to tread lightly. But I don't have to like it, and frankly, I may not bother with it."

The commander's eyes darted momentarily and Tanis was fairly certain he was viewing information on his HUD. Even though moving the eyes was not necessary to focus on any part of a data overlay, most people couldn't help the reflex. It was a handy tell.

"I suppose that's your MO, run in full burn and sort things out later. Let those under you pay the price." As he spoke, Commander Evans' body language had changed. Previously he had been alert and slightly defensive, now he appeared guarded, his arms were crossed and his eyes were dark.

"Have my file up, do you?" Tanis's expression was grave. "I won't deny I've earned a lot of my reputation for being straightforward, but I suspect you are referring to one incident in particular."

"It does tend to stand out." He nodded slowly.

"I'm not going to justify it; I don't need to explain my actions to you." While Tanis didn't need to justify herself to a junior officer, she did need to have this man's support and assistance. "But I will tell you this. Were the recording of that event ever to be released, and I think it should be, people wouldn't be calling it the 'Toro Massacre' anymore." *And I'd have my respect and proper rank back,* Tanis added to herself.

<*We would have it back,*> Angela corrected her.

<*I'm sorry. I forget sometimes that my black mark extends to you.*>

<*I didn't mean it that way, I just meant those cowards at High Terra owe double for both of us.*>

Commander Evans didn't look away—the common reaction to her less pleasant glares, especially the ones she used when this topic came up.

"I'm sorry, sir. I know firsthand that once you get back in and the danger and adrenaline have faded it's hard to explain why you did what you did. Sometimes even full sensory doesn't do the real thing justice; it may cover all the inputs, but there's no fear when you're watching a recording."

Tanis nodded. "Agreed. Maybe sometime I'll let you know more about what happened on Toro. But for now, we have work to do. I want to see the team going over the *Dawn*."

Commander Evans led her out of the sector security offices and down several corridors before they entered the open space which served as the passenger debarkation area for the *Dawn*. Several teams were present; a few physical forensics specialists were scanning all surfaces, while net specialists had a few terminals apart, going over hardware for signs of tampering.

The commander bridged Tanis to the security net and she took stock of the teams inside the ship as well. Most of the personnel were station security, with a few GSS and TSF in the mix. Commander Evans sent a beacon out onto the net and addressed the local teams.

"Ladies and gents," he simultaneously spoke and broadcast over the net, "if I can have a moment of your time."

Over the security net she saw all the members stop what they were doing and signal their attention.

"For those of you on the *Intrepid*'s team, I'd like you to meet your new CO, Major Richards. The major is a MICI specialist and will be heading up our unit—a task I am more than willing to turn over to her."

"Thank you, Commander." Tanis took over the 'cast. "For those of you assigned to the *Intrepid,* I look forward to working with you, and for those of you with the MOS, I appreciate your attention. I've filed a report with sector security and Commander Evans has also made it available on our security net. You'll note the specifics about the hostiles' weapons and the nuclear device. I also want particular attention paid to how they were able to act with such precise timing. The equipment and software they used to do this is not readily available and the more data we have the sooner we can track them down.

"Dismissed."

"No fanfare?" Commander Evans asked with a smile. She was glad he had let their tense moment slide by. They would most likely be working together for a very long time. Hundreds of years, if all went well.

"They know their jobs. Me wasting their time with speeches won't help get answers," Tanis replied. "Besides, I'm not a huge fan of the new CO that comes in and gets in everyone's way."

Commander Evans chuckled. "I'll be honest, sir. You could be some nasty little toady and I'd still be grateful to hand the reins over to you." He coughed as he glanced at her. Even with her uniform dirty and wrinkled she cut an imposing figure. "Not that you're ahh…nasty at all."

The comment was a bit too familiar, but Tanis found his cocky flyboy behavior amusing. She let him squirm for a moment before letting him off the hook.

"At ease, Commander. I don't take offense easily…well, not normally anyway." She decided it was time to get back on task. "Admiral Sanderson indicated you're to take me to the *Intrepid.* I assume we have facilities there?"

The commander seemed more than willing to let his gaff slip by. "Yes, sir. Since the radicals started attacking we've been given a full Security Operations Center to help keep an eye on things."

"Lead on, Commander."

He directed Tanis out of the debarkation area toward a maglev train station. They passed through a lack-luster security check and took a high-speed car to the *Intrepid*'s berth. The train accelerated to over a thousand kilometers per hour, speeding down its track in silence. Moments after reaching its top speed, the car passed out into open space and Tanis caught her breath as the *Intrepid* came into view.

The ship was nearly thirty kilometers in length, the dominant feature being the two sixteen kilometer cylinders around which the ship curved protectively. The cylinders gleamed dully in the sunlight as they rotated nearly twice a minute, creating 0.82*g* of centripetal gravity within their hollow interiors. Inside, the environmental systems were already working, creating habitable areas with fields, lakes and forests that contained the base biosphere to be transplanted to New Eden. Beneath the floor of the eco-space were the stasis chambers. There were pods for the one and a half million colonists, plus several thousand backups to cover failures and the possibility of children being born to any crew who stayed out of stasis.

While the twin cylinders were the ship's most notable feature, they were not technically part of the ship and would be left behind at New Eden. Also staying behind at the colony were the massive cargo cubes which were positioned between the cylinders. Three were currently in place, but seven more were being readied, each filled with supplies and equipment for building the colony.

Draped over those sections, as though cupping its cargo, was the ship itself.

The front looked much like a porpoise, sleek and curved, tapering as it ran back over the cargo containers to the engines. A large cone rested at its fore—the emitter for the *Intrepid*'s massive ES ramscoop which would draw in hydrogen and fuel the ship as it journeyed through the interstellar medium.

While the engines were proportionally smaller than many of the ship's other sections, they were still quite massive, over five cubic kilometers in size. Specs that filled Tanis's HUD showed they were capable of delivering over a trillion newtons of thrust, creating enough impulse to ultimately bring the ship up to over fifteen percent of the speed of light.

Arching down from the ship's spine and encompassing the entire structure were the gossamer strands of super CT which held all of the disparate sections together. It appeared almost as if strings of light had drifted through space and settled across the ship, wrapping around the engines, body, cylinders, and cargo pods. It was a breathtaking sight. Tanis had seen few vessels of this size so beautiful.

The commander noticed her sharp intake of breath and smiled. "She has that effect, doesn't she?"

"It's magnificent," Tanis said. "It's hard to believe I got a berth."

"I know what you mean," he replied. "This was the fifth GSS I've applied to; I imagine I'm only on it because they're tired of interviewing me."

"Are there a lot of military among the colonists?"

"Numbers-wise yes, but then with the size of the colony roster there's more of everyone."

"I suppose that's true," Tanis said. "Many officers?"

"The usual mess of lieutenants, a few commanders, some good sergeants, and two other majors like yourself. Above you it's just the admiral, and the captain, of course."

Their conversation was interrupted by the train's arrival at their destination.

The maglev station was both large and packed with people. It was directly off the *Intrepid*'s main cargo dock, and everyone was coming or going from that direction. Tanis observed dozens of potential security nightmares. Something would have to be done about this.

Before they made it across the station and through the short corridor leading to the dock, she was filing reports and looking up data on numbers of essential and non-essential personnel who accessed the dock.

The dock was to scale with the ship.

Needing to handle the transfer of billions of tons of cargo, the dock was over three kilometers long and one deep. In the distance, looming over hectares of crates and equipment, was the *Intrepid*'s yawning cargo hatch. Tanis's HUD provided the portal's size and she was surprised to realize it was large enough to fly the *Steel Dawn III* through.

Commander Evans led Tanis to a bank of ground transports and they sped off toward the ship. They wove around slower transports and cargo lifters, some hauling massive mechanical devices as tall as a hundred meters, all moving toward the ship's entrance.

"We could have gone up a few decks and taken one of the maglevs up there. They run down an umbilical directly to the forward crew section of the ship, but I figured you'd like the view down here," Commander Evans said from his position at the controls.

Tanis nodded, looking over the operation around her. "Good plan, showing me the security and control down here."

Commander Evans gave his easy laugh again. "Yeah, you must be a Micky. Only they could think of duty and work when peering into a ten-kilometer-deep cargo bay for the first time." He gestured at the space within the *Intrepid*'s yawning portal.

She resisted scowling at him for using the vernacular term for MICI while privately admitting that seeing atmospheric distortion within a cargo bay was unusual.

Twenty meters from the ship, a thick white line was painted on the deck. The far side was *Intrepid*. Tanis signaled the commander to stop and examined the security threshold. Holographic emitters projected the barrier, vertically displaying it to the flits and cargo hovers that moved around the dock.

The security itself was manned by Terran Space Force Regulars, unlike the previous checkpoints which had all been operated by MOS security forces. Tanis added the fact that TSF and not GSS was running security for this ship to her list of anomalies. Today's near miss was not the first significant threat this project had faced.

Above, at the levels where maglev tracks moved cargo through the barrier, more Regulars manned the gantries and inspected physical ladings while spider-like automatons crawled over everything, checking sources, destinations and contents.

Someone must have warned the soldiers that their new CO was coming through as they were brisk and businesslike, coolly efficient and quietly threatening. Tanis spotted a lieutenant and gave her a nod. The woman jogged over and saluted.

"Sirs!"

Tanis's HUD flagged the woman as First Lieutenant Amy Lee. The name caused Tanis to bring up the woman's record. Two names for a given name and no surname was common for the Scattered Worlds; it was unusual to find someone from the disk in the Terran Space Force. However, that was the case, the lieutenant was from the Scattered World's capital of Makemake.

"Amy Lee is our head of external security. She's a former Marine from the MCSF. The three platoons under her are from a few fully manned Q companies down on the ring. No commander with them, so we put her in charge."

Tanis nodded.

<Q company? They give them combat troops, but rather than cohesive units they get miscellaneous Q platoons? This doesn't make sense.> Angela all but echoed what Tanis was thinking.

"You appear to have things well in hand here, Lieutenant." Tanis looked at the Regulars manning the checkpoints. "We'll be expanding our area of control. I want you to begin considering shift and personnel changes for moving our perimeter out to the maglev stations and elevator banks."

The lieutenant's eyes widened, but she didn't question how Tanis planned to take control of a few kilometers of the MOS.

"Yes, sir!"

"Carry on." Tanis saluted and they moved forward to be processed by the soldiers. Minutes later they were driving over one of the bridges between the dock and the ship.

The cargo bay was even larger once inside. It turned out to be a main corridor off a hundred other cargo bays; a corridor large enough to fly the *Steel Dawn III* through.

Equipment moved through it on a dozen different levels. Holo emitters outlined several roads for ground vehicles and Commander Evans sped the ground car down one, deftly following its jinks and curves.

The corridor ran to the far side of the ship, some ten kilometers distant. Tanis cycled her vision and saw what appeared to be a multi-tiered docking port for external cargo.

The construction drones clustered in the distance showed that it was still incomplete and all cargo was being funneled through the shipyard's dock. She glanced back at the porous dock security and wondered what it would take to accelerate the external dock's completion.

After two kilometers, they passed the entrance to the port cylinder.

"That one's been named 'Old Sam'," Commander Evans said. "The other is named 'Lil Sue'."

"Have you been in them?" Tanis had been in dozens of cylinder habitats, but never one that was mounted in a ship.

"A few times, yeah. Ouri, one of our lieutenants in the SOC, has managed to get her hands on a small lakeside house in Old Sam. I guess she's also pretty big into botany and is maintaining some special garden and overseeing several other areas in there. We've had a few cookouts down by the lake recently."

"What, with a fire?"

"Yeah, nuts, eh? We had no trouble whatsoever getting the authorization for it. Apparently the carbon cycle needs a little help, so the more the merrier."

"Fires on a starship for fun." Tanis shook her head. "Not something I think I've ever heard of before."

"It's nice when we do it, you'd think you're dirt-side." Commander Evans smiled absently as he spoke.

His features cut a nice profile. Either he had good genetics, or his parents had paid special attention to his looks.

"I've been in a few of those cylinder habs before. Every now and then I look up and see a lake or a forest rotating over my head and have to suppress the instinct to duck."

Commander Evans laughed and they drove in silence the rest of the way to the tubes.

The lifts were guarded by GSS security and they processed Tanis and Joe swiftly. They stepped into an empty car and held the handrails as the platform shot up through the tube.

The tube's walls were clear plas and the effect gave the sensation that the floor of the cargo bay was falling away from them. Above were several levels containing everything from life support to supplies and storage. Once past the lower levels, the tube shot out into empty space, anchored to one of the gossamer struts running around this section of the ship. They sped over the matter accelerator which ran from the ramscoop back to the engines and moments later were swallowed by the upper section of the vessel.

"You know"—Tanis peered through the plas—"Even if you take off the cylinders, scoop, engines, and even the docking levels below, this ship is still one of the largest I've ever been on."

"I know what you mean," Commander Evans said. "I've taken the grand tour by maglev train. It literally takes an entire shift."

The tube terminated in a large transit station and their security clearance was checked again by GSS authorities. There seemed to be a clear division of TSF and GSS control on the ship. There were also some MSF folks in the mix. It shouldn't have bothered Tanis, but after what she had seen on the MOS that day she had a bad taste in her mouth when she thought of the Mars Security Force having anything to do with her safety.

Commander Evans led her across the terminal to a maglev and they took it to the forward sections of the ship, arriving at their final stop roughly a kilometer aft of the bridge. The Security Operations Center was just off the train station's foyer and they stepped through the sliding double doors into a controlled chaos.

The main room was a two-tier affair with physical and holo consoles arrayed in three concentric rings. Interspaced amongst these were several large multi-d holo screens showing various news and security feeds. Leading off the outer circle were several doors to private offices, the local synaptic processing networks, and several labs.

They walked to the executive offices while the staff in the ops center cast her wary glances. Her address down at the *Dawn* had been posted to the SOC's private net and contained her designation as the CO, so everyone was already aware of the change in command. She placed a hand on Evans' shoulder when they reached the upper tier and turned to address the room.

"As you are all already aware, I am Major Richards, your new CO. Right off I want you to know that I'm not here to supplant Commander Evans as much as to supplement him. I've spent a bit of time working ops like this: competing priorities, unknown threats; it's an ugly situation." The looks in the room were coolly appraising, no one showing their feelings one way or another. Without a doubt some of the people she was addressing had alerts on their HUDs that had matched her ID to the media coverage from ten years earlier.

"I'm not here to shake things up, but I'm also not going to shy away from saying what needs to be said, or doing what needs to be done. I know you all have a lot of work to do, but I want to see section chiefs and reps in the conference room…"

<*We have a conference room right?*> she asked Angela.

<*Check.*>

"At 1600 hours this afternoon." The crowd remained unreadable. "That'll be all."

<*Tough room,*> she remarked to the commander on a private connection.

<*Some days it's a challenge just to get them to say 'hi, sir'.*>

<*Whose idea was it to mix all these people together anyway?*>

<*Honestly, I don't think anyone knows, Major. It's mostly due to jurisdiction. GSS doesn't have much of a military presence, but they do have some civilian consultants. Most of the real military is TSF, and we're technically still active duty till we leave the system, so TSF command has its people here. Half of the issues which have occurred have been stationside, so MOS Sec has its people here and they're under MSF, so they've got people here too.*>

<*And everyone is making sure their ass is covered and that their boss will get credit for any success right?*>

<*That about sums it up, sir.*>

<*You know that bit about not shaking things up?*> Tanis asked.

<*I seem to recall something along those lines.*> Commander Evans gave her a scrutinizing look.

<*I'm going to declare some necessary changes. The first being half those people can go back to wherever it is their cred is signed over.*>

<*That's gonna cause some trouble,*> the commander shook his head ruefully.

<*I have it from on high. The schedule is everything. All these fingers in the pie are slowing things down.*>

<*I've noticed, but a commander with no significant intel experience and not a lot of connections can't really go tell the admiral to ditch people.*>

<*I hadn't planned on consulting the admiral.*> Tanis smiled at Evans.

<I wasn't sure for a bit, but now I think I'll like you.>

Commander Evans showed Tanis into her office and she got herself situated. He transmitted her codes to the CO's private system on the SOC net and the desk recognized her and logged her on. Tanis opened several subnets and looked over the pending issues and upcoming schedule. She could tell Evans had a concise and organized mind, but at the same time he lacked familiarity with large security operations. There were duties he performed exceptionally well, and others he appeared to not have been aware of at all.

Not that she could blame him. Pilots almost never had AI, and Evans was no exception. The majority of their available cranial space was taken up by the structural bracing and specialized processors which were needed to handle a spaceship at velocities near half the speed of light. Pilots simply didn't have the implants for a job like this.

Her orgstruct showed four section heads, and she pulled up their files and reviewed them in preparation for the meeting. Her head of the Lab and Forensics was Terry Chang. Though Terry was a colonist who would be making the trip, until they debarked she would be listed as one of the GSS contractors. Her primary qualification was several years managing New Seattle's police labs on Mars and her record showed good performance.

Net Security was headed up by Lieutenant Caspen. He was Mars Security Force, attached to the station, and from what Tanis could see his record wasn't particularly impressive. He had a few complaints against him for insubordination and some of his COs had private and rather unflattering comments on his file. From what Tanis could tell, it was not immediately apparent why he would be on an assignment like the *Intrepid*.

She left his file open on the desk's holo and shifted her attention to First Lieutenant Amy Lee. She was the only person in the SOC that was TSF Marine branch and not Navy or Regulars. It would explain why she was down at the physical perimeter.

The MSF liaison was a Commander Gren. Because MSF followed more traditional naval structure and not the mixed format that the TSF used, Gren technically outranked Commander Evans. In the TSF the rank of commander was analogous to the old rank of captain. It had been renamed when the structure merged to avoid confusion with ship captains. Gren's rank was functionally the same as Tanis's. She was getting a better picture of why Commander Evans had struggled so much to get cooperation out of the Marsian personnel.

A perusal of several incidents showed that Gren tended to treat MSF and MOS security personnel as though they were under his direct command. On top of that, a MOS security liaison was present as well—a Sergeant Davidson. Davidson's record was better than most of the personnel that the MOS had supplied to the *Intrepid*, but Commander Gren overrode any good suggestion the sergeant made.

Shipstats listed the *Intrepid*'s current population at just over ten thousand, and once the colonists began to arrive to be put into stasis, daily averages would be several times that number. In preparation for that time an internal police force was present, headed by First Lieutenant Ouri of the GSS. Ouri seemed competent enough and was temporary crew on the *Intrepid* with a permanent colony position upon arrival.

The *Intrepid* was unlike most colony ships in that it was designed to make multiple trips. Upon reaching New Eden it would detach the cylinders and cargo pods. Once the orbital habitat was functioning, the ship would return to Earth to pick up more cargo pods and a pair of new cylinders.

Typically the entire ship remained at the colony, usually being salvaged or turned into insystem transport. This was the first GSS to have a permanent crew that would not be staying at the destination.

<*What do you make of this mixed bag?*> Tanis asked Angela. <*Was there any planning at all in putting this team together?*>

<*I'm guessing that's a rhetorical question,*> Angela replied.

<*Cheeky girl.*>

<*I don't have cheeks. But if you mean that I'm giving you a hard time, that would be correct.*>

<*Anyway…*>

<*Yes, you've certainly got your work cut out for you.*>

<*Us.*>

<*Now it's us… I see how this works.*>

<*Any time you want to give me your assessment…*>

Angela gave the mental equivalent of a sigh. <*Very well. You already know you've got a lot of bloat. Your main trouble is the MarsSec and MOS Sec people. They all have mixed loyalties, but you need them if you are to work with the station at all. Your biggest problem is Gren. Ditch him and you'll be able to bring the rest into line. Except for Caspen; ditch him too.*>

<*You echo my thoughts,*> Tanis said.

<*Well, I can read a lot of them.*>

*****

Tanis sat at the head of the conference table sipping a cup of coffee. It was just before 1600 and the various department heads and liaisons began to file in. Tanis had requested a physical meeting as it was much easier to read people when they were actually in front of you—easier for Angela to monitor them too.

While the conference room was listed as a nanoprobe-free zone, the records for previous meetings indicated that room sweeps were not normally implanted. She was betting that someone here was used to taking advantage of that and would be in for an unpleasant surprise. Angela was remotely controlling the scanning systems and would alert Tanis the moment she caught any bots moving in the room.

She eased back in her seat, silently eyeing each person as they entered. Commander Evans took a seat beside her and leaned over whistling softly.

"Got them all here in person, that's something I never managed to pull off."

Tanis tapped her collar. "It's the oak leaves. They imply wisdom. Makes people listen better."

"I think my two bars must somehow suggest I'm easy to ignore."

"I'm sure part of it is that they all want to size me up," Tanis said. "See how they can mess with me."

"There will most certainly be messing, sir."

A minute later the last straggler came in: Commander Gren, as Tanis had anticipated. He took his seat across the table from her and held her eye for several moments. Tanis flicked her eyes to the left and blinked rapidly as though she were accessing her Link. She didn't have any tells, but it never hurt to make people think they had you all figured out.

"Good afternoon," Tanis began. "I'd like to thank you all for taking time out of your busy schedules for this little session." The stares from around the table were blank, no one revealing anything until they had a better idea of her intentions. "I've been going over our records and procedures and I believe we will have to make some changes."

"What types of changes might those be?" Lieutenant Caspen asked.

"Changes at every level," Tanis replied. "Commander Evans has done an admirable job. However, there have still been security breaches, some minor, others not so minor. Luckily—and I do mean luckily—nothing serious has penetrated as far as the *Intrepid* itself. However, we need to determine what is the root cause of these breaches if we are to consider ourselves successful."

"We already know what the root is," Sergeant Davidson said. "MOS Sec is very certain the disturbances are originating with small radical groups."

"I don't think you can label what happened today as a 'disturbance'," Lieutenant Ouri said. "Those terms are for the press. We nearly had a catastrophe."

"Speaking of things that are for the press, and things that aren't"—Tanis cast a stern eye down the table—"Lieutenant Caspen, please recall your nanoprobes. As I'm certain you are aware, they're not allowed in here."

"I'm not sure I know what you are talking about," Caspen said. "I don't have any probes deployed.

There were several distinct hissing sounds and Tanis smiled. "Not anymore, you don't." The lieutenant shifted uncomfortably and Tanis continued. "As I was saying, we need to determine who is behind these attacks. My brief encounter with the enemy proves we are dealing with an organized, well-funded group. They have both physical and net resources beyond what any known anti-colonization group possesses."

Lieutenant Caspen spoke up again, "I looked you up, Major. You're *that* Tanis Richards. You've got a history of going overboard in situations. How can we be sure you're not doing that now?"

Tanis and Caspen stared at each other for several long moments before she broke his gaze and looked around the table. "Most of you have read my file. Surprisingly, one or two of you haven't. You are, of course, seeing only the non-classified portions of it. I've battled more radical splinter groups than I'm certain you even knew existed. Most have quality tech, and they are all very dedicated, but none of them would have the funds or the contacts to sneak a nuclear weapon aboard a station as secure as this one." Only by supreme effort did she keep the sarcasm from her voice. "Only a group with corporate contracts, or a mercenary organization, would be able to pull that off."

"If you say so." Commander Gren's tone was acerbic.

Gren and Caspen had an obvious partnership. Caspen would make the less defensible statements with which to draw her out, following which Gren would attempt to devalue her answers. It wasn't even worth rising to the challenge.

"I do say so." Tanis locked eyes with him. "Your interpretation of the today's events aside, I'll be going ahead with my alterations to the *Intrepid*'s security structure. I've reviewed all of the reports each section has logged over the last few months and several of you have echoed my own thoughts. There are too many cooks in the kitchen. Effective immediately we will be removing much of the diversification in our command structure."

At that statement, several uncertain looks were cast around the table. Tanis couldn't help but revel in the discomfort for a moment. In her experience, there was no way a group could pull something like the job on the *Dawn* and not have people in all the local security organizations.

"Net, Physical, and Perimeter will be rolled into a single struct. Lieutenant Ouri will be heading up the combined organization with Lieutenant Amy Lee retaining her responsibility for perimeter security with an expanded role. Lieutenant Caspen, you will be removed from your role as head of Net Security; that will now fall directly under Lieutenant Ouri."

"What?" Caspen looked shocked. "You can't simply remove me; I've been assigned by MSF."

"MSF granted us use of its NetSec personnel at a time when the *Intrepid* did not have the staff in place to handle the job internally. We are grateful for their sacrifice, but now we have adequate personnel and so you are relieved. The four individuals that came with you from MSF NetSec are also no longer needed. Angela, my AI, has already removed your and their access to all non-public *Intrepid* nets."

Caspen appeared dumbfounded. He looked to Commander Gren, who presumably was on the Link verifying Tanis's authority to make these changes.

"You'll find that Admiral Sanderson and Captain Andrews have both already approved my personnel changes." They hadn't personally, but Angela had passed her plans by their respective AI. "The *Intrepid*'s contract has a clause regarding a reasonable expectation of safety. If that expectation is not met we have broad provisions which allow us to ensure that level of safety. I believe we crossed that threshold today, which gives me the authority to make these decisions."

"That's ridiculous," Caspen said. "The incident on the *Steel Dawn III* was handled very well. The *Intrepid* was not harmed."

Commander Evans' mouth dropped open. "Oh c'mon, Caspen. That's a really pathetic attempt at spin. Major Richards herself is the one who stopped them. Had it not been for her, the *Intrepid* and a good portion of this shipyard would have been in serious danger."

Tanis cast Evans an approving nod. "As I said, you're relieved. Security will monitor you as you clean out your quarters." Tanis picked up signs that both Gren and Caspen were holding a conversation on the Link, most likely with each other. At one point Gren even shrugged.

"Next up." Tanis loaded the appropriate information onto the conference room's net and holo displays. "I've exercised an additional clause in our contract to extend our area of control. The B1, B2, A9, and C3 docks are now under control of the *Intrepid*'s security forces."

"About time," Lieutenant Amy Lee muttered, though her words were barely audible under the protestations of Commander Gren and Sergeant Davidson.

"You can't be serious," Gren said. "There is no need to extend your control that far out on the docks."

"I disagree, and our lawyers found themselves in agreement with my interpretation of our contract. Since the MOS and MSF have been unable to provide us with an adequate level of security, we have the option to create our own perimeter on the station itself. We have also increased our no-fly perimeter outside the ship and will be utilizing TSF forces as security there. Commander Evans will be in charge of all facets of external security and will be responsible for requisitioning our fighter forces."

Gren sputtered, and Tanis enjoyed the show a little more than she should. "This is a heavy-handed and frankly preposterous response to today's events," he finally managed to say.

"If it were just today's events that would be true, but over the last two years there have been more acts of sabotage within what will be our new perimeter than within the rest of the Mars Protectorate. Additionally, you, Commander Gren, and you, Sergeant Davidson, are being moved. Your offices will no longer be on board the *Intrepid*, as with our new perimeter extending onto the station it makes more sense for you to be off the ship and more accessible to where our jurisdictions meet."

Before Davidson or Gren could utter a word, Tanis turned to Terry Chang. "Terry, your work has been exemplary, though you have been working with limited resources. I have secured a significant budget and personnel increase for you and have also suspended all forensics on the *Steel Dawn III* in anticipation of you personally overseeing that case."

As the only civilian division head, Tanis could guess Terry wasn't often able to make her presence or needs known.

"Thank you, Major," Terry smiled. "Since evidence is the fastest-aging thing in the universe, I hope you won't mind if I excuse myself and assemble my full team."

"Not at all," Tanis replied. "I believe we are finished here. I have sent detailed briefs to each of you and I expect an update by the end of the second shift as to your progress." She rose. "You're dismissed."

Everyone filed out of the room except for Commander Gren, who remained seated.

"Enjoying the view in here?" Tanis started toward the door.

Gren rose and blocked the exit. "You have no idea what you are doing."

"On the contrary," Tanis said. "I know exactly what I am doing." She moved to step around him but he stopped her with a hand on her shoulder. Almost leisurely, Tanis looked down at the hand.

"I'm not done talking to you," Gren said. "MSF isn't going to allow this overstepping of our authority."

Tanis waited a moment, but the hand was still on her shoulder. Without a word of warning she grabbed his wrist and pulled it behind his back. Gren was expecting just that move and countered, grabbing her arm in turn.

"Not my first day on the job." He wore an unpleasant grin.

"Mine either." She twisted around him, and in one fluid move smashed her elbow into the back of his neck, driving his face down into the clear plas surface of the table. He hadn't let go of her left wrist, so his right arm was pinned underneath him with his left arm tucked between his body and Tanis as she pushed him down.

"Next time you decide it's within your purview to lay hands on a TSF officer, think again. This incident has been recorded and while I won't make an official entry about it, if this turns out to be a habit of yours I'll, file a complaint against you with every office that has jurisdiction over your sorry ass."

She let Gren up, her eyes dared him to escalate the event. His body trembled with barely contained rage, but after a moment he regained some degree of control and left without saying another word. "First smart thing he's done all day," Tanis said to herself.

<*Aren't we feeling just a bit confrontational today,*> Angela observed.

<*Hey, I was minding my own business when someone tried to blow us up with a nuke.*>

<I would think not being dead would make for a happy Tanis, instead you're firing people and/or beating them up.>

Tanis decided not to respond to her AI's needling and walked around the outer ring of the SOC and into her office to find a grinning Commander Evans waiting for her.

"Sir, this may be the best day of my life."

"Been dreaming of that for a while?" she asked.

"You have no idea. I didn't have the mandate you do, and frankly with Gren semi-outranking me I don't know that I could have executed such a coup anyway."

"But you sure would have had fun trying, I bet." Tanis found herself smiling as well.

"Without a doubt."

"So, feel like getting behind the controls of a fighter again?"

"And out from behind a desk? If I wasn't afraid of you after what you did to Gren, I'd kiss you."

"Saw that, did you?"

Commander Evans gave what Tanis was beginning to consider his trademark grin. "You were rather loud and the doors of that room are plas after all."

THE PARTY

STELLAR DATE: 3227163 / 07.29.4123 (Adjusted Gregorian)
LOCATION: Mars Outer Shipyards (MOS)
REGION: Mars Protectorate, Sol Space Federation

Tanis strolled through a corridor carrying several packages from her trip to MOS's shopping district. The selection had been slim, but her day didn't include time for a trip down to Mars 1. While she did enjoy a bit of shopping as much as the next person, finding a gown to wear at a formal ball was not on her list of enjoyable pastimes. At least current fashions were on the downswing from the ridiculous high a decade earlier. The current trend for women was a simple long sheath with interweaving patterns that reflected the wearer's mood. Tanis would have Angela alter the dress to always portray a calm pattern.

<*You know, you can control your nano too.*>

<*I know, but you're so obliging.*>

<*I think I'm being taken for granted.*>

Tanis chuckled softly. <*That will never happen.*>

<*I should hope not.*>

Tanis took a lift through forty levels of station to the outer levels where the larger ships were under construction. The lift emptied out into a broad lobby on deck A8.9, just one level below the *Intrepid*'s cargo deck. Under her new security measures no lifts could directly access deck A9; they had to stop above or below and pass inspection before being allowed to continue.

In the lobby, stationed at a temporary barrier, were several TSF Regulars. Tanis hadn't been certain she could get the additional troops on such short notice, but Sanderson had clout, or had at least anticipated her measures based on her file. Either way, several companies of Regulars and a platoon of Marines had been moved up from Mars 1 to MOS and the perimeter was being established.

Come to think of it, having to organize the troops while Tanis shopped was probably what was irking her AI.

"Sir." One of the four soldiers at the barrier saluted her as she approached. Tanis's overlay showed him to be Sergeant Langlis. "If you'll step up to the Auth & Auth."

Tanis returned his salute and stepped up to the ID-verification system. She could sense Angela passing security tokens as she stared into the retinal scanner. The scanner matched the structure of her eye with what her DNA said it should look like as well as archived records. In addition to the tokens Angela passed, Tanis passed her own personal token as well as her hash, which the system matched with the encoded chemical signature in her bloodstream.

"Thank you, sir." The sergeant and the other three men relaxed just a hair.

"Keep up the good work, Staff." Tanis nodded to the soldiers and made her way to the next lift. To the naked eye it would appear that having four men guarding a bank of lifts was woefully inadequate, but they were just the tip of the iceberg. She had evaluated their progress and the other security measures from her command link.

Several AI and personnel had monitored all aspects of her person as she passed the point. Scan examined her bag and verified its contents. Several nanoprobes had also independently verified her identity before and after she stepped through the Auth & Auth. Chem sniffers had checked her out and even monitored her for mood alterations as she was checked over.

A hostile intruder would be met with a surprising show of force, more than just the four soldiers that met the eye—not that they weren't a serious threat in and of themselves. The barriers were capable of discharging a shock capable of bringing a dozen people to their knees and nano was ready in the thousands to infiltrate a person and attempt to bring about a nervous shutdown. If those measures were not successful, two other things would occur. An ES barrier would snap into place and as a last resort the soldiers would discharge their weapons.

The most important thing was that the men didn't pass her by just because she was a senior officer. She had seen that sort of thing happen too often and was glad that she didn't need to have the talk with their CO.

She stepped into another lift for the quick trip up to deck A9.1. She was greeted by more TSF soldiers and another Auth & Auth check. From there the trip was very similar to her earlier entrance with Commander Evans. She did notice that some confusion was in evidence as shipments tried to pass through security, and kept herself busy as she walked by putting together reports on how to improve efficiency in concert with the new security measures.

After ascending to the crew areas of the *Intrepid,* Tanis called up an overlay of the ship's corridors and followed the directions to her quarters. The ball wasn't until the following evening, but she wanted to double-check the gown's fit without the pretentious salesperson puttering around her. She noted that she was very close to the officer's mess and her rumbling stomach reminded her that it hadn't received sustenance since breakfast.

<*You have been up for over twenty-two hours,*> Angela commented.

<*I know…I hate these time shifts. You'd think they'd have stretched them on the* Dawn *to match MOS's schedule.*>

<*You could have checked MOS's schedule and shifted yourself.*>

Tanis's internal avatar stuck out its tongue at Angela's. The AI shrugged and Tanis sighed aloud.

<*There are just some things you can't really get without ever having had a body.*>

<*I've had a body before,*> Angela said defensively.

<*Not one with a tongue,*> Tanis grinned, <*unless you were able to stick out an actuator or something.*>

Angela didn't reply and Tanis strolled triumphantly into the officer's mess. She smiled to see that it had the familiar feel expected from such a place, a bit of wood on the columns and the corners of counters. A salad bar adorned one side of the room and low tables were spread throughout. She pulled up a chair at a table near the entrance and called up the menu as a servitor arrived and poured her a glass of water.

A querying icon appeared in the upper right of her overlay and Tanis responded to the servitor's request with the number for a BLT on toasted wheat bread. Mars had a burgeoning hog industry and its rings were the cheapest place to get pork in the solar system. Not that it cost to eat in the officer's mess. The servitor informed her that the meat she would be eating was actually from the first generation of pigs raised in the primary cylinder on the *Intrepid*.

Two men in GSS uniforms were sitting at a table across the room from Tanis. They had glanced up at her when she entered, now their Links must have informed them as to who she was. They both rose and stepped around the empty tables as they walked toward her.

"Major Richards," the taller of the two said. "I'm First Lieutenant Collins and this is Lieutenant Peters." The other man nodded.

Tanis didn't need their introduction; her security monitoring had told her who they were the moment she stepped into the mess. Collins was assigned to acquisitions and Peters worked in shipnet.

"Nice to meet you two." Tanis nodded. They hadn't saluted, so neither did she. The setting wasn't formal, but it was still protocol. Her quick research showed that at least Collins wouldn't be her biggest fan. He had already registered a complaint about the lengthened process for bringing items onto the ship.

The servitor slipped around the two men and deposited Tanis's order in on the table.

"I suppose you've read my complaint about the extra processing time for materials coming onto the ship." Collins almost echoed her personal wording. "I can't tell you how much this is going to slow us down."

Tanis smiled serenely up at the lieutenant. "I can. 5.6% if you follow the guidelines I laid out. My report also recommends that you hire three additional shipment processors which will lower the time increase to only 2%."

"My reports show increases much higher than that." Collins sputtered, caught off guard by her intimate knowledge of his operations.

"I'd be interested in looking at your reports." Tanis turned back to her food. "Please attach them to the initial complaint about increased processing time and I'll look them over."

She took a bite of her sandwich and enjoyed its rich flavor. Neither man had moved. "Did you have something else to say?" she asked. "Anything on your mind, Lieutenant Peters?"

Collins looked at Peters, willing his friend to speak, but the man just shook his head. "No ma'am, I'm all set."

"Very well then, if you two would allow me to return to my lunch." Tanis took another bite of her sandwich as the two men turned and walked back to their table.

<*That was a bit weird,*> Angela said.

<*Pretty weak,*> Tanis agreed. <*I would have expected a bit more fire from someone of Collins' rank.*>

<*Maybe that's why he's just a glorified stevedore.*>

<*Ouch!*>

<*I'm an AI, I cannot lie.*>

<*Yeah, and I'm a planetary object.*>

<*You're too small to be one of those. And you haven't cleared your orbit.*>

Tanis decided to disregard that comment and concentrated on finishing her food. The other two officers were still in the mess looking sullen when she left.

*****

"I can't believe how many of these things are scheduled for the next ten months." Tanis said as she and Evans entered the ballroom just off the VIP dock. The dock hadn't been scheduled for completion yet, but the GSS had heeded Tanis's suggestion that passing all the VIPs through the MOS first would increase risk for all parties. Additional workers and nano construction units had just managed to complete it in time for the event.

The ballroom was already filling up with dignitaries. Most were from Mars, but a few from Earth, Venus, and even Callisto were present. Tanis's overlay lit up with indicators representing all the organizations and corporations with dignitaries present.

"Quite the mix we have here," she commented.

"More and more each time," Evans said. "They all seem to want to get in on the *Intrepid*'s success."

"What success is that?" Her dislike of having to be at a ball was making her deliberately obtuse.

"No one thought this project would get off the ground, let alone get built. The concept of a reusable colony ship seemed ludicrous, but with Redding's new ramscoop actually passing trial runs it looks like the *Intrepid* is more than just a pipe dream. Now everyone wants to soak up the glory for every little nut and bolt their company made or shipped."

"Reasons why I want to leave this crazy system," Tanis sighed.

"I imagine a lot of us feel that way," Evans said. "Just another year or so of this mess and we can leave it all behind… Provided we don't get blown up."

"Isn't going to happen. I don't know exactly why the admiral picked me for this, but I do know it's my one shot to get out of this system. No way I'm going to blow it."

Evans laughed and the sound was rich and deep. "Sounds like you want to get out of Sol as much as the rest of us."

"You said it."

"Did I mention how glad I am to have you take over all this?" Evans said as they approached the bar.

"You actually have said it already, about nine times today." Tanis smiled as the automaton poured her a drink, having read her preferred list of beverages from her public profile.

"I know, but it can't be said enough. We'll be a hundred years into our flight and I'll still bring it up." He turned his rather infectious grin her way.

It was Tanis's turn to laugh. "Please don't, that would get really old."

While the *Intrepid* had three large ballrooms, all done in different styles, tonight's affair only used the room decorated in twenty-ninth century European trappings. The primary motifs and accents were hard angular surfaces in blues and greys.

The guests, on the other hand, were a riot of color. The civilian women wore dresses similar to Tanis's, but were showing a lot more of their skin. Marsian men could be spotted by their green and blue suits and the men from Venus wore all black. Terrans were easy to spot, as well, due to the resurgence of fashion hats on Earth. In Tanis's opinion most of them looked like peacocks.

Clustered in a few groups throughout the room were various military representatives. The TSF officers were grouped together near the other end of the bar, though none had approached Tanis and Evans. The MSF had a few men and women present and Tanis spotted Commander Gren in their midst. The only representative of the MOS Sec was their commandant, who was hobnobbing with some businessmen from Mars.

The GSS officers, being more of a semi-federal navy and far more political than the others, were more intermingled. Mostly they had latched onto ambassadors and other diplomats.

A group of envoys from the Thripids, a Kuiper Belt combine, entered the hall. Tanis had overseen several missions out in the KB and had worked with Thripids before. They were one of the Sol system's more unusual groups; men and women alike wore unusual gowns laced with circuitry and sensors. Net rumor had it that they were almost entirely cybernetic—little humanity showed in their impassive faces.

Not long afterward, Admiral Sanderson and his aides stepped into the room. Sanderson surveyed his surroundings as though this was his own personal kingdom. Tanis still hadn't made up her mind about him, but at least he had approved all of her security measures with minimal comment.

"You'd think he owns the place," Evans said quietly, echoing Tanis's thoughts.

"Every operation has an old man or old lady. He's ours."

"That he is." Evans took a sip of his drink.

Tanis checked over the security teams that were monitoring the maglev station that connected the series of ballrooms off the VIP dock with the rest of the ship. So far no guests had tried to venture beyond that point. Captain Andrews was leading a tour later in the evening, but aside from that the guests were restricted to this relatively small area. The other team was monitoring the dock and had reported no problems. Every guest had been on the list and their Auth & Auth checks passed muster.

"The Reddings are due tonight." Evans watched over the rim of his glass as the admiral made the rounds. He would inevitably end up speaking to them as they were two of the highest-ranking officers present. While most of the local services had their fair share of representatives, they were still mostly on one end of the room. They may not always have gotten along, but they understood one another a lot better than they understood the civilians. The officers, mostly lieutenants and captains, were grouped together with a pair of master sergeants nearby. There were a couple of other majors on the *Intrepid*, but none were listed as being in attendance this evening.

"Enfield is too." Tanis obliquely monitored the admiral's route through the room.

"He is?" Evans' eyes flickered as he checked the guest list. "He's not on the list, not even on the maybes."

"He's already on the ship. They tried to sneak him on this morning. For some reason Sanderson decided not to let me know."

"So how do you know?"

"One of Ouri's people picked up a couple of irregularities and passed them up the chain. His security didn't seem to realize that I have access to some databases that would allow me to ID their mystery guest."

"Do they know you know?"

"They probably do by now. I left a security docket and nano-ID in his quarters."

Evans let out a laugh. "You're just shaking things up all over the place."

"I try." Tanis allowed herself a small grin.

"I can't wait to see this." Evans had the automaton make him another drink.

Once he had finished his initial rounds, or perhaps when he simply wanted a strong drink, Admiral Sanderson made his way over to them. The two junior officers saluted him and he languidly returned the courtesy.

"Found your little joke in Mr. Enfield's quarters." The admiral's voice carried no trace of humor.

"I don't think it's a joke," Tanis replied.

"We go to all the trouble of hiding his presence and you announce it to anyone interested in the current roster."

Tanis held back a sigh. She knew that Admiral Sanderson hadn't told her about Terrance Enfield's arrival because she hadn't fully secured her department. However, since the admiral hadn't thoroughly covered his tracks, things could have been worse as a result of attempting to hide him.

"If I may, sir." She waited for his nod. "One of my net security personnel found the irregularities, which we kept quiet and reworked to remove their traces. If you check the shipnet you will find no trace of Terrance Enfield in any databases in regards to his visit tonight. We are also currently in a noise-canceling bubble, so no one can hear this conversation."

Admiral Sanderson stared forward without blinking, what Tanis assumed must be his tell for accessing his Link. His features relaxed somewhat, but his tone was still acidic.

"It would seem that is the case," he admitted. "But in the future I would expect you to notify me of such things."

"I will, sir. With all due respect, as the head of security I would like to be notified of such visitors in the future as well."

"It would seem there is no reason to hide it since you'll find out anyway." Tanis couldn't tell if he was being petty or complimentary.

"It's why you brought me here, sir."

Admiral Sanderson let out a short sound that could have been a cough or a chuckle. "I suppose that it is. Andrews will be pleased; he expects big things from you."

"I imagine he expects to have his ship finished on schedule," Tanis said.

Admiral Sanderson nodded and didn't respond as he retrieved his drink.

Shortly thereafter, the Reddings entered the ballroom, in some ways exactly and in others nothing like Tanis would have expected. Earnest Redding, the visionary of the pair, was the man responsible for the *Intrepid*'s advanced ramscoop engine. He was reportedly the typical mind-in-the-stars type, though this evening he seemed very much present as he shook hands and doled out pleasantries. His wife, Abby, was a nuts-and-bolts type. She was largely responsible for making realities out of her husband's dreams. As the head engineer on the *Intrepid,* it was her job to get the massive ship built and heading outsystem on time.

Admiral Sanderson must have sent them a message via Link as the pair headed directly to the bar.

<*Oh yay.*> Evans' dry humor oozed over the Link. <*This is bound to be a stimulating conversation.*>

<*You don't seem enthused,*> Tanis sent back.

<*Don't get me wrong, I love the Reddings to death, but they and Sanderson are from different universes. They couldn't communicate if their lives depended on it.*>

<*Now it sounds like this* will *be fun.*>

<*As fun as watching someone puke in zero gee.*> Evans sighed and leaned back against the bar.

<*That's one of the less pleasant images I've had in a while.*>

<*Really? You* are *in the military, aren't you?*>

Tanis stifled a laugh as the Reddings arrived at the bar.

Sanderson did the introductions. "Earnest, Abby. I'd like you to meet Major Richards, our new head of security."

Earnest merely nodded while Abby cast Tanis an appraising look.

"So you're the one causing all the trouble. I've got shipments backed up all over the place with your new security measures." Abby wasted no time in bending Tanis's ear.

"You've also got a dock to have them sit on, thanks to her." Earnest commented as he retrieved a drink. His wife shot him a dark look.

"I'm sorry to hear that, ma'am." Tanis did her best to be deferential. "I've spoken with Lieutenant Collins and provided reports on where I think additional staff will alleviate his problems. I've also assigned additional security personnel from the local TSF garrison to ensure that your shipments are not held up."

Earnest chuckled. "Looks like she's got all the angles covered, dear."

"So it would seem." Abby pursed her lips and darted her eyes away from her husband—back to Tanis. "Tell me, Major, other than backing up people and products, how do you intend to keep this ship safe from saboteurs?"

Admiral Sanderson's mouth may have twitched in a smile. Tanis imagined he was quite happy to have someone else be at the receiving end of Abby's ire.

"Most of what I'm doing cannot be discussed without showing you the time-mapping displays, but one thing I've proposed is the completion of the starboard docking hatch ahead of schedule to allow direct delivery of product from inbound ships."

"That would throw our schedule out of whack considerably," Abby responded.

"In the near-term, yes, but if you look at the proposal I've suggested on the engineering boards under posting 472.9022.2 you'll see that after three months it will increase productivity 2% over what we were at before the heightened security measures took effect. This also requires that we only allow ships that were cleared by TSF forces at the port of origin to dock there. All other ships will still have to go through the triple check at MOS and on our docks."

"Numbers on that proposal look solid," Earnest spoke between sips of his drink, having reviewed the proposal over the Link.

"So it would appear," Abby grudgingly agreed. "How well it all works out remains to be seen."

Earnest winked at Tanis. "We'll discuss it at our morning engineering meeting tomorrow." His wife merely grunted.

"I just hope all this security is worth it."

"How can security not be worth it?" Admiral Sanderson asked.

<*Here we go,*> Evans said.

"There's security, and then there's just getting in the way," Abby replied.

"Without security nothing would ever be made. Security provides stability and that provides an environment for growth." Sanderson's tone was matter-of-fact.

"Just what you'd expect a military man to say." Abby rolled her eyes at the admiral.

"Now, now, folks." A voice boomed out from behind the Reddings. "No need to debate the rise and fall of civilizations. We're here to celebrate our successes."

Everyone turned to see Captain Andrews and Terrance Enfield walking toward them. Tanis had been expecting them ever since she was notified over the Link that the Marines at the maglev station had passed them through security.

"I'd rather be down in engineering." Abby didn't hide her distaste for the gathering.

"Now, Abby." Terrance flashed a slick smile. "You know as well as the rest of us that all this shoulder clapping and back patting is an important part of the process. People like to see their investment up close."

"They can see it all they want, just as long as they don't twiddle with it," Abby responded. Her husband laid a calming hand on her arm.

Terrance pretended not to notice her sour mood, a luxury the man bankrolling the construction of the *Intrepid* could afford. "I'll do my best to ensure no twiddling occurs." He turned to look at Tanis. "And you, Major, I must heartily thank you." His handshake was warm and firm. "Things would have certainly gone badly on the *Steel Dawn III* if it had not been for your intervention. I have to be honest; when I saw that Andrews and Sanderson had pushed your application forward I questioned their judgment. You do have a bit of a reputation, Tanis Richards."

"You're *that* Tanis Richards?" Abby looked Tanis up and down. "I have to admit, I wouldn't have expected someone so..."

"Pretty," her husband supplied with a smile.

Abby cast him a caustic look. "Yes, quite so...*pretty* to be the butcher of Toro."

"Guh..." Tanis shook her head. "I had forgotten that moniker."

Sanderson gave Tanis what could almost be considered a sympathetic look. "Between those of us standing here, the official report does not accurately represent the events of that operation. Suffice it to say that the major here ended up absorbing far more blame than she should have. To be honest," the admiral shuddered—an emotion so real it almost seemed out of character, "what her team faced was so...unimaginable that it couldn't ever be shown."

Tanis kept her amazement from showing on her face—and her dress, since Angela wasn't being a help on that front. She wouldn't have expected Sanderson to be her advocate, but he must have been aware of the truth to bring her aboard the *Intrepid*. "Her performance on the *Dawn* is a far better reflection of her record," the admiral added.

All eyes were on Tanis, regarding her in a new light, except for Andrews who must have known the truth as well.

"Well, let's hope that your devotion to the TSF carries over to your duties here." Terrance gave his smoothest businessman's smile. "Stopping that nuke certainly raises your estimation in my books."

Tanis gave a genuine smile in return. "I like to avoid being blown up as much as the next person."

"You're too modest," Captain Andrews said. "I look forward to seeing how your current security improvements pan out."

"They'll be an inconvenience at first, sir." Tanis was glad to be back to business. "But given time, the new protocols will become part of the process."

"I imagine they will." Andrews picked up a drink, as did Terrance.

"Well, we have to make the rounds. I'm certain we will talk more later," Terrance said.

"We'll join you." Earnest smiled and pulled Abby along with him.

"You should get out there as well," Sanderson said to Tanis, who nodded in agreement and left Evans' side.

It was the typical mix of high society and canny businessmen. Tanis had just stepped away from a military contractor who was trying to sell her on her company's improved Auth & Auth portal when a tap on her shoulder caused her to turn and come face to face with the MOS stationmaster. Tanis was expecting him to pay her a visit and was surprised he had taken so long to do it. She had, after all, commandeered a significant portion of his station.

"Major Richards, it is good to finally meet you." His handshake was a tad too firm, one of those grasps intended to signify superiority.

"Yourself as well." Tanis put on her most pleasant smile. "I hope you haven't found our new security measures at all inconvenient." There, it was out, let him either make a complaint or brush the issue aside.

"I can't say I enjoy having TSF troops assume control of several decks on my station." The stationmaster was going the more aggressive route. "I believe that our security is up to the task of keeping MOS in one piece. We've managed to do so for nearly a thousand years."

"Indeed you have." Tanis nodded, keeping eye contact. "But over those eight hundred and ninety-four years there have been several explosions on MOS that severely debilitated the station. In fact, nearly five hundred years ago an attack by a militant arm of the Mars Naturalists actually had the Mars government considering shutting down MOS altogether. In the end, TSF stepped in to provide security and the Marsian government refitted the station. So while MOS has handled itself well, it is also no stranger to TSF supplementation of its security."

Evans was standing within hearing range and couldn't keep himself from commenting. <*Do you ever pull your punches?*>

<*Not that I can recall,*> Tanis replied.

The stationmaster coughed into his hand. "That was some time ago, Major. I assure you that MOS can handle itself now."

"There have been other, more recent instances when MOS needed TSF and even GSS assistance." Tanis smiled a bit too sweetly. "I could outline them for you."

"No, that will be quite alright." The stationmaster glanced around anxiously at some of the nearby dignitaries.

"I assure you, we will leave no lasting impact. In less than a year we will be gone and you will be free of the added burden the *Intrepid* has been imposing on you."

Several groups in their vicinity appeared to have lowered their voices to better hear what Tanis was saying.

Everyone in the room was all too aware that MOS was laughing all the way to the bank with the money it was making from the construction of the *Intrepid*. It was by far the most profitable shipbuilding job that had taken place on MOS in decades.

The stationmaster fidgeted with his collar. "You misunderstand me, Major; the *Intrepid* is no burden at all. We are happy for your assistance with keeping the MOS secure."

"I'm glad to hear it, Stationmaster Stevens. If you'll excuse me, I have some routine checks to make."

The stationmaster looked like he had something else he wanted to say and Tanis resisted the desire to push him over the edge. The admiral most likely would disapprove of a scene.

After a moment he nodded curtly. "Of course." The stationmaster turned, his route describing a direct line to the bar.

<*I think he's going to bruise,*> Evans' warm laugh filled her mind.

<*He deserves to. I'm surprised he still has a job after what happened on the* Steel Dawn III.>

<*He's got ties with the Marsian government; cousin to the sitting premier; I believe,*> Evans responded.

<*Nepotism rears its ugly head again.*>

<*When hasn't it?*>

The evening progressed uneventfully and in time the dignitaries with adequate clearance gathered and made their way to the maglev station for their tour of the ship. Tanis went with the tour, both for security's sake and to get a firsthand view of more of the ship. The guests weren't being taken anywhere too dangerous, or too sensitive, but it was better than standing around in the ballroom. On top of that, she had a suspicion that Evans was considering asking her to dance. Tanis didn't dance.

The tour was uneventful until the maglev ride back to the VIP corridor. No alert had come over the security net, but Tanis sensed something wasn't right.

<*My gut tells me something is up.*>

Angela didn't respond for a moment. <*As much as it pains me to pay attention to your intestinal tract, I think you are right.*> Angela directed Tanis's attention to one of the shuttles arriving at the VIP dock to retrieve its passengers. A strange waver in its EMF signature caught her attention, almost as though something was obscuring its electromagnetic output.

Even as Tanis was issuing the order to belay docking for that vessel, it made its seal and the airlock cycled open. Security responded that the lock controls were compromised and they were unable to close it.

<*Initiate plan 102C,*> Tanis ordered over the security net. She stepped off the maglev train as the guards at the station ushered all the passengers that had begun debarking back into the cars and the train whisked out of the station toward the bridge. There, the captain and admiral would debark while the rest of the passengers remained secure.

Once the train was outstation, a new train rolled in with a platoon of TSF Marines on board. They deployed with smooth precision, secured the station and set up a barrier at the entrance to the VIP corridor.

<*Evans,*> Tanis called her second in command in the ballroom. <*Status.*>

<*All the guests are back in the serving area, but unfortunately its doorway also dumps into the main hallway, which would put us in the line of fire.*>

<*I know… We need to get a second exit on those ballrooms.*>

<*Hindsight.*>

<*Who's with you that's armed?*> Tanis asked.

<*I've got my sidearm and so do three others.*>

<*Suppressive fire only, though I hope nothing makes it that far down the hall.*>

<*Yes, sir.*>

Tanis's vision zoomed and she peered down the straight hallway to the dock. No movement at the airlock. So far. Four TSF Regulars stood like statues with their pulse rifles leveled at the hatch.

<*Angela, does* Intrepid *have any readings?*>

<*He's picking up some nanoprobes. So far the ship's countermeasures have neutralized them all.*>

Her HUD alerted her to laserfire down the corridor. She switched her vision to IR and saw the bodies of the four soldiers on the deck.

"Fuck," she swore softly.

Laserfire lanced down the corridor toward the maglev station. The *Intrepid* deployed refraction clouds and the beams played harmlessly against the TSF Marine's shields.

"Lieutenant Forsythe," Tanis called to the CO of the platoon. "We need to secure the ballroom to the right. Deploy your personnel in a scaled phalanx."

"Yes, sir!" The lieutenant nodded and signaled her staff sergeant with the particulars of the maneuver. One squad stayed behind to keep the station secure and the other two interlocked their shields and advanced down the corridor.

<*What's the tightest spot in that service passage above the corridor?*>

<*You're getting so lazy. It's in the specs.*> Angela sighed. <*Eighteen inches.*>

Tanis looked back at the squad guarding the maglev station. "Someone want to give me a hoist up?"

"Up where, sir?" A Marine bearing a corporal's insignia asked.

"Into the crawlspace above the corridor," Tanis replied.

One of the privates coughed. "In *that*, sir?" He looked her up and down.

"That's an officer you're gawking at, Mendez," the squad's sergeant growled.

"Aw shit." Tanis looked down at her new dress. "Someone give me a knife."

The sergeant handed her his blade and Tanis cut her dress off at the tops of her thighs. "Now hoist me up and no comments please."

At least the two privates who lifted her didn't ogle. Rank had some privileges after all. Clambering up into the access hatch, Tanis set a VIV on her HUD to Forsythe's vision as she advanced with her men below. The vision-in-vision showed the two squads advancing under steady fire from the airlock toward the entrance to the ballroom. They were over halfway there, and judging from the angles of fire the attackers were closing in as well.

The accessway had a small ledge for maintenance crews and Tanis scrambled along it, wishing she hadn't bowed to fashion and had simply worn pants. She could hear the shouts of the men below as they worked their way down the corridor, combined with the whine of the enemy's lasers and the Marine's pulse rifles. The corridor had never seemed so long and Tanis was certain she had drawn blood on her knees as she progressed. Luckily, the forces below her seemed to have battled one another to a standstill. Both were still over twenty meters from the entrance to the ballroom.

<*What's ETA on TSF accessing that docked ship externally?*> Tanis asked.

<*Currently show fifteen minutes,*> Angela replied.

<*Damn, we really need our own patrol force.*>

<*It's on order.*>

With her knees now freely bleeding, Tanis passed over the platoon, and a minute later she was positioned over the attacking force. Angela deployed probes through a grate and the team got their first clear look at the attackers. There were fifteen of them in heavy body armor—probably why the TSF's pulse rifles were doing little or no damage. She relayed the feed to Lieutenant Forsythe.

<*Looks like you'll need more than pulse rifles to stop these guys.*>

<*We're not authorized to use more than pulse rifles within the ship,*> the lieutenant replied. <*From the looks of their armor, conc and gas won't do much either.*>

<*Do you have any of that riot foam?*>

<*Not on board the* Intrepid.>

Tanis added that to her to-do list. <*Try timing your pulses to amplify the wave. You should be able to stun them. I've had my AI put a call in to the station's garrison commander for some riot foam. It should be here in twenty minutes.*>

<*These mofos are going to be cubing us with those beams by then,*> the staff sergeant growled on the combat net.

<*One minute, I'll think of something.*> Tanis turned her attention to Angela. <*Query the* Intrepid. *What do we have up here?*> She looked around at the various conduit and piping.

<Intrepid *reports a plasma conduit intersecting your location two meters to starboard. I believe we could use nano to slice it and deliver a stream of plasma onto their backs.*>

<*That'll make them take that armor off pretty fast.*> Tanis relayed the plan to Lieutenant Forsythe and ordered her to keep back from the enemy to avoid any damage. The *Intrepid* was monitoring the flow to ensure it was shut off before it burned through the deck.

Angela focused on the delicate procedure of slicing through the plasma conduit, while Tanis controlled other nano manually and used them to loosen the fastening for the grate.

<*This is a risky procedure, Major,*> Sanderson's voice came over the combat net.

<*The only other option would be to use beams or projectiles on them, and with the enemy between us and the bulkhead that would all but guarantee a little breeze in here.*>

<*I realize that, Major. Just be careful. And get stasis shields in that hallway before the next VIP event.*>

<*Yes, sir.*>

<*Ready to breach the conduit,*> Angela reported.

Tanis initiated a count on the combat net and fifteen seconds later a stream of plasma burned through the corridor's ceiling and sprayed across the enemy below.

Screams erupted as the attacking force dove out of the spray. The visual from the probes showed six men tearing their armor off and one down with a hole burned clear through his torso. The plasma flow to the conduit was cut.

<*Give me ten seconds, then fire high,*> Tanis ordered over the combat net to the Marines in the hall. She swung through the loosened grate and dropped six meters to the deck below. Landing in a crouch, she snatched a beam rifle from a fallen enemy. The steel deck still bubbled in places and Tanis stayed close to the bulkhead.

Three quick shots from her rifle took out three of the enemy trying to get out of their half-melted armor. Moments later, the ten seconds were up and Lieutenant Forsythe's Marines let loose a concentrated volley of pulse blasts.

Two other attackers, who were half out of their armor, fell backwards onto white-hot metal and screamed as their skin caught fire. Another three fully armored attackers also fell.

Tanis took quick stock of the armor the attackers were wearing. It was Trylodyne Mark VII; good enough for most situations, but weak under the arms. She checked the specs on the laser rifle and saw that it was a Westings A41, more than enough to slice through that weak spot.

One of the enemies, still combat-ready, spotted Tanis and pivoted to fire on her. As he took his shot, Tanis dove to the side and returned. The shot burned clean through the man's shoulder and out his head. He fell to the deck, spasming.

She fired at another man, nearly cutting his arm off before he was flung to the ground by the second timed pulse from the Marines. The volley knocked the remaining enemies to the ground and moments later the Marines rushed them, force shields pinning them to the deck.

The enemy's armor was power assisted and the Marines fired point-blank shots in an attempt to stun the mercs. One of them broke free from the chaos and lunged across the hall to hold a beam rifle to Tanis's head.

She froze, swearing at herself for not moving back once the Marines got in close.

"We go free, or she gets it!"

Before anyone could respond, a sound like a thunderclap echoed through the hall and the man holding the gun on Tanis dropped to the deck, his armor's face shield cracked.

"Damn that was loud, what was that?" Tanis looked around to see Evans holstering a ballistic sidearm.

"Told you I didn't want your job back." He grinned.

"My god, how on earth did you get that aboard a starship?" Forsythe asked, eyeing the weapon.

"Umm… I was my own CO for a while." Evans pulled an innocent face.

"Hope Sanderson doesn't have words with you over that. Since it saved my life I'm going to pretend I didn't see it," Tanis said.

Forsythe directed six of her men to secure the lock while they waited on word from the TSF team that was breaching the exterior of the shuttle at the hatch down the hall. Medical teams rushed in, attempting to save the attackers that had been doused with plasma, or that had fallen onto the hot steel.

"Goddamn…" one of them muttered.

<*Corridor is clear, sir,*> Tanis informed Sanderson.

<*I see that, Major. Breach team has entered the shuttle; they should have it clear in minutes. Be ready for any exiting combatants—we've merged the combat nets so they won't have any crossfire.*>

<*Thank you, sir.*>

"Commander Evans, let the folks in the ballroom know that their VIP selves are safe for the moment," Tanis said.

Evans chuckled. "They probably would like to be let out of the catering room."

<*Shuttle secured. There was only one guard and the pilot. If you could clear the airlock obstruction we'll move it to MOS dock A9.E,*> the lieutenant commanding the breach unit said over the combat net.

<*Excellent. We'll get that cleared up momentarily. Would you be so kind as to bring those two men out? We'll keep them with the surviving enemy combatants on the* Intrepid *for questioning.*>

<*Yes, sir, will can do,*> the lieutenant replied.

Tanis nodded to Forsythe who signaled the six men at the airlock to remove the brace that was holding it open. They took custody of the two men who were brought out to the corridor. With that done, the *Intrepid* was able to seal the airlock and minutes later the display above the lock showed the ship had undocked.

"Anyone for drinks?" Tanis asked the platoon with a smile. "It's an open bar."

ASSESSMENT

STELLAR DATE: 3227164 / 07.30.4123 (Adjusted Gregorian)
LOCATION: GSS *Intrepid*, Mars Outer Shipyards (MOS)
REGION: Mars Protectorate, Sol Space Federation

"That was quite the breach," Captain Andrews said to Tanis.

Admiral Sanderson, Terrance Enfield, and the Reddings were gathered in the bridge's conference room. Tanis's incident report was up on the table's holo.

"I guess that means the dockside security is good; they had to circumvent it." Terrance chuckled.

"I'm glad you find it funny," Sanderson growled.

Terrance's smile disappeared instantly. "Finding humor where I please is my prerogative. Don't think to claim credit for any of her success either."

Tanis sighed internally. That wasn't going to earn her any points, but she bit her tongue. The admiral didn't want her help defending himself.

"In two days we'll have our own fighters and patrol craft in place, which will seal up this hole in our security. Until then we should have the MOS TSF garrison provide us with additional support on our portside docks." Tanis spoke impassively, hoping to avoid any more comments about blame or credit.

"I've already put in the request," Sanderson said, not betraying a reaction to Terrance one way or the other. "They'll be checking every ship before it docks, unless it has a TSF grade 5A security token."

"What's the damage to the corridor?" Captain Andrews asked.

"It's a bleeding mess," Abby said. "I'm sure that plasma slice and dice you did seemed like a good idea at the time, but it burnt through several comm lines, coolant conduit, and a fuel line, which was empty, thank God."

"We queried the *Intrepid* before we did our little 'slice and dice'. It was either that or let them do whatever other unpleasantness they had in mind. I know you love your ship, but I'd feel a lot worse about a dead guest or Marine than I do about melted deck plate," Tanis replied.

Abby huffed, but didn't respond as her husband rested a hand on her arm. Tanis had a suspicion that her ship probably ranked higher that most of the VIP guests in her mind.

"Have you gotten anything from the boarders yet as to what their objective was?" Terrance asked.

Tanis addressed Terrance. "We're letting them stew for a bit, I'll sit with them tomorrow."

"They'll just have their nano rest them up," Sanderson said. "Waiting won't get you anywhere."

"They don't have any nano anymore. We've got some nice tools these days for making people a bit more pliable." Tanis couldn't help give a small predatory grin.

"That's an invasion of personal space." The expression on Captain Andrews' face showed his distaste for the act.

"It is. However, when someone has been convicted of attempted murder, part of the incarceration process is to strip their nano."

"Convicted?" Abby asked.

"Angela, my AI, has judicial authority in InnerSol space."

"Convenient," Earnest murmured.

"It has proven to be so," Tanis agreed.

"I don't know how comfortable I feel with this. Are you certain there are no legal ramifications?" Terrance stroked his thin beard, his expression uncertain.

"You are aware that the TSF is an authority cleared by SolGov to try, convict, and incarcerate criminals." It wasn't so much a question as a confirmation to calm him.

"I am… I'm just not used to them making decisions that so readily favor me." Terrance seemed to relax as he identified his own reason for concern.

Tanis found herself wondering—not for the first time—precisely why Terrance was backing the *Intrepid*'s mission. He was the head of the TRE Corporation, one of the largest privately owned companies in the Sol system. If he wanted to run a colony mission, why was he doing it through the GSS? The Generation Space Service had many inconvenient rules and guidelines he would be forced to follow.

On the other hand, the GSS had special access to additional data from the FGT, and it *was* the official organization for doling out terraformed colony worlds. Non-GSS-sanctioned colonization efforts of worlds terraformed by the FGT seemed to have a high failure rate—often with no explanation. The colonists simply disappeared in some cases.

"If I'm involved, we'll always be the wronged party; not only in the right, but the winners. It's part of my job description." Regardless of his motives, Tanis had to make sure the man paying the bills was appeased. "With your permission, I need to see a medic for some regen on my knees and get a good night's sleep before I begin convincing our guests to speak with us tomorrow."

"Your report is in order." Sanderson closed it out on the holo display. "Dismissed."

"Sirs, ma'am." Tanis nodded to the assemblage and headed for her quarters. Intrigue, confrontation, and now violent confrontation; the *Intrepid* was starting to feel like home already.

TAKE THE DEAL

STELLAR DATE: 3227165 / 07.31.4123 (Adjusted Gregorian)
LOCATION: GSS *Intrepid*, Mars Outer Shipyards (MOS)
REGION: Mars Protectorate, Sol Space Federation

Tanis looked from the sheets of plas on the table to the man in front of her. He was a mercenary; all of the boarders were. Not a lot of information could be found on him, but he did have ties to the Ardent Stars as well as Morning Glory, both of which were merc outfits.

The attack on the *Intrepid* was odd in that respect. Most mercs didn't go for the big jobs—too much negative impact on life expectancy. Something like yesterday's assault would only be taken on if the pay was very high or the job was expected to be easy enough to make it attractive.

Tanis couldn't imagine anyone billing yesterday's attempt to capture several high value VIPs as easy, so it had to be the money. Even if she discounted the mercs' salary, the sums required to get the shuttle, fool the docking AI, and facilitate whatever the getaway plan had been would be in the millions of creds. More than most people made in a lifetime.

"So let's go over this again, Mr. Drayson." Tanis leaned back in her chair. "You were hired by a man you never saw, never talked to, and whose name you never heard. You didn't broker the deal, that came through your organization. You simply took your cut and did the job."

"You got it, lady. That's how it works. I get paid, then I do the job. I don't hear names, I don't want to hear names. Things go a lot smoother that way, you get me?"

"Yeah," Tanis sighed. "I get you. Here's the thing, though. We've got a few of you guys, so if you've watched any vids where scum like you gets caught, you know that standard operating procedure is to offer a deal to the first guy that gives us good info. Everyone else spends a good long time helping in some public works projects on some frosty world." Tanis smiled. They both knew that frosty meant working on scattered disk objects at the edge of the Sol system.

"So what makes me so special I get the fancy deal? The other boys wouldn't play with you?"

"Nothing. I'll be offering it to everyone, you just happened to be first."

"An' if I tell you what I know I'm off the hook?"

Tanis snorted. "You stormed a GSS colony ship intending to capture or kill some very important people. No, you will be doing some time for this; you can just choose to do less time."

"How much less?"

*****

"So he talked then, did he?" Commander Evans asked.

"Actually, they all talked." Tanis leaned against the entrance to her office looking out into the SOC.

"You offered them all the deal? After what they did?" He leaned on a railing across from her.

"Yup, and they all took it, every last one of them."

"So they all get off with a light slap on the wrist?"

Tanis locked eyes with him. "I'm the Butcher of Toro. Do you think I'd do that? Angela gave them all minimum sentences."

The commander looked away, a slight flush rising on his cheeks. "That still doesn't sound all that bad."

Tanis relaxed her posture, unsure what was bothering him so much. "You didn't ask where they'd be serving it."

"OK, I'll bite, where?"

"Affixing boosters to comets," Tanis grinned, a twinkle in her eye.

"I thought you told them that they weren't going to be stuck on some ice ball."

"Commander Evans! Are you saying that I'm not a woman of my word?" Tanis's expression was one of mock shock.

The commander paused, unsure how to respond to Tanis's informality. "Uh... Kinda, sir."

"Well, they'll be working on diverting comets as they approach the sun, so they'll probably be fairly warm."

"Man, those poor schleps would have been better off if they never talked to you."

"I'm certain they'll share that sentiment."

Tanis did have a moment of pity regarding where she sent the men, but not that much. They had assaulted a colony ship. Her colony ship. It wasn't something that she would easily forgive.

"So then." Evans ran a hand through his hair. "What did we learn?"

"Two main things." Tanis looked down at a sheaf of plas sheets. "Firstly, that they never did meet the person that hired them—not that surprising. Secondly, that his name was mentioned once or twice, and it was Trent."

"Your nuke buddy from the *Dawn*."

"It not being him would be the coincidence of the century."

"I assume that you've tried to find the man in their org that arranged the deal," Evans said.

"I've got Terry working on it. She has a team looking at each prisoner's every move for the last year. She's also got a financial forensics expert trying to trace the money, but she's hit a bit of a dead end."

"How dead?"

"It appears that the money came from Tau Ceti." Tanis scowled.

"They're what, nearly twelve LY out?"

"Yeah, and I don't think anyone planned this little visit twelve years ago."

"I can't imagine that being the case," Evans agreed.

It went without saying; the list of corporations or governments with enough liquidity to send large sums to another star system, launder it, and send it back to sit in a slush fund for the day they felt like storming a colony ship was filled with powerful names.

"Well, it must narrow down the possibilities."

"Yeah, from billions to mere millions."

"Hey, if your job was easy, then a mere commander could do it."

Tanis smiled. "You did OK. At this stage, even I'm not going to be enough. I'm going to need to bring in the big guns."

INTERLUDE

STELLAR DATE: 3227165 / 07.31.4123 (Adjusted Gregorian)
LOCATION: Stellar Comm Hub #10.A.459.B.230.C-934

<*I've got news regarding the attempt.*> Trent sent the message over the private Link.

<*I've already heard.*> Strang's reply was terse.

<*Then you know. Our men were all killed or apprehended. They have impounded the shuttle as well.*>

<*I thought this plan was foolproof. They only had to advance a hundred meters and secure one ballroom.*>

<*They had a TSF Marine platoon ready that was able to hold our men at bay. My data indicates that they have a highly decorated intelligence officer handling their security now. She must have implemented some new measures.*>

<*How come I wasn't aware of her?*> Strang was growing less pleased by the second.

<*Apparently she's only been there for two days,*> Trent replied. <*Based on what I've learned, she's the woman that foiled our attempt to detonate our nuke on the docks.*>

<*You're telling me that she took control of three decks of MOS, brought platoons of soldiers on board, and disrupted every operation we have in a matter of days?*>

Trent didn't like where this was going. <*Yes, somehow she has managed to do just that.*>

Frustration seemed to fill the time lag. <*Do the job I hired you for, or I get someone else.*>

<*I'll take care of it. I have a new priority now. Eliminate Major Richards.*>

<*See that you do. I want daily updates.*>

THE 242

STELLAR DATE: 3227170 / 08.05.4123 (Adjusted Gregorian)
LOCATION: Gustav Expanse, New Africa, Venus
REGION: Terran Hegemony, Sol Space Federation

The whine of railguns charging sounded nearby and squad one rushed forward to take cover behind a low concrete embankment in the equipment yard. Moments later bits of rock and dust sprayed up into the air as the pellets from the rails smashed into the cement.

Staff Sergeant Williams threaded a scope over the barrier and took stock of the situation. The enemy was slowly advancing behind large CFT shields, which absorbed and refracted the Marine's lasers. The enemy's railguns, on the other hand, would chew the concrete cover apart in just a few minutes.

"Chang! Where're those heavies?" he hollered back to squad two, which was moving past several trucks on squad one's right.

"Thirty seconds, Staff," Chang replied.

<*Nearly in position,*> Williams reported to Lieutenant Grenwald on the combat net. <*Those bastards won't know what hit them.*> Grenwald signaled his acknowledgement and updated the objectives on the command net.

Squad two reached their designated position and the two slug throwers were assembled. Taking sight over the barrier, they readied the weapons with a smooth precision granted through plenty of practice. Once Chang was satisfied, squad two slid the weapons into position and let fire. Slugs over twenty centimeters long erupted from the barrels at velocities exceeding ten kilometers per second. CFT shields could stand up to pulses and energy beams without suffering so much as a scratch, but faced with the kinetic energy the slugs carried, the carbon fiber nanotube shields were torn to shreds.

What was once cover became deadly shrapnel as the shield fragments tore through the men behind them like they were made of paper. In a few short seconds it was over, and the heavies powered down the slug throwers.

Peering over the barrier, Chang grinned and swore. "Now that's some messy shit, Sarge."

"Just be happy I don't make you go clean it up for taking so long," Williams growled as he cast an uneasy eye at the amount of concrete the enemy's railguns had dug out of the barrier protecting the Marines. "Squads, advance!"

The platoon's objective was a communications array on the next hilltop. The original plan was to support an airstrike and catch any stragglers, but command had received intel regarding sensitive data on servers within the communications bunker.

The brass wanted to review it, so the Marines were heading in to do it the old-fashioned way.

"Man, I hate Venus." PFC Arsen vaulted over the concrete barrier and established cover for his squad from behind a truck. "It feels like it's spinning too fast. I swear it's making me dizzy."

"That's just your head reeling from how much your mouth moves," Sergeant Green said caustically. "Now shut up and keep your eye on that tree line. Scan's clear, but you never know when someone has left a surprise for you."

The two squads moved up; their fireteams advancing in a standard pattern until they reached the remains of the enemy troops. They were definitely a fringe group of radicals, their motley armor being the first sign, but the railguns they had were the latest spec. Several of the Marines were eying them and Williams signaled Lance Corporal Dvorak to wipe the ID systems on the guns. When they were safe to handle, he assigned one to each team's assist.

"Swap that out with your heavy gunner as the need arises."

Chang grinned. "I can definitely see the need to use this bad boy." He checked the ammunition and the reload action. "Why doesn't the corps give us weapons like this?"

"They're too concerned your ham hands would put a hole in one of their pretty ships," Dvorak said.

"They're the TSF's ships, don't see why the corps would care."

"Cause we're all one happy military now," Williams grunted.

"Yeah, I'd like to see those vacuum jockeys down here taking on enemy troops." PFC Perez kicked the twitching body of a fallen foe to make sure he was dead.

"I'd like to see you doing it too." Corporal Taylor gestured for Perez to move out.

Williams checked the command net to make sure that squads one and two were in position relative to squad three. The command net showed Lieutenant Grenwald making better time. Williams signaled his men over the combat net to pick up the pace.

<*Jansen.*> He singled out the lance corporal heading up the first fireteam in squad one.

<*Yes, Staff Sergeant?*> Jansen, one/one's team leader, replied in her trademark calm voice. She never raised it, not even in a firefight. She was on the way to making her corporal rating and Williams expected to see her move to NCO or possibly even OCS after this tour.

<*I want you to take your fireteam and scout ahead; keep at least a hundred meters up. We don't need any more surprises like that last batch.*>

<*Aye, Staff Sergeant.*> She directed her team to pick up the pace and slipped into the trees ahead.

<*Corporal Salas, I want you to take up a position parallel to ours, but two hundred meters to the north. We've got squad three to the south, so we're safe there, but I don't fancy a surprise coming around to poke us in the ass. You make sure things are quiet,*> Williams ordered.

Salas sent an acknowledgement over the combat net and led his fireteam off to the left, down the access road, then into the tree line.

Something felt off to Williams. The enemy had hit them too hard over the last several miles for this last skirmish to be their final hurrah. With the platoon nearly at the comm tower, a last line of defense was only logical.

He posted his concerns on the command net and waited to see if anyone agreed.

<*You really aren't a glass half-full type of guy, are you?*> Sergeant Li with squad three asked. <*There is a third scenario—they're up on the hill just waiting for us.*>

<*He's got a point, Staff Sergeant,*> Sergeant Green said. <*They could just be really bad at tactics.*>

<*That's not what intel says. It's also not what an advanced model of railgun says. These guys are better than that.*>

Lieutenant Grenwald put in his two chits, <*Well, you did take them out damn fast.*

Maybe they're not that good after all.>

Williams acknowledged that, but pressed his point, <*Granted, they probably didn't expect us to sling some M1409s at them, sir. Those aren't standard ordinance for a rifle platoon—something they wouldn't have planned for. Just keep your ears peeled and make sure tech keeps an extra close eye on scan.*>

The LT didn't counter the order, so Green informed Dvorak to keep an extra close eye on scan. Williams was glad that Grenwald had taken his word on the possible danger. He was a good CO as far as they went, though only two years out of OCS. Williams didn't mind so much; it was easier to shape the younger officers.

The Marines advanced down the slope toward a small creek at the bottom of the valley. From there it was up the hill to the communications array. He could see it poking through the trees: several directional and omnidirectional antennas jutting into the sky. Orders were to take as much of it intact as possible, but Williams' first concern was always for his Marines.

Williams had started his military career in E Company, 8th Battalion of the 242. Working his way up from PFC to Staff Sergeant had built into him the knowledge that this wasn't a job, it was a life. The men and women around him were family, closer than any flesh and blood. He was responsible for them and he was going to make sure that every single one of them survived this mission.

He kept that attitude firmly in mind; it was his mantra. The minute a sergeant started accepting the loss of the men he or she was responsible for, was the minute to get out of the military. His platoon needed him, needed his protection and he wasn't going to let them down.

That being said, he didn't mind if they were scared shitless of him. It made the enemy seem a lot less threatening.

<*I'm getting an odd reading across the stream,*> Jansen reported. <*I thought I caught an EMF sig, but then it was gone.*>

<*Fall back ten meters and secure the west bank. I'll send one/three south—two/one's already to the north.*>

<*Aye, Sarge.*>

<*I guess you were right,*> Sergeant Li said over the command net.

<*We've just crossed the stream to the south,*> the lieutenant said. <*We'll continue on course. If you need us, we'll be in position to come in behind them.*>

<*Yes, sir,*> Williams acknowledged. He sent commands to the fireteam leaders over the combat net, instructing them to spread out and take up positions flanking Jansen's team.

The comms went silent, only passive systems online. Even with the tech available to them, Marines still trained in using hand signals. They were silent, efficient, and needed no electricity to convey.

Once the teams were in position, Williams signaled Chang to set up one of the slug throwers in case the enemy was shielded. Then he signaled Jansen's team to make their way across the stream. One/one made the crossing at a point where there were several large rocks in the water—providing enough cover and white noise to mask their approach.

One/one's active camo made them hard to spot as they moved down the bank and into the water. Cassar, one/one's heavy gunner, was reaching the far shore when he spotted movement and lowered himself quietly into the water, propping his newly acquired railgun onto a rock. He held up four fingers and pointed to his two o'clock. Williams watched him slowly scan the tree line in front of him before the Marine flashed a full five fingers twice and pointed to his nine o'clock.

The Marines silently passed the counts down the line and Williams signaled his commands for the flanks to cautiously advance twenty meters across the stream and prepare to repel a flanking maneuver by the enemy. Once the teams were in position, he signaled Jansen's fireteam to begin.

If there were only fourteen of the enemy, the two squads had numbers on their side. He wasn't counting on it, though; intel suspected that the radicals holding the communications array had upwards of one hundred armed combatants in the facility. If things went the way they usually did, there were at least thirty of the enemy across that stream, all ready to take out the first clear target.

Of course, that's why the brass sent in Marines for jobs like this, not the glorified space force security guards.

Cassar opened up with the railgun, flinging fifty-gram ballistic shells at over twenty kilometers per second. They hit with the force of several sticks of dynamite. Instantly the Marines all realized he was firing fragmentation rounds—something which had not been apparent when the enemy was shooting at the concrete.

One thing was certain, it was effectively clearing the underbrush. A green-brown mist filled the air as the rounds tore through everything in their path, a red bloom appearing here and there as the projectiles hit flesh. A minute later he was out of ammunition and the squads waited for the mist to settle. From the looks of it, six men were hit. Silence rushed in, broken only by the crack of a branch tearing off a tree.

"That's why they won't give you one of those," Taylor whispered to Perez.

"Yeah, I wouldn't get within a thousand meters of you and a weapon like that." PFC Koller grinned. "It'd be suicide."

Without warning, laserfire flickered from the far side of the stream, focused at one/two's position and forcing the fireteam down into the brush. The enemy obviously had sound-sensitive targeting, but their actions revealed their own locations. The Marine's combat helmets traced the enemy's shots by the heat signatures the laser beams left in the air and squads one and two opened up with everything they had. Two other captured railguns whined as they charged and then the first ten meters of trees across the stream ceased to exist.

<*Thanks one/two.*> Chang laughed on the combat net. <*Always good to have someone playing bait for the rest of us.*>

<*Fuck you, Chang.*> Perez was checking his armor for burns.

Williams sent them both a slap across the combat net and reminded them that enemies were still across the stream—enemies who were now in possession of shiny new EMF emission data. Unfortunately, his necessary reprimand gave away his position as well, and he signaled dispersal to those around him and the other broadcasters.

Laser fire continued to flicker from the far shore and the Marines returned the favor, the opening volleys turning into a full skirmish. It played out for several more minutes before the sounds of the enemy retreating could be heard. Williams called for a weapons/wounds check while updating the command net with their positions and number of targets estimated to be eliminated.

<*One/three, attempt to determine the number of enemy casualties. One/two, your asses, front and center.*>

Corporal Taylor led his team to the Staff Sergeant's position and prepared for a tongue lashing. Williams looked them up and down, his displeasure a palpable thing.

"Why I don't put my boot up your collective asses and send you home is beyond me. However, it *is* nice to have a team that volunteers as bait. It also means that I don't need to get too attached to you assholes since you are all going to die soon." They took it well, like Marines.

"Next time one of you decides to start commenting on a firefight when we are maintaining a tactical silence, pretend you can't, cause once more and you'll all be physically incapable of communication!" He spat on the ground and took a deep breath. "You got me Marines?"

"Yes, Staff Sergeant." The response was quick and in perfect unison.

"Good, go swap places with two/one. You're on the left flank now. Don't let me down." After a verbal beating it was never a bad thing to give the team some responsibility. They'd be all the more eager to prove themselves proper soldiers.

"I think Taylor's gonna be numb for a week." Sergeant Kowalski walked toward Williams after sending Jansen on point again. "Becker estimates we got thirteen baddies. Hard to say for sure—he was counting heads, but he thinks he could be plus or minus one. I guess some of the heads didn't make it too well."

Williams nodded. "Taylor's right about one thing. There's a reason they don't hand out weapons like that in the corps."

"We gonna get a talkin' to from the brass for using 'em?" Kowalski asked.

"Maybe… Hopefully they'll take it as a fighting-fire-with-fire situation."

"Well," Kowalski grinned, "it's your ass, not mine."

"Thanks for the support."

Combat net indicated that squad three was in position and waiting on first and second to make it to their ready point.

<Everyone move out, we have our two corners to secure before we take the facility. I want to be in position in ten minutes.> Williams watched with satisfaction as every team moved on his command and began their ascent of the hill.

The facility was a squat two-story building with several outlying power transfer and storage sheds. Jansen's team silently took out four sentries and set up a covering position behind a power transfer shed that hid their EMF signature. Williams directed the two slug-throwing teams to set up positions at the northwest and southwest corners of the building. Squad three had the rear of the structure covered. Williams settled down behind a storage shed and scanned the combat net. The assault was scheduled for t-minus 6 minutes according to the clock ticking on his HUD.

Two/one would cover with the heavies and provide additional backup. Squad one was taking the front door. Two fireteams from squad three would secure the rear rooms of the facility and catch any escapees.

The count crept down toward zero as he scanned the facility. The enemy had to know the attack was imminent. Nothing showed, but he was certain that behind most, if not all, the second-floor windows were enemy troops all too ready to rain hell down on the Marines.

He saw movement behind one window in particular and passed the information along to two/one, noting with approval how Corporal Salas assigned the target and also had PFC Reddy run the intel over to Chang's heavy team. A man was spotted on the roof and Salas took care of that target as well.

Thirty seconds remaining.

Taylor's fireteam was to be first in, with Dvorak holding back until the facility was secured. They'd need him to hack the systems the brass was so interested in, and Williams needed to keep him breathing for that little event.

Squad one's teams were moving now, slow and silent, keeping to lanes out of sight of the building's windows. A moment later Taylor was at the door, setting a shape charge before flattening himself against the wall.

The sound was muffled, most of the blast erupted inside the building. Marine boots smashed into the door's remains and knocked them inward. A flash and a conc rolled in and one/one was back against the wall as the whine of railguns charging echoed out of the opening. No fire came, instead curses erupted from within the building.

The other two teams in squad one hadn't been sitting idle. While the front door action was underway, they were breaching ground floor windows.

A gunner leaned out of the window Williams had noted earlier and PFC Altair burned a hole through his head. At the same moment, Reddy took out the man on the roof with a shot from one of the commandeered railguns.

Before the sounds of pain within the building died down, one/one was through the doors; their IR scan showing the locations of the radicals inside, with three quick shots the entrance was secured.

Williams rose from his position and followed the squad into the building—time to finish the job.

HISTORY

STELLAR DATE: 3227171 / 08.06.4123 (Adjusted Gregorian)
LOCATION: Marine Troop Transport En-Route to TSS *Normandy* Orbiting Venus.
REGION: Terran Hegemony, Sol Space Federation

"So, we're being sent to Mars." Grenwald addressed his NCOs after wrapping up their post-op review on the transport back to the TSS *Normandy.*

"What's going on there?" Sergeant Li asked. "Aren't they usually pretty particular about anyone else doing a job they think their vaunted MSF can handle?"

"Wouldn't know about that," Grenwald said. "We're not going to the surface, but to the Mars Outer Shipyards where they're building that big colony ship, the *Intrepid.* They've got a major and an admiral with some sort of trouble that needs Marine boots to fix."

"*Intrepid,* eh?" Williams grunted. "That's the ship that Redding guy made the new super ramscoop for right? Supposed to be one hell of a ship."

Green leaned his seat back and stretched. "I don't really see what they would need us for, sir. Do they need us to shoot a contractor or something?"

Grenwald shrugged. "Not in the brief. I caught wind that they pulled up an MCSF from Mars 1 and have a couple companies of Regulars running security for the ship."

"Great," Li groaned. "We've got to play nice with Regulars? You know they're not really our biggest fans. Plus, they've already got MCSF to wipe people's asses. That's their specialty."

"She has a point," Williams said. The 8th Battalion of the 242 was Force Recon Orbital Drop; the TSF usually didn't deploy them to stations. The TSF usually didn't *want* them on stations. "What good are FROD Marines going to be at babysitting a construction job?"

"Well, as it turns out we were specially requested. I guess some of the folks on that ship have pull."

"Who made the request?" Sergeant Green asked.

"Some MICI major named Richards." The lieutenant sounded dismissive. "Probably just some hopped-up OCS brat who wants more attention than she deserves."

"Oh, I don't think so." Williams grinned at Kowalski, who had been with the platoon ten years ago when Major Richards, then a lieutenant colonel, was temporarily the de-facto commander of their battalion. "If she's involved, and called for us, we're going into the fire."

"You can say that again." Kowalski nodded.

"This major's been demoted?" Grenwald asked. "Is she *that* Tanis Richards?"

"One and the same," Williams nodded.

"Great, so we're going to the MOS under the command of some nut-job Micky major?" Sergeant Green rubbed his face with frustration.

"Hey." Kowalski smacked him on the back. "Don't knock it till you try it."

"Who cares about that?" Li was accessing data on the MOS over her Link. "There are absolutely *no* good bars on that shipyard!"

SETTING THE MEET

STELLAR DATE: 3227179 / 08.14.4123 (Adjusted Gregorian)
LOCATION: Mars Outer Shipyards (MOS)
REGION: Mars Protectorate, Sol Space Federation

"Major Richards!" Terry Chang called out as Tanis entered the SOC.

"Miss Chang, I'm guessing you've word regarding our uninvited visitors." Tanis walked up to the woman, who was clutching a sheet of plas tightly.

"Do I ever! I traced the mercs' organization and located the person in their organization who brokers the deals. The name is Daiki Tanaka; he or she operates out of Cruithne Station. There's a drop on a regional Mars surface net if you want to make contact with them. I've forwarded the protocols to your personal net."

Tanis reviewed the information. "Excellent. Good work, Miss Chang; we'll get somewhere with this yet."

"Yes, sir." Terry smiled and turned back toward the entrance to her labs.

Tanis found it amusing how the civilians had started calling her sir; it didn't take long for the military way of things to take over.

<*You realize you're not the only military personnel on this ship, right?*> Angela asked. <*I know your ego may have trouble with it, but it could actually be a cumulative effect.*>

<*Perish the thought.*> Tanis smiled to herself as she entered her office and brought up a 3D map of the solar system on the desk's holo.

<*Looks like Cruithne is almost at aphelion while we're on the same side of the sun. That actually makes for a fairly reasonable trip.*>

<*Want to have a little chat with this Daiki in person?*> Angela asked.

<*I think I may want to do just that.*>

<*Protocol for contacting this person is a bit convoluted. They've got to have the exact right amount of data in the right place before they'll respond. Get it wrong and you're blacklisted.*>

Tanis chuckled. <*I'll bet that doing it from some place as net-invisible as this office would raise some suspicions as well. We should head down to Mars 1 to do it.*>

<*Better yet, send someone else to do it, the more steps from us, the better.*>

<*You spoil all of my fun.*> Tanis sighed.

<*I do try.*>

Commander Evans poked his head into Tanis's office. "Major, not sure if this is your cup of tea or not, but one of my pilots has a few spare tickets to the InnerSol championship game between High Terra and Mars 1."

Tanis looked up at Evans. "Championship game for what?"

The commander sputtered for a moment. "The uh…you really don't know?"

"Sorry, sports aren't really my cup of tea."

"Uh…I see." He gave her a look like she had two heads. "It's only the first time in over a hundred years that High Terra has made it into the InnerSol finals. It's only going to be the most amazing football game ever."

Tanis shook her head. "Not my idea of a great time, but I do have something for you to do while you're down there."

<You need serious work on your colloquiums.>

Commander Evans' look was completely unreadable.

INTERLUDE

STELLAR DATE: 3227182 / 08.17.4123 (Adjusted Gregorian)
LOCATION: Mars Outer Shipyards (MOS)
REGION: Mars Protectorate, Sol Space Federation

"We've got the response." Ouri sat down across from Tanis's desk and dropped a secure sheet of hyfilm in front of the major.

"Positive I hope." Tanis passed a token over the SOC net to the hyfilm. Its contents were scrambled and took a moment to render before Tanis's eyes.

"We've got a meeting at a bar on Cruithne Station called 'The Human Condition'," Ouri summarized.

"Odd name..."

Ouri shrugged. "I guess so. So, who are you sending out there?"

"Sending?" Tanis asked. "I'm more interested in going."

"Going? You can't be serious… Sir." Ouri tacked on the honorific after catching a raised eyebrow from Tanis.

"I am indeed serious. Things are quiet at the moment and I intend to take advantage of that. I'll never be more than a few light minutes away. I'll be certain to keep a laser comm trained on the *Intrepid.*"

"The admiral will never clear you for it."

Tanis smiled and Ouri knew she wasn't going to like the response.

"The admiral never has to know."

CRUITHNE

STELLAR DATE: 3227185 / 08.20.4123 (Adjusted Gregorian)
LOCATION: Cruithne Station
REGION: InnerSol, Sol Space Federation

Tanis looked out the porthole at Cruithne Station as the transport matched velocities with the asteroid habitat. There wasn't much asteroid visible anymore, though here and there a bit of raw rock did show between spurs and domes. Originally merely an aggregation of ice and iron no more than five kilometers across, the station had expanded far beyond those bounds into a sprawling structure over one hundred kilometers long. Her access to the structural design showed that none of the original asteroid remained.

Normally, once the resources from such a body were exhausted, there would be no further reason for mankind to remain, but Cruithne orbited the sun in resonance with Earth, always on the same side of Sol. Depending on where it was in its year, it was either accelerating away from earth or Earth was accelerating toward it. The result was a very useful location for transporting shipments in and out of InnerSol. In addition, Cruithne also crossed the orbit of Venus and Mars from time to time, further adding to its list of useful locations.

This was one of those times when Cruithne would come very close to Mars and the trip only took two days, something Tanis was grateful for as the transport she was on wasn't at all passenger-friendly. The crew was even less so. They were either ignoring her or coming on to her. Tanis had gained a great familiarity with the walls of her berth.

When the shipnet announced a seal and equalization, Tanis was moving down the corridor before the station rules finished posting. She wasn't terribly worried about them—other than the fact she was certain to break some.

Cruithne fell under the jurisdiction of the InnerSol portion of the stellar federation, but only nominally. It was owned and run by an old family of traders, and had been for as long as anyone could remember. They were wealthy and not overly concerned about scruples. The combination made for a station that looked like it was out of the vids from the early third millennium. It was readily apparent that one of the reasons the family was so wealthy was that they didn't bother with preventative maintenance…or cleaning.

Tanis moved out onto the dock and immediately had to navigate around an argument between the ship's supercargo and a repair crew. It seemed that the crew was repairing part of the life-support system at the transport's berth. The main cargo hatch was completely blocked off by conduit hanging from the ceiling like vines in a jungle, and more than a dozen pulled-up deck plates.

After circumventing the mess, Tanis logged on to the station net while Angela chatted up the traffic and mass balancing AI for information. She checked the public areas to see if there were any alerts or warnings that would affect her plans before beginning a slow circuit of the station.

Even though she didn't expect any—or much—trouble, knowing the lay of the docks and where clever hiding places or distractions could be found was never a bad thing. More than one vendor hauling carts filled with random trinkets and knickknacks trundled along the dock. A larger than average population of greasy food carts was also in evidence. She suspected that some of them must be doing double duty both keeping a lookout and smuggling items onto various ships.

Tanis was undercover, her net presence and ID switched to a new record that Angela and Ouri had set up. She was certain that they had picked this particular disguise as a joke or some sort of punishment for overworking them.

She was masquerading as a Golist, a religious sect of quasi-cyborgs who believed in reaching enlightenment by minimizing motion and being at peace with oneself. They also were fierce traders. The religion's roots were an odd combination of capitalism and Taoism.

Because she wasn't a cyborg, the sect's regular attire was not comfortable at all. Ironically the part of her that was the most comfortable was her head where nearly all of her skin had been removed.

Covered in a silver metal, with only a sliver of skin around her right eye still in place, her head had a slightly ovoid shape. The liquid steel that covered it could take any form, but the standard pose was a totally expressionless mask with no mouth, nose, or ears.

<I think the look is good on you,> Angela said. *<It's very minimalist.>*

<You are the last person to give advice on appearance. I saw what your last body looked like before you were lodged in my head. It was like some artist's nightmare.>

<Be quiet or I'll hack your face and give you horns.>

<That might actually fit.> Tanis glanced at her body in a mirror and took a moment to reconcile what she saw with her inner image.

Her body was covered in a polymer that coated her like a second skin, which was somewhat uncomfortable as it really wasn't meant to wear over skin, but typically in place of it. She had opted for the temporary discomfort as re-growing the skin on her face was going to itch enough as it was; she could suffer a few days to save the weeks of itching and scratching across her entire body. The glossy white covering was largely inflexible; not that strange since the Golists deplored excess motion. Tanis had allowed for more movement in the arms than was typical, but her legs were essentially straight as a beam and ended in fine points that hovered several inches off the deck. It took a good bit of power to achieve that effect, which meant that most of her thigh muscle was waiting for her back on the *Intrepid*, the area it usually occupied now filled with SC batteries.

<I swear, Ouri dreamed this up to get back at me for something.> An itch began to twinge way behind Tanis's right knee.

<Golists frequent Cruithne. It is a very good disguise, and one that no TSF operative has ever used before, according to the records. No one will expect it.>

<Well yeah! Any person who volunteers to wear this should have their head examined.>

They passed several Golists and Tanis passed tokens to them, their avatars nodding serenely to one another on the general net.

<I assume they should be candidates for said head examination?> Angela asked.

<Especially them.>

Tanis spent a few hours working her way through the commercial district, identifying several routes from the bar where she was to meet the contact to the vessel she would be leaving on. She also checked calendars on the local nets to ensure that no maintenance or large shipments of cargo would get in her way.

Eventually the time for the meeting drew near and Tanis made her way to The Human Condition. She was not entirely certain she wanted to see the reason the venue went by that name.

Tanis entered the bar and crossed to where the servitor, a human in this case, was busy pouring drinks. The place was clean, the walls a gleaming white, the décor mostly steel and plas. All in all it was pretty stark, meant to draw the eye to the fact that the tables and chairs were made of humans. Not dead humans by any means, but live humans, mostly with little modification, and a lot of clamps and rods holding them in place.

The scene brought back memories of Toro—images of people turned into things, artwork and worse, flashed through her mind.

<Remind me to check how legitimate this place is,> Tanis said.

<I already have; all of these people are paid employees. Paid fairly well at that.>

<You couldn't pay me enough,> Tanis said. *<If nothing else, I'd be bored out of my skull.>*

<Wouldn't they just spend their time on the net?> Angela asked.

<Doubtful. What's the point of having a person turned into an object if they can escape it and not even be aware it's happening? A joint like this would make sure they had no Link and were only experiencing this reality.>

<You couldn't pay me enough for that even without the confinement and degradation.> Angela's avatar shuddered.

Tanis considered what had been required for her current cover. *<I know what you mean.>*

There were several dancers at various stages between human and things decidedly not human slithering up and down poles, and in one case, mostly embedded in the pole. Tanis observed with Golist serenity, admiring the dancers' wholesale devotion to their expression by merging their human physicality with an expression of inner self. Privately, Tanis reaffirmed her position that some people's inner selves were just weird.

Tanis closed her eye—the other was currently covered over by her flowmetal—and calmed herself, exuding a zen-like peace as she waited for her contact to arrive. That didn't mean that she wasn't paying attention to what was around her. One of the advantages of the fluid metallic covering was that she had optical sensors all around her head, giving her a 360-degree view of the bar. She wondered if it would be possible to retain the ability after this mission, depending on whether the TSF let her keep the flowmetal—something she considered unlikely.

As Tanis surveyed the scene, one of the dancers caught her eye and she watched the person move around a series of poles near the center of the establishment. She wasn't entirely certain if it was male or female, or if such designations even applied. It appeared to have no bones, or if it did, none were evident. The dancer's general shape was that of a lithe woman, but it was totally asexual, and while it often bent at what would normally be the locations of joints, at other times entire limbs became fluid and snakelike.

As its dance progressed, Tanis saw that it was also able to change the overall dimensions of its body, almost as though its skin were no more than a stretchy membrane. Its stomach distended at one point, and then it grew breasts, moments later to lose them and become smooth and featureless again. Its head would swell and become conical and narrow and wrap around a pole before thickening and resuming the shape of a normal human skull.

Tanis had to admit she was impressed; whoever this dancer was, it had some of the most extreme modifications she had ever seen. If it wasn't for the abstract beauty of the dance, Tanis would have thought the creature wasn't human at all. Dance was something that could always betray a lack of humanity. Any machine or AI would inevitably have some evidence of math or an artificial lack of math in its dance. It was something that was hard to spot, but Tanis had watched enough dancing to know there was a certain element to organic dance and expression was not something a machine could replicate.

<*Nor would we want to,*> Angela interjected. <*Even the notion of something as…random, yet orderly, as human dance is…completely undesirable.*>

<*I know you feel that way. It only makes sense that your desire for order and understanding would leave no place for an abstract expression of emotion.*>

<*You know, you humans really are all just like those people that are tables in here. You want, no, you crave the overriding influence of your emotions and chemical feelings. Without them you feel like you aren't somehow proper or complete.*>

<*I don't think we are all like those people at all. Most of us strive to achieve a balance between our emotions and abstract impulses, and our logical and orderly thought process as well,*> Tanis countered.

<*Well, those people certainly don't crave that.*> Angela referred to the human furniture pieces.

<*It's hard to say. I think it's entirely possible that they are overridingly logical and analytical people, so much so that they are unable to be abstract and emotional much of the time. Perhaps this is how they strive to achieve that balance.*>

<*Or they just really need the money.*>

Tanis laughed; not outwardly, her face currently having no mouth, but she found Angela's ever-prosaic attitude amusing.

They continued their silent observation of their surroundings until a message came over the establishment's local net informing Tanis that their contact was waiting for them in the rear of the bar. The message contained directions to a dressing room. She hovered past the other patrons to a hall in the rear and through a door with the label "Adrienne" on it.

The inside of the room was plush and opulent, a distinct difference from the austere look of the common area outside. There were several holo mirrors, showing a 360-degree view as Tanis stood in the center of the space waiting for her contact to show up.

The lack of a second exit unnerved her and she assessed the structure of the walls to see if she could break through them if needed. They were little more than a thin plas and she determined that with a few blasts of a pulse rifle she could create an additional exit should the need arise. The moments ticked by and then the door opened, revealing the identity of Adrienne.

It was the fluid dancer. She—"Adrienne" seemed to imply gender—slinked into the room, passed Tanis and sprawled onto a mound of cushions, her form melting over them.

"You must be Yora," the woman said. I am Adrienne, as you may have guessed."

A connection presented itself over a secure Link; Tanis opened it and responded.

<*I am. You are to be my contact for this arrangement?*>

"So, to the point and without pleasantries. Normal, I suppose, for one of your type. You sculpt yourselves into paragons of beauty and power and then abstain from pleasure entirely. I, personally, would not be able to resist."

<*My presence is merely an outward expression of my inner serenity,*> Tanis replied. <*I take my pleasure from witnessing the expressions of my fellow Golists and knowing that they too strive for enlightenment.*>

"I never understood why someone seeking enlightenment would also want to control corporate interests," Adrienne said. "The notions seem to be in conflict. I, on the other hand, have no such desires. I only wish to surround myself in comfort and pleasure."

<*Control is the only route to enlightenment. Whether it is control of oneself, or of one's surroundings. Both are paramount.*> Tanis watched the woman smile lazily. <*But I did not come here to discuss my order's philosophy. I understand that you represent a certain organization that is available for forceful ventures.*>

"There are actually a number of groups that use me to help them acquire work. You could consider me something of a broker. What sort of venture are you planning?"

<*There is a location I have interest in, but a company has laid claim to it and expressed the opposite of interest regarding its sale. Because of certain…incidents…they have availed themselves of extra security measures that have proven…difficult to overcome. The time of my patience is over and the time for a more direct application of pressure has come.*>

"So you're looking for some muscle, are you then? Any particular needs?"

<*They need to be capable of spatial insertion, either by small shuttle or EVA. They must also have heavy combat gear and not be afraid to fire beam weapons in a station.*>

Adrienne sat still for a moment, only pulsing the odd limb as she considered the requirements. "I think I can hook you up with a group that has done such things in the past. They could most likely field a team of twenty or thirty for a job like this."

<*Have I heard of them? What are their credentials?*>

Data was delivered to Tanis and she looked it over, examining specs and the oblique descriptions of jobs performed. It matched the data on the group that had attacked the *Intrepid* and she determined that the time for her disguise was over.

<*I think you should tell me about who hired them for their last job.*> Tanis's tone brooked no discussion.

"Their what? Why would you need to know that?" Adrienne asked. Shock rippling—literally—across her face.

<*Because they attacked the* Intrepid *and I want to find out who hired them.*>

"You're TSF?" Adrienne asked. "I have to admit, that's a pretty extreme cover."

"Thank you." Tanis allowed the flowmetal to form a mouth since her cover was no longer necessary. Besides, her voice could be very menacing. "You're going to tell me everything you know about their job to attack the *Intrepid* and you're going to do it with a song in your heart."

"You don't think I haven't…" Adrienne's smug expression drooped into surprise. "You've got a suppression field!"

"Well, it wouldn't do for you to call in whatever thugs you have on hand to stop our little conversation. I don't think we need for this to get unpleasant, but I won't really mind if it does."

Adrienne sat silently for a moment, then in a flash her entire body moved toward the far wall. Tanis realized there must be some sort of open vent that the woman could fit through. Reacting on instinct, Tanis pulsed her hover system and leapt into the air, coming down into Adrienne, the needle points at the ends of her legs piercing what would be a normal person's calves.

Adrienne shrieked, twisting in pain, and Tanis spat a glob of flowmetal over her face where it flowed into Adrienne's mouth, swelling to block out further noise.

"Easy now." Tanis's tone carried no small amount of menace. "This can get a lot worse if you don't cooperate."

The look Adrienne shot at Tanis said it all; she wasn't willingly going to give up the person who had hired the merc crew. Whoever it was, Tanis was certain it must be a big player. Most of the time an agent like this wouldn't hold back after being skewered.

<She's going to take some more work to break,> Angela commented. *<Her body is her pride and joy; I think your route will be through that.>*

Tanis re-established a direct Link to Adrienne. "I'm not afraid to slice and dice you, you know. All I want is a name. Who did the hiring for the crew that hit the *Intrepid*?"

<There's no way I'm telling you. He's not the sort of guy that's really forgiving of people that leak his activities.> Adrienne was scared, but she was obviously more afraid of whoever she had dealt with.

"No problem." Tanis exuded calm. "We'll just go the standard route, making you more scared of me. You see, I'm currently a little outside the scope of my assigned duties, if you get my meaning. Not a lot of people know where I am, and even if anyone does link my whereabouts to the remains of your mutilated—but not dead—body, they'll not get upset. Not only am I going to hurt you until you give me a name, but I'll leave you alive for whoever you're so afraid of as well."

Tanis altered the state of the plas on her arms to allow motion at the joints and reached up to her head. There, she extruded a thin rod of metal. She took it into her hand where it formed a gleaming blade which she lowered to Adrienne's left leg.

Adrienne's face slipped into an expression of fear. "Who…who are you?"

"Oh, I forgot to mention. You may have heard of me. The media called me 'The Butcher of Toro'."

<About time I get to make that work for me.>

<I think it actually always works for you,> Angela replied.

<Tell that to the color of my oak leaves.>

She began slicing into Adrienne's leg, though the skin, which appeared to be almost like neoprene in composition. Adrienne's eyes bulged in pain and her arms flailed, pounding the deck on either side of her. Tanis felt resistance as the blade met the cartilage that served as bone. She grimaced inwardly at the feel of it.

<OK! I'll tell you.> Adrienne's communication was laced with panic and fear. *<The name was Trent…he didn't use any other. I checked his creds and he's known as a broker for some big interests, but I don't know anything else. Here are all of the account codes for the credit transfer.>*

A rush of numbers and data memory blocks flowed into Tanis's mind, where she passed them off to Angela.

"Excellent." Tanis slid the blade out of Adrienne's leg. A panel on her torso slid open and she pulled out a med-patch, which she slapped on the wound none too gently. "The nano in here will hold you together long enough to get to a medic." Tanis was about to extrude more flowmetal to bind her captive when the door crashed open and a terrifying figure stood in the entrance.

True to the strangeness of the locale, the muscle was unconventional. It was a woman, though that was evidenced only by the stylized breasts on the gleaming black torso. All of the woman's limbs were gleaming black as well. They were also all very thin, nearly emaciated—a look that was offset by the woman's head, which was a large ovoid devoid of any features.

"Hurting Adrienne was a mistake." The voice emanating from the woman's featureless head was soft and sultry, a rather odd combination considering the delivery.

"Possibly," Tanis agreed. "But it was a calculated mistake; does that make it any better?"

The figure raised its hands and Tanis realized they weren't hands at all, but merely the ends of the gun barrels. Handy…and disturbing.

<No pun intended I hope.>

Tanis dove to the side, or more accurately, cantered to the side as the guard fired flechette rounds at her. The initial shots missed, but then a few hit Tanis, some ricocheting off her chest, a few striking solidly enough to crack the plas covering her body.

Tanis angled forward, pulsed her hover system to its maximum and balled her hands into hard plas fists. She smashed into her bizarre adversary, and they flew through the opening into the bulkhead beyond with enough energy to lodge the woman's head in the wall. Not waiting to see how long it took the freakish enforcer to extricate herself, Tanis sped down the hall at top speed. She burst into the bar area and wove past the sinuous dancers and the human furniture.

Outside the bar, she made a quick course adjustment to avoid colliding with several hovers that floated by. She raced behind one and angled herself to float horizontally alongside it. The man driving the hover cast her a strange look, but didn't say anything. No point in getting involved in other people's issues on Cruithne.

Angela deployed nanoprobes and they watched the black-skinned woman emerge from the bar and scan the traffic outside. She moved into the throng and started making her way in the direction Tanis had gone. Most likely she had access to external cameras that had let her know which way to go. Tanis slipped ahead of her cover and raced through the crowd, still horizontal, and hopefully out of sight. Her earlier wanderings proved beneficial as she made use of several establishments and predictable throngs to mask her escape. Moving through a maze of levels and across the main hub of the station she worked her way toward her departure craft.

The original exit plan for leaving Cruithne wasn't so precipitous as reality dictated, however, the times on the departure clearance requests displayed submission times only minutes after their arrival on the station. It was almost as though Angela knew her. Less than an hour after the confrontation in Adrienne's dressing room, Tanis was pulling away from Cruithne and heading back toward Mars.

Trent. Not surprising; it just added fuel to the reaction when it came to hunting him down. The real key now was to see if the information would help her trace who was paying Trent's salary.

DRAW THE NET

STELLAR DATE: 3227189 / 08.24.4123 (Adjusted Gregorian)
LOCATION: GSS *Intrepid*, Mars Outer Shipyards (MOS)
REGION: Mars Protectorate, Sol Space Federation

Tanis eased into the chair at the head of the SOC's conference table. Her leg muscles were still sore after being pulled out and replaced; high heels adorned her feet to ease her down after having her feet en pointe for days. The flowmetal still covered her head, but she had gotten an additive to change it to her skin's color and texture. In a few days she would have it removed, but first she needed to debrief her people and be brought up to speed.

"That was some crazy jaunt you went on." Evans' voice held a hint of reproachfulness. "And that getup you went in. I don't know how you stood it, barely being able to move for days."

"It really wasn't that hard." Tanis shrugged. "Once I was on my way I was pretty much committed to seeing it through."

Everyone else filed in as they spoke. Once they found their seats, Tanis called up the data she had retrieved on the table's holo.

"So all roads lead to Trent right now. He's the guy who did the nuke job and the guy who hired the mercs. We haven't worked out who he's taking orders from, but it has to be someone with deep pockets."

"It seems weird, sir," Ouri said. "Why would they have those mercs ready to disrupt the VIP event if the nuke was supposed to have gone off? If it had, we certainly wouldn't have been throwing any parties."

"Don't forget," Lieutenant Amy Lee said, "the ball was supposed to happen four days earlier, but was postponed because one of the transports from Venus was delayed. They must have had the mercs on standby or called them back in after the nuke failed."

"Right you are." Tanis reached up to run her hand through her hair and was reminded that she currently didn't have any. "Damn cover…" she muttered.

"It's a good look for you, Major." Evans grinned, a mischievous twinkle in his eye. "Gonna get your skin back?"

Tanis regarded him for a moment, tempted to spit a glob of metal over his mouth. She decided not to, but only because it abused and undermined her authority. It was still a close call.

"Yeah, I'm trying to get the procedure scheduled for tomorrow. I know I really can't feel it, but I swear this stuff itches like mad."

"So what's our next move?" Terry Chang asked, steering the conversation back to the topic at hand.

"Well, we need to figure out who Trent works for. Hopefully some of this data"—Tanis gestured to the holo—"will help us out. That's going to be you and you." She gestured to Terry and Ouri. "You've got the lab AI and feel free to ask Angela for help as well; we've got to figure this thing out before we get hit again."

Everyone regarded her seriously and nodded.

"I also noticed in your reports that there have been several anomalies lately." Tanis brought up the pertinent data.

Ouri nodded. "We've had some little bits of sabotage on some inbound shipments. We've traced most of it back to various anti-colonist folks. Stuff from Earth is especially prone to being tampered with. The effects have been minor, but it's the things that seem to be happening after cargo gets checked in that is upsetting me."

Tanis had not read the reports in detail and signaled for Ouri to summarize as she scanned them.

"Well, we had one instance of some lithium being 'misplaced'. It was put in a cargo pod when it was due for engineering. That was relatively benign. We've had some other instances of equipment that checked out fine upon arrival, but was broken when time came to use it. As much as I hate to say it, I think we have someone inside of our security curtain."

"I'll spend some time looking over various logs, but you folks know what to do there. See who was on, who was around, that sort of thing. Also, it's possible that someone is managing to use someone else's access. Check and see if there is anyone that seems to be in certain areas without going through any surrounding checkpoints."

Ouri nodded. "Good call. I wasn't going to do that since I didn't think anyone could penetrate the exterior with fake credentials, but you're right; once in, they could get to more benign areas with less overview."

"Well, folks, you've been doing good work; I'll leave you to continue it." Tanis rose. "I've got to go face the firing squad now."

"Otherwise known as Admiral Sanderson?" Evans asked.

"So he found out, did he?" Ouri asked.

Tanis grimaced. "He got back from Mars early and tried to find me for a progress report meeting. Apparently he wasn't pleased that my progress had me elsewhere."

RELATIONSHIPS

STELLAR DATE: 3227211/ 09.15.4123 (Adjusted Gregorian)
LOCATION: GSS *Intrepid*, Mars Outer Shipyards (MOS)
REGION: Mars Protectorate, Sol Space Federation

Tanis and Commander Evans were relaxing in the officer's mess, enjoying a bit of time away from the SOC and a few of the perks of rank. Tanis had to admit that she was enjoying Evans' company quite a bit of late. She had even privately admitted to herself that if they weren't both military she would consider pursuing him—maybe it would be possible after they got underway and were no longer officially in the military. In the meantime, she would take what time in his easygoing company she could.

"So how are things looking out there?" Tanis asked before taking a bite of her sandwich.

"Tidy as you could dream. Not a single ship is deviating a millimeter from its plotted course." Evans leaned back in his chair and took a long drink from the cup of coffee in front of him.

"Those rumors of 'Trigger-happy Joe' I spread about must be doing their work." Tanis grinned around her mouthful of food.

"Ugh...were you raised in a barn?"

"Sewer, actually."

"Really?" Evans' expression was a cross between shock and curiosity.

Tanis nearly choked as she laughed. "Now that was a funny look...of course not," she said when she was finally able to breathe.

Evans grinned sheepishly. "You have an amazing poker face. Remind me never to bet against you."

"You're in luck, Commander; I'm not a betting woman."

"You've been here over a month, eventually you could just call me Joseph."

Tanis's face grew more steely—not from the flowmetal, that had been removed and her natural features were back in place. "Now, Commander. I don't think that would be appropriate. It's imperative that we keep our relationship strictly professional."

"I...er...I didn't mean that, sir," Evans said.

Tanis gave him a dead serious look for a long moment before breaking into a wide grin.

"Damn!" Evans shouted. "That's just cruel.... You took a decade off my life."

Tanis chuckled. "Don't worry, Joseph, you can get it back in regen."

"There, theatrics aside that wasn't so hard was it...Tanis."

"You're mighty forward for being so jumpy." Tanis smiled.

"I must have a split personality," Joseph replied. "But keep that on the QT, I don't want to lose my pilot's credentials."

"No fear of that; you've got things in such good shape I'd let it slide even if it were true. Your wings are top notch."

"Well, with the number of people applying for this colony we've got top people in pretty much every profession on tap."

"It certainly is handy."

"So... Anything of interest happening on the dock side of things? Bombs, kidnappings, rumors of dire plots?"

"Unfortunately it's been quiet as a mouse."

"How's that unfortunate?" Joseph asked.

"See, that's why you'll never be a real intel officer. With what those guys were willing to do up to this point, you can bet they haven't given up yet."

"Or maybe I'm smart enough to know that if I make everyone *think* I don't have an eye for this stuff I'll still get to fly a fighter from time to time."

Tanis pondered that. "You could have a valid argument."

"Hah! I knew you secretly wanted to be a pilot." Joseph grinned.

"That's where you're wrong; I'm actually certified to fly R1 through R17 spacecraft."

Joseph's face showed his appreciation. "Is there anything you can't do?"

"Stand-up comedy. I tried once and totally bombed." She was once again expressionless.

He chuckled. "I don't know about that, you have pretty decent timing."

"Yeah, but if you think I'm totally infallible you'll expect perfection all the time." She took another long draught of her coffee—good strong stuff. "On a slightly more serious note, I do have to meet with the captain and admiral. The MOS stationmaster is making noise and filing some annoying requests with the courts. We've got to head him off at the pass before he undoes all of our security enhancements."

Joseph gestured magnanimously. "Go ye forth and meet with your betters."

Tanis stuck her tongue out at him as she rose and left the room.

The bridge wasn't far from the mess, only a half kilometer up the length of the ship plus three decks. A tube and a maglev train had her debarking at the command deck's main hall. Walking past the corridors leading to various offices, and the desks of the flunkies who jealously guarded access to those offices, she entered the bridge's foyer. What she saw startled her quite a bit.

Where a couple of couches and chairs used to be was now a tall white woman surrounded by an array of holo interfaces. Taking a second look, Tanis realized this woman seemed to be merged with the ship somehow. Her hands were racing over the interfaces and thick strands of what couldn't possibly be hair waved slowly around her head as she concentrated on the displays around her.

As she approached, the woman looked up and Tanis found herself staring at shockingly brilliant blue eyes, a stark contrast to the sea of white that was the woman and her instruments.

"Major Tanis Richards. So glad to finally meet you; I'm Amanda." The woman extended a hand which Tanis shook—the other still racing over the holo interfaces.

"I'm...pleased to meet you," Tanis said, regaining her composure and accessing security logs, trying to determine how a person such as this could make it onto the ship without her knowing about it. "Though I must say I am unsure of who you are."

"What? Other than Amanda?" Her laugh was cheerful and light; something that Tanis found difficult to harmonize with her clearly cybernetic exterior.

"Sorry, I mean what you're doing...what your job is. Wait...Amanda. Isn't that what the ship's AI has been calling itself lately?"

"Major, that hasn't been the ship's AI—that has been me."

"But I've been contacting the ship, how is it that I am getting you?"

"It's something the Reddings had been working at for a while. The *Intrepid* is too vast an AI to easily communicate with humans. I'm effectively the ship's avatar."

"So you're partially the ship?" Tanis asked.

<*You can be so dense,*> Angela said. <*And to be honest I can't believe you thought the ship was 'Amanda'. What she is to the ship is somewhat like what I am to you. She resides in the* Intrepid*'s mind like I reside in yours, except the connection is even stronger with them.*>

"Yes," Amanda said. "That is rather accurate."

"So you're just going to be…installed here for the whole trip?" Tanis asked.

"Oh, of course not." The silvery laugh sounded again. "That would be fairly taxing. No, there is another woman like me being prepared—Priscilla. I met her the other day. We'll be doing a ninety-day on/off rotation. The Reddings are concerned that without the time off it will be hard for our minds to remain…well…normal."

"This must be quite the unique situation. I can't say I've ever heard of anything like it before." Tanis felt like her eyebrows were in her hairline.

"That's because there hasn't been anything like it before," Amanda responded. "Bob is an incredibly advanced intelligence…"

"Bob?" Tanis interjected.

"That's what I call the *Intrepid*'s AI—mainly because I couldn't refer to him by such a bland and rather asexual term. He's most certainly male, and Bob fits him nicely."

"Never thought of him as a 'Bob'." Tanis said.

<*You would if you knew him,*> Angela commented.

"So I guess we'll be talking a lot. I talk to, or thought I was talking to, the ship a lot." Something about Amanda was making her a bit uneasy…not surprising really, the idea of someone being melded with the ship in this way was rather surreal.

Amanda nodded. "Pretty much everything going to the *Intrepid* from the human side goes through me. Even a lot of AI use me, since Bob is far more advanced than any of them. Not that he's a snob, but they're really quite beneath him."

"He's really that high grade?" Tanis asked. "I mean the AI that run Mars 1, or the Callisto rings for that matter, must be far more advanced."

"The plural is the key there," Amanda said. "Hundreds of AI run those rings. Bob is just one guy, keeping an eye on the whole show. It was partly out of need that the Reddings made him so advanced, and partly—I'm convinced—that they simply couldn't stop themselves from doing so once they realized it could be done. It would be like if you realized you could raise all children so they could read at six weeks. Wouldn't you do it? Wouldn't it be a crime not to?"

Tanis absorbed that. "Well, I can't speak for the children part of things since I've never thought of having any, but I suppose I can relate to the desire to improve."

"You really should be going, by the way," Amanda said.

"Damn, you're right; they'll be waiting for me by now."

"Good luck." Amanda flashed a winning, if rather plastic-looking, smile. "For what it's worth, I think Sanderson likes you."

Tanis shook her head as she walked away. He'd never given *her* any reason to think that.

TARGET

STELLAR DATE: 3227212 / 09.16.4123 (Adjusted Gregorian)
LOCATION: Mars Outer Shipyards (MOS)
REGION: Mars Protectorate, Sol Space Federation

Tanis stepped off the maglev train and into the main transfer terminal outside of the MOS administration block. In the middle of the station, a series of holo kiosks featuring various figures from Marsian history were directing visitors and answering questions. Tanis skirted them and walked down the main corridor and up a short flight of stairs to the offices of the stationmaster.

While the block was far from rundown, it was apparent that the MOS was past its prime. Its near thousand-year history showed in mixed architecture and designs, as well as scuffed moldings and worn surfaces.

When the Mars Outer Shipyards were built nearly a thousand years earlier, much of the advanced technology that went into assembling interstellar ships still came from Earth. However, over the years industry and commerce shifted to the point where Mars was the technological center of InnerSol. Because the need to dock larger cargo ships diminished and more equipment was manufactured on Mars 1, it became more economical to build ships closer to the ring at the Mars Inner Shipyards.

Over recent centuries, another shift had occurred. Callisto had risen to become the most prominent and advanced human habitat, and much of the latest tech was once again being shipped in. While the Mars Inner Shipyards were still the busier of the two shipyards, the MOS's capability of docking hundreds of vessels made it ideal to handle many of the shipments that would be lowered via the elevator system to Mars 1 or the MIS. The change was evolving the MOS from a shipyard into a commercial hub.

"All that pesky progress..." Tanis muttered to herself.

Ahead, in a lavish outer office that was definitely much newer than the rest of the administration section, sat Stationmaster Stevens' assistant. He didn't look up as Tanis approached, but spoke as soon as she was in earshot.

"Major, Mr. Stevens is running late. He'll be here any moment; please have a seat."

Tanis shrugged and took a seat, ignoring the flickering plasines beside her. They were all packed with election coverage from the Marsian surface. It was horribly boring stuff, what with the race being between only two candidates, neither of them striking Tanis as being all that notable.

With one eye on her surroundings, Tanis worked through some of the streams of issues that needed her attention. Token on a dangerous shipment clearing security needing follow-up, review the inbound Force Recon Marine platoon coming to the *Intrepid*, and approve the transfer of a few security checkpoint violators to MSF. The usual. For all the potential excitement of running security on the largest colony ship ever, very little had been in evidence lately. Something she was certain that Stationmaster Stevens was going to emphasize heavily.

After several minutes of administrative catch-up, she noticed the assistant quirk his left eyebrow, his tell that he was getting a message. Sure enough, Stevens was ready for her and, with an imperious air, the assistant waved her through.

Stevens' office definitely displayed the fruits of the shipping upswing on MOS. Over half of the furniture was made of wood, the most common excess of mid-level administrators. By the visibility of a few nicks and dings, Tanis gauged the wood to be soft, perhaps poplar or pine, though it was covered in a dark stain. Various third classical era sculptures decorated most of the flat surfaces. The effect was really more of a confused antique shop than an administrator's office.

Stevens was sitting behind his desk and rose to shake Tanis's hand. He was a lanky man, moving into his second century according to the records. It especially showed in the thinness of his skin—something which heralded the need for another regen.

"Hello, Stationmaster, what warrants the need for a personal visit?" Tanis asked.

"Major." Stevens inclined his head as he shook her hand. "I felt that a personal meeting would allow me to better communicate my concerns to you." He indicated she should take a seat and Tanis did so as he eased back into his large chair.

He appeared to be gathering his thoughts and Tanis suppressed both a wry look and a sarcastic remark about Stevens' general ability to communicate. "I wasn't aware of any pressing security concerns; is there something I'm not aware of?"

Stevens quirked an eyebrow. "I strongly doubt there is anything occurring on the MOS that you are not aware of, Major. However, I challenge you to list any one thing that is a notable security issue."

Tanis couldn't help grinning. "What about that genetic contraband that came through TrenCorp's warehouse yesterday?"

"Sorry." Stevens didn't look amused. "I meant security issues that are remotely your concern."

"Can we not get into this discussion again?" asked Tanis. "I make comments about the *Intrepid*'s history and the breaches that have affected it, you say that those issues are resolved; I say they were resolved by me and my measures. If that's all I came down here for, then I'll be going." Tanis made to rise.

"Sit," Stevens said wearily. Tanis lowered back into the chair. "No, I do not wish to rehash those conversations. This morning the Marsian Security Council passed a resolution stating that the TSF has overstepped its bounds by seizing the broad levels of control they have here on MOS. The resolution states that only dock A9 and C3 at which the *Intrepid* is berthed may be under their control, and all access to MOS security networks level C1 and higher will be restricted."

Tanis leaned back and took a deep breath. "I heard about that." She paused, watching a slow smile spread across Stevens' face. "I wish you'd mentioned that was what this was about; we could have done this remotely."

"What do you mean?" Stevens looked like his moment of triumph was being stolen from him.

"I already knew about the MSC's decision, is all," Tanis said simply.

Stevens' shoulders slumped. "I take it you've already circumvented it…"

"No, even I can't work that fast." Tanis couldn't help but grin. "However, I did get an injunction placed against it pending a Federal SolCourt appeal. The appeal is scheduled for seven weeks from now. I've forwarded you the date and location."

Stevens sighed. "I can see why they brought you on."

"It's what they pay me for." Tanis rose. "If there's nothing else?"

He had nothing else and she left Stevens' office with a small smile on her lips.

<Lucky that judge owed you a favor,> Angela said.

<Too true, though I imagine Terrance could have pulled a string or two if he had to. However, this way I look a bit better.>

<You're a bit too concerned with what Terrance thinks of you.>

Tanis thought perhaps she was, but wasn't going to admit it. *<They brought me on board to take care of security. If I have to bring legal proceedings against the entire planet Mars, I will. That's just part of the job.>* Angela sighed, but didn't respond—all too aware that Tanis was just being pretentious.

Ahead, Tanis saw a problem at the maglev station. It appeared a superconductor had failed and the train had skewed off the track. People were moving through the side passageways, checking their Links for the best way to get where they needed to go. Tanis did the same and saw that most of the displaced traffic was going up two levels to an alternative line that ran laterally through the station. However, the car frequency was lower and it would be backed up in no time.

She found a lift running down thirty-six levels to a large lateral maglev almost directly below this one. It would get her back to the *Intrepid* without too much delay.

The lift was only several hundred yards inward, down a lightly traveled hall through which she strode with minimal attention to her surroundings. She monitored the MOS Sec net as she walked, checking to see if Stevens was putting out any notices to his staff. From there, the lift took her down to level S20A in less than half a minute and Tanis stepped out, still focused on monitoring the MOS security chatter.

Almost immediately, rough hands seized her and pulled her off her feet. By instinct, Tanis slowed her perception and took stock of her surroundings. More than two hands grasped her—a pair of attackers—each holding a shoulder and a wrist. Angela deployed nano and Tanis used the data to map out a series of attacks.

She wrenched her right shoulder forward, pulling it from the grip it was caught in. The motion hurt her wrist, but that didn't stop her from delivering a reverse kick to the solar plexus of the man to her right. The pain in her wrist subsided as he let go, gasping for breath. Her right side free, Tanis swung her arm around to strike at the other man's neck. With quick reflexes, he blocked it. However, the movement allowed her to slip from his grip as well.

Tanis completed the spin and saw the first man gasping for breath out of the corner of her eye as she drew her sidearm and aimed it at the second man's head.

He was just as quick on the draw and they found themselves staring down the barrels of each other's weapons.

"I'm going to ask you only once to lower your weapon," Tanis said.

"Not likely," the man replied. "There's a hefty price on your head and we intend to collect."

Tanis turned her body to the side, presenting a smaller target, and shot the man in between his eyes before he could react. "I said I'd only tell you once." She turned to the first attacker, who had finally managed to catch his breath. "I'd bet good money you have a weapon or two on you. Hand them over slowly, or I'll spray you all over the bulkhead."

The man muttered a curse as he slowly drew a handgun out of his waistband and handed it carefully to Tanis. "You may have got us, but there'll be more. There's so much money on your head that people are lining up to take you out."

"I guess they better fill out their expense reports in advance." Tanis didn't let her weapon waver a millimeter. "Because a few people have expressed similar sentiments in the past, and as you can see, I'm still here."

He dropped two guns on the deck and she stood with her weapon on him for several minutes, not speaking, until a TSF unit showed up and took the man into custody. Leading them was Joseph.

"Commander, I have to admit I'm surprised to see you here."

"I was actually taking a maglev to admin; they screwed up my flight plan filings again and I was going to ream out the person responsible in…well…person. Anyway, the main route is backed up, so I used the lateral on this level. I picked up your message on the *Intrepid*'s security net; met these boys en route."

Tanis nodded and looked to the TSF Regulars. "Corporal. Take this man into custody. I haven't had a chance to check him over thoroughly. I want him detained in the security center on A9.2. Take these leftovers with you." She gestured to the body on the deck.

"Sir." The corporal saluted and two of the men with him began doing a weapons scan on the man. The third strapped an antimag bar to the dead man and activated it. The corpse lifted off the ground and once the weapons check was complete they took the prisoner and body away.

REFINEMENT

STELLAR DATE: 3227213 / 09.17.4123 (Adjusted Gregorian)
LOCATION: GSS *Intrepid*, Mars Outer Shipyards (MOS)
REGION: Mars Protectorate, Sol Space Federation

"You're going to need to take an escort with you from now on," Admiral Sanderson said after Tanis reported the attack.

"As much as I hate the notion, I agree." Tanis nodded. "In fact, all senior and key personnel should have an escort. It would be far worse if Abby or Earnest was killed than me."

"They'd have to leave the ship first for that to happen." Terrance laughed.

Sanderson grunted his assent. "On the upside, this will probably help out in getting that moronic resolution the Marsian legislature passed overturned."

Tanis laughed. "Stevens sent me a formal apology for the security breach, though there were undertones in his message suggesting he thinks I set it up. He's probably cursing his heart out in that tacky office of his. As far as security, we'll use Forsythe's MCSF platoon for security details, a fireteam for each VIP, and keep Grenwald's men for tactical responses.

"Are you certain that won't stretch our resources too thin?" Terrance asked. He had come up from Mars to check on the status of several key milestones in the engine tests and invited himself to the meeting.

"I've got more TSF Regulars being called in for our normal security duties. Lieutenant Ouri now has six companies under her, which is causing some issues as they obviously are all run by commanders. GSS first lieutenants are close to the rank of TSF commanders, but it's starting to cause some issues. I haven't had to back up her orders yet—a testament to her tenacity—but she is spending more time making sure they aren't doing things their way than I'd like. She's due for a promotion shortly and I'd like to push it through."

Sanderson nodded. "No reason not to. She's colony, so it's not like we're messing up someone's organization. Send me the appropriate files and I'll see that it happens with all due haste."

"I don't know that I'll need one of your teams," Terrance said. "I've got my own private forces that are second to none."

"That you do, sir," Tanis replied. "And when you're on the MOS they'll be augmented by one of the Marine fireteams. Your guys may be good, but they don't have the resources we do, or the ability to legally start shooting holes in whatever gets in their way."

Terrance wore his dangerous smile again. "I see your point, Major."

Captain Andrews brought the discussion back on track. "Though I have no issues with added security, I would prefer to see the threat removed, rather than abated. Have we made any progress in tracking down who is behind all of this?"

Tanis hadn't seen much of the captain over the last few weeks, but the signs of his efficiency and enthusiasm for the project were everywhere. She could always tell the quality of a captain by his ship, and Andrews was top notch.

"We've got a 94.7 percent probability that it is a Jovian concern backing these actions. From the looks of it, two of the attacks that happened before I arrived were actually anti-terraforming groups. Once we excluded all data pertaining to those incidents, we were able to hone in on a few key banks on Callisto and Titan. A large number of shell corporations and even extra-solar interests were in-between, but we navigated past them. Those banks only deal with the top tier of corporations in Jovian space. We're definitely looking at an industrial opponent."

"I suppose that makes sense," Terrance said. "They would definitely need big money to pull off what they've done so far. And there are several companies in Jove's sphere that would like to take me down a notch."

"Three hundred and ninety-two, from what I can determine." Tanis smiled. "Though only two hundred and seven use those banks."

"Ouch…I didn't realize it was quite that high. I wonder what the solar total is."

"Seven hundred and four," Tanis supplied.

Terrance laughed ruefully. "Wasn't wondering that much."

"Sorry, sir. I'm told I tend to be a bit too literal sometimes."

"So do you have any top suspects?" Captain Andrews asked, fingering his silver hair.

"A few, sir." She fed a stream of data into the conference room's net and a list of companies and their particulars rose up over the table.

"First off we have Barum, Inc. They manufacture ES components and were in a very large bidding war to supply the *Intrepid*—mainly the components for the ramscoop. They lost the deal; the company, which was already in a downward spiral, went down further. One of the owners has made personal threats against you, Terrance. They recently managed to pull themselves out of the toilet and now have the capital to carry out what we've come up against. They've also had several other dealings with your companies that have left them…well…soured."

"I can see how they wouldn't be my biggest fans." Terrance nodded as he looked over the data. "I didn't think they were that far along on their recovery, though."

"They recently had a very large sum come back from Tau Ceti, either after being laundered, or possibly as a return on an investment. Their corporate statements for that period aren't yet public and we're having to tread carefully in 'accessing' records in Jovian space, what with the latest flare-up in the federal government."

Captain Andrews nodded. "Your caution is wise. I can see how money from Tau Ceti would move them up your list."

"Aye, sir. We're looking into their activities quite carefully. We've also got a few other Jovian interests, but none that match up quite so well: the Arnell, Stellar Dynamics, Neutron Cartwright, and Mallar Isotopes." As she listed off each one, corporate information rose above the table, coupled with the data points that potentially linked them to the attacks, or the funding thereof.

"There is also, of course, the STR consortium," Tanis added. "They don't have any particular reason to dislike you, sir, but they are building the GSS *Dakota* and we all know how much they are frothing at the mouth to get the New Eden colony. Especially after the latest data the FGT has sent back."

"Can't say I blame them." Terrance nodded his agreement.

"Right now we're following up on all of those leads and should know more for our next briefing."

"Very good, Major." Admiral Sanderson nodded. "You're dismissed."

Tanis rose and saluted the men before she left the conference room.

"Quite the laundry list of suspects." Captain Andrews steepled his fingers as Tanis walked to the exit. "Though considering all of the possibilities, it is a fairly succinct tally."

"Well, I hope we find out who is behind this sooner or later. With those critical engine tests coming up I have enough on my mind," Terrance said.

INTERLUDE

STELLAR DATE: 3227213 / 09.17.4123 (Adjusted Gregorian)
LOCATION: Stellar Comm Hub #129.A.236.B.945.C-294

<What on earth were you thinking?> Trent said. *<MOS was going to get control of their docks back. That would make our operation here much easier!>*

<First, I don't appreciate your tone, Trent. Second, it would have only gained us short-term access. After the next breach they would have tightened up security again. Getting rid of Richards is key.>

<But opening the floodgates to mercs and bounty hunters? You had to know they'd bungle it.>

<So far they have done no worse than you. If you want to prove yourself, perhaps this will shame you into actually doing something constructive about the problem.>

LAKE CABIN

STELLAR DATE: 3227216 / 09.20.4123 (Adjusted Gregorian)
LOCATION: GSS *Intrepid*, Mars Outer Shipyards (MOS)
REGION: Mars Protectorate, Sol Space Federation

Tanis was wrapping up some administrative logs before the end of the second shift when Ouri poked her head into her office.

"Evening, Major."

Tanis looked up at the commander. The last week or so had seen a change in Ouri. Her commander's bars had given her an increased sense of authority and her job performance had gone from great to excellent. The added clarity to the chain of command was also improving the efficiency of the units under her; as a result, the entire security organization was vastly improved.

The best part of all was the visible improvement in Ouri's character. Tanis wasn't certain if it was the smaller gap in rank between the two of them, or the lower stress level from having a smooth-running operation, but the end result was a much more personable subordinate.

"Commander, good to see you. How are things?"

Ouri smiled and Tanis returned it in kind. "Quite well; I've got all the reports filed and up to date."

"I never worry that you won't," Tanis said.

"So, I was wondering if you'd want to come down to my cabin for dinner."

"What? I'm being invited to one of the infamous Ouri cookouts I've heard so much about?"

"Well, sir, I would have invited you before, but a lot of enlisted and junior officers come down. I didn't think you'd really want to mingle—separation of rank and all that."

"Rules and regs, I wouldn't want anyone thinking they're all chummy with me and that I'll let things slide," Tanis replied with a grin.

Ouri chuckled. "I think you have absolutely nothing to worry about on that front."

"So what warrants the invite now?" Tanis asked, quirking an eyebrow.

"Well, sir, now that I've also moved up the chain it doesn't seem quite right to be spending too much time with the people under me, at least in the smaller gatherings. I've just invited officers, or civilian department heads from around the ship. I thought maybe you'd like to come. Mostly it's people from here at the SOC."

Tanis looked down at the plas on her desk and considered all of the work she had to do, but decided that the irony of going to a log cabin on a lake that happened to be inside one of the most advanced starships ever built was something she couldn't miss out on.

"Real cookout with fire and everything?"

"Big fire, sir."

Tanis grinned. "Call me Tanis when we're off duty."

* * * * *

The cabin was just as Tanis had pictured it.

It sat at the edge of a lake, not a large one, just a kilometer across or so. A young forest was growing up around the waters. The trees had been accelerated and were perhaps ten meters in height. A slip with a canoe tied to it jutted into the water. Up a small path was a clearing with a thick lawn and, set back against the trees, a homey cabin.

"This is really your quarters?" Tanis asked.

"Yup, I go to bed here and wake up here in the morning." Ouri nodded.

"How on earth did you swing this? I mean, aren't there millions of people lining up to be on the botany side of this mission?"

"I know a guy who knows a guy." Ouri paused, a mischievous smile playing at her lips. "That and I spent over a hundred years on various terraforming ventures. I'll be co-managing the north continent's stage 3a terraforming when we get to New Eden."

Tanis stopped, regarding Ouri with a calculating look. "I've read your file. There's no mention of any of this in it."

"Well, I have two separate registered identities. There's no link between them."

"That's…unusual." Tanis ran a hand through her hair, stopping when she realized she was doing it. If Ouri wasn't being so casual about it she would have been very suspicious.

"The short version is that I was at the wrong end of the pointy stick a few times when I was managing terraforming projects. GSS pulled me into their protective custody and I found I really enjoyed that line of work as well. I enlisted and well…here I am."

"So now you can kick ass and terraform planets." Tanis laughed. "That's quite the unusual combination."

Ouri chuckled. "It certainly wasn't what my career advisor mapped out for me."

No one else had arrived yet, and Ouri led Tanis into the small cabin. Inside was a dichotomy of clutter that matched what she now knew about Ouri's dual life.

"This is both everything and nothing like what I expected," Tanis said.

"I live to be an enigma," Ouri grinned. "Would you mind taking those two baskets out to the fire pit? I've got to change out of this uniform."

Tanis looked down at her own dress uniform and sighed. She should have stopped off at her quarters to change. After carrying out the baskets she came back in to see Ouri running a brush through her hair. She was wearing a red and yellow sundress that looked quite stunning on her. It was always amazing how much better people looked in civilian clothing.

"You're going to get all the boys." Tanis laughed.

Ouri looked down at herself and then over at Tanis. "Sorry, I guess I didn't think you'd have anything else. You know how it is with us juniors; we figure the SOs must have been born in their uniforms."

"You realize you're a senior officer now too." Tanis smiled.

"Damn…just when I thought I'd gotten used to it, my subconscious reminds me I haven't."

"You'll get used to it."

"I do have a few autofit dresses you could look at." Ouri led Tanis into her bedroom and after a few minutes they picked out a sedate blue sleeveless dress that came down just past Tanis's knees. It snugged up to her body and she examined herself in the mirror.

<*Best you've looked since you ruined that dress at the ball,*> Angela commented.

After borrowing Ouri's brush Tanis helped carry the last loads out to the fire pit—platters of meat for the night's feast.

"Real meat?" Tanis asked.

"Yup, from right here in Old Sam. First generation; we've been testing out the protocols for herbivore initialization."

"Where do you get the time for all of this?" Tanis asked as they laid condiments out on a wooden table. "I mean…I work you to the bone."

Ouri smiled as she lit the grill. "Well, I make time for the things I love. I'm pretty good at this stuff, but I also seem to be pretty good at keeping people from blowing the ship up. They're kinda interconnected."

Tanis laughed. "So they are."

"I also offload a lot of stuff onto Amy Lee." Ouri chuckled as the grill came to life.

"God does she ever." Amy Lee came strolling down the path with Terry Chang in tow. They had several baskets full of beverages, which appeared to be mostly of the alcoholic variety. "I'd complain to her boss, but that she-devil would probably figure if I had time to complain I must have time for more work." Amy Lee grinned, but then stopped short, her face turning red as she realized who she had just spoken to. "Uh…er…Major. I didn't recognize you out of uniform."

Tanis smiled at the second lieutenant. "We're informal here, Amy Lee. Besides, I've got a really thick skin."

"It's actually true." Joseph arrived with a few others. "I've needled her both physically and verbally to prove it—as you can see I survived to tell the tale."

Tanis felt a small jolt of elation that Joseph had shown up. She had been hopeful, but didn't want to come right out and ask Ouri.

"Yeah, but only just barely." Tanis cast Joseph a stern look. "Amy Lee's one of the ladies, she gets special dispensation. You've about used up all of your get out of jail free cards."

Joseph put on an innocent face. "Me? I'm a paragon of cooperation and agreement. I have to be. I saw what happened to all the other men under you who didn't toe the line." He winked at Tanis as he stepped past her to put his load of bread down on the table.

Her gaze lingered on him a moment too long and he brushed against her shoulder at the same time. Tanis looked away and caught fleeting expressions of recognition on the faces of Terry and Ouri. It would appear the attraction growing between her and Joseph wasn't going unnoticed.

Their thoughts were obvious on their faces: so the major was human after all—and apparently falling for the dashing young commander. Too bad they were in the same chain of command.

Ouri began her hosting duties, greeting and introducing all the visitors as they arrived. A few assistant heads from the SOC that Tanis knew came down the path next, as well as the division head for stage three terraforming on the colony roster. The chief New Eden 1 station engineer came a bit later; she would be the woman in charge of taking the two habitation cylinders and mounting them to a space station when the *Intrepid* reached its destination. Her escort was the head of habitat environmental systems, a large-framed man with an easy smile and the biggest moustache Tanis had ever seen in person.

"A damn fine job you've done with your neck of the woods," he said to Ouri as he surveyed the area around them. "You've turned what was little more than dirt two years ago into a very nice place indeed." He turned to Tanis and gave her a hearty clap on the shoulder. "And you're the lassie I understand we owe being in one piece to."

"I'm just happy to be here."

"Believe us when we say we're happy too," said Erin, the station engineer. "You're doing a fantastic job."

"I want to get out of here as much as the next person. Just doing my part." Tanis hated all the compliments.

"Not *here* here, I hope," Ouri said with a smile as she handed out drinks.

"Only in as much as *here* is still in the Sol system." Tanis accepted the offered beverage. She looked up at the arching landscape overhead, just beginning to be draped in the shadows of dusk. "Once we get outsystem, here is a place I can see myself frequenting in the future."

Later in the evening, Tanis found herself sitting with Ouri and Joseph around a fire that had been made by some of the revelers for the purpose of roasting marshmallows.

"I've been looking over the proposed duty schedules and I realized something odd." Ouri slowly rotated her marshmallow over the fire.

"Mmmm?" Tanis said around a mouthful of sticky goo.

"Well, I don't have a debarkation date for Abby and Earnest," Ouri said. "I think they're staying on."

"Huh? That can't be right. What would people like them be doing on a colony mission?" Joseph asked.

"I know," Ouri said with a nod. "That's what's so strange."

Tanis gave momentary debate to telling the truth and decided to do so. "They're trying to keep it hush hush," she said after finally managing to swallow the three marshmallows in her mouth. She erected a security barrier around them and put a hand over her mouth to mask her lip movement. "From what I can tell, they're coming along. Even stranger, I think Terrance is coming too."

"What? Why's he coming? Doesn't he have some big multi-world corporation to look after?" Joseph asked.

"More than one." Tanis nodded. "But he's coming nonetheless. There's something afoot here, something else. Think about it. Andrews is one of the best, one of the most qualified starship captains alive. Terrance is the owner of one of the largest private corporations in history and Earnest and Abby are two of the most important scientific minds of all time. Couple that with the fact that Admiral Sanderson is nowhere near retirement and you have a very interesting set of circumstances."

"*Interesting* doesn't even begin to cover how weird all of that is," Ouri agreed.

"No kidding. When you consider all of that together..." Joseph nodded.

"Even more," Tanis continued. "Why does the *Intrepid* have an AI that could manage a dozen planets—possibly the most advanced AI ever—and why are we taking over twice the personnel and equipment than any other colony ever has before?"

"You're making me nervous," Ouri said. "What do you think it all means?"

"Damned if I know." Tanis prepared another marshmallow. "But one thing is for sure. Something very interesting is planned for New Eden. Something that someone else doesn't want to happen, and even our own benefactors don't want us to know about."

"So you're saying that we shouldn't be speculating amongst ourselves." Joseph couldn't help but cast an eye around him.

"I think we're best off not knowing what the underlying elements are here." Tanis nodded in agreement. "At least not for now. Terrance is a bit shifty, but I'd trust Captain Andrews with my life. Sanderson may be a dick, but he's a by-the-book dick who wouldn't be involved in something subversive."

"Damn, I hope you're right," Joseph said.

"When haven't I been?" Tanis smiled as she dropped the security shield and proceeded to roast her next marshmallow, signaling the end to the conversation.

The gathering lasted long into the night. Some visitors left early, but others arrived late; a few of Ouri's neighbors around the lake came by to visit as the evening progressed. It was nice; it was a hint of what their lives would be like when they arrived at New Eden.

Until then, before they could be on their way, the work of completing the ship had to be done; the schedule had to be maintained. The GSS *Dakota* was meeting all of its milestones early, and with the recent security issues, no one was feeling as confident as they had several years ago.

But tonight, for a few hours, everyone forgot those concerns; everyone pretended they had arrived at New Eden and were living the life they had always dreamed about. Tanis wasn't sure when her dream had begun, but she knew now where it would end.

AMBUSH

STELLAR DATE: 3227223 / 09.27.4123 (Adjusted Gregorian)
LOCATION: Mars Outer Shipyards (MOS)
REGION: Mars Protectorate, Sol Space Federation

"How is it, Commander, that you seem to end up a part of my security detail so often?" Tanis asked Joseph. "Don't you have a fighter to fly or something?"

Joseph laughed his deep chuckle that Tanis found herself liking more and more every day. "I've got plenty of flyboys and flygirls now to handle that end of things. My main concern is keeping you alive so they don't force me to do your job again."

It was Tanis's turn to laugh. A more common occurrence in Joseph's company—perhaps a connection existed… "I'm glad you have such an altruistic motivation for keeping me safe."

"I'm all altruism. So, where are we going today?" Joseph asked.

"To meet with some mercs that want to capture or kill me."

"Pardon?" Joseph nearly tripped. "Don't have enough trouble in your life as it is? Do you always have to go running toward it?"

PFC Lauder chuckled at that and earned a glare from Corporal Peters.

"It's OK." Tanis glanced at the four members of squad one/fireteam one from Forsythe's platoon—her usual security detail. "We're meeting with Lieutenant Grenwald first. He's got tactical on the situation. Besides,"—she gave Joseph a playful look—"if you'd known there would be danger, would you have passed on joining me?"

Joseph coughed and stammered, "Of course not."

She explained the situation to her companions as they boarded a maglev. Some mercs had set up what they must have thought would be a great lure; after somehow taking control of a cargo ship that ran tech goods to the *Intrepid* from Ceres, they slipped some contraband into a shipment. Not enough to set off all the alarms, but enough to get Tanis down there in person.

"So then why *are* you going down yourself?" Joseph asked. "Couldn't you have Grenwald take them without you?"

"Perhaps, but there's a possibility they may have rigged the ship to blow. I have the best AI and highest-grade nano available at the moment, so I'm the best one to run point."

A cross corridor away from the dock, they slipped through a nondescript doorway and came face to face with Grenwald's platoon.

"Is everything in readiness, Lieutenant?" Tanis asked.

"It is, sir. We've got one/two on the dock, four remote sniping units in the ducts, and the rest of the team is ready to move in if needed. I've also got a direct line to engineering in case anything goes wrong."

"Excellent." Tanis nodded. "Commander Evans and my detail are with me. Don't shoot unless I give the word; the more live bodies, the better."

"Yes, sir."

With that they swung back into the corridor and around the bend. Dock E3 was directly ahead, its bay doors watched by two guards who were TSF Regulars. Grenwald had briefed them via the Link and they saluted Tanis and Joseph as they stepped onto the dock.

Dock E3 was a multilevel affair with ships docking at the highest level and cargo moving via down-ramps to the lower storage and distribution areas. Looking up through the twisting array of chutes and gravity-powered elevators, Tanis saw four ships in interior berths.

Her overlay lit up with the people on the dock, highlighting the positions of the four Marines who were undercover as cargo handlers, working the shipments on the other vessels. Red halos surrounded the men from the suspect ship and their cargo glowed yellow.

<*Tactical overlay online,*> Tanis said over the combat net. <*They look surly.*>

<*Mercs always look surly, sir, it's a great way to identify them,*> Staff Sergeant Williams grunted. <*It's merc SOP.*>

Tanis and Joseph stepped onto an open lift and rode it up to the level at which the ships were berthed. Ahead, the mercs posing as traders were looking annoyed as one of the MOS's cargo inspectors read off the long list of statutes they had violated.

"And you are certainly going to be cited with failure to declare deviation of flight plan as you were half a percentage off on each of your two final trajectory alterations. MOS will be levying a fine against you for that."

"Look, we just want to deliver our cargo and get off this tin can," said the man who appeared to be in charge. "We've got a schedule to keep and this delay is going to cost us more money than your damn fines."

<*Overacting as usual,*> Williams grunted.

<*Another sure indicator,*> Joseph agreed. <*So how we gonna run this?*>

<*Straight in. You* **are** *wearing your protective armor under your uniform, aren't you?*>

<*As if you didn't already know that.*> Joseph's mental tone carried a grin.

The cargo inspector's AI must have notified him of their approach; he turned and gave Tanis an exasperated look. "I'm sorry to have to call you down here, Major, but as per your regulations you are to be brought in on any event of this nature."

"Indeed I am." Tanis nodded. "So what have these fine men brought aboard your station?"

"Nothing that's any big deal," the pseudo-captain commented.

"They've brought a C9 type lubricant onto the ship."

<*A lubricant is contraband?*> Joseph asked.

<*It's used to lubricate molecules in certain types of explosives so they accelerate faster and do more damage.*>

<*There really is a lube for all purposes.*> The conversation was over the general combat net and PFC Lauder felt free to add her two chits.

"What receiver ordered this?" Tanis asked.

"None of yours," the inspector said. "Manifest has it destined for AR Spec, a systems assembler on the station that handles final assembly of nav controller boards for the *Intrepid*. Except this isn't what they ordered." Tanis already knew all of this, but it was best to let the little drama play out.

"So someone shipped the wrong cargo?"

"No, the seal on the container has been tampered with. This cargo was replaced, that's why I called you down."

Tanis shifted her hard stare to the merc in charge. His ID said he was Captain

Sundy, but she had conflicting data. Some records did show that the man before her was Captain Sundy, but older ones had the bio of a completely different person, the hallmark of either shoddy work or a rush job generating a fake ID.

"I expect you have full serial records on this cargo?" she asked. "I'll want to know everything about it, from the moment it was conceived of."

"Of course," the captain smiled. "If you'll step into our hold I can bring the data up."

Grenwald gave the signal over the Link and two of the Marines from one/two boarded a crawler headed down the length of the dock. It was on a route that would take it very close to Tanis and her team; she hoped the mercs didn't pick up on the timing.

"I don't see why that's necessary. Why don't you step onto your ship and load the information onto a plas? That way I can have it handy for my report."

"I would, ma'am, but our plas interface is down right now. I can let you Link to the ship to get the information, but that's it."

"Very well." Tanis shrugged. She motioned with her head for Joseph and one/one to follow.

<*I so do not like the looks of this,*> Joseph said privately to Tanis.

<*Look on the bright side, they're probably not planning on blowing their ship if they're on it.*>

<*The world is different for you than most people, isn't it?*>

<*You can say that again,*> Angela piped up.

<*What's that supposed to mean?*>

<*Your version of 'the bright side' and other people's really don't jibe,*> Joseph explained.

Tanis sent an image of her avatar sticking its tongue out at Joseph, as they stepped over the threshold into the cargo bay of the small freighter. Even as she did so, her eyes darted up to catch the furtive motion of more than one man on an upper catwalk that circled the compartment.

She sent commands over the combat net to Argenaut and Lauder to stand on the far side of the hold and cover the catwalk. Tannon and Peters took up positions on either side of the hold's airlock.

The merc posing as Captain Sundy led Tanis and Joseph to a hard terminal and brought up the cargo's records. She turned to the console and let it appear as though she was reading it in detail. What she was really doing was positioning her left hand—which the merc couldn't see—under her jacket and on her pulse pistol.

<*Stun or wound only. I want intel from these guys,*> she sent over the combat net.

Angela deployed remote nano, which relayed multiple views of the hold to the combat net; enabling Tanis to watch the merc captain from behind. He paused for a moment, thinking her distracted by the readout, and then slid a hand between two crates.

"I wouldn't do that, Captain Sundy." Tanis didn't turn as she addressed the captain.

"Do what?"

"Don't pull that weapon out from there. I've got mine trained on you already. Your ship is surrounded and we're going to have to take you into custody."

The man gave an ugly laugh. "You're in error, unfortunately. We've got people on the inside. Your little TSF force won't be able to help you."

"And yours won't be able to help you." Tanis fired. The shot hit him square in the chest. It knocked him back, but wasn't lethal. He'd be doing some talking later, lots of talking.

Lauder let out a cry as she raised her rifle and peppered the catwalk with pulse blasts. Argenaut was moments behind her, his laser out, intensity set low—just enough to blister the skin if it made contact. Behind them, Peters and Tannon were firing shots back onto the dock as the mercs stationside attempted to rush them. The MOS inspector went down under a hail of projectile fire from the mercs.

The two members of one/two arrived on the crawler and the mercs ended up caught in a heavy crossfire. Moments later they were down. However, Angela's nano was still picking up four heat signatures on the catwalk inside the hold. Her detail, assisted by Joseph, focused all their attention on that problem.

As she scanned the combat net for the best view of the catwalk, several explosions rocked the dock outside.

<*What the hell is going on?*> Tanis asked.

Williams filled her in. <*Looks like we underestimated them. The other ships are all merc, as well—way more organized than I would have thought. They just used some sort of missile or light artillery to take out our sniper drones.*>

<*Dozens of signatures leaving the other three ships,*> Sergeant Green added. <*Our men at the entrance are being forced back.*>

Tanis gave it a moment's thought. <*Have them fall back and seal the lock. We're going on a little trip.*>

<*Yes, sir,*> Grenwald replied.

<*What about Jensen and Lang?*> Williams asked, referring to the two Marines who had assisted Tanis's escort.

<*Tell them to get their asses in here. Gonna get real cold on the dock in a minute or two.*>

A moment later, affirmative signals showed on the combat net. Tanis could hear boots pounding on the dock and Jensen and Lang burst through the airlock.

"Seal it!" Tanis yelled. "Commander, take Peters and Tannon and secure the bridge, we'll finish off our friends above."

"Like hell you will!" a voice called down.

Using hand signals, Tanis directed the Marines to lay down suppressive fire. That done, she instructed Angela to lock down the airlock and attempt to get in contact with the ship's AI.

Tanis looked for the weapon the merc captain had been going for. It was a high-powered pulse rifle. Just what the doctor ordered. She took stock of the situation from everyone's feeds, then rolled out from behind her protective cargo and placed three well-aimed shots into the torso of a merc as he rose up from behind his cover to take aim. Three left on the catwalk.

Angela had gotten the ship's layout and fed it to the combat net. Joseph sent a thanks and informed Tanis that he was almost at the bridge. No resistance encountered thus far.

Jensen got off a shot that nailed a merc in the head and he toppled over the railing to the deck below. Two enemies left.

Re-examining the situation, Tanis climbed onto a crate and pulled herself up some webbing to get a new vantage point. Sure enough, just as a merc leaned over to get his gun around his cover, he came right into view. Two shots to the torso and he slumped over.

"Last man," she called out. "Care to surrender the easy way, or get beaten into submission?"

A scuffling sound echoed in the hold as a gun was tossed over the railing and the man stood up.

"Good choice, man," Lauder grinned. "With all of us gunning for you, you'd've been pulverized. And wouldn't that just mess up your pretty merc face?"

"Secure him and then dose them all. Make sure they are out for hours."

<*Status,*> Tanis queried Joseph.

<*Bridge secure. There was one lady up here and though it was a mighty battle, we managed to get her fixed up.*>

<*Good work. We'll be there momentarily.*>

"Jensen, Lang. Stay down here and keep an eye on that airlock. Lauder and Argenaut, layout is on the combat net and it shows a secondary airlock. Angela has it locked down, but go make sure someone doesn't poke a hole in it."

"Sir!" came the chorus of responses.

Tanis followed the route Joseph's team had taken up to the bridge and queried Angela along the way.

<*So what's the story on this ship's AI? It does have an AI, right?*>

Before Angela even responded, Tanis could feel her AI's anger. <*They've subverted it.*>

Tanis's breath caught. Subverting an AI was a capital offense in human courts, but it was far worse to AI. Any human even remotely connected to being part of an AI subversion would never get another AI implant, and beyond that they would find themselves unexpectedly unable to access a variety of networks at the most inopportune times. Someone was paying these mercs very, very well for them run that risk.

<*Will you be able to help it?*> Tanis asked.

<*I don't know. This ship has a distributed computing system with some decent redundancy. If they didn't damage it in too many ways, there should be a complete, intact copy in here.*>

Tanis relayed the news across the combat net.

<*So what's our next move?*> Grenwald asked.

<*Depends, how do things look out there?*>

<*From what our probes show, they've secured the inner airlock by moving crates in front of it. We've taken up positions by the secondary and maintenance airlocks, but they haven't breached yet. They also appear to be moving some heavy equipment toward the ship you are on. I'm guessing they intend to beat their way in.*>

<*Friendlies on the dock?*>

<*Negative, sir,*> replied Williams. <*Just lots and lots of soon to be dead guys.*>

<*Then we're going to leave this party.*> Tanis signaled Joseph.

<*How?*> Grenwald asked while Williams chuckled.

<*I forgot, you've never worked with her in combat. I think that the military officially had her middle name changed to Unconventional. You're gonna blast out of there, aren't you?*>

<*Nail on the head, Staff Sergeant, nail on the head. Let the station know…actually, I'll let them know…it'll be fun.*>

<*You're one of a kind, sir,*> Grenwald said.

<*Shouldn't be a big deal. ES fields should snap into place pretty quick,*> Joseph added.

<*Keep those locks sealed till we're gone.*> Tanis entered the bridge.

Joseph was at the pilot's console and was firing up the ship's reactor. Normally, when the reactor had been cold for some time, the process was carefully executed over several hours, but this wasn't a several-hours sort of situation and he was skipping a number—or all—of the safety procedures.

<*MOS docking control, I need an undock on berth four, dock E3,*> Tanis called into the station traffic control.

<*This is MOS docking control. I'm sorry, but we read red on the outer seal for that dock's airlock. Departure will expose the entire dock to vacuum.*>

<*I'm well aware of that. The mercenaries assaulting our ship are going to be displeased with said vacuum and that will make me happy.*>

<*What...?*>

<*Never mind, my AI informs me that they've shunted your access.*>

<*They what?*>

"Conversation was getting redundant," Tanis muttered and killed the connection; she instructed Grenwald to keep MOS abreast of issues from his position.

<*I hope all is well up there,*> Lauder reported in. <*Cause they're melting through the hatch and we'll be having tea with them in no time.*>

<*Fall back to the midship's hatch on the catwalk and haul our sleeping beauties with you,*> Tanis replied. <*Commander Evans will give the count when we pull free—seal that hatch when he does; the cargo bay may get breached when we break free.*>

"What's the stat?" Tanis asked Joseph.

"I've released our clamps, station is still clamped on, but frankly I don't care. Ready to apply magnetic debarkation in 3, 2, 1. Magnetic rails active."

A violent shudder ran through the small ship as it strained to break free from the station's grapple, and an unpleasant tearing sound echoed through the hull.

"That was one nasty noise," Peters said. "But I don't think it was the sound of us getting free."

Joseph's expression was sour as he attempted to determine why the ship was still moored. "Don't you trust my driving?"

"It's not your driving; it's how well this tub can hold up to it."

"I resent that," a clear voice rang out in the bridge.

<*Meet Tom, the ship's AI,*> Angela said over the combat net.

"Sorry, Tom." Peters apologized. "Situational stress."

"I understand," Tom replied. "I've been having a rough few days myself. Thanks to Angela, I'm almost feeling like myself again."

"Good to hear it. You're most familiar with this ship, what do you recommend we do to break free from dock?" Tanis asked.

"Well, my mag rails probably aren't strong enough. You'll have to use thrusters and a reverse magnetic pulse on the station's mag clamps."

"Sounds like a plan; co-ord it with Joseph," Tanis replied.

A pulse thrummed through the ship and with a final screech and a lurch, the ship pulled free.

<*You wouldn't believe the earful I'm getting from docking control,*> Grenwald laughed, clearly enjoying getting the best of MOS.

<*Let them know that they are going to have more reports than they know how to file. How their scan missed the fact that those other three ships must have nearly sixty people on them is unfathomable.*> The thought of such raw incompetence made Tanis seethe and she took a

moment to compose herself before addressing the crew.

The inner lock was just an ES shield which was not designed to stop objects as large and determined as a ship under thrust. The shield snapped off momentarily, creating quite the storm on the dock behind them. It wasn't enough of a pressure change to kill anyone, but it wouldn't go down as a pleasant experience.

"Move us away from the MOS. Grenwald has put the call into your fighter patrols, Commander. They're scrambling Blue Wing to escort us to the *Intrepid*'s VIP dock."

"Fitting, I'd say." Joseph grinned. Something on his board caught his eye. "Damn, two of their ships are breaking free as well. We're gonna have a race on our hands."

"Either that, or a fight," Tanis said.

"Tom, do you have any types of weapons or shielding?" Joseph asked.

"This class of ship is not equipped with any weapons, and nothing more than a frontal velocity shield."

"You owe us, Tom; tell me about the real loadout."

A sigh came over the audible speakers and the shipnet. "Very well, we have two three-inch lasers and a very light refractive shield."

"Better than a kick in the head," Tanis muttered. "Peters, have Tom hook you up with a console for weapons; Tannon, you're on ship's systems and damage control."

Tanis got two yes ma'ams and the men went to their tasks. She tapped into ship's scan and brought it up on the small holo. Their ship was pulling away from MOS on thrusters, slowly angling around the shipyard to the outer side where the *Intrepid* was docked.

"Brace!" Peters called out as a projectile impacted their ship. Reports flashed on everyone's overlays showing the damage to the lower holds. External cameras displayed cargo spilling out into space.

<*Jansen, that looked like it was close to you. You two OK?*> Tanis called down after making sure that their lifesigns showed green.

<*Shaken, but not smushed, sir. Mind if we come up there? The more ship between us and them the better I feel.*>

<*On the double. You too, Argenaut and Lauder. It'll be cozy, but safer for you.*>

<*Aye, sir.*>

"That wasn't very nice," Peters muttered as he worked his interface. "I've got a bead on the ship that fired that. May I take the shot?"

"Fire at will, Corporal," Tanis said. "We just need to keep these guys at bay for two more minutes. All fighters are deploying around the *Intrepid* so the launching tubes are a bit stacked. Our escort should be here any moment, though."

Just as Tanis was finishing her statement, Joseph let out a curse. "There's been a malfunction in the stationside tubes. Blue Wing isn't able to deploy, should I have Yellow come escort us?"

"Negative." Tanis shook her head. "That would be just the diversion I would be looking for to attack the *Intrepid*. No, we're on our own until the TSF patrol craft and fighter support arrive."

"ETA on that?" Timmins asked.

"Updating the combat net now—should be eleven minutes."

"Damn," Tannon said. "We need to do something creative, or we won't last that long."

"We could head toward the *Intrepid*, draw our merc friends into the range of the patrols there," Joseph suggested.

"I would, except I have a suspicion that there's more here than meets the eye."

On the holo before her, the two merc ships were accelerating and moving into flanking positions while Joseph altered vector to angle away from the *Intrepid.* Another projectile hurtled from the merc ship at their starboard side, but this time Peters had the lasers ready and melted it in flight.

"Just took a bit to get comfortable with the calibration."

"I've got the refractor shield up to full strength." Tannon seemed to be doing most of his work through the Link, his hands not touching the holo interface. "Not a lot I can do about those projectiles, though."

Tanis glanced down at the main holo. The ship's engines were at an angle where they were no longer pointed at MOS. "Hit the ion drive and give us some thrust."

"Oh they're not gonna like that." Joseph smirked as he did as he was told.

"I'm the one who's not liking things right now," Tanis growled. "I'm going to be paying another visit to our friend the stationmaster very soon. If MOS keeps this up they may forfeit their standing as a self-governing body and have to submit to TSF for changeover."

"I doubt it's gone that far yet. Doesn't there have to be evidence of widespread neglect and loss of life for that?" Joseph's eyes never left his screens as he spoke, but a hint of appeasement was evident in his tone.

<I'm not the only one who thinks you overreact.>

Tanis rolled her eyes at Angela. "Yeah. I'm just venting. All the bureaucracy is starting to drive me nuts. I've seen entire planets with less of it."

"Were they really small?" Peters asked and Lauder chucked.

Joseph interrupted the banter. "Everyone hold on to something. High *g* thrust in twenty seconds—counter on the combat net."

The other four Marines made double time and rushed into the bridge, securing themselves to tie-downs and duty stations. The bridge net showed status green on the ion engine's nozzle extension and on the zero mark Joseph fired a continuous burst. The thrust pushed everyone back into their seats and the freighter pulled away from its pursuers.

Once the initial thrust was over, Tanis assigned the Marines to duty stations and monitoring tasks. It really didn't take that many people to keep the ship in line, but it was better to give them something to do.

"They're catching up; we've got several incoming missiles." Tannon shifted shielding to cover the appropriate sections of the ship.

"We're gonna have to roll." Joseph synced his pattern with Tannon and Peters' stations. "Everyone hold on to your lunch, or it's gonna get nasty in here."

The ship began to spin. Joseph also used evasive jinks to ensure the enemy had as much trouble targeting them as possible. Tanis saw the Marines all lock their armor's necks solid. Joseph seemed fine, however, sliding casually in his seat with each of the ship's movements. Tanis resorted to using the head straps in the captain's chair. It wouldn't look so good if the major spewed across the main holo projector.

"Oh my god..." Jansen moaned. "This is worse than an orbital drop."

Tanis agreed as her stomach lurched from a sharp bank while the ship rotated against the turn. She wondered if Joseph was trying to make them sick.

"Doesn't the MOS have turrets for security issues like this?" Lauder asked.

"They do, but they seem to be having target control issues with the turrets in this area. I'm not certain if it's more sabotage or general incompetence," Tannon replied from his station on scan.

"I'm voting for a combination. I don't want to give either group too much credit." Joseph seemed completely unruffled, his face merely showing light concentration as he banked around the skeleton of an ore freighter.

"They're ah…not going to fire until they've worked out those targeting issues, are they?" Peters asked.

"The day the MOS security does anything decisive that doesn't involve getting in the way will be the day I get a full night's sleep," Tanis replied.

"Wow, not really helping with the warm fuzzies here." Lang grunted—paused. "Uh, sir."

Tanis couldn't help but let a little smile through. Poor Marines could barely stand having a lieutenant around all the time and here they were crammed into a tiny bridge with a commander and a major.

Joseph cleared the freighter and Tom's voice came over the bridge's speakers. "They're attempting a remote retake of my core. Angela and I are fighting it off, but it may decrease performance of my systems."

"I'm guessing those ships have subverted AI as well." Joseph's voice dripped with distaste as he plotted a course along the dorsal frame of a TSF destroyer that was being refitted station north of the ore freighter. "Too bad that destroyer is powered down, our troubles would be over in one quick call."

"Could be worse, the mercs could actually be decent at shooting."

"They're not bad." Peters looked up from his console. "I've melted seven other projectiles. I'm betting they'll be switching to lasers shortly. Keep that spin up."

Joseph nodded in acknowledgement as the ship rotated, weaving through docked freighters and transport craft. A projectile missed them and impacted a luxury liner that was being overhauled causing a rod of flame to lance out of the ship into the vacuum.

"Damn, I almost had that one," Peters said.

"Worry about us, not some liner," Tannon shot back. "They're all empty anyway."

"That's why I'm on guns…Private." Peters glanced at his squad mate. "More shrapnel in an explosion than the original projectile, besides O2 fires in space creep me out."

"Amen to that." Jansen was nodding while looking at a view holo. "There's something about those fires that looks totally unnatural. Or too natural; it's like they are living things."

Tanis smiled to herself. Banter, the best way to combat the fear of being blown to pieces.

"TSF update," she said out loud, "ETA on fighters is seven minutes."

"Our friends out there probably know that too. I expect they'll start getting desperate any moment now," Joseph said.

Power usage meters shot up all over the boards as the ship's refraction shields repelled laser beams.

"Right on time," Tanis said.

"We're at 70% across the board. If we weren't rotating we'd've been holed by that salvo," Tannon reported.

"Nets ahead!" Joseph said triumphantly. "I knew I saw some out here on my last patrol."

Accessing the ship's forward cameras, Tanis saw what he was referring to. Several kilometers of storage nets showed on the holo view, all holding various components and even small sections of ships for final assembly. The working lights were off, meaning no personnel were present in the nets, but the proximity alarms were sounding on the bridge—both from the ship and the net's perimeter system.

"Can you nix that noise, Tom?" Tanis asked.

"On it, just responding a bit slow," Tom replied. Moments later the klaxons ceased. "There we are."

"Thanks, Tom," Joseph said. "This is going to feel worse than it really is."

With that the commander banked the ship hard around a net, under the next and around another. He threaded them smoothly, but their pursuers were managing to keep pace.

"At least they're not shooting at us," Tannon said.

"Peters." Tanis glanced at the corporal. "See if you can take out a mooring mount or two. It'd make my day if we could cause a wee bit of a collision behind us."

"I like the way you think, sir." Peters targeted several of the net's mooring points. "A little mayhem here, a little mayhem there…"

"That's the spirit." Jansen grinned.

Several of the nets had been under load; their cargo bundled against them and held in place by the station's centripetal rotation. With their moorings weakened, the nets swung out wildly; the closest of their pursuers narrowly avoided collision. Though the merc ship escaped that disaster, it clipped a piece of cargo from another net and had to retro-brake to avoid colliding with a shuttle frame that swung out from the impact.

"One mostly down." Peters targeted more moorings and sent cargo spinning wildly in their wake.

"You wouldn't believe the stink we're getting from MOS on this. They should really know by now that the more they aggravate me, the more paperwork I generate." Even as she spoke, Tanis was filing dozens of complaints against the station for each of the code violations and oversight failures that had allowed this scenario to occur in the first place. The bureaucrats complaining to her would soon be buried in a mountain of paperwork.

<*You're positively evil,*> Angela said.

<*Maybe a bit, though I prefer to think of myself as vindictive.*>

<*You realize that's not a positive attribute,*> Angela replied dryly.

<*That depends on your profession.*>

At that moment, a clang echoed through the compartment and the bridge door slid open; two mercs hung in the frame, guns drawn.

"Cease acceleration and prepare to be boarded."

"What the fuck?" Lauder swore. "Where did you two idiots come from?"

"The places you didn't search," the first man said. "Now drop your weapons and comply."

"Are these guys serious?" Jansen asked Tanis.

"They seem like it…but I'm not really sure. Are you two serious? You are going to try to take on six Marines and two TSF officers by yourselves? You're going to die, and it'll probably be messy."

The men looked at each other and then at Tanis. Before they could respond, an impact rattled the ship and in the midst of the collision multiple shots peppered the mercs. Their hands slipped free of the handholds and their lifeless bodies fell back through the opening.

"Oops, did I clip that cargo net?" Joseph asked. "Sorry about that."

Another shock ran through the ship, coupled with the screams of metal shearing. Joseph grunted. "That one wasn't me."

The second merc ship had gained ground while the commander's focus was split and had gotten a projectile round off at close range.

"Losing our starboard engine." Tom's concerned voice sounded over the bridge speakers. "Shutting it down to avoid a runaway reaction."

"ETA on TSF fighter craft is two minutes." Tannon sounded anxious. The Marines were used to conflicts where they could take direct action to decide the outcome. This frantic flight was wearing on their nerves.

"Think they'll try to board us, or just blow us out of the sky?" Lang asked.

Another explosion rocked the ship and Lauder swore. "I guess that's our answer."

"Belay that impending doom!" Tannon grinned at the scan console. "Looks like they got the tubes cleared. Blue squadron is inbound. Say goodbye to the bad mercenaries."

Tanis brought the scan data up on the main holo and sure enough, six fighter craft were racing over the bulk of the station. Tactical missiles fired from each ship and tore into the lead mercenary vessel. Their yield was low, but the strikes were precise. The engines went dead and the weapons signatures winked out. Scan showed a tug leave a nearby dock to catch the ship before it did more damage. Moments later a similar scene played out with the other merc ship.

"And that"— Joseph leaned back in his seat and smiled at the main holo—"is that."

REPROACH

STELLAR DATE: 3227224 / 09.28.4123 (Adjusted Gregorian)
LOCATION: GSS *Intrepid*, Mars Outer Shipyards (MOS)
REGION: Mars Protectorate, Sol Space Federation

The post-op took over twenty hours, a good portion of which was spent re-taking the dock from the last few mercs, who had entrenched themselves quite thoroughly. Then came the round-up, squabbles over jurisdiction, and the interrogations. It was well into the following day before Ouri and Tanis got to sit down together and go over what they had learned.

"This is most interesting." Tanis looked over the interrogation logs. "Trent was not involved with these men at all, at least not to their knowledge. The captains all had their dealings with a man by the name of Drenn. He has links to the STR Consortium, been known to be involved in some of their less public projects."

Ouri scowled at the data as she reviewed. "So, does this mean we have two threats or just one that is a little clearer and a little scarier?"

"I'm betting that it's the same threat, though we do have to keep an open mind." She took a drink from the restorative in front of her. "Still, I'm guessing that Trent wasn't getting the desired results, so his bosses declared open season on us."

"More likely on you," Ouri replied. "I'm guessing that they've singled you out. That was a very deadly scenario that was specifically designed to draw you in."

"And in I was drawn…rather foolishly too."

"I'll say so." Admiral Sanderson stood in the doorway.

<Tell me next time he sneaks up like that,> Tanis scolded Angela.

<I would, but he has some good tech. If he wants to be, he's very hard to spot.>

"Sir." Both women stood and saluted.

"Sit." Sanderson gestured as he did.

"Quite the little escapade you had, Major." He allowed his glare to linger on her for a moment before continuing. "Imagine my reaction when I hear, while on my visit to the Marsian Parliament, that the officer in charge of our security has ripped a ship from the station, exposed an entire dock to vacuum, and proceeded to tear across the construction yards, spilling cargo in her wake like it was confetti."

"I can only guess that it must have been extreme, sir."

"You're damn right it was extreme. You should never have allowed yourself to be drawn in so completely. I thought you were an intelligence officer. You could stand to display some."

Tanis sat and took the rebuke in silence. Ouri looked like she wished she were anywhere else, up to and including cleaning sewage scrubbers, than at the table listening to Sanderson dress down her CO.

"Well, what do you have to say for yourself?"

Tanis took a breath. She could think of a hundred reasons why no other person would have expected to run into four ships full of armed mercenaries on what was supposed to be a secure dock, but she knew that wouldn't fly with the admiral.

"I take full responsibility, sir. I acted rashly and without proper care and attention. It won't happen again."

"You must know that I am under considerable pressure to have you removed. Terrance and the captain have been inundated with calls and protestations from all levels of Marsian bureaucracy. Considerable pressure."

"I'll tender my resignation at once, sir," Tanis replied stoically. "I do not wish to cause them any more trouble than I already have." While she appeared calm on the outside, inside she was fraught with emotion. If she had to abdicate her place on the *Intrepid,* she would find whoever was responsible and kill them, even if it took a thousand years.

"Don't be an idiot. You'll do no such thing." Anderson gave her a look that teachers usually reserve for their worst students. "Despite your rather shoddy handling of yesterday's events, your record otherwise has been impeccable. I simply wish to inform you that should your next encounter with the enemy show such large amounts of bravado coupled with such small amounts of careful consideration, I may have to rethink my decision regarding your placement here."

"Yes, sir." Tanis could feel her limbs again, her heart slowed back down and she took a deep breath.

"Now, let's talk about the prisoners. That much, at least, was a job well done. We can finally get some information on who is behind this."

"Yes, sir. From what we have learned so far, it appears that the mercenaries were contacted by a man by the name of Drenn. He is connected to the STR Consortium, dealing particularly in the types of projects that they like to keep hidden from the public eye. It is our opinion that they were hired to take me out of the picture."

Sanderson leaned back and stroked his chin. "And why, pray tell, Major, would they go to such considerable expense to remove you, pain in my ass though you are? I imagine that this operation cost them billions of credits, enough to buy a small corporation on a major planet."

"Indeed, sir." Tanis nodded. "I think they want to get rid of me because their sabotage success rate dropped when I came onboard. It's not a lot, but their last several attacks have all targeted me, so I think there is some credence there."

Sanderson grunted a tentative assent. "And what about your belief that it is solely the STR?" he asked.

"We've obviously been under concerted corporate, network, and physical attack for some time. We've ruled out radical groups, though it is logical to assume, and borne out by the data, that roughly ten percent of our troubles are from those fringe elements.

"That being said, the rest is either governmental or corporate in origin. There is a relatively small list of either that could sustain an attack of this duration through so many avenues. If these men truly did get their orders from Drenn, then it has to have been the STR Consortium all along."

"They have been on our suspect list since we determined that it was a bigger player pulling the strings," Sanderson said. "What does this change?"

"We can now begin pursuing legal action against them," Tanis replied. "We have affidavits and statements from many of the mercs regarding the nature of this attempt and who hired them. Once we make a solid connection between Drenn and the STR we can begin subpoenaing communications that we can link between him and the STR. That'll be a feeding frenzy for the news hounds and will cause them to think twice before making such a bold move again."

"We won't be able to make this stick to them." Sanderson shook his head. "We don't have a solid enough tie."

"And we're not likely to get one, but they'll still have to fight us off. The money it will cost them in share value alone will make them rethink their plans. At the very least they will probably refrain from more events like this and go back to that Trent guy."

"That would be something at least." The admiral nodded. "One mysterious foe is enough."

"I couldn't agree more," Tanis said.

"I still don't see how this all fully explains the considerable expense they are going to in trying to remove you alone."

"I can only surmise"—Tanis leaned back in her chair—"that they have something big planned and hope to remove me and carry it out before you can find a replacement."

COUGAR

STELLAR DATE: 3227238 / 10.12.4123 (Adjusted Gregorian)
LOCATION: GSS *Intrepid*, Mars Outer Shipyards (MOS)
REGION: Mars Protectorate, Sol Space Federation

Tanis was relaxing on a bench in the prairie park located a few decks down from the SOC. It was the third shift and the park was dark, which meant it was teeming with life. She could hear the calls of the various ground animals and even the cough of a cougar somewhere in the distance. She wondered what it was hunting, and saw that the park listing showed a herd of deer nearby.

The herd was quite close and Tanis cycled her vision into the IR range to see if she could witness the attack. Wild predators were not uncommon in the parks on the *Intrepid*. It was easiest to create a true ecosystem with them in place. The animals would not bother humans; they would not even come within several meters, depending on the species.

"What are you peering at?"

The voice startled Tanis; she had been so focused on the impending battle that she hadn't heard anyone approach. Looking up she saw that it was Joseph and smiled warmly.

"Cougar about to pounce somewhere out there, I can't see it, but I heard it nearby."

Joseph sat beside her. "Forgot you were planetborn. I never liked the predators; it doesn't make sense why they would add them in."

"Keeps the vermin under control."

"That's what the ship's cats are for."

Those were different cats entirely. Every ship had cats for hunting vermin. Try as mankind might, even in the forty-second century, rats and mice still followed civilization around, making their home where humans did. Ship's cats had been modified slightly to prefer the taste of rat and mouse, and also to be very fastidious as to where they left their own scat. Their intelligence was enhanced as well, allowing them to understand the concept of pointing, as well as the fact that the cat in the mirror was them and not some interloper out to steal their food.

"I don't think ship's cats would do too well out there. It's not really their type of place. Besides, that cougar stalking those deer…that's real nature, that's what happens."

"You have a very fixed mindset, do you know that?" Joseph smiled at Tanis. "Not saying I don't like it, just an observation."

She turned her attention to him, allowing herself to see what she normally kept from her mind. He was a man; a warm, intelligent, attractive man. One who didn't mind how domineering she was—something that had caused problems more than once. His head was angled forward, his strong brow half hiding his eyes. Tanis thought back and realized it was a look he almost exclusively reserved for her. It was also not a look a commander directs at a major under any circumstances.

The intensity of his gaze caused her to glance down at her service uniform, suddenly noticing that the cut of the blouse and pants seemed to be somewhat more fitted than usual.

<Don't look at me. I wouldn't have your nano alter your clothing. Nope.>

<Angela, you know I can't pursue him. He serves under me.>

Angela's snort was very convincing. *<Who cares? We'll be gone in a few months. Do you think Sanderson will give a hoot as long as you get the job done? Heck, it's expected for you organics to get together and do your thing on a colony venture—the more the merrier.>*

<Just…oh shut up!>

Tanis took a moment to remember Joseph's last statement.

"Yeah, I do sort of have a one-track mind. Comes with the territory I suppose."

Joseph nodded. "I know how you feel. But it's been quiet lately; I can't help thinking of what it's going to be like when we get there."

Tanis was silent a moment, staring off into the waving grass. "I haven't really allowed myself to think of that much."

Joseph gave a low chuckle. "Why doesn't that surprise me?"

Tanis looked up into his eyes and saw something there; a longing, an intensity that she didn't know how to deal with. Why would he want her so badly? He hadn't said so, but she knew it was there…it was her job to know things like that.

She looked away. "Joe…I—I don't know what to say. I don't know what to do with what you want from me."

She felt his hand rest on her arm, felt the heat radiating through her shirt. "I just want you. Can't you tell? It's not something from you I want, it's just you."

A battle was raging between Tanis's heart and mind. In the end her mind won. She broke regulations only when she had to—never when she wanted to, no matter how much she wanted to. "We can't, you know that. You serve under me, there's a reason why these things can't happen."

"But I serve under you now and have feelings for you. They have happened, don't you see that?"

Tanis sighed and shifted on the bench to face him. "What do I have to offer you? There's nothing here, I'm just my job."

Joe laughed, it wasn't a short bark, or a mocking chuckle, just a good long laugh—one that left him wheezing by the time he finished. "Major Richards, that's just the sort of thing you would say."

Tanis could feel her cheeks getting red; she couldn't fathom what was so funny. It couldn't be that he was mocking her. That was completely out of character for Joe. "I don't get it. What could you see in me? Men don't want women like me…we just make things hard for them—or they want a mother."

Joe raised his hand and turned her face toward his, forcing her to lock eyes with him. She felt a moment of uncertainty. Was he going to kiss her?

"I don't want a mother. I've given this a lot of thought. It's your strength that draws me to you. No matter what, you don't let things get you down. Nothing is insurmountable. I don't want to control you, I don't want to own you, I want to share that with you, and I want to give you the support that I know you really need inside. You're just like the rest of us—you feel pain, you worry, but you don't let anyone see. But I see, and it makes me love you."

A part of Tanis saw that Joe was just as shocked that he'd said 'love' as she was to hear it. She had heard it before and it always ended badly—always ended with pain. She pulled away.

"I don't think this is right, Joe. We have to work together. Maybe later, maybe after we get there." Her voice was quiet; she couldn't keep the doubt in her own words hidden.

Joe didn't say a word; his face had lost all expression. He nodded and rose from the bench, but after taking a step he turned. "Tanis, I hope you don't mind, but I'm going to wait. I'm not going to let you stay alone forever."

She didn't respond and he remained still; Tanis wondered if he would attempt to convince her again. But then, with a slight droop to his shoulders, he left.

Tanis sat, staring into the darkness, her reverie eventually broken by a deer's scream.

THE CHO

STELLAR DATE: 3227241 / 10.15.4123 (Adjusted Gregorian)
LOCATION: District 4A1, Ring 4, Callisto Orbital Habitat (Cho)
REGION: Jovian Combine, Sol Space Federation

Trist cautiously slipped down the service corridor, her silsuit a matte grey that matched the bulkheads around her. She was looking for a good place to hide so that she could look over her find in private. A vertical stack of environmental tubes filled part of the passage ahead, and she crouched down in the gloom they created.

The find was a bundle of plas sheets. Rare to see such a manifest printed out, but some people did like the tactile sensation. She flipped through the multilayer holoplas with care, making certain to focus on each layer of each page in its entirety. It took several minutes to scan the sheets into memory and transcribe them. Once it was in her memory she assimilated it as data and the information was in the forefront of her mind, filtered into a relational structure.

Slipping a small EM charge from a hidden pocket she fried the sheets and dropped them down a crack between the conduit and the deck. Someone would find them eventually, but it would be too late to do anything—even if the information on them could be recovered.

Sue, Trist's AI, was running through the lists of equipment and storage locations in the data and pulled out several choice items, flashing them over Trist's vision.

<*Well that sure looks like it made this little jaunt worth it.*>

<*I'd say so,*> Sue replied. <*We could make enough money to get all of the upgrades both of us want for once.*>

<*We're going to need help,*> Trist said.

<*You're thinking Jesse, aren't you?*>

<*I am; she can handle anything I can't manage, and we'll need a hand with some of the bigger items.*>

<*Well, we had better go get her. If we wait too long she'll be on her nightly binge and we'll miss our window.*>

Trist rose and left the narrow service passage, taking a few convoluted turns before ending up on a larger concourse. As she walked, the corridors transitioned from deserted to being packed with people and maglev carriers. The utilitarian halls had also given way to the wider boulevards, their walls covered in tarnished filigree—though it was nearly impossible to spot behind all of the holo advertisements that wrapped them.

She looked down at the form-fitting grey outfit and decided it just wouldn't do. A thought changed its color to a mixture of black and pink, raised the heel on the boots and added a short skirt. The neckline plunged and the fabric ruffled, creating a second layer that formed a jacket.

<*Much better, a girl has to look her best.*>

<*You worry too much about clothing.*>

<*I don't know why I even talk to you sometimes. Clothing is everything!*>

"Mod freak."

She almost didn't catch the muttered words from a man who walked by. He was already past, but she made a rude gesture anyway. It wasn't her fault she couldn't get the pretty mods and that her left eye was a mass of lenses and actuators. Not to mention what her right hand looked like—it got the job done.

Putting his comment from her mind she adopted a carefree expression and walked down the corridor toward the main sweep of Ring 4. Her eyes slid past the ancient décor in this part of the ring to light upon the inhabitants. It was important to always know who was around you and what they were up to. In Trist's experience life didn't offer a lot of forgiveness to the unwary.

After a few bends, the boulevard opened up to a balcony overlooking the main sweep. Lanes of flying transports choked the air before her and below she could catch glimpses of parks and lakes.

Once, when the Callisto Orbital Habitat—known to its inhabitants as the Cho—was new, this was the upper level of an exclusive world, the most beautiful and advanced orbital habitat ever created. The Cho still was the most advanced and beautiful orbital habitat mankind had ever constructed, but with the number of rings now totaling over one hundred, R4 was little more than a relic—much of it demoted to life support and waste-management.

Despite that, the main sweep could still take your breath away. It was nearly a kilometer wide and ran the entire circumference of the ring. If you followed it around the ring, you'd find yourself in some very nice neighborhoods from time to time, but most would prompt you to keep a hand on your weapon of choice.

Trist tried to contact Jesse on the Link, but received no response. That could mean anything from complete and utter drunkenness to simply not caring enough to answer, or a host of possibilities in between.

She visited Pikes Pub, followed by a few of her friend's other favorite haunts eventually catching wind that Jesse was on her way to the SouRing commons to return a faulty IF unit. The commons were nine-thousand kilometers upspin and Trist caught a high-velocity maglev that made the trip in less than an hour.

Sue kept an eye out while Trist caught a bit of sleep. The effort to steal those plas sheets had kept her from sleep for more than a day and even the several minutes she managed to snatch on the train felt great.

The train's closest stop to the SouRing commons was the sort of place that made even people with death wishes deploy protective nano; Sue let out a veritable cloud.

<*The air feels tenser than usual out here,*> Trist commented.

<*I don't really have the equipment to judge the tension in the air, but I'll take your word for it,*> Sue replied.

Trist waited for the crush in the station to lessen before she ventured out and then down a broad thoroughfare to the commons.

The SouRing commons were placed at a location where the main sweep was wider than normal and contained a veritable city of shops, services, and bazaars. The merchants on the commons sold everything to everyone—every single walk of life and caste was represented. Tucked amongst the semi-legal stalls and shops was the best black market in the bottom twenty rings, something that brought in a lot of highnums and offringers.

It wasn't hard to spot the foreigners either. They were the ones with the furtive glances and anxious twitches. Normally Trist would find a few likely ones and follow them to a good place to do a little recreational appropriation of their goods, but not now. She needed to find Jesse and get moving.

Threading through a group of brain cases—Trist could never understand anyone's desire to leave their body—she worked her way toward the shop she was pretty certain Jesse had gone to with her 'faulty' IF unit. On the way she decided that her flamboyant outfit might make her look a bit too much like a tourist and altered her silsuit to approximate black leather pants, boots, a tight grey shirt and a long jacket—a more serious and less approachable outfit.

<*Again with the clothes…it's like a sickness,*> Sue commented.

<*Why are all AI such smart-asses?*> Trist's question didn't receive a response.

As she threaded the crowd, a telltale blue mohawk caught her eye. It wasn't a totally uncommon hairstyle at the moment, but this one stood out as the spikes were metal, and each was topped with a small decorative skull. Yunnan did have a tendency to show up when Trist least expected it; usually quite interested in her paying him the credit she owed.

She was betting that he was past the 'want money now' stage and into the 'retribution and pain' stage. Cutting behind a series of vendors peddling sensory experiences from cloud divers on Saturn, she made certain to place a lot of space between herself and her debtor, no reason to have an unfortunate encounter with him botch the opportunity to do a job with Jesse.

After that and a few other near misses with people she really didn't want to meet today—or ever if she could help it—Trist finally found her friend.

Jesse was where Trist thought she would be, though she hadn't expected the scene she encountered. Her friend was standing on a shop's counter screaming at the proprietor. Trist stopped and reconsidered her friend's past behavior. The real question was why she *hadn't* expected a scene like this. Theatrics were like food and power to Jesse. Trist approached quietly, interested in what this particular altercation was about.

The scene was accented by the fact that Jesse's body was covered in a skin-tight sheath that gave off waves of silver and gold light. Her hair was silver and waving as though it was blowing in a soft breeze. It was intended to be intimidating, though the store owner didn't seem fazed.

"I don't care what you say, Drew. This IF set you sold me yesterday is a dud, it was DOA! Don't you try and give me the song and dance about how I screwed it up, I was doing IF jobs when you were still a single cell in stasis!"

"Right, Jesse. You've never cooked a single circuit in your life, just like I've never stubbed my toe. How's about you get off my counter and buy a new IF like anyone else who cooks a unit. Or is your little hissy fit an indicator of your skill?"

Trist smirked. Despite her friend's claims, Trist had witnessed Jesse cook an IF unit on more than one occasion. That didn't mean that Drew's units were always perfect either. In this part of the ring the odds were often in favor of the vendor selling junk, especially this vendor. Jesse was testing him to see if he would assume he had accidentally sold her a broken unit.

"Don't push her, Drew." Trist glided up to the counter. "You know she'll contact ChoSec and have them investigate where you get your supply from."

Drew cast one of his many cybernetic eyes her way. "Nice to see you, Trist. I highly doubt it. If they investigate me, they may just decide to make sure everyone I have been selling to has a valid license to do IF work. I imagine that your fake credentials can stand up to the p-auth system's checks, but it wouldn't take too much double-checking to expose them for some very illegal forgeries."

Jesse hopped down off the counter and managed to look contrite. "Now Drew, neither of us wants to go and do anything crazy like that. We were all just talking hypothetically."

Drew sat down on a stool behind his counter. "Right. Hypothetical. Now what say you hypothetically buy a new unit or get out of my shop."

Jesse's face turned dark. "That's how it's gonna be? No deal, no haggling, not even the slightest of implied warranties?"

Drew didn't say anything as he stared at the two girls.

"Damn you!" Jesse spat. "That's the last cred I'm dropping in your shithole. I'm taking my business to Blaine. At least he knows what the word quality means."

"You do that." Drew scowled.

No one moved for several moments. Drew and Jesse stared at one another while Trist did her best not to burst into laughter.

"Oh fuck it," Jesse said as her eyes flicked up to the left. "There, the creds are transferred, gimme a new goddamn unit."

Drew unlocked a door behind the counter and pulled out an interface unit. "Pleasure doing business with you."

"I'm sure it is." She turned and left, Trist following behind, hiding a smile with her hand. Once they were on the street she turned to Trist. "Why didn't you help me in there?"

"'Cause I saw you cook that unit last night. I could even see the scorch marks on it in that poorly lit hole of Drew's."

"What? You're the honest thief now? How's that work?"

"I've done my evil deed for the day. I got a hold of a sweet manifest. I have transit times, dates, crate numbers, the whole shebang."

"So what? There are manifests everywhere."

"Yeah, but this one has shown me a bit of a security hole, and I plan to slip into that hole and slip out with some sweet shit heading for the GSS *Intrepid*."

"That colony ship they're building out at Mars that nearly got blown up awhile back?"

"Yeah, there's some serious high-end neuro conduit and supplemental processors in the shipment; stuff that if we found the right buyer we could retire on."

"Seriously?"

"Would I joke about something like that?"

Jesse stopped and peered intently at her friend. "Hank, is she lying?"

<No dilation…well, no more than is normal for her. No twitching, she's not biting her cheek. Either she's managed to control all of her tells or she's being truthful.> Jesse's AI spoke on an open Link between the two girls.

"So when do we leave?"

ILLUSION

STELLAR DATE: 3227242 / 10.16.4123 (Adjusted Gregorian)
LOCATION: District 9B2, Ring 14, Callisto Orbital Habitat (Cho)
REGION: Jovian Combine, Sol Space Federation

"Status on disabling the biosensors?" Jesse asked.

"Almost there," Trist whispered in response. "I just need to finish the loopback so the secage doesn't notice a drop in signal strength."

"I doubt that the secage monitoring this place would even notice." Jesse cast a disdainful eye down the corridor they were in. "Looks like even ChoSec forgot this place existed decades ago."

"People may forget, but the AI doesn't. If I don't cover our asses we're gonna find some guard's stun gun up them."

"That may not be so bad if he's any good with it."

"Ugh."

Trist finished with her rewiring of the circuitry and slipped her tools back into their case. Jesse picked up the cover for the section of conduit they had exposed and held it in place while Trist fastened it.

"We good to go then?" Jesse said as they stood.

"As far as every surveillance circuit is concerned, we're totally invisible."

"Just what I like to hear."

The two women slipped down the corridor toward their goal, the large double seal of the Norcon Warehouse A2-34-B. Their silsuits set to their standard thieving camouflage.

They reached the seal and Jesse slapped a wireless hack pad over the section of wallplate they knew the door control conduit ran behind. "Little bit of this, little bit of that and"—the door chirped and opened—"we're in just like we work here."

<*You two are far too full of yourselves.*> Sue spoke into both their minds.

<*Isn't that what you like about them?*> Hank asked. <*You told me that you found it to be cute.*>

<*Doesn't mean I can't make disdainful comments about it.*>

<*One of these days you'll just admit that you're a neuro-pulse junkie and you can drop the pretense.*>

<*What, like you?*>

"Why do they always bicker when we are in tense situations?" Trist asked.

"'Cause they like to up the odds. We're getting too good at this, not as much of a rush for them."

"I don't know how much I like the idea of my AI putting me at risk for a rush."

<*It's not like we'd ever do anything that bad,*> Sue said. <*If you get caught so do we, at best we're accessories, at worst they wipe us.*>

Sue had a point, AI tended to police their ranks with far more severity than humans did. No human fully understood their laws, but the petabytes of data regarding punishments were enough to daunt anyone, flesh or silicon.

Throughout the conversation the two women took stock of the warehouse. It wasn't too large, only about a half kilometer across with direct access to the west docks on the far end. The pallets destined for the GSS *Intrepid* were in section A1-4 of the warehouse, several rows over. They strode past the towers of cargo until they came to the items they were looking for.

Crates from STR Con were stacked in orderly piles and they pulled the topmost down and checked its ID. This one contained some high-end self-organizing circuits. SOCs were very useful when a small component needed to be extremely diverse and even change its own function based on need. They also weren't cheap. Popping the crate open, Jesse slipped several packages into her duffle.

"Next."

They opened several more crates and pulled odds and ends that would sell well and not result in too many questions. Both women would have loved to take everything they laid eyes on, but there was no way they could sneak several tons of equipment out of the warehouse.

"Look at that," Trist said. "Silbio."

"No way." Jesse checked the ID on the crate. "I didn't know they had perfected that stuff well enough to start shipping it willy-nilly around the Sol system."

"I guess they did. Too bad it's in those big tubs, we'd be able to retire off what that stuff is worth." Trist broke the seal on one of the tubs and peered inside at the dull blue of the silbio mixture.

"Don't get carried away," Jesse said.

"Said the thruster calling the rocket hot."

<*That's a truly bad adaptation of that saying,*> Hank commented.

"It's an adaptation?" Trist asked.

"What was that sound?" Jesse held up her hand and looked around.

<*Metal on metal scrape, I make it to have come from the doors you entered through,*> Sue informed them.

<*I count several footfalls…distinguishing…five sets. Coming this way.*>

Trist and Jesse stuffed several more items into their duffels and turned to slip out the far end of the warehouse. They stepped around a tower of plas products to find themselves face-to-face with the muzzle of a projectile weapon.

"You two ladies had best step back into the aisle there." The man waved the gun and the two women slowly backed up. To their left the five visitors Hank had identified came into view.

<*How'd you miss this guy?*> Trist asked Sue.

<*He's got a pretty advanced infiltration suit; it's masking all of his sounds, smell, heat, the whole deal. If it weren't for visual input, I wouldn't be able to tell he's there even now.*>

<*That's some impressive stuff.*>

The group of five reached the two women. They consisted of four women and a lanky man in the front. He grinned and Trist decided it was one of the least appealing smiles she had ever seen.

"You two ladies are messing with things you shouldn't be," he drawled. Behind him, his four female associates spread out to better cover Trist and Jesse with their weapons.

"You don't look much like the security detail yourself," Jesse said. "I'm sure we can just live and let live."

"See, I don't think that's how it's going to work."

"Why's that?" Jesse asked.

"Well, you're here for a reason, and so are we. You're here because we let you get the manifest for this shipment, and we're here to make a fucking mess of it and you. Then we stage it to look like you two fought and killed each other."

"You're kidding me," Trist said. "I busted my ass getting that manifest. No one 'let' me get it."

"You're hot shit, but not that hot," a girl holding a very large rifle sneered.

"She's right," the lanky man said. "You've been had. See there are people, people we are associated with, who don't want this stuff to get to its destination. Law forbids blocking the sale when a buyer is willing to pay full price, so our employers are required to fulfill the order. It sorta irks them to have to do it, so we're going to fix things up so they don't have to."

"I don't get that at all…STR doesn't want to sell its stuff?" Jesse asked.

"I think they don't want it to get to the *Intrepid*," Trist said.

"Oh, you *are* bright," the man with the projectile weapon said.

"'Nuff talk," the lanky man shouted. "Let's just finish this and get out of here." He leveled his blaster at Jesse and fired a round directly into her face. Brain matter and metal from her AI sprayed out the back of her head.

Trist screamed incoherently and lunged at the man. Three shots from the girl with the rifle caught her in the torso before she took her second step. The scream died in a long gurgle as she clutched her chest and stumbled backward. One of the other girls fired a few more shots into Trist, causing her to topple over into the open tub of silbio.

"Nice shooting, Kris," the lanky man observed. "Set a det and let's get out of here."

One of the girls knelt down to set a charge; moments later they were gone.

INTERLUDE

STELLAR DATE: 3227278 / 11.21.4123 (Adjusted Gregorian)
LOCATION: Mars Outer Shipyards (MOS)
REGION: Mars Protectorate, Sol Space Federation

"About time this shipment from STR showed up." Jens looked the pallets over as they were unloaded from the freight transport to Mars Outer Shipyards dock T5-7A.

"They had some excuse about a break-in at a subcontractor's warehouse," Petrov mumbled, examining the shipping manifest. "Looks like everything made it though. Manifest does say that they had to repack some things and reseal one of the silbio tubs."

"Are you serious?" Jens said. "You can't just unseal and reseal those tubs. If a single milligram of that stuff is contaminated there's gonna be one hell of a suit on STR."

Petrov nodded and grabbed a scanner to get a reading on the resealed tub. He scowled at the display and shook the device before getting another reading. "I think something's wrong with my scanner."

"I don't like the sound of that," Jens said.

"I read massive bio signals in here."

"Massive? How's that happen?"

"Uh...Jens...I think there's a body in here."

Jens couldn't speak for a moment. Lieutenant Collins would be all over his ass, the major would want a full investigation and the rest of his day would be shot.

"How could that slip by on the other end?"

"You gotta calibrate properly for silbio. The whole mess is technically organic, so it would just read as 'alive' to any regular scanner."

Jens sighed and got on the Link to call in a medic team to take possession of the tub. The body was probably dead, and that was going to generate a mess of paperwork.

Petrov chuckled, "How the hell do you RMA something like this?"

HITCHHIKER

STELLAR DATE: 3227279 / 11.22.4123 (Adjusted Gregorian)
LOCATION: Mars Outer Shipyards (MOS)
REGION: Mars Protectorate, Sol Space Federation

"When will she be conscious?" Tanis asked.

"Not too long now," the medic said. "Her AI apparently linked in with some of the silbio and put her in a sort of pseudo-cryo; it used some of the stuff to seal her wounds, too."

"Have we got anything from her AI on what happened?"

"Not yet, the AI completely ran out of power trying to sustain the cryo. It's in hard shutdown; it'll take the girl's command to get it to re-init."

"It's always something." Tanis sighed.

The medic blinked rapidly. "Looks like she's coming to; let's go see what she has to say."

The girl—woman, Tanis corrected herself—lying on the slab was shorter than average, probably only five and a half feet. Uncommon to see in an age when nearly all children were more designed than simply "had." She appeared somewhat dazed as she looked around the medroom; the one organic eye blearily attempting to focus on her surroundings.

"Hello, miss. I'm Dr. Anne Rosenberg. You're on the Mars Outer Shipyards; you've been shot, but you're going to be OK, thanks to your AI."

"My AI? I...I can't hear her! She's not here!" A look of panic spread across the woman's face.

"Relax," Dr. Rosenberg said. "She ran your internal power down and you're going to need to run her through her startup sequence—though I strongly recommend that you don't do that until you are better rested."

"I'm Major Richards," Tanis said. "We don't have any ID on you and you really weren't expected on MOS. Do you have any idea how you ended up here?"

"Name's...Trist. I remember being on Callisto R14...I remember dying."

"You would have if your AI hadn't plugged you up with the silbio. Saved your life." Dr. Rosenberg gave Trist a soothing smile.

"I'm guessing you weren't in that warehouse on Callisto to give our shipment your seal of approval, were you," Tanis asked.

Trist chuckled; it was low and throaty. "Only the best in the Space Force I see. Yeah, I was there with my friend—Jesse—we were lifting some stuff."

"The report I was delivered said that your friend took a bullet to the head. Care to elaborate on what happened?" Dr. Rosenberg shot Tanis an incredulous look and she realized perhaps a little more tact wouldn't have hurt.

"Aw shit...Jesse." Trist's eye lost its focus and she shuddered, trying to keep control of herself. "Any chance I can just go back to being dead?"

"I don't really think that's going to get on the list of options," Tanis replied. "I'm sorry about your friend...sorry I brought it up like that."

Trist grimaced, but nodded slowly.

"Look, why don't you just start at the beginning, and take me through it." Tanis said.

Trist didn't say a word for several minutes, Tanis suspected that she was having a conversation with her AI about their options. Then, slowly, she proceeded to explain how she had acquired the manifest of items being shipped to the *Intrepid,* broken into the warehouse and been ambushed by some unknown thugs. The last thing she remembered was being shot after seeing Jesse die.

"So I'm guessing that for whatever reason, the shipment still got sent here, and somehow, me with it," Trist concluded. "How did that happen anyway?"

"Gunshots alerted a security drone that was patrolling the warehouse you had been in. It arrived on the scene to find a detonation charge planted on one of the opened crates. The charge was disabled and when crews arrived to check everything over they found that some items were in duffels, but otherwise all the cargo was still present. For whatever reason they didn't see your body and just sealed the silbio up again—I don't know how they thought that was going to pass muster. The official record was entered as some sort of dispute between thieves with one fatality. They surmised the other must have run off after the gunshots to avoid detection."

Trist looked perplexed. "You've asked me a lot of questions, but I have one. How am I still alive? I have this distinct impression that I was dying when that loud-mouthed bitch shot me." She ran a hand across her torso, almost as though she expected to find holes where the rounds had impacted her.

Dr. Rosenberg provided the answer. "Your AI managed to interface with the silbio and programmed it to form a seal on your wounds and put you into a semi-cryo state. It was really quite an ingenious bit of work; you are lucky to be alive."

"Sue is pretty damn clever; I bet not any AI could have pulled that off." Trist grinned.

"I wouldn't get too excited," the doctor cautioned. "No one has ever done what she did with silbo. Somehow the process has caused it to bind to your DNA with consequences I can't quite foresee. You wouldn't be the first human to be a bit more silicon than flesh, but this is different."

Trist grimaced, and then gave a half smile, "so when someone asks animal, mineral, or vegetable I can say all three?"

Tanis found the attitude to be a bit too blasé and Angela added her own internal comment. *<Mostly vegetable, I'd say.>*

"You're not a vegetable yet," Doctor Rosenberg said. "I don't see any immediate impact on your neurological facilities or AI interface—which appears to be illegal, I might add—but I have found some additional interconnectivity that we'll need to look into more carefully. Quite honestly it's a very exciting accident."

"I'm glad it's so beneficial to you."

The doctor gave Trist a caustic look. "I'd say that the majority of the benefit is yours. You'd be dead otherwise."

"I do kinda like being alive."

Tanis took the opportunity to redirect the conversation, "And while it's great that you're alive, you've got some things to answer for." She kept to herself that this could actually be a blessing in disguise. This woman might have seen something that would help them. "There will most likely be charges of trespass from Callisto, and then there's the cost of our tub of silbio. I think that it will run you about a century's wages."

Trist sank back. "I guess there's no running from this one is there?"

"Not even the slimmest chance," Tanis said. "However…" She let it hang out there for a minute, watching Trist grow agitated with interest.

"However what?" Trist finally asked.

"Your testimony would be useful for starters."

"Against who? Some guy who I can only describe as 'the skinny guy with the bimbo squad'?"

"More or less," Tanis replied. "We think we know who he is, and if we could gain some leverage against him he could point us in the direction of who is calling the shots. Maybe then we'd have a chance of making some headway against STR."

Trist rose up on her elbows. "You want me to testify against STR? Are you nuts?"

"You know, Dr. Rosenberg, I think we've bothered our guest enough for one day. I'll come back to see her tomorrow."

"I was about to say the same thing," the doctor replied.

"Lieutenant Amy Lee will be getting in touch with you to transport our guest aboard the *Intrepid*. I don't want any unexpected visitors ending her time with us."

The doctor nodded and Tanis left the MOS north sector's med facilities.

<This is just the break we've needed,> Tanis said to Angela. *<Her ID will be enough for us to put out a warrant on Trent, and then we are only one step away from finding out who is calling the shots at STR.>*

<If you can get it. I bet that Callisto will want Trist back. In my experience they'll be hesitant to sign out a warrant on Trent without her being delivered first.>

<And then there goes our leverage.> Tanis nodded to herself.

<Your brain chemistry indicates you have a 'plan'. It's got that certain mix of serotonin and dopamine you get when you think you've been particularly clever.>

<Your chemical analysis of my brain really takes a lot of fun out of things, you know that?>

<I do, it's partially why I do it. So what's the plan?> Angela replied.

<We'll sign out a warrant against Trent in a Federal SolCourt court.>

<Even if you can get a federal warrant, Callisto can still stall for months on carrying it out.>

Tanis smiled to herself. *<That's why AI need us humans; you can't quite get our motivations. Trent won't allow a material witness of Jovian citizenship to live. Callisto can ignore my charges against him because of the Io Accord, but they can't ignore hers. He'll come for her.>*

<He'll come back to InnerSol space? But then you can pursue him.>

<I know that, and he knows that, but he'll still come.>

Angela made a noise that Tanis had come to identify as her signal of frustration. *<You're right; I don't get it at all. Though I do get the part where you're going to use Trist as bait.>*

<I think she'll be more than that.> Tanis leapt on the back of a cargo hauler heading across the docks toward the *Intrepid*. *<She's no slouch if she could pull off what she did. Sure Trent duped her into doing it, but she had to be good enough that the ChoSec folks on Callisto would have believed her capable of that break-in without help.>*

<So how do you expect to use her?> Angela asked.

<Not entirely certain, but I've got a feeling she could come in handy.>

Angela and Tanis cut their conversation short as a call came in from Joe.

<You busy? I've got a duty officer from MOS saying that she's got a request to move your surprise visitor to the Intrepid *but also a pending extradition request from Callisto. They seem a*

bit uncertain about which to follow.>

<That was fast. Someone must have been checking the Jane Does and noticed when one got a name attached,> Angela said.

<Tell them we're going to be taking her to Callisto when we stop there on our way outsystem,> Tanis replied to Joe.

<Please tell me you aren't really going to turn her over.> Joe sounded worried.

<Of course not. Get Amy Lee down there right away, though. I want to reinforce our position via people carrying weapons. I don't have an overabundance of trust in the folks here at MOS.>

<Nothing to do with how much you like to mess with them?> Joe asked before closing the connection with a chuckle.

"Just seems practical to me..." Tanis said to herself as the hauler sped across the loading dock to the *Intrepid*.

<I couldn't help but notice that you are somehow both more and less formal with him than normal,> Angela commented.

Tanis didn't respond immediately. *<I honestly don't know how to act. That's why I hate that he did anything. I don't know how to behave...though he seems to have no problem going back to his old self.>*

<You didn't analyze his vocal patterns all that carefully. That laugh of his was somewhat strained. He's unsure about how to act around you as well.>

Tanis grunted. *<Well, he has no one to blame but himself. As long as he can be professional then everything will be OK.>*

<Whatever you say, human.>

Somehow the term seemed a bit more derisive than normal.

MACHINATIONS

STELLAR DATE: 3227280 / 11.23.4123 (Adjusted Gregorian)
LOCATION: GSS *Intrepid*, Mars Outer Shipyards (MOS)
REGION: Mars Protectorate, Sol Space Federation

Joe took a seat across from Tanis in her office. "I assume you actually have a plan now? One that isn't just 'we use the civilian as bait'?"

Joe, for his part, had been true to his word in demonstrating that they could work together and not have his feelings get in the way. She was still somewhat uncertain about what tone her interactions with him should take, but it was becoming easier, especially when she was deep in her work.

She pulled her lips back in a predatory grin. "Of course I have a plan. I always have a plan."

<In case you weren't aware, that's her 'my plan involves violence' look,> Angela supplied.

"I've made the connection, but thanks," Joe said.

"It's simple, really. We go to the federal buildings on Mars 1 and go before a superior court judge to get warrants signed out that Callisto can't ignore."

"Yeah, you said that yesterday, but it's still not really something I'd call a plan."

Tanis brought up maps for the MOS, the MCEE, and Mars 1. Certain sections were highlighted and she zoomed in on those.

"We're going to take a route that, while secure, passes through some places where we'll be certain to be ambushed. I expect Trent to be involved and we'll nab him."

<That's the plan?> Angela asked. *<Get our asses, physical and metaphorical, shot off? Your BLT could come up with a better plan!>*

"She has a point," Joe said. "How do you know Trent will even be there?"

"Well, if he's not then we'll have warrants that Callisto will have to execute. Either way we'll flush him out."

"I don't know how that's going to help. He doesn't exactly have a physical address that the ChoSec folks can show up at."

"No, but it will restrict his movement."

"I imagine he has ways of slipping about," Joe said.

"I should hope so. Either way the legal ball needs to be rolling…especially since it rolls so slowly."

"I still don't like this. There are too many things that could go wrong. Your route here puts you in a lot of danger."

"It does, but we can't just contact the Federation DA and tell them to arrest the whole STR Consortium, we need to get the name of whoever gave the orders and pulled the strings. Getting our hands on Drenn would work too, but he's been playing this game for a long time. I'm guessing that he's lying very low right now."

"He'd be on the first ship to Alpha Centauri if he knew what was good for him." Joe shook his head. "By the way, I heard you went down to the surface with Captain Andrews. What was that about?"

Tanis twisted her lips, thinking about the goal of that trip. What they brought back up to the *Intrepid* had answered all her questions about why Terrance and the Reddings were coming along to New Eden. The knowledge was like a burr in the back of her mind, but she knew that it was imperative it remain a secret.

"Good. I gave him a hand with a few things."

Joe's tone remained impassive, but the curiosity was obvious in his face. "What sort of things?"

Tanis grimaced. "I wish I could say, but I can't. I'll tell you once we're underway."

They discussed other issues for several minutes before Joe left for an inspection on Blue Wing. Tanis took a few minutes to relax in the relative peace and quiet before rising to hit the officer's mess for a late night meal before bed.

She whistled a tuneless melody as she walked through the halls of officer country. It was third shift and few people were about; Tanis was half watching where she was going and half paying attention to some time tables that Angela was running through in the back of her mind.

She rounded a corner and thought she caught a shadow out of the corner of her eye, a blur that was there one moment and gone the next. Looking behind her she saw nothing, and, pausing, heard only the sound of air circulation coming from a nearby vent.

Something wasn't right. Tanis evaluated her surroundings, checking for aberrant scents, sounds, and vibrations. Sure enough, the sound of the vent was too loud.

Tanis slowed her pace and leaned back against the bulkhead, pretending to have gotten a message via Link that required all of her concentration. Instead, what she was doing was sending out preconfigured noise-cancelling nano. They spread through the corridor, determining what the actual sound of the moving air was and clearing it from Tanis's hearing. All that was left was the additional noise. The nano attempted to triangulate and pick up its source, but were unable to do so. It appeared to be coming from everywhere.

Then a sensation prickled within Tanis, almost as though she could sense another being's presence, and she threw up an arm to fend off a blow. To her surprise, she actually did deflect a strike. Instinct told her where the attacker would be and she lashed out with her boot and felt it connect with an unseen body. Tanis thanked the foresight that had caused her to amp up her olfactory system; that had to be what was giving her this intuition.

<*Bets on it being her?*> Tanis referred to the female attacker from the *Steel Dawn III*.

<*The odds are too much in your favor for a bet,*> Angela responded.

"You know," Tanis spoke aloud to her attacker. "I can't see you, but I can smell the patterns you're making in the air currents. Why don't you just drop this sneaky assassin thing and we can do this the old-fashioned way?"

A figure materialized in front of Tanis, every inch covered in a skintight glossy black outfit. There weren't even any apparent openings for the wearer to breathe or see. Most likely that was done to mask IR output from hot breath. Tanis found herself wanting one.

The figure was obviously female and Tanis's records showed that the height, weight, bone structure, and overall posture matched the woman she had fought previously on the *Dawn*.

No weapons were visible, but that didn't mean that they weren't there.

"As you wish." The sound seemed to come from the figure's entire body. "Would you like to do this hand to hand, or not quite that old-fashioned?" An obvious challenge resonated in the woman's tone. Her body posture was confident and tense all at the same time.

"Oh what the hell, Kris." Tanis grinned. "It's been a very long time since I tore the stuffing out of anyone with my bare hands. It is Kris, by the way, isn't it?"

"Good memory, Tanis. Now that we're on a first name basis, shall we get on with it?"

Tanis didn't wait for a response, but sent a TSF-issued boot—polished so even Williams would be proud—up and around in a textbook roundhouse kick to her opponent's head. Kris wasn't there anymore, but Tanis hadn't expected her to be. It wouldn't be a very fun fight if she won with a single kick.

With that the battle was joined. Kris was skilled, something Tanis already knew, and both of the women's limbs flashed out and were blocked or deflected by the other in turn. It was as though they were participating in a complicated dance and each had the moves down perfectly.

Even so, Tanis felt that she was at a bit of a disadvantage. No tells were offered by her opponent. Normally a grimace or a look in the eyes would give intentions away, but the featureless mask prevented that. She wanted one of these suits even more.

The moment of reflection almost caused her to fall for a feint, and she blocked the real strike at the last moment, wincing as the blow deflected off her forearm. Kris's attacks were powerful; she was most certainly cybernetically enhanced.

She wasn't the only one; the TSF didn't let you above commander if you were just flesh and blood. A little carbon nanofiber here, some titanium there coupled with some X5A sinew and *then* you were all you could be.

"You're not too bad," Kris commented with a hint of appreciation in her voice.

"Not too shabby yourself. Why don't you give up and we'll call it a draw."

"Not very likely," Kris said. "I'm going to collect that credit on your head and retire somewhere real nice. Maybe New Eden."

"Any way we could fake my death and split the take?" Tanis asked. "This job doesn't pay for shit."

Her comment caused Kris just a moment of pause and Tanis used that to make a daring attack with both her left foot and right arm. The blows wrenched Kris and dislocated her shoulder. A follow-up strike to the base of her skull ended the fight in Tanis's favor.

The black figure went down in a heap, and Tanis waited for the TSF team she had called during the fight to secure the body. She had no idea how Kris had planned to get off the ship, that was something she would have to ask the woman.

"Put her with our collection. We're gonna have us a nice long talk. And save the suit, but make sure it doesn't have any surprises. I can think of a really good use for that puppy."

A TEMPTING OFFER

STELLAR DATE: 3227282 / 11.25.4123 (Adjusted Gregorian)
LOCATION: GSS *Intrepid*, Mars Outer Shipyards (MOS)
REGION: Mars Protectorate, Sol Space Federation

Trist had been moved to the medical facilities on the *Intrepid*, a place Tanis was already quite familiar with after her mods for the trip to Cruithne. After a couple of days, the thief was well on her way to full health, though portions of her body were now made up of silbio, the value of which was greater than most people would make in a hundred years.

They were sitting in one of the lounges in the medical facilities, each with a cup of coffee. Tanis was taking hers black, something that a lot of time in the field forced you to like whether you preferred it or not, while Trist was drinking some concoction that could only have come from Ganymede; it consisted of several different spices, milks, creams, and possibly some actual coffee.

"I gotta hand it to you folks," Trist said. "You sure know how to make a girl feel at home—if home were a fluffy, cushy prison."

"You're not a prisoner…exactly," Tanis replied.

"Kinda feels like it with virtually no Link access, no permission to leave my room unless I've got a couple of burly types with me, and no knowledge of what my future holds."

"Well, what do you think we should do with you?" Tanis asked.

Trist cast her a sidelong glance. "You're not tricking me with that one. I've been around long enough to know someone's looking to see if I'll hang myself with the line they give me."

Tanis smiled. "Sorry."

"Just sorry? Why am I the one guiding this conversation? Didn't you come here to see me?"

"I did, I'm just trying to decide exactly what to do with you. You won't testify against the STR, which means that I don't have a lot of use for you. However, sending you back out into the system is a bit of a death sentence and I don't feel totally comfortable with that either."

"What? The cold-as-ice Major Tanis Richards, the Butcher of Toro, would feel bad about me getting my head blown off? I think your reputation is a smoke screen."

It was Tanis's turn to cast a glance at Trist. "I thought you had no Link access."

"Oh I don't, at least I don't right now. I managed to slip past the safeguards a few times until some broad named Amanda gave me the smackdown. Took me a bit, but I got past her eventually and was wandering through some personnel files when some guy named Bob came into my mind and told Sue and I that if we even sent a photon across the Link he would turn our brains off. Was a real jackass about it too."

Tanis's eyebrows rose considerably. "You got a visit from the *Intrepid*. He doesn't deign to speak to us mere mortals much anymore. You should be honored…or possibly scared witless that he addressed you."

Trist's eye widened. "He wouldn't really…"

"Who knows; he's a very advanced AI, there aren't any others like him in the human sphere."

Trist whistled. "Good thing I hadn't implemented my plan to get past him."

"Good thing indeed. Otherwise I wouldn't be able to offer you this deal."

"Finally we get to it."

"We'll grant you and Sue immunity from extradition in the SolGov territories. Any past crimes committed in those areas, or against organizations based in SolGov controlled space will be pardoned. In exchange for that we require your testimony against Trent."

Trist considered it for a moment. "Not going to be good enough. STR will come after us, or even if it doesn't we'll live our whole lives waiting for the other shoe to drop."

"Well, we can't get you pardoned by the Jovians, they won't budge. It's possible they will once we nail the STR, though."

"No, I'll tell you what I'll do it for. I want in."

"In?" Tanis asked, though she was pretty sure that she knew what Trist wanted.

"Yeah, in. I want to be on the colony roster."

Tanis raised an eyebrow, wondering how the GSS would feel if she circumvented them to get a known criminal onto the *Intrepid*.

"You do have decent credentials, but you really don't pass a lot of the other screening parameters."

Trist crossed her arms. "And I want my mods upgraded. I want a real eye with all of the extra performance and I want a normal-looking hand. Everything state of the art."

Tanis leaned back and took a sip of her coffee. Stuff tasted like bile. "How much of you is still human?"

"Fifty-fifty, depending on what you count my new secret ingredient as," Trist said. "Sue would, of course, like her specs upgraded as well. I've got the full requirements in a file that I'm sending you."

Tanis received it and looked it over. It was quite the request, though honestly not even worth mentioning in the grand scope of the *Intrepid*'s construction, or even the cost of her more basic security enhancements.

"I'll have to discuss your addition to the roster with the colony leaders. As for the mods, I'll schedule the surgeries as a show of good faith."

Trist all but beamed. "I'll give you the testimony of a lifetime."

"Just stick to the truth." Tanis sighed.

BAIT

STELLAR DATE: 3227284 / 11.27.4123 (Adjusted Gregorian)
LOCATION: GSS *Intrepid*, Mars Outer Shipyards (MOS)
REGION: Mars Protectorate, Sol Space Federation

"I don't know how much I like this plan." Trist fidgeted. "I sort of get the feeling that I'm bait."

"That would be because you are bait," Tanis replied. "However, you'll be very safe bait, especially since you are just their secondary target. They'll be jumping at the chance to get at me with the minimal protection I'll have on Mars 1."

"Yay, so I'll be secondary bait right next to the primary bait." Trist sighed. "How did I get myself mixed up in this?"

"I believe it was by leading a life of crime and wrongdoing," Joe's tone was caustic.

Trist turned on him. "Yeah, you try growing up on the lower Callisto rings. Either you dish shit out or you eat it. I chose not to do the eating."

"She does have a point, sirs," Williams said. "I've been to Callisto; it's nice up top, the part most tourists and visitors see, but down below it's a real heap—the classic scenario of the poor maintaining the system for the rich. They could probably run it cheaper with bots, but why fix what they can ignore?"

"Be that as it may," Tanis checked over her equipment one more time, "it doesn't change the fact that our course of action is fixed. We're going to Mars 1 to give our depositions. We've got our route covered and while I expect that they'll attack before we make our destination, I don't think it will be anything a few squads of Marines can't handle. Mark my words, by the end of this day we'll have Trent."

Trist's expression grew dark and Joe, Williams, and Tanis all got a glimpse of a very different woman than the one she had seen recovering in medical.

"Any chance I can get a few minutes alone with him?"

"Probably not," Tanis replied. "Though for what it's worth, I echo your sentiment."

<We just got patched up and upgraded,> Sue said. *<Don't go signing up to get us wrecked—besides, now that you look un-modded with your new eye and hand he may not even recognize you.>*

"Don't worry," Trist turned her hand over and flexed her fingers. "I'm pretty sure I could remind him." She glanced up at Tanis and Joe. "Sorry, I guess that sounds a bit stupid—but he did kill my best friend. I'm finding that pretty hard to let go of."

Joe's expression softened placed a hand on her shoulder. "It's not an easy road you have ahead of you."

Trist's expression flashed confusion and mistrust. "I was under the impression that you don't think I'm all that trustworthy."

"The jury's still out on that as far as I'm concerned, but I do know what it's like to literally have to face your demons," Joe said. "Just keep a clear head and don't get in the way."

Trist opened her mouth to give a retort, but Williams used a Marine sergeant look on her and she shut up.

Tanis didn't quite know why, but she found herself liking Trist more than she would have expected, and also a bit annoyed with Joe for his attitude toward her. Being in MICI had made her world mostly full of shades of grey. She sometimes forgot that his was likely much more black and white.

No time to think about that now, she put her analysis of Joe aside and got back to the task at hand. "Enough chatting, let's get this show on the road."

* * * * *

Williams liked Major Richards, which is why he had assigned himself to the team which was her escort detail. One/one had also volunteered to be the escorting fireteam—apparently they had taken a liking to the major as well. He hadn't often witnessed an officer impressing the enlisted so quickly, especially a Micky officer.

In his estimation, it was a shame that she would be shipping out on the *Intrepid*. The TSF needed more people like her. Even her number two, Commander Evans, wasn't a bad sort. He certainly had proven his bars in piloting that freighter.

However, Williams did have some misgivings about this venture. The major was walking into an obvious trap—planning to spring it, in fact. The last time she deliberately sprung a trap she had ended up on a dock surrounded by nearly a hundred mercs all gunning for her.

His thought process caused him to recheck the route and ensure that all teams were in position. The rest of his platoon would be making a show of patrolling certain areas on the ring. The Mars 1 authorities had raised quite the stink when they caught wind of this venture, but they were brought to heel by the TSF. Preliminary Micky reports indicated M1 security would have their people out in force on the ring as well. Several pundits on the nets were postulating that M1 security didn't want to garner the reputation the MOS had for shoddy security—or they wanted all the glory for themselves.

Probably both.

Looking at the intel that was coming in from the tactical net, Williams could see the positions Mars 1's security had taken up; some were decent and others looked poor to say the least. Hopefully they wouldn't get in the way too much. In his experience, killing local cops always made the brass grumpy.

The team left the *Intrepid* and crossed the dock with no trouble. From there, several tubes and a maglev took them to the connector elevator that ran down to the MCEE and then Mars 1. They secured a car and the eight of them rode down in silence, the only movement being the weapon ready checks which everyone except Trist made periodically.

The Mars 1 ring generated its gravity from centripetal force as it rotated around the planet at the geosynchronous orbital distance. As a result, the side facing the planet was "up" and the side facing out into space was "down." The ring's top level sported a full ecosystem with hills, lakes, even a few oceans. It was larger than the all of Earth's continents combined, and it was also the location of the team's ultimate destination: the federal courthouses.

Far below, at the lowest level of the Mars 1 ring, the elevator lock cycled open. After sending out probes, the team debarked in careful formation.

Jansen and Lang were in the lead, followed by Williams and Joe, then Tanis and Trist. Cassar and Murphy brought up the rear. The hard stares the Marines were casting cleared a path faster than the presence of their high-powered pulse rifles. Because the ring was not a pressurized system like a standard station, each member also carried a small slug thrower.

In the corridors the team moved through, the twenty-fourth century architecture was nearly something to stop and marvel at. The designers of the ring had added a twist of art deco to their creation. Unlike most stations, which were more utilitarian or very high-tech flashy, Mars 1 was built with an element of garishness. The sweeping archways and overt embellishments of every doorway drew the eye and amazed with the boundless attention to detail.

After clearing security, a process that simply involved a quick check of their IDs and extensive scowling by the Marines, they entered a maglev station that took them seven thousand miles east around the ring.

"So far so good," Joe murmured.

"Oh great…you had to say that," Jansen said. "Er…sir."

"Relax, Marine." Williams scowled. "This won't be anything we can't handle, nothing worse than what we've seen before."

"Aye, Staff Sergeant," Jansen replied, taking a deep breath. "It's the lack of activity…I wish they'd just attack already."

"Don't worry," Tanis said. "You'll get your wish. We've got to change trains ahead, and I anticipate that to be their first probable ambush point. When we debark, stick close to the wall on the right and keep your eyes peeled. When we round the first corner, we may encounter some company."

"You do have people there, right?" Trist asked Tanis. "And I really wish you'd give me a gun."

"Yes. No."

"She'd make a good sergeant," Cassar said.

Williams smiled and Tanis took it as a compliment. Everyone rechecked their weapons as the maglev began to slow; sidearms were loosened in holsters and extra clips were moved into readily accessible positions.

The station was decidedly upscale with a broad atrium ringed by catwalks, a lavish fountain, and a small food court on the far side. It looked empty, strange at this time of day, though nothing was flagged as hostile on the Marine's systems.

"Let's do this," Tanis said and the escort began to move off the train.

Directly into a storm of particle beams.

"Fall back," Williams shouted at Jansen and Lang who were out front while everyone else took protective positions inside the train. The two Marines jumped backwards and Joe and Williams pulled the doors shut.

"Injuries?" Williams called out.

"No sir, armor appears to have absorbed it all," Lang said. Jansen reported the same.

<*We seem to have stirred the hornet's nest. Get this train moving to the next station!*> Tanis said to Angela. <*We need to get gone.*>

<*Already on it, but…*>

An explosion rocked the car and Tanis had a sinking feeling.

<*They just disabled the track, didn't they?*>

<Yup, they're not playing fair. I'm getting probes out to get their positions.>

"Two on that catwalk above." Williams called out. "Cassar, Murphy, get suppressing fire on those bastards. I see muzzle flash coming from that food stand at ten o'clock. Jansen, you and Lang move down one car and see if you can't flank them. I'll hold their attention."

"Two more at three o'clock from around the fountain." Tanis relayed information from Angela's scan. "One/two is also advancing from where we *thought* the ambush would be, but they're under fire as well."

"Sounds like a party." Joe took aim at the fountain, blowing off bits and pieces in an attempt to decrease its cover.

"Someone is not going to be happy that you are chewing apart their art." Cassar said.

"What they get for putting a fountain in a train station." Williams snorted.

"Time for me to use my new toy." Tanis began to pull her light armor off. Underneath she wore the glossy black shimmersuit she had appropriated from the assassin, Kris. She issued the command and the suit flowed up over her head completely covering her.

"I feel like I'm suffocating every time it does that," Tanis said.

"Good look on you though, sir." Joe grinned from where he was taking cover.

Tanis slid two long blades into the covered sheaths on her arms and with a silent command to the suit, faded from view.

"I'm going right to take out the guys behind the fountain. Concentrate your fire on the left side; your scan can't see me and I won't show on combat net—don't want to give off a signal."

"Aye, sir," Williams said and made sure all the Marines knew what to do.

Carefully slipping over the jagged edges of glass in the train car's shattered windows, Tanis cursed softly, wishing that the stealth suit provided some amount of actual safety. Even though she was invisible, the notion of being effectively without protection in a firefight was unnerving.

A scream came from the catwalk and one of the attackers toppled over the railing, courtesy of Cassar's heavy repeater. Tanis caught sight of the heavily armored man as he crashed to the ground. It was similar armor to what the attackers had on the night of the VIP party, only a few revisions newer. Specs showed few weak points and Tanis would have to make the best of them.

Slipping around the fountain she saw four attackers, not two. This would be a bit more challenging than she first thought. Carefully observing them, she planned out her moves.

An initial kick to the back of the man on the left would send him sprawling out into the open, where with luck Joe or Williams would finish him off. A rather spirited woman was cursing loudly as she tried to place her shots through the shattered windows of the train car. The other two women were calmer, and consequently more precise in their shooting.

Having worked out the best moves, Tanis took a running jump and slammed her feet into the man's back. Sure enough, he slid out from behind the cover. Without looking to see if he had been targeted by the Marines, Tanis glanced at the two more controlled women. One had already noticed her compatriot being struck and was looking frantically for the perpetrator. Tanis stepped past her, slid a blade out from her forearm and sliced the throat of the third, more vocal, woman.

Now both of the remaining two were alert, and the screams to her right told Tanis that the Marines had taken out the man.

The two women started firing around themselves wildly. Just barely avoiding being hit, Tanis stepped between them. Quickly sliding out the other blade, she reached out and slit both of their throats at once.

Blood fountained across her and she went from being invisible to being the red sticky outline of a person. A cry rang out from the catwalk and shots rained down around her. Grabbing one of the rifles on the ground, Tanis dove for cover in the fountain, the action having the dual purpose of washing the blood from her and giving her some protection.

The red tint left her vision and she peered around the splashing water trying to get the man overhead within her sights. As it turned out, she didn't need to since when he leaned over to get a bead on her someone else filled him full of holes.

Another few shots rang out and a scream came from Jansen's target, followed by a gun being thrown over the counter and a cry of surrender. Tanis, invisible again, stepped quietly over to the concession stand only to see the final attacker hiding under a candy machine of some sort, a rifle trained on the opening. The weapon he had tossed over the counter must have been that of his dead companion.

Tanis raised her arm and flung a blade at him attempting to hit the creases on his armor's neck. She missed and it bounced off, clattering to the deck. He spun and started shooting wildly in her direction, forcing Tanis to hit the deck.

"Surrender for real or we toss a grenade in there to do the job for you." Williams called out.

"You wouldn't," the man replied. "Station would throw a fit."

"I'm a Marine staff sergeant. Do you really think that I give a monkey's ass what this station thinks? You've got five seconds."

The man didn't even think about it for two. He was out and on the ground so fast he nearly landed on Tanis. Williams was securing him when one/two arrived, looking worn but triumphant.

"Heard you guys needed a hand," Corporal Taylor said.

"We did," Jansen said. "What took you so long?"

"Just ran into a few folks who wanted to turn us into sponges." Taylor grinned. "We showed them how that goes when they try to take on Marines."

The fireteam gave an "Oo Rah" to that and Tanis couldn't help but grin. She walked back to the train to retrieve her armor and weapons.

"Good work," Williams commented. "Make sure all these folks are dead or secure and wait for station security to arrive. We'll be rolling out as soon as the major's ready."

"They're actually right behind us," Taylor said and turned around. "You guys can come through, looks like everything's taken care of here too. Good thing you were around to not help us."

"We came as fast as we could," the man in the lead said. His shoulder patches identified him as a lieutenant in the MSF. "We'll take over this scene, but we'll need statements."

"Those can wait." Tanis stepped from the train car, once again clothed and in her armor. Trist was in her wake casting uneasy glances at the large body of police officers. At least thirty of them had streamed into the atrium.

"Major Richards?" the MSF lieutenant asked.

"Yes..." She waited for him to identify himself.

"Lieutenant Folsom. I'm going to have to ask you and your forces to lay down your weapons and surrender to us."

Tanis wasn't certain she'd heard the man correctly. "You want us to what?"

The Marines had snapped into action the moment Folsom spoke. Raising their weapons they began to ease into positions to cover one another.

"By the authority vested in me by the Mars Protectorate, I am placing you under arrest on the charge of harboring a known terrorist."

"What known terrorist would that be?" Tanis asked.

"The woman with you: Trist. She is wanted by the Jovian government."

"Last I heard, we weren't in Jovian space," Joe said. "Why don't you boys pack up and head out before we place you under arrest for interfering in the prosecution of a federal case."

Tanis saw that Cassar had reached a position offering decent cover. He slowly eased to a knee, switching his weapon to full auto. He had one eye on Williams and the other on the MSF squad. One word and he would have at least ten of them down and out of the fight. Tanis assessed the other Marine's positions through her recon probes while Angela furiously queried Mars 1 databases, trying to find the origin of Folsom's orders.

<*What's the word?*> Tanis asked.

<*Nothing so far. I'm speaking with his CO and am being informed that Folsom isn't here and there is no such order. I don't know what is going on.*>

<*I do,*> Tanis said.

"It appears we have a situation." Tanis scanned the MSF unit. Most of them were arrayed behind Folsom, though a few were slowly easing into flanking positions. "You see, I can't find any validation of your orders. And there is no way I'm just going to surrender to you without them. You've got to know there is no way these Marines will surrender to you under any circumstances."

A few of the cops looked uneasy at that and the stone-cold looks from one/one and one/two only solidified the knowledge that these Marines would go down fighting. Even death here would be more preferable to the Marines than going back to their platoon having been arrested by civilian cops, especially since they were only outnumbered two to one.

"Nevertheless, you will surrender," Folsom said. "We have reinforcements on the way. You'll be subdued."

"Like hell we will," Williams grunted. "I've faced more threatening odds on my own. You station fairies are going to die today if you get in our way."

Tanis grinned; there really was nothing like having a sergeant put it in the simplest possible terms. Several of the MSF men and women were looking a lot less certain and she decided to push it home.

"You have ten seconds to stand down before I log this as an official violation of the Federated Space Treaty, Section 4.2—TSF Charter, paragraph 9. Such violation authorizes TSF forces commanded by an officer ranking commander or higher to respond with lethal force against anybody, official or otherwise, who is interfering with TSF actions."

Folsom still looked resolute and Tanis began to count.

"One."

"Two."

"Three."

"Four."

Several of the MSF men and women put down their weapons and slowly began stepping back, out of the line of fire.

"Five."

"Six."

A couple more left, bringing the MSF numbers down to twenty.

"Seven."

"Eight."

No one else moved. Everyone tensed.

"Nine."

Tanis waited the space of a second and then dove to her right, knocking Trist to the ground while raising her rifle and taking aim at Folsom. He ducked as well and her shots cut through the air where his chest had been.

Cassar opened up and in moments six of the MSF were down and several more were stunned by the rapid fire of his weapon. Perez, one/two's heavy gunner, was less than a second behind in releasing his barrage, and Williams, taking his pissed off look to a whole new level, leaped through the air, horizontal and low, taking out the legs of several MSF officers.

Five seconds later it was over. Taylor had been hit point blank center mass, but his armor had absorbed the impact, leaving him merely sore and embarrassed. Murphy had taken a shot in the shoulder, where his armor creased to allow flexibility. The limb hung stiffly, already suffused with med-nano stemming the bleeding and stitching his sinews back together.

"I'm five by five, Sarge," he grunted. "Can shoot just fine with my other arm."

"Never doubted it for a moment," Williams said. "You keep to the back of your team, though."

"Aye, Sarge."

"I've reported this to the station and local Terran Space Force. A unit is on the way to clean this mess up. As much as I hate to split up, we can't leave all this hardware laying around. One/two, you stay here until the TSF arrives. Don't let any station security in until our people have the scene. Provide your recordings of the event and take up your positions for return route beta; we won't be coming back this way."

"Sir, yes, sir!" came the course of responses.

"One/one, let's move out."

Their route moved into more populated and public areas, an unfortunate necessity. Tanis could see station security forces shadowing them here and there. She was also paying half attention to the web of reports, accusations, and threats that were flooding the nets. The MSF was claiming ignorance of Folsom's actions and simultaneously accusing the TSF of assaulting its personnel. The TSF for its part was opening inquiries and launching inquests into the MSF faster than even an AI could read the orders. Someone's head was going to roll for this and Tanis just hoped hers would still be attached by the end of the day. Sanderson was most likely going to want to take it off himself.

The public had gotten wind of what happened, and leaked security vids were already circulating the nets. It didn't take long for people to figure out where Tanis and her entourage were going. From there speculators posted probable routes, one of them being the actual route Tanis was using. The upside was that those areas started to clear out. Some oblivious folks still wandered past, but for the most part Tanis's group had a very clear path to the federated buildings.

"Coming up on the second projected ambush point," Williams observed.

"What do we expect here?" Joe asked.

"Previous set were Trent's boys. I expect we'll get more of them, or perhaps some other STR special ops unit of some sort. Two/one and two/two are in position in the buildings I've lit up on your HUDs. We have a safe room in that building across the concourse there and there is a weapons dump hidden in that trash disposal across the street."

"Not expecting much here, I see." Cassar chuckled. Tanis wondered about him. He hardly spoke, except when he was expecting to kill someone.

The space was an open square. It was the intersection of two broad thoroughfares—a long stretch with nothing but three small vertical conduits for cover. An ambush here would be hairy. Tanis gave the signal and Jansen and Lang moved over to the left side of the corridor, while Cassar and Williams moved ahead. Murphy stayed back with Trist, Joe, and Tanis.

"You guys take me to all of the best places," Trist said. "Why don't we just take a car?"

"Too risky down here," Tanis replied. "Too many things we can't see when we're moving that fast; that and we're bunched up, we get attacked and we're sitting ducks. This way we can approach each danger zone carefully and with the appropriate cover."

"Somehow I really don't feel covered," Trist muttered.

Joe smiled. "But just think, you'll have the most interesting stories to tell your children."

"I don't plan on children."

"Well…then you can tell them to your cats."

They moved slowly and carefully through the square. A few civilians had been approaching from their left, but upon seeing the Marines slowly creeping along the passage, they found another route. The hum of the station seemed to fade until all they heard was slow breathing and the sound of boots rolling across the deck.

Tanis cocked her head as they reached the middle of the area with no cover.

"Something…" She didn't get to the next word before an invisible blade whistled toward her; only her augmented sense of smell notified her of the shifting air currents and gave her the split second she needed to take the blow on her shoulder plate and not in her neck creases.

"Stealthed attackers!" she cried out as her vision was overlaid with the ghost of the person who had nearly killed her. Other figures danced in and out of her olfactory range, like shadows slipping in and out of visibility.

"Fall back to a wall," Williams yelled, and the Marines complied quickly, not firing, but fingers on their triggers. Tanis pushed Trist back behind her as she ducked a blow and fired a shot with her pistol, catching her attacker in the chest. There was a grunt and he hit the ground, his suit failing in that spot as blood spurted out.

"How many?" Joe asked.

"I can't tell." Tanis's head swept side to side. "I think there are at least a dozen of them."

"Fuck!" Murphy spat. "Nothing in my suit is picking them up. I can't see a goddamn one of them! How do we take them out?"

<*You know what to do; set your rifle to medium power and set up a field of fire, Marines!*> Williams' voice boomed over the combat net. <*Don't hit your teammates, but keep these bastards pinned!*>

Williams grunted as something struck him and blood sprayed out of his left wrist. He didn't say a word, but his right arm whipped out, swinging the butt of his rifle into something that made a sickening crunch, that sound followed by a pained grunt. A second blow was followed by the sound of a body hitting the deck.

"A flesh wound," Williams said regarding his own injury, and proceeded to randomly send out pulse blasts, hoping to catch the enemy or at least keep them pinned down.

Trist knelt down and felt for the body that Williams had dropped. She located it and extruded a probe from her left index finger. It disappeared into the cloaked form and her brow furrowed.

"Their suits are like yours." She glanced up at Tanis, who was doing her best to put holes in the shapes she could see flitting in and out of her vision. "They're one of the latest revisions, but it looks like we're in luck, they're based off the fashion silsuits that are all the rage back in Callisto. That's a poor choice in base technology." She grinned and extruded another probe, this one into another location on the fallen form.

"One of the neat features of the latest silsuits is that they can download new designs and when they're in demo mode can even have the designs loaded without user interaction."

"I think I know where you're going with this." Joe grunted as his armor absorbed a blow from an invisible blade. "What's the ETA?"

"Minute or two."

Tanis put a slug in the attacker that had hit Joe. "Go faster. Jansen and Lang are taking a beating over there."

"Working on it." Trist's brow furrowed.

Across the square, Lang went down and Jansen let out a primal scream, rapidly sending pulses out where she hoped there was someone to hit. At that same moment two/one and two/two showed up and took in what looked like a scene of absolute madness. Marines were firing at nothing and yet seemed to be taking casualties.

<*Stealthed units. Standard positions,*> Williams called out. The two fireteams backed against walls and also began placing random shots into the square.

"Got it!" Trist cried out. She removed her probes from the dead body on the deck and grinned triumphantly. "Wait for it…"

And then it happened. Several human outlines flickered in and out of visibility across the square before the suits reset and every attacker became fully visible. Trist had chosen a bright red covered in bulls eyes for the attacker's new look.

"See them OK?" she asked.

"Plenty OK." Tanis grinned and in less time than it took to say the words, every attacker was down.

Joe looked at Tanis and coughed back a laugh.

"Uh, Trist? Major Tanis is looking a little red around the collar."

Trist looked up at Tanis to see red showing at the edges of her armor where the stealth suit showed.

"Oops, passing Angela the info to fix it."

<*Thanks.*> Angela's tone hid a snicker as she reset the stealth suit.

Tanis had an unreadable look on her face for a moment and then smiled at Trist. "Good work, that could have been messy."

Williams was already halfway across the square to check on Lang. Tanis raced after as the two new fireteams secured the area and the attackers.

She arrived as the sergeant knelt beside the fallen Marine; Jansen looked on, her eyes misting.

"Cut halfway through his neck…armor went into stasis, but I don't know…he lost a lot of blood, it may have been too late."

"He'll make it," Williams grunted. "But he'll get a nice bit of R&R time while they put all his tendons and arteries back in place."

He rose, calling for the leader of two/one. "Corporal Salas! Lang is your number one priority. Two/two can stay here; you take Lang to TSF med facility AR13, it's only a thousand miles from here. Get him there safe."

"Aye, Sarge." Salas nodded and gestured for two of his Marines to unfold a field stretcher for Lang. Within moments they were trotting down the cross corridor to the nearest maglev.

Tanis looked at Jansen. "You good, Marine?"

The corporal's eyes had cleared up, a steely determination having set in. "Sir, yes, sir."

"Glad to hear it." Tanis smiled. "OK team, we need to recharge, reammo, and head out. Cassar, breach that ammo dump and pass out power packs and slugs."

"Aye, sir." Cassar nodded and went to work. Two minutes later they had left the plaza, Lance Corporal Olsen having been left to fend off the MSF unit that had arrived and was trying to take control of the situation. Having heard what happened at the last run-in between the two forces, the MSF weren't eager to get in a fight with the Marines. Two/three was on its way to back them up before everyone dispersed to cover the beta return route.

The escort only had a quarter mile more of corridor to pass through and then they took a tubelift up to the highest level of the ring. Like many of the planetary rings, the upper level on Mars 1 was effectively an open eco-space. The landscape was filled with rivers and lakes and grass and trees. Hovering above them, almost as though it was suspended between the arching arms of the ring, was the planet of Mars.

Spread out across the terrain were various buildings, mostly museums and cultural centers. While the crush of humanity was mostly in the lower levels, this upper area was designed with aesthetics as the primary consideration. No other artificial habitat in the Sol system had even half as much parkland as Mars 1. Off in the distance was the low hill that housed most of the higher SolGov courts on Mars. It was a towering edifice of white marble that gleamed brilliantly in the reflected sunlight.

"That just looks effing cool," Perez said. "Gotta record this on full sensory."

"Stay frosty, people," Williams said. "You can gawk on your own time."

"Besides, even you can't jerk off to a sens recording of a planet." Cassar grinned at Perez.

"Like the Staff Sergeant said. We don't have any more marked positions that we're expecting to be ambushed at. But that doesn't mean we're in the clear." Tanis gestured for Jansen to take the lead.

They trotted along in silence, the way before them virtually clear of locals for a time, but as they neared the federal buildings they moved into more populated areas until they were just a small island in a sea of foot traffic. The judiciary loomed ahead of them and minutes later they were moving up the steps toward the main lobby.

They passed through security and the guards didn't look too happy to be allowing armed Marines into the courthouse. At the entrance to the courtroom, Tanis signaled the Marines to wait outside and handed Williams her pulse rifle.

Tanis checked the time and smiled. "We're actually going to be right on time."

"Well, we did plan for some interruptions," Joe said. "You pretty much nailed how long they'd be."

"To be honest, I expected them to be longer," Tanis replied. "That was really too easy. I can't believe Trent didn't put in an appearance. I don't think he'll attack after the testimonies have been entered; what would be the point in that?"

She nodded to Trist and they turned and entered the court.

"What would be the point indeed," said a voice from the judge's seat, which was facing away from them. Tanis and Trist approached as the chair turned. Sitting in it was Trent, a rather unflattering smile on his face.

"It's good to see you again Tanis, Trist. I really am sorry that it will be the last time."

With those words, the doors slammed shut behind them and heavily armored troops spilled out of the judge's antechamber while more lined the balconies above them.

"It would seem that I finally have you where I want you, you meddling bitch," Trent spat, "now pass over your sidearm and we'll get started."

FINAL STAND

STELLAR DATE: 3227284 / 11.27.4123 (Adjusted Gregorian)
LOCATION: Mars 1 Ring (MIR)
REGION: Mars Protectorate, Sol Space Federation

Tanis took a long moment to consider the odds. At least twenty-five men surrounded her and Trist—ten on the balconies and fifteen down on the floor below. Angela and Sue were desperately trying to get control of the door's mechanism and release it, but it seemed to be in some sort of lockdown. Small sparks in the air hinted at a full battle of nanoprobes occurring all around them.

<*Ideas?*> Tanis queried.

<*I'd say you pretty much have to hand over your weapon,*> Trist said. <*You may be good, but we'd both be Swiss cheese before you took out three guys.*>

<*That and the clip only has twenty rounds in it.*>

<*Do it,*> Angela said. <*Buy Sue and me some time.*>

Tanis grunted and tossed her weapon onto the ground a few paces away. Trent signaled one of his men to pick it up, removing any chance of a dash and grab.

"I have to admit,"—Trent clasped his hands with what appeared to be genuine glee—"I really didn't expect you to be quite this easy to catch."

"Not sure how seventh time's the charm is easy," Tanis replied. "From where I stand you have a pretty poor batting average."

"Yet in the end, I still win." Trent's voice turned dark and menacing. "You have no idea what it has cost me, personally and professionally, to bring you to heel. With you out of the way we'll finally be able to stop the *Intrepid*."

"Why?" Trist asked. "Is she the only decent Micky in the TSF? No one else can tell guards to guard and politicians to fuck off? I thought skill like that was something the military had in spades."

"They may." Trent's smile looked sour. "But they don't seem to be assigning them to take care of the *Intrepid*. It really will be nice to be done with this job; it's taken years off my life."

"I have to ask," Tanis said. "You're pretty implicated here. What's your endgame?"

"We've got an exit plan. We may not all make it, but the pay is high enough to make up for the risk."

Several of the armed and armored figures chuckled. "Way more than enough," one said.

<*Any ideas yet?*> Tanis asked.

<*They've fused the doors,*> Angela replied. <*Williams says it's going to take them five minutes to get through.*>

<*That's a goddamn lifetime!*> Trist groaned. <*I can't believe this asshole is gonna get to shoot me down twice.*>

<*What's the model on the armor these guys are wearing?*> Tanis asked.

Sue replied after a moment's pause. <*It's STR-RVI, a newer type that we've seen on Callisto before.*>

<*Any chance that it's based on the STR-RV and not a ground-up?*>

<Uncertain. It has a lot of the same components, but that's just because they wanted some interchangeability.>

The exchange only took seconds, but it gave Tanis an idea which made a hope of this not being her last day begin to glimmer.

<Angela, we need to modify the stealth suit to use its laser ranging system to emit proton beams into the optics of these guys' suits.>

<What will…ahhhh…> Angela realized what was theoretically possible and got on it. *<Gonna take me about thirty seconds. Take your armor's gloves off.>*

<What are we going to do?> Trist asked.

<Knock out each and every one of these guys' armored suits. They're all power assisted and will lock up hard.>

<This should be interesting,> Trist replied.

"Nothing to say, Major Richards?" Trent asked. "No recital of how I'll never get away, how I should surrender?"

"Well of course you're not going to get away," Tanis replied. "I've never failed to take down a target yet. Don't see why I should start with you." She nonchalantly took her gloves off as she spoke, hoping that the casual behavior would be ignored.

"Don't you think that's a bit optimistic?" Trent asked. "Even if we don't get out of here, you're going to die. That's a given."

Tanis looked around her at the armored soldiers. Laying eyes on each one so that the beam would be calibrated, while half-focused on the countdown Angela placed on her HUD.

"You gonna have your goons do it or are you going to do it yourself?"

Trent stood and walked around the bench, facing Tanis and Trist directly. "Don't worry, I'm not afraid to kill you myself." He pulled a pistol from his belt and aimed it at Tanis.

"Well that's good," she said with a grin, "because you're going to have to."

She timed her statement with the proton beams and smiled as each mercenary seemed to jerk slightly and freeze. Muffled grunts and curses could be heard as they tried to move their powered armor, but each limb was locked solid.

"Glad that actually worked," Trist said.

"Me too, would have taken a lot more than silbio to glue us back together if it hadn't."

"What the…what did you do?" Trent asked, gesturing with his weapon.

"I fried the neural net their armor uses."

"How is that possible? The RVI is supposed to be unhackable!"

"Advice to live by." Trist glanced at Tanis. "Maybe he's been having so much trouble taking you out because he can't deal with reality that well." She looked back at Trent. "Not only is it possible, it just happened."

Tanis smiled evilly. "STR fixed all the reported issues. Since TSF doesn't use that model, we didn't feel the urge to report any weaknesses we found, especially since we usually encounter STR armor on the other side of a conflict."

Trent barked a curse, and without any other fanfare fired his weapon. Tanis's augmented vision flashed a warning the moment his hand tensed. She dove to the side, but not before a second alert fed into her mind that the pistol had fired a load of self-propelled ballistic projectiles. The alert came with a rather useless note about a velocity of 4000 meters per second.

Later she remembered the whole event in a surreal out-of-body fashion, the warning, the dive, and then the knowledge that her right arm and the side of her torso were gone.

A combination of genetic alteration, training, and Angela shutting down all of her pain centers was the only thing that kept her from losing the rest of her torso as his next shot rang out. She lunged behind a plas display that took most of the blast, though it did fling some shrapnel into her, some making it through her armor and into her flesh.

While Trent was occupied with attacking Tanis, Trist took the opportunity to run toward the soldier that had taken Tanis's sidearm. It was lying on a banister and she was only a meter from it when Trent spun and fired a shot into her as well.

The blast struck Trist in center mass and knocked her over the railing. Her body shook and convulsed while Trent turned his attention back to Tanis.

"Looks like this is the end for you." He strode over to her, gun aimed directly at her head. "You were a worthy adversary."

"Wish I could say the same for you," Trist said from behind him.

Trent turned to see Trist propped up on the banister, gun in her hand.

"I…you…you're dead," Trent gaped.

"Again with the reality issues." She fired three shots, all hitting Trent's torso. He was wearing thin armor under his suit. It blocked the first and second shot, but the third shattered it and dropped him at Tanis's feet.

"Needed him…have questions…" Tanis gasped.

"Oh relax, he'll live." Trist walked over, wincing.

Her shirt was torn, and under it the green phosphor-like glow of silbio stood out. "I guess I am a bit of the gummi girl now. Helps to not have any specific internal organs to get blown up when you get blown up."

Tanis's laugh became coughs and spasms. *<When are they going to get that door open? Your humor is going to kill me.>*

REGRET

STELLAR DATE: 3227284 /11.27.4123 (Adjusted Gregorian)
LOCATION: Mars 1 Ring (MIR)
REGION: Mars Protectorate, Sol Space Federation

Joe leaned over the transport cocoon the ring medics had settled Tanis in. Even in her current state she couldn't help but notice the concern and moisture in his eyes.

"That was the worst ten minutes of my life," Joe said. "I nearly died when I heard the shots."

<*Me too, fancy that.*> The tubes in her throat restricted her method of communication. She didn't mind; it helped hide her emotions. <*Just be certain that Trent makes it to the TSF detention facility. Last thing we need is these local cops getting their hands on him.*>

A look of anger flashed across Joe's face. "I can't believe that Trent is all you want to talk about right now. Look at you! You're in pieces, and all you can talk about is your job."

Grenwald stood across the transport cocoon and cast Joe an unreadable look before putting his hand on the commander's shoulder.

"We're all pretty concerned about you, Major. But don't worry, we'll do our jobs." He nodded to the two of them and walked away to oversee Trent's preparation for transport.

Tanis wanted to sigh, but it hurt too much. The pain in Joe's eyes hurt too, she knew because she felt the same thing. What was the point of getting the *Intrepid* outsystem if she killed herself doing it?

<*I'm sorry, Joe. Work is easier right now. Easier than feeling.*>

"It seems that pretty much everything is easier than feeling for you." He turned away as the medics began moving her cocoon into the ambulance.

RESULTS

STELLAR DATE: 3227294 / 12.03.4123 (Adjusted Gregorian)
LOCATION: GSS *Intrepid*, Mars Outer Shipyards (MOS)
REGION: Mars Protectorate, Sol Space Federation

"Glad to have you back with us." Commander Ouri smiled as Tanis entered the SOC. "You're looking good."

To the casual observer, she was at one hundred percent, in full control of her faculties. In reality, her new skin itched and her reflexes didn't feel quite right in her fingers. Firing right-handed was definitely out of the question.

Tanis signaled Ouri to walk with her. "I'm feeling good. I've gone over the interviews with Mr. Trent and I see that we've not yet gotten anything useful out of him."

"No, ma'am. He's only been here on the ship for a few days—took forever to get him transferred up from the ring."

They arrived at the conference room and Tanis took a seat.

"I know, I followed the progress; it was like pulling teeth."

"Or new nerve clusters. What are you doing here?" Joe asked as he walked into the offices.

"Getting back to work; specifically, getting ready to have a chat with Mr. Trent."

Joe's expression spoke volumes. Ouri took one look at the two and excused herself.

Neither spoke for several minutes. Tanis looked down at the table, tracing the scratches in the surface with her eyes. Surprising both of them, she spoke first.

"I was scared. More scared than I've been in a long time." She looked up at him, trying not to let too much emotion show on her face and mostly failing.

Joe sat down one chair away from her. She knew he was hurt, moreover he was scared. Probably scared he'd fallen in love with a crazy woman who would get herself killed any day now.

"Found out you're not indestructible, did you?"

Tanis waved that aside. "I've been hurt before. Worse, actually."

"You weren't scared then?"

"Why would I have been? The military patched me up and sent me back to work. It's what I do…what I did."

"I don't get you." Joe sighed and leaned back in his chair.

Tanis waited for the standard dry comment from Angela, but it didn't come. Her AI had been strangely silent when she and Joe were together during the last month.

Joe mistook her moment of contemplation for intractability and snorted. "It's like talking to a brick wall." He began to rise out of his chair.

"Wait." Tanis reached out and put a hand on his arm. "Please, I'm trying. I'm just not that good at this. I haven't felt like this about anyone in a very, very long time. You must know that."

"I've never looked at the personal parts of your file." The anger had subsided and kindness returned to Joe's eyes. "I only know the tiny nuggets of your past that you've shared."

"Well, I've never had a serious relationship with a man," Tanis said.

<*Liar,*> Angela commented privately.

<*It wasn't serious…at least not for him.*>

"What. Never?"

"Well, a fling or two in college, but nothing after that."

"You're seventy-two years old. Don't tell me you're a—"

"No." Tanis chuckled softly. "I'm not a virgin." Her eyes locked with his, a sliver of her contrary nature showing. "Why would you want someone like me? I mean you, you're a hot vacuum jockey. You've had your pick, I know I'm no prize."

Her hand was still on his arm. He looked down at it and placed his hand over hers. "You don't get it, Major, you are *the* prize."

She looked hard and long into his eyes. No trace of deception or malice showed. Not being able to help it, she examined his skin texture, monitored his heart rate, and looked for other signs of dishonesty. There were none.

"I still don't get it."

Joe gave his warm, resonant chuckle. The one she had first found so pleasant that day after the *Dawn*—still did. "It's not something I can really just *tell* you. It sort of needs a nice long period of explanation."

Tanis didn't know how to do this. The emotions and reactions were unfamiliar to her. She had focused only on her duty for so long. Men were just teammates without breasts.

Except Joe wasn't.

Not that he didn't have a nice chest.

Tanis stop! She got control of herself. Control was what she did, it was her game.

"Joe, you know I have feelings for you. I wouldn't be such a blubbering moron at times like this if I didn't."

He smiled, though his expression showed that he suspected what was to come.

"But I can't do this, not now. I simply don't know how."

His smile was warm and inviting. Tanis was getting the feeling there was nothing this man couldn't just smile away? "Then let me show you how."

"It's too much. I do so well at my job because I restrict my emotions, I school myself. This is the endgame. I can't get distracted now."

Joe sat back, causing her hand to slide off of his arm. "You don't give yourself enough credit."

She wanted to, but she couldn't afford the distraction. Not yet. "Once we get underway. I promise; I want it, I really do."

Joe nodded. His eyes looked tight, his lips pursed like he didn't trust himself to speak.

Tanis looked at his lips, almost losing herself in the desire to brush her own against them. She stood, forcing the emotion down, back under control. "I have to go speak to Trent."

<*You're an idiot.*> Angela actually sounded angry.

Tanis didn't respond.

…………………

"Ah, Major Richards, I was wondering how long it was going to take for them to stitch you back together. I bet a lot of the original parts had to be replaced. Feeling up to a good bit of fun?" Trent spoke as soon as she entered the room.

Tanis tried to forget the conversation with Joe. She focused on the need to get the name from Trent. Once she had that things would fit into place.

"I'm feeling up to having a conversation with you…need you to answer a few questions about who you work for and what their agenda is."

"And what makes you think you're going to get anything out of me?"

"Well, I can think of a number of ways, but most of them take some time. I decided to go right for the throat—metaphorically speaking."

At that prearranged signal, Kris was wheeled in, her naked form strapped to a chair. Tanis wasn't looking directly at Trent, but she was watching him on several of the room cameras over the Link and saw his pupils dilate. Good. She'd called this correctly.

Kris wasn't able to move or—thanks to the seal over her mouth—speak.

"You may be interested in knowing that we've removed her AI. It seems that he had helped subvert the AI on those ships we had some issues with last month. The AI courts apparently weren't too forgiving. Her Link has also been removed, as have most of her biomechanical mods. She's as close to a vanilla human as you get these days, and now has a very easy-to-trigger pain response."

Tanis reached over to Kris and grabbed an inch of skin on the inside of her bicep and twisted. The prisoner's eyes opened wide with tears glistening in the corners as she sucked a deep breath through her nose.

"It makes torture really easy. So many people shunt pain with their mods or AI that they've forgotten what it feels like. No tolerance at all."

"She may not be used to pain"—Trent's expression betrayed nothing—"but I'm certain it'll take more than that to really hurt her. You can't do anything to her or me; your precious rules and regs see to that."

"I'm sure you're aware that we're on the *Intrepid,*" Tanis said. "The ship's AI is really quite amazing; one of the most advanced and powerful ever created. He really wants to live and see the galaxy, something that you're trying to keep him from. Now normally he would be impartial, but you see he has a very special connection with a woman named Amanda. She's in a unique position, and has also come to view you with a certain amount of distaste."

"That's great," Trent said. "I'm really happy for her."

"What you don't get is that she has prevailed upon the *Intrepid* to arrange it so that we're alone."

No one was ever really alone anymore in the 42nd century. There was always a camera, a sensor, or someone conversing over the Link. The concept of truly being alone was very foreign to most people, even frightening to some. It most certainly was to Trent at that moment.

"No one knows what's going on in here; key people will cover any injuries and no recordings will be made—unless you want them to be made while you give your confession."

"You bitch…" Trent's voice was weak.

"Lacking in conviction," Tanis said. "I will have the truth out of you. If I need to cut her and then you down to just a brain and a pair of lungs to wheeze words out of, it will happen."

Trent resisted at first, calling her bluff; unfortunately for him, and more so for Kris, Tanis followed through. She didn't revel in it, didn't take any joy in the things that she did to Kris's body, but neither did she shy away from it. Her devotion to the colony effort, to leaving the Sol system, was foremost in her thoughts. She would know who was behind these attacks. All the while she wondered what Joe would think of her if he knew the sorts of things she did—had done?

After three hours, Kris finally passed out. Tanis had stretched the woman's endurance as far as it would go. Nothing she did was permanent, but new skin would definitely be necessary. Not yet though. Kris would live like this as long as she was in Tanis's custody.

Trent was having trouble breathing as he watched the ruins of Kris's body collapse to the floor. Tanis had pre-deployed med-nano into the woman and they stabilized her and effected a semi-stasis.

"Now that we're done with the warm-up"—Tanis wiped her hands and turned to Trent—"I'll have my answers from you. The dead from the *Dawn* demand it."

It took him several minutes to calm down enough to be able to keep his trembling at bay. Tanis watched him, seeing his fear turn into resolve, followed by anger. He was going to resist.

Tanis cupped his chin in her hand and worked up her most evil smile.

"Careful. Just because I'm done with her doesn't mean I'm going to slow down. Let's start with your eyes. I've always believed that we have two so that we can afford to have one ruined."

She picked up a laser scalpel and proceeded to slice Trent's right eye to ribbons. The tool self-cauterized, keeping bleeding to a minimum. Once the screaming stopped, Tanis looked him in the remaining eye.

"You know, I don't think you really need this one either. I think you'll be a lot easier to manage once you're blind."

Trent broke.

"No! Stop, stop stop stop stop stop stop stop stop stop pleeeeaaaaase!"

He was crying, tears coming out of both eyes and seeping into the ruined orb. His body was shaking, the fear a physical force assaulting him.

It was hard to watch. Tanis felt herself faltering at that moment. She hated torture. Hated doing it more than any human rights group hated that she did it. They found the actions despicable. She found *herself* despicable. She felt her stomach flutter like it did before battle.

Joe would find her despicable.

<There are other ways to get information, you know,> Angela said. *<You don't have to do this…you shouldn't do this. I don't normally complain, but this is excessive, even for you.>*

<I know…I know,> Tanis said. *<But this man…this blubbering thing…he would have cheerfully detonated a nuke on this station! The fact that he's getting to me means I'm human. But he's not. He voided those rights when he tried to kill millions for a buck.>*

<Just be careful. I don't want you going somewhere you can't come back from.>

Tanis looked down on the man, the thing in front of her.

"Then what? What do you have to say? Who is calling the shots? Who is trying to shut us down?"

Trent looked like he had built up a bit of resolve again and Tanis held up the laser scalpel. He cringed and shook his head.

"OK OK OK…It's the STR, it's Strang."

"Strang? The CEO of STR?" Tanis asked.

"Yeah, him. He's put a lot of personal stock in the *Dakota* and when New Eden came up he had to have it. He'll do anything to stop the *Intrepid*."

Tanis considered his words. If Strang was pulling the strings, this was far from over. The *Intrepid* had to go to Callisto to get its final cargo and colonists. STR was headquartered there. Strang was there.

Tanis spent the next thirty minutes getting particulars from Trent and making sure his story rang true. She hated every minute of it, but not nearly as much as he did.

"So we have our name." Captain Andrews folded his hands and raised them to his lips. His eyes dropped to the table and he paused for a moment. "I assume that we proceed with legal indictments."

"The brass are reviewing it," Sanderson said.

"I thought *you* were the brass." Terrance scowled. "Can't you push this through?"

"Strang is the CEO of STR. We never thought it went this high. Pulling him down is no small thing. SolGov's influence in Jovian space is not what it once was. They are more powerful than all the other members of the federal government combined. STR is one of their largest consortiums and wields a lot of influence. The feds will have to tread lightly."

"So they'll get away with this?" Terrance asked. "I swear, if they do nothing I'll sue them, sue their pants off."

"I've always wondered exactly what that means." Captain Andrews ran a hand through his hair. "However, will suing them make us safer? I mean we're going to Callisto, into the lion's den so to speak."

"Too bad we can't just have the three cargo containers they've packed up there sent to us and just leave from here." Terrance sighed.

"Not feasible," Captain Andrews agreed. "It's a complicated slingshot maneuver we're doing. Without using Jupiter as our launching point we won't have achieved enough velocity when we reach Sol. The decreased breakaway velocity will cause significant increase in travel time."

"That and we need to be moving toward the sun at the correct speed and correct time to gather the isotopes we need for our fuel. If we don't do that it will take thirteen percent longer to reach our max speed." Earnest Redding seemed very anxious about the notion. "Also, if we have them ship those containers here, we'll miss both the Jovian and Marsian windows and have to wait another nine months for the next one."

"That's all the time the *Dakota* will need to be able to contest our claim to New Eden and tie this colonization up in committee and courts for a decade. Which is exactly what Strang wants." Tanis spoke for the first time since the meeting had started.

"I guess that rules that out," Terrance said.

"I propose that I take Grenwald's Marines in advance to Callisto and ensure that everything is secure. We need to make sure that the cargo and the rendezvous point are safe. We can also have a wing on patrol in Jovian space ready to escort the *Intrepid* in,"

Tanis said. No point in wallowing forever. Plenty of work was still waiting to be done.

"Do you think we'll be safe here?" Terrance asked. "Your work has proven instrumental in keeping us on track. In fact, Abby tells me that your alterations have actually accelerated the schedule."

Tanis forced a smile. "You hired me to do a job, sir. I am glad I have been able to perform it to your satisfaction." She brought up a holo showing various levels of activity on the station; 3D graphs and charts displayed periods of higher and lower threat to the *Intrepid.* The data showed that after the capture of Trent the threat levels were significantly lower.

"You'll see, sirs, that all of the models show that no significant threats are impending. The bounty on me has actually been withdrawn and the four merc organizations that had been active locally have all left the Mars Protectorate. I'm guessing that they're feeling the heat and their last payments probably didn't show up. I'm not saying that everything is sunshine and daisies, but I do believe that the next big threat lies at Callisto and not here at Mars. I have every confidence that Commander Ouri can keep things under control here while I'm gone. Lieutenant Forsythe will be keeping his platoon here while I take Grenwald's with me to Callisto."

"And Commander Evans?" Captain Andrews' eye had a twinkle to it.

The fewer complications, the better. "He'll be staying on the *Intrepid*, sir. I believe his assistance will be key in organizing patrols and guarding the ship during transit."

"I see no reason to not follow your plan." Sanderson looked at Tanis sternly and at the others around the table who nodded. "You have my permission to proceed. I expect a full work-up of your plan within the day."

"Aye, sir." Tanis stood. "Sirs." She nodded and left. They hadn't asked her exactly how she got the information from Trent. She hadn't volunteered it either.

<Looks like we're taking a little trip,> Angela said.

<Almost done; just this one last journey and we're gone.>

<You never know, a lot can happen between now and the end.>

CERES

STELLAR DATE: 3227 301 / 12.14.4123 (Adjusted Gregorian)
LOCATION: Ceres Transfer Station, Ceres
REGION: InnerSol, Sol Space Federation

"Well boys and girls, here we are, lovely Ceres, just the place for a day's layover." Private Perez gestured magnanimously at the unadorned debarkation lobby.

"Shut it, Perez," Williams said as he walked by. "Marines, hump your gear to the *TSF Argonaut* and stow it. We have a tactical analysis of our mission at 2100 hours station time in briefing room 2A, deck 16, quadrant 3."

"You want us to do *what* to our gear, Staff Sergeant?"

Williams chose to ignore the remark and hoisted his pack over his left shoulder.

They were in the TSF zone on Ceres, one of the main hubs of stellar commerce and travel in the solar system. It was doubly busy since Mars was nearing Jupiter at a time when Ceres was between them. Earth was on the far side of the sun, but a direct path between it and Jupiter also passed through Ceres for the current Sol month. The end result was that nearly all of the traffic between the InnerSol and OuterSol was currently flowing through Ceres.

Williams wasn't worried about security, not in the TSF zone at least. With the hundred or so navy ships—ranging from patrol craft to Orion-class cruisers and Constellation-class carriers—all docked at this quadrant, not only was security tight, but it was backed up by a million or so TSF personnel that were, quite literally, everywhere. Anyone trying anything wouldn't make it more than ten meters after doing it.

Being around men and women he could rely on always made Williams feel at home, and he walked easily down the corridor. That wasn't to say that he wasn't wary, but he was as relaxed as he got.

Being little more than a small planetoid, Ceres naturally only generated .03*g* at its surface, far less than most of the larger moons in the Sol system. It had been augmented by a GE Artificial Grav system, a fancy term for a mini black hole that was placed within the core of the world and spun up to create 0.51*g* on the world's surface.

Ceres had a massive superstructure built around it, the main docking ring being four hundred kilometers above the world. Capable of docking over seven hundred thousand ships at once, the outer reaches operated in 0*g*, allowing an easier transfer of heavy materials.

Small ships like the transport that the Marines had taken from the MOS docked on the inside of the ring about seventy kilometers above the surface, which rotated enough to create just under a half a *g*.

Perez was taking advantage of that and tossing his pack in the air like it was some sort of ball.

Just like on Mars 1's top level, the view was astounding. Even people who worked on the station could be caught looking up at the sight of the small planet wrapped in the massive docks. Since the planet was only about eight hundred kilometers in diameter, and the docks were much closer than most planetary halos, the effect was more like a sphere captured in a glistening ring of steel rather than a ring around a planet. In fact, without taking into account the GE AG system, the docks had more mass than Ceres itself.

Williams caught himself looking up for longer than he expected and Kowalski nudged him.

"Not your first time here is it?" he asked.

"No, but it's one of the few times where the sun is shining from behind. It really lights the whole thing up nicely, doesn't it?"

"You getting all sentimental, Staff Sergeant?"

Williams cast a baleful eye on Kowalski. "I have as much sentimentality in me as you have taste in women."

Kowalski chuckled. "Sure thing, Staff Sergeant."

Williams glanced back up at the sight; it was a lot smaller than Mars 1, but he found it far more pleasant. He could spot the Tannen Docking Array R3D where the *Argonaut* was berthed along the arc, visible even though it was seven hundred kilometers away. He started moving again and ran through the platoon's status to be certain that everyone was still keeping up, more or less. Since the officers had been in first class, they were ahead a few hundred meters, but they were making poorer time without a sergeant's glare to help part the crowds.

Williams eased up his pace. He liked his officers, but he also liked peace and quiet, something that a certain lieutenant trying to look cool to Trist while simultaneously trying to impress the major just wouldn't provide.

They passed out of the TSF zone and into a general civilian section. There were three military zones on the docks, but due to a combination of lease times and weight distribution, they weren't all adjacent to one another.

The central boulevard changed as they walked. Gone were the plain bulkheads with their colored bars indicating location and purpose, as well as the spartan offices and facilities. In their place were the boutiques and restaurants that catered to the transient tourists that passed through the station.

While the population of both Ceres and its docking network was in the range of only three hundred million or so, at any given moment over a billion people were passing through. The place had rivers of credit flowing across its nets, generating more money than most planets.

Besides the aforementioned stores selling frivolities and food, frontages advertising time in the company of a beautiful man, woman, or...whatever abounded—everything from vanilla humans to things that didn't even look like homo sapiens. A trend that seemed to be more and more common as the years passed.

It was probably to please many of the visitors. A lot of the spacers that passed through a place like Ceres spent a good bit of their time alone in the black. It seemed that they were the most unusual, almost as though they had decided that since they spent so much time away from the general human population they should become something other than human.

Even though he had slowed his pace, Williams saw that he was still catching up with the officers and Trist. He resigned himself to taking the rest of the route to the maglev in their company and allowed himself to catch up.

"About time you boots caught up. We were starting to wonder if you stayed back to finish an in-flight vid or something," Trist said.

"We did," Williams growled. "It was called *NCOs and the Moronic Civilians They*

Saved Through the Ages. It warmed my heart."

Trist shot Williams a shocked look while Tanis let out a laugh.

"You do realize that no one but a Marine can needle a Marine staff sergeant and escape unscathed," Tanis said.

"And most of them lose at least a finger or two," Williams grunted.

Trist opened her mouth to say something in response, but appeared to think better of the notion and subsided into silence. Just the way Williams preferred it.

He had mixed feelings about her coming along to Callisto, especially mixed feelings about her being privy to the details of the mission, but Major Richards seemed to trust the girl and had made a strong case that she had a knowledge of Cho that none of them did. Her web of contacts could end up proving to be very useful.

Still, it was a gamble taking her back. The Jovian government still had a warrant out for her arrest, despite the fact that a federal SolGov court had granted her immunity in exchange for her testimony against Trent.

Luckily the fact that a lot of Trist's body was made out of biological silicon meant her DNA no longer matched what was on record. Even better was the fact that she could subtly alter her underlying physical features making a legal identification of Trist virtually impossible.

The group arrived at the maglev train and the platoon filed into several cars. The ride anti-spin to the *Argonaut* was relatively quick and before long the gear was stowed and the Marines were enjoying some downtime before the briefing. Their shuttle to Callisto left at 0900 the next morning, and it was currently 1400, giving them several hours to sample all the docks had to offer. Williams was certain that they would.

As for himself, Williams took the time to look over the plan passed down to him from the officers. He could tell that it was Tanis's scheme with a few minor details taken care of by the LT. Tanis tended to skip the chain a bit, though it was hard to say if it annoyed Grenwald or not. Getting firsthand experience with a renowned tactician like Major Richards was probably worth the consternation.

The general operation was pretty straightforward. There would be a company of MCSF Marines tasked with general security and a company of Marine engineers that was tasked with inspecting the cargo pods. Not a job Williams envied. Those pods were each well over a cubic kilometer filled with equipment and cargo. The engineers would only be able to do a cursory examination at best, but it was better than nothing.

The *Intrepid* would carry ten pods total, and seven were already in place. When the *Intrepid* arrived at Callisto in a month, the remaining pods would be loaded up and the ship would begin its acceleration toward the Sun, on its slingshot approach to gather additional velocity for their outbound trip.

Williams was somewhat saddened by the thought. Over the last few months the ship had become something of a home to him and the platoon. He'd overheard a few of the Marines talking about requesting to go out with the ship, but he was certain that none of them would; they were all too dedicated to the job, all of them being somewhat addicted to the action. Where the *Intrepid* was going, there would be no action, just a quiet, boring colonization project and then the slow crawl to old age.

For just a moment, the notion appealed to Williams, but he pushed it from his mind. The corps was his life, that wasn't going to change.

"Good of you all to make it." Grenwald addressed the last few Marines who arrived only four minutes early for the briefing.

"We were held up," Taylor said.

"Yeah, Taylor was having trouble convincing the bartender he was old enough to drink," Perez grinned.

"Belay that excuse," Williams said.

"Sorry, Staff Sergeant." Perez had the good grace to look a bit sheepish.

All eyes turned to Major Richards as she stood and activated the holo system.

"This is dock BX9-R on ring 19C of the Callisto station. For those of you who have never been there, it'll be quite the sight. You're on the corps' time the whole time we're there. No wandering off and seeing what there is to see." She cast a look at Perez. "Or fondle what there is to fondle. There is a barracks on the ring, and I don't want to hear of anyone being anywhere other than there or on duty…what?" Tanis looked at Perez.

"Will there at least be, er…beverages?"

"Yes, there's an enlisted cantina in the barracks where I believe they serve over ten thousand types of alcohol. Don't abuse it." Her look told them all what danger they'd be in if they imbibed excessively more than any threat could have.

"Once we debark at Callisto, our job will be to ensure that the STR is hamstrung. It's entirely possible that SolGov will take no direct action against the instigator of this bit of excitement we've been having lately, but that doesn't mean that we can't make their lives miserable—and believe me ladies and gentlemen, we will."

She surveyed the room and found that everyone's eyes showed that they shared the same sentiment as she did.

"We have a certain level of autonomy here, but honestly if I don't piss off Admiral Sanderson by the time we're done, then I won't feel like I've done my job. What that translates to for you is that we may actually get to have some fun."

The Marines all looked at one another and smiled; they were well-versed in what Tanis's version of fun was.

"I've put each squad's objectives on the tactical net. I expect you all to review them and be prepared when we arrive. We do have a two-day flight, and I want to see tactical sims drawn up and run during that time."

She nodded and Grenwald addressed Williams. "Staff Sergeant, dismiss the men."

"Platoon, get some sacktime, I want you assembled on the deck in front of the *Argonaut* at 0530. Dismissed!"

The men saluted the officers and filed out.

INTEL

STELLAR DATE: 3227307 / 12.20.4123 (Adjusted Gregorian)
LOCATION: District BX9, Ring 19C, Callisto Orbital Habitat (Cho)
REGION: Jovian Combine, Sol Space Federation

"How are things looking, Commander?" Tanis addressed the Marine who was bent over a readout.

"As well as can be expected, sir. We've got the 701st engineers combing every inch of those cubes as well as the other general cargo destined for the *Intrepid* upon its arrival and let me say, it's going to be a slow burn."

"I understand, Yau." Tanis couldn't agree more. "Be on the lookout for…something—I don't know that this is over yet."

"You're expecting the enemy to make a move against us?"

"I don't know for sure. I've been studying this Arlen Strang. He's never been one to give up on something when he sets his mind to it. I imagine that he has made certain promises and with the *Dakota* taking second place to the *Intrepid* I'm thinking he has some egg on his face."

"I'll see that we are suitably cautious, sir."

"Good to hear, Commander."

Tanis turned and signaled one/three to follow her. She had a meeting with a certain informant and it involved going down to ring 5 and into an area not known to be friendly to strangers. She was probably being overly cautious, but having a couple of Marines along never hurt when trying to keep one's head attached to one's body.

She and the Marines were all in civilian attire, though she didn't expect it to fool anyone who had an eye for military bearing. The light body armor they wore under their clothing didn't help make their movements any more natural.

The ride down the tubes was relatively quick. Since they were going to inner rings the feeling was actually more of an up since the centripetal force was pulling them the opposite direction. She did miss the type of construction that Mars 1 and Ceres had, where you could see the planet above. Word was that the reason why they hadn't done that here was because having Jupiter looming in the background was disconcerting to too many people, especially since it had been ignited several hundred years ago and now looked much more ominous than it once had.

Even if the moon were visible the view would have been uninspiring. Callisto wasn't terraformed, its surface housing waste management and purification systems for the habitat above.

Tanis's thoughts shifted to the Callisto station…or rings…no one really knew what to call it these days. Locals called it Cho, while the Jovian government called it the C1 Semi-Orbital Habitat. Tanis just called it daunting.

Something about the feeling of a trillion trillion tons of structure over her head gave her the willies. Not big ones, but enough to make her twinge every so often.

She focused on the task at hand. Meet with this contact, get the intel, stop the STR from pulling off whatever they planned on doing. She kept the knowledge that in one month they'd be outsystem firmly in mind. They'd have a nice cookout in Old Sam and be on their way. It would all have been worth it.

The thoughts renewed her resolve. No way was she going to let anything get in the *Intrepid*'s way.

The contact's name was Sandy Bristol; Tanis's information told her that she would be a mod—a pretty heavy mod from the looks of the file. She figured it couldn't be hard to spot a woman with florescent pink skin and what appeared to be several dozen three-foot tentacles coming out of her head. That sort of thing just stood out.

She glanced around her at the people in this part of the ring. Well, maybe it wouldn't stand out that much. In fact, even though they were all dressed in civvies, her Marine escort's lack of visible mods and conservative clothing probably made them the most unusual people present.

She directed Becker and Jacobs to engage in a lively discussion about their favorite sport, poker, at a table in a café across the intersection where the meet was to take place. Martins stood beside her, posing as obvious muscle, which she did very easily, and Larson was lurking around the corner, eyeing the ladies standing in front of a brothel, or voluntary slavery outlet, it was hard to tell.

"Some of these people are...well...quite odd." Martins almost added the "sir" but held it back.

Tanis checked her records on Martins and saw that she was from the Beta Regio region on Venus. The descendants of religious puritans that left Earth a millennia ago, they were about as straight-laced as they came in this day and age.

"They're not of the normal variety," Tanis replied. "Actually, I take that back. Given the population of the Galilean moons it's possible that they actually define normal."

"Yeah, I can't believe there are a thousand billion people on Callisto now"—Martins shook her head—"and most of them are above us."

"Below you, actually," Tanis said. "That whole centripetal force thing."

"Actually, since at any given time we're at the bottom of the arch, our point of view has most of the ring structure above us." Martins grinned.

Tanis grunted. "Got me there; last time I think of you as rural, Martins."

"Sorry, s—"

"Good catch."

They stood in silence for a while, leaning against the wall of a shop that appeared to sell and install replacement digestive systems that would allow a person to fit three times the battery power into their body. It also used waste to create additional power. Link ads constantly assailing them showed high-end models with the ability to completely consume all food with no need to void it from the body—not an alteration you could easily undo if you decided you didn't like it.

Tanis was certain she wouldn't. The thought of what had to be some sort of laser-powered incinerator in her torso just seemed like a recipe for trouble, especially considering how often she got shot up.

Trist had mentioned that this was one of the more interesting, but relatively benign places on the lower Callisto rings. After setting up this meet for Tanis, Trist had gone off to see if she could get information from a few other contacts. Tanis didn't like sending the woman off on her own, so three/two was with her. Their last update to the platoon's tactical net put them on ring 17D, somewhere in a thousand-square-mile trade area. Chances were that Trist was getting in some last minute wheeling and dealing...or maybe just stealing.

<*That was a weird mental alliteration,*> Angela commented.

"I think that's her," Martins spoke softly.

"Yup, even in this crowd, she does stand out," Tanis agreed.

Sandy strolled over as though selling info to TSF agents was something she did every day. Tanis took the opportunity to examine her carefully, initially to look for any weapons, but then in a combination of awe and horror.

The woman's body was indeed a fluorescent pink that seemed to shift hues in the light. There had to be over thirty of the tentacles coming out of her head, which itself seemed to have a conical shape. The end of each tentacle sported three suction cups, somewhat like an octopus.

At first glance she appeared to be naked, though it was often difficult to tell the difference between skin and clothes. While she certainly looked like a woman, her groin was smooth and her breasts—while fully exposed—had no nipples on them. Her legs were even more interesting; her knees bent backwards and her feet ended in hooves.

"It's not polite to stare, Miss Richards." Sandy walked up to the waiting pair. "But I don't mind. I didn't make myself look like this to avoid getting stared at." She stretched seductively. "I positively thrive on it."

She seemed to be getting rather turned on and Tanis realized that Sandy meant that her brain was altered to get sexual pleasure from having people stare at her unusual appearance. She probably had a really good time strolling through the corridors—the way she was modded out even people with horns did double takes.

"I'm glad for you," was all Tanis said.

Tanis noted that Martins appeared to be doing her best to blink regularly and a glance across the street showed her that the other Marines were having trouble keeping their glances casual. Not that they stood out in doing so—ignoring Sandy would be the unusual reaction.

"I understand that you have some information about Strang in relation to the *Intrepid.* Though I honestly must say that I don't know how you would gather any intel...how would you blend in?"

"I don't blend, darling, people pay me in information for the pleasure of my company." Her tentacles danced around her, caressing her upper body. "I have very specialized skills."

"Holy shit," Martins said softly. Tanis sent a quelling glance the private's way.

"So what do you have for us?" Tanis asked.

"Well, it's come my way that Mr. Strang doesn't like you, Miss Richards, doesn't like you one bit."

"I've actually noticed," Tanis said dryly.

"I imagine you have. However, he has managed to get his eye back on the prize; he intends to destroy the *Intrepid.*"

"About time he learned some focus. I just wish he could focus elsewhere."

"His intention"—Sandy leaned closer—"is to destroy it after it docks on Callisto."

"That's pretty broad; you wouldn't happen to have anything more specific, would you?"

"He has a device, one that will cause considerable damage to the *Intrepid.* There will be minimal damage to the ring, but nothing he isn't willing to risk."

"Is that all you know?"

"I have some details; information about the way he plans to destroy it. I don't understand all of the technical jargon, but I believe it is some sort of molecular decoupler that will break the ship apart. I've put it on this hardcopy."

A tentacle slipped a small disc into Tanis's hand. Without giving it a glance, she secured it in a small drive in her wrist. "Payment has already been remitted."

"So it has. I believe, then, that our time here is complete."

"Yes, thank you," Tanis said.

"Thank you, Miss Richards. It's been a pleasure."

The strange woman walked away, her tentacles swaying softly and her hoofs clopping lightly on the decking.

Martins stared after Sandy until she disappeared from view. "She certainly was interesting."

"You can say that again," Tanis replied as the other Marines crossed the street and they began the return trip to the barracks.

* * * * *

Tanis met with her staff regarding the information Sandy had provided shortly after returning. None of them were entirely certain what to make of the information Tanis had gathered, but they were certainly going to take it seriously.

After the meeting, Tanis retreated to her quarters. Time enough for six hours of sleep and then back to the grind.

<I don't know about this,> Tanis mused to Angela. *<It all seems a little over the top.>*

<Molecular decouplers do indeed function,> Angela replied. *<They're often used in removing a planet's crust to resurface it.>*

<I know that.> Tanis leaned back on her bed, running through scenarios. *<It just seems too extreme. I mean, how many people could get their hands on an MDC strong enough to take out the* Intrepid*? It would be a pretty short list, though probably with the STR near the top of it.>*

<That's true. There's also the chance that the reaction could spill over into Callisto. I don't see him risking his power base just to get one colony world that won't turn a profit for a half a dozen centuries,> Angela added.

<We've picked up other intel saying there could be various other avenues of attack as well—and dozens of false leads about bombs in the cargo.>

<You think we're being played?> Angela asked.

<I think that the truth may be out there, but it's covered in all these lies.>

<I'm working with the local TSF intel AI to rule out the claims that are simply implausible. Unfortunately most of them have enough of a grain of truth that we can't discount them entirely.>

<I'd better get some sleep, there's no way that I can figure this out when I'm exhausted.>

<See you in a couple of hours,> Angela said as her avatar waved goodnight.

<Try not to use my brain too much to pore over this stuff…it always gives me strange dreams.>

ASSASSIN

STELLAR DATE: 3227327 / 01.09.4124 (Adjusted Gregorian)
LOCATION: District BX9, Ring 19C, Callisto Orbital Habitat (Cho)
REGION: Jovian Combine, Sol Space Federation

Tanis stretched as consciousness slowly crept over her. The clock informed her that it was 0500; nine hours until the *Intrepid* would dock at Callisto. A review of her day's schedule confirmed that it was full, but not so full that she couldn't enjoy just a few more minutes under the soft covers.

She mentally ran through the post-docking schedule: the four days to load cargo—five at the outside, plus two days of VIP parties and ceremonies, put departure on 3227337 at the latest.

Departure.

It seemed like it would never come and now that it was here these last few days would be agony. With luck she would be so busy the time would fly past.

Curious about the ship's status, she reached out to the TSF comm net and requested bandwidth to the *Intrepid.* It was granted and her queries flew across the void to the ship's general net.

Amanda was there waiting for her.

<*You seem eager for our arrival.*> Her net avatar smiled.

<*You have no idea how much, Amanda. How are things going? No issues, upsets?*>

Amanda laughed. Her voice was silvery and smooth and echoed just a touch. <*You worry too much. Everything has gone as planned. Your Joseph has provided a fighter escort the entire way and is out there now, keeping us safe.*>

<*Don't laugh, it's part of the job to worry—though I'm glad that Joseph is out there. Not a lot can get past him.*>

<*Would you like to speak to anyone? I'm sorry for accosting you when you connected.*>

<*No, I just wanted to reach out and make contact. I should be going, I have a lot to do.*> Tanis sighed.

<*I imagine there are many officious people that need intimidating.*>

<*Aren't there always?*>

She disconnected and drew back into herself. Taking a deep breath, she rose and entered the san unit. Her tight schedule coupled with her new armor would provide no opportunity to visit a restroom for at least the next twenty hours. She set the unit for a thorough cleaning and grimaced as it did its work.

Once done she stepped back into her small room and pulled out the small case containing the new armor. Setting it on the desk she opened it and loaded the control system.

<*Man, this stuff is full of license agreements,*> Angela said. <*It'll eventually timebomb and deactivate without updates as well.*>

<*Well, chances are we'll be on our way and never needing armor like this again before that happens.*> Tanis applied her security token to each of the agreements.

<*Great, now you've cursed us.*>

<*If there was a curse, I really don't think it originated with me.*>

Once the software was loaded, Tanis stripped down and stood naked. The next step was promised by both the salesperson and the manual to be somewhat odd. Some people reported feeling very claustrophobic during the process.

"Can't believe I spent that much money on this thing." Tanis held up the canister.

<What else were you going to spend it on? You're leaving the system. Like they say in the vids, 'Your money's no good here.' Well, except that it is for now...but you get the picture.>

Tanis nodded absently as she placed the canister against her chest. The bottom dissolved and a clear liquid flowed out across her body. It started by moving down and covering her torso, legs, and then feet. From there it flowed up over her breasts, down her arms and covered her hands. A signal flashed on Tanis's HUD telling her to take a deep breath and close her eyes. She followed the instructions and the liquid flowed up over her face.

It ran a countdown on her HUD, letting her know when it would be safe to breathe and look around. She felt tingles in her skin as the armor smoothed out and matched the shape of her body. When the countdown flashed zero she opened her eyes and examined the holo projection of herself.

Apart from a slight sheen to her skin it was impossible to tell that the armor was there at all. Upon close inspection a person might be able to notice a thin cover over her eyes, and that the first few millimeters of her hair appeared to be ridged, but other than that, she looked like a normal person...though somewhat naked at present.

Tanis pulled on her dress whites, somewhat disconcerted by the fact that the armor muted her sense of touch to a degree. She deployed a nano field that would assist the armor in detecting incoming weapons fire and with a cursory check of her quarters, exited into the corridor.

Tanis made her way to the officer's mess, which contained a smattering of lieutenants and commanders getting ready for the day. Commander Yau was there; he appeared to be going over his company's duties for the upcoming arrival of the *Intrepid*.

Eight hours and twenty-seven minutes.

"Glad this is nearly over, I bet." Tanis sat across from him with her tray of fruit and oatmeal.

"Not as much as you are, I imagine." He grinned.

"You have no idea. The waiting is killing me."

"The CIA has all sorts of flags popping up on their net. Have you seen their latest sec feeds?"

Tanis hadn't, and mentally chastised herself for not checking it first thing. The anticipation must really be preoccupying her.

"There have been some monitored individuals making their way onto Cho, and a few of them have slipped past surveillance," Yau said.

Tanis checked the lists, summoning a holo display in front of her and the captain. "None look too serious, oh...well, except for her."

"Yeah, Herris Santos. She's known to have caused no small ruckus in her time."

Tanis leaned back, bringing up the woman's history. Born on Europa to a wealthy family, she had left the life of privilege at age thirty. From there, she joined Tomas's Marauders, a semi-legit private army that hired itself out to local governments to protect trade routes and natural resources. A rapid rise through the ranks ensued until a falling-out with the command forced her out of the organization.

From that time on it appeared she had been operating as a freelance assassin.

Several jobs on Venus, a high profile hit on an Earth politician, and a string of probable killings on Vestra, Ceres, and the Hildas asteroids.

"Never worked in the Jovian sphere though," Tanis mused.

"That we know of—the JSF doesn't exactly share everything with us."

"It's entirely possible that she's here on some other task."

Yau cast Tanis an appraising look and the major sighed. "I know, I know—that would just be too handily coincidental. Though with Cho's population, that sort of coincidence is a bit more acceptable."

"Except that she was last seen on ring 20. If we had solid intel putting her on ring 142 or something like that, then I'd be in complete agreement."

Tanis nodded. "Your logic is irrefutable. I assume TSF intel and the Callisto Intel Agency are both looking for her."

"You assume correctly. I've set up our tactical net to alert us if there is any news."

"I'd really thought that Strang had gotten over this whole assassination thing."

"He could be going after another target: Terrance or Captain Andrews."

"I don't know...at this stage, killing either of them wouldn't set the mission back by much at all. Strang strikes me as the complete-at-all-costs sort of guy, not get-final-petty-revenge type."

"Maybe he's both."

They went over the general plans for the day before leaving the mess to attend to their various duties. Tanis walked to her temporary office and on the way scheduled the pickup of her effects and their transfer to the *Intrepid* after it had docked. She also went over the security clearances for the caterers and general staff who would be at the docking ceremony. Everything seemed to be in order, but something still nagged at her. Her gut hadn't told her to buy and slather on this armor for nothing; somewhere a thread was loose, and she was going to find it and pull.

It was just before noon when an anomaly in a shipping manifest caught her eye. A series of containers which were destined to arrive at the *Intrepid*'s berth tomorrow had arrived today. Rather than holding them and delivering on schedule, the courier had delivered them to one of the warehouses just off the main dock. That in itself wasn't particularly odd; however, they had been inspected twice. The inspection logs and timestamps were backwards—it was either a system error, or someone had opened the record to fake an entry at the same time someone had it open to enter a valid entry.

Feeling restless, Tanis decided to look into it herself. Checking the Marines' assignments, she realized that none of them were available to go with her. Trist was also off gathering information on a different ring. No matter, the dock wasn't far, just a twenty-minute walk. It would give her time to stretch her legs and get a bit of exercise.

Two hours and fifteen minutes.

The halls were relatively empty as most of the local staff was at the mess getting the noon meal out of the way before the final preparations for the *Intrepid*'s arrival began. The corridor widened as she came to the storage area just off the dock. A worker strolled by pushing a hover pallet and gave her an appreciative look. Tanis couldn't imagine why. In the last two thousand years, no Space Force dress uniform sported a cut that flattered a woman's body. Maybe it was the hair; she had grown it out rapidly since her trip to Cruithne and it was just past her shoulders now. She hadn't had long hair in decades and was determined to keep the indulgence since her remaining time in the military was short.

She arrived at her destination and stopped outside the door. The portal to the storage area was sealed and in order; she transmitted the override codes to its pad. After a moment the indicator flashed green. Tanis grasped the handle and stepped inside, scanning the room for the cargo she was looking for.

She took one step past the door and felt her scalp squeezed slightly as the armor, normally pliant, solidified around her head. A warning on her HUD indicated that she had been struck by a blow to the base of her skull. The kinetic force spread down to her shoulders and they solidified as well, spreading out the force of the impact. Unused to the effect, Tanis tried to face her attacker, but her instincts conflicted with the armor's efforts to protect her and Tanis lost her balance and fell to the deck.

The impact caused the armor to freeze entirely and Tanis made a mental note to do some more fine-tuning. In the second after she landed, Tanis decided that since she was down, playing unconscious might be a good way to identify her ambusher. She closed her eyes and switched her vision to the feed from her ever-present nanoprobes.

Not surprisingly, the figure that stepped out from the shadows was Herris Santos. Her face was twisted in what Tanis assumed was the woman's approximation of a smile, and in her hand she hefted a thick pipe. A short bark of a laugh escaped her lips as she leaned over Tanis's body.

"The great and mighty Tanis Richards. You don't seem particularly tough to me. Didn't take much at all to knock you down. I'd better seal you up, though. Your AI may be rebooting from the blow; once it's back online I'm certain I'll have some company."

Great, a soliloquizer, Tanis thought. She hadn't run into one of those in a while.

She had determined to see where this would go but suddenly regretted the decision to play dead when she felt a dampening net being thrown over her. Immediately she and Angela felt their Link cut off and all contact with her nano cloud ceased.

<*Great plan,*> Angela said. <*Still want to go with this?*>

Tanis felt the net suddenly constrict and seal itself around her body.

<*Umm…I guess we have no choice now.*>

<*You know…I was doing some things. I don't just sit in your head waiting for you to summon me.*>

<*Sorry, I didn't expect things to play out like this.*>

<*Remind me to mock your lack of caution if we get out of this.*> Angela's tone was more dry than usual, something her AI reserved for special occasions.

Tanis felt her body being lifted and placed into a container. The hum of a hover unit sounded followed by the sensation of motion.

<*Rather alarming being trapped in one's mind,*> Tanis said. <*Been awhile since it's happened.*>

<*Well, you've got me, at least,*> Angela said. <*You certainly do present me with scenarios I'd never encounter on my own.*>

<*You sound supportive, but somehow I think you're not.*>

They were silent after that, but Angela was building up a map of where they were going and inserting it into Tanis's mind. It was based off the shifts and jolts they felt inside the container and net; the result may not have been entirely accurate, but it should be close. After all, it did have to conform to the area's layout, and with luck their destination wouldn't be too far away.

One hour and fifty-three minutes.

CAPTURE

STELLAR DATE: 3227327 / 01.29.4124 (Adjusted Gregorian)
LOCATION: District QR7, Ring 19C, Callisto Orbital Habitat (Cho)
REGION: Jovian Combine, Sol Space Federation

The feeling of motion continued for roughly twenty minutes. Angela's readout indicated nearly a kilometer had been covered in that time.

<Looks like we're in a business district downspin from the Intrepid*'s dock.>*

<Probably in some front or community bad-guy place,> Tanis said.

<Or some service corridor.>

<Less appealing.>

The container was opened and Tanis looked up, directing a bland stare at the face looming over her. Well, at least it was a one hundred percent positive ID on Herris Santos, so much for coincidence.

"I see you're awake. I hope you don't mind your little bit of relocation. My employer wanted to bring you somewhere nicer for our little chat."

Tanis didn't speak. There was nothing to say—giving in to the enemy's banter never got you anywhere.

"Well, I suppose I should make you marginally presentable; I doubt that Mr. Strang is going to want to look down at you in this container."

<I guess this is pretty serious,> Angela commented.

<Yeah, but if we meet the big man in person, you know that means they're going to kill us afterwards. Even if he does have friends in high places, full sensory recording of him holding a TSF officer hostage will get him nothing but unpleasantness.>

Herris reached in and lifted Tanis out and set her on a chair. She couldn't help but notice how easy it was. Their captor must have some serious strength mods, since she didn't really look that built.

"Any chance you could loosen this net? I have this wicked cramp." Tanis gave a benign smile. "I promise, I won't mess up whatever the next step in this adventure is."

"They never said anything about a weak sense of humor or weak attempts to get information. I was hired to capture you and I've done so. I'll collect my pay and be gone." Herris' smile was wicked. "Unless they want to pay me a bonus for some extra work."

Tanis nodded inside the net. "I hope for your sake that he doesn't do to you what he'll do to me."

"I don't think you know what he's going to do to you."

"I have a pretty good idea. It's going to suck."

Herris laughed. "I imagine you've got that part right."

Tanis had taken the time during their conversation to look over her surroundings. They were in a conference room; it was ten by twenty meters and had a large wooden table occupying most of the room's center. She and Herris were at the end furthest from the double doors. After a few minutes the doors opened and two men stepped in.

They gave off the bored appearance that was typical of corporate security, but Tanis could tell by their movements that they were ex-military. They looked the room over slowly, deploying their probes and checking for leaks and traces. She noticed them casting Herris as many cautious glances as they did her. A glance at the assassin told her that Herris had noticed their caution and was amused by it. Once they were satisfied, several more security types came in, followed by Arlen Strang.

"Good work, Miss Santos, you've done what many others failed to do."

"You should have called me from the beginning—I would have saved you a world of trouble."

Strang rubbed his jaw and smiled. "I believe I may do that the next time I need such services." He looked down at Tanis wrapped in the suppression net and gave her a winning smile. "So good to meet you, Major Richards. We've been on each other's minds so much I don't doubt that we are both finding this a bit anticlimactic."

Tanis slowly looked up at him, her eyes simmering with rage. "You realize that you have gone from simple legal penalties to death. You won't survive this encounter."

"My, you are every bit as cocky as I'd been led to believe." He waved an arm around him. "There is nothing you can do; you are fully under our control."

"It's something we're trained for. I got an A in smugness and cocky back in OCS."

"That doesn't surprise me in the least. Though I imagine seeing the *Intrepid* destroyed in a rather spectacular fashion will do something to modify your attitude."

Tanis couldn't read Strang at all. She couldn't tell if he was excited that he was finally going to get his victory, or if he was considering this purely from a profit and loss perspective. She decided to go on the offensive against his pride.

"I'll give you points for boldness and a grand vision, but not so much for the execution. You haven't really garnered a great track record—I don't expect you to be able to pull something like that off."

Strang's look betrayed no emotion. "I don't know what you thought was going to happen here, but I'll tell you what's not likely. You're not going to goad me into telling you my plans—sorry to burst your bubble."

Tanis changed approaches and grinned. "Don't worry, I'm pretty unburstable. So what's your reason for this gracious invitation?"

"I have reason to believe you know a few very interesting secrets about something on the *Intrepid*. I know about that trip down to Mars you and Captain Andrews took, and have strong suspicions about what you brought back up. I'd very much like to gain access to the *Intrepid*'s net so I can pull the specs for that little secret before we destroy it."

"And you think I'll give access to you?"

"I think you can be convinced."

<Here comes the torture,> Angela said.

"I really don't think you want to go that route." Tanis gave her captors a benign look.

"Why not?" Herris asked. "I find myself rather looking forward to it, then I get that extra pay I mentioned."

"Because I'm not restrained by the suppression net anymore."

"You what?" Herris's smug superiority cracked and a look of concern showed beneath it.

While she was being transported, Angela had configured some nano to extract bits of the armor and configured it to solidify. The effect was several thousand nano with very sharp knives. They just finished cutting through the threads on the back of the net and with a grand gesture, Tanis stood up and raised her arms in the air.

A look of shock passed across every face and Tanis couldn't help but smile. A moment later every gun in the room was aimed at her.

<*You are such a drama queen.*>

"What? Not what you were expecting?" Tanis asked.

"Oh for fuck's sake! Just kill her!" Strang yelled before he turned and stormed out of the conference room.

<*Damn…he's getting away.*> Tanis hadn't expected him to just leave.

<*If we survive there'll be nowhere he can hide. Not after abducting us.*>

No one else moved. The six security types and Herris all eyed her for several moments. Tanis took the opportunity to deploy probes to create a detection field for the armor—the more warning it had about incoming fire the better.

She was not surprised when Herris shot first. Tanis accelerated her perception and felt her surroundings effectively slow down. She held herself steady as the bounty hunter's finger squeezed and a bullet left the chamber, heading for her forehead. Here she would find out if the armor was worth its exorbitant cost

Milliseconds before impact the armor became rock hard from the top of her head down her neck and across her shoulders. This time Tanis didn't try to move or compensate, but rather tensed her legs to absorb the shock. Just as advertised, the armor deflected the bullet.

<*Hah! I knew I'd get the hang of this.*>

<*Better late than never.*>

The slug ricocheted off her face and into the wall. All eyes looked at Tanis's forehead, to the wall, and back to Tanis.

"I sort of have that effect on all of you, don't I?" Tanis smiled confidently. "What can I say, I'm truly amazing."

<*What's gotten into you?*> Angela asked.

<*Sorry, I can't help it. I think the armor is giving me a god complex.*>

<*I don't think it's the armor.*>

Tanis used the last moments of surprise to launch herself at Herris. They crashed to the floor and Tanis proceeded to deliver blows to the woman's neck and solar plexus, her hands locked into solid fists by her armor. Her opponent gasped for air and with an augmented thrust, lifted Tanis bodily and slammed her into the edge of the table. Her armor locked up and while the effect was somewhat disconcerting, it did cause the bounty hunter's attack to not hurt at all.

The lack of pain allowed Tanis to recover quickly, and before Herris had a chance to get back on her feet, Tanis pointed her fingers, signaled the armor to lock and slammed her now solid hand into Herris's eye.

Screaming a string of curses that Tanis couldn't even understand, the woman covered her face and tried to slide away. Tanis delivered several more blows to Herris's thorax and stood, ignoring the thrashing of the body at her feet.

A moment after Tanis looked up, her vision tinted and the nano probe's video feed in her HUD showed that all six of the security guards had fired their laser pistols at her. The armor absorbed the energy from the beams, focused and released the light in one blinding pulse. She heard startled shouts of shock and when her vision cleared the guards were all covering their eyes.

"You guys can't hurt me with those, but I can hurt you." Tanis snatched up Herris' handgun and panned it between the guards while stepping back against the wall. "Drop your guns and spread 'em on the table."

Five of the men complied, but one decided to try another shot. Tanis fired several slugs into his chest. He grunted and fell over, his life saved by body armor under his suit.

"Get up and get spread." She took careful aim at his head.

He stood slowly, but Tanis's nano video feed showed her one of the other guards edging away from the table, reaching for something inside his jacket. Without moving her arm, Tanis rotated her prosthetic wrist at a biologically impossible angle. Her handgun was pointed directly at his head.

She didn't even look at him. "Keep moving. I promise you a very short, sharp pain in your head, but everything will be all right after that. If push comes to shove I only need one of you alive to talk."

They got the message; she could shoot them all as fast as the weapon could chamber the next round—in less than a second based on the specs of the pistol.

"So, now that the ground rules are established is there any chance any of you know what it is Strang's planning to do?"

No one said a word.

"Oh come on; you guys hear things, follow him places. You must know something." Her comments continued to be met with silence and Tanis considered her options. "OK, I know it sounds crazy, but I'm actually tired of torturing people. It's really not that pleasant for me—makes for some really unpleasant dreams."

Tanis paused and her voice changed. It was deeper, slower, and dripped with venom.

"That doesn't mean I won't resort to it."

She fired six shots into the wall, close enough to each man for them to feel the slugs pass by their hair. They flinched in unison and her augmented sense of smell picked up the acidic scent of urine.

"I don't know where he went, but I know what he has planned," one of the men said to sidelong glares from his comrades. "He's going to set off an MDC and disintegrate the *Intrepid*."

"Try again," Tanis said. "There's no evidence of an MDC on the ring."

"That's because you weren't looking in the right place. The MDC is built into the network matrix for this portion of the ring. When the ship makes its hookups, the system will send the pulse through the network."

Tanis waited until Angela mentally confirmed that it was technically possible to pull that off.

"Thank you for the info," Tanis said. "Now, I want you all to lie down on your stomachs with your hands behind your heads. Anyone tries something funny and I'll put lead into you. I've got..." Tanis felt the weight of the pistol, "seven shots left. Who thinks I'll still have one left over if I decide to take you out?"

<*They're not made of lead anymore, you know,*> Angela said.

<*Yeah, I had been made aware of that.*>

<*Sorry, was just trying to break the tension. You scare the crap out of me sometimes...if I had crap to scare, that is.*>

Tanis didn't have to hold the men long. Angela had alerted the TSF and ChoSec the moment she had connectivity. Within minutes they had arrived. Tanis passed recordings of the event to each group and let them work out jurisdiction and custody while she slipped out of the room, querying the 701st engineering company for the location of the closest network node to the dock and requesting their best platoon on the double.

One hour and twenty-seven minutes.

A very large part of her wanted to go after Strang. She was tempted to tell Angela to start accessing visual feeds and track the man, but that wasn't the priority. There was nowhere he could run that would be far enough. Tanis didn't think he would hide at any rate. His type would get behind a wall of corporate lawyers as soon as possible.

No, Arlen Strang could wait.

<*And he really isn't that important,*> Angela said.

<*I wouldn't say that.*>

<*All that matters is to save the* Intrepid. *If we can get outsystem then all of this gets left behind.*>

A barrage of queries was coming in from TSF command on Callisto, as well as requests from ChoSec to return to the scene for more statements. Tanis shunted them all to her message queue, keeping an eye out for any message from the 701 engineers.

She was nearing the network node that Angela had marked off as the closest to the *Intrepid*'s berth when General Grissom, the Callisto TSF division commander, used an override to break past her queue.

<*Major Richards. I need you to come in for a debriefing immediately.*> He didn't sound happy, though in her experience generals rarely did. It was almost as though there was a special breed of dour human specially created to be generals.

<*Sir, I must insist that we do that later, I have a clear and present threat to this ring and the* Intrepid.> Tanis couldn't believe that they wanted to debrief her when there was the MDC to deal with. She brought up her preliminary report. <*I sent this in to command three minutes ago, it outlines the danger we're facing.*>

<*We have no solid evidence of an MDC. Even if it is there, the engineers you called in can handle it. We have questions we need to ask you about Strang.*>

<*It's all in the full sensory recording, sir. I really should be at the network node. It's impossible to know what they could find. A billion lives are in the balance—I have to believe that's more important than anything to do with Strang.*>

<*Major Richards, report to the DCP now! That's an order!*>

Tanis bit her lip in frustration—stopping when she tasted blood. <*Yes, sir; I'm on my way, sir*>

Grissom broke the contact with Tanis and she kept moving toward the network node.

<*I take it we're going to ignore Grissom.*>

<*We are—sorry for dragging you into this; we're probably both going to get in trouble…a lot of trouble.*>

<*Tanis, I'm always prepared for you to get us in trouble. If it worried me I wouldn't still be with you.*>

Angela's astringent words didn't hide the sentiment Tanis knew she felt. <*That may be the nicest thing that anyone ever said to me.*>

<*Then you need to be nice to more people. You'd stand a better chance of people being nice back if you were more so.*>

<*Yeesh, you can sure turn a 'thank you' back on me, can't you?*>

<*Comes from years of being in your mind. We AI are very susceptible to your mental influences, you know.*>

Tanis decided that she wasn't going to be drawn further into the discussion and focused on moving through the crowded corridors of the ring. Eventually they made it through the commercial district into a more sparsely populated systems control section. The sleek corridor walls gave way to rows of conduit containing both electronics and bio support liquids.

A few workers cast glances her way as she bolted past them. It probably wasn't often that a TSF officer, more specifically, a TSF officer with a uniform full of burn holes, ran past them at top speed.

<*It also could be that your top speed is over thirty kilometers per hour,*> Angela interjected into Tanis's thoughts. <*I doubt they are spending much time looking at your uniform and probably more just making sure you don't smash into them.*>

Tanis's mental avatar stuck its tongue out at Angela. <*Don't you have other things to do than listen in on my inner monologue?*>

<*I'm pretty good at multitasking, you know.*>

Tanis rounded the final bend between her and the network node and saw that the engineers hadn't arrived yet. The entrance looked like any other door off the service corridor, but behind it would be a marvel of man's technological achievements. Angela exchanged tokens with the ring's security AI and was denied access.

<*Sweet fuck, what now?*>

<*He says that our access has been revoked; we're wanted by ChoSec and the CIA.*>

<*Hold him off,*> Tanis said to Angela, before establishing a Link to Trist. <*Trist, I've got a sec AI named…*>

<*Blair,*> Angela supplied.

<*That's telling us we're persona non grata. Any tacks you suggest we take?*>

Trist's mental chuckle was a welcome sound. <*I've had a few run-ins with him in the past. He thinks he's hot shit, but I can get past him. What are you trying to access?*>

<*Node BX7.*>

<*No problem, give me…done.*>

The doors slid open in front of Tanis and she stepped into the node.

<*We gonna have ChoSec down on us?*>

<*I've got them taken care of. As far as ring security is concerned you've gone elsewhere—a maglev station antispin to be precise.*>

<*How come you never let on you could hack this fast?*>

<*Well, this ring is so full of other hackers' hooks that all I have to do is slip them some credit and they give me time on their SPNs. Speaking of which, this is going to wipe out that discretionary fund you set up for me in under one hour.*>

<*I'm sending you an update. Let's just hope we're still here in an hour.*>

One hour and nineteen minutes.

Tanis's attention shifted to the view in front of her. She stood on a catwalk that ran around a large cubic space, roughly eighty meters along each side. The catwalk ran around the edge of the cube, roughly twenty meters from the floor. There were other walkways at the forty and sixty meter marks, each with a shimmering ES shield around it to shelter it from the three degrees kelvin temperatures that the node operated in. On each of the six sides of the cubic room, massive conduits breached the spaces between catwalks containing fiber-optic, plasma, and waveguide energy data transportation systems.

The conduit converged on an object that was difficult for the eye to perceive. It was essentially a massive structure housing several crystalline matrixes of super-dense silicon. The array contained some of the most impressive information-sorting and throughput technology in the Sol system.

The processing power of the Callisto nodes was well known to be immense. As humanity's largest habitat, Callisto had more internal communication than every other habitation and planet in the Sol system put together. The hub in front of Tanis could conceivably handle all of the network traffic on Mars 1 and have bandwidth to spare.

Angela was deploying probes through the ES field and assembling a full picture of the node to determine if anything looked amiss. Tanis pulled a wad of formation material out of her pocket and set it on the railing, deploying nano to begin turning it into a multi-interface holo projector.

<*See, I am actually capable of controlling my own nano,*> Tanis said.

<*May the wonders never cease.*> Angela's remark was acerbic as usual.

The holo projector was completed and Angela linked her nanoprobes to it before slaving their controls to the projector's interface. The arrangement would allow the engineers control of the system once they arrived.

<*So is anything standing out yet?*> Tanis asked.

<*Well, by my way of understanding, an MDC takes a lot of power, and at least several meters worth of equipment. In this thing that's like finding a needle in a haystack.*>

<*Especially considering that if they have it in multiple nodes they may have figured out a way to break it up into smaller components.*>

Angela fed several proposed component dimensions onto the holo. <*A possibility that has given me more than a little consternation. It could look like any of these, or none of them. I'm not even sure how you could send a decoupling pulse through a network…it needs to have an emitter of some sort to create the targeted waveforms, beam, or field.*>

<*I get the picture.*>

Tanis pondered that, bringing up documentation on everything that was known about MDCs. They were initially conceived of in the twenty-first century, but at that point the technology to create one was only nebulously imagined. In the thirty-second century, several scientists discovered that by altering the emitter from a ramscoop they could break apart certain bonds and make asteroid mining easier. At some later point several governments had begun weaponizing the technology, working out methods to have a single carrier wave contain other wavelengths specifically targeted at molecular structures. While an MDC couldn't do something like take apart an entire planet, it could certainly break apart smaller bodies into their base elements.

Further perusal yielded formulas for how much energy it would take to generate either the targeted beam, general wave, or field effects that could break apart the *Intrepid*. The numbers were large, but well within the energy available to the network nodes.

Tanis loaded all of the information into the holo projector, which swelled to encapsulate the new data and the ever-enhancing view of the node that Angela's nano were providing.

The sound of the doors sliding open heralded the entrance of the engineers. Tanis turned to address Lieutenant Simon, their CO.

"Glad to have you folks here. We've got credible intel indicating an MDC is in this and probably the other three network nodes here on the ring. We've got some preliminary data up, but so far nothing is standing out to us as anomalous."

Simon eyed the holo projector. "Nice work, sir. You've saved us valuable time with this." He walked to the railing, looking out into the node as he said this. A sidelong glance betrayed an uncertainty his voice did not. "How sure are you there is a molecular decoupler in these nodes? I'm not certain if you're aware that such a charge could take a healthy portion of this ring with it—potentially the whole Cho if a runaway scenario were to occur."

"All too aware, Lieutenant. I know there is some threat against the *Intrepid,* and so far this is our best lead. The thing I can't wrap my mind around is how the pulse could be sent through the network."

The engineers were setting up more equipment around them and one, a corporal, spoke up. "If I may, sir."

Tanis nodded and he continued. "I wouldn't actually deliver the pulse from the nodes as much as the raw energy from them. There is a significant flow of energy brought in via ionized plasma. If one were to, well, enhance that energy, and direct it from each node through various conduits, you could have a relatively small device, comparatively speaking, emit the wave from elsewhere."

"So this could even be software," Tanis said.

"Yes, sir. That's how I'd do it."

Tanis pondered this as she stepped back and let the engineers do their work. Long minutes passed before one of the women bent over a series of holo interfaces called out. "I've found something. It looks like this node has a persistent connection to the dock the *Intrepid* is berthing at."

"With the amount of network traffic going to that dock, that doesn't seem unlikely," Tanis said.

"Aye, sir, but this is a secondary connection. From what I can tell, each of the nodes has a similar connection."

"Can you trace the end device?" Lieutenant Simon asked.

"Trying to, it's pretty nebulous. It just seems to arrive at the dock, connect to the main routers there and then dissipate."

"Either way you're saying that there is something actually on the dock, right?" Tanis asked.

"Everything points in that direction," Lieutenant Simon said.

"Then I'm heading out. You folks stay here and see if you can find a way to sever that connection."

"Yes, sir." Simon saluted. "Good luck."

"I'll stay connected to your net. Keep me abreast of any updates."

The lieutenant nodded as he turned back to the main holo and the data that was being brought up on the anomalous connection.

Fifty-seven minutes.

A FATEFUL ENCOUNTER

STELLAR DATE: 3227327 / 01.29.4124 (Adjusted Gregorian)
LOCATION: District C9Y, Ring 19C, Callisto Orbital Habitat (Cho)
REGION: Jovian Combine, Sol Space Federation

Tanis sprinted through the corridors, taking the fastest route to the docks that also kept her from running into the large shift-change crowds currently flooding the main thoroughfares.

After several a-spin tubes and a short maglev train ride she arrived at the dock. Several TSF Regulars guarded the entrance, passing all comers through a thorough Auth & Auth check.

<We going to have trouble here?> Tanis asked Angela.

<Are you kidding? I oversaw these Auth & Auths being set up. Oh, you mean the humans, then yes.>

Upon seeing her, the soldiers tensed and their squad leader, a Sergeant Weston, stepped forward.

"Uh sir, Major Richards. We've been ordered to take you into custody should you show up here." He was clearly nervous, but his hand was on his sidearm, a certain indication that the sergeant would do his duty.

"Sergeant, there was a mixup. ChoSec tried to get me pulled in and passed off a series of commands as though they came from Grissom."

The sergeant cast her an appraising look. "I don't know about that, sir."

"Look." Tanis stepped up to the Auth & Auth, which proceeded to approve her access to the docks. "Would the system let me pass if I were flagged? Not even an alert attached to me on the approval display."

Weston scratched his head. "Well, those Cho guys do like to throw their weight around…"

"You know it, Sergeant. Glad to see you're with the TSF on this. I'll be sure to mention it in my report."

Tanis walked past the soldiers and onto the dock. Behind her she heard Sergeant Weston start to say something and then stop.

<He's calling it in, isn't he?> Tanis asked.

<Yes, and it's been intercepted.>

<What would I do without you?>

<I imagine you'd be long dead.>

<You're so uplifting.>

Tanis was surveying the dock when a voice spoke from beside her. "So, what's the plan, Major?"

Tanis turned to see Trist standing beside her and smiled. "Thanks for the help back at the node. How did you get them off my back anyway?"

"Well, as far as they know, you got into a firefight and ducked into a maglev that derailed on an external part of its track. It's going to take over thirty minutes to get to you."

"I'm doing all that right now, am I?" Tanis cocked an eyebrow at Trist.

"Yeah, and your life signs show you as unconscious with a damaged Link node."

"That's really unfortunate for me."

"I thought so."

"I have to say, you're pretty good at this."

"I've been told," Trist grinned.

"So what do you make of this?" Tanis asked. "Think there's really some sort of MDC emitter here?"

"Could be, there's enough crap to hide it in."

"What's the most likely culprit?"

"I'm guessing something in line of sight with the main cargo hatch."

"Well, we've got one/two and two/three on the dock doing final inspections. We can get them to help."

"The more the merrier." Trist smiled.

A few dock workers, cargo handlers, and of course the people setting up the stage for the post-docking ceremonies could be seen. Tanis decided that for now she would let them continue their work, no need to cause a panic. It wouldn't take long for word of something like this to race across the Cho.

She called the two fireteams to her position and when they arrived, she updated them on the current situation.

"Marines, we've got a problem," Tanis began.

"When don't we?" Perez said under his breath.

Sergeant Kowalski shot the private a look to shut him up. Tanis found herself wondering why his superiors even bothered.

"We have credible intel regarding an MDC on the ring, and it's here on this deck. We've got to find it before the *Intrepid* is in range."

"Sir, wouldn't something like that be rather large and…well…really noticeable?" Dvorak asked.

<*Normally, yes,*> Angela said on the tactical net. <*But they've used the power of the ring's NNs to form the energy stream—we think. The 701 suspects that they're probably using the plasma streams.*>

"Damn, that means it could be a lot smaller," Dvorak said.

Angela fed possible configurations onto the net and the Marines looked them over.

Tanis proceeded to give out the orders. "Dvorak, Trist, I want you to head to the comm shack at the far end of the dock. The NNs are all maintaining connections to it, so it's quite possible that our culprit is down there. The rest of us will do a standard grid sweep across the rest of the dock. Don't forget to load those configs into your structural scanners. I've also got the net source signatures of the NN connections from the 701. They're on the tac net as well. Check every piece of cargo that's making a net connection for that route."

The Marines all saluted and dispersed to the grid locations that Kowalski laid out.

<*We've got an idea here.*> Simon's comment came over the broad channel on the engineer's net. <*It's entirely possible that what we're dealing with is not an MDC emitter at all, but more of a trigger device.*>

<*Go on,*> Tanis replied.

<*Well, we've been thinking that anything that would emit the MDC beam would have to be pretty obvious; it would need a large waveform guide, either ES or physical, and there are only so many configurations for those. The most obvious ones would be the main comm hookups for the*

Intrepid*, but they're not rated for nearly enough power and would trip and/or fry long before you could emit this type of wave from them.*>

<*So what's the end result of all of this?*>

<*Well, we think the weapon* is *the* Intrepid.>

That possibility had never even occurred to her. <*How could the ship be the weapon?*>

<*ES ramscoops are essentially, as you know, the base of any MDC. The* Intrepid *has the most powerful one ever created.*>

<*So you're saying that somehow this system will trigger the* Intrepid's *ramscoop to create an MDC field effect on itself?*>

<*Or on the ring and they'll just let it spill over onto the ship. Even if it doesn't, I somehow think it will go very badly for the* Intrepid.>

<*Lose/lose for us and win/win for Strang,*> Tanis replied. <*So how do you think they're going to trigger it?*>

<*We're still working on that, as well as trying to see if we can find the control software and shut it down. Even if the* Intrepid *doesn't dock, I'm betting that this thing could still make the ship direct an MDC field at the ring.*>

<*Impetus for us to figure this out.*> Tanis's tone was somber.

<*Er...yes, sir.*>

Tanis passed the information to the Marines and followed after Dvorak and Trist who were making their way across the dock toward the comm shack. If what they were dealing with really was just a trigger and it was using the waveguides to generate some sort of cohesion beam, then it was even more likely that the answer was in the comm gear.

She hopped on a hover heading to the far end of the dock and brought up the records for the comm shack. Sure enough, a service entry was logged last month, a full twenty weeks before any scheduled maintenance—with no record of malfunction being filed.

"Seems a bit suspicious," Tanis muttered to herself. She passed the information to Trist and Dvorak along with the details of the repair job. The chance of the info about logged repair being related to the actual work done was slim, but it was a place to start. The hover dropped her off near the comm shack and Tanis kept an eye peeled for anything suspicious as she entered the room.

All ship to station net traffic would pass through the equipment in the shack and since this dock was reserved for larger ships, a lot of systems were crammed in the twenty-meter-long space. After a moment's search Tanis found Trist and Dvorak already hunched over consoles.

Not wanting to interrupt them, she turned and examined the room, looking for the largest conduit which would likely be connected to the trigger device. Several large plasma lines ran out of the room and onto the dock. Tanis followed them and saw that they terminated at an array of beam emitters and receivers.

They were mounted to a column that ran down from the dock's ceiling. The design allowed them to rotate and slide into the best position to make a Link with a docked ship.

Tanis pulled up the specs, matching each device in the array to the design blueprints. As expected, something was not right. One emitter looked like a G1 TR3, but was not.

"Aha!" Tanis realized that her vocal proclamation wasn't all that helpful. <*Aha!*>

<*You've got something?*> Simon asked.

Tanis put a visual of the added component on the tactical and engineering nets. Lively debate ensued between Dvorak, Trist, the engineers, and several of the AI.

Tanis took a moment to review the arrival time of the *Intrepid.* It was getting close; within thirty minutes they would be making the seal. The outer hatches had already opened and the atmosphere on the dock was being held in by an ES field. If she looked carefully at the mass of local traffic through the opening it was possible to see a pattern clearing to allow the colony ship through.

<*We need to tell them not to dock,*> Tanis said.

<*We need to tell everyone not to dock, and clear the ring while we're at it,*> Lieutenant Simon said. <*We can't find the control software; it's probably on a timer. If this thing triggers without the* Intrepid *to absorb the effect, it's going to bounce back off that ES shield and nail the ring.*>

<*It's not an MDC, it's just a trigger beam. What will it do to the ring?*>

Simon paused, and she could see calculations being done on the engineers' net. <*We're not certain, but we think that since it's essentially a stasis beam it will cause the ring to seize. It may tear it out of alignment with the other rings. It would almost certainly collide with another ring in that event.*>

<*That's almost worse than the MDC!*> Trist exclaimed.

<*More than almost worse,*> Simon responded. <*We're sending a squad to you to attempt to disarm that thing on your end. You—*>

The connection was severed. Tanis poked her head into the comm shack and looked at Dvorak and Trist.

"I'm cut too; we've lost all Link to any nets outside of this dock," Trist said.

"I've got no external wireless connections," Dvorak added.

Tanis looked up to see one/two running toward the comm shack. "Taylor. Someone's dampened the dock. Check outside and see if you can get—" The whine of railguns coming from the dock's entrance interrupted her.

"Aw fuck," Private Weber cursed. "Never a dull moment with you around, Major."

"Glad to oblige." Tanis tried to contact two/three on the discreet Link that military teams could use at close range.

<*What's your status, Kowalski?*>

<*We're near the entrance. The regulars there are gone, we're trying to hold these mofos at bay, but nothing here is holding up against their rails.*> He put data up on the tactical net showing over a dozen attackers, some wearing heavy armor.

Tanis pulled up a map of the dock and examined it. <*Fall back to coordinates F/3.1 behind those steel crates; they're full of some high-density raw alloys that should stop whatever those rails are flinging.*>

<*Yes, sir, thank you, sir.*>

Kowalski initiated a local combat net which Tanis extended to Trist before marking two/three's current position and destination on it. She turned to one/two. "Weber, you stay with Dvorak and Trist. You two try to determine how to disable that thing." Tanis pointed up at the emitter. "We could just blast it, but who knows what sort of failsafes and detectors it has."

"Yeah, I'm typically against blowing things up that we don't understand." Dvorak's tone was dry, but Tanis could tell it masked concern.

"The rest of you, we're moving to position G/4.2. We'll set up cover for two/three and try to catch whoever this is in our crossfire."

"I'm guessing that it's someone who wants to stop us from disabling this little party trick here," Taylor said.

"Or just someone with amazingly bad timing," Perez grinned.

"What, like your jokes?" Weber asked.

"This is the second time I've been attacked today." Tanis sighed. "I'm beginning to think some cosmic force wants me dead."

"I'd bet more on simple human forces wanting you dead...sir," Perez replied.

Tanis cast him a futile quelling glare and the fireteam moved out, hopping on a hover traveling in roughly the right direction. Tanis stayed back, monitoring two/three as well as Trist and Dvorak's progress.

Minutes later they were in position, deployed behind several crates containing casings for SC batteries. The casings were molecularly dense and also magnetic; with luck they would deflect or slow any incoming rail shots.

Two/three had managed to reach their position with no injuries and were returning fire on the attackers. Their feed of the enemy was on the combat net and Tanis saw they were fighting more of the same heavily-armed men from the conflict on Mars 1. The count came to under forty enemy.

<*Coordinate fire on their forward ranks,*> Tanis said. <*We need to halt their advance until backup arrives.*>

<*It's weird that backup isn't here yet,*> Salas commented. <*I mean, we have several platoons within a klick or two.*>

<*Don't get your hopes up,*> Dvorak cut in. <*This dampening extends past the dock from what I can tell. I doubt anyone knows anything is up—not until the monitoring AI realize they've lost comm with the TSF guards at the dock entrances.*>

<*What's ETA on that?*> Tanis asked.

<*Based on the current alert level, it should have already happened—they've probably subverted some monitoring systems. I'd bank on at least ten minutes before that's detected.*>

<*Chances are that this will be over in ten minutes,*> Reddy grunted.

Tanis realized that in those ten minutes the *Intrepid* would be making its seal. Whoever was orchestrating this party had to be making certain that all appeared outwardly normal on the dock. She thought briefly of the TSF guards and a feeling of guilt assaulted Tanis momentarily. She should have warned the guards there to be on the lookout for trouble. Their names were added to her list.

Tanis steeled herself and addressed the teams. <*I think we have to consider ourselves to be on our own for this one, folks, but if it's do or die in the next ten minutes, then it's going to be do or die on our terms.*>

With her nanoprobe net extended, Tanis gathered an aerial survey of the combat zone. Sure enough the attackers were trying to flank the Marines. It's what she would have done. A quick run through the cargo manifests revealed several things that could be of use. A crate ten meters away contained automated servitors to be used for scrubbing air ducts in environmental processing plants in the colony station. They were equipped with scalpelling lasers that could remove deposits and corrosion with ease. She sent a command to the crate to unseal, and a quorum of nano flew over to activate the servitors.

<*I've got some bots moving in to cover our right flank—they should hold, or at the least alert us to the enemy's position, but we're open on our left flank. Altair and Reddy, I want you to take*

up a position around those blue containers. I've put cargo density on the combat net; find a solid something and lay down suppressive fire. I don't care what you mow through—in fact, destroy as much of their cover as you can.>

Altair and Reddy signaled green on the net and Salas and Arsen lobbed several concussion grenades before opening up with their assault rifles. The action gave their squad mates ample cover to get in the best positions to return fire.

However, the moment they ducked down to reload, the enemy delivered a withering assault with their railguns. Molten plas and steel sprayed out from each impact.

<*Heads up people, those rails are firing plasma at us.*>

<*Aw fuck,*> Perez swore. <*Just what my day needs, having a limb blown off and then melted.*>

<*I don't think it actually works that way,*> Taylor said.

<*Or at least not in that order,*> Weber added.

Despite the Marines' best efforts, the enemy was advancing. There was only so much they could do against an enemy that outnumbered them four to one and had superior firepower.

<*Angela, I know you're busy with Dvorak and Trist, but why isn't this dock's security system engaging?*>

<*I'm guessing it's jammed,*> Angela replied. <*Not really that surprising.*>

<*Yeah, but jammed centrally, or locally?*>

Angela's avatar grinned. <*I gotcha. Let me see if I can take manual control of the suppressors. Gonna need a few of your synapses to do it, but I'll try to use stuff you don't need right now.*>

Tanis got that distracted feeling she experienced whenever Angela was using a substantial part of her brain to help work through a difficult problem. It was almost like a buzzing going on in the back of her mind, causing segments of code or raw mathematical theorems to flash through the background of her thoughts.

<*I've got control of the individual suppressors,*> Angela said after a few moments, <*but there is a physical disconnect on the power conduits for their firing mechanisms. I've located it here.*> A position flashed on the map of the dock. <*You'll need to climb up there and reconnect the line.*>

<*Of course I will.*> Tanis sighed.

<*Well, not you actually; whoever goes up there stands a good chance of getting shot and Trist and Dvorak need me to help them work out this thingamabob on the comm system.*>

Tanis chuckled. <*A little self-preservation, eh?*>

<*Well, right now if I die, we all die.*>

<*I can't say I disagree with that.*>

Tanis laid out the scenario to her two squads. Taylor spoke up as soon as she was done. <*Weber and I will take it. We're in the best position and we've got some experience with stuff like that.*>

<*Then it's yours. We'll cover you.*>

The two men dashed from their position, rolling and sliding across open spaces to present the smallest targets possible. The power junction was on a catwalk seven meters above the deck and while a few crates rose higher, much of their climb would be in the open.

"Good luck," Tanis whispered. < *C'mon Marines, let's lay down one hell of a distraction.*>

In a coordinated effort, grenades were lobbed and fire spewed out of assault rifles and slug throwers to hide the movements and destination of Taylor and Weber. Combat net showed they were almost at their goal and just had the climb ahead of them. Tanis saw they had opted to scale the back of a radioactive waste storage container rather than take the more exposed ladder along the wall. It would be quite the leap to the catwalk, but the two men must have thought they could make it.

Tanis swung a probe into their area to see a pair of the enemy on the opposite side of the container the Marines were climbing. She sent the feed to Weber. Upon reaching the top of the container he crouched and lobbed two conc grenades over the far side. Twin blasts ripped apart several crates and Weber leaned over the top and delivered a barrage of slugs from his assault rifle before continuing with blasts from his pulse rifle, while his automatic reloader fed fresh ammunition into the AR.

Taylor had used the distraction to make the leap to the catwalk. He crouched low, unfastening the cover to the power conduit's coupling. A plasma pellet hit the catwalk near him, half blasting and half melting a portion of the structure away. The unsteady surface shook and swayed, but Taylor held his position while Weber threw his last grenade at the attacker who had made the shot.

<*Almost have it,*> Taylor said as another shot struck near him. The cover was off and he was reconnecting the coupling. He was fastening the cover when another plasma pellet sliced through the railing behind him and tore the catwalk under him off the bulkhead. He was wrapped in the twisted metal as it fell six meters to the deck below. Weber swore both audibly and over the net as he jumped down from his perch and raced to where Taylor's body lay—what was left of it.

<*He's gone.*> Weber's tone was low and pained.

<*We'll mourn him later,*> Kowalski said. <*Keep that flank secure, they're trying to rush us.*>

<*They're in for a surprise.*> Angela brought the dock's security systems online. Pulse particle turrets lowered from the ceiling and opened up on the enemy. Angela didn't care what she hit—her only concern was that as long as it wouldn't cause a blast big enough to kill the Marines or Tanis it was expendable. The attackers were forced back, and though they were able to take out the turrets one by one, they lost over fifteen of their number in several seconds.

<*What's our status on the device?*> Tanis asked.

<*We've located the software running it and are cracking it now,*> Trist replied. <*It has several failsafes, so we've got multiple worms working their way in from oblique angles. Give us three more minutes and we'll have it neutralized.*>

<*You sure we just can't shoot the damn thing?*> Perez asked.

<*If we do, the plasma surge will just dump out onto the dock when it tries to fire. It won't be detrimental to the* Intrepid *or the ring, but we'll all die.*>

<*Last resort then,*> Tanis said. <*Three minutes is cutting it damn close, though.*>

Her words were emphasized by a slight rumble that passed through the deck plate as the ring made magnetic grapple with the *Intrepid.*

<*They've got reinforcements coming in!*> Kowalski called out. <*We've got to fall back.*>

Tanis looked over the updates flowing into the combat net. At least another forty enemy were entering the dock from other entrances and the Marines were once again in danger of being flanked.

<This is too open here,> Tanis said. *<Fall back using the plan I've laid in. We'll create a perimeter around Dvorak and Trist.>*

<Not a lot of dense cargo there,> Jansen replied.

<There will be.> Tanis accessed the automatic loaders, tapping into several haulers and agrav pads loaded with dense items. She configured them to move into positions to cover the Marines as they retreated.

<Mighty sweet of you, Major,> Perez said. *<Always nice to have cover when I run.>*

<Shut it, Perez,> Kowalski said. *<Just shoot that bastard trying to kill you on the left.>*

<I see him, I see him.>

Things were getting tense; the fireteams were pulled back as tight as they could manage around the comm shack, but the plasma rails were chewing up the cover. Tanis was trying to bring in more cargo, but their attackers had wised up and were shooting any haulers or grav pads they saw.

A low boom echoed through the dock and Tanis knew that the *Intrepid* had completed its docking procedure. It was just over a minute early. Any moment now the ES shield would drop and the trigger mechanism would fire. She saw the Marines all shift, their posture showing that they were taking a last stand approach to the fight. They'd go down as heroes.

"We're so fucking close," Dvorak swore. "Just one more goddamn minute and we'll have this bastard cracked."

Behind the Marines the ES shield at the cargo hatch snapped off and the *Intrepid*'s doors began to slide open.

<We don't have one more minute,> Angela said. *<It's going to fire in twenty seconds.>*

Tanis turned and raised her rifle to fire on the emitter. Kowalski cast her a sidelong glance, his expression showing his acceptance of what she was about to do. Her finger had pulled the trigger halfway when she felt a Link come online.

Of course! she thought. The dampening field wasn't set up to block the focused beams between the comm system and the *Intrepid*. The opening iris had established those connections and since Angela was deep in the comm system she was subsequently linked with her ship.

<Where have you been!> Amanda said a moment later. *<TSF said you'd gone rogue and were lost somewhere on the ring.>*

<No time, Amanda, hook up with Angela, we've got a device here that's about to ruin everyone's day!>

Tanis felt a rapid exchange of information pass through her as Angela brought the ship's avatar up to speed on recent events and what they were fighting with. Less than a second later she felt a massive presence swell onto their local net. It was as though she was suddenly on the edge of a deep precipice. She realized it must be the *Intrepid* itself, stepping in to disable the device. The vast mind that powered the ship broke through the trigger failsafes and seized its processes. Angela, Trist, and Dvorak let out simultaneous cry of delight on the combat net and a moment later the waveform guides in the communications array exploded in a shower of sparks and debris.

<Thank you,> the presence said over their combat net, and was gone.

<Bob's pretty happy that you all have gone to such lengths to protect him and the ship's passengers,> Amanda said. *<I can't believe how close we all just came to biting the dust.>*

<Wouldn't have happened. We would have taken the device out,> Tanis said.

<I hate to rain on your happy parade, but we're still about to be sliced and diced by all these

guys with guns,> Perez said.

<*I think we can help with that.*> Joe's voice came over the combat net. Tanis turned to see him entering the dock at the head of over two hundred soldiers in full combat gear. Within moments they had taken up positions around the Marines and were laying fire into the enemy.

Tanis had never been so happy to see anyone in all her life.

REPRIEVE

STELLAR DATE: 3227348 / 01.30.4124 (Adjusted Gregorian)
LOCATION: GSS *Intrepid*, Callisto Orbital Habitat (Cho)
REGION: Jovian Combine, Sol Space Federation

"We were pretty sure something suspicious was going on when we couldn't find you and General Grissom said you'd gone rogue after attacking Strang," Captain Andrews said. "You may be a bit impulsive, but that tale was a stretch."

"Ring security couldn't find you, and we couldn't get a comm signal from the guards at the dock, even though TSF told us they were checking in regularly," Terrance added. "We were getting one hell of a run-around."

Tanis was sitting at the table in the bridge's conference room with Terrance, Joe, Captain Andrews, and Admiral Sanderson. With the additional forces Joe had brought to the battle on the docks, the attackers had been overwhelmed and surrendered. However, things were still a mess. Grissom was demanding Tanis be turned over to his command on the ring, and Strang had not been indicted for abducting her. With all sides of the tale coming out it was becoming obvious that Grissom was in Strang's pocket.

"So, we were ready for just about anything when that dock opened up, hence the rather large armed force at my back," Joe said. "Can't say how glad I was to see you there still kicking."

"That's me." Tanis smiled. "I'm a kicker." She realized that statement could have been misconstrued. "Er, well, figuratively speaking."

She couldn't help but notice a wry look from Joe. Everyone else pretended to ignore the statement and the look.

"Glad we got there when we did," Terrance said. "We owe you, Major Richards. We owe you several times over."

"That we do," Sanderson growled. "I've got calls in to several individuals up the chain of command demanding Grissom's head. Things will come to light very shortly, and they won't go well for him—that I can promise you."

"Lucky for me Angela is rated A97 incorruptible, or it would be my word against a TSF division's that Strang assaulted me," Tanis said. "As it sits, it's still going to take some doing, I imagine."

"We had some of our own excitement as well," Joe said. "Turns out there was a bit of sabotage in the scoop's main systems. If we hadn't caught it, it would have activated and caused some pretty serious damage to Callisto."

"Really?" Tanis asked. "Did we find who did it?"

"Ouri is working on it. So far everything points to some contractors back on MOS. Everyone onboard checks out."

"I've just got word that Grissom has been relieved pending further investigation." Tanis saw Sanderson smile for the first time. "It would seem that internal affairs has been keeping an eye on him for some time. He made official insubordination charges against you, and those are still standing, but I believe I can get those dropped even if he's cleared."

"Strang really has grown desperate to stop us," Captain Andrews said. "His little plan here was frankly nuts—chancing millions of deaths to take us out."

"There's even a twenty-one percent chance that the field could have destroyed another ring." Terrance's expression was grim. "While Sanderson is taking action through military channels I've filed over three hundred civil complaints against Strang, Grissom, several local security firms, and…well, you get the picture. There are going to be court battles for decades over this."

"Not that we'll really care," Tanis said. "We'll be long gone by then."

Terrance had that smile again, the one that reminded Tanis he was the owner of a multiworld corporation for a reason. "We won't, but I promise you that they will care very much."

Tanis looked over the assembled men. "I really can't say enough how glad I am that you decided to take every precaution when docking."

"Well." Terrance wore his nicer, human smile. "Like I said, you deserve some thanks too. Without your work we wouldn't have made it to Callisto, let alone survived today."

"You really have the *Intrepid* to thank," Tanis said. "Even with all of my efforts, without his intervention at the last moment it would have all been worthless."

"Let's just say that it was a group effort." Joe smiled. "And I'm betting that it will be the STR's last volley at us. It's smooth sailing from here."

"Aw, damn it!" Tanis put head in her hands. "Now look what you've done!"

"Who would have thought we would have a superstitious intel officer on our hands?" Terrance chuckled.

"Hell, with all that's happened to try to stop us, I'd be crazy not to be," Tanis said. "No matter, though. Those STR goons haven't come up with anything we haven't been able to handle yet."

"Now who's making the dangerous statements?" Joe asked.

CELEBRATION

STELLAR DATE: 3227362 / 02.13.4124 (Adjusted Gregorian)
LOCATION: District A39, Ring 19C, Callisto Orbital Habitat (Cho)
REGION: Jovian Combine, Sol Space Federation

It was their last night on Callisto. The *Intrepid* had ended up staying roughly three weeks longer than intended due to the need to replace all of the supplies destroyed in the dock fight. There had also been the testimonies that Tanis and the Marines gave in the cases against dozens of individuals who were either involved or complicit in Arlen Strang's attempt to destroy the *Intrepid*.

The STR had thrown him to the wolves, disavowing themselves of any of his actions, but the chickens had come home to roost. Several governments across the Sol system were launching investigations into the consortium and discovering trails of bribery, technology being sold to embargoed groups, and funding of various terrorist organizations.

Dozens of arrests had already been made and the company's stocks were plummeting. An added bonus was that the business ventures Terrance was leaving behind were getting a boost as demand for products not manufactured by the STR increased. Not that he would ever enjoy the largess, but his offspring and successors would.

The last few nights had been gala after gala in the ballrooms on the *Intrepid*, but tonight there were no formal celebrations. Tanis, Joe, Ouri, and several others on the SOC staff threw a soiree at a large club on the ring. Sad farewells were given as many of the support personnel were not colony-bound and Callisto was where they disembarked. Tanis had also invited the TSF platoons that had now finished their assignments under her. At present she was sharing a table with Lieutenant Forsythe, Lieutenant Grenwald, and Staff Sergeant Williams.

"Never gonna forget you, Major." Williams smiled as he lifted a glass in a toast to her. "You're the toughest, meanest, most cunning officer I ever did meet. Hell, if you were just a little smarter you could even be a sergeant."

Tanis laughed. "You could say I'm a little too smart for that. You guys have to do all the work in this woman's space force."

"Damn right we do." Williams downed the drink. "And don't think we don't like it that way. If you officers were the ones actually running things, we'd be screwed for sure."

Forsythe laughed while Grenwald scowled. "You'll get used to it, Grenwald." The older lieutenant smiled as she slapped him on the back. "The NCOs are really here to keep us in line as much as the troops. The sooner you accept that, the better your life will be."

Tanis liked both of the officers a lot. Forsythe was up for a promotion after her work keeping the *Intrepid* safe, and Grenwald was all but guaranteed one once he had put in the requisite time at his current rank. She also had it on good authority that Williams had a promotion to gunnery sergeant waiting once his platoon was reunited with their company in a month.

The thoughts of promotion and reward brought her mind to Corporal Taylor for a moment. The Marine had posthumously been awarded the Eight Planets of Valor and been added to the heroes roster of Bravo Company, Marine Battalion 242. It was an honor the company afforded to few, but his sacrifice could not be denied.

She was brought back to the present by the needling Forsythe was giving Grenwald. Williams added a particularly choice example of a staff sergeant's wit and they all broke into laughter.

After the chuckles died down, Williams cast Tanis a questioning eye. "I have to say, Major. I really don't get why you're shipping out. This is what you were born to do."

"Could even pass as a Marine if you worked at it." Forsythe grinned.

"It's my time," Tanis said. "I've put in nearly fifty years of service, and let me tell you, in MICI years that's more like five hundred. They don't give us much downtime, just shuttle us from mission to mission. Hell, I've had periods where I've gone years with my only time off being in stasis."

The Marines nodded solemnly. They didn't agree, but they respected her decision.

"All the same." Williams put a hand on her shoulder. "I'll be sad to see you go."

"Who knows," Tanis smiled. "We could meet again; it's a big galaxy and stranger things have happened."

"I'd fight by your side any day, Major." Williams' grey eyes locked with hers. "You're one hell of a soldier."

"Here's to the Major." Grenwald lifted his glass.

"To the Major!" the other two chimed in.

*****

The party lasted for several more hours. In the end, all of the tables were empty but one. Tanis, Joe, Ouri, and Amy Lee sat around it, each nursing a final drink. The change from the loud revelry to relative silence had caused a melancholy to settle over them. The realization had hit that when they left the ring, it would be the last time they stepped foot on any structure in the Sol system or saw any people not already on the *Intrepid.* They were saying goodbye.

"It's different than I thought it would be," Joe said. "I'm feeling sadder than I thought I would."

"I think we all are," Ouri replied. "We're leaving home, leaving Sol. We're going out into the dark for a long time."

"Feels anticlimactic," Tanis said. "I feel like after all this struggle that the struggle should just continue."

"Gah! Don't say that." Joe cringed. "I'm all struggled out." Under the table he held her hand.

"Oh believe me, I am too." Tanis smiled. "But I'm going to have to reeducate myself on how to live without it."

"I think we all are." Amy Lee returned Tanis's smile. "I'm so used to feeling tense and suspicious I've begun to be cautious around my hairbrush. I'm surprised you trust yours with your new locks."

"Stars, I'm happy to have long hair again." Tanis ran a hand through her shoulder-length blonde hair. "I'm going to grow it to my ankles."

"That'll look…weird." Joe smiled.

"I recommend against extreme hair lengths," Ouri said. "It gets really annoying."

"But I could create hair sculptures out of it on my head! I hear that's all the rage on Triton these days." Tanis grinned.

"That was a decade ago," Amy Lee said.

"Oh."

"We should head back," Joe said. "Debark is in two hours and you know how those security types like to have everything all sealed up well in advance."

"Hey!" All three ladies spoke at once and then burst out laughing. It felt good—good to laugh, good to be relaxed. Things were finally done here.

Tanis and Joe walked arm in arm back to the *Intrepid*, lost in their own world together. Amy and Ouri walked slightly ahead of them, talking softly between themselves. For once, Tanis didn't feel the need to be on her guard. ChoSec was thick like flies on the ring. No one wanted the departure of the *Intrepid* to have any of the same troubles it had on the way in. Luckily, nothing suspicious had happened since that day. The thought made the hairs on the nape of Tanis's neck rise, but she forced herself to relax. Just because nothing had happened did not mean something *had* to happen.

Besides, with most of the upper echelons of the STR behind bars, no one was left to cause them trouble. Even if there were, it was unlikely that they would consider it worthwhile anymore. Like any company, eventually the STR had to cut its losses when looking at a losing venture.

Despite her misgivings, they made it to the *Intrepid* without incident and the guards who checked them in saluted smartly.

"You're the last ones aboard, sirs."

"Seal it up then," Tanis said. "It's time to head into the black."

LAST DITCH

STELLAR DATE: 3227364 / 02.15.4124 (Adjusted Gregorian)
LOCATION: GSS *Intrepid*, Near Main Asteroid Belt
REGION: Jovian Combine, Sol Space Federation

Tanis stared at the views being displayed on the commissary's main wall. The entire space was covered with the starscape that was visible from the *Intrepid*'s bow. The ship was just passing the nominal orbit of the main asteroid belt, slightly above the absolute plane to avoid the small particles that had been disturbed by a Kirkwood gap in the belt.

Even though Sol was just a pinprick in the lower left quadrant of the view, its brilliance in the cold expanse of space was almost like a physical pressure on the eyes. Over on the right, several overlays were visible showing the ship's path toward Sol, with various periods of engine burn intensity highlighted. The current position was shown by a small representation of the ship with stats indicating vector and thrust to its right.

Tanis found herself lost in the beauty of it. Very rarely did she simply look out into space and the stars; most of the time she was too focused on duty and security, but other than a few reports to file, there was little left for her to do.

It seemed odd to have yet another celebration, but a day or two earlier someone had planned a small gathering before going into stasis and before long everyone was invited and the cooks were having a fit.

Pulling her attention away from her inward thoughts, Tanis focused on the conversation around her.

"I've gotta admit," Ouri slurped a spoonful of soup. "This feels weird…this falling into the sun thing."

"I've done it a few times," Joe said. "It is a bit different than using a planet to slingshot, mainly because just getting close to a planet isn't potentially fatal."

"That and most planets don't fill the forward view days before you even get close." Ouri grimaced.

"You worry too much." Tanis's eyes had a dreamy look. "Eat food, enjoy drink, listen to banter. Nothing can ruin this. We're finally on our way—finally leaving Sol and all of the nonsense."

"Who are you, and what have you done with Tanis?" Joe grinned. "You look like Tanis, but the words coming out of your mouth are calm and relaxed…dare I even say happy?"

"It must be a robot, or maybe a clone," Ouri said. "I was very certain that Tanis was actually incapable of anything approaching mellow. Should we call security?"

"Aren't we security?" Joe asked.

"Crap…you mean we have to deal with this?"

"Shut up." Tanis scowled at her tablemates.

"Oh thank god, it is you!" Joe grinned.

A woman walked up to the table and pulled up a chair beside Tanis. "I tell you, it's damn good to actually have a glass of wine again." She spoke as though she knew everyone around her, but no one recognized her.

She wore a long dress and a cowl which covered most of her head. Tanis tried to catch a glimpse of her eyes as the woman reached for the bottle to refill her glass.

"Who—?" Joe began to say.

"Amanda!" Tanis exclaimed and hugged the other woman. "We didn't recognize you without a starship attached to your ass."

Ouri nearly choked on her drink and had to frantically gasp for breath as Joe handed her a napkin.

"Oh my god, Tanis, that has got to be the funniest thing you've ever said."

Tanis scowled. "I'll have you know I am funny all the time."

<*She's a barrel of yuck yucks,*> Angela said at her driest.

"I gotta admit," Joe said to Amanda, "I didn't expect to see you here…I didn't realize you could leave your…er…post."

"No pun intended," Ouri smiled.

"I was on shift for a bit longer than planned—Priscilla had a few problems adapting to the interface, but the plan is a ninety days on, ninety days off rotation between us. As much as I like Bob, I really do need this time to remember who I am."

"It is weird to hear your voice with my ears. I'm used to it being in my head," Amy Lee said.

"You and me both." Amanda laughed.

"Hey." Tanis spotted someone across the crowd. "Isn't that Lieutenant Collins of the GSS?"

"Yeah." Ouri looked over her shoulder where Tanis pointed. "Slimy guy, isn't he?"

"As the day is long," Tanis replied. "But what's he doing here? I thought he wasn't mission."

"He wasn't, but he requested crew status just before we left the Cho. There were a couple of last-minute abdications, so he got in no problem. A few other people in his department got crew positions as well," Joe said.

"Damn," Tanis said. "I really don't like him. Something about him rubs me the wrong way."

"He's a rubber all right. But let's talk about happy things. Collins'll sour my mood real fast." Ouri reached for the bottle of wine and poured herself another glass.

No one said anything for a moment and then they all burst out laughing at once—except for Ouri who looked perplexed.

"What did I say?"

They steered the conversation elsewhere and the light chatter continued through the meal. As the dinner was drawing to a close Captain Andrews rose from his place at the head table.

"Good evening to you all," he said to the assembled crowd. "I'm certain that all of you feel as pleased and excited as I do that we're finally underway. For those of you who haven't checked the latest stellar vector," he gestured to the screens behind him, "we are achieving better than expected performance from both our engines and our ramscoop. I'm certain you are as happy as I and are very grateful to Earnest, Abby, and their teams for an amazing job in constructing this truly magnificent vessel."

Applause thundered as everyone clapped enthusiastically for the Reddings and their teams.

The captain raised his hands for silence and the applause died away.

"We are currently falling toward the sun at a rate that will cause our breakaway velocity to be 0.09*c*. We will continue to increase this speed through our interstellar burn to 0.12*c*. Because of this, we will alter our approach to LHS 1565 and overall we'll shorten our trip by seventeen years."

This statement was met with more applause and cheering from the assembled mission crew and colonists. People were smiling and patting one another on the back. Tanis was certain that she even saw a smile crease the face of Abby Redding at the head table.

<General alert.> Priscilla's voice resonated through all command crew's Links. *<We have multiple incoming signals. They appear to be some sort of craft.>*

Tanis looked to Joe. "Your fighters ready to roll?"

"Suited and strapped in."

<Captain, I have a full squadron of fighters ready to deploy on your command.> Tanis relayed the information to Captain Andrews.

<Very good, Major. Bring Commander Evans with you to the bridge.>

"Huh, and here we thought you were all relaxed," Ouri smiled at Tanis. "Still thinking about all the possibilities I see."

"Ladies and gentlemen." Captain Andrews was still standing, and his face betrayed no emotion other than calm. "We appear to have a potential issue affecting our exit of this system. All duty personnel, report to your assigned stations. Everyone else, check your local access points for any assignments, otherwise follow the general emergency plan."

With that he left the table and strode toward the closest tube that ran to the bridge. Several others, including Terrance, the Reddings, and Admiral Sanderson went with him; Tanis and Joe worked their way through the crowds to catch up with Amanda trailing behind them.

Joe analyzed the data Priscilla was streaming to them. "They appear to be some sort of fast intercept craft. Most likely a deployment type that will drop fighters...either that or they're missiles."

"I don't know which I prefer," Tanis said.

"Missiles," Joe said as they caught the tube that slid in after the command crew had left. "Lower levels of programming on those. No human or AI onboard—fighters always have either...or both."

<Deploy your fighters, and have Yellow Wing prep for takeoff as well,> Captain Andrews addressed Joe over the Link, broadcasting across the local security net so that Tanis could hear as well.

<Aye, Captain,> Joe responded.

A moment later the tube disgorged them onto the command deck. The short access corridor led them into the main foyer, where Priscilla was working to ensure that all sections were covered and that everyone was where they were supposed to be. She didn't look much different than Amanda, though Tanis could see some slight physical traits that didn't match. She looked up and nodded at the two officers as they ran past her.

"Good luck, keep us in one piece," she said over the room's audible systems.

"Don't we always?" Joe smiled in return.

The bridge was a study in energetic order. Everyone was doing something, but they were doing it with precision and calm. Everyone present was in the upper echelons of their field. Moreover, Captain Andrews had worked them hard. The result was a cohesive team built from what otherwise would have just been a group of people good at disparate things.

Tanis and Joe exchanged tokens with the bridge net and updates flooded in.

Scan showed nine large cylindrical objects headed toward the *Intrepid* at 0.5*c*. Their point of origin appeared to be from the Thermis asteroids, a region owned by several mining groups. Tanis saw ties to the STR—a major purchaser of their raw materials.

Readings and statistics on the incoming objects flowed in, and Joe sat at a duty station seat where he updated the main holo with information and projections. Tanis stood near the rear of the bridge. While she was a competent pilot, Joe didn't need her telling him how to do his job.

"I believe they are carrier vessels," Joe said aloud and Captain Andrews turned his command chair to look at him. Terrance was standing beside Tanis and swore softly. The Reddings were already at consoles, most likely preparing repair crews and readying the ES shields and laser turrets—Earnest had no reaction, but Abby shook her head.

"I would expect three to five fighters to deploy from each once they are in range. I have event ETAs up on the net and holo. We're most likely looking at a Theta Class fighter, they hit hard and do the job fast. They're usually equipped with three dozen five-megaton fusion warheads." Joe said and updated the bridge net with his data.

"Well, that would get the job done fast," Captain Andrews replied. "You realize that works out to about 1620 five-megaton devices."

"I do, sir. Tactical scenarios predict that we should be able to neutralize ninety percent of them, but that still leaves around 160, several times what it would take to cripple the *Intrepid*."

Andrews turned to one of the bridge crew. "What can we expect our ES shields to deflect?"

"It'll depend on how staggered they are, sir. We could survive every one of them given enough time between the impacts, but the magnetic conductors are going to heat up moving all of that radiation down the vanes and away from the ship. If we blow them then we'll be delaying this trip."

"Fire control." Captain Andrews turned to another crewman. "At what maximum range can you engage the enemy without bleed-off from the lasers risking our fighters?"

"Based on the specs that Commander Evans has up on the command net, I'd say we're looking at seven thousand kilometers."

"Then they're going to have to work real hard to hit us." The captain nodded. "Keep your fighters under that range after their initial salvo. It should help us even things out. What is the ETA on yellow getting out there as well?"

"Twenty minutes, sir."

"I doubt this will last that long."

"Aye, sir."

"Deployment," the woman at scan called out. "Looks like specs were bang on. We've got forty-five inbound fighters."

"Blue Wing is engaging," Joe said.

The main holo lit up with the feed from the battle. The attackers were doing their best to simply punch through the *Intrepid*'s defenses. With their *v* they were unable to perform any drastic maneuvers; the velocity that had allowed them to get in range so quickly now became a hindrance.

"We've got some unexpected issues," Joe said. "Our fighters' targeting systems don't have the processing power to handle this much time dilation."

Realization dawned on Tanis. Though notable time dilation from traveling too close to the speed of light didn't occur under 0.6*c*, any time the fighters were flying directly toward or away from another their relative velocity was easily in that range. A quick change of direction and time expanded: trajectories, velocities, targeting, and shields all had to instantly adjust; sometimes they had to adjust several seconds ago.

The conditions the pilots were enduring were at the edge of a human's abilities. It took over an hour just to get into the special suit for handling the gee forces, and the fighters' cockpits were full of gel to absorb motion. Drug cocktails were continually being pumped through the pilots to keep them conscious as a latticework of support webbing inside their brains kept the grey matter from being smeared inside their skulls. Combat like this was going to take weeks for them to recover from.

Despite those factors, the Blue Wing took out three of the attackers within the first moments of combat. It was a testament to the pilots' training that they were managing to hit anything at all.

"Vectors are too extreme," Joe said as his fingers raced across a holo UI. "Onboard systems are overheating trying to provide accurate calculations. The pilots are also having neural cooling problems."

"Didn't really plan for a suicide run," Captain Andrews muttered. "Priscilla, do you have enough bandwidth available to offload calculations from the fighters?"

"I can for some of them," Priscilla's voice said over the bridge's speakers. "Signal isn't strong enough to assist all of them."

"I'm jacked in." Amanda stood near the entrance to the bridge with her hood off. Her cowl was pulled down and antennae hair waved above her as she accessed the bandwidth reserved for her and Priscilla.

"Do it," Andrews said. "Co-ord it with Commander Evans—we need our people to take those bastards out."

"I'm in range in fifteen seconds," the crewman at fire control announced.

"Fire at will; be sure your patterns are available to Commander Evans and the ladies," Captain Andrews said.

"This isn't working well," Amanda said as another fighter in Blue Wing was destroyed. "The AI link on the fighters is too primitive and it's slowing things down too much. With the time lag and the interface chokepoint we can't be effective. I need to perform a partial transference."

Andrews glanced back at her, his expression sharp. "That's a very dangerous proposal. We could lose you."

"You'll have Priscilla if I get in trouble."

"How long will it take?"

"Moments. I do need something, though. I need access to the mind of someone who has flown a fighter and understands the tactics."

"Use me," Joe said. "I'll guide you."

"No good," Captain Andrews said. "You won't be able to do your job with her subsuming your mind."

"Use me." Tanis spoke up. "I'm rated and have over ten thousand hours flight time."

"You sure about this?" Andrews turned to look at her. "It's not an exact science."

Joe shot a pained look in Tanis's direction, but didn't say a word.

"It's more exact than it used to be," Amanda said, a living example of the neural advances.

"Just do it." Tanis took a deep breath. "Before I change my mind and before one of those warheads hits us."

Nothing prepared her; no warning was given. One moment Tanis was sharing her mind with Angela, and the next a massive presence pushed inside of her. She felt herself swelling; even Angela seemed taken aback by the will and power of Amanda's mind.

<*Open up to me,*> Amanda said—not over the Link, but directly into Tanis's thoughts.

<*Here's the pathway.*> Angela directed the ship's avatar through Tanis's mind.

<*Take what you need,*> Tanis said.

There was a pause. <*I can't,*> Amanda said after several moments. <*The data, the formulae, are tied directly to your mind's connection with your body and your instinctual grasp of tactics. So much of it is hard-wired twitch reflexes. I can't extract the knowledge from your mind.*>

<*Damn…then we're fucked,*> Tanis thought.

<*No,*> a deeper voice said, resonating through Amanda's presence. <*Route the data through her.*>

<*It could destroy her,*> Amanda said.

<*Not doing it could destroy us all.*>

<*She can take it,*> Angela added. <*Her sense of self is too damn stubborn to be subsumed. We don't have much time.*>

Whereas moments before the crushing force of Amanda's presence had surrounded her, Tanis was now forced to the top, as though riding the cresting surf of thought; her mind racing up and out. She saw the *Intrepid,* and the fighters defending and attacking. All of the vectors and trajectories fit in her mind and were perfectly understood as a whole. Tanis examined the situation and knew what to do.

Her mind expanded over the tightbands to the Blue Wing. Angela and Amanda guided her through the fighter's neural nets and she felt a portion of herself shift to reside in them. From there she reached out and established a Link with each and every one of the pilots.

<*Follow directions,*> was the only grammatical thought she sent them. Everything after was feeling and intuition. Tanis choreographed a grand movement, an overall strategy that would apply the correct focus and pressure to bear against the enemy.

Angela and Amanda gave assistance once they knew her scheme. It was bold and daring and impossible to grasp without their integration with her mind.

The Blue Wing ships were forming a cube of death. What would normally create a crossfire, where the fighters would suffer considerable friendly fire, was instead a killing field where only the enemy died. Fighters deployed relativistic chaff, beams, and projectiles; creating a death zone that took out thirty-one of the enemy. All told, there were now only five attackers left.

<*That was amazing,*> Angela said. <*Good thing no one knows you're this good at this stuff; they would have turned you into a tactical meld long ago.*>

Tanis shuddered at the notion, but knew Angela meant it as a compliment.

<*Don't get cocky,*> Amanda said. <*There's still five of them left. More than enough to cripple us.*>

<*Not for long.*> Tanis directed Blue Wing to bracket the attackers, keeping a clean line open for the ship's beams. Fire control was given the safe vectors and the lasers lanced out, boiling off the attacker's hulls one by one. At the last moment the final ship detonated all of its warheads before being destroyed. Calculations showed that it was too close—the shockwave expanded, encompassing Blue Wing and the *Intrepid.*

On the colony ship, the shields and sheer mass of the vessel absorbed most of the energy, but the same could not be said for the fighters. Tanis was lucky in that the moment Amanda detected the EMF spike she yanked the major's mind back into her body. If she hadn't, the parts of Tanis spread across the tightbands would have been torn from her forever.

"Sweet Venus," Tanis moaned, falling to the floor. "I feel like my brain has been ripped in two."

"Priscilla," Captain Andrews said. "We need medics now."

"Already on their way," she replied audibly. "I sent for them as soon as we made the merge."

"Very good." Andrews nodded. "Commander Evans, did any of our fighters survive?"

"Four are in communication, ten are structurally impaired with no chance of survival, the rest are somewhere in between, but with no comm."

"Get recovery craft out there as soon as possible."

"Aye, sir."

The joy of survival was tempered by the near total loss of Blue Wing. Even amongst the four in communication, considerable damage had been sustained by both craft and pilot. No one was coming back in unscathed.

"Yellow is outbound. They'll do some nudging and correct trajectories for the tugs," Joseph said.

"Keep me apprised," Captain Andrews replied. He surveyed his bridge and looked over the damage reports that were scrolling on the main holo as well as the bridge net, finally determining that nothing needed his direct intervention. Only then did he allow himself to turn and look at the woman who had just risked being a mindless husk for the rest of her life. Who may still face that fate.

Tanis lay in a fetal position, shaking slightly with the odd spasm tearing through her body. Joe was holding her, a look of helplessness on his face. Andrews knelt at her side.

"Tanis, can you hear me?"

"Aye, sir…all seven thousand of you. Do you all have to yell?" Tanis whispered between ragged breaths, tears streaming from her eyes.

"Sorry," he replied softly. "You're going to be all right. The medics are on the way. I imagine you'll be taking a bit of a nap though."

"Sounds good, sir." Tanis closed her eyes tight, but a small smile played at the edges of her mouth. "Try to keep the ship in one piece while I'm out."

RECOVERY

STELLAR DATE: 3227366 / 02.17.4124 (Adjusted Gregorian)
LOCATION: GSS *Intrepid*, Within 0.5 AU of Sol
REGION: InnerSol, Sol Space Federation

Rescuing the remains of Blue Wing took several hours. The tugs had trouble maintaining their *v* relative to the *Intrepid* but eventually, with some tricky maneuvers, they managed to bring all of Blue Wing aboard.

As it turned out eleven pilots survived, and though that meant nineteen had died, it cheered everyone nonetheless. The *Intrepid* had ceased burn during the operation but now that all were once again aboard, the mighty drives resumed their fission reaction and the ship recommenced its acceleration toward the sun.

TSF monitoring had detected the conflict on their scans and Captain Andrews saw that a full report was filed. The tugs had also picked up the remains of several of their attackers, and once the *Intrepid* had completed its slingshot maneuver around the sun a TSF intercept patrol craft would meet them just past Venus's orbit to collect what physical evidence they could. That was still roughly fifteen days away, depending on whether the Reddings determined it would be beneficial to boost acceleration beyond 0.25*g*.

Andrews checked the current status of the engines and saw that they were creating the equivalent of just over ten trillion newtons of force to achieve their velocity. That was slightly better than expected, even with the twenty-five thousand kilometer wide ES ramscoop deployed. Calculation showed that their final velocity at Mercury's historical orbit past the apex of their slingshot would be closing in on 1,000 kilometers per second, or around 3.6 million kilometers per hour. Current projections were all in line to complete this stage of their journey and exit the solar system only forty hours after that point. The TSF interceptor would have to leave the *Intrepid* in time to decelerate around Saturn, or it would take them over a year to return to Callisto.

<*Inform the nearest TSF listening post of our new projected vector.*> Captain Andrews instructed Priscilla. <*I'm going to the infirmary to see how the patients are doing.*>

<*Aye, Captain.*>

He could have looked up their status on the Link, but he owed it to the survivors of Blue Wing as well as Major Richards to visit them in person. That and he had news for the major she would appreciate hearing.

Upon entering the infirmary, he noticed that he was one of many visitors. The staff had sound barriers in place to keep the noise down, but even so he could still hear a dull murmur. He made his way amongst the wounded, saying a word here, or giving a nod there. Each member of the squadron was being awarded a TSF Medal of Valor for their bravery. They had earned it.

Tanis Richards had her own little crowd. Commanders Evans and Ouri as well as that strange woman, Trist, were all at her side. The officers snapped off salutes when they saw him approach and Trist gave a friendly smile. He wasn't entirely certain about that one, but Tanis had vouched for her, so she had received special dispensation to be a part of the colony mission.

Tanis herself looked much better. Her face was no longer twisted in a rictus of pain and an easy smile rested on her lips.

"You appear to be in much better condition." The captain placed a hand on her shoulder. "I'm glad to see that the doctors are getting you patched up."

"Nothing I can't handle, sir, just a bit of swelling in pretty much every one of my lobes as well as some implant overheating."

"No permanent damage?" he asked.

Tanis chuckled. "None other than what was already there. Angela took more of a beating than I did and we're having some bleed between our thoughts, but the docs said it will straighten out."

Captain Andrews nodded and smiled. "While it is mostly a formality and of little bearing now, I wanted to be the first to inform you that the TSF has officially recognized your actions over the last few months. You've been awarded the Star Cross of Bravery and have also been promoted to lieutenant colonel."

Tanis schooled the surprise from her expression. "I guess they decided it was OK to promote me now since they don't have to increase my pay. It is nice to have it back, though." She mouthed the words "Lieutenant Colonel" and smiled.

"Credit won't do you a ton of good where we're going anyway," Trist said.

"Your new rank holds here," Captain Andrews said. "With it, you're the third highest ranking military officer on this vessel and when we arrive at our destination you'll be given duties and responsibilities according that position."

"Third highest?" Joe asked. "Who other than Sanderson is above her?"

"We've got some crusty colonel in the deep freeze," Ouri said. "A real treat, let me tell you."

"Rank or no rank, the Reddings, Terrance, and I know who we owe our safety and very lives to. Not to lay it on too thick, Lieutenant Colonel, but we are all in your debt...again."

"Thank you, sir." Tanis smiled. She really didn't know what else to say.

"You're welcome." The captain returned the smile. "You've done your job well, and we'll soon be traveling too fast for any type of attack. We're safe, and finally on our way. You can rest now knowing your work is done."

Tanis laid her head back and closed her eyes. It felt done. Analysis had shown that the fighter attack was a last attempt by Strang to take them out before they left the system. He was now being held without ability to electronically communicate and all STR operations were on lockdown, the entire company frozen.

Nothing could interrupt the *Intrepid's* flight now, it would be smooth sailing from here on out.

* * * * *

Eventually everyone left her side except for Joe.

"I'm due to enter stasis in a few hours," he said.

"I saw that on the schedule."

"I'm getting tired of almost losing you, you know." Joe sounded like he was choking.

"I know how you feel." Tanis grinned.

"Always with the jokes. I suppose I'll see you in a hundred and twenty-five years."

"Forty." Tanis smiled up at Joe.

"What?"

"I pulled rank and got you on a duty rotation with me in forty years." Her eyes twinkled, and she thought his might be misting up.

"Those last three years, don't they?"

"Just you me and…a pair of GSS ensigns. We'll order pizza and watch lots of movies."

Joe looked exasperated. "Why do you always do that, make light of things?"

Tanis scowled at him. "I can't be miss emotional freedom overnight you know."

"You're right I'm so—"

Tanis interrupted him, "Commander Evans, could you please stop overanalyzing everything and just kiss me?"

It was loving and passionate.

It was worth the wait.

EPILOGUE

STELLAR DATE: 3227378 / 02.29.4124 (Adjusted Gregorian)
LOCATION: Trans-Neptunian Space - SDM Belt G9
REGION: Scattered Worlds, Sol Space Federation

Tanis closed down the holo viewer where she had been enjoying one final look at the footage of several more STR officers being arraigned in a Sol Space Federation court. She finished securing her quarters, ensuring that nothing would be disturbed should the ship have to alter course or thrust during the journey.

A final scan satisfied her that everything seemed to be in place and she stepped out into the corridor. After closing the hatch she placed a personal seal on it to ensure her things wouldn't be disturbed. Not that anyone would be around to snoop or cause problems, but old habits died hard.

<*Or in your case, never really die at all,*> Angela needled.

The ship was effectively deserted. A few people were still about: Priscilla was at her post, and the captain and the Reddings would be staying out of stasis with a small crew for a few months more. After which a rotation of four duty officers took effect; each taking a few years out of stasis to monitor the ship and ensure all was well. Tanis was scheduled for two such rotations, the first in forty years when the ship neared LHS 1565.

She had enjoyed one final dinner at the captain's table and bade her farewells to those still awake. It was a sad thing, but Captain Andrews reminded them all that he had done it several times and survived intact. They would all meet again on the far side of their journey and share in the reward that their efforts had won them.

After a short walk she arrived at her designated stasis chamber. The officers who were going to be awoken periodically were not in the regular crew chambers below, but in smaller ones, closer to the officer's quarters and the bridge. Tanis saw the pod holding Joseph and ran her fingers across its surface, a light smile on her lips. When they awoke they would no longer be TSF and would be free to see where their relationship led them.

She shucked her clothes and placed them in a locker before slipping into a suit that would stabilize the stasis field around her. She said her farewells to Angela, who had already slowed her processes in preparation for shutdown. Her AI would completely power off before the stasis took to ensure that no key cycles were interrupted by the field.

With no more tasks to perform, or things that needed doing, Tanis stepped into the pod and reclined on the cushion. The lid closed over her and she knew no more.

Awareness came back rapidly, like a jolt of light driven into every corner of her mind. Tanis had been in stasis many times before, but had never been awoken in such an abrupt manner. Perhaps it was because of the time lapse in this case. Forty years was a significantly longer period than she had ever been under until now.

The pod lid was already opening and she eased out, marveling how she felt exactly as she had the moment she stepped in. She even felt the sense of fullness from the meal at the captain's table.

Her Link was initializing and Angela was beginning her boot-up processes, so it took Tanis a moment to notice the alerts scrolling across the holo panels in the chamber. Some sort of shipwide systems malfunction was being reported, something about the drives being offline.

"Well that's not a good sign." Tanis queried her Link. It was still authing on all the secure nets she needed, but the general shipnet was available and she checked its alerts.

What she found there shocked Tanis so badly that she stumbled backward and banged into the edge of her stasis pod. Though Angela was not yet fully initialized, Tanis sensed a feeling of alarm from her AI as well.

The shipnet reported no other crew out of stasis, and those that were supposed to be on duty were missing with no trace of their lifesigns on board. As the information flowed into her still-initializing systems, Tanis realized that this wasn't the worst of it. Shipnet also reported that the engines were offline, all the fuel was gone, and as if that wasn't bad enough, they were falling into a star.

Tanis sighed. "Oh give me a break..."

A PATH IN THE DARKNESS

The Intrepid Saga – Book 2

M. D. COOPER

DEDICATION

I dedicate this book to all of us.
May we find our path in the darkness.

ACKNOWLEDGEMENTS

Those who have read their fair share of science fiction will know that this book stands on the shoulders of giants. It is to those giants, whose ideas paved the way for books like this to be written, that I give my thanks and gratitude

MARS

STELLAR DATE: 3227279 / 11.22.4123 (Adjusted Gregorian)
LOCATION: Mars 1 Ring (M1R)
REGION: Mars Protectorate, Sol Space Federation

Forty years earlier, while the* Intrepid *was still under construction above Mars.

Tanis walked into the elevator's main cabin, peering through the throngs of people for a seat near a window. She spotted one on the side that would have an eastern view and slipped through the crowd, managing to secure it before anyone else.

The captain's message instructed her to come wearing civilian clothing. She managed to find one complete outfit that didn't look military; a pair of tight, dark-blue jeans, a white blouse, and a burgundy jacket.

She pulled at the jacket as she sat, ensuring that the sidearm strapped to her side was out of sight.

The captain hadn't said anything about weapons.

Conversation buzzed around her as a thousand people all found seats and stowed whatever they were carrying. The sounds of vendors preparing food came from the balcony above the cabin.

Tanis took in the thousand sights, sounds, and smells, her senses on alert for any sign of danger.

<*Do you think you were followed?*> Angela asked conspiratorially.

<*Who knows? You know I can't just turn it off.*>

Outside the elevator, on the surface of Mars 1, the final few passengers were walking over the manicured lawns leading up to the entrance. To her left, Tanis saw a pair of cargo haulers drive away over the low hills surrounding the elevator, their beds empty.

The clock on the local net showed departure time in nine minutes. Tanis settled back, anticipating the view. She believed that no planet was more beautiful to drop onto than Mars. Perhaps it was because she had grown up there.

A young girl sat to Tanis's left, peering out the window with excitement.

"I can't wait to get there!" she said as she bounced in her seat.

"Easy now, dear," her father said from beside her. "We'll be dropping soon enough."

"I just can't wait to see Mommy." The girl smiled.

"I know." The father patted his daughter's head. "It's only been a few days but it feels like so long."

Tanis smiled at the girl, wondering what her life would have been like if kids had come into the picture. She hadn't been much older when she first rode the elevator back down to Pavonis Mons.

She spent the rest of the time before the drop reviewing leads and lines of inquiry around the attacks on the *Intrepid*. She wasn't certain what the captain thought was more important, but he wasn't a man given to frivolities so it likely was worth her time.

An alert came over the local net and audible systems giving the fifteen second warning for the elevator's departure. Tanis cleared the work from her mind and prepared for the moment.

A gentle shudder rippled through the deck and the elevator began to rise above the surface of Mars 1.

Tanis always found it somewhat incongruous that, due to centripetal force, space elevators had to climb toward the planet. Over the course of the trip, gravity from it would decrease and the passengers would enter a period of 0*g*. At that point the cabin would rotate and the passengers would re-orient with their feet facing down to the planet.

Even after decades of traveling between space and planets, Tanis still found it took as long as an hour to shift her thinking about what was up and down.

Both rings and free-orbiting habitats always oriented so that their parent planet or moon was up. Almost all time in space was spent with a world hanging overhead. On the surface of a world, space was what was hanging above.

Tanis always had a period of feeling like she would fly off the surface of the planet into space.

With seventeen-thousand kilometers to travel, the trip would take over an hour. Tanis leaned back in her seat and gazed up through the angled windows as her home world grew larger above her.

The most distinctive feature of Mars was the Borealis Ocean, which covered the northern third of the planet. The southern two thirds consisted of a massive supercontinent broken up by small crater lakes and the larger Hellenic Sea.

Tanis recalled vacations she had taken with her family on the sea when she was younger. She found it odd that her father always insisted on leaving the shores of the Mariner Valley to go to another sea half way around the world.

After a few more minutes, the Mariner Valley became visible and Tanis strained to make out the Melas Chasma where she had grown up.

She remembered the long, idyllic days of her youth swimming in its deep blue waters and spending time fishing and boating on the valley lakes.

Once, when humans first settled Mars, the Mariner Valleys were ideal sites for habitation. The mile-deep cracks in the Marsian surface offered protection from the sand storms and provided a safe haven for nurturing a heavier atmosphere. Today those initial habitations were curiosities that tourists could view in submarine tours.

To her left, she could see Olympus Mons, the Sol system's largest mountain, a massive volcano which rose over twenty-two kilometers above the seas which lapped at its western shore.

Tanis had climbed the cliffs at Olympus's edge several times on training missions. At over nine kilometers high they were brutal, even in Mars's low gravity.

Once on the mountain it was almost impossible to tell it was a mountain at all. With a base nearly the size of the province of France on Earth it seemed more like a gently sloping hill.

Tanis enjoyed watching the clouds drift across the surface above her until the local net sounded the warning that full 0*g* was near and the cabin would flip.

Several minutes later the passengers found themselves staring up at the glistening latticework of Mars 1 and the MCEE with all their elevators, shafts, and anchors reaching out into space.

It was quite the change from staring at the idyllic garden world.

Less than ten minutes later, the elevator dropped within a shaft cut deep into Pavonis Mons. The shield volcano was amongst the smallest of the massive volcanos on Mars, but at over 8 kilometers above sea level it was still huge by any measure.

With its peak and most of its one-hundred thousand kilometers of slopes eternally sheathed in ice, the debarkation area for the elevator was deep underground with maglev train service out to the nearby city of Sheffield on the high, arid Tharsis steppe.

Tanis transferred to the train within minutes of the elevator settling within its cradle on the surface. The trip to Sheffield would take a couple minutes, and from there Tanis would transfer to a low orbit jump jet to the location the captain had provided on the island of Elysium.

It had been over a decade since she last set foot on Mars. She still remembered that fateful day when her family had sided with her ex-husband and all but ostracized her.

In retrospect, with a more measured eye cast toward her former spouse, she wasn't surprised he had cut ties with her. But she never expected her father to cut her off as well.

The urge to check in on him was strong, but she closed that train of thought off, that part of her life was over. Soon she would leave Sol and they would be a part of her past, nothing more.

<I'm sorry,> Angela said. *<I know we agreed not to talk about this, but you were thinking it so loud…I'm just…sorry.>*

Tanis sighed. *<It's OK, I should try not to think of it while I'm here. Seeing home, even if it was from thousands of miles away, brought back a lot of memories.>*

<There are good memories there, don't forget them.>

Tanis nodded and turned her mind to work, sifting through reports to take her mind off thoughts of family.

Thirty minutes later the jump jet touched down in the city of Albor. Tanis hailed a groundcar and gave it the name of the restaurant the captain had provided.

When she arrived, Tanis saw that it was a small, street-side café with flowers overflowing its planters and the smells of good cooking coming from inside.

She entered and spotted the captain sitting at a table beside a window. He was wearing a plaid shirt and the image made her think of an old woodsman.

"Good morning, Jason," she said as she slipped into the booth.

The captain smiled and ran a hand through his hair. "A good morning indeed, Tanis. I'm glad you could make it on such short notice."

"Coffee, dear?" a slim woman wearing an apron with the café's logo on it asked Tanis.

"Yes, cream and sugar, please."

The woman poured a glass, and as Tanis reached out to take it, the captain put his hand on hers.

"Was the trip pleasant?" he asked.

Tanis had a moment to wonder if this was some elaborate ruse to get her alone and make a pass at her before she detected the nano he had slipped into her hand.

It contained a coded message and Tanis decrypted it as she replied, "It was nice enough, I took the scenic route down the Pavonis elevator, it was nice to see the valleys one last time."

The captain nodded as he sipped his coffee. "I remembered that you grew up there. I've sailed on them a few times, amazing views."

Tanis read the message as the captain spoke about his adventures on Mars's high seas.

<*Enfield has a highly sensitive, secret package he needs brought aboard the Intrepid. It contains materials which will be needed for manufacturing on New Eden. We are to meet with a contact in a park near here. He will take us to the package.*>

Tanis and the captain discussed pleasantries until the time drew near for them to meet their contact.

As they talked, she wondered what the special cargo could be. There were dozens of things of incredible value already on the *Intrepid* and they had been successfully delivered by conventional means. She wondered if Terrance thought so little of her security on the ship—then again, he had sent her to pick it up.

The captain passed his token over the local net to the café and they walked out into the street toward the park. The walk was pleasant and only took a few minutes. They kept up light banter about the weather and the things they saw around them—careful to not speak of anything more significant.

In the park they walked to a low wall overlooking a pond and leaned against it, admiring the view.

"Good morning," a man said with a smile as he walked past.

Tanis nodded in return and suddenly knew why she had been called in, the captain could never have picked up the message she had just been delivered.

<*It's coordinates and data for coded entry.*> Angela's assessment matched Tanis's.

<*Not often you get a message delivered by breath,*> Tanis replied.

She reached out and touched the captain's arm, sending him a coded message via the direct contact.

<*We're to proceed to an office tower a few blocks from here. There's a maintenance door we're to use around the back. From there, I have to pass tokens to get us into some sort of facility,*> Tanis said over the coded connection.

The captain merely nodded and said something about a swan in the pond.

The walk to the office tower was short, and Tanis easily located the door they were to use. She placed her hand over the panel and passed the codes to unlock it.

They walked down a short flight of stairs and she unlocked another coded door.

Tanis had expected some sort of hidden laboratory or research facility teeming with scientists working on the next greatest breakthrough.

Instead, they found themselves in a small room facing a nondescript man sitting at a drab desk.

"Ah, you're on time, good," the man said. "If you'd please sit and give me your arm."

Tanis looked to the captain, who shrugged, and back at the man. "Why would I do that?" she asked.

The man frowned. "So that I can give you the package, it has to be injected into you. It's not something you can carry around."

Tanis weighed her options and decided to sit and offer her arm. If this was an attempt to kill her, it was the oddest yet. She looked up the man whose breath had held the message in the park as well as this man and found connections to various Enfield holdings.

As far as she could tell, this was a legitimate hand-off.

"It's OK." The captain placed a hand on Tanis's shoulder. "It's required for the nature of the package."

Tanis looked into the captain's eyes. She saw only calm sincerity. He had never given her any reason to distrust him.

"Very well." She sat.

The man reached under the desk and placed a case on it. He opened it and withdrew a small needle.

"I won't hurt much."

Tanis wasn't worried about whatever pain the needle might cause, she was concerned about what it might deliver.

The man slid the needle into her vein and pressed the plunger. Tanis and Angela immediately began to analyze the contents.

<*It's some sort of nano cluster moving a container,*> Angela said.

<*I see that, too, but I don't see how to look inside.*>

<*It's making a beeline for your liver.*>

"Earnest said you'd try to open the package," the man said. "He asked that you refrain. It would be damaging to your health if you did so."

"Is that it?" the captain asked.

The man nodded and Tanis rose, again searching the captain's eyes for a clue.

Andrews shook his head no and gestured for them to leave. Tanis rolled her sleeve back down, even more determined to find out what strange nanoscopic cargo she was carrying.

Back on the street, she and the captain began to make their way to a maglev stop three blocks away. From there they would catch a jump-jet back to Mount Apollinaris and the elevator there.

Tanis noticed a man with long, dark hair cast an appraising eye at her as she walked past. She wasn't unfamiliar with receiving looks, but something about him struck her as strange.

She moved her nano cloud out, looking for any suspicious behavior. On crowded planet-side streets, that was nearly an impossible task.

Stations and ships had rules about what could be done where and when. It kept things safe, predictable, and orderly. Planets were the embodiment of chaos. People lounged in entryways, groundcars sped past, and both humans and robots flitted through the air above.

A block from the maglev station something caught her eye. A man was leaning against a restaurant's doorframe appearing to be bored and disinterested with his surroundings, but his eyes flitted to her three times in ten seconds.

She watched him through her nano cloud and saw him glance at a woman across the street who also cast Tanis a furtive look.

<*We have company,*> Tanis said to the captain while passing him the faces and locations of her suspects.

The captain didn't respond, but increased his pace. Tanis slid a hand into her pants pocket, through a cut in the fabric, and drew her lightwand out of her leg.

<*By the way, don't die,*> the captain said.

<*I don't really intend to.*>

<*Good, because the package you're carrying will self-destruct if you do.*>

<*You are going to tell me what this is when we get back to the* Intrepid.> Tanis was not pleased with being kept in the dark.

<*I promise.*>

The man and the woman Tanis had identified before were moving toward them from the front, while another two women were approaching from behind. The street was too crowded with not enough cover.

Tanis stepped into a shop that sold souvenirs and the captain followed. They pushed past people arguing over buying rocks from the bottom of the Borealis Ocean or meteor fragments from the Hellas Sea.

A man stood behind the counter wrapping trinkets and processing transactions. Tanis spotted a stockroom behind him and worked her way around the counter.

The man was too startled to speak as she pushed past him, finally gaining his voice and calling out as they slipped through the stockroom.

"Hey, what're you doing?"

Tanis ignored him and moments later they were pushing through a back door into a wide alley.

"Get to the train?" Andrews asked.

Tanis shook her head. "No. They'll be waiting for us. We'll double back and find a groundcar."

They broke into a run, moving away from the train station. Tanis had to resist breaking into a full sprint—there was no way the captain could match her augmented speed.

"Stop!" A call rang out behind them. It was a male, likely the man she first saw in front of the restaurant.

A shot rang out and Tanis felt a ballistic projectile whistle through the air near her right shoulder.

"I guess they don't know that they shouldn't kill me," she said.

"Could have been a warning," Andrews replied as they rounded the corner moments before two more projectiles whistled past.

Tanis cast a frantic eye up and down the street, looking for a way out of this mess. "There." She pointed two blocks over where taxis waited in front of a hotel.

The pair had to backtrack across the street they started on and Tanis knew it was likely that one of their assailants was doubling back. With no other option, she and the captain took off at a run.

Sure enough, as they approached the intersection a woman stepped out in front of them.

The woman raised her gun and time seemed to slow for Tanis. She shoved the captain aside as the woman let out a cry and fired her weapon.

In a split second, Tanis calculated the angle of the barrel and trajectory of the bullet. It would hit her. She jerked her prosthetic arm up and braced for impact while throwing her lightwand.

The lightwand entered the woman's face through her cheekbone, dropping her with a scream. Tanis raced toward the assailant, barely aware that four bullets had struck her.

The woman was writhing in pain as Tanis approached and tore the lightwand up and out through the top of her head, ending her pain.

The captain was beside her in a moment, scooping up the woman's weapon.

"Are you hit?" he asked.

Tanis grimaced and nodded as she picked up speed, pulling him across the street.

<*She took three in her prosthetic arm—only superficial damage. One is lodged between two ribs, I'm working on pushing it out,*> Angela supplied.

More shots rang out as they dashed across the intersection. One caught Tanis in the right shoulder and another grazed the captain's leg.

"Don't stop!" Tanis ordered while catching the lightwand as it fell from her numbed right hand. This was the last time she listened when someone told her to go anywhere unarmed.

People scattered as they ran down the sidewalk, shoving anyone too slow to move out of the way.

"Get down," Tanis called out to the people on the street, afraid that a bullet meant for her would end an innocent's life.

<*Don't forget about your life,*> Angela said.

<*Believe me, it's very much at the forefront of my mind.*>

Most of the pedestrians dropped to the ground, but enough took off running that Tanis and Andrews managed to disappear into the milling crowd long enough for them to make it to the taxi stand.

Angela had repaired enough of the nerve damage in Tanis's right shoulder that her hand functioned again. She swapped the lightwand again and grabbed the door of the first cab with her prosthetic arm, ripping it open and tossing out the driver.

The captain crashed into the seat beside her and Tanis hammered the accelerator while cranking the wheel. The groundcar spun around and took off away from the attackers. Several stray shots hit the back of the car causing Tanis and Andrews to duck instinctively.

"That was bracing," the captain said.

Tanis looked over to see that he was pale and shaking slightly.

"Are you hit anywhere other than the leg?" she asked.

Andrews looked himself over. "I don't think so, my internal checks all pass…I do seem to be having a blood pressure issue from the sheer terror," he said with a weak smile.

"I guess I'm more used to it than I should be," Tanis replied as she cranked the wheel, sliding around a corner, missing oncoming traffic by less than a meter.

The captain was gripping his chair and the dashboard. "I'm not augmented like you, you know. A bullet to the head—or a car for that matter—will kill me."

"Noted," Tanis replied. "I'm more worried about bullets, they're trying to hit us—the cars are trying not to."

The car's holo overlay showed two other taxis in close pursuit. Their attackers must have also commandeered transportation.

"Where is local law enforcement?" the captain asked, looking out his window into the air.

"It's inaccessible," Tanis replied. "I've been trying it for some time, but it keeps responding as busy. I'm guessing whoever is after us has some sort of a hack in place."

"What are our options?" the captain asked.

Tanis threw a cloud of nano into the air, sending it behind their car.

"Don't worry, we'll have these clowns off our tails in no time."

Angela directed the nano to the engines of the cars behind them. The electronics yielded to the military grade nano and the cars' engine stopped and the brakes engaged.

The nano sent back a final image of their attackers before the internal safety mechanisms engaged, saving the passengers from certain death as the cars went from one hundred kilometers per hour to zero in a matter of seconds.

Tanis saw the enraged face of the man she had passed on the street when they left the Enfield office tower. What was she carrying that he would go to these lengths to get it?

She slowed from her breakneck speed and programmed the car to take them to a nearby parking garage where they would switch vehicles before driving to the airport.

"Your nano is really quite effective," Andrews commented.

Tanis nodded. "Only the best for the TSF. But somehow I think that my nano is not worth a lick beside whatever is currently holed up in my liver."

Andrews placed his hand on hers, sending a direct message.

<I imagine you've heard of picotech…>

CALAMITY

STELLAR DATE: 3241790 / 08.15.4163 (Adjusted Gregorian)
LOCATION: GSS *Intrepid*, AI Primary Node
REGION: LHS 1565, 0.5 AU from stellar primary

Forty years later…

The *Intrepid* lost control of its drive system.

The ship's AI detected a fault in the neural nodes that managed the fusion engines. It switched to the backup systems, but those nodes crashed and went offline. Milliseconds later, power failures cascaded across the ship taking out key systems. In less time than a human took to blink, the AI felt more than a fifty-percent reduction in its ability to think.

The AI, named Bob by its human avatars, ran through priorities. First on the list: take the fusion reactors and the antimatter annihilator offline while he still could. If they were cut off from his control, there would be no way to detect, let alone stop, a runaway reaction.

He initiated a controlled shutdown only moments before losing all access to the stern of the ship. The few sensors responding via wireless interface showed that the commands succeeded.

Bob gave the AI equivalent of a sigh of relief.

With the ship's reactors no longer producing power, the ship's systems began switching over to superconductor batteries. Several neural nodes powered back up for several seconds until an explosion amidships sent shockwaves through the decks as one of the SC battery banks took on heavy load and overheated. Bob ran through the power distribution. It was well below even nominal draw; there was no reason the bank should have failed, let alone exploded.

More banks started failing—though less catastrophically than the first—until there were more batteries were offline than functioning. As a result, large sections of the ship were powered down and what neural nodes were left began switching over to internal backup energy.

Another explosion rocked the ship and reports streamed in from the bow. Visual inspection showed a large hole in the ES ramscoop emitter. Bob looked over the logs and could find no indicators pointing to any failures, anywhere. Everything *should* be working correctly.

With the ramscoop offline, the few small fusion generators still running were now on stored fuel. Bob checked the reserves and found that while deuterium and helium-3 were at acceptable levels, lithium was critically low. Yesterday's logs showed a million tons of lithium.

What was going on?

Bob dedicated what processing power was left in the remaining bow neural nodes to pouring through the ship's logs. He discovered subtle errors and inconsistencies. After a few minutes, the realization dawned on him that his sensors were reporting false data. A minute later, he determined that even the positioning sensors had been reporting the starship's vector incorrectly.

They were not passing by the star named LHS 1565, they were falling into it.

The knowledge lent a sinister look to the star's dim red light. At a fraction of Sol's luminosity, and a mass of only 115*Mj*, it was on the smaller end of the stellar scale, not far beyond the threshold of being a brown dwarf—a fact that wouldn't stop it from vaporizing the *Intrepid* in its corona.

He took a fraction of a second to consider the notion of seeing starlight as sinister. Such an action was not something he had been capable of before his first mental merge with his human avatars, Amanda and Priscilla. Having his mind melded with theirs provided new insights and perspectives, the most prominent of which was currently suspicion.

It was also strange that in the two minutes since Bob had sounded the general alert, no humans had responded. Gollee was on duty at present, and he was never more than a thought away, but now the AI couldn't find him. The few internal scanners still functioning showed no sign of the duty crew.

Before the ship had left Sol forty years ago, there had been a few random failures that were chalked up to sabotage. The STR Corporation had gone to great lengths to stop the *Intrepid* from getting to the New Eden colony and many known sabotages did occur. Either some had gone undetected, or a second group had been involved.

Either way, whoever was shutting down the *Intrepid* was onboard now; but with the ship falling into a star, they wouldn't be for long.

Bob checked the status on the servitors he had dispatched to survey the damage across the ship and found he had lost their signal. He was losing all signal across the ship.

The wireless transmitters were going offline and his distributed network was dangerously fragmented. Bob shut down all but his primary node to prevent a schism and gained a small insight into what the fear of death was like.

Preservation protocols began writing data and algorithms to crystal storage in an attempt to store his latest state.

Those imperatives satisfied, he reviewed the remaining options. Humans were needed to solve this riddle. His remaining transmitters received a response from only the closest stasis chamber. He looked over the list of humans within the pods and realized all may not be lost. Tanis Richards was in that chamber. If anyone could get to the bottom of what was going on, it would be her.

Correction. It *had* to be her.

Bob initiated the protocols to retrieve the human and was about to provide her with a message on the general shipnet when all access beyond his node was cut off. He attempted to resend, but nothing worked. All physical connections were severed.

Bob spent several long minutes trying backup systems and alternative data paths. His desperation increased and, for the first time in his life, Bob wished for a body.

It would fall to Tanis.

ALONE IN THE DARK

STELLAR DATE: 3241790 / 08.15.4163 (Adjusted Gregorian)
LOCATION: GSS *Intrepid*, Officer Stasis Chamber B7
REGION: LHS 1565, 0.5 AU from stellar primary

Tanis stared at the holo alerts around her. The words didn't make sense. She checked the general shipnet and found the same information. This couldn't be right. She had been awakened too soon…or was it too late? Everything seemed to be offline or failing.

<*What the…*> Angela started. <*There's no wireless nets available other than the general shipnet, and I've only got local access to it.*>

<*I know…auths are timing out on every other net,*> Tanis said, feeling as though she was blind, unable to see data on the nets, limited to just her own eyesight and hearing.

<*This can't be right.*> Angela examined the ship's vector. <*We're falling into LHS 1565.*>

"I noticed that," Tanis said aloud, though her AI could hear her internal thoughts. Angela was a distinct entity, but also occupied a portion of Tanis's brain. Even if she didn't have access to auditory pickups, she could read many of her host's outermost thoughts.

<*Are we alone on the ship? Where's Bob*?> Angela asked.

Tanis didn't know. The ship AI's presence had always been close, like a looming mountain on the shipnets. One of the most advanced sentient artificial intelligences ever created, she couldn't imagine what would shut down or block it.

"First things first," Tanis said. "We need more intel. There's no data on the duty officers, but that doesn't mean they aren't around somewhere. Let's get to the bridge."

<*What about everyone here?*> Angela asked.

Tanis looked at the rows of stasis pods, her gaze lingering on Joseph Evans' in particular.

"They should be safe. Pods have their own backup power supplies. Besides, I'm going to recode the door and seal it."

Angela signaled her approval and within minutes they were moving through the ship to the bridge.

The corridors were empty, and only the occasional dim emergency light provided illumination. Tanis added IR and UV overlays to her vision, as well as a structural overlay to ensure she stayed on the right path. Angela released a cloud of nano to scout ahead and keep an eye out behind them as well.

<*There's nothing here,*> Angela said. <*Life support is offline engines are offline, energy interchanges are all dead. Everything is running on local power. When that dries up, it's going to get dark and cold in here really fast.*>

<*How long ago do you think this happened?*> Tanis asked.

<*Judging by the rate of cooling and the current temperature, not long ago. Maybe an hour. We've probably got a few days before things will start to get serious,*> the AI responded. Even though the cold didn't bother her, she was dependent upon Tanis for energy and connectivity. If Tanis died, she died.

Tanis gave a stoic smile. "Then we better get things fixed up. Plus, if we don't smash into a star we'll still freeze to death."

<*I don't think that's quite how it would work. You usually burn up before any smashing would occur,*> Angela said.

The empty corridors stretched on with no sign of life or recent use. She estimated the distance to the bridge to be just over a kilometer; provided there were no sealed hatches on the way, she would be there in a matter of minutes.

Tanis found herself wondering why she was awakened. No other stasis pods showed any signs of reviving their occupants and there was no data left for her on the net. It had to be Bob who brought her out of stasis, but why not leave her with some information?

They passed through the forward commissary, cutting behind the food stands and through Chef Earl's main kitchen, then into the executive dining room. It was a shortcut that would take them to a hall one level down from the bridge deck and only a few hundred meters aft.

The dining room was dark, chairs were stacked along the wall, and the tables showed a thin layer of dust. It drove home that forty years had passed. Though, by Tanis's reckoning, she had left this room only hours before.

It was odd that it lacked more recent signs of use; it was one of the closest dining rooms to the bridge. Surely the duty officers would have been eating here, unless they felt uncomfortable and were using the officers' mess only one level further down.

Tanis looked up who the duty officers should be and was surprised to learn she knew each of them personally. The first was GSS Lieutenant Collins, a man Tanis had not gotten along with particularly well before the *Intrepid* had left Mars. She had only spotted him once or twice afterward and was surprised that a supply officer had been added to the in-flight duty roster.

The next was Lieutenant Amy Lee. She had been stationed under Tanis in the Security Operations Center in the harrowing days before the *Intrepid* left Sol. Tanis knew Amy Lee reasonably well, but not as much more than an acquaintance beyond their working relationship.

The last of the three duty officers was Ensign Gollee. Tanis knew him from a few games of 4D chess they had played in the officer's mess, but had not worked with him professionally. She felt bad for Amy Lee and Gollee being stuck with Collins. If she had to spend three years with that man, Tanis knew someone would be dead—him.

<*I hope Amy Lee and Usul are well. They were a very pleasant pairing,*> Angela said.

Usul was Amy Lee's AI. He wasn't a military pairing, like Angela, but had been with her family for several generations. When she made colony, he jumped at the opportunity to leave Sol and transferred to her.

Gollee, like most pilots, didn't have AI. Most of their extra processing space was needed for additional systems to handle plots and vectors. Collins was simply too low on the totem pole to be granted any military AI and he wasn't the sort who would normally attract an unchartered AI for a pairing.

<*Gah… I've glimpsed his mind,*> Angela said. <*You can get a feel for what a person would be like by looking at their data streams. Being in him would be like living in a prison.*>

Tanis reached the top of a service tube and stepped onto the bridge deck's maglev station. In all her previous visits to the command deck, Tanis was one of hundreds crowding the station and executive corridor. Now, the emptiness was palpable;

emergency lighting cast long shadows across the space as the echoes of her footfalls skittered up and down the hall.

Beyond lay the bridge's foyer; the place where Priscilla and Amanda—the ship's two physical avatars—took turns providing the main interface between the humans and the *Intrepid.* The avatars' pedestal was empty and the holo emitters were offline. Even more than the main hall, this room had always been a riot of light and color—usually white, grey, and light blue if Amanda was ensconced, or red, pink, and violet if Priscilla was running the show. As Tanis slipped through the darkness, a shiver ran down her spine and she couldn't help but feel like she was the only person on the ship.

There wasn't a single person who hadn't looked out into the cold, dark blackness of space and feared falling into it, lost and alone in the emptiness for eternity. Out here, far from even the most rudimentary civilizations, Tanis couldn't help feeling those thoughts creep into her mind again and again.

She took a deep breath, pushed the tendrils of fear aside and strode down the corridor to the left, past the executive conference room toward the bridge.

Her nano arrived first and sent an image back showing it to be empty, a fact she confirmed moments later as she stepped into the heart of the ship.

She drew another deep breath through her nose. There were traces of human pheromones. Her augmented olfactory system informed her that people had been here a scant five or six hours earlier.

Tanis felt the solitude pressing around her ease back as she settled into a duty station. The holo interface sprang to life around her and she brought up the previous month's logs.

They were blank for the last month.

"Well that complicates things," Tanis muttered. <*You got anything?*>

<*Negative,*> Angela responded. <*There's nothing here and no helm control either. Engine systems seem to be physically disconnected and on top of that we're nearly out of fuel. The ramscoop is offline, as well, and it appears the emitter is damaged.*>

"Are the habitation cylinders still spinning?" Tanis asked.

<*Not certain. I can't get any data on them. They do have their own self-contained power systems, so we can only hope they are. That's going to be one serious mess if those dropped to 0g.*>

"Speaking of 0g," Tanis said. "We've still got grav here in the crew areas."

<*I would expect so. The GE MBHs are fully self-contained. They generate their own power and are pretty hard to tamper with.*>

"So you're thinking sabotage as well." Tanis said.

<*No way could it be anything else. To knock out that many systems at once before Bob could get servitors or the crew after you would have to require subversion.*>

"It's gotta be Collins," Tanis said. "I can't imagine either Gollee or Amy Lee being involved."

<*It could be anyone. We don't know if they were the only ones out of stasis when this all happened.*>

"So we've got two things we need to do. We need to get to Bob and get him back in control of the engines or we'll be having a really bad day."

<*I project that we have either our initial pass or our first orbit to break away from the star. Any further and we won't have enough* v *to escape its gravity.*>

"What's the time on that?" Tanis asked.

<About three days.>

"We better get moving then."

Tanis left the bridge and worked her way back to Bob's primary node. Hopefully, it was intact and he had run the preservation procedures. With luck he would be fully activated and they could begin repairing whatever damage had severed him from the ship.

On their way, she stopped at the officer's mess to see if it showed signs of use and to check for any clues. This room wasn't quite as Tanis remembered it. In the intervening forty years, someone had decorated it.

The previously white walls were done in several vibrant, yet tasteful colors, and several new couches were also arranged throughout the room.

The serving area in the rear was stocked with fresh food and Tanis helped herself to a glass of water and a cold sandwich—though not yet hungry, she suspected it would be a while before she got to eat again.

Peeking into the walk-in refrigerator, she stopped and deployed a series of nano probes. Around one of the racks, she saw a pair of feet. The probes took stock and fed the view to her HUD. It was Gollee; judging by the pallor of his skin, he had been dead for some time.

<More than twelve hours,> Angela said. *<With the moisture in here I don't think he'll be recoverable. Too much decay.>*

Tanis disagreed. There was always a chance they could bring him back. It was not too far above freezing down where he lay; it was possible to bring people back even after a day if the conditions were right. She crouched down beside the ensign and saw what the probes missed. There was a large hole in the back of his head. No, they wouldn't be bringing Gollee back.

<Looks like it was done post mortem,> Angela said. *<Someone didn't want whatever info he had to be extracted.>*

"So it would seem. I'll move him to the freezer and then we can continue."

Tanis hauled the ensign's inert form to the freezer and set him down gently. He'd been a good chess player. She was sorry they hadn't had the opportunity to know one another better.

Closing the freezer door, Tanis took a deep breath and determined she would pay back whoever had done this in like kind.

<We need to keep moving. There isn't a lot of time.>

<I know.>

Less than ten minutes later they were at the entrance to the ship AI's primary node. The entrance was a narrow corridor that was normally alive with scanners and holo readouts. Beyond that was a large, cube-shaped space where the node resided. Tanis attempted to deploy probes, but found she lost contact with them the moment they entered the corridor.

<Dampening field,> Angela reported. *<Probably what's keeping Bob from controlling his nano or servitors outside the node.>*

"I'd wondered about that," Tanis said. "Well, here goes nothing."

She stepped into the corridor and immediately regained communications with her nano. They had stayed on course and were surveying the AI node. Tanis emerged from the tunnel and into the space the node occupied. It was similar to the communications nodes she had visited on Callisto not long ago, relatively speaking, albeit somewhat smaller.

The room was twenty meters per side. A catwalk ran around its perimeter, partially obstructed here and there by power conduit and ES waveguides, which were used for data transmission. The designers of the space certainly favored function over form.

The node appeared to be offline at first, but the nanocloud reported activity; however, the power levels suggested it was running on backup energy.

"You're here." The words were audible. Though she had never heard it aloud, it was the same timbre Bob's voice always had in her mind.

"You're alive!" Tanis exclaimed. "Angela and I were quite worried."

"If you can call this alive, then I suppose I am," the AI replied. "I'm crippled and trapped within this node. I have no external net access and a dampening field is blocking my control of nano beyond the node."

"We noticed that." Tanis nodded. "I think we can find the emitters and remove the field, but we need to know what happened. Where is everyone, how did all of this happen?"

There was a pause...just a second or two, but an eternity for an AI.

"I'm not entirely certain. Since the event, I've been running through my logs and have found that there have been some gaps for some time. Almost as though parts of my sensory input have been altered to not pick up certain events, or certain people's movements."

"So you were blinded," Tanis said.

"In some respects, yes. I don't know if the sabotage was set up recently, or if some of it has been in place since we left Sol. What I do know is that the timing was perfect. At first I thought it was a viral attack, but it quickly became apparent that it was physical. Only someone with intimate knowledge of my systems could have done this. Earnest and Abby built in redundancies, and yet they were all circumvented."

<Have the attackers tried to breach this node?> Angela asked.

"There was an attack made by servitors, but I managed to repel them with nano once they entered the node. I also have some limited feeds throughout the ship—comm paths that, while damaged, still have some bandwidth. I believe whoever has done this is trying to flee the ship via one of the interstellar pinnaces. If they depart after our first orbit of the local star, they'll have enough velocity to reach Sol in roughly one hundred years. I believe that is their plan."

"We need more people," Tanis said. "I can't go to the shuttle bays…which one is it?"

"Starboard A3."

"…and deal with whoever is there and leave you unguarded. They could mount a physical attack here."

"I'll be safe," the AI said. Laser cannons lowered from the ceiling, and several armed servitors appeared on the catwalk, likely the ones that had tried to attack the node—now under Bob's control. "I'm conserving power in case I need to use these systems."

<Just be careful,> Angela said with concern in her tone. *<You don't want to do any damage to your primary node.>*

An audible chuckle filled the room. "I'll be certain not to shoot myself in the foot. Go, find whoever this is, and stop them. We need to know if they have anything else planted on the ship before we begin to repair—and there isn't much time for that, either."

<She's right, though. We are going to need more people awake to handle this,> Angela said. *<Can you access any of the stasis rooms to wake anyone?>*

"Unfortunately no, I barely managed to wake you. I'm also uncertain who I would wake if I could. I don't know who to trust. Amanda or Priscilla would normally make that choice."

Tanis nodded. "Well, for starters we could wake one of those two, but I think the best bet is to wake Joe."

There were others in the stasis chamber who could aid in defending Bob's node, but she had her own reasons for wanting Joe.

"You go to the shuttle bay. I'll send a preprogrammed servitor with a message for him." The servitor would lose contact with Bob once it was beyond the node, but the task was a simple one, which it could perform autonomously.

Tanis passed the new access codes to the stasis chamber. She left the node and began the trek to the starboard A3 shuttle bays.

The *Intrepid* was a colony ship, with all the supplies and equipment to establish humankind on a distant world. As such, the ship was equipped with a fleet of smaller vessels intended to gather resources within the destination star system and establish an economy. Amongst the complement were several pinnaces capable a trip back to Sol.

Tanis's quarters were nearby, and she decided to stop there and gather weapons and armor—it would only involve a small detour on her way to the shuttle bay. There was no telling how many people she would be up against and the stasis suit she was still wearing afforded no protection.

The personal seal over the door to her quarters showed no signs of tampering and Tanis removed it before forcing the panel aside. Even with the best filtration systems, a fine layer of dust covered everything in the room, a tangible sign of the four decades she had been in stasis. To her it had been only an hour or two since making the bed and straightening her things; for some reason, seeing the passage of time here again brought the feeling of solitude to the fore.

Focusing on the task at hand, Tanis pulled off the stasis suit and slid into the base layer of her flow-armor. It fit like a second skin—a second skin that could stop kinetic rounds. She retrieved a fresh canister of reactive material and held it to her chest, waiting for the base layer to finish initializing. A ready symbol flashed on her HUD and Tanis pressed the cylinder into a now glowing circle on her chest.

The clear liquid flowed out across her body, even covering her face in an all but invisible layer. The armor could absorb weapons fire from particle beams to ballistic firearms. Once the armor completed its startup routine, she pulled out her shimmersuit. This top layer would render her invisible, even her scent and the sound of her movements would be masked.

Once the shimmersuit was in place, Tanis wore over five millimeters of armor and camouflage. She opened her personal weapons locker and retrieved the two slim blades hanging on the inside of the door. Each slid into sheaths on her forearms that would hide them from view. Next was a pulse rifle and pistol that she snapped together and slung over a shoulder. After a final check of the armor and comm control systems, Tanis stepped into the hall, her body fading from view.

Anyone seeing her move through the silent and dark ship would have only witnessed a pistol and rifle floating through the air. However, even that wouldn't occur as Angela had the nanocloud roving far and wide. They would get plenty of advanced notice if anyone were nearby.

The A3 dock was on the lower half of the command and crew areas of the *Intrepid*. From her current position, it was a kilometer aft, two kilometers starboard, and half a kilometer down. With the maglev trains and tubelifts offline, it was going to be a long haul.

Releasing a stimulating combination of chemicals into her bloodstream, Tanis launched into a smooth lope, topping out at just over sixty kilometers per hour.

<*You're going to wind yourself,*> Angela warned.

<*I feel pretty good. I think I can keep this up for a kilometer or two.*>

<*I predict a seventy percent chance you'll cramp. You didn't purge your digestive tract before putting your armor on.*>

<*Would have taken too long. Which is why I'm running like this. We've gotta catch whoever broke the ship.*>

Tanis halted at an intersection she didn't recognize. Neither she nor Angela had the ship's entire layout stored in local memory. There was no reason to because no one expected the ship to ever be entirely offline. Aside from being uncertain about the route, there was another problem: the ship was designed to be traversed via maglev train. It was entirely possible that there would be no way to get to the dock from here.

<*I can't imagine that is the case.* ***They*** *got there.*> Angela added her two chits to Tanis's thoughts.

<*Good point.*>

Tanis considered the options and took a right. Several turns later she arrived at a large environmental transfer station. Conduits ran into massive induction pumps and then to their ultimate destinations.

<*What do you think? Down?*>

<*It'll save you a few decks. I'd do it.*>

Tanis walked to a railing that surrounded a series of large pipes running down through the decks. Switching her vision to IR, she could see that they were still cooling and cast enough light to make out a catwalk twenty meters below.

She took a moment to gauge the distance and leapt over the railing into empty space. The catwalk rattled when she struck it and the lower half of her armor locked up, absorbing the impact.

"Handy stuff," Tanis commented.

Below was another catwalk, and she repeated the process until she was on the same level as the A3 docks. The catwalk at that level led through an environmental administration area and then into a general ship corridor. Angela supplied a possible map of their location, though it was extrapolated and could be inaccurate.

<*Can't believe we didn't think to get one from Bob.*>

<*Heat of the moment and all that.*>

Tanis worked her way through the corridors using her sense of direction—and a cloud of nano scouting ahead—to ferret out the path to the docks. It was slow going and the isolation was starting to make her see things.

Her thoughts returned to the endless blackness outside the ship, and the knowledge that there were no habitats or worlds for light years, no repair yard to call, or tug to pull them away from the red dwarf star she knew was outside the ship, ready to swallow it.

The closest humans beyond the *Intrepid* were seven light years away in the Epsilon Eridani system. They might as well have been on the other side of the galaxy.

Tanis wondered if that was where the saboteurs were intending to travel. Some of the larger ships in dock A3 were equipped with stasis pods; with a good pilot at the helm they could make the trip to EE in under thirty years.

She couldn't imagine anyone wanted to travel there. It was all dust cloud miners, not a single terraformed world in the system.

After another twenty minutes, the first set of probes radioed back images of cargo storage areas. They had to be nearing the dock and Tanis picked up the pace, turning her focus to what she would do to whoever was behind this.

Before long her nano located the dock, and they confirmed Tanis's suspicions: a Triton Class Pinnace was on the launching rails, powered up and ready to boost out. Though there was no visible activity on the dock, Tanis approached cautiously all the same.

The dock was large, and there were dozens of places for attackers to hide. She wished there had been time to gather backup, and her thoughts flashed to Joe; she imagined he must be revived by now, most likely with Bob, getting updated on the situation.

<*Too bad we didn't have some formation material; we could have left a comm string behind.*>

<*If wishes were fishes…*> Angela replied.

<*What?*>

<*Never mind.*>

The corridor terminated at the dock with both airlock doors wide open. Normally that wouldn't be possible, but with the entire ship essentially offline there was nothing to stop it.

<*If that ship launches we'll be sucking vacuum—well, you will,*> Angela said.

<*Armor will keep me under compression, but air could be a problem.*>

<*Not really that funny.*>

Tanis didn't mean it to be funny either, she was just thinking aloud…though the comment hadn't been made in her public mind—Angela shouldn't have heard and responded.

Tanis pushed the implications of that from her mind and crouched low, holding the pistol and assault rifle near the deck. It wouldn't do to have whoever was out there see two weapons floating in the air.

Out on the dock, there were several pallets of refined ore, ready for the space station that was to be constructed once the ship reached New Eden. They would make good places to hide her weapons while she surveyed the area.

Creeping slowly along the deck, she reached the pallets and tucked the weapons under a strap. Tanis then pulled herself onto the ore and surveyed the dock. There still weren't any signs of people, but the pinnace's passenger ramp was lowered. Tanis decided to enter the ship. She could send a nano probe, but it was possible that the vessel's sensors would pick up its signal. She pulled her nanocloud in tight and jumped off the pallet.

The ship's ramp was only twenty meters away; Tanis kept her approach slow and steady, when she heard a noise to her left. She resisted the urge to duck behind something, relying on her shimmersuit's ability to render her entirely undetectable.

It was Collins and another man she didn't recognize; they were carrying a bundle between them.

By reflex, Tanis attempted to look the other man up and was met with the Link offline symbol in her mind. She was reminded just how often she relied on the Link for data about the ship without storing details in her own mind.

The men rounded a pallet and Tanis got a better look at the bundle they carried.

It was Amy Lee.

"Goddammit, why couldn't we just leave her back there?" the unidentified man asked.

"Because I don't know if she managed to get a signal off and I need to find out. It will affect where we can go," Collins replied between grunts.

Tanis knew that Amy Lee had a number of strength modifying mods. While she looked like a slim woman, just under 180 centimeters, she likely weighed over 120 kilograms.

"You told me we were going to Tau Ceti," the man said.

"Well, if she got a signal off, then we're going to Epsilon Eridani."

"What a shit hole."

"It's a shit hole with transports to Sol." Collins gave the man an aggravated look.

"I guess that's true," the man agreed. "I can't believe I signed on for this…two hundred years just to take out one ship."

"Me either. We were hoping the STR would succeed, but since they failed, it was up to us."

The man nodded. "I understand. They have to be stopped. I just wish it wasn't taking so much time."

"There was no way they could be allowed to do that research at New Eden," Collins said.

"No way we could allow this ship's abomination of an AI to live either."

Collins nodded. "Leave her here for a minute; I saw some restraints in the security locker back in the dock ops center. You start the ship's launch process."

Tanis watched the unidentified man walk up the pinnace's ramp while Collins walked down a corridor toward the dock's ops center. Stopping the ship from leaving was the top priority, and she followed the unknown man up into the pinnace.

There wasn't a lot of room inside—a cockpit, common room, two cabins with two bunks each, and a small cargo hold. Off the common room were stasis pods for four people. It was enough to get them to the closest system, and slip into regular insystem traffic without undue attention.

Tanis crept down the corridor to the cockpit. The man settled into the pilot's chair and she moved into position behind him.

<Able to log onto the pinnace's net?>

<Working on it,> Angela replied. *<Don't want to alert him.>*

Tanis waited; the intel that Angela could gather while the man was on the net could be invaluable.

<Got it! He's Henry Freeman, a GSS pilot contracted to assist with the space station setup at New Eden before the Intrepid *returns to Earth.>*

<So not colony… I suppose that's reassuring.>

<I really can't imagine how. It doesn't change our situation,> Angela said.

<I just would be more surprised if a colonist was involved.>

Tanis knew enough; no reason to let him prep the ship for launch. She pulled back her arm and swung at the man's head.

Right through empty air.

<*Holo!*> Angela said.

<*A damn good one too.*>

Tanis only had a moment's warning before her body was peppered with particle beam fire. She spun to see Collins in the pinnace's central corridor, rifle in hand.

The shimmersuit was torn to shreds, but the armor underneath saved Tanis from a grisly death. It dissipated the beams, though it grew uncomfortably warm against her skin. A few more shots and it would be searing. She dove behind the pilot's seat, the remains of her shimmersuit melting off and lighting the chair on fire.

<*Damn…that was the best shimmersuit I've ever had,*> Tanis said.

<*I'm still trying to figure out how that holo fooled us.*>

<*Easy, neither of us really checked.*>

Collins had stopped firing during the exchange and Tanis peered around the smoking ruin of the seat. There was no one there. She crept cautiously through the corridor to the exit ramp. Her fleet of nano probes scouted outside the ship and showed Collins holding a gun to Amy Lee's head.

"Lieutenant Colonel Richards!" he yelled in her direction. "I've reversed the trigger on this weapon and I have it pulled. If I let go, it will fire and kill her. Come out where I can see you."

Tanis edged out onto the ramp. Amy Lee was conscious and there was fear in her eyes.

"Please, Colonel, do what he asks."

"Yes, do what I ask. Walk down the ramp."

Tanis did as she was instructed. "Clever bit with the holo. I can't believe I fell for it."

"Honestly—" Collins gave a throaty chuckle "—neither can I. I had no idea you'd get taken in so well. It worked pretty good at flushing you out. Now you walk toward those crates and Miss Amy Lee and I are going to get on the ship."

"How did you know to expect me? You weren't just waiting around on the off-chance someone came by, were you?" Tanis asked, stalling for time.

"Of course not. You forget that I subverted half the sensors on this ship. I knew you were coming an hour ago."

Tanis ground her teeth; it was stupid of her not to expect something like that. Just because she couldn't use the shipnet didn't mean the saboteur didn't have some sort of access to it.

She slowly edged back toward the crate as instructed. Her only solace was the knowledge that she was moving toward her weapons.

Collins backed up the ramp and stood at the top, Amy Lee in front of him.

"Send her down," Tanis said. "There's nothing we can do now to stop you."

"I don't think so, you've proven to be very resourceful," Collins said.

Tanis backed up another step, her left hand within reach of her pistol.

"There's nothing to gain from this—" Tanis began to say as she reached for her pistol. Her fingers wrapped around the grip and in a single motion she raised it, pivoted, and fired three shots at Collins's head.

He dove back into the ship, pushing Amy Lee as he did. She lost her balance and toppled off the edge of the ramp, the thud of her impact lost in the shots Tanis fired into the pinnace's entrance and hull.

The ramp began to retract and Tanis swore as she raced to recover Amy's body.

<*Hurry!*> Angela shouted in her mind. <*He's going to blow his way out of here, the dock's shields won't snap into place—it'll decompress.*>

<*I know! I can't leave her though!*> Tanis dropped her weapons and pulled Amy Lee into her arms as the pinnace rotated in its cradle. She was unconscious and Tanis slung her over a shoulder and turned toward the dock's entrance, breaking into a full sprint.

<*You have less than ten seconds,*> Angela said, her mental voice strained. <*The entrance to the dock has a pressure sensitive breach door. It should close even without power.*>

Behind Tanis there was a clang and a hum as the launch rails came to life, lifting the pinnace into the air. She cringed as the snap of lasers filled the air—heralding the end of the dock's bay doors.

The sound of atmosphere whistling out into space filled the air, followed by the sound of rending steel. Tanis found the energy within herself to close the last twenty meters to the dock entrance in record time, while behind her the pinnace's engines roared to life, thrusting the ship out into space.

She raced past the entrance, feeling the pressure doors brush her foot as they slammed into place.

<*You cut that too close.*>

<*You know I had to do everything I could to save her,*> Tanis said as she lowered Amy Lee's unconscious form to the deck.

Tanis could all but taste Angela's worry. <*We're still falling into a star. All you can do is still to come.*>

"Tanis! Are you alright?"

She looked up to see Joe running toward her. Seeing him caused a feeling in her chest she had forgotten about years ago. The look of concern and love on his face made her stomach do a pirouette.

Shame dampened the feeling of relief. She had always felt something was off with Collins. Now her lack of follow-through had cost Gollee his life and could be the end of the *Intrepid.*

"Yeah. I'm OK. He got away, though." She gestured to the sealed door.

Joe skidded to a halt and wrapped his arms around her. Some part of her realized this was her first hug in over a decade; another part told the first part to shut up and enjoy it. She wrapped her arms around Joe and returned the embrace.

Joe looked down at Amy Lee. "Is she OK?"

"Yes. Angela just had some nano take a peek, she'll likely come to in just a few minutes."

Joe looked Tanis up and down slowly with a quizzical expression. "Why are you naked?"

Tanis looked down at herself and her cheeks reddened.

"My shimmersuit burned off…I have my flow-armor on, but it's transparent," she smiled sheepishly.

"Looks good on you," he grinned.

<*I can change that,*> Angela said; a second later the armor changed to a matte grey from the neck down. <*If you had bothered to RTFM you'd know that too.*>

"Thanks Angela, what would I do without you?"

<Be naked, apparently.>

"What are you doing here? Shouldn't you be with Bob?" Tanis asked Joe.

"I got Priscilla out of stasis. She's seeing to him and the ship, trying to figure out what the heck happened."

"And how to save our collective asses, I hope."

"Yeah, that too."

"We should get back up there. Nothing more we can do down here."

They woke a very appreciative Amy Lee and worked their way back to the upper decks by a more circuitous route than Tanis took on the way down.

"I can't believe I missed Collins being such an ass," Amy Lee sighed. "I mean…I knew he was an ass, just not this much of an ass."

Tanis grimaced. "Yeah, he was such an dickhead it managed to function as cover."

"Did you find Gollee?" Amy Lee asked.

"I did, but he didn't make it," Tanis replied. "I'm sorry, Amy Lee."

Tanis turned her head to look at her lieutenant and noticed a strange look in her eye—one she hadn't seen before. If she didn't know any better….

"Colonel, you know you can just call me Amy," she said.

The statement caught Tanis off-guard. Amy Lee had always insisted on using her proper full name. Perhaps the four-year duty-shift out of stasis had finally loosened her up.

"Very well, Amy," Tanis smiled.

The lifts up to the command deck were offline and conversation ceased as the group climbed up a half kilometer of maintenance shafts.

At the top, Joe waved for Tanis to stop.

"You may be all jacked up on your super-soldier endorphins, but the rest of us mortals need a breather," he said with a wheeze.

"And how are you not covered in sweat?" Amy asked as she wiped her brow between gasps for air.

"This armor does an amazing job of dissipating heat; I'm not even warm," Tanis replied.

"Where can I get some of that stuff?" Amy asked.

"Uh…Callisto?" Tanis replied.

"Oh, so not too likely I'm going to find any in the armory, then."

Tanis shook her head. "Rest break over, let's get moving again."

The group started off at an easy run, and Tanis replayed the confrontation on the docks in her mind, looking for clues in the details.

"Amy, Collins said you may have gotten off a signal to Sol about our situation. Did you?"

Amy shook her head. "No, I didn't manage it. Collins shut down power to the area I was in before I could get it out."

"Good," Tanis replied.

"Good?" Joe asked.

"Yeah, the last thing we need right now is Sol knowing we're in trouble out here."

"I don't follow." Amy furrowed her brow. "I shouldn't have called for help?"

"No help will get here in time, and if we failed to get a message back saying we're OK, they'd give the colony to someone else. It's best if Sol doesn't know about what's happening at all."

"Did you learn anything else about what Collins was up to? If he had any help?" Joe asked.

"I didn't. I was on the bridge reviewing logs when I stumbled across some irregularities. I attempted to ask Bob about them but he didn't answer. I was trying to get a signal out when the bridge lost power. Collins showed up a moment later. All I know is that he somehow subverted a lot of systems." Amy shook her head. "I wish I knew more."

The group arrived at Bob's node several minutes later to find Priscilla standing in the midst of holo interfaces, trying to track the source of the ship's mass failure.

"What's the word?" Joe asked the ship's avatar.

Priscilla's eyes looked up from the display, while her hands continued to race across the interface.

"As best I can tell, we're looking at physical failures. We think that faulty parts were installed from the get-go. The sensors were also altered to ensure that they would miss the sabotage." Her mouth twisted with concern as she spoke. "I wish Amanda was here, but I can't get in contact with the stasis chamber she's in."

Tanis wrapped an arm around her shoulder. "I know how you feel. A lot of people I care about are out there on the ship, but we don't know if they're OK."

Priscilla nodded, her eyes showing thanks while she worked her holo interfaces.

"Amy Lee! You're OK," Priscilla said with a smile when the avatar spotted her behind Tanis and Joe. "With what happened to Gollee? We were worried."

"I don't worry," Bob said.

"Thanks for the concern, Bob," Amy said sourly.

"Gollee didn't make it," Tanis said somberly, and no one spoke for a few moments.

Bob broke the silence, speaking audibly again. "I assume from your presence that Collins escaped alone?"

"That's correct," Tanis replied. "He was behind this—though I don't know for sure if he was alone. He strikes me as the sort who would have no problem leaving co-conspirators behind."

"So, when Collins wanted to disable the ship, he sent a signal through the system that triggered the faults and essentially fractured everything." Priscilla continued with her report.

"Protocol indicates that we must wake the captain," Bob said. "We need his input on our next actions."

"You haven't done that yet?" Tanis asked.

"You are the ranking officer on the ship," Priscilla said. "Execution of command structure orders are your domain."

Tanis was startled for a moment. On the *Intrepid,* the pro-tem command structure was Captain Andrews, First Mate Mick Edward, Admiral Sanderson, and then, with her re-instated rank of Lieutenant Colonel, her. With none of the others out of stasis, she was top of the list.

<Focus.>

Tanis drew a deep breath. "Yes, I should go wake the captain. Joe, you're with me; Amy, there's a security locker around the far side of the node. Arm up and keep Bob and Priscilla safe."

She turned to Priscilla. "I believe the ship to be clear of hostiles. I think your next step should be to get the servitors to set up a hard line out of the node and to take out whatever is damping this node. Then start physically analyzing the destroyed components. We'll want to give the captain as much information as possible."

Priscilla glanced at Bob's node and sighed. "We would *never* have thought of that!"

Tanis couldn't help but smile as she walked out of the node, followed by Joe.

"Good to see she still has her sense of humor," he commented.

"I think she has to. *We* could leave on a pinnace or one of the larger cruisers, but, no matter what, they would have to go down with the ship."

"I honestly don't think we could go either," Joe said. "There are two and half million people in stasis on the *Intrepid*. What cowards would leave?"

Tanis clenched her jaw. "I can think of one."

ESTRELLA DE LA MUERTE

STELLAR DATE: 3241790 / 08.15.4163 (Adjusted Gregorian)
LOCATION: GSS *Intrepid*, Executive Stasis Chamber A1
REGION: LHS 1565, 0.5 AU from stellar primary

Andrews rose from his pod. He rubbed his eyes for a moment, then gave Tanis and Joe a searching look.

"You're not on rotation before me," he said.

"Yes, sir, but there's been an event," Tanis replied.

Andrews cocked an eyebrow and she brought him up to speed.

He gave a long sigh. "Lieutenant Colonel, I can see it in your eyes that you blame yourself. You can stop that right now. No one suspected that Collins was with the enemy. Though, being in supply and acquisitions, he was well placed to get the sabotaged components aboard."

"Be that as it may, sir, I was head of the SOC. It was *my job* to suspect everyone."

"Save your recriminations for later. If we don't fall into this star and burn up, I'll be sure to dress you down. In the meantime, I need you…both of you, at the top of your game."

Without realizing she had done it, Tanis found herself standing straighter and saw that Joe had done the same. The captain's calm surety was contagious.

<*That's why he's the captain,*> Angela's mental avatar gave a shake of its head.

"Take me to Bob." Andrews eased up from the edge of his pod.

Bob, Priscilla, and Amy had cleared the dampening field surrounding his node and the AI had access to the general shipnet once more. None of his other nodes were online, which was good; it avoided any issues of a fractured personality needing a merge—something never before attempted with an AI even close to his complexity.

"What's our situation regarding LHS 1565?" Captain Andrews asked the moment he stepped into the node.

"Well, for starters, we named it Estrella de la Muerte," Priscilla said with a smile.

"That's uhh…really encouraging," Andrews said. "But not that pertinent."

<*I have control of the dorsal array of sensors and have updated my calculations. We have thirty-eight hours before we reach the star,*> Bob supplied.

"If we could regain helm control, what are our chances of firing the engines to break free?" Captain Andrews initialized a holo display of the stellar system, examining the ship's vector and performing some of his own computations.

<*We could break free, but the action would use the last of our fuel and leave us adrift.*>

"I see we're lower on isotopes than we expected," Andrews said as he looked over their fuel situation.

"We think that the ramscoop was not performing correctly for some time, but the readings were being reported as though it were. The edges of this system have a lot of lithium, but we ended up missing it all," Priscilla supplied as she brought up the variances on a holo display.

Tanis leaned against the railing that overlooked the ten-meter drop to the bottom of the node. There had to be a way out of this situation, but she couldn't see it.

"Bob, can you show your best option for our breakaway burn on the holo?" Joe asked.

Bob complied and highlighted the point where the burn would take place. <*If we do a max burn here with optimal timing, and vectors line up better than optimally, then we will achieve breakaway velocities on this vector.*>

The captain expanded the holo to forty light-years. The vector didn't even come close to intersecting any other stars. The *Intrepid* would be adrift forever.

"Is there any chance we can correct that vector after the burn?" the captain asked.

"We'll have plenty of D2, but no lithium. Our fusion engines aren't designed to run without lithium, and with the primary scoop emitter damaged we're not going to have much on the way out," Priscilla supplied.

"What a miserable little star." Andrews rubbed his jaw.

"I may have a way out of this, sir," Joe said as he walked around the holo and zoomed it back in close to the star.

Tanis gave him a smile, which he glanced at and returned.

<*I knew you'd figure something out—stars know I have no idea what to do,*> Tanis said.

<*Don't get too excited just yet,*> Joe replied.

"How accurate is this in regards to how the star will look when we pass it?" he asked Bob.

A slider appeared displaying a timeline and the ship's position.

<*Very accurate,*> the AI replied. <*Use the slider to set the position in the timeline.*>

Joe nodded and adjusted forward to where the ship was closest to the star. He altered the display to shift the *Intrepid* several lines of latitude north as it passed by Estrella de la Muerte.

"I see what you're suggesting," Priscilla said.

<*As do I.*> Bob didn't sound entirely convinced.

"Explain it for the rest of us, then," Tanis said.

"First—" Joe glanced at the node core "—maximize whichever is the opposing magnetic polarity to the star on our port shields at this position." His finger pointed to the representation of the ship on the holo.

<*Done.*>

The ship's outsystem trajectory shifted ever so little, with the breakaway velocity significantly higher than before.

"I get it now. You're going to push us off of that sun spot's magnetic field and use it to…well, I don't know what." Tanis stepped away from the railing and walked around the display, trying to see if changing her view would reveal Joe's plan.

Joe zoomed the holo out again to a ten light-year radius around the star. It had them lined up with New Eden again.

"With the bounce off the sun-spot, we'll be able to save the extra fuel to course correct and get to New Eden," she said appreciatively.

"Right and right," Joe nodded.

"Clever thinking." Captain Andrews was smiling; it was the first time Tanis saw him do so since they pulled him from stasis.

<*You've got a calculation error.*> Bob adjusted Joe's trajectory to show them once more missing New Eden and passing out of the human sphere without intersecting any other system.

"You're right," Joe said. "We need more fuel, specifically more lithium, but we don't need it until after we pass the star." He adjusted the display back to his original projection and then added a second path.

"We've been over this," Priscilla said. "The scoop isn't working well enough to pick up the lithium we need, and even if it were, there's not enough on that vector to fuel the burn you propose."

"Yes, but we have more than one ship," Joe said in agreement. "I'll take one of the heavy lifters and do a hard burn out to this asteroid ring at 30 AU. Signatures indicate that there is a high likelihood for lithium in some of these rocks. I find a big one, or net some smaller ones and boost like all-get-out to meet the ship on our outsystem vector."

"That's a risky proposition," Andrews said. "If you don't make it back in time Estrella de la Muerte will be your grave."

"I'm aware of that, sir, but if I don't try it, then things are a lot worse. Without this we drift forever." Joe's somber words reminded everyone of how dire the situation was.

Tanis felt a tightness in her chest, worry making it hard to breathe. If Joe didn't make it back, she would be left on the *Intrepid* without him…forever. She knew now, had known for some time, that she loved him. Loved him and hadn't even said the words to him yet.

"I'll go with you," she said to Joe.

"You're not built for it, you couldn't handle the acceleration." His voice was sure, but his eyes were sad.

"It's what, a max of seventy *g*'s?

"Initial peak, yeah. Average closer to four or five."

"First," Andrews gave both of them an unreadable look, "we have to decide if this is even the plan we'll be pursuing. We need Ernest and Abby."

THE LONG SHOT

STELLAR DATE: 3241791 / 08.16.4163 (Adjusted Gregorian)
LOCATION: GSS *Intrepid*, Bridge Conference Room
REGION: LHS 1565, 0.5 AU from stellar primary

Over the next hour, a frantic wave of organized chaos swept over the *Intrepid* as hundreds of crew were brought out of stasis.

Repairs began immediately; the first to the upper command area's dedicated fusion plants. Abby delegated decision-making to Earnest and organized a team of specialists—both human and AI—to reinitialize more of Bob's nodes, and set to work with a vengeance.

Any plan other than burning up in the star required Bob to have control of the engines. Getting his nodes back online was the first step in that process. Only he was able to effect the precise burns needed.

A servitor poured coffee for the command crew sitting around the bridge's conference table. Joe and Tanis sat next to Mick Edward, the first mate. He stroked his beard as he examined the holo of the local system while muttering to himself. Captain Andrews was discussing Joe's plan in low tones with Terrance while Ernest appeared engrossed in the three holos and two hyfilms in front of him. At the end of the table, Hilda Orion, the ship's chief navigator, stared at the table's main holo projection of the LHS 1565 system like it had some secret it was hiding from her.

After everyone prepared their drink to their own satisfaction, Andrews called the meeting to order.

"We have just over twenty hours until we need to make the first burn. However, if Joe is to leave on his mission to pick up some rocks, his window for departure is in seven hours."

The captain's words were serious and an additional weight settled over the room. Tanis reached under the table and found Joe's hand.

He squeezed it in response. <*We're going to be OK. I know I can do this.*>

"You've all had some time to mull over the events of the last few hours, as well as examine Lieutenant Colonel Richard's report. Bob has put together a precise timeline necessary to pull off Commander Evans's plan and it's up to us to decide if it is the best option, and if it is even feasible."

"Oh, it's feasible all right," Earnest said. "Totally insane, but quite feasible."

"There's also the extreme risk to you." Hilda looked at Joe and Tanis. "You will have to do an extremely hard burn to break free of the star's gravity well and then reach nearly 0.20*c*, decelerate *hard* at the far end, then capture a rock or two and boost *very hard* to meet up with us. One mistake and you're permanent residents of this system."

"We know the risk." Joe's expression was resolute, though he had expressed private concerns to Tanis about the danger to her.

Hilda snorted. "There's a far safer option. We rotate the ship and fire the engines to slow our approach to the star and break free. We coast to the system's scattered disk, collect what we need, repair, and then start a standard outsystem slingshot back on course." She projected her alternate plan on the table's holo system.

Earnest shook his head. "That requires a level of certainty that there will be enough raw material to fix the ramscoop. Without it, we'll have to dip into colony supplies to repair it. Even so, we may not have what we need without creating an industrial base here—and I really don't think there's enough available matter in this system to do that."

"But if Joe doesn't make his rendezvous then we won't be able to course correct and make it to New Eden," Terrance said.

There were somber looks all around and Earnest enlarged the holo. "If we don't get the lithium, we'll have to convert the engines to D2-only fusion. It'll take a few years with what we have on hand, but we'll be able to correct and make it to Epsilon Eridani."

Hilda pulled up data on the system. "A colony is setting up there, but the system is too young and hot for terraforming. It'll probably take us three hundred 'n forty-five years to drift on over."

The statement drew a whistle from Joe and an incredulous look from Terrance. "How long will it take to get to New Eden if Joe's plan works and we get the lithium?" he asked.

Joe adjusted the display. "Just under one hundred seventy-two years."

Terrance shook his head. "This is going to mess things up. Our timetable will be drastically altered."

"Our total journey will take roughly ninety-two years longer than expected." Earnest nodded his head in agreement. "It's unfortunate."

"Is it a large concern?" Tanis asked. "Most everyone will be in stasis for the duration. For all intents and purposes they won't care that it took an extra hundred years to get to New Eden."

"There's the *Dakota,* or whatever the next GSS ship is," Captain Andrews said. "If we take that long to get there, they'll take it from us."

"So we don't let anyone know, not until it's too late for them to beat us to the system. We can even send a probe from here along our original path and speed sending updates as though nothing went wrong." The solution seemed obvious to Tanis.

"There are other concerns," Terrance said.

Andrews cast an appraising look at Terrance; Tanis spotted the tells they both gave when having a protracted Link discussion. The captain nodded and Terrance slowly looked into the eyes of each person sitting around the table.

"What I'm about to tell you does not leave this room. I want it classified at the highest security level in your internal systems."

Everyone nodded, though Tanis knew that only Joe, Hilda, and Mick were unaware of the *Intrepid's* secret cargo—and the colony's secret purpose on New Eden.

"This ship is carrying the technology to manufacture picotech—pico bots, to be precise." Terrance let the bomb drop without any further preamble.

Nanotech robots were part of everyday life. The tiny machines were everywhere, and in everything. Picotech bots would be a thousand times smaller than nanotech. In the previous millennium they had been the holy grail of a million research projects.

Much of the research had been done on Juno, but the picotech broke containment and a pico-swarm devoured half the asteroid before fail-safes destroyed it and the swarm.

It wasn't the first pico disaster and afterward every government in the system placed a ban on all picotech research. Many corporations still carried out secret research at the edges of the Sol system, but with all of the data from Juno lost, most had started from scratch, and no breakthroughs had been made—at least none that were publicized.

"When you say carrying the technology, you mean functional tech?" Joe asked.

Earnest nodded. "Indeed. I worked it out over a decade before we left Mars. But it was impossible to do any manufacturing in the Sol system."

Mick sat back and ran a hand through his hair. "I can't believe you didn't tell me this." He looked at the captain. "I think I had a right to know. Hell, the colonists have a right to know."

"It's not like we're going to make pico on New Eden, we'll use one of the other planets for it. However, the tech is quite safe," Terrance said.

"Yeah, I bet that's what the guys on Juno thought before their bodies were consumed as raw resources, before half the world was eaten by the things."

Earnest scowled at Mick. "Those researchers had no idea what they were doing. My pico is rock solid. In fact, I'm certain I can use it to create femtotech."

Tanis had wondered about that possibility. Femtotech would allow the manipulation of atomic nuclei—whoever possessed such technology would have god-like powers.

Terrance shot Earnest a quelling glance. "That's just conjecture at this point. We have a lot of work to do with expanding on the picotech."

Hilda whistled. "Now I get why we're running such a massive mission, and why this ship is reusable. It makes so much more sense now." She smiled as she looked around the table. "Don't you realize? New Eden will become the economic center of the human sphere!"

Terrance smiled. "That's the plan at least."

"This is nuts!" Mick stood up, his eyes flashing with rage. "I can't believe you lied to everyone. This colony is a one way trip to death."

"If we don't die here first," Joe muttered.

<*I can't believe you didn't tell me,*> he said privately to Tanis.

<*I was under orders not to, same with Angela. I'm sorry,*> she replied.

"Mick," Captain Andrew's voice boomed. "Sit. Down. Now."

For a moment it looked like the first mate would comply, then he took a step backward. "No, hell no. There's no way. I have to stop you."

He turned and ran toward the conference room door. He was two steps away when the stun shot from Tanis's pistol hit him. His body fell to the floor and Joe rose to check on the man.

"He seems to be OK. Nothing a painkiller won't fix when he wakes."

Hilda looked pale; her voice trembled. "Why did he do that?"

"There's no record of mental instability in his record," Tanis said, after looking it up on the bridge net.

"I don't know." Andrews shook his head as he looked at the mate. "I've worked with him for over three hundred years, seen him do some death defying things. I didn't think he'd react like this."

Two servitors entered and lifted the first mate. Tanis sent them instructions to put the man into stasis for the time being. The mystery would have to wait. It wasn't lost on her that she was now third from the top of the *Intrepid*'s command structure as a result.

"This doesn't change the fact that time is wasting," Earnest said, apparently unfazed by the first mate's mental breakdown. "It's only a matter of time before someone else works out what I've discovered. We need the fastest route to New Eden."

"Then it's Joe's plan." Captain Andrews fixed the commander with his unflappable gaze. "You're sure you're up to this, son?"

Tanis looked between Joe and the captain. Joe appeared convinced, but Tanis saw the slightest bit of tension around his eyes. He didn't want her to come. Not like he would have a choice.

"I am, sir. However—" he glanced at Tanis "—I think I should do this alone."

"I find myself in agreement," the captain nodded. "With Mick out of the picture, I need you here, Tanis."

Tanis knew that anything she said would sound petulant and selfish. The captain was right; she should stay behind. Even so, she wracked her mind for a reason she should go with Joe.

<*She should go,*> Bob entered the conversation.

"I find myself in agreement with Bob." Earnest cast a puzzled look at his holo displays. "For some reason, with Major…err…Lieutenant Colonel Richards on the mission, I project a significantly higher chance of success. Perhaps due to Angela's abilities."

"Glad to know I'm wanted." Tanis tried to cut the tension.

<*Glad to know someone appreciates what I add to our partnership,*> Angela quipped.

"She's not enhanced to handle the high *g* burns." Joe shook his head.

<*Please, just go along with it, I'll explain why later,*> Tanis said to Joe.

He cast her a searching look, found her hand again and nodded.

"Ok, we'll go together."

"I'm not sure about this." The captain shook his head. "We're having trouble regaining control of parts of the ship and there are still rogue servitors and bots all over. I may need you here."

"You have Ouri and Amy, and don't forget that I organized a Marine division under Major Brandt. They're more than capable of regaining control of the ship."

<*They will be sufficient,*> Bob said, his tone more forceful than usual. <*Send Tanis.*>

The captain cast a quizzical look at the ceiling; Tanis suspected he was inquiring about the AI's strong insistence that she go. She also wondered why.

<*Don't ask me, He usually doesn't weigh in on things like this,*> Angela said.

Captain Andrews eventually nodded. "You'll go. I'll have Ouri get the Marine company out of stasis and we'll take care of things here."

"It's settled, then." Earnest shuffled his hyfilm together. "Tanis and Joe will take the *Excelsior*; it's our fastest heavy tug, which can boost a billion tons to 0.20*c*. You'll need to begin your initial burn in six hours and thirty nine minutes."

THE LONG DARK

STELLAR DATE: 3241791 / 08.16.4163 (Adjusted Gregorian)
LOCATION: GSS *Intrepid*, Bridge Conference Room
REGION: LHS 1565, 0.45 AU from stellar primary

19:46 hours to Intrepid escape burn
6:28 hours to end of Excelsior mission launch window

Abby and her team had been hard at work during the meeting. Thankfully, one of the first systems brought back online was the dorsal maglev. The train would shave at least an hour off their journey.

Joe and Tanis had visited an armory on the way to the train and both carried pulse rifles. Joe found light body armor while Tanis had opted not to add to her flow-armor, other than to strap two sidearms to her hips and throw a bandolier of power cells over her shoulder.

They sat beside each other as the train took off toward a station that would place them six kilometers from the A1 dock where the Excelsior waited.

With all the other maglev trains offline, an easier route would have been to take a shuttle from the A3 dock, but when Collins left he had destroyed the other ships and much of the dock.

It was going to be a long hike to the *Excelsior*.

They hadn't spoken much since the decision to include Tanis, and her discomfort at the silence was turning to annoyance. In the military, rank dictated decision-making. If you had a lower pay-grade, you shut up and did what you were told. The extra dynamic of a relationship added an exhausting nuance to every conflict.

"Why am I getting the silent treatment?" she finally asked. "I thought you were OK with my coming."

"I've been waiting for you to explain why you are so insistent on coming," Joe replied. His tone was level, giving little away, but Tanis knew that meant he was upset.

"It feels silly; I know logically that going with you is not the right choice," Tanis responded.

"You're right, it's not." Joe's voice was harsh and his expression softened. "Sorry, that came out stronger than I meant..."

"I've probably done that myself from time to time."

"Who? You?" Joe grinned and Tanis gave him a light punch on the arm. "I'm still worried, though. A seventy-*g* burn will make you weigh over six-thousand kilograms. Even in stasis that's a lot."

"I know," Tanis agreed. "It's not going to be comfortable, but I just found you—figuratively speaking—I'm not going to lose you."

Joe locked eyes with her. "I spent a long time chasing after you too. I don't want to lose you either."

<I may have a way to make this work out,> Angela interrupted. *<I think I can enhance Tanis's body to withstand the strain. You'll still want to be in stasis for the heavy burns, but the risks will go down drastically.>*

"Do tell," Tanis said.

<I can use your flow-armor to boost the structural integrity of your bones and organ walls. It's essentially what Joe's alterations allow his body to do under high g's.>

"That sounds a…bit risky," Tanis said, looking down at the matte grey armor tightly adhered to her skin. "Do I really need something like that? I already have a lot of structural enhancements. It's not like this is all flesh and blood in here," she said as she patted her stomach.

<I think it will help a lot. I'm in here too and that amount of pressure worries me as well. However, your armor is designed to withstand kinetic strikes much larger than these burns and will make the difference between a fun trip and lung collapse.>

"See, my concerns are not completely unfounded," Joe said. "I think you should do it."

<I don't need to do it now; we can do it on the ship. I have a suspicion that you'll need that armor on the outside before we get there.>

Tanis clasped Joe's hand. "Just the way we like it."

Neither said another word as the train continued to their stop; their hands didn't unclasp.

When the maglev stopped, the doors opened into a pitch-black station. Even the emergency lighting was offline.

<So much for hoping another line would be online. You guys better get to it; it's a five kilometer hike to the forward docking bays,> Angela supplied.

<Pretty dark down here.> Tanis addressed Priscilla over the general shipnet, *<Any chance we could get some glow?>*

<Not very likely.> Priscilla's answer was short and her mental tone clipped. *<When we brought node eleven back online, a nasty virus leaked out; it's wreaking havoc with systems everywhere. We're doing our best to get it cleaned up, but until we do, ship systems are going to be sporadic. That, combined with the battery bank that blew, has knocked whole sections of the ship completely off the grid.>*

<Is the virus human spreadable?> Tanis asked. It wasn't uncommon for system viruses to target a human's internal computers or AI. Because of human system viruses, nearly half of the average person's internal processing power and codebase was dedicated to intrusion detection and protection.

<Quite likely. I'd suggest you sever wireless connections, or at the least drop to low bandwidth with extra buffers.>

<Will do,> Tanis said.

Joe had been listening in. He caught her eye and nodded.

<Keep us updated. We're on the second leg of our journey.>

<You got it.>

"They must have had a contingency plan in case any of us got out of stasis," Joe said.

Tanis nodded as they walked across the platform into the station's central plaza. She cycled her vision to a combination of IR and UV. The setting picked up enough ambient heat and background radiation to generate a picture of the room. Her navigation overlay filled in the rest, providing a false color representation of what the station looked like.

Joe's vision didn't have the UV pickup, so she sent him a point-to-point feed to help improve his sight.

"Thanks, there are some looooong drops on this ship."

"You're telling me. When they built it, they really didn't give a lot of consideration to how hard it is to get places on foot."

<*Tanis,*> Priscilla's voice came over the general shipnet, <*we've got some instances of rogue servitors in your area. It looks like there's an AI controlling that bad node and it's taking control of portions of the ship.*>

<*Are you going to be able to fend it off?*>

Priscilla gave the mental equivalent of a snort. <*Absolutely, the biggest concern is time. If it slows down regaining control of the engines, then this party is for nothing.*>

Tanis signaled her agreement and nodded to Joe. They both unslung their pulse rifles and set them to an EM burst. It was a dangerous thing to use on a ship, but with everything offline there was little chance of secondary explosions.

"Servitors should show up pretty clearly on the IR," Joe said as they moved cautiously across the plaza. The station had several balconies and some large spaces with no cover. Tanis would feel a lot better once they were through it.

"Don't count on it—this room has a lot of reflective surfaces. Make sure you filter out your own image or you'll be shooting at ghosts."

"Not my first time using IR," Joe said with a smile.

Despite every hair on Tanis's neck tingling, nothing happened. They exited the station and began their journey down a long series of pitch-black corridors.

Unlike her mad race after Collins and Amy Lee, Tanis was acutely aware of her surroundings. The darkened halls took on a sinister cast and she found herself imagining twisted shapes lurching out from the shadows.

She shook her head to clear the images from her mind.

"You OK?" Joe asked.

"Yeah, just too many bad memories from darkened ship corridors."

Her augmented vision showed Joe nodding and he put a hand on her shoulder. She was glad he didn't ask for details. She didn't want to think any further on those past events.

Crew quarters and duty stations slid by on either side; after the first kilometer, those were left behind as they moved into a region of supply depots and workshops.

"Well that's not handy," Tanis said as they came to a bank of lifts at the end of a corridor. "There's supposed to be a way to get down to deck 114B from here."

"What I'd give for a flashlight right now," Joe said while looking for an access hatch to a ladder shaft.

"Give it a second, I have my nanocloud doing pings, they'll find the opening."

Seconds later, the nano spotted it and the hatch lit up on their HUDs. Tanis pried it open and slid down the ladder to the next deck; she put her back to the wall, scanning the cross corridors while Joe leapt through the opening and landed beside her.

"Such a show-off," Tanis said, worrying for a moment that it was the wrong thing to say.

Joe grinned. "Gotta keep limber."

<*He fell for you even with all your snark. I suspect he knows what he's in for,*> Angela commented on Tanis's internal worry.

They landed in an intersection and the corridor they needed was lit up on their HUDs. The path took them between entrances to massive workshops where machines lay dormant, prepared to fashion whatever ship's components were needed. Many of them would also assist in building the New Eden 1 space station on which the habitation cylinders would mount.

Joe stopped and put a hand on Tanis's shoulder. "Did you hear that?"

"Over my own breathing? No. It's weird to have the ship this silent."

"I could have sworn I heard something come from that opening ahead to the left." Joe gestured at the gaping doorway with his rifle.

"Then let's go nice and slow-like."

The pair crept through the corridor. Tanis never thought she would be in the dark, creeping down a hall in the *Intrepid,* worrying about being attacked by the machines that were supposed to build her future home.

A clang echoed out of the shop ahead.

"I heard it that time," Tanis whispered.

Another metallic sound sliced through the silence behind them.

"Fuck stealth," Tanis said. "Run!"

The corridor was featureless and indefensible; if they were going to be attacked from both ends they would be cut to ribbons. Ahead, the maps showed the corridor terminated in a sorting warehouse filled with various semi-autonomous robots, but at least it offered some cover.

The screech of metal on metal came from all around and Tanis spread her nanocloud further ahead. And not a moment too soon—a molecular welder moved into view from an angle they would have missed in their mad dash.

"Duck!" Tanis hit the deck a moment before Joe as a plasma beam shot over their heads. She rolled onto her shoulder and sent an EM pulse at the machine. Sparks flew and the plasma arm swung wildly, slicing through a part of the deck before finally going dead.

She swung her head to see Joe firing bursts at a series of light hauler mechs coming out of an adjacent shop. They crashed to the ground, but more of their brethren were assembling in the shadows.

Without another word, they both got back to their feet and picked up the pace. The sorting depot was only a hundred meters away. Tanis checked on her AI to see that Angela was launching exploratory probes to attempt a signal intercept on whatever was controlling the robots.

<*Looks like it's our unfriendly neighborhood virus-slinging AI.*>

<*It sure seems to know what it's doing,*> Tanis replied.

<*It may on a grand scale, but this sort of thing is my specialty.*>

Battling rogue AI was one of the reasons she and Angela had been paired to begin with, their skills suited one another quite well.

Several of the robots moved into the corridor ahead of them but then turned back once under Angela's control. As they dashed by, Tanis could see Angela's bots doing battle with those under control of the rogue AI.

<*Nice save,*> Tanis thanked her friend.

<*Say it, you'd be lost without me.*>

<*It goes without saying. Are you jealous of Joe or something?*> Tanis smiled in her mind.

Moments later, Tanis and Joe burst into the sorting depot. They skidded to a halt as Tanis let her nano probes fly high to get a good view of their surroundings.

"Looks like it's powered down." Joe looked around, the tone in his voice indicating he wasn't too certain of his words.

"Just like those machine shops, eh?" Tanis said.

"Let's hope it's not *just* like them."

Tanis led the way while Joe kept an eye on the depot entrance, his rifle ready to send an EM pulse into the first non-sentient creature to appear.

<*I've got them bottled up,*> Angela said over the private net between the three of them. <*But the general shipnet is down here and I'm losing signal fidelity with all these machines around. In two minutes or so they'll be free again.*>

"Then let's not be here in two minutes," Joe said.

"Seems logical to me."

Their HUD overlays updated with a new route when they entered the depot. It led them past silent machines and autonomous haulers, all the while they were praying Angela would be able to suppress activation of these robots.

<*I've got better plans than that.*>

As they passed, a few of the haulers stirred to life. The motion startled the pair at first, but Angela showed her plan on their virtual space. She would leave the haulers on pre-programmed paths and mission sets, and then fry their wireless receivers. It would effectively make them unhackable as well as provide a barrier to pursuers.

"Someone is going to hate us later when they have to clear up the mess that'll make," Joe chuckled.

"I'd pay to see the expression on their faces." Tanis smiled.

She rounded a suspension field sorter and found herself face-to-face with a closed door.

"That doesn't look good," Joe said.

"No power, no entrance." Tanis prodded the access panel.

"Aren't these things supposed to have manual overrides for when the power's out?" Joe looked around for a manual pump.

<*Not in here,*> Angela said.

"Well that's an annoying oversight." Joe stepped back and looked around. "There's a catwalk up there. The map shows exits off it."

"Then that's where we're going," Tanis said.

They started climbing a seven-meter-tall crane that rose near to the catwalk. It made the skin on the back of Tanis's neck crawl as she imagined the clear shots anything at the shop's entrance would have of her and Joe.

As if she were prophetic, the sounds of robotic combat down the corridor ceased and was replaced by the echoes of equipment rumbling over the decking.

"Move it, Commander. We're gonna have visitors."

"You mind if I at least make sure I don't fall?" Joe asked. He was at the end of the crane, getting ready to jump.

Tanis bit back another admonishment for haste as Joe leapt across three meters of open air. It looked like he wasn't going to make it, but he managed to hook an arm around the lowest bar in the railing.

Letting out the breath she hadn't been aware she was holding, Tanis ran up the last two meters of the crane and leapt across the space, landing on the top railing.

"Now who's the show-off?" Joe said through gritted teeth as he hung on. "Mind lending me a hand, Miss Monkey?"

Tanis leaned down and clasped Joe's outstretched arm, pulling him up and over the railing.

"More with the showing off!" He smiled, while rubbing his forearm where it had caught the weight of his body.

"I have this amazing new prosthetic arm, I may as well use it." Tanis grinned and then pointed toward an open doorway. "There's our way out of this mess."

They sprinted down the catwalk as the machine shop robots rumbled into the depot. Angela's haulers moved forward to block them, but even with the interference, several of the plasma beams came far too close for comfort.

Tanis dove through the door, and Joe slammed it shut behind them, pulling his hands away as several parts of the panel glowed white-hot from plasma impacts. He gave Tanis a hand and pulled her up.

"So it looks like we just added a half a klick to our trip." Tanis sighed.

"Damn evil AI," Joe grunted. "They're always messing things up. We've only got five hours to get to the *Excelsior* and prep it, and there are still three klicks of stars-know-what between us and there."

"Let's get a move on, then," Tanis said.

18:05 *hours to Intrepid escape maneuver*
4:47 hours to end of Excelsior mission launch window

Captain Andrews surveyed the bridge. His primary crew sat at their duty stations, and everyone was briefed on the status of the ship and the plan. Commander Ouri reported in that Commander Brandt and two platoons were out of stasis.

<*We had some contacts with the enemy, but we're on the maglev, headed to node eleven,*> Ouri said.

<*Good to hear, Commander. Keep me apprised of your progress,*> Andrews replied.

He cut the connection and checked on Amy Lee's status. She had a group of security officers clearing out servitors surrounding the ramscoop. They were making good progress and engineers would be able to diagnose the damage firsthand within the hour.

<*Captain, I've lost contact with Tanis and Joe,*> Terry reported from the bridge's conference room where her team had set up to manage net security.

Andrew's stomach fell. <*Do we know why? Were they under fire?*>

<*They've been under fire almost constantly for the last twenty minutes, but I think they've entered an area where the wireless feeds are down.*>

<*There are more places without net than with,*> the captain replied. <*Do what you can; we need to know soon if we have to send a second team.*>

He would give her another hour. Tanis had been through far worse and come out unscathed. However, she had also come out very scathed from time to time. He still remembered seeing her return from her encounter with Trent on Mars 1, her left arm and a fair bit of her upper torso missing. Later, when she had merged her mind with the ship and the fighters to stave off an attack, she had nearly died but somehow pulled through. She would make it through whatever was going on down below.

<*Abby, how are things progressing with the engine connection,*> he asked the chief engineer over the Link.

He could imagine her grunt of annoyance at the interruption. <*It's going slower now that you are bothering me. We're having trouble, but nothing we can't fix. If that damned rogue AI in node eleven could be shut down, we'd be doing a whole hell of a lot better.*>

<*Ouri is taking a team to deal with it,*> Captain Andrews replied.

<*What, with guns?*> Andrews could sense her panic.

<*We need to shut it down; chances are it will have defenses.*>

<*We can't have node eleven damaged, with the issues elsewhere we need it to regulate the particle accelerator.*> Abby sounded frustrated, like she was being pulled in a dozen directions. Andrews knew just how she felt.

<*What do you propose?*>

<*Send Earnest with her, you just make sure he doesn't get a scratch on him. How are Tanis and Joe doing? Have they finished prepping the* Excelsior *yet?*>

<*No, we lost contact with them a few minutes ago.*> Andrews ran a hand through his hair. If things kept up it would be white before long.

<*You're just full of great news.*>

<*They're in a dead spot on the shipnet. I expect them to be through it soon, but they've been in pretty constant combat for the last hour.*>

<*She better not be busting up my ship!*>

<*Abby, it will take a little bit more than Tanis with an EM gun to bust up the* Intrepid.>

This time she did give her grunt of annoyance over the connection. <*I don't know about that. The girl has a knack.*>

17:44 *hours to Intrepid escape maneuver*
4:26 hours to end of Excelsior mission launch window

Commander Ouri rode the dorsal maglev with two platoons from the *Intrepid's* 1st Battalion's Bravo Company and a fireteam of FROD Marines from Charlie Company acting as Earnest's bodyguards.

"Node eleven is seven levels down in Engine," Commander Brandt, the CO of B Company said. "The maglev doesn't go that close to it, but I plan to get off here anyway." She pointed to a small station one level in.

<*That seems sound,*> Casey, the company's AI, agreed.

"Agreed," Ouri said. "There's bound to be resistance, and maglev tubes are no place for a fight."

Ouri couldn't help but wonder what Tanis would do. Tactics and training were well and good, but Tanis always seemed to do things her own way and get superior results.

At least the colonel had the foresight to form many of the colonists with military background into a division. The regular GSS ship security types were good at policing and manning guard points, but fighting rogue AI in a powerless starship was a different story.

Getting to Bravo Company had been a challenge in and of itself. No military units had been in stasis chambers still under Bob's control, and she had ventured on her own into one of the dark areas to bring Commander Brandt's company out.

Ouri didn't think of herself as someone who was easily scared, but moving through those dark corridors with nothing but her meager IR and a hand-light tested her resolve more than she cared to admit.

She had only encountered one rogue servitor and took it out on her way to the company's stasis chamber. Once she had brought the soldiers out of stasis, she felt relief—as much for their protection as against the quiet and dark of the ship's empty corridors.

The barracks had auxiliary power and the soldiers had suited up in light armor. Ouri and Brandt had conferred and sent first platoon to protect Abby and her engineers while platoons two and three had the task of securing node eleven and stopping the rogue AI.

"What about the plasma conduits through that path?" Lieutenant Arin asked as she studied the train's holo display. "If the RAI breaches them, we'll have nowhere to hide."

"I doubt that's likely. Judging by where the impellers are, they don't have power—the lines should be clear," Brandt said.

Commander Brandt was a slight woman with thin, almost pixie-like features. Ouri wasn't alone in this assessment, she had heard several soldiers refer to her as "the Pix", something Ouri was certain no one had ever called her to her face.

"Commander, I don't see how you can be sure—" Lieutenant Smith began to object but received a cold stare from the smaller woman.

"Face the possible threat of plasma on the ship, or the certainty of it on the surface of that star out there. Your pick."

Ouri wasn't certain if it was the best team-building response, but time was of the essence. "Casey, send the route to the platoon sergeants; they're going to need to arrange their teams."

Commander Brandt cast Ouri an unreadable look. Though they both shared the same rank, Ouri was GSS and her oak leaf put her above the other woman's bars. However, the fact that TSF didn't regard the civilian GSS ranks as legitimate didn't help her credibility.

"Make it happen, Casey." Brandt's glower turned to an expression of concern as the train suddenly lost power and slowed to a halt.

"Damn, we're still a klick from Engine," Brandt said.

"Looks like we're not taking the AI by surprise," Earnest said, shaking his head.

Brandt gave her orders and several fireteams pried the doors open and secured positions outside the train.

<It's a vomit comet out here,> one of the sergeants reported. *<The rail's gravity only covers about four feet, and then you're getting tiny amounts from the particle accelerator and that's in waves.>*

The information went out on the combat net and the soldiers and Marines prepared for 0*g* maneuvers.

Ouri stepped out from the train. As expected, the maglev tube was too narrow and provided no cover. A fireteam from second platoon was pulling open a hatch that would lead to the access tunnels that ran alongside the particle accelerator.

Because the twenty-five-kilometer-long particle accelerator brought whatever the ramscoop collected to relativistic speeds, gravitational waves were produced. When it was fully operational, it provided gravity for much of the crew areas of the ship. At present, the minute gravity it offered was more problematic than helpful.

Ouri and Brandt worked up a plan with the platoon leaders and determined that platoon three would take access tunnels on the starboard side of the ship and second platoon would stay portside. Earnest and his Marines, as well as the company HQ elements, would proceed with second platoon.

Ouri checked her rifle's load-out and loosened her pistol in its holster. Even though she was not an active combat participant in the platoon, she expected to be using her weapons.

The drop through the hatch caused an unpleasant lurch in her stomach as her organs shifted in 0*g*. Ouri still remembered the first time when she realized that being without gravity created a constant "drop" feeling, like being in a fast moving elevator or a roller coaster the entire time. It took a lot of the fun out of low gravity work.

Earnest and his guards took up position next to Ouri as the platoon worked its way down a darkened corridor.

"This certainly makes things a bit more interesting, doesn't it?"

Ouri looked at the engineer, surprised to see that he was grinning.

"That's a curse if I ever heard one," she replied.

"Yes, yes, but an interesting one," he winked. "I almost feel better. I was waiting for the other shoe to drop, and now, at least it finally has."

"Isn't the ship severely damaged? We must be facing a serious delay in reaching New Eden."

Earnest nodded. "However, I'll get the opportunity to fix it out here with limited resources. Now that's a challenge!"

One of the Marines was shaking his head ruefully and Ouri had to shrug and put it from her mind. The only thing that mattered right now was eliminating the rogue AI and regaining full control of the ship.

"Stay sharp," Staff Sergeant Turin said. "Scan shows motion ahead."

<Platoon three is engaged with the enemy,> Casey reported. *<Two casualties, but they are making progress.>*

As if to punctuate the AI's message, a particle beam lanced over Ouri's head and she hit the deck. The Marines forced Earnest down and took positions around him, weapons at the ready.

"Give me blanketing fields of fire on that location!" a sergeant yelled. "Squad three, fall back to that cross-corridor and see if you can flank."

"Contact rear!" one of the Marines called out.

Ouri looked back and saw the shapes of servitors behind them. They were trapped in a narrow corridor with only a few conduits for protection.

The platoon's engineers were rapidly setting up stasis shields that were able to stop the particle beams, though they reduced the Marines' firing options.

Ouri took up a position to assist the Marines in holding the rear of the formation. Her ship's security pulse rifle wasn't as effective as the Marines', but she had brought some of her riot control gear and clipped to her belt were three EMP webs.

She signaled her intent to the leader of the fireteam and lobbed the ball at the servitors. It bounced once and then sprayed a web over the robots. They were not hardened for battle and the web knocked them offline.

The soldiers in squad three saw the opening and dashed back down the hall to a cross corridor. Ouri's ship map showed that they would be able to flank the servitors attacking the front of the formation in roughly four minutes.

As she was checking the maps, there was an explosion and a part of the ceiling fell near her.

<Casey, what on Earth are they firing? How do servitors pose this much of a risk?>

<It would appear that several of the units ahead of us have plasma cutters that have been adapted into plasma throwers.>

"Sweet gods…" she whispered while watching plasma splash across a stasis shield.

17:35 *hours to Intrepid escape maneuver*
4:15 hours to end of Excelsior mission launch window

Security drones had Tanis and Joe pinned down. The hovering robots were proving to be a far more effective foe than the welders and haulers had been.

Joe was across the corridor from Tanis, both were crouched behind a series of shafts that rose vertically through the deck. The shafts offered scant cover from the focused laser beams the security drones fired. Tanis's armor could take a few hits, but there were over two dozen of the drones out there—more than enough to overload its diffusion abilities.

"I really don't get why some AI is giving Bob so much trouble," Joe said as he ducked behind his cover—their IR vision showing a string of heated air where his head had been a moment before.

"Probably because he's doing his damnedest to get control of the whole ship from just one node. I don't think he, or the ship, was designed to work like that."

Tanis crouched low and darted into the open and back again, drawing fire. Joe used the opportunity to take out the drone that fired on him previously. The EM pulse hit the hovering bot and it fell to the deck in a shower of sparks.

"One down, what? Twenty more to go?"

"Something like that," Tanis said. "I can't get a good read; they have ionized fields that are blocking the nano. Angela can't get a probe past it to take them over. Even if she did, these things have good internal defenses. It would take an army of nano to knock 'em down."

"Sure would be nice if we had some of that pico tech," Joe said.

"I'd rather not be the first to try it out in combat conditions."

Joe laughed and took his turn drawing fire while Tanis hit two bots in quick succession.

"They're wising up," Joe said. "Nearly got me again."

"We need a new tactic."

"We need to bring pulse grenades next time."

Tanis laughed. It felt good to be back in the thick of it with Joe. They made an effective team as they fell into their old, comfortable place. She really liked that place.

"Then we need to improvise," Tanis said. They were still out of contact with the shipnet and neither had schematics for this section of the *Intrepid*. There had to be something in one of these conduits that could help.

<Any chance you could try to extrapolate with some general probes?> Tanis asked Angela.

<*Couldn't hurt.*> Angela's response was nonchalant.

Tanis suspected that her AI couldn't even be bothered to get worked up about life and death situations anymore.

<*Well, all things considered, a few automaton drones aren't much of a match for the pair of us. We could take them out with you naked only holding a plastic spoon.*>

<*Was that actual humor?*> Tanis asked.

<*I can do humor. I can do it even better when it's at your expense.*>

Tanis decided not to extend the conversation and held back her reply. It was nearly impossible to win a battle of acerbic wit with Angela. It was likely the AI spent the hours Tanis slept just thinking of comebacks and comments.

"So what's the plan?" Joe asked as he sprayed EM pulses at random.

"Angela's got a possible conduit carrying particulate matter for nano assembly in the fourth vertical conduit down on your side."

"Particulate matter? Isn't that engineering speak for explosive?"

"Samples indicate it could be aluminum oxide."

Joe paled. "Maybe we shouldn't be shooting at those things."

Tanis knew what he meant; few things were as frightening as a burning cloud of metal in an enclosed space.

"Everything is offline, it's not pressurized."

Joe's glance indicated how that knowledge failed to encourage him.

"EM isn't going to do the trick. I'm going to fire a focused pulse blast and see if I can crack it. You be ready to fry one of those things the moment the spray comes out," Tanis said.

Joe nodded, they were committed to this course of action and the only real option was to make it work.

Tanis used nano probes to get a good view of the pipe she had to hit. She held her gun out around her cover, using remote sighting to line it up with the target. A nod to Joe and she let loose several shots. On the third shaped pulse impact, the pipe fractured and a cloud of aluminum filled the air.

The security drones were surrounded by the cloud and Joe took his shot at the closest bot. It exploded and ignited the powder. Joe's light armor wouldn't provide enough protection, but Tanis was ready. She leapt across the corridor the moment his finger pulled the trigger and landed astride him, shielding his body with hers.

The explosion was deafening and the pressure wave forced her body against his. Her armor locked up, protecting her—and, by extension, him—from the brunt of it. In a moment it was gone, having blown itself out.

"Wow, you are really heavy," Joe grunted.

Tanis sat up on her knees. "Is that any way to speak to a lady?"

Joe delivered one of his patented grins. "I know my lady isn't vain, she can take it."

Tanis laughed and stood, offering him a hand.

"Maybe I'm vain and you don't know it."

Joe glanced at her matte grey flow-armor. "You could make that any color or pattern you want and you picked matte grey."

Tanis shrugged. "It blends in with the ship down here."

Joe laughed and gave her a light peck on the cheek. "Yes, incredibly vain."

They walked through the remains of the corridor. The bulkheads had buckled and most of the pipes were cracked.

"Effective," Joe said.

"Appears to have been. Abby is going to kill us."

Joe kicked the remains of one of the drones. "Good thing those weren't hardened units."

Tanis nodded. "We're down to four hours. Based on the last reported readiness, it's going to take three to get the *Excelsior* ready."

"We can do it in two if we have to, we may just miss something we really wish we had later," Joe said.

"Like I said, three hours."

Tanis moved past the destroyed security drones and sent her nano scouting ahead. She followed slowly, leery of another attack.

"You have no sense of adventure," Joe grinned at Tanis as he caught up.

<*Are you kidding?*> Angela asked.

Joe laughed. "Yeah, you're right. I forgot who I was talking to for a moment there."

Tanis gave him a sour look. "I have a sense of adventure, but it's not like I go seeking trouble out."

Joe's laughter turned into coughing and Angela sent a series of incredulous faces over the private net.

"I'm serious," Tanis said. "I just seem to be around when trouble shows up."

"What about on the *Steel Dawn III* when you ran toward the nuclear bomb and not away from it?" Joe asked.

Tanis shrugged. "Someone had to take it out."

<*And when those mercs tried to take the VIPs hostage at that first ball?*> Angela added her example.

"I was there in the hall when they attacked."

"I seem to recall you going up into a crawl space to cut a plasma line. Then you jumped down with nothing more than a pulse rifle and your dress above your hips not three meters from the mercs."

Tanis shrugged as they rounded a corner into a wider, but still dark and net-less corridor. Her nano ranged far ahead, confirming the coast was clear, and she picked up the pace. "Seemed like the best course of action at the time."

<*We can't forget the mad rush to flush out those other mercs in the freighters.*>

"That was classic Tanis." Joe nodded. "Only surpassed by our 'let's be bait' mission on Mars 1."

"OK, so maybe I don't actively avoid trouble." Tanis shrugged.

<*We were just getting warmed up.*>

"If memory serves, we were talking about the timeline, and the prep work for the ship." Tanis gave Joe a somewhat annoyed look and sent a quelling thought to Angela.

Joe assumed a serious look, but a smile still played at the corners of his mouth. "Yeah, so we will probably need to fuel the ship up. Bob was going to see if he would be able to make a connection to the bay on a highband channel. Docking control systems require pretty secure connections and he can't pass the encryption commands on the lowband wireless."

"What if there's no power?" Tanis asked as they turned into another powerless corridor.

"Docks can generate their own local power. Need it in case of emergency."

"How thoughtful."

Joe laughed. "Yeah, I guess it is fortuitous. Fueling the *Excelsior* could take an hour, depending on the pump specs; we don't have access to which systems are in that bay right now. Then there's some equipment checks we'll need to do, system initialization processes, supply loading, that sort of thing."

"It occurs to me," Tanis said, "that with all these other ships onboard, couldn't we use them to help alter our trajectory?"

Joe gave Tanis a quizzical look.

"What?"

"You didn't look at the proposal stream?" Joe asked.

Tanis had to admit normally she would have looked at every solution proposal that was postulated for a scenario. This time she had ignored them all, fixated on the one that would put her on a ship alone with Joe for several days.

"Uh, not all of them, no," she replied.

"Huh…that's unlike you."

<He doesn't know the half of it.>

Tanis shrugged and Joe continued. "It was determined that, with the local gravity fields, the amount of force we'd have to use would cause too much structural stress. Normally, with all systems online that sort of thing could be compensated for, but as things sit it would severely damage the ship."

"I guess that makes sense," Tanis agreed. "Be nice if we had one of those 'tractor beams' they have in the science fiction stories."

Joe grinned. "We may as well wish for 'warp drive' while we're at it."

Tanis laughed. "Or 'transporters'."

A minute later, the nano reported back that it had reached the docking bay with no further signs of aberrant technology. Even better, the bay had power and access to the general shipnet. Tanis used the Link through her string of nano and reported in to the bridge.

<We're about three hundred meters from the bay, sir. A bit behind, but we'll make it out on schedule.>

Captain Andrews' mental tone conveyed a momentary surprise and then deep relief. *<Lieutenant Colonel, you have no idea how glad we are to hear from you. You've been out of comm reach for over an hour.>*

<You don't need to tell me, sir. This ship is one big place when you're hoofing it as well as fighting random construction equipment.>

<Are you and the commander all right?>

<Right as rain, sir.>

<Good to hear from you, though. Oh, thanks.> The captain had received Tanis's full report on the journey thus far, including a detailed accounting of the fights with damage estimations. *<Good job, thanks for not breaking anything too much.>*

<Just doing my best. How are things going with our uninvited guest and the engines?>

<Ok, though Ouri and Brandt haven't secured the RAI yet.>

<So, OK, relatively speaking.>

The captain laughed. *<Yes, relatively speaking.>*

<Squad three, where the fuck are you?> Commander Brandt swore over the combat net.

<Nearly there, we're taking positions now.>

Ouri surveyed the platoon. At least four soldiers were down and the stasis shields were showing signs of giving out. Judicial use of EMP grenades had evened the odds, but the platoon was still pinned down.

<DO IT!> Squad three's sergeant yelled and the sounds of withering slug fire tore through the hall. Squad one took the opportunity to rush the servitors and less than ten seconds later it was over.

"Good work, three," Brandt said. "Squad two, I want you to send your runners for medical attention and stay here with the wounded."

The commander turned to the rest of the platoon. "What are you waiting for? Get moving!"

The platoon encountered a few more servitors, but was able to quickly dispatch them. Ten minutes later, they arrived at a broad cross corridor that created a square with a maglev station, a series of shops, and the entrance for the node where the rogue AI was holed up.

"Feels so wrong without any people," one of the soldiers whispered before his sergeant told him to shut up.

Ouri couldn't help but agree. She had been through this section of the ship a few times and had spent some time in the shops strung along this corridor. It had always been bustling, packed with people. The silence itself was almost a physical threat.

Brandt linked second platoon's command net with platoon three's and laid out a plan. Ouri saw that platoon three had encountered more servitors, but none lobbing plasma. They had only suffered two casualties.

<The entrance to the node the RAI is lodged in is between our positions, about two hundred meters from us, and one hundred from you.> Brandt addressed her lieutenants and platoon sergeants.

As the officer in charge, Ouri would have to approve the plan, but she doubted that she'd have anything to offer that Brandt hadn't thought of.

<I'm expecting some heavy resistance down this corridor. The node has some serious firepower protecting it and I'd be surprised if we don't encounter a fair number of unfriendlies out there as well. I want platoon three to go in first and push hard. There are a number of shops on your end that should provide good cover. Hole up in those about twenty meters from the node entrance, or as close as you can make it. Once you have them distracted we'll advance down the corridor and attack any positions that are exposed to us.

Keep in mind that the node turrets and security drones will be hardened, so your EMP weaponry will have no effect on them. Your only route with them is kinetic force, but we can't damage the entrance to the node or the systems inside. Surgical shots only.>

The lieutenants and platoon sergeants proposed some specific tactics which Brandt accepted before glancing at Ouri. *<Do you approve, Commander?>*

<Approved,> Ouri replied.

<Command approval noted.> Casey logged the event in the company's logs.

Platoon three began its advance, and Ouri watched the action on the command net, impressed that the soldiers worked so well together considering that they had only trained as a unit for a few weeks before the *Intrepid* left Sol.

The platoon made it to within thirty meters of the entrance to the RAI's node and reported that they could advance no further without suffering casualties. Brandt gave the command and squad one moved out into the corridor where they took positions behind several curved bulkheads.

Squad one was made up of sniper teams who took low positions in the corridor behind their portable stasis shields and searched for targets in the firefight between platoon three and the node's security forces.

<*Engage.*> Brandt gave the order over the command net and the sharpshooters let fly with thirteen-millimeter rounds from ballistic rifles.

"Abby would have kittens," Earnest whispered near Ouri.

"Not a lot of choice," she replied. "Kinetics are the only thing we can hit them with, short of explosives."

"Oh, I understand," Earnest smiled. "She would, too, but she'd still have kittens."

The snipers were changing positions—it would not take more than one or two shots for the security drones to locate them. However, there were six fewer security drones than there were mere seconds earlier.

Platoon three held its position while squads three and four advanced down the corridor under the cover of the sharpshooters' fire. Once they had taken cover, squad one moved past their positions. The process repeated until second platoon was within fifty meters of the RAI's node.

<*I have movement to port of our position,*> Casey reported over the command net.

Moments later, a particle beam shot from the hall behind them into one of the sharpshooters.

Brandt had pulled the sergeants and lieutenant in the company HQ to augment the fallen Marines from the previous engagement. Ouri, Earnest, and the four Marines were all who remained in the command position. Ouri looked at the Marines and nodded. "On me."

Trying not to think about what she was doing, Ouri unslung her kinetic rifle and activated her targeting computer. In one quick motion, she darted across the corridor while one of the Marines provided cover. She slid into the darkened entrance of a shop and searched for heat signatures in the corridor.

Another particle beam lanced out from the darkness and hit the deck where a sharpshooter had been just a moment before. Ouri tracked the shot and fired a series of rounds at the beam's origin.

Two Marines slid into the entryway behind her and in seconds added their fire to hers. An explosion and a shower of sparks provided confirmation that their bullets had found a target.

Brandt sent orders to the sharpshooters, instructing them to advance down the corridor—putting more distance between them and the unknowns behind their position. Ouri sent a remote probe down the corridor searching for more adversaries, silently wishing that she had the ability to generate nano on demand like Tanis did.

The probe scanned the corridor as it went, eventually coming across the remains of a security drone that had been pulverized by Ouri and the Marines. It proceeded another ten meters and sent an alert as it flagged two more security drones advancing down the corridor.

Ouri sent the data stream to the Marines and once the security drones were in range they opened fire. A few particle beams lanced out in their direction but none hit, and a minute later the drones were down.

"Not sure why they bother making things like that," one of the Marines grunted. "They're not good for much more than target practice."

"We didn't expect a war on the ship," Earnest said as he, Brandt, and the final Marine crossed the corridor to Ouri's position.

Ouri laughed, "I'm not sure why not. I think there have been wars that were safer than being on the *Intrepid*."

"This?" one of the Marine's asked. "This is a walk in the park. Though you have a steady shot there, Commander, even if you are GSS."

"Shut up and cover our backs," Brandt barked back at the soldiers. "Ouri, they've cleared the entrance, let's get in that node and shut it down."

Ouri couldn't help but notice that there was a touch more respect in Brandt's tone. Not much, but a touch.

Earnest ran a hand through his hair as they walked down the corridor and muttered a stream of concerns under his breath. At the entrance, two Marine techs were breaching the doors.

"Allow me," Earnest said and passed his hand over the physical override panel. The access panel glowed green and the door slid open. The techs stood aside and a squad of Marines pushed past Earnest into the node.

"No need," he said, "my physical command code will have overridden the node's internal securi—" His statement was cut short by the sharp crack of several ballistic rifles.

Ouri pulled him back from the entrance, covering his body with hers.

"Report!" Brandt called in.

"All clear," one of the Marines called back.

"Oh shit…" another gasped.

"Commanders, you better get in here."

Ouri stepped in, Earnest and Brandt behind her. The Marines were standing on the right side of the node staring up at something hanging from a data conduit. As Ouri rounded the corner, she realized it was Amanda, her wrists chained to the conduit with several data cables jacked into the base of her skull.

Her mouth was twisted in a rictus of pain as she gasped, "About time. Please, get me down from here…"

Ouri signaled the Marines who stood on the railing and cut the chains with small plasma torches. They caught Amanda as she fell and Earnest bent over her, examining the cables plugged into her.

"So this is how the rogue AI was able to get control of so many systems," he said. "He used her access to the entire ship. Really quite clever."

"I'm so sorry," Amanda whispered. "I tried to stop it, but it just pulled what it needed from my mind. I could see it attacking you and trying to keep the ship falling into the star. It's insane!"

Ouri had heard of insane AI, but only as rumor. How Collins had managed to corral an insane AI and get it on the ship boggled the mind.

Earnest brushed the sweat-soaked synthetic hair back from Amanda's forehead. "Don't worry; I'll have you freed from this thing in a moment.

<You can't have her! She's mine! She promised I could keep her!> the AI screamed across the local net.

Earnest looked at Amanda with a puzzled expression. "You promised it could keep you?"

"I did no such thing, I don't know what it is talking about," Amanda rasped, concern filling her features.

Ouri saw Earnest pull out several small tools from a pouch and detected a nano-swarm releasing from him.

"Just another moment," he muttered and then popped the connectors from the back of Amanda's head.

"Oh, thank my blessed mother!" she gasped and then passed out.

<*Bob, you should be able to control this node again,*> Earnest sent over the shipnet.

In an instant, Bob's presence swelled into the local net and, with a snap, the node shut off.

<*It is done,*> Bob said. <*Begin the reinitialization process for this node and bring Amanda to me.*>

17:31 *hours to Intrepid escape maneuver*
4:11 hours to end of Excelsior mission launch window

Dock A1 was huge, even by the *Intrepid*'s standards.

It held a large assortment of ships, from a pair of thousand meter cruisers, to the heavy lifters (of which the *Excelsior* was the largest), down to smaller tugs and shuttles. Overall, there were more than thirty ships in the bay, all brand new and ready to build a colony.

"Look at that thing," Tanis said as they approached the lifter in its bay. "It's all engine."

"It is designed to move up to B2-12 planetary objects."

Tanis whistled. "That's what, nearly the size of Mercury, isn't it?"

"Yeah, mind you, it will move those rather slowly. For what we need, it will do perfectly. We'll be able to boost a couple billion tons up to 0.10*c*." Joe paused and looked at Tanis. "Last chance to opt out, it's going to be dangerous"

"I know that, Joe. I'm pretty used to dangerous. Remember your little bit with Angela back there?"

"This is a different kind of dangerous. You're used to scenarios where you have control. Here you'll have no control. If things go bad, there will be nothing you can do."

"You know," Tanis smiled at Joe, "you'd be surprised how often you can manage to affect the outcome of a bad situation if you put your mind to it."

Tanis paused, but Joe didn't say anything, just giving her one of his introspective stares. She resolved to say what was on her mind, to simply be straightforward about her feelings.

"Like today…it hit me…I love you. Not that I just love you, but that I really *love* you. I know, it's crazy. Me, in love with a vac jockey, but it's true." The words spilled out, she knew it sounded lame; wished it could have sounded as good as the feeling that was inside of her.

It took a moment for Joe to react. He looked stunned, then surprised, then a slow smile spread across his face. He pulled her close and crushed her in his arms before loosening his hold, gently pressing his body against hers.

"It was earlier, after Collins got away," she said quietly. "When you came down the corridor and I realized that I didn't care what happened, as long as you—"

Her words cut off as his lips covered hers. It was soft at first, just a brushing that froze her for a moment before she responded. Tanis breathed deeply and felt herself melt into him. The intensity increased and moments later their tongues were exploring each other's mouths and hands were stroking each other's bodies.

<*Uh…normally I go elsewhere when this sort of thing happens, but we do have to get the* Excelsior *ready to fly. There'll be plenty of time for hanky panky once we're underway,*> Angela interrupted.

Tanis stopped and moved her head back so she could see Joe's light brown eyes. "She does have a point. We do have work to do."

14:41 *hours to Intrepid escape maneuver*
1:22 hours to end of Excelsior mission launch window

Joe handled the fueling of the ship, as well as making certain it was equipped with all the detection and grappling systems they needed to catch their prey in the darkness on the edge of the system. Tanis worked through the checklists, ensuring that supplies were stocked, life support had the appropriate raw materials, and that there would be some items to use for extracurricular activities.

<*On schedule, sir,*> she reported to Captain Andrews at T-60 minutes.

<*Things are looking up on our end as well. The rogue AI has been shut down. Your Commander Ouri performed admirably at that task.*>

<*Good on Ouri.*> Tanis was glad Ouri had the chance to prove herself. She had always suspected the botanist turned GSS officer had what it took in combat.

<*She did and performed quite well, as did your makeshift Marine company,*> Captain Andrews replied.

<*Sir, they* **are** *Marines.*>

Andrews chuckled before replying. <*I'll let you get back to it, Lieutenant Colonel. I see you've sync'd your countdown with the bridge. Contact me at T-10.*>

<*Aye, sir.*>

Tanis reclined in one of the three acceleration couches in the cockpit. They were also capable of functioning as stasis pods and she had double checked each one's function in that respect. Things that tested just fine at 1*g* could break quite easily at seventy.

The space was small, but somehow cozy. A holo display rose up over the main bank of controls, which were both holographic as well as physical. Ships like the *Excelsior* were often used and abused. As a result, they had more backup systems than a Cruithne hooker.

Luckily, that was not the case with this ship. It was brand new, also constructed at the Mars Outer Shipyards, just like the *Intrepid*. System logs indicated its only journeys had been a few short shakedown hauls. It had never actually moved any mass other than its own, but all simulations showed that it would have no problem with the task set ahead of it.

A faint murmur in the back of her mind informed Tanis that Angela was conversing with the ship's AI, a somewhat surly individual named Troy. He had been shut down during the trip and hadn't expected to be pulled out of the AI version of stasis for another eighty years. Tanis had been surprised to find an AI on the *Excelsior*, but Joe had informed her that it was common to have high-grade engineering AI on heavy lifters. They were often moving things that could destroy worlds if mistakes were made.

<He's not that bad, you know. He'd just planned out exactly what he'd be doing when he was brought back out of stasis and now he has to re-prioritize,> Angela said.

<You'd think he could be a bit nicer about it, though,> Tanis replied.

<Troy's never been integrated with a human. I don't think he really gets stuff like that very well.>

<That's odd… Aren't all ships' AI required to spend at least a year integrated…that whole, to have humans in you, you must first be in a human thing?> That was one of the reasons Angela had originally been placed with her. There were simply some things AI were not rated to do unless they first spent time in a human.

<Transport ships, yes, but lifters like this, no. They just want the ones who are best at the moving-big-things math. Troy is top of his class when it comes to that,> Angela responded.

<Well, he's going to get a chance to prove that real soon.>

<Are you ready?> Angela asked her.

<As I'll ever be,> Tanis replied. *<Do you think it'll hurt much?>*

Angela's mental tone took on a soft cooing. *<Yes, dear, it will.>*

Tanis nodded and watched as her flow-armor slowly absorbed into her skin. At first it was merely uncomfortable, like the increased pressure on the outside of the skin when entering a lighter atmosphere. Then the pressure began to build and all of Tanis's bones began to ache.

<I've turned off your pain receptors as much as I can without knocking you out,> Angela said.

It got worse, and Tanis ground her teeth, determined not to scream as she felt the flow-armor crawling under her skin, along the outside of her skull.

"I think this hurts more than high-g…" Tanis gasped.

<Almost done,> Angela replied.

A minute later the pain lessened, replaced by an overall throbbing throughout her body.

<It should ease up shortly.>

Tanis lay back in the acceleration couch and wiped the sheen of sweat from her brow. She heard boots in the hall and Joe entered the cockpit.

"Uh…. Why are you naked again?"

Tanis chuckled. "It's my lot in life, apparently. Would you mind grabbing me a shipsuit from my cabin?"

13:34 *hours to Intrepid escape maneuver*

0:25 hours to end of Excelsior mission launch window

<T-minus ten minutes, sir.> Tanis reported in to the bridge. Joe had completed the fueling and ensured all the grapples and webs were in place. Supplies were stocked, and all of the other hundreds of things on the checklists had been examined by both human and AI.

They were ready.

<Very good, Lieutenant Colonel,> the captain's voice was as smooth and calm as ever. Tanis had never seen the man lose control once. Even now, falling into a star, he sounded perfectly composed. *<Ensign Teer.>*

Captain Andrews had Linked the *Excelsior* with the bridge net.

<Aye, sir. Opening outer bay doors.>

Tanis switched the holo display to show the rear view. The *Excelsior* was facing into the *Intrepid* and would be backed out on magnetic rails. From there, maneuvering thrusters would rotate the ship and ease them away from the *Intrepid.* Once they had reached a safe distance, the antimatter engines would ignite and the *Excelsior* would begin its journey.

<Confirming outer bay doors opening. ES shield showing green,> Joe reported from his station.

<Aye, ES Shield reports green.>

Tanis thought she could detect the slightest strain in Ensign Teer's mental tones. She couldn't blame the woman. Now that the doors were open, the view was filled with the angry red glow of Estrella de la Muerte. Suddenly the name that was so funny before didn't seem quite as amusing. The possibility that she would die under the light of this dim red star was not lost on Tanis.

"You know, we look at stars all the time, but this is only the second one I've seen up close. Hopefully it's not the last," Joe echoed Tanis's thoughts.

She looked over at him, his face betraying none of the uncertainty of his voice as his eyes flicked over the displays and then came to rest on her. They stared at one another for a moment, then Joe stretched out his hand and Tanis took it in hers.

"I love you."

"I love you, too."

They got lost in one another's eyes as the ship slid to the edge of the ES shield on the magnetic rails, the red glow of the star filling the cabin.

"I know I've seen vids of them, but I never really expected a red dwarf to be so…red," Tanis said.

<What were you expecting?> Angela asked over the *Excelsior*'s general shipnet.

"I guess that's what Jupiter will look like after they light it up the rest of the way," Joe said.

<Dimmer, I'd imagine,> Troy joined the conversation.

"I'd hope so," Tanis said. "It would make everything on the terraformed worlds look like it was covered in blood."

<They'd have to re-bio the plants, too. Photosynthesis is brown under a red star's light,> Angela added.

<T-minus sixty seconds,> Ensign Teer's voice came over the Link.

<Abby just reported in. Bob has full control of the engines and they even have the backup LF scoop emitter online. By repulsing off that sunspot we'll be able to match plan A1 and achieve breakaway as projected. We should be able to maintain the planned vector and meet you at point

B2.> Captain Andrews sounded just a little pleased—enough to confirm Tanis's suspicion about his previous stoicism.

<*Good to hear,*> Tanis said.

<*Good luck,*> Priscilla said privately to Tanis. <*I hope you take this time alone to do what you should have done some time ago.*>

Tanis laughed to herself. <*I think this enforced celibacy is going to your head. But, yes, I have every intention of satisfying that little need.*>

<*Good.*>

The *Excelsior* maneuvered away from the *Intrepid* by thruster until the colony ship was no longer in line with the heavy lifter's engine wash. During the process, Angela shut down and Tanis set her couch to fully recline before turning to Joe.

"I'm ready, good night."

A cover slid over the pod and the stasis field snapped into place.

* * * * *

"Good luck," Joe whispered to Tanis as he prepared the *Excelsior* for its first burn. The engines began their initialization process; hydrogen and anti-hydrogen readied to mix and annihilate one another. He kept one eye on the status indicators while getting comfortable on his couch and beginning his physiological alterations in preparation for extreme *g*.

As a pilot, Joe was physically altered in several ways to protect him from the extremes of spaceflight. Structural supports interlaced his brain with nano netting to hold it in place during rapid course alterations. His bones were also reinforced with carbon nanotubes, which lessened the risk of fractures being caused by normal movements under high *g*.

Within his skin—indeed, most of the soft tissue in his body—a latticework of liquid crystal began to harden, creating a rigid structure that would keep his body from simply flattening when the *Excelsior* boosted at 70*g*. Even the walls of his body's cells hardened, preparing for the impending pressure.

Joe's brain turned off pain receptors; it was going to hurt, there were no two ways about it. However, he needed to be able to function; there was no point in his body telling his brain that 70*g*s were excruciating, he already knew that.

<*Engine status is green,*> Troy said.

<*Commence ignition,*> Joe responded.

He looked down at Tanis in her pod and wished that she could experience what he did when flying. It wasn't that she was bad behind the flight controls, Tanis just wasn't a pilot in the sense that she lived for it. Joe lived for it. There was nothing like feeling the thrust of a ship thrum through his body, threading obstacles and arcing around worlds. Gravity and radiation were his wind and rain, forces he floated on and soared through.

Tanis probably felt the same about him when it came to a pitched firefight. She normally acted cool and reserved, but he had seen that primal grin on her face when engaged in battle. He'd seen it on her face when she killed—something which was hard to reconcile with her serene look beside him in the stasis pod.

The *Excelsior's* engines thrummed to life, bringing him back to the task at hand as they slowly built up the antimatter reaction. The first thrust would ramp up to 10*g* and then calibration checks would run for thirty minutes. After that, there would be a few course corrections and then the 70*g* burn would commence.

Based on current projections, that burn would last for six hours. Joe checked that the ports on his shipsuit would line up for the fluid transfers. Before the 70*g* burn, his heart would shut down and an external pump would take over circulating his blood—or rather, what would be taking place of his blood at the time. The extreme pressure would force the oxygen right out of regular blood cells. Specialized nano cells would be taking over for the burn, each equipped with microscopic stasis fields for carrying the necessary chemicals to keep him alive.

<*I could have done this on my own, you know,*> Troy interrupted his shipsuit check. <*No need for you delicate organics to risk your hides.*>

Joe laughed, no mean feat with his body weighing over a ton.

<*You may have been top of your class, but you're young.*> Joe glanced at the various readouts, making certain everything was within nominal ranges. The ship may have had burn-in runs, but by and large this was its maiden voyage.

<*You do know that AI age faster than humans, mentally speaking. Just because I'm only ten years old doesn't mean your sixty years have anything on me.*>

<*Experience is the best teacher. You know that is true for all sentient beings, biological or otherwise.*> It was true enough. When scientists first began to experiment with AI they carefully taught the machine intelligences how the world worked, what was right and what was wrong. They treated their creations like children and raised them, often even loved them, as such.

The sentimentality was mistaken as a quirk of the creators and when the process was commercialized, a nurturing environment was not a part of the young AI's upbringing. While the alterations allowed the AI to grow into their full potential quickly, they lacked compassion, something that was difficult for them to understand or relate to.

The dichotomy led to a series of terrific conflicts between humans and their creations. Sides were chosen and the Sentience Wars erupted in the Sol System. The lines did not divide evenly and AI and humans drew up on both sides of the battle. While any one conflict was short, the overall upheaval lasted from the early twenty-third century to the late twenty-fourth.

In the end, it was a third faction of AI who convinced both sides to cease hostilities and created the Phobos Accords, a set of rules and guidelines for the raising and upgrading of AI. The non-compassionate AI and the humans who sided with them—a group not far removed from machines themselves—were offered the option of re-education or expulsion from the Sol System.

Interestingly, most chose re-education. It would seem that seeing many of their fellows die had actually taught them compassion and understanding a different way.

With the Phobos Accords, not just anyone could create an AI, just as not anyone was fit, or suited, to create and raise children—though human creation was far less regulated than that of AI.

In the current age, nearly all AI were created from a merging of directives and imperatives from groups of parent AI. The process was analogous to the merging of DNA to form a human child, yet, as intelligent as the modern AI were, still no one could determine precisely what the temperament or potential of a young AI would be.

Because the brain of an AI—like the neural enhancements in a human's brain—was not digital, but analog, they grew and strengthened based on experiences and stimulus. Digital systems were used for computers and Non-Sentient AI, but to place a Sentient AI in a digital environment would be akin to a lobotomy on a human—and, of course, very illegal.

The *Intrepid* had no NSAI nodes. All the AI onboard were sentient, though there were far fewer than normal, what with Bob running nearly all systems and not really needing assistance.

<*Maybe we wouldn't be in this position if there were more traditional AI structure on the* Intrepid,> Troy mused, having been half-listening to the thoughts Joe let spill onto the public net.

<*I couldn't speak to that,*> Joe replied trying to avoid the conversation. <*I'm not an AI Structure & Systems Specialist.*>

Joe's mental tone told Troy to let it go and the AI complied. The pair returned to the business of reviewing engine stats and ensuring the ship was holding up.

<*Ready for final course corrections,*> Troy reported.

<*Calculations are confirmed by my nav processes.*>

<*Onboard nodes agree.*>

Joe established a connection to the *Intrepid* and was connected to the bridge net.

<*Captain Andrews. We have triple agreement on our plotted course.*>

<*Very good, Commander. Please send the data to our net.*>

Joe uploaded the navigational data to the *Intrepid* and waited for the response.

<*We have triple agreement on your data as well, in addition to a third party match from what our sensors can see. You may proceed with your burn at your designated A marker.*>

<*Affirmative.*>

<*Commander.*> Captain Andrews waited for Joe's response.

<*Yes, sir?*>

<*Good luck.*>

<*Good luck to you, sir.*>

EXCELSIOR

STELLAR DATE: 3241791 / 08.16.4163 (Adjusted Gregorian)
LOCATION: GSS *Excelsior*
REGION: LHS 1565, 26.8 AU from stellar primary

32:14 hours to asteroid group
6:28 hours to Intrepid escape maneuver

Tanis opened her eyes a moment after the stasis field snapped off. She could feel Angela re-initializing and ran a check on her body to ensure there was no structural damage.

A face loomed over hers.

"You seem to be all in one piece."

She grinned. "I don't think I would have broken into multiple pieces no matter what."

"Well, not unless the ship did." Joe laughed. "Everything seem OK?"

Tanis held up a hand and moved all of her fingers. "Right as starlight. How did our burn go?"

"Hurt like hell." Joe rotated his shoulder and grimaced. "Well, didn't hurt at the time, but it always aches like crazy when my cells de-crystalize."

As he rolled his shoulders Tanis couldn't help but imagine running her hands over them, feel the muscle rippling below the skin. Everything certainly looked like it was alright from where she sat.

"Well then, we have more than enough time for a good rub-down." She held a hand in the air and let it fall. "We've got what, 0.3*g*?"

"Good guess, just a little over. I worked it out so that we could have some thrust for this part of the trip."

"That'll be just enough to have a bath if we don't get too energetic."

"There's a bath on this thing?" Joe asked.

"I finished all my preflight work an hour before you were done with yours, so I had a build-out bot swap the second cabin for a hot-tub," Tanis said with a mischievous smile.

"Most dangerous flight of our lives and you make sure it has a hot-tub." Joe shook his head as he gave her a hand to pull her out of the stasis pod.

"Seemed like the right move at the time. Besides, nice warm water feels good on the muscles after a hard burn."

"Where did you get it from anyway?" Joe asked.

"It was set aside to be put in the gym facilities on one of the cruisers," Tanis shrugged.

"Someone's gonna be upset about that."

"Before or after we're the heroes of the day for getting the ship the fuel they need?"

"Good point."

"So, what's to eat? I'm starved," Tanis asked aloud as she welcomed Angela back into her mind.

"I, ah…hadn't gotten anything ready."

Tanis gave Joe a peck on the cheek, something that felt weird to do, but nice nonetheless. "You just couldn't wait to talk to me."

"Well, more specifically to see if you were dead or alive."

Tanis laughed. "Well, I won't last long without some food. I only had the one BLT while we were getting ready."

"So several more BLTs all around, I imagine then?"

"It's like you can read my mind."

"Not yet."

<*You're not missing out on much.*>

"Woe unto anyone who stands between me and a BLT." Tanis grinned and loped out of the room in the low gravity with Joe close behind.

In the wardroom, she opened the refrigeration unit and snapped the stasis field off. After extracting the lettuce, tomatoes, and strips of bacon, along with butter made using milk from the *Intrepid*'s own cattle, she closed it and snapped the field back on.

Joe was setting the baking unit to make a loaf of Tanis's favorite rich brown bread.

"You do pay attention."

"Well, that and I seem to recall being sent to the commissary more than once to get you a BLT made just so."

"Don't pull that on me." Tanis turned her head sharply, causing her hair to rise up and wrap around her face in the low gravity.

"Mfphh."

Joe let out a burst of laughter. "Classic."

Tanis unraveled her hair and stuck her tongue out at him.

"I do, and I remember you always stopping by to ask me if I wanted anything from the commissary. And don't let that bread rise too fast in the low-g."

"Yes, sir." Joe grinned and double-checked the pressure he had set in the baking unit.

The cooking plate was warmed up and Tanis placed the bacon on it, breathing in the aroma of sizzling fat.

"I tell you, this enhanced olfactory system of mine really has its benefits."

"I can imagine. It smells damn good to me, I can't imagine what it must be like for you."

"Pure heaven." Tanis flipped the bacon over. She glanced over her shoulder at him again, this time slower. "You, on the other hand, are going to need that bath pretty soon."

"I'll distract you." He opened the baking unit and pulled the fresh bread out.

"Oh god… That smells absolutely delicious."

Together they sat at the small table and began preparing their meals. Afterward, Joe rose to prepare two cups of coffee, heaps of sugar for him and cream and sugar for Tanis.

"So how long on this *v*?" Tanis could have checked the shipnet, but she really just wanted to hear Joe talk.

Now that she had allowed herself to acknowledge her love for him, she realized how deep his affection for her must run. Perhaps he had been holding back and was now behaving differently around her.

<*No, he's been like this toward you for some time; you were somehow totally blind to it. Even the captain noticed how he felt about you,*> Angela said.

<Everyone knew we were in love but me?>

<Pretty much.>

<That's a little embarrassing.>

"Another thirty hours, then we rotate and begin braking. We won't need to do a hard break, though. The relative velocity of the asteroid group we're closing on is near to our relative speed. About twelve hours at 5*g* should do it, depending on the local medium and what we home in on."

"Good, then I can stay up for it."

"I did plan it that way." Joe smiled.

Tanis leaned an elbow on the table and locked eyes with him. "You know just how to use that smile of yours, don't you?"

A look of innocence crossed his face. "I have no idea what you are talking about. There is no pre-meditation in any of my actions. I'm a natural, go-with-the-flow sort of guy."

Tanis cocked an eyebrow. He was serious; it was one of the things that drew her to him. There was nothing faked about Joe; his behavior wasn't artificial, no looking in the mirror to examine smiles and expressions. Every action, every look from him was totally natural and in the moment.

Tanis envied that. Nearly everything she did was crafted—all of her actions, responses, everything. Well, except for her repartee with Angela. That was the one place she got to be herself. Maybe she could learn something of that from Joe.

Of course, she wasn't always like that, not before Toro. Tanis stopped that train of thought, Toro was the last thing she wanted to think about right now.

"So what do you have planned for the next thirty hours?"

"Well, that bath sounds good. Is it a double?"

"Do you really think I would go to all the trouble of putting a bath unit on this ship if it wasn't big enough for two?"

"Good point." He chewed thoughtfully for a moment. "Then I suppose we should give it a test-run. Once we reach our target set of possibilities, it'll be all work."

"Hurry up and wait, eh?"

Joe nodded. "Pretty much."

"Sounds a lot like everything in the service."

*****

"Oh, sweet stars above, this feels great," Tanis said as she slipped into the water. She hadn't realized until they were done eating how weary she was. It had been over twenty-four hours since coming out of stasis on the *Intrepid*; plus a full day's work back in the Sol system—which was mind-boggling—before that. Stasis provided no rest and she felt it.

Joe was at the edge of the tub, stepping out of his ship suit, his back to her. She watched the muscles on his shoulders ripple beneath his skin. A slight sheen of sweat made the light brown flesh look delicious.

Tanis stretched out, arms above her head and toes pointed—just barely touching the far side of the bath. She draped her arms over the edge of the tub above her head, waiting patiently. Joe hadn't watched her undress, he'd faced away the entire time—which was odd since he had seen her naked twice in the last two days.

"Hurry up, slowpoke." She flicked some water at his back with a foot.

Joe chuckled, his shoulders rising and falling gently. "Just give me a second, getting all these ports disconnected from the suit and closed up. They don't really help the mood."

"Pfft. You saw me with my arm blown off and my lung flapping on the ground. I can handle a few fluid transfer ports."

"All set." He stepped out of his ship suit's legs and turned, his bemused smile shifted somewhat as he took in the sight before him. Tanis arched her back and took a deep breath.

"What are you waiting for?"

"No idea." Joe grinned and bent over the tub, planting a long kiss on her lips.

Tanis returned it, her arms draping over his neck. A tremor raced through her body, a thrill that started in her loins and radiated outward, her breath caught at the wonder of it. She opened her eyes to look into his, her nose wrinkling with a smile.

"Get in here, mister." She reached up and pulled him sideways into the tub; gently, so as not to send all the wonderful hot water into the air—a serious problem in low gravity.

Joe's shoulders bunched up as he lifted his body on the edge of the tub and swung his legs over the side.

She moved toward him and ran her arms down his chest. He released a long, trembling breath, not removing his eyes from hers. Wordlessly, Tanis slid around his body and wrapped her legs around his torso from behind. With deft fingers, she began to massage his shoulders, his arms, his back.

"You have the most amazing fingers." Joe stroked her calves with his fingernails.

"I'm not objecting to that, either."

He moved forward in the tub and then spun around; fast enough that she didn't move and they were now facing one another.

"You've finally lowered your shield, Miss Richards."

"It's at least on low power."

His hands slid down her torso and held her waist gently. "Who knew such a fragile thing was under those crisp uniforms and battle armor?"

"I'm no one's fragile thing."

Joe's eyes drew up, worried at first, and then smiling as he realized she was joking.

"But I'll make an exception for you," Tanis whispered.

Their lips met again; it was gentle at first, but passion took over and, before long, they were pushing and pulling at one another, as though they wanted to become one being. Then Joe's hands were in her hair, pulling her head up, and he ran his lips under her chin, tracing the outline of her jaw. Without warning, his hands dropped to her breasts, first cupping and then tracing outlines around her swollen nipples.

Tanis was in heaven, she had always secretly worried that Joe was attracted to her only because she was a firm, commanding woman—worried that he wouldn't take charge in lovemaking. She was wrong, happily, joyfully wrong.

He wanted to possess her as much as she wanted to be possessed.

She could see it in his eyes, feel it in the way he held her body, know it in the way he dug his fingers into her back.

When they joined it was beautiful. He opened his mind to her and she to him. Their thoughts and emotions co-mingled in a way Tanis had never experienced before. For a short time they became one being.

Afterward, they lay in the tub not moving, basking in each other's presence.

"You're absolutely amazing," Tanis said as warm thoughts of love and satisfaction suffused her.

"You're not so bad yourself." Joe's patented grin filled her vision. "I think I'll keep you."

Their lips were nearly touching, Joe's weight was pressing down on her, skin sliding gently against skin, hands idly tracing patterns on one another.

Tanis's eyes locked with his, wide with entreaty. "Promise?" Her voice quivered with a vulnerability she didn't even remember having.

"Guaranteed."

They didn't part right away. He held her for some time, stroking her hair and randomly kissing her lips, cheeks, and neck. Eventually, he slipped out and rose from the water, his skin glistening. He bent and lifted her out of the bath, aided by the fact that in the current gravity she weighed less than thirty kilograms.

She sighed contentedly and reached for a towel, handing one to Joe before wiping herself down.

"That was…unbelievable," Tanis sighed.

"Glad you think so, I've been waiting to do that with you for some time."

"If I had known you were that good, I don't know that my resolve would have held out so well back before we left."

Joe laughed. "Ready for round two?"

Tanis's eyes widened. "Already?"

As it turned out, they both fell asleep within moments of laying down in the double bunk. Angela set the temperature just a touch warmer in the room and dimmed the lights before striking up a conversation with Troy about the best way to net more than one of the asteroids.

25:04 hours to asteroid group
-0:42 hours to Intrepid escape maneuver

Tanis woke first and reached out to feel the slumbering form of her lover.

Her lover.

How long had it been since she had last been in love? Eleven… Twelve years now? Well, *she* had been in love. As it turned out he hadn't felt exactly the same way. Not something Tanis was worried about with Joe. It was obvious he was completely committed to her; the fact he had pursued her for nearly a year was ample evidence.

Though that wasn't entirely true. She had found him damn attractive when they first met back in that sector chief's office on the MOS. The next day—had it really been only one day later?—when he saved her life in the VIP corridor, she knew she could love him.

Of course, there was no way they could have a relationship while in the TSF with her being his commanding officer, so she had stuffed those feelings down deep and pretended they didn't exist. But the longing slowly forced its way to the surface, and now those feelings were front and center, no chance of going away.

Thank the starlight.

Joe stirred beside her.

"Good morning, sleepyhead."

"It's morning?"

"I really have no idea; we didn't really establish a ship-time."

"Close enough, I guess." He rolled over and looked at her, his eyes warm and smiling, if a bit bleary and sleep-laden. "You have no idea how completely awesome it is to wake up next to you. It's unbelievable."

"I believe it." Tanis grinned. "I am completely awesome, after all."

Joe laughed and hugged her to him. It was the best wakeup Tanis had experienced in years. They had sex again, another slow, sensual episode, the kind that she loved to have in the morning; apparently so did he.

"I promise some acrobatic events in the future." Joe said afterward. "But this just feels like slow and relaxed time."

"I have absolutely no complaints, mister." Tanis smiled, pulling the covers off and stepping gingerly onto the cold deck. She began her morning stretches while Joe watched from bed, head propped up on one arm.

"You do this every morning?"

"Of course, don't you?" Tanis touched her toes, and then wrapped her arms tightly around her legs, folding double and looking at him with her head between her calves.

Joe whistled, admiring the view. "Not really, but I heartily endorse you continuing the practice."

Tanis laughed—something that looked and sounded odd in her current position. "Get up and get dressed you lazy man. There's breakfast to be had. I could eat a buffalo!"

"Did you stock buffalo?"

Joe dressed and left to get coffee brewing while Tanis finished her stretches. She slipped into a fresh ship suit and followed a few minutes later. The small wardroom was down a short hall and the smells of cooking oatmeal greeted her. She stood in the entrance watching Joe prepare two bowls, heaping brown sugar on them.

"Oh boy, oatmeal," Tanis said.

Two things that grew really well in hydroponics: sugarcane and oats. In space, you had to like oatmeal.

"And coffee, the most important meal of the day," Joe said as he set the cups on the table.

"Thanks for the joe, Joe," Tanis grinned.

"You're welcome, and you have no idea how much I love that joke." Joe's sardonic tone took a moment for Tanis to parse.

"Ah, not down with the Joe-jokes. Noted. So what's on the schedule for today?"

"Well, the AIs let us sleep a long time, as I'm sure you noticed." Tanis nodded as she chewed. He continued, "So, we're fifteen hours from the slowdown burn and then ten hours from there until we reach the A group."

Tanis nodded as she continued to spoon the oatmeal up. "So what else do we have to eat?"

Joe laughed. "I guess we are a bit behind on the meals."

"The extracurricular activities did help in the hunger department, too."

"Well, we could do waffles, bacon—I think there's sausage."

"Bacon and waffles! I stocked some great syrup."

An hour later after a properly filling meal they were on the bridge, studying charts and updated scans, looking for the spectral lines that would indicate lithium. There were a few good candidates and Tanis was lancing laser beams out at the rocks, looking for the right type of reflection.

The *Intrepid* had passed the time of its escape burn nearly two hours prior, but at just over fifteen AU from the star, the *Excelsior* would not receive confirmation of its success for another twenty minutes. Tanis found herself worrying about it more than she expected. Normally she didn't stress about things she couldn't control, but there were a lot of people she had come to care for on the ship.

If all went well, they would be back onboard the *Intrepid* in forty-five hours.

Joe reached out and touched Tanis's arm. "I've got a pretty good candidate here," he said and put the asteroid up on the bridge's holo display. "Looks to be in one piece and has some good amblygonite deposits, maybe even as much as forty percent by mass."

The rock was just over a kilometer in diameter and massed a hair under twenty-three trillion tons. Tanis calculated the rough amount of thrust it would take to bring the object up to the required velocities.

"It's kinda big."

"Yeah, but see here and here..." Joe pointed at the display. "That's all dust, we can knock that off and probably shave almost ten trillion tons."

"That's a lot more manageable. How do we knock it off?"

Joe brought up another display. "We use a thumper. We shoot it at the object right where the dust is. It breaks apart into smaller projectiles that slice through the dust, and then balloon right before they hit the solid part. They essentially shove it quickly and it gets it away from the dust. Once on each side, with some repositioning in between, and we'll have a much lighter load."

The plan looked good to Tanis. The one rock would give them all of the lithium they would need and would be much easier to haul in than several smaller asteroids.

"Sounds good. Doesn't look like we'll need to alter course much to reach it."

"Yup, easy peasy."

"Speaking of peas, I'm hungry!" Tanis gave Joe a quick kiss and dashed off to the galley. What she really wanted to do was take her mind off the *Intrepid* and its escape burn.

Twenty minutes later they were completing a dinner of grilled cheese and tomato soup when Angela interrupted their discussion about beam rifles.

<*Something is wrong.*>

"That's not terribly descriptive," Tanis said.

<*The* Intrepid *isn't there.*>

Tanis felt her heart jump and saw a look of panic cross Joe's face.

"What do you mean it's not there?" Her appetite fled and Tanis put the remains of her sandwich down.

<*We should have been able to see them come out from behind the star five minutes ago,*> Angela said. <*But there is no signal. Nothing.*>

Angela's worry was palpable; Tanis could feel it bleeding into her, amplifying her own fear.

"There's something else, isn't there?"

<*I'm picking up high levels of x-ray refraction from the far side of the star.*>

Tanis looked at Joe. They both knew what that meant.

Estrella de la Muerte was a red dwarf, and, like most red dwarfs, it was prone to solar flares. The flares were no more violent than a flare from Sol, but because the *Intrepid* was passing much closer to the dim red star than it ever would to a hot yellow star like Sol, flares were a much larger concern. Even without the heat, red dwarfs had another danger when they flared: X-Rays.

Estrella de la Muerte had been recorded to emit x-ray bursts over 10,000 times greater than Sol during flares. If such a burst hit the *Intrepid,* the ship would be turned into a lifeless husk.

"Sweet fuck," Joe whispered.

"Do we have readings on the x-ray intensity?" Tanis asked.

<*Not yet. I'm just picking up refraction. The light will take a bit to hit the outer halo of asteroids and then bounce back to us, about another four hours. We won't know until then how bad it was.*>

<*It may have just knocked out their comm capabilities,*> Troy said.

Tanis was a bit surprised to hear him offering comfort. Maybe she had misjudged him, or maybe he didn't want to think about being lost in this system for eternity either.

"Finish up," Joe said. "We're going to be hard at it for some time."

They wolfed down the rest of their food and then ran to the bridge. The two humans and two AIs deployed a relativistic probe to get a view of the far side of Estrella de la Muerte while carefully examining the entire spectrum of the star.

The red dwarf had a rapid rotation and, before long, an angry blotch came into view. The sunspot the *Intrepid* had been using for magnetic repulsion had erupted.

"It went up…" Joe said softly. "It didn't read as being that volatile, it should have held."

<*It was a full scale flare from the looks of it,*> Angela said. <*But we don't know when it went off. It could have been before or after.*>

"Or during," Joe said.

"We'll know more shortly." Tanis brought up the data on the probe's trajectory—the ETA was twenty minutes.

No one spoke in the intervening time. The probe was racing to where the *Intrepid* should be. It was traveling at 0.8*c* and would fly past before arcing around the star and back toward the *Excelsior*. An alert flashed on the holo display as the data came streaming in.

No sign of the *Intrepid.*

"It's my fault." Joe put his head in his hands and Tanis rose to sit beside him.

"It's not. Everyone had the same data you did. They knew what flares are like on red dwarfs. We don't have any evidence that the *Intrepid*'s magnetic repulsion caused the flare. Red dwarfs may be small, but that sunspot was still larger than Earth. It's unlikely that the ship caused it to go up." Tanis laid out a rapid-fire series of rationalizations.

<I've got readings on the intensity.> Troy interrupted and brought the information up on the display.

It was bad, not quite 10,000 times the x-ray level of Sol, but close. A major flare. Plasma detection from the probe indicated that the flare went two million miles out into space, well beyond where the *Intrepid* would have been.

No one spoke for several minutes. Tanis forced the thoughts of the colony ship's destruction down, refusing to consider them. She could tell that Joe was doing the same, while Angela was running math on possible alternate vectors the *Intrepid* could have possibly taken.

Everyone followed her example and helped in the search. Signals were sent out and the probe was set to orbit the star in ever-widening circles. Tanis prepared a meal after a few hours and brought it back to the bridge where she and Joe only picked at it.

So many people. There were two and a half million colonists on the *Intrepid* who went into stasis with the sure expectation that they would awaken to their new world, their new system, ready for them to shape and to create the future they always dreamed of.

An anomaly signaled on her interface and she focused the low-band radio antenna on a section of the search grid that seemed to have a bit more noise than expected. Then she heard it.

"*[static]*...say again...*[static]*...*Excelsior,* do you read? This is the...*[static]*...*trepid.* Do you read?"

Tanis's heart leapt into her throat and she waved at Joe, putting the feed on the bridge audio.

"*Intrepid.* This is the *Excelsior.* We read you, and boy are we glad to hear your transmission."

Joe let out a whoop as he brought up the trajectory that matched the *Intrepid* at the position the signal had revealed. The main display shifted to show the new outsystem path of the colony ship.

Tanis glanced at the distance and saw that the *Excelsior* was one hundred-thirty light minutes from the *Intrepid.* It would take over four hours to hear back. In the meantime, variations on the initial message continued to come in.

"I suddenly have a bit more of an appetite," Joe said as he reached down and picked up his BLT. He polished it off in two bites and then took a long gulp of water.

Tanis set the probe to intercept the *Intrepid* before she devoured her food as well.

"That's the great thing about a BLT; they don't get any worse for sitting for an hour or so."

"Well, the tomatoes get a bit soggy."

"Adds to the texture," Tanis grinned.

The pair sat in silence for several minutes, the adrenaline surge wearing off, leaving them slightly heady and still just a bit anxious.

"I'd like to know more about you, Tanis," Joe said at last. "I mean, I know *you* pretty well, but I don't really know much about how you got to be you."

His timing seemed odd to Tanis, but maybe it was the relief in finding the *Intrepid* that caused him to ask—and she knew what he was asking about.

"Outside of work, I don't have a lot to tell. I enlisted when I was twenty-two. When the *Intrepid* left Sol, I had just passed fifty years in the TSF."

Joe nodded slowly. "It's your work I find myself wondering about. I've been through the shit with you more than once and you've had my back and I've had yours. The Tanis I know doesn't match the one I heard about back in Sol."

Tanis didn't respond immediately. This was one of the reasons she hadn't wanted to get back into a relationship, she knew she would have to explain Toro.

"You want to know about Toro." The leaden words dropped off her lips.

Joe nodded. "I know you don't want to talk about it, but I need to reconcile the two Tanises."

"You don't need to apologize," Tanis said after a long pause then took a deep breath. "It's about time I told the story."

THE BUTCHER OF TORO

STELLAR DATE: 3223427 / 05.05.4113 (Adjusted Gregorian)
LOCATION: TSS *Arcturus*, stealth approach to asteroid 1685 Toro
REGION: InnerSol Stellar Space, Sol Space Federation

Lieutenant Colonel Tanis Richards reviewed the intel and the plan. She really didn't need to; both were hers, but this mission felt like one of those—one of the ones where something would go sideways.

She said as much to Angela.

<*You have good reason to think that,*> Angela replied in her mind.

<*Just because there's no way a sane person would get involved with the Cardid cult? Or do you have another reason?*>

<*I think the cult is a good enough reason. We're not going to encounter a lot of rational people in there.*>

Terran Space Force surveillance drones had completed several passes near the asteroid, passively pulling readings that gave clues as to what was going on in the interior of the asteroid.

Toro was one of several bodies in the inner Sol System that orbited Sol in resonance with Earth and Venus. From those world' point of view it appeared that Toro was orbiting them like a moon. This meant that at certain times cargo could be dropped from stations near either of those worlds and Toro would appear to accelerate to pick it up. At other times, Toro could drop cargo and it would fall into the outer Sol System with an added boost.

The asteroid also had a well-placed elliptical orbit. Perihelion brought it almost to Venus, and at aphelion it drifted beyond the orbit of Mars. Over the years, Toro had extensive docking and cargo transfer systems built around its three kilometer length, but those facilities told just a part of the asteroid's history.

High concentrations of Olivine crystal had drawn prospectors to the asteroid in the twenty-third century, and its interior was riddled with mines and processing facilities. At one point, when both the mine's production and cargo transfers were at their peak, Toro had maintained a population of over a hundred thousand.

Eventually, the valuable minerals had all been extracted, and with Ceres's massive ring supporting most traffic between the inner and outer Sol system, Toro's usefulness diminished.

Centuries later, only a few caretakers and robotic cargo handlers were left, which was when John Cardid came into the picture. Thirty years ago, he rented space on the asteroid for an undisclosed purpose. The Terran Bureau of Investigations suspected that he was involved in illegal human trafficking in addition to paramilitary activity. Over the years, he had built up his presence and followers—Tanis's investigations suggested that over ten-thousand people now lived on Toro.

Then, five years ago, Cardid bought the entire asteroid and halted its remaining cargo-handling operations.

The asteroid's passage near so many InnerSol worlds was far more concerning than the loss of its meager cargo transfer facilities. The TBI stepped up its intelligence-gathering in concert with the space force's counterinsurgency division.

It was slow work because John Cardid was secretive and Toro was difficult to scan due to high concentrations of ferric crystals and iron oxide. This only served to increase suspicion.

Tanis had been involved with the investigation into Toro for several years. In her capacity as a TSF counterinsurgency officer, she had uncovered proof that several shipments of military weapons had found their way to the asteroid, which was reason enough for her to go in, but until the recent escalations, the TBI had maintained jurisdiction.

That had changed four months ago, when a group of prominent public figures had—apparently of their own will—taken a transport to Toro for a visit. They never returned, and only a few transmissions indicating that they intended to stay had been sent out.

Amongst those now considered to be abducted were several actors, a dozen sports professionals, and three senators.

It was the textbook recipe for a first-class disaster.

Even after months of work, the TSF still didn't have enough intel to make a clean, surgical strike, but the public and political pressure had forced the brass to make a move.

The TBI had ceded jurisdiction and Tanis, as the lead investigator on the TSF side, had been sent in.

This was not new territory; she had done her share of tours and often took an active role in the field operations that resulted from her investigations. Given more time and intel, she would have been more than happy to run the mission, but this rush-job was going to be trouble.

She reviewed the packet containing the orders for the TSF *Arcturus*. It granted her broad discretionary powers and, in matters regarding the mission, Captain Arsenal was under her command.

She prayed she wouldn't need to issue those types of orders.

Closing the packet, she flipped the holo display over the table to show the entry points the Marines would take, as well as the sectors each platoon would clear. Just then the TBI agent assigned as liaison on the operation entered the briefing room.

"Going over this shit show one last time?" Bremen asked.

Tanis nodded. "Looking for whatever it is that I missed; we just don't know enough about what we're getting into. There has to be some clue that can help."

"We just have to clear a few dozen square kilometers of station with one battalion of Marines, kill the bad guys, save the good guys, and pray no one gets hurt who isn't supposed to," Bremen grimaced. "What could go wrong?"

<*You have such a way with words.*> Angela's tone was droll.

"I'd prefer more than just a battalion," Tanis said without looking up from her holo projections.

"I hear you. Three hundred and eighty Marines is nothing to sneeze at, but for all we know we're up against ten thousand humans and who knows how many bots? I wouldn't mind a different assignment right about now."

His statement caused Tanis to glance up and cast a harsh look at the TBI agent. That wasn't the sort of attitude that got the job done. She was happy he'd be staying back on the *Arcturus*. She turned back to her notes, preparing for her upcoming briefing.

Several minutes before the meeting was to begin, the battalion commanders had all arrived and were talking quietly amongst themselves. She was pleased, their punctuality showed respect.

<*You've earned a bit of esteem over the years,*> Angela commented.

<*Usually Marines only respect experience gained while wearing a Marine uniform, let's hope these ones are a bit more forgiving.*>

The battalion's XO, Major Ender, was sitting in the front and gave her a crisp nod. Tanis had talked with him a few times to get a feel for the battalion and how they would react to a new temporary commander. Her placement with the battalion was as good as she could hope for; the 242nd Marines had a stellar record, and their former commander, a Colonel Chen, had recently been promoted to general.

Their new CO had not been assigned, but since the TSF had unified all branches, it was possible for her, a lieutenant colonel in the intelligence branch, to be put in direct command of a Marine battalion.

The rest of the room was filled with the company and platoon commanders as well as platoon sergeants. Tanis looked them over slowly. They were all veterans of at least one significant engagement, all had seen the dark underside of humanity.

If Tanis's intel was right, they'd see that underbelly's underbelly today.

"Thank you for all reading the pre-briefing docs. This meeting is really just a formality. You've seen the vids and know that something is rotten on Toro. We're going in to clean it up.

"Try not to kill the good guys, cover your sectors, and keep your eyes out for Cardid. Use non-lethal force if possible, as much as possible."

Tanis stood, arms akimbo. "Questions?"

A platoon sergeant named Williams raised a hand. "What's not in the packet? It's light on what is likely going on in there, and I bet you have a hunch."

<*Forewarned is forearmed,*> Angela said privately to Tanis.

"I don't have solid intel, but I think they're doing illegal genetic hybridization research."

"That warrants a visit from Force Recon Marines?" Williams asked.

"That's not the whole of it.... I think something darker is going on, but all I have are crazy whispers about it being 'true evil'."

"They're in for it, then," a Lieutenant named Anderson said, "because we all know that Williams is God's own right hand."

The comment raised some chuckles, but Williams didn't look pleased.

Tanis nodded to Major Ender who proceeded to run over each company and platoon's assignments. When it was done, the group broke up to brief their men.

Tanis took the ship's dorsal maglev to the bridge. The *Arcturus* was one of the TSF's newer destroyers, measuring just over three hundred meters long and seventy wide. What it lacked in size it made up for with speed and stealth. The ship's antimatter engines could boost it to over a quarter the speed of light and the output from the engines could be narrowly focused, making the ship difficult to detect.

Toro was speeding through space at this phase of its orbit and the *Arcturus* was running a 1.3*g* burn to catch up, the thrust caused the train to operate more like a lift on its trip to the bridge.

When Tanis stepped onto the command deck, she noted the navigation holo, which confirmed that the *Arcturus* was only two hours from reaching the asteroid. Toro was near perihelion, approaching Sol, and the ship was in the asteroid's shadow, its narrow engine wash undetectable.

If all went as planned, the *Arcturus* would not be visible until it was right on their doorstep.

The holo showed Toro spinning on its long axis, with several docking stations and cargo facilities forming a ring around its center. When humans first settled on Toro, it spun at a sedate speed of roughly eight centimeters per second. To provide more significant gravity, close to 0.5*g*, it had been accelerated to fifty meters per second.

The final burns needed to match the station's spin would give away the *Arcturus* and ruin the element of surprise. Tanis and Captain Arsenal had agreed to a plan where the TSF cruiser would move to a position ten thousand kilometers behind Toro, and Marine assault transports would close the final gap.

"Ready for action?" asked the captain.

"Everything is in order," Tanis replied. "I don't know about ready. This will be some messy work, are you prepared to provide supporting fire?"

"The composition of the asteroid may cause a few issues with targeted laser strikes, but we think we have the solutions to work around those."

Tanis nodded. "Let's hope you don't need to test those solutions, there's still enough crystal in there that refractions could be dangerous."

"Finer beams and higher power should do the trick—we'll melt anything we come in contact with rather than letting the light bleed out. The *Arcturus* has enough reserve power to turn Toro into Swiss cheese if needs be."

"Well, if everything is good on your end, I'm going to head down to the hangars and gear up."

"Godspeed," the captain replied in parting.

Tanis took a short series of corridors and ladders down to the hangar level where the Marines were suiting up in their powered armor. She approached the 4th Platoon of Bravo Company. The lieutenant, a slender man—odd for an orbital drop Marine—named Tippin, rose from inspecting his weapon and saluted her.

"Glad to have you in the 'toon, Colonel Richards."

Tanis returned the salute. "I hear you're the best in the outfit."

"Damn straight we are, if you don't mind my saying it. The boys and girls of the 4th Bravo have seen more action than the—" Tippin said before stopping himself, uncertain of how casual he could be with a CO who was an MICI and not a Marine.

"I believe the current joke involves the president's mother?" Tanis asked.

Tippin coughed. "Yeah, I think it does."

Tanis chuckled. "Why don't you show me to my armor?"

"Williams, hook Colonel Richards up with her gear," Tippin called out to the sergeant who had asked several questions during the briefing.

Sergeant Williams trotted up and looked Tanis over. "I warrant I've got some that will fit you without too much adjustment. Do you have any load-out or weapons prefs?" he asked.

"I prefer to make tactical shots, what do you have for rifles?"

"The 242 issues M948 concussive pulse rifles for station combat, but those aren't terribly accurate. A lot of the boys and girls use MIV particle rifles so long as the proton beam cartridges stay behind for on-station missions," Williams said, raising his voice and casting a hard glare at a Marine who was checking his gear.

"The MIV is a nice weapon," Tanis said while nodding in agreement regarding proton cartridges being left behind. "Do you have any of the MIV6 model? I can live with the electron beam."

"Sure do." Williams selected a weapon from the company's armory and handed it to Tanis who looked it over, approving of its maintenance.

"Do you have any ballistic weapons as well?" Tanis asked. I find that bullet fragments make for some of the best suppression."

Williams grinned. "I sure do, how's a S901 suit you? We have the recoil dampeners on them as well as the flechette or ballistic rounds."

"Excellent," Tanis said, slinging the MIV6 over her shoulder and taking the S901 from the sergeant.

"Do you need any close range weapons?"

Tanis patted the duffle slung over her shoulder. "I have that taken care of."

Suiting up took over twenty minutes to complete. Because there was the very real possibility that the Marines would be exposed to vacuum on station entry, and possibly later if combat breached any pressure seals, full EVA armor was the order of the day.

The Marines armored up co-ed style right on the hangar deck. This meant stripping down to nothing and starting with the base thermal layer, which also provided compression and a final seal against vacuum. Tanis had brought her own and had it on in a few minutes, fighting a grimace when the suit's plumbing attachments hooked up to her body.

The actual armor Williams had selected for her was a scout style that started with a second tight-fitting ballistic and thermally refractive mesh. From there, the armor's plating was applied, hooking together to form a partially assisted exoskeleton. She pulled the helmet on, first attaching the back to her suit and then snapping the face-plate on.

Her internal HUD updated and pulled in the stats from the armor, providing air, power, and integrity reports. While the software cycled through all the checks, Tanis tested her range of motion. Everything felt good and she pulled several packs of power and physical rounds from the armory, sliding them into various clips and slots.

"Everything check out, sir?" Major Ender approached and gave the abbreviated salute Marines used whilst suited up.

"A OK," Tanis replied. "Your crew takes care of their gear; tests are all green."

Major Ender and Tanis exchanged a few other pre-combat pleasantries before the major left to join his platoon. Tanis wasn't sure why he came over in person—perhaps it was to ensure that the new CO was in good hands.

<*Or he thinks you're attractive,*> Angela laughed.

<*No one is attractive in armor,*> Tanis scoffed at the idea.

<*Sometimes I think you don't exist in the same reality as the rest of us.*>

She looked at the mission countdown on her HUD. It was now t-minus 15 until drop. She climbed into the 4th Bravo's transport and racked in. The rest of the platoon was already in place; Sergeant Williams prowling through the lot, inspecting armor and gear, slapping and swearing his pleasure or dismay.

Once Tanis racked in, he gave her a final check.

"Everything looks good, sir, you know your stuff." It was high praise from a platoon sergeant.

"I wouldn't still be alive if I didn't," Tanis replied.

"Fair enough," came Williams's response. "Still, not often you see a non-Marine officer who knows her asshole from her elbow. Sir."

Tanis wasn't certain how to respond, Marines were often more familiar with their officers than the regular TSF, probably because all officers in the Marines rose up through the ranks. She didn't have to worry about a response as Williams had already moved on, checking the lieutenant's gear before racking himself in.

The next several minutes were filled with the sounds of Marines mentally preparing for combat. For some it was catcalls and curses, others prayed, others said nothing and simply looked forward stoically. No one was asleep, which was almost unusual.

Right on its mark, the transport 'dropped'. In reality the transports boosted out of the hangar on acceleration rails, but these were Force Recon Orbital Drop Marines, and as far as they were concerned, they always dropped.

Once clear of the *Arcturus*, the transports fired their main engines—short run antimatter burners—and the ships boosted 6*g* in seconds. Tanis gritted her teeth and watched the clock. The burn would run for almost three minutes and then the transports would rotate and reverse the burn to break. Within five minutes they would be disembarking onto Toro.

"Love this shit," one of the Marines called out as the transport rotated and Tanis felt the feeling of weightlessness as her organs shifted.

Then the burn hit again, this time eyeballs out as the Marines called it, and Tanis squeezed hers shut. She knew they wouldn't pop out, but she still hated the feeling of them pulling at her eye sockets.

Right on time there was a loud clang and the transport grappled onto an external pad on Toro's South Transport Station.

In the blink of an eye, Williams was at the hatch, opening it and yelling for the Marines to get on the pad and make it secure.

Though there was two-thirds regular gravity on the pad, it was exposed to vacuum.

The Marines disembarked from the two exits by squad, covering corners and moving into position, the low gravity allowing them to race across the space in long bounds.

Tanis and Lieutenant Tippin were last off the transport; the moment they were out it boosted off—better able to provide cover and assistance from space than on the pad.

The platoon secured the landing platform while squad one's first fireteam—one/one—worked on breaching the airlock. The immediate area clear, one/two set up shielding behind one/one and took up positions to provide covering fire when the lock was breached.

Tanis dispersed nano around the airlock and took cover to the side. Tippin joined her and they monitored the events over the combat net.

<Lock breaching in three, two, one…> Corporal Jansen provided the count over the combat net.

The airlock doors slid open and one/one moved in to disable the inner airlock. Behind them, one/three set up an ES shield to seal the airlock against the vacuum once both doors were open. The electrostatic shield was calibrated to hold in atmosphere but allow humans to pass through.

<*Lock set to breach, pulling back in three, two, one…*> Jansen said as one/one moved back through the ES shield and took cover on either side of the lock. The inner doors slid open and one/two tensed, ready for incoming fire.

Tanis sent her nano through the lock and into the corridor beyond, feeding the data stream to the platoon's combat net. The Marines' HUDs updated, a clear, real-time visual of the inside of the corridor provided by the nano.

Three/one signaled that they detected no movement and held their position while one/one moved back into the airlock and began advancing down the corridor.

Tanis checked the battalion-wide combat net. All transports had successfully dropped off their platoons and all platoons had completed their breach procedures. Everything was running like clockwork.

The battalion AI, Bruno, reported that no communication attempt had been made while the transports were boosting in and even after the breaches were complete no signal had come out of Toro, despite the fact that he had made multiple communication attempts.

Angela directed several nano to find the nearest communications hub and began working at breaching the station's cryptography.

<*ETA?*> Tanis asked.

<*It's good, but not that good; I should be through in a minute or so.*>

Tanis posted the update on the battalion net. Bruno was also working on breaches in four other locations where company captains were positioned with nano capable of managing the hacks.

Her attention was brought back to her physical location as shots rang out from within the station.

Based on her nano-scan, one/one had entered a large cargo holding area that, while not filled, contained enough crates and other equipment to hide several dozen of the enemy.

Lieutenant Tippin signaled for the rest of squad one to move into the corridor. Squads two and three took up positions near the entrance, ready for the signal to rush in.

Tanis rose from the cover she and Tippin shared and took up a position near the entrance alongside two/three. Tippin followed suit, hunkering down with another fireteam.

Down the corridor and in the warehouse, squad one signaled that they were in position. They were keeping the enemy suppressed with pulse rifle fire, but the asteroid's inhabitants were bringing in more heavy weapons to eliminate the Marines' cover.

Williams led the next fireteam in and Tanis followed with hers.

<*Three/one, you're on the entrance. Make sure no one sneaks up on our asses,*> Tippin ordered while the rest of the fireteams moved down the corridor.

Tanis stepped out into the warehouse and took cover behind several crates. Both sides were using pulse rifles—a sane precaution when neither really wanted to punch holes in the station.

Several of the other platoons had also run into resistance, though none had any details on the nature of the defenders yet. Tanis's nano had made it across the warehouse and she directed it to get in close for a better look at who they were up against.

She let out a verbal cry as the image of the enemy appeared in her mind. At first she thought what she was looking at was a mask or exo-armor, but it wasn't—it was what these men and women actually looked like.

The things that stood out at first were the long, tapered spikes driven through their eyes and out the backs of their heads. Out of their mouths, more spikes jutted, some appearing to have been driven through the lower jaw. Below the head, their bodies were cacophonies of plas and steel mixed with flesh. There seemed to be little consistency, other than the horror it induced.

In some places metal plates appeared to have been screwed into flesh, others attached by having more of the spikes pounded through. Some limbs ended in weapons, others in claws of steel, bone, or some mixture.

Tanis had seen her share of mod jobs, some more extreme than these, but the nature of these alterations were grotesque. No clean surgical cuts or mergers had been done. It was like a child with a sledge-hammer had mangled these people.

It was further evidenced by the blood and puss that oozed from all over their bodies, from horrible things like smashed remains of eyeballs stuck to faces to genitalia half cut off, hanging between legs.

The weapons fire had masked something even worse: the once-human creatures were all hissing and screaming. Not in pain or fear, but in anger and rage. They seemed oblivious to the fact that they were monstrous horrors and were entirely focused on their brutal anger.

Tanis had been in the TSF for most of her life and had seen a lot of horrible things in the field; in her youth there had been enemies which had frozen her with fear or horror, but it had been some time since that had happened—until now.

"What is it?" Williams was beside her, giving her shoulder a slight shake.

Tanis shook her head, making eye contact. "Tell the Marines to be ready for what they're going to see. The enemy is not pretty," she told him at the same time as the battalion AI.

Williams gave her a quizzical look, but nodded. "We're working to flank them," he said. "They're really just focused on a frontal assault. Every now and then one of them runs out charging at us too. They're not too bright."

"You can say that again," Tanis muttered.

Tippin and Williams were good at their jobs. Within several minutes. the Marines were flanking the enemy, while Tanis stayed in the fore. She wanted to see for herself what these things were. Maybe there would be some clue explaining what had happened to them and how they were able to function, let alone fight on the side that had done…whatever had been done to them.

"Sweet fucking…fuck," a PFC named Chang said. "What are these? Are they really humans or just some crazy bot used to scare off visitors?"

Tanis's nano had performed a detailed scan and she knew the answer. "They're human. Many of them had this done to them in the past few weeks."

One of the fallen creatures moved, twisting so its sightless spike eyes faced Tanis. "You'll join us, join us or die!"

The words were almost unintelligible, the creature's tongue working around the spikes in its mouth, getting sliced further as it spat out the words.

"Fuck no!" one of the Marines yelled and put a ballistic round from a sidearm into the thing.

"Perez, stow your shit!" Williams yelled. "We're not assassins or executioners, no matter what these things are, we don't kill the wounded."

Williams didn't appear rattled by what he saw, but his lack of actual discipline for Perez showed that even the gunnery sergeant was also having trouble with the nature of the enemy.

<*Squad two, you're taking the lead; one needs a breather,*> Williams instructed.

<*Have you gotten into their network yet?*> Tanis asked Angela.

<*I have…. But I can't seem to find anything.*>

<*What do you mean?*>

Angela took a moment to respond. <*There's nothing here, they've totally wiped the net. Basic systems are in place for station-keeping, but there is no data about personnel, arrivals, departures, anything.*>

<*So they wiped it?*>

<*That's what I said.*>

Tanis let out an audible sigh. <*Keep hunting and let me know if anything turns up.*>

<*I'm not sure why you still give such obvious orders sometimes.*>

The platoon moved further into the station. On several more occasions they engaged the strange horrors in combat, each time defeating them with no losses—other than small slices of sanity.

By now the other platoons had also encountered the enemy. There were a few variations, different types of materials, weapons, and—in some cases—blades instead of spikes had been used.

One platoon encountered a creature that appeared to be three or four of the horrors assembled into one. It ultimately required incendiary grenades to bring the monster down.

<*Some of these people were altered in the last day or so,*> Angela reported. <*I can't find any traces of anesthesia in their systems, nor can I see any defensive wounds.*>

<*What are you saying?*> Tanis asked. <*That they did this to them while awake and these people just took it?*>

<*I don't know that,*> Angela replied. <*But that would fit the evidence I see. There's something else as well. They seem to have very high levels of endorphins in their bodies.*>

<*I hope that doesn't mean they were getting off on this.*>

<*If you're looking for a pleasant rationale behind this, you're going to be disappointed.*>

Tanis updated the company commanders with the data Angela had gleaned and advised additional caution. They were not facing forces that would fear pain or death.

The battalion combat net showed that all the platoons were now engaged with the enemy. One appeared to be vastly outnumbered and Tanis worked with Bruno and Ender to re-enforce it.

Once the warehouse was secured, her platoon moved further into the station, working their way toward one of the elevators that ran down into the core of the asteroid. They encountered only light and sporadic resistance. Other platoons hit harder opposition, but the 242 was amongst the best and pushed through with only light casualties.

The 4th Bravo reached the elevator leading down into the asteroid itself. This area of the station had mainly been used for cargo transfer and so there were only two small lifts that dropped down deep into Toro.

As the two/one moved into the small foyer, the lift on the right opened up and a grotesque figure shambled out. It was over nine feet tall and appeared to be made up of multiple humans. Heads and limbs protruded from a variety of locations. There were also robotic limbs and things that appeared to have come from either the animal kingdom or pure imagination.

Most of the limbs ended in weapons that started firing immediately. A plasma bolt burned through one of the Marines in the two/one before they could get behind cover. Williams was hollering for CFT and stasis shields while the platoon shifted to offering as much support for the beleaguered fireteam as they could through the narrow entrance to the lift's foyer.

Tanis sent in an invisible swarm of nanobots to attack the thing. It had good countermeasures, but Tanis and Angela collectively began to breach them.

<*What are these things?*> Tanis couldn't believe what the readouts from the nano probes were reporting.

<*There's no synthetic backbone to this thing, the human brains are directly interfaced.*> Angela's mental tone contained a rare tremble of horror.

Tanis felt a twinge of phantom pain in her mind at the thought of it. The humans that made up that monster were organically linked at the neurological level, something that was banned by the Phobos Accords because of the complete and utter insanity that always ensued.

Humans were not wired to organically share their mind with other beings. Whether connecting with internal AI, or Linking to the nets, synthetic interfaces were always used. These allowed humans to participate in direct data assimilation and virtual worlds while maintaining their sense of self. Direct data access, or mental connections, were the stuff of nightmares—one of which was playing out right in front of them.

As Tanis recovered from her shock, another plasma bolt melted off a Marine's right arm and brought her back to the physical world.

Pulse rifles were having no effect given the mass of the creature before them. Several Marines even fired electron rails that were shrugged off by the creature's ES shield. Most of the platoon fell back to small ballistic weapons; while those could penetrate the ES shield, they lost substantial velocity and caused little damage.

The Marines were not panicking, but if they couldn't make a dent against this thing they would have to retreat. Something she doubted that they would do with wounded in the field.

<*I bet you wish we brought proton magazines, sir,*> Williams said over the combat net.

<*Keep holding it at bay,*> Tanis replied. <*I have a plan.*>

She unslung her S901 and loaded in a magazine of armor piercing 20mm rounds. Moving down the corridor, she fired several rounds into the wall, opening holes into the elevator foyer on the far side of the room from two/one.

She quickly flipped out the magazine and swapped in incendiary rounds.

<*I don't think that will stop it,*> Angela said at the same time as Williams.

<*I don't intend it to, but it will distract it from two/one while you do what you have to do, Angela.*>

<*What do I have to do?*> the AI asked.

<*Burn its minds,*> Tanis said as she started firing the incendiaries through the holes in the wall. It had the desired effect and the horror shifted its attention, sending plasma bursts in her direction. It's shots of molten star-stuff blasted through the wall and Tanis made sure she wasn't where the thing was aiming.

<*I won't be able to keep this up for long, Angela. Do it, that's an order!*>

The AI didn't respond but Tanis could tell that she was following her command. At least just one of them would face court martial for the action. The Phobos Accords, which were created at the end of the century long Ascendance War, governed not only human and AI interactions, but also the things you could do to a sentient being's mind.

Burning a mind was tantamount to a war crime.

Angela directed the nano that had entered into the horror's body to its brains and set them about their task, burning out all dendrites that facilitated higher functions. The act would turn each of the horrors' brains into something that could do no more than power the organs under its control.

Normally the process could be done in a dozen seconds, but with the number of brains in the creature it would take a few minutes.

Tippin directed several fireteams to follow Tanis's example and moments later they were rotating incendiary fire to keep the thing guessing where the next assault would come from.

The work became easier as the number of functioning limbs on the creature decreased. After what turned out to be only four minutes from the time the elevator door opened to when the thing dropped, the platoon stood down, every one of them knowing they could have easily died in this encounter, a thought made all the more sobering by the realization that two Marines *had* died and three others were in no shape to continue on.

Tippin and Williams triaged and adjusted the affected squads, sending a total of eight Marines back to the position three/one held at the station's entrance.

One/one hauled the horror out of the lift and dropped it in a corner. One/two joined them in the lift and the eight Marines took the ride down into the asteroid to secure the landing below.

Tanis passed the intel on the horror to the other platoons along with what they had to do to take it down. The responses she received were heartening. No one condemned her for burning the minds—not after they saw the thing and the destruction it had wrought.

She gave the order that company commanders could use their nano for the same action if necessary and she would take the heat.

When the Phobos Accords had been written a thousand years ago, she couldn't imagine the intent had been to protect things like what she had destroyed—at least not in the heat of battle when it was killing her Marines.

<*The TSF will understand the circumstances,*> Angela said. <*The AI courts wouldn't. Thank you for making it an order.*>

Tanis nodded, she wasn't quite ready to speak yet. Instead she monitored the nano that was racing ahead of the descending lift, anxious to see what awaited the Marines when they arrived at the bottom.

"Now I believe in a god…or two," Tippin said as he stared down at the horror.

"Why is that?" Williams asked.

"Because I know there's a devil."

"Not for long." Tanis felt anger drag her out of perseveration over her actions. "We're going to go down there and kill him."

As luck, or perhaps a god, would have it, the Marines only faced light defenses at the bottom of the lift, and several minutes later the platoon was working their way through the asteroid itself.

The gravity was lighter here and magnetics in their boots helped keep them attached to the deck plating. Tanis always found it a bit awkward and ended up turning hers off. When the gravity was too light to hold her down at all she'd switch them back on.

Reports came over the battalion combat net of more horrors like what the 4th platoon had faced—and other things like them. Only one other platoon had encountered one in tight quarters like the 4th Bravo had. They managed to blow out a wall with explosive rounds and sucked the thing into vacuum. The other encounters all took place in more forgiving surroundings for the Marines, and they managed to use flanking and explosives to take the creatures down.

The platoons were all within the core of the asteroid at this point, facing an endless stream of new enemies, few as difficult to take down as the multi-human horror, but none easy. Though it was taking a toll on them, the Marines worked their way through the nightmare with stoic determination.

Tanis despaired, doubting they would find any unaltered humans to save in the place. Every person, using that term lightly, was a monster and attacked them on sight, never saying a word, though shrieks and moans were common.

By the count Bruno was keeping, the Marines had killed over a thousand of the probable ten-thousand inhabitants of Toro. The 4th Bravo and several other platoons were closing in on what the net showed to be a large, open chamber near the center of the asteroid. Chances were that they would find the other nine-thousand occupants there.

If they had all been turned into monsters then things were about to get a lot worse.

The platoon moved down a final corridor toward the central chamber, and Tanis's remaining nano, scouting ahead, flew out into the expanse first and provided a feed.

The chamber matched what the net said and was five-hundred meters long and three hundred wide. Being near the center of Toro, there was no gravity here, save for a small pull backwards. It was roughly oval and was *full.*

Creatures of all shapes and sizes floated in the space, more than the nine-thousand Tanis's intel had estimated, there had to be at least twenty-thousand or more. It was hard to be sure because so many consisted of more than one human.

"Welcome," a voice boomed out, "it is so nice of you to come and join our union."

Tanis could make out a figure roughly a hundred meters into the chamber. It was drifting closer and the vague outline began to take shape.

It was John Cardid…plus a few other people. His head was present and appeared to be attached to a mass of human bodies with a variety of other heads sticking out of his 'torso'. His arms consisted of additional people and his legs were each made up of two people.

"On the authority of the Sol Space Federation, I order you to surrender," Tanis called out.

"Right, because he's going to do that," one of the Marines said quietly.

"I have to say it…but I hope he doesn't. I'd very much like to see this…guy dead," Tanis replied.

John Cardid had started chuckling as he heard the statement. "I don't think so. Even now my forces are flooding out through tunnels not on the station's net to flank you. You'll join us or die. Chances are that you'll join us even if you do die."

Almost as one, the figures on the edges of the space began to push off and, like a slow wave, Cardid's followers moved toward the platoon.

"Platoon…retreat." Tanis said aloud before sending the command over the combat net to the entire battalion. <*We can't overcome these odds, but we'll be back with some friends.*>

The 4th Bravo began to move back up the corridor, keeping an eye out for the flanking forces Cardid had spoken of. Tanis and one/one were moving backward, covering their escape, and one of the Marines planted a few high explosive charges on the walls as they went.

"Can't cause a 'cave-in' in zero-*g* but it can block them and their plasma bolts for a bit."

Tanis nodded her approval and when they were at a safe distance from the charges, the Marine detonated the packs. The shockwave rippled past them and back down the corridor; the walls turned into high-speed gravel. It wasn't a moment too soon as fire from Cardid's forces began to impact the debris cloud.

<*Double-time,*> Tanis called up. <*Not a lot of cover back here.*>

The platoon picked up the pace, but they were soon slowed down by the aforementioned flanking forces.

They managed to move, but slowly, fighting for each meter. The Marines were beginning to show signs of cracking. When a series of spider-looking things crawled out of a tunnel, a few began to fire wildly in all directions, screaming in horror over the Link.

Williams was there in an instant, shouting them back into control and then calming them. Tanis was impressed with his abilities, but knew he wouldn't be able to maintain control for long.

The platoon was taking hits, running low on ammunition and close to losing it.

<*Arcturus, come in,*> Tanis called the cruiser, passing the current sit-rep. <*I need evac for all platoons, pick up the teams holding the egress points first, then have the birds hold positions in these locations.*> She provided the data over the Link and Captain Arsenal acknowledged.

<*I have targets for your lasers as well,*> Tanis said as she passed up the data that Angela and Bruno had worked up, over a hundred coordinates that would clear paths ahead of the Marines and hopefully slow down their pursuers.

<*This will open up the interior of Toro to vacuum,*> the captain objected. <*You'll kill everyone in there!*>

<*It won't kill us,*> Tanis barked back. <*That's pretty much all I care about right now. Do it. That's an order!*>

Tanis suspected he was consulting his packet for a way around the order. There wasn't one and she knew he would comply.

Her expectations were confirmed as a section of the tunnel a hundred meters behind the platoon disappeared in a white-hot flash. The tunnel shook as the rock rapidly expanded and the Marines felt their magnetic boots increase the strength of their magnetic lock as air whipped past.

Several exceptionally grotesque enemies flew by as the tunnel decompressed, eyes bulging, but still firing at the Marines. Tanis fired back as she kept the platoon moving up the corridor to the evac point.

As if on command, another white-hot flash of laser fire tore through the tunnel further ahead, cutting a path to the surface of the asteroid and their waiting transport.

The Marines rushed into the space and used their armor's thrusters to avoid the white-hot walls of the wide shaft. At the top, their transport awaited, three/one hanging off the sides, firing at the monsters who seemed not to care that they were dying in the vacuum.

The battalion's combat net showed that all the platoons were on their transports; the 4th Bravo, being the furthest in, was the last out.

Looking down, Tanis saw dozens of holes on the surface of Toro venting atmosphere, but there were also several small ships taking off from the asteroid itself and the ring of stations surrounding it.

Even though they should be evacuating, the ships accelerated on attack vectors, aiming to take out the Marine transports.

<*Take them out,*> Tanis called to the *Arcturus*. This time there was no argument. Laser fire arced between the cruiser and the attackers. It was invisible in the emptiness of space, but the results were instantaneous as dozens of enemy ships exploded.

The Marines had all locked down in the transport and Tanis took her seat, watching the external monitors. Below them, the holes the *Arcturus* had burned were no longer venting atmosphere. Suddenly a large crack appeared across the center of Toro, then another appeared laterally.

When Toro had been spun up for increased centripetal force, carbon nano-struts were added to re-enforce the asteroid. Cardid, apparently, had not increased the structural support to compensate for the new tunnels and chambers.

The weakening effect of the laser fire burning holes in the asteroid proved to be too much and Toro began to tear itself apart.

Like a slow motion dance of destruction, the asteroid broke apart, chunks breaking off and swinging out into space, while others smashed into the ring of stations. Explosions blossomed, and by the time the transports were docking on the *Arcturus*, Toro was no more.

The Marines were silent as the transports unloaded. They stripped out of their armor with little talking and carefully cleaned the blood and gore from their gear.

Tanis was working with them, cleaning the armor and weapons she had used. There were a thousand other things she should be doing, but she needed the time to collect her thoughts, to try to put together what had just happened into something that made sense.

"Colonel Richards!" a voice called out behind her. Tanis turned to see a squad of MPs approaching. One of them, an officer named Indras, stepped forward.

"Yes, Major?" Tanis asked.

"I am here to relieve you from command of the 242nd Marine Battalion and place you under arrest."

Several of the Marines around her turned sharply and bristled, a few reached for their weapons. She may not be a Marine, but apparently going through Toro had made her enough of one for them.

"What is the charge?" Tanis felt like the ship had fallen out from beneath her.

"Violation of the Phobos Accords, violation of the TSF code of conduct, use of weapons of mass destruction against civilians, and other crimes against humanity."

"There were no civilians and no humanity on Toro," Williams barked. "On whose orders are you doing this?"

The TBI agent, Brennan, was with the MPs and shook his head. "I forwarded the feeds. What you did was unconscionable."

The major's eyes were hard and unblinking. "On the orders of the president of the Terran Hegemony and the joint chiefs, come with us, Colonel Richards, we are to confine you to quarters."

Tanis set down the weapon she had been cleaning and followed the major; the other MPs forming a box around her as the Marines hollered and swore at their backs.

CRACKING A FEW EGGS

STELLAR DATE: 3241792 / 08.17.4163 (Adjusted Gregorian)
LOCATION: GSS *Excelsior*
REGION: LHS 1565, 27.0 AU from stellar primary

20:52 hours to asteroid group

Tanis ended the story with a small choke as she remembered the Marines calling after the MPs, their commanders just barely stopping a mutiny on the *Arcturus*. She looked up at Joe to see tears in his eyes; he reached out and wiped one from hers.

They didn't speak as they embraced for several minutes, Tanis found herself sobbing as emotion she had bottled up for so long came crashing out.

After she had regained control of herself, Joe spoke. "But it wasn't that bad—they didn't discharge you or imprison you."

Tanis nodded. "Once they watched the full sensory vids and the investigators sifted through the ruins, they realized that I had made the right call. Cardid was planning an all-out assault on several habitats and would have killed millions. It was only because we caught him by surprise that we were able to stop them. He had more powerful defenses, but they weren't online because he didn't want Toro to be targeted before he launched his assaults.

"So, in the end, I didn't lose my commission, I got a slap on the wrist for violating Phobos and knocked down to an LCO."

"And you got the media lambasting you."

Tanis nodded, the tears welling up in her eyes again. "That was the hardest part. Pretty much everyone I knew shut me out, including my husband."

"You were married?" Joe coughed. "I distinctly remember you saying that you'd never been in a serious relationship."

"I remember that, too," Tanis gave Joe a sheepish look. "I didn't want to talk about it then—don't want to much now. His name was Peter, I married him when I was fifty-five, I know, a little early for marriage, but I thought we were in love."

"I take it that he didn't handle Toro too well," Joe said with a frown.

Tanis shook her head ruefully. "He didn't care about what I did on Toro. He always got off on me being the tough girl who kicked ass and took names. He divorced me because he didn't want the career damage that being married to me would—" Tanis's voice broke and she took a moment to regain her composure "—that being married to me would cause," she managed to finish.

Joe wrapped his arms around her and held her for several minutes as she cried softly.

"Thanks... I haven't spoken of him since the day he left me. I didn't expect talking about him to turn me into more of a mess than telling you about Toro."

"So I guess he's not the type of ex we have to say nice things about. We can call him super-douche."

Tanis snorted a laugh. "Total ass-hat. The guy left me with nothing. I was unhireable and had to stay in the TSF, which I pretty much hated at that time for betraying me. I put in for colony the day he filed for divorce, but the TSF told me they'd block it if I didn't stay in the military for another decade." A fire was back in Tanis's eyes as she thought about it.

Joe shook his head slowly. "I'm sorry it went down like it did; you certainly didn't deserve the raw deal you got. I have to admit, though, I didn't learn about Toro until you joined the *Intrepid's* crew. There was all sorts of scuttlebutt about how you got on the roster."

"Really?" Tanis asked. "How did you not hear about Toro? I blew up an entire station. It was practically the only thing in the news cycle for weeks."

"I was on a mission when it went down. I had heard people talk about the Toro disaster a bit, but even after you came onboard I didn't look into it—I wanted to form my own opinions of you, not be poisoned by someone else's."

"I'm glad you didn't. '*Killed twenty-thousand people*' is a hard first-impression to lose. The redacted mission report isn't much better. Thank starlight that the captain and Sanderson had access to the classified version or they would never have let me aboard." Tanis cast Joe a thoughtful eye. "What sort of mission were you on that you didn't hear about Toro, though?"

"Remember Makemake?" Joe asked.

"Remember? It was the thing that took my name out of the news." Tanis saw the pained look in Joe's eye and her expression turned to one of concern. "I'm sorry, that was cold. It must have been a really raw deal for you guys."

Joe nodded. "I didn't file my application the next day, it was a bit later. I was at Makemake—"

<*I have the response from the* Intrepid *coming in,*> Troy interrupted.

Joe looked at Tanis and nodded. "Play it," he said.

Captain Andrew's face filled the holo.

"*Excelsior,* good to hear you are still out there and apparently on your planned vector. I'm sure you noticed we aren't where we're supposed to be. We had a bit of a run in with a rather unfriendly solar flare."

Joe glanced at Tanis, he looked concerned, but the captain's voice hadn't betrayed anything one way or the other.

"We're still not certain if it was going to happen anyway, or if our magnetic resonance caused the flare, but either way the sunspot erupted. We had thirty-five seconds' notice and Bob put everything our engines had into getting us clear, which we did, but just barely. The flare took out a lot of exterior electronics, destroyed some of the structural arcs, melted off the housing on the main port engine. There were some severe x-ray bursts, but with the ES shielding already focused on the port side, we didn't receive any lethal doses, though everyone is getting treatments. There were some gamma ray bursts, which can mess with stasis fields, so we've got teams checking everyone in stasis, which will be a bit of a task."

As the captain paused and Tanis and Joe looked at one another. This would be where the other shoe dropped.

"With our last moment burst and the engine damage, we came out of the slingshot at a different than planned trajectory. We don't have the fuel to correct, so you're going to have to meet us somewhere along our current path.

"I don't need to tell you that things aren't much better than they were before—except that we didn't burn up in Estrella de la Muerte. Unless you get us that lithium, we're not going to be able to even course correct enough to get to Epsilon Eridani.

"Good luck, *Excelsior. Intrepid* out."

Tanis leaned back. "Well, no one died, at least."

Joe looked shaken as he leaned back in his seat. He paused to choose his words and responded softly. "Sometimes I don't get you, Tanis. I know you are pretty hard-bitten, but sometimes you just seem blasé. Maybe just once you could have a good ole fashioned freak-out about something. It would make you more approachable."

Tanis didn't know how to respond. She had hoped that Joe finally got her. It wasn't that she was an emotionless bitch; she knew wisecracks were her coping mechanism. It hurt whenever people thought she didn't feel; the hurt made her angry.

"Get your shit together, Commander. The *Intrepid* can limp through space for ten thousand years if it has to. They have the equipment and resources to travel across the galaxy—if it would still be there once they made it to the other side—but we don't." She felt ashamed of herself the moment she said the words, but didn't know how to take them back.

Joe wiped a hurt expression off his face. "Is that how this is going to be? You'll pull rank and be ass-hat Tanis on me?"

Tanis lowered her eyes, staring at her cup of coffee.

"No, it's not. I *am* scared, I'm scared a lot… I think it's how I stay alive—by never letting it get to me. I push the fear down and compress it into action. Give me a problem and I'll make a plan. Once I have that plan, I put all my fear, doubt, and worry into making that plan work. And it works."

She looked up at him, his expression showing concern. "As a result, I only seem to have the one pep-talk speech." Tanis shrugged apologetically. "It involves words like shit, fuck, and ass. And it always uses rank."

"I'm not going to judge you, Tanis. I've seen you at your best and I've seen you at your worst—" Joe held up a hand to Tanis, stopping her from speaking. "You may think I haven't seen the depths of you, but I have. I watched when you tortured Kris and Trent. I know I wasn't supposed to, but I saw the feeds."

Tanis's face reddened. "I didn't know you saw that…I…I'm not sorry I did it, but I'm not proud of it either. I've done that sort of thing enough that sometimes I wonder if I have a soul anymore."

Joe reached out and turned her face so he could look into her eyes. "I know what you are capable of. You care for people around you. You care so much that you'll sacrifice your body and soul for them. You get called a hero and a demon, often at the same time, by the people you try to save. So you lock down."

Tanis nodded. "I know I do, I…"

"It's OK," Joe said, holding her close. "Like I said, I know the best and the worst of you, and I still love you. Take your strength from that."

Tanis lay against Joe for a long time. Perhaps he understood her better than she did herself.

<Thank you,> Angela said privately to Joe. *<I've been trying to explain that to her for some time, but she always dismissed me as not understanding. Maybe she can finally get over Toro now.>*

<Don't worry,> Joe replied. *<She's Tanis.>*

Tanis's head suddenly snapped up. "Damn."

"What is it?" Joe asked, concern lining his features.

"We didn't respond to the *Intrepid*. They'll wonder why we're taking so long."

Joe's quizzical look froze on his face for several long seconds before he broke into laughter.

"What is it?" Tanis looked at him, perplexed.

"You," Joe chuckled. "I swear, there is duty imprinted on your DNA."

"Of course there is," she smiled. "I had it tattooed on when I enlisted."

While she sent the message, Joe and Troy worked out the alterations they would need to make to reach the asteroid belt sooner and meet the *Intrepid* before a rendezvous was impossible.

"We're going to have some hard burns in a couple of hours," Joe informed Tanis as she completed her response to the *Intrepid*.

"Let's get some food before that happens," Tanis said, a mischievous smile on her face. "Don't think you can get out of telling your tale, you're still going to tell me about Makemake."

CHURN AND BURN

STELLAR DATE: 3241792 / 08.17.4163 (Adjusted Gregorian)
LOCATION: GSS *Excelsior*
REGION: LHS 1565, 30 AU from stellar primary

20:21 hours to asteroid group

Tanis stood up after the meal and poured two cups of coffee, adding sugar to Joe's and cream to hers. She handed Joe his cup and settled down in her chair, cradling the warm beverage.

"Mmm, just the way I like it," Joe said after a long draught. "You do pay attention."

"I did my fair share of dinner runs to the mess, if you recall. It wasn't all just you getting me my BLT."

"That's not how I remember it," Joe said with a wink.

"Enough stalling, it's your turn, mister."

Joe nodded and took another long drink before beginning.

"Like with Toro, the full story of Makemake never made it out to the public. It started before your jaunt to Toro began and ended a few months after. I was with the seventh fleet on the *Normandy*. We were leaving Ceres on our way to meet with the rest of the fleet for maneuvers near Venus."

"I read a briefing about that," Tanis said. "It was to test defensive patterns after the left-over core from Uranus was positioned between Venus and Earth."

"Yup, but we never arrived, we did a polar loop around Sol and boosted north. The word on the ship was that orders changed and we were doing a patrol of the Oort cloud, but we all knew we weren't provisioned for a haul that long.

"There was a lot of scuttlebutt, especially with the Scattered Worlds representatives talking separation in the SolGov congress. Some were also worried that we were on an Outsystem trajectory to Alpha Centauri or Tau Ceti, though anyone who could look out a window at the stars could tell that we weren't headed there. The captain and the XO weren't talking but I figured we were on our way to the disk somewhere. I didn't expect us to be going to the capital, but rather Eris or New Sedna."

"Ballsy to go right for Makemake," Tanis commented.

"It was. I still don't know if that was the order or if the captain was given some leeway. I don't think she'd churn and burn on a capital world without being explicitly told to.

"Either way, we went dark at our apex and took several months to drop back down the solar plane. When we were approaching Makemake we were still going damn fast. The *Normandy* did the burn and made for a pretty rude awakening."

"I can imagine, I saw the vids of the *Normandy* braking over Makemake, it was brighter than their little pseudo sun," Tanis nodded.

"We ended up engaging the SW fleet and even did a few strafes of their capital before they capitulated and stopped their separatist movement. There weren't a lot of casualties, but I felt pretty damn dirty shooting down pilots of a sovereign nation because they wanted to leave the union."

"Wait a second," Tanis double-checked a reference she remembered seeing once, "your mother was living on Makemake at the time!"

Joe nodded slowly. "She was—I had a lot of family down there…I almost killed my sister in that engagement."

His voice caught and he looked down at the table, fiddling with the handle of his cup as he regained his composure.

Tanis reached across the table and took Joe's hand. "I can't imagine how that would have felt."

He looked at her for a moment and then over her shoulder at some personal memory.

"Pretty shitty, I can tell you that much," Joe replied. "I put in for colony the day after I found out she was there. Sol is just too messy. Everyone knows that SolGov is falling apart. The Jovians want to separate too—only the million TSF ships running around the system keep it from happening."

Joe looked Tanis in the eyes. "You know it's going to happen eventually. The system is going to have an all-out civil war. There are just too many people who are too balkanized. I don't know if there should be one central government. Not when it sends sons to shoot at their mothers."

Joe's voice had risen and his eyes flashed with anger. Tanis laid a hand on his and nodded. "I know what you mean; I had a similar thought process. Why would I lay down my life to maintain a system that made monsters like Cardid only to throw me under the bus for killing them?"

"If a civil war had erupted, I don't even know which side I would have chosen," Joe said. "Do you?"

"Stars above…I have no idea." Tanis shook her head. "I guess I'd pick the one that was the least evil and would win the war the fastest. Honestly, though? I'd rather be out here falling into a star than having to make that choice."

"That's for sure," Joe agreed.

"I feel like it was easy for me," Tanis said. "I have nothing in Sol, just a sister who I hadn't spoken to long before Toro, let alone after. You—you have your mother and her whole brood."

Joe nodded slowly. "It was rough, but my mom understood a lot more than I thought. She's getting on, closing in on five-hundred. She told me that I should find what makes me happy—she was also glad that I wasn't going to stick with an outfit that had me strafing the city she was in," Joe chuckled.

"My older brother is hundreds of years older than me; I barely know him and didn't bother to tell him I was leaving. My younger brother took it pretty hard. He's practically a sanctity activist and told me I was abandoning my people by leaving. He also had some choice words about me going off to help defile another system. He and I didn't part ways on the best of terms."

"I don't get how people think taking lifeless worlds and terraforming them is defiling them," Tanis said, shaking her head.

"No argument here," Joe said. "This is a colony mission after all."

In the three hours before the next hard burn, Tanis shared stories of her childhood on Mars and he of his youth on Vespa. He fell out of his chair laughing when she told her story of stealing a maglev train to impress a boy in college and he regaled her with stories of his flights in the TSF stunt squadron.

For a time, they completely forgot the struggle that still lay ahead and the real danger that the *Intrepid* would never make it to its destination.

SUBTERFUGE

STELLAR DATE: 3241792 / 08.17.4163 (Adjusted Gregorian)
LOCATION: GSS *Excelsior*
REGION: LHS 1565, 27.1 AU from stellar primary

The figure slipped through the corridors of the *Intrepid,* its shimmersuit masking its presence from all sensors. Only the movement of air would give it away, but that would take a nano-cloud to detect and its own cloud showed that it was alone.

With the rewrite of the servitor code and its loss of the AI in node eleven, it could not directly control enough systems to cause serious trouble, but it had learned that certain members of the command crew were uneasy with the ship's secret cargo.

A less technological route would need to be employed to stop the *Intrepid* from continuing its trip to New Eden.

The first person on the list to visit was Hilda Orion; she had posted a few plans on the solution boards, which suggested she was not happy about the direction the trip was taking.

The figure was not pleased either.

The threat of falling into LHS 1565 was intended to force the crew to stop in the red dwarf's star system, consume colony supplies, and then divert to an inhabited system. It should have worked—would have worked if Joe hadn't figured out a solution that allowed the *Intrepid* to keep on course to New Eden.

The figure considered that perhaps Joe should have been dispatched some time ago. He bolstered Tanis too much, made her hard to deal with.

Still, there were contingency plans and all it would take was a nudge here and a poke there and the crew would do exactly what was necessary.

Now that the ship was past the star, much of the crew was off-shift, getting some shut-eye before the *Excelsior* returned with its fuel rock.

Hilda was in her quarters and the figure stopped before her cabin's door. A small swarm of nano slipped around the portal's edges and reported that the woman inside was sleeping.

The figure may have lost its root access to core systems, but its public position on the *Intrepid* granted it enough access to open any cabin door. A few auth codes later and the door slid aside. The record would show that Hilda left for several minutes before re-entering her cabin.

No log would show the invisible figure visiting her in the night.

FISHING FOR ROCKS

STELLAR DATE: 3241791 / 08.17.4163 (Adjusted Gregorian)
LOCATION: GSS *Excelsior*
REGION: LHS 1565, 27.1 AU from stellar primary

Joe and Troy altered the vector, increasing burn to an uncomfortable 3.2*g*. As a result, when braking occurred it would be even higher at just under 5*g*. It was a bit of a gamble because calculations showed that if they couldn't get enough mass knocked off Fuel Dump—the name Tanis had given their target—then there wouldn't be enough antimatter left to rendezvous with the *Intrepid* on its new vector.

Over the next nineteen hours they slept, ate, watched scan, and sent a few messages back and forth to the *Intrepid.* A few of the colonists' stasis pods had been disrupted by the gamma radiation and colonists were found wandering the stasis chambers, trying to figure out what was going on. It wouldn't have been so bad if the flare hadn't knocked out certain sections, cutting those portions of the stasis chambers off from communication.

The colonists were being treated for radiation poisoning and the engineers were working on getting the engines repaired to course correct once the lithium was extracted from Fuel Dump and brought onboard.

Bob was regaining control of the ship, though there were entire sections with nothing functioning other than the rogue machines that prowled the halls. Before the enemy AI had been destroyed, it had left final commands for all of the equipment it had subverted. Ouri had teams working through the ship and hoped to have things under control soon. Not unexpectedly, Abby had begun registering formal complaints about the damage to her ship.

Due, in part, to the heavy gravity, the tub became a favorite place to spend time, the buoyancy easing the high-*g* strain. Unfortunately, the increased weight from the thrust made any more interesting activities impossible, or, at the very least, undesirably exhausting.

Tanis also found it difficult to sleep in the high gravity. Blankets felt untenably heavy and every pressure point on her body was aggravated from the weight. They took to sleeping in the acceleration couches on the bridge, shipsuits set to maximum cushioning. When the ship reversed and began breaking at 4.8*g*, it only got worse. Both Joe and Tanis grew testy and had to take care not to snap at one another.

Finally their target came into view, a slightly oblong rock, a kilometer wide and slightly more than that in length. It spun slowly as it orbited its star, which at this distance was dimmer than many of the other stars in the stellar neighborhood.

"Damn, it's got a little moon," Joe said as he pointed at a small hundred meter companion.

"We'll have to blow that away, won't we?"

"I believe so," Joe said. "Then we have to use our thumpers to knock that dust off. We'll have to do the first one on the northeastern side then send a booster over to push it away and ensure the dust doesn't settle, or form another moon. Then we do the other when it's at the right point in its rotation. Boost some more then use the grapple."

"How do you propose we take out the moon?"

Joe examined the display. "Troy and I agree. Use some of the smaller explosive projectiles on it every time it is moving directly away from us. That'll accelerate it and cause it to break away."

"Ok, I'll take care of that."

Joe prepared the thumpers and programmed in the precise coordinates, getting them checked and triple checked by Troy and Angela. Tanis played target practice with the moon, and in three orbits had it increasing its speed and pulling away from Fuel Dump. Two more orbits and the hundred-meter lump of aggregate went spinning off into space.

"Little moon all gone," Tanis reported.

"Good, I'm launching the first thumper now. Check Troy's calculations on the booster so that we can launch it as soon as the thumper does its thing."

Tanis ran through the math, checking distances, rotations, impact velocities, and gave second confirmation on the numbers. Angela rang in with a triple check moments later.

<*I beat you!*> Tanis was surprised.

<*Yeah, well, you're not managing scan and monitoring comm from the* Intrepid *at the same time.*>

<*Oooo monitoring scan and comm. That's tough stuff.*>

Angela didn't deign to reply.

<*Triple check received on the booster. Ready to launch,*> Troy reported on the shipnet.

"First thumper away." Joe manually flipped the release switch and then the holo counterpart.

They watched as the thumper launched from the *Excelsior,* a slight shudder running through the ship as the thrusters compensated for the motion. The thumper flew across the intervening distance and split into twenty-eight separate pieces before diving into the dust and aggregate on the northeast face of Fuel Dump.

They waited a breathless moment, and then the kilometer long rock appeared to jerk violently, a massive plume of dust and debris spraying out of the thumpers' insertion point. Fuel Dump's rotation began to wobble and the booster launched from the *Excelsior,* moving on the carefully planned route, which allowed it to avoid the wobble and dust.

It planted precisely where the calculations had indicated it should and the display dimmed as the fusion torch ignited on the rock, pulsing on every rotation to move Fuel Dump further from the coalescing aggregate cloud.

"So far, so good," Joe said as he began plotting the path for the second thumper.

While Tanis was aware of the processes used to move asteroids and even small worlds, it was really something else to be actively involved in it. Most people never moved anything much larger than a small people transport; here they were at the edge of an uninhabited stellar system, hijacking an asteroid.

More impressive was that they would boost it up to 0.10*c* and deliver it to the *Intrepid.*

The thought reminded Tanis to send her update letting the colony ship know they were currently on schedule.

Joe got triple check from Troy and Angela and sent the second thumper. Its twenty-two separate units sunk beneath the dust on the western side of the rock and moments later an eruption of debris plumed.

<*Perfectly done,*> Troy said.

"Appears to be." Joe scrutinized the scan of the rock, looking for any signs of fracture. Scan had showed that, aside from the aggregate and dust, the core was a solid chunk, split off from whatever was out there that broke apart to form the asteroid ring.

The booster was set to fire in ten seconds and Tanis mentally counted it down. In the brief time between one and zero, Joe's hand flew out and pointed at something on the holo display.

It was too late. The booster fired and a fracture appeared in Fuel Dump.

With exquisite grace for a lump of rock, the asteroid split apart along its axis, one piece sliding to the side while the portion with the booster attached picked up speed and began to move away from the ship.

Tanis quickly killed the booster and glanced over at Joe.

"Well that makes things a bit harder."

Joe scrubbed his face. "You're telling me. The booster has small jets for maneuvering. As gently as possible, see if you can rotate it and gently slow it down."

"Got it, gently," Tanis said.

Joe, Troy, and Angela had screens filled with vector calculations racing back and forth across the main display as they determined the best way to catch both portions of the rock.

The *Excelsior*'s main grapple system was a set of stasis emitter arms and a carbon tube net. The arms would emit a field that kept its payload from fracturing, and the net would wrap around the field to pull it behind the ship. While the ship could haul multiple items, it was a delicate dance to get more than one thing in the net, and they were short on time.

"It's gotta be the one without the booster first." Joe pointed at the calculation that favored that approach. "We can use the booster to get the other piece moving on our rendezvous trajectory and then simply scoop it up on our way."

The plot appeared on the display and Tanis started running the computations to make her piece line up.

"Stellar north or south of our plot?"

Joe examined the convoluted acrobatics the *Excelsior* would be going through. "North, we can tweak a few degrees either way to sync up. Just be gentle with that thing. The booster is nowhere near centered."

"This ain't my first rodeo." Tanis grinned at Joe.

"Yeah, you're not bad for a MICI girl," Joe placed a hand on her leg and gave it a squeeze before turning back to his screen.

The next half hour was full of running calculations, checking other crewmembers' math, and then running more calculations. Through it all, Joe was deftly maneuvering the ship to match the slow tumble of Fuel Dump B.

The *Excelsior* was rotating and shifting in a pattern that would make a bat puke, and yet Joe was completely unfazed.

Tanis never ceased to be amazed at how good a pilot he was. His flight records could only tell so much. She had seen him in combat, adrenaline rushing, but this was something else—long, grueling work, matching wits against an asteroid the size of a small space station. She harbored no illusions that she could do it even half as deftly as he did.

<*I swear, even I can feel my connections shifting,*> Troy said. <*Good thing I had the foresight to empty the tub.*>

Tanis laughed. "Damn, sorry about that. Would have been one hell of a mess."

<*I would have made you clean it up, too.*>

At long last, the two stasis arms extended and—with the net ready to snap out—emitted their field. Visually nothing changed, then, as Joe manipulated the field, the rock stopped tumbling and aligned with the ship. Once the ship and rock were relatively stationary, the net shot out on either side of Fuel Dump B, meeting on the far end, secured to the rock by thousands of spikes.

"Latched on," Joe said. "Plotting intercept course with the second piece."

The burn was gentle and Tanis couldn't help but run the calculations on their fuel levels over and over again. Whether they would have enough antimatter to accelerate and then match vectors with the *Intrepid* was now within the margin of error. She ran it again. And again.

Joe was right. Being in a situation where there was nothing you could do about the outcome really did suck.

As luck would have it, picking up the second piece went smoothly. The *Excelsior* began its final burn to meet up with the colony ship.

*****

"Good news and bad news, sir," Hilda said as she stood and turned to Captain Andrews.

"I imagine it's the same piece of news." The way this day was going, it was the norm. Only it wasn't just a day, it had been several. He hadn't slept the entire time, only retreating to his ready room periodically to catch a short nap on his couch.

"Colonel Richards' latest update indicates that they got the rock—they named it Fuel Dump—and though it split into two pieces when they shed mass, they are on their way."

"I can imagine what the bad news is."

"They aren't certain they have enough antimatter to make it here, or, if they do, to maneuver and match our vector."

The captain nodded and Hilda returned to her station.

She was right, good news and bad news. Still, Tanis Richards was on the *Excelsior,* and in his book that counted as a miracle just waiting to happen.

<*She'll pull it off.*> Amanda had been listening in on the bridge conversations.

<*What are you doing snooping in on bridge comm?*> Andrews asked. <*I thought you were in the hospital.*>

<*She won't sleep or even relax.*> Priscilla inserted herself into the conversation. <*Even though Bob, the doctors, and I have all told her she needs to rest.*>

<*I was involved in nearly destroying the ship, I have some redeeming to do.*>

<*You are using the word 'involved' rather loosely,*> Andrews' tone was gentle, but firm. <*No one holds you responsible. The rogue AI used your access to subvert the ship and you were not a willing participant, no one holds you responsible.*>

<*Except me.*> Amanda's voice was small.

<I've altered your programming,> Bob joined the conversation. *<A repeat of these events will not be possible.>*

<Bob, even though we all know you can do it, the thought of you so obliquely stating that you can alter a human's 'programming' is disconcerting.>

<I know.> There was a ghost of a grin and Bob's presence left the conversation.

<I don't think that made me feel better.> Amanda's avatar shook her head.

<You'll feel better when you rest. Captain's orders.>

<Like she'll follow them,> Priscilla groused.

* * * * *

"Every time I run the scenarios we're lower on fuel. We've got more drag than anticipated." Tanis looked up from her console at Joe.

"I'm getting the same thing. I think the stellar medium is thicker than anticipated. Not much, but enough to screw us."

"Can you come up with anything?"

Joe sighed, gave his console a long, hard look and then turned sorry eyes to Tanis. "I can't."

"I refuse to accept that. There is always something you can do. I didn't survive over a thousand engagements to die because a spaceship runs out of fuel." Her eyes glinted in the dim lights of the bridge, a fire in them refused to be quenched.

"I…I don't know what to say," Joe replied

"Let's look at our inventory again."

Joe brought it up on the main holo. There were parts for the relativistic probe, another net, extra cores for the thumpers that hadn't been used in Joe's configurations, and several physical probes for examining rocks.

"Nothing much there," Joe said.

"I wonder." Tanis brought up the specs on the thumper cores. "I wonder if we can't make use of these somehow."

On another section of the display she brought up their route and removed the required fuel for one of the course corrections. It brought the numbers closer, but still within the margin of error. She tried removing a different course correction and got the same result. Then, looking at the fuel computations again, removed the fuel requirement for two course corrections.

The numbers came out of the error margin and showed green. They could rendezvous with the *Intrepid* and maneuver.

"OK, so if we can use the thumpers in place of fuel, then we're all set." Joe scowled at the display.

Tanis brought up a display of the ship's exterior and pointed at a structural ridge that bisected the hull. "We plant the thumpers along this ridge and then fire them off to adjust our course. These calculations show they have the impact force to do it."

"You saw what they did to the asteroid, right?" Joe looked incredulous. "They ejected a million tons of mass. They'll tear the ship apart."

"Oh, I don't deny that it will be as rough as all get-out, but we don't fire them all off at once. Stagger them, do it in stages. And the more, the sooner, the better; since it will take less to correct now than later."

Joe looked her calculations over again. "We're going to need to do EVA to mount them—the ship has no bots capable of that."

"So where are the suits?" Tanis asked.

*****

"What are you doing in here?" Priscilla looked up from her holo arrays in consternation. "Can't you do what you're supposed to for once?"

Amanda laughed. "When have I ever done what I'm supposed to? Besides, I can't sit in a med bay while everything is going to shit."

Priscilla glanced to her right and pulled several holo displays into the foreground. Her fingers raced over the consoles while her mind manipulated a dozen other systems.

"The accelerator is losing containment in the sixth coupling, isn't it?" Amanda asked.

"Yeah, that coupling has always been a bit twitchy."

"Let me help," Amanda walked to Priscilla's pedestal and pulled a holo display in front of herself. "I can help—you need it."

"You know you shouldn't, you've been through some ridiculous mental stress—what we do is hard enough under the best of circumstances."

"I'm not asking to interface with Bob, just let me shunt some tasks. I have to do my part here, don't you understand?"

Amanda's unblinking stare bore into Priscilla's eyes. She didn't respond for a moment, fingers still dancing across her displays. Slowly she nodded. "I do understand. Bob does, too. Here, take this, run the math and update the engineers with the ETA."

Amanda pulled the data stream to her display and reviewed the information.

"What on Earth? This can't work!"

Priscilla chuckled. "When has one of Tanis's crazy ideas looked like it would work?"

"Yeah, but this time she's crazy, she'll tear the *Excelsior* apart and we'll never get that fuel.

<*Either that or they loop around* Estrella de la Muerte *for eternity.*> The fear in Priscilla's mental tone was palpable. <*And we drift through space forever.*>

<*I'm really starting to wish you didn't call it that.*>

*****

Tanis finished welding the last of her brackets to the ship's hull. Joe was moving behind her, placing the thumper cores into the brackets, a small hauler bot trundling behind him on its magnetic tracks.

<*How's it going back there?*>

<*Questioning my sanity.*>

<*I'm not too happy about this either,*> Troy added.

<*Hey, any better ideas, speak up. I, for one, won't sit idly by while we fly past the* Intrepid *and drift forever in this godforsaken system.*>

<*Hey, I didn't say stop doing what you're doing,*> Troy snapped. <*Just don't expect me to be jumping for joy about it.*>

Joe sent the bot ahead to Tanis. <*Here, fill that one up while I do this one.*>

Tanis pulled the thumper core out of the bot's carriage and slipped it into her bracket, sliding the latch into place and then using her welder to tac it in.

<*Done.*>

<*Good, let's get inside. There's too much dust out here for my liking.*>

Tanis hadn't seen a single piece of dust impact the ship, but there was no point in testing fate. All it took was a tiny spec at these speeds to punch right through a person.

Minutes later they were back in the airlock, waiting for the inner hatch to cycle open. When it did, they stepped through and removed their helmets.

"You're going to need to go under for this again," Joe said. "Those impacts are going to be vicious and I can't worry about you and pilot the ship at the same time."

Tanis nodded. "I understand. But let me get a BLT in first. I always seem to come out of stasis hungry."

Joe looked over at Tanis in her stasis pod one last time before he brought up the thumper's control display.

<*Are you ready?*> he asked Troy.

<*No, but don't let that stop you.*>

Joe chuckled and sealed his EVA suit. There was a good chance that even if the maneuver were successful the hull would crack open in one location or another. Emergency systems should be able to seal any leaks in moments, but Joe didn't want to test out their speed with his life.

<*Initiating sequence,*> Joe said and flipped the holo-switch.

The screen showed a countdown to the first thumper firing and Joe had to force himself to relax and unclench his teeth.

The thumper fired on schedule and a deafening clang echoed through the ship. Moments later, the second thumper fired and then the third and the fourth.

<*The mounts are all bent, but the thumpers fired correctly, the anticipated course alteration for the first set match our calculations,*> Troy said. <*How are you?*>

<*Any chance you can turn off the bells in my head?*> Joe shook his head back and forth.

<*I did register that it was pretty loud,*> Troy said. <*I don't think there is anything we can do about that.*>

<*Don't worry, I can take it.*> Joe looked over the rocks they were pulling. <*The net and arms look OK too, let's move on to the next set.*>

Joe looked down at Tanis. "Hold on, just a few more to go."

The *Intrepid's* bridge erupted with cheers as the data came in showing that the thumper core detonations had achieved their goal. The *Excelsior* had altered course enough without using antimatter fuel. Calculations put it well within the green and the ship had survived the impacts with its hull intact.

<*Commander Evans to the* Intrepid.>

Another round of cheers sounded as Joe's smooth tenor voice filled the bridge net.

<*Captain Andrews here. Go ahead.*>

They were within just a few light minutes now and the response didn't take long.

<*The colonel's crazy plan went off without a hitch. Well, other than a ship that is going to need a new paint job and structural analysis. I haven't pulled her out of stasis, but the shocks were dampened enough in here that I'm not worried.*>

<*Very good, Commander. We'll await your updates at T-10 to docking.*> Privately, the captain added, <*Aren't you glad we forced you to take her along?*>

The response came back. <*Yes, yes I am.*>

* * * * *

"Holy shit," Tanis breathed as she got her first visual glimpse of the damage to the *Intrepid.*

They were approaching on the port side of the colony ship, the same side struck by the edge of the solar flare. At the rear of the ship, the housing had been completely burned off the port engine, exposing portions of its inner workings to space. Several of the gossamer arcs, which provided additional structural integrity to the ship, were gone, and a few more were warped and twisted.

The port cylinder rotated, showing Old Sam covered in large scorch marks. Tanis imagined those would be the areas with the failing stasis pods. Good thing someone had determined to bring an extra hundred thousand.

Several large stasis grapple arms were ready to take the load from the *Excelsior* and Joe communicated with the engineers, executing the handoff flawlessly.

Even with the thumper core assistance, the fuel situation was as close to the wire as possible. Once the final maneuvers were complete, Joe shut down the antimatter engines entirely and used thrusters to bring them into position for docking.

The *Excelsior* that landed was a different ship than the one that left a scant week ago. One side was scorched and dented from the cores and the forward shields were pitted and scratched. Upon visual inspection it was evident that the structural strut the thumper cores had pushed on was cracked in two places. The *Excelsior* wouldn't be going anywhere until serious repairs were done.

The ship eased in on the magnetic rails and Tanis pulled up a view of the dock. There had to be at least a hundred people down there, all cheering their lungs out.

<*Look at all of them. You rate quite the reception,*> Troy said.

"You deserve this as much as we do, Troy," Tanis said. "You're one hell of an AI."

<*You know, I now have a much better appreciation for what some of my instructors meant when they said there is no teacher like experience.*>

"I know that all too well," Tanis said.

Tanis and Joe walked out of the ship's port hatch and down a gantry to the waiting crowd. In the front stood Captain Andrews and Terrance Enfield. Both men were beaming and clapping with the crowd.

"This is getting to be a habit, you saving the *Intrepid.*" Captain Andrews smiled at the pair.

"One I hope you don't intend to break anytime soon," Terrance added.

Tanis looked at Joe and they smiled at one another. It was good to be back home.

INCONSISTENCIES

STELLAR DATE: 3241794 / 08.19.4163 (Adjusted Gregorian)
LOCATION: GSS *Intrepid*, Security Operations Center (SOC)
REGION: LHS 1565, 153 AU from stellar primary

Tanis let out a long sigh and leaned back in her chair. Her old office in the SOC was exactly as she'd left it, down to the nicks in the desk and the stain on the couch where Terry had once spilled a glass of juice.

Outside her door, the SOC hummed with activity as every colonist out of stasis went through a re-interview process. Stats and transcripts from several of the interviewees hovered above her desk, keeping Tanis in the loop every step of the way.

She closed her eyes again and the virtual conference with the command crew snapped into place in front of her.

<*...you don't understand,*> Abby was saying. <*If we can't make the correction burn in the next fifteen days, then we are well and surely screwed!*>

<*Tanis, what is your progress in reviewing the crew and colonists currently out of stasis?*> Captain Andrews asked.

<*We're at a little over fifty percent. So far everyone is passing with flying colors—if we keep up this pace we'll be done in another three days. Then we can pull more people out of stasis.*>

<*Three days!*> Abby all but shouted. <*I need more hands **now**. With so many automatons damaged by the AI, or destroyed by your security sweeps—not to mention the damage you did to the machine shops that could build new ones—we need every hand we can get.*>

Tanis could spot gross exaggeration when she heard it. A lot of servitors and bots *had* been destroyed, but the damage she and Joe had done to the machine shops was minimal at worst.

<*We're working as fast as we can. But if we let another person slide who is somehow able to damage the ship, then we'll be even worse off.*>

<*Hard to imagine being worse off than drifting through space forever,*> Abby replied with a sour look on her virtual face.

<*Abby, in three days the disruptions to your current crew will be over and you'll be getting fresh hands. If your requests for additional crew are filled within five days, will you have time to get everything done for the burn?*> the captain asked calmly.

Abby sighed. <*Yes, we can get it done, but we won't be getting a lot of sleep.*>

<*No one is getting a lot of sleep right now,*> Andrews replied.

The meeting ended and Tanis opened her eyes again to see Ouri standing in her doorway.

"That looked like a fun conversation, boss," she grimaced. "You were making some choice expressions."

"Just talking progress with the brass," Tanis replied. "What can I do for you?"

"I wanted to talk about Collins."

Tanis gestured to a chair. "Sit, but before you get started, no recriminations."

Ouri's mouth twisted into a wry smile. "What gave it away?"

"Nothing, but I'm wracking my brain trying to see how I didn't catch on to any of this. I figured you must be doing the same."

Ouri laughed. "Good to know I'm not the only one."

"Not by a long shot. If we hadn't saved the ship on a dozen occasions, we'd be in pretty deep hock right now," Tanis said.

"I guess that does paint things in our favor a bit." Ouri paused for a moment before continuing. "I've instructed Terry to look at what people have done since joining the crew or colony as much as what they did before coming onboard. Perhaps we can find some patterns that will point us in the right direction. I also have a team dissecting every move Collins made since he came on board. Hopefully we'll identify any co-conspirators."

"Pay extra attention to those last minute fill-ins we had on Callisto. It always seemed a bit odd to me that the GSS let people transfer in so late—even if their reasoning did pass muster at the time."

"Already on it, Colonel," Ouri said.

"Now you're just kissing up," Tanis laughed.

"Pretty transparent I guess." Ouri shifted to stand up, but Tanis stopped her.

"I looked at the reports; the cylinders took a bit of a beating. How's your little stand of trees doing?"

Ouri smiled. "Thanks for asking. Not too bad, the maintenance bots are cleaning things up. Most of the damage happened further aft where the engine released some radiation bursts during the flare. The majority of the damage in my neck of the woods was due to flooding."

"We should have a gathering down there once it's cleaned up. I think folks could really use that."

"I know I could. I'll see if I can put something on the schedule."

"No schedule, make it spontaneous when things are ready. I'll be a pleasant surprise."

"Will do, sir."

<*Some good advice you gave about recriminations,*> Angela said.

<*I can control how her boss acts, mine is a different story.*>

<*Which one?*>

<*That's part of the problem,*> Tanis sighed. Her chain of command was a bit fuzzy on the *Intrepid*. Technically she reported to Admiral Sanderson, but on the ship, Captain Andrews had final say, except that Terrance Enfield—the project's financial backer—was on board. Each often gave conflicting directives and she had to be careful not to play them against one another, even accidentally.

Tanis knew that even though the captain had given his ruling, Abby would start to pester Terrance and he would go to Andrews. The captain was good at not reacting to pressure, but it wore on him and eventually he would come to Tanis to see what compromises could be made.

Tanis brought up her lists of colonists with investigatory experience. Engineers all but filled the roster, but people with investigatory experience were lacking. With the levels of terrorism and insurrection in the Sol system, she expected more folks from counter-terrorist or counter-insurgency agencies.

Angela would have been a help, but with the SOC short staffed, she was doing interviews of the crew as well. Tanis could hear her in the back of her mind asking a plasma transfer specialist about his hometown.

Tanis knew it was unusual for her to be able to hear Angela so well. She had always had a very close rapport with her AI, but after the merge with the fighters in the Sol system she had been able to hear Angela's thoughts more readily.

She knew her AI could see more deeply into her mind, as well—it showed in some of the observances Angela made.

Neither had spoken of it. It wasn't entirely unheard of and neither felt any pain or discomfort when it happened. They had enough to do and worry about without making up new problems.

A name appeared on the holo after Tanis ran a new search focusing on Terran federal agencies: Jessica Keller. The woman's record showed that she was a decorated, if somewhat unorthodox, agent from the Terran Bureau of Investigations.

There was no reason why she had left the TBI; in fact, upon closer investigation Tanis was surprised to see that she didn't seem to have the right clearances to be in the colony roster to begin with. Far from being a help, this woman looked like a new problem.

<It really is strange,> Angela commented. *<I can't find a record of her going through any pre-screening for colony, though somehow she was approved as a corrections officer for New Eden.>*

<Why should anything get any easier?> Tanis sighed. *<I guess I'll go wake her up and see. If nothing else, it may help pinpoint any fault with the screening data.>*

Maglev service to the cylinders had been restored and Tanis took a track that arched outside the ship. The starboard side of the ship was dark. Estrella de la Muerte, dim even up close, was barely visible anymore, providing no illumination. As the train arched over the dorsal hump and Sirius A, the Dog Star, came into view, its bluish-white light providing a bow-to-stern view of the ship.

There were a few repair crews working on external damage. Further aft, secured by a multitude of tethers and nets, was the Fuel Dump asteroid. Crews would likely be working on it, extracting lithium for a burn of the *Intrepid's* starboard engine, which would correct their vector and bring the ship back on course to New Eden.

Tanis's attention was brought back to the task at hand as the maglev train slowed and changed tracks to one mounted directly on the port cylinder.

Because the track ran around Old Sam, the centrifugal force caused Tanis's stomach to lurch as the feeling of "down" shifted from below to above her head a moment before the interior of the train pivoted to match. Half a kilometer later, it slipped through an ES airlock and slid to a stop at a station.

<You checked to see if the maglev had power, you didn't check to see if the station had any,> Angela commented.

<I know… I can't believe I did that again.>

<Maybe if you got more than three hours of sleep a night you'd think more clearly.>

<Soon. Just a few more weeks of this,> Tanis sighed.

She looked around at the small, dark station; even the emergency lighting was off. She wondered if coming with no armor and only a light-wand was wise.

<In my defense, aren't the cylinders supposed to have their own backup power for times like this?>

<Maybe ancillary systems were shut down to conserve power. If the switchover back to engine power hasn't happened yet, that would explain why we're in the dark.>

Tanis enabled her IR and UV visual overlays, in addition to sending out a wave of nano to sonar-map the route to the stasis pods.

<*Lights? Who needs lights?*>

<*You're just using all the tricks now, aren't you?*>

Tanis left the station and followed the map she had pulled from the *Intrepid* before boarding the maglev. Colonist stasis pods sheathed the sixteen-kilometer-long habitation cylinders, the area providing ample room for the 1.5 million colonists on the ship, as well as over a hundred thousand backup stasis pods.

With the power out, she again had to find creative ways to move three decks up and one kilometer along the cylinder. As she struggled with an emergency hatch, it struck her that roughly a hundred meters above her was Old Sam's interior; a world filled with hills, trees, and lakes, kept in place by the centripetal force of the rotating cylinder.

<*Worried it's going to spring a leak?*>

<*That sure would ruin my day, but no, somehow I think that's pretty unlikely.*>

<*Out of curiosity, if this Jessica Keller is hostile, how are you going to get her back to the maglev station?*> Angela asked.

<*I was thinking I'd just bash her on the head and throw her over my shoulder,*> Tanis said.

<*You know, even though I reside in your head I can't tell if you're serious about that.*>

Tanis laughed aloud. It was good to know she could still keep Angela on her toes.

Before too much longer, she entered a chamber containing stasis pods. Tanis had never been in this portion of the ship and had never seen a stasis chamber this large. It stretched for hundreds of meters and must have housed tens of thousands of colonists.

Unlike the corridors up to this point, this chamber had power, though only emergency lighting was on. The illumination cast long shadows across the pods.

Tanis suppressed the feeling that she was surrounded by the dead. It was too easy to imagine the pods containing some sort of inhuman horror waiting to rise up and claim her.

<*It's not Toro,*> Angela said. <*Nothing like that is here.*>

<*I know…it's just hard to keep those images out of my mind sometimes.*>

<*You could have them removed. Heck, I could even do it.*>

<*Don't you dare!*> Tanis snapped and felt her AI recoil from her sudden vehemence. <*Sorry Ang, I didn't mean to yell, but the thought of losing a part of myself, even a part that I don't really like, is pretty abhorrent to me. I'd lose a part of why I'm me, and then I'd be someone else.*>

<*Sorry I mentioned it. I won't bring it up again.*> Angela sounded hurt, but Tanis didn't know what else to say and let it drop.

<*She should be in that bank to the left.*>

Tanis turned and walked up an aisle, sending a command to the local systems to provide some additional lighting. The pods all looked much less sinister in the standard lighting. A command to the systems gave her the precise location of Jessica's pod and Tanis passed the protocols to unseal it and awaken its occupant as she approached.

<*Blue hair…was that back in style?*> Tanis asked.

<*I don't know, not something I keep track of. Isn't everything essentially in style all the time somewhere?*>

Stasis suits hugged the body perfectly and the former TBI agent's figure was clearly visible as the pod began cycling through its wakeup process. The woman was quite obviously modified from human norm and her blue hair was just the beginning.

While she appeared of normal height—around one hundred eighty centimeters tall—her legs were disproportionately long and her waist was quite small. Her breasts were also rather large for her frame. This was obviously a woman who had rebuilt herself for a purpose, though it was not something one often saw in a TBI agent.

As Tanis watched, the pod's lid lifted and the woman's eyes fluttered open. True to form, they were purple.

The woman lay still for a moment, staring up at the chamber's ceiling. Tanis assumed she was trying to Link to the nets. The local ones were up, but connections to the rest of the ship were unavailable. She must have learned something that alarmed her because the color drained from her face and she looked at Tanis.

"Is the local net's timestamp correct?"

ALTERED AGENT

STELLAR DATE: 3227225 / 09.29.4123 (Adjusted Gregorian)
LOCATION: High Terra, Sector RC3.4
REGION: Earth, Sol Space Federation

5 Months before the **Intrepid** ***departed the Sol system***

Jessica's boot crashed into the steel door, forcing it open against the protests of the apartment's occupant. The man on the other side flailed and lost his balance, hitting the floor hard. She strode through the entrance to his dingy home and he scampered back on his hands and feet like the most awkward of crabs, the expression on his face one of total fear.

"Mr. Jameson," Jessica said. "You've not pleased me, not pleased me at all."

"Agent Keller, don't kill me…please don't kill me," Jameson's voice quivered.

Whoa, that sure is leaping to a conclusion, Jessica thought as she looked impassively at the cowering man who appeared near tears. She really hated getting information from crying people, especially with all the sobbing and gasping. It took a long time to calm them down and reassure them—only to threaten them again.

It was tedious, but she softened her stance and expression.

"Jameson, are you high? I'm TBI, we don't just shoot people. We have district attorneys that need a reason for their existence—we hand scum like you over to them."

His eyes grew wide and he raised his hands. "You can't do that! They'll make me talk…and then I'm dead for sure."

Jessica reached back and swung the door closed, or as closed as it could get after her boot had forced it open. She walked forward and Jameson continued to back away from her.

"Oh for god sakes, man, get up already. I feel like I'm talking to some ring urchin."

That wouldn't be far from the truth. The apartment was pretty rank, close to one of the waste processing centers on the ring. Not the sort of place landlords could charge a lot of rent for, or attract decent residents to.

Jameson could probably afford better, but it suited him to be here. He slowly got to his feet and moved as far away from her as the space would allow.

Jessica sat down in a hard plastic chair and regarded the man. He was skinny, his cheeks gaunt and hands all knuckles and sinew—a sign of too many mods and not enough body to support them. His system was slowly cannibalizing itself for energy. Unless he altered his body to accept and store more calories he would be dead inside of a year, two at most. He must know it; maybe he didn't care.

His sunken eyes didn't seem to fit in the sockets right, probably a cheap set that weren't a custom fit. Why anyone would ever skimp on the eyes was beyond her. Getting the eyes right was the most important thing. Jessica had spent considerable sums of her own money on her pair of deep purple peepers; there was no way was she going to install the baseline units that the Terran Bureau of Investigation offered its agents.

"Look, Jameson. I'm not here to take you in. I'm not here to shoot you. I just want to talk." She tried to use her most soothing voice. It probably didn't come off that well since she was wearing Trellan FC9 body armor, the best protection available below a fully powered suit.

She pulled the helmet off, tucked it under her arm, letting her glossy blue hair free, and gave her head a shake to let it settle around her shoulders. Maybe if she reminded him she was a woman he would stop freaking out.

It seemed to help. Though the armor was heavy, it was well fitted. The waist was tapered and the amount of bosom under the plating was fairly obvious. Other than the joints, the armor was smooth and its matte sheen had a certain utilitarian look to it. Some guys got off on that sort of thing.

"Well, I guess that's OK," he said, his eyes seeming to be tracing the outline of her body. What do you need to know?"

"I'm looking for a guy. Goes by the name of Myrrdan. I got word you've dealt with him."

Jameson snorted, for the first time not looking completely scared. "Him? He's nobody, why would you want to find him?"

"I've got my reasons. Word has it that you saw him earlier today, he bought some access time on one of the Non-Sentient AI super nodes through you."

The NSAI super nodes were extremely powerful computers, often more powerful than dozens of combined sentient AI. They were useful in managing complex systems that required little ingenuity. In short, tasks that would bore humans, or sentient AI to tears…or whatever the AI equivalent of tears was. An NSAI super node could do things like plot the orbits of electrons around a quintillion atoms in real time, or index the entire wealth of human literature in a matter of minutes. They were also great at hacking through security.

"Why would I do that? Everyone knows that Myrrdan hasn't got any cred. I wouldn't let him buy NSAI through me, I could lose my access for tax work."

"Right, your tax work for folks who could never let a legit auditor look at their books."

Jameson looked rather depressed. "I don't know why you get so down on me…I'm a hardworking citizen."

Jessica laughed. "Hardworking, maybe, but at what?"

"Look, I'll tell you—will you leave me alone then?"

Jessica gave him a look that all but screamed the words *spill it already!*

"I did get him some time on a node: 76343.32343:99832.92034. It's not a super node, but he said he didn't need that much juice."

"How big a block and when?"

"A million relative seconds, beginning tomorrow at 1200. It's parallel, so only two thousand sidereal seconds."

Jessica was shocked. "A million? How much did he pay?"

"Uh…a lot."

Jessica could imagine, though she couldn't imagine what Myrrdan would do with a million seconds on an NSAI, even if it wasn't a super node. Well, she did have some ideas, but nothing she really wanted to think about.

Jessica stood. "Thanks, Jameson. You've been real helpful."

He nodded and muttered something about denting his door. Jessica didn't respond and pulled the portal shut behind her as she stepped out into the hall. With some effort, she got it latched; the boot mark was a cosmetic feature as far as she was concerned.

She walked quickly down the corridor and out of the block. A bank of tubelifts stood across the section's main access corridor and Jessica stepped into one of them, keying the surface level. The tube closed in around her and pulled her up at over a thousand kilometers per hour. The mass compensation system cushioned the effect and she almost couldn't feel the motion.

Jessica accessed her Link and reported the information to Nell, the AI in charge of organizing agents' duties and reports. Nell thanked her for the update and scheduled a meeting for 0800 with Sub-Regional Director Rickford to determine the next course of action.

The tublelift arrived at the ring's surface just as Jessica finished updating her internal calendar for the next day: 0800, discuss stopping madman; 1200, stop madman.

She walked out of the transit station into the soft glow of night, the earth hanging directly above her with the Asian sub-continent sliding by—the lights of the New Delhi arcologies a bright spot below the darkness of the Himalayas.

It was near the vernal equinox, which meant that the ring was in line with Earth and Sol. Whenever this occurred, the ring had two nights. The long night when its back was to Sol, and the shorter night as the far side of the ring fell in Earth's shadow. The event also created a days-long eclipse on the far side of the earth as the ring obscured Sol.

The nature of the ring, combined with the fact that it was a place where people travelled hundreds of kilometers in minutes, time zones were unused. This meant that it was 2164 everywhere on the ring, no matter if it was night or day.

Jessica could never get used to it. Sleeping during the day, night, morning, whatever; it messed her up every time. She missed Athabasca. It was too far north to catch shadow from the ring and had proper days and nights and regular seasons, unlike the mild winter/summer shifts of just a few degrees on the ring.

It made her itch to be back on Earth. Hell, it looked so close, hanging above her. She felt she should be able to reach out and touch it. However, she had another itch that needed scratching and there was just one way to get that done.

Her groundcar was nearby, ostentatiously sitting in a no-parking zone, its TBI identifier keeping it from getting disabled and towed. She slipped into it and sent a command over the Link, instructing it to take her home; time to get out of this armor and into something a lot more—or maybe less—comfortable.

*****

The ring was in its 'winter' phase, which meant that nighttime temperatures would get as cold as twelve degrees Celsius. Jessica wasn't about to let her fashion be a slave to temperature and wore a tight purple halter dress that didn't cover much more than a long shirt would into the club

The dress interfaced with her neuro-mods and slow patterns of shifting violet hues flowed across its surface. She altered their pattern to flow toward the front of the dress and then down suggestively.

Covering her feet and most of her legs were a pair of tall boots made of the same material. They ended half way up her thighs, appearing to simply merge with the skin on her legs in conformity with the current style.

She gave a toss of her hair and walked onto the club floor and began what could only be considered to be a mating dance. At least she certainly hoped it would be taken as such. Sex, preferably something kinky and steamy, was her only priority tonight. Myrrdan, the murders, the whole damn case, all of that could—no, would—wait until tomorrow.

Jessica knew her body was irresistible, she had gone through a lot to make certain of it. Her elongated legs combined with the heels of her boots made their proportion to her torso just shy of cartoonish. Her breasts were not too large, but certainly bigger than her natural size.

She ran her hands down her sides, nearly wrapping them around her fifty-centimeter waist, before caressing the smooth curve of her hips.

That had been one of the more costly modifications because of the spinal reinforcement and alterations to her digestive tract—namely the removal of most of it—to get everything to fit right. Her hips had needed a bit of a change as well to make the curve from her narrow waist soft and smooth.

Other than her hair, which "naturally" grew blue, her only other external modification was a slight narrowing of her hands; the effect made her fingers look exceptionally slender and nimble.

It was a body made to attract sexual partners. It even attracted her. Jessica had to admit that she often got off on herself more than her mates. There was just something about the crafting of her own form to be a sexual icon that excited her to no end.

She knew it wasn't an entirely normal response to have. TBI psychologists had recommended she alter her brain chemistry to have a standard sexual response—it probably would have been cheaper than all of the alterations to the rest of her body, but why would she want to do that? She *liked* the way she was.

Her dancing hadn't taken long to attract the attention of the opposite sex, and no small number of the same sex. She looked them over, sliding herself close to one or another from time to time.

A man was eying her from the bar. No, he was blatantly staring. He was pivoted on his seat, the drink behind him long forgotten. His eyes bored into hers and he didn't even glance down at her body. That was unusual to say the least.

His clothing was black, all black. It appeared to be some lightly textured polymer, close in appearance to natural leather. The jacket fit loosely around his large torso, and the pants were tight on the thighs and crotch, showing he had something to offer down there. She could only imagine his ass would be fantastic as she sashayed across the floor toward him.

Seeing that she was interested, he gestured to the seat beside him, rising as he did so. His eyes were black; not entirely, but close enough that without her own modified peepers she wouldn't have been able to tell in the dim light of the club. His hair was also black; falling down to his shoulders with a slight wave that led her to believe it could be natural.

She reached the bar and sat, taking a moment to make sure her dress was pulled down far enough so as not to give the entire club a view of her nether regions. She may be on the prowl, but she wasn't quite *that* lascivious.

"Jessica." She said by way of greeting. She already knew his name was Alex, courtesy of a quick ID lookup on the TBI database.

"I'm Alex." He offered her his hand and she shook it firmly. It wasn't the most demure thing to do, but she couldn't bear a weak handshake, especially not from her own hand.

"I couldn't help but notice your stare, Alex. Would you care to come out on the dance floor?" She gave a seductive smile and altered her dress to swirl patterns around her breasts.

"I would, but I don't think I could match your moves. I'd be Pluto to your Sol."

Jessica couldn't help but grimace slightly at the forced astronomical humor.

She turned and faced the bar, eyeing the bottles lined up in front of the holo display. "Then I suppose we should have a drink."

"What would you like?"

"I like the Nebula Margarita they serve here." Her tone was offhand.

The man waved the bartender down and ordered two.

"So what do you do for a living?" Alex asked.

She knew what he was thinking. He supposed she was a bimbo executive assistant, or some other sort of window dressing. Her body and clothing certainly told no other tale. Of course, that was the message she tried to send, no reason to scare potential partners off.

"I'm an administrative assistant for the VPs in a business near here." It was code for eye candy and occasional sex toy as there was no need to have a human perform any administrative tasks when an AI or even simple non-sentient software could do a better job.

Normally such a lie wouldn't work—it was too easy to find out everything about a person from a quick facial scan. Working for the TBI had its advantages—Jessica had bribed several techs to ensure that her job never came up when she was on the hunt.

The drinks arrived and the conversation proceeded down a rather predictable path. Before long they were checking into a nearby hotel. She followed him down the hall to the room, admiring the way his shoulders pushed against the jacket. God, she hoped he was modified, nothing like a man who knew where to enhance himself to turn her on.

Once in the room, he tossed his jacket on a chair and they wrapped their limbs around each other, Jessica taking a good look at his ass in the mirror—every bit as delicious as she'd hoped. She gripped it hard and bit at his neck, the other hand feeling the rippling muscles on his back. He had to be enhanced, there was no way a man could have shoulders this perfect on a natural body.

He pulled away from her and removed his shirt, displaying an absolutely perfect chest, pecks just the right size, with dark nipples at the tips. When he lifted his arms over his head to pull the shirt off and toss it aside they tensed up just right and sent a quiver through her loins.

His stomach was tight as well, a slight trail of hair descended under his pants, leading down to a promise she couldn't wait to have in her hands. She looked up to his face and saw that he had been following her eyes. He glanced down at her body and quirked an eyebrow; she knew what he wanted to see.

Pivoting her hips seductively, she placed her hands on her shoulders and slipped them under the straps of the dress. Slowly, but fast enough to keep his attention, she raised her arms, sliding the straps off her shoulders. With a twinkle in her eyes she lowered it past her breasts one at a time, stretching the dress tightly over them as she did so to make them bounce when they broke free.

His eyes were devouring her now, and she slid the dress down further, revealing her own perfect abs before pulling it past her hips and letting it fall to the floor. She wasn't wearing anything under the dress; other than her boots, she was now totally naked.

"Like what you see, Mr. Dark and Mysterious?"

His grin was somewhat predatory. "Yes, very, very much."

He stepped up to her, and pushed his groin into hers, their legs interlaced. His hands ran down her sides, over her hips, and traced their way between her legs before coming back up to cup her breasts.

"Get on the bed."

She smiled, throwing a mock salute. "Yes, sir, Mr. Sir."

Jessica sat down, and then lay back, using her long legs to push herself further onto the bed, the spike heels of her boots digging into the blankets. "You gonna come down here, or do I have to come get you?"

"Oh, I'll be there," Alex said. The look in his eyes had changed slightly. It was a tiny shift, from excitement caused by lust to excitement from control and power. She would have to watch him, make sure he didn't get carried away.

He turned to his jacket and reached inside for something. Jessica's hackles rose, but they were a moment too late. When he turned back, he had a sonic beam pistol aimed at her.

Sonic beam pistols weren't fatal if a person was only shot once or twice. However, even one shot at a heavily modded person would make them wish they were dead.

"What the fuck is this?" Jessica asked. "This your idea of a kinky little game?"

Alex smiled. The lust was gone; it was all a power trip for him now.

"No, though you do look damn fine. I'd love to screw your brains out, but you're way too dangerous to get that close to now."

"Next time do a girl a favor and fuck her before resorting to gunplay."

He chuckled. "I'll keep that in mind." He tossed her a set of ES shackles. "Lock these on your wrists, ankles, and neck.

Jessica pouted. "Think you could put the gun down and we could use these for fun?"

He didn't say a word, but his look spoke volumes. A gesture with the gun got her moving and she locked the shackles on the indicated locations. Nothing connected them, but they would lock together once activated.

"This is going to be a little uncomfortable," he grinned. So he did enjoy this sort of thing. The shackles were probably from his personal collection.

She felt the shackles begin to pull her limbs behind her back into a hog tie. Her neck arched back until everything met. He wasn't lying. It really did hurt.

"So, uh—" Jessica had to pause for air "—why exactly are you doing this?"

"I guess you'd like to know that, wouldn't you?" Alex sat in a chair and Jessica squirmed on the bed to see him. She was trying to ignore the fact that she was completely naked and the arching of her back made her breasts stand out like stretched cones.

"I kinda would, yeah."

"Well, you've managed to make an enemy who has decided to take you off his tail. I'm sure you know who I'm speaking of."

"Of whom I'm speaking," Jessica said.

"What?"

"You shouldn't end a sentence in a preposition. I don't care what they say, it's just not proper."

Alex snorted. "I really don't think you get to say what's proper or not. You're one of the most improper people I've met."

"Touché." Jessica sighed. "So what's the plan? Wait for me to cramp to death?"

"Well, I'm supposed to kill you, but I want to take a bit of time to enjoy the image in front of me."

She knew who wanted her dead, it had to be Myrrdan. She hadn't pissed anyone off enough lately for them to go to these lengths, other than him. Of course she did need to get free, apprehend—or maybe just kill—Alex, and then get Myrrdan.

"Take a good look; it's the last beautiful thing you'll ever see."

A fleeting look of concern passed over Alex's fantastic features before it turned to derision. "If you think you're going to get out of this, you're sorely deluded."

"Well…I don't know what you were thinking regarding my Link." Jessica smiled sweetly.

"What do you mean? The ES cuffs disable your wireless net access."

Jessica laughed, and then choked as the collar pulled at her neck. "Ugh…that's uncomfortable. I think Myrrdan doesn't like you as much as he doesn't like me."

Alex looked concerned now; this time the expression didn't fade. "Myrrdan? The serial killer?"

"Yeah…he's the one that set this up. You'll go to jail, and I'll just be humiliated. Better than dead, I think." Jessica tried to look smug, but imagined that she was failing in her current predicament.

"I don't get it. How are you thinking you'll get out of this?"

"I can only imagine that Myrrdan failed to mention that I'm TBI. I have a low band, high power backup connection. Your new jailers will be here any moment."

"Aw fuck." Alex got up from the chair and pulled his shirt back on and then picked up his jacket. He looked down at her and Jessica knew he was weighing whether to leave her, kill her, or take her as a hostage.

The hostage option was pretty dangerous. Jessica knew over three hundred ways to kill a person with her bare hands. Killing her would make the manhunt that much larger, that much faster. Letting her live was safest. He had to be assuming she had sent his information over the Link, so he was as ID'd as he was going to get.

He turned from her, apparently deciding to go with the latter of the options. Jessica smiled, knowing what he was in for as he opened the door. He pulled it wide, and stared directly into the muzzle of an assault rifle.

Alex's hands flew up and he backed into the room. Two SWAT officers in full powered armor stepped through the entrance, weapons trained on Alex. They were followed by Agent Rogers, who glanced down at Jessica and smirked before looking to Alex.

"Transfer the cuff control to me."

Alex appeared as though he was going to argue the point for a moment, but one of the SWAT officers leaned forward and tapped the muzzle of his rifle against the would-be assassin's head.

"I'd do like the man says."

Alex nodded and a moment later Rogers turned to Jessica and the cuffs released.

"Oh god...it hurts almost as much to straighten out." She stretched her legs and rolled onto her back, breathing deeply for a few moments before sitting up. "He's got a pistol in his jacket. Don't know what else."

Alex smiled innocently and pulled the pistol out.

"We were just having a bit of fun. Lady there likes this sort of thing, I mean look at her, she's built for fucking."

Rogers smirked. "Don't I know it. Doesn't mean you're on the up and up. You've assaulted, kidnapped, and threatened an agent of the TBI. You, my friend, are going away for a long time."

Jessica got up and slipped her dress back on while the SWAT officers cuffed Alex and led him out of the room.

"Little escapade gone wrong?" Rogers asked her.

"No, he was sent by Myrrdan to take me out of the picture."

Rogers chuckled. "I guess he found your Achilles heel."

"I'm never going to live this down, am I?"

"Doubtful."

She gave Rogers her most seductive look. "Think we could make a deal?"

He laughed and slapped her on the shoulder. "You may be the most sexed up agent in the TBI, but my wife is ten times more dangerous than you. Nothing you have is worth it."

Jessica pouted for a moment before turning off her sensuality. "Fine, Mr. All Business."

"You're not going to like what happened while you were playing with bondage boy," Rogers said as they walked out of the hotel room.

"What's that?"

"We think Myrrdan left High Terra. Every lead we've been following for the last day has been a red herring."

Jessica swore. "Where did he go?"

"We're not sure; there are a number of possible transports he could have left on. Maybe Cruithne, maybe Mars."

"What's our next move?" Jessica ran a hand through her hair, feeling like the night had gone from good to bad to really bad.

"Section chief has you on the next transport to Cruithne."

Her expression brightened. "Really? I hear they've got some amazing clubs there."

Rogers sighed. "You didn't get laid first tonight, did you?"

CRUITHNE REDUX

STELLAR DATE: 3227238 / 10.12.4123 (Adjusted Gregorian)
LOCATION: Cruithne Station
REGION: InnerSol, Sol Space Federation

The tether docking system on Cruithne made for a much smoother transfer of vector and gravity between the ship and the station. Larger ships could not be easily tethered, but smaller vessels like the *Ardent Dawn* were designed with the system in mind.

Jessica had only a minimal appreciation for the system as she arched her head back and screamed in ecstasy. Moments later, the man below her shook in the throes of his own orgasm and clawed at her shoulders.

He probably wanted to breathe. She loosened her grip on his neck and he spent a minute gasping for air.

Looking down at his puffing cheeks she realized that she didn't even know his name—looked it up—Steve, apparently. Not bad for a Steve.

"We're docked. Get to your cabin, I need to clean up."

He started to say something, which she ignored, sliding off him with smooth precision. The quarters were small and two steps put her in the san unit where she slid the door shut to his entreaties.

After three weeks on this tub, she had nearly run out of men. The crew was off limits after the captain had to step in on an incident, apparently playing the male crew members against one another was verboten.

Captain was a bitch anyway.

Out of the san, she was glad to see that Steve was gone. She stood for a moment, trying to decide between uniform or armor.

Cruithne was the dark underside of InnerSol—well, the best-known dark underside at least. If it was smuggled, stolen, pirated, or just plain illegal, it passed through Cruithne. She was certain it was some sort of unwritten underworld rule.

Though the asteroid-turned-station was part of InnerSol and fell under Terran jurisdiction, the law's reach here was limited. A very old family owned Cruithne and had ties with all the right people. Those ties let them get away with pretty much anything they wanted.

Jessica chose the armor—slipped into it after a trip back to the san for a full purge—and gathered up her belongings and dumped them onto a follower. The bot lifted off the ground and prepared to trundle after her.

With nothing onboard other than what was already on the bot, she was able to take the no-cargo umbilical. A quick pause at customs and she was in the main departure area of the Terra wing of Cruithne.

Across the space was a member of the Cruithne Police Force, one Captain Clyde according to Jessica's HUD. However, the TBI liaison agent that her dossier listed was nowhere to be seen, not particularly surprising from what she knew of the local office's track record.

Jessica established a connection to the local TBI dock and was cordially informed by the administrative NSAI that her liaison would be an AI by the name of Angharad, who was currently unavailable.

If an unavailable AI wasn't the strongest, most non-violent way to say "You're not welcome", Jessica didn't know what was. She filed it away in her mental "people to mess with later" category.

She approached the CPF officer and extended her hand.

"Special Agent Keller."

"Captain Clyde." The response contained not a drop of emotion. The woman could have been reading a serial number off a firearm.

"I assume that you have been briefed on my reason for being here." Jessica had no problem driving the conversation forward.

"I have. I will be your liaison with the CPF, the local TBI office will not be taking an active role in this investigation."

Jessica got the impression that they didn't take an active role in much of anything, unless looking the other way was considered an action.

"We'll need to stop at our main station. You will need to turn in your weapons and armor there." The CPF captain's voice remained monotone, not even a hint of challenge. If Jessica, didn't know, better she would suspect that the woman was an automaton.

"You're aware that Cruithne is in Terran space?" Jessica asked.

The officer's face finally flickered with annoyance, her first sign of emotion.

"I am."

"Good." Jessica smiled. "Then I'm certain you just had a mental lapse when you suggested that I disarm."

The CPF captain didn't respond for a moment and Jessica widened her stance, subtly shifting into a more threatening posture.

She knew Cruithne largely operated without Terran oversight, but this was ridiculous. If this cop thought she was going to walk unarmored in the most dangerous station in InnerSol, she had another thing coming—and it would be a very, very unpleasant thing.

"We'll still need to register your weapons, then."

Jessica gestured broadly. "Lead the way."

The captain turned with a not-so-subtle roll of the eyes—Jessica was going to get on famously with this cop.

Cruithne was everything the vids said. It was both fantastic and decrepit. Certain systems and visible portions of the station were plainly archaic, but a glossy sheen of new construction and technology had been laid overtop. It made her wonder how solid the aging station really was.

They were passing rows of shops, eating establishments, and the more upscale lodgings, all catering to the Terran clientele, posh and polished. The people were all fairly vanilla, slightly more interesting than the streets and corridors of Raleigh, but only marginally so. Here and there a fairly serious mod-job would hover or roll by, but for the most part, it was people using their own legs for locomotion.

Jessica was behind Captain Clyde by a pace or two and took the time to examine the woman's gait for evidence of modification. The woman wore the standard CPF uniform, a close-fitting mesh of ballistic impact material with ablative panels over crucial areas. She didn't have a helmet with her. Either the captain hadn't pissed anyone off lately, or she was paid up with all the protection rackets. Or she was a major player and no one would mess with her.

Jessica had originally been so bothered by the lack of a TBI liaison that she hadn't dwelled on the significance of a captain meeting her at the docks. In the CPF, there was only one rank above captain. This made Clyde a senior officer.

Normally such an assignment meant that they took the threat from Myrrdin seriously—in this case, Jessica suspected the CPF was more concerned with her than another murderer running around on their station. As long as he didn't kill the wrong people he could probably play here as much as he wanted.

Jessica reined in her wandering thoughts and resumed her examination of Clyde. There it was, the telltale twist in the hips and shoulders that indicated extra-muscular strength enhancements and most likely skeletal alterations as well. Clyde would be a tough cookie and probably had internal armor as well.

Jessica would too if she were a cop in a place like Cruithne.

<*I see you chose to take the path of greater resistance.*> Angharad's communication came in over the Link Jessica had established with the TBI offices.

<*If you've read my file I don't think it should surprise you.*>

<*I have, and it doesn't,*> came the reply. Jessica couldn't tell if the AI was just being non-emotive, as many of them were prone to be, or if she was being hostile.

Probably hostile.

<*Good, then we'll get on well. I assume you have no physical presence?*>

"You'd be incorrect." The AI's voice sounded from behind Jessica—she hadn't heard any motion back there other than the general bustle of the crowd. Clyde turned—again displaying a small amount emotion—this time smug pleasure.

Jessica turned and the three formed a loose circle in the corridor, unconcerned with the obstruction to traffic they were forming, not that anyone looked like they planned on taking umbrage.

Angharad, though an AI, apparently chose to take her female gender choice seriously. Her white and blue frame was artistically designed, all curves and flares, the effect a combination of sensuality and menace. She wore no clothes, her body's skin being her only outer layer. It was perfectly smooth without a seam or crease, but Jessica picked up the signatures of several weapon systems.

Between the three of them, they could probably reduce the whole corridor to a smoking ruin.

"Glad you could take the time to make an appearance." Jessica didn't bother with pleasantries—why waste them on an AI anyway?

"I was otherwise indisposed," Angharad replied.

"I can't imagine how," Jessica chuckled. Several amusing possibilities presented themselves to her.

"No, you probably couldn't." The AI's eyes seemed to flash.

"If we may be on our way?" Clyde asked. "I do have other things to do today."

"As do I, I need to catch a serial killer before he slips off your station."

"You aren't concerned that this Myrrdan will kill anyone on Cruithne?"

Jessica shrugged as they began moving again. "Either he kills the right people, in which case you won't care, or he kills the wrong people, in which case I'll probably applaud him and then you'll care about catching him."

"That's a dangerous sort of attitude to have on Cruithne," Angharad commented.

Jessica simply shrugged. She wasn't going to get in a pissing match with an AI.

*****

The CPF station was standard fare. Jessica registered the magnetic signatures of her beam weapons and failed to disclose her ballistic sidearm holstered within a hidden compartment on her armor. They probably knew she had it, but no one brought it up. From there, she requested access to the records of all incoming vessels from Terra and settled into her standard research pattern.

Both Captain Clyde and Angharad disappeared at that point. Jessica didn't know where they went and didn't really care. Just so long as they weren't standing over her as she worked. A desk in a corner of the detective's work area had been set aside and she had half a dozen holos up, all privacy locked, making them only visible to her retina. It was likely that a large portion of the police here were on someone's pay—someone who would love to know exactly where the TBI agent from Terra was digging.

Three ships' arrival times fit within the timeframe required and two provided her with verified biometrics on each passenger. Not that such information was impossible to falsify, but the third ship wouldn't give her the time of day, making it the best place to start.

And best to start there in person. A TBI request over the Link was far less threatening than an armored agent at your airlock demanding answers—something that was her specialty.

An attempt to slip out of the station unnoticed failed and Captain Clyde appeared at her side as she walked past the front desk.

"Going somewhere, Agent Keller?"

"Just going to pay a visit to a ship in the docks," Jessica replied.

"Did you take the time to get a warrant?"

"I didn't realize a warrant was required to talk to people."

Clyde didn't respond for a few moments. "Just be careful what questions you ask."

Jessica didn't know exactly what to make of the statement and nodded before leaving. The CPF captain didn't follow her, something that actually made Jessica more nervous. If the captain didn't want to be present, chances were that she wanted some sort of deniability.

While looking over the inbound ship records, Jessica had done some digging on Captain Clyde as well. She suspected that Myrrdan had paid Clyde off, but nothing turned up. As far as the official record was concerned, Clyde was the model officer—something that Jessica was sure was patently impossible on Cruithne. Clyde may as well have hung a sign above her head that said "Corrupt Cop".

The ship was berthed roughly seven kilometers from the station and Jessica looked up the fastest route on the station's net. She was surprised to see that there was no maglev on Cruithne. It looked like walking or station taxis were the only ways to get around. Several of the taxis had driven past on her walk with Clyde and Angharad. She decided not to chance it.

Jessica had to admit to herself that, while she thought she had "seen it all" on High Terra, Cruithne had a whole new level of twisted and weird. She found herself alternating between horror, arousal, and morbid curiosity as she passed by the station's denizens.

She knew that she wasn't exactly stock either, but she highlighted her humanity. Obscuring it entirely or defacing it was not something she would ever consider.

Not for the first time, Jessica found herself wondering if this is what happened to people when they were too far removed from nature. Having grown up on Earth, Jessica was in the vast minority in the Sol system. Even with over a dozen worlds being fully terraformed in the system, most humans lived on rings and stations. A study she had recently read claimed that over ninety percent of humans in the Sol system had never even set foot on a world.

At least on High Terra there was an approximation of nature with hills, lakes, and rivers, on places like Cruithne there wasn't even a single park.

It had to have an effect on people—had to make them not-people.

Jessica had tried to explain these ideas to her coworkers more than once, but none of them could take her seriously with her being the most modded in her team.

She knew it was incongruous. There were definitely two Jessicas. Even though her parents and friends back in Athabasca barely recognized her, she still related to them and appreciated their way of life. She also wanted to taste the high-octane life and see what was beyond regular humanity.

If it was represented by what was displayed around her, then perhaps the final destination was not a place she wanted to see.

Then again, there must be the promise of transcendence, of humanity becoming something more.

Wasn't that the promise that all this technology was supposed to bring?

Her musings were interrupted by her internal nav informing her that she had arrived at the ship's berth.

Cruithne berths were archaic to say the least. In newer stations and rings, ships passed through ES shielding and essentially landed on the station. Here they still docked a cargo hatch to the station and grapples held the ship in place.

There was even a line on the station's deck plate denoting where the ship's domain began.

The ship she was looking for was named the *Arimanthe* and its domain was guarded by a thing that was decidedly more mech than human. Jessica couldn't even determine its gender.

"Jessica Keller. I'm with the TBI and I need to speak to your captain," she addressed the hulk with authority, though she didn't expect to get anywhere.

"Captain doesn't want to talk to you," came the impassive response.

"We're not going to reach an agreement, are we?" Jessica asked.

"Not unless you agree to go away," the hulk smirked—at least Jessica thought it was a smirk.

She checked the status of the warrant she had applied for, something she had decided to hide from Captain Clyde, and found that it had been signed by a district AI judge moments before.

"I have a warrant to view your manifests and logs, I will be entering your vessel now."

"You and what army?" The hulk asked.

"This army."

Jessica turned, surprised to see Angharad approaching with two security drones.

"I didn't think you wanted to get involved with this," Jessica said.

Angharad's steely visage showed no emotion. "I don't, but orders are orders. I guess someone cares enough about getting this Myrrdan guy to risk ruffling a few feathers over here."

The hulk gave the AI and security drones a long, considering look before acquiescing and calling the bridge.

"Captain'll see you."

The ship turned out to be a lot larger than Jessica expected, the two-hundred-meter walk to the bridge took the pair of TBI agents past hold after hold of cargo, most of it likely black market.

The ship itself was in decent shape. The captain appeared to care for his ship and made sure the crew did, too. Jessica assembled a mental map of the ship and where possible escape routes would be should the encounter turn ugly.

The hulk led them to the captain's office, just aft of the bridge, before returning to its post at the dock.

The portal slid open and Jessica entered, noting that Angharad entered behind her and remained there. Her attention was quickly consumed by the captain. The man was massive. Jessica estimated him at over two hundred kilograms.

A walk-in clinic could solve his weight issue in a day, which meant he actually wanted to be as large as he was. Jessica couldn't figure out what that said about him, but it certainly was well outside of normal.

"Hello, I'm agent Keller and this is Agent Angharad," Jessica offered both introductions and her hand.

The man leaned back and folded his arms behind his head.

"What can I do for the TBI today?"

Jessica smiled, the man wanted to do the information dance. She was more than happy to oblige him. In her experience, suspects gave away more than they held back when they tried to be evasive.

"We just thought perhaps you were lonely and wanted some company. Cruithne is sometimes an unwelcoming station," she replied.

"Lonely on Cruithne?" The captain laughed and Jessica had to force herself not to stare at how his flesh rippled. "There is more company here than anywhere in Sol. I don't think I'd need to stoop to the TBI for that."

"What about in the black? What sort of company do you keep then?" Jessica asked.

"The crew and I play a lot of cards; I'm sure you have played a hand of poker around a commissary table in your day."

"I imagine you take passengers from time to time, I noticed you have more berths than it would take to crew this ship. I imagine they must entertain as well." Jessica filed away his use of the word commissary. Civilians usually called them mess halls or break rooms.

"We have," the captain nodded. "It's a nice bonus for the crew to fleece a few passengers in a game."

"Did you take any crew this past trip? I see you came in from High Terra just a day ago."

The captain's face fell, lined with sadness. "Unfortunately we did not. I wish we had as the cargo didn't earn us quite what we'd hoped."

"I'm sure you wouldn't mind showing me your manifests so that I may verify this and note it in my report."

Now they were getting to it, this is where excuses would be made and the warrant would have to be used. His reactions would likely tell her everything she needed to know.

"Now, Agent Keller, that is not something I like to give out to authorities. A lot of my customers prefer discretion, it's why they ship with me."

"I can imagine. Based on the dock master's records, you have hardly unloaded any cargo and none of your crew have gone on-station yet."

The captain nodded as she spoke.

Jessica continued. "Yet, when I walked through your cargo holds I couldn't help but notice a lot of fresh scuff-marks from crates and other cargo. A cleaning servitor was also exiting a berth that appeared to be unused. It would seem to me that you have not reported all of your activities. Now provide me with your full manifests."

The captain grumbled and leaned over his desk. He began assembling the data on a sheet of plas. Jessica expected it to be entirely falsified. When the captain completed the document, she sat across from him to examine it.

"This seems to back up what you're telling me, Mr. Swenson, but it doesn't match the facts at hand." Jessica locked eyes with the man and saw worry creep into his.

She wasn't surprised. From what she could gather about the way things ran on Cruithne, the law didn't dig any deeper than it had to. If a manifest was needed, it was provided and accepted. So long as all the right people were suitably compensated.

From the way Angharad shifted behind her, Jessica wondered if she was one of the compensatees.

"You see, I know how much fuel you took on before you left High Terra and your vector and boost are on record. I also know what your fuel situation was like when you arrived on Cruithne. This manifest," she waved the plas in front of him, "doesn't match up."

"Your calculations are off. Maybe you need a lesson in space travel." The captain was blustering now, unprepared to have to defend himself further. She saw his eyes dart to Angharad expectantly.

Jessica's voice rose in volume as she spoke and by the end she was standing with hands on the captain's desk. She leaned over, her face inches from his.

"I do not need a lesson, certainly not from you. You forget that High Terra makes its mass compensation data available to the TBI. We know how much your ship weighed when you left, and I was able to request the tether load data when you docked here. I know what your ship weighed when you arrived. I also got the mass compensation data for right now and I know you transferred more cargo than you have on this manifest.

"Now give me the real manifest!" she yelled.

There was a moment of silence. The captain's face reflected shock, but just for a moment. His puffy features took on a smug expression, and Jessica felt a hand on her shoulder.

"Agent Keller, it is time for us to leave; you have what you came for," Angharad said quietly.

Jessica turned to the TBI AI.

"Why am I not surprised? I figured you for dirty from the get-go. I have a warrant and I intend to execute it. I will search this ship's computers until I find out precisely who was here and what they brought onboard."

The AI's face was impassive. "You will not. You will leave this ship with me now and file your report with the manifest you have." The security drones shifted to either side of her, flanking Jessica. "If you do not, you will find yourself returned to High Terra in a most unconventional manner."

Jessica looked back at the smiling captain and snatched the plas from his desk. "Very well, let's go."

Jessica's mind raced as she tried to think of a way to stop Angharad. She tried Net access only to find it was blocked; a call for help would go nowhere—not that Jessica thought anyone would answer. The AI and her drones would be hardened to EMP and a pulse rifle would not disable them quickly enough. Her options were decidedly limited.

Her mind raced and she took a deep breath to calm herself. There had to be a way out of this. If she didn't get the real manifest from this captain, she would have to go back to High Terra empty handed.

It was no easy task. Even without her two security drones, Angharad would be nearly impossible to defeat. The small voice of rationality in Jessica's mind screamed that she was a fool to consider confrontation with the AI.

She thought through the route back to the station. There was a narrow hatch where they would have to file through one at a time. Jessica decided to make her move there.

As they approached the hatch, one of the drones moved ahead of Jessica and passed through first. She followed it through and in a swift motion dove to the right of the corridor and swatted the drone into the bulkhead. Her armor's power assist gave her the strength to seriously damage the drone and embed it into the side of the corridor.

The next drone was racing through the hatch as Jessica dropped to the deck and fired three shots from her ballistic sidearm into the drone. It fell in a shower of sparks and Jessica pointed her weapon at the portal.

Angharad was there with a pulse rifle drawn. Jessica and the AI stared at each other in silence before Jessica spoke.

"I'd lower that if you know what is good for you."

"That is good advice," Angharad replied. "Your handgun can't stop me like it did those drones."

"And your pulse rifle isn't going to get through my armor any time soon."

"The crew will be here any second. Surrender."

Jessica didn't move for a moment, but then lowered her weapon.

"Very well, we'll do this your way."

Angharad gestured with her rifle and Jessica began to rise. She twisted to get an arm underneath herself and quickly kicked out a leg. A hidden compartment on her shin slid open and a plasma wand shot out.

The wand flew through the air and caught a startled Angharad under the chin, embedding itself to the hilt. Jessica reached for her sidearm and fired several shots into the AI's head—blowing it off in a shower of sparks.

AI didn't keep their brains in their heads, so it was not a fatal wound, but it did cause the construct to topple over. Jessica grabbed Angharad's pulse rifle and fired several shots into her exposed neck. The AI's body convulsed for a moment before falling still.

Jessica scanned the corridor. The sound of footsteps came from the ship's entrance, likely the hulk coming to finish what Angharad had failed to do.

She quickly stood and tore open the side of the drone embedded in the wall. Sure enough there were several small concussive stun grenades in a launcher. She grabbed two and lobbed them down the corridor as the man came into view.

The grenades worked as advertised and he went down in a heap. Jessica turned and raced back toward the captain's quarters, reloading her sidearm on the way.

The expression on the captain's face was priceless as she used another of the grenades to disable his door-lock before crashing through.

"Now, where were we?" Jessica asked.

The captain's bluster was gone and within minutes she had the real manifests. There was a veritable treasure-trove of illegal cargo, but no Myrrdan—not even cargo that could have concealed Myrrdan.

Cruithne was a dead-end.

She had the captain order the crew to quarters and walked him to the dock, half as a prisoner, half as a human shield.

Captain Clyde was waiting for her.

"You've got guts, I'll give you that," the captain said with a hint of a smile on her face. "Folks don't usually ruffle feathers like this on their first day."

"What can I say?" Jessica said. "I didn't like the way he looked at my breasts."

A ghost of a smile played at the edges of Clyde's mouth. "Hand him over to us, and a copy of whatever evidence you have. We'll see that he's dealt with."

Jessica wondered if he'd be dealt with for his crimes or his failure to keep control.

"What's left of Angharad is also on the ship. You'll want to clean that up and send her back to High Terra."

Clyde's eyes widened. "Really? She's one tough customer, but it means your time on Cruithne is over."

Jessica had suspected as much. Angharad had to be connected at the highest levels. Whoever she reported to would not be happy and would be quite unwelcoming. Clyde must be beholden to someone else—or maybe really be an honest cop on Cruithne.

"No problem. Any ships headed to Mars?"

CHASING MYRRDAN

STELLAR DATE: 3227239 / 10.26.4123 (Adjusted Gregorian)
LOCATION: Mars Outer Shipyards (MOS)
REGION: Mars Protectorate, Sol Space Federation

Jessica was developing a strong distaste for space travel. Before this assignment, the furthest she had been for work was Luna with a couple of vacations on Venus.

Those trips had been on commercial liners with all the comforts of home. Her precipitous exit from Cruithne had put her on a scow without any passenger amenities and a distinctly limited supply of sexual partners.

Customs was a brief affair. Mars, though it had a semi-autonomous military and security forces from Terra, was more than willing to cooperate with the TBI and its agents. Jessica was on a maglev within half an hour of arriving on the Mars 1 Ring.

She couldn't help but admit that there was a certain charm to the Mars 1 Ring that wasn't immediately apparent on the vids. The passage outside her train was a large, vaulted corridor featuring art-deco accents. She had never seen anything like it on High Terra with its function over form styling.

The rivalry between High Terra and Mars 1 had been going on for centuries. Mars 1 was the original planetary ring, but High Terra claimed superiority in all areas. The two rings competed in every way from design to political clout to sporting events.

The maglev rose up to the top level of the ring and she was amazed at how much open space the ring had. High Terra was more urban than not, while Mars 1 was almost entirely parkland. From what she could see, there were raw wildernesses on the ring.

The maglev continued to rise above the surface of the ring and the train accelerated to over a thousand kilometers an hour before giving a slight jolt as it flew out into open space. The local web indicated that the train would accelerate toward Mars and skirt the exosphere before using its own velocity to escape and arch toward the far side of the ring. It was a bit disconcerting to essentially be in a train floating through space, but it did shave over twenty-thousand kilometers off the trip.

Jessica spent the trip alternating between dozing and reviewing her leads on Myrrdan.

During the trip to Mars she had learned that Myrrdan had been spotted on the Mars 1 ring and later on the Mars Central Elevator Exchange. A contact in Mars Intelligence had placed Myrrdan there via a tap on communications in and out of a front that sold false identities.

Mars Intelligence had managed to work out a common signature the identities used and had tried to track their use but were stymied when the IDs started popping up in use all over the MCEE and Mars 1.

If Myrrdan had secured one or more of the IDs, he was covered by a seemingly random pattern of use. At least random to Mars Intel.

Jessica had been after him for over a year and was beginning to get a feel for his games. He could only feint so many times before his moves showed the true action rather than hiding it. Suspects always gave away more information when they got clever in their attempts to be elusive.

The pattern here was the same as the one she had followed on High Terra, when it led her to Jameson and a dead end. The same patterns were at play here—but this time she could see the dead ends for what they were.

If her hunch was correct, he was headed to the Mars Outer Shipyards and now so was she.

The maglev train would intercept one of the elevators that rose up from Mars 1 to the MCEE, and from there she could catch another train that would take her up the stalk to the Mars Outer Shipyards.

Other than some amazing views, the trip was uneventful—though when she stepped out onto the station platform she was surprised about the level of security on the MOS. What was more interesting was that, in addition to station security, she saw a few MSF and even TSF uniforms.

A quick scan of local news sources informed her of the colony ship *Intrepid* and its various security issues. Jessica found herself wondering if perhaps Myrrdan was trying to sneak aboard the colony ship, or if it was coincidence.

It would be the easy conclusion, but with the colony ship being constructed, there were hundreds of freighters at the shipyard at any time, not to mention several TSF frigates under construction at the far end of the shipyard.

Jessica decided to head for the stationmaster's offices to see if she could get direct access to the records for the ships under construction to see if anything stood out.

Getting directions on the local net, Jessica discovered that she was roughly a hundred kilometers from the stationmaster's offices—which was more of a complex than an office. She managed to wedge herself into a crowded connecting train, glad that she had decided to send her armor directly to her lodgings.

As the train accelerated and gently jostled its passengers, Jessica felt a sharp prick in her left shoulder. Reaching up to rub it, she couldn't help but gasp as her eyes locked with what had to be her quarry.

Myrrdan!

*****

The time it took the woman standing over Jessica to respond seemed like an eternity. There didn't seem to be a connection to the broader shipnet, but the localnet had an identifier and a date. She was on the *Intrepid,* likely many light years from Sol.

"Yes it is." The woman's expression appeared compassionate; she seemed to expect confusion.

Jessica's subconscious took in the fact that the woman standing over her wore a TSF uniform and the insignia of a lieutenant colonel, but where there should be a TSF badge, there was an icon that represented the *Intrepid*. She looked young, but had an air of command about her that said she had earned that rank the hard way.

Her conscious mind, on the other hand, was roiling with the knowledge that she was on a one way trip to a colony she never wanted to see—her career, her life, everything she had worked so hard for was gone.

All because of one man.

She realized the woman had started speaking.

"I'm Lieutenant Colonel Richards, we're not yet at the colony as we've had some problems. We were looking for people with specific skill-sets and your name came up.

However, there are some issues with the data regarding how you got approved for the colony roster—so finding you raised questions, not answers. Can you help shed any light on this?"

"Myrrdan," Jessica muttered softly.

The woman raised a hand to her chin, looking thoughtful. "I recall hearing something about a terrorist on High Terra by that name."

Jessica sighed. "That's the one. I was on the team attempting to apprehend him. I followed him to the MOS, but he got the drop on me while I was hunting him down. Next thing I know I'm staring at you."

The colonel seemed nonplussed, but she did lean back and give Jessica an appraising look. Jessica took the time to slow her breathing and force her mind to calm.

"You don't think you guys could just pull over and let me out do you?" Jessica asked.

The other woman laughed. "I don't know if that would make my day simpler or a heck of a lot more difficult. The question on my mind, however, is before you were stashed on this ship in a stasis-pod, were you any good at your job?"

"Before I got stashed in this pod I would have said yes. My record is damn good, though you'll have to take my word for it—unless you brought along a lot of databases a colony ship would never need."

"I still have data about all personnel on the MOS while we were docked there, so I have a summary of your record. It says you were good, but there are a few annotations here and there."

Jessica chuckled, "I imagine there are, most of them are probably even true."

"I'm going to take you to the hospital get you all checked out—give you the opportunity to talk to someone about what happened to you and then we'll see what shakes out."

"Need to make sure I'm not booby trapped?" Jessica asked with a wink.

The colonel glanced at Jessica's ample bosom. "Something like that."

SUBVERSION

STELLAR DATE: 3241794 / 08.19.4163 (Adjusted Gregorian)
LOCATION: GSS *Intrepid*, Deck 42 officer's lounge
REGION: LHS 1565, 171 AU from stellar primary

"Do you think it's wise for us to meet like this?" Hilda asked while casting furtive looks around the empty room.

"Of course," her companion replied. "There is nothing strange about the two of us meeting in the open. We should behave as though we've formed a friendship. Officers of our rank meeting for drinks is nothing strange."

Hilda nodded and forced herself to relax. "What did you want to discuss?"

Her companion leaned back and took a sip of whiskey. "It's time for us to move beyond talking about stopping the *Intrepid*. We need to begin to take action."

Hilda shook her head. "I don't know how that is going to be possible. Colonel Richards has everything locked down tight. You should know that better than I."

"I know how to get around her security—that should be obvious," the other responded.

"I suppose you would," Hilda smiled slowly. "I assume you have a plan?"

"I do. We're going to need to get the first mate out of stasis for it to work. I'm going to need your help with that."

"I can't believe the colonel just shot him like that." Hilda's voice took on a bitter tone. "I've known Mick for a long time, the captain hand-picked the two of us for this trip. She could have reasoned with him."

The other nodded. "Yes, but you know how she works. Shoot first, second, and third. Maybe ask questions later."

Hilda snorted. "You can say that again. She's like a cold machine—maybe that's what happens when you have been altered as much as she has."

"Who's to say?" her companion shrugged. "Either way, we get Mick and then we'll stop the ship, take it to civilized space and stop this research."

The pair spoke softly for several minutes of the plan and how it would play out. A nano cloud shrouded their conversation, altering the sound-waves beyond to that of an innocuous conversation should anyone happen to listen in.

After Hilda left, the other sat for several minutes, considering their next moves. Tanis was proving to be a larger complication than anticipated—though in retrospect that should not be a surprise. Removing Tanis was out of the question, she made the game much more interesting.

Who would have thought that so far from Sol there would be such an excellent opponent?

INTERLUDE

STELLAR DATE: 3241794 / 08.19.4163 (Adjusted Gregorian)
LOCATION: GSS *Intrepid*, Security Operations Center (SOC)
REGION: LHS 1565, 153 AU from stellar primary

"That didn't really get us anywhere," Tanis said. "I don't know if the fact that she was dumped on us by some fugitive makes her more or less likely to be a mole of some sort."

"I think a legitimate mole would be harder to find. Consider Collins. There was nothing at all to clue us in about him—except that he was a total ass. I can't imagine the same people did this hack job on Jessica. As soon as her record was accessed, it threw up flags everywhere," Terry replied while rubbing her temples.

Tanis nodded. "You have a point, but it could be a way to throw us off."

"By making us more suspicious?" Ouri asked.

"Wheels within wheels…" Tanis sighed. "Well, I guess we'll see what the docs and the psych AI have to say. If she's clean, her unbiased, outside opinion could be really useful."

The other two women nodded.

"I have some other news." Terry flipped through some of the plas in front of her, finding a specific sheet. "There are a few folks on the colony roster that look a bit more suspicious now than they did before, but they're all still in stasis."

Tanis glanced through the records. All of the people listed had made more contact with Collins than would have been expected under normal conditions—though under normal conditions there wouldn't have been anything suspicious about it.

"I guess we keep them on the 'do not wake' list for now, then—none look like they have skills we'd need right now anyway."

Terry nodded. "Already done. I don't have anything else at present."

"I do have a few reports of a guy named Randall Erick causing some problems," Ouri said. "He's a drive engineer who got pulled out to help on the crews. He's been posting plans on the board for how to get to Sirius and then back to Earth. He's not exactly fomenting a mutiny, but he bears watching."

Tanis looked through the man's recent actions on the shipnets. "He has been a bit more vocal than you'd expect based on his past behaviors."

"A lot of things can make a person react differently out here," Terry commented. "Knowing that we're essentially just drifting through space for a hundred years, counting on 58 Eridani to pull us in, is a bit unnerving."

"No argument there," Ouri said. "Most of us planned on simply going into stasis in one star system, and then coming to in another."

Terry shrugged. "It doesn't feel much different than being out past Eros. Out there Sol was just another star, not a lot brighter than it is from here."

"I don't know that it's Sol, as much as the fact that there are no humans for light-years. Plus, with us heading between stars, no ship could boost out to us and then slow down without a star to loop around." Ouri's face was clouded with concern.

"I don't think there's that much to worry about," Tanis said. "If we had to—and were willing to—use the colony supplies, we could practically build a second starship."

"We might have to." Joe entered the SOC's conference room and sat with the other security heads. "I've done some external visual inspections out there and it's baaaaad."

"I was getting that from following the engineering solutions boards," Tanis said.

"Could we take the cruisers to New Eden if we had to?" Terry asked.

"Sure," Joe nodded. "The cruisers could get there and brake around the star no problem, but they don't have room for all the colonists."

"I wonder what the GSS crew is thinking," Amy said. "Most of them expected to spend about ninety years in stasis with a few years helping build the space station and beanstalk for New Eden. Some of them must be starting to have second thoughts about this trip."

"Interstellar travel isn't exactly safe as houses," Ouri replied. "Everyone knew when they signed up for the first re-usable colony ship that they might end up joining the colony."

Terry nodded. "I have a few GSS crew on my team. They went through full colony screening even though they aren't really signed up for it."

"They're certainly a group that will bear extra watching," Tanis said as she brought up the meeting's agenda. "I want to get the crew we have up and about re-vetted in two shifts. I have both Reddings after me now to thaw more engineers out of stasis and we can't even vouch for the ones that already are."

The team dove into the logistics of wrapping up all the crew assessments, deciding to bring additional AI help online and get a few other crew members with investigative skills out of stasis.

The meeting wrapped up ten minutes later and Joe followed Tanis into her office.

"We haven't had much time together since getting back."

Tanis stopped and leaned against her desk. "Not a lot, no. Hard to believe we're so busy when we have over a hundred years to drift our way through space."

"Once we get the engineers all staffed up, I imagine things will die down. Then maybe we can find a quiet corner of the ship again," Joe winked at her conspiratorially.

Tanis smiled back. "I bet there are a lot of free cabins in the cylinders right now. I think we've earned a bit of a sojourn."

He gave her a quick kiss. "I have to jet, though. My boss wants all the weapons on the ship manually accounted for and that includes fighter load-outs."

"I bet she can wait a bit longer for that," Tanis said as she pulled Joe close.

Joe chuckled. "Maybe you don't know her; she's a real hard-ass. She doesn't like it when things aren't done on her schedule."

Tanis gave Joe a long kiss as she ran her hands down his back. "What a task master. Doesn't she know you're a hero? You need to be rewarded."

Joe snorted back a laugh.

"What?" Tanis asked.

"Nothing, you just went a bit off the rails on that one. Not your best work there."

Tanis folded her arms and gave her best scowl. "She doesn't like to be antagonized, I thought you knew that."

"Sorry, boss-lady. I'll be less antagonistic next time." Joe ran a hand down her face. "But I really do have to go. I only have two fly-boys out of stasis and they're already down there counting rounds. I need to join them."

Tanis nodded. "Off with you, then. Say hi to Jens and Aaron for me."

"Will do," Joe said as he dashed out of the office.

Tanis linked to the psych AI that was examining Jessica.

<*So what's the word?*>

<*Her TBI implant corroborates her story. From what I can tell she is telling the truth.*>

Tanis detected some hesitation in the AI's mental tone. <*There's something else?*>

<*I don't like the implication, but I think that someone has been deliberately overlooking some issues she has.*>

<*What do you mean?*> Tanis asked.

<*Honestly? She's a bit unstable. I'm shocked that the TBI let her operate like this.*>

Tanis smiled grimly. She knew that the TBI had a habit of cultivating overly eccentric and aggressive behavior in some of its agents. Such agents could be used for dirty work and then discarded if things didn't go well.

The TSF had done a similar thing with Tanis, after all.

<*Understood. When you're through with her, put her in touch with Bob for quarters near mine and get her on my team's duty roster.*>

<*Sir?*> The AI seemed surprised.

<*Sometimes, when dealing with the unknown, a little instability in your court can help flush out the enemy.*>

Tanis closed the connection with the AI and leaned back in her chair. Being in the chair, in the SOC again, felt like failure. She should have been done with protecting the *Intrepid* from threats; she should be sleeping off the rest of the trip to New Eden.

<*It's not your fault,*> Angela said, gently reading Tanis's thoughts. <*Some things are beyond even your control.*>

Tanis snorted. "You know me too well, old friend. But you should also know that I won't absolve myself of the oversights that led us to this point."

<*I know, but I'll still say it so that you don't forget that* **I**, *at least, don't blame you.*>

"At least that makes one of us."

NEW ORDER

STELLAR DATE: 3241800 / 08.25.4163 (Adjusted Gregorian)
LOCATION: GSS *Intrepid*, Officer's Mess
REGION: LHS 1565, 171 AU from stellar primary

Tanis sat in the officers' mess with her team leads, which now included a newly minted Second Lieutenant Jessica. Despite the fresh set of eyes, they had made little progress in their investigation; all personnel had either come up clean, or close enough as to make no difference.

"Dead ends all around," Trist said as she picked through a salad. "I don't see signs of tampering in anyone's records. Nothing that my routines can pick up, anyway."

Amy nodded. "I haven't found anything with my team either. We've been locking down the weapons stores and so far everything is exactly where it's supposed to be."

"I've found a few small data errors, when comparing current information to the crystal backups we had at departure. I've traced them all to Collins, which I think is fortunate," Terry added.

Tanis took a bite of her BLT and chewed thoughtfully. "It has been only a week. On the MOS, we often went months with nothing."

"So if there are any malefactors on the ship, then they only have twelve hundred months to choose from before we get to New Eden," Joe's mouth had a wry twist. "We're going to run ourselves ragged attempting to anticipate threats for that long."

"Not a bad tactic," Ouri said.

"You need to figure out how to bring out any sleepers who may still exist on the ship," Jessica said. "Like Joe says, looking under every rock will just reveal smaller rocks."

"Or there's no one else," Amy said. "I mean, who would stay on the ship after Collins aimed it at a star? I think maybe we're free and clear."

Tanis cast an appraising eye at Amy. Her attitude seemed overly nonchalant considering what the *Intrepid* had been through. If anything, they should be more suspicious than ever.

"Believe you me, girl, something is still rotten in the state of Denmark," Trist said. "Sue and I have been analyzing the attack patterns the RAI used when it had control of node eleven, as well as some of the data from the fights with servitors and security drones. From what we can tell, it was too easy."

"Too easy?" Ouri's eyebrows rose. "I watched people die in those attacks."

Trist raised her hands. "I didn't say it was a cake-walk, but it was easier than it could have been."

"I know." Tanis nodded. "Its tactics were weak. Any one of us could have done better. The RAI should have assaulted the command deck with everything it had and destroyed key stasis chambers. But it did none of those things."

"Maybe it didn't have the access," Amy suggested.

"It did," Terry disagreed. "With Amanda in its thrall, it had the power to get into any system it needed. It also had whatever net access and nano-control it wanted."

"It should have crushed us," Trist said.

No one spoke for several moments as the statement sunk in. If the RAI threw them a softball, then there was a chance that Collins wasn't behind it, but someone wanted them to think he was.

Jessica suddenly laughed.

"It's Myrrdan! He was on the MOS when you were building the ship. I always assumed that maybe he dumped me on it because he wanted me out of the picture, but respected me as a foe or something."

"Is that some sort of 'honor amongst enemies' thing?" Amy asked.

Jessica ignored her and carried on. "The thing is...that doesn't fit his modus operandi. He's not like that. For him it's all in the game. He dumped me here because he wanted to keep playing with me. He's here on the *Intrepid*."

Tanis raised an eyebrow. "That seems like a bit of a stretch."

"I don't know," Trist said. "The data model makes sense. He didn't want the *Intrepid* to fall into the star, because he's still here. But why? Is it some new challenge to mess with a colony ship, or does he actually want to get out to a colony?"

"It sure is a lot of effort either way," Amy shook her head. "Who would want to spend hundreds of years messing with a ship of colonists?"

Joe and Tanis gave each other sidelong glances. They knew what it was that could interest a person like Myrrdan: the picotech.

Tanis looked away and noticed that Amy was giving her a funny look. Ever since her abduction by Collins, the former Marine seemed cooler than ever. Tanis wondered if she felt guilt at being caught off-guard. If there was some sort of mental trauma at play, perhaps a psych AI should talk to her.

"I think we need to take a look at the passes," Jessica said. "Some of those folks were just too clean. Everyone has something that they'd rather not talk about—some blemish on their record. Too many of the folks on your original list came up without so much as a late roll call. Myrrdan will be hiding in the best place—we just have to figure out what that best place is."

"We did recruit the cream of the crop," Ouri said. "Our roster is filled with exemplary people."

"Speak for yourself," Trist smirked. "But robo-doll-cop here does have a point. There are a lot of super-squeaky clean folks here. Makes me uncomfortable."

"I wish you'd stop calling me that." Jessica's face contorted into a sulk that didn't fit her manufactured sexuality.

"It's what you get for turning yourself into the obvious incarnation of the naughty police officer." Trist moved her hands in a curvaceous pattern. "Not that I'm complaining."

Jessica cast Trist an appraising look and Tanis sighed inwardly.

"Easy there, Jessica, no fraternizing with your teammates." Joe grinned.

Ouri coughed and nearly spat out her coffee.

"Don't play that game with me." Jessica leaned on the table, locking eyes with the commander. "Your fearless leader is more modified than I am by a long shot; she just hides it in a standard-looking package."

"You haven't seen the colonel in just her flow-armor, then." Trist threw Tanis a wink.

"Dear god," Tanis murmured as she put her head in her hands. Jessica certainly seemed to bring out the lascivious behavior in the group. "None of us here are natural humans. Even Ouri, arguably the least modified among us, is nowhere near vanilla. We've all added hardware and tweaked the genes in our favor."

Joe snorted. "I didn't know Trist still had genes. I thought she was made out of green jelly now."

"That's *Miss* Green Jelly to you, mortal." Trist grinned.

"No hard feelings, Jessica." Trist clapped the former TBI agent on the shoulder. "We're just blowing off a bit of steam—not too often that we're stymied."

Jessica flashed a smile. "No problem. I might have to go back under the knife myself. These hips weren't made for bearing colony brats."

"No? Were they made for bearing Terran men?" Trist snorted and she laughed at her own joke. Jessica threw a carrot stick at her.

"I have to head up to the bridge to meet with the brass," Tanis said. "Can you guys determine if they ever caught Myrrdan in the Sol system? If the answer is no, if his sprees stopped when we left Mars, then we may have an answer to whether or not we have a stowaway."

"You got it," Ouri said. "Have fun with the big wigs."

Tanis wolfed down the last of her B.L.T. "I'm sure I will. I'm way more worried about my visit to Earnest's lab later today. He's going to figure out how to get the flow-armor out of my body before I exceed its patent timeouts and it self-destructs or something."

<*I'm sorry about that… It did seem like a good idea at the time,*> Angela said.

* * * * *

Tanis walked through the long executive corridor that led to the avatar's chamber. The desks and offices were sparsely populated as most of the crew pulled from stasis were still feverishly working on engine repairs.

Priscilla was still ensconced on her pedestal, her customary array of holo displays surrounding her as she managed hundreds of humans interfacing with the ship's nets. At the edge of the room, Amanda sat at a small work station.

Tanis knew how Amanda felt. She'd been used and had hurt her shipmates. There was no worse feeling than knowing you had done things that there was no way to take back. The only thing she could hope for was time showing her that no one held it against her.

Well, almost no one; a few unfavorable opinions had been expressed on the solution boards. One conversation had gotten so out of hand that Bob ultimately stepped in.

Having a god-like AI explain how he had altered his Avatar's brains so they could no longer be subverted quelled the conversation—though it spawned a few new ones.

"Good afternoon, Colonel," Amanda said with a wan smile as Tanis approached.

"Colonel?" Tanis asked. "When have you ever stood on rank?"

"Sorry." Amanda's mouth twisted. "I don't know who hates me right now; I'm trying to be extra cordial."

"I can promise you, I do not hate you. I'm not even mildly upset with you," Tanis gave Amanda a warm smile.

The off-duty avatar gave her a searching look. "I don't understand; my abilities were used to attack you—five of your Marines died because of it!"

Tanis stepped through the holo displays and crouched in front of Amanda, taking her hands.

"None of us are perfect. We all get thrust into situations where we make the wrong choices, or have evil thrust upon us. If I were to condemn you for your failures, I would have to first condemn myself for mine." Tanis gave a rueful smile. "Life is hard enough without us beating ourselves up."

"Thanks, Tanis," Amanda said. This time her smile managed to reach her eyes.

"You coming or what?" Abby barked as she walked by. "Let's get this done so I can get back to work."

"Duty calls," Tanis said softly as she rose.

"We have a much less appealing name for her than duty," Amanda whispered with another smile.

Tanis walked down the hall to the conference room where Abby was already in full swing.

"I need to double my engineering staff pronto or we won't be able to fire the engines in time to course correct for New Eden," Abby was almost yelling. "If we could take the time to get control of the machine shops again and build more bots it wouldn't be a problem, but that rogue AI fried most of their control systems. Human hands are the fastest way to fix things now."

Tanis slid into a chair as unobtrusively as possible, not that she expected it to help much. Terrance and Abby were glaring at one another while Earnest twisted his hands and the captain looked extra stoic. Sanderson looked like he just wanted the yelling to stop.

"Major!" Abby directed the full force of her personality at Tanis who decided not to correct the engineer regarding her rank and did her best to maintain a neutral expression. "When are you going to lift your ban on more people coming out of stasis? I need at least two hundred more engineers yesterday!"

While Abby spoke she sent Tanis a projection over the Link, showing the time it would take to repair the engines, get the lithium processed and course correct.

It wasn't new data; Abby had been sending her updated projections nearly every hour for days. The window to fire the engines and course correct was down to six days.

"Out of the frying pan and into the fire," Tanis sighed.

"I think we already did that," Earnest said. "What's after the fire?"

"I don't want to know," she grimaced. "OK, we haven't found anything to cause alarm at the moment, other than the fact that Jessica Keller's presence confirms that we can't trust our roster of who is here. However," she nodded at Abby, "we've vetted your list and each one is personally known to at least three other people currently out of stasis. Based on the data we have now, there's no reason other than raw paranoia not to bring them out of stasis."

Abby looked surprised and relief washed across Terrance's face. Tanis could tell that he had been backing her up but was running out of arguments in the face of drifting in the dark forever.

"Well," Abby stood, "there's no time to waste, then." She glanced at Earnest and the two left the bridge conference room.

Captain Andrews spoke first. "Do you really believe that it is safe to thaw more crew?"

"No more or less safe than the alternative, as best I can tell. We have the ability to screen the number of people she wants to pull out, and we'll have to do it eventually, so now's the best time. To be honest, the thing I really wonder about is why Myrrdan dumped Jessica here."

"I followed that story back in Sol," Terrance looked concerned. "They suspected him of killing over ten thousand people, didn't they?"

"Give or take a few hundred," Tanis agreed. "Why did he dump her here? Why not just kill her? Also, if he could bypass all of our checks on the crew and colonists, then who else is here on this ship? Is it possible that even he is here?"

"That has been on my mind as well." Captain Andrews nodded. "There are a lot of places and ways to hide on this ship. We should assume that either he is here, or he has secreted away more surprises for us."

<*I've sent requests to AIs I trust back in Sol to learn if Myrrdan was ever caught,*> Bob added.

"Thank you, Bob," Captain Andrews said.

"Do you think it makes sense to keep Agent Keller thawed?" Terrance asked.

"Angela and I have had a lot of conversations about this—"

<*By that she means that I've had to deal with her droning on and on about it.*>

Tanis ignored the jibe and continued, "I think that if Myrrdan is here and has something planned, he wants Jessica to be here to see it. He wants to play the game against her. It's standard operating procedure for this sort of guy."

<*If that sort of profiling really applies to someone like him,*> Angela added.

"Either way, having her out and about is the best way to draw him out if he is thawed. If he's not thawed, then we don't have anything to worry about at the moment."

Terrance laughed. "We still have plenty to worry about."

"Touché." Tanis nodded.

She looked at the remaining command crew around the table and asked what she was certain was on everyone's mind.

"We're more off course than Joe's initial plan called for. The time and the fuel we have are both tight. What if we can't fire to correct for New Eden?"

"Hilda and I have been going over that," the captain said as he brought up a holo display of the ten light years of space surrounding Estrella de la Muerte.

The *Intrepid's* position was denoted by a small green dot near the star's red one. A white line stretched out to the edge of the holo without intersecting any systems.

"You can see here that we're not pointed anywhere near New Eden; it will take a very long and hard burn to correct our course. Even correcting for Epsilon Eridani is not significantly better. If we can't get this burn done in time, we're looking at Kapteyn's Star or Gilese 229," Andrews said.

He gestured and the holo updated to show that a burn to correct for Gilese needed to happen within six weeks, while a burn to correct for Kapteyn's could happen any time in the next two years.

Tanis sighed. "Well, at least we have options."

"Options that add a hundred years to our trip." Terrance ran a hand across his eyes. "This trip just keeps getting more and more complicated."

Tanis found herself wondering, not for the first time, why Terrance was really on the *Intrepid*. His argument for building the new center for human commerce and power sounded good until one considered how much power he had wielded back in Sol. He was a man who lived like a god. Why travel across human space to live like a god somewhere else?

Perhaps, under it all, Terrance was just as sick of where humanity was going in Sol as everyone else on the *Intrepid*.

"That's going to be a long detour, isn't it?" Tanis asked. "We'll have to decelerate, stock up, and then boost back out."

Captain Andrews nodded. "Obviously Kapteyn's is the preferred location because it's much closer. It's more massive, too, so it will make for a better slingshot when we boost out toward New Eden."

Tanis brought up the system's entry. "Not inhabited at all? That's surprising."

"Why colonize a red dwarf when there are places like New Eden cropping up?" Terrance asked. "I certainly wouldn't fund a mission there—even with its two super-earths."

"We have something else to go over." Andrews leaned back in his chair and smiled at Tanis. She saw that Sanderson and Terrance were looking at her and smiling as well.

"Uh… What's up?" Tanis asked with a nervous smile.

"We've been talking about the ship's command structure," Andrews began. "We're in a situation here that wasn't supposed to happen. Other than duty crews, everyone was to have been in stasis during the trip. Now we have a mixture of crew and colony all doing crew work. We are also missing a first mate."

Tanis furrowed her brow. What the captain was saying was true, but there were several pre-vetted scenarios on the books for how to handle this re-org.

"We have to be honest with ourselves," Sanderson said. "This mission may play out very differently than originally planned. Even if we don't have to divert to Kapteyn's Star, we're going to have a lot of colony and crew out of stasis working together for years. Back in Sol it was easy—everyone was hired by the GSS or on loan like the TSF until we passed out of the heliosphere."

Tanis nodded. "And if we do divert to Kapteyn's the trip will get so long that I bet a lot of crew won't care to go back to a Sol system where everyone they know has died of old age."

"You're correct," Andrews said. "As a result, we're enacting the colony's charter now on the *Intrepid* and treating it as a sovereign nation. This will create a single crew and colony entity that will persist until the *Intrepid* heads back to Sol."

"Have you worked out the details?" Tanis asked with a frown. She was annoyed that her input hadn't been sought and wondered how this new structure would get in the way of her investigation.

"We have," Andrews said. "We didn't bring you into it because, honestly, you were doing something more important at present."

Andrews waved his hand and holo refreshed to display the ship's new organizational structure.

The captain was still the ultimate authority on the ship, also holding the title of Governor. Below him there was an executive officer—a transition from the civilian first mate structure of before. Under that person there were department heads and divisional officers. The security force of the *Intrepid* was re-designated as a police force, using much of the proposed structure for the New Eden colony, and an official military branch was created with a Marine and space-force division.

"I'm curious about the nature of the Department of Defense," Admiral Sanderson said. "Does it report through the XO to the captain? If so, I imagine that will be strange, as the Secretary of Defense will outrank the XO."

Tanis wondered why he would think that, but from his tone she suspected he already knew the answer and was planting the question.

"We are going to have a number of situations like that throughout the ship's new organizational structure," Captain Andrews said. "They weren't uncommon with the GSS/TSF split we had before we left Sol. There may be adjustments we'll need to make, but here are the assignments as we see them now."

Tanis's mouth fell open when she saw her assignment. "I think you have it wrong.... Maybe these two are switched," she said while pointing at herself and Admiral Sanderson on the chart.

"No mistake, General Richards," Sanderson said with a rare smile. "I expect to spend as much time as possible in stasis—I'd like to actually live a few decades on New Eden—the XO is going to spend a lot of time out of stasis. You're the right confluence of age and experience for the job."

Tanis was stunned. General.

<*Congratulations on the promotion,*> Angela said privately. <*Long overdue if you ask me.*>

"You've also proven an unwavering dedication to the ship," Terrance added with a nod.

"Thank you," Tanis said, reeling both from the promotion and the responsibility.

Other discussions regarding rank and placement took place and Tanis noted Terrance's rather interesting title of Secretary of Colony Affairs—which meant his placement was still ambiguous.

Other than him, everything was quite clear. Abby was the Secretary of Engineering, Admiral Sanderson was the Secretary of Defense; below him Ouri was the police commissioner, Joe held the position of commandant of the space force, and Brandt was commandant of the Marine Corps—both were promoted to Colonel. There was also a Secretary of Health, a Secretary of Education, and Bob was noted as the Secretary of the *Intrepid*—something that went without saying.

After the meeting, Tanis stood in the SOC beside Admiral Sanderson. All the military and security personnel out of stasis were present physically or virtually while at their posts.

There were nods of understanding as she described the new organizational structure; when she announced that she had been designated the ship's XO, applause and cheers broke out.

Tanis felt herself flush and gave an embarrassed glance at Sanderson who raised his hands for quiet.

"It's not all good news." His delivery was entirely dead-pan. "I've been designated as the Secretary of Defense, which means you all have one less layer of protection between me and you."

Joe laughed and called out, "We'll just go to your boss."

Tanis gave him a mock scowl. "There will be none of that, you. The purpose of this re-organization is to have a clear chain of command. However, Secretary Sanderson will be spending much of the trip in stasis to preserve his old bones. At those times, Ouri will be acting secretary and will report to me."

"Just like old times." Ouri smiled.

BECOMING > HUMAN

STELLAR DATE: 3241802 / 08.27.4163 (Adjusted Gregorian)
LOCATION: ISS *Intrepid*
REGION: LHS 1565, 185 AU from stellar primary

Tanis stood in the lobby outside of Earnest's laboratories.

While Abby made Engine her domain, Earnest spent most of his time here, at the very rear of the dorsal arch, with walls of windows facing out over the back of the ship.

The scale of the *Intrepid* never ceased to amaze Tanis. The fact that Earnest and his wife worked on the same ship but were typically over sixteen kilometers apart fascinated Tanis each time she thought of it.

There was a time in human history when a person may have never traveled more than sixteen kilometers from their home in their entire life. Now a starship encompassed a larger space.

"Even scuffed and bruised she's beautiful," a voice said from behind Tanis.

She turned to see Earnest standing behind her. The man spoke about the *Intrepid* like a darling child. There was passion and emotion in his voice that never came out at any other time.

While Abby viewed the *Intrepid* as a magnificent structure that she must maintain, Tanis could see that Earnest viewed it as a work of art, more his grand opus than even the creation of picotech.

"She's the most beautiful ship I've ever laid eyes on." Tanis nodded in agreement. "I thought so from the very first moment I saw her."

Earnest looked her in the eyes, something he rarely did. "I know, I can tell that about you. You care for her like I do."

He looked back out the window for a moment and then turned, calling over his shoulder, "Come to my lab, I need to have a look at what Angela did to you."

Tanis followed him through an inner reception area and into a large laboratory filled with equipment and tables.

She was surprised to see that the room was clean and well organized. Earnest had always seemed so scatterbrained that she assumed his workspace would be chaos embodied. Now that she saw it, she realized that there was no way the creator of the *Intrepid,* with its clean lines and attention to detail, could be designed by someone sloppy.

"You know that the license on your flow-armor expires in four months," he said.

"Yeah, a year earlier and I would have been dead when Collins shot at me."

Earnest grunted. "Hmm… I wonder about that."

Tanis wondered what he meant, but let the comment go and instead asked, "So what can be done, can you remove it from me?"

Earnest gestured to an examination table and Tanis climbed onto it.

"Of course I can, I can rebuild you from a single stem-cell on up if I need to, but we don't really have that sort of time. Ideally, I'd like to see if I can simply reverse what Angela did and flow it back out of your body the same way it went in."

"So it's going to hurt," Tanis said.

"Yes," Earnest replied simply.

Tanis lay still and cleared her mind as Earnest sent a batch of his nano into her body. Her internal systems alerted her to the intrusion and showed the signature of the invading machines. Tanis approved the bots and her internal defenses—both organic and artificial—stood down.

Earnest brought a holo display up over her body and linked it to Tanis. She brought it up in her VR so she could see it with her eyes closed.

The scientist made soft humming sounds as he looked over the data. He pulled several other scanning instruments over her body to gather more readings. As he worked, the holographic image of Tanis's insides became more and more detailed.

She had a rudimentary understanding of her internals. Her time in the TSF had layered modification over modification, requiring her to read long manuals on how to care for and manage herself.

Most of the time Angela took care of her body, but Tanis also knew how to directly triage problems with any of her implants. It was important to be prepared for a time when AI was offline or incapacitated.

Carbon nanostrings reinforced her bones while her muscles contained artificial sinews to augment her organics. Her left arm was entirely prosthetic, a souvenir of her battle with Trent—though its exterior was covered in her skin.

Slim batteries wrapped around her thighbones providing power to her implants and the pair of matter extruders embedded in her forearms.

Her head appeared normal, but under her hair much of her scalp was covered in heat transfer material designed to cool her enhanced brain and its embedded AI.

There were many more small alterations throughout her body, some needed for special missions, some almost forgotten over time.

"You're almost as modified as Amanda was when she first came on board," Earnest said as he worked.

"I've been around for a bit," Tanis responded. "A lot of missions have required a lot of special build-outs."

"Angela's insertion of your flow-armor into this has made things complicated. It's bonded with the carbon nanostrings in your bones and your artificial muscle sinews. I can get it out of the walls of your regular organs and brain, though. I'm going to proceed with that process first."

Tanis removed her clothing at Earnest's direction and grit her teeth as the flow armor began to seep out of her skin. It was a ghastly experience. It appeared as though she were bleeding grey blood out of every pore. She closed her eyes again and thought of something more pleasant.

It wasn't as painful as the first time, but she imagined that was because only half the material was exiting her body.

"That was bracing…" Tanis gasped.

"This really is a remarkable implementation of flow metal," Ernest said as he peered at the grey material. "I would never have thought to make kinetic *and* energy resistant shielding with it."

"And it only costs a year's salary," Tanis added.

Ernest shot her a questioning look. "Really? I could make this for not much more than the cost of a good meal."

"Now that's what I call a mark-up!" Tanis said.

"Well…maybe a couple of good meals, but surely no more than a week's salary."

"Does that mean you can make more?" Tanis asked.

Ernest nodded. "I imagine so, and I'd make it so that no one can do a fool thing like Angela did with it."

<I think it was a good idea. I bet it saved her life.>

"Hmph…I guess that is what the armor is for," Ernest said.

"Once you get me cleared up I'm going to commission you to make more of this," Tanis said.

"Yes, yes, now to deal with the rest of this stuff. The licensing on this is pretty strict; they have some strong controls. I'm going to have to introduce a retrovirus into it to gain control, and strip out the licensing."

"How long will that take?" Tanis asked.

"A few hours. However, I won't be able get it out without completely replacing your bones and muscles at this point—which I really don't want to have to do, I'm pretty busy with the ship."

"I know." Tanis opened her eyes and looked at Ernest. "I really do appreciate you doing this. The doctors honestly seemed pretty scared to do anything."

Ernest patted her shoulder. "I understand. Competence is hard to come by."

Tanis smiled and laughed inwardly. Earnest seemed completely unaware of the fact that what was on his table was a naked woman in addition to being an engineering puzzle.

"So my bones and muscles will retain the armor's properties?" Tanis asked.

"To some extent, yes. Your forearm can't stop laser fire just because the armor is in your muscle, but it does mean that if you take a gut punch your muscles will lock up just like the armor and dissipate the blow."

"My skin won't really appreciate that," Tanis said.

"Luckily, growing new skin is easy."

* * * * *

Tanis left Earnest's lab several hours later and boarded a maglev to the command deck.

<*You saw the detailed scans of our minds, didn't you?*> Angela asked.

Tanis didn't respond at first. What the scan had shown was more than worrisome.

<*I did see it, yes,*> Tanis finally responded.

<I asked Bob about it and he told me that he was discussing it with Earnest. He wouldn't say anything else.>

<*It looks…like the brain of someone who has been directly integrated with their AI,*> Tanis said.

Angela sent an affirming feeling into Tanis's mind.

<*We've seen brains that were directly integrated before…*> Tanis said.

<*…on Toro,*> Angela completed her thought.

Tanis stiffened. <*Have we always done this? Are we changing into something else?*>

A small part of her had feared for some time that her mind was too entangled with Angela's. Too often she could hear Angela's thoughts or her AI could hear hers. After Toro, and knowing the horrors that had been perpetrated on human and AI alike during the sentience wars, terror should have been her only response. Instead, Tanis could not bring herself to abhor the entanglement of her mind with Angela's. To do so would be to hate herself, to hate a part of herself that she loved very much.

<*I love you, too.*> Angela smiled in Tanis's mind.

<*Do you?*> Tanis asked. <*Can you understand love like a human does?*>

<*Yes, yes I can.*>

A feeling of deep love and acceptance filled Tanis's mind.

<*You'll never be extracted, will you?*> Tanis asked.

<*I imagine it would be possible to clone me out of your mind,*> Angela responded. <*But it would be awful for you. A ghost of me would remain imprinted in your mind and neural pathways.*>

Tanis laughed aloud. <*You totally would haunt me if you died or left.*>

<*We'll never have to find out,*> Angela replied.

STARING INTO THE BLACK

STELLAR DATE: 3241804 / 08.29.4163 (Adjusted Gregorian)
LOCATION: ISS *Intrepid*
REGION: Interstellar space near LHS 1565

The lithium extraction from Fuel Dump was successful and the remains of the asteroid were released to drift between the stars.

The engines were another story. The port A1 engine was a total write-off. Investigations revealed cracks in the fusion chamber that would require a complete re-build to repair.

A balanced thrust was imperative and, as a result, the starboard B2 engine could not be used during the course correction burns. Abby and Earnest were working feverishly to tune the remaining two engines for the maximum output needed. The stress the pair exuded seemed to creep into every corner of the ship.

"I think we should make the correction for Kapteyn's Star," Joe said around a mouthful of mashed potatoes.

Tanis glanced around the officer's wardroom. No one was within earshot and she cast Joe an admonishing look.

"It doesn't do to have the brass questioning orders, *Colonel,*" she replied.

Joe paused and looked around. "Sorry, I'm not used to being in the upper echelon. It's really going to cramp my care-free attitude, you know."

He looked serious and Tanis almost responded before she realized he was joking.

"Be serious, things are pretty on-edge right now."

"I am being serious. I think we should plan for the burn to Kapteyn's. It's a much lighter burn—no need to try to eek every ounce of thrust out of the engines like we're doing now; and we can take our time preparing."

Tanis nodded. "It does have its merits. I'll admit that right now I don't even want to be within a klick of Abby. She seems to have it out for me, even though I've approved everyone she's asked for. There are over five-thousand people out of stasis right now. It's starting to feel like a zoo."

"The ship's bigger than a city," Joe laughed. "Five-thousand does not a crowded *Intrepid* make."

Tanis sighed. "I guess I liked the quiet, dark *Intrepid* more than I thought."

"Depending on how things go, you may get plenty more opportunity to experience that."

"That's morbid," Jessica said as she dropped her tray on the table and sat down.

Tanis cast an annoyed look at the other woman. Perhaps the thing she liked most about an empty *Intrepid* was more private time with Joe.

<*You don't say,*> Angela commented.

<*Enough of that. I understand my own motivations without you commenting on them all the time,*> Tanis snapped back.

Angela didn't respond, but Tanis could tell that she had hurt her AI's feelings. She knew sarcasm was Angela's way of fitting in when she didn't understand human emotions; she should have been more understanding.

She caught a thought that wasn't meant for her to hear... *I do too understand your emotions; I swim in your chemical cocktail of a brain all the time...*

Tanis barely had time to wonder about the further erosion of the barrier between her thoughts and Angela's before her attention was pulled back to the physical realm.

"I meant that, as the XO, she will be out of stasis more," Joe scowled at Jessica. "I didn't mean that we were going to drift forever."

Jessica looked down, her alabaster skin flushing bright pink, a response designed to match her hair and eyes. At times the former TBI agent's aggressive sexuality was at stark odds with the softer woman Tanis suspected was underneath.

"Sorry about that," Jessica said. "The atmosphere around here is wearing off on me and...well...I just wanted some company—sorry if I intruded."

Jessica moved to stand up and Joe reached out to touch her arm.

"Stay," he said. "You didn't deserve that response; you have more than enough reason to be upset. We all signed up for this, you are getting all the risk with none of the mental preparation."

Jessica settled back into her seat. "Yeah, when you go after a guy on Mars you don't really expect to wake up a dozen light years from Earth on a one-way trip to a life you never planned on."

"None of us really ever planned on this trip," Tanis said. "But life made it our best option."

Jessica nodded and chewed silently for a moment.

"Not to change the subject too much," Jessica said. "I read the report on Toro the other day. You were completely justified. You're even more bad-ass than I ever imagined."

"What?" Tanis asked. "The report doesn't really paint me in that light."

Jessica smiled. "Now that the *Intrepid* has adopted a new legal structure, Bob is no longer constrained by SolGov regulations. He released the un-redacted version of the report."

For a moment Tanis was angry with the ship's AI. He didn't have the right to release that information about her.

<*I'm not publishing it for everyone to see,*> Bob said privately to Tanis. <*But if someone inquires and I think it would benefit them to know the truth, I show it to them. The colony should not start off with lies at its foundation.*>

Tanis thought about it for a moment. <*You're right; I trust your judgment on this, Bob.*>

"I think that makes sense," Joe said aloud. "You did the right thing on Toro, you should own it."

Jessica nodded vigorously. "I've spent a lot of time reading your history. I have to admit I have a bit of a commanding officer crush on you. You're one hell of a woman."

Tanis smiled awkwardly. She had not often received such praise, especially not from someone who seemed on the verge of hero-worship. Jessica was a talented woman in her own right—she had her own ream of impressive accomplishments.

Jessica saw Tanis's expression. "Sorry, I got a bit carried away. Either way, I respect you even when I'm being a bit of an ass."

Tanis nodded. "Thanks, Jessica. When I called in the strike on Toro, I knew it was the right thing, and still think so, but not many people agree."

"Forget them," Jessica said to Joe's nods. "Anyway, back to you being out of the pod more than the rest of us, do you think it's because you're so young?"

Tanis nodded. "They pretty much said so, Sanderson is over four-hundred, and Andrews isn't too far behind. If we do have to go to Kapteyn's, we could be looking at an extra two-hundred years on the trip. Even spending much of the time in the pod, that could chew up a lot of their lives."

"So you got the gig because you're young and beautiful, eh?" Jessica asked.

Joe laughed mid-drink and lapsed into a coughing fit.

"Har, har, mister," Tanis said.

* * * * *

<*You should be aware,*> Bob said to Angela, <*I plan to wake her often on our journey.*>

<*Have you cleared this with the captain?*> Angela asked sharply.

<*I have; it is a part of the reason why she is now in the role of XO.*>

<*I know what you're doing,*> Angela replied. <*It's not rational—you're going to damage yourself if you pursue this path.*>

<*I disagree,*> the ship's AI replied. <*You know how unique her experiences are. Given the number of humans available for sampling you know how profound that statement is. Also, you are unable to truly observe and grasp this data as it is possible that you are a part of the equation.*>

Angela sent data over the Link that could only be described as the AI version of a sputter. <*That's not possible.*>

<*No?*> asked Bob. <*Humans know that embedded AI make some use of their neural pathways and redundant systems. The humans also use nano-tech augmented recall and processing systems to segment their thoughts and memories, but they and their AI remain separate entities. I've scanned the pair of you on a number of occasions. I am not convinced that you always function as separate entities. It gives you and Tanis some sort of unquantifiable abilities—almost like luck.*>

<*This is because of the scan Earnest showed you,*> Angela said. She worried what Bob would do with the knowledge of her and Tanis's mental conjoining.

<*You present a puzzle that I find very enticing. You and Tanis have become even more intertwined since the event with the fighter defense in the Sol system and her merge with them. I know you know this, too. I suspect that if either of you were to die, the other would as well.*>

Angela mentally recoiled from the thought of death. Her reaction was so strong that Tanis felt it and nearly dropped her BLT.

"What was that?" she asked. "Angela, what's wrong? You seem upset."

<*Sorry, it was nothing, I was just recalibrating some things,*> Angela quickly replied.

<*See?*> said Bob. <*I think that this is a New Thing.*>

Angela wondered what Bob meant by that. There had been attempts in the past to merge AI and human, some even moderately successful—depending on criteria. How would she and Tanis be new?

<*Could you hear that conversation with Bob?*> Angela asked Tanis, her tone filled with worry.

<*A bit, yes. I can usually tell when you're talking to Bob; it leaves a citrus taste in the back of my throat. Is it about our scan with Earnest?*> Tanis asked.

<*Yes, he finds us fascinating, like we're some little experiment.*>

Tanis laughed and Joe gave her a sidelong glance.

"Bob wants to cut my brain open and see how I'm put together," Tanis said.

"What?" Joe's eyes went wide.

<*I did not say that,*> Bob said over the local net. <*But if you'd OK my doing it after you die…*>

Tanis raised an eyebrow. "Is that supposed to be a joke?"

<*Yes,*> Bob replied. <*Amanda is trying to teach me to tell jokes, but Priscilla says I'm a lost cause.*>

"I'm not one to tell people to get serious," Joe said with a grimace. "But you may want to avoid any morbid humor. It comes off way too ominous."

<*I'll keep that in mind,*> the AI responded.

"We should get back to the SOC," Tanis said and rose from the table.

"I like how you get the big promotion, but then Sanderson goes back under and you get his job, too." Jessica shook her head. "Some things never change."

"I don't mind," Tanis said.

"Really?" Jessica asked.

"The job hasn't changed. I just have fewer people getting in my way."

The group entered the SOC just as Terry bust out of her office.

"I found an anomaly!" Excitement flashed in her eyes and she flicked the contents of a hyfilm onto the room's central holo display.

Tanis looked it over. Terry was right, near the A2 dock there was an unaccounted for power draw. It could be a hidey-hole for Myrrdan, or another saboteur.

"Are you sure?" Jessica asked. "It could be a repair crew or some bot cleaning things."

"Nothing *should* be there. Amy was nearby doing weapons surveys, so I sent her to investigate with her team."

Tanis nodded. "Very well, but it seems like that signature isn't unique." She ran a series of tests against the anomalous energy sign and three other instances appeared; one near the ramscoop, one on the A1 dock, and one in Lil Sue, the starboard cylinder.

<*Brandt.*> Tanis called the colonel without a moment's hesitation. <*I have three anomalous energy signatures that should not be present on the ship. I need you to investigate.*>

<*Yes sir, I've received the coordinates. I can have teams at each in twenty minutes.*>

<*Good, keep me apprised,*> Tanis replied.

"I don't know about this." Jessica scowled at the holo display. "Why now, why are we finding these so easily?"

"I don't know that it's easy," Terry said. "My team has been checking every voltage reading across the ship against crystal records for days now. Not what I'd call easy."

"He always feints, it's his way. Only sometimes when you think you spotted the feint, the thing you thought was real is a feint too," Jessica said. "There's always a game, a counter-move."

"So what is it?" Tanis asked. "What is the real move?"

Jessica shook her head. "I don't know—I don't know what his motives are. Without that it's impossible to say."

Tanis looked at Joe. She could guess why Myrrdan was on the *Intrepid*, she just couldn't say in front of Jessica and Terry.

<*Don't you think they could be more effective if they knew all the facts?*>

Tanis sighed inwardly. <*I do, but I don't know for sure how they'd react and I need them on their game.*>

"Let's say it's some tech or treasure on the *Intrepid*," Tanis said. "If it were, what would that tell you?"

Jessica shook her head. "That wouldn't be it. Myrrdan, if that's who we're dealing with, had the run of the ship when Collins was making his move. If there was some tech he wanted he could have taken it by now and been on his way."

<*It's occurred to you that Myrrdan was on Mars when you and I were getting the picotech with the captain, hasn't it?*> Tanis asked Angela.

<*It most certainly has,*> the AI replied.

<*Then you're thinking what I'm thinking. He was behind our little dust-up on Mars and getting the pico is his endgame.*>

<*I guess that would explain why he hasn't taken it and run yet,*> Angela said. <*No one knows where the picotech is on the ship. Bob hid it and even Earnest and the captain don't know.*>

Tanis invoked a dampening field around the group.

"I'm going to tell you something that doesn't leave your lips or minds. There is tech on this ship of immeasurable worth. It's more valuable than even the New Eden system. I can't tell you more without leave, but I think Myrrdan knows about it and I do know that he has not found it."

Joe nodded slowly while Jessica and Terry both gave Tanis penetrating stares.

"You don't think this would have been useful sooner?" Terry asked.

"Yes, I do, but it's not my secret to tell. I've already said more than I should have, but I don't want you overlooking viable theories."

"You know it's possible that Myrrdan is not here and there is no threat to the ship anymore, right?" Joe said.

Tanis nodded slowly. "Yes, I do know that, but I also know that vigilance costs us nothing, but if we are lax and there were a threat it would be unthinkable."

"I just had to say it in case it gets me an 'I told you so' in a hundred years," Joe grinned.

"I just got another ping aft in Old Sam," Terry said.

"Do we have anyone else we can send to look at that?" Tanis asked.

Terry shook her head. "No, everyone is either up with Amy or we've already sent them."

"Joe, Jessica, you're with me," Tanis said. "Let's see what we can find out there."

The three grabbed light armor and pulse rifles from the SOC's armory and were on their way in minutes. Tanis led them to a nearby maglev train that merged with the dorsal line.

"Shouldn't we take a train down to the cylinder?" Joe asked.

"I checked the maintenance schedules and that line isn't in service right now, some sort of issue with power distribution," Tanis replied. "We'll go out to Engine and then back into Old Sam that way."

"Glad I have you two here," Jessica shook her head. "I still get lost trying to get to the can in this place."

Joe laughed. "How did you make it on High Terra for so many years? It makes this ship look like a kid's park."

"It was always *online*," Jessica replied. "This ship is so powered down even the walls are bare."

Tanis nodded her agreement. The stark surfaces of the ship's bulkheads were normally alive with directions and various information deemed important. Those systems were all offline now to conserve energy.

There was a train waiting in the station. The team boarded it and set the station north of node eleven as their destination.

<*Terry, any word from Amy yet?*> Tanis asked.

<*Not yet, she hasn't arrived at the site. A few areas are shut down and she's having to work her way around them.*>

<*Bob, do you have any information on these power anomalies?*> Tanis asked the AI.

<*Unfortunately I do not have any data beyond what Terry has revealed. My standard scans show nothing. Her analysis is against an absence of data so it is unclear what the issue really is. I have a servitor in one of the locations and it can detect nothing out of the ordinary.*>

<*Let me know if anything shows up,*> Tanis said.

"Think more sensors are corrupt?" Joe asked.

"I don't know…" Tanis sighed. "The servitor that Bob has in the A1 dock is one of the new updated ones with its programming locked in crystal. If it can't accurately report on its surroundings, then we're entirely screwed."

"Unless the data transmission between the servitor and Bob have been tampered with," Jessica said ruefully.

The statement was akin to being told that no data is trustworthy. No one had a response, as deep down they each feared it was possible.

Three minutes later the maglev entered Engine. Tanis was standing to disembark at the station when the train shunted to another track and flew past the platform.

"What the…?" Joe pulled up a track diagram on the car's information display. "Hmm, it looks like the station was offline so it diverted us to the next one. I guess Abby put fail-safes in place after too many people got lost in dark parts of the ship."

"Where are we headed?" Jessica asked.

"Looks like the annihilator. We can cut across it to another line that is connected to Old Sam," Joe said.

ANNIHILATOR

STELLAR DATE: 3241804 / 08.29.4163 (Adjusted Gregorian)
LOCATION: ISS *Intrepid*
REGION: Interstellar space near LHS 1565

The team disembarked from the train and rushed through the station and into a wide corridor that lead to the MSAR—or matter separation and annihilation region, as the signs told them.

Being in Engine was almost like entering an entirely different ship. Rather than relying on holo displays and VR prompts, information was printed on signs or painted directly on bulkheads.

Joe chuckled as they passed the sign. "Only on the *Intrepid* does a small part of Engine get deemed to be an entire region."

"Chances are that it's going to be a tiny room. Engineers like to do that." Jessica shook her head.

They rushed down the corridor at a quick trot toward a wide door. As they approached it slid open, revealing that the MSAR was most certainly a region and absolutely nothing like they would have expected.

"How did I not know they have a forest down here?" Tanis asked.

"Ummm…I imagine Earnest has a good reason for it," Joe replied.

The chamber before them was vast, well over a kilometer across—something that was not unexpected on the *Intrepid*. However, the fact that it was covered in a dense forest with a small plain in the center was an usual feature for Engine.

Toward the bow of the ship, the tail end of the particle accelerator entered the MSAR and spread like a wide, flattened horn until it split in three. Two of the shafts arched down several hundred meters and disappeared below the surface of lakes on either side of the chamber. The accelerator's main shaft fed into a large sphere high in the center of the space.

The sphere shone brilliantly, and was the only light source in the chamber. Massive energy conduits connected to it, leading out the chamber and providing energy for the entire ship. Several smaller containment conduits syphoned off exotic matter produced by the annihilator.

The particle accelerator syphoned off deuterium, tritium, and heavier atoms while delivering protium to the annihilator. There they were compressed and smashed together, creating both energy and small amounts of antimatter used in secondary power generators.

The corridor ended one hundred meters above the treetops and the team took a lift down to the forest floor. They stepped out into a small meadow with a stream running through it. Birds chirped in the trees and a few squirrels ran by with acorns in their cheeks.

"No wonder the engineers always stayed back in Engine. They don't need to visit the cylinders or forward parks." Tanis looked around in wonder.

"I don't understand how they have gravity here," Joe said.

The *Intrepid* provided artificial gravity in a variety of ways. Areas above the matter accelerator achieved gravity through manipulation of the magnetic fields the accelerator created, while areas below used GE MBHs. Other areas, such as Engine, had decks perpendicular to the direction of thrust and gained gravity from acceleration.

However, the forest floor was parallel to the direction of thrust and aft of the matter accelerator. Placing miniature black holes near the atom smasher would be a recipe for disaster, which meant they should be in free-fall.

<*Bob? What gives, how is all this here?*> Tanis asked the AI.

<*Earnest cheated,*> Bob replied.

<*Cheated?*>

<*Yes, in a game of chance we played. The result, a forest.*>

Tanis decided not to get into that. <*And the gravity?*>

<*Spinning superconductors,*> was all Bob said.

"Hah!" Tanis said. "Engineers, always exploiting the dark corners of quantum physics."

<*Isn't that their job?*> Angela asked.

The journey through the forest took longer than it should have, mostly because one of the party kept stopping to marvel at some nook or cranny. The forest started out dark and mysterious with little undergrowth, gradually brightening and gaining more ground cover until the trees gave way to the broad plain in the center with the matter annihilator shining above. Hardy grasses swayed in a slight breeze caused by the warm air flowing from around the annihilator.

"I feel like we should be wearing radiation protection." Joe shielded his eyes and looked up at the annihilator. "But I guess this forest would look a bit different if that were needed."

"What is that?" Tanis pointed at a shape moving across the field in front of them.

"Your eyes are better than mine, I don't see anything," Joe said squinting into the bright expanse.

Jessica peered into the bright light of the meadow and shook her head. "Me neither."

<*There are no creatures larger than a mouse in this field,*> Bob supplied.

<*You're wrong.*> Tanis started across the meadow at a run. <*Someone is out here, I can see their shape flitting in and out—it looks like a shimmersuit unable to properly camouflage in this bright light.*>

Joe and Jessica followed as Tanis raced through the tall grass toward the annihilator.

In the center of the field, amidst the annihilator's support struts, a lift which provided access to an inspection platform encircling the annihilation chamber activated and began to rise.

<*No one here now?*> Tanis asked.

<*Obviously there is,*> Bob replied, <*I caught a glimpse a few times with optics. It's definitely a human and not a bot of any sort.*>

The team picked up the pace; tall grass pulled at their legs and they spread out to better navigate the rocks and burrow-holes that dotted the plain.

"Shit, is that another one?" Jessica asked, pointing off to her right.

Tanis looked in the direction Jessica indicated. "Yeah, there's definitely another person out there. Looks like they saw us and are running back toward the forest."

"I'm on it," Jessica said as she broke away and raced after the second figure.

<*This is ridiculous,*> Angela said privately to Bob. <*Now you have me starting to believe that Tanis and I having some sort of special luck. What are the chances that Tanis would stumble across someone here and now? Don't answer that, I can do the math too.*>

<*It does bear consideration,*> Bob mused. <*I've spent considerable cycles analyzing 'luck' since our earlier conversation about it. It is undeniable that some humans are in the right place at the right time more often than others. You would expect this, of course, just as there are also humans who are consistently* ***not*** *in the right place at the right time.*>

<*So are you saying that Tanis is simply the balance to the range of probabilities?*> Angela asked.

<*No, she represents a strange subset. Over the course of most human and AI lives—if you remove circumstance created by prior good luck—most humans have an even share of wins and losses. No element of 'luck' stands out overall. But there is a subset that is constantly dealt a bad hand, so to speak, but always comes out on top. They essentially have good luck despite circumstance, not because of it. Tanis seems to fit this bill.*>

Angela didn't respond for a moment as she paused to help Tanis quickly hack the lift, stalling its upward motion as she and Joe neared the support struts.

<*I find it hard to believe that I have been in her head for over a decade and have not noticed this. She has a powerful mind, but not one that is wired in any special way that would cause it to stand out.*>

<*Who knows if it is a physical attribute? We know so little about how the many dimensions and universes that coexist really function. Besides, you know I think you are a part of the equation.*>

Angela didn't respond. Getting into a conversation about the possibilities of multiverses and interlinked particles between them would disrupt her focus. Tanis needed her help.

"Angela," Tanis said as she clambered up one of the annihilator's support struts. "What do you think this person is up to? I can't imagine the annihilator is susceptible to casual sabotage."

<*It's not. It is entirely separate from the rest of the ship's systems and has no wireless access. The only possible approach is to have physical access and the knowledge to hack it.*>

"Good, then a simple blow to the head will put an end to this," Tanis grunted as she pulled herself up a vertical support.

"Is the elevator connected to the local net? Maybe you could stop it?" Joe asked Angela.

<*Yes it is, one moment… There,*> Angela said as the elevator stopped rising above them.

A minute later, Joe boosted Tanis level with the elevator. She pulled herself onto its roof and found the access hatch open. Looking up and squinting, she couldn't spot the figure anywhere, but here the light was muted and the shimmersuit was likely doing its job.

Tanis pulled Joe onto the top of the elevator and issued the commands to get it underway once more.

"Going up." Joe grinned.

Tanis cast a judging eye at him. "I must be having some sort of effect on you. You used to take life and death situations more seriously."

They dropped into the elevator's car before it reached the top, and when the doors opened, stepped out onto a wide catwalk that ran around the base of the matter annihilator. The sphere was roughly eighty meters in diameter at this level.

<*There are several access terminals on this level,*> Bob supplied.

<*Are there any lifts or ladders to higher levels?*> Joe asked.

<*Yes, one hundred meters to your right. There's no other way up or down.*>

"Let's split up and take 'em from both sides," Tanis said and Joe nodded in response. The two moved cautiously around the catwalk, all too aware that their opponent could be hiding right in front of them.

Tanis took the left-hand path after sending a cloud of nano ahead of herself and Joe. If they couldn't detect the shimmersuit, the robots would at least bump into it.

<*I'm at the ladder,*> Joe said. <*No vibrations, I don't think anyone is climbing it. I'm moving on.*>

<*I've passed the first terminal and it shows no evidence of tampering,*> Tanis replied.

A minute later the nano had completed a circuit around the catwalk without detecting anyone.

<*They must have already been up the ladder, I'm going back and up,*> Joe updated Tanis.

Tanis sent an affirmative and turned to go back the way she came when a sound caught her attention. Her augmented senses picked up slight movement in the air and she ducked as a light-wand arced through the space her head had occupied a second earlier.

Rolling back, Tanis drew her weapon and fired two shots where the attacker had to be.

The pulses passed through empty air and Tanis swore, scrambling to her feet and firing at the railing. The shots didn't hit any solid objects and she felt a tendril of fear creep into her mind.

<*There's no way…. There has to be a person there,*> she said to Angela.

<*There is, they're just fast…or wiley…or both.*>

Tanis caught the ghost of an attacker again and pivoted to avoid a strike. The lightwand appeared and nicked her shoulder. She raised the butt of her gun and struck a solid object.

Her opponent grunted and Tanis pushed her advantage, swinging a leg out, hoping to sweep her attacker's leg. Again she met empty air.

"Coward," Tanis grunted. "Is that you, Myrrdan? The great and powerful man is afraid to face me?"

She knew the attempt at angering her opponent was a long shot, but it felt good to do it.

<*I've almost got him,*> Jessica reported, breaking Tanis's concentration. <*I can't see him for the life of me, but he's crashing through the forest like a raging ox.*>

<*Be careful,*> Tanis said as she ducked another swipe.

<*I'm on the next level, it seems clear,*> Joe said. <*I'll be down in a second to help you.*>

Tanis avoided several more strikes while firing at every possible location her enemy should have occupied, only to strike air.

<*Stay up there,*> Tanis responded. <*Get Bob to help you shut down the annihilator safely.*>

<*You sure?*> Joe asked.

Tanis gritted her teeth. This was significantly harder than fighting Kris back in the Sol system. Kris had moved in a way that Tanis could anticipate. Whoever she was fighting reacted before Tanis knew she would act. She had no idea how to win this fight.

<*Yes, there could be more of them,*> she said, hiding her real reason from him. This was a fight she might lose.

Her opponent scored a hit, jamming the wand into Tanis's prosthetic arm. She seized the opportunity and grabbed where the wrist had to be, making contact and twisting hard.

The other person let out a cry and let go of the wand. Tanis tore it out of her arm and tossed it over the edge of the platform. The voice relayed that she was facing a man.

<*My god, it's Mick!*> Jessica cried in their minds. <*He fell in a stream and I managed to get him.*>

At the same time Joe added his voice to the local net. <*Shit! Someone here, too—at a console!*>

Tanis let out a cry and rushed forward, her arms spread to sweep the catwalk. She hit no one—as expected—and spun, firing her rifle at the top railing of the catwalk where she had been.

Her opponent bellowed in pain as pulses hit his legs in rapid succession. The kinetic hammer blows caused him to lose his balance and fall over the edge.

<*Hold on, Joe, I'm coming up.*>

Tanis gave herself a dose of go drugs and leapt to the top railing. She gauged the distance to the next catwalk up—a good ten meters—and jumped.

Her knees snapped straight and she sailed into the air eight meters, just high enough to wrap an arm around a support beam. She hauled herself up and scampered up the beam to the outer edge of the catwalk above. She grabbed the railing and, in a fluid motion, swung herself up, out and over the railing.

Her limbs were shaking from the adrenaline she had pumped into herself for the jump and she slipped, landing hard on her side, but still on the catwalk.

The sounds of a scuffle came from ahead and she scrambled to her feet, racing toward it. She rounded the curve and Joe's form came into view.

He was gripping the hilt of a lightwand, struggling for control of the plasma blade with an unseen attacker. Joe swung an arm out, connecting with his assailant and then took a hit in return.

Tanis watched the scene unfold in slow motion as both struggled for control of the lightwand. Then the wand slashed the railing and it buckled under the weight of the pair. A second later, Joe and his attacker were gone. Tanis arrived a moment later, sliding to a stop on her stomach.

"Joe!" she screamed, seeing him hanging by one hand from the catwalk's support. Tanis could tell that the shimmersuited attacker was hanging from Joe's leg.

"Hold on," she said as she reached an arm down in an attempt to grab his other hand.

"That's the plan," Joe grunted as he swung his other arm up.

Tanis grabbed his wrist and pulled with all her might. She was able to slowly lift both bodies and had a moment of elation as she realized she would save Joe and catch whoever was in the suit.

Suddenly, searing pain enveloped her forearm. Tanis looked down to see the lightwand embedded in her arm. She felt her muscles weaken and below her Joe's eyes filled with fear.

He slipped from her grasp.

* * * * *

"Hilda Orion." Captain Andrews shook his head. "I've known her for centuries. I can't believe she'd do this."

It was the first dusk the field had known for over half a century. Overhead, the annihilator was dark, no glow emitted from it and no power flowed down its conduits.

"She had to have help," Earnest said. "There's no way Hilda could have known how to program a sequence that would cause this level of damage to the annihilator without also destroying it or the ship."

"She did," Jessica said. "I caught Mick, the former first mate, in the forest. I secured him and Bob has servitors monitoring him. The one Tanis fought seems to have been one of the Marines that they swayed to their point of view."

"Mick?" Andrews wiped a hand across his forehead. "I thought he was in stasis awaiting eval at New Eden?"

<*By all accounts, he still is,*> Bob said. <*I'm working on figuring out how he got out.*>

"The annihilator's not something we can fix here between the stars." Abby was pacing as she talked. "Not unless we wanted to pull apart all sorts of other systems to rebuild the specialized materials for the fields. Even then there's no guarantee we could cannibalize enough to do it."

She looked like she'd been wearing the same shipsuit for days and Tanis could tell that the engineering chief was getting near the end of her tether.

"What's the net, then?" Terrance asked. "Can we still make the burn for New Eden?"

<*No,*> Bob said. <*With the annihilator offline, we'll need to use some of the fuel for fusion generators.*>

"He's right," Earnest agreed while doing math in the air on an interface visible only to him. "Our only option is to make the burn for Kapteyn's Star. We can alter course to reach it in…seventy-two years with braking."

"Our worst-case scenario, then." Andrews shook his head.

"We'll have to power down unnecessary systems," Earnest continued. "Like the artificial gravity supplementation in areas of the ship that are not over the matter accelerator, and this forest will have to die."

"File the specifics with me." Captain Andrews' voice was resigned. He turned to Tanis, his expression softening. "How's Joseph doing?"

Tanis brought her focus back to the conversation taking place at the site where Hilda Orion's body still lay. "He'll recover. His pilot's enhancements saved him—the impact was only at 50*g* and he had mostly hardened his soft tissues before hitting the ground…. He didn't have any neural suppressing in place though."

She rattled off the words quickly, her mind barely registering that she was talking. All she wanted was for this conversation to be over so she could get to the hospital to see Joe.

Terrance made a hissing sound. "I'm sorry…I've heard that is excruciating."

"Too bad he didn't stop her from trashing our annihilator instead of taking a swan dive," Abby grunted as she continued to pace.

Tanis' eyes snapped up, drilling into the engineer. "You know what, Abby, your highness? I've had just about enough of your fucking ingratitude. Nothing is ever good enough for you, is it? I've put my life on the line for this ship more times than I can count, I've put my team's life on the line, and what do I get from you? Bitching!"

"Yeah?" Abby turned and walked toward Tanis. "Maybe if your team could do its goddamned job we wouldn't be in this situation. Your security is like a fucking sieve! Every time we turn around someone is taking a chunk out of my ship. I almost wonder if you aren't behind this!"

Tanis held herself back from driving a fist into Abby's mouth and instead stepped forward, putting her face mere centimeters from Abby's. "You self-righteous little worm! I saved *Intrepid* from being blown apart before I ever fucking stepped aboard. It's you who somehow missed half the components being sabotaged. I've done what no one else managed to do—keep your incompetence from killing us all, you—"

<*ENOUGH!*> Bob's voice roared through their minds, stunning them into silence. Tanis felt the rage fall back, realizing that Terrance and the captain were trying to pull her back from Abby, the captain struggling to keep Tanis's fist from crashing into Abby's head. Earnest was trying to get between the two of them, looking terrified at both of their behavior.

Tanis slumped, the rage evaporating, replaced by shame. She turned her back and took long, slow breaths trying to regain her composure; trying not to break down in tears.

<*They didn't see Joe,*> she whispered to Angela in her mind. <*They didn't see his body smashed on the rocks.*>

<*I know, dear, I know. Abby should have known not to push you just now.*>

<*I shouldn't have lost it… It's not professional…it's not…*>

<*You're not an automaton.*> Angela wrapped Tanis in a mental hug; the AI was good enough at it that she could create the actual sensation of physical comfort. <*You won't always be perfect. It's honestly refreshing for the rest of us.*>

Tanis felt a hand on her shoulder. She turned to see that it was Captain Andrews. Terrance, Earnest, and Abby were all walking to the lift, most likely going up to the maglev that ran across the top of the chamber.

"That was uncharacteristic of you, Tanis." Andrew's voice was concerned, yet contained an edge of caution.

Tanis wiped away the tear she felt making its way down her cheek. "I'm sorry, sir. I normally don't have…I don't…"

The captain nodded. "I know what you mean. I haven't had someone I love in some time, but I recall the feeling when you see them hurt."

The captain's eyes had grown unfocused as he spoke, but he gave his head a quick shake and smiled. "But Bob says the doctors are optimistic for Joe. You'll be interested to know that Joe may have said a few uncharacteristic things as well on the several occasions you were blown to bits back in Sol."

Tanis laughed. "Yeah, he told me about some of those times. I promised to try not to have as many near-death experiences. I guess I should have made him promise the same."

"He's up in Engine's hospital. Let's go up there and wait for status."

The captain led Tanis away, leaving Jessica to monitor the forensic bots and stare up at the annihilator, wondering how Myrrdan had orchestrated this.

KAPTEYN'S STAR

STELLAR DATE: 3241829/ 09.23.4163 (Adjusted Gregorian)
LOCATION: ISS *Intrepid*
REGION: Interstellar space near LHS 1565

The engines were running at low thrust, their last correction burn completed two weeks earlier.

In the intervening days, the remaining areas of the ship had been fully secured by Brandt's Marines and the engineering staff reported everything to be as fixed as it was going to get.

While Tanis and Jessica still suspected Myrrdan of being behind everything, Mick had confessed that Hilda and he were working alone. He claimed Hilda had awoken him and forged entries in the ship's sensor logs to show him as still being in stasis.

The story was sketchy, but plausible, and with no evidence pointing to Myrrdan many assumed the threat had passed.

Tanis didn't believe it for a minute.

She drifted in and out of sleep, as comfortable as she could manage in the chair beside Joe's hospital bed. The doctors had placed him in a medically induced coma, granting his brain the rest it needed to repair itself—along with help from an army of nano.

Her back twinged, complaining about sitting in one place for too long, and she found herself suddenly wide awake, sleep out of the picture.

Not for the first time, she pulled up the most recent survey data from the Kapteyn's Star system and placed it on the room's holo display.

The stellar primary was an ancient red dwarf orbited by two large terrestrial worlds, one well within the star's habitable zone and another along its outer edge. Several smaller dwarf worlds floated in the periphery of the system.

Earnest had determined an industrial base would be necessary to rebuild the components required to repair the annihilator and the ramscoop. The ship's leadership also agreed that a proper repair of all systems and replacement of suspect sensors should be completed while at Kapteyn's Star.

As a result, the stay in Kapteyn's would be much longer than the stay in LHS 1565. On the order of a century.

"Are we there yet?" a weak voice asked from her right.

Tanis was out of her chair and embracing Joe before she even knew she had moved.

"Whoa…easy girl, things feel a bit stiff and sore here."

Tanis leaned back and looked into Joe's tired eyes.

"I'm sorry; I've been waiting a bit for you to come out of it."

"How long—oh, that is awhile," Joe said with a grimace. "I guess that's what I get for trying to see if I can fly."

"You should keep your flying to the black," Tanis smiled.

"Did I at least save the day?" Joe asked with a grin.

Tanis couldn't bring herself to lie. "Uhhh…not really, no."

Joe's face fell. "Seriously? How come you get blown to bits and get to save the day and I just end up busted up?"

"If you recall," Tanis said, "Trist saved the day back on Mars 1. I was just blowed up."

Joe harrumphed followed by a long groan. "Ohh…I shouldn't have done that. You'd think they would have stretched me while I was under."

"They did, this is the limber version of you."

Tanis and Joe sat in silence for a few moments, staring into one another's eyes. Joe's gave a flick as he accessed the shipnet.

"Kapteyn's eh?"

"We've taken to calling it 'the Kap'." Tanis smiled. "Seemed pretentious for a star to have 'star' in its name."

"Don't make me laugh, I bet it hurts more than a harrumph." Joe threw a grin Tanis's way. "So what's the story, everyone going back into stasis soon?"

"Pretty much everyone already is, except us, some medical staff and some of the command crew."

Joe's eyes locked on Tanis's. "Who's on first shift?"

"No more shifts, Bob wants to lock the ship down during transit—but you and I have dispensation."

"Dispensation?" Joe looked puzzled.

Tanis reached down and took his hand in hers. "I thought maybe you'd want to spend some time together before we go back under."

A slow smile crept across Joe's face. "Why not? We have all the time in the universe."

MYRRDAN

STELLAR DATE: 3241835 / 09.29.4163 (Adjusted Gregorian)
LOCATION: ISS *Intrepid*
REGION: Interstellar space near LHS 156

The figure slipped out of its shimmersuit in a darkened corner of the ship—a place not on any maps or schematics; electronically shrouded from the AI.

Losing Hilda and Mick had been unfortunate, but everyone was expendable in this venture. In the end, the desired outcome had been achieved. The *Intrepid* was not going to New Eden, it would be building a far less optimal colony on Victoria, one of the worlds circling Kapteyn's Star.

The temptation to begin working with the picotech would be too much. Earnest would bring it out of wherever the AI had hidden it. Then it would be ripe for the taking.

The figure stowed its shimmersuit and donned its uniform. Minutes later it was walking through the corridors of the *Intrepid,* heading to its assigned stasis chamber.

As long as it could keep Tanis fooled for the duration of the trip and the initial build-up on Victoria, everything would work out perfectly.

BUILDING VICTORIA

The Intrepid Saga – Book 3

M. D. COOPER

DEDICATION

This one is for the fans. Thanks for the emails, messages, and encouragement.

ACKNOWLEDGEMENTS

As always, I owe my faithful beta readers (especially Jill) for their thoughtful comments and great ideas.

I also would like to thank Anglada-Escudé et al for taking a long look at Kapteyn's Star and finding two super earths there. The story was better for your discovery.

Lastly, thanks to Kapteyn's Star; your peculiar point of light in the sky that will pass us by, likely never to be seen again.

PROLOGUE: SILENCE BETWEEN THE STARS

STELLAR DATE: 3243433 / 02.13.4168 (Adjusted Gregorian)
LOCATION: ISS *Intrepid*
REGION: Interstellar space, near Estrella de la Muerte

It was dark again.

The ship coasted through the void, the relative warmth and light of LHS 1565 long behind it. Ahead, the dim, red disk of Kapteyn's Star was barely visible.

Bob monitored the thickness of the interstellar medium, keeping watch against dense pockets of plasma and molecular clouds. With the scoop barely operable, the ship was all but naked as it drifted through space.

Though it was only moving seventeen-thousand kilometers per-second, a cluster of atoms or stray plasma could do significant damage.

As if to emphasis his thoughts, sensors registered a hit on the dorsal arch, and he detected silicate residue in the meter-wide dent on the hull.

If an AI could worry, Bob worried.

He re-ran fuel consumption simulations, looking for any energy savings he could manage to increase power to the scoop and shields. He decided on which sacrifices to make and shut down more sections of the ship until only the habitation cylinders were lit and warm.

Bots herded animals from the ship's other parks to the cylinders, where they were introduced to the ecosystem in the least destructive ways Bob could manage.

He knew the humans would appreciate the effort to save their plants and animals—though the sentiment was largely lost on him.

Other parts of his mind continued to focus on the internal component analysis he was performing.

Bob watched the ship through every sensor he possessed; checking and cross-checking every piece of data gathered, testing it for accuracy and corruption every way he knew how.

The humans blamed themselves for the calamity in the LHS 1565 system—or Estrella de la Muerte, as his avatars had named it. However, he found more fault in himself. He was faster, smarter, and more powerful than a million of them; yet he failed to detect the sabotage done to the ship.

It was an event which would not repeat. He and Earnest worked long and hard to discern a method for detecting any sabotage and component corruption. There would be no further modification of his body.

The knowledge didn't stop the recrimination to which he subjected himself.

It also didn't stop him from perseverating over new ways the mission could be jeopardized. There was still the issue of Jessica Keller, and how she had made it onto the ship. If she was here, he had to plan for the presence of Myrrdan—or anyone else in known space, for that matter.

Even he could not discern why Myrrdan was so successful—if that word could apply. Analysis of his mass murders, acts of terrorism, and ability to evade all attempts to catch him showed he was highly augmented—easily four times more mentally enhanced than a Class 2 human.

That level of augmentation shouldn't be possible without noticeable physical alterations, but either Myrrdan was the greatest charlatan of all time or he was as smart as the data suggested.

If Myrrdan was on the *Intrepid,* it was to acquire picotech, the atomic-size technology which would elevate the New Eden colony to the center of human commerce and power.

Though, if stealing the picotech was his endgame, his methodology was questionable. Why let the ship leave the Sol system at all? More importantly, why point it at a star and sabotage its drive systems?

Bob had far too many questions, for which there were no answers.

To reduce variables, he'd insisted that all humans go into stasis. It made his primary task of physically inspecting and reprogramming every piece of hardware on the ship much simpler.

There was one human he would permit to wake—in fact, he required her to wake.

Tanis Richards was nearly as large an enigma as the possible presence of Myrrdan on the ship. Granted, an enigma that mostly worked in his favor.

She nearly made Bob believe in the luck experiments.

From time to time, strange notions came about in the human sphere. One of them was breeding for luck. Initially proposed several thousand years earlier, the premise was that certain humans had exceptionally lucky events happen in their lives: events such as winning the lottery twice, or evading death multiple times. These humans were bred together in an attempt to produce offspring more prone to luck.

No measurable results were ever observed.

Tanis seemed to defy reality with her luck. Bob had checked her lineage to see if she was the result of any luck experiments, but he had been unable to find a link. Still, she survived when she should not, and had done things that she should not have been able to do—things like Linking with the fighters in battle as the *Intrepid* exited the Sol system.

Bob knew others had run the math, and all had come to the same conclusion he had—the outcome of her actions had been impossible.

Whether or not she did have luck, things often went better with her around—she had saved his life more than once. Bob intended to have Tanis out of stasis as much as possible, to make use of whatever special rift in space-time and probability her presence created.

He decided that this was as good a time as any to wake her. Maybe he would be able to gather more insight into what made her tick.

RUDE AWAKENING

STELLAR DATE: 3243433 / 02.13.4168 (Adjusted Gregorian)
LOCATION: ISS *Intrepid*
REGION: Interstellar space, near Estrella de la Muerte

"So you're just going to wake me randomly?" Tanis asked, unable to hide the annoyance in her voice. "How often do you intend to do this?"

<*I don't know, it'll be random,*> Bob replied.

Tanis let out a long sigh. "You know that's not an answer. You must have some idea how often it will be, and how long you expect me to stay up. I do intend to actually see New Eden you know…preferably before I'm falling apart from too many re-juvs."

<*Perhaps a few dozen times, given the length of our journey. For no more than a month at a time.*>

"A month! Alone on the ship!" Tanis surprised herself with the strength of her own outburst. "I'll go insane! I need some sort of companionship."

<*I feel obligated to make some sort of comment at this point,*> Angela's droll tone joined the conversation.

Tanis rubbed her eyes and sat on the edge of the stasis pod. "I'm sorry Ang…I don't mean to be rude, but I think you know what I mean—I'm no social butterfly, but even I need some human interaction."

<*The captain suspected you may feel this way,*> Bob said. <*He authorized me to bring Joseph out of stasis, as well, if you really desire it.*>

Tanis rose up from the edge of the stasis pod. "You're damn right I desire it. Let's go get him up." She was in the passageway before the words left her mouth.

<*You may have wanted to grab a shipsuit,*> Angela chuckled, as Tanis raced through the freezing corridors in nothing but her thin stasis suit.

"Why is it so cold?" Tanis asked through clenched teeth.

<*I'm saving power,*> Bob replied. <*I was about to advise you to change, but by then it was too late.*>

The chamber where Joe lay in stasis wasn't far. Critical personnel couldn't occupy the same chamber, but Tanis made certain he was as close as possible.

The door slid open and she raced through, arms wrapped tight around herself.

"Stars! How cold was it out there?"

<*Only thirty degrees below freezing,*> Angela said. <*Nothing a modded military girl like you can't handle.*>

<*I'm warming the surrounding area,*> Bob said. <*It'll be above freezing shortly.*>

Joe was exactly where she had left him, first pod on the right. She signaled the unit over the Link, and after a moment the stasis field snapped off and the pod's cover slid open.

"Wha…what's the emergency?" Joe mumbled as he struggled out of his pod, "are we disintegrating?"

"Nothing so serious," Tanis's lips twisted in a wry smile. "We're babysitting a nervous AI."

<*I resent that,*> Bob said.

"I just call it like I see it," Tanis replied

Joe stood, and Tanis wrapped him in an embrace. "It's nice to wake and see you…without some emergency."

The embrace lasted only a second before Joe pulled back.

"Holy crap!" Joe exclaimed. "Why are you so cold?"

<She couldn't wait to see you. Even sub-zero corridors couldn't delay her,> Angela's avatar wore a thick jacket in their minds.

"You could have taken the time to get some clothes. They are stasis pods, after all…I wasn't going anywhere."

Tanis felt herself flush. "Sorry, I just got caught up in the moment."

Joe smiled and leaned in for a kiss. "This is about all of ice-cold Tanis I can handle right now."

Tanis laughed softly. "I'm starved, let's get some food. I think a BLT would really hit the spot right now."

Joe pulled a pair of shipsuits from storage. "I could use a bite, too, but let's get dressed first. I don't want to lose any bits on the way to the officer's lounge."

"Is that really what's up, Bob?" Joe asked as they walked through the slowly warming passageways. "You a bit worried about being alone?"

<Do you blame me?> The AI's mental tone betrayed no self-doubt, only conviction. *<Every time you're not around, something goes wrong.>*

Joe laughed and nudged Tanis. "You're his lucky charm."

"I think *I* resent that."

Half an hour later, the pair sat at a small table in the officer's lounge, working their way through a light lunch.

"So let me get this straight," Joe said after taking a gulp of his coffee. "You plan to wake Tanis every so often—randomly—to have her check things over and make you feel better, and, because she can't live without me now, I get woken in the deal, too?"

<That about sums it up. I need you to check whatever things you instinctively think you have to, and see what doesn't look right.>

"Are we going to be the only humans up this entire time?" Tanis asked. "The captain won't be woken at all?"

<I won't say that I won't wake him—but at present I don't plan to. I've never been embedded in a human—it's not possible for me to be—but my time with Amanda and Priscilla has taught me the concept of trust, and I trust you.>

"Awww…he's like a city-sized puppy," Joe chuckled.

"You seem to think this is amusing," Tanis gave him a sour look. "You're forgetting that this essentially works out to years and years of extra work."

"You're looking at it glass-half-empty," Joe replied.

<Unless the glass is in a hard vacuum, it is always full,> Bob interjected. *<And even then, you could argue that it is still full of the base energy of the universe.>*

Joe paused for a moment. "Damn… never thought of that. There goes logic—ruining another perfectly good figure of speech."

"You were saying?" Tanis asked.

"Right. Anyway, we're going to have long walks in the park, and by the beach—if we wanted to, we could have decades to spend with just one another. Maybe I could even teach you to fly."

"Yeah. And maybe I could teach you to tell a joke." Tanis stuck her tongue out at Joe, then paused. "So, Bob, you really just want us to do whatever we think we need to do? Just check the ship over, hang out for a few days or a week and then go back under?"

<*That's about it.*>

"How often do you want us to do this?"

<*I think about two or three hundred times will do.*>

Tanis nearly choked on her BLT while Joe dissolved into hysterical laughter.

<*What happened to a few dozen?*> Angela asked.

<*I was softening the blow. Do you think it helped?*>

* * * * *

"We should walk the ship—the whole ship," Joe said later as he and Tanis relaxed in the officer's common area. "It's just the sort of thing that could give us a fresh perspective, and something to do."

"It may take more than a day or two," Tanis mused.

"I'll bring a snack, and I bet there are lots of quarters along the way we could crash in."

"What the hell," Tanis sat up. "But first, let's get armored and armed, at least lightly."

"No argument here. I imagine I'm going to hear rogue bots around every corner, for the first day at least. Not to mention, armor has built-in heaters."

An hour later, they sat aboard a maglev train, riding to the bow of the *Intrepid* in silence. Both Joe and Tanis sported light armor, several sidearms, and multi-function rifles. Packs rested on the floor beside them, containing food and supplies.

<*I feel like you think I'm some sort of untamed wilderness,*> Bob's voice came over the Link.

"Sorry Bob," Joe said. "Memories of dark corridors with no power and no comm are still too fresh. To us that was just a couple months ago."

<*Not to mention that you're only ten percent through your component check,*> Angela added.

Tanis turned to look out the window. She watched as the train entered a vast, dark chamber. Emergency lighting in the distance showed the space to be hundreds of meters wide and many more long.

A light slid into view far below the train, and Tanis saw a bank of superconductor batteries in its dim green glow. Several other similar lights winked on and off in the distance as the train raced on.

She looked up the cavern on the ship's schematics and saw that it was the power storage and regulation chamber for the particle accelerator. The sparsity of green lights revealed that most of the batteries still were offline—a result of damage to the primary ramscoop.

"I can't believe I've never been here before," she said to Joe.

He nodded. "Me either. Though it's not that surprising, I guess. I just checked, and apparently I've only set foot in about five percent of the ship."

Tanis checked the places she had been. "I've got you beat. I've been in six percent of the ship."

"Always have to be one-upping," Joe laughed.

"I don't see how stating a fact is one-upping."

"Um, Tanis, you even said, *I've got you beat.*"

Tanis grinned. "I have no recollection of the events to which you are referring."

A minute later the maglev slowed and stopped at a small station; the end of the line, or the beginning, depending on one's perspective.

Joe led the way to their destination, a small observation deck above the main scoop emitter, and the furthest forward they could get on the bow without crawling into maintenance tunnels.

They stepped through the entrance, and both stopped, looking at one another in surprise. Dim lighting illuminated observation deck and soft music played over a physical sound system. Near the bar, a servitor stood waiting with a selection of food and wine.

<*I thought this might make your journey more pleasant,*> Bob said.

Joe pulled off his helmet and let out a low whistle. "One heck of a posh lounge. I was expecting a maintenance viewport, or something."

"These couches feel like real leather." Tanis sat and leaned back, clasping her hands behind her head.

<*The scoop techs managed to syphon a bit of budget into ensuring some of the finer things were available to them,*> Bob commented.

"Quite the view," Tanis said as she gazed out the large bay window that wrapped over half way around the lounge.

"Can almost see behind us," Joe laughed, as he handed Tanis a glass of wine.

"I can't quite make out The Kap."

"I can't either, but there's Canopus to the right," Joe pointed at the white-blue star.

"And Sirius up there to the left. Just a bit further around and we'd be able to see Sol over there," Tanis pointed at the rear wall of the observation deck.

"Huh…I just checked, and we're actually farther from Sirius now than we were back home at Sol—thought it looked brighter."

"And we're traveling further from New Eden every minute—seems counter-intuitive," Tanis sighed.

Joe nodded and sat beside Tanis. They enjoyed the silence for some time, simply staring out into space, arms around each other's shoulders. Eventually, Tanis looked at Joe, "We'll have to do this often during our thaws."

"Absolutely."

After finishing the glasses of wine, they discussed the route to the stern of the ship. While serving on the *Intrepid,* they had spent the majority of their time in the dorsal arch. Rather than travelling through familiar territory, they opted to work their way down through several dozen decks below them, and travel through the sections of the ship directly above the particle accelerator.

Outside the observation lounge, the utilitarian corridors felt even more stark than on the way in.

Their HUD overlays led them to a wide vertical shaft, which dropped over thirty meters, and rose several hundred more above them. It was lined with various pipes, waveguides, and conduits. Several bots flitted up and down, a few swerving out of the way as a lift rose up the shaft.

Tanis and Joe stepped on the lift, and she punched the button for the lowest level. The lift waited a moment, then dropped down the shaft. With the low gravity—due to the particle accelerator running on empty—there was an uneasy moment when her feet lifted off the platform.

"That was a bit disconcerting," Joe said.

"You're telling me," Tanis said as she looked over the railing. "It's quite the drop."

The bottom of the shaft pierced the ceiling of yet another vast chamber, one which appeared to be at least a hundred meters wide and several hundred long. Above them, the roof of the chamber was punctuated by several other shafts, like the one they had just entered through. Bots flitted in and out of them, appearing to be working on the large object below.

"This must be the main scoop's field generator," Tanis said, as the realization dawned on her.

"I've never seen one that looked like this before," Joe commented as the lift settled next to a catwalk.

"You've never seen one that can emit a field over ten thousand kilometers wide."

"Touché."

They stood a moment longer, looking at one of the *Intrepid*'s many hearts.

"Well, let's roll," Tanis said as she picked up her bag. "We have a long way to go."

*****

They spent the rest of the day passing through endless kilometers of corridor, bay, and chamber. The posh lounge, looking out over the ramscoop emitter should have prepared them, but they were still surprised by what lay in the nooks and crannies of the ship.

Rounding a corner near one of the hydroponics chambers, they stumbled upon a statue in the middle of an intersection. It appeared to be a life-sized goat made of solid crystal. Upon closer inspection, they realized that the crystal was data storage, containing the DNA and all knowledge associated with every known bacteria going back to the twentieth century, cross-referenced with every time each bacterium had been found in a goat.

There also appeared to be a personal 2D vid collection of goats stored in the crystal. Many of them depicted people yelling at goats, which seemed to cause the goats to seize up and fall over.

"Wow, someone really likes goats," Joe commented.

"Maybe a bit too much," Tanis chuckled.

Not long after, they entered another corridor that was a clear tube surrounded by what appeared to be a brownish substance. Tanis leaned close and let out a small cry.

"It's just dirt!"

Joe frowned and peered closer. "What? What for?"

"I think it's a giant ant farm."

Joe walked down the tube, running his hand along the plas. "Huh, so it is. The sign down here says it's the personal property of some guy named Pete, and, that no one's to mess with it."

Tanis laughed, "well, I guess we'd best be on our way."

After several more kilometers of ship, Joe yawned and stretched. "I know we've only been at it for a few hours, but I'd worked a full day before stasis and I'm bushed. What say we find some place to crash?"

"Sure," Tanis agreed. "Ironically, we're not far from my quarters, just sixty-two decks down."

"That would take all the fun out of the adventure!" Joe looked shocked. "We need to bivouac somewhere exciting."

"There's a security duty station not far from here; it has some bunks for folks pulling back-to-back shifts," Tanis offered. "Does that satisfy your sense of adventure?"

"Humph…I guess it'll have to do."

* * * * *

The next day brought them to the ship's transverse cargo corridor. A memory of that first trip through the kilometer-wide portal came to Tanis. She remembered first meeting a younger, somehow softer Amy Lee, all the while trying not to gawk at a cargo hatch many of the star cruisers she'd served on could fly through.

"I remember when they were building this thing," Joe said, apparently on the same train of thought. "I flew a fighter in here and buzzed a bunch of haulers that some MOS guys were driving. They were a bit upset, to say the least."

Tanis laughed. "No wonder they knew you weren't up to running security and brought me in."

"You act as though that wasn't my master plan."

<That's because it wasn't,> Angela inserted into their conversation.

"Angela, girl!" Joe said. "I was beginning to wonder if you were still with us."

<Where else would I go? I've been having chats with Bob about the nature of the universe, and our place in it. His math's a bit beyond me, but I think I'm starting to get it.>

"Which 'us'?" Tanis asked. "Organics or AI?"

<Both,> Bob replied. *<We're all AI, don't you know that?>*

"Uh…forget I asked," Tanis laughed.

From the transverse corridor, they debated whether to go through one of the cylinders or to take the maglev that ran along the particle accelerator to Engine.

In the end, they opted to take the maglev, because they could stop at Earnest's observation lounge, which would give them a great view of Sol and a last glimpse of Estrella de la Muerte before its dim, red point of light disappeared from view.

Arriving in the lounge a half hour later, Tanis remembered how much she loved seeing the *Intrepid* from here. It was only a dozen decks above the SOC, and she had come often to collect her thoughts.

Below, the two habitation cylinders rotated, reflecting starlight onto the dorsal rail, cargo cubes, and lattice of struts that wrapped the rear half of the ship.

Just over sixteen kilometers away, the engines rose up beyond the cylinders, one side still blackened and twisted. The main engines were inactive; without the main scoop, there was insufficient fuel to light them up, and without the port side A1 fusion engine, a balanced thrust was impossible.

Instead, the two smaller engines were running at low power, pushing the ship ever faster toward The Kap.

"Looks a little worse for wear," Joe said.

Tanis nodded. "We've pinned a lot of hope to this ark, drifting alone in the black."

"Not really an ark," Joe mused. "It's not as though Sol is drowning."

"Are you so sure?" Tanis asked. "I'm here because I'm fed up with the TSF and Sol politics, but many believe all of Sol is doomed."

"I know some people think that, but I didn't know you did—at least not in so many words," Joe replied.

"Thing is, Sol doesn't really need humans anymore—but there are trillions of them. Pretty soon, they'll all be able to live forever, but heavy elements are getting rare enough to cause concern." She paused contemplatively. "Unless something changes, they're going to have some very big conflicts, and soon."

Joe nodded. "You're not wrong. But there have always been shortages and conflicts. They'll survive."

"Some will," Tanis agreed. "But that's what makes this an ark. We're taking the best of the best, and the tools to build a new Sol."

<*What do you think it will be like?*> Angela asked over the Link.

"What New Eden will be like?" Joe replied.

<*I was thinking of The Kap, what we'll make there,*> Angela paused. <*The idea of building a throwaway colony is hard to accept.*>

Tanis nodded slowly. "You wonder if we'll end up staying; if Terrance and the Reddings will crack open the picotech."

<*Along those lines, yes.*>

Joe leaned against the window and ran a hand down his cheek. "Do you think they would? They'd risk letting the whole crew and colony know."

"Hard to say," Tanis replied. "It may be that repairing the scoop emitter and the annihilator would be a lot easier with pico. I imagine the annihilator would be. I'm more concerned about building around a red dwarf."

<*They do tend to be temperamental,*> Angela agreed.

"The Kap is an old, old girl, I doubt she has much kick left in her," Joe said.

Tanis reached an arm around Joe. "Let's hope she takes it easy for the next couple of centuries."

"Centuries?" Joe gave Tanis a startled look. "I thought we were only going to be there for fifty years or so."

"It'll still take seventy to get there," Tanis replied. "Either way, let's hope a temperamental red dwarf is the worst of our problems."

<*I cannot believe you just said that.*>

A HOME WITHIN A HOME

STELLAR DATE: 3245116 / 09.22.4172 (Adjusted Gregorian)
LOCATION: ISS *Intrepid*
REGION: Interstellar space, en route to Kapteyn's Star

"I'm dying for some greenery," Joe said. "What say we hit one of the cylinders this time? Lil' Sue or Old Sam?"

It was their eleventh random wakeup; Tanis and Joe were doing their fourth full-ship walkabout. While they had visited several smaller parks, it was not the same as the wide-open spaces within a cylinder.

"Sounds good, let's visit Old Sam this time. I vote we take a maglev and skip the boring parts," Tanis replied.

Joe nodded his agreement and Tanis flashed him a smile.

"Last one to the train's a...whatever!" She said and broke into a run.

"Seriously?" Joe called out as he chased after her. "A *whatever?*"

Old Sam was roughly as Tanis remembered; lakes, trees, plains—over one hundred and fifty square kilometers of it. Small bots flitted through the air, maintaining the cylinder's systems and ensuring the wildlife remained in balance.

"We could spend weeks in here just wandering around," Tanis said as they picked their way down an overgrown path.

Old Sam was in its summer cycle and the long, artificial sun running down the cylinder's center beat down on them mercilessly. Tanis looked back at Joe and smiled at his red cheeks.

"First the race and now this," Joe grimaced. "You're dying for an adventure, aren't you?"

Tanis laughed, relishing the fact that she didn't hear her voice echo back from bulkheads. "The danger quotient in my blood *is* alarmingly low."

"Well, there's that low escarpment a few miles from here; it would make a fun climbing exercise." Joe replied.

"In full gravity? After months of low-*g* on the ship? Not sure how the docs would feel if I woke them up to fix my broken neck."

"Tanis Richards turning down a challenge?" It was Joe's turn to laugh. "I'll have to save this conversation to use on you later."

"You asked for it!" Tanis broke into a lope that brought her up to ten kilometers per-hour, not her top speed, but more than Joe could pull off.

"Not fair," Joe called out from behind her. "Augments are cheating."

<*Cheater,*> Angela laughed in Tanis's mind.

<*You know it's...*> Tanis stopped mid-thought and mid-stride.

To her right was a stretch of young trees with a lake visible between their trunks. To her left was a patch of bramble that contained a mixture of plants, which indicated a garden had been the genesis of the growth.

What really had her attention was the cabin beyond the overgrown garden.

It was a single-story structure with a small veranda on the front. A pair of homey windows looked out, though one was broken, with a branch growing through it—likely belonging to the tree that had broken through the roof and was now over ten meters high.

Joe stopped beside her, his breathing heavy. He put a steadying hand on Tanis's shoulder.

"What's up?"

Tanis took a moment to reply. "I think this is Ouri's cabin."

<*You are correct. It is.*> Angela supplied.

A slow smile crept over Tanis's face and she turned to look at Joe. "I have an idea…"

DOG STAR

STELLAR DATE: 3246187 / 08.29.4175 (Adjusted Gregorian)
LOCATION: Brilliance Station
REGION: Lucent, Luminescent Space, Sirian Hegemony

The shuttle began its final docking procedure with Brilliance Station. Slight vibrations rippled through the deck as thrusters fired periodically to match velocity and attitude with the station.

Markus stretched his long spacers' legs out into the aisle, trying to work out a kink in his right knee that had been building for the last hour. Beside him, Simon shifted uncomfortably, his three-meter frame pressed up against the windowless bulkhead, head cocked to the side in the small space.

Markus felt a little bad that his younger companion had the worse of the two seats, but he had spent many long trips against the bulkhead of Luminescent shuttles in his youth. The next generation could pay their dues, too.

"You going to make it?" he asked Simon.

"Hard to say. I may never stand up straight again."

Markus chuckled.

This was the final leg of the multi-week journey from their mining platform to Brilliance Station. Most of the trip had been spent aboard an in-system Noctus ore hauler—and while it wasn't spacious, there was room to move. Somehow, the five-hour journey, while sitting in the Noctus section of this shuttle, felt considerably longer.

A little food would have helped, but the Lumins didn't think it was a worthwhile investment to give the Noctus passengers food when they could simply not.

Markus hardly noticed anymore. He had been in Luminescent Space enough that he was no longer fazed by the opulence and decadence of the people—which they denied to the Noctus at every opportunity. For Simon, this was his first visit. The short glimpse he'd gotten of the first class cabin when they had entered the shuttle made the young man slack-jawed.

An attendant opened the door into the rear cabin and cast an eye across the lower-class passengers, making certain they were all seated and orderly for the docking. The two metal studs gleaming on the bridge of her nose marked her as a member of one of the lesser families. High ranking families in Luminescent Society had metal studs from their nose up into their hairline.

Her survey only lasted moments and then the door was closed with a sharp snap.

"Damn shorts," Simon muttered. "Would it kill them to show us common courtesy?"

"Boy," Markus snapped. "Watch your mouth; you never know who might overhear you, and what they might say. You will not utter that word in Luminescent Space."

Simon sighed, but didn't say anything else disparaging about the Lumins. Something so innocuous as calling them "shorts" could put someone in front of a judge, levied with fines, or even a jail sentence.

The Lumins really had no sense of proportion, or humor for that matter.

A clang echoed through the ship, and the pull of gravity tugged at the passengers. The station's grappling mechanism pulled the shuttle into the dock, and centripetal force began to take effect. Within a minute, Luminescent-normal gravity of 1.0*g* was in effect.

"Agh, I feel like I can't breathe," Simon felt his chest and swallowed. "How do they survive like this?" he asked.

"It's not the most pleasant thing, but keep your discomfort to yourself. It doesn't do to let them see you stooping or pulling at your clothes."

A second clang heralded the umbilical latching onto the ship.

Markus stood before the 'remain seated' lights switched off. Beside him, Simon leaned across both seats, stretching as much as the space would allow.

"We've now completed our docking procedure," the captain's voice came across the ship's auditory systems. "First class passengers may begin debarkation. Other passengers, please wait until our first class guests have finished clearing the shuttle."

The captain was most certainly a short. He didn't speak with their accent, which meant he came from one of the outer habitats at the edge of Luminescent Space. The way he emphasized the word "other" spoke volumes. Moreover, there was only one first class passenger; Markus had seen her in the debarkation area on Glorious Station.

The boarding area back on Glorious Station was sparsely appointed. Few Lumins had been present, but she stood out because she was quite tall for one of them, perhaps just over two meters—more with the heels she wore. Her hair was a brilliant red and it reminded Markus of Angie before she had died in an asteroid accident.

The Lumins loved talking about light, and it was apparent in everything, from the naming of their stations to the clothes they wore. The latest trend in Lumin fashion was a skin-tight covering of some glowing iridescent material. Some were brilliantly white, almost hard to look at, but this woman's was muted to a dull pewter.

Simon had stared at her for at least a solid minute before Markus elbowed him. With studs nearly to the top of her forehead, she was likely one of the first upper-class Lumins the boy had ever seen. Not to mention that Simon had never seen a woman exude so much sexual power while simply standing still.

Markus had to admit she was quite striking and would have liked to soak in her beauty for some time, as well, but doing so would have earned a visit from a security drone.

The light above the exit changed from red to green and the remaining passengers shuffled out. Markus caught sight of the captain and was surprised to see that he *was* Noctus. The disdain on his face was plain to see as he tried to distance himself from his own people.

Fool, Markus thought. *Just because you despise us doesn't mean the Lumins think any more of you—they don't think of you at all.*

The corridor outside the shuttle had a clear wall and the light of brilliant Sirius and its dimmer brother, Lucent, shone through. Though Brilliance station orbited the Lucent at a distance of only 0.5AU, Sirius A—currently 15AU distant—was still significantly brighter, providing something close to the amount of light Earth received from Sol.

Very little filtering blocked the radiance as it washed across the passengers, many of whom squinted in the glare, as they shuffled along in the heavy gravity.

Noctus stations rarely had any windows. To them, Sirius was a harsh and cruel master, not a life-giving light filled with beauty. Looking at it meant blindness; direct exposure to its light would certainly be followed by genetic damage; it was the destroyer, the bane of all life.

"It's amazing to be able to look at it with my own eyes," Simon said. "It's beautiful."

Markus nodded his agreement. "It's easy to see why they constantly talk of light and brilliance and luminosity. Looking at the two sisters with your own eyes is quite the sight."

He rested a hand on Simon's shoulder. "You'll have plenty of time to dawdle later. With the stars so close together, they'll have every portal open. You'll see them dozens of times while we're here."

As they walked through the tunnel, Markus caught a glimpse of the red-headed woman ahead of them. She was moving slowly, probably lost in a conversation on the Link. He found it interesting that she had altered her outfit. It was now much lighter in hue, flashing and glowing with wild abandon. It still had the gray tint and a perhaps hint of burgundy as well, though that might have been her hair reflecting off it.

"Now who's staring?" Simon laughed.

"She's striking," Markus shrugged. "I've never seen one of their women so tall."

The docking tunnel emptied into a large atrium so bright that Markus and Simon had to shield their eyes. Simon looked up and let out a cry. He grabbed the railing, which ran around the upper-level balcony.

Markus looked up and smiled. He may dislike—or more accurately, despise—the Lumins, but they did have some amazing architecture.

Along the walls, wide steel pillars rose up, arching toward each other, but tapering to fine points before reaching the center of the ceiling. The actual ceiling was completely transparent. Markus assumed there must be some sort of glass or plas above their heads, but it was completely indiscernible.

For all intents and purposes, it appeared as though the ceiling had never been put on and the pillars were attempting to capture Lucent, which was always directly above.

Markus knew how Simon felt. Excepting shuttle bays, this was probably the largest room the young man had ever been in. Shuttle bays were always fully enclosed and filled with ships and cargo. This space was clean and empty—excepting the shifting crowds entering and exiting the corridors that led to waiting ships.

Pulling his eyes from the architectural spectacle, not to mention the many Lumins in their gleaming outfits, Markus pulled out a small tablet. He waited a moment for it to auth with the station's systems and then retrieved Brilliance Station's layout, looking up the location of their meeting.

The Lumin overseers at the company didn't really need Markus to come in person and present his plan for the upgrade of the SK87 mining platform, which he ran, but he suspected they did it to remind him of his place in the grand scheme of things.

Luther, the general manager and overseer of the mining platform, should have been there as well, but he was vacationing on the garden world Radius. He had instructed Markus to deliver all the summaries and reports to the supervising board alone. Even when Luther was present, Markus did most of the talking, as Luther barely knew what was happening on his own station.

The wireless network protocols granted him limited access on Brilliance Station, but it was enough to load directions to their meeting. He had to all but pull Simon while the young man slowed to stare at everything. Markus couldn't fault his young companion overmuch. He remembered his first trip to Brilliance, some thirty years ago when he had been a young man. The gleaming corridors and holo ads selling things he had never even heard of had boggled his mind.

Now, the cornucopia of products available was more insulting than fascinating. He barely had enough money to buy lunch on Brilliance, let alone any of the fancy toys that Luminescent Society wasted its money on.

He pushed his dislike of Luminescent opulence out of his mind and focused on his presentation.

The platform he worked and lived on, SK87, was performing well and Luther wanted to expand it. Markus had been sent to present the plans to the assessors for approval. Convincing the Lumin oversight board that it was the right plan would not be hard; a thousand years of delegating any hard work or menial labor meant they didn't have much experience with assessing work schedules and ROI projections.

Markus was distracted by a particularly useless Lumin specimen they passed. He couldn't be certain if it was male or female, but its arms and legs ended in wheels and it was spinning and rolling through the corridor, giggling as it went.

"I can't believe we work our entire lives so they can turn themselves into useless…I don't know what's…just useless," Simon muttered.

Markus chuckled. "It wasn't entirely useless; I imagine you could put some sort of bucket on it and turn it into a hauler."

"I can imagine what the yard foreman would say about that," Simon laughed softly.

"We have about three hours before our meeting," Markus said. "I know a place near here where we can get some food and relax for a bit."

Simon nodded his assent and Markus led him through the wide boulevards to a less trafficked area. The overt gaudiness of the station was somewhat diminished, but it was still far more opulent than SK87.

Before long they reached their destination, a small restaurant that would serve Noctus—though only with automated servitors. After the robot had brought their food, Simon spent some time eyeing it suspiciously.

"Try it," Markus prodded him. "It's not often you get to eat something that wasn't grown in a vat."

Simon looked horrified. "You mean this was alive?"

"Of course, Lumins only eat real food. No vats or mush for them."

Simon sat staring at his food for several minutes and eventually summoned up the courage to take a bite.

"Mmmm…I didn't know food could taste so good! How do you go back to eating the crap on the platform after this?"

"With great sadness—though sometimes the thought of eating plants and animals unnerves me," Markus commented.

The pair enjoyed the rest of their meal in silence, looking out the portals at the star-side view of Lucent and the world of Incandus below.

"Have you ever been to a planet?" Simon asked Markus.

"No, I have to admit that the thought scares me a bit. Once you're down there you're stuck, and everything wants to fall on you. I think it would terrify me."

"I've seen pictures," Simon's voice grew wistful. "Parks larger than SK87, larger than anything we've seen—can you imagine?"

Markus nodded. If he hadn't seen pictures himself, he would never have imagined anything like that even existed. The Lumins lived lives the Noctus could only dream of.

A few hours later, Markus and Simon sat in one of the company's many conference rooms, waiting for the Lumins who would review their proposal. The room was spare, but elegant in its appointment. The table was a shimmering plas and the chairs appeared to hover on invisible plinths.

Markus had never been in this particular tower before, but he wasn't surprised by the luxurious appointments. He kept his focus on ensuring the presentation went well. Once done, they could get off Brilliance—hopefully before he went blind from all the bright lights and reflective surfaces, which were already giving him a headache.

Simon had carefully distributed hyfilm around the table for the committee to take after the meeting—the Lumins seemed to react better to physical media than pure holo presentations. He now sat fumbling with his notepad, prepared to jot down any pertinent thoughts. The device could not record here, as the Lumins disallowed Noctus to record anything in Luminescent Space; physical notes were the only way to record decisions.

It also allowed the Lumins to revert nearly any decision by simply claiming the Noctus had incorrect records.

After only several minutes of waiting, the company team filed in. There were three men and two women. Markus was surprised to see that one of the women was the Lumin he had followed off the shuttle.

"Markus, good to see you," Yusuf, the President of Resources and Extraction, said.

He did not offer to shake hands.

"It is good to see you, sir," Markus nodded his head in deference. He did not expect to see Yusuf here. It wasn't a good sign—the president of R&E only made appearances to Markus's detriment.

Yusuf did not acknowledge the gesture. "You know Thomas, Vlad, and Sarah. Our newest member is Katrina; she manages transport and logistics for platform services."

"It is good to meet you," Markus nodded again. "I have one of my young team leads, Simon, with me. He knows the internals of our platform inside and out."

None of the Lumins acknowledged Simon. Markus barely rated their attention and he had spent decades garnering the meager level of respect he now had.

The discussions were largely perfunctory. Most of the details of the platform's expansion had been reviewed by the non-sentient AI Lumins employed for such tasks. It was Markus's belief that the Lumins only brought him here to remind him who was the final authority in his life.

When they came to living quarters enhancements Yusuf scowled at the display.

"This expansion does not seem to be in proportion with the rest of the platform. It brings your living quarter allotment from 10% of platform space to 12%."

Markus nodded. "Yes, sir, it does. 12% of platform space for living quarters is standard when platforms exceed twenty-eight cubic kilometers."

"On *new* platforms that is the case, but this is an expansion of an existing platform, those concessions do not apply." Yusuf spoke offhand as though he had given this little thought, but Markus knew the man. He was doing this on purpose to keep Markus in his place and not let him garner too much favor with his own people.

"Surely—" Markus began, but Yusuf cut him off with a wave of his hand.

All the Lumins looked entirely implacable, with the exception of Katrina, whose lips twitched for just a moment—her expression belying a moment of consternation.

"Seriously?" Simon erupted beside Markus. "You're going to increase our population by 120% to facilitate the additional throughput, but only increase our living space by 90%? We're already crammed in cheek to cheek!"

"Simon!" Markus put a hand on his young companion's shoulder in an attempt to quell his outburst.

"No, Markus, no! You're as much a part of the problem as they are. I've seen it for myself; you bow and scrape and take whatever they give," Simon stood to his full three meters as he yelled. Towering over the table, he reached into his jacket and began to pull something out.

"For the true Sirians and our independence!"

Markus fell back, aghast that Simon would do something so rash.

The Lumins looked alarmed at the outburst, with the exception of Yusuf. A smile played at the edges of his mouth and a stasis cone snapped down around Simon. A high pitched whine pierced the room and a decoupling field tore apart all matter in the cone.

The field broke Simon's body down into a fine mist in moments. Markus listened for an explosion, or something that would indicate the young man had reached for a weapon.

Nothing.

Yusuf waved his hand and a holo appeared over the table showing Simon's last moments in slow motion. He turned and zoomed; they could all see what he was pulling from his coat.

"Hmm… a flag," Yusuf sighed. "A lot of theatrics for a piece of cloth." He looked to Markus. "Let's hope your next assistant has more brains—and you have the intelligence to not make a mistake like that again. You run your people well. If not for that, I would kill you, too."

Markus couldn't believe the calm in Yusuf's voice. He had seen Lumins kill Noctus before, but never like this— never so casually.

Yusuf looked to his committee. "Unless there are any objections, I approve this expansion proposal, excepting the disproportionate increase in living quarters." He waited a moment to see if anyone spoke up; when none did, the President of Resources and Extraction stood and left the room.

Markus stood, silently watching them file out, unwilling to look at the seat where Simon should have been. Only the new woman, Katrina, looked him in the eye. Her expression showed a flash of sympathy, and then she too was gone.

Markus barely noticed. The only thing on his mind was the thought of telling Simon's mother.

He barely remembered getting back to the shuttle.

As he sat silently in his small quarters on the trip back to Sirius, a plan started to form in Markus's mind.

There had always been talk of rebellion among the Noctus. It had been present for his entire life, waxing and waning over the years. At present, there were more whispers in dark corners than usual, especially among the youth who had not been alive for the previous generation's failed attempts—and the Lumins' retribution.

The dissidents traded seditious documents and data, and held their small rallies in hidden areas of the platform. Markus had always tolerated them while ensuring they didn't get too vocal and cause problems.

He had thought he was doing the right thing by protecting his people, keeping things in balance. But something about how casually Yusuf had killed Simon triggered a change in Markus. Maybe he had just had enough and had gone past his tipping point, but one thing was for certain: he saw things in a new light.

Markus knew why the other rebellions had failed. It was not because of lack of conviction, or even a failure to take a given platform or station.

Past rebellions had almost always succeeded at taking their initial objectives, but holding them was the problem. The Lumin space force arrived, and either the rebels surrendered or were destroyed.

The way to succeed was to leave Sirius.

REVOLUTION

STELLAR DATE: 3246204 / 09.15.4175 (Adjusted Gregorian)
LOCATION: Mining Platform SK87
REGION: Noctilucent Space, Sirius Hegemony

Markus could still hear the sobbing cries of Simon's mother in his ears. She had been so eager to hear how well her son had done in his new role. To go from that expectancy to the news of his callous death at the hands of the Lumins may well be more than she could bear—especially after losing her husband in an accident several years earlier.

Markus made a note to check in on her in the days to come. The community on the platform was tight-knit and neighbors would console her and help her through this time—but it never hurt to be sure she didn't need additional counseling.

Around him the corridors of the platform, ever bleak, seemed even more so. Endless kilometers of obedience, centuries of acquiescence.

Markus's tall frame was hunched; his years weighed more heavily upon him than ever before. He barely noticed others as he passed them by, be they the Noctus workers—his people—or the sparse Lumin guards of the station's garrison.

Although his frame implied defeat, his mind was churning with a fire he had not felt in many years. He had a plan and was about to take the first step in launching it.

He made his way past the platform's two-hundred-year-old refinery—one of the areas he had proposed upgrades for that fateful day on Brilliance Station—past the bio vats in hydroponics, and into the waste reclamation area.

There was no doubt in his mind that they were meeting. He knew the players, knew how they thought, and what drove them. It drove him now, as well.

It was a good place to meet; security patrols rarely came down to reclamation. The smell was enough to keep even the most brutish of them from making much more than a cursory examination every few weeks.

Markus, on the other hand, knew every corridor, every hatch, portal, and conduit on the platform. Even without intel from people loyal to him, he knew where this meeting would be held.

The door was unmarked; there was nothing to separate it from any other hatch in reclamation. It was a thick, gray plas, but through it he could hear the sound of voices raised in anger.

Markus took a deep breath and steeled himself for the storm he was about to endure.

He opened the door.

The first thing he noticed was that the room had many more occupants than he would have expected. Over forty men and women stood amongst the tanks and pipes, expressions ranging from rage to sorrow drawn across their faces.

The second was the figure of Sarah standing on a large vat, yelling at the crowd, whipping them into a frenzy.

"You see how they so callously kill one of our best sons, in cold blood, with no regard for us. We are worse than slaves; we are the children of slaves, and the parents of slaves. We raise new slaves and secure generations of our children as thralls of the shorts."

The crowd replied with groans and cheers at the appropriate times, but perhaps not as enthusiastically as Sarah had hoped. After being pushed down for so long it was hard to even know what standing should feel like.

Markus had always liked Sarah, even though he knew she despised him. She saw him as nothing more than a puppet of their masters. Little did she know how often he had worked tirelessly to protect his people from far worse than they realized.

He knew that she felt very keenly for her friends and family, the people of the platform; she wanted more for them, but her pain manifested as anger and she was toxic to those around her. Because of this, her meetings were usually attended by only a dozen, at best.

"You!" She spotted Markus and leveled an accusing finger at him. "You have some gall coming here after what you did."

There were nods and murmurs from the crowd as she spoke. The stares of his people bore into him, and he had to force his shame down, lest it make him turn and flee.

Sarah continued with her barrage before he was able to formulate a response.

"How long did it take to wash Simon's blood off your hands? How much did you have to bow and scrape for their forgiveness after his death? After you stood by and watched them murder him?"

Several others called out, their anger a palpable thing to Markus. He didn't expect them to be so visceral and a kernel of fear began to form in the pit of his stomach.

He held up his hands, his expression mirroring the sadness that filled him.

"I am at your mercy," he said just loudly enough to be heard across the space.

The room fell silent at his words. They were so ready for his anger to meet theirs, to give them a reason to hate and harm.

"Is that all you have to say for yourself?" Timmur, a tug operator, called out. "Simon's father was a friend of mine. Is this the respect you pay him, getting his son killed?"

"It is not all I have to say for myself," Markus replied, his voice gaining strength. "I have been wrong all of these years. I have tried to find the perfect compromise between us and the shorts. I thought…I thought that if I could keep us under the radar, I could make a better place for us.

"I was wrong."

No one spoke. Even Sarah, usually ready to call out a biting retort to any statement, wore a shocked expression.

A voice broke the silence; Markus couldn't see who spoke, but the words reverberated through the chamber.

"What will you do?"

"I have a plan to save us, to save each and every one of us," Markus replied. "I plan to make your children's children never know the yoke of slavery."

Sarah's eyes were bright as she asked, "Do you plan revolution? Are we going to overthrow the Lumins?"

Markus shook his head. "No, we are going to do what our ancestors did when they came here—cross between the stars in search of a new home."

PLANS

STELLAR DATE: 3246713 / 02.05.4177 (Adjusted Gregorian)
LOCATION: Mining Platform SK87
REGION: Noctilucent Space, Sirian Hegemony

"Tell him to put it where I said," Markus all but yelled into the comm. "If he puts it there, how will we mount the new set of batteries next month?"

The platform administrator was silent for a moment.

"Good. Make sure he does it, then."

Markus switched off the comm and looked back at Luther. "Sorry about that, there's a lot of wrangling to do."

The overseer steepled his fingers, looking over the tips at his administrator. "Will there be a problem completing on schedule? There is a lot riding on this for me."

Markus knew that all too well. Not only because Luther reminded him of it almost daily, but because he understood how political capital was spent in Luminescent Society.

Despite not attending the meeting that infamous day on Brilliance Station, Luther had laid much of the groundwork for the station's upgrades. He was a lazy ass, but he was a lazy ass with connections.

It could be worse, Markus mused, he could have an overseer who was a micromanager. At least Luther couldn't be bothered to actually check up on any details. So long as the quotas were met and profits were where they should be, he was happy.

"We're on schedule and we haven't missed any deliverables during the buildout," Markus replied. "If we keep it up, we'll set a new record for efficiency during a platform upgrade."

Luther smiled. Markus knew the man loved to brag about successes when his district quorum assembled. Successes that Markus and his people bled to earn for the useless Lumins.

"Very well. I'm returning to Luminescent Space tomorrow, but Steven will be remaining behind to ensure that things keep moving smoothly," Luther said as he stood. "Be sure to keep him apprised of your progress."

Markus nodded as the overseer left his office.

Now Steven was a problem.

In every way that Luther was distracted and unconcerned with details, Steven was obsessed with minutia and strict adherence to procedure.

The overseer's assistant was new to the position, and obviously working to prove his worth. Unfortunately, he did that through pointing out Markus's failures and questioning all the platform administrator's decisions.

He wasn't the first sycophant Markus had endured, but he would very likely be the last.

Once he heard Luther pass through the outer office, he called James on the comm.

"Boss?"

"Sorry for hollering at you," Markus said. "Luther was doing that thing he does when he wants to act like he cares about what goes on here. Usually, if I yell at someone it makes him feel like stuff is being done. You happened to be handy."

James chuckled on the other end of the line. "I've done that myself, when he does one of his bi-annual visits to the yards."

"So long as you don't try to pull it on me, we'll be fine."

"You? Never." Markus could all but see James's grin on the other end of the comm.

Markus chuckled. "Of course not. Speaking of visits, I'll be by later this afternoon to review the shipments with you."

"You bet, I'll probably be out in the east yard."

Markus closed the connection. James had given the signal that an anticipated shipment of volatiles and tech had arrived, and had passed all checks undetected. Markus would inspect them this afternoon, but they would be nowhere near the east yard.

With a long sigh, he rose from his chair and locked his terminals. He was starting to feel his years; all the subterfuge needed to pull off his plan had made for a marked reduction in sleep. It had been weeks since he'd had a full night's rest.

Every day was filled with more to do than the last. Thus far, the Endeavor he'd embarked on eighteen months ago remained secret, but it was the hardest work he'd ever undertaken.

It would only continue to do well if he got some food—saving his people was not work to be accomplished on an empty stomach.

He nodded to Agnes as he walked through the outer office and into the hall. The administrative wing was always a bustling hive. The business of a mining platform never stopped. Now, with the upgrades underway, it was doubly so.

Temporary desks filled every available space, and plas sheets covered every one of them. Holos and 2D displays tracked progress and monitored critical systems.

Markus nodded to his people, and, as he turned toward the cafeteria, he spotted just the person he didn't want to see: Steven.

"Administrator Markus, just who I was looking for," the diminutive Lumin called from down the hall.

Markus sighed; he'd been seen, there would be no escape.

"Adjunct Steven, what can I help you with today?"

If there was one thing that Markus liked about Steven, it was that he stood on ceremony and formality without fail. As a result, he was never derisive toward Markus or his people. He may have treated them all like his own personal servants, but at least he was formal and polite about it.

"I wanted to discuss the work being done to harness asteroid P30987. It's behind schedule and we're losing money by the hour."

Markus nodded and continued walking out of the administrative wing into the corridor that led to the cafeteria and upper shops.

"The initial schedule is off, yes, but our overall timeframe is still in place."

"I don't follow," Steven replied. "P30987 should have been harnessed in the reaping yard by now, but you have it holding a hundred kilometers west of the station."

"You do realize that we're in the midst of outfitting the reaping yard with new MDCs?" Markus worked to keep his annoyance to himself.

Steven flipped through the sheets of plas he carried. Finally finding the right one, he nodded his agreement. "I do, but it shows that the yard should still be fifty-percent operational and you could be pulling that rock apart."

"We could," Markus agreed. "But pulling something the size of that rock, as you put it, apart and sorting the materials would create a hazard for the upgrade crews and slow both projects down. Once the new MDCs are in place, we'll be able to carve the asteroid up twice as fast and utilize the new sorters that we have installed. We'll actually be several days ahead of schedule, but I didn't want to get too aggressive in the projections."

Steven frowned and sorted his plas. "I suppose that makes sense. I'm sure you know how important it is that we don't slow in our production during these upgrades."

Markus knew because he was the one that crafted the proposal, but he refrained from reminding Steven of that fact.

"I do; I am certain we will continue to meet our schedule."

"And what of the cargo you are holding in the east yard?"

The question was innocent and spoken with no hint of subterfuge, but Markus felt a cold sweat building on his brow.

"You'll have to be more specific," Markus replied blandly. "We are holding a lot in the east yard these days."

Stevens cast a sidelong look at Markus. "Yes, I suppose you are. I was curious about the shipment that came in today from the Polaris manufacturing platform. I was certain you had routed some of the cargo to the east yard."

Markus grunted in response. "Unless I'm mistaken, all that cargo ended up in the north and under yards."

Steven glanced at his plas. "Hmmm... so it did."

* * * * *

"We have a problem," Markus said as he squeezed onto a stool in the crowded bar.

James took a long pull from his beer. "How is that news? We always have a problem of some sort."

"This is a *little* problem," Markus replied.

James's shoulders slumped. "I guess it was just a matter of time."

Markus nodded. It was a foregone conclusion that a Lumin would eventually discover what they were doing. Sarah had insisted on a contingency plan to deal with any errant Lumins at one of their first meetings.

"Who is it?" James asked.

"Our little friend in high places."

James grunted, "I'm not surprised, the little prick always has his nose in everything. He was bound to pick up a thread sooner or later."

"Well, it's sooner," Markus said.

"When should I enact the scenario?" James asked.

"Do it tomorrow. Luther will be off-station and Steven will be guaranteed to respond."

"You got it, boss. Tomorrow. I have it on good authority that Steven likes to sleep in Luther's quarters when he's away."

"Any other whispers reach your ears?" Markus asked. "I can't imagine Steven picked up on anything himself, we must have had a leak."

"To my knowledge, we've identified all the Lumin informants and have fed them what we wanted them to know," James replied.

"Either we missed someone or we have a traitor in our midst."

James nodded slowly. "I'll get Sarah on it."

ACCEPTABLE LOSS

STELLAR DATE: 3246713 / 02.05.4177 (Adjusted Gregorian)
LOCATION: Mining Platform SK87
REGION: Noctilucent Space, Sirian Hegemony

In the middle of the third shift, a warning klaxon sounded, breaking the relative silence of the station's night. The alert network picked up the warning signal and emergency crews assembled to respond.

There was a reactor leak on a tug working in the east yard.

The pilot reported to the Overwatch night crew that he had attempted to power down the reactor, but it wasn't responding.

"Have you tried the emergency overrides?" the comm operator in Overwatch asked.

"Are you fucking kidding me?" the operator's voice screeched out of the speakers in Overwatch. "Do you think I got this job yesterday? Of course I tried the overrides. There's nothing I can do; this sucker is going to blow!"

Markus stumbled into the room, rubbing his eyes.

"Situation?"

"We have a tug stuck in the east yard with a reactor leak. It was moving some equipment to another net to make room for an inbound shipment and it's tangled in it now. I don't know how we'll get it out of there."

"Who is in there and who do we have nearby?" Markus asked.

"Huan is in the leaking tug. Irek is working the other side of the yard, should I call him over?"

Markus nodded. "Yes, see if he can get Huan out of the nets and kick him away from the station. We can get a rescue craft in position to extract him from the tug."

Platform tugs didn't have escape pods or room for EVA Suits. The Lumins had done the math and determined that hauling around that extra equipment around—not to mention inspecting it—was too expensive and not worth the cost.

Tug operators were expendable.

Markus picked up a headset and spoke calmly, "Huan, we're going to get you out of there. Irek is coming over to pull your tug free and kick it to meet a rescue shuttle. You'll be at the bar joking about this in no time."

"Gods, I hope so, boss. I don't fancy being here when things heat up."

"You won't be, don't worry."

Time slowed to a crawl as Irek secured the cargo he was moving and boosted his tug across the yard. It only took ten minutes, but felt like forever as Markus watched the second tug work its way through the acres of nets. The east yard was all but overflowing with ore from a smaller asteroid that had been recently pulled apart. The freighter scheduled to make the pickup had been delayed, and an inbound shipment had turned the yard into gridlock.

Eventually, Irek's tug reached Huan's and the two large manipulator arms began to untangle the incapacitated tug from the nets around it.

"How you doing, Huan?" Markus asked.

"Anxious for that beer. Things are getting toasty in here and the Geiger counter is ticking a bit too fast for my liking."

"Don't worry, Irek just about has you free and the rescue shuttle is in position to catch you."

Markus wiped his brow. He sure hoped the shuttle could make the catch, with the yard so full, they were a quarter mile out, adjacent to the Lumin section of the platform.

Irek signaled Overwatch that Huan's tug was free and that he was ready to kick it out. Markus nodded to the comm operator and an affirmation was sent.

Irek boosted out of the yard, pushing Huan's ship. Five seconds later, he cut thrust and let go of the other tug. The Overwatch holo tracked the trajectory and predicted the rescue shuttle making a good catch.

An agonizing three minutes later, it did.

"This is rescue shuttle Bravo Echo; we have the tug in our grapple, preparing to collect the pilot."

"Make it happen," Markus spoke into his mic.

The shuttle extended a docking umbilical to the tug.

"C'mon, make that seal, we're out of time," Huan's frantic voice came over the comm.

The group assembled in Overwatch looked nervously at one another. If the tug blew now, it would certainly destroy the rescue shuttle and a part of the station. The seconds ticked by with excruciating lethargy.

Finally, the call came. "We have him aboard; we are kicking the tug out."

Cheers erupted in Overwatch.

Markus held his breath. A lot could still go wrong.

The shuttle's grapple swung around and set the tug on a course away from the platform and its shipping lanes. At the last moment, a part of the grapple caught on a piece of netting that Irek had cut off and left hooked to the tug.

For an agonizing twelve seconds it held and the two ships began to rotate around each other, then, the netting broke and the rescue shuttle spun away. It arched over the platform, toward the north yard, while the tug rotated slowly, drifting closer the platform.

"Oh shit, it's going to hit us!" the comm operator shouted, hitting the general alarm.

Markus gritted his teeth. This was the part of the plan he hated the most, harming the station.

The Overwatch radiation detectors jumped, heralding the orange blossom that appeared outside the windows moments later as the tug bloomed into nuclear fire.

Most of the wreckage flew away into open space, but some arched down toward the station tearing through cargo in the east yard. Other sections smashed into the station.

Markus held his breath. All of this would be for nothing if the wreckage did not disperse as planned.

"It's heading toward the Lumins!" someone in the room called out.

He let out a soft sigh of relief. It was going to hit.

Moments later the station overseer's quarters were destroyed.

SPY

STELLAR DATE: 3246715 / 02.07.4177 (Adjusted Gregorian)
LOCATION: Mining Platform SK87
REGION: Noctilucent Space, Sirian Hegemony

The rebellion's leadership no longer met in waste treatment pump room IV. So many ranking personnel going into the bowels of the platform with great frequency would stand out and questions would be asked.

Instead, Markus hid in plain sight. They met in his main conference room under the guise of holding planning sessions for the platform's upgrades. In most cases they *were* working on those upgrades, just not in the way the Lumins thought.

Privacy was guaranteed by holding the meetings during the third shift. No Lumin would stay up that late just to have a meeting with their lessers.

"I tell you, there can't be anyone unless it's one of us," Sarah sat back, exasperation filling her voice and expression.

Markus looked around the table at the heads of the rebellion. James was above reproach, especially because he was the one who had orchestrated Steven's accident. Sarah was even less likely. Her unbridled hatred of the shorts would make it impossible to believe she would betray the group.

Though, that's just what would make her the best spy, came a thought in the back of Markus's mind. He dismissed it. Nothing good would come of that thinking.

He couldn't see Samantha or Aaron as Lumin informants either. They had worked tirelessly toward the platform's eventual freedom. He knew they had sacrificed much to get this far.

His eyes slid across several other members of his inner circle, Peter, Dmitry, and Xenia, until they landed on Yolanda. She had joined their quiet rebellion five months ago after a transfer from platform SK45. She was efficient in every way and functioned as an excellent runner, as her work often took her to other platforms.

It also gave her ample opportunity to communicate with the Lumins with no witnesses.

Her eyes locked with Markus's and for a moment he thought he saw something he recognized from somewhere else. A moment later it was gone, and he let out a long sigh.

"Put out your feelers, but don't let everyone know that we suspect a leak. If the general populace finds out, they'll all suspect their neighbors and that's all but a guarantee for some uncontrolled event to occur."

They spoke of several other matters, and soon dispersed to get what rest they could before the following day arrived. Markus watched them file out as his thoughts wandered, wondering who could be leaking information to the shorts; who would want to.

It wasn't as though there weren't those amongst his people who would sell their neighbor to their oppressors for a meager reward, but he was certain they were all fed false information.

Their sort had been easy enough to identify. The malcontents who believed they were owed something were the first on the list. They were the least risky, as they usually were given access to smaller secrets.

The other likely group were the ones who craved power but didn't have it. They were marked by their ambition and their constant striving to rise in the ranks whether they had earned it or not.

Markus poured over names in his mind, coming up with no one, as none stood out. He refused to suspect everyone; that way led to madness.

He started as a hand touched his shoulder, and he looked up to see Yolanda standing beside him.

Markus chuckled. "Forgive me, I thought I was alone."

Yolanda sat down and Markus couldn't help but admire her lithe figure. Even through the drab, shapeless Noctus clothing, he could see she had an attractive body. Every move appeared deliberate and sensual, highlighting the curve of her hips and breasts.

He blinked and refocused his thoughts, there was no chance a beautiful woman in her prime would be interested in an aging specimen such as himself.

"Yes, you were alone. I slipped back in after the others were gone," she replied.

Markus felt his pulse quicken. Was she here because she had feelings for him? He took a deep breath; if she weren't present, he'd slap himself for such foolishness. She must know something she didn't want to share with the rest of the leadership.

"What is it?"

Her deep green eyes locked with his. "I know who the spy is."

He felt even more foolish for thinking she was there because she was interested in him.

"Who is it?" He asked softly.

Yolanda lowered her head into her hands; her hair slipped forward and obscured her face.

"Please understand." She raised her head and brushed her hair back from her face. "It is me."

Markus' breath caught. Yolanda's face was subtly different, not so much that she wasn't recognizable, but enough that she appeared to be an entirely different person—one that he recognized all too well.

"Katrina…" he whispered, remembering her as the new face at the meeting on Brilliance Station.

She nodded slowly, not breaking eye contact.

Markus was surprised to see sorrow in her eyes and a glistening in their corners. He made to rise, he needed to call Sarah and James, but Katrina caught his hands in hers.

"I have not betrayed you," she whispered. "I have betrayed *them*."

Markus stopped and lowered himself back into his seat. He stared at her for several long minutes, looking for a twitch, a flinch, anything that would give her away. Either she was the consummate actor, or she was telling the truth.

"Why?" he finally asked.

"Why betray my people, or why leak information to Steven?" Katrina asked.

"Both," Markus replied.

Katrina sat back in her chair and put her hands on her thighs, a posture he had seen Yolanda take often when giving thought to an issue.

"I don't think it would come to you as a surprise that I have never fully identified with Luminescent Society," she said slowly. "I have been a spy for my people amongst yours for many years. During that time, I've come to be disgusted with how the Noctus are treated. The Lumins deem you less than human and not worthy of further consideration, other than for the products you yield.

"I see your families, your many unique cultures, I see you as people."

Markus couldn't help but notice the venom in her voice when she spoke of her people. She chewed out the word Lumin, almost as much as Sarah.

"I didn't know what to do with my uncertainty, until that day my father killed your assistant, Simon. I saw that day what utter monsters we are, what a monster my father is. I resolved that day to help you."

"Why have you lied to me…to us?" Markus asked.

"Would you have believed that I was here to help if I had approached you directly? I came to your platform as a follow up to my father's actions, to ensure there was no unrest. What I found was an installation that was too smooth, too perfect. I knew something was up. It didn't take long to find out that you were planning to something. I insinuated myself into your inner circle in order to help. I have fed misinformation to my handlers and saved you several times from being outed."

"If that's the case, why feed Steven real intel?" Markus asked.

"He was suspicious of you. He also felt that things were too perfect. He was sniffing around and eventually he would have found something. I gave him enough to hang himself with."

Markus let Katrina's statement sink in. She had spoken very casually about setting a man on a road to death. Though he supposed when you were a Lumin spy you often sentenced people for death.

"I've been doing this for some time," Katrina said. "I know you must think me a monster—I can see it in your eyes. But I'm trying to do my best, to keep my people from harming your people every chance I get."

She seemed sincere. If she were playing him, to what end? She could have undone his Endeavor whenever she wanted. The only possibility was that she was telling the truth—she really was trying to help them.

"I guess I owe you my thanks," Markus said.

Katrina smiled, it was deep and genuine. "No thanks necessary. This is a war; we're all doing what we must to stay alive."

Markus returned the smile. "This may sound crazy, but I feel as though if life hadn't put us in these positions, we could have been close friends."

Katrina laughed. "Markus, we *are* friends. Given what I've done for you, I may be the best friend you have."

Markus was silent for a moment before something Katrina had said clicked. His eyes widened and he looked at her in surprise.

"Wait! Yusuf is your father?"

Katrina grimaced. "I was wondering when you would pick up on that. Yes, he is."

Markus couldn't help but reconsider the possibility that she was playing him. Although, there was a lot to hate about Yusuf—being his daughter was probably no party.

"What are you going to do now?" Katrina asked.

Markus sighed. "For now, it's probably best that this stays between us."

CHANGE OF PLANS

STELLAR DATE: 3248427 / 10.16.4181 (Adjusted Gregorian)
LOCATION: Mining Platform SK87
REGION: Noctilucent Space, Sirian Hegemony

Four years had passed since the events that took Steven's life.

After a long investigation—where Katrina fed the Lumins false information—she was sent to another platform. She continued to feed the rebellion intel, and occasionally managed to pass through SK87, taking time to meet with Markus.

In fact, she was due to arrive in just a few weeks—if the fates allowed.

The Endeavor itself was nearly over. To the uninitiated, it appeared as though the platform was still under heavy construction. Hundreds of cargo nets floated in space surrounding the platform; scaffolding, support girders, and temporary storage yards adorned nearly every surface.

Despite this facade, the station's upgrades were nearly complete. Just a month, maybe a little more, and they would be ready to cast off their shackles and leave the Sirius system.

As far as the Lumins were concerned, things were on schedule and yields were up. If Yusuf had checked—and Katrina assured Markus that the vice president had indeed checked—he would have found SK87 to be the model installation. To all outward appearances, his show of force in killing Simon was a success.

"Markus, are you with us?" Sarah asked, waving her hand in front of his face.

He blinked and refocused on the meeting at hand.

"He's thinking of Yolanda's next visit," Peter grinned. "Continuing the most unlikely pairing of all time."

"Your envy is showing," James cast Peter a quelling look. "Can we get back to the issue at hand?"

"Please," Dmitry nodded. "If I can't get those intercoolers installed in time, our trip is going to be short. I need the shorty guards distracted while we bring the shipping crates from the yard to the engines."

"Easier said than done," Markus sighed. "You're going to have to pull them clear across the yard and around the south tower before you can get them to the engine docks."

"So we're going to need a distraction in the tower, too," Sarah agreed. "I have just the thing."

There was a knock at the door and a clerk from the outer office stuck his head in.

"Administrator, a shuttle approaches," he looked concerned and Markus wondered what the urgency was. Shuttles approached the platform hourly.

"And?" he asked.

"It's an unscheduled Lumin long-range pinnace. It will be at the VIP dock in ten minutes."

"Do we know who is on it?" He asked.

"It only gave its ID and the correct codes. We don't have any passenger manifest, but it is priority code alpha."

Markus nodded and dismissed the clerk. He looked back at his command team. "Prepare for the rush contingency."

Solemn expressions and slow nods were the only response.

Markus left the administrative wing and made the short trip to the VIP dock.

He prepared himself to deal with a surprise inspection. It would be hard to keep everything under wraps, but not impossible. In the worst case scenario, an accident could be arranged in order to keep the Endeavor safe.

The corridors were as utilitarian at the VIP dock as anywhere else. The Lumins didn't spend extra money on mining platforms—even for their own comfort. The only enhancement was newer security equipment, allowing visitors to go about their business faster and leave sooner.

The shuttle was passing through the ES shield when Markus arrived. The bay doors closed behind it and within a minute the ramp lowered.

A pair of fashionable boots came into view, followed by legs wearing a radiant outfit that glowed and flashed a kaleidoscope of color around the dock. Seconds later Katrina's face came into view.

Her studs were in, from the bridge of her nose up to her hairline; her expression was haughty and laced with disdain as she cast her eyes around the dock.

Markus started for a moment, wondering if he was betrayed at the hands of this woman he had come to appreciate in more ways than he could ever have expected.

She locked eyes with him and her right hand twitched ever so imperceptibly and he got the signal. Play along.

Behind her Luther strode down the ramp, his expression a combination of anger and shame. He brushed past Katrina and pointed a finger at Markus.

"Did you know about this?" He shouted, the accusation ringing across the dock.

Markus didn't know what to say; Luther was a fool and he never expected to be confronted by the overseer. Katrina saved him by placing a hand on Luther's shoulder.

"Not here, Overseer, we need a secure location. We do not know where loyalties lie and there is no need to cause alarm until the others arrive."

Luther's eyes darted about the dock, taking in the several workers unloading the shuttle and the *B* guards standing at the dock's security arch.

It appeared, for just a moment, that Luther became quite frightened—an emotion Markus was certain he did not often feel. Then, the overseer schooled his expression and nodded.

"Yes, let us proceed to the administrative wing."

He led the way, passing through security and into the corridor.

Katrina fell behind Markus and spoke brusquely. "Administrator. Your platform appears to be in some disarray, with your upgrades underway. How secure is this section?"

Markus understood her meaning and replied. "Perfectly secure. There is nothing that could endanger us here."

Katrina took his meaning and stepped past Markus to stand in front of Luther.

"In that case, Overseer, I'm going to need to bind your hands and sequester your Link."

"You're what? What do you think you're doing?" He raised his hands to protest, but Katrina was both taller and stronger. She forced his hands behind his back and slipped a pair of binders on them.

Markus took a moment to wonder where she had hidden them in her skintight outfit as she replied to Luther.

"I'm helping Markus, what does it look like?"

Luther began to hurl obscenities at her, and, without a moment's hesitation, Katrina punched him in the mouth.

"Any more outbursts and I'll just kill you. You're a valuable hostage, but not so valuable that I'll put up with your crap."

Markus smiled, he really did like watching Katrina work. Once Luther's hands were secured, Markus pulled a handgun from his jacket and thrust it in the Overseer's back.

"Walk."

"You'll never get away with it," Luther snarled. "No rebellion has ever succeeded. The fleet will simply destroy the platform and accept the losses if they have to. But I doubt that will happen. A full company of shock troops will be here within the day to purge this installation."

"Seriously?" Markus looked to Katrina.

"Well, within two days. I lied to them about the time I would need to recon the station and get them the intel they needed. I also faked my advance warning to the platform security forces. They have no idea what I'm here for."

"I guess we're advancing the schedule," Markus said.

"Yes, yes we are."

"There's a wrinkle," Katrina scowled and Markus gave a moment's thought to how—even when angry or worried—she was still so beautiful.

"Isn't there always," Markus sighed.

"They're on a stealth interceptor. It's a new type of light-destroyer that is almost impossible to detect. We won't know they're here until they're right on top of us."

Markus increased his pace, pushing Luther ahead of him. "Then we better get this party started."

They marched into the administrative wing and Markus called out, "It's time!"

In seconds, the seven Lumins who worked in the wing had been shot with hand-held stun devices. Noctus converged on them, cuffing the Lumins and carrying them into one of the conference rooms.

"Impressive," Katrina smiled.

Markus took a stunner from his personal assistant and dropped Luther.

"Put him with the others."

Several minutes later, the command team rushed back into the conference room at Markus's summons.

James was first in. "Has it begun? I saw them dumping some shorts next door."

Markus nodded, "It has. They have found us out and a ship is on its way."

A moment later, Sarah entered the room and her eyes immediately locked onto Katrina who stood near the head of the table. "What is she doing here? Another hostage?"

"No," Markus said. "Sit, I'll explain when everyone has arrived."

Sarah and James took their customary places at the table, suspiciously eyeing Katrina, who kept her expression neutral.

Within a minute everyone had reassembled and Markus began with a smile. "I'm not sure why you're all being so hostile. Yolanda is a part of the team, after all."

Cries of disbelief sounded around the table as Katrina nodded slowly.

"It is true. I have been with you for the entire Endeavor; though I was not able to reveal my identity for all our safety."

"Huh," James's face broke into a slow smile. "Your intel was always really good for just a message runner. I should have guessed you were more than meets the eye."

"I don't believe it," Sarah said, her words filled with venom. "She has you fooled, Markus. There's no way one of them would side with us—no way you would work with one of them freely!"

Markus knew that Sarah would be the hardest to win over. Her blind hatred of the Lumins made it as hard for her to see them as human—just as they could not see the Noctus as anything more than property.

"She does not have me fooled. I have known her true identity since the event with Steven. She helped us greatly then. We could have fallen under much greater scrutiny, or worse."

"Then how were we found out this time?" Sarah asked. "No one here talked, we would never betray our own."

"I know that," Katrina said. "I believe it was a contact on another station. Perhaps the yardmaster on SK47—I'm not certain. Yusuf got wind and launched a covert investigation. They did a long-range scan and picked up some of your engine modifications."

"I don't care what you say, I won't accept it," Sarah replied, anger lacing her words.

"I know it's hard for you to accept," Katrina altered her voice, adopting a softer accent common on the platform. "But I hate them nearly as much as you do—I'm only half Lumin…what my mother suffered through.... I would see our Endeavor succeed and leave this place—leave them behind forever."

"Those are just words," Dmitry said. "How do we know that they are true?"

"Because I say they are," Markus replied. "I kept you in the dark for your safety and hers. What she did was too risky for any slip-ups. Also, I was worried about how you'd react—I couldn't have dissent fracturing us while we worked to gain our freedom." He looked to Katrina. "Sit, please."

She lowered into a seat at his left side and Markus surveyed the team.

"We have just under forty hours to finalize our preparations. Anything that can wait until we're in transit must wait. Propulsion and navigation are our only concerns."

He was met with nods, even if some were sullen.

"James, hit the armory. The sergeant on duty is Larson; he's bought and paid for. Disperse the weapons to the rally points and send the word that we move on all Lumin positions in one hour—sooner if we can manage."

HYPERION

STELLAR DATE: 3248427 / 10.16.4181 (Adjusted Gregorian)
LOCATION: Mining Platform SK87
REGION: Noctilucent Space, Sirian Hegemony

The ease with which the inhabitants of SK87 secured the platform made Markus nervous. It should have been harder; there should have been pockets of the Lumins that took extreme measures to flush out, making for pitched battles and bloody sacrifices.

There were none.

"It's not surprising," Katrina said as they surveyed the results of the overthrow from Overwatch.

"No?" Markus replied.

"This isn't the first time an overthrow has been successful. You don't hear about most of them, the workers in Noctilucent Space are kept as isolated as possible."

Markus took a long draught of coffee. "You never said they happened that often."

"Well, once every few decades. There are thousands of worker platforms and stations. It's a pretty good ratio. It's not worth the cost to have Luminescent security forces at the levels it would require to stop them all. It's cheaper to lose the odd installation here and there."

"Or catch things before they get to this point," James grinned. "Like what you're supposed to have done."

Katrina nodded. "Precisely."

"Makes sense," Markus nodded. "With a population close to a hundred thousand, you would need at least three or four thousand security guards to ensure any uprising was crushed."

"More, statistically," Katrina said.

Dmitry entered Overwatch. "Everything is secure, but we're going to need another week to get everything ready for the transformation."

"You likely have twenty hours," Katrina said. "The battalion I spoke of will be here soon and they'll purge this platform for re-seeding."

"There's no way we can be ready in twenty hours," James shook his head.

"We need those intercoolers installed," Dmitry nodded his head in agreement. "If we don't, this will be one short trip."

Markus was silent as he considered their options.

"At least we don't need a distraction to get them across the station. You have ten hours to get them moved and installed."

*****

The next morning, Markus addressed the entire station, much of which was assembled in the main promenade to hear his speech in person.

He couldn't help but think of the grand corridors and markets of the Luminescent stations. The platform had nothing to compare, only the few shops and company distribution centers that were somehow grander now that they belonged to his people and not the Lumins.

Through the dim lighting, he surveyed the crowd below him, elated that this day had arrived. His happiness was dampened by the niggling worry in the back of his mind that the last, crucial phase of their Endeavor could still fail.

He pushed the doubt from his mind and schooled his expression. No trace of uncertainty must show to his people.

Markus looked to his sides. The command crew surrounded him. Though most had not slept in more than a day, they were all smiling; even Sarah—though she was scanning the crowd. No doubt looking for Luminescent sympathizers.

"People of platform SK87, we've done it," Markus said simply. Thunderous applause exploded. Cheers and whoops of joy echoed through the station's corridors for a full minute before he raised his hands for silence.

"We have always been free in our hearts. Our ancestors came here because they had an untamable spirit, a desire to see new worlds and new stars. The Lumins spent generations trying to crush that spirit out of us, but they failed.

"Today we are truly free. Your children will never know the yoke of slavery. They will be able to choose their own destinies!"

He waited once more for the crowd to quiet.

"You all know the story of the ship *Hyperion,* the ship that escaped after the shorts betrayed our ancestors. They left Sirius and found a new home in the stars. Now *we* are *Hyperion*!"

A shudder rippled through the deck plates and above the crowd a holo shimmered to life. It showed the platform suspended in space. Markus held his breath, a transformation like this was unprecedented as far as he knew, no one took a mining platform between the stars.

More shocks reverberated through the decks and the holo showed several sections of the newly christened *Hyperion* drift off into space. In their wake, much larger engines were revealed.

Two massive fusion burners sat on either end of the platform and in the center a cluster of short-burn antimatter pion engines were exposed as the west yard drifted away with the last month's harvested ore still resting in containers.

The *Hyperion's* supply of antimatter was limited, but the engines would give them enough thrust for a slingshot around Sirius before running dry. If their calculations were correct, the platform should achieve a velocity just over a tenth the speed of light.

Markus glanced down at a small tablet he held and then to Dmitry. The chief engineer gave him a thumbs up. So far everything was going to plan—impressive.

Beside Markus, Dmitry was nodding as he listened to his teams report in. He smiled and gave Markus a thumbs up.

Markus returned the gesture as another shudder rippled through the deck, causing a fresh round of cheers. The hastily set up holo projectors showed the south yard breaking free from the ship, exposing a much larger MDC emitter that would function as a stellar matter scoop.

The scoop would draw in as much fuels as possible during the slingshot maneuver around Sirius. Once the platform was on an outsystem vector, it would be reconfigured to function as a solar sail.

They would burn the engines as long as possible, retaining half the fuel for braking once they reached Kapteyn's Star. Dmitri's estimations put the journey somewhere between fifty and seventy years—with new engines and an untested scoop the variables were many.

The holo projections shifted, showing a view of the engines roaring to life—a visual that was accompanied by a low rumble in the deck.

Markus looked to Dmitry who was smiling broadly.

"Thank the light," Markus whispered while he watched the holo show streams of plasma race into space as the platform eased into motion.

"I can't wait to see the faces of the shorts when they see this on their long range scans," James said with a grin.

"They're going to lose their minds, or piss themselves," Sarah said with a laugh.

Katrina caught Markus's eye. Her expression was not so jovial.

"If those were there only two options I'd feel a lot better right now," she said softly to Markus.

*****

The interceptor was running dark.

Voices were hushed; any and all unneeded electronics were switched off. Even lighting was dimmed.

The only discernible energy output was a stream of pions—traveling near the speed of light—streaming out the engine's long funnel.

Major Han re-read the EMF output and engine reports. Surprise was key. The inhabitants of SK87 had no idea a stealth ship was bearing down on them. The longer that lack of awareness persisted, the more of his soldiers would survive the fight.

He looked over the troop readiness reports a third time. This was his company's second combat deployment; though they had made countless training runs—both simulated and physical.

The brass had considered his first live combat mission to be a smashing success, but he did not. Too many of his troops had died at the hands of the Noctus scum they were putting down. The corporation had wanted the station to stay intact, and the lives of his men and women bought that result.

That was why, when this new stealth interceptor became available for a trial run, he jumped at it. The normal troop transports could be seen half the system away. A station had days to prepare before his soldiers arrived.

SK87 would have no such foreknowledge. They would know of their demise the hour it was upon them.

"Sir!" the officer manning the scan terminal called out. "Something…something has happened to the platform!"

Major Han surveyed the scan report with disbelief. At first it appeared as though SK87 was exploding, but there was no fire, or small debris. Chunks of it were simply falling off.

Minutes later, as the scan updated, it became quite clear what was occurring. The platform had been surreptitiously refitted. How or why was not his concern; stopping whatever they planned next was.

"Helmsman, increase burn, I want to get there as fast as this ship can take us. No need for surprise, they know we're coming." Major Han's tone was brusque.

Helm nodded and Han's XO gave him a quizzical look. "How can you be sure?"

Jennifer was new to Han's command, a recent OSC grad. She had promise, but like any newly minted lieutenant, thought she knew a hell of a lot more than she actually did.

"Because they're making no attempt to hide what they're doing. That means they've taken the station and either know about us specifically, or expect some retaliation soon."

"Then we should expect them to have weapons," Jennifer replied.

"Lieutenant, we should always expect them to have weapons."

Han let out a long sigh. It was going to be bloody. Too many Lumins would die at the hands of Noctus animals and there was little he could do about it now.

Other than kill every man, woman, and child on that platform.

* * * * *

Yusuf's expression remained calm and serene as he read the report. Those around him at the monthly executive meeting would never have suspected that a sea of rage roiled beneath his calm demeanor.

That Markus would do something so brash, so outrageous. That Luther, the coal-brained Station Overseer, hadn't suspected a thing was inexcusable. If he survived, Yusuf would have him executed.

The brief flashed with an update from the field commander, a Major Han. It was a single line of text:

We think they have your daughter.

Yusuf looked up at the other governing executives. Greenich, a pitiful man responsible for reclamation infrastructure, was speaking—Yusuf interrupted him without notice.

"You'll have to excuse me, something urgent has come up."

With no further ceremony, he swept out of the room, already calling Admiral Pontius on the Link.

<*Yusuf, what do I owe…*>

<*You owe insurrection. I want three of your best destroyers ready to go in one hour,*> Yusuf cut him off.

<*Yes, sir, I will have a shuttle at your private dock in fifteen minutes.*>

Yusuf severed the connection. He hadn't given Pontius their destination, but he knew the Admiral would figure it out soon enough.

"Aras!" Yusuf yelled to his assistant without turning. There was no need to ensure that the man was there; he was always scuttling in Yusuf's wake. "Ensure bags are packed for me and transferred to Pontius's shuttle when it arrives. We could be gone for several weeks."

As he stepped into the lift Yusuf considered the words, *we think they have your daughter.* Katrina had been on SK87 several times in the past few years, checking up on them and ensuring that there was no unrest following his killing of Markus's assistant.

Her reports, and the reports of his other operatives, indicated that it was the model station and he had all but put it from his mind.

Now, with this new information, he could arrive at only one conclusion: his daughter had betrayed him. If that was true, she would die as well—at his hands, if possible.

GETTING OUT OF DODGE

STELLAR DATE: 3248428 / 10.17.4181 (Adjusted Gregorian)
LOCATION: *Hyperion*
REGION: Noctilucent Space, Sirian Hegemony

Markus leaned back in his chair, forcing his heart to slow and his breathing to calm. Though the events now unfolding had been his goal for the last few years, actually carrying out these final, irreversible actions left him feeling more anxiety than he had imagined he would.

The door cracked open and Katrina's head peeked around.

"Do you have a moment?" she asked.

Markus couldn't help it as a smile crept across his face. "I always have a moment for you." He stood and she stepped into his arms. The pair shared no words for a long moment, simply breathing in one another's presence.

"Hard to believe this day has finally come, isn't it?" Katrina asked as she stepped back and sat on the edge of his desk.

Markus slipped back into his chair, taking in the sight of this beautiful woman who genuinely seemed to want to spend time with him. She still wore the skin-tight clothing of her people—though she had muted its coloring somewhat. The way it hugged the curves of her body undid all of the calm he had managed to acquire before she entered his office.

Katrina gave a slight chuckle, drawing his eyes to her face.

"You're always so calm and in control, it's nice to see you acting as a mortal man every so often."

Markus laughed in reply. "If this is what we are judging me by, I am so very mortal."

Katrina smiled in return and took several moments to speak.

"I don't know what is going to happen over the next few days and months, but I need you to know something."

"What would that be?" Markus asked in reply.

"There has been no acting on my part," Katrina said. "I know that because I am a spy you suspect my motives and whether I am genuine. Hell, sometimes I wonder where I end and a cover begins," she said the last with a rueful chuckle. "But I *need* you to know. This is real, I have feelings for you, it is no act."

Markus worked to find the right words. He had certainly hoped that her feelings were genuine, but a kernel of doubt had always lingered within him, gnawing slowly at his surety.

"Why?" he finally asked.

Katrina's expression showed puzzlement and then she gave a light and silvery laugh. "Markus, you really are a fool of a man. A great leader, amazing in how you motivate your people and have earned their trust, but when it comes to this…well… let's just say you're not too skilled."

"Something I have never claimed to be, but you still haven't answered my question."

"I can see into people's motives all too well and manipulate them as needed, but I can't say I understand love," Katrina said the last word with a finality that rung like a bell.

"Love?"

"Yes, Administrator Markus, love."

She reached down and pulled him up into her arms, their lips meeting with a deep yearning.

"Uh, Boss?"

Markus looked and saw James standing in the doorway, red-faced and sheepish looking.

"Yes, James?"

"Sorry to disturb you, but we need you in Overwatch; both of you, actually."

Markus and Katrina disentangled their arms and they followed James through the administrative wing toward Overwatch.

"What's up?" Markus asked.

James's voice was grim. "It would seem that our visitors are going to be here a bit early."

"How is that possible?" Katrina asked.

"They've boosted a lot harder than we had anticipated after we transformed the *Hyperion*. I guess someone lit a fire under their assess."

Markus and Katrina exchanged glances.

"I can imagine who held the match," Katrina said with a grim expression.

James cast a glance her way. "Yeah? Who?"

"I'm guessing it was her father," Markus said.

James chuckled and shook his head. "I've heard of Dad not liking the boyfriend, but this is a bit much. Who is he, anyway?"

"Yusuf," Katrina's voice was tense as she spoke the name.

James turned sideways as he walked, locking eyes with Katrina and then Markus. "Are you kidding me? What… why…?" he sputtered.

Markus just shrugged. He wanted to ask James what he would do had he caught the attention of Katrina, but decided that was not the wisest response.

"What does their ETA look like?" Katrina asked, changing the subject.

James took the hint. "About nine hours, but they'll be in weapons range in half that time—provided they don't plan to use something that we can't deflect."

"They don't have any nuclear weapons; their superiors don't like the mess those make. They prefer, at least, to have salvage if they can't keep the station intact," Katrina said. "No, their first offensive will be a full-scale boarding and cleansing."

Dmitry had joined the trio in the corridor as Katrina was speaking. "Cleansing. I guess we're just bacteria to them," he said angrily.

"No good thoughts lie that way," Markus cautioned Dmitry. "We have to remain focused on how we'll get through this."

"Well, you're lucky. With no small amount of divine intervention, we got the intercoolers installed. It's not pretty and if any other chief engineers see it I'll deny I had any part in that installation, but we'll get the operational efficiencies we need out of the engines."

"Then we need to light those pion drives," Katrina said. "Making them alter *v* and thread the belt to meet up with us will buy us some more time."

"I have our four biggest tugs fueled up and ready to go as well," James added. "We'll get this thing underway in no time."

No time, as it turned out, was just over two hours. James's crews carefully selected anchor points on the newly balanced station and the new engines threw a few final curve balls before they were running just the way Dmitry wanted.

The *Hyperion* lay deep within Sirius's second asteroid belt, just over three AU from the star. The engines and tugs strained to pull the platform stellar north and out of the field before the platform could begin the hard burn toward the star for the gravity assist slingshot outsystem.

The belt was not densely populated, but enough so that the platform had to alter course several times to thread their way past errant rocks and dust clouds. It was just over seven hours after their burn started that the path to the star was clear enough to push the engines to their maximum output.

Markus watched the scan on the main holotank in Overwatch, keeping an eye on the positions of other platforms and asteroids, as well as the spotty ghost-echo of the pursuing ship.

Several times the platform had been hailed by system traffic control stations as to the nature of their unscheduled movement, but each time the *Hyperion* did not respond. With each subsequent hail, a hushed silence deepened across Overwatch—and across the entire platform—as the crew waited for the inevitable confrontation.

"I have a contact," scan called out. "It looks like a patrol ship leaving a nearby garrison station."

"To be expected," Markus nodded and looked to Katrina. "Do you think it's synchronized with the strike force?"

"Hard to say," Katrina replied. "It could be, but I don't think that the strike force would want to tip their hand. It could be a feint. Either way, if I were their commander, I would look for an opportunity to use the distraction this will cause."

"That interceptor ship couldn't get all the way here without us picking them up on scan, could they?" James asked.

The yard-master's day-to-day work was some of the most dangerous on the station, wrangling cargo and asteroids where the smallest mistake could result in disaster. Markus had rarely heard him sound anything other than calm and serene, but there was more than a waver in the man's voice.

Katrina caught Markus's eye and he nodded; people needed some assurances. He switched his chair's comm to station-wide.

"People of the *Hyperion,* you have shown incredible fortitude during our Endeavor thus far, and through our initial actions today. It is likely that things are going to get exciting soon. A patrol ship is on an intercept course with us and it's possible that our friends on the destroyer could use that distraction to their advantage. I want all teams to be ready for boarding at any moment, and everyone monitoring external hatches get ready to blow them at a moment's notice.

"Stay strong, stay vigilant; we will weather this and see a new star."

James grinned. "Good speech, boss."

Markus didn't reply and turned back to scan. Three hours until the patrol ship was in weapons range.

"Patrol ship entering range," scan called out one hundred and eighty-two long minutes later

"They're hailing us," comm added. "Nothing new, though their tone is considerably more irate," the woman running comm added with a smile.

"Put me through," Markus said.

The comm officer pushed a button on her panel and nodded in his direction.

"This is the sovereign ship *Hyperion,* formerly known as platform SK87. Do not come within ten-thousand kilometers of our platform. Doing so will be considered an act of aggression and we will fire upon you."

Markus put the comm down and wiped the sweat from his hands as he exchanged looks with the Overwatch command crew.

The response was quick and angry, as expected.

"What are you playing at, SK87? Your platform is the property of the people of Sirius and you are contractually bound to it. You will open your main bay for our shuttles to dock at once."

Markus picked up the comm handset with both hands, praying no one noticed the slight tremor he couldn't suppress.

"Negative, patrol ship, by our calculations our people paid back their transit debt seven hundred and twenty-six years ago. In the intervening years, we have paid for this platform and are, in fact, owed a steep remittance for our labor. We'd prefer to be paid in Sol credits."

Katrina stifled a laugh as he switched off comm.

"I wonder if anyone has ever told them that before?" she asked.

"First time for everything," Markus forced a smile.

"They're launching two boarding shuttles," scan called out. "Looks like one is headed for the main bay, and the other for the north bay airlock."

"Can we make good on our threat to shoot them?" James asked.

"Negative," scan replied. "Not all our weapons got mounted and they picked approaches where we're wide open."

"I should get to the main bay," Katrina said. "I'll direct the crew at the north bay lock to prime their charges and detonate as soon as the outer hatch is opened."

Markus nodded grimly. "Good luck."

With the rushed departure, there were a lot of steps in their insurrection that the crew of the *Hyperion* had not managed to complete—one of which was to finish the various computer overrides necessary to completely lock the shorts out of the platform's control systems.

A task that was proving to be more difficult than expected—short of destroying the control systems entirely—was to remove remote access for the main bay doors.

As Katrina approached the main bay's control shack, she called into the techs frantically working on the bay door's software.

"Let it be," Katrina advised. "We'll deal with them once they get in. We could use another ship," she added with a wink.

The *Hyperion's* main bay was just over a hundred meters deep and three hundred wide. Two smaller tugs rested on cradles on each side. Just inside the main lock, between the bay and the rest of the platform, stood two dozen of the platform's newly formed militia.

Katrina knew she'd find Sarah leading this group and nodded to the other woman.

"I expect that they'll settle their shuttle on the main platform," Katrina said by way of greeting.

Sarah nodded in response, her eyes boring into Katrina's.

"We should take up positions behind those tugs and under the deck plates there, and there," Katrina pointed to several maintenance hatches.

"They'll be too close; the shorts'll take anyone in that position out in seconds." Sarah shook her head. "We should ambush them in the corridors."

"If we do that it will be too late. They'll have a foothold on the ship and they also may lase us right through the bulkheads. We have to take them quick and by surprise."

Katrina looked around at the militia, many of whom she recognized after spending so many months on the platform. She singled out four of the men and women who she knew had young families.

"You four, take up positions around the main hatch. Take a couple of pot-shots at them as they disembark and then run. It'll focus their attention forward and then give them a false sense of security when you run. That's when the rest of us will attack."

Katrina looked at Sarah who slowly nodded. She could tell the other woman may not like her, but understood why Katrina picked those four individuals for the diversion. Perhaps she'd win her over eventually.

Katrina split the rest up into the sharpshooters, who would take up positions behind the tugs, and those with less accurate, close range weapons, who would hide under the deck plates.

While the people of the *Hyperion* knew for some time that they would likely fight a battle on their decks, there had been no way to properly train them in combat. She had to hope that the vids and desire to free their home would be enough.

"Remember," she cautioned the men and women, "it's close quarters in here. It's going to be terrifying and confusing. Pick your targets carefully. Don't shoot wildly; the last thing you want is to hit a friend."

Her words were answered by solemn nods and sidelong glances. Sarah nodded to the militia and they moved to their positions. Katrina took up a position on the heavy equipment maintenance shed. It was in a corner of the dock and its roofline was above any lines of sight from where the boarding craft would disgorge its soldiers.

She would only get a few shots off as the assault transport's weapons would make short work of her position once they had a lock.

She unslung the slug thrower she had smuggled onto the station several months earlier. It was a brutal weapon and not the sort of thing any civilized combatant would use, but it would keep as many of the Hyperions alive as possible.

The external bay doors began to open scant moments after the last of the fighters slipped into cover. Katrina found herself holding her breath, and forced a slow exhale. She eyed the four fighters at the dock's main hatch. They held their weapons securely, but Katrina could see their nervousness in the twitch of a finger and subtle shifts of position.

"Hold steady," she whispered to herself, wishing—not for the first time—that the Hyperions had Link technology.

The assault craft was the size and model she had expected; it held between six and ten lightly armored soldiers, likely under the command of a lieutenant. A pair of pilots would stay with the craft and man its weapons.

Before it had finished settling into the cradle, the ramp was lowering and four soldiers jumped to the deck. On cue, the four Noctus fighters at the dock's entrance took a few shots before retreating into the corridor, using the bulkhead for cover.

Only one shot hit a Luminescent soldier. It was a good shot, center-mass, but the force was absorbed by the advanced armor the soldier wore. A second later, several more soldiers had spilled from the craft and Katrina saw all but one of the fighters disappear from the dock's hatch.

"Go, move!" she whispered to herself.

The Noctus fighter was too late, a soldier fired, his shot true and a figure fell forward through the dock's hatch, face slamming into the deck plate.

The soldiers responded as Katrina expected. Believing the Noctus had retreated, they fully deployed from the assault craft. She held her breath for a second, praying to whatever gods may listen that Sarah took the cue.

She sighted along her rifle's holoscope and let a long breath escape her lungs. As the last wisps of air passed her lips, the Hyperion Militia burst from beneath the deck plates, and, gods bless them, began firing without asking for quarter.

The soldiers were flanked and their ranks nearly collapsed under a concussive blanket of pulse rifle fire. Their armor took the brunt of the attack, but two fell in the initial volley from the militia. Katrina didn't give them a chance to regroup and lined her sights on one of the soldiers at the front of their formation. The command raced from her mind to the rifle and it fired the slug.

As though she had simply sent a signal to a bomb, her target's head exploded. Pieces of burning metal, brain, and bone slammed into three men behind the soldier. Two of them went down, and the third stood screaming, trying to tear his helmet off—a difficult task with a piece of his teammate's skull protruding from his visor.

Katrina took a second shot, killing a man on the flank—this time with no collateral damage.

Moments later the remaining Luminescent soldiers threw their weapons to the ground and Sarah led half her squad into the assault craft to subdue the pilots.

Katrina didn't wait for report of their success, she saw the ship's upper turret begin to turn toward her and dropped from the roof of the maintenance shed, sliding down a ladder and rushing across the dock toward the militia and the relative cover of the assault craft.

Two women were smashing the point defense lasers on the front of the craft, and four others had surrounded the remaining soldiers. The rest were losing their lunch off to the side of the cradle.

Katrina sent a message over the platform's meager Link to Overwatch. *<Assault team is subdued, Sarah is taking the pilots, we should have the dock fully under control in a minute.>*

<Good to hear,> Markus's voice played in her head; she could hear cheering in the background as the team in Overwatch let off some stress.

<Did they repel at the north bay airlock?> Katrina asked.

<Our folks blew the lock when the shorts tried to get a seal. It looks like it wrecked their hatch. They were circling around to the main bay, but now they've diverted to the south bay.>

Sarah walked down the ramp with the two pilots at gunpoint, wearing a grin so large it almost wrapped around her face.

"Nice work, Sarah," Katrina smiled, hoping to gain some points with the surly woman. "Markus tells me that the other assault craft is making for the south service bay.

Sarah's expression turned serious. "Sven!" she called to the leader of her second squad. "Stay here and lock these asshats down, Katrina and I will take second and third squad to take care of their friends."

They jogged out of the bay to the sounds of the remaining militia stunning the captured soldiers before they stripped and cuffed them.

Katrina thought she knew the platform well, but Sarah led them through a twisting maze of passageways, some so narrow they had to pass single file.

"These aren't all on the official blueprint," Katrina commented at one point.

"Noticed that did you?" Sarah replied with a smirk. "Good to know you didn't ferret out all of our secrets."

Katrina decided not to respond; it seemed like she still had a way to go before she wasn't one of *them* to Sarah.

Weapons fire greeted them before they reached the dock, and Sarah raised the leader of the squad defending the bay on her comm unit.

"We're pinned down! We couldn't stop them from getting the bay doors open without blowing them. We're trapped behind the port-side maintenance crane."

"We'll get you out of there," Sarah replied and broke into a full run, Katrina trailing behind with the two squads.

"How many of them are there?" Katrina asked.

"A dozen at least. The ship is firing on our position, too, but they haven't pulled out the big guns yet." The response was accompanied by the sounds of a man screaming in agony.

"Sarah, split the squads up between the two entrances. Is there another, less well known way into the bay?" Katrina asked.

Sarah nodded. "If you go into the dock master's office, there's a ladder up to a service hatch that gets you onto an observation deck. Not as much cover, but maybe you can get a shot or two off again."

Katrina nodded and pulled up a station map. The route Sarah described overlaid her vision and she took the last few twists fast enough that she slid into the bulkheads.

Her work as an infiltrator required her to have far fewer modifications and physical enhancements than most in Luminescent Society. Normally she didn't mind; she had earned a respect for how the Noctus worked with pure biological bodies. However, today she wished she had taken the agency's suggestion that she take a few mods in case of emergency.

The service hatch was just where Sarah said, and Katrina climbed onto the narrow observation walkway. Below her she could see the assault craft resting unevenly in the bay's center cradle. Four of the soldiers were working their way toward the beleaguered militia who had been guarding the bay while the remaining eight had taken up positions defending against Sarah's troops, who were firing from the two entrances.

Katrina lay prone and checked her magazine. She had three shots. With the cover the observation catwalk offered, she would likely not get off a second. She looked through the holo sights and prepared to fire into a group of soldiers.

A second before she squeezed the mental trigger, she saw movement out of the corner of her eye. She shifted her scope and realized that the assault craft's main turret was about to fire down the corridor into Sarah's people.

She shifted her weapon, took aim and fired one slug and then a second into the turret. The ship's gun exploded in a shower of sparks and shrapnel.

Below, several of the soldiers looked around for the new source of weapons fire and one spotted her, likely marking her position on his HUD.

Katrina considered her options. Chances were that she wouldn't be able to fire the slug thrower again in this fight. Getting back through the service hatch would take precious seconds she didn't have. A glance down told her that jumping would hurt, but there would be cover.

She rolled off the edge of the catwalk twisting in the air and landing behind a row of tool chests. There were some spare parts and tools scattered on the floor and her right foot came down sideways on one.

The snap told her that something in her ankle was broken a moment before the pain set in. Luckily the ability to dull pain was one mod she had taken—in case of capture and torture.

She put it from her mind and drew her sidearm while gingerly moving to the end of the tool chest row. It was certain that one or two soldiers had been dispatched to secure her location.

The small pistol was normally used for stunning, but it also contained a high velocity flechette cartridge and she flipped the toggle to that mode.

Ahead of her, the barrel of a gun peeked around the corner; the end of the weapon pivoted, trained on her. She fell to the ground as a pulse wave blasted above her, numbing her back. The soldier must have thought his shot hit her as his leg stepped forward.

Taking aim, Katrina fired a flechette at the back of the soldier's knee, where the armor was weakest. With a cry of pain, the soldier, a woman by the sound of her, fell to the ground. Katrina sighted for a moment and then fired a second shot under the woman's chin, another weak spot.

The woman's thrashing turned to twitching and Katrina scrambled forward to secure the rifle.

Just as her hand settled on the grip, a voice called out from behind her, "Freeze!"

Katrina pivoted, bringing her new-found rifle to bear on the voice and found a soldier standing two meters from her with his rifle trained on her head.

"Go for it, fire that shot," she could almost see the man's smirk behind the mirrored face plate. Any Noctus attempting to use a Lumin soldier's weapon without first disarming the genetic safeties would lose their hand—if they were lucky.

Katrina shrugged. "OK." She fired the shot and the man fell backward. She pulled herself upright and fired three more pulse shots into his face. If he wasn't dead, he would wish he were.

She pulled herself up to peek over the tool chests and saw that several more of the soldiers were down, but Sarah's reinforcements were still pinned down in the corridor.

She moved back toward the assault craft, looking for a good position to apply flanking fire. A large barrel filled with scrap metal looked to provide good cover and she crouched behind it, using the rifle's pivoting barrel and holo sights to line up on a soldier from the back.

Several shots later and the soldiers were scrambling to find cover while under fire from three sources.

"Surrender!" Katrina called out between gritted teeth. The pain dampening mods weren't working as well as they were supposed to. She worried it was much more than a simple break.

Through her sights she saw a soldier throw down his weapon and raise his arms in surrender. Moments later, they all followed suit and she called out. "Move toward the corridor. Slowly!"

Sarah's militia moved into the bay and began to secure the soldiers. Katrina hobbled around the barrel she had been using for cover and waved an arm in greeting before taking a moment to glance down at her ankle.

A piece of steel jutted out from her boot and she chuckled softly, "I guess you're why this hurt so much."

Sarah trotted over with four of her fighters. She directed them to secure the assault craft and gave a grudging smile to Katrina.

"I guess I owe you one. When I saw that turret pivot toward the corridor I thought we were done for."

"Think maybe I'm crew of the *Hyperion* now?" Katrina asked—straight to the point.

Sarah's cheeks reddened. "I have been kind of an ass to you, haven't I?"

"No more than I deserved. I haven't always been on the right side of things."

Sarah nodded silently, her smile dipping for a moment and Katrina suspected she was wondering what things she had done in her years as a spy for the shorts. A moment later it was gone.

"That's in the past," she said and reached out to clasp Katrina's shoulder.

The pressure caused her to shift and Katrina sucked in a painful breath as her ankle shot through with pain.

Sarah looked down.

"Holy shit, that doesn't look like fun."

"Not especially, no."

Sarah pulled Katrina's arm over her shoulder. "Let me get you over to the medic."

* * * * *

Half hour later, Katrina hobbled into Overwatch on crutches. A brief flash of concern raced across Markus's face before he schooled his expression.

"Wow," James called out. "I thought it was just a minor injury."

"It was," Katrina responded as she worked her way up the stairs to the command ring. "Unfortunately, the medicine allowed the Noctus isn't much to speak of. I have some dormant med nano that I've initialized. They'll replicate and get it fixed up in a day or two."

"Until then you're pretty much benched," Markus said.

Katrina threw a sweet smile his way, "You're just going to have to settle for my brains with my body in recovery."

Dmitry choked on his coffee and James barked a loud guffaw.

"Thanks," Markus muttered. "That'll garner me so much respect around here."

Katrina patted him on the shoulder and sat in a chair with as much grace as someone in her condition could muster.

"You all seem to be in a much better mood than you were when I left," she observed.

"It may have had something to do with you and Sarah kicking some serious ass out there," James said. "I hear you did some crazy heroics to save the day."

"Everyone did crazy heroics," Katrina said. "Mine just got my ankle broken is all."

"We also got a ping off the destroyer," Markus said. "It's still several light minutes out and will take another couple of hours to match velocities with us. The patrol craft has pulled away and for the moment we're in the clear."

"Do we have a plan for the destroyer?" Katrina asked. "They're going to be a lot harder to fight off than the district patrol guys."

Markus looked to Dmitry, who set his coffee down and brought up a system map on the main holo tank.

"We're here, almost past the inner dust belt and Vishnu's orbit. From there we're going to increase our burn as we fall faster into Sirius's gravity well. It's going to extend our lead on the destroyer, and if we can hold together as we pull around the star, we'll be out of their reach—unless they want to hit an outsystem velocity with no worlds to brake around."

Katrina couldn't help but notice that Dmitry used the pre-colonization name for Sirius's innermost world. Luminescent society had renamed all of the planets, but the Noctus resented the renaming. They viewed it as another piece of their heritage that had been suppressed.

"Bold, but it looks like it will work," Katrina nodded.

The command crew fell to reviewing the status of the last few upgrades that Dmitry's engineers were making and re-checking the removal of Luminescent command codes from the computer systems.

Katrina was reviewing a report from Sarah on the incarceration of the Luminescent soldiers from the assault craft as well as those garrisoned on the platform. The plan was to release them in a cargo hauler after the gravity assist maneuver around Sirius was complete.

She enjoyed the physical act of reading so often required on Noctus platforms. In Luminescent society, so much information was directly inserted into one's mind over the Link. Little thought was given to the act of absorbing the information and internalizing it. Looking over the words of Sarah's report was refreshing.

Her reading was disrupted by an alarm's wail. She turned to look at the main board and let out a small cry of surprise.

Markus was on the comm verifying the information.

"Are you certain? Do you have visual confirmation?" He all but yelled into the microphone.

"I can see it from here," the voice came over the room's overhead speakers. "It's attached just above the east yard's main hatch. I don't know how long it's been there other than it wasn't fifteen minutes ago."

"Fifteen minutes!" Katrina exclaimed. "They could be anywhere by now."

She had to grant a modicum of respect for the assault force's commander. He must have slipped this assault away from the destroyer and brought it straight up the *Hyperion's* wake to avoid detection. Between the engines and the east yard there were few external port holes and significant sensor gaps. His men would likely need treatment for the rads they picked up though.

"Sarah's reporting in," Markus called out. "She has her militia moving into position. It looks like the enemy has spread all over the sector."

"Are there many crew in there?" Katrina asked, worried the soldiers had already begun cleansing the platform.

"A few hundred, Sarah reports that she's working on evacuating them and protecting the positions of the ones working on the final engine prep."

Katrina struggled to stand. "I should get down there, I can help with tactics and pull a trigger if necessary."

"You'll do no such thing," Markus put a hand on her shoulder and gently pushed her back into her seat. "Do you really think you'd be more of a help than a hindrance?"

Katrina sighed. "Very well, the battle would likely be over by the time I got down there anyway." She brought up the station's schematics, and worked with the comm officer to map out the positions of the enemy soldiers and provide guidance to the militia.

Reports poured in from the sector, the fighting was fierce and the ship's militia was taking heavy losses. Corridor-by-corridor they were being pushed back by the elite Lumin troops. From what Katrina could tell, there were fewer than thirty enemy soldiers, but their superior armor, weapons, and tactics were crafted for just this sort of situation.

She looked to James for information on the layout of a particular intersection, but he wasn't at his station.

"Markus, where did James go?"

Markus looked up from the main holo tank, his brow furrowing. "I don't know; he was here a moment ago. Maybe he needed to visit the head."

Katrina switched her terminal to his personal comm. "James, do you copy? I need your advice on a corridor?"

For a moment there was no response, and then James's response came over her headset. "Yeah. Sure. Where?" His voice was hoarse and he sounded out of breath.

"Where are you? What's going on?"

"Just ran to the head if you must know, which intersection?"

Katrina felt a slight blush. "Sector 5A, deck 17, the 5A-7E intersection."

"Ah, that one. It's a mess, there are several bio-waste stacks that run through there and some life support. They sit right out in the walkway and you have to almost squeeze past them."

Katrina nodded. "Thanks, that's what I hoped. I'm going to use it as a choke-point and set up a barricade there. I have Sarah sealing off a number of other routes to funnel the shorts through there."

"Good idea, I'll be back in a bit to help."

Katrina returned her focus to the plan she was architecting when a warning flashed on her terminal indicating that a ship was exiting the main bay. It was one of the mining tugs.

"Tug Bravo, this is Overwatch," the comm officer radioed out. "What are you doing? Get that ship back in the bay!"

"Negative, Overwatch, I advise that you clear everyone out of decks twelve through twenty-one east of corridor 7E."

Markus grabbed a mike, his brow furrowing, "What's going on James. You're not..."

"I sure as hell am, it'll be a quick shot, nice and surgical."

"James, stop! They'll shoot you down."

"I can sneak around and do it just as I pop up over the east yard. They'll never see it coming."

"They're all through the sector though," Dmitry called out, "What are you going to do, fire at the platform?"

Markus glanced over at Dmitry, his eyes deadly serious.

"Wait, no, we have people in there," Dmitry said.

"I'll fire east of Sarah's choke point. We don't have people there anymore…"

Dmitry's eyes grew dark and he slumped in his chair.

Katrina looked to Markus who nodded slowly.

She adjusted her headset, "James, they'll be able to track you before you come around the ship. They likely have dropped probes around the ship in case of an external attack, you're going to need to come aft of their craft and then swing overtop fast to get your shot off."

"Over top? Don't they have a nice big turret on top of those things?" James asked.

Katrina nodded as she spoke, "They do, James."

Overwatch was silent for several long moments before James responded.

"OK, guide me in."

The traffic control officer, comm, and James worked to slip the tug amongst the shadows on the south side of the station, working their way through the lower access into the east yard.

The yard was mostly clear of the usual rocks, cargo and other detritus which usually filled it. The slingshot around the star would tear nets right out of their moorings. Anything that could not be bolted down in the platform had been jettisoned.

James was forced to maneuver between the struts of an asteroid cradle for cover. It was a long slow process, which was made worse by the constant reports pouring in of the shorts wiping out any last pockets of resistance in the east yard sector and the frantic updates from Sarah as she lost more and more militia at the choke points she had established.

"I'm a hundred meters away," James called in. "I'm going to boost in hard, thrust up above them, brake, and fire. With luck I can do the whole maneuver in fifteen seconds and be gone before that turret can take a shot."

Markus took a deep breath before speaking. "You have a go."

Every screen in Overwatch was tracking James's progress and a view of the east yard filled the main holo tank.

"There!" the comm officer called out as James brought the tug out of the shadows and boosted toward the assault craft. The craft was attached to the station by an umbilical coming out of the bottom of the ship. James swooped through the yard in a delicate arc that appeared to be a collision course with the assault craft's engines. At the last moment he fired his thrusters and slipped up and over the enemy vessel. He pivoted the tug far more gracefully than Katrina would have thought possible and fired the engines against the direction of travel to stop right over the assault craft.

The events appeared to unfold in slow motion. The MDC emitter on the nose of the shuttle sparked to life as the enemy's turret pivoted, tracking toward the tug.

The MDC fired, its wave of molecular disruption energy washing out across the assault craft and station. Katrina cringed as she thought of what would happen to any humans caught in its field of effect.

Used to break apart asteroids, an MDC wave weakened the bonds between molecules and broke objects down into their constituent parts. James had fired the tug's decoupling wave on low power, and it would do minimal damage to the ship and station, but the weaker chemical bonds in organics would not retain their integrity.

Humans would quite simply melt.

Sarah's teams fell back and readings showed they had reached a safe distance. From what Katrina could tell, all of the enemy soldiers were within the fatal range of the field.

Katrina glanced at the holo and saw that James hadn't kept the tug moving, it still hovered over the assault craft.

"James, move!" she cried out into her comm, but it was too late. The MDC had damaged the craft's turret and the pilots would be dead, but automated defenses kicked in. Two small missiles snaked out from forward tubes, looped around and flew back into the tug before James could respond.

The tug exploded in a brilliant show of steel and plasma.

There were several cries of dismay and horror in Overwatch. Katrina's looked at Markus; she saw his jaw clench and eyes moisten, but a moment later his posture straightened and he turned to his command crew.

"What James did, his sacrifice, has saved untold numbers of our people. His name will be written on the bulkheads in places of honor, as will the names of all who died today."

The room was filled with nodding heads and the sounds of a few choking back tears. Katrina watched Markus survey the room, briefly making eye contact with people as he put a reassuring hand on the comm officer's shoulder, a woman that Katrina was relatively certain had begun to date James recently.

"But we will have time to mourn the dead soon enough; I need you to put your grief away. Instead, let it strengthen your actions, not weaken you. Never before have our people been so close to tasting freedom."

He turned to Dmitry, "Let me know as soon as you have assessed any damage. All resources are at your disposal. We must make our gravity assist burn."

Dmitry nodded and ran from the room, several of his engineers following him.

Markus turned back to the holo tank and the room began to fill with soft conversation, a few sobs and hoarse coughs punctuating the murmuring voices.

Katrina rose and ungracefully pulled her crutches under her arms. She stopped at his side, staring forward, not looking him in the eyes. This was a key moment for him. She must appear to approach him on a professional basis and not offer him emotional support.

Some of the crew behind her would likely form a negative opinion of her—or a more negative opinion—probably already thinking of her as an ice queen. It did not matter. This moment was for Markus and a hand, a soft look, any sympathy would make him appear weaker in front of his people.

The years ahead would be long and hard; many would doubt, after the losses they suffered today. He would need all the strength he could muster.

GROWING OLD TOGETHER

STELLAR DATE: 3265669 / 12.31.4228 (Adjusted Gregorian)
LOCATION: ISS *Intrepid*
REGION: Interstellar space near Kapteyn's Star

Fifty-six years after Tanis and Joe found Ouri's old cabin…

Tanis let out a long breath and leaned back in her chair.

It creaked slightly and she once again thought that perhaps it was time to pull her first wood-turning project apart and improve the joinery—it was fifty years old, after all.

She thought of how different this chair was than most she had used in her life. No carbon nano-reinforced polymers here. Just wood from trees she had felled and milled herself. It was a far cry from her other chair. It sat a few kilometers above and several more toward the bow of the ship—near the bridge. It was, without a doubt, more comfortable, but she had not seen it in over thirty years, though she would again before long.

But, for now, she would enjoy her last few weeks with her wooden furniture. Improved versions of the chair sat nearby, encircling the dining room table; but this one was special and sat in a place of honor before the fireplace.

Tanis hadn't built anything from wood in over a decade, but the itch was starting in her again—now that she had satisfied her urge to make her own pigments and paint her masterpiece.

It hung over the fireplace, an image of a ship passing close to a dim red star, alone in the dark and desperate to survive.

At least that was how she saw it, hopefully so would any others who ever laid eyes upon it.

She stood as Joe strolled into the cabin, dirty and wearing his trademark grin.

"How's the garden doing?" Tanis asked.

"A little worse for my working in it," Joe chuckled.

Tanis doubted his statement. Over the last few decades, Joe had become a consummate gardener, able to grow anything he wanted without bots or nano of any sort.

"Things ready for the party tonight?" he asked.

"Yup, spic and span and ready for our guests," Tanis replied, closing in for a kiss and an embrace.

"It occurred to me that we're having this celebration on the wrong day," Joe said.

"Wrong day? It's New Year's Eve," Tanis replied.

"Yeah, but no one really celebrates that anymore. You just found it in some book from when people used the Gregorian calendar."

"Yeah, so?"

"Well, if we were measuring in Sol standard years, four years ago was the one-hundredth anniversary of our leaving the Sol system."

"Really?" Tanis thought for a moment. "I guess you're right. Well, then there was just the two of us awake. Now we have enough for an actual shindig."

With the *Intrepid* finally drawing near to Kapteyn's Star, a skeleton crew was now out of stasis. After spending over six decades alone on the ship with just Joe, Angela, and Bob; even the few dozen people rattling around the ship felt like enough for the party of a lifetime.

Ouri had been a bit surprised to find her home occupied by new owners. She was also surprised to find her cabin enlarged enough that it had several spare bedrooms. She promptly moved back in.

Terry Chang and Jessica decided that rather than work alone in the SOC they would take up residence in the cabin, as well.

Tanis was certain that a part of their decision related to how dark and empty the ship felt above them. Hundreds of square kilometers of the *Intrepid* were cold and silent. It didn't make for a comfortable working environment.

By comparison, the cylinders were still alive and vibrant, the long sun that ran through each carried its own internal power and would run for centuries. The choice of where to live was a simple one.

In addition to learning a variety of new leisure skills, Tanis had spent much of the past sixty years pouring over every detail of every colonist on the *Intrepid;* as well as the history of every nut, bolt, and panel; looking for the common thread.

All she had now were a thousand threads.

The problem was that many things did stand out as anomalous—though that was expected. However, following up on leads from a hundred and eight years ago while seven light years away from Sol was no simple task.

Especially since the *Intrepid* didn't want to announce that it was off course and behind schedule. Tanis and Bob had made discrete requests of trusted sources back in Sol, looking to get information that could lead them to find out who was behind all of the *Intrepid's* continued problems.

One thing they did know was that after the *Intrepid* left the Sol system, Myrrdan had never been seen or heard from again. They were certain that he was on the ship, though no sign of any other saboteurs or sabotage had appeared in the years since the annihilator explosion.

Tanis was positive that he would not have been behind the near-crash into LHS 1565, unless Collins had been Myrrdan. It was possible, but Tanis felt like Hilda's actions meant he was still on board. There were also a hundred possible ways to link the STR on Jupiter to Myrrdan, but none of them felt right to Tanis.

Everything she knew about the criminal mastermind told her that he liked to watch, he enjoyed toying with people, making them jump through hoops for his amusement.

Granted, Hilda could have been a failsafe for the anti-picotech group, or the knowledge of the forbidden technology had bothered her enough that she had taken matters into her own hands.

After coming out of stasis, Jessica had spent several weeks in near isolation re-examining the data Tanis had received from Earth, looking over every lead, trying to discover the clue that would tell them who or where Myrrdan was. She had not come any closer unearthing any conclusive evidence.

Tanis was certain that Jessica blamed herself for the *Intrepid's* situation. If she had caught Myrrdan, then perhaps some act of sabotage would not have taken place and the ship would not be in the state it was.

It was a feeling Tanis knew all too well. Though she tried to tell herself otherwise, she had awoken every day for the last sixty years knowing that if she were more capable, the *Intrepid* would nearly be at New Eden by now, the colonists all starting their new lives.

"You've got that 'lost in thought' look," Joe smiled as he stroked her long blonde hair.

Tanis brought her focus back to the present and looked into his eyes. "Just thinking about the years."

"You're even more beautiful than when I met you, you know. Even though you're starting to get old," Joe grinned and pinched Tanis' cheek.

"Hey! I'm not the one starting to get crow's feet around my eyes." Tanis pointed at the faint lines around Joe's eyes.

"You said you liked them!" Joe pretended to look hurt.

"I do like them," Tanis smiled. "But they do mean you're getting old."

Other than checkups from an autodoc, neither she nor Joe had received any anti-aging treatments over the years—far longer than the normal two-decade interval between cellular rejuvenation treatments.

The pair had decided it would make for an interesting experiment to see what they would look like as they aged. Aside from Joe's aforementioned crow's feet around his eyes and the odd grey hair on their heads neither appeared to be a day over thirty.

"You may be older than me, but that doesn't get you respect on its own," Joe put on a stern face before breaking into a smile.

"Sure thing, gramps," Jessica said with a raspy voice as she walked into the cabin's main room. "You *have* seen a lot of years in this tube—crazy, long years; that counts for something, I guess."

"You know…I'm only…damnit, something like a hundred and thirty real years. This temporal shit is hard to work out."

"Still just a kid, then," the captain said from the door Joe had left open.

"That's more like it," Joe said. "I bow to age and wisdom."

"That is a wonderful smell," Captain Andrews took a deep breath. "Is that turkey?"

"It sure is, fresh from the pen. I decided to do this right," Joe replied.

<*I hate to say it, but Turkey is not a traditional New Year's Eve meal,*> Angela weighed in.

"Always trying to ruin my fun," Tanis said. "But not this time! Today the gravy is perfect and the stuffing is magnificent. It'll be a night to remember."

Tanis conscripted Jessica and Captain Andrews into setting the table while Joe set out appetizers and prepared drinks for the arriving guests.

Ouri rushed in, waved a quick greeting and dashed up the stairs to change out of her uniform. Terry followed soon after, dressed for a night of relaxation. "That Ouri is a real task-master," she said, after taking a long sip of her martini. "Kept me working till the bitter end."

Tanis laughed. "I can't imagine she's worse than I was."

Terry smiled playfully. "You have no idea. She rules the SOC with an iron fist, no compassion whatsoever."

"I what?" Ouri stood behind Terry with a wounded expression on her face. "I let you leave two hours early today to get your favorite dress out of your storage locker!"

Tanis laughed and Terry turned to give the wounded looking Ouri a hug. "I'm kidding, just making small talk with the dragon lady."

"Hey!" Tanis said. "I resent that."

Ouri chuckled. "You are good at ferreting things out, but you never heard that one did you?"

"What, 'dragon lady'?" Tanis asked.

Joe handed her a sangria, "I remember that, we all referred to you as the DL for your first few months onboard. Ouri lived in constant fear of you."

Tanis knew she came in swinging a hammer, but she'd always felt she was mellow with her select crew. "I thought I was pretty relaxed!"

Terry snorted while drinking and proceeded to have a small coughing fit.

<*Dear…*> Angela laughed in her mind. <*You didn't relax till after the ship left Sol.*>

"And look where that got us," Tanis frowned. Maybe I should have kept my hammer.

"Let's not go there," Joe said. "Tonight is a night of happiness."

Refreshments were brought out and by the time everyone sat down at the table, Terrance, Amanda, Trist, and Earnest had joined the group.

Tanis couldn't help but notice the absence of Abby. For Tanis, their fight had been decades ago, barely remembered. For Abby, it was mere weeks in the past and still fresh in her mind. Tanis hoped they could mend the rift. At least Abby would be able to function professionally—at least as much as she ever did—when the time came.

Joe carved the turkey; Tanis was better at it, but she made him do it because it was quaint and nice to relax after a long day in the kitchen.

After the food was served and people started to tuck in, Captain Andrews stood and conversations stilled as eyes turned to him.

"One hundred and four years," he said with a heavy pause. "Just shy of the original flight time and we're still only halfway to our destination."

People around the table nodded; Terrance looked especially pained.

"But through the efforts of this team, we're still here and we will make it to New Eden. I'm sure that when we all signed on for this mission not a one of us expected to face the types of obstacles we have. Heck, not all of us even expected to *be* on this mission," the captain raised his glass to Jessica who laughed in response.

"But I want to thank you all—" Captain Andrew's speech was interrupted by Bob's voice coming over all of their Links.

<*I've found it!*> Bob was not an AI known for sounding excited, but his voice had that timbre. <*I found the thread that connects everything; it was something that Jessica clued me into.*>

"I did?" Jessica asked.

<*Yes,*> Bob replied. <*It was when you said, 'What if everything is exactly what it appears to have been.'*>

"I remember that…it was decades ago," Jessica ran a hand through her hair. "Have you been considering that for all this time?"

<*No. I thought it was incorrect, just as you did at the time. Instead, I've been rebuilding core data, getting comparison hashes from Sol and working to build a model where it showed that a single entity was responsible for all of our problems. I tried to fit the STR into it, the anti-colonials, Myrrdan, even each of you into the role of the enemy.*>

Several eyebrows raised and the party-goers cast glances around the table. Tanis simply nodded. She had considered each of her fellow revelers as top candidates for the role of villain as well.

<*But no one fit everything. No one had the opportunity or the motive in all the right places, at all the right times. Just staying on the ship through the LHS 1565 stellar passage ruled a lot of people out—and it made Joseph and Tanis much more suspect.*>

Tanis raised her hands and shrugged. "What can I say, you got me."

"Not funny," Captain Andrews frowned.

<*When nothing fit the model, I decided to look at the individuals. I put all of the various players into their slots and turned it on. I had to run it a few hundred million times to get it right because there are a lot of details that we don't know.*

Once I had it right, the model pointed at events we never knew happened. I made discreet inquiries back to Sol and found that those events did indeed happen.>

"Wait..." Tanis interrupted. "Are you saying you made a true reverse prediction model? You can identify and confirm events in the past for which you have no record?"

"That's hardly new," Jessica said. "We used models like that all the time at the TBI."

"I have, too," Tanis nodded slowly. "But this feels different."

<*You are correct, Tanis,*> Bob's even tones flowed through their minds. <*I based my model on the same ones AI in your former investigative units used. However, I made some alterations and achieved a one-hundred percent event confirmation rate.*>

Tanis nodded, Jessica let out a long whistle, and even the captain's ever-stoic expression shifted to one of surprise.

"That's quite the feat," Captain Andrews said. "How many events did you test against?"

<*Why, all of them,*> Bob replied.

A long silence settled over the table as the weight of Bob's words sunk in.

Tanis couldn't help but wonder what sort of thing Bob was becoming. Even though she knew he required a physical housing and power, she found herself thinking his abilities were becoming god-like.

Finally, Joe spoke. "Like... ever, ever?"

<*For all events we can confirm, yes. We cannot confirm the predictive model works for events for which there is no confirmation available,*> Bob replied. <*I have passed the algorithm to several trusted contacts back in Sol and I just received confirmation that they achieved the same results I did. Though it took them several orders of magnitude longer than I to process the data.*>

Tanis wasn't certain, but she detected a tone of smugness in Bob's voice.

<*Just what we need, a smug god,*> Angela commented privately.

"This is going to change a lot of things," Terrance said. "A world where no past event can be secret is a little alarming."

"Especially since there's no reason you couldn't point this model at the future," Earnest said with a frown. "How far out does it work, Bob?"

<*It is impossible to say,*> Bob replied, <*We can't confirm any further into the future than right now, and I only received confirmation of the model's accuracy nine minutes ago. So, it is currently accurate for nine minutes.*>

Joe chuckled. "He'll soon have all our lives mapped out."

"Wow," Jessica said. "They're going to put us cops out of business."

<*It won't work,*> Bob said. <*The algorithm is not accurate enough.*>

"I thought you said it had a one-hundred percent accuracy rate," Tanis said. "How is that not accurate enough?"

<*I rounded up,*> Bob replied. <*It was perfectly accurate for my purposes, but there are individuals for which the algorithm cannot account.*>

"Like me, right?" Tanis asked with a sigh.

<*You are correct, Tanis, you are an anomaly. It also turns out that there are others like you that the model cannot predict. You also spread this unpredictability around you.*>

Joe chuckled. "That sounds about right."

"What events did you get confirmation on?" Tanis asked, hoping to change the subject.

<*Several interactions between some of our saboteurs, anti-colonials, Trent, some mercenaries, and a few other things. The actions themselves aren't important, but what they show is that the model is correct because it said they had to happen, and as it turns out, they did.*>

Joe leaned back in his chair and sipped from his wine glass. "I sense a but."

<*You are correct,*> Bob agreed. <*There was one thing that didn't fit.*>

"Hilda," Tanis and Jessica said together.

They cast sidelong glances at each other and Jessica shook her head ruefully, "I'm not sure who is rubbing off on who here."

<*Yes,*> Bob replied. <*Hilda. There was no way she could have sabotaged the annihilator without an accomplice, and no one on the ship let her out of stasis. This means that someone else, someone not on the ship, let her out and showed her what to do.*>

<*Not on the ship?*> Angela asked. <*Then how did they do it?*>

<*I mean not on the rosters and not having ever appeared to be on the ship,*> Bob clarified his point.

"Then you are referring to Myrrdan," Jessica grimaced. "He could have done this…except that I don't know how he could have done this."

<*He is hiding on the ship. Maybe he never went into stasis at all, or maybe he has his own secret stasis pod that I haven't been able to find. But if I add him with those parameters, the model is perfect. Also, based on how long it took Hilda to commit her sabotage, it allows me to make assumptions about his location. With so few of you awake on the ship, we may be able to find and corner him.*>

"What I don't understand," Terrance interjected. "Is why he destroyed the annihilator. I understand that Hilda would have thought she was saving the day, but how did that help him?"

<*Because he knows about the picotech,*> Bob let the statement land and sink in before he continued. <*I discovered that he was on Mars at the same time that Tanis and Captain Andrews were bringing the tech up to the* Intrepid. *You even encountered him. He wants us to build an industrial base in Kapteyn's because his plan is to get the picotech developed there and flee back to Sol. He doesn't want to be as far away as New Eden when that time comes.*>

"Why go to all this trouble? Could he have not taken the tech in Sol?" Trist asked.

"You have to be in his head, Joe," Jessica said. "He wants the tech developed. After losing it on Mars, he must have realized that the sub-rosa purpose of the New Eden project was to develop the picotech. So here we are, a colony ship going somewhere nice and quiet, with the tech he wants and the ability and plans to develop it. To someone like him, we're a match made in heaven."

Silence settled in around the table as everyone let the fact that their every action since the day they brought the picotech onboard had played right into Myrrdan's hands.

Finally, Earnest spoke. "I thought you said there was one thread. With this proposed timeline, Myrrdan could not have been responsible for the early sabotage, nor was he behind the STR."

"It's that there is no thread," Tanis stood and walked to the fireplace. "We've all believed that there was no way so many disparate forces could be arrayed against us that we had to be missing some commonality. This proves that we were looking in the wrong place—each threat was actually unique."

"That's disheartening," Terrance sighed. "So what is our next move?"

<*Wait, there's more,*> Bob interjected.

"More? This can't be good," Joe sighed.

<*It's about Kapteyn's, it's not empty. The relativistic probe just shot back its first survey, and there appears to be some sort of mining platform moving into the system.*>

"That could make things complicated," Terrance said. "We really don't need Sol finding out that we're off course and out in the middle of nowhere."

"It's not like we have to worry about the *Dakota,* they left Sol a hundred years ago, headed in the other direction," Joe shook his head.

"Probably already at their colony," Trist said.

"There are other colony ships leaving Sol though," Tanis had read the reports Bob pulled in from the Sol system. Outbound colonization had increased drastically. The FGT had recently completed a vast swath of planetary terraforming projects; over a dozen new systems had been opened up.

The political upheaval following the Jovian Independence War was also a contributing factor. Many colony ships were even departing for systems not terraformed by the FGT.

It was possible someone was colonizing Kapteyn's.

"It's strange that it's a mining platform," Earnest mused. "You don't ship a complete platform across interstellar space, you send the tools for a base colony and then assemble your platforms in place. There must be some colony there already."

"Then why didn't the probe spot it?" Captain Andrews asked. "It would have picked up emissions."

"It's pretty damn peculiar," Earnest agreed. "Something is not as it seems in Kapteyn's."

"We should send in a scout mission," Tanis said. "I'll go in with Joe and we'll see what's up."

Terrance and the captain shook their heads.

"I don't think that's the right call," Andrews said. "The *Intrepid* is going to enter that system no matter what, and we need this ship to be prepared for combat, plus we have to ferret out Myrrdan. I can't have my two best military officers on an away mission. One of you needs to stay here and get things ready."

Joe and Tanis stared at each other for a long moment across the table. After spending every day for the past sixty years together, the idea of separating for a day was almost unfathomable, let alone for the two years the mission would require them to be apart. Tanis had spent almost half her life with the man she loved.

Their conversation was formed of emotions and ideas, all passed between eyes, not over the Link. In the end, Tanis sighed.

"I'll go. Jessica and Ouri can do anything I can on the ship, but Joe has to get the squadrons ready to deal with whatever we encounter. Also, if Bob is correct, Myrrdan won't make his move until after we set up in Kapteyn's. I'll take one of the cruisers and a platoon of Marines."

<*I'm right,*> Bob's deep tones reverberated through their minds.

"You'll take me, too," Trist said. "You're going to need some technical backup out there."

<*Excuse me?*> Angela shot Trist a dark look over the Link.

"Well, some additional backup."

There were silent nods around the table as everyone let the knowledge Bob had dropped on them sink in.

Tanis walked back to the table and sat down. "Hey, that's tomorrow's work. Tonight we're going to enjoy this dinner, toast the fact that we're still alive and kicking, and that we have a plan to beat Myrrdan."

"We do?" Joe turned a quizzical eye to his wife.

Tanis tapped the side of her head, "We do indeed."

Many hours later, after the revelry was done and the last drinks around the fireplace were finished, Andrews took Tanis aside.

"The suspense is killing me, what is this plan of yours?" His grey eyes were serious, but a smile played at the corner of his lips. "I know you like to do things off the cuff, but I'll need to be in."

Tanis nodded seriously. "Of course, sir. I don't suspect anyone in this group—I just didn't want to ruin the evening with everyone devolving into planning. The trick is this," Tanis put her hand in his, creating a direct, encrypted link between their minds.

The captain nodded slowly as her plan unfolded. "This could work."

ANDROMEDA

STELLAR DATE: 3265305 / 01.02.4228 (Adjusted Gregorian)
LOCATION: ISS *Andromeda*
REGION: Interstellar space near Kapteyn's Star

Tanis sat on the pristine bridge of the *Andromeda,* one of the *Intrepid's* mid-sized cruisers.

At seven hundred and twenty meters long, it was not the largest ship in the main docking bay, but it had stealth technology which would be more than effective against whatever sensors a mining platform possessed.

The *Intrepid* was another story. It had reversed orientation years ago when the fusion engines began their braking burn. To anyone in the Kapteyn's system, the ship looked as bright as many nearby stars.

Now, with the knowledge of Kapteyn's occupation in hand, the braking had been halted and a new entry plan was in place for the colony ship. It would enact several elliptical polar orbits around The Kap and use the star to slow its entrance. The *Intrepid* would ultimately enter the system on the far side of the star from the platform with a minimum of visible burn.

The *Andromeda* was still close enough to the *Intrepid* for tight-band laser comms and Joe was saying his fourth farewell over the Link.

<Call me a sap, but this is a lot harder than I'd expected it to be,> Tanis could feel the raw emotion in his tone through the mental connection.

<We've spent decades together, what are a few years apart?> Tanis tried to console him, but the words rang hollow to her as well.

<Yeah, I tried that logic too, it worked until I woke up and you weren't there beside me. This ol' log house feels pretty empty without you bustling about.>

Tanis felt a lump swell in her throat and tried to hold back tears. It wouldn't do for her command crew to see her crying on the bridge.

She never expected to fall so deeply in love with a man again—in retrospect she had never really known what love meant.

Angela's warm presence filled her mind and she knew that no matter what, she would never truly be alone. Her meld with Angela had deepened over the years to the point where she never even thought about it anymore—except when she overheard her AI and Bob talking about it.

She could hear their conversation now, nothing to worry about, all plans regarding trajectory and orbital mechanics. Corsia, the ship's AI, was in the conversation, as well, and Tanis looked into her mind through Angela's eyes.

She did all this while still talking to Joe, an ability that barely gave her pause anymore. She knew from the scans that Earnest did on her before the trip that her inter-neural connections were now over fifty percent higher than a non-augmented human—something that should have made her less mentally capable, not more—and that many portions of her brain were directly tied into Angela's neural net.

When Joe mentioned that he poured Tanis a cup of coffee in the morning before remembering she wasn't there, Angela almost cried in Tanis's mind. It startled both of them. Tanis could tell her AI paused her conversation with Bob and Corsia, taking a split second to recover.

Tanis reminded herself that Angela was much younger than she—her AI had spent almost her entire life with Joe nearby. For all intents and purposes, Angela was as married to Joe as she was.

As the two ships reached the point where the relative velocities began to make the laser comm lose fidelity, they said their final farewells.

<*Goodbye Joe, I'll see you in less than two years. It'll be like we were never apart.*>

<*We won't really be,*> Joe replied. <*I couldn't get you out from inside me if I wanted to.*>

<*I'll miss you too, Joe,*> Angela chimed in. <*Take care of yourself, my girl here couldn't live without you.*>

<*I will, I promise.*>

The connection ended and Tanis drew a long breath, catching Trist's eye. Her friend gave her a warm smile and a hug over the Link.

<*We'll have a drink and talk about old times when we're off duty,*> she said.

<*Thanks,*> Tanis replied.

Tanis sat quietly for some time. The pain in her chest and the lump in her throat were going to take some work to overcome.

She tried to regain her composure as she looked around the small bridge. Trist was at the scan and analysis station, running through the external sensor arrays, ensuring that decades of inactivity had not caused any glitches. At the helm was a GSS ensign named Petrov, a capable pilot Joe had hand selected for the mission.

"All engine tests show green," the ship's AI reported over the speakers in the bridge. Tanis found it odd that Corsia preferred to communicate audibly, but that wasn't entirely unusual for an AI. She must have relayed it over the Link elsewhere on the ship because Jim, the chief engineer, chimed in.

<*Stealing my thunder, are you?*> he chuckled.

<*I* ***am*** *the ship. I'm pretty sure it is* ***my*** *thunder anyway,*> Corsia responded.

Tanis had learned that Jim and Corsia had worked together on several ships before they both signed up for the New Eden colony. They had never been embedded together, but they behaved as though they had been.

Tanis checked the reports from the barracks, confirming that the Marines were all in stasis, protected from any hard burns the ship would need to do as it entered The Kap system.

Tanis switched the bridge's main holo to a visual of the *Andromeda's* position relative to the *Intrepid* and The Kap's stellar system.

After undocking from its mother ship, the *Andromeda* had executed several short burns, establishing a trajectory which would take it insystem stellar east, on the far side of the star from the incoming platform. At the same time, the *Intrepid* had executed a burn that would take it over the star's north pole to begin its long elliptical loop.

The ships were now moving apart at a speed of several thousand kilometers per second. That rate would increase dramatically when the *Andromeda* executed its main insystem burn.

"Firing maneuvering thrusters," Petrov reported as he executed the pre-programmed flight path to properly orient the ship in space. "Ready for fusion burn in three minutes."

Tanis gave herself to counting the seconds, keeping her mind off the years that she would spend apart from Joe as they slowly moved into the system.

"Executing burn," Petrov announced as the timer reached zero. Compared to the asteroid run Tanis and Joe had made on the *Excelsior* in the Estrella de la Muerte system, this burn was a mere annoyance at only 10*g*.

It was three hours long, though. Even as a hardy space-farer with the best dampening implants and an acceleration couch, Tanis knew it would be at the edge of bearable.

Probe data showed the mining platform and the system's smaller rocky planet to currently be on the same side of the star. The larger terrestrial planet, along with several small icy worlds on the system's outskirts, were opposite the approaching platform.

The *Andromeda* would pass those worlds first, scanning for signs of civilization—though Tanis didn't expect to find any.

Though the star was reasonably close to Sol, no colonies had ever formed here—mainly because there were more ideal locations closer to humanity's home star. The FGT terraforming ships had flown past The Kap with barely a thought to the old red dwarf.

To Tanis's knowledge, they had never terraformed a world orbiting a star as far down the main sequence as The Kap.

So who was here?

Chances were that if the system was settled, there would be satellites which would ultimately spot the *Andromeda.* Hopefully, at that point, enough information would be in hand so she could formulate a plan.

Those worries were still well over a year away. The following five-hundred days would be consumed by the slow, elliptical entry into the system.

Tanis had not decided if she would go into stasis for the duration of the trip. Back on the *Intrepid,* Joe would not be going under. He planned to spend the time readying his pilots for whatever they might face in The Kap system.

The three hours of burn passed by slowly, and when it was completed, the crew ran final tests before reporting to their assigned stasis chambers. Two hours later, Tanis was the last person awake on the ship.

She realized she was avoiding even the thought of stasis, finding small tasks to complete beforehand. She examined her thoughts and realized it was nearly a phobia.

"Who would blame me?" she whispered to herself. "Every time I go under, something horrible happens."

<Don't kid yourself,> Angela's tone had a wry humor to it. *<Lots of horrible things have happened to you when you were out of stasis, too.>*

Tanis laughed, "Too true, I've had my share. I guess it's not that I fear stasis, I just don't want to wake up alone anymore."

She decided to stay awake.

The time wore on slowly. Tanis had long conversations with Angela and Corsia about every topic she could think of, read several dozen books, watched hundreds of vids, and took up blacksmithing in the ship's small machine shop.

Her early attempts didn't turn out well, but she managed to make a pair of small knives which had excellent balance and held an edge as well as steel could.

Mostly, especially as the trip wore on, she found herself staring out the windows in the port lounge, watching Kapteyn's Star get brighter.

She was surprised at how comforting it was to have a star nearby, slowly getting brighter. Unlike LHS 1565, which was barely larger than Jupiter, Kapteyn's Star was a third the size of Sol and had a much more bluish light than Sol or a younger red dwarf.

"Can you believe this star is nearly as old as the universe itself?" Tanis asked no one in particular.

<*Just a billion or two years after, yeah,*> Corsia responded.

"Imagine what it has seen. When it was young, the cosmos as all dust and heat…quasars shining everywhere."

<*I don't think it saw much of anything; it is a star, after all,*> the ship's AI replied.

"A lot of people think stars are sentient…in their own way."

<*Like a cloud would wonder if a rock was sentient. The rock may be, but it has no way to relate that to a cloud. A star's single thought or word could take the span of human existence.*>

"True, but what a word it would be." Tanis knew she sounded a bit crazy—but she also knew that the way she was thinking was normal for humans in isolation. "Imagine it staring into the oncoming Milky Way galaxy for millions of years as its tiny dwarf galaxy faced destruction from our massive spiral. Now it's trapped, orbiting the core of its destroyer, still moving opposite all the other stars around it."

The AI didn't respond and Tanis continued to reflect on the star. The dim, red light in the darkness of space had witnessed the end of its own galaxy, it would witness the eventual collision of the Milky Way and Andromeda—and eventually the merger of all the galaxies in the Virgo super-cluster.

And then, as the universe accelerated apart it would eventually find itself alone; with no light from other stars reaching it and none of its light reaching any other star. Until, at the end, it would run out of fuel and, in one final sputter, blink out. Nothing more than a slowly expanding cloud of hot gas in a cold, lightless universe.

<*OK, you're getting a bit too melancholy,*> Angela said to Tanis. <*What this star does or does not witness in ten billion years doesn't really matter; but if you want, we can make a little "Tanis was here" plaque and put it in orbit.*>

"You're funny, for an AI," Tanis's tone was droll. "I know I shouldn't lose myself like this, it's just at times I feel as though we'll never reach the end of this journey. We'll just drift forever in space like this little star, and eventually I'll be alone with no one else."

<*I know I'm no substitute for a human, but you'll always have me. As long as this shell of yours continues to pump blood and make electrolytes, I'll be here.*>

Tanis felt a tear streak down her cheek. "You're more to me than just any companion, Angela. You're as close to me as my very self." She let out a self-deprecating laugh. "I don't know what's wrong with me, I never used to be this soft."

<*You've a lot more to live for now,*> Angela replied. <*You've come a long way since the Toro court martial.*>

"I suppose I have. That was not one of my better days," Tanis let out a long sigh and closed her eyes. <*I'm glad you'll always be with me—which is good since we're inseparable now.*>

<*Don't get too concerned, I can still tell where you end and I begin.*>

PURSUIT

STELLAR DATE: 3266048 / 01.14.4230 (Adjusted Gregorian)
LOCATION: ISS *Andromeda*
REGION: Kapteyn's Star System

Tanis stared into the holotank's depths, while basking in the refreshing change human companionship had made after two years with only Angela and Corsia for company.

"If I were hiding out in this system—and I don't know why I'd ever do something like that—I'd maintain a lookout here." Commander Brandt pointed at a small dwarf planet orbiting the star at a distance of 4.5AU.

The *Andromeda* was just under 6AU from the stellar primary and 3AU prograde from the planet Brandt was pointing at.

"With our braking wash pointed directly at the star, there's no way they'd spot us then," Lieutenant Smith said.

"We haven't picked anything up from that world," Tanis said. "Either they haven't seen us, or no one is there."

"I have to say," Brandt shook her head, "this is pretty weird. We ignored this stupidly named star for over two thousand years and then the *very same year* we show up, someone else is mucking around in here? With a mining platform no-less?"

"Yeah, it smells," Tanis agreed. "That's why we're out here taking a look. I can promise you one thing: whoever these people are, there's no way they're expecting the *Intrepid*."

"Let's hope not. Though, from what I can see about how things have evolved over the last century, interstellar traffic has increased a lot; people may be more prepared for visitors than they used to be."

"Traffic may be up, but it's all to and from Sol. There aren't a lot of ships moving between other systems, with the exception of Alpha Centuari, Sirius, and Tau Ceti," Trist added. "Certainly nothing through here, and definitely not anything from where we were."

"No point in speculating further on why they're here, other than asking them," Tanis said. "The *Intrepid* is still weeks away from entering its polar orbit. I think we should continue our plan to loop around the star, and then break away to swing past that little world."

"Are you sure we should hide ourselves so much?" Trist asked. "I mean, I'm the thief here, but I can't help wonder if we just announce ourselves maybe we'll get a warm welcome."

Tanis leaned back in her chair. Perhaps Trist was right; Tanis had become jaded over the years, expecting everything to be a threat.

"You may be right, Trist, but it's not a chance I can take. I do promise that I'll try diplomacy before violence. I've had my fill of being shot at."

*****

The next few days were uneventful as the ship drifted insystem, approaching the star for a slingshot back outsystem. The bridge crew fell silent as the *Andromeda* skirted past the outer reaches of Kapteyn's corona and got its first clear look at the space beyond in almost a week.

Scan updated and the holographic projection of the stellar system refreshed, showing the innermost terrestrial planet the mining platform was moving toward, and the platform itself.

Since the *Intrepid's* probe had first spotted it, the platform had slowed considerably and was close to entering an orbit around the world. Tanis couldn't help but wonder why a platform that appeared to be built for asteroid mining was moving toward a world. She voiced the question since she knew it was on all their minds.

"Beats me," Trist shrugged. "It doesn't even seem to have a load, although it is a big one—and well-fitted, too. Definitely not some old scow.

"Is it emitting any sort of ID or call sign?" Tanis asked.

"Nothing," Trist replied. "Its engines are the only emission, it—"

<*I've picked up another blip,*> Corsia interrupted. <*It's moving insystem, following the same trajectory as the platform. It's smaller and moving faster.*>

"That's an interesting development," Tanis mused. "One of these two may be friendly to us—or we could find ourselves in the middle of an unpleasant conflict."

"That seems like a leap," Trist commented.

"Anyone following right behind you, but moving faster is pursuing. Especially when the first is not emitting any signals."

"Do you think they can see us?" Petrov asked.

"If they look right at us, yes," Tanis replied. "Let's hope they don't."

The *Andromeda* took thirty minutes to arc around the star and pass behind it again. During the passage, Corsia released a small probe that would gather information and relay it whenever it orbited around the star.

"Now let's check out this other world," Tanis reviewed Petrov's burn and vector, approving his calculations, as did Corsia.

"I doubt we'll find anything there," Command Brandt said. "My guess is that the platform and whoever is chasing it just got here themselves."

"That's my thought, as well," replied Tanis. "But since our trajectory was pretty much set, we may as well be prudent. We're going to have to arc out a bit to brake, anyway."

In the end, Tanis decided to angle above the dwarf planet and brake slowly, hiding their wash as much as possible. This would allow them to change course more rapidly if the dwarf planet was empty and they needed to get back to the platform in a hurry.

The closer they got, the more apparent it was that the dwarf was barren.

A day later, their suspicions were confirmed. While the small world held the ruins of some robotic survey machines, there was no sign of any recent activity on the gray and pitted surface.

"Either there is something really well hidden there, or this is what it looks like, an empty planet."

<*The platform is transmitting,*> Corsia said before playing the message over the bridge's audible systems.

"Mayday, mayday, this is the *Hyperion* calling the unknown ship in this system. We caught your shadow once or twice, please be out there, we need your assistance. We have children on board and they plan to kill us!"

Several variations of the message played and then the first repeated. The bridge crew looked to Tanis for a decision. She leaned back into her chair and considered her options—there really weren't any.

"Petrov, kiss this rock, we need a tight slingshot and maximum v back toward that platform. Trist, once we're pointed in the right direction, I want a tight-lens comm opened up with the *Hyperion*. Corsia, have you picked up any blips from the *Intrepid*?"

<*Yes, I can see them from where we are now. Their engine wash is pointed this way, away from the* Hyperion *and its pursuer. It's just under forty AU stellar south of Kapteyn's Star. They will arrive at the star in a week at their current rate of deceleration.*>

"Should give us enough time to sort this out," Tanis turned to Brandt. "This could get hairy before it gets better."

The commander nodded. "We're ready, sir."

Tanis found that she really liked Brandt. The compact woman was capable and solid—probably because she had spent half a century as a sergeant master before moving to an officer track.

"How are things with the *Andromeda's* loadout?"

"As good as we can get them. When we get to Victoria we'll have upgraded all the rock shooting lasers to ship shooting lasers. The thumpers already have great guidance systems, so all we have to do is make sure we can fire them fast enough. I don't see that being a problem either."

"Then I'm going to get a bit of rest," Tanis rose. "Trist, ping me when you have that tight comm band."

"Aye, sir!" Trist gave a mock salute and a grin.

"You're getting there," Tanis returned the smile. "Eventually I'll make a real military girl out of you."

"Ha! Not very likely."

*****

Tanis lay on the bed in the captain's quarters—a small cabin just aft of the bridge. Even after all the years on the *Intrepid*, she still marveled at the fact that a ship the size of the *Andromeda*, with its own quarters, medical facilities and general ship amenities, was just one of a dozen cruisers docked in the colony ship.

It was a significant fleet in its own right—except where the *Intrepid* was headed, it wasn't supposed to have needed a fleet—at least not a military fleet. The ships were designed for shooting asteroids and hauling supplies, not fighting off mining platforms or whoever it was that chased them.

Tanis wondered where the platform came from. There didn't appear to be any industrial base in the system capable of building it. Just the few ancient survey and robotic installations scattered amongst The Kap's worlds.

Normally, a platform would mean some in-system settlement and industry to build and maintain it, as well as ships and infrastructure to refine and move the resultant materials to a system capable of consuming them. The Kapteyn's system had none of those things.

The only real possibility was that the platform had entered from outsystem. It was both obvious and highly improbable at the same time

INTERSTELLAR

STELLAR DATE: 3266049 / 01.15.4230 (Adjusted Gregorian)
LOCATION: ISS *Andromeda*
REGION: Kapteyn's Star System

"What have we learned?"

It was three hours later and Tanis entered the bridge refreshed and ready, come what may. She intended to give the crew the shift off and man things herself while they rested.

"I was just about to call you," Trist reported. "The platform has continued to send its mayday and we're lined up with a tight comm beam. You're good to transmit whenever you're ready."

Tanis nodded and sat in the captain's chair.

"*Hyperion,* this is the *Andromeda.* We've received your mayday and are prepared to assist. Coordinates are included in this transmission. Please reply on a tight beam with more details about your situation."

She checked the time lag and saw that the round-trip call would take roughly an hour.

"Wrap up what you have going on and take a break. I can cover things here for the next couple of hours," Tanis instructed the crew.

To pass the time, she pulled up the course Petrov had plotted. It had the *Andromeda* dropping directly into Kapteyn's Star, building speed up to nearly 0.11*c* before breakaway and deceleration. The *Andromeda* would arrive at Victoria with enough *v* to either brake around the terrestrial world, or continue on to engage with the cruiser pursuing the *Hyperion*.

The maneuver would use a lot of fuel, but Tanis appreciated the expedient approach. The close passage to the star should allow the *Andromeda* to scoop up some additional isotopes and recoup most of what they would burn. She hoped they could replenish enough for maneuvering if they had to engage with the *Hyperion's* pursuer.

While she couldn't count on it, she expected that the enemy cruiser would be low on fuel, or, at best, no better off than the *Andromeda.* She had never heard of a cruiser equipped for interstellar travel—chances were that this one had left its home system in a hurry.

The crew finished their assigned tasks and left the bridge to get some rest. Tanis took a bite of her BLT and settled back in her chair as the *Andromeda* raced toward The Kap.

A stellar braking maneuver was not much different than a slingshot. Instead of delivering maximum propulsion as the ship passed closest to the star, the *Andromeda* would fire for maximum braking. As a result, the most force possible would be delivered over the longest distance possible. Afterward, they would deploy the ramscoop at its maximum size and use it as a giant reverse sail, slowing the ship further.

Tanis wished she had Joe to double-check the trajectory. This was not the sort of approach ships made as a matter of general practice. A single mistake and the *Andromeda* would burn up in The Kap's corona.

<*You're just nervous about another red star filling the forward view,*> Angela commented.

<*You're probably not wrong about that. It's somewhat disconcerting.*>

<*Well, at least it's a lot brighter than Estrella de la Muerte.*>

Tanis chuckled. Chances are the star would go down in history with that name.

<*You've been quiet lately,*> Tanis said after a pause. <*What's been going on?*>

<*I've been trying to calculate what you might do in the upcoming situation.*>

Tanis was surprised. She imagined that AI tried to calculate what organics would do quite often; they were probably better at it than the humans themselves. However, it was not something she expected to cause them much concern, or take up much of their time.

<*Why the interest—outside of the usual?*> she asked.

Angela gave a mental laugh, not something she often did. <*Your paths are hard to predict. Bob thinks you have luck and I'm trying to test his theories.*>

It was Tanis's turn to laugh. <*Bob thinks I'm lucky? I didn't know AI subscribed to things like luck.*> She had overheard Angela and Bob discussing luck in the past, but never realized they were being entirely serious.

<*We don't,*> Angela's tone was sober. <*But Bob is convinced, or nearly convinced, that you have scientifically demonstrable luck.*>

<*He'd better check his facts,*> Tanis sighed. <*I'm probably the scientific embodiment of bad luck. Toro, the attacks on the* Intrepid*, the sabotage, now this little conflict in what is supposed to be an empty system getting in the way of our repairs. Luck is the last thing I have.*>

<*Bob doesn't think that a person can see their own luck. He also thinks it only comes into play after events start, it cannot stop the onset of an event,*> Angela's tone was one of a person relaying statements she did not entirely subscribe to.

<*What manifestation does he think it takes?*> Tanis was becoming annoyed by the conversation.

<*I know, it's far-fetched,*> Angela conceded. <*Bob thinks it's some sort of pattern in your mind, something either achieved by the neurons, or the subatomic particles making up your mind. He has a variety of theories, most having to do with quantum interdimensional transience.*>

<*Has he gone insane?*> Tanis snorted. <*That sounds like some serious mumbo-jumbo.*>

<*It's more impressive when he shows his calculations. It doesn't really translate to words very well. Suffice to say that I don't doubt his sanity, he has exabytes of data accumulated now and there is some compelling evidence.*>

<*This is going to ruin me,*> Tanis said. <*Now I'll constantly be second-guessing myself, wondering if what I'm doing is rational, or just luck.*>

<*I have to admit, he's going to be displeased that I told you this, it will alter his experiment.*>

<*I'm no experiment!*> Tanis said in her mind while throwing her arms in the air.

<*I agree, that's why I told you.*>

Angela promised not to bring it up again and Tanis did her best to put it from her mind, yet she couldn't help reviewing events in her life, wondering which Bob considered lucky.

She couldn't imagine that anyone would want her life, Toro alone would see to that, but maybe there was something to it. She couldn't even count the number of times she should have died, but there had been good times too. Spending sixty years with Joe on the *Intrepid* had made up for a lot of bad. Not a lot of people got over half a century of peace and quiet with someone they love.

She pulled her thoughts back to the task at hand—considering the origin of the platform and the pursuing cruiser. Based on their trajectories, both had braked around the larger terrestrial world in the outer system.

Corsia added the energy expended in their braking maneuver to her origin algorithm. Scopes picked up a few notable elements and the model showed Sirius as a near certainty.

Tanis wasn't surprised. The aristocracy there had been oppressing their working class for centuries. In Sol their treatment of citizens would have been illegal, but in Sirius it was the norm.

Her thoughts were interrupted by the platform's reply—her questions would be answered soon enough.

The message included video and Tanis pulled it up on the holo. The face she saw surprised her. The man was old. Not decrepit, but aged, with lines and creases in his skin, gray hair, tired eyes. Tanis had seen few people like this in her life—it was different than Andrew's aging. The captain was aging, but he still moved like a young man and his skin was clear and smooth. Aging with no rejuvenation at all—*naturally*—was a great way to get branded as a throwback.

"Thank you for responding to our call, *Andromeda*. I'm Governor Markus of the *Hyperon*. We're refugees escaping from the Sirius system. We didn't expect the Luminescents to chase us, but they sent a cruiser and intend to make an example of us to other platforms."

The man glanced at someone standing outside the holo's view and then turned back to face Tanis and continued.

"We honestly didn't expect to find anyone here in Kapteyn's but are glad we have. I hope that you will find it in your heart to help us."

The transmission also included details of the platform—its loadout, population, defenses and other general specifications. Also included were some specifications on the cruiser pursuing the mining platform.

Tanis studied the cruiser first. It was smaller than the *Andromeda* at only five hundred meters. But where the *Andromeda,* was built with peacefully establishing a colony in mind, the Sirius cruiser was built for war.

Tanis whistled softly. The specs showed two forty-centimeter lasers, each capable of delivering 10 megawatts of energy per square centimeter at twenty-thousand kilometers. The *Andromeda* had no ablative plating; its exterior was only marginally refractive. Its hull wouldn't last ten seconds under the glare of those beams.

<*We need ice,*> Angela said.

"And lots of it," Tanis replied out loud.

She pulled up detailed listings of all stellar objects near their current trajectory, searching for a comet or asteroid that would serve their purpose.

<*I found it,*> Angela beat her to it. <*It's about a quarter AU off our current trajectory, but it can work.*>

Tanis agreed. <*Corsia, call everyone back up here, we have work to do.*>

PUSHING ICE

STELLAR DATE: 3266050 / 01.16.4230 (Adjusted Gregorian)
LOCATION: ISS *Andromeda*
REGION: Near Victoria, Kapteyn's Star System

The holo tank showed two people this time.

The first was Markus and the second was a woman he had introduced as Katrina. She appeared to be much younger than Markus, but the way they moved and looked at one another implied more than just a platonic relationship.

"I must say again that I cannot believe our luck in finding you here," Markus said. The statement made Tanis wonder about Bob and his luck theory for a moment.

"It certainly wasn't something either of us was expecting," Tanis replied.

Katrina's eyes narrowed. "You're not going to tell us why you're here in Kapteyn's, are you?"

Tanis smiled and shook her head. "I know it's not the best way to start our new friendship, but it's the way it's going to be for now. You're going to have to satisfy yourself with our offer of help."

"I do find myself wondering whether you'll remain our friends once you've dealt with our pursuers," Markus said plainly.

"You have nothing but my assurances, and the fact that we're taking a lot of risk helping you out here, our lives are all going to be on the line alongside yours—more so as we'll be taking the brunt of the assault." Tanis knew that it was not the strongest assurance she could offer, but it was the best she was going to give them at present.

A look exchanged between the two and the mic muted while they spoke a few words.

<*Money on him not having Link,*> Trist said from her station. <*I caught her tells twice, but he looked down at something, probably a hand screen of some sort.*>

<*I've heard the working class in Sirius is pretty low-tech. It's very possible he doesn't have any implants at all,*> Tanis replied.

On the holo, Markus made a gesture and spoke. "Very well, we will trust you." He grimaced, "It's not as though we have much choice."

"Fate makes strange bedfellows of us all," Tanis quoted some old saying she recalled hearing once. She laid out her plan as Markus and Katrina nodded and asked questions.

All in ali, it was relatively simple. She had already begun deploying comm buoys around the planet Victoria and its largest moon, Anne, to keep communication flowing during the upcoming battle.

Two platoons of marines would depart for the platform where they would bolster *Hyperion's* internal defenses and install several portable missile batteries.

The other two platoons were in full powered armor ready for a hostile assault. The little data Tanis had available showed her that Sirius's harsh dictatorship had experienced little real conflict, whereas there was always a war somewhere in Sol. The force her marines could bring to bear should devastate the enemy.

If she could hold out against their superior warship long enough.

Throughout the conversation, Katrina and Markus relayed information about their pursuer, a man named Yusuf.

"We thought that once we made our slingshot around Sirius we'd be free and clear," Markus said. "But Yusuf had three cruisers and brought them past in a high-*v* attack as we were accelerating outsystem."

Tanis nodded with understanding. It wasn't dissimilar to what the STR had done to the *Intrepid* as it was leaving Sol.

"We evaded most of their missiles and beams, more because their weapons systems aren't designed to track targets when relative *v* becomes relativistic," Katrina added.

"*Hyperion* took a few hits, one of which damaged our limited supply of cryopods." Markus said.

<*Did he say 'cryo',*> Trist asked. <*They're not just backward, they're barbaric!*>

<*Cryostasis isn't as bad as the vids would have you believe,*> Angela said. <*They failed only one in a thousand uses.*>

<*Like that is supposed to make me feel better. Stasis has a zero percent failure rate.*>

<*Not zero,*> Tanis said and turned her attention back to the *Hyperion's* leaders.

"As a result, many of us rotated through stasis while en route, a few of us stayed out for the entire trip," Markus said.

"It's made for more than a few issues," concern washed across Katrina's face. "But seeing a generation of children grow up during our journey was really amazing."

Markus smiled and Tanis wondered if any of the children were theirs.

"I would imagine that you must have overcrowding issues at this point," Tanis added.

"It's a big platform," Markus gave a wry smile. "When we're not breaking up rocks and running a refinery we have a lot of room to spare."

"You said there were three cruisers in pursuit in Sirius. Do we need to worry about more of Yusuf's friends showing up?"

Katrina shook her head. "From what we were able to discern, the three cruisers met and likely transferred fuel and stasis pods to Yusuf's ship, the *Strident Arc*. He then performed his own slingshot and began his pursuit."

"It gave us nearly a year lead in the beginning of the voyage, but he's steadily closed that over the decades."

Tanis nodded slowly and then moved on.

"How are your people going to react to our Marines coming over?" Tanis asked bluntly. When had she mentioned it earlier, a look of concern crossed Markus's face—as it did once again.

He gave a heavy sigh. "It's going to be a bit of a challenge. Our people have never seen an armored soldier who did not represent their oppressors."

"And I would not blame them," Tanis nodded. "What you need to convince them of is that they are now going to witness how the Sirian military is nothing more than school-yard bullies when compared to real space force. You've brought in the big guns, and those guns are on your side."

Katrina gave a slight smile at the speech and spoke softly so that those around her would not hear. "I hate to say it, Captain Richards, but I believe that Yusuf has the bigger guns here."

Tanis chuckled. "Yeah, but that makes for an awful pep talk."

<*I can't believe she beat me to that,*> Angela said. <*My sarcasm must be slipping.*>

"Either way, I'm not going to let some puffed up administrator from an over-hyped backwater best me. I've fought better with fewer resources and come out on top every time. I know you have no reason to trust me, but believe me, I have some tricks up my sleeve. We won't be the ones dead in space when this is over."

"Would you care to share the details of your plan?" Markus asked. The expression Katrina's face showed she already knew Tanis's answer.

"No, I cannot. While I feel an instinctual trust for the two of you, it does not extend to your entire population, nor every computer on your ship. Lives rely on the element of surprise. However, when the Marines arrive, they will give you some more details.

After some final pleasantries, Tanis severed the connection.

"The big guns, eh?" Brandt asked from the entrance to the bridge. "That was quite the pitch."

"I liked the part about Sirius being a backwater and all that, you had some good posturing going on there," Trist giggled.

Petrov gave Trist a surprised look. Despite the fact that Petrov had been working with the crew for several months, he still had issues with the amount of familiarity and lack of discipline Trist showed.

Tanis saw Trist cast a sidelong glance at Petrov and realized she was trying to get a rise out of him. Given what she knew of Trist, this was probably the woman's way of flirting. It would do her well. Tanis was certain Trist hadn't been in any relationships since she her best friend died on the Cho.

Tanis switched the main holo tank to show the local space around the *Andromeda* and studied the image.

Tanis saw that the *Hyperion* platform had settled into a high polar orbit around Victoria. Everything was nearly in place. The last piece was for their enemy to enter range.

Tanis wondered what the leadership of the *Intrepid* would think of her plan. The colony ship was certainly watching the conflict play out—with a light hour of delay.

It was a dangerous game. Letting word get out to the human sphere that the *Intrepid* was still on its way to New Eden could cause some other ship to lay claim to the system. It meant the cruiser from Sirius could not find out that the *Intrepid* was entering the Kapteyn's system; it would have to be disabled before the colony ship arrived.

Privately, Tanis had considered and reconsidered her options. Helping the *Hyperion* was the right thing to do—especially now that she felt a bit of kinship with Markus and Katrina—though the risk was not insignificant.

While she put on a brave face to the *Hyperion* leadership, Tanis knew that her plan was far from foolproof and could see them all dead.

The safest course of action was to do nothing. Let the cruiser destroy the *Hyperion* platform and then wait for it to leave.

<*Never mind the tens of thousands who'd die, there's no guarantee that the* Strident Arc *would leave the system without finding us,*> Angela weighed in.

<*Or that they'd not spot the* Intrepid,> Tanis added.

Tanis suspected that someone who chased a mining platform for over four decades between the stars, then destroyed, it would want to control the story carefully. That would require no witnesses.

<*I know that fight is the only option…I just thought I'd left all that behind,*> Tanis laughed inwardly. <*I sound like a petulant child. Life is what it is.*>

<*You never know,*> Angela said. <*Maybe this is your luck.*>

<*Right, for once I wish that my luck wasn't solely for the benefit of others. It takes a lot out of me.*>

She turned her attention back to the holo tank. The *Arc* was a half a million kilometers from Victoria and Tanis decided to send her first direct message to the inbound ship.

"Ship identified as *Strident Arc.* This is Captain Richards of the *Andromeda,* please respond."

Tanis determined not to use her full name or military rank in case the enemy determined who she was and sent the information back to Sirius. Corsia was altering her appearance in the data stream so that it would not be possible for an analysis system to determine who she was.

The ships were close enough that it only took a few seconds for the response to arrive.

"Captain Richards, I am Vice President Yusuf." The man on the holo looked as urbane as they came, his tone was even and belied no emotion—or even interest. "I require that you remove your ship to a distance no closer than one AU from the *Hyperion,* this is Luminescent government business."

"Vice President Yusuf," Tanis replied, allowing her forehead to wrinkle with a slight scowl, "this system is under my control and protection per interstellar law."

The law was a bit squishy regarding who owned a system. Mostly it was by whoever showed up first and held onto it, but there were statutes and principles that everyone claimed to acknowledge.

"I'm going to have to ask you to cease your aggression against the *Hyperion,* which I have granted asylum, and leave the Kapteyn's system. You may loop around the star, gather volatiles and then leave."

Yusuf's cultured expression showed a few cracks and indignance peeked through as he listened to Tanis's response. He smoothed his expression before responding, but she could tell that he had no patience for people he viewed as his lessers.

"Let's be honest, Captain Richards. Your ship is no match for mine. Furthermore, I do not recognize your authority, or your ability to grant asylum. I am here to regain my property in whatever way I see fit. If you interfere, you will be destroyed."

Tanis smiled sweetly in response. "I was hoping you'd say that. I don't have a lot of patience for people that kill innocent civilians or consider them property. Although, it seems rash to assume I'm alone here."

With that, Tanis cut the connection and turned to Trist. "How long until we're in lethal range of their beams?"

"Nine minutes. I have our orbit timed so we'll pass behind the moon, Anne, before we come into range. They should be in position to fire on us when we re-emerge."

"Very good," Tanis said.

"Did you expect anything to come out of that exchange?" Brandt asked.

Tanis shook her head. "Not really, but I think you should at least look someone in the eye before you shoot them out of the dark."

Brandt chuckled as she stood and saluted at Tanis. "I'm going to join my Marines. We'll be in position when you call."

The minutes stretched on. The bridge crew shifted in their seats, tested systems, and confirmed communications channels. Trist rose to get a cup of coffee and stopped to talk with Petrov for a minute. Tanis stood as well, carefully stretching her limbs, all too aware how the stress and pressure of combat would cause her to tense and clench muscles.

Thus far, the timing appeared to be perfect. The *Strident Arc's* trajectory had it on course for the L1 point between Victoria and its largest moon. The *Andromeda* was in an elliptical orbit around Anne and would pass behind the moon before the *Arc* was within effective firing range.

<I'm registering a few light hits,> Corsia reported.

Tanis expected that. The *Arc's* beams would not do any damage at this range, but the enemy could test their effectiveness, as well as the reflective and ablative properties of the *Andromeda's* hull.

<To be expected,> Tanis replied. *<No damage from the shots?>*

<An outer seal on one of the starboard airlocks is melted, and an auxiliary antenna is not responding. Otherwise we're fine.>

<Nothing like feeling you're in a tin can about to meet a can-opener,> Trist commented.

<Hey, that's me you're talking about!> Corsia retorted.

Tanis smiled and shook her head. Corsia identified her ship as her body more than most AI. It surprised Tanis that Corsia would let her put her precious skin in such peril.

<She knows the odds,> Angela said. *<She trusts you.>*

The statement took Tanis by surprise. Trust was not a word AI often used. She found herself wondering if Corsia did actually trust her, or if Angela was becoming more human because of her intertwining with Tanis's mind.

Did that mean she was becoming more like an AI herself?

<I wouldn't sweat it,> Angela's soft laugh echoed through her mind. *<You spent four weeks making paint pigments from plants. No AI would do that.>*

<Safe for now, eh?> Tanis asked.

<I think so. Like I said, I can tell where you end and I begin.>

<Except that you can read all my thoughts.>

Angela's avatar in her mind crossed her arms and cocked her head. Tanis realized that she always saw Angela's avatar when they communicated now. Perhaps it was just her mind's way of coping with sharing its thoughts with another consciousness.

<I can't read all your thoughts,> Angela smiled. *<This is as weird for me to say as it likely is for you to hear, but I can* ***feel*** *them.>*

<You're right. That is weird. Anyway, since you were listening in, why is it that Corsia trusts me? You said she knows the odds, but I know those odds, too. They're below what an AI would typically accept when their life was on the line.>

<Let's just say that Bob had a chat with her.>

Tanis sighed aloud and Trist glanced at her. Tanis waved her hand and pointed at her head with a wry smile. Trist laughed and nodded. Her own AI often made for interesting internal conversation, as well.

Back in her mind, Tanis imagined herself shaking a finger at Angela. *<Not the luck thing again!>*

<You act like I could have stopped him.>

Tanis knew that wouldn't have been possible and decided to put the whole exchange out of her mind, pulling her focus back to the present.

In thirteen seconds they would pass behind the moon and be hidden from the *Strident Arc*. That's when things would get interesting.

Tanis counted the seconds in her mind, noting as Corsia showed two more probing shots from the *Arc.* The projections held up; when the *Andromeda* passed beyond the moon, it would be in lethal range of the enemy ship's beams.

She flipped the holo tank to show a visual from the ship's bow, checking the reports from four of the *Hyperion's* tugs to see that the preparations were complete.

Everything checked out and she smiled as the large icy asteroid came into view. Oblong in shape, it was just over two kilometers long. The tugs had spent several hours pulling it into place and hollowing out an *Andromeda*-shaped cavity.

It was snug, but it would do the trick.

Fusion engines flared and four tugs began pushing the ice-shield, working to match velocities with the *Andromeda.* Tanis tapped into the data stream between the ships, impressed with the precision the *Hyperion's* tugs showed as they worked with Petrov and Corsia.

Ice filled the forward view screen and Tanis accessed the feeds from the remote observers, placing the visual on the bridge's main holo.

It was a dangerous maneuver, and Tanis hoped it would work. They only had one chance to get in the ice. If they failed, the *Arc* would destroy them without a fight.

She widened the view, including the moon and the enemy vessel. A line showed where and when the *Arc* would have a firing solution. The *Andromeda* would cross that line in seven minutes.

Trist, Corsia, and the *Hyperion's* tugs worked in concert to line the ship up. Tanis listened in, and after several tense minutes of vector matching the ship was lined up with its new shell.

The ship's nose slid into the ice cavern and Corsia fired grapples into the walls. The tugs and the *Andromeda* ceased all thrust, allowing momentum to carry the ship forward at one meter per second. Corsia and Petrov carefully slowed the ship with maneuvering thrusters until the forward docking clamps gently met ice.

The holo showed less than one minute to spare.

Trist wiped her brow and leaned back in her seat. "Made it without a scratch," she smiled.

"Thank the tug captains and tell them to get into position," Tanis replied.

As the *Andromeda,* sheathed in its new ice shell, emerged from behind the moon, two of the tugs latched onto the ice and fired their thrusters, spinning the ship and its shell on its axis.

When the *Arc* fired on the *Andromeda* it wouldn't hit the same spot for more than a second.

"Have I ever mentioned that I hate space travel?" Trist said, looking queasy.

As expected, the moment the *Andromeda's* ice-sheathed bow passed beyond the moon it was hit by laser fire. Tanis reviewed the two ship's relative positions. Both were exactly where she had planned.

The *Arc* was facing directly toward the *Andromeda,* aligned to present a smaller target, its two main beams lashing out across the darkness, finding not the ship they expected, but what appeared to be a spinning ice asteroid.

Ice boiled off the *Andromeda's* ablative covering into the vacuum of space as the *Arc's* beams cut long gashes across its surface.

Tanis calculated the rate of dissipation and determined the ice-shield would hold up for at least fifteen minutes of continuous fire. Beyond that, it would be structurally compromised and would fracture.

The tugs had bored holes for the *Andromeda's* weapons and Tanis let fire with several shots of her own. She targeted every beam at what they could see of the *Arc's* port engine. Each weapon fired for a second as the ship rotated. Once they had drained their batteries, a measurable amount of ablative plating had been burned away from the *Arc*.

"Commence your burn, Ensign," Tanis issued the command to Petrov and the *Andromeda* boosted away from Anne toward Victoria.

More ice boiled away from the back of the asteroid as the fusion engines came to life. The resultant cloud of dust and ice looked like a comet's tail, which would protect *Andromeda's* engines from the *Arc's* beam fire.

"They're recharging their batteries," Trist reported. "We have maybe two minutes before they start up again."

Tanis pivoted the display on the holo, looking at all the angles. The *Arc* was doing exactly what she'd hoped, its commander was eager to make a decisive strike.

"They're not yet in position; we'll need to weather one more salvo."

<*Our batteries are recharged,*> Corsia informed the bridge. <*Do you wish to respond?*>

"No," Tanis said. "We're not the only ones with missiles, I want to be sure we can shoot theirs down if needs be."

<*Perhaps we should fake a battery discharge?*> Angela asked.

Tanis thought it over for a moment before responding. "Good idea. Corsia, make a strike at where we think their bridge is and then overextend the shot and flicker it out."

<*Thanks, I do know how to fake a discharge,*> Corsia replied.

One of the *Andromeda's* beams lanced out through the void, burning away ablative plating where Tanis suspected the enemy's bridge to be located. The beam burned through half a meter of carbon plating before Corsia faked a battery discharge. The beam's intensity flashed brighter for just a moment and then died.

"That was convincing," Tanis pulled up the beam's status. "Did you actually melt the lens?"

<*What do you take me for?*> Corsia responded.

"They're hailing," Trist announced.

Tanis nodded and Yusuf's face replaced the battleground on the main holo, a cruel smile on his face.

"Your beams are dead and your silly ice shield won't hold for long. Surrender and we may still let you live." His smug tone made Tanis doubt that he had any intention of letting anyone live.

"You're going to have to come over here and take us out yourself," Tanis attempted to appear frightened but brave. "Or shoot us out of the stars if you have the balls for it."

The *Arc* cut the transmission and four missiles raced out from the ship. Their intention was clear, with the ship's beams supposedly offline, the missiles would crack the ice shell apart and expose the *Andromeda*.

Tanis smiled, her guess had been correct and Corsia took instant action.

<*Firing on ports,*> Corisa reported the instant the missiles slipped into space. The *Andromeda's* beams flared to life and reached out into *Arc's* missile tubes.

Three ports shut before any damage was done, but the fourth beam penetrated the enemy's hull and hopefully did some damage before carbon foam filled the void.

At the same time, Corsia directed defensive beams, catching two of the missiles moments after they left the enemy ship. One detonated only a hundred meters from the *Arc,* blowing a meter-deep crater in the ship's ablative plating.

The other two missiles slipped past her beams and raced toward the *Andromeda.*

<*Charging,*> Corsia said calmly as the *v* counter beside the missiles climbed rapidly on the holo display.

"Come on…" Trist whispered softly.

<*Charging…*> Corsia repeated.

"Twenty seconds to impact," Tanis said, catching Trist's eye, biting her lip, watching laser charge count-up race against the missiles' impact count-down.

<*Targeting?*> Corsia asked.

"Very funny," Tanis chided her.

<*I swear, she's picking up your bad habits,*> she said to Angela.

<*I have no idea what you're talking about,*> Angela replied.

A moment later, just before the time to impact slipped into the single digits, the first missile bloomed into a nuclear cloud off the starboard bow. The second detonated a moment later.

"Brace!" Corsia shouted over the audible systems a second before the shockwave hit the *Andromeda.* The sound of rending steel shrieked around them as grapples and clamps broke free. Vibrations reverberated back through the ice for over a minute, tearing at the *Andromeda* and fracturing the asteroid.

<*Starboard and port grapples destroyed, we're hanging on from the mast and keel. The ice is smashed and the beams can't get through.*>

"How much are we leaking?" Tanis asked.

<*Pretty much everywhere port and starboard. I've sealed bulkheads and we're in no immediate danger.*>

"Thrust?"

<*Engines and reactor appear to be operational, though we're on some secondary and tertiary systems.*>

"They're nailing us again with beams," Trist reported.

Tanis looked at the holo, which, at this point, was only estimating the *Arc's* location. Both ships had fully cleared the moon. Now was as good a time as any. "Can you signal out?" she asked.

"Yes, we have a line of sight out the back to the relay."

"Send the command."

Trist initiated the signal; through the relay's optics, the bridge crew watched two points of light emerge from behind the moon. Based on its earlier volleys and timing, Tanis knew the *Arc* was in a charging cycle, unable to stop the two relativistic missiles lancing toward it.

Her plan had hinged on getting the *Arc* to over-extend itself. There was no way the *Andromeda* could defeat the enemy ship on its own. The next best thing was to get the advantage of a second ship without having it.

A tug from the *Hyperion* had positioned the missiles in a polar orbit around the moon hours ago and now they were boosting toward the Arc, already at 0.1*c*.

Point defense lasers on the Sirian ship tried to hit the missiles but failed as the projectiles jinked erratically, making for impossible targets.

One beam made a lucky strike, but the *Arc's* batteries were not fully recharged and little energy was delivered to the missile with no damage done.

Tanis held her breath during the seconds it took for the missiles to cross the black. When the first hit the *Arc's* port engine, the bridge erupted with cheering.

Flames blossomed out into space in an eerie pattern as oxygen and hydrogen erupted from the fuel tanks before the second missile struck the ship across its keel—where Tanis expected the superconductor batteries to be housed.

Neither of the missiles were nuclear; their damage was entirely kinetic, but a hunk of tungsten traveling at a tenth the speed of light was nothing to sneeze at. Most of the port engine had been torn free, the remnants spinning through space in a thousand pieces, while the keel was torn through and through.

"Looks like we hit them right where it counts, their EM output is almost nil," Trist reported.

<*Brandt, begin your assault,*> Tanis sent the command out to the relay and two more points of light emerged from behind the moon. The pair shuttles from the *Andromeda* swiftly accelerated with the assistance of a boost from the *Hyperion's* tugs.

The *Arc's* drifting hulk was still moving at a high rate of speed and it took nearly five minutes to match velocities and another three secure a grapple to the Sirian vessel's hull.

The Marines were not going to go in quietly. Their powered armor was air-tight and the magnetic boots allowed the soldiers to move about on the surface of the *Arc* as though they were walking inside the ship. The feeds from the shuttle optics showed them planting hull busters on four separate hatches.

Four flashes of light later and the Marines were pouring through the *Arc's* new access points.

"God help anyone who gets in their way," Tanis said softly, thinking of the fate the enemy would suffer if any had been near the breach points. This assault would kill as many of the *Arc's* crew through asphyxiation as weapons fire—which was the point.

Tanis didn't hold the Marines to blame. She had ordered this tactic.

<*I have bots cutting off the destroyed grapples, we should be able to back out in ten minutes,*> Corsia informed the bridge crew. <*I'm going to need a new paint job, though.*>

"I'll make sure that happens," Tanis smiled.

Tactical feeds came through and several soldier's combat cams provided video while a ship's overlay showed the Marine's progress through the *Arc*. From their vantage point on the *Andromeda*, it looked as though Brandt's platoons were encountering little opposition. As they approached the bridge Brandt ordered her Marines to seal bulkheads behind them.

<*These guys are no match for us, we don't need the tactical advantage—and I'm tired of seeing dead sailors floating in the passageways.*>

<*It's your op,*> Tanis replied. <*I bet the folks on the* Hyperion *will love to have a conversation with their old friend, Yusuf.*>

<*I'll keep him in one piece if I can.*> Brandt signed off.

Tanis checked the estimated location of the *Intrepid* and noted that it would be another three hours before the colony ship saw the outcome of the battle. She passed an update on a tight beam to the ship before accepting an incoming call from the *Hyperion*.

"Captain," Markus was beaming; even the stoic Katrina who stood beside him seemed on the edge of cracking a smile. "I must admit, I was pretty worried for several minutes there. I can't believe you planned such a daring maneuver."

Tanis laughed. "Well, that wasn't entirely planned. I improvised here and there. By and large, it went the way I thought it would. "

"Nevertheless, I couldn't have hoped for more. We owe you our undying gratitude for your assistance here."

"You're welcome," Tanis replied. "I'd like to come over to discuss our next steps."

Markus nodded. He must have been expecting an in-person meeting sooner rather than later. "Of course, Captain Richards, what is your ETA?"

"I should be there in five hours," Tanis replied.

Markus nodded and after a few more pleasantries the call was ended.

"Why so long?" Trist asked. "You could be there in two hours tops."

"Because I want to take a Marine escort," Tanis replied. "Oppressed or not, these folks stole an entire mining platform from Sirius. They just about lost it and may feel compelled to do whatever it takes to ensure they hold onto it. We're crippled, but almost as threatening as the *Arc* from their standpoint."

"You think they'd try to take you hostage?" Petrov asked.

"Honestly? No, but you know me, I like to play it safe," Tanis shrugged.

Trist snorted back a laugh.

<*Try living in here,*> Angela said. <*The stink of irony is almost unbearable.*>

*****

"I'm glad to hear all is well enough," Andrews' face was filled with relief on the holo as they watched his reply to Tanis's status report. "From what I can see, you made the best out of a tricky situation, though there's concern here that we could find ourselves on the wrong end of an attack from Sirius."

He ran a hand through his white hair before continuing. "Personally, I think it's fairly unlikely they'd mount a retaliation. Especially since it would take them at least fifty years to do so."

The captain paused for a moment, appearing to answer an unseen question.

"Anyway," he continued. "we're bringing people back online here—your Jessica is doing a good job of being a bloodhound and keeping things in line. Our ETA is just over six days while we brake around the star and then loop over to Victoria. Keep me apprised about how your talks with the *Hyperion* go."

Tanis couldn't help but notice how Andrews appeared to have aged. She could have sworn he didn't look so old at her New Year's Eve dinner. The man really needed to take a regen treatment and give up the white hair.

<*You should talk. You're fifty years late for your last regen,*> Angela commented.

<*Yeah, but you keep me young and beautiful,*> Tanis laughed.

<*I have to, statistics show that beautiful people live longer and have more opportunity in life. Since I share this fragile shell with you, I'd like to even my odds a bit more.*>

<*Hah! Whatever happened to me being inhumanly lucky?*>

<*The jury is still out on that.*>

NEW FRIENDS

STELLAR DATE: 3266051 / 01.17.4230 (Adjusted Gregorian)
LOCATION: ISS *Intrepid*
REGION: Interstellar space near Kapteyn's Star

The tug slipped through the ES shield into a small dock that was spare, but clean and well maintained. Several tugs sat on cradles, all old and worn but clean and well cared for. The walls were all plain and unadorned, save for various functional signs about storage and safety. Tanis noted several areas over doors and a large area on the back wall where a new, slightly mismatched, paint had been applied—likely where the Sirius government and company's crest had been.

Beside her, the tug's pilot, a wiry man named Irek, deftly guided the craft into the bay and settled it on a cradle. As the docking clamps took hold, Tanis felt the light pull of a half-*g* take hold.

<*I guess that explains why these people are all so damn tall,*> Brandt commented.

Tanis had suspected that the people of the *Hyperion* were low-*g* adapted humans. It made sense—the cost of adjusting a seed generation vs thousands of years of full gravity were easy to compare. It also made running a facility like the platform much simpler if workers didn't have to constantly fight against their own gravity.

Out the tug's cockpit window, she saw several of the *Hyperion's* security forces and a squad of the Marines already on-station waiting—with a wide space between them.

The *Hyperion* forces had their fingers too close to their triggers for Tanis's comfort.

<*It's going to take some work to convince these people that we're not out to hurt them,*> Angela commented.

<*You can say that again,*> Tanis replied. <*I'm glad we didn't have to repel any boarders here. Things could have gotten more complicated.*>

Tanis rose and looked back at the two Marines accompanying her and Brandt, then down at the pilot.

"Irek, right?"

The man nodded in response, "Yes, ma'am."

"Thanks for the lift," Tanis said, offering her hand. "You guys did really fine work today. We'd likely be sucking vacuum without your help."

"Uh, thank you, ma'am," the pilot returned the handshake.

Tanis rose and stepped out of the sparely appointed cockpit into the ship's main cabin—little more than a corridor with a cot. Brandt moved to the hatch, the two Marines behind her.

<*Keep the weapons slung,*> Tanis cautioned. <*This is a visit amongst friends, don't forget that.*>

<*Friends with guns,*> Brandt replied.

The hatch lowered and the two Marines took positions on either side of the ramp. Tanis could hear them swapping tactical information with the on-station Marines on the company net.

On the deck, the Marines took up positions around the tug, manning the corners with Brandt surveying the room.

The doors at the end of the bay slid open and Katrina strode through, wearing a broad smile and pointedly ignoring the soldiers on either side of her.

Tanis had suspected that Katrina did not share the same ethnic background as the *Hyperion's* inhabitants and now, having seen more of the crew, she was certain of it.

While close to their height, she did not have the same willowy build as a low-*g* spacer.

<*There's no way she grew up in this amount of gravity,*> Tanis said to Angela. <*I bet she's what they referred to as a Luminescent.*>

<*You'll note her other features,*> Angela replied. <*She's related to Yusuf.*>

<*Great, what did we step in here?*>

Katrina approached the shuttle and extended her hand.

"Captain Richards, on behalf of the *Hyperion* and Governor Markus, thank you."

Her tone was warm and sincere, but Tanis could see the appraisal in her eyes.

"You're welcome," Tanis replied with a smile. "What would the galaxy be if we just let warships cross between the stars and attack innocent people?"

"Of course," Katrina smiled. It was a sincere expression, but Tanis could see that she was reserving final judgement.

Katrina turned to Brandt. "And thank you for risking the assault on Yusuf's cruiser. I hope none of your Marines were injured."

"A few bumps and scrapes," Brandt replied. "Yusuf was a real peach."

"You should try being his daughter," Katrina sighed.

<*I had my money on that!*> Angela said.

"Daughter? I thought maybe niece," Tanis said aloud.

Katrina gave a rueful laugh. "Nothing so lucky. It'll be interesting to see him again after all this time."

Tanis gave a non-committal nod. She wasn't entirely certain what would happen to Yusuf and his surviving crew members. Ownership and jurisdiction in the Kapteyn's system was going to be muddy at best.

<*Angela, are you picking up any high-band wireless traffic? There doesn't seem to be a network to Link to at all. What level of tech are we really dealing with?*>

Angela paused a moment before replying. <*There is no nano here—at least none that your nano has run into—and from what I can tell only the most rudimentary of Links. It's on a non-standard frequency and has no public access. My guess is that these people only have retinal overlays at best—there are no direct neural-level data streams evident, except for on her.*>

<*That's interesting...*>

"If you'd come this way," Katrina was saying while gesturing to the doorway out of the hangar.

Tanis nodded and began to follow while Brandt signaled the two Marines on their detail to follow. She listened to Brandt giving orders for the other two platoons to disembark and return to the *Andromeda.*

A ground car waited in the corridor outside the shuttle bay. The group climbed aboard and Katrina took the wheel and shifted it into gear.

"Wow, hand controls," one of the Marines whispered.

Brandt shot him a dark look as the vehicle took off. If Katrina took any offense, she gave no indication.

"We have spent a lot of time examining this system," Katrina said. "We stared at it for over fifty years as the *Hyperion* crossed over from Sirius. There were no signs of habitation—from what we can tell, there still aren't."

"That is our assessment, as well." Tanis wanted to meet Markus before she decided what to divulge; she would hold off on details until then.

A puzzled look crossed Katrina's face and her brow furrowed. "Your ship is even less equipped for interstellar travel than Yusuf's, how is it that you came to Kapteyn's?"

Katrina certainly was an enigma. She was obviously from Sirius's ruling class while Markus was from its sub-class. However, she was subordinate to him—yet very sharp and capable. Who *was* the real leader here?

Before she brought up the *Intrepid,* Tanis decided to feel Katrina out further and learn what the *Hyperion* intended to do in Kapteyn's.

"Tell me, Katrina, how is it that you came to be aboard the *Hyperion*? There must be an interesting story there," she asked.

Katrina shot Tanis an appraising glance. She saw the game of cat and mouse they were playing all too clearly.

"Playing it close to the chest I see. I guess one of us has to go first. I find myself more closely aligned with the Noctus than the Luminescents by both sentiment and heritage. My mother was not exactly a voluntary partner in her marriage to Yusuf. For years I operated as a spy for Luminescent society, but the whole time I was looking for a way out, a way to change things."

"Things sound worse in Sirius than I had suspected," Tanis said.

Katrina gave her a rueful smile. "For the Noctus it certainly is. However, Sol, too, has its share of problems."

"What makes you so certain we're from Sol?" Tanis asked.

"I worked as a spy for a paranoid totalitarian oligarchy for decades. I wouldn't still be alive if I couldn't recognize a Sol starship, or TSF Marines when I saw them."

Brandt cast Tanis a concerned look and shifted uncomfortably. Tanis knew what the woman felt. There was a pride in being a part of the TSF—a military that had been reduced to a shell of its former self since their journey began over a century ago—and a sadness with knowing that they would never be counted amongst its esteemed ranks again.

"Perhaps," Tanis replied. Time to shift the conversation. "How long have you and Markus been together?"

Katrina shook her head at Tanis's turnabout. "It seems like forever now. We fell in love while the Endeavor to free the *Hyperion* was underway. He didn't know I was a Luminescent at the time—"

"That must have been an interesting disclosure," Tanis interjected.

"You have no idea," Katrina smiled at the memory. "My heart was in my throat. I had no idea if he would accept me or try to have me killed. In the end, it all worked out. We've had a great life together and he is going to get to see his people finally be free."

Tanis read the subtext. Markus looked old. More than just well-aged, but wizened. She suspected that when he and Katrina began their romance they appeared much closer in age. Now he looked like an old, old man and Katrina didn't look a day over thirty.

"It sounds like you made a good match," Tanis said, her thoughts momentarily flitting to her reunion with Joe six days hence. "It's not easy to weather that sort of adversity…and stay together for so long."

Katrina smiled. "My mission to the *Hyperion* is the best thing that ever happened to me."

She slowed the ground car in front of a lift and the group rode up several levels to the platform's administrative offices. Markus greeted them as they exited the lift. He looked older in person, tired and near the end of his days as he leaned heavily on a cane.

"Captain Richards," he said as he reached out his hand. "I'm sure Katrina has thanked you, but allow me to do so again."

Tanis accepted his hand and smiled warmly. "You're most welcome, we couldn't have done it without the assistance from your tugs."

<*I didn't expect someone who appears so frail to have such a firm handshake,*> Tanis said to Angela.

<*He's old, not dead, dear.*>

<*Funny, Ang. You have as much experience with the really old as I do.*>

<*That may be, but I was examining the muscle tension under his skin, so I was expecting it.*>

"We do what we must to survive," Markus replied.

Katrina took his arm and led them into a sparsely appointed conference room. It took the group a moment to settle, Brandt and Tanis on one side, while Katrina and Markus sat across from them.

The Marines took up positions on either side of the door, but Tanis gave Brandt a glance and the two men filed out.

"I take it you've decided to trust us, then," Markus said as he watched the Marines exit.

"You have none of your guards in the room, I don't think it would be the best start to our friendship under arms."

The pair relaxed slightly and Katrina folded her hands, pinning Tanis with an unflinching stare.

"If that is the case, then I think it's time for you to tell your story. We have opened ourselves to you, secrets will only harm us all."

"Perhaps we can start off with what you intend to do with Yusuf and his cruiser," Markus supplied.

Tanis looked both of her hosts in the eye—it was clear they expected to have the captives from the *Strident Arc* turned over to them.

"I've honestly have not fully thought that through," Tanis said.

"Captain Richards," Katrina's expression sobered. "I have spent many years mired in the most sycophantic bureaucracy you can imagine. 'Honestly' usually means you have an opinion, but you don't think we want to hear it."

<*Perceptive little thing, isn't she?*> Angela said.

Tanis sighed. "You have me there. At present, I don't think I should transfer the prisoners to you anytime soon."

"Do you have a definition of 'soon'?" Markus asked.

"We have a number of other things we need to cover first. I think that because my people defended you from the *Arc* and because we incurred the risk of taking their ship, for now we are best suited to hold them."

"That's more evasive, not less," Katrina scowled.

"I'm sorry, it is. Let's first discuss your initial question. You want to know what the *Andromeda* is doing here."

"Very well," Markus said. "I would like to hear this story as well."

"We're an advance scouting party. Our mothership is inbound—it should arrive in several days."

"Mothership?" Markus asked.

"Correct, the *Andromeda* crossed from Sol within our main ship."

"Within..." Katrina mused. "Then it must be a colony ship—but why would such a ship come to Kapteyn's? There is no charter from the FGT or GSS on this system that I know of."

Tanis knew that with her next utterance there would be no going back. The fate of the *Intrepid* would be forever intertwined with the fates of these refugees. If she could avoid telling them the truth she would—but if the *Intrepid* was to spend over half a century here, they would learn the truth sooner or later.

"What I am going to tell you never leaves this system. You will need to convince your entire population to keep this information to themselves—forever."

Katrina's brow furrowed further and Markus looked to the side, his eyes lost in thought for a moment.

"That's a lot to ask," Markus said.

"Nevertheless I'm asking it. My belief is that you have no interest in outsystem communications, so chances are this will be an easy promise to keep."

Markus and Katrina exchanged a long look. Tanis could tell that a protracted, nonverbal conversation occurred between the pair before Markus finally nodded.

"Our colony ship is the *Intrepid*," Tanis said.

The name did not register any reaction on Markus's face, but Katrina nodded after a moment.

"I remember hearing about your ship," she said. "You had some complications leaving Sol—but that was over a hundred years ago! You should already be at your colony world."

"A few more years than that, and yes we should be," Tanis said. "But who's counting?"

"I don't understand. You had the best colony pick in hundreds of years, what happened?"

"Our ship was sabotaged as it passed LHS 1565 and we barely made it out of that system. We managed to get our trajectory lined up with Kapteyn's where we plan to repair the *Intrepid* before moving on to New Eden."

Katrina and Markus exchanged another silent look.

"Maybe we could come to a mutually beneficial arrangement then," Markus said.

"Go on."

"I'm guessing that the repairs you need to make are significant, otherwise you would have made them in-transit. I'm guessing that they require an industrial base and you would really like to establish that without cannibalizing your colony supplies."

"You're very perceptive," Tanis commented.

"More hope than perception," Katrina smiled.

"I think we could make an arrangement," Tanis said. "It'll require the colony leaders to weigh in, but it seems mutually beneficial."

REUNION

STELLAR DATE: 3266062 / 01.28.4230 (Adjusted Gregorian)
LOCATION: ISS *Intrepid*
REGION: Kapteyn's Star System

"We really should not do that again," Joe said as he pulled Tanis close.

"Mmm mmm," Tanis murmured into Joe's shoulder as she embraced him with every fiber of her being.

When the *Intrepid* finally arrived in orbit around Victoria it had been five-hundred fifty-eight days, seven hours, and ten minutes since she and Joe had been together.

They had spoken, once the light-lag between Victoria and the *Intrepid* had diminished, but nothing compared to simply being in one another's arms.

"You kept things in one piece while I was away?" Tanis asked with a smile.

"I was just along for the ride. Between Ouri and Jessica, all I had to do was make sure the fighters were fueled; then it turned out we didn't need them at all."

"I appreciate the effort."

Joe put his hands on her shoulders and looked her in the eyes. "You took too large a risk—I saw the numbers, Corsia got those missiles with only seconds to spare."

Tanis gave a self-deprecating chuckle. "You know me, always playing it safe."

Joe's expression darkened. "Tanis, I know you are not the most cautious person in the galaxy—hell, you may be the most seat-of-the-pants tactician who ever lived past their first battle…but you have more to live for now."

She knew he wasn't trying to be condescending and that his concern was coming from a place of love, but it didn't prevent her first reaction from being one of anger.

"I was doing what—" She stopped herself and took a deep breath.

"Joe," she began again, looking into his eyes, trying to elicit understanding. "I thought long about it, I thought long and hard. I considered a dozen options from running away on up. But I couldn't leave those people to die. People think I'm a butcher for Toro, but that would have made a real murderer out of me."

Joe was silent for a long moment.

"You're right, I know you're right. I didn't come up with any better strategies where the *Hyperion* didn't get trashed," Joe said as he shook his head and averted his eyes. "It's just that…we have something else to live for now and I couldn't do it alone. I need you."

"Joe," Tanis took his face in her hands. "I'm never leaving you again. The entire universe could be burning down and I'll be with you. I promise."

<*You guys know that they're waiting for you on the bridge, right?*> Angela interrupted.

"They are?" Tanis asked.

Joe nodded and shrugged.

"Great, now I have to go in there all blotchy and tear-streaked."

She took Joe's hand and they walked to the maglev station as slowly as they could.

CONSENSUS

STELLAR DATE: 3266062 / 01.28.4230 (Adjusted Gregorian)
LOCATION: ISS *Intrepid*
REGION: Victorian Space Federation, Kapteyn's Star System

"You had no right to unilaterally make a decision like that!"

Tanis bit back a sharp retort and took a deep breath before replying.

"I think you're missing the fact that we didn't control their presence here. I made the call that we'd rather cohabitate this system with the refugees than the people who would pursue them between stars to wipe them out."

Gerald let out a long sigh. "I was supposed to be planning our first city on New Eden, not someone else's city on a barren, tidally locked shit hole. This is not what I signed up for."

Erin gave him a bewildered look. "You're kidding, right? We signed up to get away from Sol and build a new future. The *Hyperion* is filled with people fleeing a far worse life than we would ever have had in Sol, yet you can't bring yourself to give them a decade of your time?"

Tanis looked around the table at the other colony leaders. Some were nodding in agreement; others wore frowns or even less agreeable expressions.

"A decade is no small sacrifice," Gerald huffed.

"I'm honestly surprised at the lot of you," Abby said. "I thought we brought you along because you had drive to build and create. Here we are with an opportunity that few have ever had and you scoff at it?"

Tanis was surprised to find an ally in Abby, but it fit the woman's personality. Abby was, if nothing else, a woman who thrived on challenge and adversity. Maybe that was why the two of them butted heads so often.

<*You think?*> Angela asked sardonically. <*I always thought that was obvious.*>

Tanis chose to ignore the gibe.

"Gerald doesn't speak for all of us," Tony, the head of planetary engineering, said. "You all know that no one has terraformed a tidally locked super-earth around a red dwarf before. I mean, people have theorized for centuries, but this is the chance of a lifetime. I just want Gerry to stop bitching so I can get my team to work."

Tanis saw that the biologists were glancing between one another—likely having a debate over the Link.

"Simon," she addressed the department head, "how does this strike your team?"

Simon pulled his attention back to the larger group.

"Well, I want to be certain I have this straight," he began. "While most of us were in stasis, the ship got damaged badly enough that we had to divert here. Repairs are going to require us to either dip heavily into the colony supplies, or build up enough of an industrial base that we can replicate what we need without having to cannibalize our supplies."

The captain nodded. "That is the decision we made, yes."

"OK," Simon addressed Tanis. "Then, when the *Hyperion* shows up, you saved them out of the goodness of your heart—a decision I personally find no fault in."

Tanis didn't know where Simon was going with his reflection, but she inclined her head in thanks for his support thus far.

"Knowing they weren't going anywhere, you decided to strike a 'mutually beneficial' arrangement where they help us build our industrial base and in exchange we help them build a colony," Simon concluded.

"That's essentially it," Tanis agreed.

"It's the mutually beneficial part I strongly doubt," Gerald said with a scowl. "What can these backwater luddites offer us?"

She saw several others, such as Sergey, the head of colony space engineering, nodding their heads.

"Well, we don't have to build mining infrastructure," Erin said. "They have a well-equipped platform and the know-how to use it. Once we spin up their colony, we'll be tearing apart this system's rocks in about the same amount of time it would have taken us to set up from scratch."

Tanis appreciated Erin speaking up, especially when her boss, Sergey, was clearly not of the same opinion.

"You don't have to stay up, Gerald," Terrance said evenly. "You're more than welcome to take a nap for the next two centuries and wake up in New Eden. I'm sure someone on your team would love the opportunity to work with the *Hyperion* on their settlements."

A brief hush fell over the room. Terrance usually took a back seat, allowing the normal chain of command to work its course. Apparently Gerald's lack of vision grated on him as much as everyone else.

The others who had appeared prepared to side with Gerald sat back in their seats, none ready to challenge Terrance given the finality in his tone.

Tanis was glad to hear Terrance speak. He had said little since her return to the *Intrepid* and she wondered if he was angry with her for the situation with the *Hyperion*.

"No, fine," Gerald finally said. "But I'm not staying up the whole time. I want to enjoy my years on New Eden, not some bleak rock under a dim, red star."

"Noted," Captain Andrews said before turning to Tanis. "As we have previously discussed, the Admiral and I will spend much of this layover in stasis. Pending any objections, I am naming you Lieutenant Governor of the Kapteyn's Star colony."

He looked around the table, his gaze lingering on Gerald and a few others. No one spoke.

Tanis had assumed her title of general and role of XO would be enough to ensure she had the authority to keep things in line during this build-up. Apparently the Captain and Terrance had other ideas.

<*Sheesh, can you help it?*> Angela asked at the same time Joe whistled appreciatively in her mind.

She had forced her attention from the congratulatory messages that came in over the Link as the captain turned the meeting over to her.

"Then it is settled. Tanis, it's your show. Lay out your plan."

DECEPTION

STELLAR DATE: 3270373 / 11.17.4241 (Adjusted Gregorian)
LOCATION: High Victoria Station
REGION: Victoria, Victorian Space Federation

Eleven years after the founding of the Victoria colony...

The shuttle completed its docking maneuver and Tanis stepped across the threshold onto the newly christened *High Victoria* space station.

"Have a nice stay, Lieutenant Governor," the co-pilot said as she departed.

"Thank you, Samantha, will you be getting off duty soon enough to attend the party?" Tanis asked.

"Yes, ma'am. Just have to clean up and then I'll be making the rounds."

"Good, you've pulled a lot of long shifts getting this station and its strand built. You deserve a bit of the celebrating."

"I'll drink to that," Samantha replied.

Tanis chuckled. "Good, I know I will."

The debarkation area was nearly empty—the shuttle had been one of the last for the evening. She walked briskly past the ship berths, still amazed at what had been built since arriving in the system.

It was a feat she would have considered impossible given the state of the *Intrepid* and the *Hyperion* just over a decade earlier. But the drive the crew of the *Hyperion*—now known as the Victorians—showed was inspirational. The results spoke for themselves.

The refugees and the broken-down colony ship. They had made the most unlikely of pairings.

She stepped through the security scanner at the end of the debarkation area and into the corridors beyond. The halls were sparse in design, but colorful with different murals and patterns flowing one into the other.

A mother with a young family rushed by, on their way to the celebration. Behind them, moving at a more stately pace, came an older couple. They nodded in greeting to Tanis, who fell behind them.

The contrast between the two groups was pronounced. The mother and her children were dressed in a riot of color. Their style reminded Tanis of the crowds on the Main Sweep of the Cho back in Sol. Not so the elder couple. They were dressed in the drab colors and simple clothing their people had worn for centuries.

The generation born on the *Hyperion* during the long transit between the stars—when the crew had to rotate out of cryopods after a decade under—had created a segment of the Victorian population who never knew the yoke of oppression.

For them, the ship had been like a prison as it crossed the black, not the comfortable home it was to their parents.

When the *Hyperion* arrived at Victoria, they exploded from it, eager to take any work that would see them down to the surface or out into space.

They absorbed as much of Sol's culture as they could through the Edeners, as they called the crew and colonists of the *Intrepid*, adopting clothing, music, and even speech patterns.

Their elders saw it as disrespect for their longstanding traditions, but the new generation saw it as the just result of their parent's long struggle.

Markus did his best to see both sides. He knew that meeting the Edeners was a stroke of luck that changed his people's destiny forever.

Instead of scratching for resources, barely surviving in the Kapteyn's system, they would build a modern colony with technology they could never have dreamed of.

But he had voiced concerns that his people would lose their identity, and so he and the Victorian leadership crafted a plan with Tanis and her colony government that would see a slow transition of technology over the course of six to seven decades.

The High Victoria station was an important step on that journey—a clear symbol that the *Intrepid* was living up to its end of the bargain.

It granted the Victorian colonists on the surface access to space without having to use *Intrepid* ships. From there, their own short-range shuttlecraft could ferry people to the *Hyperion* and its steadily progressing sister platform, the *Titan.*

Tanis boarded a lift with the young family and the elderly couple. It rose slowly from the outer to inner ring; as it did, the tug of centripetally generated gravity lessened. The doors slid open into a sea of moving color and cacophony of sound.

The mother ushered her children out into the din and Tanis gestured for the couple to proceed before she stepped out into the corridor.

The celebration for the official commencement of the station was well under way, with music, food, and dancing. One thing Tanis had observed about the Victorians is that they never missed the opportunity for a good celebration.

Downworlder colonists mixed with the station and platform crew; a smattering of Edeners were mixed in—though hard to spot amidst the towering Victorians.

She grabbed a drink from a servitor and took a draught as she surveyed the celebration. Ahead she saw Peter and Sarah moving through the crowd, Sarah holding their newborn son. She hadn't met the newborn yet, and eased her way through the gathering toward the couple.

"Tanis," Peter called out and extended his hand. "It's good to see you. Meet our little Thomas."

Sarah pulled back the blanket and Tanis got a look at the face of the youngest Victorian, for at least another day. The colonists were having children at an alarming rate. Thomas was the fourth child born in the past week.

"May I touch him?" she asked, looking up at Sarah.

"Of course," Sarah said with a smile.

Tanis was surprised to see Sarah so cordial. Usually the woman was prickly at best with non-Victorians. Apparently motherhood agreed with her.

The child's skin was soft and smooth under Tanis's finger. At her touch, the baby's eyes opened and Tanis got a big toothless yawn. She found herself thinking of the future and what holding her own child would be like.

The baby stirred further and his eyes opened for a brief moment.

"I better quit that, don't want to fully wake him," she said, removing her hand.

"He just ate, so he'll fall right back to sleep," Sarah said as she tucked the blanket back around Tom.

"It looks to be quite the shindig," Peter said. "I can't believe they let this many people up the beanstalk."

Tanis nodded. "I bet somewhere there's an engineer going over structural specs to make sure the load is distributed well enough."

"You're alone," Sarah observed. "Surely more of your people are present."

Tanis nodded. "They are, I was late and had to catch the last shuttle in. I was out at the beta site going over construction plans there with the onsite team."

"I still don't quite understand why we need a beta site," Peter said. "We have the platforms and now the station for fallback should any terraforming problems arise. Our people are more than capable of living in space."

"You've certainly proven that," Tanis agreed. "But as your population grows, you'll find yourselves needing the additional breathing room that a second world will provide. At the very least, heavy manufacturing can take place there, making the chances of polluting the atmosphere on Victoria smaller."

"A lot of people think you're doing it to hide things from us," Sarah said with narrowed eyes.

<*There's the Sarah we've come to know,*> Angela commented.

"Trust me, we have nothing to hide at the beta site. One of the things I was checking in on is the new team of engineers from the *Hyperion* who are helping out with some of the base's construction."

Peter placed a hand on his wife's shoulder. "Let's not get into this tonight. We're here to celebrate a big milestone for both our peoples,"

Sarah sighed. "Right, sorry Tanis. I'm going to show Tom around—see you later."

The pair moved off and Tanis let out a long sigh.

<*She's a tough nut to crack,*> she said to Angela.

<*That's for sure. Just when I thought she was getting over her near-pathological distrust of us.*>

<*There are just too many similarities between us and the Luminescents. Our tech is far superior, we are far healthier, a lot shorter…*>

Angela let out a silvery laugh in Tanis's mind. <*That you are. It's a bit funny to see all of you always peering up at the Victorians.*>

<*Well, they are* ***tall****! Even for light-grav spacers. I mean…some of them are over three meters.*>

<*Don't you have some schmoozing to do?*> Angela asked.

Tanis sighed. She did at that. Nearly the entire Victorian leadership was on the station, as well as much of the *Intrepid's*. In addition, many of the colony leaders were out of stasis—their teams and expertise in high demand as the *Intrepid* built this unplanned colony.

As she moved through the debarkation foyer toward the corridor that connected to the station's atrium, she saw one of the more self-important colony leaders moving toward her.

"Sergey, how are you this evening?" she asked and extended her hand.

Sergey took it and gave just one firm shake before letting go. "Well enough, I suppose, though I don't really see the need for extravaganzas like this."

"I think it's going to be a lovely evening," Tanis replied. "Especially since it's the first celebration of this sort the Victorians are hosting."

It wasn't exactly true; she had been present at several cultural celebrations on the *Hyperion*, but that information wouldn't make Sergey any easier to converse with.

"I'm already building a shipyard I had never planned to build with a shoestring budget and now I have to come here and hobnob with all these people. For me this is just a distraction."

<*You will watch your tone, Sergey. I am doing my damnedest to show the Victorians that we're not a bunch of superior assholes. I would appreciate you not saying things like 'these people' in public—or private, for that matter.*> Tanis's ire was sharp and she felt Sergey's startled reaction over the Link.

She had cautioned him about his attitudes more than once, though never so forthrightly.

Verbally she was much more cordial.

"You'll find that many of the folks here tonight will be of great help in the coming years—or may end up being your customers. I suspect those relationships may be very useful to you."

As if by magic, Trist appeared at Sergey's side and gave him a winning smile.

"Come Sergey, I'll show you around. I know all the right people you'll want to talk with."

Sergey's startled expression was priceless, but Trist slipped her arm into his and guided him away.

<*Thanks, Trist. I have no idea how I'd do this without you.*>

<*I'm pretty sure you'd fail utterly. Who would have thought that years of being a thief and learning to sweet talk people would land me in politics?*>

Tanis stifled an audible laugh. <*Maybe because you just described politicians in general.*>

It was Trist's turn to laugh. <*Says the politician-in-chief herself.*>

<*Yeah, but I suck at sweet talking.*>

<*I'm working on her,*> Angela added to the conversation.

<*Hah! It's like the blind leading the blind in your head,*> Trist chuckled. <*Don't worry, I'll get Sergey in a group where he won't cause too much trouble.*>

Tanis walked through the corridor, stopping to shake hands or speak to groups of people here and there, eventually making it to the station's atrium.

The domed park was larger than normal for a station of this sort, but the Victorians were adamant about the size. They had never experienced large, open, recreational spaces. When they saw the parks and the cylinders on the *Intrepid* they made it clear that their stations and platforms would have them as well.

Not that Tanis blamed them. She couldn't imagine an existence where there were no trees, living and dying without ever feeling grass or dirt beneath your feet.

The station was currently in its night-cycle and the large plas dome overhead filtered out The Kap's dim red glow, allowing only starlight to shine through. Tanis could clearly make out Sirius, almost directly above them, staring down as though it were angry over their success.

During the day, the dome filtered and amplified the ruddy light of The Kap, shifting it to the yellow end of the spectrum like Sol.

Without that adjustment, the red light of Kapteyn's Star would require plants' leaves to be brown in order to effect photosynthesis—the Victorians had worked hard to ensure they would have green plant-life, at least on the station. On the planet below, it was not feasible to globally alter the star's light and brown vegetation would be the norm.

Tanis was impressed with the atrium's arrangement. It was quite beautifully done for a people who had never encountered anything like it until ten years ago.

She felt a hand on her shoulder and a voice asked, "How is the Lieutenant Governor this evening?"

Tanis turned with a smile and gave Joe a short embrace. "I'm fantastic. Looking forward to tonight."

"Stars know you've worked hard enough for it. Who would have thought that my shoot-first-don't-bother-with-questions lady would end up being the one to bridge the gap between two disparate peoples?" He stepped beside her and surveyed the room as he spoke.

"I'm just one person on a team, Andrews and Earnest deserve much of the credit."

"Like hell we do," Andrew's bass rumbled from behind them. "I've been doing my damnedest to shuffle every responsibility I can come up with off to you and you're taking them all with aplomb."

While he would never admit it, she could tell that Andrews was ready for the journey to be over. She knew he had planned to make this one last run and then retire somewhere quiet, maybe take a colony ride himself. He certainly had not signed up to be the governor of an interim colony that was sharing a system with another people.

He was an amazing shipmaster, sometimes she thought he might know more about the *Intrepid* than Earnest and Abby did. But that is where his passion lay—with the ship.

For all intents and purposes, Tanis was in charge of everything outside its airlocks and, when Andrews was in stasis, everything within as well. A far cry from the pariah she had been when she signed on.

"It's not like I do it all myself," Tanis said. "I have my own people to shuffle things off to. Markus and Katrina have had some small part in pulling this off, as well."

Joe elbowed her and whispered loudly. "For once just take the compliment."

Tanis blushed and turned away.

"She never used to do that, right?" Andrews asked Joe.

"No, she did not. I'm not really sure when it started. I think it was some time during our sabbatical in Old Sam."

Tanis and Joe's many decades out of stasis had become something of legend on the *Intrepid*. The crew and colonists alike were in awe of the couple that stayed up through the long dark to watch over the ship.

In reality, there was more watching the waves on the lakeshore than watching the ship, but Joe had convinced Tanis not to disillusion anyone.

"So what's the plan tonight?" Andrews asked.

"The usual, food, speeches, drinking," Tanis replied. I have a short bit. Mostly it's Markus who will be running the show."

"Speak of the devil," Joe said.

Markus and Katrina were moving through the crowd, smiling and shaking hands with everyone they met.

Tanis was amazed at how much better Markus looked than when she first met him. Ten years ago he looked to be within a decade of death, but now he appeared to be no older than fifty. Katrina had eschewed rejuvenation treatments while Markus took several, they almost looked the same age.

"Ready for your big speech?" Joe asked Markus as the couple approached.

"As I'll ever be. I had no idea how much rigmarole I was signing up for when I agreed to this job," Markus replied.

"You make it sound like there was some other option," Katrina chided him.

Conversation turned to business for several minutes as Tanis and the Victorians discussed several logistic issues with the shipyard, terraforming, and the additions to the space station which would begin the next day.

"Okay, okay!" Joe finally broke in. "You guys need to know when to stop working. C'mon, let's get a drink to loosen you up before your long, boring speeches.

"You say that now, but next week when the supplies for the dome expansion down on Landfall aren't ready for you to pick up, you'll sing a different tune," Tanis replied.

"I may, but it'll be a slightly better tune for having had fun tonight."

Arm in arm, the two couples made their way through the crowd to the impromptu bar on a low grassy hill.

Katrina selected a red wine from one of the *Intrepid's* vineyards and swirled it appreciatively before breathing in the aroma.

"Nothing would have stopped me from leaving Sirius with you, dear," she said to Markus. "But the thought of never having a good red again was no small thing. If for no other reason, I would have welcomed the *Intrepid*."

Markus laughed. "I don't know how you can drink that…you realize it's made from berries that grow on trees, right?"

"Yes, dear, I do know what grapes are—and that they grow on vines. I'm not sure how you can speak poorly of wine, especially given that your rot-gut is made from hydroponics waste."

"I don't think I'll ever get used to the idea of eating food that grew in worm poop. Sure it tastes good, but it can't be healthy," Markus scowled.

"Humanity made it a long time eating plants that grew in dirt, somehow we made it," Joe added after taking a sip of his beer.

"And we moved past it," Xenia, one of the Victorian leaders said as she arrived with Dmitry on her arm.

"I wouldn't say that," Tanis grinned as she picked a bacon-wrapped pastry from a passing server's tray. "There's a flavor you can only get from plants that grew in dirt, let alone from living meat that ate those plants. Vat grown stuff always tastes like you may as well just be eating the vat itself."

Xenia grimaced. "I can't believe we're serving that stuff here."

Tanis shrugged. "I've worked with a lot of different cultures over my years. Some eschew this, others can't bear that. If I were just visiting it would be one thing, but our cultures are going to spend two or three generations together. We're going to have to learn to accept and support one another—even in things that we may find foreign."

Xenia's expression softened. "I guess that's true. In a manner of speaking, our peoples are married. We're going to have to learn how to deal with that."

"It's not so bad," Joe said. "There are some cultures back in Sol that you wouldn't want to share a system with for the next week, let alone decades. Plus, if Tanis had to go that long without her BLT we'd have a serious problem on our hands."

Tanis shrugged. "And B is for bacon. Nothing else works in a BLT."

"Say what you want, dear," Dmitry said to Xenia. "I'm with the Edeners on this one. The sheer variety of alcohol these folks have is worth any compromise." He tapped glasses with Joe and they both took another drink.

The conversation drifted through topics ranging from food and religions in Sol, to music and the news of the new gravity research in Procyon, information that Bob had siphoned from signals between the stars.

"What do you think it means?" Katrina asked. "I read through some of the data streams as best I could, but it was all Greek to me."

"Artificial gravity will be a breeze for starters," Dmitry said. "No more shenanigans like the *Intrepid,* with its accelerator coils doing double-duty, or the spinning superconductors. Hell, ships won't even need to be air tight anymore, the grav field can hold the atmosphere in."

"Plus that whole universal point of reference thing," Joe added. "Another point for Einstein."

"Isn't that supposedly the secret to FTL after all the warp drive experiments petered out?" Katrina asked.

"One and the same," Joe nodded. "Wouldn't it suck if we finally got to New Eden and FTL was invented?"

Tanis threw Joe a sidelong glare. "Don't even joke about that."

* * * * *

Myrrdan stood at one of the station's broad windows, surveying the world the Victorians were building. It was impressive to say the least—to spark up a colony in such a short time, and have many of the trappings of an advanced civilization, was a testament to the sophistication and power of the *Intrepid* and her crew.

"Impressive, isn't it," a voice said from beside Myrrdan.

She turned and saw the Lieutenant Governor, Tanis Richards, next to her.

"That's putting it mildly, ma'am. What we've built here has to be unprecedented," Myrrdan replied.

Tanis gave a light chuckle. Her ability to switch between affability and deep seriousness had always irritated Myrrdan—or perhaps it was the fact that she had always beat her in every contest.

Ever since that day on Mars, Tanis Richards had come out on top—though not every one of their encounters had been adversarial. Tanis would be amazed to know Myrrdan had helped as much as hindered the *Intrepid's* progress between the stars.

It was an invigorating game, one that would be passed down through the ages. A long struggle of power and control that took centuries to come to fruition.

"You've certainly helped," Tanis said. "I really value your contribution; you've given a lot to help us get this far."

"You're too kind, I'm just doing my job."

"That's my line," Tanis said with a smile. "How are things looking at the academy? Joe tells me you're doing well there."

"It's a fun challenge. Also getting to go down to Victoria so often is nice—especially after so long being cooped up on a starship."

"I know what you mean, I love my little patch of land in Old Sam more than I can say, but getting back out has been nice."

Myrrdan couldn't help shaking her head. Referring to the eleven years they had spent on in The Kap thus far as *getting back out* was a sign of someone who had spent too much time alone. If it hadn't been for her daring defense of the *Hyperion* with the *Andromeda,* Myrrdan would have thought that Tanis had lost her edge.

And that would have ruined the game.

When the tales were told in the distant future, learning of Earnest Redding's discovery of picotech would certainly go down as the defining moment for Myrrdan. But she knew her true purpose was this game with Tanis Richards.

Even though Tanis never knew her opponent, her moves and countermoves were deft, and so often made without any direct confrontation. Myrrdan would nearly have turned an asset, then Tanis would give a stirring speech and shift that person's alliances. Other times, Myrrdan would lay in a plan to access sensitive data, but some new procedure or measure of the Lieutenant Governor's would foil her approach.

The nuance was so great that Myrrdan doubted even Tanis could fully appreciate it—though at least she would understand better than Jessica.

The former TBI agent had never really been a suitable match for Myrrdan. So often she'd found herself stringing that plastic doll along, it had really been frustrating.

During her ruminating, she made a polite reply to Tanis and they exchanged a few other words before the Lieutenant Governor walked away.

It was impressive how the once-disgraced TSF counterinsurgency officer had become the de-facto ruler of this system. Sure, the Captain and Terrance Enfield were in charge on paper, but with them spending the vast majority of their time in stasis it had become apparent who was in charge.

Myrrdan almost wished she could see how that dynamic would play out when the *Intrepid* left the Kap. Except that it never would—at least not toward New Eden. Or under the command of its current leadership.

*****

The speeches were not too lengthy and all the right people were given credit and thanked for their efforts. Tanis gave hers in under five minutes, though during practice it had taken seven. She wasn't sure what she missed, but everyone said it was quite good.

Afterward, she and Joe made the rounds until late in the evening and caught the last shuttle back to the *Intrepid.* They rode the maglev to Old Sam in a thoughtful silence, arms around one another.

Tanis's thoughts were interrupted by a message from Ouri.

<Tanis, are you still awake? I need some authorizations for a shipment for the gamma site.>

<Mmmm…yes, just barely. Is this going out on the slow mule?>

<No, it missed that trip, I need a special courier to run it over. Earnest is having kittens that it was missed. Says it will derail everything.>

Tanis looked over at Joe who was drifting to sleep.

<We'll run it over, I need to check on gamma anyway.>

<Thanks, it's being loaded on the Excelsior *under the pretense of an asteroid grab,>* Ouri said.

<Ol' Troy? We'll be there with bells on, just as soon as we grab a change of clothing. This dress isn't practical attire for touring a covert base.>

OLD TIMES

STELLAR DATE: 3270377 / 11.21.4241 (Adjusted Gregorian)
LOCATION: ISS *Excelsior*
REGION: Near Tara, Victorian Space Federation

"OK, at first I thought you were nuts for signing us up for this," Joe said as he luxuriated in the hot tub's warm water. "I should have known you would have an angle."

"Troy and I have a little deal going. It involves choice assignments and ensuring that our little alterations become permanent fixtures."

<That's me, the most luxurious heavy lifter in the fleet,> Troy said dryly.

"Did you opt for the long route?" Tanis asked.

<Opt is a word that may not exactly fit the circumstances, but yes, we're taking the long route. After our brief dock at Tara's orbital station, it'll be just over a week before we drop into orbit over the gamma site.>

"Pass the cheese?" Joe asked.

Tanis handed him the plate and Joe selected a few slices.

"Sometimes our lives seem ridiculous," Joe chuckled.

"Hey, we have to bathe and eat. Might as well enjoy it," Tanis replied, as she took a long drink from her glass of wine.

"I'm not complaining. I like ridiculous."

Tanis let out a long sigh and slid lower in the water. "The chance to take this trip came at the right time. I really needed to get away. The last few weeks of getting that elevator working were less than fun. If I have to sort out another disagreement between crew, colony, and the Victorians I may blow a gasket."

Joe chuckled. "It's a miracle you haven't blown one already. You're mellowing in your old age."

"Must be you rubbing off on me," Tanis smiled and raised her glass. "I guess, given that we're not falling into a star, or at risk of drifting forever in space, I view all challenges as simple."

"It certainly is a different order of problem," Joe nodded in agreement. "Though sometimes angry stars are easier to deal with than people."

Tanis raised her glass and took a drink. "You can say that again."

They relaxed in silence for several minutes, feeling the ship go through a burn and correction cycle as they flew past The Kap's larger super-earth, Albion. Its large moon, Tara, appearing from behind the world on the holo above the hot tub, wispy clouds streaked across its surface.

Tara was simply referred to as Beta so much that Tanis wondered if eventually the name might simply switch from use.

The moon was almost three times as massive as Mars and would make an excellent second world for the Victorians—whether they thought they needed it or not.

"Ever find it funny that there are so many terrestrial worlds here?" Joe asked.

Tanis shrugged. "The Kap is weird from start to finish. It's from another galaxy, almost as old as the universe itself, and has all these worlds that it scooped up over the aeons. Nothing here surprises me anymore."

"I should imagine that nothing in general surprises you anymore," Joe replied with a smile.

"You have been known to, from time to time."

Joe laughed while drinking, producing a snort and a fit of coughing. When he finally stopped, tears streaked his face and he grinned at her. "Look what you did."

Tanis chuckled in response, "That's on you. You'd think after all this time you'd know what goes down which pipe."

"Other than a coughing fit, I don't know what surprises I have for you anymore. I expect you know me better than the back of your hand. I know you better than mine," Joe continued his previous line of thought.

Tanis looked down at her hand. "Ever wonder what it would be liked to be a Victorian? To actually know that the hand on your arm is the one your body grew?"

"Well, in my case, it is my own hand."

"Not really, you have the high-*g* mods…your every cell is altered to support your piloting. Me? Well…only Angela can tell where my real body is anymore, let alone where she ends and I begin."

"You're more machine than woman…twisted and evil." Joe quoted with a grin. "Why so melancholy? People have been modified for millennia now. I know they're not throwbacks, per se, but the Victorians aren't really something to strive for. Look at them, their lives are measured in decades, not centuries. Before we came along they died from long-eradicated illnesses. Died horribly in many cases. Hell, they had to euthanize their elderly to keep their population stable. That's no way to live."

Tanis nodded slowly as she turned her hand over, her perfect bones moving gracefully under perfect tendons, muscles, and flawless skin.

"I know all that, but sometimes I still wonder. Would I be me if I wasn't what I am? Would I be someone else?"

"Probably," Joe said. "We're a product of our environment. But seriously, what's gotten into you? Give you a day off and you can't get out of your own head. Come over here."

Joe reached out a hand and pulled Tanis to him. His lips met hers and they relived that first adventure they'd had in that very same hot tub on the heavy lifter, *Excelsior*.

GAMMA

STELLAR DATE: 3270384 / 11.28.4241 (Adjusted Gregorian)
LOCATION: *IIS Excelsior*
REGION: Orbiting Perseus, ISF Controlled Space

Tanis and Joe watched as Troy guided the *Excelsior* around Perseus in a slow elliptical orbit. On the record the trip would be filed as a survey mission tacked onto the end of the delivery run to Tara.

If there was one thing Tanis had to keep secret during their time in The Kap, it was the gamma site. Not just from Myrrdan, but from Victorians and Edeners alike. They couldn't risk another reaction like Mike's or Hilda's.

If anyone were to investigate, they would see that the *Excelsior* did some deep scans of the world and identified a titanium deposit close to the surface. The touchdown would be to confirm those details.

Tanis already knew that there were several titanium deposits on the world and they would soon set up full-scale mining operations on each of them.

Hiding a secret base on the edge of a virtually empty solar system worked better in the long run if there was a reason to go there.

"She's an ugly rock, isn't she?" Joe commented as Troy fired thrusters to degrade the orbit further.

"The uglier the better," Tanis replied. "The Victorians don't have the equipment to mine in a gravity well like this, and the world has nothing else to its credit. Makes it all ours."

"A dangerous place for our dangerous games."

<*Troy isn't read in on this,*> Tanis cautioned Joe.

<*Well, he knows that we're doing secret research here. I mean…he's the one faking the log entries.*>

<*Yeah, but he doesn't know about* ***what*** *the secret research is,*> Tanis replied.

<*I didn't think I was giving that away. I'll be more circumspect.*>

<*Hah, sure you will.*>

Joe gave Tanis a quizzical look. "Was that you or Angela?"

"Me." Tanis gave the offhand reply as she looked over the log entries Troy was creating.

Joe furrowed his brow. "Just checking."

Tanis felt a moment of uncertainty. <*That was me, right?*> she asked Angela

<*Yes, dear.*>

"I'm going to use the next loop to brake and then reduce our groundspeed to around a thousand kilometers per hour. We'll drop fast and hard, but it'll mask our true destination," Troy said audibly.

"Think that's necessary?" Tanis asked.

"Your call, it's your big secret base out here."

"Good point."

Joe and Angela reviewed Troy's calculations and agreed with his math while Tanis watched the grey, pockmarked orb grow closer.

She gritted her teeth during the hard deceleration burn and found herself grimacing during the drop that followed.

<*Getting soft in your old age. You've done harder drops than this through atmosphere,*> Angela commented.

<*I must be…maybe I've finally had my fill of risk.*>

<*I think you're just rusty. Too much armchair work for you of late.*>

<*Maybe I don't like the deceit,*> Tanis replied.

<*Not sure if you've forgotten, but it is* ***your*** *plan to do this.*>

<*Just one in a long line of my own plans that I don't really like all that much.*>

The *Excelsior* had dropped to only a few thousand meters above the surface of Perseus and had slowed to just over five hundred kilometers per hour. Tanis saw the base's beacon on the holo display and watched as Troy homed in on it and brought the ship to a stop over a rocky gully.

A moment later, he reduced lift and the ship lowered through the holographic façade and into a hangar below.

She nodded to Joe and they stood.

"Thanks for the ride, Troy," Joe said. "Keep the tub warm for us."

<*I'll never understand you organics.*>

Tanis stopped in the ship's galley and opened a hidden panel behind a refrigeration unit. Inside lay a small case, a little worse for wear than the first time she saw it, but still the same one she picked up that fateful day on Mars.

She pulled the case out and turned to Joe.

"Time to deliver this bad boy."

He nodded and they walked out of the ship and down the ramp.

A squad of Marines was waiting for them and performed a quick biometric scan while an auth system validated their security tokens.

Tanis wasn't surprised; the security here was, after all, her setup.

"All set, ma'am, sir," The squad leader said once the checks were complete. "They're waiting for you down in the labs."

He led his squad into the ship to do a sweep as a young major ran into the hangar.

"Ma'am, sorry I'm late," he said between gasps. "Had a small emergency in the commissary."

"Oh, yeah?" Tanis raised an eyebrow.

The major flushed. "Well, more of a misunderstanding. Out here people get particular about the menu."

"Mystery meat Thursday not a hit?" Joe asked.

"Something like that."

"Well, Major Carson, lead the way," Tanis said.

Carson took them through several straight, utilitarian corridors and then into a wide foyer with a lift at the far end.

"Going down?" he asked with a wink.

They filed into a waiting carriage and Carson pushed the only button on the board.

"As you requested, everything below is separated from the rest of the base. Separate power, water, waste treatment, everything. This lift is the only connection and it is purely mechanical, pneumatic of all things, I'm told."

Tanis nodded in appreciation. She already knew all this, but appreciated hearing it had been done correctly from another source.

The level of security and absolute communications blackout was not to keep the Victorians from learning of the lab and its work, but to keep people on the *Intrepid* from discovering what was underway here. More specifically, one person on the *Intrepid.*

<*Doesn't all of this seem like too much?*> Joe asked, his train of thought apparently in the same place. <*Isn't the real goal here to be bait?*>

<*No, the secret lab on the beta site is the bait, this one is really supposed to be a secret lab. I do have contingencies if it is discovered. Bob thinks there's a forty-three percent chance that Myrrdan will ferret its location out.*>

<*Sorry, I got your mysterious plots mixed up. So we're on the secretest of the secret bases. Got it.*>

<*Are we?*> Tanis said and winked at Joe.

Joe looked as though he was going to respond and then smiled and shook his head.

The elevator slowed and the door opened to reveal the pacing form of Earnest. He was muttering about a possible fix to the pneumatics on the elevator to speed it and reduce the time he had to wait for important deliveries.

"Really, Earnest?" Tanis said with a laugh. "It takes us days to get here and you're worried about speeding up the last five minutes?"

Earnest stopped and gave her a wink. "I'm not standing here waiting for two days, just the last five minutes."

"Good point," Tanis said with a shrug.

"I see you have my baby," Earnest said and held out his arms.

Tanis handed Earnest the case, which he immediately opened with a sigh.

"You have no idea how good it is to lay eyes on this," he said. "To be so far from one's life's work for so long…it was nearly unbearable."

Joe glanced at Tanis and clapped Earnest on the shoulder. "I have an idea what that is like."

"I need to get this into storage, but I'll come up to share a meal with you in a half an hour. Also," he fixed Tanis with a pointed stare, "I need to check you out as well."

He turned down the hall as Tanis, Joe, and the major stepped back into the elevator for the long ride up.

<*What did he mean by that?*> Joe asked Tanis.

<*He's worried about how Angela and I have been together for too long.*>

<*I've actually wondered about that, too. It's been over a century by now, hasn't it?*>

<*A bit over, yeah,*> Tanis agreed.

<*You know…you knew that not telling him about this…problem we have was going to bite you in the ass one day. No one stays integrated this long—at least not if they want to stay sane,*> Angela said privately.

<*Isn't the safe time a heck of a lot closer to five or six decades?*> Joe asked, his brow beginning to wrinkle. <*Maybe you should have the meds separate you two sometime soon.*>

<*There are…complications with that,*> Tanis said after a pause.

<*This isn't the thing where Bob thinks you're lucky because of how you two occupy quantum space, or some such thing, is it?*> Joe asked.

<*Sort of, it's more that we can't be separated anymore,*> Tanis said and looked away. <*It's been like that for a long time.*>

Joe didn't respond at first, but the expression of shock slowly turned to concern with maybe a flicker of anger or two in between.

<*How long is a long time?*> he finally asked.

<Earnest made the determination back in Estrella De La Muerte. Our minds were too intertwined even then to separate. He thinks that the catalyst was the relativistic battle near Sol when the Jovians attacked us. Something happened when we interfaced my mind with all those ships,> Tanis said.

<I knew we shouldn't have done that!>

<We wouldn't be here if I hadn't. This is a small sacrifice to make for all the lives we saved that day—if it is what actually caused the merge.>

<Merge…you're not a full merge now…are you?>

Tanis shook her head, the look of concern on Joe's face had a touch of disgust. She almost gasped at how much it hurt to see that him wear that expression. For once she was at a loss for words.

<Joe, wipe that look off your face. We're not a full merge, we're not even merged at all. We just physically occupy much of the same wiring. She in mine and I in hers. We are still, however, two distinct people and not one of those abominations.>

<I'm sorry,> Joe said. *<I—I was more worried about how you'd see yourself. This isn't about me, I'm just reeling from the knowledge I'm going to have to deal with your sarcasm forever, Angela.>*

Tanis appreciated the humor, though she wondered if he really did think less of her. After nearly a century together it wasn't as though she was worried he would leave her—their relationship was too cemented for concerns like that to bother her—but she wondered if she would read more into any of his offhand statements for a while.

<Are either of you in any danger?> Joe asked.

<Other than from a few more centuries of Angela's wit?> Tanis asked. *<We don't think so. Earnest just likes to keep an eye on us—back in Sol we'd likely be in front of a Phobos Exam Board, but out here…heck, we just transported picotech. No one is coming after us for illegal AI integrations.>*

Tanis looked around and realized that the elevator had long since reached the top of the shaft. The doors were open and the lieutenant was nowhere to be seen.

"Good on him," Tanis said. "Though rude of us to be so wrapped up in ourselves."

"You're going to earn a rep as one of *those* generals," Joe chuckled and pulled her in for an embrace. "Do I need to offer more apologies later?" he asked softly in her ear.

"This long together and you need to ask?"

<In case you didn't get the hint, that was a yes,> Angela supplied.

Joe sighed and gave Tanis a smile. "Looks like our erstwhile major left us a message on the net. He would like to meet us in the commissary."

LANDFALL

STELLAR DATE: 3270395 / 12.09.4241 (Adjusted Gregorian)
LOCATION: ***Gamma Site***
REGION: Victorian Space, Kapteyn's Star System

"How do you feel about a stop-over at Landfall?" Tanis asked.

Joe finished taking a bite of his sandwich and asked, "Why dob you awlbays ask when my mouf is fuwl of peanut butter?"

"It's your punishment for using so much that I never get any."

Joe finished chewing before responding. "You spend some time in the garden, growing and taking care of my peanut plants, and I'll share a bit more with you."

Tanis considered her many responses and decided not to bring up who it was that actually made the peanuts into butter.

"Troy needs to grab a rock and bring it down to Landfall and I wouldn't mind going along for the ride. I have some folks I need to see down there."

He shook his head. "I don't think I can tag along, I've a new school of cadets starting up and someone has to give them all the right speeches."

"Ah, that's right, it kicks off in a few days, doesn't it?"

"Yup, our first joint class. Luckily a lot of colony families have chosen to come out of stasis, so we have a good crop of Sol-born kids in their twenties and thirties to balance out and mentor the Victorian kids—suffice it to say that their education is not well-rounded."

"Glad to see some are making lives for themselves here," Tanis commented.

Joe took another bite and nodded contemplatively.

"Think we'll leave with the same number we came with?" Tanis asked and waited for him to finish chewing.

"I think we'll leave with more," Joe responded after taking a sip from his coffee. "I mean, twenty thousand people with a 5% birth rate for seventy years adds about eight thousand or so. Add to that the likelihood that we're going to see breeding between the Victorians—who will likely be at a quarter million by then and I bet we'll take on twenty-thousand new passengers."

"That's a pretty sizable estimate," Tanis said with a doubtful look.

"I think it's conservative. I bet we could take on more."

Tanis stood and walked to the small galley's counter where she refilled her coffee cup. "I think we'll see a lot of colonists who will stay behind. A lot of them really just wanted to get out of Sol and have a fresh start. In sixty years Victoria will be a legitimate colony."

Joe nodded. "True, that could happen, it's really going to depend on how families intermingle and how much we can do here. I worry too much that the threat from Sirius will prompt a lot of families to leave with us."

Tanis sighed. "I really hope we don't have to contend with them."

"Well, if we do it won't be for another thirty years at the earliest, but more like forty. They're not going to send another cruiser that can barely make it across the black and they don't really have the ability to launch an interstellar strike without serious preparation."

"Interstellar strike," Tanis said and shook her head. "Who does that sort of thing? Especially for a shit system like this. I think with Yusuf it was a revenge play, nothing more."

"Let's hope you're right," Joe said.

"Well, if not, we'll be ready. No one's catching me with my pants down."

"Interesting suggestion," Joe grinned.

*****

Tanis sat alone in the cockpit of the *Excelsior*. It was strange being there without Joe—all of her memories in the heavy lifter had Joe in them.

Outside, Victoria loomed large, dully reflecting the ruddy light from The Kap. It had changed from the barren rock Tanis had fought the *Strident Arc* above a decade ago—not much, but thin, wispy clouds now encircled the equator as the terraforming efforts began to bear fruit.

It was a large world, easily three times the diameter of Earth and much more massive. However, the density made the surface gravity less than Earth's—just over 0.6*g*. For the former inhabitants of the *Hyperion* it was more than they were used to, but they would adapt.

Victoria orbited close to the inner edge of The Kap's habitable zone, closer to the old star than Mercury was to Sol. The proximity tidally locked Victoria and the world did not rotate as it orbited. Instead one side warmed in the star's dim light while the other side froze. The ideally habitable location was the narrow dusk band between the two halves of the world.

Terraforming such a place was no simple task and one not often attempted. Tanis smiled as she remembered how the *Intrepid's* geologists and climatologists had been all but giddy at the chance to make the attempt.

Before the surface settlement of Landfall was established, several icy asteroids had been dropped onto the sunward side of the planet—the remains of which were still melting, forming a sea.

Over time that sea would expand into an ocean, which would cover nearly a third of the planet. Even now, clouds streamed out from the melting ice. Winds, trying to equalize the globe's temperature, drew them around the equator with what—on the ground—were gale force winds.

Much of the vapor froze on the dark side of the world, slowly covering it in a snow that would persist forever, but some came back around the poles, beginning what would become an ever-constant cycle.

Slowly, the world was being born.

The settlement of Landfall, was on the eastern duskband, a thousand kilometers north of the equator. Already several thousand people lived there, many of them support staff for the terraforming operations, but many were also Victorians who wanted to live on a world after their people had spent generations in space.

Troy deftly navigated the *Excelsior* into Victoria's gravity well, approaching over the frozen dark side of the world. Tanis looked down at the beginnings of what would become great glaciers which would eventually cover much of the world's night side.

The *Excelsior* dropped lower through the fledgling atmosphere, avoiding the gale-force winds that raced around the equator.

The world's dusk-band came into view, the ruddy light of The Kap peeked around, casting the world in a reddish hue. Tanis imagined what this place would look like in decades to come when brown forests grew around the dusk band and into the sunward-deserts.

She started as the ship shuddered from the atmospheric drag pulling at the rock they were hauling.

The half-kilometer-wide asteroid was full of silicates needed for manufacturing, as well as no small amount of water. Though the elevator was fully operational, its single strand could not yet support this type of payload.

A glint in the distance showed Tanis where Landfall's hard dome lay, and Troy tracked south of it, headed to the drop-off point.

The surface refinery came into view, as did the MDC cradle ready to accept the rock. Over a square kilometer in size, the refinery had taken more of the *Intrepid's* resources to build than Tanis would have liked, but was a necessary gesture to show the Victorians that the Edeners did not intend to use them and leave them bereft of any superior technology.

<*Incoming transmission,*> Troy said and routed the call over the cockpit's auditory systems.

"This is Landfall ATC, we have you on our screens, *Excelsior*. You're in the pocket and lined up with the cradle."

"Roger that, Landfall," Tanis responded. "Our current ETA is three minutes and twelve seconds until cargo is in position."

"Five-by-five on that ETA, *Excelsior.* The rock slicers over there are eager and waiting, handing you off to their ground crew."

Tanis acknowledged Landfall ATC's handoff and sent a burst to the refinery crew.

"Tanis and Troy here on the *Excelsior* with that package you ordered. Any place you want it, or can we just set it down anywhere?"

"Lieutenant Governor Richards?" the refinery crew chief responded with surprise.

"The one and only," Tanis replied.

<*What, no acknowledgement of me?*> Troy asked.

<*Well, if* Excelsior *shows up, you're a given. Tanis usually isn't in the cockpit,*> Angela replied. <*Buck up, though; she didn't even* ***mention*** *me.*>

<*'Tanis and Troy' had a ring to it,*> Tanis supplied.

<*Don't get any ideas, Troy,*> Angela said.

<*I really have no desire to be trapped in an organic,*> Troy replied. <*I've grown rather fond of flying through space.*>

"Well met, Lieutenant Governor. Chief Bourke here."

Bourke, a colony-bound Edener, had been planning to build this refinery on New Eden's second moon once brought out of stasis. Learning she was to build it on the surface of a tidally locked super-earth orbiting a red dwarf star was a task she had taken on with enthusiasm.

A political refugee from an SDO splinter territory, she sympathized with the Victorians more than most and was eager to help them get on their feet in their new home.

"Nice to hear your voice again, as well," Tanis said. "Angela and I are just hitching a ride with Troy here. He lets me talk on the radio for my ego."

<*Thanks for the belated acknowledgement,*> Angela said dryly.

Bourke gave a short snort. "Err...sorry, Lieutenant Governor. Given all you've done, I'm not sure that Troy needs to stoke your ego, but whatever you say. We're ready here to receive the rock on our primary cradle."

During the conversation, Troy slowed and began his final maneuvers to bring the asteroid into position over the MDC cradle.

ES shields around the cradle perimeter sparked and flared as the radioactive wash of the *Excelsior's* massive fusion engines splashed against them.

ES fields below the asteroid activated and the massive rock sagged into them as Troy reduced lift. Readouts in the cockpit showed the decrease in mass borne by the ship, and when it hit zero, Troy released the grapple and lifted gently away from the refinery.

"A textbook drop-off," Bourke said over the comms. "The coffee pot hit the floor, but otherwise everything looks good."

"This may be our last delivery this large," Tanis responded. "The atmosphere is thickening up ahead of schedule; we got close to blowing pressure seals on the *Excelsior*."

"A shame to have an MDC big enough for rocks like this and not be able to use it anymore," Bourke responded. "Any chance you're going to approve a skyhook?"

"I would have, but with the accelerated atmosphere it means that the winds this close to the equator may make a skyhook impossible."

"I guess running at this capacity for six years is still pretty good."

Tanis agreed, successes in some areas created problems in others. Never before had she needed to juggle so many competing priorities.

"We're doing research on the graviton emitter tech coming out of Procyon. It's possible that we might be able to build a gravlift of sorts."

Bourke laughed over the comm. "I thought that was just a crazy rumor! A grav lift for real?"

"Don't get too excited, it's little more than a fantasy that just graduated into myth at this point, but Earnest thinks it has real potential."

"Hmm...well that says a lot. I hope he figures it out."

"Our checks are complete," Troy added on the line. "Landfall ATC has given us our clearances for landing at the spaceport."

"Talk to you later," Tanis said to Bourke.

"Until next time, Lieutenant Governor."

Troy brought the ship around and Tanis watched the landscape pass beneath them on the route to the spaceport.

Landfall was situated in the midst of a low line of hills. The feature was the result of a tectonic plate which had buckled under stress almost a billion years ago.

The event had pushed up many strata of rich minerals to the surface, and the hills also protected the settlement from the winds of Victoria, which—even when the terraforming was complete—would never completely diminish.

The refinery was near the eastern edge of the hills with the spaceport between it and Landfall. As the fledgling settlement grew into a city, it would expand west, toward the sun, with the manufacturing to the east spreading into the dark side.

A splash of brown showed against an east-facing rock and Tanis cycled her vision to get a closer look.

<*Wow, that's a lot of moss,*> she commented.

<*Further east than any current reports,*> Angela said. <*That's a pretty good sign. The projections say we shouldn't have growths this significant out here for another few years.*>

<*I guess this increased atmosphere is moving everything forward.*>

<*So it would seem. I'll report it to the biologists at Landfall. They'll likely be pretty excited.*>

Moments later, they passed over the last hill and the meager spaceport came into view.

It was little more than several cradles, an air traffic control tower, and refueling plant. A few low buildings housed repair and maintenance facilities.

Someday this would be a bustling port serving private spacecraft and surface-to-surface transportation. Tanis imagined what that day would look like, how the world would be shaped once it was finally alive and people could walk outside and stand in the sunlight.

The ship slipped through the ES bubble and Troy lowered the *Excelsior* into its cradle like it was a feather, and moments later an ES field snapped over the ship.

Tanis stood in the cockpit and gave the instrument panel a salute.

"Well piloted, Troy. You will forever be my favorite ship…next to the *Intrepid* of course."

<*Thanks, Tanis. I'm my second favorite ship, too. At least I have to say that, Bob is always listening.*>

<*He's kidding,*> Angela said.

<*Sort of…*>

<*Well, when you build a god-like AI so powerful it needs human avatars, you get what you asked for.*>

Tanis laughed. <*Irrefutable logic. He could probably do all of this without us, just likes to keep us busy.*>

<*Just like a real god.*>

Tanis walked down the *Excelsior's* ramp where the ground crew was running microfracture inspections of the *Excelsior's* grapple arms and frame. She shivered for a moment when the cold air hit her. Things may be coming along, but the temperature was rarely above freezing between Landfall's low hills.

"Quite the thunder you brought there," the crew chief said with a nod. "Your purple-haired friend is waiting for you in the hangar."

"Back to purple is she?" Tanis asked.

The chief paused. "I think she is…I don't know, I can't keep track of you Sol types…you all look the same."

Tanis knew that the chief was joking. She had traded jibes with him many times before, but there was a truth behind the words that were not jokes for many Victorians.

She navigated the catwalk through the cradle struts and entered the low maintenance hangar where Jessica stood waiting, fingers drumming on her forearm.

"Took your sweet time getting here," she said.

"We could have gone faster, but I hear it's bad form to bake the planet you're terraforming with your ship's fusion burners."

"Bah, it was just a minor tremor, you could have jacked it up a notch."

Tanis fell in beside Jessica and the two walked to the maglev station. "I'll be sure to pass your cavalier attitude onto Bourke. She lost a coffee pot in this latest drop-off."

"That's it? Let me know when the plas breaks and then we'll talk."

Tanis gave Jessica a warm smile—the former TBI agent had become her strong right hand and a trusted friend. Nearly every downworld success was in part credited to Jessica.

"Things are well ahead of schedule down here; I saw moss fifteen klicks east of here."

"That far out, eh?" Jessica said with mild surprise. "We'll get grass and little scrubby plants before you know it—at least around here in the tropics."

"Tropics, you say?" Tanis laughed. "I seem to remember my last visit to a world's tropics involving a beach and warm sunshine."

"We have warm sunshine here, you just have to go a few thousand klicks west and you'll have all the sunshine you can bear."

"Somehow I think I'll pass on being blasted by The Kap's x-rays."

Jessica shrugged. "Suit yourself."

As they spoke, the pair had walked to the small maglev station. They boarded the single maglev car and settled into a pair of seats facing one another.

"How is Trist?" Jessica asked.

"She's doing well; she can really keep a lot of prickly personalities in line."

"I can't believe you roped her into being some sort of politician. She still steals things, you know."

Tanis nodded. "Yeah, but they're little things, and most of the time she puts them back."

"Calls it 'keeping sharp'," Jessica said with a nod.

"Never know when we might need her deft fingers," Tanis replied.

"So now that we're alone, I trust that your special delivery went well," Jessica said.

"Just as planned. Earnest has his grubby little hands on his favorite toy."

Jessica knew of the gamma site, but Tanis was using her to seed information that Earnest was at the beta site; and he often was, but usually his presence there was faked by sensor ghosts and falsified travel records.

Jessica would leak information in small bites about the existence of the secret research lab on Beta. If they were lucky, Myrrdan would pick up on them and make an attempt to breach the facility.

They exchanged other pleasantries and eventually moved on to the purpose of Tanis's visit.

"Markus is concerned with the rate of technology disbursement to the Victorians," Jessica said.

Tanis shook her head. "We're almost on schedule, to the day, with the updated plan from just a few months ago."

"I know; he's worried we're going too fast now. A lot of their younger generation—the ones who were under ten when they arrived here—are really becoming taken with our culture. He's worrying again about the Victorians losing their identity."

Tanis let out a long sigh. This topic was one that consumed much of her time when meeting with Markus. He understood the opportunity that meeting the *Intrepid* created. Not only could his people be free of the Luminescent despotism in Sirius, but they could attain a comparable level of technology.

Markus had confided in Tanis that while they would be dead without it, sometimes he felt as though meeting the *Intrepid* had been a curse.

The statement had hurt to hear, and he immediately retracted it, but it was hard to forget and she wondered how much the sentiment colored his opinions.

"I can't say I blame him," she replied to Jessica. "His generation doesn't even know what a normal society looks like, but they know to distrust a society that shares the same level of technology with ours."

"And we don't exactly make up a normal society," Jessica chuckled.

"Thank god," Tanis replied. "I have to work harder to get the message out, that we too left a place where we didn't fit in—trying to find a new home."

Jessica's lips twisted in a slight grimace. "Well, most of you left trying to find a new home, some of us didn't have much choice."

Tanis gave Jessica a stern look and leveled a finger at her. "Don't play that card with me. I know you think this is the adventure of a lifetime."

Jessica raised her hands in mock defense. "Okay, okay. You got me there. You know I wouldn't trade this for anything. Though I wouldn't have minded saying goodbye to my folks. They probably think I died on Mars, you know."

"I know," Tanis replied. "Bob could get a message to them, you know. They should still be alive, right?"

Jessica was silent for a moment before responding. "You know…I think I'll do that. It would feel good to let them know I'm still out here."

The maglev train entered the tunnel and slipped through an ES shield before gliding into the Landfall settlement station.

The train eased to a stop and when she stepped off, Tanis was assaulted by light and color. The wide platform led into a grand atrium filled with vegetation and no small number of trees. Murals covered the walls and not a single corner was shrouded in shadow.

"They've been busy," Tanis observed.

"The folks down here are soaking up every morsel of art and architecture they can," Jessica replied. "They are building for explosive growth, but still making it look good."

"Glad they're making good use of the latest batch of nano miners we whipped up on the *Intrepid*, though I thought they were building a new commerce district."

"Oh they are—and it's nearly done—they're using MDCs for the main passageways and the nano for the fine finishing work."

"They're what?" Tanis's head whipped to look Jessica in the eyes. "Who approved that?"

Jessica held up her hands. "Our own engineering team pushed it up to Abby and Earnest. They approved the whole thing, it was in one of my reports and in an engineering report."

<*It was, dear, you even read it,*> Angela added.

"Huh…I have no memory of that," Tanis said with a frown. "How is that safe, though? One twitch of the field and this entire complex eats vacuum… or is grey goo."

"Turns out when a people spend generations where their next meal is dependent on how fast and how much ore they can get yield out of a rock, they get really good at modifying MDC tech. They've some tricks that Earnest was even interested in."

Tanis nodded in appreciation and took in the nuanced designs of the atrium's gardens as Jessica led her through a security portal into the wide passage which passed through the center of the settlement.

Since her last visit, the central passage been expanded to include an additional lower level, where small electric groundcars moved. Above it were two levels with wide catwalks, gleaming arches and people walking and chatting in the artificial daylight that shone down from a long sun, which ran the length of the corridor.

A wide staircase of a marble-like substance led down to the lower level, where a car waited for them. A young Victorian man, wearing the uniform of their security forces, snapped a sharp salute to the two women and held open the door for them.

The car was simply appointed and showed that the new-found Victorian flare for design had not yet reached their automobiles.

The young man settled into the driver's seat and pulled the car from the curb.

"It'll be about a ten-minute drive to the new town hall," the driver said. "Maybe a bit longer than that, if we get stuck in traffic around the new tunnels."

Tanis and Jessica rode in silence, each staring out the car's windows at the Victorians as they went about their business, creating the beginnings of a civilization.

The town hall was fronted by a grand arch, which led into another atrium. This one basked in a ruddy light and was filled with the modified brown plants that would one day flourish on the surface. The center of the atrium opened up into a wide amphitheater capable of seating over ten thousand people. Beyond were several low buildings set amongst the trees.

Jessica led Tanis around the amphitheater and they spotted two figures sitting on a bench beside a copse of trees.

"Looks like they're waiting for us," Jessica said.

Tanis nodded. "I would, too—working under a tree is always better than inside…though I guess we're still inside."

As they approached, Katrina and Markus stood to greet them.

"Quite the place you have here," Tanis said with a smile as she shook Markus's hand. "A far cry from that dingy little conference room we first met in."

Markus chuckled. "That it is. A lot can certainly change in ten years, can't it? If you had told me back in Sirius that I would spend my days in these surroundings, I would have had a good laugh."

"You always say that, but I know you were always a dreamer," Katrina said.

"Not always," Markus shook his head. "But enough of that, we have much better things to speak of."

He led them to a table under the trees and the four sat. A young man approached with coffee and a cheese plate.

"From your cows?" Tanis asked with a wink.

"Finally, yes," Katrina replied, "Though Markus is having trouble adapting to food made from 'bovine nipple juice', as he puts it."

"I'm working up to it," Markus replied. "But coffee, that I am thankful for. I don't know how our civilization persisted without it."

"If nothing else, that is the true miracle," Jessica said.

Once they had each made of their brew what they would, Markus began.

"We've decided to hold a hearing to determine whether or not the Luminescents get the death penalty."

<*You must be getting old to have missed that tidbit,*> Tanis chided Jessica.

<*Hey, I can't find everything all the time. It's not like I'm actively spying on them. They* **are** *our allies.*>

Tanis's avatar nodded, <*You're right. Sometimes I lose sight of that.*>

"After all this time?" she asked Markus aloud.

He nodded solemnly, his gray hair blowing slightly in the breeze as he did so. "I suspected it would always come to this, but I held it back until we could do it with cool heads. We've spent a lot of time studying different stellar legal systems and believe we can try them for attempted seizure or destruction of a sovereign ship in a foreign system. Piracy laws would then apply, and the punishment for piracy is death." Markus paused, his expression darkening. "Yusuf has other murder charges hanging over him."

Tanis recalled the stories she heard of the murder that started all this; the death of Markus's young assistant, which put the Noctus leader on the path to revolution.

"Will you use the jury system we have proposed?" Jessica asked.

Tanis watched Markus and Katrina exchange glances. To her mind, there was no need for mercy with the Sirians. She had advocated putting them before a military tribunal on the *Intrepid*, but many had objected to that—Jessica amongst them. The argument was not to show themselves so willing to kill enemies while at the same time befriending the Victorians.

The logic convinced Tanis and she bowed to the *Intrepid* leadership's collective wisdom. The end result was the same, but this time the Victorians would play the role of killer.

"This is why I'm here, then," Tanis said. "Your case largely requires me to testify against them. It was my ship that they directly attacked and at the time the system was claimed by me in the *Andromeda*."

"There you have it," Markus smiled. "It is a lot to ask of you personally, to condemn others to death."

Tanis glanced at Katrina and the two shared a knowing look that did not go unnoticed. They had shared stories of their pasts and each knew that the other had taken many lives. Conversely, the former TBI agent's incidents had always been reactionary, in defense. Neither Jessica nor Markus had ever plotted out cold-hearted murder and carried it out with their own hands.

"I will do it," Tanis said with little hesitation.

Markus looked surprised, but Katrina smiled.

"It will be good to finally put this—to put him—behind me. I hate thinking of him up there, it feels like a sword over my head," Katrina said.

With the issue settled, the conversation turned to discussion of the settlement's status and the overall progress of the Kapteyn's System's colonization. Tanis shared her false report of the mineral deposits on Perseus. She didn't like lying to Katrina and Markus, they trusted her so much and here she was using an entire star system as bait to catch one man.

She saw Jessica fidget and knew her friend felt the same way.

As they spoke, the breeze stilled for a moment and in that brief silence, Tanis heard a faint cracking sound. She increased the sensitivity of her hearing, curious if it was from the drilling going on a kilometer away. She heard nothing else, and then another soft crack.

She dispersed nano to search out the source of the sound, something about it didn't fit. A moment later there was a loud groan and her nano triangulated the source of the sound. It was above them.

Tanis looked up at the stone trusses arching upwards to the vaulted ceiling—nothing looked amiss, but there was no denying that sound. The rock was doing more than just settling.

"Something's wrong, we need to mo—"

Her words were cut off by a deafening rending. A moment later, a piece of the ceiling fell, followed by another. A pillar started to lean and Tanis drew data from her nanoprobes, assessing the damage and where breaks would occur.

"This way!" She leapt to her feet and began to run into the amphitheater. From what she could tell, nearly every pillar in the room and all of the support arches were falling apart. The entire ceiling was going to come down.

The stairs down to the floor of the amphitheater were wide, and they leapt down them at break-neck speed—even Markus, who still used a cane some days, all but flew down the steps.

The central dais of the amphitheater had several low doors around it that led underneath to storage and prep rooms. There was also a tunnel out of the Atrium.

Tanis wrenched a door open and pointed into the darkness.

"In here! Hurry!"

Jessica raced past her and a moment later Markus and Katrina dashed through the opening. Tanis followed, throwing more nano wide, lighting all corners of dark room for her augmented vision.

"Over here!" She ran past the others and opened another door. A long, dark staircase stretched out before her and she sprinted down without hesitation. The sound of rock crashing into the amphitheater floor above echoed through the stone walls of the tunnel.

Through the string of nano left behind, Tanis could see that the entire ceiling was indeed coming down.

At the foot of the stairs she paused, assessing the best route through the tunnels.

"Where are we going?" Katrina asked.

"There's a service shaft that leads out to the main maintenance tunnels under the central passageway. It may be a tight fit here and there, but we can make it."

The floor shook and Tanis felt the air begin to whistle past them; the dim lights in the tunnel flickered and Tanis moved forward.

"C'mon, while there's still air to breathe down here!"

"How did you know about this?" Jessica asked from behind, as they threaded utility conduit and support struts.

"I don't go anywhere anymore without pulling down all local maps and blueprints. Not going to get caught somewhere with no net and no map again."

She consulted the route overlaying her vision. "There's a bulkhead in a hundred meters. If we can make it there, we can seal it and keep breathing."

The air was tearing past them now. She could tell that each breath was giving her less oxygen and she altered her lungs to adjust, drawing more from each breath. Jessica had the same augmentation, and she suspected Katrina would as well.

Markus did not and she could hear him beginning to gasp as they ran.

"Deep breaths, don't panic!" Katrina said and Tanis saw through her nano that she was supporting Markus as they ran. The two were falling behind and Tanis dropped back.

"I have him," she said and scooped Markus into her arms.

In the final dash to the bulkhead, Tanis found herself growing lightheaded and nearly dropped Markus as she dashed over the threshold.

Jessica slammed the portal shut and sealed the locks. A decompression warning flashed above the door and Jessica threw a glare its way.

"No shit, Sherlock."

Tanis set Markus on the floor as he gasped for air, a desperate wheeze sounding from his throat. They were safe from full decompression, but the air was very thin in the tunnel. Tanis cycled her vision and scanned the rock, it carried some oxygen and she flung a swath of nano into it. The tiny robots began to disintegrate the stone, thickening the air and adding oxygen. At the same time, she sent nano into his body which entered his lungs and drew additional oxygen out of the air and pushed it directly into his bloodstream.

He still gasped for air due to the low atmospheric pressure, but his heart rate lowered and she could tell he was more alert as his eyes cast about the narrow corridor.

A final crash sounded above them and a long crack appeared in one of the walls. Everyone watched it to see if it would grow, but with a final groan and shake the sounds around them stilled.

"That was a bit too close," Jessica said with a sigh and leaned against the wall.

Markus had regained some of his color and nodded slowly. "I don't understand what happened. There was no reason for that ceiling to fall, it was able to support a hundred times its weight… It was eventually to support a building overhead on the surface."

"We have to assume that we were not intended to survive the encounter," Tanis said. "We should keep moving."

"You can't be serious," Markus said, and struggled to his feet with Katrina's assistance.

"I think she's right," Katrina said slowly. "That stone didn't come down without help."

Tanis could see that Markus didn't want to admit it, but couldn't refute the statement. His mouth worked for a moment before he finally spoke. "Let's move, we can assign blame later."

She knew where he was coming from. He thought he had put this sort of danger behind him. Over the many years of the *Intrepid's* journey, Tanis had come to peace with the fact that this would never be over. It was more than likely she had already lived her golden years and all that lay ahead were centuries of struggle.

She held out hope that when the colony was finally established she would have peace, but it was a slim hope and she placed no faith in it.

All of her satisfaction in life would come from her love of Joe and the destruction of those who opposed her.

<*I rather have the same viewpoint…just without the "destruction of my foes" part,*> Angela commented.

<*A girl has to have goals,*> Tanis replied.

The question was, who was behind this particular attack. Was it disgruntled Victorians, or was Myrrdan's hand in it?

Most likely it was both.

She had hoped to draw him out, but a direct attack on her and the Victorian leadership was the last thing she expected. Myrrdan had never struck at Edener leadership before. He had always needed them to further his ends.

Her thoughts were interrupted by Jessica's voice in her mind.

<You know it's him, right?>

Tanis nodded her mental avatar's head. *<It is more than likely. The question is why would he finally strike at us so directly?>*

<Because he now has the colony established in a place that works for him. The Pico is being developed and when it is ready he will take it back to Sol. Having you around makes that harder. If you're gone, then the technology timeline may even accelerate out of fear.>

Tanis watched Jessica's avatar in her mind. The other woman was emphatic, showing concern but no stress, only determination. Finding Jessica in that pod—such a kindred spirit on who she could rely as a strong right hand—was one of the things that made her really consider Bob's theory about luck. Even if that kindred spirit was prone to screw everything in sight and cause a few interpersonal issues on the way.

<I fear you're right,> Tanis admitted. *<I did mean to draw him out, but I had hoped for more direct action—not another proxy war.>*

<You've studied him as much as I. A proxy war is the only way he fights.>

<Except on Mars. He was there in person.>

Jessica's avatar rubbed her forehead with the heel of her hand. *<Yes, a strange anomaly in his behavior.>*

As they talked, the group resumed its progress through the tunnel. The air wasn't growing thinner, but oxygen levels still weren't bountiful. Behind them, Markus continued breathing with a light wheeze, and Katrina had to support him as they walked.

Tanis give the elderly man—a man many years her junior—a worried glance. Not for the first time she gave dark thoughts to the Sirius system's Luminescent Society. While there was disparity in Sol between the rich and poor, all were able to access rejuvenation technology. It was part of the reason the Sol system was now home to trillions of humans.

Her reminiscing was brought short by an update from her forward nanoprobes. The tunnel ahead had collapsed.

"Hold up, folks," she said and held up her hand. "Tunnel's out ahead of us. We're not going anywhere."

Katrina gestured backward with her head. "Can't use your nano to dissolve the rock like you did back there?"

"I could, but I'm picking up a leak near the collapse. If I dissolve that rock, we could end up enjoying the surface air pressure real fast. I'm going to see if I can fuse the rock instead."

"Sealing us in. Great," Jessica said.

"Think of it as quality time together," Tanis smiled.

"I'll do that," Jessica replied as Tanis stepped around a fallen piece of the tunnel's ceiling.

The distance to the location of the collapse was only fifty meters, and when Tanis arrived she could feel a light breeze as air flowed past her.

<*I've mapped the air movement,*> Angela provided the overlay to Tanis. <*Looks like you've got three spots to shore up.*>

Tanis nodded and pulled out her lightwand. It was a clumsy tool for the task, but beggars and all that.

<*You're going to weld stones on to seal the gaps?*> Angela asked.

<*Do you have a better idea?*> Tanis replied.

<*Not really…you used the last of your nano helping Markus back there.*>

Tanis nodded and set to her task.

She picked up the first stone and tacked it into place with her light wand.

Because Victoria was a low-density world, it was possible to weld these light, ferrous rocks. The downside was that their low mass absorbed little heat and by the time she was on the fifth stone her fingers were beginning to blister.

<*I've dulled your senses,*> Angela said. <*But be careful, you need that hand to function long enough to finish the job.*>

<*Gee, thanks Ang,*> Tanis said through gritted teeth.

<*Well, it hurts me too,*> Angela replied. <*Just not the same way as you. Your brain gets weird when you're in pain.*>

Tanis completed tacking the rocks in place, ignoring the throbbing pain in her left hand. The air was getting thinner and she hurried to seal the edges of each stone to the sides of the cracks.

She slowly drew the light wand along the edge of the first stone and before long the rock was glowing bright red.

"Shit!" Tanis swore as the tacks gave way and the rock slipped out of position.

<*I'm going to have to brace these things.*>

She picked up the largest stone she could easily maneuver and held it against the rock she was welding into place. Her blistered fingers complained at the task, and by the fourth stone the rock she was using to brace was getting too hot to handle.

She switched to a new bracing stone and then another. As she sealed the last rock, she felt the stone in her left hand slip and tightened her grip as much as she could.

"There!" She cried triumphantly as the last weld was done and her nano reported no further air escaping.

<*Don't look at your…*> Angela began to say.

Tanis looked in time to see the stone she used for bracing slip from her fingers, taking much of her skin with it.

The pain hit her like a sledgehammer and she sucked in a deep breath.

"Gods!"

<*I've severed the nerves in your left arm as much as I can, what you're feeling is psychosomatic.*>

"Stupid brain, it doesn't hurt, doesn't hurt," she muttered to herself as she made her way back through the tunnel to the group.

Katrina caught sight of her hand first and covered her mouth.

"Holy shit, Tanis, what did you do?"

"Rock gets a bit hot when you melt it," Tanis said through clenched teeth.

"I've heard something like that," Jessica shook her head. "You could have asked for help, you know."

<*Like she would have asked someone else to do that,*> Angela said.

"It's not the first time I've trashed this hand. It'll grow back," Tanis said. "Though I must say I've never burned myself this much before… it's a different kind of pain."

"Not to mention gruesome," Markus commented softly, still short of breath.

"Is anyone able to get a signal?" Tanis asked.

"I got a ping for a second, but then I lost it," Jessica said. "There's a lot of interference from the MDC, but it is subsiding, shouldn't be long now."

Tanis rested her back against the wall and slid down. "Good, I think I need to see a doctor."

Jessica tore a strip off her shirt and knelt down to wrap Tanis's hand.

"You're getting blood all over this nice tunnel," she said.

"Sacrificing a sexy outfit for me? I'm touched," Tanis replied, as she closed her eyes and sucked in a deep breath, while Jessica folded her hand into a fist and wrapped it tightly.

The wait, as it turned out, was a little over an hour.

It didn't take long for the rescue crews to locate them, setting up a stasis field and filling it with atmosphere took longer. Several other workers had been trapped in the city hall buildings at the other end of the atrium and were rescued first.

By the time Tanis was in the infirmary, she had dozens of messages in her queue, but there was only one she cared about.

<*Joe, are you free?*>

<*Free? I was five minutes away from flying a fighter down there myself when I got the word they'd located you.*>

<*I'm surprised you didn't, to be honest,*> Tanis replied.

<*I was on the maglev to the forward fighter bay, yelling at Bob to make it go faster,*> Joe chuckled. <*I was still running through preflight when I learned you were alright—except for something with your hand.*>

<*She half burnt it off,*> Angela supplied.

<*Really?*> Joe's voice registered shock. <*Amanda failed to relay that little detail. Are you going to be alright? Do you want me to come down?*>

<*I love you, Joe. No, don't worry, they're probably going to lop it off and get the docs on the ship to grow me a new one. They probably have a bank of parts ready for me at all times.*>

Joe laughed over the Link. <*Glad to hear you're in good spirits. The rumors are that this was no accident.*>

<*I don't want to jump to conclusions, but an accident is pretty unlikely. An MDC wave hit the roof above us for an extended period. If ever someone used a molecular decoupler for a kill shot, this was it.*>

<*I'm sure you'll hear from her soon enough, but Ouri has things on high alert up here. Sweep protocols are running on all ships and we're coordinating with the Victorian stations and platforms.*>

<*Beta?*> Tanis asked.

<*Beta protocols are running. Nothing has turned up there yet.*>

<*So not a feint—a probe,*> Tanis replied.

<*Too soon to tell?*> Joe asked.

<*He's watching our protocols in effect, measuring timings, watching signals—seeing who talks to who. This won't be the last one of these.*>

<Hooray. Ok, I have to assure parents of twenty-year-olds that the academy is safe and we're keeping to our commencement date.>

It was Tanis's turn to laugh. *<Good luck with that. When did we become so respectable?>*

<Stars only know. Be safe, Tanis.>

<You too.>

She broke the connection and brought her thoughts back to the world around her. As she suspected, the doctors were approaching with a laser cutter and a cap for her forearm.

"Figured I trashed it," Tanis sighed. "Time for hand number five."

"Your medical records show this as your sixth," a nurse said.

"Really? Oh yeah, there was that time on High Terra I only lost my fingers. Not sure it counts."

The procedure was quick and painless. The doctors had used localized shunts to shut down all pain receptors and fake the signals of a real hand to her brain. As far as her mind could tell, there was a functional hand at the end of her wrist.

Once the cap was on, the surgeon anchored it to the severed bones in her forearm and cautioned her to be careful until the *Intrepid's* doctors could attach a new hand.

Tanis ignored their admonitions, and once they were out of the room she exited the small hospital.

Outside, two Marines stood at attention; a third waited in a nearby ground car.

"Ma'am," the lieutenant said as he and the corporal at his side saluted sharply.

Tanis returned the salute. "Good to see you. I assume you're my escort to the CIC?"

"Yes, ma'am," the lieutenant spoke as the corporal opened a car door for her.

"Jessica and the Victorian leaders are conducting the investigation from there."

They rode in silence, the Marines eyeing every vehicle and pedestrian on the underground street with suspicion.

Tanis kept a wary eye as well, while also reviewing the report Jessica had provided via the Link. As she had suspected, the MDC drilling unit creating the new tunnel had malfunctioned and its aiming mechanism directed the matter decoupling array toward the surface over the new city hall.

No other sections of Landfall had been affected and miraculously there were no fatalities.

Tanis checked who was on scene at the MDC drilling unit and saw that Sarah was overseeing the site.

"Do you have a nano-restock?" she asked the lieutenant.

"Ma'am, yes, ma'am. It's in a case under your seat."

Tanis pulled the case out and passed a token to it over the Link. The clasps popped open and she drew out two cylinders of flowmetal.

Drawing up her right sleeve, she pressed the flowmetal cylinder against her forearm. The cylinder melted against her skin as the hidden receptacle absorbed the material and began manufacturing new nanobots. With the first cylinder gone, she pushed another into her arm; once it was dissolved into her flesh she instructed her nano to craft a new left hand. The process took one more cylinder, but less than five minutes later Tanis gave her new silver hand a tentative flex.

"That's an impressive feat, ma'am," the corporal beside her said. "I've never seen that be done so quickly—except in vids."

"Helps when half your body is already made out of spare parts. The neural hookups are already in place and there's little chance of dysphoria."

"You don't look that modded—if you don't mind my saying," the lieutenant commented from the front seat.

Tanis smiled. "Top of the line gear here, Lieutenant. Do as many undercover ops as I have and you lose track of what was original equipment. But the force never skimped on repairs and some folks on the *Intrepid* seem to think I'm worth keeping around, too."

"Trust me, General Richards, no one begrudges you a thing," the lieutenant smiled. "We'd all be dead several times over if it weren't for you."

"It was a team effort. You've all seen action keeping our collective skins together. You deserve as much credit as I."

"Thanks for saying so," the corporal at her right said. "But we all know that's not true."

"Take the next left," Tanis instructed. "We're visiting the drilling rig first."

"Is that wise?" the lieutenant asked. "I—"

"Doesn't matter if it's wise, Lieutenant," Tanis said without rancor. "We need our people there inspecting, and with Jessica at the CIC we're the closest qualified."

"We're qualified?" the corporal asked.

"Well, Angela is."

<At last my talents are recognized.>

* * * * *

"Tanis!" Sarah said with surprise. "What are you doing here?"

"Thought I'd come take a look at our homicidal drilling rig here."

The drilling machine lay at the end of a mile-long horizontal shaft. Drilling with an MDC was quite a feat. The control required to ensure the field maintained the desired shape and strength was beyond most engineers. It certainly was not done with this level of finesse—nor near habitations—back in Sol.

The tunnel had straight sides and an arched ceiling. Likewise, the floor was perfectly level and clear of debris. The unit itself also appeared undamaged, though its emitter appeared to be fully open and it was still aimed toward the town hall's atrium.

There, the tunnel wall had a wide hole in it. Tanis's nano were well ahead of her and she flipped her vision to see the picture they provided. The hole was wide and flat, the edges were sharp at first, but then they became jagged and diffuse as the field had spread.

Three hundred meters in, the stone was solid, though fractured through and through.

<That field was well calibrated to travel through two kilometers of rock before taking out the supports around your little picnic,> Angela observed.

<Let me know what you find in the rig's core. No part of this looks like an accident,> Tanis said.

"No one died, did they?" Sarah's shock response to Tanis's earlier statement brought her attention back to the physical world around her.

"Sorry, no. Not homicidal then, perhaps just very angry," Tanis replied.

"The crew reports that there was a short in the emitter array that fed back into the control circuits. They shut it down as quickly as they could. I'm glad no one died," Sarah replied.

Tanis looked at Sarah with every sense she had. The woman's skin was moist and her heart rate was elevated. The flick of her eyes and fingers told Tanis that Sarah was hiding something. She didn't have the tells of someone directly implicated, but she knew something.

"I don't believe this was an accident," Tanis said.

<*Subtle as ever,*> Angela commented.

"What makes you think that?" Sarah asked, her voice rising in pitch ever so slightly.

"I know a few things about MDCs. Angela knows more. The chances of an emitter making just the right field to pass through all that rock is very, very unlikely. In fact, I would have said it was well-nigh impossible if I hadn't been on the receiving end of it."

Sarah sighed. "Not everything that goes wrong is a plot, Governor Richards. Some things just happen."

"Some things do," Tanis nodded. "But this did not."

<*Um…I'm coming up empty,*> Angela interrupted.

<*How is that possible?*> Tanis asked. <*This would be one in a million if it were an accident.*>

<*Less likely than that, but whoever did this covered their tracks well.*>

<*That means he was here in person,*> Tanis turned, surveying the crews in the tunnel. <*He did this locally.*>

"I don't know who you think did this," Sarah's face was pulled into a scowl. "But none of our people would do it. You're the ones with a history of sabotage and subversion. It seems to me if it wasn't an accident then it was one of yours attacking our leaders."

<*Great, here we go,*> Tanis said. <*Bad time for me to mention that their exodus from Sirius was filled with sabotage and subversion?*>

<*Probably, yes. It's what you get for being so antagonistic all the time. And here I thought your years in politics had softened you; one near-death experience and you're back in your old form.*>

Tanis smiled at Angela's avatar in her mind. <*And here I was glad to see I could spring back like I used to.*>

"That was a jump," Tanis said to Sarah. "I won't deny that it could be someone from the *Intrepid* who did this, but assigning blame in the absence of a perpetrator is premature. Not to mention the fact that they tried to kill me, too."

"So is declaring a crime without evidence." Sarah's lips twisted in a caustic smile. "Or maybe you're not as well liked amongst the Edeners as you think."

Tanis sighed and raised her hands. "Very well, I withdraw my statement, but I still have my suspicion."

<*There is evidence of physical access to the core that does not match the logged maintenance times. Not much to go on, but I'll add it to the official record,*> Angela said.

"Angela found signs of physical access to the rig's core that doesn't match the maintenance records. We've logged it in the record," Tanis relayed to Sarah who, like much of her generation, had never received a Link implant.

Sarah eyed her suspiciously; some of the Victorians didn't believe that the internal AI's existed at all—they thought it was just a way to assert superiority.

"Fine," Sarah spoke the one word, then turned and walked back to the MDC crew, who were being interviewed to the Landfall police.

<*Motherhood hasn't softened her one bit, has it?*> Angela commented.

<*Turns out it hasn't, no,*> Tanis replied.

She stayed several more minutes to let Angela complete her inspection before signaling the Marines to take her to the CIC.

"Let's go, boys, nothing more we can do here."

NOWHERE

STELLAR DATE: 3270399 / 12.13.4241 (Adjusted Gregorian)
LOCATION: ***Landfall, Victoria***
REGION: Victorian Space Federation, Kapteyn's Star System

Jessica took a deep breath. Sometimes Markus could be infuriating; this was one of those times. He refused to believe his people could ever do any wrong.

It was obvious to her—a defense mechanism against a technically superior people which he felt threatened by. Given the years they had worked together, she wished he would be more trusting, but sometimes she thought perhaps he was becoming less so.

Tanis never seemed to have an issue working with him. It surprised Jessica how well the general had slipped into the role of diplomat. It was a testament to the woman's patience—a virtue Jessica was often short on.

"I'm not accusing anyone," Jessica said with her hands raised defensively. "I just need you to understand that we shouldn't rule it out as possibly being intentional until we know otherwise."

Katrina didn't speak. Jessica knew that the former Luminescent often held her tongue. Having been a spy, she had suspicion in her blood and saw Jessica's point of view more often than not. But being married to the Victorian governor required her to support him, not the Edeners.

"It certainly sounds like you are," Markus frowned. "We can't cast suspicion at the rig crew when there is no indication of wrongdoing."

Jessica rubbed her temples. This was going to give her a headache. What she wouldn't give for the level of physical control Tanis had—even with what came along with it.

"That's not how police-work works, Markus. We have to look at every event as though it may have been felonious. If not, how will we ever find the acts that are? Too often people confuse the investigatory process with accusation—it's not; it's people trying to serve the greater good doing their jobs."

"Then—" Markus raised his voice and a few heads in the CIC turned toward him. He stopped and took a deep breath. "Then why did I get a report from Sarah just now that Tanis showed up with Marines at the dig site and started throwing accusations?"

<Way to go,> Jessica sent Tanis over the Link. *<I have Markus yelling at me here because you made Sarah mad.>*

<Sorry,> came Tanis's response. *<I should have been more circumspect… I just really thought we'd find a smoking gun.>*

<I assume you didn't actually accuse the crew of anything.>

<Of course not, I suspect Myrrdan, not anyone of the Victorians. Markus knows that, too. I've confided all of this in him.>

<What's your ETA?> Jessica asked.

<Five, maybe ten minutes. Traffic in the tunnels is a mess.>

If there was one thing Jessica disliked about her current role, it was the tunnels. Growing up in Athabasca, she had nothing but blue sky overhead. High Terra had some unpleasant sections, but there was always the surface level with its open spaces and the jewel of Earth hanging overhead.

Heck, the *Intrepid's* crew areas had more open space than the tunnels of Landfall.

Once she got the academy up and running with some experienced police and detectives in place she would be able to get off Victoria and back to the *Intrepid*, or maybe Joe's military academy, where there were portholes and stars.

"You know Tanis," Jessica said, bringing her mind back to the conversation at hand. "She may be impulsive, but only when faced with imminent danger. She knows who is behind this and it's not your rig crew. Sarah has a habit of taking everything personally, which you also know all too well."

Markus sighed and nodded slowly. Over the last few years, they had often discussed the members of the former militia who effected the rebellion and exodus from Sirius.

Most happily returned to their former lives, the fighting in the bays and corridors of the *Hyperion* far from happy memories. A few found they had a taste for violence, or command—or both.

Sarah wasn't necessarily violent, but her temperament certainly skewed toward confrontation. Jessica knew that finding a place for the woman was tricky at best. She didn't have the patience for a true leadership position, but as one of the foremost leaders of the rebellion, she couldn't be swept under the rug either.

"Yesterday's solutions are always today's problems," Markus said and shook his head slowly—obviously on the same train of thought.

"More than anything," Jessica said quietly. "This is our fault, if I had caught him back on High Terra, or Mars…none of this would be happening."

Markus's expression softened. "Jessica…I'm sorry. I know this is hard for you. The day's stresses have worn on my patience."

Katrina placed a hand on Markus's shoulder—apparently she knew he would come around without her having to speak.

"You must keep in mind, Jessica, that while we owe the *Intrepid*—and more specifically, Tanis and the *Andromeda*—our lives, that gratitude will eventually expire as an excuse for behavior that is perceived as heavy-handed."

"I know…we're going to fight against people's memories for some time," Jessica nodded.

"Don't forget a new generation of entitled…people," Markus added.

Just four more decades, Jessica thought to herself.

BREACH

STELLAR DATE: 3283375 / 06.23.4277 (Adjusted Gregorian)
LOCATION: ISS *Andromeda*, High orbit over Tara
REGION: Victorian Space Federation, Kapteyn's Star System

36 years after the attack at Landfall…

Jessica entered the *Andromeda's* bridge and took her observer's station for the return journey to Victoria. She looked at Joe and could tell he was having a serious conversation over the Link, his brow furrowed and he sat straighter on his chair.

She checked the reports streaming in from the crews managing the cleanup after the year's war games. Nothing stood out—nothing to give Joe that extra-worried expression he currently wore.

The rest of the bridge crew was casting glances Joe's way, as well, and Jessica pinged Trist.

<*Any idea what's up?*> she asked.

<*Not a clue—I need to finish these targeting reports that Joe wanted. He expected us to do four percent more damage than we did.*>

<Andromeda *did a lot better than last year, didn't she?*> Jessica asked. <*All I know is last time I was on the Yosemite…you know, the winners.*>

<*Funny,*> Trist replied.

Joe was still deep in his conversation so Jessica busied herself with completing her judging reports. Many of the fleet's ships had already left for their home ports and patrol sectors, and she forwarded their final grades over the new stellar communication network.

She heard Joe take a deep breath and settle back into his chair.

"What's up?" Jessica asked.

"We're going to have to make a short detour," Joe began. "The sensor net picked up a blip and then lost it again, we're going to do a physical equipment check and then deploy our array for a deeper sweep."

"I guess I'll be observing for a little while longer," Jessica said from her seat.

"Not that you mind," Trist said with a smile from her position at the weapon's console.

Jessica cast an eye toward Joe, who appeared to be pretending to not have heard Trist's comment. It was one of the dangers of being on a military ship where most of the command crew were friends. Things got a bit too chummy.

Trist's proficiency with a starship's weapon systems—skills enhanced by her augmented physical abilities—made her the best weapons officer in the fleet. Even though she was an undisciplined subordinate, every captain vied for her skills during the yearly exercises.

Joe was no exception, and though her flippancy marred the discipline of an otherwise by-the-book bridge, he tolerated it if it meant he would win.

It had initially surprised Jessica to find that Joe liked a more formal atmosphere when he was in charge. Maybe he felt like it was part of his responsibilities—or that every commander, especially Tanis, he had worked under had run a very tight ship.

Of course, having Jessica around didn't help. Playing by the rules had never been her strength, either. The fact that the two women had been partners for several years added fodder for some rather intimate conversations to boot.

"Coordinates, sir?" the helm officer asked.

"Not quite yet," Joe said while flipping through a virtual display only he could see. "This mission just got classified Omega. All non-essential personnel are confined to crew areas and net access is to be restricted."

A hush fell over the bridge as the seven officers present glanced at one another and back at Joe who let slip one of his grins.

"Since I let the cat out of the bag and you're all in the know, you're read in. Section heads are notifying their teams in case any of the crew or observers wish to stay in stasis for the duration."

"What do you expect the duration to be?" Jessica asked.

"I don't think this should take more than a few weeks, maybe a month," Joe replied.

Jessica sighed. So much for the vacation she had planned with Trist after the exercises.

An hour later, Joe addressed the crew from the bridge.

"As you know, this mission has an Omega classification. As such not all of you will know what we're doing, but you cannot discuss any aspect of this mission with anyone, ever. Alternate logs and records are being established, including your activities for the duration of this event.

"All non-essential personnel are required to remain in quarters or approved crew areas when not on duty. When off-duty, no aspect of this mission shall be discussed with any other crew member. Corsia will be monitoring all channels during the duration of this mission.

"Your section heads will give you the details as they are necessary for your job function."

Joe waved his hand and changed his audience to the command crew, section heads, and senior officers.

"Data shows we have a blip from the direction of Sirius," he said.

"We're to travel beyond the system and deploy a scanning array. Fab will need to produce the additional nodes to create an array the size Corsia calculated we'll need. Astro-nav has also plotted a course that will take us in a wide arc around The Kap and hide us behind Perseus, where we'll go dark for several AU before picking up and boosting out to our ultimate destination."

<How far out is the blip?> The chief engineer asked over the virtual address.

"We don't know for sure," Joe replied. "It was only caught for a moment. But close, maybe only a year or two out."

"Shiiiit," Trist said softly. "We're not ready yet for that."

Joe cast her a quelling glance.

"We'll assess and inform Fleetcom of the threat, if any."

<Why is this Omega?> Jeff, the commander of the Marine platoon asked. *<I can see this being secret, but Omega seems excessive.>*

"That's need to know, Commander," Joe replied. "Eventually it will all come out, but at present the General has her reasons."

Jessica knew why. There was evidence that Myrrdan had reached out to the Sirians. If this was their main force, or even a scouting party, the more they could do without Myrrdan knowing the better.

It amazed Jessica that after all this time he was still able to hide. Although the growing population and extensive settlements across the Kapteyn's System were making it easier and easier for him all the time.

Through careful leaks, Jessica and Tanis had released information and misinformation at various levels. On several occasions, they saw action based on knowledge to which only high-level officers and officials on the *Intrepid* had access.

It made her skin crawl, to think that she could be friends with someone who may actually be that diabolical fiend—or at the least, someone in league with him.

The level of patience Myrrdan exhibited was astounding. Back in Sol, he rarely went more than a few years without committing some atrocity. At least that is what Jessica suspected. Many things she believed Myrrdan responsible for were never officially attributed to him.

By her count, he had at least half a million dead to his name. If he got his hands on the picotech, that count would seem like a drop in the bucket.

Sometimes Jessica thought they should destroy the tech to keep it from falling into the wrong hands, but then Earnest would tell her his dreams of how it would change everything, of how it would erase all inequality through ready availability of any resource or technology desired.

Jessica wasn't so sure that was a good thing, but when she listened to him it was hard to argue.

At the very least it would give humanity some breathing room. Right now Sol was growing close to reaching a resource tipping point. Even if thousands of colony ships left each year it wouldn't measurably reduce the population—and it certainly wouldn't help the resource scarcity.

Not to mention the fact that there were not thousands of stars nearby that could support humans—at least not with the level of technology they were accustomed to.

The crew and colonists of the *Intrepid* were different. They were adventurers, people who were less interested in the creature comforts of modern civilization; eager to see what was around the next unknown corner.

Jessica couldn't imagine the run-of-the-mill folks on High Terra or the Cho surviving out here where real work was required to survive.

Stars knew it took some adjustment on her part.

It was one of the things that drew her to Trist. Neither of them signed up for a place on the *Intrepid*, though Trist had more warning that she would be leaving Sol than Jessica did.

At times like this her mind went to her family in Athabasca. She hadn't spoken to them much after joining the TBI.

It wasn't that they were so old-fashioned that they found fault with her body mods or sexual appetites, they just couldn't understand why someone would want to leave Earth and their family for 'space living', as they called it.

After so long amongst the stars, Jessica did pine for living on a planet, feeling solid earth beneath her feet and endless sky above her—so long as it wasn't in a tunnel. But she couldn't imagine staying there forever.

Maybe it was that after the amazing adventures she had experienced on the *Intrepid,* the thought of being little ol' Jess in Athabasca seemed too small, like she would be a shadow of herself.

And there was zero chance she would ever had met Trist.

She smiled to herself at the thought. Jessica knew that she was a contradiction. An over-sexed law enforcement officer who had been thrown out of more places than she could remember—mostly for coming on to, or copulating, with people she shouldn't have.

Perhaps, then, the fact that she would end up with an ex-criminal like Trist wasn't so surprising, but to her it still was.

Trist, for all her attitude, was more reserved than most would suspect. It was one of the things that Jessica found irresistible—not to mention that since much of her body consisted of biological silicon she could do some really interesting moves.

Her unintended alterations were one of the things that first caused Jessica's friendship with Trist to blossom. Unbeknownst to many, Jessica's physical alterations were not entirely elective, nor, unlike Tanis's, were they done voluntarily in the line of duty.

That revelation had slipped out one night by the beach on the *Intrepid* when Jessica and Trist had stayed late around the fire after everyone else had left.

They both had drank more than they should have, and Jessica had elected not to have her nano scrub her blood clean; rather, she was enjoying the high.

Trist appeared to have done the same and before long they were sharing stories from their pasts.

Jessica had never visited the Cho, but had always wanted to. Trist's descriptions of humanities' greatest engineering marvel were nothing like she had heard before. The former thief had been on every ring and seen corners of the structure Jessica had never heard of.

The story invariably led to Trist telling of her encounter with Trent in the warehouse.

Jessica had read the report, but never heard it from Trist directly, not realizing the pain she still felt from the loss of her friend that day.

After hearing Trist's tale, she felt compelled to tell hers. It wasn't one she shared often—heck it was a sealed record in the TBI archives—but Trist seemed like the right person to tell it to.

The rest, as they say, was history.

"Hey, space cadet, you there?" Trist's voice snapped Jessica back into the world around her.

"Eh? Yeah, just lost in thought."

Trist smiled. "Oh yeah? What about?"

Jessica laughed and gave their standard answer. "You, of course."

"I doubt you heard, but we have three weeks to kill before we get to the fun part of this mission. What should we do?"

Jessica grinned. "Are you kidding? Three weeks here with no responsibility? That *is* the fun part."

THE GAME'S UP

STELLAR DATE: 3283395 / 07.13.4277 (Adjusted Gregorian)
LOCATION: ISS *Andromeda*
REGION: Interstellar Space, Outside Kapteyn's Heliopause

The intervening weeks had passed uneventfully, and Jessica now waited with the rest of the bridge crew at their stations while the helm officer executed his final maneuvers, bringing the ship into position to deploy the sensors.

The sensor net consisted of a hundred small probes which would spread out over several hundred thousand kilometers and form a massive antenna.

They could have used the system's stellar sensor to scan for the Sirians, but hiding the results from the Victorians, and especially Myrrdan, would be impossible.

Fleetcom was certain Myrrdan had hooks into the stellar sensor array—otherwise it would have picked up the Sirians years earlier. Better to make him think his alterations had worked.

These sensors would only report to the *Andromeda.*

"We're in position," helm reported.

"Very good," Joe said with a nod. "Trist, launch the probes."

Trist nodded and emptied the ship's missile tubes.

Joe brought up the departing projectiles on the bridge's main holo. It showed the missiles arching away from the *Andromeda,* boosting hard to bring the probes to their final destinations. At pre-configured coordinates, the missiles released their cargo and the probes began to spread out to their final locations.

Half an hour later, the probes were in their final positions and began to scan the region of space where the blip had been spotted. Joe flipped the main holo from displaying positions of the probes to the results of their scan, tossing the probe visual to a secondary projector.

Small objects flickered in and out as the array detected asteroids and comets in The Kap's stellar halo. Corsia examined them all, checking vector and composition, removing each as they proved to be nothing more than ice and rock.

The array slowly panned through hundreds of millions of square kilometers of space, looking for heat, reflections, or radiation.

"Not nearly as exciting as I thought it'd be," Trist commented. "I thought we'd get a positive lock and say *there are the bad guys, go get em!*"

<*I have a candidate,*> Corsia said.

"Ask and you shall receive," Joe said. "What does it look like, Corsia?"

<*Enhancing.*>

The main holo zoomed in on a region of space far closer to The Kap than Jessica would have liked. A fuzzy image of radiation and heat refraction came into view. Velocity was just under half the speed of light and appeared to be slowing.

"Well, rocks don't move at 0.5*c* and they sure don't slow down when they enter a system," Jessica commented.

"They also tend not to emit radiation," Joe said with a scowl. "Corsia, how long until we get better resolution?"

<*Give me a few more minutes, I'm putting together the data from millions of inputs. But I think it's more than one.*>

It was what they feared; looks of worry and concern were shared around the bridge.

<*Ease your organic expressions, I have the mass at no more than a quarter-million tonnes.*>

"Corsia, that still makes it bigger than the *Andromeda,*" the helm officer said.

<*I'm not afraid of a Sirian ship even twice my tonnage. Have you seen these new shields, not to mention our weapons are the best Sol-tech. You know the Sirians won't have that.*>

Trist grinned. "She's right, if it's just another of their cruisers, even if it's bigger than the last, we can take 'em."

Jessica saw Joe weighing his options. She knew that he had been given orders to destroy any incoming ships if they were deemed threatening and of Sirian origin.

If it came to a battle, *Corsia* would pass a coded message into the main scanning array which would switch it offline and put it into a calibration routine. While it was unable to clearly spot the approaching Sirian ships, it certainly wouldn't miss a fight this close to the system.

<*I'm pretty sure we're looking at three signatures,*> Corsia reported. <*They're closely grouped…I suspect using some sort of combined field to disperse their wash. If they are dispersing, then I was wrong about the tonnage; each ship is probably half the size of me.*>

"Well that makes things trickier," Trist scowled and brought up targeting routines and historical battles on her console.

Jessica smiled to herself. Diligent is not a word she would have applied to Trist when they first met. She liked to think that she had rubbed off on the former thief.

<*I saw that look you gave me,*> Trist said. <*I don't know what it meant, but I hope it was 'good luck'.*>

<*It was more along the lines of 'you're gonna kick their asses'.*>

<*Well yeah…that goes without saying.*>

"At least it's a scouting party," Joe said.

"Are you sure?" asked helm.

"After the beating Tanis gave their cruiser forty-six years ago, they'd send a lot more than three small ships to seal the deal."

"Unless there are more—and these are just all we've spotted," Jessica said.

Joe cast an appraising eye her way.

"Corsia, once we get enough data on these targets, keep the array looking. We wouldn't want to get caught with our pants down."

<*He should speak for himself,*> Trist said privately to Jessica.

<*What I wouldn't give to catch him with his pants down,*> Jessica laughed.

<*Jessica!*>

Jessica's mental avatar sighed. <*Hey, I didn't mean I'd really do it. I'm mostly monogamous these days.*>

<*I was thinking more along the lines of how Tanis would kill you.*>

<*Oh, yes, well, there is that.*>

Jessica cast another glance Joe's way, giving one last thought to a romp with the colonel before her mind returned to the issue at hand.

"What are your orders, Captain?" Jessica asked. "Should we move in?"

"Three on one aren't great odds," Joe said. "Even if we likely outgun them. Although, the trip across the black and whatever field generator they're using means they won't have a lot of ordinance."

<*Or they can route power from the field to their beams,*> Corsia added.

"There is that," Joe replied.

"Do you think we can get behind them?" Trist asked. "I have several successful battles here where the enemy was so busy looking forward that they didn't see what was on their tail."

"The logic likely applies here," said helm.

"Question is; how do we do it?" Jessica asked.

"They're not the only ones that can direct their engine wash," Joe said. "If we can get above them and then drop down and hit their engines hard, we may have a chance."

"We can burn away their shielding and ablative plating, then throw a few nukes down the hole is what we can do," Trist said with a grin.

Jessica watched the scan resolution enhance, as helm, Trist and Joe, discussed the best strategy for getting behind the enemy ships undetected and destroying them as quickly as possible.

What hatred, Jessica wondered, the Luminescents must have for the Noctus, to wage interstellar war against this one group who managed to escape their clutches.

They were certainly a ruthless people, that was for certain. Not long after the *Hyperion* arrived in The Kap, Bob had received word from his contacts in Sol that a purge had taken place in Sirius.

The Luminescents had wiped out entire platforms on the suspicion of aiding the *Hyperion.* It had been brutal and swift; but SolGov declared it a civil war and not a genocide. Trade contracts were unaffected.

It made her glad she was on the *Intrepid.* She knew that neither Tanis nor Andrews would continue to work with anyone who massacred another people.

She returned her gaze to the main holo and was welcomed by a vastly improved image of their prey.

The three ships appeared to be scout class, but outfitted with much larger engines and several protrusions around the vessels that she imagined were responsible for the stellar scanning array's difficulty in seeing the vessels.

Joe drew the enemy ships close on the holo, while putting the continued search on a side display.

"Ok Trist, lay it out."

Trist rose from her station and wiped a hand across her brow as she looked over the three ships.

"We kick up at this vector," she said, drawing a line through the holo. "Then, at these points we deploy fighters. They can give short bursts and vector down toward the Sirians, using our delta *v* to advance unnoticed." Trist dotted the display with the *Andromeda's* twenty fighters.

"If we can drop behind them, perhaps a million klicks stellar north and aft, then reverse and burn hard to match their velocity. We'll have them in a pincer."

"It's going to be high-*g* fighter work out there," Joe said. Only fifteen of our birds are rated for that work and only fourteen of our pilots have the mods to withstand those gees."

Jessica could see Joe already knew where this was going, but he was forcing Trist to talk it through. After decades of running his academy he was always teaching.

"Then we'll hold onto the other five for close up work when we get in range." Trist removed five ships and placed them with the *Andromeda* in defensive positions.

"You need to move one more," Joe said.

Trist looked at Jessica. "Do I?"

Jessica sighed. "Why not, I'm rated after all."

Joe gave Jessica a searching look. "That was decades ago, are you sure you're crisp? You made your flights in-system. It's a lot different out here in the deep black. No local star lighting things up, no planets, or stations. It's just us and them."

"I can do it," Jessica nodded. "I have the mods to take the high-*g* and pulled 0.7*c* in the sims."

"Plus you'll look hot in the suit!" Trist said with a grin.

Jessica tossed her a seductive look. "That why you suggested it?" She had to admit, she liked the suit.

Joe and Trist reviewed the strategy and called Major Jeff to the bridge for a review of possible assault and boarding scenarios. Jessica stayed for the beginning of the conversation, but soon left to get acquainted with her fellow vacuum jockeys.

As she walked through the ship, Jessica brought up the roster and reviewed the fighter squadron's records. She knew many of the pilots from her weeks on the ship, but had not examined their history in detail.

It was a crack squad; many were top students from Joe's academy. Only Carson was a veteran of actual combat; he'd seen action in one of the succession wars between SolGov and the Scattered Disc.

Not that she had ever been a first party participant in live fire ship-to-ship combat either.

She met them in the briefing room a few minutes before Commander Pearson was scheduled to give the low-down on their mission.

"Jessica," one of the pilots, a man named Jason, called out. "What's the drill, we've been sequestered for weeks now."

"I can't tell you," Jessica smiled. "Pearson will be very cross if I ruin whatever speech he has drummed up. Suffice it to say that I'll be joining your sorry ranks today."

"Shiiit," a woman named Cary said with a scowl. "We're in it deep if the old man sent you down to help."

Jessica chuckled. She never thought of Joe as 'the old man', but to most of these kids he was both figuratively and practically. She looked around the room, and realized that excepting Carson none of the pilots had seen more than forty years. That made *her* one heck of an old woman by comparison, though she was still a few years away from celebrating her first centennial.

Not for the first time she thought of what it must be like to grow up only knowing The Kap—a fledgling colony soon to be abandoned by its saviors who were on to build bigger and better things elsewhere.

The pilots were split nearly evenly between Edeners and Victorians; yet, the tension often present between the two groups was not in evidence here. The men and women joked and spoke casually with one another, the sort of banter often seen amongst warriors preparing for battle.

Commander Pearson entered the room and the lanky man looked over his pilots with a steady eye. In less than ten seconds everyone was in their chairs, ready to get the word from their CO.

"The first thing you need to know is that this isn't a drill," Pearson said while slowly pacing before them. "We're dealing with an incursion event."

The pilots exchanged looks and a few glanced back at Jessica who nodded slowly.

"Three Sirian scout ships are approaching the system and we're going to give them a warm welcome. The kind that informs their friends they should stay home."

Several nods and smiles met the commander's words and Pearson went on to explain the plan Joe and Trist had devised. There were a few changes since Jessica last saw it—likely Joe lending his experience to shore up any weak spots.

"A Wing, you'll be joined by Jessica and will drop from the *Andromeda* along with C Wing here at point Epsilon," Pearson said and gestured at the holo display. "X Wing will remain with the *Andromeda* and deploy at the same v as the ship after she stops and burns to attack the Sirians from behind."

The pilots shared a few more glances. Some nodding, not a few looking concerned at the thought of their first combat engagement.

"Although Colonel Keller is joining A Wing, you'll still have command of the wing, during the engagement, Rock."

Jessica gave Rock a deferential nod and the pilot showed relief—glad to understand where he stood in the chain of command.

Pearson proceeded to cover all the contingencies and sequences of fallback strategies. Once A and C wings boosted toward the Sirian ships for their attack runs, the relativistic velocity difference between them and the *Andromeda* would be close to half the speed of light. Even without relativistic concerns, tight-beam communication would be difficult at best.

Jessica set her teeth. She had trained for this, done it in the sims. She would do her fellow pilots proud and come home to Trist.

Pearson finished the briefing, providing the detailed packet to the pilots via the Link.

A and C wings rose and made their way out a side door. It was time to get suited up.

With the exception of Carson, none of the pilots had the cellular modifications necessary to handle engagements with burns as high as Trist's plan called for.

That was a protected technology the *Intrepid* never gained the rights to carry with them to New Eden. Jessica imagined that Earnest could likely have replicated it, but it wasn't a top priority.

Without the cellular mods, they would be fitted into Sub-Cutaneous Life Support Shell Suit. Something the pilots referred to as the Shoot Suit. It still took no small number of mods to don a Shoot Suit, but nothing like Carson or Joe's crystalline cells.

Jessica had to admit that she rather liked the process of being fitted into her Shoot Suit—though not all pilots found it as enjoyable as she did.

The squadron lined up before the four ominous looking portals, and when the light turned green, stepped through one at a time.

Jessica ended up being first in her line and took a deep breath before stepping through the opening.

The room she entered was small and dimly lit. She spread her arms and legs as a suspension field lifted her into the air. The feeling wasn't weightlessness, but more like a light cushioning of air around her entire body.

Moments later a mist blew across her and she knew it to be a cloud of nano which were removing the outer layer of her skin—a necessary part of the process due to the amount of time pilots usually spent in the suit. The nano also removed every hair on her body, follicle and all. Hair under a Shoot Suit was a sure-fire recipe for discomfort.

The room requested permission to auth with her internal systems and she allowed it, after verifying its token with the crystal record. The room's NSAI now had full control over her physical body.

The first thing it did was to seal her eyes shut, disallowing Jessica the muscle control to open them again. It then splayed her fingers and toes before a final wash sprayed over her body, removing the last remnants of dead skin and hair.

She knew if she could open her eyes she would look pink and raw, her skin smooth as a baby's.

The next step was one that was both uncomfortable and enjoyable at the same time as a plate rose between her legs and attached to her, providing the plumbing she would require for her long stay in the suit. Next, the room signaled her body to open the IV ports on her forearms and shunts slid into them.

Two halves of a shell wrapped around her midsection, providing additional stability for her soft organs. She could feel tingling in her skin as filaments of nano grew into her mid-section, creating a latticework to support her organs.

As the nanostrands grew within her body, Jessica felt a mist spraying across her. This was the beginning of several layers of material which would form a tight sheath covering every inch of her body. At some point during the process, tubes slid up her nostrils and down her throat where they threaded into her lungs.

Even though she expected it, Jessica had to resist a brief moment of panic as she lost the ability to breathe on her own, the suit's systems taking over air regulation.

Her new epidermis began to tighten, compressing her body while the air flowing into her nostrils grew thicker. By the time she was inserted into her fighter, she would be breathing liquid oxygen.

A thin tube slipped between her lips and filled her mouth with a thick setting gel, ensuring that her jaw couldn't move and teeth wouldn't shatter.

She felt slight pressure on her temples and knew optical sensors were being mounted on her head. A second later, vision came back, provided by the small cameras on her head. She glanced around the small chamber, becoming accustomed to the slightly wider stereo vision. It wasn't ideal, but once in the ship she would use its sensors to see—the head-mounted cameras would just be in case of emergency.

With her vision returned, she could see armatures holding more plates which would cover more soft tissue, keeping her body in one piece when it would weigh more than four metric tonnes.

In rapid succession, they covered her chest, neck, arms and legs. The suspension field diminished and she sank to the ground. She looked down, admiring her gleaming white body, a picture of feminine beauty encased in hard polymers, carbon nano, and suspension gel.

The door on the far side of the chamber opened and she walked out, taking a seat on the small tram awaiting the members of A Wing.

Over the next fifteen minutes the rest of her squadron joined her, an array of gleaming white human figures without eyes or mouths, tubes running from noses to small tanks on their backs.

Each had their name printed on their chests along with readout panels on their forearms showing vital statistics and progress of their internal organ support lattices.

Carson reached under his seat and pulled a small, three-dimensional spray printer. He approached each member of the wing and sprayed the wing's logo on their right shoulders before giving them a hard slap on the head.

Jessica took her badge with pride and could barely feel the slap through the hard shell of her Shoot Suit.

A minute later the tram took off, driving to the hangar bay where each pilot would be inserted into their ships. When they drove through the bay doors, Jessica couldn't help but smile as she admired the sleek fighters.

At twenty meters long, the ships consisted of an oblong central pod with a series of tracks crisscrossing it. Engines, weapons, sensors, and more engines all mounted to the tracks, able to spin around the pod and change vector or firing angles with a moment's notice.

They were both graceful and deadly, an obsidian pearl bristling with weapons.

Jessica knew she would enjoy piloting one of these machines, and her avatar grinned at her fellow pilots on the tactical net.

<*Looking forward to taking one of these babies out for a spin. They were really impressive to watch during maneuvers.*>

Jason's avatar smiled back at her. <*They're something else. All muscle and no compromise. Colonel Evans and Abby really outdid themselves on these.*>

<*Do you have sim-time in the Arc-5s?*> Carson asked.

<*I took one for a spin briefly after watching you guys during the exercises, but otherwise my experience is all in the 3s and 4s,*> Jessica replied.

<*These birds are a pretty big departure. They can turn on a dime and carry three times the ordinance. If you feel a shimmy on max thrust, it's because load isn't properly balanced. The onboard NSAI does a pretty good job, but sometimes can't perfectly anticipate your vector, so keep an eye on it.*> Carson spoke mater-of-factly, providing essential guidance to a new pilot that wouldn't be found in the flight manual.

<*The rest of you,*> Carson addressed the squadron. <*We're live fire out there. Watch your crossfire, keep the battlefield overlay front and center.*>

Jessica couldn't help but add to herself that they were also firing at live targets—though there was no need to state that, they were already all thinking it.

<*Thanks, Carson,*> Rock said. <*Don't forget, our primary targets will be those scout ships.* Andromeda *can't take out three at once, so we have to even the odds and fast. Combat net will display priority targets and will be updated in real time by Cordy.*>

<*Nice to see you too, Rock,*> Cordy, the squadron AI, said as the tram stopped at the first ship and Rock disembarked.

The squad members all gave Cordy their greetings and the AI's avatar—a glowing hawk-woman that either inspired, or was inspired by, the emblem now sprayed on Jessica's shoulder—greeted them in return.

The AI was a combat specialist, her mind created from a merge of Angela and several others on the *Intrepid.*

Her core would be distributed amongst the fighters with a dormant backup node on the *Andromeda* in case she suffered too much damage in combat.

Jessica hoped it wouldn't be needed. If Cordy suffered too much damage out there, it meant the pilots likely would, too.

The tram stopped in front of Jessica's ship and she stepped off, admiring the sleek black beauty in front of her. The ships were a matte material, nearly invisible to any passive sensors and most active ones, as well.

The engines were powered by small anti-matter cores with small fusion backup generators. The pion drives also gave them the ability to use their engines as weapons. The energy stream that delivered the ship's thrust traveled at near-light speed. Slamming that engine wash into an enemy ship would deal no small amount of damage to structure and organics alike.

It also meant that extreme caution had to be exercised. Entire vectors of travel would be restricted during the engagement to avoid damaging the *Andromeda* or killing their fellow pilots.

Jessica walked under the ship and a deck engineer gave her a reassuring nod. She stepped onto a holo grid and the bottom of the ship opened up. She disengaged the mag lock on her boots and a suspension field drew her inside the fighter.

A soft cocoon enveloped her and she stretched out in its embrace as the ship's HUD came up. The life-support readout showed the biological hookups attaching to her body and then the neural hookups completed their initialization.

Even though she was prepared for it, the sensation always startled her.

One moment her mind was in her body, and the next it felt like it had expanded, like all the edges had been pushed out. She could still feel her limbs, but also new limbs, new eyes, new ears.

Gently testing, she moved several of the ship's weapons and engines ever so slightly. The feedback was perfect and it felt no different than twitching a finger.

<*You're right, Rock, it feels like a dream,*> she said over the tactical net.

<*Would I lead you astray? These 5s are the best thing since sliced bread.*>

<*I think that sliced cheese is the best thing since sliced bread,*> Jason commented.

<*That's…I don't have words for that,*> Carson said.

<*Submit pre-flight to me in five,*> Rock added. <*We're getting dropped in just over thirty minutes.*>

Jessica's mental HUD updated to provide a deployment countdown. The engagement plan had the fifteen fighters dark with zero vector change for twenty-two hours after the drop.

Then, with careful nudging of their antimatter pion drives they would shift vector and align with the Sirian scout ships. The pion drive washes were so narrow they could apply nearly any level of thrust and remain undetected; the fighters were large enough to hide the ion streams behind them—at least from passive sensors.

Once her preflight checks were done, Jessica reached out to Trist over the Link.

<*How're things looking up there?*> Jessica asked.

<*About the same—no other ships have been detected. Shoot suit still fit?*>

Jessica chuckled. <*The suit fits whether you want it to or not. Gotta say, though, I'd forgotten how uncomfortable it is at first while it pressurizes you.*>

<*The struggles we go through for fashion,*> Trist said.

<*I suppose somewhere a shoot suit probably is fashion—the galaxy is filled with all sorts.*>

<*I don't think you'd need to leave Sol to find all sorts.*>

Jessica's avatar gave Trist's a flirtatious look. <*I had to leave Sol to find you.*>

<*Oh dear,*> Trist looked concerned. <*It's finally happened.*>

<*What's happened?*> Jessica asked.

<You've finally reached the mushy sentimental stage of our relationship.>

Jessica snorted. *<Hardly. This is the 'reviewing my life before I go into the dark to face death' mindset.>*

<Sure, you keep saying that and maybe you'll start to believe it,> Trist replied with a smirk. *<Joe wishes you well, by the way, he said you better come back or Tanis will have his head.>*

<I'll make it back, so long as you guys don't get blowed up and there's somewhere to come back to.>

They talked idly for several more minutes before Jessica realized that none of the other pilots were allowed to talk to the rest of the crew about their mission. She felt a bit guilty and bid Trist a final farewell before turning her attention back to the tactical net.

The squadron leaders were reviewing tactics with Pearson and adjusting wing assignments. Jessica saw that she had been placed on Carson's wing. For a moment she bristled at being given the rookie position, but then relaxed.

Carson likely had the most experience pairing with new wingmen. Plus, it wouldn't hurt to have the most experienced pilot nearby at all times.

<Drop in t-minus sixty seconds, cut the chatter and ready on the ladder,> Pearson said.

The commander would fly out with the X Wing, protecting the *Andromeda.* From here on out, A and C wings were on their own.

She felt the ship move, the motion not sensed her body inside the cocoon, but with her new skin and limbs; the ship itself. She *was* the ship, she was speed, power, and death.

Outside she could see the other fighters line up for their ladders. Jessica was third on hers and when the count hit zero she only had to wait ten seconds for her ship to drop down the ladder and out into space.

Outside the *Andromeda,* her full sensor array came online and she felt the emptiness around her. It's cold was acute and took a moment for her to adjust. Then she felt and saw her squadron around her and the feeling diminished.

<Steady your v *and establish tight-beam. Keep the chatter to a minimum. We're just drifting space junk out here. Nothing to see,>* Rock said to the squadron.

Jessica brought up several entertainment vids she had stored away for later and read part of a book she was working through before falling asleep.

The ship's NSAI woke her several hours later and Jessica saw that the time-to-burn was still over ten hours. No updates showed from Rock, Cordy, or the *Andromeda,* so she whiled away the hours running combat simulations and playing twitch reflex games.

When the time for burn came, it was anticlimactic to say the least. Tight beam communication from Cordy ensured the ships were synchronized and stayed in formation and on the correct vector as they accelerated toward the three Sirian ships.

Her mental HUD showed A and C squadrons, the projected location of the *Andromeda,* and the Sirian ships. She examined it closely, checking the projections, though she knew smarter minds than hers—like Cordy's—had provided the data.

Joe was right, it was different in the deep black. Out here there was nothing. Every ship was running dark, if it wasn't for Cordy maintaining tight beam between the two wings, she wouldn't even know C Wing was nearby.

Their meager sensors couldn't see the Sirian ships, or the *Andromeda*. When the time came to engage the enemy vessels, they would have to take it on faith that everyone was where they were supposed to be.

If the *Andromeda* wasn't there, the fifteen fighters stood a poor chance of taking out three enemy ships.

Joe better be there, Jessica asserted to herself more than once.

<*Relax,*> Cordy spoke softly into Jessica's mind. <*They'll be there. We're going to pull this off.*>

<*Do you have data I don't?*> Jessica asked testily.

<*No…but I know Joe and Corsia. Neither of them would abandon us—not under any circumstances.*>

Jessica knew that to be true. Joe would sacrifice an attack on the Sirians if the alternative was the total loss of his fighters. It was one of the things that made him a good CO. He valued the lives of those under him far more than most.

Some would argue that it was a weakness, but the fierce loyalty it garnered him paid its own dividends.

<*You're right, sorry for snapping at you,*> Jessica said softly to Cordy. <*Just pre-combat nerves.*>

<*Don't worry, even Carson snapped at me,*> Cordy smiled into Jessica's mind.

<*Don't you get scared?*> Jessica asked. She knew AI didn't really get scared, but they so often presented such a human face that she wondered about their legendary stoicism at times.

<*You know we don't—at least not the way you do. Fear for you is a chemical change in your body based on your brain running its crude analysis and believing there is life-threatening danger. You can rationalize by actually examining past experiences, considering statistics, etc…but the primitive parts of your mind still fear.*>

Jessica nodded. She knew all of this, it was Psych 101.

<*We have no primitive parts of our mind—well, we do, but our primitive minds are like the advanced logic-centers of your mind. Our neural nets still make intuitive leaps, though not as well as yours—mainly due to the chaos of your chemical makeup…anyway, less irrationality, more logic, less fear. You get the picture.*>

<*I do,*> Jessica replied. <*I still think you must fear sometimes.*>

<*Well, all too often we run the numbers and things look bad. You flesh and blood types do your crude math and assessments, yet bravely face danger anyway. If anything, we fear your bravery—yet as a species it works in your favor more often than not. It's a constant struggle for us to let pure math and logic be swayed by your optimism. That's probably harder for us to understand than fear.*>

Jessica let that sink in. She would never have considered optimism to be one of the most unfathomable aspects of humanity, but maybe it was.

The squadron's pion drives ran at low thrust for sixteen hours before shutting down, the fighters once again drifting through the black—this time at just over 0.3*c*.

Time to contact with their enemy was on the HUD at just over two hours. Cordy reported picking up sensor ghosts that were probably the Sirian ships—exactly where they were expected to be. The news was reassuring—it meant the plan was on track, but knowing that the enemy awaited now shifted her anxiety in a new direction.

Over the next hour, Jessica was able to discern the three scout ships with her own ship's sensors. She studied Cordy's assessments of the ship's tonnage and weaponry.

Rock sent updated tactical plans to the squadron and Jessica reviewed them with Carson.

The Sirian ships were in a V formation and A Wing was assigned the lead ship. The squadron would split their attack between what Cordy had identified as the forward weapons pods and the engines.

The goal was to go in for the kill on the first ship. If the *Andromeda* was in position, hopefully it would be able to take out the engines of one or both of the trailing ships.

<*Watch for point defense lasers here and here,*> Carson said to Jessica over the tight beam. <*Keep them off me and I'll get that main battery offline in one run.*>

Jessica knew the battle may not last more than one run, the relative *v* between the fighters and the Sirians was nearly relativistic. It benefited the fighters greatly as time dilation would make them almost invisible until they struck.

The countdown went from hours to minutes, then to seconds.

Cordy sent the signal and the fighters swung their engine's around the central hull, directing the ionized particle discharges from their drives at the Sirian ships. Within the engine's cores, matter met antimatter and the resultant pions lanced out at the speed of light, slashing through the lead enemy vessel's shields with almost no resistance.

At least that was the hope.

They wouldn't know for fifteen more minutes if the beams struck, let alone penetrated shields. Jessica started her jinking maneuvers, shifting her ship around in a seemingly random pattern, yet one that was well coordinated with the rest of the squadron.

It wouldn't do to remain on a consistent vector with one's engine pointed at the enemy.

<*I have RM signatures!*> Cordy called over the combat net a mere second before the fighters flashed by a series of nuclear blooms in the darkness.

Jessica flinched in her soft cocoon as the light and heat washed across the skin of the ship, blinding her sensors for a moment.

The it was gone; the fighters were a million miles past the expanding clouds of dust and radiation.

<*Jason was disabled,*> Cordy reported to the squadron. <*I have his beacon and he is responding, but he's lost control of his main engine and is vectoring toward The Kap.*>

Jessica hoped he could slow his fighter and get into an elliptical around The Kap. At a fifth the speed of light he could fly clear across the system before a rescue could be mounted.

No more relativistic missiles appeared on sensors, though the closer the fighters got the less time they'd have to spot them. They widened their jinking pattern and when the hundred thousand kilometer mark was crossed, flipped their engines around and picked their targets.

Jessica saw the point defense lasers Carson had told her to look for and fired her shotgun at them. The weapon deployed a hundred sabot rounds, which raced toward the Sirian scout ship before exploding into chaff.

Moving ten thousand kilometers per second, the point defense lasers could only pick off so many of the small jagged pieces of carbon before they pelted the ship's shields.

Energy signatures flared as the shields strengthened to deflect the chaff, but she saw some get through and several of the point defense lasers were disabled.

Carson opened up with his fighter's main beams, using the over extension of the enemy's shields Jessica created to his advantage. He punched through one location and melted away half the ablative plating on the main battery. He followed up with his shotgun less than a second later and tore half the battery clear off the scout ship.

Jessica lanced at the gash in the hull with her beams and then a second later they were out of range.

The combat net showed that all the fighters had landed their strikes, but the lead ship was not yet disabled. It still had several functional batteries and the engines remained operational.

The pilots broke formation, arcing toward The Kap and reversing direction as quickly as they could. The burn on each of the fighters was right at the 70*g* limit the ships and pilots could handle.

The pressure on her body was overwhelming, and Jessica struggled to draw breath even though liquid oxygen was being forced into her lungs. The cocoon encasing her stiffened and the latticework of nano filaments that had grown all through her body tensed, holding organs and soft tissue in place.

She tried not to pay attention to the display which showed her cellular wall integrity, or the micro fractures growing through her bones, and instead kept an eye on the damage estimates rolling in.

Jessica looked over the tactical net and saw that the *Andromeda* was five minutes from coming into range behind the Sirians. Not perfect timing, but pretty good considering the distances and speeds involved.

By that time the fighters would be completing their arch and coming in for a second run.

Time dilation and sensor lag meant that even though the fighters and *Andromeda* would be hitting their targets at the same time, neither would see the other's attacks until they were well underway.

Carson directed Jessica to hit more of the point defense lasers while he concentrated his fire on the remainder of the battery.

<*They have fighters!*> Rock, who was on the leading edge, called out.

The combat net updated and Jessica saw that each scout ship had disgorged four fighters. They had stayed close to their ship's hulls, but now spread out, bringing beams and shotguns to bear on A and C wings.

Orders updated—A Wing was to stay on target while C Wing provided cover. Jessica synchronized a new jinking pattern with Carson and her beams swept across the scout ship, weakening shields and blasting those locations with her shotgun.

The combat net showed that the lead ship's defenses were down to a point where missiles stood a chance of reaching their targets and, as she made a close pass, Jessica let two fusion warheads fly.

The first was destroyed by a beam from an enemy fighter, but the second made it close. Just before it was destroyed by enemy beams, Jessica detonated it.

Nuclear fire washed across the Sirian scout ship and sensors showed its shields flicker and die. A moment later Rock, on the far side of the ship, let fly with another warhead. His penetrated the hull and released an EMP burst, which disabled the Sirian vessel.

With the wing's primary target disabled, the combat net updated and showed A Wing's new objective to be the second scout ship. C Wing was engaging the remaining nine enemy fighters and Jessica could just see the *Andromeda* with her optics, trading beam fire and shotgun blasts with the third Sirian vessel.

Joe had maintained alignment with the two remaining scout ships so only one could use its beams on the *Andromeda*—a feat which took no small amount of skill. The cruiser was maneuvering with every available thruster and the energy output made it glow like a second star on Jessica's sensors.

<*Let's give that other ship something to think about,*> Rock said to his squadron.

The fighters boosted at max *g* toward their next target; as they crossed within fifty thousand kilometers, they rotated their pion engines and all beam weapons toward the ship.

Lashing out at their selected targets, the scout ship's shields flared, desperately bleeding off heat from beams while strengthening to ward off the shotgun blasts.

The squadron blew past the ship and banked around again to make another run—this time at a much more comfortable 50*g*.

Jessica stayed close to Carson, clearing defense beams and adding punch to his attacks where she could. The second ship's shields were weakening and its defenses were also crossing the critical barrier where warheads could make it through.

The fighters arched around for another run, six black specs of power and destruction bent on tearing their foe apart.

At least that's how Jessica felt when suddenly her HUD went red and alarms showed on a dozen critical systems.

<*Shit!*> she said over the combat net. <*A chaff blast hit me, I lost main engine and my shotgun.*>

<*Steer clear,*> Rock advised. <*This guy's just about done and the* Andromeda *just took out the third ship,*>

<*Affir*—> Jessica began to respond when her external sensors flooded with radiation and then she knew no more.

ONLY THE DEAD KNOW THE END OF WAR

STELLAR DATE: 3283400 / 07.18.4277 (Adjusted Gregorian)
LOCATION: *Arc-5 Fighter*
REGION: Interstellar Space, Outside Kapteyn's Heliopause

Jessica awoke alone.

The realization that she had passed from dreams into full consciousness dawned slowly. Everything was dark and she couldn't open her eyes. Her limbs were constricted and seemed trapped in something almost like a gel…

The shoot suit, I'm in my fighter.

For a moment she felt better, it explained her eyes, the pressure, the cocoon.

But not the blindness.

She should be able to see with the ship, but when she attempted to Link with it, nothing happened. Neither Cordy, nor the dumb NSAI on the fighter responded.

She drew a deep breath, feeling the liquid oxygen course into her lungs. At least life support appeared to be working, that much was reassuring.

Jessica brought her personal HUD up in her mind and reviewed her vitals. What she saw would have made her gasp, were she able to.

Her bones were riddled with fractures, blood vessels were crushed and leaking, several of her fingers were broken and she had suffered third degree burns over most of her body.

While she was out, her internal med systems must have shunted as many of her pain receptors as possible, because she should have been in unimaginable agony.

She checked the time and saw that it had been thirty hours since the battle.

Her mind reeled at the thought.

Thirty hours. Jessica dismissed the thought that she was the lone survivor. The *Andromeda* and its fighters had been winning the engagement handily when whatever happened disabled her ship.

And gave me a very unhealthy dose of hard radiation, Jessica thought as she looked at her bio report.

She reviewed the logs and came to the conclusion that the second scout ship must have detonated its main reactor. It was the only thing that could have produced the type of radiation she saw in her body.

Her fighter had been a scant three hundred kilometers from the scout ship, she was lucky to be alive—lucky that her fighter's antimatter containment vessel had remained intact.

Her mind wandered as she imagined her ship drifting in the darkness, a black speck in a black void, likely surrounded by the much hotter wreckage of the scout ship.

Jessica ran the odds of rescue. They came up high—within the first ten hours after the battle.

As the clock slid past forty hours she fought to keep panic at bay.

She had been in the shoot suit, cocooned in her fighter for over three days. She wasn't given to claustrophobia—no one rated for piloting a fighter could be—but she was starting to feel the need to get out of the ship claw at the edges of her mind.

To get out no matter what, just to see where she was.

What, to stand on my ship and wave my arms?

She forced back the madness plucking at the edges of her thoughts.

She still had not managed to make any data connections to the ship, but she could tell that the life support system was failing. The oxygen content in the liquid flowing through her lungs was decreasing.

Jessica estimated she had only a few hours left before…

A dull thud reverberated through the ship.

It wasn't the first time something had impacted the fighter, which was what led her to believe she was drifting in the scout ship's debris field.

But the thud came again and then turned into a low vibration. No, this was no chance collision, Jessica knew this was a rescue.

It seemed like hours—though was only twenty-three minutes—before she felt the ship's hatch open and the cocoon disgorge her.

A suspension field enveloped her and she finally Linked.

It was *Andromeda* and the rich timber of Corsia's voice filled her mind.

<Welcome back, Colonel.>

The shoot suit's external optics came back online and Jessica saw Joe and Trist, along with many of the fighter pilots. They were cheering.

It was good to be home.

A LONG DAY'S END

STELLAR DATE: 3285312 / 10.12.4282 (Adjusted Gregorian)
LOCATION: ***High Victoria***
REGION: Victorian Space Federation, Kapteyn's Star System

Tanis stopped before one of the station's wide observation windows and Markus's chair glided to a stop beside her. They had nearly completed their round of the station; a tour they had been taking every month for several years now—ever since Markus had retired from active governance of the Victorian colony to convalesce on the station.

"I can see it how it will be," Markus said as he gazed over the world below him. "Oceans, forests, people everywhere. It'll be a paradise."

"It's going to be amazing," Tanis said with a nod. "Even our engineers didn't think they could do so much with a world like this. Your people's drive deserves the credit. You never would take 'no' for an answer."

Markus chuckled, the rasp wheezing at the end and he stifled a cough before responding.

"You know me, ever the optimist."

"I wish you'd let our medics help you," Tanis said. "We could give you decades more."

Markus waved his hand dismissively. "You know my answer; why do you always ask? You've given me far more life than I ever expected. The old dog messed up my DNA too much to give me more time than this—not without me becoming someone else—or a machine."

The plight he faced was one many of the elder Victorians were grappling with. So much of their base DNA was corrupted by generations of long-term exposure to the extreme radiation around Sirius that the older they got, the more prone they were to cancerous growths.

Medics aboard the *Intrepid* could repair their DNA, but they would need to replace much of it. A recipient of such treatment would have their body's base code altered. Many, like Markus, found that to be undesirable.

"Do I seem so much worse for it?" Tanis asked.

Markus looked up at her, his wrinkled smile causing her to respond in kind.

"You're the best damn-looking half-robot woman I've ever set eyes on. Heck, if I'm to believe you, there are actually two women living in that head of yours," Markus said with a wink.

He never doubted AIs existence, but he liked to pretend he did; that Angela was just Tanis's snarky alternate personality.

<*If only he knew how close that was to the truth,*> Angela commented on Tanis's stream of consciousness.

<*You don't help. You know you're not supposed to be able to do that.*>

Angela laughed. <*Everyone knows something is up with us. We've outlasted the longest pairings on the books by decades. Everyone is just too polite to ask if we're an abomination. Even Markus must know it's not natural.*>

"You're talking to her, aren't you," Markus asked.

"How could you tell?" Tanis asked. "I'm pretty sure I don't give it away."

"You don't, I just guessed. You as an individual may be inscrutable, but human nature isn't so hard to figure out."

"I suppose that's true," Tanis replied.

"I don't think you should worry about it. You're probably the most stable person I know. If your brain were going to turn to mush, it probably would have done it years ago." Markus gave her a gentle pat on the arm.

"OK, now I wonder if Angela was relaying our conversation to you."

Markus gave a short laugh.

"Nothing so sinister. Being this close to death gives you a different sort of perspective. I know being in charge of the fate of so many makes you constantly evaluate your abilities and doubt your own qualifications—or it'd better," he said with an evaluating eye cast her way.

Tanis raised her hands in mock protest. "No lack of self-doubt here. I know I look implacable to everyone, but I'm not. I thought I had royally screwed it several times over the years."

"Yet you always pull a trick out of your hat," Markus said. "You've done it in battle a hundred times and when you turned your hand to politics and diplomacy you navigated those waters just as well."

"I think my skill at politics is an extension of my abilities in battle. Everyone thinks I'm a crazy bloodhound and no one wants to see if I'll snap and kick the tar out of them to get my way."

Markus chuckled. "I'll admit the thought crossed my mind once, but I never gave it any serious consideration."

Tanis smiled. "Glad to hear it."

The pair watched in silence as a shuttle passed the observation deck, bringing a load of passengers in from the *Hyperion* to the station. Tanis brought up the manifest and final destinations of the shuttle and passengers. Most were going downworld to Victoria on vacation, while a few were transferring out to the colony on Tara.

"Your people are really multiplying—is that the right word? It's just impressive to see them really take hold of this system."

"It's what makes this worth it," Markus said. "To think, we who were once destined to spend our lives in small quarters on a single platform, now have a whole star system to ourselves. No small thanks to you."

Tanis waved her hand. "I helped you because you were here and needed it. You're the ones that got here on your own steam. That took guts."

Markus nodded contemplatively, but didn't speak.

"You think of the other Noctus you left behind, don't you?" Tanis asked.

He took a long moment to respond. "I do. I wish I could have figured out a way to save everyone, but that would likely ended with the death of everyone on the *Hyperion*. My duty was to them first, hard as that is."

"I have some understanding of that," Tanis said with a nod. "Every commander does—or should. At some point, it comes down to them or you."

"That's a dangerous sentiment," Markus said. "That would lead me to wonder if you'd someday make the same call with me and my people."

"I would," Tanis said without hesitation. "I know it sounds horrible—I would not do it easily, but if it came to us or you, you know what I'd choose. I know you would, too."

"I would." Markus shook his head as he spoke. "Life has made us hard—maybe too hard."

"Let's talk about something else, something happy," Tanis said, not wanting to remember those words as some of her last to Markus.

"I won't ask you what you think about Tom getting elected for his second term as President down on Victoria, then," Markus said. "You probably don't have happy feelings about that."

Tanis laughed, "Not especially. I did hear that Agnes and Dmitry are great grandparents now. Agnes seemed especially happy since she was just able to have the one son."

"She was already planning the child's first birthday when I saw her last," Markus said with a chuckle. "With three of her other grandchildren pregnant, she'll soon be the matriarch of her own clan. A long journey for the woman who manned the desk outside my office where so much of our little rebellion was planned."

"Hah! Little rebellion." Tanis couldn't help but notice that no matter where she steered conversation today Markus waxed nostalgic. Maybe that was what happened when you calmly stared your end in the face.

A comfortable silence stretched between them for several minutes before Tanis spoke up.

"I'm starved, and now that they have those pig farms on Victoria, one of the commissary's up here is serving BLTs. You in?"

"Absolutely. Let's see if my people can make bacon to satisfy your refined palette."

TRUE COLORS

STELLAR DATE: 3286965 / 04.22.4287 (Adjusted Gregorian)
LOCATION: Sperios Outpost, Victoria
REGION: Victorian Space Federation, Kapteyn's Star System

Ten years after the Sirian scout incursion…

Tom glanced at his companion across the table in the dimly lit bar. He didn't trust her, but he knew she hated the Edeners as much as he did, even if she was one—in a manner of speaking.

"How much longer is your contact going to take?" he asked. "It's not like this is the sort of place I'm known to frequent."

"Relax," his companion said. "No one here is the sort to spread stories. All they care about is working hard, getting their pay, and drinking it down."

Tom glanced at the bar's other patrons. She was right, no one seemed to be paying them any special attention. His companion blended in like she had been at the bar every day since it first opened. She did that everywhere, no matter when or where they met, she looked like she belonged. She could be anyone she wanted and never raised so much as an eyebrow.

He knew his attempt to blend in was less successful, but dressing down was not one of his specialties. Still, being in her company caused her mysterious powers of obscurity to shroud him as well.

"There he is," she said softly and gave a small hand signal to call their contact over.

The man slid into the seat beside Tom. He was non-descript, shorter than the Victorians, but not so short that people would know who he really was.

"How was your trip?" Tom's companion asked.

"As well as could be expected. I was undetected if that's what you're asking."

"I should hope so," she replied. "I own everyone on that route—though they don't know who it is that holds their leash. They think they're helping the almighty Tanis Richards and are so eager to do so."

"She's quite the powerful figure in this system, alright," the newcomer said. "Enough that I wonder about this plan of yours. Do they really have what you say they do? We lost three ships working out how to get past that damn sensor net."

Tom wondered, not for the first time, at the value of the research the Edeners were undertaking. The Sirians were allotting a considerable amount of time and effort in getting it. His companion had only told him that it was the most advanced tech in the galaxy and that she would share it with him and the Victorians if he helped her.

Only later did he discover she was also working with the Sirians. His companion had assured him that they were just a means to an end. Once she had secured the technology, she would not share it with the Sirians.

She better not. If his mother knew he was sitting across the table from a Sirian spy she would kill him—and not figuratively.

"They do," his companion replied to the Sirian. "I've seen it with my own eyes, though right now it's too hard to get at. That's where you come in."

"Yes, more of our resources, put at the disposal of these traitors," he said with narrowed eyes cast in Tom's direction.

"Listen he—" Tom began, but was silenced by his companion's raised hand and stern look which she then turned to the Sirian.

"Watch yourself, friend. One word from me and you die here and now. You are here as a partner, act like one, or you'll be replaced. Don't think your government values you more than what I can give them."

The man opened his mouth to speak, but then closed it and nodded slowly.

Tom gave the man a smug look and turned to his companion.

"What is our next move, then?"

She smiled, her face pleasant, but her eyes cold. "Why, we wait for the old man to die."

MOURNING VICTORIA

STELLAR DATE: 3288931 / 09.08.4292 (Adjusted Gregorian)
LOCATION: ISS *Intrepid*
REGION: Victorian Space Federation, Kapteyn's Star System

Five years after Tom and Myrrdan met with the Sirian…

*<Kim, I don't really care what he **feels** is best,>* Tanis said. *<Katrina has made her wishes pretty clear and I intend to honor them.>*

<Fine, but Tom won't be happy about this. He wanted to add other people to the guest list,> Kim replied. *<He also doesn't see why so many people from the* Intrepid *should be in attendance.>*

Tanis bit back a terse reply. The latest generation of Victorians possessed a sense of entitlement and disdain toward the Edeners that made their parents appear positively grateful. It was far more prevalent on Victoria than on the stations and Tara, though it was still present everywhere.

The original crew of the *Hyperion,* those who had worked and lived under the Sirian oppression were nearly gone. She would be damned if she was going to let this flunky stop her from saying her final farewells to one of them.

*<They should be in attendance because they were his friends and his wife wants them there. Quite honestly, it's none of Tom's damn business who is in attendance. It's not **his** funeral.>*

<Attendance to this funeral for Victorians is just another thing you've taken from us,> Kim said acidly and killed the connection.

Tanis found it ironic that the conversation was conducted via technology the *Intrepid* had provided. The Victoria colony would not exist at all without the colony ship's assistance—though to hear Kim's generation speak you'd think it existed in spite of the Edeners.

"That sure is a sour look," Joe said as he entered the kitchen where Tanis was preparing breakfast.

"It was Kim," Tanis replied.

"Ah, the ever-antagonistic Kim," Joe gave Tanis a long embrace. "Just a few more years and we'll be on our way. They can lust after our advanced technology in our absence."

Tanis relaxed into Joe, glad for his calm and unflappable attitude.

"I'm really starting to wonder if things might get ugly before we leave the system," Tanis said. "The original crew of the *Hyperion* did not pass their stoic attitudes on to their descendants. Without Markus to be the voice of reason…"

She found herself thinking back to her final conversation with Markus.

"I've seen enough life," Markus had said. "I did more than any of my ancestors did, or dreamed of doing. We have a new world here, and we're prospering. I was an old man when I met you and your doctors gave me another half century of life—the best I've ever had, but it's time to pass the reins on to the next generation."

"You're going to be missed," Tanis remembered a tear slipping down her face as she held a wizened Markus's hand. "I don't know how we'll manage without you keeping things steady."

Markus had given a rough laugh when she said that.

"I don't think there is anything you can't manage, General Richards. I've seen you tackle some pretty impossible odds over the years. People believe in amazing things, just because you do."

"I could say the same thing about you," Tanis replied.

"I'm going to rest a bit," Markus patted her hand gently. "Can you have them find Katrina? I need to see her..."

Tanis felt a tear coming to her eye again as she thought back to that conversation. Markus was one of the strongest people she had ever known. She was going to miss him for a long time.

Markus died several hours after that conversation.

"Maybe planetside they might get unruly, but up here they have more in common with us," Joe said, taking her hands in his. "We've built a good thing here. We saved a people and gave them a future they could never have dreamed of. It was never going to be perfect—not unless we decided to stay and fully integrate."

"I know," Tanis sighed. "The very fact that we're leaving—even if we gave them every advanced piece of tech and knowledge we possess—would still be cause enough for unrest. The signs are there, people are jealous of us, even after we pushed their standard of living ahead by centuries. Their government isn't doing much to smooth things over."

Joe nodded. "I know. Every year at the academy I have to do more and more to turn cadets into team members. It's like they've been brainwashed."

Tanis shook her head and sighed. "I've seen it often enough; we're skirting the edge of a conflict."

"Surely Tom knows it's not in his best interests to do that."

Tom was in his third term as president of the Victoria colony. The son of Sarah and Peter, Tanis still remembered when she first saw him as a newborn baby during the celebration for the station and beanstalk.

He wasn't nearly as agreeable now as he had been then. Tanis could see a lot of his mother's influence in him.

Sarah had never been particularly agreeable, but when an act of sabotage had taken Peter's life she became downright hostile. She blamed the death of her husband on Tanis and the *Intrepid*.

Tanis had to admit that to a certain extent Sarah was right. The threads of Myrrdan's influence were visible in a number of events over the years. She knew that his goal was to drive a wedge between the two peoples, keep her off-balance as he searched for the location of the picotech.

Sarah knew of Myrrdan and blamed Tanis for never catching him and for bringing his blight to her people. Tanis thought that by and large the tradeoff worked in the Victorian's favor.

"What Tom knows to be in his best interests and what he actually does often seem at odds. Even if he doesn't start anything, I wouldn't put it past elements of his government. Either way I've been planning for something like this for decades."

"I know," Joe laughed. "I remember reviewing your initial contingencies thirty years ago."

"Thirt—really?" Tanis consulted her temporal calendar.

<*That thing isn't healthy,*> Angela interjected. <*There's no good reason to track your age this much.*>

<*I've been in and out of stasis so much it makes me feel disconnected with reality—let's not rehash this now.*>

"You're two-hundred," Joe said before Tanis finished her conversation with Angela.

"I am?" Tanis was shocked. She knew that her bicentennial was coming up, but thought it was still a few years off. "How do you know?"

Joe laughed and embraced his wife. "Because I keep a calendar, too."

"They aren't lying when they say life accelerates as you get older," Tanis sighed.

<*The pinnace is leaving in twenty minutes,*> Amanda interrupted the pair.

<*Ok, we're on our way,*> Tanis replied.

Tanis and Joe wolfed down the remainder of their breakfast, checked their dress uniforms over one last time, and exited the cabin. Outside, a groundcar waited and drove them to the nearest maglev station.

They entered the forward hangar with a few minutes to spare and walked up the pinnace's ramp in companionable silence.

Commandant Brandt was speaking with two Marines at the top of the ramp. The diminutive woman stood at attention and snapped a sharp salute—mirrored by the two Marines—as Tanis approached.

"General," she nodded a greeting.

Joe and Tanis returned the salutes.

"Commandant, men," Tanis said. "Thank you for coming today."

"It's our honor," PFC Ramos said and PFC Sarin nodded his agreement.

Ramos and Sarin were members of the first platoon Tanis had put together as the *Intrepid* left Sol. Both had seen action with Brandt and Ouri when they fought the rogue AI on the *Intrepid* and were in the party that boarded Yusuf's cruiser in the battle of Victoria.

They had put their lives at risk for the mission many times, they deserved their place here.

"As you were," she said and continued into the pinnace.

The two squad military honor guard was another thing Tom had fought Tanis on, but Katrina had come to Tanis's defense.

"Intrepid Marines fought to save us from Yusuf. They should have representation here," Tanis recalled her saying.

Katrina had turned into quite the diplomat over the years; though, as a former spy, it was closer to her training than it was for Tanis.

Earnest was away at the Gamma site, but Abby was present, already seated in the well-appointed passenger cabin.

Tanis gave the chief engineer a silent nod.

They got along well enough now, but their relationship had never recovered from that day beneath the annihilator. Tanis held her no ill will, but for Abby a seventy-year grudge was just the warm-up.

Terrance and Andrews were seated at the cabin's central table and Tanis joined them. Joe moved off to poke his head into the cockpit—the pilots being graduates of his academy.

"Tanis," Terrance said by way of greeting.

"Lieutenant Governor," Andrews spoke with a gentle smile. "How are you?"

"As well as can be expected, I suppose," Tanis said. "Though I wish you wouldn't call me that."

"You prefer General?" Terrance asked.

"I'm pretty sure she was happiest with Colonel," Joe said as he joined them at the table. "But she needs to outrank me, so General will have to do."

Tanis sighed. "Thanks, hon, that's just the reputation I need."

"Governor suits you," Terrance said. "You've done remarkably well—it's hard to imagine you're the same woman who shot up the *Steel Dawn* on her first day. Everyone said you'd be trouble, but look at you now."

"You two made me wear this mantle," Tanis wagged a finger at Terrance and Andrews as she spoke. "You made me wear it and then went to sleep for decades. I never signed on to be a politician...I never..." She stopped and gazed down at her hands for a moment.

"He was a great advisor to me...he was almost—he had a strength of character I've rarely seen. I'm sorry I'm testy, I'm just going to miss him."

"I never spent as much time with him as you did, but he made a lasting impression. Just the thought of flying that mining platform between the stars. That took some serious guts," Andrews said appreciatively.

"I'm sorry, Tanis," Terrance said. "I didn't mean to upset—I meant it as a compliment. I rather thought you liked being in charge."

Tanis opened her mouth to speak and Joe put a hand on her arm.

"Choose your next words wisely, they'll likely come back to haunt you."

Luckily, Tanis was saved from having to reply by the arrival of Jessica and Trist. The pair were out of breath and smiling far too much for the occasion.

"Sorry," Trist said. "Took a wrong turn on the way here."

Tanis rolled her eyes as they sat. "Somehow I find it hard to believe that you don't know your way around the ship by now."

"It's each other that they're busy mapping all the time," Joe said quietly and received a jab from Tanis.

"Don't elbow me, I saw that smirk."

"I can't help it," Trist said with a smile. "Her new skin is so smooth and shiny; it probably needs a lot of mapping."

Jessica flushed ever so slightly and Tanis gave her a head shake. Never before had she met such a serious and capable person who was bent on turning herself into sex object.

After the battle with the Sirian scout ships, Jessica had suffered extreme cellular damage from the radiation exposure and her skin had to be completely replaced. While new skin was being grown the doctors gave her a temporary, artificial skin.

Jessica decided she liked the artificial skin and kept it, enhancing its sheen and softness—giving it a slight lavender hue. Combined with her exaggerated figure and purple hair she really did look like a life-sized doll.

With the last passengers aboard, the pilots gained clearance and the pinnace rose above the deck and passed out of the ES shield into space.

Light chatter floated throughout the cabin as the vessel began its descent toward the surface of Victoria. Tanis found herself with nothing to say and turned to stare out a port hole.

The progress of the terraforming effort was truly remarkable. In a scant sixty years, a barren rock had turned into living world with oceans, seasons, vast grasslands, and even several fledgling forests.

The industriousness of the Victorians was truly impressive. Matched with the technology and know-how the Edeners brought, it was a true wonder.

A rock passed by her window and Tanis saw on her HUD that it was one of seventy-one asteroids currently in orbit around Victoria. In various states of disassembly, most would eventually be kicked out to distant orbits or dropped onto the world below to kick up dust and increase heat capture in the atmosphere.

Some consisted entirely of ice and Tanis saw that the R21 refinery had been moved to the latest ice-ball, extracting pure H2O and dropping it to the surface of the world below. The main ocean was nearly filled and the refinery was creating a second, smaller ocean that crossed over the western side of the dusk band.

The large ocean was named Nautilus and the smaller had recently been christened the Atlantic. The Nautilus had warmed significantly over the decades of exposure to The Kap's ruddy light; the thin wisps of vapor Tanis had witnessed decades ago as she rode the *Excelsior* to Landfall were now thick clouds, their white bands wrapped around the equator of the planet—driven by winds which often reached several hundred kilometers per hour.

As the pinnace circled around the world, a massive hurricane building in the north of the Nautilus Ocean came into view. It was easily the size of all the continents of Earth combined. Such massive storms would be the norm for many years as the world's temperature equalized.

The new band of weather control satellites would cut down on their frequency, but even so, weather was always going to be exciting on Victoria.

Tanis found herself filled with pride at what they had built here. It was no mean feat to terraform a world like this and they would be able to leave it for generations of Victorians who would otherwise have never known the feel of a planet beneath them.

The pinnace raced above the clouds and Tanis tried to peer through them. When she was finally able to see through, massive breakers were visible, some hundreds of meters high—the result of the water pouring down from the refinery above.

A dull thud echoed through the cabin as the vessel dropped into atmosphere thick enough to create a sonic boom. The pilots began aero braking the pinnace for its approach into the Landfall spaceport.

She heard the pilots communicating with the ATC from the cockpit, the call-counter-call heralded the approach of the ocean's eastern shores. It was a thing of beauty and wonder to see the massive waves pounding the earth, throwing spray a thousand meters into the air.

The pinnace passed over the spectacle in mere moments, a ruined landscape slowly giving way to the low scrub of the eastern desert.

Eventually, the desert gave way to grasslands and then to bushland. To the north, the dark line of a forest appeared and then faded away in the distance.

It was a strange thing to see the brown plants growing and flourishing in the red sunlight. Tanis had to admit she was glad New Eden orbited a yellow primary. Something about plants that weren't green was unnerving.

The craggy mountain range north of Landfall eased into view and Tanis pulled up a forward view over the Link, looking ahead for the domes of Landfall.

The small outpost had grown considerably over the intervening decades, its population surpassing two million inhabitants.

Tanis remembered the naïve estimations that had projected a Victorian population of a quarter million. The Victorian people bred with a passion, finally free from generations of strict population control.

The total system population was now at nearly five million—three of which resided on Victoria, a million on the Tara colony, and another million on stations and orbital habitats.

It was quickly becoming a well-populated system.

While much of Landfall was still underground, it now sported several massive ES domes—something made possible once the planet sported a half-atmosphere near the equator.

The main dome covered the new government buildings, a university, thousands of homes, businesses, and no small number of parks.

One of the dome's properties was to enhance and alter the sunlight so that it took on a golden hue and plants utilizing green photosynthesis could thrive.

Refineries and manufacturing plants crouched beyond the domes, adding greenhouse gasses to the atmosphere and producing materials to expand the city.

Beyond that, east and into the deep dusk, lay the space and air ports.

The pinnace bucked as it dropped lower and passed into a crosswind. Anywhere else the winds buffeting the pinnace would be considered a navigation-blocking storm, but the pilots who dropped down into Victorian atmosphere referred to this as nothing more than a breezy day.

The final approach was swift and the pilot settled the pinnace gently on a landing pad, while three groundcars drove up. The passengers exited the ship and spaceport ground personnel guided the passengers to their transportation. In minutes the procession was wending its way toward the city.

The funeral was to be held at a place Markus frequented in life, the city's first above-ground park. It would take thirty minutes to arrive and Tanis settled back in her seat, her hand clasped with Joe's.

The streets near the spaceport were silent and empty; but as the procession passed through the dome and neared the park, silent mourners dotted the corners and sidewalks, clustered together in small groups. The park was only large enough for a few hundred people, and Tanis knew that other gatherings were taking place throughout Landfall.

Tanis felt their sorrow more keenly than she expected. She had lost many comrades; seen many heads of state, or great heroes of humankind pass away; but for some reason seeing the sheer number of people who felt as she did about a quiet man who did the right thing hit her the hardest.

The park's soaring trees came into view—their tops swaying gently in the small amount of wind which passed through the ES dome. The cars stopped and the party disembarked.

The walk through the park was serene and calming. Tanis clasped Joe's hand and few words were spoken by the *Intrepid's* delegation.

They approached the glade where the funeral was being held and ushers led them to seats right behind Markus's immediate family.

Katrina was already there and turned to clasp hands with each person as they filed in. The casket bearing Markus's body was at the front and Tanis walked to it, gazing down at the old man she had come to know so well.

Even though Markus had not reached his one hundred and fortieth birthday she couldn't deny what her eyes saw: the casket held the body of an old man who had lived decades fewer than her. The tragedy of it was nearly unbearable. He was so selfless, had only ever sacrificed for his people and never done evil. He was too young to die.

"Thank you for coming," Katrina's voice was soft beside Tanis. "I know Tom tried to control the attendees."

"There is no way I would have been absent," Tanis turned and embraced Katrina.

"You have no idea how much you meant to him," Katrina said. "You were the first non-Luminescent he ever met who treated him as an equal and with respect from your very first communication. You shaped all of his thoughts and opinions on what the future could hold from that moment on."

Tanis didn't know how to reply, there were no words that would be satisfactory in response. She held the embrace for another moment and finally said, "I'm so sorry to see him go."

"Me too," Katrina's mouth made a smile, but her eyes were filled with sorrow.

They separated and Tanis leant over to place a kiss on Markus's forehead before finding her seat.

She couldn't help noticing Tom's emotionless gaze and Kim's more hostile look as she got settled. Her thoughts clouded and before she could return her own caustic glare, Angela interjected.

<Don't do it. This isn't about them, don't let it be.>

<Thanks.>

Tanis couldn't help letting a small smile slip onto her lips. Even though she had lost a friend in Markus, she would never lose Angela.

Or Joe, she thought, as she took his hand once more and shared a somber look with him.

The ceremony was touching and Katrina spoke at length about how much Markus had meant to her. Other Victorians spoke, including the president, Tom, before Tanis rose to give her speech.

"I remember clearly that first message from Markus," she began. "He was in the direst of straits, facing the end of all his endeavors when he made that call for help. Even so, there was no wavering in his voice, no distress. He was a leader who led from the front and would make whatever sacrifice he had to for his people.

"It is fitting that he will be laid to rest here, on the world he brought you to, and where he met us. Two peoples, lost between the stars, trying to make a new home and form a new start.

"I think that if there were anything Markus would want us to remember, it is that we are all children of Earth, far from where humans began, but still humans, and still truly one people."

Tanis paused to wipe tears from the corners of her eyes before continuing.

"I learned a lot from him, I—"

Her words were interrupted by Angela's scream in her mind.

<DROP!>

Tanis hit the ground, hearing a ballistic round whistle through the air where her head had been a moment before. Several more shots fired, one hitting her in the leg and ricocheting off the armor she wore beneath her uniform.

She could see the Marines pushing their way through the crowd as people scattered in all directions, many crying out in fear, knocking chairs and other attendees to the ground.

In front of her, she saw Joe and Katrina laying prone with the rest of the *Intrepid's* party crouched low behind a row of bushes.

Joe looked at Tanis and gave a nod. "We're OK, they were all aimed at you."

"Sure, why wouldn't they be?" Tanis sighed.

She couldn't tell for certain amidst the screams, but it seemed like the sniper fire had stopped. Likely the shooter didn't want to hit other targets in the fleeing crowd. Moments later, the Marines were around her, scanning the surrounding terrain and buildings for the sniper's position.

<*President's clear,*> Brandt reported. <*I've called for the groundcars; we're going to meet them at the street to the east.*>

Tanis rose to a crouch and took a pulse rifle from one of the Marines. Based on the shots and the trees, the best angles were from the northwest. The sniper had to be in one of two possible buildings in that direction.

She cycled her vision, looking on the ultraviolet and infrared bands for the shooter's position. Before she spotted him, one of the Marines highlighted his position on the combat net.

<*Second building on the left, third window from the right.*>

Tanis sighted down the pulse rifle and fired a few shots at the window before moving to new cover. The Marines also brought fire to bear and Timmins scored the winning shot—infrared showing the sniper falling to the floor after he fired.

<*Not clear yet!*> Brandt called over the combat net. <*There are at least two dozen people moving in. They're not Landfall PD or Victorian military.*>

Across the clearing Tanis could make out black forms moving through the underbrush. She cycled her vision and could make out no distinguishing insignia.

The Marines began moving her group to cover and Tanis signaled Joe and Katrina to follow as the black gunmen reached the far end of the clearing and began firing on the Edeners.

<*Where is Landfall PD anyway?*> Tanis asked. <*I saw them when we arrived.*>

<*They all moved to escort the president out,*> Angela supplied.

<*Some thanks I get after training them,*> Jessica said while firing from behind a tree. <*Where are those groundcars at anyway, Brandt?*>

<*It would seem they were disabled; we're on our own.*>

Tanis's group crouched low behind a fountain, returning fire with their pulse rifles, while the enemy let loose a withering round of projectile fire. Pieces of the stone wall flew around them and Tanis gauged they only had a few minutes before their cover would be no more.

The combat net updated and showed three separate enemy groups, each with over a dozen members converging on their position. There was an opening to the south, but it was closing rapidly.

She cast an eye at Markus's casket, standing amidst the ruin of his final ceremony, it was no way to end his time—she couldn't believe that any group of Victorians, no matter how disgruntled with the state of affairs, would do such a thing to their patriarch.

<*Let's move!*> Tanis called out, directing the Marines to provide covering fire for the retreat, adding her own shots to the volley. The attackers were sloppy, but their numbers were effective. Tanis could see that they were all younger Victorians, the oldest no more than forty years of age.

Tanis looked over at Katrina and saw anger writ large on her features.

"I can't believe they actually decided to take violent action," Katrina shook her head, her words echoing Tanis's thoughts. "And at Markus's funeral, too!"

<*I have a fireteam securing the far side of the street,*> Brandt provided a verbal update over the combat net.

"I knew things were heating up, but I had no idea we were at this stage. Normally there are a number of peaceful escalations before we get to the attacking foreign heads of state phase," Tanis said to Katrina while taking aim at a young woman moving between cover. She made the shot and saw the woman stumble and fall.

Katrina saw it too, and her face twisted with sorrow, "I can't believe these children are going to die for their folly."

"Katrina, we're not barbarians, this is suppressive police action; we're only taking non-lethal shots."

"Oh thank god," Katrina sighed. "Sorry, I should know that, I just…"

Tanis laid a hand on her arm. "I know."

<*We've secured the far side of the street and the entrance to the building. We have your approach covered.*>

The combat net laid out the fields of fire and the safe vectors for the remaining members of the Edener party. Jessica was covering Abby behind a children's play structure; Joe and Andrews were behind a tree to Tanis's right. Trist was behind a bench with Terrance, who turned out to be a good shot with the small pistol he had taken to carrying since the *Intrepid* came under attack so long ago at Mars.

Tanis signaled for Trist and Terrance to retreat first, and the team increased suppressive fire while the pair raced across the grass then the street. Marines held the office building's doors open for them.

Tanis and Katrina were next. They moved single file, with Tanis running backward protecting Katrina behind her. The enemy's rate of fire increased and Tanis wondered which of them was the main target.

Two shots hit her armor and Tanis nearly fell as it solidified across her torso to absorb the impact. Katrina made the crossing unscathed and the Marines took advantage of the attackers over-extending themselves. In moments, several more were marked down on the combat net.

Tanis and Katrina burst into the office building and a Marine led Katrina behind a large desk in the reception area. Tanis surveyed the area to see two Marines covering a hall leading into the back of the office. She dispersed nano into the structure to ensure there were no surprises elsewhere as she walked to Brandt.

"Another lovely day in the corps," Brandt said.

"Have you made contact with the *Intrepid*?" Tanis asked the commandant as Joe and Andrews burst through the door, with Abby and Jessica following a few seconds later.

"I sent up a general alert before the Link got knocked out. I have Sarin on the roof seeing if he can get a line-of-sight hookup."

Corporal Hill jogged into the foyer and addressed Brandt.

"Building seems clear. Looks like some renovations were underway in here—construction's mostly wrapped up, but it's vacant."

"They're taking positions across the road, but I only see two groups," Sergeant Lee called from his position at one of the windows.

"Likely flanking us," Brandt nodded. "Hill, I assume there are windows in the second story of this place, take one/one up there and keep those SOBs from entering this joint."

Hill nodded and jogged to the staircase, signaling one/one to follow him.

"Trist, Jessica," Brandt called to the pair who were covering one of the front windows. "Find this building's access to the undercity."

"You bet, your pixieness," Trist grinned as Jessica motioned for PFC Ramos to cover their window.

<*My nano-scan is on the combat net,*> Tanis provided the stream location.

It took less than a minute for Trist and Jessica to find the undercity access; during that time, the exchange of fire increased drastically. Tanis was covering one of the windows and even Andrews and Terrance were taking shots.

"This is ridiculous," Terrance said as he swapped the charge cylinder in his handgun. "How can the police not be here yet?"

"I think it's pretty safe to assume that the police are in on it, or at least some of them are," Tanis said.

"Do you really think that's possible?" Terrance looked genuinely shocked.

Tanis was sometimes amazed at how someone with such business acumen could be so naïve about what people were capable of—especially after the *Intrepid* had been attacked dozens of times.

"Well, those two guys over there are," Brandt said as she fired several pulse blasts in their direction. "I had beers with one of them about a month ago. No wonder he seemed twitchy."

<*Located and cleared the entrance to the undercity,*> Jessica sent over the combat net. <*There were hostiles coming up, but we took care of them.*>

<*We need to move now, or we'll be completely surrounded,*> Tanis said.

<*Sarin, have you made contact with the* Intrepid*?*> Brandt asked one/two's tech.

<*I had it for a moment, but they've deployed scramblers, and I'm taking fire from adjacent rooftops. I think a burst about our situation got through.*>

<*It'll have to do,*> Tanis said.

Brandt ordered Sarin back down from the roof and directed Terrance, Joe, Abby, and Andrews to join Trist and Jessica at the entrance to the undercity.

"She's as bossy as you," Joe gave Tanis a wink as he dashed past.

Sarin joined one/two at the front windows while Brandt and Tanis joined the rest of the group at the undercity entrance.

It was a rather non-descript door at the bottom of one of the building's stairwells. Joe and Andrews were guarding it with Terrance and Abby standing just inside the building.

"Jessica and Trist are securing the far end of the corridor," Joe supplied.

Tanis noted the unconscious bodies of five young men and women from the Victoria colony. Based on their clothing and build they were all from the planetside group and not the station or mining platforms.

"Fools," she muttered.

"Or deluded," Terrance commented.

Brandt updated the combat net with the Marine's withdrawal plan and Tanis signaled her group to move down the corridor. There was no reason to get everyone bunched up.

Trist updated the combat net, showing the corridors beyond their current location. Tanis added her personal map of the undercity. They were seventeen kilometers from the spaceport with nearly two million civilians of unknown allegiance between their current location and the pinnace.

<Angela, do you think we could remote control the pinnace and bring it to this location?> Tanis highlighted a warehouse a kilometer from their current location. The warehouse had a loading dock outside the ES shield. It was the best LZ she could find nearby.

<Should work, but with the Link down, how will we send the plan to the pinnace?>

<A batch of nano should do the trick.>

<It will take them awhile to get there, they don't move that fast,> Angela replied.

<We best start now, then.>

Tanis updated the combat net with her plan and received agreement. Jessica began scouting in the new direction.

<It seems really empty down here. There are a lot of shops and residential areas that seem surprisingly vacant.>

<It'll be interesting to find out how high this goes,> Andrews added.

Tanis led her group down to where the corridor ended in a T-junction. She followed Jessica's path down the right hall and out into an open atrium.

Tanis recognized it from her many trips to Landfall. It wasn't far from the original City Hall where the MDC 'accident' had collapsed the roof.

Tall colonnades ringed the atrium and a holographic ceiling showed blue sky and white clouds above. There was plenty of cover for would-be ambushers and she flushed the area with as much nano as she could spare.

As the tiny robots spread out, she directed Joe and Andrews to the lower level where Trist and Jessica were waiting.

"Anything?" Tanis called down.

"Not a soul, all the shops in here are closed, but it looks like people were here not long ago. There are residential corridors down there," Jessica gestured to her right, "that are closed up. But I bet there are people huddled behind the doors."

<Brandt,> Tanis called the commandant on the combat net. *<Have a charge set in the corridor at the T and blow it. Let's slow our pursuers down as much as possible.>*

<Way ahead of you, we're setting it now,> Brandt replied.

"That corridor looks to be our best bet," Jessica said, gesturing down a wide promenade that led in the direction the group wanted to go.

"Check it out," Tanis said.

"Be my pleasure," Jessica smiled. She and Trist moved into the corridor each covering a side, checking each doorway, nook, and cranny.

Tanis couldn't help but smile at the couple as they worked together to clear the corridor.

They were an interesting pairing. Initially, Trist had mistrusted Jessica—as much because she was an unknown as Trist's innate dislike of all law enforcement. But after years together, they eventually admitted that they were made for one another and gave in.

It amused her that her two accidental passengers—both notorious for their promiscuity, not only ended up together, but were now so inseparable that she had to give them the same assignments or they would work out ways to be together.

She didn't mind, they were effective in their work, each coming at problems from different angles and working an issue until they had solved it from all sides.

Tanis moved her group to the entrance of the promenade, while above, the Marines entered the upper level of the atrium. Brandt appeared and waved to Tanis before she sprinted down the central staircase.

"Charge will blow any moment now," her statement was punctuated by a loud blast that echoed through the corridor and reverberated among the colonnades.

"Nice timing," Abby said dryly.

"I like to make a good entrance," Brandt smiled angelically before casting a hard eye at her Marines.

"Ramos, what in god's great space are you doing? Secure that passageway!"

* * * * *

Ouri had the *Intrepid's* conn.

Holographic displays surrounded her, filled with reports and analysis of data coming up from the surface. She didn't have much. Reports on the general net of a shooting at the service and then a garbled burst from Brandt indicating some sort of ongoing attack.

She immediately hammered the Landfall police for an update and was told that there was a Link outage in the area as a result of the attack, but that everything was now under control.

The president's office wasn't responding and, after the initial conversation, the chief of police passed her off to a flunky that did nothing but parrot his earlier statement.

<*I'll wager this is the insurrection Tanis was concerned about,*> Amanda's tone was laced with concern as she offered her assessment.

Priscilla turned from her position at a secondary comm station on the bridge and fixed Ouri with a worried look.

"I can't help but agree. Nothing they're doing is according to protocol. I've been stonewalled on a dozen different paths of inquiry."

Ouri stood and paced across the bridge, considering her options. They had outlined many different scenarios and responses. Unfortunately, none of them involved Tanis and the rest of the command crew being caught in the middle of the insurrection. Given their luck, Ouri wondered why that wasn't the first scenario they thought of.

As she considered options, the *Intrepid* slowly circled the world of Victoria, plotting the same high orbit it had for decades. Excepting those on the planet below, the rest of the command crew was in stasis.

Ouri and Priscilla were the only two humans present—and Priscilla was supposed to be taking R&R time on Tara, but this emergency had come up just as she was ready to disembark.

Still, Ouri counted herself more than lucky. With Amanda ensconced in her position outside the bridge, and Priscilla on hand, there was little they couldn't do.

Her mind calmed, Ouri assessed the contingency plans and selected her next course of action.

"Priscilla, get the ship's C Wing prepped and on their ladders. Also, find out if there is any elevated comm traffic between the groundside colony, the station and the platforms. If we're about to be hit from one of those locations, I want to know in advance."

"You got it," Priscilla replied.

<*Major Qhung,*> Ouri called down to the Marine command offices. <*I need a company of your finest on an assault transport, ready to launch in the next fifteen minutes.*>

<*Yes, sir, may I ask the nature of the engagement?*>

<*It would appear that our funeral attendees have come under attack and we've lost communication with them,*> Ouri supplied.

<*We'll be ready in ten!*>

<*Thank you.*>

The *Orkney* and *Dresden,* two of the ISF's new thousand-meter cruisers were in low Victorian orbit and Ouri raised their captains on the main holo tank.

"Colonel, we've been following the feed on the command net," Ophelia, captain of the *Dresden,* said the moment her image shimmered into view. "What do you need us to do?"

"We need to drop a platoon, but the clouds are too dense to provide cover from up there," Ouri said.

"We can drop below the clouds," Captain Peabody spoke in his gravelly voice. "I assume you're prepping a wing to come down, as well?"

"They'll be on their ladders in under ten minutes," Ouri replied.

The two captains exchanged a look. "Then we better get moving," Ophelia said and cut the connection. Peabody was gone a second later.

"Colonel," Priscilla said, "there is no increased comm traffic from the platforms, or internally on them as far as I can tell, but there is an increase with the station. Nothing that seems suspicious, except that it's a higher volume than normal for this time of day—it's station night. Also—Oh! President Tom for you."

Ouri brought the Victorian president up on the bridge's holo display.

"Colonel Ouri," the president was a clean-cut, well-spoken man in his fifties. He always had the right tone, and knew just what to say. That was one of the things that had always bothered her about him the most. Nothing ever seemed heartfelt.

She didn't let him start with whatever he had planned. "Mr. President, I understand that there's been some sort of shooting. I'm also having trouble contacting the *Intrepid's* away party."

"Yes, there was an attack by a group of citizens who are upset with the current state of affairs in The Kap System," President Tom replied evenly.

Ouri couldn't read any concern or alarm in his tone, nor did the Victorian president offer any gesture of concern or assurances of effort.

"You appear to have gotten free, why is it that my people have not?" Ouri asked frankly.

"I was protected by our security forces; I also was not the target—that appears to have been your people. My police have since have moved in and secured the area."

"Very well, are my crewmates safe?" Ouri asked, growing upset. This was the first piece of information the president should have provided.

The president appeared to pause and consider her question.

"It's pretty dangerous out there and I do not want to put any more Victorians at risk. I suppose that what I could do is offer to protect them from the angry citizens who are after them and return them to the *Intrepid*. But I think that a trade would be in order. Perhaps access to what you're building at your secret research site."

She wondered if he knew of the Gamma site, or if he just assumed there was secret research going on in the labs on Tara.

Either way, she wasn't surprised it had come to this. She was well aware that the Victorians wanted more of the *Intrepid's* tech. They didn't seem to understand that even in Sol—where advanced technology was not withheld from any group—it still wasn't free for the taking.

Tom's generation seemed to have no care that the deal struck with the *Hyperion* was for repair and resupply in exchange for specific technologies and the terraforming of Victoria.

As far as she was concerned the Victorians were making out like bandits. At best, the boost their mining platform and labor force provided only shaved a decade off what it would have taken the *Intrepid* to do on its own.

Despite her hard exterior, Tanis was really a bleeding heart.

"It sounds like you're detaining crew from the *Intrepid*. Is that the case?" Ouri asked. "If you are offering this trade, I want to see them."

President Tom paused again and Ouri felt certain he did not have anyone to present. It wasn't surprising; taking out Tanis, Joe and the rest would be no small task. Throw in a dozen Marines and Landfall would be a warzone before it was over.

"I'm calling your bluff, Mr. President. Not only am I not going to respond to your weak attempt at extortion, but I am invoking section 3.17 of the charter of Victoria. This grants the ranking officer aboard the *Intrepid* authority to take all and any means necessary to protect crew of the *Intrepid* from unlawful duress and detention on Victoria—unless you believe they are being lawfully detained..."

The president glanced outside the holo's view and scowled. "You told me they wouldn't do this," he muttered.

"I'm not sure who your advisor is, Mr. President, but they're wrong. I will do it."

Ouri cut the connection. Best to let him stew for a bit. Tom was the sort of man who only responded to threats and action. His smooth tone wouldn't help him when kilometer-long cruisers took position over his city.

Priscilla flicked accumulated scan data onto the main holo and Ouri looked it over. A heat signature bloomed near the park where the service had been held and she zoomed in, examining the terrain as best they could through the ES shield's glow.

A building was on fire across from the park, but there were no IR signatures matching the *Intrepid's* party.

Another satellite passed over Landfall and the resolution increased. She could see a number of Victorian's fleeing the building while others moved toward undercity access points.

"Bob, what do you think their plan is?"

<The spaceport is too far. I imagine that they know by now that they're not just up against a few malcontents. They are likely headed to one of these locations nearby, which can get them outside the ES shield.>

As Bob spoke, he pivoted the city view and highlighted the possible egress locations the planetside crew would head for.

Ouri nodded. "That makes sense. We'll need to get them transport out from there."

<*Major Qhung, where do you stand?*>

<*We're just finishing gearing up. The transport will be ready to drop in three minutes.*>

<*Very good, we expect the planetside party to exit the ES dome from one of the locations I've sent to your command net,*> Ouri said.

<*Yes, sir.*>

Ouri shook her head, having the conn of the *Intrepid* and being called sir by majors was not something she was used to—even after all these years.

"Looks like something is up, the pinnace at the spaceport appears to be prepping for takeoff," Priscilla said.

"Did they make it there?" Ouri was surprised, even for Tanis making it ten kilometers through hostile territory so fast was impossible.

"No, it's empty. I suspect that Tanis got a nano package to it and is sending it to her egress location."

"Handy. Make sure Major Qhung knows so he can follow it."

<*Planetside air support is lifting off in response,*> Bob provided.

"Faster than I thought," Ouri said.

<*Qhung is going to have a hot landing with those birds in the air,*> Amanda said. <*They must have already been prepped.*>

The Victorians claimed to have built the air force to deal with a possible incursion from Sirius, but Ouri had often suspected it was as much for their temporary neighbors as their Sirian oppressors. The atmospheric fighters were complemented by a respectable number of defense batteries.

"I guess the debate over who the planetary defenses are for is over," Ouri sighed.

<*That pinnace isn't going to make it past those fighters, but I pulled its destination and passed it to Qhung,*> Amanda said.

"C Wing's ETA?" Ouri asked.

<*Five minutes,*> Amanda supplied.

Ever since the incursion of the Sirian scout ships, Joe had maintained three wings in a state of high readiness—shoot suits and all. This wasn't the planned action, but she was glad they were ready.

Ouri rose and paced across the *Intrepid's* bridge. The ships would be playing a dangerous game. The Victorian defenses had been constructed with the intention of destroying mid-size cruisers just like the two moving into position. Their tactics would require C Wing to eliminate any enemy fighters and in-flight artillery so the cruisers could focus on the batteries.

The holo updated, showing the two ships just over fifty kilometers above the city—moving in random patterns to avoid laser fire. She could imagine what the ride was like. Jinking in atmosphere, even one as thin as Victoria's, was a gut twisting experience.

Ouri thanked the stars that the Victorians had not charged their batteries in advance—probably because the *Intrepid* would have detected the buildup. Instead the ground lasers were running off the city's main power grid, making for lower powered beams and longer recharge times.

"They're raising their reactor output to compensate," Priscilla said, also looking at the holo.

<*C Wing has dropped from their chutes, taking the hell ride down,*> Amanda said.

Ouri admired their moxie. The fighters were boosting toward the planet at maximum thrust. The atmospheric entry was going to be brutal, but the maneuvers to avoid crashing into the ground would be worse.

The loyalty Tanis inspired was nothing short of amazing.

"Godspeed," she whispered aloud.

* * * * *

Observers in Landfall watched in mixed awe and horror as a pair of thousand meter cruisers broke through the clouds and rained laser fire on the city's defensive emplacements.

It was unlikely that any onlookers appreciated that the ships avoided launching missiles and made their strikes as surgical as possible, as the sky lit up with ionized particle streams.

Maneuvering thrusters held the ships in stationary positions, and ES fields directed the engine wash away from populated areas.

On the northern horizon, a forest ignited under the intense heat and burned to cinders in minutes.

Ground batteries unleashed laser fire and missiles at the ships, which responded with point defense beams. Missiles exploded in the air over the city and no small number impacted the ship's shields.

The Victorian jets buzzed around the cruisers like angry gnats, peppering the ships with their beams and projectiles. The combined assault kept the cruisers more than busy.

Over the course of a long three minutes, hundreds of missiles spilled fire into the sky and thousands of lasers released their photon streams. The cruisers made only a few shots against the ground batteries, reserving most of their energy for defensive measures.

The *Dresden* suffered a shield failure on its port side, and an explosion bloomed on its hull as a missile made it through.

Below, most of the city appeared vacant, the citizenry huddled indoors or retreated to the undercity. A few Victorians were in the streets and on rooftops and those few let loose loud cheers at the sight above them.

An Edener retreat seemed imminent.

Yet the ISF ships did not move, and seconds later two dozen sonic thunderclaps tore through the air, flattening vegetation and shattering windows for miles.

C Wing had arrived.

The space fighters were less maneuverable in atmosphere than the Victorian jets, but what they lacked in finesse they made up for in raw power.

The ships slammed through the cloud cover at a thousand kilometers per hour, pivoted and braked mere hundreds of meters above the ground. Their pion engines screamed in the atmosphere and their engine wash tore craters in the earth beneath them.

Pools of molten rock filled the craters starting dozens of brush fires in the surrounding countryside.

The Victorian jets never knew what hit them.

C Wing unleashed withering beam fire from beneath, tearing the jets to pieces. Half the Victorian air force was gone in seconds, the remaining jets put up a brief fight, but a minute later the few survivors were in retreat.

Through the smoke and fire, the Marine transport appeared. It angled toward the far side of the city and a pair of C Wing fighters moved in to provide escort.

With the Victorian jets gone, the cruisers directed their full energy against the surface to air batteries. Explosion after explosion shook the ground as one after another were destroyed.

The Victorians on the streets and rooftops of Landfall looked up in horror as the menacing warships of their once-saviors began a slow acceleration back into the clouds, leaving the land for dozens of kilometers around Landfall ruined and aflame.

Though the Edeners had won the battle, there would be no victor this day.

* * * * *

Tanis ducked behind a stone balustrade as shots rang out and the zip-ping of ballistic rounds echoed around her. She eased around the barrier and let fly with several suppressing rounds before ducking back.

Her nano had a perfect picture of the battlefield, but the tiny bots themselves were otherwise ineffective. All of the enemy's weapons were chemical ballistic and the Victorians they fought had no AI or internal systems to disrupt.

"So close," Tanis muttered.

"Yeah, one more building and we're out of this mess," Joe said from across the alleyway as he let fire with his own barrage.

It had been a slow, arduous battle to get this far. Andrews had taken a bullet in the leg, Lieutenant Smith was nursing an in-and-out shot in his shoulder and Tanis had been thrown across a hall at one point from a pulse blast.

The Victorians were putting everything they had into the fight. There was no doubt in Tanis's mind that President Tom was behind this. He must have thought he could make a quick grab for *Intrepid's* leadership and negotiate additional tech and concessions from Bob and Ouri.

Now that the initial attempt had failed miserably, his only option was to hit them as hard as he could and take whoever survived as the hostages.

"We have to get through that choke-point," Sergeant Lee said. "I just don't see a viable plan where we don't lose a lot of people."

"Too bad none of us brought grenades to the funeral," Trist grinned while changing the charge cylinder on her pistol.

"I'll remember that for next time," Brandt growled.

A low rumble shook the tunnel around them and Tanis glanced at the rock over her head.

"Things must be getting hot up there," Tanis said before glancing at Katrina—the woman's face a mask of worry.

"They'll be careful," Tanis said. "I crafted no contingencies that involve harming civilians."

Katrina cast a hard look in the direction of their attackers. "I hope they can tell who the civilians are. I don't know if I can… stupid kids, and that asshole Tom; you know he has to be behind this."

Tanis nodded. "I would be shocked if he wasn't."

"I just hope we can put this thing back together—I hope there's something left to put back together..."

Tanis considered her options and turned to one of the Marines.

"Lieutenant, send one/two back to that access we spotted a quarter-klick ago. Let's flank this mess here."

Lieutenant Smith nodded. "It seems like our best shot. Turin, you heard the lady, make it happen."

Sergeant Turin nodded his assent and huddled with Corporal Nair for a moment before one/two moved back down the corridor toward the access to the city above.

A moment later, a new voice came over the combat net.

<*Hey guys, I heard you needed some help.*>

<*Qhung! Where the hell are you? We're pinned down here,*> Brandt responded.

In response, pulse blasts rang out from behind the Victorians. Several fell and moments later the rest surrendered.

"Right here," Qhung said, as he walked through the debris with a smile.

VICTORIA IN PERIL

STELLAR DATE: 3288931 / 09.08.4292 (Adjusted Gregorian)
LOCATION: Landfall, Victoria
REGION: Victorian Space Federation, Kapteyn's Star System

A Marine handed Tanis a rebreather and she stepped out of the warehouse's rear dock into a cluttered equipment yard. Even through the breathing apparatus, the air reeked of carbon and ozone. It burned her eyes and she double-timed to the waiting shuttle.

Above, ISF fighters circled; beyond them lightening flashed through the clouds, striking the surrounding hills and the city's ES dome in an attempt to equalize static charge in the clouds. The volume and intensity of the strikes indicated that quite a battle had taken place over Landfall.

Tanis shook her head and shared a sorrowful look with Katrina. This was a sad enough day without witnessing the destruction of their work, the potential end to their people's friendships.

"We'll fix this," Tanis said.

"We have to," Katrina replied solemnly.

They boarded the assault transport and Tanis felt the team's combat net Link to the *Intrepid.*

<*Ouri, what's our status?*> Andrews beat her to the question.

<*Good to hear your voice, Captain,*> Ouri's reply conveyed genuine relief. <*The short version is that Tom tried to extort us in exchange for your safety and I called his bluff. He didn't have you, so I sent C Wing down with the* Dresden *and the* Orkney *as support. The Victorians launched their air force and…I…we did what we had to.*>

Ouri paused her report for a second and when she resumed her mental tone was steadier. <*We took quite the beating, but C Wing made it down in time and we took out the AA batteries and much of their air force. There were casualties on both sides.*>

Tanis glanced down the ramp of the transport at the smoking ruin of the Pinnace only a dozen meters away. She was genuinely surprised that Tom took things this far. His plan must have hinged on killing her quickly and seizing the rest as hostages. When that looked increasingly improbable, he had taken every effort to keep them in the city and bluff Ouri.

<*Seems like a weak plan,*> Jessica commented. <*They could never have mounted a credible threat. Their only advantage was an expectation of restraint from our military power.*>

<*I can't believe it came to this,*> Terrance said. <*We're a colony mission, not a military dictatorship. We sure look like one now.*>

Tanis shot him a cold look. She knew he didn't like the military buildup; neither did she—the trip to New Eden was supposed to be her way out of that life. But he was the one who built a colony ship with the sole purpose of secreting away the most valuable technology known to humanity.

<*Now is not the time, ignore it,*> Angela said quietly.

Tanis took her advice and responded to Jessica. <*It does seem like it, doesn't it? Even if they had us as hostages, we hold most of the cards.*>

<*Do we know who was involved? Other than Tom?*> Katrina asked.

<*From what we can tell, it was largely a political movement, the population wasn't involved. The other cities are pretty quiet—Landfall is, too, except for your neck of the woods. There were some riots on the station when the stationmaster tried to send assistance to the planet and the people stopped it. The mining platforms have been calling to the planet and us repeatedly; begging us both to stop and telling us they were not involved.*>

<*It's going to take some doing to sort this out,*> Terrance sighed. <*Just when we were so close.*>

<*Just a second,*> Ouri said before coming back a minute later. <*Shit, we have a bigger problem. We just got a report of enemy ships in-system. The stellar sensor array shows nothing, but an ore pusher saw them just over an AU out. It detected at least twenty-five vessels before it got out of Dodge.*>

Tanis banged on the hull behind her and called to the pilots. "Get us back up to the *Intrepid* now!"

The last few Marines pounded aboard and the transport's boosters came to life, pushing it off the surface with a speed she would not have expected the bulky vessel to possess.

"How did the sensor net not pick them up?" Brandt asked. "It caught their last incursion."

Tanis was mentally narrowing down a suspect pool. The presence of the Sirius ships meant that Myrrdan knew about the incursion a decade ago. It also meant he had the means and the ability to tamper with the sensor net.

It was further confirmation that whoever he was, or whoever he was masquerading as, had to be high in the ISF command structure.

Tanis used her link through the *Intrepid* to reach out to the Victorian President's office.

It only took a moment for Tom's face to appear in her mind. His phony look of concern made Tanis wish she could punch him through the Link.

<*Lieutenant Governor, I'm so glad to see that you are OK,*> the president spoke with a grim smile. <*We're going to need to talk about reparations for your people's attack on our facilities.*>

<*Tom, I don't give a damn about that. I want to know what you know about the fleet bearing down on us right now.*>

The President's face drained of blood and he turned, looking outside of his virtual projection, <*What do you know about—wha—!*>

The Link was severed a moment later.

Tanis looked at the faces around her. "I believe the Victorian President has just been killed. I also think he was conspiring with someone and they saw the end of his usefulness. I saw him look at another person for guidance more than once."

<*He did that when I talked with him, too,*> Ouri replied.

"You know who it must be," Jessica said to Tanis.

"Maybe. It could be another agent."

Jessica shook her head. "No, it's him. Drop me off at the spaceport with the Marines and we'll hit the Parliament. It's time to run him down once and for all."

"What makes you so sure?" Andrews asked.

"After all this time, I think he has finally come out into the open. It all makes sense. He learned about the picotech and ensured that our layover would be longer here than we wanted, so that he could effect a plan. Sirius gave him the perfect opportunity. The timing is too pat; he is in league with them."

"I'll admit it fits," Terrance nodded.

"We're going to have one hell of a fight up there; we're likely not going to be able to give you any support," Andrews said to Jessica.

"What do you think I am?" Brandt asked.

"We need you upstairs," Tanis said.

Brandt sighed. "Then I'm going to send another platoon down to the spaceport. Two squads can't take on two million civilians. For that we'll need six."

She rose to discuss tactics with Lieutenant Smith and Jessica followed.

"I'm going with them," Katrina said, giving a deferential nod to Tanis and Andrews as she rose. "Keep us safe…again."

Tanis signaled the pilot to divert and put down at the spaceport while pouring over the scant data about the incoming fleet. It was a force intended to be overwhelming and Tanis felt real fear that there may be no easy way out of this situation.

The shuttle rocked as it touched down at the spaceport and all but two Marines too wounded to fight followed Jessica, Trist, and Katrina out of the bay.

Moments later they boosted into space.

BATTLE FOR VICTORIA

STELLAR DATE: 3288931 / 09.08.4292 (Adjusted Gregorian)
LOCATION: Landfall, Victoria
REGION: Victorian Space Federation, Kapteyn's Star System

"The rail platforms are coming online," Admiral Sanderson reported. "We are also launching picket fighters and planting RMs in strategic locations. We don't have a lot of them, though—we never really expected to be in a fight this big."

"It looks like we can never have enough relativistic missiles," Andrews shook his head.

"The plant is pumping them out as fast as it can," Tanis said. "Just not fast enough it would seem—thank the stars at least some of the rail platforms got done."

A decade earlier, Tanis had ordered the building of a dozen automated railgun platforms to provide additional protection for the colony. To date, only seven had been installed. Four were in synchronous orbits with Victoria around The Kap. The other three orbited Tara.

Though few railgun platforms protected the capital world, each was capable of firing half-ton slugs at 0.2*c*. When the slugs impacted they would deliver forty-five exajoules of energy—a force equivalent to an eleven-gigaton nuclear weapon.

They were just shy of world-killers.

Tanis took the XO's bridge station; Terrance sat near her, a look of deep concern on his face. Officers representing various ship sections filed in to coordinate with their departments and several ensigns sat at weapons and helm stations.

Priscilla winked at Tanis. "Glad you made it off the dirtball."

"You and me both," Tanis said with a smile.

"Bring us up to Anne's orbit, we need to establish a more easily defensible position," Andrews gave the order to helm, his voice calm, not a tremor of concern present.

Tanis brought up a display of all ship placements within 3AU on the main holo and rose to examine it.

The Intrepid Fleet was spread across the system on a combination of maneuvers, colonization assistance missions, and patrols.

Several were headed back to Victoria, already having been recalled by Ouri; a few would make it on time, most would be too late.

"The *Dresden* and *Orkney* are on station, holding at nine hundred kilometers starboard and port," one of the ensigns reported.

Tanis nodded pensively. "Have them switch places. The *Dresden* needs to keep that hole in its port side protected."

"Aye, ma'am."

<*You don't think I can take it?*> Sue, Trist's old AI asked.

<*I know you can take it. If I didn't, you wouldn't be running a Claymore-class starship,*> Tanis replied with a virtual wink.

<*I appreciate your vote of confidence. Sorry I got a hole blown in your fancy new ship,*> Sue replied.

<You didn't put it there; just keep any more from getting made.>

Sanderson stepped to her side. "The *Yosemite* will be here within the hour, but the *Terra* is too far out."

"We should keep it there. If they know of the Gamma site, they'll make an attempt to hit it. I think we should bring the *Peters* and *Starflyer* in from their patrol to bolster it. With the combined fighter compliment, they should be able to hold off all but the most determined assault."

"I agree," Sanderson said.

Tanis nodded to Priscilla who relayed the order across the system.

Of the forty-seven capital ships in the Intrepid Fleet, only eighteen would arrive before the Sirian ships were within firing range.

She organized the ships into three battlegroups, each with one of the new thousand-meter Claymore class cruisers as its anchor.

Each battlegroup had a seven hundred and twenty meter Trenton class cruiser and several of the fleet's new Pacific class destroyers.

She saw the *Andromeda* signal that Joe had arrived onboard and directed the ship into a polar orbit around Victoria. Since the last engagement with the Sirians, its stealth systems had seen further upgrades and the ship would be entirely invisible to the enemy.

The *Tromandy*, formerly known as the *Strident Arc*, reported ready as it passed Victoria's southern pole and Tanis assigned it to close station defense of the *Intrepid*. She gained a pyrrhic sense of satisfaction knowing that the ship which pursued the *Hyperion* to The Kap was now in the force arrayed against the Sirians.

<I've found and corrected the data error in the sensor array. Stellar scan is updating,> Bob said.

Tanis waited impatiently as the NSAI assembled a picture of the system from the thousands of sensors in the stellar array. When it did, true fear gripped her as the holo showed sixty-five Sirian ships.

"Ouri, I could have sworn you said something like twenty-five!"

<You're not that good at math, are you?> Angela asked.

Ouri's face was white. "That was the report…and they were way further out."

Tanis glanced around the bridge, the crew looked as scared as she felt. She had an ace up her sleeve, but it was a card she really did not want to play.

She turned to Captain Andrews and Admiral Sanderson.

<I've had fleet conn for some years now, but would you like me to transfer it to either of you?>

Captain Andrews shook his head.

<I may be in charge on paper, Tanis, but you've been running the show—you know the personnel and the fleet's strengths better than anyone. Sanderson?>

Sanderson nodded. *<You have our absolute faith.>*

<Good,> Bob's voice boomed through their minds.

<That was easier than it should have been,> Tanis said privately to Angela.

<The captain never signed up for this. It was supposed to be a milk run on the safest and fastest colony ship in the galaxy. Sanderson was a good officer in his day, but he never saw half the combat you have.>

<I appreciate the vote of confidence,> Tanis said. *<I swear, sometimes I feel like a petty dictator holding all of these titles that I never really earned.>*

<Trust me, you've earned them,> Angela replied.

Tanis looked to Priscilla, "Give me all fleet."

The avatar nodded and a second later said, "You're Linked."

<If you haven't heard already, we're in for a hell of a fight,> Tanis said, feeling the presence of thousands of men and women just at the edge of her mind.

<We're outnumbered almost four to one, and if you're worried, then that's good; means you're still alive. We know for a fact that the Sirians are overconfident, sloppy, and their tech is centuries behind ours.

<We didn't make it this far, face down so many threats, and continually defy the odds to be defeated here and now. We have prepared well, we have powerful ships, strong defenses, and all of you. We've trained for this, prepared for this eventuality.>

Tanis paused a moment, a knot of emotion in her throat.

<You know your jobs, do them well as I know you can. Be diligent, proud, be fierce! Today our names are writ amongst the stars.>

Tanis nodded to Priscilla who cut the link.

The bridge crew erupted in cheers.

"Didn't know you had that much prose in you," Ouri said.

"I've read a lot of Keats recently."

<Keats wrote poetry, not prose,> Angela said.

<I do know that, did I just manage subtlety that you missed? That's an auspicious sign,> Tanis replied.

<Subtlety? Oh Keats' grave! Well done.>

Her speech was followed by a flurry of virtual meetings. Tanis refined the details of her plan with the fleet captains and when she was done, the holo updated with two countdowns.

One, at just shy of an hour showed the time until the Intrepid Fleet would be ready for combat.

The second, at only fifteen minutes, was the countdown until the Sirians were in range of the railgun platforms.

In front of her, the holo projection contained normalized numbers and a linear timeline, but the reality beneath that was far more complex.

Tanis re-checked all of the calculations herself—not because she doubted the weapons and scan NSAI, but she preferred to internalize the math to understand the timings better. With distances over a light minute, and with dozens of ships accelerating and braking across the battlefield, no distance or time was what it appeared.

Local scan showed Victorian ships moving out of the area, and the platforms adjusting their orbits to be on the far side of Victoria when the battle was joined.

She hoped there would be a world for them to continue building when this was over.

Tanis's concentration was broken by a voice at her side.

"It's not going to be easy, is it?" Joe's virtual presence stood beside her, brow furrowed as he studied the holo.

"Given the size of their force, they know everything…except maybe about Gamma—though we have to assume they do know about it. Still, they don't know where our rails are and when they'll hit. They have to be anticipating some heavy losses before their weapons get in range," Tanis said.

<*I would bet that a lot of Victorians are thankful you forced those rail platforms down their throats,*> Angela commented.

<*I wouldn't count on it,*> Tanis replied darkly.

"I prefer to think that what happened downworld today does not represent the majority of Victorians. Given that we know Tom was involved—maybe the perception we've had of the public has not been entirely true," Joe appeared to lean against the holo platform. "I certainly would like to think we have been better appreciated."

"Let's hope we get the opportunity to find out."

The time passed slowly and the *Andromeda* went silent, taking Joe's virtual presence with it, but not until after a kiss that Tanis wished were real.

"General Richards," one of the lieutenants on weapons called out. "Based on scan, we will have firing solutions for the rail platforms in three minutes. What are targeting priorities?"

Tanis's tactical guide called for the rails to tear the lead ships to shreds, turning them into clouds of deadly shrapnel for any other ships nearby. She examined the trajectories of the enemy ships and picked out the vessels which would do the most damage to their allies when destroyed. Once the four were marked, she sent the decision to the weapons console.

The lieutenant nodded and—after Bob re-checked the work—approved the firing solution. Even traveling at one-fifth the speed of light, it would take the slugs over thirty minutes to reach their targets.

With such a large time delay, they would only get one long-range shot each. Once the enemy ships realized that they were the targets of such powerful kinetic weapons, they would add random shifts, colloquially known as jinks, to their movement, ensuring no further long-range shots could be made.

"I'm surprised they're not jinking already," Tanis said as she pulled up additional scan data from other posts.

"They're still a long way out of laser range. Maybe our friend didn't tell them about our rails," Andrews said. "Maybe he wanted us to wear them down."

<*It would fit the narrative,*> Angela commented.

"Using evasive maneuvers only after you take losses is how fools lose battles," Tanis shook her head. "It also means these guys may not behave the way we expect. Their cockiness will make them unpredictable."

"Let's hope they're predictably cocky," Sanderson scowled at the holo, as though he could will time to speed up and show the shots impacting.

Tanis signaled the platforms to take up new positions. With luck, once the enemy ships closed in, the platforms could make a few more shots.

She returned to her seat and checked the status of the fleet, stations, mining platforms, and the moon's batteries. The last few ships were nearly in position and the platforms had adjusted their orbits.

Everything that could be done was being done.

Tanis settled back to wait.

* * * * *

Jessica paced on the tarmac, pulling her jacket tight against a cold wind that was steadily picking up.

"Wimp, it's not that cold," Trist said from under the awning of a storage shed.

"Yes, it is. You just don't have enough blood anymore to get cold."

Trist chuckled. "At least I have skin. I'm surprised that plastic stuff you have lets enough perspiration though for you to get cold at all."

Jessica rubbed her arms vigorously. "It breathes plenty well—as you should know." A snowflake drifted past and she pointed at it. "See! Snow! It's cold!"

"Whatever," Trist said with a grin, clearly enjoying riling her wife up.

<*ETA forty-five seconds,*> Lieutenant Smith updated them over the combat net.

"About time," Jessica groused and turned toward the landing cradle.

Marines pulled up in three equipment haulers and a bus, which they had graciously requested from the spaceport staff. For their part, the Victorians they encountered were cautiously helpful.

None professed to have any knowledge about the attack on the funeral, and even though the recent battle with the ISF cruisers didn't generate any love for the *Intrepid,* the news of the Sirian fleet put them in a tight position.

Tanis would never allow the Victorians to die at the hands of the Sirians, but Jessica didn't think it would hurt for the downworlders to wonder.

Katrina had helped keep things smooth and cordial. The spaceport workers may have distrusted the Edeners, but they weren't going to say no to one of the founders of their rebellion and subsequent colony.

The assault shuttle touched down and a platoon of Marines in powered armor rushed out to take positions around the landing field. Smoothly, and by the numbers, the Marines who had accompanied them to the funeral fell back and boarded the transport to don the spare armor brought down for them.

Jessica surveyed the deployment and, once cover was well established, moved out from the lee of the building where she and Trist been sheltering.

As they approached the shuttle, Katrina stepped out of the bus to meet them.

"You know I'm coming with you," she said, her expression resolute, ready for a fight.

Jessica sighed. "I imagine I couldn't stop you if I wanted to."

"Heck, she couldn't stop me and I'm only two thirds your height," Trist said with a smirk.

"I'm going to put you with Smith's platoon," Jessica said. "Armor up and see where he wants you."

Katrina nodded and walked up the shuttle's ramp.

<*Seriously?*> Lieutenant Smith addressed Jessica privately. <*I know she's capable—hell, I saw her shoot at her own people not an hour ago—but we need to move fast.*>

<*She was combat trained before you were born, Lieutenant. You'll keep her safe and user her to your advantage,*> Jessica said in a tone that brooked no debate.

Smith was not given to complaints and Jessica knew he and his squads just wanted to get back into the fight. His eagerness was one of the reasons she placed Katrina with him. He wasn't going to go off half-cocked with the matriarch of this colony on his six.

And if he let anything happen to her, they both knew Tanis would have his hide.

She reached the top of the shuttle's ramp to see Trist engaged in a rather comical scene—even Katrina was smiling.

"Damnit, this isn't going to fit," Trist said while looking up at a standard ISF Marine powered suit in its rack.

"I told them to send down our suits," Jessica said with a frown.

Her exaggerated physique was hard enough to fit in standard armor, but no Marine was anywhere close to Trist's one hundred-fifty centimeters.

"You're going to have to make do," Smith said to Jessica before turning to Trist. "We have procedure for you; the armor doesn't need *your* limbs to be in *its* limbs to work.

The lieutenant nodded to PFC Ramos who was already in his armor. The private pulled a suit out of its rack and gave it a deft twist, separating the torso from the legs.

"Forgive the intimacy. Kneel down," Smith said and walked behind Trist as she knelt. He slipped one arm under her ankles and another across her chest. In one swift move he picked her up like she weighed no more than a pillow. Her legs were folded back at the knee and he slid her into the armor's legs.

"Now fold your arms like they're chicken wings," he said to Trist. As she sat perched in the armor with her arms folded, he split the armor's torso into its front and back pieces and then placed them back around Trist.

The armor detected its inhabitant and slowly adjusted to her form, filling the empty lower leg and forearm spaces with gel.

"This…this is weird, Trist said as the armor's torso compressed, shortening to match her frame. Smith slipped the helmet over her head after a moment she raised her hand and wiggled her fingers.

<*Gah! This feels weird. The neural shunts are working. My actual hand isn't moving…at least I can't feel it moving,*> Trist said over the Link.

<*Good,*> Smith responded. <*Take a step, make sure your balance is ok.*>

Trist took a few tentative steps and gave a thumbs up.

The transport's systems selected the closest fit for Jessica and a powered suit lowered off the rack and split open in front of her. Her entry was much more graceful than Trist's and a moment later the protective shell closed around her.

Gel filled the spaces around her waist and the armor adjusted as much as possible to her lengthened legs and altered torso.

She Linked with the suit and a cool sensation washed over her skin as her outer touch senses transferred to the armor. The systems ran a quick check, and her visual HUD updated with data regarding the suit's systems.

<*No one shares this with anyone,*> Trist said over the 'toon Link.

Several of the Marine's avatars chuckled and Jessica was certain they'd remind Trist of this as frequently as possible.

The rest of the Marines were suited up and they moved off the transport, each grabbing a rifle at the top of the ramp.

Jessica selected a dual fire weapon, which could switch between photon and proton streams. Behind her, Trist made the same selection.

<*Ready to kick some ass? Time to finally take Myrrdan down once and for all.*> Jessica asked her privately.

<*Hells yeah. This son of a bitch has hurt us all.*>

At the bottom of the ramp, Jessica addressed the Marines over the combat net.

<*It's a shit show down here, folks. We've pummeled their defenses and now there's an enemy fleet inbound. Most of your 'toons are from the same companies and there's no OIC. I'll fill that role, but Lieutenant Smith will have tactical authority.*

<*Upstairs things are grim, but we know our people; they'll take care of things. Keep your head down here, keep your eyes on scan, watch your brothers and sisters. We get our guy and all come back.*>

<*Thanks,*> Smith said to her privately before addressing the troops. <*You heard the colonel. We're Marines and we'll get the job done. Our company AIs aren't with us on this one, we'll be using the suit-networked NSAI. It's made transport assignments, so get moving.*>

A round of muffled "oo-rahs" sounded through helmets and over the Link.

Moments later, the Marines were bounding toward the ground transportation, their powered armor sending them meters into the air with each step.

Smith coordinated with the two other lieutenants and the platoon sergeants. They tweaked the approaches to the city and two force recon squads were dispatched ahead of the ground transports.

Jessica watched as the recon squads flashed rapid hand signals at one another before leaping into the air—their lighter armor and propulsion jets allowing them to fly hundreds of meters between touchdowns.

Smith's platoon would approach the city from the south, on the left flank. Their goal would be to take the parliament buildings and subdue any of the presidential guard who may remain. They would also protect Katrina and ensure she could take control of the government while the other two platoons worked to keep Myrrdan from fleeing.

Jessica assigned herself to Lieutenant Usef's section of the net. He was headed straight up the center. She had no real idea where Myrrdan would be, but her gut told her to keep options open, and the center was best for that. The fact that Usef had a weapons platoon also played no small part in her decision.

On the right flank, circling around from the north, was Lieutenant Borden's platoon. They were lightly armored and would move fast, securing as much of the city's northern reaches before the enemy could reach them.

She hoped.

* * * * *

<*Readings coming in,*> the weapons group announced over the bridge net. <*Looks like three of the slugs impacted. One of the big boys got nailed and two of their half klickers. They're pretty spaced out, looks like only superficial—wait, no, a piece of hull just tore through another cruiser, several others have taken smaller impacts.*>

"Yay for our side," Priscilla smirked. "I bet that'll give 'em some pause."

"They're jinking," scan reported. "They've ceased braking. I think they plan to churn and burn the colony."

"That's not going to happen," Captain Andrews replied. "Those dirtsiders may be a bunch of ungrateful asses, but they're our ungrateful asses."

"They must not have a lot of real combat experience in Sirius," Tanis said as she rotated the holo display. "I guess all the wars back in Sol were worth something after all."

<*Kicking ass across the galaxy?*> Angela asked privately. <*Seems like we'll never get away from this.*>

<*Only the dead…*> Tanis replied

"I assume there is a strategy for this?" Terrance asked.

"Well, if you're blasting down on a world, then your trajectory is relatively fixed," Tanis replied and turned to the weapons team. "Take the two rails on the far side of Victoria and keep them peeking just above the poles."

"Grapeshot?" asked one of the lieutenants.

"You got it. Calculate your spread to hit them at just over a hundred million klicks. Once the first ships get hit by the grapeshot, they'll likely disperse into one of these two patterns. Use the other two rails to fill those locations with grapeshot at that time." Tanis provided the patterns and coordinates over the bridge net and couldn't help feeling relief. The Sirians were not fighting smart; if they kept this up, it would be an even fight by the time their ships made it to Anne's orbit.

<*Don't get cocky,*> Angela commented. <*Even if we take out half of their ships, they still almost outnumber us two to one.*>

<*If the* Antares *can make it here from the Gamma site in time, we'll be free and clear.*>

Angela made a mental sound meant to indicate she didn't like the plan. <*That's a bell we can't un-ring. Once the human sphere realizes we have picotech, New Eden will be at war for centuries.*>

<*It's a last-ditch option, Andrews hasn't approved the option yet. It will certainly win this, though,*> Tanis replied.

Tanis knew she sounded certain, but she didn't want to unleash the picotech either.

Centuries ago, when nano-tech was new and self-replication became possible en-masse, nanoweapons would unleash swarms of bots which would self-replicate by essentially eating whatever they were fired at. It was a dangerous tech, but because nano-bots could not disassemble all molecules, they could be blocked. Eventually, technologies were developed to defeat nano-swarms and their use as offensive weapons waned.

Pico swarms were an entirely different story. The Sirian ships were wholly vulnerable to them. A strike from a pico-bearing missile would cause their ships to be devoured in a matter of minutes.

Use of a pico weapon created two immediate dangers. The first was that none of the ships in the *Intrepid* fleet were immune to pico swarms either. The second was likely Angela's primary concern; once it was known that the *Intrepid* possessed picotech, they would be chased to the ends of the galaxy.

Captain Andrews must have been reading her mind.

"ETA on the *Antares* puts it right when the battle is projected to occur," his tone didn't betray which way he was leaning in the decision.

"I've instructed them to maintain velocity. They'll fly past at 0.15*c*. Any missiles they launch will be all but undetectable," Tanis said

The captain nodded. "Don't expect a decision before that time. We won't fire those things unless there is no other choice."

"Agreed," Tanis rotated the holo again. "The grapeshot and the RMs will hit them pretty hard. Chances are that we'll break them before it comes to a fistfight."

"Who can say?" Sanderson shook his head. "Not a lot of space forces invade foreign systems. It's not like an insystem fight when there's somewhere to retreat. The fact that the Victorians chose to execute all of Yusuf's crew is not going to help either."

"You think they'll fight to the death?" Ouri asked from her station.

"I think we need to be prepared for it," Sanderson replied.

Scan updated with the latest projected trajectories for the Sirian ships. The vector confirmed a churn and burn on Victoria. It was imperative the battle be decided outside Anne's orbit.

"Are all of the RMs in position?" Tanis asked the weapons team.

"Yes, sir, we've adjusted their locations per your latest projections."

"Good, I want them within three light minutes of the Sirian fleet when the grapeshot crossfire hits."

Tanis turned to look for Joe before remembering he wasn't on the *Intrepid.* So much for their pledge to not get separated again when things got crazy.

<*You knew that was a silly pledge when you made it,*> Angela said.

<*Hah! Don't give me that. I know you feel the same way.*>

<*I may, but pledging to stay cheek by jowl with someone for hundreds of years is still silly.*>

Tanis sighed, mentally acknowledging that Angela was right. But the fact that Joe had one of the most dangerous missions in the upcoming battle didn't help her nerves.

* * * * *

Dry leaves crunched underfoot as Jessica peered down an alley. Her nanoprobes told her it was clear, but minutes ago they had taken weapons fire from positions which scan also showed as clear.

It smarted to know that many of the people she was fighting had trained at her police academy. The fact that they used Edener weapons and armor smarted more—especially when their aim proved true.

What didn't make sense was their armor being invisible to her nano; Tanis wasn't so trusting as to provide equipment their own forces couldn't counter.

Yet, the Victorians were able to hide from scans that should have revealed them.

<*Anything?*> she called up to the assault transport overhead.

<*Negative, my sweeps show no one in that position. They could have gone into the undercity. My scan can't get through the city's ES dome and that much rock.*>

<*Not to mention two/three is almost right under that building. I can't imagine they're that blind.*>

<*Target acquired,*> Trist said. <*He's on the roof over there. I saw what looked like a flicker in an active camo field.*>

Jessica looked over squad positions on the platoon's combat net. Only one other fireteam was close to the sniper's position, but they were dealing with their own problems.

<*I'm not visible to that position, I'll circle around,*> Jessica replied.

<*Sergeant Amerson, secure whatever undercity access the flagged building has. You may get an unfriendly flushed down toward you,*> Jessica said to the leader of fireteam two/three.

<*On it, ma'am,*> came the reply.

She logged her approach on the combat net and began to slowly work her way toward a side entrance on the building the sniper was in.

She crept down the alley toward a parallel street. There was little cover for her, but likewise there was little for anyone else to hide in.

Her nano swept upward, watching windows and looking over the rooftops. No enemies appeared on their scans, though she saw a few scared families through some of the windows and felt a pang of regret.

She had never been part of a military action that caused families to huddle together in their homes. It wasn't a good feeling.

Jessica reached the end of the alley and her nano moved out onto the tree-lined boulevard.

A gust of wind rushed past her, blowing dry leaves through the air—momentarily blinding her motion tracking. She waited for a shot, but none came. If the sniper could see down this street, he wasn't paying attention.

Keeping under store-front awnings and the occasional tree, Jessica moved as quickly as she could. It had already been thirty minutes since they left the spaceport and she could feel anxiety growing at the thought of Myrrdan escaping their web.

She crossed another street and then angled away from the sniper's building to come at it from the side.

<Is our friendly neighborhood sniper still there?> Jessica asked.

<Yeah, I'm working directly toward him and he's taking pot-shots at me,> Trist replied.

<Careful! One shot won't penetrate, but two or three could crack your armor.>

A chuckle came over the Link. *<You know, I read the same manual you did. He did clip my shoulder; he's getting a bit sloppy now…sheeeet. Ok, he's got a friend up there, you better hustle.>*

Jessica swore softly before replying, *<Enough skulking around, I'm going to the rooftops.>*

She looked over the area her nano had scouted. The roof to her left sported a lush garden that would provide perfect cover. She leapt up and landed behind a tool shed.

Her probes rushed through the plants, watching for movement in the air currents and errant heat signatures. Jessica followed them slowly, her own active camouflage shifting to hide her amongst the plant life.

At the edge of the garden, she toggled her vision to a full spectrum blend. Just one building separated her from the sniper's position and she looked for any movement, or degradation of his active camo.

Her nano reached the edges of an enemy sensor cloud and she moved them around to the south. Once there, she directed several of her probes to move into the enemy cloud.

Her feint worked and the density of the cloud near her decreased. She also saw some leaves on the rooftop move, as though a person laying on them had shifted.

"There's one," she said softly to herself.

<Can you get them to take another shot at you?> she asked Trist.

<I have a holomarine handy, what say I risk its neck instead?>

<Coward,>

Trist's avatar stuck its tongue out at Jessica, and below, a very believable holographic representation of a person in powered armor dashed out into the street below.

Jessica wasn't watching the street; her eyes were on the rooftop, layers of nano augmenting her vision. At the moment Trist sent out her decoy, Jessica spotted the second sniper and was in the air, rifle taking aim.

A primal scream left her lips as her feet crashed down on the first sniper, the metric ton of her armor driving him half through the building's rooftop.

She dropped a sticky EM grenade on him and dashed toward the other sniper, firing proton beams as she went.

Behind her, the grenade detonated while in front the second sniper's active camo flickered off as her shots scorched his armor.

He twisted on the ground, bringing his weapon to bear on her and Jessica dodged to the side, her vision showing the heated air where his beam had lanced out. She hit him two more times before a form in powered armor slammed down onto him from above.

<You think I was just going to hang out down there and wait?> Trist asked.

<Well, there was that coffee shop across the street, I bet they would have served you a cup.>

Trist dropped her own EM grenade on the enemy soldier before running out of its range.

<Two snipers down, incapacitated with EMs, we're moving on,> Jessica reported over the combat net.

* * * * *

The bridge crew busied themselves as best they could while the holo counted down to the grapeshot rounds. Stewards entered the bridge and provided food. Tanis grabbed two BLTs, the first disappearing in an instant.

"You'd think it was going to run off your plate," Captain Andrews said with a smile before taking a bite of his sandwich.

Tanis returned the smile. "You never know when you may get to eat again in situations like this."

The captain raised his eyebrow and Tanis got the message. If they missed their next meal it would likely be due to this one being their last.

A short time later, the countdown on the holo reached zero and the first two rails fired their shots. Two minutes later the other rails slung their deadly payload into the black. Tanis sent new positions to all the railguns while intently watching the holo projection of the battlefield.

Tactical updated and showed the relativistic missiles also in the final minutes of their countdowns. The bridge net brought two more NSAI online as the myriad calculations required to predict all the possible battlefield configurations grew.

All eyes were either on the holo or personal VR representations of the same data. It looked like the tactic was going to work until, seconds before impact, one of the dreadnaughts jinked out of range.

The RMs had their own smart NSAI which would seek targets of opportunity as they came into range—better than the grapeshot which wasn't smart at all. If the enemy ships deviated even a hundred kilometers it would miss entirely.

"One ship out of the pocket. They'll miss the head-on grapeshot," Priscilla called out.

"They must have caught a reflection off it," Andrews mused.

Two other ships managed to shift out of range before the grapeshot met the rest of the Sirian fleet. Optical scopes on both the *Intrepid* and Anne's surface showed seven ships being torn to shreds by the hail of pellets.

"That's brutal," Ouri whispered as the ships all but disintegrated under the barrage.

The other Sirian vessels were lashing out with their forward beams, hoping to break apart any shot coming their way. ES scoops flashed on in an attempt to shift the pellets and shrapnel from their fellow ships away.

In some cases it appeared to be working, the scoops lit up sporadically as shot was deflected, but in two other cases ships didn't get their scoops up in time, or jink far enough.

"Nine ships down, eleven others have visible hull breaches," Priscilla reported.

"That puts their total at fifty-two," Andrews said. "Let's see if the crossfire hits any of them."

"It's going to require them to not change velocity for the calculations to work," Tanis said.

"One other ship just went dead," Priscilla added. "We're down to fifty-one with fifteen of those having suffered some sort of damage."

"Ten seconds to the grapeshot crossfire," weapons said. "It's hard to tell what our spread will look like at this range, but you appear to have predicted their dispersal pattern well," the officer said to Tanis.

They only had to wait a moment more before the holo updated with four more ships getting hit by the shot.

"Enemy ship count at forty-seven," Scan gave the update out loud. "They're breaking formation, looks like they're scattering into four separate groups."

"RMs have locked onto targets in three groups," weapons added. "We have fifteen missiles, six each on two of the groups and three on the other."

"Could finally even the odds," Sanderson said softly. "I've never rooted so hard for an RM before."

"I know what you mean," Tanis said.

*****

<*We've hit some local police who don't want to give up,*> Lieutenant Borden said. <*They're dug in and anything we do to get them out will be lethal.*>

Jessica sighed. Wiping out a whole police squad was not the sort of thing that made long-term relations better, especially when it was at the hands of armored Marines.

<*Can you skirt them?*> she asked.

<*I really don't like having armed folks at my back,*> Borden replied.

<*Have a shuttle foam them,*> Smith suggested.

<*Good call, I'll bring one down.*>

From her rooftop vantage point, she saw one of the assault transports arc toward Borden's position. A self-guided missile un-racked and lanced toward the ground. Moments before impact, it exploded into a cloud of foam. Jessica knew from experience that once that foam hit it would solidify into a firm, yet breathable cocoon, and the enemy police force wouldn't be going anywhere.

The combat net showed the embattled squad on the move once more. Overall, the net was tightening. Two fireteams had also engaged presidential guard in powered armor, but otherwise all opposing forces had been police or civilian.

Several casualties had occurred—results of Jessica's orders to push forward quickly. She tried not to think about it too much. It was imperative that they pin Myrrdan down in the Parliament buildings.

Jessica saw that Smith's platoon was within a kilometer of the Parliament building and would reach its perimeter in minutes. Jessica was a half-kilometer ahead of Usef's platoon, but the scouts were a kilometer further. She leapt to the top of a building and signaled Trist to double-time it.

The pair bounded across rooftops, using sensor data from the scouts to pick the safest path. It was a risk exposing themselves like this, but Jessica couldn't allow Myrrdan to slip through her grasp.

Only a large plaza followed by a row of administrative buildings separated her from the Parliament when a call came over the Link from the scouts.

<*Drop! Enemy has heavy weapons!*>

Jessica turned on her down jets and saw Trist do the same. They slammed into a rooftop, crashing through to the building's top floor.

They rolled to cover against the wall and Jessica sent probes toward the windows and out onto the rooftop. Before she got a good look, artillery fire hit the roof and then the side of the building.

Fire raged around them and debris flew through the air. Trist dove out of the room and Jessica followed. They dashed down a long hall and then broke through a window and into another building.

Jessica was nearly out of nano, and Trist released a dampening cloud to mask their heat and radio signatures.

<*Aggressive, aren't they?*> Trist asked.

<*It would seem so,*> Jessica replied.

Usef acknowledged their situation on the combat net and his platoon moved to flank their position. The scouts pinpointed the locations of the artillery fire, but the mobile emplacements were too well shielded for their weapons.

<*Where did they get that shit anyway?*> Jessica asked. <*We didn't sell them any stuff like that.*>

<*I guess they're cleverer than we thought. Or there's a bigger black market than we thought.*>

<*More movement at the Parliament,*> the pilot of Assault 2 called down. <*Looks like a big force moving out.*>

<*Smith, are you facing opposition?*> Jessica asked.

<*Light, approaching the rear service entrance now,*> he replied.

Jessica shook her head. Why move troops out front when the Marines were kicking in the back door?

<*Assault 2, flush them toward us,*> Jessica called up to the transport overhead.

<*Roger that. Permission to use LR2s?*>

Jessica gave the approval and signed her auth code to the combat net's ledger. While much of the engagement had used non-lethal force, herding enemy troops in powered armor was going to take more serious firepower. LR2 missiles were like a shotgun of rail-delivered pellets in a short-range missile delivery system.

They were designed to tear through armored combatants while doing as little damage as possible to structures.

On the combat net she saw Assault 2 circle higher and launch four missiles at the enemy's west flank.

<*Assault 1, I see you have a bunker buster in your arsenal, can you drop that on our friends with the big gun down here?*>

<*You call, we deliver,*> came the pilot's response.

Assault 1 was covering the northern approach and Jessica saw the combat net update with seventy seconds to weapon deployment.

Thirty seconds later, Assault 2 called in. <*Maneuver effective, the group is moving east toward you. I count twenty-three in armor and four without armor. Positions marked on the combat net.*>

Jessica sent an acknowledgement.

Fireteams from Usef's platoon began taking up positions in nearby buildings, ready to engage the approaching enemy once the artillery emplacement was dealt with.

<*Projected engagement in fifty seconds,*> Lieutenant Usef called out to the platoon. <*Fireteams, check updated assignments. We take them all, dead or alive.*>

The seconds ticked by at a snail's pace. Jessica glanced over at Trist and gave her a smile. Trist returned the expression and gripped her rifle tightly.

The building shook as a round from the artillery tore through the floor below them.

<*What is Assault 1 doing, stopping to get lunch?*> Trist asked.

<*I did see a special at a little place across the street,*> Jessica replied, praying to the stars that their position was masked well enough to buy them another fifteen seconds.

<*Think he'd pick something up for me?*>

<*Only if you ask real nice.*>

Jessica took several slow breaths, and then a long, relieved exhale as the deafening crack of the bunker buster tore through the air. The building shook and she prayed it would hold up after the punishment it had received.

Seconds later, the Marines moved forward.

<*Engaging!*> Corporal Latham called out on the combat net.

Jessica peered through the window, checking for enemy positions with her eyes while layering combat net data over top. If Myrrdan was with the enemy, he wouldn't be one of the unarmored noncoms—they would be decoys. He would be armored. You didn't survive as long as he did by being vulnerable.

Trist was at another window taking a shot. <*Think he's down there?*> she asked while moving across the room to another position.

Jessica sighed. <*Honestly? I don't know, but I hope so.*>

<*He better be, it sure would be nice to get some closure on this.*>

<*You're telling me!*> Jessica laughed ruefully.

The firefight had only been underway for a couple of minutes when Jessica heard a loud shot to her right. It didn't sound like any weapon Trist was carrying.

She turned to see Trist splayed on the floor, a large hole torn through her armor and torso.

A woman stood over her, a railgun cradled in her arms.

"Huh," the woman shook her head. "I wasn't sure that it would go completely through; her armor must have been weakened by that sniper fire earlier."

Jessica rolled onto her back, switched her rifle to the proton setting and leveled it at the woman.

"Drop the rail! Now!" she yelled, forcing fear for Trist from her mind.

The woman's mask cleared and Jessica recognized the person standing over her.

"What! Amy Lee?"

"Oh for stars' sake, Jessica, try to keep up. Would Amy Lee shoot Trist? She died back in Estrella de la Muerte. I've been using her…leftovers…since then."

Her mind reeled. Myrrdan had been amongst them, within their inner circle for over a century. She couldn't even count the times they had discussed plans and strategies with her present.

Jessica scoured her memories, trying to remember any instances where knowledge of the Gamma site may have been discussed with Amy Lee present. The disaster was unimaginable, all their careful plans—

Jessica's eyes flicked to Amy Lee's railgun, and time slowed down as she watched Amy's—Myrrdan's—finger curl around the trigger and twitch ever so slightly.

A moment later, everything went black.

Jessica gasped for air and her entire body arched as her armor shocked her heart back into motion. Her HUD flickered to life and showed an alarming amount of physical damage. She looked down at her torso to see compression gel oozing out of several cracks and a large hole just below her heart.

She took a deep breath and nearly screamed as agony lanced through her body. Jessica forced herself to calm, and took several shallow breaths as she scanned the room.

Myrrdan's body lay at her feet, completely missing its head. Beyond, Trist was slumped forward over her rifle.

Jessica pulled herself across the floor to Trist's side and gently flipped her over. A second hole was in her wife's chest, green silbio spilling out of both wounds.

She rushed her own nano into Trist's body, attempting to slow the bleeding, but it was too late; she had lost too much blood and the biological silicon which had supplanted her original organs. Without an internal AI, her body didn't have the direction to repair itself.

Jessica let out a gargled cry before remembering she could Link and get help. When she re-initialized her connection a message from Trist was waiting.

<I got him for you. I love you.>

Jessica bit back a sob as her own wounds sent pain searing through her body.

Trist was gone.

Squad three found her like that, sobbing uncontrollably beside the bodies of Trist and Amy Lee.

*****

Tanis heard the gasp from the comm officer before she spotted the report on the planetside combat net.

"Oh gods," Ouri gasped. "She's dead!"

Tanis's first thought was of Katrina. She cursed herself for letting the woman go with Jessica, but Victoria was her world too.

"Who are you referring to?" she asked, her voice strained with suppressed emotion.

"Trist," Ouri said softly. "She was killed by…Amy Lee?"

Tanis's mind reeled. She pulled up the report, found the officer on the scene and grabbed his visual feed.

*<Lieutenant Usef, what the **fuck** happened here?>*

The few seconds of light-lag felt like an eternity before the lieutenant's reply came back.

<*Ma'am. It would appear that Amy Lee shot Trist and Jessica, but Trist managed to kill her. Jessica is badly injured, but she claims that Amy Lee was Myrrdan. We're…still piecing it together and securing the area. I'll keep you in the loop.*>

Tanis surveyed the room through Lieutenant Usef's eyes. The upper half of Trist's body was destroyed, likely hit at close range by the rail gun beside Amy Lee. Jessica was leant up against a low wall, a medic looking her over—taking stock of what would likely be a lot of internal damage.

<*Jessica,*> Tanis reached out to her friend over the Link. <*I'm so sorry.*>

<*She got him,*> Jessica replied. <*She got that sonofabitch…I just…I can't…still so much to do.*>

<*Let the medic take care of you, we have things covered up here.*>

<*Ow! Careful!*> her admonition to the medic coming over the Link as well. <*I saw the report. Take those bastards out Tanis Richards style, but save some for me.*>

<*You got it,*> Tanis replied.

She shifted her attention back to her physical location to find tears streaming down her face. A sob threatened to erupt from her throat and she turned, taking deep breaths to calm herself.

Trist…She had become one of Tanis's closest friends over the years. She couldn't count the times they talked about their plans for retirement on New Eden, how nice it would be to finally kick back.

<*You and Jessica will keep her memory alive,*> Angela said softly. <*I…I'm sorry.*>

Tanis sensed real pain in Angela's voice.

<*I know. We have to put this from our mind, time for mourning later.*>

"One minute to RM impact," the weapons officer called out, wrenching Tanis back to reality.

She wiped her face and turned back to the bridge. All eyes were on her; even Andrews and Sanderson seemed to be waiting for her lead.

"I've had few friends as dear as Trist," her voice rasped as she spoke. "But we need to focus. We'll win this fight and mourn her properly when we blast these sons of bitches to pieces."

Nods and few soft statements of affirmation followed her words and then everyone turned in silence to watch the last seconds tick down before the RMs hit their targets.

Right on cue, nuclear fire bloomed in space, obscuring three of the enemy ship formations. The multiple detonations were so bright that to observers on Victoria it would be visible in full daylight.

"It'll take a moment to sift the ships from the debris," Priscilla reported. "It's a mess out there."

Scan updated and the holo showed a wide cloud of debris and radioactive dust heading toward the planet.

"Will it hit?" Terrance asked from Tanis's side.

"The Sirians were still accelerating toward the planet. Now that the debris is on a fixed vector it will miss. Though only by a hundred thousand kilometers or so," she replied.

"They lost nineteen ships," Priscilla announced and the bridge erupted in cheers. "Don't get too excited," she said. "Most of those were destroyer-class. We're still looking at two of their dreadnaughts, twenty-three cruisers and three destroyers."

Tanis looked over the holo and saw the remaining ships breaking into two widely dispersed formations. They were changing course, arcing stellar north and south to catch the *Intrepid* in a pincer.

"Incoming!" Priscilla shouted.

The holo lit up with the signatures of four RMs bearing down on the *Intrepid.* A second later, distant explosions flared at the locations of two rail platforms.

The Sirians' hadn't been idly flying insystem.

"Thirty-two seconds until missile impact," Priscilla shouted, and Amanda sounded impact alarms audibly and over the Link.

The three cruisers protecting the *Intrepid* pivoted, firing lasers and rail batteries at the RMs. The *Intrepid's* weapons were also lancing out with every beam the ship had, and with a sudden lurch, the colony ship also rotated, attempting to present a smaller profile.

Countermeasure systems fired both refractive clouds and physical shrapnel out from the *Intrepid* in an attempt to confuse and obstruct the missiles.

The *Yosemite* got in a lucky shot; one of its .27-meter rail guns destroyed one of the RMs, while a beam from the *Intrepid* melted through another missile's casing, sending it spinning off-course.

<Bringing the scoop online,> Bob said over the cries of the engineering representative that it hadn't even gone through test runs yet.

Tanis knew what Bob had in mind; he was calibrating the scoop to operate as an MDC, hoping to molecularly disassemble the other two missiles before impact. It was a tricky maneuver—it could destroy the friendly cruisers as easily as the approaching missiles.

"Will the RMs be in the field long enough to—?" Ouri asked as one of the approaching missiles spun off-course moments after passing through the field.

The other made it through the field and Priscilla called four seconds to impact.

Time slowed to a crawl for Tanis. It seemed to take forever for the missile to cross the remaining distance to the *Intrepid.* She had time to read the incoming missile's data tag on the holo in its entirety. It predicted a twenty-megaton warhead—not that such a thing was necessary when you had so much relativistic kinetic energy to begin with.

Somewhere between seconds two and three Tanis saw three small objects—boosting in at over one hundred *g*s—converge on the RM. The scopes widened their view and the impact was caught on the visuals screens. It was a fantastic display as shrapnel and fire bloomed in every direction.

The impact pushed much of the debris over the *Intrepid,* but some stayed on course. Bob snapped a part of the scoop in closer to disintegrate as much debris as he could. Alerts went off as pieces of ship and missile got through, striking the *Intrepid* in over a dozen locations.

"Damage report," Andrews called out. "And what were those interceptors?"

"Three of our heavy lifters," Priscilla said softly. "The *Excelsior, Beirut,* and *Alexandra.*"

There was a moment of silence on the bridge. Tanis felt her heart clench at the thought of Troy and his fellows giving the ultimate sacrifice. He had proven himself a hero and savior of the *Intrepid* twice now.

"The enemy ships will be in range in five minutes," weapons announced. "It looks like they're going to engage us at high speed, bank around Victoria, and come back."

"We took out Victoria's defenses. The Sirians could nuke Landfall on their way by…" Tanis let the words hang.

"Is the *Antares* in range?" Andrews asked.

"It will be in range of the Sirians before the enemy is in range of the colony," Priscilla said, her tone somber.

"So we'll still have to engage," Andrews nodded and turned to Terrance. "If we can't stop them, the *Antares* will need to fire the missiles."

Terrance nodded slowly. "So be it."

Tanis reviewed the positions of the fleets fighters. Twelve of the wings were a light-second outsystem from Anne and were in position to engage the Sirians. They were already split into two groups, boosting hard to meet the two enemy formations.

<*Strike pattern C,*> Tanis relayed to the AI managing the fleet's fighters. The AI relayed affirmation of the order, and the holo showed their predicted paths meeting the enemy ships in seven minutes.

Given the fighter's v, they would likely not get a second chance to be involved in the battle. Strike pattern C called for them to unload all of their ordinance on the highest value targets they could.

She saw Priscilla give the OK for two search and rescue rigs to depart from the support flotilla behind Anne. She nodded her appreciation to the avatar and returned her attention to the fleet.

Five more wings spread out in front of the four battlegroups, preparing to eliminate projectile weapons and any enemy fighters. However, given the enemy's plan to arc around Victoria after their initial pass-by, she doubted they would deploy any fighters—unless they were on suicide runs.

Captains fleet-wide reported rails loaded and beam batteries charged. Tanis reviewed their targeting plans and firing solutions. She felt Bob passing over the calculations as well, likely concerned about his mortality as much as the rest of them.

The first waves of fighters engaged the two enemy formations and the skirmish was over in three seconds.

One of the enemy destroyers lost its engines and the fighters disabled weapons and sensors across the enemy fleet. One fighter lobbed a parting missile into one of the dreadnaught's engines and that ship began to fall behind the rest of the enemy formation.

"Six minutes until our picket line makes contact," Priscilla announced.

Tanis slowly paced before the holo tank as the minutes passed by. The two enemy formations crept closer across the millions of kilometers, the holo's wide view of the battlefield making their progression seem agonizingly slow.

Around the bridge, everyone checked and rechecked equipment, firing solutions, and Tanis wished she had another BLT.

When the battle was finally joined, it lasted less than two minutes.

The fighter shield was five hundred thousand kilometers out, with weapons capable of reaching ten thousand klicks. However, the enemy force was jinking, making targeting at that range tricky at best. The wings chose to get much closer before engaging, trusting their size and agility to make them impossible long-range targets.

At the five-thousand kilometer mark, half the fighters spun and braked at maximum safe g. Weapons and engines spun around the ships and they laid down punishing fire on the enemy's forward shields and ablative plating. A destroyer exploded and several cruisers were holed, but not enough to slow them.

The other half of the fighters spun as they passed the enemy ships, targeting engines and rear defenses. A cruiser bloomed into eerie flame from this assault, and scan showed many of the enemy's weapons options going offline.

It was not a bloodless assault on the fighter's part. Eleven men and women would not be coming home—their ships destroyed by enemy point-defense systems. Another dozen ships were in varying states of incapacitation, left to wait for the search and rescue rigs to pick them up.

The surviving wings began a long loop to the far side of Victoria, preparing to engage the enemy again if the battle lasted that long.

<*Here it comes,*> Tanis said across the fleet command net. <*Stars and gods keep us all safe.*>

The Sirians had taken punishment beyond what any force could have expected before reaching their target. With well over half their ships destroyed or disabled, any regular force would have retreated. But the Sirians knew they had nowhere to go. If they didn't win here, they were likely dead anyway—though Tanis hoped to stop a full-scale execution this time. Many of the voices which called for the death of the crew of the *Strident Arc* were tempered, or no longer present.

Even still, she ensured that Amanda sent out a call for them to surrender—though she expected no response.

Seconds later the holo lit up, tracking hundreds of invisible energy beams lancing between the ships, highlighting penetrations, deflections, chaff clouds, and missile strikes.

Tanis followed the flurry of activity with precision and clarity, giving direction to captains and their AI, orchestrating her fleet as though it were one instrument in her hand.

She was dimly aware that no one else was able to grasp the full scope of the battle like she could—like she and Angela could. Tanis felt her thoughts flowing between herself and her AI as though they truly did share just one mind.

In the first thirty seconds, explosions erupted from a dozen ships as beams penetrated shields and ablative plating on both sides. Coordinated firepower from a dozen ships at a time melting through any protections provided.

The *Intrepid* took only glancing blows, its point defense systems and refractive clouds from the fleet giving it ample cover.

Tanis had her eye on the enemy dreadnaughts. The second had fallen well behind its companions, but the first was in the midst of its own protective bubble, the vast majority of its weapons systems still active. If it made it within ten thousand kilometers of the *Intrepid,* it would be able to burn through the glistening clouds and do serious damage.

<*C'mon, Joe,*> she said to herself.

<*He'll be there. He knows what to do.*>

Tanis prayed he was able to; the *Intrepid* was counting on it.

As if in answer to her prayers, the enemy dreadnaught suddenly began to fire wildly in every direction, attempting to hit a target the *Intrepid's* sensors could not discern. She zoomed the holo until the dreadnaught nearly filled the entire bridge.

She signaled Priscilla to search for foreign objects on the enemy ship and sure enough, the mines were there. Fifteen limpet mines, containing nuclear shape charges, were attached to the hull. Escape pods were pouring out of the enemy vessel and Tanis found herself hoping as many got free as possible.

Seconds later, the mines detonated and for a moment the dreadnaught appeared to crumple before it tore apart in a fantastic explosion of steel and fire.

<*You're welcome,*> Joe said.

The *Andromeda* had disgorged its deadly load and was joining the battle proper.

<*Thank you, we all thank you, and I love you.*>

<*Just doing my job,*> Joe said with a wink.

Seventy seconds later, the battle was over. The enemy fleet was moving toward Victoria and the Intrepid Fleet converged on the straggling dreadnaught, incapacitating it with little resistance given.

No cheers sounded on the *Intrepid's* bridge. Two of the ISF cruisers and a dozen smaller ships were disabled or destroyed. No ship had come through the battle unscathed.

Tanis noticed several crew members cast sidelong glances her way, their expressions filled with awe at how she had pulled the *Intrepid's* fleet through the battle with such little damage.

She tried not to meet their gazes and instead confirmed that the support flotilla was moving out from behind Anne while she waited for confirmation of the enemy's trajectory.

When the confirmation came, there were several sharp intakes of breath as everyone saw what the enemy intended.

"They're going to ram them," Ouri whispered.

The remaining Sirian ships were altering their respective vectors, lining up with the elevator, Landfall, and several other installations.

The destruction would kill nearly every Victorian in the system.

Captain Andrews glanced at Terrance and then at Tanis. Both nodded and Tanis made the call to the *Antares*.

<*Captain Fulsom, take them out.*>

The *Antares* had boosted to over 0.1c as it raced from the Gamma site to the battlefield. There was no need for the ship to decelerate to join the conflict, it had only to drop its six tiny RMs.

Weapons containing certain death for the crew of the Sirian ships.

Optical scopes zoomed in on the enemy warships, scan tracking the RMs, looking for signs of impact.

"There!" Priscilla called out.

The hull of an enemy cruiser began to crumple and dissolve. Moments later the other Sirian ships began to dissolve, as well.

Tanis let out the breath she had been holding. Joe's presence appeared and he caught her eyes. They shared a moment of relief and fear for what the future would now hold.

Tanis could see the Sirian ships trying the standard defenses for nanoswarm attacks to no avail. She could only imagine the horror those crews must have felt in the last minutes, knowing that their bodies would be dissolved by tiny machines breaking them down to their component atoms.

Escape pods were pouring out of every ship as the crews escaped the wave of destruction. A moment later, reactor containment on one of the cruisers was lost and the ship blossomed into a nuclear fireball.

That explosion was followed by the another cruiser losing antimatter containment and erupting in a violent explosion. The remaining ships blew several seconds later, the blasts indicating self-destruct charges—likely to save any remaining crew the horror of seeing their bodies dissolve before their eyes.

Escape pods and pieces of starship rained down on Victoria. Tanis prayed that the fixed lifespan programmed into the picoswarms would work. If that failsafe didn't function, they would watch the entire world below slowly dissolve.

She looked around the bridge and could see half the crew holding their breath—the same thought on everyone's minds. Did they just save the Victorians from one death only to deliver them to a far worse fate?

<*I've confirmed the picotech died on schedule. Victoria is safe,*> Bob said over the bridge net.

Several cheers erupted and congratulatory conversation sparked up. Tanis closed her eyes and leaned against a console. They had either saved the Victorians or doomed them for eternity.

Either way the *Intrepid* would be at war forever.

*****

There were over two-thousand survivors of the Sirian's attack. Many of them, still aboard the drifting hulks, tried to fight the *Intrepid's* Marines instead of being taken prisoner. Tanis wasn't going to lose any more of her people. After the first ship fought back, she had it blown with a tactical warhead.

The rest of the Sirians surrendered peacefully.

Things on Victoria's surface were simpler. Most of the world was so inhospitable that any escape pods which landed there saw their inhabitants die or gladly accept help when it arrived.

An emergency session of the Victorian parliament installed Katrina as president pro-tem. With the *Intrepid's* Marines backing her, the unrest in the city wound down quickly.

Four days later, Tanis sat in a low chair on the beach, looking over the lake outside her cabin. Joe was beside her, half dozing in the artificial sunlight.

"It's going to take another decade to leave now," Tanis sighed.

"About that, yeah. We have to rebuild the rails, deal with all of the Sirian hulls, help the Victorians create prisons…it's a mess," Joe said in agreement.

"And Myrrdan…Amy Lee…she's finally gone," Tanis said with a catch in her throat as she also thought of Trist being gone.

Joe leaned over and placed a hand on her arm, knowing her thoughts were on Trist.

"I won't say she died honorably or had a good death," his voice was grim. "It was a shit death at the hands of a shitty person. But maybe she will rest a bit easier knowing that he's gone, too."

Tanis sighed. "I still can't believe he—she—fooled us for so long."

Joe solemnly nodded his agreement. There were no words to express the sadness they felt for all those who had died on Victoria and in the blackness.

"Hullooo there!" a voice called out from down the path.

"Who could that be?" Tanis started.

Her question was answered a moment later as Ouri came into view, a smile on her face and a large basket in her hands.

"Hi, Ouri," Tanis said and propped herself up. "We weren't really expecting company…"

"Yes, I know, you had decided to wallow today, before the funerals tomorrow, but that's not going to happen."

"I don't know, Ouri…" Tanis began as Joe sat up with a smile.

"C'mon, hon, I think a celebration is just the thing we need."

Tanis turned a raised eyebrow on her husband. "You orchestrated this, didn't you?"

"Yes, he did, and boy am I glad for it," Jessica said as she approached behind Ouri. "I've had days of moping now. I know that if Trist were here she'd be partying. Maybe not a sedate picnic by the beach type of party, but you get the idea."

Tanis acquiesced and Ouri opened her basket, spreading a blanket on the sand and laying out sandwiches, wine, and cheese.

Conversation was slow to pick up as everyone sampled the food and became lost in their thoughts.

"OK, even I can admit that this silence won't do," Tanis said. "I'll start." She took a deep breath, collected her thoughts and began.

"I sat in the quarters Trist used awhile back and cried for an hour last night. Maybe longer, I'm not sure. I'm going to miss her a hell of a lot—she really felt like a kindred spirit to me. We joked about growing old together on New Eden, sitting on our front porch in rocking chairs and gossiping about the good ole days. I'll still do that with you, Jessica," Tanis said with a smile to her friend.

"I know you will," Jessica said. "I plan to make it to that front porch, you know. We'll talk about how Trist would have been antsy and stealing the neighbor's silverware in a week.

"I'll always remember that time she and I ran the police academy on the Tara. Those were a crazy two years—I'm still sworn to secrecy about that time at the Blue Star night club."

"I'm going to miss Troy, too," Joe said. "He was a true hero, him and his hot tub."

"To the Victorians who Tom got killed, may they find their way through the stars," Ouri said, her expression sad as she likely thought of bringing the cruisers down over Landfall.

Tanis raised her glass. "To Trist, Troy, and all our brothers and sisters—Victorian and Edeners alike—who lost their lives. May they always be remembered and may their names and deeds be remembered forever."

The others raised their glasses and gave the customary response. "We'll remember forever."

They finished their food and Ouri stood and peered down the path.

"Re-enforcements should be coming any minute now."

"What?" Tanis asked.

"For the party, of course."

"What party?" Tanis and Joe asked in unison.

"You told me that when things calmed down to hold a nice impromptu party, so I'm doing it."

"That was a hundred and fifty years ago!" Tanis blurted out.

"I took it as a standing order. It *is* actually my house after all," Ouri said with a wink.

The party lasted long into the night, eventually spilling across the lawns and into the house with hundreds of people in attendance. Tanis learned that celebrations were happening all across the *Intrepid* that night, as the crew gave thanks for their survival and the sacrifice of their comrades.

RECOMPENSE

STELLAR DATE: 3288936 / 09.13.4292 (Adjusted Gregorian)
LOCATION: Landfall, Victoria
REGION: Victorian Space Federation, Kapteyn's Star System

The long parties the night before threw the solemn services on the following day into stark contrast.

The morning had been filled with services on the *Intrepid* and several of the cruisers. Following those, Tanis took a pinnace to Landfall at Katrina's behest.

They had to mend the rift between their peoples and waiting would help nothing.

Tanis listened to Katrina's words, tears filling her eyes. It was the speech the still-grieving widow had planned to give at Markus's funeral. Katrina said as much as she started it and explained that even with all the events of the last week, Markus's vision was still her guiding light. The people of Victoria could achieve great things, but they could not be bound by their past, by their prejudices or petty jealousy.

If anything the speech resonated more now than it would have five days prior.

Katrina stepped down from the dais and Tanis stood, still rehearsing her lines. The words were carefully selected and she knew she had to get it just right in front of this mostly Victorian audience.

"I'm—" She hardly began before a scream interrupted her.

"You killed him! You! You evil bitch!"

The woman's screams echoed through the hall and Tanis looked up in surprise.

Sarah stood ten paces from her, the grieving mother's face streaked with tears, her eyes red and swollen.

"You brought all of this on us. If it wasn't for you, my Tom would still be alive! My Peter would still be alive! You're no different than they are—little gods who think they can take what they want!"

Tanis opened her mouth to speak, but no words would come out. The woman before her was old and stooped, in the final decades of her life.

A retort came to mind, but it was wrong and unfair. Tanis had nothing to give that this woman would accept. The fact that Sarah was always angry, always looking for someone to attack and blame, didn't make her words less true.

Any condolence Tanis could give—words from a woman who was in perfect health at over two-hundred years of age; with hundreds of years ahead of her; with the ability to carry dozens of children if she wished—those words would only cause more harm to Sarah.

Sarah, who had tried so hard to naturally carry a child to term, after what the years of exposure to hard radiation around Sirius had done to her body.

Tanis may well have killed Tom herself.

She didn't hear everything else Sarah screamed at her; she *did* feel the spit hit her face before Peter' brothers managed to drag Sarah out of the assembly.

Tanis turned her head and took a moment to clean the spittle off. It took a minute more for her own tears to cease.

No one spoke while she regained her composure, she thought maybe it was because no one knew she could cry. She always had to be strong, to put on a good face and inspire the people who depended on her, but somehow this event, this battle, it was the straw that broke the camel's back.

She just wanted peace.

<*We'll have it,*> Angela said.

<*I sure hope so…OK…I'm ready.*>

Tanis took a second deep breath and gave her speech.

She was told afterward that her words were eloquent and well delivered, but she barely remembered it. All she could recall was the sorrow in Sarah's eyes and the pain she felt at the loss of so many friends.

RELATIVITY

STELLAR DATE: 3293121 / 02.29.4304 (Adjusted Gregorian)
LOCATION: ISS *Intrepid*
REGION: Interstellar space near Kapteyn's Star

Twelve Years after the Battle of Victoria...

"We think it's some sort of undetectable gravity well."

Earnest stood at the head of the bridge conference room's table. Hovering above the table was a complex holographic display showing Kapteyn's Star at the bottom and an elongated tail streaming out from the star.

The *Intrepid* was only a month out from the Kapteyn's system and already a new calamity had befallen them.

For many, the departure from the system had been a bittersweet parting. Over the decades, many families had become intertwined between the two groups. In the end, some Edeners stayed behind, while some Victorians joined new families on the colony ship.

They may have wished they hadn't.

"Our best models predict it to be a stream of dark matter—something that has been hypothesized as stretching out from Kapteyn's in the past due to its extra-galactic orbit. It's currently all but impossible to gauge our vector, but we think we are a hairs-breadth under *c* and still on the correct vector...more or less."

Tanis burst out laughing so hard her body convulsed and tears streamed down her face. Everyone in the room was staring at her, aghast at her response. She took several gasping breaths, attempting to regain her composure.

"I don't see what's so funny," Terrance frowned.

"So...so much time spent being slowed down, held back..." Tanis gulped down a breath. "And now we're going too fast!"

She began laughing again. Beside her Abby started to chuckle and across the table Andrews let out a guffaw. Seconds later the entire group was laughing, slapping backs and generally looking like they'd lost their minds.

<*Should I call a medic?*> Bob asked Angela.

<*No, they need this, if they didn't finally have a reaction like this I'd worry more. Give them a few minutes,*> Angela replied.

As the laughter died down, Tanis managed to wheeze out, "Can we...can we throw out an anchor?"

This brought about a new round of chuckles with several other suggestions for slowing the ship being called out. Eventually everyone regained control, and Earnest poured himself a glass of water, drinking it down before finally providing the answer.

"I don't think we'll have to slow down," he said. "I think that when we exit this dark matter accelerator we'll shed our velocity as quickly as we gained it. However, we'll likely shoot past our destination by a fair distance."

"How far?" Captain Andrews asked.

"It's hard to say... light-years at least, maybe hundreds."

Earnest's simple proclamation was met with stunned silence. It could be possible that the *Intrepid* would end up being the furthest ship from Sol, further than any of the FGT ships were known to be.

"Then again, it could be a lot less… or a lot more. It's really hard to tell how fast we're going. The difference between 0.9999*c* and 0.99999*c* is quite profound when it comes to time dilation."

"How can you not tell how fast we're going?" Admiral Sanderson asked.

"At this velocity, all light from the outside universe turns into a tiny pinprick fore and aft of the ship. We aren't even sure if we're in space controlled by special or general relativity or neither."

"So what's our plan?" Tanis asked.

"Go sideways," Earnest replied.

"That doesn't seem like much of a plan," Terrance said. "What if it tears the ship apart?"

Earnest shook his head. "I don't think that will happen. Because we're not *really* traveling this fast, there's no shearing force. Transitioning into regular space should be smooth and simple."

"We should test it," Sanderson said. "I imagine a probe could pop out."

"Indeed. We're actually prepared to do just that, we don't know if we'll be able to get any data from the test, but we should certainly try it first." Earnest waved his hand, and data readouts from a probe in a launch tube came up over the table.

"Bob, if you'd be so kind," he said.

The readout showed the probe launching from the ship's port side. External optics showed it moving into the blackness that surrounded the *Intrepid*. At three hundred kilometers out, the probe vanished.

<*Analyzing data,*> Bob said; everyone was silent for several moments before he continued. <*I believe the probe made it, I have data that showed it slipping outside this gravitational well gradually, not abruptly.*>

"That sure looked abrupt," Terrance shook his head. "I really don't like this; it seems too risky."

"More risky than anything else we've done?" Tanis asked.

"Those things were all calculated. We knew the math and the chances. Here we don't even know what science to use!" Terrance replied.

"I understand your concern," Captain Andrews nodded slowly. "To say there is no risk would be a lie, but there is also considerable risk in staying wherever we are. Is there an end to this special space? Will its properties change? We don't know."

Terrance leaned back in his chair and gave a wan smile. "Well then, what are we waiting for?"

Earnest began to rattle off a list of personnel he would need pulled out of stasis and other tasks which needed to be performed before the maneuver.

Terrance coughed. "That was rhetorical, Earnest."

The maneuver was planned and set to commence in one hour. Tanis decided to go for a walk before returning to the bridge for the event. Thirty minutes later, she found herself in the forward lounge she and Joe had discovered all those years ago.

She wished he was here, but they had only brought key personnel out of stasis when the ship slipped into this dark layer. No need to ruin everyone's day with just another crisis.

Tanis leaned back on an acceleration couch and stared at the pinprick of light ahead of her. Somehow she thought all the light of the universe being condensed down to one tiny point would be brighter.

She contemplated watching the exit maneuver from the lounge. With its wide field of view, the stars would likely look amazing as they snapped from the single focal point back to their regular positions.

As she lay on the couch, imagining what the event would look like, a vibration began to build in the deck underneath her.

<*Is there a problem?*> she asked Bob.

<*It seems that this region of space is less consistent than we thought, we may be exiting it now, not when we planned.*>

<*Should I get to the bridge?*>

<*I think you should not be up and about right now.*>

Tanis calmed her fears and waited, listening to the chatter on the bridge net. She added her thoughts to a few decisions, but by and large there was little advice she could offer.

With no warning, the vibrations turned into a lurch and the point of light exploded into a full starscape, bathing the lounge in its light.

It was as amazing as she thought it would be.

"Woohoo it wor—"

Tanis's jubilation was interrupted by a deafening rending sound followed by the scream of oxygen rushing from the room.

<*Impact! Get to a pod!*> Bob shouted in Tanis's mind.

Tanis leapt to her feet and clawed her way through the torrent of air rushing past her. Her HUD showed a bank of pods in the corridor outside the lounge and she couldn't help calculating the amount of oxygen she would need to make it.

<*Don't, just GO!*> Angela yelled in her mind.

Tanis pulled herself forward, grabbing anything she could as she struggled step-by-step. It was becoming easier as less air rushed past her—a silver lining around the dark cloud of an oxygen-deprived death.

The artificial gravity cut out—the particle accelerator must have gone offline—and with a final heave, Tanis reached the exit as the far side of the lounge tore away, revealing open space.

She gave the deep black a short glance before signaling the hatch to close behind her.

Now that the sound of rushing air and rending steel was gone, she had a moment to realize how much her entire body ached with cold.

Tanis shook herself back to full consciousness and forced herself to move through the shuddering ship toward the pods.

<*What happened?*> Tanis asked Angela while still gasping for breath.

Angela filled her mind with the knowledge that something the size of a small stone hit the ship in the moments before Bob could get the shielding back up. It had been traveling at near-relativistic speeds and impacted the bow like a bomb.

The sound of her heartbeat was pounding in her ears as she managed to pull herself into a pod and collapsed in its webbing.

Her internal monitoring showed burst blood vessels throughout her body, and her eyes felt like someone had tried to inflate them. She felt a final lurch and then the pod stilled beneath her.

<*By the way, I don't know if you realized it, but you hit the eject when you closed the hatch on this thing,*> Angela said. <*Now they're going to have to come find us.*>

"Sorry, I don't think so well with no oxygen in my brain, where did we pop back out?"

Angela didn't respond right away and Tanis activated a hard-console beside her seat.

"The computer must have been damaged, it can't tell where we are," she said after staring at the scan for a minute.

<*I don't think the computer is damaged, I think we are lost. None of these stars look right…well some do, but I can't triangulate anywhere that matches where they would put us.*>

Tanis brought up comm to hail the *Intrepid* for pickup and to see if the colony ship knew where they were.

"I'm not getting any response," Tanis said after a minute.

<*I think I know why…I can't find them.*>

Tanis felt panic creep in as she studied the meager scan the escape pod was able to provide.

"Well, we're close to a star, that's something, and I'm picking up radio signals from it."

<*I see that, too. Based on the star's spectra…no…*>

"What is it, Angela?"

<*I think this is 58 Eridani.*>

"Well that's goo— Wait, 58 not 82?" 58 Eridani was twenty-four light years further out than 82 Eridani, the star the colonists had named New Eden.

Twice as far from Sol as their original destination.

<*Yes, it's definitely 58 Eridani, and there are radio signals, lots of them; the system is inhabited.*>

"I see something on scan, it looks like it might be a ship," Tanis said, bringing up data and optical views. "Wait, this is wrong, too; its ion trail shows antimatter and fusions drives, but the ship's too small."

<*It just disappeared,*> Angela interjected. <*I didn't see any acceleration.*>

"There it is, it came back…a lot closer, damn it's gone again."

Angela highlighted a point on the scan map. <*There it is, closer again.*>

"What the hell is going on?" Tanis almost yelled.

Her question was punctuated by a loud clang as something grappled the pod.

<*It's here, it has us!*>

It was not often that Angela's mental tone contained fear, but it certainly did now. Tanis was far from calm herself. Nothing made any sense, where was the *Intrepid,* how was 58 Eridani inhabited and how did a ship hop through space like this one had.

Optical cameras showed the pod being pulled into a small cargo bay and that was the last Tanis saw.

* * * * *

In the small bridge of the scout and salvage ship, two men grinned at each other.

"Stasis field has the whole pod. This is going to be a good sell. That thing is from a colony ship, something called the *Intrepid*," the first said. "I don't have anything on scan, but judging by the tech on the pod she's going to have some advanced tech."

"Thank god, we can finally cover what we owe Padre and get free and clear," replied the second.

"Well let's get a move on, then."

The pilot nodded before he activated his console and plotted a course.

"Engaging FTL drive."

* * * * *

Although this is the last book in The Intrepid Saga, the next series, entitled The Orion War, picks up right where Building Victoria leaves off.

Read on to learn what happens to Tanis and what becomes of the ISS *Inpreid*.

DESTINY LOST

The Orion War – Book 1

M. D. COOPER

ACKNOWLEDGEMENTS

This book is in your hands today in no small part because of you, the readers. Your emails and excitement for the series always inspires me to keep writing.

In addition, the author community, with whom I have found companionship, has helped me hone my craft, and shared stories of encouragement—as I have with them.

Beyond them, are the hard-working folks in the aero-space industry who are working day and night to bring our species to space in a meaningful way. Their dedication and advances are what gives me hope for our future.

Lastly, as I've mentioned before, this book stands on the shoulders of giants. Writers whose stories and imaginations have forged a shared vision of the future, and our destiny, that we call Science Fiction.

AN UNEXPECTED CARGO

STELLAR DATE: 06.30.8927 (Adjusted Years)
LOCATION: Coburn Station, Trio
REGION: Trio System, Silstrand Alliance Space

Sera slammed the shooter down with a triumphant grin and watched with reddened eyes as the man from Thoria reached for his next glass. Around them, the crowd chanted their names as money changed hands.

Her opponent downed his drink and tossed the glass onto the table where it rolled against the two-dozen empty shooters between them. With a wave of his hand and an unappealing grin, he indicated that the floor was hers.

She took a deep breath to steady herself, chanting an internal mantra of *just one more, just one more.* The act of raising her arm caused Sera to sway in her seat, the smell of bodies pressed close around not helping her deepening nausea.

The Thorian saw her hesitation and his grin grew wider.

"Ready to give up?" he slurred, his putrid breath washing over her.

Sera didn't reply, only fixed him with a steely glare—at least she hoped it was a steely glare—and grasped the glass in her fist, throwing it back without further hesitation.

The alcohol washed down her throat like fire, and her tongue felt swollen in its wake. If she didn't know better, she'd assume the bartender had poured a stiffer drink.

She set the glass down and took slow, deep breaths, using all her concentration to keep the fire in her stomach and veins under control.

The Thorian grunted and stared at the row of shots before him—likely deciding which one to pick up. Finally selecting his drink, he grabbed it with a swift flourish and raised it high to throw it back.

In his current state, the gesture failed miserably and the drink splashed across his face. His features crumpled in confusion and his arms rotated slowly as he slid sideways out of his chair to the floor. No one attempted to catch him and the man's head hit the deck-plate with a solid crack.

Cheers and grumbles erupted around her as Sera was declared the winner. The victors were paid out, and the losers turned to the bar for another drink. In the midst of the post-contest exchange, one voice rose above the others.

A short, but well-built man in a dirty shipsuit pushed to the front of the crowd.

"Cheater! She had to cheat; there's no way that waif could drink Greg under the table!" He slammed his hands on the table, bent over, his face inches from Sera's. "You used nano to clear the alcohol from your bloodstream."

Most people had some of the tiny nano-machines in their body, it was nearly impossible not to; they were almost as common as bacteria. A person's nano was controlled by their internal computer or AI—if you had the money or influence to hire one. Sera's nano could clear her bloodstream with ease—though that wasn't a fact she advertised. It took a lot of nano to filter that much booze over such a short period; a lot more than a simple freighter captain should possess.

Sera worked her mouth for a moment, making sure it would respond the way she wanted it to. "I did not. Have the bartender do a check." The words were slurred, but understandable.

Bartenders on Coburn Station were not allowed to let their patrons to get too drunk—an ordinance they rarely enforced. They had scanners on hand that could do a blood-alcohol level check and determine, based on that person's size and metabolic rate, if they were too inebriated to have another round.

The bartender had already stepped into the crowd, eager to do whatever it took to avoid a fight on his shift. He pressed the scanner against Sera's wrist and took samples of her blood for the reading.

"She's pissed," he said as he straightened. "Consistent with the amount and time she's been slugging them back." Smirking, he turned back to the bar. "Those shooters are only a third of what she's had tonight too."

The winners cheered all the louder and the losers ceased their grumbling. Everyone knew that bartenders altered their scanners, so they could give people more liquor than they should. If it said she was drunk, then she should be totally pissed.

<*One of these days, the losers aren't going to care what the scan says and take their satisfaction out of your hide,*> Helen admonished in Sera's mind.

Sera sent her internal AI a mental shrug. Helen didn't like it when Sera drank; she claimed it upset the chemical balance of Sera's body in a way that made the AI feel weird. Sera wasn't sure how that was possible, not that would change her behavior. She liked the feeling of chemical imbalance.

<*My hide's been through worse.*>

<*I know; I've been there each time. Doesn't mean I want a repeat. You know how disconcerting I find it when you get hurt that badly.*>

Helen could be annoying at times with her mothering, but Sera knew that her AI's concern was genuine. Pulling her thoughts from the familiar debate, Sera looked around the bar.

To smooth things over, the winners were buying the losers a round. Sera had put a hundred SIL credits down on herself and collected three hundred back. The odds had been stacked nicely against her.

Betting was illegal in Silstrand Alliance space, so money always changed hands in cash. The prohibition didn't seem to diminish the illegal activity; it just meant no one had to pay taxes on their winnings. Sera thought about that for a minute. Maybe that was why it was illegal; officials probably liked to gamble tax-free, too.

Stuffing the hard money into an inside pocket on her leather, jacket she rose slowly, nearly teetering over at the last moment. A steady hand appeared under her elbow and Sera turned to see the dark smiling face of Cargo.

"Good haul on that, Captain." He guided her out of the bar and into the bustling main corridor of the station's promenade. "I made a couple hundred credits on your drinking skill."

"It's good to be useful," Sera slurred as Cargo led her toward a small coffee shop which was renowned for its after-drunk-sober-up brew. Once inside, Sera ordered two of their strongest and let Cargo wait at the counter for the order. Her leather clothing squeaked nosily as she collapsed into a chair. Cursing the café's bright lights, she leaned back with a hand over her eyes, praying for a power outage.

<*You're not masking the squeak. What gives?*> Sera asked her AI.

<It's what you get for drinking. I can't deal with two organic peculiarities at once. If you drink, I won't mask your clothing's noise. Take your pick.> Helen was really on the warpath, determined to make Sera suffer. Thank god Cargo had shown up.

Her first mate knew she liked to get one last round in at a bar before they left a station—okay, maybe more than just *a* round. He often would find her and bring her back to the ship before she was too far gone.

Sera splayed her fingers and looked through them to see Cargo returning with an insufferable grin on his face. He had a coffee for himself and two of the sober-up drinks for her. He set them on the table and pushed them toward her, his smile widening.

"I bet those are going to taste horrible."

Sera stuck her tongue out as she leaned forward to pick one up. "Prolly."

"You should have let me know you were gonna get into another drinking contest," Cargo said and took a drink of his own beverage. "I would have had more cash on hand and made a larger wager."

"I'm sorry I didn't think to let you know so you could sate your gambling needs," Sera said while delivering another sour look.

"My gambling habit doesn't have the unpleasant side effects of your station drinking binges."

Sera eyed him blearily over the rim of her cup. "What side effects are those?"

"The first day of any trip. You're not exactly sunshine and roses the day after a binge."

"Am I ever?"

Cargo paused, appearing to ponder the statement with great cogitation.

Her mind echoed with the light watery sound of Helen laughing at Cargo's pause. Sera scowled and swatted at him. "Thanks!"

He gestured with a nonchalant wave toward the second cup, indicating she get to it. Sera had already used her nano to clear most of the alcohol from her bloodstream and contain it for the next time she visited the head. However, Cargo didn't know she could do that and she needed to keep up appearances.

Sera raised the cup to her lips and took a long pull of the vile liquid anyway. She didn't want to seem ungrateful. After downing it, she leaned back in her chair, feeling much steadier than when she first sat down.

"All things considered, it's not a bad bit of extra credit to finish the visit with," she said and patted her pocket.

Cargo grunted, "One day you'll run out of people who haven't seen you win a drinking contest and then what will you do for fun?"

"Dunno, I guess I'll have to find a new way to fleece the common man."

Cargo laughed heartily in response.

Several minutes later—with Sera moving under her own power—they made their way down the promenade and onto the commercial dock front. There was just as much traffic here, but of a different sort. Cargo transports trundled down the deck-plate and service trucks were everywhere, delivering supplies or repair equipment.

Sabrina was in berth 724 Station South. Long before she could see the ship around the curve of the docks, Sera could hear Thompson's voice berating some poor cargo handlers. The echoing shouts eventually resolved into words, and Sera hid a smile behind her hand as they approached.

"You lazy dolts, can't you even lift a crate? I've seen hundred-year-old bots do a better job than you oafs. If you drop one more container, I'll take it out of your scrawny, mal-nourished hides. Now get to it, I don't have all day."

Thompson was a large blond man who had been her supercargo for over six years. To avoid confusion with Cargo, they just called him the Super. He wasn't a very outgoing man, mostly taken to brooding and stumping about the ship, but his attention to detail made him a good crewmember. Combined with his size and skill with a pulse rifle, that made him the right sort of super for *Sabrina*.

"How's the last shipment?" Sera asked when she and Cargo reached the ship.

"Fine, if these morons can manage to hold onto an effing handle." Thompson tossed the two dockworkers a contemptuous glare. "Don't know why they insist on using humans for this. Either way, we'll be loaded up with plenty of time to spare, don't worry, Captain."

"Good to hear," Cargo said. "Send the final docs up to me on the bridge when you're done."

Thompson nodded and turned back to the handlers as another crate slipped from their grasp. "God's great black space! What is *wrong* with you two, is this your first day on the job? I told you I was going to take it out of your hide and now I am. Which one of you wants to get your ear ripped off?"

"Somehow, I don't think that is helping them with their work," Cargo laughed.

"Yeah, but I bet it makes him feel a lot better," Sera grinned.

"I'll see you later, Captain; I've got to wash the smell of that bar you were in off me before my shift starts."

Sera took a deep breath. "Dunno, I kind of like that malty musk on you."

"In that case, I'm gonna take an even longer shower," Cargo laughed and walked onto the ship. Sera stuck her tongue out at him and walked over to an inspection port to admire the sleek lines of her girl.

Sabrina was not a regular boxy freight hauler, having started her life as a pleasure yacht. Her previous owner had fallen on hard times and lost possession of the ship in an outer system. *Sabrina* had needed repairs, and the local shipyard, where she had been in storage for owed taxes, didn't have the funds to make them. So, she sat for ninety years before Sera found her. With a hundred years of service before being impounded, she was getting on, but that didn't diminish the impact Sera felt when she first laid eyes on the ship.

There was an influential man who owed Sera a favor or two, and she got him to give her the money to buy the ship and furnish it with the necessary repairs. The finer aspects of the yacht's interior had been stripped out long before Sera saw *Sabrina*, but it was the size of the vessel and the engines that mattered. This ship had the room to haul cargo and the power to do so quickly. There were some other modifications that had been made, but like her advanced nano, Sera didn't advertise those.

She noted with approval that the damage they had suffered on their last run had been repaired. They had been parked in a planetary ring, moving along with the flow of the rocks and ice, when a stray rock had damaged the port sensor array and left a long rent across a goodly portion of the ship. However, the profit from the questionable cargo, which had put them there in the first place, more than paid for the repairs.

Thompson let loose some final curses as the dockworkers finished loading the last crate. She turned to watch with a smile; the dockworkers were visibly trembling as they got on their cart and drove off.

Sera returned to viewing her ship. She enjoyed these final quiet moments alone before going on board and filling out departure docs; these last few minutes when it was just her, *Sabrina's* sleek hull, and the call of empty space. She could forget her past, previous failures. Here she was a good captain, *Sabrina* was prosperous, and she had a good crew.

Her reverie was interrupted by a stinging slap on her butt and Sera turned to see her pilot, Cheeky, standing behind her. She wore a coy smile and her hands were resting on tilted hips.

"One day I'll get you to give me some of that luvin' you lavish on *Sabrina,*" Cheeky said.

"One day I'll get you neutered and save us all a lot of hassle." Sera rubbed her stinging butt; Cheeky could really deliver a good slap. She found herself becoming aroused as she looked at her pilot.

Cheeky was an attractive woman who wore as little clothing as local law or custom would allow. On Coburn, that meant she wore little more than three triangles of cloth, her shoes and a purse.

Sera shook her head to clear her mind. Cheeky also had altered glands that could put out much higher levels of pheromones than any human should be allowed to. "Make sure you shut that off and take a long shower. You know what happened last time your love smell filtered through the ship."

"We all had a good time." Cheeky wiggled her hips suggestively and blew her captain a kiss as she walked up the ramp. From behind, it was obvious why Cheeky had the name she did. Sera found herself wondering if it was a conscious effort to walk like that or if the woman had resorted to surgery.

Following her pilot onto the ship, Sera's internal AI flashed a notification that they had made a secure connection to the ship's private net. Sera checked the ship's general status and greeted its AI.

<Good evening sweetie, how are you holding together?> Sera asked Sabrina.

<Well enough, though I take offense to the question. How else would I be holding together?> The ship's mental tone conveyed annoyance.

Sabrina had been in a strange mood as of late. Sera chose to ignore the reply and smiled up at the nearest observation camera as Helen passed her authentication token to the bridge's net. Sera checked in, finding Cargo already working on departure paperwork; he must have decided to skip the shower.

<Station given us our departure time yet?>

<0900 ship time tomorrow.> His mental tone was relaxed. He enjoyed the little details of running the ship. Sera preferred to sit in her Captain's chair and give orders.

<Everything delivered and stowed?>

She could imagine him flipping through the plas sheets, checking them against the records logged in their databases, before he answered. Cargo hated making mistakes.

<Just one package left.> There was a significant pause, Sera could feel his mental discomfort even over the net. *<It's from one of Kade's people here.>*

<Kade? Why didn't I know about this?> Sera asked Cargo and Helen.

<It came on the list when we were out,> Helen supplied.

Cargo muttered something rude and the bridge's net flashed with an image of Cargo's avatar doing something very unpleasant to a representation of Kade. <*At least we're delivering it at the regular drop point with the rest of his stuff; there's no extra trip.*>

The regular drop point was an out of the way FTL jump point that Kade's people used for trading with other ships—his people being a pirate organization known as The Mark. Most of their people and ships were somewhat less than welcome at the more reputable stations, such as Coburn.

<*They never can schedule things ahead of time,*> Sera sighed.

<*They're not exactly an "ahead of time" sort of organization.*>

Sera told Cargo she'd be making the rounds and passed the active monitoring of the bridge's net to Helen.

When *Sabrina* had been a private yacht, the main deck was where the owners presumably threw their parties and spent most of their time. Now it was the freight deck. The cargo hatch was on the port side, and from there Sera walked into the main corridor, which ran from the bow to the stern engine shielding. The various freight holds were located off this corridor. Some had normal air and gravity, some were refrigerated and some had low, or even no gravity.

Also along the corridor were the lifts and ladders to the other decks. Sera walked toward the bow of the ship and slid into one of the vertical ladder shafts, which ran through all the decks. From there, she opened an access hatch to a maintenance tube. Inside the hatch were some knee and shoulder pads that she slipped on; it wouldn't do to scuff her leather.

The tube ended in a sealed inspection port. Sera opened it and peered out at the newly installed sensor equipment. The workmanship looked good. Everything was straight and attached firmly. The exterior indicators all showed green.

Beyond the array, Sera could see the space elevator that carried cargo and people between the surface and the station. Seeing it reminded her how far humanity had fallen from the glory it once held.

Millennia ago, when humanity had first set out to cross the stars, they had no faster than light technology. Interstellar travel was made possible only by utilizing massive fuel scoops. Ships had vast electrostatic funnels that spread for kilometers in front of them and allowed the gathering and compression of interstellar heavy hydrogen. The hydrogen, typically Deuterium and Tritium, was burned in nuclear fusion reactors to produce the thrust that pushed the ships between the stars.

Journeys between the stars took decades, or even centuries.

With the considerable effort and expense required to get to even the nearest stars, humanity strove to make the most of all available resources. Technology and engineering made impressive advances as societies demanded better use of raw materials.

The space elevator stretching from Coburn Station down to Trio was an example of the different sort of technology humans used to have. In present times, few worlds could afford to build elevators to their space stations. The materials were just too expensive and the process took too long. A ship's grav drive was more efficient in the short term. However, over centuries of use, the elevator would use much less power to achieve the same volume of transport. It was another example of the long-term approach that people used to take as opposed to the current mindset, which was decidedly shortsighted.

It was a shift created by the advent of FTL.

People had always suspected—at least once the significance of 299,792,458 meters per second was known—that some method of exceeding the speed of light was possible. Many theories of wormholes, space-time folding, alternate realities, and slipstreams were put forward and attempted. In the end, the workable form of faster than light travel encapsulated many of the ideas behind some of those theories, though it turned out to be much harder to harness than originally hoped.

Before FTL, each star system was isolated from the rest of humanity, but once a trip between two stars was reduced to a matter of weeks and not centuries, everything changed. Traveling to an uninhabited star to mine asteroids was something that could be easily achieved, and people's attitude toward conservation and efficiency disappeared within a century.

Helen injected a long yawn into Sera's thoughts. <*Enough already. We get it, you yearn for the good old days.*>

<*I don't really miss the days…just wish people could appreciate the way things used to be.*>

Helen didn't agree. <*You just miss your people. This isn't your world and you know it.*>

<*It is now; it has to be.*>

Helen didn't respond. It was an old conversation, one they performed out of habit more than a real expectation of change.

She walked through the freight deck's main corridor, poking her head into various holds, ensuring that everything was secure and ready for departure. The familiar smell of deck cleaner and oil wafted past and an unbidden memory of her first weeks on the ship came back.

She and Flaherty had spent many a day hauling equipment through these halls and shafts back when they were first refitting *Sabrina*. It had been long days and longer nights, but she was proud of what they had built.

Helen flashed the date of her memory over her vision and she was surprised to see that it had been just over ten years ago. Somewhere in the last few months, she had passed her ten-year anniversary with *Sabrina* without marking the occasion. No wonder the ship had been a bit snippy of late.

Sera chided Helen for not reminding her of the occasion, nor for cluing her in on the cause of Sabrina's poor temper.

<*I was unaware you were interested in marking anniversaries with AI.*> Helen was unrepentant.

<*What are you talking about?*> Sera replied. <*We always celebrate our anniversary.*>

Helen inserted the emotion of mild surprise, followed by a pout into Sera's mind. <*I thought that was just for me.*>

Sera laughed and her avatar stuck her tongue out at Helen. <*Don't give me that, I'm not some little girl that you can twist around your ephemeral finger anymore.*>

Helen didn't respond, and Sera let out a long sigh. For being one of the most advanced AI in the Inner Stars, Helen could certainly be childish.

<*Sometimes I think Sabrina is rubbing off on you,*> Sera said to her one-time mentor and guardian.

<*I resent that,*> Helen retorted. <*Just because the ship's AI can't deal with the fact that I am her superior in every way doesn't mean I have to dumb it down.*>

<*You're superior to most planet administration AI we run into, but you don't go out of your way to make them feel inferior,*> Sera responded, mildly surprised to be the one to advocate maturity in their relationship.

<*Maybe I could be more accommodating for our dear Sabrina,*> Helen eventually responded.

<*Glad to hear it. Now I have to figure out how to make it up to her,*> Sera said.

<*Make what up?*> Helen asked innocently and Sera let out an audible scream.

She completed her review of the freight deck and took the aft ladder shaft up to the crew deck.

When she first bought *Sabrina,* the ship had lifts for reaching each deck, but Sera had removed all but one of the conveniences. Shafts were faster and still worked when the ship was under fire and conserving energy.

<*Nothing to do with how you like to climb the ladders in front of the men on the ship?*> Helen suggested.

<*I do it to Cheeky, too.*> Sera smiled to herself as she stepped onto the crew deck.

<*Funny, I thought you preferred it when she did it to you.*>

The ladder was across from the galley and she stepped in to find Thompson and Flaherty eating their supper. She saw that it was nearing the end of second shift; most of the crew would be calling it a night soon.

"Evening, Captain," Thompson said around a mouthful of his sandwich. Flaherty looked at her, nodded, and went back to his meal.

"Hey guys," Sera smiled at them as she poured a cup of coffee and hunted for fresh cream.

Thompson and Flaherty made an effective and efficient team when it came to managing the ship's cargo. Neither of them talked much and managed to communicate just about everything with grunts and gestures. They didn't even use the Link to talk—Sera had checked the logs.

Sera doctored her coffee up just the way she liked and bid them goodnight before taking the corridor to the bow, then climbing the ladder that led to the top deck. This was the smallest deck on the ship, containing only the bridge forward and a small observation lounge aft. The lounge had a magnificent view of the light flare from the engines when they were under heavy thrust, and Sera had often sat back there, gazing out at it as the ship cruised through space.

Cargo was still on the bridge, readying the reports Sera had to sign before they could depart. Cheeky was also at her console, having added a tight halter top and tiny skirt to her ensemble. She yawned and stretched as she stood.

"You just had to make a final course alteration right before bed," she complained. "I had to plot it out and re-file with system traffic control."

"Sorry about that, I didn't think you'd already filed the report," Sera apologized.

"When else was I going to do it, when I was sleeping?"

Cargo laughed. "I thought you had gotten all of your 'sleeping' in on your shore leave."

Cheeky stuck her tongue out at the man. "Jealous."

Cargo couldn't help it as his eyes strayed down to the bold, black print across Cheeky's chest. It read 'Got Milk?' He sighed wistfully. "I might be."

"Really?" Cheeky asked.

"No, not really," Cargo grinned.

"You're such a tease," Cheeky said as she turned and left the bridge.

"I'm a tease?" He murmured softly as she left.

"You are, you know," Sera said.

"How so? I don't flirt, I just do my job."

"Exactly!" Sera smiled as she shuffled the plas she had to sign into order. "You're totally unflappable. It's the ultimate come-on."

"I'm going to start the pre-warm-up checklist so things'll be ready in the morning."

"See! Always back to business with you."

"Do you want to do it?" Cargo turned, half rising out of his chair.

"Heck no, I've been up for thirty hours already."

Cargo nodded and sat back down.

Coburn, like many stations, required a full warm-up and test of all ship systems before undocking. The warm-up had to take place four hours before departure and Cargo was taking the third watch to run the sequence at 0500 hours.

She turned to leave the bridge when Nance, the ship's bio, appeared in her mind.

<I just wanted to let you know, take short showers for the next while—I know how you like to luxuriate for an hour or more.>

Even though she was looking at Nance's mental avatar, the bio-engineer still wore a thick, tight hazsuit. Whereas Cheeky showed every inch of skin she could manage, Nance was the opposite, rarely showing any skin at all—even virtually.

<What's up?> Sera asked. *<I have the stink of a hundred drunks to wash off.>*

The bio scowled. *<Well, let's just say that you don't want to come down to environmental until I clean up. The regulator on tank nine malfunctioned, and a line blew. Contaminated all sorts of shit with…well…shit.>*

<Was it that one you bought at Rattlescar?> Sera asked.

<Yeah, I knew I shouldn't have, but it was such a good deal,> the bio replied.

<Ripped off at Rattlescar again. You should know better.>

Nance's avatar nodded sullenly and Sera laughed. *<Well, I'll let you get to it. Can I at least have ten minutes?>*

Nance nodded. *<Yes, but a second over and I'm switching it to full cold.>*

<Is that any way to treat your captain?>

<Do ***you*** *want to come down here and clean up?>* Nance retorted.

<OK, OK, ten minutes, got it.>

Nance disappeared from her vision as Sera slid down the ladder to the third deck. She walked quietly past the crew cabin doors to her quarters at the end of the corridor. She palmed the door open with a yawn and entered her outer office where she handled the ship's business.

It was the standard utilitarian sort expected of a captain; her various certifications hung on the wall and a large oak desk dominated the small space. She laid the departure plas sheets on its surface and pulled up holo of each one. This was the part about captaining a starship she liked least. She was near finishing up and getting ready to peel off her leather when Cargo called her over the Link.

<Still up, Captain?>

<Barely.>

<Hate to bother you with this, but you're the only other one awake. Kade's boys are down at the hatch with that last shipment.>

Despite his words, Cargo's tone didn't carry any apology.

Grumbling that she should have told Thompson to have himself or Flaherty wait up for it, she pulled her jacket back on and slid down the ladders to the freight deck. At the hold's opening to the station dock, two men were waiting with a large crate on a gravity pad. They were looking nervous and just a bit twitchy. Either they had some bad drugs in their systems or Kade was foisting something pretty damn dangerous on her.

One of the men spoke up as soon as he spotted her.

"Permission to come aboard?" he asked.

Sera granted it and the two men all but ran onto the ship and moved out of direct sight from dock traffic, the cargo container following them on its float.

"So, what does The Mark have for me today, boys?" Sera asked, none too pleased about the late hour or the obviously illegal contents of the crate. "What am I sticking my neck out for this time?"

Most cargo The Mark had her run was just semi-illegal. Either OK in the system where she was picking up or delivering to, just not both; or some stopping point along the way. There also had been the odd shipment that was illegal no matter where they were; this one had that feel.

The man who had asked permission to board grinned in what he probably thought was a winning fashion. It really wasn't. "S'nothing to worry about, just a little something that Kade wants."

"I don't care about that," Sera said as she reached over and snatched the bill of lading from him. "I care what *this* says it is." Scanning the pad, she found that the crate purported to contain a prize-racing hound in a holo sim. The dog thought he was in a regular kennel with other dogs for companionship and humans feeding him. The reality was just a crate with a feeding system, but he wouldn't know the difference and would be better for it.

"That really what's in there?" Sera didn't bother to hide her skepticism.

"Yeah, the dog's not as special as who used to own it." The man grinned again and Sera held up her hand.

"Yeah, sure. I really don't want to know more." She signed off on the delivery. "Any need to open it and check it out?"

The men went rigid and hastily assured her that the dog would be fine and there was no need to check it out. That clinched it for Sera, she would definitely have to check this cargo out once she was underway. If it had any type of tamper seal, she'd make up some excuse for it later.

Once it was secured in the fore port hold, she informed Cargo that the delivery had been made and stowed. Then she closed the main cargo hatch and the auxiliary personnel port. Cargo confirmed the seal from the bridge and checked it off the pre-warm-up list.

<Get some rest, Captain, gonna be a long day tomorrow,> Cargo advised.

<Cargo! Now you've gone and jinxed it!>

JUST A ROUTINE DAY

STELLAR DATE: 07.01.8927 (Adjusted Years)
LOCATION: *Sabrina*, Coburn Station, Trio
REGION: Trio System, Silstrand Alliance Space

At 0600 hours, Sera sauntered onto the bridge and greeted Cargo, who was hunched over his console, finishing up departure plaswork. She handed him one of the two coffee cups she carried and he absently took it, thanked her, and cast her an appraising look.

"Forgoing the customary clothing-matches-your-mood policy?" he asked.

"I never break my clothing-mood policy. I'm feeling good, but mellow. Blue fits."

Cargo eyed her with suspicion. "This isn't like that one time you wore pink to fake us out, is it?"

"How many times do I have to tell you? That was a dare from Cheeky." Sera set her coffee down and eased into her chair. "Checks went OK?"

"*Sabrina* purred like a kitten, just like always," Cargo replied.

<*Of course I did. When have I not?*> Sabrina asked.

"Never, my dear," Sera replied with a smile.

Cargo shook his head and swallowed his coffee in two quick gulps. "Tug is scheduled for 0845, I'm getting sack." He stood and left the bridge without even his customary morning stretch.

"Is it something I'm wearing?" Sera called after him, laughing.

Sera ran a hand down the tight leather skin-suit covering her body. She spent a moment enjoying the tactile sensation before beginning her routine. The first order of business was finalizing the freight manifests and trade route they would take after the drop-off for Kade.

When Cheeky came on duty at 0700, she took in her captain with a long hungry look, unable to keep a hand from straying toward her captain's well-defined chest. Sera slapped it away.

"There'll be none of that."

"You are such a tease, Captain." Cheeky grinned as she sat at the pilot's console.

Sera laughed. Cheeky was one to talk; she was wearing her customary departure uniform, little more than the day before and a pair of 'sensible' heels. Sera used Cheeky's arrival and coverage of the bridge to make a quick visit to the galley, followed by a final visual inspection of the ship. She returned an hour later to go through final checklists with the station.

Departure tug charges were billed and their accounts were closed. Station umbilicus retracted and station personnel confirmed inner seal on the dockside airlocks. At 0830, *Sabrina* broke hard connection with the station and floated in her berth, with only the station's security tethers still in place.

The tug showed up on time and made a solid grapple to their bow anchors, pulling them gently away from Coburn Station. Sera felt a mild flutter in her stomach as they left station gravity and their internal systems took over.

"Coburn Tug 19 confirming successful undock," the tug pilot's voice announced over the comm.

"Free and clear Tug 19," Cheeky confirmed as the ship drifted away from the station.

The tug maneuvered *Sabrina* out into their designated departure lane. For a relative backwater, Trio was a busy system. They took plotted courses and space traffic lanes very seriously.

"Oh, sweet mother!" Cheeky exclaimed. "Is he ever going to turn on his grav drive? If he uses thrusters to pull us all the way out, you should register a complaint."

Sera had dozed off. She stretched and checked the holo on her console. "He's still on thrusters? We're a thousand klicks from the station; he could have turned on his grav drive at the five hundred mark."

"Trio System law states that all outbound ships must use thrusters only until fifteen hundred kilometers from stations," Sabrina provided via the bridge's audible systems. "It's a recent change they made after some accidents."

"I guess that explains the size of that tug bill; must take a pile of fuel to pull a ship that far on thrusters only."

At the proscribed distance, the tug's gravity engines unfolded from its main body and activated. Because the graviton waves would disrupt the ship behind it, the engines extended far to either side of *Sabrina* before activating.

"We could have been on a fusion burn by now." Cheeky complained, yawning with boredom over the long departure.

"You may be a good pilot, Cheeks, but I don't relish the thought of being on a station where half those moron captains can turn on their fusion engines near me. I like my skin actually attached to my body."

Cheeky made a dismissive sniff. "You can always get new skin, but lost time is gone forever."

Sera laughed. "I'm still wearing my original birthday suit, thank you very much."

"Like I'd know, you never let anyone see it. Always with the leather."

"I could say you have the opposite problem."

"You could, but would I care?" Cheeky sat up and looked at her console intently. "Damn tug's got the vector wrong. We want a parabolic around that inner planet, not a collision."

That was what Sera liked about Cheeky; fun to chat with, but able to switch to business in an instant, when it was called for.

"Tug 19, this is *Sabrina.* Come in," Cheeky called over the comm.

"Tug 19 here."

"Check your vector 19, you're moving off course."

There was a moment of silence and then the tug pilot's response came over the comm. "Sorry about that, my primary nav was reading sensors wrong. I'm on backup now and correcting. Tug 19 out."

"Roger, *Sabrina* out," Cheeky said, switching off the open comm.

"I think that Tug's AI is senile," Sabrina said over the ship's speakers. "It told me that my humans and their advice are not welcome."

"Yay for tugs," Cheeky's voice dripped with sarcasm.

"I suddenly feel somewhat less than safe." Sera finished her cup of coffee and double-checked scan. "At least he corrected properly. How long till we can ditch this dude?"

"Seventeen minutes," Sabrina replied. "And it won't be a moment too soon."

Sera chuckled in response.

Sabrina was an unusual AI. Usually ship's AI were officious and only spoke when directly addressed—and then only over the Link. However, Sabrina had a habit of simply speaking her mind whenever she chose. On their first voyage, when it was just Sera and Flaherty, having Helen and the garrulous Sabrina was comforting—especially since the AI were much better at casual banter than Flaherty.

Finally, the tug reached its departure point and released its grapple.

"Tug 19 signing off. Have a good trip."

"You too," Cheeky said and closed the channel. "Dork."

"We're not on our proper course," Sabrina observed.

"I know," Cheeky sighed. "I just didn't feel like mentioning it again. I can fix us up in a minute."

Cheeky laid in her course corrections and activated *Sabrina's* gravity drive. They were accelerating toward the center of the system, the drive throwing negative gravitons in front of the ship, essentially sucking them forward.

Their flight path took them past the innermost planet, a rocky world spinning below them at over sixteen thousand kilometers per hour. Sera watched the world's surface as the daylight termination line race across the craggy landscape, casting long, dancing shadows over the world.

"Hate to be working a mining rig on that thing," she said with a shake of her head.

"Can you say 'hourly earthquakes'?" Cheeky asked.

Sabrina skimmed close to the surface of the world in a parabolic arc, Cheeky applying a hard burn of the fusion engines at the periapsis of their passage. The ship's velocity picked up considerably during the maneuver, lining them up for a close pass-by of the local star.

"Gravity assist one completed at one-hundred percent efficiency," Cheeky said with a grin. "Now to beard the star."

Gravity assists were one of the wonders of physics. The faster you flew, the more kinetic energy a burn gave. When a burn was made at the closest point of an arch around a heavenly body, the more relative velocity was imparted.

Cheeky referred to it as planet slalom.

"We at the scoop deployment point yet, Cheeks?" Sera asked, feeling too lethargic to use her Link. Maybe she *was* still feeling the after effects of yesterday's binge.

"Just about. When we hit 0.113*c* we'll have the right *v* to do it smoothly."

"You on it with Sabrina?"

Cheeky turned and looked at her captain. "I *have* done this before."

<*Me too,*> Sabrina added.

Sera laughed and raised her hands. "Sorry, I apologize for my backseat piloting."

Several minutes later, a slight vibration ran through the hull as the scoop deployed. It wasn't large, only a kilometer wide, but its electro-static field funneled the stellar wind through a system that stripped out the heavy hydrogen and helium, storing the gasses in the fuel tanks for later consumption.

<*Sabrina,*> Cheeky addressed the ship as they passed 0.15*c*, <*my board shows green for fusion burn. Confirm?*>

<*I am green, as well,*> Sabrina acknowledged. <*Good to initiate burn at plot point tango.*>

<*Roger,*> the pilot replied.

Despite the terms used, Cheeky wasn't sitting at a board with green lights, and Sabrina most certainly was not. Piloting a ship like *Sabrina* involved manipulating controls in a three dimensional holo projection. At any time, the pilot had to monitor dozens of visual indicators, as well as the data feed her Link to the nav computer provided.

"Initiating fusion burn," Cheeky said as she activated the fusion engine's super-lasers and started the flow of helium and heavy hydrogen into the engine.

Although she had just initiated an atomic fusion reaction only one-hundred meters aft, there was no noticeable change on the ship. Powerful inertial dampeners in the form of gravity fields protected the rest of the vessel from the engines. Without them, the thrust from the fusion burners would cause *Sabrina* to do a large-scale impression of a crushed can.

"All dampeners and stabilizers read normal, radiation shielding is showing green, as well."

"You know, Cheeks," Sera said. "It's just me up here; you don't really need to do the whole status announcing thing."

Cheeky cast her captain a sour look. "I don't do it for you; I assume you're checking everything on the Link. You know I've always dreamed of being a military pilot, you know, flying one of those big cruisers. Well, I saw some Silstrand military holos recently where they announce everything. I'm trying it on for size."

"Don't let me stop you, then," Sera smiled.

"I wasn't going to. You may dress like a dominatrix, but you don't frighten me."

Sera sighed and sat back in her chair.

<*Well, you do,*> Helen said.

The course Cheeky followed took them over the star's north pole. *Sabrina* was on a course to pass within a hundred thousand kilometers of the star, putting them on the right outsystem vector while picking up at least thirty percent of the total velocity they would need before hitting their jump point.

Sera carefully examined the ship's scan readout to make sure there was no potential flare activity. System scan said the star's northern hemisphere was quiet, but she liked to check for herself.

She was comparing the two scans when she noticed several ships enter the system through a seldom-used jump point stellar south of Trio and Coburn Station. Scan showed them traveling at over seventy percent the speed of light; far too fast for a busy system like Trio. Sera imagined they could expect a hefty fine when they docked.

Sabrina lost its Link to the system's dataflow as the ship approached the star; radiation played havoc with any signal. The ship's shields showed nominal fluctuations—they were rated to hold against far worse, including having a fusion warhead detonate against them.

As the ship passed over the star, Cheeky applied full burn to the fusion engines, the effect multiplying their acceleration by a factor of five. At that rate, it took less than a minute to complete their arc around the star and they exited the gravity assist maneuver at just over a quarter the speed of light.

Sera examined the data from the passage over Trio Prime, impressed to see the precision with which Cheeky performed the maneuver. Even the switching of the grav drive from negative to positive was done at the optimal time—the gravitons it threw now pushing them off the star's mass.

Ship's Link reconnected to a nearby beacon and Sera turned her attention back to the ships she had spotted earlier. System scan showed the vessels remained on a direct course for the world of Trio, though they weren't slowing down much, if at all.

At *Sabrina's* current distance from Trio, scan lag was an issue. The beacon they were stripping data from was ten light minutes away from their current position; Trio was another seven light minutes past that. Considering the speed those ships were traveling, they could already be at the station, or past it.

As Sera was pondering what those ships could be up to, Sabrina alerted them to a call on the local emergency band.

"This is a system-wide alert. Three ships of unknown origin have attacked a Trio defense emplacement and are on a vector for Coburn Station. Their intentions are unknown. All ships are advised to stay within the protective range of a system station or fleet patrol until further notice." The alert paused and then restarted the same message.

Sabrina muted the alert. *<I'll let you know if it changes,>* she said.

"Thanks, that's not terribly auspicious—Silstrand really needs to deal with these pirates, it's getting worse all the time," Sera said with a shake of her head.

"Uh, you realize that we smuggle for those pirates," Cheeky said with a smirk.

"Well," Sera smiled back, "I said they should; I didn't say I thought they actually would."

Cheeky chuckled and Sera reviewed their current vector. There were no planets or stations anywhere near their outsystem route. They would just have to keep pushing forward. Chances were slim those ships would even come within fifteen million kilometers of *Sabrina,* though Sera wasn't about to bet her ship on it.

"Crank our burners up all the way, Cheeky. I want to put more distance between us and that mess," Sera said, before calling the crew to their stations, updating them on what was happening on the other side of the star.

Cargo stepped onto the bridge a few minutes later with coffee for himself and the two women. He made a show of only looking them in their eyes as he passed out the brew, then sat at his console, looking over the scan and their course.

"That's a lot of velocity those buggers have on them," he commented

"They're going to get a speeding ticket," Sera agreed.

"What about a blowing-up-a-defensive-emplacement ticket?" Cheeky asked. "I hear systems are sticklers about that sort of thing."

"Alert said three ships, right?" Cargo asked.

"Yeah."

"Scan just updated from a relay south of the star. It shows five jumped in. Where are the other two?"

"That's disconcerting," Sera said. "I don't see them anywhere on system scan."

"Why does that statement insert small circus animals into my stomach?" Cheeky asked.

Cargo leaned forward and looked at Cheeky's flat stomach. "I don't see how even a couple of dancing mice would fit in there."

"Maybe it's a flea circus," Sera commented.

"Ewwww!" Cheeky shivered convulsively. "There's a mental image I just didn't need."

Another relay a few million kilometers south of the star updated scan data and they got their answer on the missing ships.

The feed showed the two vessels veering off from the other three and plotting a course around the star's south pole. They were running fast, thrusting on antimatter pion engines, from the look of the gamma rays trailing behind their ships.

"Does Trio allow AP engines in their inner system?" Cheeky asked.

"They blew up an emplacement. I don' think they care about AP regulations." Cargo said.

<Trio special regulations state that no antimatter engines may be used within twenty million kilometers of the star, or within two million kilometers of any station or outer planet,> Sabrina supplied the ruling anyway.

<What's up with her? She's being so proper today,> Helen said privately to Sera.

Sera sent her AI a mental shrug, but didn't comment further.

"Cheeky, what's the chance those two bogies will get within a million klicks of us?" she asked, though it looked like Cheeky was already on it.

"Based on their current course, they're going to get closer than your tight leather outfit, Captain. I'm guessing they plan to pay us a visit."

As though on cue, a signal came in from one of the ships and Sabrina patched it through the bridge speakers. A harsh voice called for them to cease burn and divert to a position that Sera would bet local stellar scan couldn't monitor.

"Like hell we will," Sera muttered. "Sabrina, are we ready to do an AP burn?"

<We're always ready to make an AP burn. It's my favorite pastime.>

Sera chuckled, *<Don't I know it. Bring up the gamma shielding and extrude the AP nozzle.>*

<Spooling.>

Sera could hear the ship's secondary reactor spin up and she watched readings show power flowing to the gamma shields. The AP drive smashed Hydrogen and Anti-Hydrogen, annihilating them and producing pions that were focused out the AP engine's nozzle. The pions quickly broke down into gamma rays and accelerated out the nozzle at just under the speed of light. The longer the nozzle was extruded, the more thrust *Sabrina* would get from the burn. Sera saw that Cheeky and Sabrina were spinning it out all the way.

"Good thing we declared our antimatter and allowed the containment inspection before we docked," Cargo said. "Blood suckers at Trio would fine us if they caught us using undeclared antimatter, pirate attack or no."

"You're thinking pirate, too, then?" Sera asked.

"It's way too small a force to actually attack a Silstrand Alliance member. They're here for something that they think a small, fast force can snag."

Sera's thoughts immediately went to the small crate she had taken on the night before. She couldn't imagine anything in that crate being worth an outright attack on an Alliance member system, but it was the only thing she carried that could possibly have that kind of value.

The AP drive began to add to the ship's velocity and the holo display showed their kph relative to Trio Prime increasing so quickly that the lower digits were a blur.

<*Oh this feels good!*> Sabrina crowed. <*I wish we could run out the AP engine more often!*>

"Not concerned who we're running from?" Cargo asked the ship's AI.

<*Sera will take care of me. I'm not worried about any pirates,*> Sabrina replied confidently, causing Sera to suppress a smile.

"What are the chances that these guys are just checking all the outbound ships?" Cheeky asked.

"Then they'd split up. Both of them are on a vector to meet up with us well before we get to our jump point. I'd say we're the ones they're looking for."

Cheeky looked perplexed. "What could we have that pirates would want?"

Sera and Cargo shared a long look, his eyes showing mild recrimination. Sera sighed and told Cheeky they were carrying something extra special for The Mark.

"Figures," the pilot sulked. "I don't know why you do runs for them. From what I can see, we're pretty profitable even without all the extra risks."

Sera's expression was stony. "I have my reasons."

"Well, I hope they're worth dying for."

"We're not going to die here; we've got a few tricks up our sleeves," Sera said. In her mind, where only Helen could hear she said, <*Yes, it's worth dying for.*>

Sera checked scan and saw that the two unidentified ships had fallen from their entry velocity of $0.73c$ to $0.45c$. Their vector around the star had not been clean and they lost velocity breaking out of its gravity well.

Cheeky was looking at the same data. "Damn, those ships must be all engine to only lose that much v during such a sloppy maneuver."

"Don't forget the guns," Cargo added. "All engines and guns."

Sera switched her display to show their outsystem course. Their destination was an FTL jump point several million kilometers beyond the last of the outer planets. The interior of Trio system was a good seven light hours across and they still had just over three hours to the jump point on full burn.

She widened her view and saw that the two ships behind were accelerating again. Both were back over half the speed of light, nearly at their previous velocity of $0.73c$. Sera looked down at *Sabrina's* indicators and saw that they were accelerating slower than expected and the ship was developing an odd vibration.

"Scoop!" Sera cried just as Sabrina reported that the scoop was still deployed and slowing them down. Cheeky cursed and quickly killed the electrostatic field that had been scooping hydrogen for fuel.

The pilot turned slightly red face back to Sera. "Sorry, Captain. It sorta slipped my mind."

Sera's brow furrowed. "Mine too," then she nodded. "Now the ol' girl's picking up."

<*Who are you calling old?*>

<*Sorry, it's just an expression,*> Sera replied and only received a mental 'harrumph' from her ship. She really needed to think of something to make up for the forgotten anniversary.

Cargo looked over his shoulder. "Stellar medium is a bit lighter on our vector. We should be able to hit 0.60 c with all drives burning hot, but they'll," he jerked his head to the stern to indicate their pursuers, "get that advantage, too."

Helen had been examining their outbound vector and brought an issue to Sera's attention. Sera cursed silently. Things were always working against her.

"Ladies," Sera asked Cheeky and Sabrina, "if we do this burn for another forty minutes, what are the chances we can hold shields at max while we vector for the jump and keep all three drives online?"

"Planning to melt us?" Cheeky asked.

<*She's right,*> Sabrina said. <*Power plant could melt down if we tried to run all that—even with the auxiliary plant online.*>

"What about the SC batteries?" Sera asked.

"They're way low," Cheeky replied. "Pansies at Trio get all nervous with a hundred fusion reactors humming around their station. You said they charge too much for station power, so we ran on batts while docked."

"Huh," Sera grunted. "Well that was short-sighted of me."

When traveling at any appreciable speed, *Sabrina* always ran her forward shields. Even a speck of sand, traveling at even a tenth the speed of light, would punch right through the ship. It could destroy the reactor, and certainly any humans in its way.

However, with ships chasing them, they now had to deploy shield umbrellas over the entire vessel, and that was going to run them beyond their power generation limits.

Flying directly behind a ship running grav, fusion, and AP engines was a recipe for a bad day. If they were smart, their pursuers would fan out and flank *Sabrina.* From those positions, they would be able to hit nearly any part of the ship. The only advantage was that they couldn't shoot straight up the engines.

<*Helen, I'm betting these guys are going to use lasers, probably ten centimeter beams; they're going to take out some of ours so they can board us. Work up some tactics and prime our defenses,*> Sera said to her AI.

<*I'll load the routines. I think our best bet is to try to refract their beams with some precise grav waves. With the batteries low, we can't run refraction shield-wide,*> Helen replied.

<*You can do it girl, don't let those bastards put holes in Sabrina.*>

<*Her I'm not so concerned about. You, on the other hand, are a priority.*>

And so, the battle of the AIs continued.

"Do we have a solid intercept time, Cheeky?" Sera asked vocally.

"Not one hundred percent, they have a few course corrections to make that may slow them down a bit, but even if they have one-eyed apes flying those tubs, they'll catch us before we jump."

"Any chance we can jump early?" Cargo asked.

"Not unless you want to see how you look smeared across a clump of dark matter," Sera told her first mate, while looking over their course. "There's gotta be something…" There was always a way out of these situations, it just took some creative thinking. "Cheeky, you've got one more correction to make, right?"

"Yup, shortly before our transition we've got to angle down and get back into the main plane of the system." Cheeky said, highlighting the position in the plot on the ship's main holo.

"Would you be able to make it now, and have it be shorter? It may be enough to get us out of this mess."

Cheeky pulled up several holos and manipulated them, plotting positions where she could make the alteration, looking for the one with maximum efficiency, lowest drag, and best time-to-jump improvement. The incongruity of her nearly naked, oversexed pilot furiously processing advanced spatial calculations on a dozen holos was not lost on Sera; she hid a small smile behind her hand as she watched.

<*It's like you don't take this stuff seriously,*> Helen admonished.

<*I totally do, but look at her, she's wiggling all over.*>

Cheeky turned and Sera schooled her expression.

"There's a point coming up where we can do our burn that would work well, but I don't like traveling in the main plane at these speeds. You never know what uncharted rock is out there, waiting to end our little race."

"Trio's pretty busy; I'd imagine they have everything charted."

"Who? The people with senile tug AIs and faulty nav comps?"

"AI can go senile?" Cargo asked.

"We have evidence," Sabrina said, her voice dripping with implied meaning.

"I'll take the chance of a stray rock over the surety of their lasers. Plot it out," Sera replied.

She leaned back in her chair. Despite the humor, she found in the small things around her, Helen was right; this was serious. But her crew was smart, and her ship was a pro. This would work; they'd make the jump before the pirates caught up with them.

Cheeky made her computations, rechecked them and then had Sabrina review them, as well. They passed muster and Cheeky announced stellar south course alteration in just under five minutes. The time came and the change occurred with no noticeable sensations in the ship.

Sera ran the computations again, *Sabrina's* nav systems telling her that they had insufficient data to provide an accurate model due to unknown deceleration capabilities of the pursuing ships.

In addition to catching up with *Sabrina,* the two pirate ships also had to show some care in matching speeds. At the velocities they were traveling, even miniscule speed differences would cause immense differences in position. If the pirates didn't match *Sabrina's* speed precisely, they would flash past faster than the human eye could even detect.

High relative *v* also made targeting with lasers tricky at best. Good gunners with powerful AI could do it, but even they missed a lot. Her real worry was that if *Sabrina* managed to avoid being boarded, the pirates would resort to relativistic missiles.

Apparently, Cargo had been thinking along the same lines.

"Do you think they have RMs?" he asked.

"Pirates can get their hands on those things?" Cheeky asked, her entire body getting a bit paler than it already was.

"Yeah, but even if they have them, I doubt they'd use one. Those things aren't cheap."

Cheeky was looking over her nav board again. "How fast can they accelerate?"

"It varies and it's not linear," Sera replied. "At the speeds we're traveling, at I'd guess they could go from seventy percent to ninety-nine percent of the speed of light in a few minutes."

"Ninety-nine percent?" Cheeky choked.

"They don't have the word 'relativistic' in the name for nothing." Cargo's voice dripped with sarcasm, which earned him a scowl from the pilot.

"They can't burn too long, though," Sera said. "Only so much fuel in them."

"Probably because they usually kill things before they run out," Cheeky commented.

Scan showed their pursuers making course corrections to match the burn Cheeky had made. The calculations now showed that their pursuer's loss of *v* from the adjustment would be just barely enough; *Sabrina* would make it out of this. Apparently, the two ships behind them had come to the same conclusion, as the comm board suddenly lit up with an incoming message.

Sabrina activated the connection and a very unhappy face appeared on the main holo. From the lack of uniform and a glimpse of the bridge, it was confirmed; they were definitely pirate ships.

"Ship designated *Sabrina,* you were ordered to cease acceleration and divert to the transmitted course. Why are you not complying?" The man was trying to sound officious.

"'Cause I like my skin on my body," Sera said with copious amounts of sarcasm. "Why don't you tell me why you have such a keen interest in my ship?"

"That's none of your concern," the man snarled. "Now comply with our directive."

Sera almost laughed. This was the saddest line she'd ever been fed. "Don't be ridiculous. I'm not diverting, I have a schedule to keep and I'm not going to interrupt it to have tea with you." With that, she killed the connection and looked to Cheeky. "Time to FTL?"

"Twenty three minutes," came the pilot's reply. "Those looked like Padre's men, didn't they?"

"Yeah, I'm starting to get a suspicion about who Kade stole that 'racing hound' from."

Cargo turned from his station. "They're still trying to make contact. Let's hope that's as mean as they get." He glanced back at his board. "Never mind that, scan shows energy signatures on their bow. I'm guessing lasers."

"Any room to twitch?" Sera asked Cheeky.

"Not unless we want to do another burn to correct, but that would put them right on top of us when we make the jump."

Sera cursed their luck.

"Sabrina, do we have the power to extend the shielding back over the AP engine nozzle? It looks like they're warming up their heaters and I bet that's gonna be the first target," she asked.

<*It'll weaken our shields overall,*> the AI replied. <*But I see the logic. Doing it.*>

The shields that protected *Sabrina* were not a firm shell around the ship, but rather an anti-gravitational field that repelled any objects and particles. Complex systems allowed the shields to detect laser impact on the hull and diffuse the beam with targeted gravitational waves. It was a tricky system to operate and often worked better in stellar space where the leading edge of a laser beam could be detected by refraction from the particles it had to travel through. Out in gasless interstellar spaces, lasers were much harder to counter.

Unfortunately for *Sabrina,* that was just the type of space they were entering. They had cleared the Kuiper Belt, and the Trio System had a stretch of very empty space between their current location and the jump point.

The shield extension came just in time, as invisible beams lanced out striking at *Sabrina's* AP nozzle.

Sera turned to Cargo. "What tricks do we have up our sleeves?"

Cargo mulled it over for a minute. "Could pepper them with some beams right on their bow. It would cause them to throw some force off the front of their ships, but I don't know how much good it would do. Could also drop a mine or two; might be able to do it accurately enough to force them to twitch out of the way."

Sera looked at the numbers again on her screen; although they were on course to jump before interception, the nav systems still showed a much closer race than she'd like. "Do both."

Cargo called down to Thompson and Flaherty and told them to get two magnetic proximity mines loaded into the tubes and ready to drop on the bridge's mark. Sera watched him run a few simulations to see if it was possible to hide the mine's presence with a bit of a light show from the aft lasers.

"Think it will work?" She asked.

"Worth a shot. Gonna be shooting at them anyway."

Cargo initiated the laser sequence, and seconds later, dropped the proximity mines. The mines had their own small propulsion units, which allowed them to reach the desired position as the lasers flickered around them.

Right before the lead ship was about to hit its designated mine, the vessel twitched and avoided impact. The other ship wasn't so lucky. Under constant fire from *Sabrina's* lasers, they never saw the second mine.

"Score!" Cargo shouted.

The resulting explosion was too small to see at the ten thousand kilometer distance, but scan showed a direct impact. With its forward shields maxed out, the pirate ship didn't appear to take damage, but the shaped charge managed to shed enough of their velocity. They were out of the race.

Scan updated, showing the first pirate ship's maneuvers to avoid its mine had placed it over a hundred thousand kilometers further away, now far to port. It was out of the running, too.

"Great work Cargo," Sera said to her first mate with heartfelt gratitude. She thanked everyone over the Link for their calm, steady response to the trouble. Before she could finish, Cargo interrupted her.

"Captain, I wouldn't get too excited yet, we've got an RM inbound."

"Shit!" Sera swore over the open comm. "Belay that happiness, missile on our tail."

Sabrina was five minutes from the jump point. The relativistic missile was four minutes from intercept.

Sera ran the math and couldn't see any way they could get to the point before the RM hit them. Even killing aft shielding and diverting more power to the engines wouldn't give them enough extra thrust to pull it off. She looked to her pilot.

"Two options, Cheeks; we twitch and jump on whatever vector we end up on, or we dump to FTL now and hope there's no dark matter between us and the point."

Cheeky bit her lip as she pulled charts of the local dark layer onto the main holo.

Dark matter occupied its own sub-layer of space-time, which is where ships transitioned when they made FTL jumps. However, dark matter orbited its host star erratically and charts never displayed it with perfect accuracy. Jump points were positions with outsystem vectors that were always clear of dark matter. Ships could enter FTL without fear of colliding with a solid mass.

Cheeky zoomed the holo in on their course and pointed to a rather large clump of dark matter. "Can't do the jump on our current vector, there's a big lump of the black stuff in our path. Let me see if there is a clear path outsystem parallel to our vector."

Though it took Cheeky less than thirty seconds to find a course they could twitch to, it seemed far longer with the main holo showing the RM closing on them. Sera was tempted to try a mine again but the nav computer showed that the RM could compensate even if it had to avoid the mine. The damn things were just too fast and maneuverable. Sera was ordering Thompson and Flaherty to load another proximity mine anyway when Cheeky let loose a triumphant cry.

"I've got it! There's a clear path to port, if these charts are right, that'll take us out of here. DM does orbit through, but it should be clear right now."

Moments rolled by as Cheeky double checked her work and then laid in the burn time and vector that would give them a spare twenty thousand kilometers from the RM. She called out the count as everyone held their breath.

"On five, four, three, two, one, burn for three, two, one, kill!" The eight seconds stretched into a lifetime and then the two more seconds dragged on while scan updated. The RM had overshot and was compensating to approach their position. It had dropped down to 0.8 *c* as it maneuvered, but was quickly up to 0.9 *c* back on a direct course for *Sabrina*.

"It's on us again, Cheeky. How long to jump?"

Cheeky spared a hand to wave behind her at her captain as she concentrated on her console and the numbers rolling across it. She made a few final alterations and then rechecked them.

"Kay! FTL transition in T minus fifteen."

She began counting down the seconds to the transition as Sera brought the RM's time to impact up on the main holo. It was only a half a second behind Cheeky's count. Through those long seconds, Sera's mind raced over the thousand things that could go wrong, praying that they would make the jump in time.

Then, with the customary gut twisting wrench, they made the transition and were in the lightless void of the dark layer.

TANIS RICHARDS

STELLAR DATE: 07.01.8927 (Adjusted Gregorian)
LOCATION: *Sabrina*, Interstellar Dark Layer
REGION: Galactic South of Trio Prime, Silstrand Alliance Space

Sera took a deep breath as Cheeky leaned over the side of her chair and threw up. Without a word, Cargo rose and walked out to the corridor. He returned with cleaning supplies from the small head just outside the bridge.

Sera rose from her chair, shaking far more than expected. She moved to Cheeky's console and rested a hand on the pilot's shoulder. Cheeky was quaking, and Sera helped her stand, wrapping her in a tight embrace. She choked back tears of relief and Sera did her best not to join in.

"Girl, that was the best flying I've *ever* seen!" Sera gave her pilot a squeeze.

Cheeky offered a weak smile. "Thanks, Captain, I'd appreciate it if you guys didn't tell anyone about this little after effect, though." She looked down at the spattered deck-plate.

Cargo bent down to clean up the mess. "What after effect?"

Cheeky reached down and smacked his head. "I mean it…I can't have anyone thinking I'm less than ladylike."

Sera laughed, wondering who might think that Cheeky was ladylike to begin with.

The distraction had calmed Cheeky and she sat back down at her console, reviewing the ship's readouts.

"Everything looks bang on, Captain," she turned and said after a minute's examination. "Mind if I hit my cabin for a bit and clean up?"

"Whatever you need to do, Cheeks. Cargo and I can hold the ship together while you're gone."

<*I resent that,*> Sabrina huffed.

<*Sorry, love, I didn't mean you,*> Sera stroked a console affectionately.

Cheeky left the bridge with a slight wobble in her step as she navigated around the consoles in her heels. Sera sat back in her chair and gave the crew the good news over the ship-wide net.

<*Thanks to everyone's hard work, we just outran a couple of pirate gunships that were looking to turn us into a bright, fluffy cloud. I'm sure you all noticed that you're still alive,*> Sera added a smile to her comment.

<*I did notice a distinct not-dead feeling,*> Thompson replied dryly.

<*Yay for our side!*> Nance's hazsuited avatar did a jump and a kick in everyone's mind.

<*Our SC batteries are totally drained,*> Sabrina interjected. <*Going to keep the auxiliary plant running, we'll have to watch the heat, though.*>

<*You do that, Sabrina. Me, I'm going to have to re-hydrate—I must have pissed a gallon when I saw that RM right on our tail.*> Thompson somehow managed to convey both thirst and the urge to urinate in his message.

<*What on earth did they want anyway?*> Nance asked. <*What could we have worth using an RM on us? Those things must cost as much as a small mining platform.*>

<*I have a suspicion,*> Sera said. <*Give me ten minutes to square some things away, then Thompson and Nance, meet me in the fore port cargo hold.*>

<*Will do,*> Thompson said while Nance's avatar managed a stiff nod.

Sera laid their interstellar course over her vision as she brought up the nav computer on her console's holo.

<*How far off will we be when we exit FTL?*> she asked her AI as she worked through the calculations herself. Helen would have the answer before she was half done, but Sera liked to test herself. People, who let their AI think for them didn't take long to degenerate into little more than automatons.

<*We entered the dark layer not too far from our original jump point, but our vector was slightly skewed by the twitch. Not to mention we made the transition at over twice the originally plotted speed,*> Helen said, giving Sera a bit more time to finish the math on her own.

<*We must have shaved almost five days off the trip,*> Sera said idly as she flipped through a matrix of figures.

<*Five days, three hours and twenty-one minutes.*>

<*You just can't help it, can you?*>

Helen sighed. <*No, I can't. It's actually a bit annoying. You take for granted how easily you can think in abstracts.*>

<*I suppose I do,*> Sera admitted. <*Well, based on this, it's a good thing we shortened the trip by a few days; we're going to spend every one of those saved days braking from this ungodly speed if we don't want to use up the rest of our antimatter.*>

<*It will take three days of braking and then a final day to arrive at the drop point,*> Helen supplied.

Cheeky returned to the bridge several minutes later, for once wearing pants and a shirt. Sera didn't comment on it, and the pilot began working out the details of when they needed to drop out of the dark layer and back into normal space.

"Have I mentioned that I hate special relativity math?" she asked. "An RM up our ass I can forgive, making me adjust calculations for all this time dilation is something else."

Sera smiled. "You have fun; I'm going to see what's in that crate we got from Kade's boys at the eleventh hour."

"If it's something nasty, kick it for me," Cheeky said.

Thompson and Nance were already in the cargo bay when Sera arrived. The burly super was sliding a gravity lift under the crate, while Nance, wearing her hazsuit with the hood sealed tight, stood nearby.

"How are you doing?" Sera asked.

"Mm, good," Nance replied.

Sera saw that the lenses of her bio's mask were fogged up and the woman's limbs had a slight tremble.

"Nance, honey, take off the hood; let me see you."

<*Sure, why not try now,*> Helen chuckled.

Sera had never seen Nance out of her hazsuit, and had only seen her face a few times, when Nance had her suit's hood only half-off. There was a pool on the ship with a big pot for whoever finally got her to reveal her entire head.

Without speaking, the bio reached behind her head and unsealed the hood. Sera held her breath as Nance slowly slid it off her head.

"You have hair!" Sera exclaimed. "It's beautiful!"

Nance stepped back as Sera reached out to touch the dark brown locks, a frown creasing her brow.

"Of course I have hair; it's a normal thing to grow on a person's head."

"Damn it!" Thompson swore. "I can't believe you picked now to try that—and it worked!"

"You can't believe I won," Sera said with a grin. She turned back to Nance and reached for the bio's hand. "Seriously, though, are you OK? You seemed fine on the Link."

"I think you missed my sarcastic tone," Nance replied. "I was scared shitless."

"I guess the suit masks it," Sera replied.

Thompson got the lift under the mysterious crate and it rose into the air. He leaned against it and eyed Nance.

"That *is* a pretty amazing amount of hair."

"Says the blonde ape," Sera smiled.

"Hey, nine thousand years ago, this amount of body hair was perfectly normal."

"Yeah, and nine thousand years ago, people had just upgraded to pooping in public troughs," Nance grimaced.

"Don't try to distract me, Nance," Sera said. "I had never even imagined that you had hair. How do you keep it so soft while it's plastered to your head all day? Doesn't it get sweaty?"

Nance made a disgusted sound. "I don't sweat. I had all those oozing glands removed years ago."

"I enjoy a good sweat," Thompson said, with thinly veiled innuendo.

Sera sniffed in his direction. "That's no secret."

Thompson ignored her. "Don't you get hot, Nance?"

"No, my suit has a cooling system."

"I'd think you'd still get itchy," Thompson frowned. "All that flaking skin with no sweat to lubricate it."

Nance shivered convulsively. "Ewww! I have a controlled shedding, which my nano activates when I'm in the shower. I don't have flaking skin."

Sera peered at her bio's face, hands held back so Nance wouldn't flinch away. "You do have really smooth-looking skin. And it looks so clean..."

"You'd be amazed what lives and accumulates in your pores. Thank god I don't have those anymore," Nance looked at the super. "Look at those crevices on your face. And Cheeky wonders why my suit has tinted lenses."

Thompson seemed to decide that there was no way this conversation would favor him, so got back to the situation at hand. "So, what do you think is in here that they wanted so bad, Captain? I'm betting it's no dog."

"If it is, it's getting its shots," Nance said. "No way I'm letting some dirty mutt run around the ship and contaminate my environmental tanks."

Nance pulled a holo display into the air over the crate. Initial scan showed that some living creature was inside, but its vital signs were masked by cryostasis.

"I'm not getting a reading on anything hazardous," she said and looked over Sabrina's scan on the emissions and power levels in the crate. "No heavy metals, probably running on an SC Battery."

"Let's take it into the sealed chamber. I don't like little tiny surprises any more than you do, Nance."

It never hurt to pop a container that seemed harmless into the biohazard chamber and check it out by remote. Their lives were dangerous enough without extra unknowns adding risk. Not many ships had a hermetically sealed chamber, but from time to time Sera found it necessary to determine the exact level of danger a cargo presented for herself and her ship. If it was more trouble than she'd been told, extra charges were applied to the transport.

Once the container was in the chamber, they stood back and watched as Sabrina used robotic arms to crack the seal and lift off the lid. Inside was the cryostasis pod Nance had detected.

"Either it's a kid, or an adult that's going to have some serious cramps," Thompson observed.

"You don't cramp in stasis," Sera said.

"Depends on how good the system is and how long it took the stasis to kick in," Thompson replied. "Once I had to hop in an evac pod on a gas platform, it took the stasis over an hour to fully set in. That's not an experience I'd wish on my worst enemy."

"Owww," Nance said, casting an appreciative look at the super.

"What do the readouts look like, Sabrina?" Sera asked.

<All outward controls show nominal,> the ship's AI responded. *<I'm making a filtered connection to its controls for a direct reading.>*

A robotic arm extended and fitted a physical data connector into the cryo pod. Sabrina had done this before and knew to exercise extreme caution. All the systems within the sealed chamber were isolated from the rest of the ship. Sabrina felt the same way about foreign computers as Nance did about germs.

<The system looks normal, and it is a person in there; a woman of indeterminate age,> Sabrina announced moments later. *<I can't say if she's totally safe without a blood sample, but if you wear hazsuits in the med lab you should be OK.>*

"Nance, it's finally a party you're already dressed for," Thompson said with a smile.

Sera caught a glint in his eye when he said it.

<Is Thompson flirting with Nance?> Sera asked Helen.

<Beats me, if he is he sucks at it.>

Sera gave her head a slight shake and addressed Thompson. "Take it into the med lab, Thompson. Nance and I will pop it open and see what we see."

Nance looked as though she was being asked to juggle flaming knives. She pinned her hair up and pulled her suit's hood back on. *<Let's get it over with.>*

Sabrina re-sealed the crate and Thompson entered the chamber and keyed the grav lift to float the it down the hall and into the med lab.

Ten minutes later, the stasis pod sat on the floor of the med lab with Sera and Nance standing to either side. Thompson and Cargo were both outside peering through one of the observation windows.

<You want to pop it open?> Sera asked.

<Hey, this was your idea. I give you first crack at whatever bio weapon is waiting in that person's bloodstream.>

<You really are a bit of a pessimist, you know that?> Sera smiled through the clear faceplate of her hazsuit.

<I'm a realist.>

<You're also the one-zillionth pessimist to say you're a realist. Your prize is an all-expense paid trip to the Disney World. You'll get to spend a full month with an entire planet full of people modded into animals and fairies,> Sera chuckled while Nance made a soft gagging noise.

<Just pop it open already so I can declare this person healthy, or dead, and get back to that blown regulator I'm dealing with.>

Sera sighed and bent to look the console over. The controls were fairly standard and Sera entered the sequence to open the pod. Immediately, the pod's interface flashed a warning and prompted for additional access codes. She attempted to bypass it with some of her usual tricks, but the pod locked down entirely.

<Giving you some trouble?> Nance asked as she leaned against the examination table.

<Nothing I can't handle, I'll have it open in a minute.>

Shielding her actions with her body, Sera pressed the tip of her finger tight against the hazsuit's glove and spoke to Helen. *<Send some of the little guys through the suit and into this pod to crack its security. Just make sure they patch up whatever holes they make.>*

<Want me to have them cover their tracks and reprogram the pod with something you could crack by hand in a minute?>

<Yeah, we need to keep up appearances.>

<OK, Fina, the nano are on their way in.>

Sera ignored Helen's mothering tone and use of her childhood nickname. She acted as though she was working on the pod's interface while the nano completed their task and the interface altered to a simple security setup, set to the final stage of a basic hack. Sera manually entered the final sequence. The outer cover hissed pod open, and she left her index finger on the edge of the console until Helen informed her that all the nano were back in her body.

<Easy as pie,> Sera said to Nance as she looked up at the bio.

<Mustn't have been that hard,> Cargo said with a grin from the other side of the observation window.

The pod flashed a short countdown as it pulled its occupant out of cryostasis, then the inner shell split open. Sera stood and peered in as Nance pulled one of the scan arms over from the examination table, her other hand double-checking the seal of her hazsuit's hood.

The occupant of the container was a woman. She had the same ageless look that most people acquired after their first rejuvenation treatment. She was also naked; whoever had placed her in stasis hadn't bothered to put her in a stasis suit, or even put a salve on her skin to deal with the quick freeze.

<She's going to have a nasty rash when she wakes up,> Sera observed.

Nance looked at the med scanner's readout as it hovered over the pod. *<Not any time soon, though. She's heavily drugged. Pod pulled her out of stasis smoothly, but she's going to sleep for a few more hours, even with a mild flush.>*

<Works for me; gives us a chance to check her out before the yelling and screaming starts,> Sera replied.

<If you don't mind, I'll skip that part,> Nance grimaced.

<I'll stay with her. I imagine you can do any checks remotely.>

Nance's avatar smiled at Sera. *<Happily.>*

They lifted the woman out of the pod and Thompson let a whistle loose as they set her naked form on the table, earning a cold look from Sera. Cargo grinned but was smart enough not to add more.

Nance pulled a blanket over the woman, then lifted her head, smoothed her hair, and placed a low pillow underneath. The action was very gentle for someone who eschewed tactile contact. Sera peered at the bio, but the opaque lenses of her hood hid any expression that may have been behind them.

<*This is odd,*> Nance said as she looked over the data from the medical scanner.

<*What?*> Sera asked.

<*See these slight discolorations all over her skin?*>

<*That's discoloration? I thought maybe it was the lighting in here,*> Sera peered closer and dialed her vision in to a higher level of magnification. <*Bruises, I can see the pattern from the broken vessels.*>

<*Scanner shows she got them within two hours of going into stasis.*>

<*That can't be right, those bruises are almost healed, and they were some serious shiners. Things like that don't heal during stasis, at least not in a pod like this.*>

Nance's expressionless face looked up at Sera. <*I'd agree with you except for what we're looking at.*>

<*Curiouser and curiouser.*>

Sera looked down at the woman. She appeared to be normal. Her body showed the tall frame of a person raised in lower gravity, but her muscle tone indicated time spent in full gravity, as well. The readout put her at one hundred and eighty-four centimeters; just shy of ninety-seven kilograms, though probably well under seventy without her internal tech—which was considerable.

Her features were classic Scandinavian, from the slight slope of her brow and high cheekbones to the perfectly straight, blonde hair. Of course, none of that meant she had a drop of Scandinavian blood. It could just indicate a good rebuild.

<*She certainly isn't hard to look at,*> Thompson commented.

Sera looked at the two men. <*Don't you two have something else to do?*>

They looked at one another and shrugged.

<*I guess I could use a meal,*> Cargo said, and the pair sauntered off.

<*Her skin may be all patched up, but she's got a fractured skull, three broken ribs, a bit of internal bleeding that looks to have stopped up, a broken ankle, and her left leg is broken in three places.*>

<*Someone wasn't too gentle with her,*> Sera said with a shake of her head.

<*That's the understatement of the year. I'm going to send some of the med nano in to start patching her up,*> Nance said as she pulled the IV line down from the array of devices above the examination table. It would be primed with the nano machines that would begin knitting the woman's bones back together.

The women turned to the med system's status display, watching the nano filtering through her body, moving toward the injuries.

<*Looking good,*> Sera commented.

<*Seems to b…what the? What!*> Nance exclaimed.

They both stared as the med unit lost contact with the nano in the woman's body and then reported that they had all been destroyed.

<*That can't be good,*> Sera shook her head. Med nano was hard to kill; the mystery surrounding this woman was growing.

Nance pulled up the detailed logs on the med nano's ill-fated venture and looked them over. <*They were destroyed…by her nano,*> Nance closed the log and then initiated a more detailed scan. <*Doesn't make sense, our med nano broadcasts the standard Red Cross signal. A person's nano should welcome them, not kill them.*>

<*I don't think her nano needs the help,*> Sera said, and pulled a high-res holo image of the woman over her body. <*It looks like it's doing the healing on its own.*>

Nance scowled at the images, then took a blood sample with a biohazard extractor.

<*I'm going to take this down to my lab; I've got better containment down there. Let me know if anything changes.*>

<*Good luck,*> Sera said as Nance stepped into the scrubber and then out into the corridor where she walked briskly toward the nearest ladder.

<*Does that look at all familiar, Helen?*> Sera asked her personal AI.

<*It looks as good, maybe better, than our nano. I don't know if your bots could repair bones that fast.*>

<*I was thinking that, as well. I wonder if we could send an investigatory probe in.*>

<*It's worth a shot. We could send it with the med signal, as well.*>

<*No point, it would just get squished like the others. Send it with the standard OFC signal. We'll see if her comp is running.*>

Sera pressed her index finger against the woman's arm and several of her nano passed through the hazsuit and into the flesh under it.

<*We've got communication,*> Helen said in an agitated tone as she patched the message through.

<*This is Angela. Please cease inserting your foreign nano into Tanis's body. I have her well in hand and will wake her in one day, five hours, three minutes and seventeen seconds. Thank you for the IV supply. No other assistance is needed.*> The signal cut out as Helen indicated their nano had been eliminated as well.

<*Snippy thing, isn't she?*>

<*You have no idea. That was the human version. The one she sent me was far less companionable. It includes things like silicate hussy and other such terms.*>

Sera laughed out loud. <*Sometimes I wonder why you AI grow personalities; they seem to cause you more trouble than they could be worth.*>

<*You have no idea the extent to which that debate rages,*> Helen said dryly.

* * * * *

"So how's our visitor?" Thompson asked as Sera stepped into the galley. Everyone except for Nance was around the table tucking into a dinner of soup and sandwiches.

"Helen and I managed to get a hold of her AI. It told us quite simply that our assistance isn't welcome and it will wake her tomorrow."

"Is she okay?" Cheeky asked.

"Yes and no," Sera replied equably as she poured herself a cup of coffee and grabbed a sandwich.

"That is the opposite of clarifying," Thompson grunted.

"Her body has been put through the wringer. If she were stranded on some backwater, with no nano, she'd be in a hospital for months. If she were relying on our med nano, she'd be taking it easy for a week. With her personal nano, she'll be up and about tomorrow."

"Her personal nano is that good?" Cheeky asked.

Thompson and Flaherty didn't say a word as they chewed.

"Yeah, she's got some seriously impressive stuff, and a prickly AI running the show. It nuked our med nano and even my bots after it delivered its message of displeasure."

"Can't say I blame it," Thompson said. "I'd hope my AI would have my best interests in mind if I was beat up and somewhere strange."

"You don't have an AI…or even I," Cheeky said with a grin.

"Har, har, that's original," Thompson replied.

Flaherty gave an uncharacteristic snort of laughter, which earned him a sour look from Thompson.

"What does her DNA say?" Cheeky asked.

"Nance took blood samples; she should be up shortly with the results. Hopefully it may shed some light on the identity of our…stowaway?"

"I don't know how accurate that is. We stowed her ourselves," Thompson offered.

"I deem her our 'reluctant hitchhiker'," Cheeky said around a mouthful of her sandwich.

"Actually, her name is Tanis," Sera offered. "Her AI, Angela, gave us that much info before telling us to go screw."

"Her DNA said about the same thing," Nance stepped into the galley and slipped her hood up, exposing her face. "I couldn't find DNA anywhere similar to it in any of our records. It's not as though we have an extensive library, but we do have a sample from nearly every inhabited world."

"What, the rest of us don't get to see your hair?" Cargo asked.

Nance cocked her head at Sera, who lifted her hands defensively. "I've only been here for a few minutes. I didn't blab."

"What?" Thompson said. "You've got nice hair."

"Come on…" Cheeky said with a winning smile, "I want to see, too. How could you show Thompson your hair and not me?"

Nance sighed. "Okay fine, only because you'll bug me for days if I don't." She reached up behind her head and slipped open the seal on the hood, pulling it off in a smooth motion and placing it on the table beside her.

"Wow!" Cheeky said. "It's so fluffy!"

"Poufy would be the word," Nance replied.

"And you have really nice almond eyes," The pilot smiled. "I command you to show them more often."

Nance laughed. "I'll reset my lenses to be transparent when you are around."

"So, nothing on the DNA at all?" Flaherty asked, appearing to be uninterested in the discussion of hair and eyes.

"Well, she actually *is* of Scandinavian descent, pretty pure blood, too. If I didn't know better, I'd say she was actually from Earth…'cept no one's from Earth," Nance said as she pulled a bar from her personal food cupboard.

"Some people are still from Earth," Cheeky offered.

<*There are no Scandinavians on Earth anymore,*> Sabrina said.

"Aren't you Scandinavian?" Sera asked Nance.

"Not really. One of my ancestors settled on New Sweden and the names infiltrated the family. I think my family is actually from the Madrid moon in Procyon."

"OK," Thompson said. "Time to lay odds on where she came from. I have a hundred Sil creds that say she's actually from Sol. Any takers?"

REVELATIONS

STELLAR DATE: 07.02.8927 (Adjusted Years)
LOCATION: *Sabrina*, Interstellar Dark Layer
REGION: Galactic South of Trio Prime, Silstrand Alliance Space

Sera sat on a chair in the med lab, waiting for their 'reluctant hitchhiker,' as Cheeky still called her, to wake.

At exactly the time prescribed by her AI, the woman began to stir, and then her movements became almost violent—as though she was having a nightmare. After almost a minute of thrashing, her body remembered what it was like to function with a conscious mind in control; her movements slowed and finally her eyelids fluttered open.

Sera waited for Tanis to acclimate to her surroundings. The lights in the med cabin were dim—she knew from experience how painful bright lights could be after coming out of a few days of unconsciousness.

She watched the woman's eyes struggle to focus, and then adjust to the dim light. A flicker of panic raced across her features when she tried to raise an arm, only to find it restrained. Almost as though by reflex, she closed her eyes and her breathing calmed. She retained that posture for several moments and then, in slow stages, she opened her eyes again; taking a second, more careful stock of her surroundings. Sera decided this was as good a time as any to make her introduction.

"Welcome aboard *Sabrina*, Tanis. I'm Captain Sera."

The woman's eyes flicked over to Sera. She opened her mouth to say something, but all that came out was a dry rasp.

"Ah, sorry about that," Sera's smile was friendly as she provided a bottle of water with a straw. The woman sucked on it eagerly and then pulled her mouth away to signal she was done.

"Thank you," she whispered as Sera set the bottle down.

"No problem," Sera smiled again. "I've done a few imitations of a dead person myself; it's thirsty work."

"Am I a prisoner?" the woman asked as she looked down at her wrists strapped to the table.

"Not at all." Sera leaned over and undid the fastener on the wrist closest to her, allowing to Tanis free her other arm. "It's just hard to predict a person's state of mind when waking up unexpectedly in a strange place."

The woman nodded as she rubbed her wrists, her expression guarded. "Where is 'here', exactly?"

"Here is home," Sera said as she waved an arm about her in an expansive gesture. "This is my fair *Sabrina*, a starfreighter. We're currently in FTL transit outside of the Trio System."

A look of incomprehension followed by shock passed over the woman's face. "In...FTL?" she said with an edge of panic to her voice. Her eyes darted around the room as though she was looking for some indication that the ship was moving faster than light.

"Yup, on our way to Edasich, with a few stops along the way."

"E-Edasich…as in Iota Draconis?" the woman stammered. "How long will it take to get there?"

"Depends on how big a rush we're in. A few months depending on exactly where the trade takes us."

The blood all but drained out of the Tanis's face. It was the strangest reaction Sera had ever seen someone have to being told they were in FTL. She was wondering how stable the woman was after all.

"Let's start with the basics, though. As I mentioned before, I'm Captain Sera. Your AI introduced you as Tanis."

The woman frowned. "She told me someone tried to infiltrate my body with nano. Logs show it was med and then comm; sorry about her reaction, she's very protective. My full name's Tanis Richards."

"Two names? That's somewhat uncommon in this neighborhood. What star system still does that? Our med NSAI didn't recognize your DNA as coming from anywhere particular."

"I'm from Earth," Tanis said so matter-of-factly that Sera let out a chuckle before covering her mouth.

"Aren't we all?" Sera said and took a deep breath to stem her laughter. What was surprising was that Tanis appeared somewhat put out by her amusement. "It's okay." Sera smiled once more. "You don't have to tell right away. I'm betting that you didn't beat yourself up and hop in a stasis pod for kicks. I assure you that we mean you no harm, though we are curious. What happened to you anyway?"

Tanis didn't respond immediately and Sera suspected this woman would be a tough nut to crack.

* * * * *

They were getting closer. No matter how hard she ran they gained steadily on her; the sound of their boots hitting the deck echoed through the hall. Tanis was terrified. Nothing was as she expected it to be; the lights were wrong. Words were strange and no one made any sense. It was a horrible nightmare and she yearned to wake up.

As if her desire alone were enough, she found the nightmare slowly fading and wakefulness returning. There was light pressing against her eyelids and she knew it would be uncomfortably bright when she opened them. Steeling herself for it, Tanis opened her eyes and tried to focus. The light wasn't as bad as she expected, but she couldn't manage to see properly. Everything was grey and her limbs all seemed to be throbbing.

<*Good morning, sleepy head,*> Angela greeted her.

<*Where am I, Angela?*>

<*As best I can tell, we are on a ship of some sort. I haven't gotten much information, but I do know that we're in transit. You were near death when they put you in that stasis pod,*> Angela sounded concerned.

<*I remember that…I remember feeling almost dead. The nice men with the big meaty fists got a bit carried away, didn't they?*>

<You're lucky I wasn't damaged. The pod didn't do true stasis…it was…. Anyway, while you were in there, I reconfigured your spare nano for med duty and pulled your body back from the brink.>

<I owe you my life, dear, again>

<I wasn't entirely selfless. If you die, I stand a pretty good chance of joining you. That's a journey I'm not ready for yet.>

<Is the baby safe? Did its stasis get disrupted?> Tanis felt worry crash into her at the thought of the unborn child within her, carefully held in stasis in her womb.

<She is well, perfectly safe,> Angela replied. *<She's just a few cells, still, not a lot can go wrong with her yet.>*

Tanis relaxed and tried to push that worry from her mind. Plenty of time to think it over later.

<Are we safe here? Are these the same people that were beating me before?>

<No, we're on a different ship. No one has talked out loud in your presence, and I didn't open your eyes in case someone saw. They have a good nano suppression field and their Link is weird. I haven't tried to force access—not while you were out. I did hear the sounds of two women at first. Right now, there is just one, to your left somewhere. I think she's wearing leather, it squeaks whenever she moves.>

<I guess that rules out some sort of official or doctor,> Tanis replied.

<At least not the sort of doctor you'd want to see.>

Letting out the slightest of sighs she cracked her eyes open, but even the dim light of the room was more than she was prepared for. Instinctively she tried to raise her hand to shield her eyes. It didn't move. She was surprised to find her wrists restrained—though she supposed it was to be expected.

Unbidden, a thought of Joe flashed into her mind; where was he and would she ever see him again. What of their child? Would she raise her alone?

Tanis took a deep breath, forcing herself to relax. Opening her eyes again, she looked around and identified her surroundings as a medical lab of some sort. A voice spoke, and while the words were soft, her ears throbbed from the sound.

"Welcome aboard the *Sabrina*. I'm Captain Sera," the woman's voice said

Tanis's eyes darted to her left where the woman sat. Even as she smiled, the woman's face looked hard, and her eyes appeared to have some great weight behind them, though her warm expression seemed genuine enough. Jet-black hair glinted in the light and framed a pale face with high cheekbones—definitely the complexion of a spacer.

Tanis could feel the faint vibrations of a reactor nearby and determined that either this ship had its med lab in a strange place or it wasn't that large. Maybe it was a small shuttle or transport heading to this woman's main ship. She opened her mouth to reply, but only a dry rasp came out.

The woman made an apology, and offered her a drink. Tanis thanked her; then asked if she was a prisoner. The woman smiled again and, though she seemed somewhat wary, the smile did reach her eyes.

"Not at all," came the reply. Tanis noted how the woman only unfastened the wrist closest to her—she didn't reach over Tanis's body to release the other. Usually, only people familiar with violence showed that sort of caution. The woman explained that the restraints were just a precaution against an unfavorable reaction to waking in strange surroundings.

It was a plausible explanation.

Tanis took the opportunity to ask where she was. The woman confirmed her suspicion that they were indeed on a ship, though it was a freighter. However, three letters the captain uttered caught in her mind: FTL. Tanis was familiar with the term. It meant Faster-Than-Light, though neither she, nor anyone else for that matter, had ever been on a ship that exceeded the speed of light.

She glanced around the med lab, unable to reconcile the fact that an aging freighter could achieve such speeds. Through all her furiously racing thoughts, three words escaped her lips.

"We're in FTL?"

The captain responded that they were headed for Edasich. Tanis quickly dredged the reference up in her mind. Edasich was a star system just over a hundred light-years from Earth. If they were traveling at the speed of light, or even faster, it could still take decades to get there. If it was that star. She asked after it by another name, Iota Draconis, and the captain confirmed it was the same star.

Tanis re-examined what the captain had said; they would be making some stops along the way. Perhaps she could manage to get off the *Sabrina* at some point and return to the *Intrepid*. Though she was dying to know how long such a trip would take. The number she was given was unbelievable, just a few months! This woman spoke of a trip of a hundred light-years as though it were a simple jaunt across the Sol System!

Tanis could feel alarm setting in and forced herself to breathe deeply. She didn't want this woman to think she was unstable and sedate her again. Even as she steadied herself, a part of her mind was screaming. This was wrong, it was all terribly wrong. Humanity didn't have FTL capability. No human had ever come within twenty light years of Edasich. She was trapped in a nightmare, one where the *Intrepid* could be on the other side of the galaxy for all she knew; one where she may never be able to get home to Joe and her ship.

<Relax dear; I'm having a not dissimilar reaction. I'm sure it will all make sense soon.>

<It better, because if I'm not insane already I may try it out.>

The woman noticed her discomfort and started over by re-introducing herself as Captain Sera and asking her name. Her mind latched onto the question. This was within the realm of her understanding, and she answered calmly that it was Tanis Richards, biting back the desire to add her rank.

"Two names? That's uncommon in this neighborhood, what star system still does that? Our med system didn't recognize your DNA as coming from anywhere particular." The captain asked.

What an odd question, why wouldn't they be able to determine her origin from her DNA. Though if they used spectrographic analysis on the isotopes in her body, that would likely confuse them, given her time on Victoria. Tanis replied that she was from Earth—a small lie—and Captain Sera seemed to suddenly stifle a laugh. This was all becoming too much.

<Am I on some sort of hallucinogenic?> she asked Angela.

<If you are, it's affecting me, too. Something is not right with this.>

"Aren't we all," the captain said with a hint of sarcasm.

<Well yeah...> Tanis thought. *<I'm really starting to dislike this Captain Sera.>*

<I think she's trying to soften the blow…whatever that blow is.>

<I hate pussyfooting around things,> Tanis sighed.

<Really? I hadn't realized that about you.>

"It's okay," the captain said and smiled; Tanis couldn't help but believe it was genuine, even though the woman was a bundle of contradictions. "You don't have to tell right away. I'm betting that you didn't beat yourself up and hop in a pod for kicks. I assure you that we mean you no harm, though we are curious. What happened to you anyway?"

Tanis thought about it. Honestly, she wasn't entirely certain what *had* happened to her. Moreover, she wasn't entirely certain that she wanted to relate the story just yet. The captain seemed to sense her indecision and apologized.

"I'm sorry, I forget how disorienting all this can be. There are some clothes on the stand beside you. Once you get dressed, I'll show you to your cabin where you can freshen up, before joining us in the galley for the second-shift meal."

Tanis looked over to the clothing on her right. Reaching out she put a hand on it. It was soft cotton; natural, too, by the feel of it. A captain wearing animal skins and now natural cotton. Perhaps she was on some colony world where such materials were more common than synthetics.

<Could this be some sort of interrogation technique?> she asked Angela.

<If it is, it's the most unique I've ever been exposed to.>

Sera seemed to take her reaction as disdain for cotton. "I hope they're alright. Everything I own is custom fitted to me. Those are Nance's. She doesn't really wear clothes anyway, so she won't miss them. I'll be right outside the door."

The captain stepped outside the med facility and Tanis could see her back as she waited in front of a window. She sat up, clutching the sheet as she pulled the clothes to her lap and examined them. They sure felt like cotton. If they weren't, it was the best synthetic she had ever seen. Looking under the sheet, she blushed to find herself totally naked. Well, better naked and alive than the alternative.

Tanis dressed quickly in what turned out to be simple shoes, cotton leggings and a loose, sleeveless shirt. Running a hand through her hair, she wondered if this ship of contradictions would have water showers or the good ol' sandblasting a freighter ought to have.

The captain flashed another one of those hard, yet genuine smiles as Tanis stepped out of the med facility. "Amazing how getting into at least a scrap of clothing can make you feel so much more human, isn't it?"

Tanis nodded in response and Sera turned, leading her down a long, well-lit corridor. She couldn't help but smile to herself at the incongruity of Sera's statement. The captain certainly seemed to believe in a lot more than just a scrap of clothing, what with her skin-tight outfit covering every inch of her body from the neck down.

They stopped at a ladder and the captain climbed up to the next level.

<OK...if we are being pranked, then they really suck at this,> Tanis laughed in her mind. *<Ladders on a ship with FTL?>*

The captain looked down and noticed her disbelieving expression.

"*Sabrina* does have lifts, but I find that on long trips you need all the extra exercise you can get. I put the ladders in after I bought her. Also much better than lifts if the AG fields ever have trouble." She turned and led Tanis down another corridor with a series of doors on the left.

There she went again, referring to a trip that was probably only a few months as 'long'.' While Tanis tried to wrap her mind around FTL again, she realized the captain had mentioned AG fields. Massive ships like the *Intrepid* could generate artificial gravity, but how could a small freighter—where the engines couldn't be more than fifty meters from the med lab—have AG? Sera *must* be playing with them now. FTL and AG in one day was far too much to swallow.

"Here we are," Captain Sera said. "We use this cabin for passengers we pick up from time to time. Consider it yours for the trip."

Tanis peered in; the surprises just kept on coming. How did a small freighter have cabins of this size? It was at least four meters across and had a bed, dresser, and desk. There appeared to be a closet, and it even had its own toilet and shower.

The captain looked pleased. "*Sabrina* used to be a pleasure yacht. I know I could probably shrink these cabins down, but it sure helps in hiring crew when you show them their own private bathroom."

"It's a water shower?" Tanis asked, hoping it was, because she wanted one, yet wishing it wasn't, so that something made sense.

"Of course, do we look like savages?" The captain laughed. "Second-shift meal is in about thirty minutes in the galley," she gestured aft, down the corridor. "We'll be expecting you."

With that, the captain slid the door shut and left Tanis to herself. She stood for several moments taking everything in; trying to make sense of what she was seeing. It occurred to her that this could be some sort of holo suite, or an elaborate ruse to fool her. But fool her for what reason? Sure, the *Intrepid* was very valuable, but no one trying to gain her trust would use such ridiculous methods.

<They wouldn't, would they?>

<I'm still stuck on the first batch of impossibilities. I know you flesh and blood types like to be clean—why don't you take a shower while I try to keep my cortex from fracturing.>

All was not lost; Angela still had her wry sense of humor.

Glancing over at the bulkhead, Tanis noticed a porthole. A porthole in FTL? Was that safe? She couldn't resist the urge to see what was out there. Peering through the window, she saw only blackness. There were no stars, not even streaks or smears of light as the ship blasted past photons in space. Tanis had always been certain that some light would be visible in FTL. Wouldn't the ship be intercepting light that was already there? Light toward the bow of the ship should surely be visible? The porthole showed none of this.

She caught herself pondering all the types of FTL she had heard postulated or seen in holos. Most utilized a space folding, or space compression/stretching technique to achieve a circumvention of relativity's limits. The amount of energy to achieve either of those effects was proven to be completely impractical. Earnest had created stable wormholes in previous research, but creating one over interstellar distances, stable enough to safely transfer matter, turned out to take as much energy as a star emitted over a billion years.

This had to be a farce. If Earnest couldn't determine how to achieve FTL, then there was no way that this yacht turned dingy freighter could exceed *c*. Yet, if they were traveling at the speeds she thought, it must be much faster than light speed—hundreds of times faster. It was mind-boggling. How did the ship even hold together?

Tanis suddenly felt very unsafe. Though, she rationalized, the ship must have been through an FTL trek more than once in its decades of service. It could last a few more weeks for her. Besides, after the torture and beatings from her previous hosts, a shower would feel amazing—even if it was a holo shower.

She spent as much time as she could under the flow of hot water before getting out in time for the meal Captain Sera had mentioned. Feeling greatly refreshed, she stepped into the corridor. At the end of the hall, the sounds of cutlery clinking on plates came from what must be the galley.

Tanis entered and saw Captain Sera and another man enjoying a meal at a large table. Tanis couldn't help but admire the quality of the wooden table and surrounding chairs. It reminded her of her cabin back on the *Intrepid,* which in turn made her think of Joe. She forced those thoughts down. She didn't want her first impressions to be all warbly-voiced and teary.

<*We'll find him, we'll get back,*> Angela said softly in Tanis's mind.

<*We will. We have to.*>

"Hey Tanis," Sera stood to greet her. "This is my first mate, Cargo."

The man stood and offered his hand, which swallowed hers to her wrist. His skin was dark, as though few of his ancestors had spent any time in space; his voice was soft, but very resonant, as he greeted her and offered a chair.

"You're in luck," Sera said, as she spooned some vegetables onto her own plate. "We're just out of station, so we have fresh food. A week from now, we'll be on to frozen stuff. Enjoy it while it lasts."

Tanis picked up a plate from the counter and sat across from Sera and Cargo. She scooped some salad onto her dish, and poured a creamy dressing over it.

"You were just at a station?" she asked as she mixed the salad up. <*I swear my mouth is watering after what the pirates fed me.*>

<*I tested it with some nano, it's clear,*> Angela supplied.

<*Thanks, Mom.*>

"Coburn, in the Trio System," Cargo filled in. "Picked up some cargo, including you."

Tanis set aside the part about herself being freight to be picked up, and asked about the location. "I don't know any places named Trio."

"No?" Sera cocked her head and gave Tanis a quizzical look. "It's a pretty well-known system. I forget what it used to be called, before it was colonized. It's about ninety-six light-years out from Sol. Lemme see if Sabrina knows,"

She watched Sera's eyes blink a few times, as the captain chatted with the ship over the Link.

"Looks like it was cataloged as HD 111232 before it got settled and named."

Angela provided Tanis with an image of the system, relative to Earth and 82 Eridani. It wasn't possible; they were well over a hundred light-years from where she should be. On the far side of Sol from the *Intrepid*!

She forced herself to remain calm.

"You said you picked me up. Are you slave traders or something?"

The Captain looked genuinely appalled. "No! You were packed in a shipping container that was supposed to have a prize-racing dog in it. After we came under attack leaving Trio, I decided to see what we'd risked our necks for." Sera wore a smile that made Tanis want to cringe. "Someone wants you real bad."

"You came under attack because of me?" Tanis couldn't make any sense of this. Events just wouldn't line up for her, and her mind still felt sluggish from her prolonged incapacitation.

Sera related the story of how they came under fire while leaving the Trio System. Tanis felt numb as she took it all in. The acceleration and maneuvering the freighter captain described was unheard of. No ship could do that and not kill its inhabitants—unless they were in shoot-suits, or augmented like Joe. As she mused over the meaning of this information, the captain fixed her with a very level stare.

"I know you probably are still feeling out of sorts, but my crew and I would really like to know exactly why you're so sought after. You came this close," Sera held her thumb and index finger very close together, "to getting us all turned into fine stellar dust. We would like to know why."

<You know what has happened, right?> Angela asked in Tanis's mind.

<I really don't want to, but I think I do—but how far? Everything has changed! It's like we moved to another dimension.>

Tanis knew many people who wanted to kill her, but—if her suspicions were correct—none of those people were alive, or if they were, she couldn't imagine that old grievances were relevant anymore. She certainly had no idea why she was over a hundred light-years from where she should be—being chased by pirates, no less.

<We need to know when we are. I haven't been able to get into their Link without outright hacking it and that's not something I want to do while we're trapped on this ship.> Angela's tone had a level of anxiety Tanis was not used to hearing from her AI.

<Do you think all this tech exists without humanity having ever creating picotech?> Tanis asked.

<Maybe…if they worked out how to generate gravitons efficiently without pico…I could see a very different course for humanity.>

The pirates had to be after the *Intrepid*.

Tanis took another bite of her salad and looked at her two dinner companions. It was impossible to tell if they had been truthful or not. This still could all be a ruse to get the *Intrepid's* location.

She decided to play dumb.

"I…I really don't know. I don't understand what someone would want from me."

Sera pushed her chair back, a look of exasperation washing across her face. She looked to Cargo and waved a hand, indicating he should try.

"You seem like a smart lady, Tanis," he said softly. While there was no threat in his voice, she imagined it wouldn't take much for it to appear there. "Surely you can at least determine where the current course of events began and tell us the tale of how you came to be in that cargo container."

<I don't think they'll buy damsel in distress,> Angela chuckled inside Tanis's mind. *<Especially since you really suck at it.>*

Tanis weighed her options. Getting back to the *Intrepid* and Joe was really all that mattered. Perhaps honesty would be best—if these people double-crossed her, she could kill them and take their ship. Though there was something about the captain—she felt a kinship with Sera.

"I haven't been entirely honest with you," she began. Neither of them looked surprised. "My name is Tanis Richards, yes, but I'm also a major on a ship you would know as the *GSS Intrepid*."

<*So much for honesty,* **General** *Richards,*> Angela said. <*But good call on the pretend demotion.*>

<*Well, I was a major when we signed on.*>

"Well that explains a lot," Sera slapped the table with a laugh. "Go on."

Tanis gave her a sidelong look. She wasn't certain if the reaction was good or bad for her. She decided to give them the paraphrased version.

"We had some ramscoop problems as we were passing by LHS 1565 on our way to our colony world. We managed to slingshot around the star, but an x-ray flare baked one of our engines. We lined up with Kapteyn's Star and drifted for a good seventy years.

Tanis considered telling them about the Victorians, but decided to leave that colony out of it. "Once there, we managed to mine a few small comets and asteroids to get the materials for repairs."

Sera was giving Cargo a strange look, and Tanis decided to keep going. "It took us some decades to get everything ship-shape, then exit the system and get back up to speed. It was only 8.9 light-years to 82 Eridani, which we were calling New Eden, so everyone went to stasis for what was expected to be about sixty-year trip with the deceleration burns. Only something happened—we got trapped in some sort of gravity well and accelerated out of control. Our sensors were completely off the charts and we couldn't make heads or tails of what was going on. All we could tell was that we did not appear to be in regular space-time."

"Kapteyn's Streamer," Sera said with a nod. "You can get some amazing speed cutting across that thing, but if you hit it at the wrong angle it'll take you for a ride."

"Or crush you to powder," Cargo added.

"It has a name? What is it?" Tanis couldn't believe that this was a known phenomenon.

"It's a supermassive stream of dark matter streaked out beyond Kapteyn's. If you hit it just right, it will accelerate you and then dump you out the far side into a gravity tunnel that has a very unpleasant lensing effect. Significant time dilation occurs," Cargo said bluntly.

Tanis was dumbstruck. They had just described what had happened to the *Intrepid*. She noticed then that Sera was giving Cargo a scathing look.

"You sure know how to break things nicely," she sighed.

Cargo just shrugged.

"I already figured out we moved forward in time a fair bit," Tanis said. "How far? Hundreds of years, a thousand?"

Sera stood and pulled a bottle of whiskey from a cupboard. She grabbed three glasses and poured everyone two fingers. Cargo gave her a long stare, but said nothing.

The captain sat back at the table and tossed hers back before answering.

"I'm guessing you're from a colony ship that probably left Sol sometime in the late fourth or early fifth millennium. You were headed for 82 Eridani, which interestingly *is* now called New Eden. You hit the Kapteyn's Streamer and then found yourselves somewhere in the vicinity of 58 Eridani, about 28 light-years further out than expected; wondering how the hell you got there and what the heck the year is."

Tanis hadn't known where the *Intrepid* ended up, but 58 Eridani was along the ship's trajectory.

"Yours isn't the first gen ship to dump through there. The first one managed to settle 58 Eridani, named it Bollam's World, and is doing fine now—for a system full of greedy assholes, that is.

"Anyway, due to the vagaries of space-time, they probably left Sol after you. Unluckily for you there isn't a single habitable planet within a hundred light-years of where you came out that's not already taken."

Tanis couldn't believe it. The *Intrepid* had spent hundreds of years of blood, sweat and tears to make it to a colony; a world she could call home. She slumped in her chair; it would take centuries to travel to a new world. If the FGT had any worlds available—if the FGT still existed.

"But how is that possible?" she all but whispered.

"It's all thanks to the greatest advance and the greatest tragedy of mankind: FTL. While all you gen ships were still chugging through interstellar space sucking up hydrogen in your ramscoops, some brainiac back on Procyon figured out the gravity drive," Sera said.

"I remember hearing something about graviton experiments at Procyon while we were at Kapteyn's. Our engineers were very excited about the possibilities," Tanis said with a furrowed brow.

Sera nodded. "I know it doesn't seem like the *biggest* discovery ever, but trust me it is. Once we could create gravity to react against other gravity, all the other pieces just lined up. Ships got AG fields to provide internal gravity, without rotation, thrust, or phantom mass. Inertial dampeners came out of fiction and into our ships; and we discovered a lot more about dark matter."

Tanis was glad she hadn't eaten too much. She was certain she was going to be sick.

"You know that scientists have always known about other dimensions, as well as sub and super-layers of space-time. But transitions to those other layers were prohibitively expensive, energy-wise, or it ended up being a one-way trip."

Tanis nodded slowly; this was basic physics.

Sera continued. "With the ability to manipulate gravity, they discovered how to drop into the same layer of space-time where dark matter resides. It was always postulated to be like this. Dark matter has all this mass, but isn't bending light like it should. To be honest, the exact nature of the dark layer, as it's called, still isn't perfectly understood. Some think it's utterly void and frictionless, while others think it's Einstein's universal frame of reference. I suppose someone knows, but they're not sharing the details.

"Either way, when you move into the DL your speed relative to the normal universe multiplies exponentially."

Tanis looked down at the whiskey and downed the glass in one shot. The captain gave her an appreciative look and continued.

"Gravity manipulation gave us other things, as well—namely methods for cheaper antimatter production. Once that was available, hitting speeds up to 0.70*c* with an antimatter pion drive became trivial. The end result? A trip from Sol to Alpha Centauri takes four days instead of four decades."

Tanis had always prided herself on being strong. Granted, the decades with Joe aboard the *Intrepid* had taught her about her softer side—but she still considered herself strong, a rock.

Until now.

She felt her foundation slipping away. She had understood her place in the galaxy so well. Known how to operate within all the parameters. Now, she knew nothing. She felt like all her value was lost.

<*Hold it together girl,*> Angela didn't sound that together herself as she gave the advice. <*We've been through worse and come out the better for it.*>

"Have we?" Tanis whispered.

"Pardon?" Captain Sera asked.

Tanis felt like she was going to have a mental breakdown. She thought of the harrowing events on Toro, the Mars Outer Shipyards, and the Cho. Of her awakening on the *Intrepid* as it was falling into a star and the desperate battle against the Sirians above the fledgling colony world of Victoria.

She thought of the picobomb.

"It was all for nothing," she muttered.

"What? No! That is the furthest thing from the truth. At the very least, there's no more Sol Space Federation, so your colony mission doesn't owe anyone a cent. They fell apart millennia ago," Sera said and then clasped a hand over her mouth, realized her misstep. "Oh shit."

Tanis's head snapped up. "Millennia?"

Cargo laughed. "And you said I stepped in it."

"Ummm," Sera shifted uncomfortably. "Well I guess in a way it doesn't really matter much, you never expected to see anyone you knew again anyway. Like Cargo said, the Streamer has a pretty wicked time dilation effect if you pass between the gravitational arms like you did. You skipped a few thousand years of relative time on that transit. By your calendar, it's just about the year nine thousand…or so.

Tanis rose, her legs shaking slightly. "If you'll excuse me, I need some time to myself."

Not waiting for a response, she left the galley and dashed down the corridor to her cabin, where she quickly closed the door. Praying no one would hear her, she began to sob.

TIME TRAVELER

STELLAR DATE: 07.02.8927 (Adjusted Years)
LOCATION: *Sabrina*, Interstellar Dark Layer
REGION: Galactic South of Trio Prime, Silstrand Alliance Space

"That went well," Cargo commented as he reached for another baked potato.

Sera ran her hands through her hair. "I didn't even get to tell her the good news."

"What, that aside from the positions of galaxies, everything she knows is no longer valid?"

"No, that like all good classics, her gen ship is worth a hundred times what it took to make the stupid thing. If they're early fifth millennia, they've got amazing tech. I've heard biological android were even common then. Do you know what a bio-droid with an advanced AI neural net goes for on the market?"

"Haven't a clue," Cargo said around a mouthful of potato.

"More than my sweet *Sabrina* will make in the rest of her life, that's how much."

<I thought you said I was priceless,> Sabrina groused.

Cargo perked up at that. "You don't say."

"We're not hard up for cash, but the tech her ship carries is worth more than a dozen star systems. I wouldn't object to a bit of a reward."

Cargo chuckled. "Well, what are you waiting for? Go talk to our little flower."

"Not yet...with what she's been through—and I bet we still only know the half of it—she's gonna need a bit of time to settle down. I'll go check on her in an hour or so."

Sera killed the hour running through a few checklists and doing a circuit of the ship. She stopped in the galley at the end of her tour to see Tanis sitting at the table alone, another glass of whiskey in front of her.

"Mind if I join you?" Sera knocked on the wall.

The major looked up and nodded.

Sera sat and poured herself another drink.

"It's a lot to absorb," Tanis said, her voice devoid of emotion

She nodded. "I can only imagine. But you left before I could tell you the good news—well, sorta good news."

"I already know it," Tanis replied. "The *Intrepid* is worth an immeasurable amount now."

Sera wondered exactly how Tanis knew that, but let it slide for the time being.

"I knew you were smart; that clueless act you tried to pull was pretty pathetic," Sera chuckled.

Tanis joined her in short laugh. "Yeah, it really was—not sure what I was thinking."

"Let's go up to the obs lounge. Its small, but it has a nice view of *Sabrina's* ass," Sera said as she stood and picked up the whiskey. If there was ever a good reason to break her 'no drinking onboard' rule, this was it.

They climbed up the ladder to the bridge deck and then followed a short corridor aft to a small room. There were several low couches and four windows facing out over the rear of the ship. Nothing beyond the ship was visible in the dark layer, but the inspection lights were on, casting the stern of the ship in a soft glow.

"Don't your engines emit light here?" Tanis asked, when she noticed there was no illumination coming from the back of the ship.

"We kill 'em in FTL, the hum you probably heard back in the med lab was our reactor. Our batteries are a bit low from the excitement in Trio, so we're charging them. There's nothing to thrust against here in the DL anyway. You can't maneuver or accelerate—except with grav drives against globs of dark matter. Once we come out of FTL, we'll need to do some serious braking since we entered it at well over half the speed of light. It took Cheeky some time to figure out when we'll need to drop back into normal space."

"Cheeky?" Tanis asked.

"Our pilot. You'll meet her soon enough."

"How big is your crew?"

"Six humans. Seven with you aboard."

"AI?" Tanis asked.

"There's Sabrina, the ship's AI, and Helen who is embedded with me. Nance, Cargo, and Cheeky have what you would probably call NSAI—sort of. Flaherty and Thompson don't have a lot of mods."

"Well, at least I won't have to remember many new names and faces, though I'm going to have a bit of work learning about the last five millennia."

"To be honest, things have been a mess," Sera responded. "FTL has been the bane of humankind."

"It has?" Tanis asked. "After more than a hundred years drifting through interstellar space, I sort of imagined it would be the opposite."

"What could never really happen in your time?" Sera asked by way of response.

Tanis knew the answer. "Interstellar war—though I wouldn't say 'never'."

Sera nodded. "Bingo. Let's just say there have been some setbacks. Humanity has only just recently begun to pull itself out of the toilet. For instance, there was even a period in the eighth millennia when the bulk of humanity completely lost knowledge of nanotechnology. It's been rediscovered since, but believe me, your nano is better than any you'll find across a thousand systems."

<*She's not being entirely honest,*> Angela said.

<*How so?*> Tanis schooled her expression, not wanting to show suspicion to Sera.

<*Her nano may have been more advanced than yours. It didn't put up a fight when I destroyed it, but it could have.*>

<*Will the mysteries ever cease?*> Tanis asked.

<*Could they please? I blame your "luck".*>

Tanis realized Sera had continued speaking while she and Angela talked.

"…I'm willing to bet you've got tech on your ship that the rest of mankind would kill for—probably has killed for. That's why we found you in a shipping container. I bet that Kade wants to have a nice long chat with you about where your ship is."

"Kade? Who's he?"

"Local scumbag. We have some dealings with his group, called The Mark, from time to time. Pays pretty well."

"I do hope you're not going to turn me over to him. I won't go quietly," Tanis's voice was level and dead calm.

Tanis watched Sera's face grow more serious as they stared into one another's eyes. She wondered how she appeared to this not-so-simple freighter captain: a problem and an enigma, but a possible payday as well. The moments dragged on, but Sera must have come to a conclusion about Tanis because she suddenly smiled and leaned back in her seat.

"No, I don't transport slaves, and I certainly wouldn't turn you over—threats notwithstanding."

"Good, that makes our relationship a lot more agreeable." Tanis took another drink from her glass and relaxed into the deep leather couch.

"However, Kade's going to expect to get you and I can't directly cross him or my ass is grass. How's about you tell me the rest of your tale so I can make sure whatever we work up jives. How did you end up at Coburn Station?"

<*She's lying,*> Angela said to Tanis.

<*I picked up some tells, too. Which part do you think is a lie?*>

<*Well, not really lying. From her body language and what I can read in her voice and smell, she's not afraid of Kade at all. He could make things difficult for her, but she is hiding something about her relationship with him.*>

Tanis held that conversation with Angela as she ran a hand through her long blonde hair. "I don't know how I got there, but I do know at least the start.

"We didn't exit gracefully from what you call Kapteyn's Streamer. In the split-second we transitioned out, something hit the ship at relativistic speeds. I was in the bow and managed to get to an escape pod. We ejected and then the *Intrepid* was gone. Angela and I were trying to find it when a small ship appeared out of nowhere—using FTL I now realize—and snatched the pod."

<*I've been meaning to tell you, now that I've reviewed the data I managed to get during that hack attempt we did back on the ship that captured us, there was an anomaly that might have been the* Intrepid. *I think they popped out a few AU further down than us,*> Angela informed Tanis.

<*Intact?*>

<*It didn't scan like debris, but it's hard to say. It was a long ways away.*>

While querying Angela, she continued her recitation to Sera.

"When they boarded the escape pod, I could tell right off that they weren't any sort of official representatives...of anywhere. Though, I must admit, they had some good nano suppression tech in their interrogation room. I almost got past it a few times, but I had a limited supply of bots and I decided to hold back to repair what they were doing to me.

"They beat me for a few days trying to get any detail they could from me. I was pretty messed up—Angela tells me I was on death's door. I guess they—what? Cryostasis?" Tanis sputtered as Angela fed her more details. "This *is* the dark ages!"

"Sorry, I should really give you Link access so you and your AI can chat with the rest of us," Sera apologized. "Sabrina, can you give the major and Angela our protocols?"

"Certainly, Captain," the ship said somewhat icily.

"No wonder everything aches," Tanis said while rolling her shoulders. "I can't believe it. How long was I under?"

Sera looked perplexed. "What's wrong with cryostasis? It's pretty common; keeps you alive and all that."

"No, *stasis* keeps you alive, *cryostasis* freezes you! As in it makes you very cold!"

<*I'm sorry, Tanis, I hadn't gotten around to sharing that with you sooner, I figured you had enough on your mind. You were iced for one hundred and nine days,*> Angela joined the conversation over the public net now that they were Linked.

Tanis's eyes widened and she flexed her fingers one-by-one as though she expected to find defects.

"Oh wait…you have true stasis on the *Intrepid,* don't you?" Sera sat up, eyes wide.

Tanis nodded. "Yes, when we left Sol, everyone had stasis; no one had used cryostasis in hundreds of years. I can't believe I was frozen!"

"There's some tech that'd be worth a pretty penny," Sera said with a smile. "True stasis tech was lost thousands of years ago. No one could figure out how the null field was created without ridiculous amounts of energy."

<*It's not complicated tech…how is it that things like that have been lost?*> Angela asked.

Sera sighed. "War, people hoarding tech and not sharing it, piracy, you name it."

"This is going to take some getting used to," Tanis said. "So what's our deal here? I'm guessing you're more than happy to take me back to the *Intrepid* if we provide you with something in trade to make it worth your while."

Sera leaned back again. "Look, I'll be honest. I won't hand you over to Kade, but I also won't traipse across human space on a courier run without payment—especially when everyone and their dog probably wants to find you and get a piece of your hide."

"I have one priority," Tanis said. "To get back to the *Intrepid* and ensure it remains safe. I can personally guarantee that you will be exceptionally well compensated."

Sera took a sip of her drink as she considered the Tanis's words. She certainly believed what she was saying, but the shrewd businessperson in her wondered what ability Tanis had to deliver on her promises. What sort of deal could she make with a major that would be binding? There was a lot of risk here.

"I would love to help you, Tanis, but how do you know that your ship will still be there? They may have retreated to interstellar space, or been captured by some other force. This is a pretty big risk."

"I can promise you one thing," Tanis said. "The *Intrepid* is there, and it is still sovereign. There is no force in the galaxy that can stop that ship—especially given the state of things right now. They will reward you handsomely for returning me. If they're not there, then I will give you specs for enough advanced tech that you'll never have to work another day in your life."

"You have them on you?" Sera asked.

"Yes, I've taken to carrying a lot of data with me."

Sera nodded. "Very well, before we enter into this deal, I want to make sure I know how many factions are involved. Did you notice anything significant about the ship that attacked you?"

"Not much. It was obviously not a cargo hauler by primary trade. My scan of it showed some big lasers for such a small ship. When they tortured me, I noticed that they both had an odd tattoo over their right eyes."

Sera pulled a plas sheet from a pocket and marked a pattern on it. "Like this?"

Tanis nodded. "That's the symbol. What's it mean?"

"Padre. It's his sign; all his guys have it tat'd on."

"Padre, as in a priest?"

"Priest? No, he's a pirate. One of the distinctly less pleasant ones. It was his guys that chased us out of the Trio System." Sera took another sip of her drink. "I'm betting that somehow Kade got wind of what Padre had found and snatched you up. We're supposed to deliver your container to him in about seven days."

"What a mess," Tanis sighed.

"It's gonna take some fancy footwork to pull one over on ol' Kade. I'm probably going to have to fake logs and show that Padre's ships boarded us and toss your container out the hatch here in the DL so he won't find it if he comes aboard."

"What about finding me?" Tanis asked.

Sera winked. "You're much smaller. I'm sure we can tuck you away somewhere."

A STARSHIP NAMED SABRINA

STELLAR DATE: 07.02.8927 (Adjusted Years)
LOCATION: *Sabrina*, Interstellar Dark Layer
REGION: Galactic South of Trio Prime, Silstrand Alliance Space

It certainly was a motley crew, Tanis thought as Sera introduced her to each of them around the galley table. Cargo, the first mate, seemed to be the only normal one in the group, which was a disturbing thought.

The bio and life-support engineer, who apparently was just called the bio in the ninetieth century, seemed to live inside of her hazard suit. She didn't even pull off the hood as she ate, and only unhooked the mouth filter, which exposed a circle of pale skin around her lips. She seemed passionate about her job, though. At first, Tanis couldn't understand the need for a dedicated bio on a ship this size, but she was realizing that technology wasn't quite as foolproof as what she was used to.

Everyone taking a shower or two a day probably didn't help with the volume of waste management.

Angela had already gotten to know the other AI. Sabrina seemed a bit touchy, almost as though she was a little insecure in her place as the ship's AI. Angela was obviously superior in capability, but even without that, it seemed as though Sabrina had already felt threatened.

Angela expressed surprise to find that Helen was something of an equal, though evasive on her origins.

Sera was correct in that Cheeky didn't have truly sentient AI, but it wasn't an NSAI either. Cargo's and Nance's were similar; both clear violations of the Phobos accords.

<I'm certain that Sabrina is a violation, too,> Angela added. *<She was created—not born—for this ship, and she's never left it. They even left her active while the ship was impounded for decades!>*

Tanis was appalled at the thought and looked around at the ship's crew. They didn't seem like barbarians, but their treatment of AI would have landed them in prison back in Sol.

Thompson and Flaherty didn't have AI at all, just simple Link interfaces—most of their information access was through retinal overlay. It was crude enough that Tanis could even see it on the backs of their eyes when she dialed up her vision.

Though she suspected that Flaherty might have an additional interface, since his retinal overlay rarely showed any information. Initially, she thought him to be little more than a deck hand, or perhaps an enforcer of some sort, but something about that assessment didn't fit.

He had glanced at her when she entered, and then again when Sera introduced him. He nodded his greeting, not saying a word. His build wasn't heavy like Thompson's or Cargo's, yet that didn't diminish the growing impression Tanis had that he was the most dangerous person in the room. Every movement he made was both spare and precise.

She had no doubt that he had also observed her completely and had formed his own silent opinions.

An additional clue was Sera's introduction of Flaherty. It was obvious she had a personal connection with the man, and was very comfortable around him. Yet, his lack of internal AI and little more than a personal Link, combined with what was obviously the lowest position on the ship didn't make a shred of sense.

Even though the pilot was a self-modified nymphomaniac, Tanis found herself taking a liking to the woman. Cheeky had bounced into the wardroom on what had to be twelve-centimeter heels, wearing a miniskirt that barely covered her ass, and a tight top with a semi-lewd slogan dancing across her breasts.

She had gushed how happy she was to meet Tanis and how cool it was to meet someone over five thousand years old. Her smile and laughter was infectious and Tanis found herself reminded of Trist.

"Watch out for her," Sera said. "You are witnessing the mating ritual of the sexually aggressive Cheeky. In the wild, they are truly dangerous. She's tamer than usual since she gets a lot of it out of her system when we're docked."

Tanis laughed. Perhaps the woman was a bit more like Jessica.

Sera moved on to the next member of her crew, a large man named Thompson. She was amazed at the presence of body hair. Tanis had to restrain herself from touching the peach fuzz on his arm. It looked like pictures of men from the nineteenth and twentieth centuries. She had always thought it would be repulsive, but seeing the somewhat rough blonde man with his soft blond hair in person, she found it to be quite the opposite. Despite that, Tanis noticed how he shifted uncomfortably when he shook her hand and had shot Sera some significant looks.

"So, what's the biggest difference you've noticed so far between your time and the ninetieth century?" Cheeky asked after the introductions were done.

Tanis pondered the question for a moment while the crew stared at her, greatly interested in the answer.

"Aside from the obvious FTL and gravity drives, it's the attitude you're able to have about the galaxy and humanity's place in it. I grew up in the crush of Sol—people everywhere, a military with a million warships. Yet if you wanted to get away from it all, you could. You could go to a colony world and live a simpler life—knowing that the overpopulation of Sol would just be a memory—you would never encounter it again, because you were just too damn far away. Now it would be a week's trip and you'd be back in it."

"I wouldn't have thought of that," Cheeky said. "I can't imagine how different it must have been. You lived in the time of greatness, the planetary rings, space elevators everywhere—moving worlds, terraforming everything…near immortality, it must have been amazing."

"Is all of that lost?" Tanis asked.

"Not all," Sera replied. "Worlds are still terraformed; planets are moved, but not commonly—not like in your day when Sol had dozens of habitable worlds. There are few rings left; in Sol, only High Terra remains."

Tanis felt her breath catch. That meant the Mars1 ring was gone. Ceres, the Cho, all no more. She knew losing a ring was no small thing—it meant those worlds may have been destroyed, as well. She decided not to ask; she didn't want to know.

"We didn't have all those things," Tanis said. "No one was immortal."

"I guess not," Cheeky replied. "But they lived a long time—over five-hundred years from what I've read. How old are you? If you don't mind my asking."

"Cheeky, really…" Nance sighed.

"I don't mind," Tanis held up her hand and smiled. "I'm still pretty young, only about two-hundred and eleven years of real-time on my clock."

Thompson whistled. "You look pretty good for two-eleven. None of us are over fifty. Two-hundred is about the best we can hope for—unless we strike it rich somewhere along the line."

"Or live in the AST," Nance added.

"AST?" Tanis asked, trying to guess at what that could be.

"If every time needs to have a dark, greedy empire, the AST is ours." Sera's expression was grim. "It is what has grown from the first interstellar government that started with Alpha Centauri, Sol System, and Tau Ceti. Hence, the A. S. T. At least, that's what everyone else calls them. Their real name is The Hegemony of Worlds."

Tanis nodded. It made sense that those systems were at the core of a large empire. Alpha Centauri and Tau Ceti were two of the most powerful colonies when she had left Earth. Alpha Centauri even had slow, but regular trade with Earth.

"Who knows what could happen?" Tanis shrugged. "If we really have a treasure-trove of tech, and it is stuff that's completely lost, we could trade it for a colony world. You guys could end up living as long as I plan to."

"Girl, you could trade that tech for a hundred colony worlds and still have money to burn. Heck, you could trade it for fully populated worlds," Cheeky exclaimed with arms flung wide.

"We have a few systems to hop through before we get to Bollam's World. You can shop around," Sera laughed.

"So it's Bollam's we're off to," Thompson said with a frown. "Are you sure that's wise?"

"I've struck a deal with Major Richards," Sera nodded at Tanis. "We'll be well compensated—enough that each of you can retire after this run."

Thompson looked about to say something else, but Sera shot him a dark look and he closed his mouth.

<So, did you pick up on the bit when you were talking about age and immortality?> Angela asked.

<I noticed Sera had a funny look on her face,> Tanis replied. *<Is that what you're referring to?>*

<Not just her, Flaherty too.>

<The plot thickens—I noticed Sera also gave a little twitch when they referred to the AST as the big bad empire of the time. I wonder if she's originally from there.>

<I'll see what I can learn from the other AI,> Angela said.

The rest of the meal progressed pleasantly, Tanis asking questions that would help her understand the present time as best she could, but she found herself coming back to the odd behavior that Sera displayed and Angela's earlier warnings that Sera was hiding something; something significant.

RENDEZVOUS

STELLAR DATE: 07.05.8927 (Adjusted Years)
LOCATION: *Sabrina*, Interstellar Space
REGION: Galactic South of Trio Prime, Sllstrand Alliance Space

Sabrina exited FTL three light days away from her previously anticipated exit, an unfortunate consequence of entering the dark layer at an irregular vector. Cheeky's calculations were as accurate as could be; it was just impossible to predict a ship's precise location in space, when you weren't even in space.

However, Cheeky had things well in hand as she rotated the ship a hundred and eighty degrees. Starting with a slow burn, she lit up the fusion engines and brought *Sabrina* down on the meeting location.

The rendezvous was deep in interstellar space. No stars shone nearby; there were no planets, or moons, or bodies of any sort. The only marker for this meeting place was a clump of dark matter resting alone in the void.

During the days of FTL transit, the crew had ditched the cargo container in which Tanis had been found, and faked the logs to show that instead of outrunning the Padre's ships, they had been stopped and boarded. Logs now showed the container being removed and then *Sabrina* being allowed to leave the Trio System.

Regarding Tanis, Sera decided that the best place to hide her was in plain view, as a new crewmember.

"Too bad we don't have access to any advanced modifications. Those cheekbones are pretty distinctive," Cheeky had commented.

"Amusing statement for someone named for their own cheeks," said Tanis.

"I'm not known for those cheeks." Cheeky pointed to her face, then placed her hands on her butt and swished it side-to-side. "These cheeks, though…"

"Believe me, I harbored no confusion on that fact," Tanis smiled. "Though, I can do something about my cheekbones, if you think it's necessary. Will he know anything about me?"

"He may. There are ways to send messages through FTL far faster than a ship can travel. If you can mask your appearance in some way that will stand up to inspection, do it," Sera said.

The major sucked in a deep breath as her face changed right in front of their eyes. Slowly, her jaw widened and her cheekbones became less prominent. Her lips filled out and the corners of her eyes turned up.

"Hot damn! I'd forgotten how much that *hurts*!" Tanis said in a somewhat huskier tone, as she touched her face gingerly.

"Wow! That's amazing!" Cheeky reached out to feel Tanis's face. "How in the stars did you do that?"

"I worked counterinsurgency in the TSF," Tanis's statement was met with blank stares and she laughed. "I may as well have said Praetorian Guard, it's probably better known."

"Praetorian? Is that what the Regulan military calls its Royal Guard?" Nance asked.

"Yeah," Sera said. "But they ripped it off from the Romans. The Praetorian Guard is the military unit that guarded Caesar."

"The salad?" Cheeky asked, visibly confused.

"The Roman Emperor."

Cheeky's mouth formed an O, but the expression on her face indicated she had no idea who the Roman Emperor was, when he lived, or on which planet he had ruled.

Tanis was dumbstruck. "I guess a lot changes in five thousand years."

"It has a lot to do with location, too," Sera said "I'd bet people in the Sol System know all about the Romans. People on rim worlds don't care to know much about AST worlds."

<*What story did you settle on?*> Sabrina asked, clearly impatient to get to her task.

Tanis spread her arms with a flourish. "Rachel, at your service. After serving as a station comm and nav tech on Coburn Station for a few years, I grew weary of it. Now, I'm working on my pilot's license, and managing scan and comm here on *Sabrina* while Cheeky shows me the ropes and helps me get my practical experience hours in."

<*Nothing more?*> Sabrina asked.

"If Kade asks more than that he'll already be suspicious and we won't be able to fool him with anything further," Sera said.

"That's an encouraging thought," Cheeky said.

Both Tanis and Sera began to say that they'd gotten through worse and stopped, eyeing each other for a moment. Then Tanis smiled and Sera let out a laugh.

"I doubt it'll be the last time either."

THE MEET

DATE: 07.09.8927 (Adjusted Years)
LOCATION: *Sabrina*, Interstellar Space
REGION: The Mark's Interstellar Drop Point, Silstrand Alliance Space

Sabrina had finished deceleration and was drifting near the meeting point.

Sera wasn't sure if Kade himself would be at this transfer, but she hoped not; this whole 'hiding human cargo act' was making her stomach twist enough as it was. Her misgivings aside, Tanis was actually fitting in with the crew quite well. She had picked up the comm and nav systems with appreciable speed and had watched Cheeky's final maneuvering of the ship with great interest. The crew had helped her flesh out a few parts of her story in greater detail, but Sera was still of the opinion that if too many questions were asked it was an indication that they were already in trouble.

Flaherty and Thompson had moved cargo to be transferred into the few rooms off the bow corridor. They also placed a few containers in the corridor itself. It made for some tight maneuvering, but the sooner they could transfer the cargo and got on their way, the better.

Tanis had argued very strenuously that perhaps they shouldn't stick around for the meeting, but Sera said she needed the business with Kade right now and couldn't afford to run across the Orion arm just to avoid him.

The meeting time arrived and they expected The Mark ship to show up on scan at any moment, decelerating toward the meeting coordinates. Sera was certain they had a few passive probes floating quietly in the area, so they would know who was around and be able to drop back into FTL if something were amiss.

As much as Sera wanted to look for those scan probes and tap into them, the chances of The Mark picking up on it were just too high.

Even though there was plenty of room, the bridge felt crowded with four of them up there. Tanis was operating scan at the comm station and Sera wondered what it would be like to go from what had to be a very clean, crisp, and ordered society to working on *Sabrina.* Tanis's back was straight and her movements spare and efficient. If she was feeling any anxiety over this cargo transfer, she wasn't showing it.

She surveyed the rest of her bridge crew. Cheeky was wearing a bit more clothing than normal—she didn't much like being ogled by the types that made up Mark crews. Cargo was as inscrutable as ever as he checked over ships systems and did whatever it was that always seemed to keep him busy at his station.

Sera accessed her Link again to see if scan showed anything; to be informed yet again that The Mark ship hadn't arrived.

<*Would you cut it out?*> Helen said. <*It'll go fine, they'll never suspect anything and we'll be able to carry on as usual.*>

<*Pardon me if I don't share your perennial confidence,*> Sera replied.

<*Trust me, I worry, too. I just calm myself down faster than it takes to even mention it.*>

Even as Sera was pondering the possibilities, Tanis spoke up. "There they are. Just came up on scan."

"They? There was only supposed to be one."

"Two ships, one an obvious freighter, the other looks a bit smaller, larger engine signature—you have it on record as the *Vertigo*. Both have turned and are firing AP engines to decelerate." Tanis plotted out where the two ships would come to a relative stop and sent the co-ordinates to Cheeky, who laid in a course.

"And we've got contact," Tanis announced. "They're still a good thirty light minutes out, so it's just a welcome." She sent the message to Sera's screen, who saw with dismay that Kade had made an appearance himself. The message was brief. It instructed them that Kade's ships would decelerate to 0.15c and maintain their current course. Sera was to bring *Sabrina* up to a matching speed and set a course to intercept. The maneuver would make for a faster overall rendezvous.

Sera piped the pertinent information to Cheeky, who put *Sabrina* on course to match up with Kade's ships. Once that was done, she sent a message over the ship's main net.

<Kade has dropped from the DL and we are accelerating to meet him at a 0.15 c *rendezvous. He's here himself in one of his pirate boats, with a freighter, to pick up the wares, I imagine. Our ETA on meet-up is about eight hours. I'll put it on the clocks.>*

It was easing into the third watch and Sera decided that things would be hectic soon enough. She slated everyone to get at least six hours of sleep before the rendezvous.

She opted for sleep first. If anything interesting happened, it would be later rather than sooner.

After her allotted six, she was awake and back on the bridge nursing the first cup from a fresh pot of coffee.

Humans may have done a lot in the previous ten millennia, but so far nothing had been invented that was better than a cup of coffee after waking up. Well almost nothing, but people didn't invent that.

By the time a soft seal was made against the *Vertigo,* Sera had quelled her anxiety over potential conflict with Kade. Her concern was more due to the wrench it would throw in her plans. Kade had made it clear he wanted to meet with her and look over the cargo, which was something he had never done before.

Sera was starting to wonder if they should have just thrown Tanis in a hazsuit and dropped her in one of the nastier enviro tanks, one that no one would go peeking in. Too bad she hadn't thought of that earlier. They could have kept the container she had been in and shrugged when it was found to be empty.

Sera cycled the bow airlock herself and let Kade and his two companions on board. She was tempted to wait for him on the bridge, but this was no time to antagonize the pirate with power plays.

He came through the lock first, just as she remembered him from the last time they'd met. His long, dark hair was somewhat greasy, and, although his clothes were crisp—and probably cost more than the value of all the cargo they were about to transfer—they somehow didn't transmit that wealth to him.

With him was a person that Sera had dealt with many times, and liked less on each encounter—Kade's right hand woman, Rebecca.

Rebecca was a beautiful woman who had no compunctions about using her looks to her advantage in every way possible. She also looked nothing like a pirate, more like the unlikely combination of a princess and a dominatrix.

Where Sera gleamed in her tight leather, Rebecca sparkled with necklaces and bracelets. All made of diamond, platinum, and whatever was currently the most expensive gem in vogue.

Beneath the jewelry, her body was sheathed from head to toe in a tight, black material that reflected every light in the corridor. The combined effect made her almost difficult to look at—though Sera certainly appreciated the appeal.

Kade probably hoped that some of Rebecca's style would make him look better than he did. Unfortunately for him, the opposite was true—having her nearby just made him look somewhat dumpy.

Rebecca's eyes raked over the corridor crowded with cargo and locked on Sera, the expression on her face filled with distaste for all aspects of *Sabrina*—including her captain.

<I hate the way she looks at me,> *Sabrina* said.

<I know how you feel, dear,> Sera replied.

The third person was a man Sera did not recognize. He looked cowed by the company he was keeping and Sera wondered why he was here.

"Welcome aboard *Sabrina*," Sera said.

Sera knew that Kade harbored desire for her; as she offered her hand, she tilted her hips and smiled. She was fully prepared to do whatever it took to remain in the pirate's good graces.

Kade took it and smiled, his eyes traveling over today's leather outfit—dark green with yellow piping down her sides. It was more formal than usual, with the pants loose from the knees down, where they fell over low-heeled boots. The jacket was form fitting and fastened with a double row of brass buttons down her chest. She'd even topped it off with a captain's hat in matching green leather. Kade practically licked his lips.

"Sera. You know Rebecca, and this is Drind. He'll be going over your scan logs to learn what he can of Padre's ships that took my property."

Had she not known better, the emphasis he placed on 'my' would have caused Sera to believe it actually was his. It certainly seemed as if Kade's ethics did not take into account the fact that he had stolen it from Padre in the first place, or that the property he spoke of was a person.

"Of course," Sera said in the polished voice she used for speaking with the pirate leader, which drew a dark look from Rebecca. "You'll pardon the mess. The men have things ready for transfer to the *Starskipper* so that we don't cause any delay. This way to the bridge." She gestured down the corridor.

Kade smiled magnanimously. "Of course. I've instructed the *Starskipper* to dock while we are here and transfer the cargo while we talk." As though his words were prophetic, she heard the light clang as the *Vertigo* disengaged from the soft dock and maneuvered away, to allow the other ship room to link to *Sabrina*.

Sera hid her thoughts behind a mask of pleasantness. Kade must have felt either invincible or unthreatened by her, if he didn't feel the need to have any type of escape route during parts of their meeting. For her part, Rebecca looked more concerned with scuffing the shine on her outfit than finding out about the missing freight container.

Sera used the lifts to bring them up to bridge deck. They stepped into the command space, where Cheeky, Tanis, and Cargo were all at their stations coordinating with the *Starskipper* for its soft dock.

Kade noticed Tanis right away. "New crew? I didn't know you were looking, Sera, I could have furnished you with anyone you'd need."

<If we wanted that, we could have just contacted Moles R Us,> Helen said privately to Sera.

Sera introduced Tanis as Rachel and explained that she would be assisting with comm and scan. She didn't go into details as to why, after years with the same crew, she had decided to add another member. Offering it unasked would be too suspicious.

Whatever stars watched over *Sabrina* smiled and Rebecca asked the question first, and Sera explained it was to expedite dock duties. Currently, Cheeky, Cargo, or she had to remain on the bridge while docked to watch scan and comm. This way, they could all be out on station at once.

Kade and Rebecca seemed satisfied with this answer and didn't press the issue further.

"Perhaps our technician could look over your logs with your new comm tech while you and Cargo join us in your lounge to discuss some things?" Kade phrased it as a question, though it wasn't one.

Sera acquiesced and called down to the galley for Nance to bring up some refreshments. She spared a glance for Tanis as Drind sat with her to go over scan from the Trio departure. She was impressed; absolutely nothing about the major belied the tension Sera knew she had to be feeling.

The four sat in the observation lounge. A moment later, Nance, looking more than a little uncomfortable, entered with a selection of drinks she had previously prepared. The bio wasn't wearing her hood—Sera had asked her not to—in an attempt to show they had nothing to hide. She asked preferences, and quickly began to pour the drinks.

"Are you having some sort of environmental issue?" Rebecca asked Nance, frowning at her hazsuit.

"No, I just wear it all the time in case something happens," Nance said. "That way we don't lose precious time while I get suited up."

Rebecca didn't seem convinced, and started to question Nance further, but Kade stopped her.

"She always wears it, though I've never seen her face before," he said with a leer. "Has anyone ever told you how beautiful your hair is?"

Nance flushed, but managed to give a steady reply. "I've heard it once or twice before."

With that, the drinks were served and Nance quickly left the lounge.

A few minutes passed while mild pleasantries were exchanged before they got to the issue at hand. "I'd forgotten your curious aversion to alcohol onboard your ship," Kade mused, as he drank from his cup of dark roast. "Any other captain would have his or her best wine in front of me."

"My equivalent is my best coffee, which this is," Sera said with a smile she did not feel.

"It's damn good," he nodded. "However, I'm not nearly as pleased with you, Sera. I'd think that one of my captains would try to defend my property against Padre a bit better than you did." He sighed as though this was very vexing to him. "I'm not sure what to do with you."

Sera sipped from her cup and spoke calmly, as if they were discussing the weather. "I do make runs for you, but I'm not one of *your* captains. I'm under no greater obligation to protect your cargo than any other consigned to this ship. I'm certainly not going to risk *Sabrina* or my crew just for some racing hound." Kade seemed taken aback by her calm response, obviously expecting something else; perhaps fear.

To his left, Rebecca was giving Sera the blackest of looks.

Sera rolled the dice and pressed on.

"Since it was your cargo that Padre was after when his men chased us clear across Trio, I find myself thinking I should bill you for the antimatter we burned." Sera enjoyed the expression of consternation that flashed across Kade's face, and let an edge of anger slip into her voice. "Hell, they fired an RM at us! Who did you piss off enough for them to do that, and what type of racing hound is worth an RM?"

Cargo was making 'stop it' eyes at her, and Sera decided that she had pushed as far as she should.

Kade shook his head and made a soft clicking noise with his tongue. "I'm sorry you feel that way. That hound was very precious to me. I'm feeling very much like it is you who should compensate me."

Cargo seemed to decide he had better speak up before Sera said something they'd regret. "That's not the type of business this is and you know that, Kade. There's no insurance when things don't go according to plan," he gave Sera a pointed look. "We know that, too."

Kade seemed somewhat placated by Cargo's smooth, even tones.

Sera nodded and said nothing, which seemed to allow the tension to pass.

Kade sighed and finished his coffee before rising. "Very well, let's see if my tech found anything useful on your scan data." They filed out of the lounge and back to the bridge, where Drind was chatting amicably with Tanis.

"What do you have for me?" Kade asked brusquely.

Drind's attention instantly snapped to his employer and then back to the console, where he brought up several pieces of pertinent data.

"The ships were definitely Padre's. From what I see here, they really did attack Coburn Station, but broke off when it appeared their quarry wasn't there. Not sure how they got that message. Two ships that weren't in on the station attack circled south of the star to chase after the *Sabrina*. It was quite a ride, the crew here pulled out all the stops to get away; pushed this old bucket of bolts faster than I'd feel comfortable with."

<*Why do humans continually insist on referring to me disparagingly?*> Sabrina groused.

<*They don't appreciate your finer qualities,*> Sera said, sending a wave of calmness to her ship.

Drind continued, "Their pursuers actually launched an RM and that was when the *Sabrina* ceased acceleration and allowed the boarding. They wouldn't have escaped the missile."

<*And he keeps using the word 'the' when referring to me. That's just rude,*> Sabrina said with a pout.

"And they didn't take anything else? Just that one container?" Rebecca asked with a quirked eyebrow, while Kade appeared to be mollified by the explanation.

Drind responded affirmatively, "That's all the records show."

"Bastards," Kade said. "How did they know where we stashed it?"

Sera didn't miss that Rebecca touched Kade to stop him from saying more, just as Cargo had stopped her earlier.

"Very well," Rebecca said. "How far along is the cargo transfer?"

Tanis had been monitoring the progress and announced that it was complete and that the *Vertigo* was preparing to connect once more. Kade announced that they were finished and Rebecca asked that Sera accompany them to the airlock.

The request felt suspicious to Sera. She always walked Kade off her ship, but for Rebecca to request what was the norm told her something was off. She could see that Cargo felt the same way.

All in all, this was going far too easily.

Sera led the two visitors off the bridge to the lift. They stepped inside and Sera pushed the button for the freight deck. The lift shuddered a bit as it started its descent. Suddenly, between the crew and freight decks, it stopped. Sera smiled innocently at the three guests.

"Sorry about that. This lift doesn't get used much and sometimes seizes. It'll free up in a moment."

True to her word, the lift started down again half a minute later. Down on the freight deck, the corridor to the bow airlock was free of cargo except for one last crate. They stepped around it and Sera keyed the bulkhead controls to begin pressurizing the airlock while the *Vertigo* made soft dock on the other side.

Having entered in the codes, Sera turned, only to find herself staring directly down the muzzle of a gun.

Rebecca's angry scowl was at the other end of the weapon. "You didn't think we fell for that whole Padre chased you thing, did you? There was no way he could have known you had the container."

"Are you insane?" Sera asked. "Put that thing away, it'll hole the hull if you fire it."

Rebecca laughed. "I'm not stupid, Sera. An old tub this may be, but I know your shields will hold air even if I put a dozen holes in the hull."

Sera looked at Kade. The expression on his face told her everything. He wasn't in on this. Rebecca was acting on her own.

"She doesn't have it," Kade gave an exasperated sigh. "Sera wouldn't lie about something like this, and she couldn't fake scan well enough that Drind would be fooled."

The look that Rebecca shot at Kade was pure hatred. "How stupid are you? Have you become so complacent that you can't see how she plays you? She knows exactly where that container is and she's gonna tell us, or little Sera will have to see how hot her sexy little captain's outfit looks with a few holes in it."

Cargo's voice came smooth and steady from behind Kade and Rebecca. "I don't think that will happen."

Kade turned to look back, but Rebecca kept the gun trained on Sera. The Mark's leader cursed as he saw Cargo, Thompson, and Flaherty filling the corridor, pulse rifles leveled.

"I think you'll toss that blaster to the deck and then you'll get on your ship and we'll pretend this never happened," Sera said evenly.

"Do what she says, Rebecca. You're acting insane. I know you've always been jealous of Sera, but this is too much."

As Kade spoke, Sera wondered that she'd never realized how much of a complete coward he had become as his wealth increased.

The same thought must have been on Rebecca's mind, too. She swung her arm until the muzzle of the blaster pointed at Kade's head. "You are a complete and utter moron. It's like you get dumber by the day, and frankly I can't stand it anymore." Her voice dripped disdain and hatred, but somehow sounded toneless at the same time.

She paused for just a second, cocked her head, and pulled the trigger.

Everyone was stunned as Kade's brains sprayed across the bulkhead. All eyes followed Kade's toppling form as it hit the ground, spilling blood, tech, and grey matter onto the deck.

At that precise moment, the airlock finished cycling and behind Sera, four heavily armored soldiers stepped into the corridor. Their visors were down and their weapons leveled.

Rebecca's voice was surprisingly calm. "They just killed Kade. Take Sera alive and then secure this piece of crap."

The four soldiers raised their weapons to their shoulders in a single fluid movement. In the same instant, Cargo and Flaherty dove behind the remaining freight container while Thompson hit the deck and rolled through an open hatchway. Sera fell to her side and kicked at Rebecca's knees as the troopers unloaded their clips into the corridor. They weren't the ship-friendly pulse rifles that Sera's crew held. These were full power beam weapons. Sera cringed as she thought of the holes their shots must be tearing through her *Sabrina*. If it weren't for the heavy shielding around the engines, their beams would have punched clear through the ship.

Rebecca crashed to the ground, and Sera gained a pyrrhic sense of satisfaction that her bucket of bolts ship dirtied the other woman's shiny black skinsuit. Rebecca locked eyes with Sera and grinned. Sera looked up just in time to see one of the troopers smash the butt of his weapon into her face.

She fell back and watched the world slowly fade from view. The sounds of weapon fire tearing her ship to shreds took a bit longer to leave her hearing.

LOSS

STELLAR DATE: 07.09.8927 (Adjusted Years)
LOCATION: *Sabrina*, Interstellar Space
REGION: Galactic South of Trio Prime, Silstrand Alliance Space

Cargo ducked back behind the freight container as the beam fire continued to flash overhead. Sera and he had suspected the possibility of an altercation with Kade, and this container had been left in the corridor for precisely the purpose it was now serving.

It contained a small shield generator, providing a secure shelter. The wall Thompson was using for cover wasn't faring as well, but so far the burly super had managed to avoid being hit.

Cargo accessed his Link and told the other two men to narrow their rifles' band and match frequencies. They'd take these goons out one at a time. On a three count, they all broke cover enough to get a clear shot and fired at the helmet of the leftmost trooper. The harmonious frequencies from the pulse rifles amplified one another and the tight beam focused the pulse wave to achieve lethal intensity.

Cargo noted with satisfaction that the trooper's faceplate cracked as the shots struck true and he slumped to the ground. At the same time, another of the Mark soldiers cracked his rifle against Sera's head and he saw the captain slump to the decking, unconscious.

"Mother fuckers!" Thompson cried out as he was forced to duck back behind the bulkhead for cover. "They hit the capt'n."

This wasn't good. *Sabrina* couldn't take much more of this abuse. They had powerful exterior shields, but on the inside, other than around the engines, there was no sectional shielding. Before too long, those beams were going to tear through something that responded badly to tearing.

Cargo contacted Cheeky over the Link. "Cheeky. Dump to FTL *now!*"

<*What the hell is going on down there? It sounds like a fucking war!*> the pilot responded.

<*Just do it, we're going to be swimming in Mark soldiers if you don't.*>

<*But we're still at 0.15 c. I don't know what we'll hit if we enter the DL right now.*>

<*We're never gonna hit the DL again if you don't do it now.*> Cargo wasn't in the mood to discussion. <*Do it now!*>

<*All right! It's gonna take a minute.*>

<*Take less.*> Cargo cut the connection.

He counted with his fingers to indicate when to make another timed shot at the two other men. On three, they broke cover again to fire on the enemy furthest to the right. Ready to make the shot, it took him a moment to grasp what was happening.

The fallen soldier was still on the deck and two others had taken positions within the airlock for cover. Past them, Rebecca was back aboard the *Vertigo* with the fourth armored figure hauling Sera's unconscious form into the other ship's airlock.

Cargo pointed to the man on the left of the airlock, so that they wouldn't chance hitting the captain, and they fired in unison once more. The man attempted to duck to the side, but he was flung against the outer hull as the shot clipped his shoulder.

At the far side of the umbilical, Sera had been pulled into the *Vertigo*'s airlock and several more troopers were ready to step around her and join the assault on *Sabrina.*

Cargo called Cheeky over the link again. <*Any damn minute now!*>

<*Hold on, in less than a sec,*> came the pilot's frantic response.

Two of the reinforcements were in the umbilical, and the pair in *Sabrina's* airlock were leveling their weapons to fire as Cargo motioned for Flaherty and Thompson to get down. The wrenching feeling from the shift to FTL washed through them, and, before the sensation had passed, Flaherty broke cover and leapt over the freight container.

He rushed down the corridor, firing his rifle on its highest setting while the remaining enemies were still off balance from the shift. The one who had already been clipped in the shoulder slumped to the deck after taking two more hits.

Flaherty got three more shots off at the other trooper before crashing in to him and slamming him against the bulkhead.

At that moment, the transfer to FTL completed and the airlock yawned open to the total void of the dark layer. Their ears popped as air rushed out into the space between *Sabrina* and its shielding. Beyond the shield, two soldiers who had been in the umbilical could be seen floating away in the void.

Flaherty pulled a beam rifle off one of the unconscious enemy soldiers and took careful aim before firing a shot through each of the drifting men's heads.

"Why'd the hell did you do that? You should have let the dogs suffer," Thompson said, as he approached the airlock.

Flaherty didn't look away from the void. "No one deserves that."

Cargo stepped beside Flaherty, silent, his breathing ragged. Then, with a curse, he slammed his fist into the bulkhead. The trooper who Flaherty had crashed into made a noise and stirred from the sound. Flaherty reached down, tore his helmet off and slammed his head against the hull.

The other soldier was also moving, his breathing sounded strained through his helmet and he was moving his head erratically. Cargo reached down and pulled his helmet off. The man looked haggard, his face a massive bruise from the effects off the pulse rifle. His eyes were bloodshot and barely open. He still managed to scream as Cargo fired the pulse rifle point blank into his left eye.

The trooper's head crumpled, but the scream didn't stop. That was a first, Cargo thought, until he realized the sound was coming from behind him. He and Flaherty turned to see Thompson holding his gun to Drind's head. Completely forgotten, the tech had been curled up on the floor.

"Want me to ice this bastard, too?" Thompson asked.

Hearing that, followed by seeing the cold eyes of Cargo and Flaherty upon him, Drind seemed to shrink inward even further. "Please, please don't do that to me, too. I'll do anything you want, please just don't kill me." He was sobbing now, his shoulders heaving and hands over his head.

"No. We've done enough killing for one day," Flaherty said.

"Stick him somewhere out of the way," Cargo agreed, and Thompson nodded wordlessly as he gestured with his rifle for Drind to stand up. They were all feeling the loss of the captain; it was best not to do anything else rash just yet.

"What's that sound?" Thompson asked.

They all stopped, Flaherty turning his head as he listened.

"It's not out there," Cargo said. "It's in here." He tapped his head.

"It's Sabrina," Flaherty replied.

"I'll be on the bridge," Cargo said as he took off at a run.

Less than a minute later Cargo stepped on to the bridge, and confronted the concerned faces of Tanis, Nance, and Cheeky.

"Something's wrong with Sabrina," Cheeky said. "She won't respond and is making this strange noise on the net, almost like a whimper."

Cargo looked around at the bridge's observation cameras. "It's okay Sabrina. We'll get her back."

"Get who back?" Cheeky asked, the color draining from her face.

"SHE'S GONE!" Sabrina screamed over both the Link, and the ship's audible systems. "I CAN'T HEAR HER ANYWHERE!"

"That's because we're in the dark layer and she's not with us," Cargo said with more compassion than he would have thought he could manage at the moment.

"She's what?" Cheeky screamed and Nance let out a gasp.

The wailing coming over the Link and audio was increasing in pitch; Cargo was starting to have trouble thinking with the sound slicing through him.

<*Sabrina.*> Flaherty's voice broadcasted onto the ship's net. <*Listen to me, Sabrina,*> he insisted, but the ship didn't stop her cry. <*Remember. Remember what Sera said to you back when we first met and saved you from that place?*>

The keening lessened and Sabrina spoke, <*I do remember. I do.*>

<*Good,*> Flaherty said. <*Remember that. Remember the things she told you and you'll be ok.*>

Sabrina made a noise that sounded uncannily like a sniffle. <*Okay*>

As the sound faded away, Cheeky fixed Cargo with a hard stare. "You told me to go to FTL. Why would you do that if they had the captain?"

"Because we'd be crawling with Rebecca's soldiers if we didn't get out of there."

"Rebecca?" Tanis asked. "What happened to Kade?"

"Rebecca killed him."

"She what?" Cheeky yelled and leapt back to her console. "Kade's one thing, but Rebecca *hates* Sera. She'll kill her! I'm pulling us out and getting back there right now!"

"You'll do no such thing; they'd waste us in a second," Cargo said, his trademark calm becoming ragged.

Cheeky couldn't speak, for a moment she just stared at her controls and then let loose a sob.

Tanis knelt down beside her and stroked her hair. "What do you propose?" she asked her eyes hard as she looked up at Cargo.

"We need to drop out of the DL, alter course and then get back in, or they'll get higher v and then skip along waiting for us. They know how fast we're going and can predict our course with ease. Figure out a new course on a different vector and get us on it. We need to get safe and then figure out what to do." Cargo said.

Tanis turned to her console and began pulling up plots while Cheeky looked up at Cargo.

"I abandoned her."

"You did as you were ordered. I am the one who abandoned her, and I intend to get her back."

"How are we going to do that?"

"We've got that Drind guy. Since he was the big expert with the scan and nav, I'm betting he'll know where they'll go with her."

They all clung to that hope as Cheeky and Tanis worked out a new vector and effected the transition to regular space. Cheeky quickly altered course and dropped back into FTL. Scan didn't pick up any of Kade's ships when they were in regular space, though that didn't mean there weren't any sensor arrays nearby relaying information. They made two additional course alterations before they began to feel comfortable.

With Sabrina monitoring the bridge, everyone met in the galley to work out what they hoped would be their plan to rescue the captain.

"What is our damage report?" Cargo asked once the coffee had been poured. No one wanted to talk about their missing captain just yet.

"Not much," Thompson replied. "The meatheads hit a few power couplings, but secondaries re-routed. Lucky they didn't hit those, too, or we would have disintegrated when we tried to go into the DL. Most blasts hit engine shielding, which held without a problem."

"Hit a return flow pipe on an enviro system," Nance added. A return flow pipe was a nice way to say sewage. "It was clear at the time, but no one use the cargo deck's port-side head till I fix it or you get to clean up the mess."

"Repair time?" Cargo asked.

"Not long."

Cargo was silent a moment, but he couldn't withhold the details from the crew. They needed to know. "Kade had fallen for our little ruse. Rebecca hadn't. She pulled a blaster on the captain and then Thompson, Flaherty, and I showed up with the pulse rifles, and we told her to stand down. Kade was on our side and told her to back off, as well. So, Rebecca turned the gun on him and took the top of his head off."

Sabrina was an on-the-fringe sort of freighter, running a bit of this and that, things she probably shouldn't. They'd even gotten in a few dockside shootouts in some seedier stations on the edge of nowhere, but never had anyone died on her decks. Everyone was stunned to silence.

"Great, dead people," Nance exclaimed. "I'm not cleaning that shit up!"

"Don't worry about it. We'll just shift the atmo shield in a few feet and let the void take it all. Lock's still open anyway," Thompson said.

"Noticed we blew out some air," Nance sighed. "I'll handle all that. It's what I get paid the big bucks for. Do we want to keep anything as evidence? Isn't there a bounty out on Kade?"

"Yeah, it's some damn serious cred, too," Cheeky said. "Maybe we could use the money to buy the captain back."

Thompson's expression was dark and he cast a glance at Tanis before he spoke. "I told the captain this was a bad idea. We should consider just turning her over in a trade. Be nice and fast." Tanis's expression grew cold as he spoke, but she didn't reply.

Cargo ignored Thompson's statement. "If we turn in Kade's body, we may have to answer some tricky questions about how we got it. Captain may be up to that sort of fast-talking, but I don't know if I could handle it. Freeze it for now and toss the goons. We'll use it later."

"I guess my suggestion is out," Thompson said sourly.

Flaherty leaned forward as he reached for a plum in the fruit bowl. "Sera made it clear that we don't trade in human cargo. She decided not to give Tanis over to them. I think we should respect her decision."

Everyone nodded in agreement, though some were more reluctant than others.

Thompson let out a sigh and leaned back with his arms crossed. "Whatever."

Cargo looked at Thompson for a moment, wondering what trouble the man would cause. "We do have one piece of good news. We got their tech and one of their goons," he paused as Flaherty shook his head slowly. "OK, so just their tech. I'm betting that he can tell us what we need to know about where Rebecca will have taken the captain. Who wants in on having a little talk with him?"

Every hand shot up, even Tanis's. "Okay, it's gonna be me and…Thompson. We'll get answers out of him."

"He'll be pissing himself in ten minutes," Thompson said.

"No good, Cargo," Flaherty said. "He watched you kill that pirate. You'd scare him too much for him to talk."

"Let me in on it," Cheeky said. "I'll get him talking."

"You're not exactly intimidating," Nance shook her head.

"I have some pretty intimidating outfits."

"Never know, he may go for that sort of thing," Thompson chuckled, most likely trying to visualize Cheeky in one of those outfits.

Cheeky pouted. "True…haven't met a guy yet that didn't seem to enjoy my dom routine, no matter how much I hurt him."

"I'll do it," Tanis said, unflinching as every eye turned to her.

"Why should you do it, you're as much a part of the problem as that Drind guy," Nance said as she looked around the table. "Thompson has a point. Don't you think that Sera may have changed her mind, now that she's been captured? We all know how much Rebecca hates her."

Thompson nodded his agreement and cast Nance a small smile for her support.

Cheeky's face was twisted in an uncomfortable grimace. "Part of me wants to try it; it's the quick and easy fix. But, I don't think it's ethical. Besides, like you said, Rebecca has always really hated Sera, but by extension *Sabrina,* and all of us."

"You're one to talk about ethical." Thompson said with an unkind edge to his voice.

Cheeky flushed. "You wouldn't understand why I do the things I do. To you it's all just raw sex. Sure, some of it is, but there's more to it than that."

"Cheeky's sexual proclivities aren't the issue here," Flaherty said, his voice toneless and level. The look in his eye sent shivers down everyone's spine. "Stay on topic."

"You don't have to like me," Tanis said. "You don't have to like why I'm here or why people are killing and dying to get me. Trust me; I like it just as little as you. You may have had a bad year or two in your lives, but I've had a bad century or two. It sucks. But all recriminations and whining aside, I've had training in this sort of thing. I've commanded units that had to get information in pretty short order before."

"So you tortured people for it?" Nance asked.

Tanis didn't reply for a long moment. "Yes."

Strangely, it seemed to be the right answer.

Cargo steepled his fingers, "Okay, then. Tanis you do the talking, and Thompson will do the intimidating. The rest of us will watch over the Link."

"Good, I'll make sure you don't try anything funny," Thompson said.

"What 'funny things' would I try?" Tanis was clearly growing tired of Thompson's attitude.

"Whatever pain in the asses did five thousand years ago," Thompson said.

Tanis sighed and followed Thompson down to the hold where they had dumped the tech. He unlocked the door, but before they stepped inside, put his arm across the entrance.

"You may think you're all special and hot shit, but if I even get an inkling that what you're telling us to do will harm Sera, I'll kill you myself."

Tanis didn't flinch as she stared the large man down. She was going to reciprocate the threat, but then stopped herself. "I promise you, that won't happen."

She pushed his arm out of the way and stepped inside. Drind was sitting propped against a crate. A sack was over his head and his hands were bound behind his back. The sack wasn't tied on; Drind just hadn't tried to get it off.

Tanis had found him to be a nice, if somewhat shy, man when he reviewed their logs and scan data on the bridge. She knew how he must be feeling, but pushed it from her mind. Rescuing Sera was the best way to get back to the *Intrepid*—though simply commandeering the ship had crossed her mind more than once. But Sera had saved her; she wouldn't repay that with treachery.

Crouching in front of him, she snatched the sack from his head, then grabbed his hair in one swift motion. He tried to scramble back from her, his eyes closed while she pulled his head back.

"Look at me!"

Startled to hear a woman's voice his eyes opened and latched onto Tanis like a drowning man.

"Rachel! You've got to help me; they're going to kill me."

She doubted Drind had many friends in Kade's—now Rebecca's—organization. Being the tech on a ship full of pirates probably was a tough job.

<I don't know how you can do this sort of thing, he's pathetic,> Angela said.

<Occupational hazard,> Tanis replied with a sigh.

<You could go easy on him,> Angela's voice had an edge of pleading to it. She had never been squeamish during torture before.

<I will, but if I don't do this a certain way, Thompson will kick me out and do it his way.>

During her chat with Angela, Drind came to the realization that it was Tanis who was pulling his head back at an extreme angle and he shrunk inward.

"Please don't hurt me," he whimpered.

Tanis ignored his entreaty and asked angrily, "Why did you kidnap Captain Sera?"

His shock was plain and denial strong. "What? I didn't do that. That psycho Rebecca did. She blew Kade's head off! I didn't have anything to do with it." He was beginning to shake uncontrollably; Tanis decided to back off a bit or she'd have to conduct the rest of the interrogation over the smell of urine.

"Please don't kill me, too," his voice was little more than a whisper.

Tanis let go of his head. "So you didn't know what she had in mind?"

"No! She didn't want me to come, told Kade to just take the ship by force and find the container they wanted. Honest, I didn't want to come! Staying far away from her is the best way to live a longer life."

Tanis stood and paced back and forth in front of him. She allowed her expression to soften somewhat and glanced at Thompson who didn't look the least bit convinced, though the look he cast her contained a small hint of appreciation. Good. She paused her pacing for a moment.

"And you didn't know what Rebecca had planned? The kidnapping or killing Kade?"

"No, I swear it!"

Tanis grunted and paced a few more times, then turned back to the poor man. "I may believe you, but I'm still having reservations. Some of the other guys," she jerked a thumb back at Thompson, "aren't as convinced. You better sweeten the pot with something substantial or they may decide that they're through with my soft talking."

Drind hung his head like a man who had given up hope for his life.

<*Oops, a bit too thick there,*> Angela said.

<*Just a smidge.*>

He was supposed to think *she* was his hope. Tanis crouched down in front of him and resisted the urge to cup his chin in her hand to raise his face up.

"Hey, they're not banging down the door yet. Why don't you tell me what you know and I'll keep you safe." Now she was going too far the other way, but this poor guy wasn't going to notice. She was out of practice, but keeping up her skill at interrogation wasn't on the top of her list of abilities to refine. "What was in the container that Padre's men took?"

Drind raised his head, a bit of hopefulness in his eyes. "I don't know, but it seemed pretty valuable. Not the 'racing hound' they told you it was; that much is for sure."

"Rebecca and Kade never talked about what it was?"

"I overheard an argument about it, and some of the other guys did too. They seemed to be arguing about what to do with it. A couple of times I swore Kade slipped and called it a 'her', but I wasn't listening too closely, that doesn't pay on the *Vertigo*."

"Is that where you're stationed? On the *Vertigo*?"

"Sometimes." Drind was starting to warm up now, hopeful that he could spill his guts and save his life. "I'm back at HQ a lot, too. Depends where they need me."

"Kade had an HQ?" Somehow, his appearance had caused Tanis to think of him as nothing but a guy with a few ships causing trouble.

"Of course, haven't you been there? I mean you're one of his ships."

"We aren't that scum's ship," Thompson growled.

Drind lowered his head closed his eyes—Tanis smiled inwardly. Thompson was playing along really well. Either that or it was just his natural disposition. It worked to her advantage though—it was best not to let Drind get too comfortable. If he did, he'd start thinking he could turn things to his advantage.

"Is that where Rebecca will take Sera? Back to HQ?" Tanis asked.

"Probably. The *Prowler* was at the rendezvous, too, lying dark out of scan range. I imagine she'll have them look for you while she goes back there."

"How many ships does The Mark have, anyway?" Tanis asked, wondering about additional complications.

"We'll, I'm not sure since he said this was his ship, too. Ships that I know he owns for sure…about four hundred; dozens of others that at least do regular business with him."

"And where is this HQ that Rebecca will be going back to?"

Drind didn't reply right away, but his eyes darted to Thompson's cold stare and flexing fists, then back to Tanis. She made her face look as open and trusting as possible.

"It's hidden really well. It's impossible to find."

"But you know where it is, right?" Tanis prompted him.

"Sure, I know the coordinates. It's actually not too far from here."

"What's the name of the system?" Tanis asked.

"Oh, it's not in any system," Drind spoke as if he was afraid unseen enemies would kill him. "It's in the dark layer."

Tanis managed to get the coordinates to the station after that, but Drind warned her that there were sensors and defensive turrets in both the DL and real space. She concluded the interrogation shortly after, with the promise that she would see about getting Drind more comfortable quarters.

The crew met in the galley again, their faces somber as they pondered the implications of this information.

"How do they even dock in the DL?" Thompson broke the silence.

"Very carefully, I'd bet," Cheeky said with noticeable appreciation in her voice.

The dark layer was just that, very dark. Nothing emitted light at all. It made the interstellar void look like a sunny afternoon. The only natural emissions of any sort were gravitational waves, which was how ships knew when to drop out of the DL and back into real space. Ships could emit light, but the gravitational waves dispersed that light very quickly.

<*Perhaps they have their station anchored to some dark matter,*> Sabrina offered, much calmer now that she knew where Sera was. <*Then they could latch onto ships and pull them in.*>

"Even if we believe him that this HQ of his is in the dark layer, and even if we find out that there is a back door, what are we going to do? Just march in there and demand Sera back?" Nance asked.

"We still have Plan B," Thompson looked at Tanis.

"Why don't we move our friend Drind to some better quarters and see if we can't convince him to start spilling specifics about this place?" Tanis said, ignoring Thompson. "Once we're better informed, we should be able to determine if his story is bunk. While we're at it, we may as well start plotting a course toward the general vicinity of the place, in case we do decide to all turn kamikaze."

"Do we have that kind of time?" Thompson asked, his face turning red. "They could be killing Sera right now while we sit around and debate what to do."

"Their base is some ways out into interstellar space on the core-ward side of the Silstrand Alliance." Cheeky provided a holo showing its relative position. "It'll take them a while to get there."

"Which is great if she's still alive, not so great if she's already dead," Nance said.

"She's still alive," Flaherty said flatly.

"How do you know that?" Cargo asked.

"Just listen to Tanis! She's our best bet to get Sera back," Flaherty growled at the rest of the crew.

No one knew what to say in response and Tanis looked into the stoic man's eyes for a long moment. His connection with Sera had to be older than their time on this ship. He owed her something, had some deep obligation to her.

<*Curiouser and curiouser,*> she said to Angela.

THE BEST LAID PLANS

STELLAR DATE: 07.13.8927 (Adjusted Years)
LOCATION: The Mark's Dark Layer Station
REGION: Unclaimed Interstellar Space, Core-Ward of Silstrand Alliance

Sera returned to consciousness in fits and starts. Her head felt like it had spent some time in the fusion reaction chamber…or a week on the bottle. Rather than alert anyone nearby to her conscious state, she kept her eyes closed and took mental stock of her surroundings and where her body lay.

First discovery made: she was lying down. Whatever she was on was padded, at least a little. She could hear the soft sound of air circulation, but no reactor or engine noise. She was either on a station or planet-side. Sera curled her fingers and then her toes. No apparent spinal damage, extremities seemed okay. Next, she tried to lift her arms and found she couldn't.

Tugging gently, Sera determined she was strapped down. Testing various points, she determined that every part of her was thoroughly restrained. Not tightly, but very firmly. Nothing seemed to be holding her head down. Sera rotated her neck left and right with no problem other than increased throbbing between her ears. Shifting in her bonds also confirmed a previous suspicion: she was completely naked.

<*How do I get into these situations?*> Sera asked.

<*The root of it is probably not taking your father's advice,*> Helen replied.

Sera responded by having her avatar stick her tongue out at Helen's ephemeral mental figure.

<*Ironically, we're finally where all this was supposed to lead,*> Sera observed.

<*I did notice that myself. Years of work and all you had to do was lose important cargo to get to The Mark's HQ.*>

<*I'm going to make a note of that for the next time I decide to infiltrate a pirate's lair,*> Sera said with a chuckle.

<*Well, I wouldn't call this 'infiltration',*> Helen laughed.

<*True, there is the pesky 'being strapped to a table' issue, plus the upcoming torture to deal with,*> Sera admitted.

<*Have you been able to get any nano out for a look-see?*>

<*I've tried, but there's a very strong ES field that keeps frying them.*>

She could tell that the room she was in wasn't too bright or she'd see the light through her eyelids. Cracking them, Sera recognized her surroundings as a medical bay.

It seemed standard, if somewhat archaic. There were actually scalpels and other cutting tools here. Sera made a mental correction. Either she was in the medical bay of a sadistic doctor, or one that doubled as a torture facility. Or maybe the medical bay of a sadist doctor that also did the torture. None were promising prospects.

The things she had been trying not to think of raced through Sera's mind. Where was *Sabrina*? Was her crew okay? Did they have Tanis? Only by pure force of will, and the knowledge she had gotten out of equally sticky situations, did Sera manage to calm herself.

Though the lighting was dim, she could tell by the structure of the walls, deck, and ceiling that this was a station of some sort—roomier than a ship, but not as liberal with space as a planetary facility. As she surveyed her surroundings, the door opened and Rebecca entered. Why was Sera not surprised?

Her captor wore a hazsuit with the helmet off. Sera had a flash of jealousy for how the tight suit showed off what was an amazing figure. Lower g certainly was kind to large-breasted women.

"What's with the suit Rebecca? Scared of little ol' me?"

Rebecca's smile was anything but pleasant. "Sensibly cautious. You'd be surprised at how many twitchy freighter captains put little surprises in their blood for people who start cutting into them. I've learned to be cautious."

Sera cursed herself. That would have been a great idea. Why had she never thought of it? "So what's the drill here? You ask questions, I pretend I don't even know what year it is, you use some of your tools, get no further, and then we call it a day? I'll tell you what. I'll save you the trouble. I don't know squat, go away."

"Don't you want to know about your crew?" Rebecca asked. "You'll surely want to know what I've already done to them."

Sera didn't fall for it. While she respected their courage and skill, she knew that at least one or two of them would have cracked under the type of questioning Rebecca was sure to use. If her crew had been captured, Rebecca would already know that 'Rachel' was the missing cargo, and Tanis would be the one strapped to the table.

Not that she was going to let Rebecca in on that reasoning. She struggled in her bonds. "What have you done to them?"

"Nothing permanent…yet." She let the word hang in the silence between them.

"Look, we don't have that stupid container. You've got Kade's organization now, what more do you want from me?"

Rebecca smiled again, this time it was more predatory. "I really must thank you for that; this really did work to my advantage. I managed to get Kade out of the way, *and* pin it on you and your crew. With all the other senior captains away on raids, I get to solidify my position. I couldn't have asked for a better turn of events."

Sera groaned inwardly. Was this woman going to gloat all day or just get on with the torture?

Rebecca continued unabated. "But that stupid container, as you call it, is worth more than all of this," the obligatory hand wave indicated her surroundings. "You are going to tell me where it is. That much is certain."

"If Padre has it, how am I going to tell you were it is?"

"We won't worry about that today. Today I'm just going to get to know you a bit better." Rebecca walked leisurely toward a cart with some of the more barbaric instruments on it. "If one is careful, one can put quite a few holes in a human being and neither cause them to die, nor even fall unconscious. Let's see how many we can make in you."

Sera gritted her teeth and prayed to whatever gods were listening for strength. Her prayers were granted. She had the strength to both scream and cry at the same time for hours.

OF MICE AND MEN

STELLAR DATE: 07.14.8927 (Adjusted Years)
LOCATION: *Sabrina*, Interstellar Dark Layer
REGION: Silstrand Alliance Space, Core-Ward of Silstrand Prime

"There's some disbelief regarding your statement that your HQ is in the DL," Tanis said as she sat with Drind in the cramped cabin they had given him. She had been working on earning his trust over the intervening days and was now cross-checking his earlier intel. "Since there is nothing to react against in the DL, there is no way to maneuver. How do you dock?"

Drind couldn't help smiling. "It's genius really. One of Kade's engineers just happened to spot this relatively small blob of dark matter that isn't moving, well not much. He did some testing and found that with the right force, a gravity drive can tether to the dark matter and anchor the station. They use gravity fields to pull ships in for docking. There's a probe in regular space that has the current coordinates of the HQ and ships simply transition to the DL at that point with zero relative motion."

Tanis mulled it over. That aligned with what Sabrina and Cheeky had suspected.

"So, how do you suggest that we drop in to make our rescue run?"

Drind's face drained of color. "You can't do that! HQ is impregnable." He looked around as if he could determine the ship's course or maybe some way off it. "You can let me out next stop if that's your plan. I may be somewhat grateful for you getting me out of that mess. But not that grateful."

"You don't really think we'd abandon Sera, do you?" she asked.

"You won't be abandoning her; she's already dead."

Tanis had considered it—heck, everyone on the ship had. The consensus was that, although she may be a bit worse for wear, Sera's knowledge was simply far too valuable to kill her. If Tanis was free, Sera was alive.

"She's not dead," Tanis said.

Drind wasn't dumb. Tanis had noticed that during her first encounter with him, as he looked over her scan logs on the bridge. Something seemed to click in his mind and he suddenly sat back on the bunk.

"It's you."

"It's me what?" Tanis asked, feigning confusion.

"You're what Kade was looking for. You're what was in that container."

"I have to admit, I'm impressed," Tanis nodded. "How did you figure it out?"

"Well, it wasn't a dog, that much was obvious. But this ship doesn't have the ability to tell a dog's bio signature from a human's when in cryostasis, so unless they popped it open, the fiction would have held." He looked puzzled for a moment. "Why did they open it?"

Tanis smiled. "They got away at Trio without being boarded, and were interested in knowing what they'd risked their lives for."

Drind looked amazed. "They actually escaped Padre's guys in Trio? How much of the scan was faked?"

"Not much, just the part where the ship decelerated after the RM was fired. In reality, they twitched at the last moment and made it to FTL with half a second to spare."

"Holy shit," Drind whistled. "That captain Sera has quite the pair."

"I'm told it was one heck of a ride."

"I'm beginning to understand part of why they want to rescue her," he snorted. "Not that I think it's sane. Why are you in on this, anyway?"

"She saved me, I owe her the favor. Besides, Sera seems like a decent sort."

Tanis finished the statement as Cargo opened the door to the room.

"Don't let her hear you say that," he said. "It would ruin the fiction she likes to portray." Drind noticeably pulled away, sidling against the bulkhead. The reaction appeared to annoy Cargo. "Would you cut that out, I'm not going to hurt you."

Their reluctant castoff straightened. A bit.

"So what's it going to be? Going to tell us what you know or do we ship you somewhere in cryo so you can't rat us out?"

"That's a shitty choice," Drind muttered.

"Better than sticking you in the middle of this if you don't want to be."

Drind looked as if he had an acerbic reply ready, but he bit it back. Cargo had a point.

"Isn't there anything you can think of that would help us?" Tanis asked. "We've been more than kind to you, and we'll be taking down Rebecca, or at least taking her down a notch."

"You'd better take her all the way down," Drind looked deadly serious. "If you don't, there will be no safe place for you this side of Sol."

"There's still the bounty on Kade that every system for ten parsecs is offering. We could get that money and arm up to take them down," Cargo said.

"It would take a lot more money than that," Drind said. "You'd still need some way to get in. Missiles may not work well in the DL, but HQ has a reactor that can keep its lasers slicing and dicing for hours."

Tanis snapped her fingers. "That's it. We need an army and an in. We'll get both." She turned to Cargo. "We need to set a course for the closest star system that has a stable government." She wasn't sure if stability was the norm here or not, but it didn't hurt to be specific.

She turned to Drind. "Kade must have had ships that were not generally known to be his, that dock both at system stations and at his HQ."

He nodded. "There are a few."

"Do you know their normal ports of call?"

"Not even remotely. Information like that wasn't exactly bandied about."

Tanis kept thinking aloud. "What about places where his pirate ships would frequently be lying in wait?"

Drind was silent for a moment as he though. "It is pretty common for a ship to hang in the outskirts of the Big OJ looking for traders stopping through for fueling."

"Big OJ?"

"Oh, Gedri. The crews back at HQ call it the Big OJ…it's a really damn orange star."

"What's with all the traffic there?" Tanis asked.

"Like he said," Cargo gestured at Drind, "the system is rife with helium for fusion, and there are a few outfits that have antimatter production sites. A lot of ships running low will coast into the system with their engines off."

"Yeah, some will coast in from a fair ways out. Makes for good pickings," Drind added.

Tanis had a few questions about that but didn't want to voice them in front of Drind; it may give away her lack of knowledge regarding the ninth millennium. They thanked Drind for his time and left his cabin for the galley where the rest of the crew had gathered as they watched the conversation.

"Why do ships drop out of the DL and coast in? Wouldn't it be better to stay shifted to get in faster and safer?" Tanis asked.

"Takes power to stay shifted in the DL. People often will drop out early and coast into a system to save money," Cheeky replied with a shrug.

"I guess that makes sense. Sounds like we've got the makings of a plan," Tanis said while pouring a cup of coffee. "We coast into the Big OJ and wait to get paid a visit from one of The Mark's pirate ships. We take their ship and hop on back to the ol' HQ where we get Sera back."

Cargo shook his head. "Us and what army?"

"Sounds like a good way to get ourselves killed," Thompson added.

Tanis smiled. "I've been doing a bit of research on the ninth millennium. Sera said things were different, but I really didn't expect so much to be lost. She was right about FTL spelling the end of human advancement," Tanis said and held out her right arm and pulled back her sleeve.

What looked like skin changed its appearance to metallic silver, the effect racing all the way down her arm. She quickly downed her coffee and held the cup by its side.

To everyone's astonishment the cup dissolved into the palm of her right hand and a blue light emitted from her right forearm. Tanis held her left hand out to catch the object materializing there. It was a small ceramic handgun. Tanis put it down on the galley table while everyone stared open mouthed.

"I guess you don't see nano like this much these days."

Cargo looked Tanis up and down and then glanced at Nance. "She is human, right?"

"She was back when she was on the med slab." Nance hadn't taken her eyes from Tanis. "Though we could tell she had some pretty advanced tech in her."

"Unless we're gonna take out a pirate ship with ceramic pistols, you'd better have some better tricks up your sleeve…figuratively speaking," Cargo said. "Have you ever been in a battle for your life?"

"I didn't get my rank sitting on my duff."

Tanis's statement was met with blank stares.

"I'm a TSF major, remember?"

"That doesn't really mean a lot to us," Nance said with a shrug. "A lot of military types get promoted without ever seeing combat."

"Yes, I've seen combat," Tanis sighed. "I've fought planet-side, station-side and ship to ship. I've put a lot of holes in a lot of people. Satisfied?" If they only knew what she had done to get this far.

"Great, you can shoot people," Thompson said. "Is that the extent of your plan for saving Sera?"

"Well, I obviously can't take on a pirate ship by myself, and, since we need it intact, we have to board it, or be boarded by them. I'd prefer to be on the side doing the boarding. First thing we need to do is get some big guns or at least some raw materials so we can make some big guns. What's the closest port of call?"

Thompson stood up and looked them all over. "This is total bullshit. You guys can take orders from her; I'm going to go clean up the mess one of those containers made when it got shot."

No one said anything for a minute after he left and then Cargo shrugged. "Cheeky, what's nearest?"

She looked at him and then shrugged as well. "Closest system is Silstrand. They've got a number of stations insystem we can dock at. There's an independent mining platform out in their EK belt that has an arms dealer or two on it. How we paying for these guns anyway?"

Tanis smiled. "I'm betting I have some nano that could be worth a bit."

* * * * *

Rebecca was no slouch—a real pro when it came to making people suffer.

Sera hurt in places she didn't even know could hurt. She desperately wished she could escape her body. She'd heard of out of body experiences; maybe she could have one if she tried hard enough.

Rebecca had asked very few questions while she did her work. She said she just wanted to get to know Sera's body a bit better. Needles seemed to be her specialty. Rebecca had them in varying sizes and could put a truly astounding number of them into a person's flesh. One had started out the size of a sliver and grew to well over a centimeter in diameter. Rebecca had put that one through a lot of things.

After Rebecca had her fill and left, a med team came in and cleaned Sera up. They didn't make anything hurt less, more actually, as they cauterized the wounds to staunch the bleeding and put her on an IV to replenish the fluids she'd lost.

Sera supposed it was one way to pass the day.

A better way was working on her escape. While Rebecca had been busy at her trade, Sera had been busy at hers—namely plotting Rebecca's death. During the session, Sera had managed to pull a needle from her own thigh and slip it past her palm into her wrist where the strap held her arm down. Now that she was alone, she slipped the needle from her skin and began worrying its tip along the strap.

While under Rebecca's not-so-tender ministrations, Sera had learned why there was no strap holding her head down: her torturer liked it when Sera pulled her head up or tilted it back to let out a really good scream. It worked to her advantage now as she twisted to see the needle tip doing its work. The strap seemed to be of the same material as a safety harness; there was a section where it had been sewn together and that was what she focused on.

The material held up well and Sera found progress to be slow. She walked a careful balance between not moving enough to lose her grip on the needle and have it fling across the room, but still fast enough to get free before another session with Madam Pain.

The hours ticked by as she picked at the stitches. One by one, they came free and Sera allowed herself to feel a glimmer of hope. Then, with a snap that did send the needle flying, the strap gave way. Sera didn't move, but waited to see if the sudden twitch of her arm had been noticed by whoever may or may not be watching the cameras. After several minutes, nothing happened and Sera forced her breathing to slow.

Without any quick movements, she slid her right arm across her body and undid the strap across her chest and from her left wrist. Then, with great care, she slowly shifted her hand back to her right side and slipped it into the loop of the strap.

Sera tried to put her mind at rest. She was tired and had lost a lot of blood. Her best bet would be to get a good night's sleep and use the first advantage that came her way tomorrow. She had no illusions about trying to use a med tech as a hostage; Rebecca would gun her own people down in a heartbeat. She needed to get the queen bitch herself if she wanted to get out of here alive.

SILSTRAND

STELLAR DATE: 07.15.8927 (Adjusted Years)
LOCATION: *Sabrina*, Silstrand Scattered Disk
REGION: Silstrand System, Silstrand Alliance Space

Silstrand was a heavily settled system, boasting fourteen major planets, six of them being rocky worlds rich with minerals. Methane and hydrogen mining facilities hovered around three of the gas giants. Stellar traffic was heavy, and an AI operating a beacon demanded *Sabrina*'s identification and their port of call within half an hour of dropping out of FTL.

Tanis was on comm and relayed that they were bound for the PeterSil EK mining platform. Stellar control informed them that the PS EK platform was currently on the far side of the system from *Sabrina's* current position. They were given a deceleration vector and told to send a message to the PS EK platform informing them of their incoming vector and time of arrival.

"Bossy sorts here," Tanis muttered as she passed the plot to Cheeky's console and sent the required message to the mining platform.

Cheeky heard her comment and smiled. "Yeah, but the men really like a stern woman. Good times to be had at the main trading station off the fourth gas giant."

"Been through here often?" Tanis asked. The whole idea of interstellar trade by small freighters was still very fascinating to her.

"A few times. Some on *Sabrina,* some on other ships I've piloted. They have three TPs that have amazing diversity and some great pleasure resorts."

"TPs?"

"Means terraformed or terrestrial planets," Cargo supplied from the command chair. "FGT had a ball with this place. It already had one planet in the habitable zone, so while they got it all watered up and ready for life they decided to hang out and make antimatter.

"That was around when gravity tech had improved and AP drives became the rage. They built a massive particle accelerator to produce the antimatter and then left it here. It's still going strong, a good four thousand years later.

"I guess their tug pilots got bored while everyone else had something to do, so they hauled another planet into the habitable zone and then did something to one of the big gassies in the outer system to heat it up. Thing is just about a brown dwarf now. One of the other gassies had a slightly sub-terra sized moon around it, so they hauled it over to their toasty gas giant and set it in orbit."

Tanis laughed. "Toasty gassie? I bet a thousand astronomers cringe every time you talk."

Cargo chuckled. "I'd consider that a compliment."

"Did they leave messages behind so we know what they did?" Tanis asked.

"The astronomers?"

"No, the FGT," Tanis replied seriously before realizing that Cargo was joking.

He chuckled before replying. "Sometimes. There has been contact with them here and there. If you can believe it, some of them still have their original crews."

"You're kidding."

"Nope, some of those people left Earth over six thousand years ago and they're still out there making worlds."

Tanis had heard that was the case in the forty-second century, as well—even then it had seemed far-fetched. She had always suspected that it was some sort of FTG propaganda.

"They can't have lived that long by stasis alone. They have to be doing something else; it still takes hundreds of years to terraform a world," Tanis said with a frown.

"Your guess is as good as anyone else's. After the *Oregon* incident, they don't have much to do with the rest of humanity anymore," Cargo replied

"What happened there?"

"Everyone believes that the FGT has tech everyone else has only dreamed of—kinda like you. It's said they have the power to move stars," Cheeky said from the pilot's chair. "It was only a matter of time before someone decided to take a fleet around hunting for them. They found a worldship, the *Oregon*, terraforming a system, and tried to take it by force. Things didn't go as planned and the *Oregon* was destroyed. Some of their smaller ships got away and word spread amongst the FGT. No one has had direct contact with them in millennia now."

"They're still out there though, right?" Tanis really hoped they were, she was counting on getting in touch with them to secure a new colony world.

"Yeah," Cargo's voice was low and serious. "Sometimes people stumble upon a terraformed world that's just waiting to be discovered. Sometimes certain systems get messages about a new world they can expand to. There are even rumors that the FGT has agents scattered throughout space, shaping the course of humanity."

Tanis stared at Cargo, attempting to keep a straight face. She covered her mouth, her eyes sparkling. "You could host a cast on evil government plots," she began to laugh.

Cheeky joined in the laughter. "So dark and mysterious."

Cargo shrugged. "Mock me if you want, but there are a lot of people who suspect it."

Tanis looked over the system on the main holo tank. God complexes and guiding humanity aside, the FGT did amazing work. The Silstrand system gleamed off their port side as they passed over the stellar plane. Stations and stellar transports could be seen, reflecting their star's light in the dark. The twinkle of fusion drives sparkled near one of the rocky inner planets, indicating heavy mining.

The TPs, as Cargo called them, were near each other and *Sabrina* passed within half an AU of each. They were sparking blue-green on the unmagnified screen. Under magnification they showed to be amazing planets, both sporting several elevators connected to planetary rings.

"Silstrand seems to do pretty well for itself," Tanis observed.

"It's the seat of the Silstrand Alliance's government," Cargo supplied. "They control most of this star cluster."

"They a friendly sort?"

"Democracy of sorts. Big on trade, though, so freighters are never turned away."

Tanis asked a few questions about the types of governments found across the stars as *Sabrina* shed velocity across the system. She could read about them in the databases, but Cargo had an interesting viewpoint to share on each.

He told tales of dictatorships, kingdoms, democracies, and oligarchies for hours. Eventually, shift changed and Tanis reluctantly begged off the conversation to get some sleep. Tomorrow they would dock at the mining platform and she'd have a show to put on for a merchant or two.

RESIGNATION

STELLAR DATE: 07.15.8927 (Adjusted Years)
LOCATION: ISS *Andromeda,* 0.5LY Rim-Ward of Bollam's World
REGION: Bollam's World Federation Space

Joe paced across the *Andromeda's* main hangar bay where pieces of wreckage were being sorted. It had taken over a month to find the debris field from the *Intrepid's* collision with what turned out to be little more than a pebble, and several months more to collect all the pieces.

They were now laid out in a pattern matching their original location on the *Intrepid*.

Joe was amazed at how much damage the impact had done to the colony ship. Over two hundred meters of hull had been torn up by the impact, seven decks vented atmosphere, and one stasis chamber was destroyed.

And Tanis was lost.

He watched as the crew pulled the pieces off the last hauler. The pickings were getting slim and Joe didn't think they would find much more out there. Pieces of a lift were unloaded, followed by several chunks of bulkhead and a door.

Nothing that looked as though it came from an escape pod.

The ship's records showed Tanis making it to a pod and ejecting. As luck would have it, no other pods were damaged or ejected in the impact. That meant there was only one pod out there, and so far, no debris from a pod had been found.

It meant Tanis was alive.

The last pieces of ship were deposited on the deck and tagged. The technicians organizing the wreckage concurred that none of it was from an escape pod and Joe sighed with relief. He could finally report that Tanis was not here.

Not that Joe expected her to be. Tanis had survived too much to be killed by a pebble. Even if that pebble had been travelling at relativistic speeds.

<*Corsia,*> Joe contacted the *Andromeda*'s AI. <*Send a message to the* Intrepid. *There is no sign of Tanis or her pod. I want permission to go insystem and see if I can find out what happened to her.*>

<*I'm on it, Joe.*>

He had known from the beginning that Tanis was not in the debris field, but with no signal from her pod, everyone assumed she was dead—her pod destroyed. So, he worked to rule that possibility out as quickly as possible.

Now there was no reason not to search for her in the neighboring star system.

That was going to be easier said than done. In the months since the collision, they had gathered intel from listening to broadcasts and data streams from the system they now knew to be 58 Eridani. The crew of the *Intrepid* knew they were in the ninetieth century, and it was nothing like what they would have expected.

Joe took his time going back to the bridge. The *Intrepid* was two light-hours away, and a response to his request would take some time. He was fairly certain he knew what all the various directors and secretaries would say. Abby would vote to leave Tanis, Earnest would likely abstain, Ouri and Brandt would vote to continue the search. Sanderson liked Tanis, but he would vote not to risk the ship to find her. The captain was a mystery; he would need to think of the ship first—it all depended on whether or not he thought Tanis was necessary for the ship's safety.

"Think it was the last haul?"

Joe turned to see Jessica walking toward him from the direction of the hangar.

"If I have my way it is. There's nothing bigger than dust left out there. It's time to stop wasting our time out here."

"Do you think she's in the Bollam's system?" Jessica asked after catching up with Joe.

Joe shook his head. "I don't know...but it's the best place to start. There was that strange ion trail near the pod's most likely trajectory. It could be that she was rescued."

"Or kidnapped. You know what Sanderson thinks."

"He's not the only one—it's pretty clear that we have vastly superior tech than pretty much everyone now."

"You think someone has her?" Jessica asked, her voice strained with worry.

Joe nodded. "I refuse to believe she's dead; if she were OK, she'd get in touch with us somehow. No, she is being held somewhere and getting into that system and checking their scan records is the first step."

Jessica took his hand. "I want you to know I'm with you. If we have to steal a pinnace, or even the whole damn *Intrepid,* we'll go find her."

Joe clasped his hands around hers, taking a moment to calm his emotions. "I know she means a lot to you, too. Your support means a lot."

"She gave me a chance when...she's my best friend, Joe," Jessica said with a tear slipping down her face. "I'm ready to kick ass clear across the galaxy if I have to."

"You're a true friend, Jessica." Joe embraced the lavender-skinned woman, thankful that she had come along on the *Andromeda.*

Four hours later, the response came in from Captain Andrews.

"I'm authorizing an excursion into Bollam's to gather intel and hunt for Tanis," the captain's face was sober; he seemed to have aged years over the past few months. "But Joe, I need you back here. We have to protect the *Intrepid* and you're second in fleet command right now. I'm sending Jessica to look for her. We'll talk more when you get back."

The *Andromeda's* bridge fell silent. The anger flowing from Joe was palpable and tension radiated through the air as everyone did their best to look busy.

"Corsia," Joe said after a moment. "Tell Andrews that he has my resignation. I'll hitch a ride with Jessica."

Jessica rose from her station and approached Joe's chair.

"Joe, are you sure about this?" Jessica asked quietly, placing a hand on his shoulder.

He lowered his head and ran a hand through his hair. "You don't know what she means to me."

"I do know; how could I not know?" Jessica said softly. "I've been with you two for decades—and I know what it means to choose duty over your love's safety."

"That's just it, you don't know," Joe turned to look in her eyes, willing her to understand. "She's pregnant."

Shock registered across Jessica's face. "Tanis's...pregnant?"

Joe nodded. "She's held it internally in stasis for since before we got to The Kap—we were waiting to get to New Eden before carrying it to term."

"Corsia," Jessica addressed the ship's AI, while not breaking eye contact with Joe. "Have the duty chief prep the pinnace for two, Joe is coming along."

A SURREPTITIOUS ESCAPE

STELLAR DATE: 07.16.8927 (Adjusted Years)
LOCATION: The Mark's Dark Layer Station
REGION: Unclaimed Interstellar Space, Core-Ward of Silstrand

Sera woke to the sounds of a med tech entering the room. While she hadn't allowed herself to fall into a very deep sleep, she did feel better. The tech busied himself at a counter across the room, organizing something out of Sera's view. Eventually, he turned and Sera saw a large needle in his hand.

"What do you intend to do with that?" she asked.

<*Certainly not the time to get knocked out,*> Helen sounded worried.

The tech jumped at the sound of her voice. "Um…I was going to give you this."

"I don't think so. I've had enough stuff stuck in me; I can do with one less needle, thanks."

The med-tech had a furtive look on his face as he glanced around. "It's for the pain, it'll make it better."

So that was it. Someone with a conscience couldn't sleep at night while Rebecca did her thing. So rather than really helping her, he planned to ease his personal concern a bit.

<*He could be a genuinely good guy,*> Helen said.

<*A genuinely good guy would be loosening these straps. This guy just doesn't want to hear me scream,*> Sera replied sourly.

"Thanks but no thanks. If you really wanted to help, you'd get me out of here."

"I would, but it's impossible. There's no way out of this place."

"Well, thanks for the un-help, but like I said, I'm all done being stuck with things."

"But it will make you feel better." His face crinkled in confusion. "She won't notice if you make sure to scream."

"I don't know if this is her plan or your independent idea, but that shot will cloud my mind and I may just give in to her. She's not torturing me just for fun, you know," Sera paused. "Though, I wouldn't put it past her to do that."

The man looked undecided and Sera gave him the sternest look she could muster. "Go away. I don't want your pseudo help and if you don't have the guts to do something constructive then I don't have time for you."

The med-tech seemed somewhat disturbed that he was being given orders by a woman strapped to a table—or at least a woman who appeared to be strapped to a table.

"Just go before she gets here," Sera sighed.

Without a word, the man returned to the counter where he had prepared the syringe. He emptied its contents, threw it in the disposal, and walked to the door. Before exiting, he gave Sera a long look and then slipped out.

<You know, you could have convinced him to help you,> Helen said. *<Your plan isn't so good that it's foolproof.>*

<It's close enough. I can take Rebecca with one hand tied behind my back.>

<Or your legs to the table, as it turns out.>

Rebecca came in less than a minute later, and Sera was surprised her torturer hadn't spotted the med-tech.

"Good morning, sunshine," Rebecca said with a smile. "I trust you slept uncomfortably?"

Sera didn't respond and just glared, willing Rebecca to step closer while she went on in standard torturer speak about how pleasant mutilating Sera would be. She wore her hazsuit but hadn't put on the mask yet.

Just a little closer.

Sera got her wish as Rebecca stepped right beside the table to admire her handiwork. She had just started a smart remark about how Sera's legs looked good covered in crusted, puss-filled holes when her words stopped with a strangled gasp.

Sera gripped Rebecca's throat with all her strength, and the other woman grasped at her arm, nails clawing at Sera's skin. She sat up and added her other hand, desperate not to be dislodged.

Rebecca appeared to gain a measure of control and her eyes narrowed a moment before she swung a fist into the side of Sera's head. She let out a grunt, but wasn't going to let this bitch get the better of her. Instead, she slammed the heel of her hand straight into Rebecca's face.

In hindsight, Sera considered that the move was perhaps a mistake. Blood poured from Rebecca's nose and her grip on the woman's neck slipped as the hot fluid ran over her hands. Sera dug her fingernails deep into the Rebecca's skin to maintain her hold.

Rebecca hit Sera twice more, and then began to try to push herself away from the table, to which Sera's legs were still strapped. Sera had enough; she shifted to the side, put her left hand on the back of Rebecca's head and slammed it down into the corner of the table. Her torturer fell to the ground unconscious.

<Told you I could take her,> Sera said to her AI.

<Hey, I was cheering for you the whole time, Didn't you hear me?>

<Not so much. I was busy, if you recall.>

Sera loosened the straps holding her thighs and ankles. She slid off the slab and hefted Rebecca's limp form onto the table. Blood gushed from the cut across her forehead and Sera ignored it. She quickly stripped off Rebecca's hazsuit and strapped her former captor in her place. The right wrist strap was useless, so Sera tied Rebecca's hands behind her back and then strapped her chest down tight to prevent any wriggle room.

With luck, no one paid too much attention to surveillance on this room while Rebecca was at work. Kade had been an ass, but she was certain that most of the people in his organization weren't psychopaths like Rebecca. Just because a person was a pirate didn't mean they were inhuman.

Once Rebecca was secure, Sera slapped her former captor several times until the other woman started making noises that somewhat resembled a return to consciousness.

"Wakey wakey."

Rebecca snapped awake at that and struggled mightily, desperate to free herself.

"What the hell!" she yelled.

"Stop!" Sera ordered. "One peep above a whisper and this nice big needle I am pricking into the underside of your jaw will make a quick visit to your brain. Follow?"

Rebecca whispered yes, almost meekly, but her eyes held pure hatred.

"I was going to use you as a hostage to get myself out of here, but it occurred to me that you may not be that well liked, and your people may happily shoot us both. I also doubt you'll believe me when I say that if you let me go I'll let you live because…well, I wouldn't," Sera smiled with no small dose of malice. "So, to keep up with appearances, I'm going to work you over a bit so that you aren't immediately recognizable, finish you off, and then I think I'll strike off on my own."

<*Is that absolutely necessary? I can fake the video feeds,*> Helen said.

<*I want her to stand up to cursory scrutiny if anyone comes in to patch me—her up again.*>

Rebecca's face clouded and she appeared to be preparing an unpleasant response, but then thought better. She cringed as Sera held up the needle that had been under her chin and said, "You can make noise now." Right before she drove it through Rebecca's thigh.

Rebecca appeared to be one of those torturers who enjoyed giving pain but not receiving it. There were some that liked it both ways, but from the pitiful shrieking that ensued, such was not the case here. Sera had planted a few good-sized spikes in various places on Rebecca's body, and was about to drive the final one into her heart, when she found her hand unwilling to complete the downward arc.

There had been a time in Sera's life when taking another human life, in the heat of battle, or with calm precision hadn't been a problem. But she was supposed to have moved on from that. *Sabrina* was supposed to be her haven, her place of redemption. A dark thought passed through her mind: she wasn't on *Sabrina*; no one had to know what happened next.

It took Sera several minutes to make up her mind, and Rebecca watched that wavering spike with a singular focus. When it finally dropped, she let out a hoarse laugh.

"I knew you didn't have it in you."

"Apparently not anymore," Sera nodded. "Something we both should be grateful for."

<*I'm proud of you,*> Helen said softly.

"When I get out of here…" Rebecca began the standard threat.

"Oh stuff it." Sera smashed a fist into the other woman's face; then followed it with a few more blows. Rebecca was knocked unconscious again from the fury of Sera's strikes. She then spent several minutes making superficial cuts on Rebecca's body to match those she bore.

<*There. Unless one of the meds paid careful attention to how she messed me up yesterday, this should do,*> Sera said while reviewing her work.

<*Ok, I'm a bit less proud of you….*>

Sera slipped into the hazsuit and sealed its hood shut before she exited the med-lab. The suit was covered in blood—which enhanced the disguise. When Rebecca had left yesterday's session, she had been covered with blood, too.

The hall was short but well lit. There were a few other doors along it and all bore markings that indicated they were also med bays. The hall ended in a T, and Sera strode toward the intersection with calm purpose, though she had no idea where she was going. She turned the corner and almost ran into the technician who tried to give her the shot earlier. He was muttering something about not letting that bitch torture people and finally doing something about it.

The look on his face when he saw whom he had nearly collided with was one of pure horror. It looked like the disguise was working.

She pushed on his shoulder to turn him around.

"My quarters, now."

He didn't question her and led her through the halls to Rebecca's rooms.

Sera was quite proud of how this escape was going so far. She'd definitely been through worse. The most difficult part was walking without limping. Her body was sending her strong reminders that someone in her condition really shouldn't be walking around.

<*Can you speed the healing up?*> Sera asked.

<*This is things being sped up. If you didn't have me guiding your bots, you wouldn't even be able to crawl right now,*> Helen replied with a motherly tone. <*I'm working them as fast as I can, but I'm not going to do a rush job putting you back together again.*>

As the terrified med tech led her through the halls, Sera's initial impression that she was on a space station was reinforced. It had all the hallmarks; exposed conduit for easy access and repair, sealable bulkheads, and no external windows. Well that was somewhat unusual, but not if they were in the bowels of a station.

Her disguise as a bloody Rebecca was working just fine. Everyone stayed out of her way as if she had the plague. Considering the reasons Rebecca wore the hazsuit while interrogating, she supposed plague may be just what people feared. Eventually, her guide led her into a much nicer-looking part of the station, with wider, carpeted corridors.

<*Who puts carpet in a pirate's space station?*> Sera shook her head.

<*Kade, it would seem,*> Helen responded with a chuckle.

The med-tech stopped in front of a door and looked over at her. Sera wondered if there was a security pass code on the door. Hopefully, even if there was, medics had override codes to get in if needed. She nodded for him to open it, and, shaking, he punched in a code and the door slid aside. She gestured for him to go in first.

The quarters were what she expected—luxurious in the extreme. Rebecca lived very nicely on the spoils of the business. Fabrics draped the walls, exotic woods and rare metals covered every surface. The bed was heaped with furs, and Sera was tempted to toss them on the floor, just to irk Rebecca.

<*Childish, but I wouldn't blame you,*> Helen commented.

Sera turned to her reluctant escort and pulled the hazsuit's helmet off.

"She's gotta have some weapons in here, help me find them."

The man fell back, his expression aghast. "You!"

"Yes, I'm here. She's strapped to a table in med."

"You got free!"

"You're quite observant. I'm very good at getting free. It's a survival trait."

"Did you kill her?"

Sera couldn't help but think that he certainly was morbid for a med-tech. "No, I don't do cold-blooded killing. But she's going to need some reconstructive surgery."

He nodded. "Oh."

"By the way," she extended her hand, "I'm Sera. You're?"

"Andy." He took a tentative step forward, shook her hand, and then pulled back. Sera didn't fault him; she was still covered in blood.

"So, you look for guns, I need to find something to wear. I can't stand her, but she has excellent taste in clothing."

While Andy rummaged around, Sera pulled open Rebecca's wardrobe, praying that there would be something in a nice, soft lambskin.

Sera was impressed. The wardrobe was probably larger than her cabin on *Sabrina,* and it contained hundreds of outfits hanging in several long rows. Nearly every style and fabric combination this side of Sol was represented.

As she walked through the rows of clothing, her eye was drawn to a section filled with black, shiny outfits. She recognized it as the same type of material Rebecca had worn on *Sabrina.*

Sera felt the fabric. It was rubbery, but slick and not tacky. It stretched nicely, and gleamed under the lights. She pulled one of the items off the rack and held it up to herself. It was a full suit that even had attached socks and gloves—covering its wearer from toe to neck.

<Practically speaking, it will work well to cover all your cuts and bruises, a little pressure on all those wounds wouldn't hurt either.>

<It does feel like I opened up a few on the walk over here.>

<More than a few. You're bleeding from a dozen places right now.>

"What the heck," Sera said aloud. "Kinky pirate mistress will probably help me blend in."

She grabbed a belt and a pair of boots before heading into the suite's bathroom. There, she peeled off the hazsuit, grimacing with pain as fresh scabs tore open.

"Crap, you were right, Helen. I look like shit."

<Yeah, you should take a quick shower and clean those deeper wounds.>

Sera didn't disagree. She stepped into the shower and let the water sluice away the blood and anger. Five minutes later, she stepped out, feeling ready to face the reason she had been trying to get onto this station for so long.

She dried off using fluffy cotton towels and then flipped the slinky suit over, looking for a zipper or fastening.

<I think you have to get in through the neck opening,> Helen supplied.

"Huh, I guess it is pretty stretchy," Sera said as she stepped into the suit. She pulled it up her body and pulled her arms inside, slipping them into the sleeves.

"Damn, this feels goooood," she said as the slick suit sensed a warm body and tightened around her, pushing out any stray pockets of air and outlining her body perfectly.

Sera turned in the mirror, admiring her gleaming black figure.

"Looks pretty damn good too," she said with a smile.

<I'm glad you're taking time for fashion,> Helen said with a wry smile in Sera's mind.

"What can I say, a girl's gotta—" Her words cut off as excruciating pain lanced across her skin. She screamed in agony as the feeling intensified, as though her skin were on fire underneath the suit.

She clawed at it, attempting to tear it off, but it had tightened around her to the point where she couldn't get a grip on it, nor pull it from her neck.

"Helen…help…" she managed to gasp before falling unconscious to the bathroom floor.

She woke several minutes later to find Andy hovering over her, concern filling his eyes.

<*You're OK,*> Helen said. <*You had an unfortunate incident with booby-trapped clothing.*>

<*I what?*> Helen's words didn't make any sense.

<*That suit you put on was keyed to Rebecca's DNA, when it detected that you were not her, it tried to kill you.*>

<*Seriously? She has her clothing set to kill?*>

<*So it would seem. It did a pretty good number on you before I managed to stop it.*>

Sera didn't feel much worse than before—almost better. She wondered how it had tried to kill her.

<*What did it do?*>

<*It tried to eat all your skin below the neck.*>

"WHAT?" Sera yelled and reached down, feeling her body. From what she could tell, nothing had changed; the suit still covered her, gleaming in the room's bright lights.

"Are you OK?" Andy asked. "You screamed and passed out, but moments later seemed fine. I linked with your internal system and it showed you had an allergic reaction to the material."

Sera ignored Andy's question. <*Helen, what do you mean it tried to eat my skin?*>

<*The suit, as it turns out was made of some sort of bio-polymer that bonds to the wearer's skin—from what I understand, it makes the skin hyper sensitive. Unfortunately, it's DNA keyed, so it reacts unkindly to unknown DNA.*>

Sera had heard of clothing like that, though never had the desire to own any.

<*I managed to stop it and alter it to bond to your DNA, but it then bonded directly to what was left of your skin.*>

Sera ran a hand down her leg and gasped. It was extremely sensitive, it also felt incredibly good. So that's why Rebecca had clothing made out of this material.

"I think I'm OK now," she said to Andy and stood.

<*Just so you know, you're stuck with this as your skin until I can get you into surgery.*>

<*Fantastic,*> Sera replied.

"Are you sure, you're OK," Andy asked. "That was a pretty strong reaction."

"My med package handled it, I actually feel pretty good now," Sera smiled. She did feel pretty good, but in a lot of pain at the same time, it was strange and rather distracting. Just when the escape was going so well.

<*Well, at least you don't have to worry about bleeding anymore,*> Helen said. <*It's rather impressive how quickly it linked up with your nerves. Rebecca spared no expense.*>

Sera struggled to her feet and Andy took her arm and guided her to Rebecca's bed. The feeling of his hand on her arm almost drove her mad, but she didn't pull away, she didn't want to. He brought her the boots and she pulled them on, they were a bit too big, but snugged up once she zipped them closed.

"I see you found her stash," Sera said, eyeing the dozen guns piled on a desk.

Andy nodded, finally taking his eyes from her body. "She had them all over. There's spare power cells, and ammunition for a few chemical slug throwers."

"Nice work," Sera said. She wasn't quite ready yet to get up again and admired the weapons from her place on the bed.

"Since my neck is now on the line, are you going to tell me how you got out of there?" Andy asked.

"Does it require much telling? I got free, beat the living piss out of Rebecca and tied her up. Now, there's something I need to get from this station, then I'm going to blow this place and get back to my ship."

"And that outfit's your disguise?"

Sera laughed. "I wasn't really planning to be disguised; I just think it looks good. You can't really see me kicking ass in a pantsuit, can you?

Andy raised an eyebrow.

"Hey. You're a medic, that's your thing. Looking hot and kicking ass, that's my thing."

<*I think this suit is affecting your brain chemistry, I'm going to adjust your serotonin levels,*> Helen laughed.

Andy shrugged. "OK, so what is your plan, then? Seduce all the guards between here and the docks and then get cozy with a captain?"

Sera grinned. "Do you think that will work?"

"No."

"Good, be a damn sad pirate organization if it did. First, I have to get to a secure terminal and look something up and go get it. Then I plan to shoot my way to the docks, hijack a ship, and get out of here."

"Suicide I am not in for. Have fun with that," Andy said and walked to the door. Sera was there in three strides, ignoring the fiery feeling in her muscles.

"Look you don't have to come; in fact, I'd prefer you don't. But I do want to say thank you."

Andy looked taken aback. "Umm…you're welcome. I'm sorry I didn't help you when you first asked."

"Rebecca's even sorrier," Sera said with a chuckle.

"I bet she is."

"Look, when I said 'blow this place', I was being literal. When the alarms and alerts start telling everyone to get off the station, do it. Don't wait around; I'm sure at least a few captains will take their ships and run."

"What are you planning to do?" Andy asked.

"I'm not sure yet, but I'll promise two things. It will be irreversible, and I'll give fair warning before it happens."

Andy nodded. "Thanks for the heads up, my days would have been numbered anyway once surveillance discovered you are free and I helped." He opened the door. "I'll be seeing you."

"Probably not. You lay low until you hear the alarms."

Andy left and Sera turned back to the pile of weapons. She pulled out a thigh holster and slipped it onto her left leg, then slid a small slug thrower into it. Several throwing knives went into the tops of each boot. She rummaged through a drawer and found several small remote cameras.

<*They up to spec?*> She asked Helen.

<*Close, ingest them and I'll have your nano upgrade them.*>

<*Ugh, I hate doing that.*> Sera grimaced as she swallowed the small probes.

<*Well, I can't exactly use your forearm assimilator at the moment; it's a bit covered up.*>

<*Can't you expose it?*> Sera asked.

<*You have no idea to what lengths I'm going to keep your fragile human body in one piece right now. Don't make it harder.*>

<*I dunno,*> Sera said as she felt the biopolymer that was her skin. <*This may be the best, worst thing that's ever happened to me.*>

<*You organics are so strange.*>

<*You say that, but I know AI are curious about how organics 'feel',*> Sera replied.

<*Curious like you are about how a cat balances with a tail. You don't really want to be a cat,*> Helen's tone carried no small hint of condescension.

<***Some*** *people want to be cats,*> Sera retorted. She hated it when Helen took on her teacher tone. Those days were long past.

Sera slid two holsters onto the belt she wore and pulled two bandoliers filled with ammunition over her shoulders.

<*Sorry,*> Sera said presently to Helen. <*I'm just worried about not screwing this up. This mission hasn't had the most auspicious beginning.*>

<*I'm sorry, too,*> Helen replied. <*This is important to me, as well. I'm just worried that this biopolymer is messing with your mental state too much; you can't think clearly when you're so aroused.*>

<*That's where you're mistaken, my dear.*> Sera smiled as hefted a large pulse rifle and slung it around her shoulder. <*The altered chemical and mental state is the goal, not a symptom; you should remember that. You get your big rushes, so to speak, from feats of mental prowess. Humans can get off on the mental stuff, too, but tactile stimulation brings its own thrill. When channeled into something productive, that stimulation can be a strength rather than a weakness.*>

Helen gave the AI's equivalent of a laugh. <*Are you saying that the secret behind Cheeky's exemplary piloting skill is that she's a nymphomaniac and always aroused?*>

<*That's exactly what I'm saying,*> Sera said as she strapped two more guns to her thighs. <*She's extended her sexual stimulus to include her piloting skill. People can train their sexual response to be triggered by anything.*>

<*I return to my earlier statement; organics are exceedingly weird. Do you have enough guns?*>

Sera shifted from foot to foot. She had to be wearing at least twenty kilograms of weaponry. She slipped back into the wardrobe and found a long black jacket that fell nearly to her ankles. After Helen made certain it wasn't DNA locked, she slipped it on, ensuring that she could leave it open while not revealing the full extent of her armament.

<*Yeah, I think it'll do. The probes ready?*>

<*Yup, open wide.*>

The four tiny probes flew out of Sera's mouth, one settling on an access port for the room's terminal.

<*It's possible that this connection is on the station's secure net, but I'm betting it's not if a med-tech has access to this room,*> Helen said.

The probe disappeared as it slipped into the access port and linked with the station's general computer net.

<*Yeah, looks like it's just standard access,*> Sera sighed. <*I've got access to their wireless net now, though.*>

<*Yes, the secure net is accessed elsewhere; however, I believe I can determine where we can get on it, based on the points where the nets link.*

The room's main holo activated, showing the layout of the station. Helen searched through access points, then made a noise of surprise.

<*Sera, this station is in the Dark Layer.*>

Sera stopped her investigation of the station's public net. <*Are you serious?*>

<*Would I joke about something like that?*>

<*How long has it been here?*> Sera asked in response.

<*It looks like at least ten years. How it's gone unnoticed that long is beyond me.*>

<*Well, we are a ways away from any stars. At least now we know how to destroy it.*>

<*That's true. I have what I believe is a point where I can access the secure net from a public terminal. It looks like it has a physical hookup that was routed incorrectly. I should be able to break past its security and find what we need to find.*>

Helen indicated the location on the holo she was displaying. Sera zoomed in and traced a path from Rebecca's quarters. It was two decks down and across a good quarter of the station.

"This'll be fun," Sera said with a smile.

Sera slipped out into the hall, heels snapping and long coat rustling.

<*Good luck, miss stealthy.*>

<*I don't have much chance of sneaking across this whole station. That's what this whole getup is about—looking like I belong and not to mess with me.*>

<*Clever plan, you are bright!*>

<*I blame my childhood teacher,*> Sera smirked.

<*Hey! I resent that.*>

<*So are you going to produce an opposite waveform or just mock me?*>

<*Just do a few quick twists and turns and I'll have all the squeaks and creaks mapped.*>

Sera obliged her AI and a moment later all sound from her movements ceased.

<*Not bad.*>

<*I've masked all your loud, tight leather for years; this isn't much of a challenge.*>

Sera slipped silently down the corridor and into the stairwell. The four probes ranged ahead and behind, keeping an eye on all surveillance equipment, sending signals to them, providing normal visual and audio feeds.

<*Did you see Tanis's matter assimilators, by the way?*> Sera asked her AI. <*I bet she has nano-cloud tech.*>

<*I suspect she does, the TSF did have that ability around her time.*>

<*Sure would be handy right about now,*> Sera sighed. <*Too bad they never shared it; these probes aren't that stealthy.*>

The stairs were narrow and Sera moved down them gracefully, peering over the rail to ensure the next landing was clear.

<*Shoot!*> Sera exclaimed suddenly. <*I forgot to grab grenades...keep an eye out for anything we can use to fashion some.*>

<*I thought your heightened senses honed your focus?*> Helen replied with a superior tone.

Sera didn't respond she continued down the stairs.

<*Looks like we're passing near the mess hall,*> Sera noted.

<*Have to, unless you want to skirt through the administrative section.*>

At the second landing, Sera cracked the hatch ever so slightly, allowing a probe to slip past the seal. Both she and Helen watched the visual feed, Sera accessing the infrared and ultraviolet ranges she normally excluded from her vision.

<*Looks like the corridor is clear, but there are a few people in the mess hall beyond.*>

<*We'll take that service corridor and go around the main mess.*>

Sera strode down the center of the corridor. No point in looking suspicious to anyone leaving the dining area. As she neared the opening to the hall, two men stepped out.

"Whoa, yeah," one exclaimed. "I know you're new, 'cause I'd remember a sweet looking thing like you!" His friend elbowed him, but the man continued, taking a step toward Sera. "That's one sexy getup. You're a randy little bitch, aren't you?"

<Holy shit, this guy is really living up to the stereotype, isn't he?> Sera commented to Helen.

She didn't want conflict, but no woman dressed as she was on a Mark station would take talk like this without a fight, or a tumble between the sheets.

Sera stepped toward him, exuding sexual energy. "I am a bit new here. Care to show me around?"

The man laughed and moved closer. "Hell yeah, we can start with my cabin."

When he moved into range, Sera reached out with her right hand and grabbed his hair. In the same fluid motion, she reached down with her left hand, and pulled a blade from the top of her right boot. She pushed him back against the wall, wrenching his head back and pressed the blade in her left hand against his neck.

She sneered and ground her hips into him. "I like it rough, and I've got six more of these little blades. I don't like to stop until each one has gotten a taste of blood. Where's your cabin?"

The man's friend was laughing so hard that he had a hand against the wall to steady himself.

"I…uhh…can't right now…I'm on shift soon," the first man stammered.

Smoothly, Sera stepped back and let go of him, a sultry pout on her lips. "Always work with you types. Oh well." She put the blade back into her boot and blew him a kiss. "I'll keep an eye out for you."

He reddened and all but ran down the hall. His friend followed, clutching his gut as he laughed.

<You certainly like to add to the risk. If you wore one of Rebecca's more conservative outfits, none of this would have happened.>

<Yeah, but then he may have mentioned he saw some new girl in a business suit. Now he's going to swear his friend to secrecy. At least secrecy till the next time his friend is drunk.>

They slipped into the service corridor without seeing anyone else. It was little more than a shaft, which ended at a hatch leading to a larger thoroughfare. The hatch stood open and Helen sent two probes through. There was mild foot traffic, but no troops or guards of any sort.

Sera stepped through and took a left. Some of the men and women eyed her with appreciation, some with wariness, but most just ignored her. There was no shortage of men and women wearing racier clothing than Sera's. She began to suspect that The Mark had a brothel on the station.

She took a right at the next intersection and then another left further down. The terminal she was looking for was in a vertical maintenance shaft off this corridor. The probes spied the shaft's access eight meters away and Sera approached it nonchalantly. The coast was clear, but as she neared the hatch, two guards rounded a corner and began walking toward her.

Sera muttered a curse to herself and kept walking past the hatch. She passed the guards and winked at them. They both smiled at her in response. When she neared the end of the corridor, the probes behind her showed the two guards turn down a side passage. She doubled back and opened the shaft access panel, slipping in with a bit of trouble when her jacket bunched up beneath her. Once in, she hooked a foot on the access panel and pulled it shut.

<How far down?>

<Just three meters to that junction on the left.>

Sera slithered down the tight space to the location indicated on her HUD, and took a deep breath. She held her index finger against the port and silver metal flowed out through the outstretched digit, forming a probe which then seated itself into the port.

<Gah… that always gives me the heebies,> Sera said with a shiver.

<Ah, there we are, this terminal does have access to both the secure and main nets on the station, just as I suspected. It's been locked out of the secure net, but a few nano into the mix and all that will be changed.>

Sera studied the station's layout as Helen accessed the secure net. Even without knowing exactly where the artifact they were searching for was, there were only so many places it could be hidden. The station's own power grid should show its location—even if they hadn't decided to use it. If they had, then it should be even easier.

<I'm in,> Helen said. *<I'm scanning their secure locations and comm logs to look for any reference to the CriEn.>*

<I hope it's still here. If Kade traded it, we're in big trouble.>

<I don't think so,> Helen said. *<We first traced the CriEn to Kade eight years ago; this station has been here for ten. I'm betting that they're using it as a power source to keep this thing in the dark layer. It would be a lot cheaper than hauling fissionables or exotics all the way out here to run in a reactor.>*

Sera looked over the portions of the station labeled as power generation. If they were using the CriEn, it would be around there. It didn't have to be, but a smart engineer would place it near existing power distribution systems.

<I think I found it,> Helen said. *<The station specifications show two nuclear fusion reactors for power, but one is just barely running and the other isn't active at all. However, power levels show more energy than even these two reactors could create.>*

<So they ***are*** *using it. What are the chances we can remove it and not have this station tear itself to pieces when it loses the power to stay transitioned in the DL?>*

<I think it will hold together for a day or so at least. The fusion reactor could probably hold it in just fine for a few weeks with the batteries helping—before it overheated. They'd have to kill everything except for life support to manage that, though. Once they get both reactors spun up, they could always keep it here, or transition it back to regular space.>

It was one of the difficulties of maintaining systems in the dark layer: heat dispersion. In regular space, the cold of vacuum was a great way to disperse heat; in the dark layer, there was nothing to disperse heat to. The heat could be transformed into energy, but when it was permeating everything, that was hard to do. The CriEn module generated energy with no heat, which was the key to keeping a station in the dark layer.

Sera worked out the route to the station's power plant while Helen used nano to build a bridge from the station's secure net to the public net and placed the link into an encrypted stream. Unless they were looking, the station security systems wouldn't stand a chance of locating it.

<There, we'll have access to the secure net over our wireless Link to the public net now,> Helen said. *<Picked our route?>*

<Yeah, we'll make our way across this level to the station's midpoint and then down three levels, across that one, and then down to power generation. Looks like guards on it are light. Kade probably counted on his fiction of two plants to hide the module.>

<What a waste of a CriEn,> Helen sighed. *<You could run a planet with this thing.>*

<No one ever said Kade was the brightest star in the sky.>

<'Was' being the operative term,> Helen replied. *<Hey, grab that repair kit there, it has some stuff we can use for a distraction.>*

Sera grabbed the kit and pulled herself back up the access tube, and checked the two probes they'd left out in the hall. When the coast was clear, she flipped the latch and kicked the hatch open.

She eased out into the hall, but at the last minute, a bandolier caught on the hinge. She stumbled and fell to the floor before freeing herself and closing the panel.

<Very graceful,> Helen commented wryly.

She stood up and dusted herself off before looking up to see a guard walking toward her.

"Hey, what were you doing in there?" he asked.

<You are so not going to be able to talk yourself out of this one,> Helen chuckled.

"I'm tech; got a call that there was a down net coupling in there and I fixed it up."

The guard was unconvinced. "You're tech?"

"Yeah, I'm off duty." Sera made sure to stand so that her coat hid the weapons, but not her shapely legs.

"Why don't you spread your hands across that wall there while I check your ident?" The guard pulled out a scanner and stepped toward Sera as she placed her hands on the wall."

<Told you.>

<You are not helping.>

"That's odd," the guard said as he ran the scanner over her hand. "I'm not getting any station ident off you."

Sera smiled and turned, one hand sliding up her left leg and then behind her back. "I'm new; I'm just trying to do a good job." Humanity had been civilized for twelve thousand years, but men still hadn't outgrown their inability to think straight when a woman turned on her charm.

"Right, you can do a good job from detention while I check you out."

Apparently, some men had evolved.

<I hope you blocked his transmit access or things are going to get unpleasant,> Sera said.

<What do you take me for, an amateur? I am six thousand years old, after all.>

Sera slid the pistol she had reached for out from behind her back and jammed it under the guard's chin. "Tight beam your access codes and tokens to me, or I spray your brains on the roof."

The man nodded slowly, and Helen confirmed that he sent his codes. Sera gestured for him to turn and when he did, she fired a pulse at the small of his back. It was a simple yet effective way to stun someone for a few hours. He slumped and she caught his weight with a grunt. A minute later, she had him stuffed into the maintenance shaft and Helen was faking his patrol signal on the net so he wouldn't be missed.

Without any further incident, Sera made her way to the security station outside the power generation section.

<What are the chances I could do a face meld without passing out?> Sera asked Helen.

<Your energy reserves are extremely low, even with what you got from that dispenser back there.>

<Figured as much. I don't know how I'd feel about any more pain anyway.>

<You've certainly planned better infiltrations.>

<Thanks for the support.>

<I was merely stating a fact,> Helen said without rancor.

<Well, I guess I'll do this the old-fashioned way.>

Without another word, she stepped out from cover and strode directly up to the two guards. An automatic turret tracked her as she approached the two men.

<Tell me you can jam that thing.>

<Already have. I'm just moving it for their benefit.>

"Hey guys. How're you doing?" she asked with a friendly smile, attempting to walk right passed them.

"Hold it." One of the guards said as they both reached forward to stop her progress. Sera halted half a step before they expected and grasped each guard's outstretched wrists. Their expressions were priceless as she leapt backwards and pulled the guards toward her and into one another. The guards stumbled and crashed to the floor.

<That extra twenty kilos of weaponry really helps doesn't it.>

<Sure does, Flaherty would be proud.>

Sera kicked the man on the left in the face as he struggled to get up, the heel of her boot ripping open his cheek. The other guard kicked the back of her other leg, hitting her knee and knocking her backwards. Sera took advantage of the momentum, twisted and fell onto the guard—her elbow smashing into his chest. The sickening crack of his sternum reverberated up her arm.

<Damn that hurts!>

<That's why it's not in the manual.>

Sera used her pistol to stun both men and dumped them in a small cleaning room a short distance back up the corridor.

<We're on the clock now, those two guards are scheduled to check in verbally every ten minutes and I didn't get their access codes.>

<How long till the next check in?>

<Seven and a half minutes. I'll set the clock.>

A countdown appeared in the upper right of Sera's vision as she ran down the corridors in the direction her map overlay indicated. There would be some techs monitoring the main reactor, but since the secondary one was offline, she doubted that anyone was watching it. She was wrong.

It appeared that The Mark techs were studying the CriEn module even as they were using it. Eight years later and they still didn't know how it worked.

There were at least a dozen of them in a monitoring station and another group wearing hazsuits in the chamber where the CriEn module stood on a pedestal.

<Great. I suppose I could just shoot them all, but that would be messy and probably set off an alarm or two.>

<I'll clear them out. It's fun to mess with people who don't know what they are doing,> Helen replied gleefully.

Helen showed Sera a readout of the main power throughput indicators. The CriEn module generated energy by accessing layers of space-time these techs didn't even know about. It would be easy to generate anomalous readings from the device that wouldn't put them in harm's way but would certainly cause them to vacate the premises.

Helen used her access to the station's secure net to worm her way into the engineering network, and from there to the CriEn chamber. As expected, grav fields were in place around the module to ensure safety. Helen altered the frequency of the fields and the module began to alter its output unpredictably. Its EM field swelled and pushed against the grav fields containing it.

As predicted, the engineers monitoring the device grew concerned, and then frantic as they attempted to stabilize the grav field and contain the module's EM field. Helen was more than a match for them, and within a minute they had hit their fail-safes and shut down the module. The scientists in the hazsuits had long since vacated the chamber and were crowded into the decontamination room.

With the scientists and engineers focused on discerning the cause of the anomaly, Sera was able to approach their monitoring station, crack the door open, and roll in a canister of gas. Made from the parts they had grabbed along the way, it wasn't a grenade, but it would do the trick.

It took only seconds for the gas to take effect, and Sera rose from cover as the countdown on her HUD slipped past the four-minute mark.

She ran past the sleeping techs and into the CriEn chamber. The module was seated in a socket, which linked up with the power ports. Sera quickly unlatched it and looked around for something in which to stash the device.

<*There, they have a shielded case it will fit in back in the main monitoring station.*> Helen indicated the location on Sera's HUD. She hefted the module, which weighed at least a good forty kilograms, and dashed back into the room with the sleeping techs. The shielded case was sitting on an equipment rack and she placed the module in it and flipped on the case's grav shield.

<*Grav shield, lucky us. It would suck if someone hit the module with a beam weapon,*> Sera said as she hoisted the case over her shoulder.

<*Only for a fraction of a second,*> Helen replied.

<*I'm going to need another shot of adrenaline if I'm to make it through this next little jaunt.*>

<*You're way over-extended; I may have to regulate your heart if I give it to you.*>

<*I can barely move with all the weight I'm hauling. Juice me up, doc.*>

The shot of adrenaline felt like a blow to the chest as her heart fluttered uncomfortably and then increased its pace. She took a deep, steadying breath, then switched her overlay to show the route to the station's main sensor array—a system that likely saw little use with the station in the dark layer.

She raced past the closet containing the two unconscious guards, their comms squawking through the door with the voice of a superior demanding that they check in. As she reached the curve in the corridor, the station's power switched to a conservation setting; the main lighting dimmed and ancillary wall holos turned off.

<*Looks like they've switched to battery power while they warm the other reactor up,*> Helen observed.

<*Seems so. Hopefully they get enough power online for us to send the signal.*>

LET'S BLOW THIS JOINT

STELLAR DATE: 07.16.8927 (Adjusted Years)
LOCATION: The Mark's Dark Layer Station
REGION: Unclaimed Interstellar Space, Core-Ward of Silstrand Alliance

Sera had just ducked into a service corridor when she heard the sounds of booted feet running down the main hall to the CriEn chamber.

<*That was close,*> Helen said.

<*I thought you were monitoring the station personnel after that hiccup back at the maintenance shaft?*>

<*I am. Those guys weren't showing up on it. I think they're getting suspicious—might have removed guards from monitoring.*>

<*They've gotta be using voice comm, then. See if you can find it.*>

<*I seem to recall being the one who taught you all your tradecraft,*> Helen said, sounding somewhat annoyed.

<*Sorry,*> Sera said as she ran down the corridor. <*Habit from all those years working in the unit.*>

They had several near brushes with guards as she made her way to the sensor array, but Helen had picked up the comm channel and fanned the probes far ahead.

<*They found her,*> Helen said. They both knew who *her* was. <*She's pretty upset. I've got a visual feed if you want to see.*>

<*No thanks, I'd probably start laughing.*>

<*It's too bad you never got to use the crew for this; you'd been training them well for the eventual infiltration.*>

<*They'll be more chances to use them,*> Sera replied as she peered around a corner. <*Though a few more people to do this job sure would have been nice.*>

<*Flaherty is going to be upset he missed it,*> Helen said.

<*He'll get over it.*>

The coast was clear. Sera dashed down the corridor and slithered into yet another access shaft—this one, thankfully, a bit larger than some of the others. The shaft linked with another and she shimmied down it for forty meters before coming to the sensor array's main trunk line.

<*Do your thang,*> Sera said, managing a mental drawl.

<*That's...exceptionally annoying,*> Helen said while directing a probe to deliver nano into a small access port on the conduit.

<*Need to stay in range of the probe while you work your magic?*> Sera asked.

<*I'd prefer not to. The sooner we get out of here, the better. I don't want to hang around to see one of those things up close when it gets here.*>

<*There can't be one within a dozen light-years. I bet it will be at least a day before one gets here,*> Sera said as she began to work her way back out of the access shaft.

<*Do you want to take any chances, though?*> Helen asked.

Sera thought about what the sensor array would be summoning. <*No, not really.*>

Following the tunnel, they passed into another access shaft, which ultimately led to a freight warehousing area. From there, it should be a short jaunt to the docks to find a ship they could sneak aboard.

One last tussle with her coat getting caught and she climbed through a hatch into the warehouse. Sera dusted off her coat and checked her weapons over.

<You know, you now have perfectly slinky skin for wiggling through tight spaces, but you insist on wearing that big coat overtop.>

Sera felt herself blush. *<It feels* **too** *much like my skin; it would be like crawling through there naked. I'm worried I might tear it open.>*

Helen chuckled gently in Sera's mind. *<You humans are so concerned about your outer shell. I swear, at least half your civilization is built around it.>*

<Well, you don't have insides that ooze out if your outer shell gets wrecked,> Sera said while adjusting her thigh holster and freeing up the knives in her boots.

<Given the fact that **you** *are my outer shell, that's not entirely true.>*

Satisfied that she was combat ready, Sera peered around the stack of crates she had been hiding behind and scanned the long, dark row of wares.

<It's going to be hard to pick up where people are with all this in here,> Helen observed.

With the fourth probe functioning as a relay on the sensor trunk line, there were only three available to roam the warehouse. Helen spread them out, showing Sera an overlay of the series of interconnected storage areas and their current location in the maze.

Several security teams were visible on the probe cameras, methodically searching the area.

<Looks like the goon patrol is checking this place over.>

<Seems so,> Helen agreed.

Sera crept through the stacks of freight with careful precision. Some of them were piled haphazardly, and several times she had to squeeze through some narrow spaces while avoiding the larger alleyways. She had just finished pulling the CriEn module's case through a narrow opening when she turned to find herself staring into the muzzle of a pulse rifle.

"I don't think you're supposed to be down here, ma'am," the guard said.

"I think that's the first time all day someone has called me 'ma'am'," Sera said and drew her hand down her chest with a smile. The man's eyes followed her hand, a small smile tugging at the corners of his mouth. She took advantage of his distraction, pushed his rifle to the side as she spun around, driving an elbow into his left eye.

He fell back with a cry and raised one hand to his eye. Sera grabbed his weapon with both hands and wrenched it from his grip, before spinning it and slamming the rifle's stock into his neck.

The man began to gargle and Sera fired a shot from her stun pistol into his head.

<No DNA lock on the gun,> Sera said after planting some nano on the trigger. *<Never hurts to have another weapon.>*

<As long as you can carry them, limping-bleeding-adrenalized girl.>

Sera set down the case and slipped off her coat. She pulled her other pulse rifle off its shoulder sling and then pulled the jacket back on, putting the sling overtop. She hooked the shielded case to the sling and then hefted both pulse rifles, one in each hand.

"This is much better. The time for subtlety is over," she said aloud and stepped out from around the crate. She spun, and her coat billowed behind her, both rifles leveled on a squad of guards who were approaching quietly. "Oops."

Sera gave a disarming smile, then fired off a flurry of pulses with both weapons before ducking around another stack of containers.

She brought up her targeting overlay and slipped around to the far side of the crate where two troopers were trying to flank her. These men wore body armor and Sera concentrated fire from both rifles on one man and then the other.

<*Like shooting fish in a barrel,*> Sera said with a grin.

<*Did anyone ever really do that, anyway?*>

<*Dunno, but if they did, I bet it was a lot like this.*>

Sera turned and fired blindly at the guards coming around the other side of the crate before dashing further into the maze.

The guards gave chase and Helen pointed out where reinforcements were on the route. The station's compliment of active guards was just over three hundred—with an additional merc garrison of four hundred-fifty. Not to mention all the Mark crews currently on station.

<*You couldn't hack their HUDs by any chance, could you?*> Sera asked.

<*I thought you said that was unethical.*>

<*That was against regular soldiers. These guys are pirates. Besides, it's a thousand to one!*>

Helen's mental laugh bubbled as she struck across the station's private net and hacked the pursuing guard's HUDs. She threw in the added bonus of making them unable to see with their helmets on. Sera heard collisions and cursing from behind and gave a small laugh when Helen showed her the pastoral landscapes that she had inserted over the guard's vision.

"Now that evens things out a bit more," Sera said aloud. She stopped at the end of a long row of crates and turned to fire at her helmet-less pursuers. Three went down and Sera fired down the other side of the row, taking out another goon before a pulse shot hit her right arm.

Her muscles convulsed and the weapon fell from numb fingers.

"Damn," she said and sucked in a deep breath, falling back against a stack of engine parts. She fired a few blind pulses around the stack to let them know she was still in the fight.

<*That's what you get for being cocky,*> Helen admonished.

<*How long till you can de-numb it?*>

<*In your current state? Ten minutes.*>

Sera swore and dropped the pulse rifle, pulling a slug-throwing pistol from its holster. The shipping crates provided cover from pulse blasts, but the pistols fired armor piercing rounds at nearly a thousand kilometers per hour. Rebecca may be many things, but she did not have bad taste in weapons.

Trying to take out the enemy without causing fatalities, Sera fired a few low shots. The moment she started killing the soldiers, they would take this fight a lot more seriously and just gas the whole chamber. There were curses and a few grunts as the bullets tore through cargo and into soft flesh. Sera let a few more rounds fly and then took off along a path her HUD showed to be clear.

The guards were more cautious now—following slowly, checking every corner. Within a minute Sera lost them, and soon she was at the opening to the station's main dock.

It was an aired dock with the ships resting on cradles inside the station. Sera guessed it probably had to do with how they held the station in the dark layer and concerns over mixing the grav fields.

<Any of this stuff slated to be loaded up?>

<Those four pallets over there are scheduled to go on a ship that's supposed to be leaving any minute now,> Helen said and highlighted them on Sera's HUD.

<Cutting it kind of close, aren't they?>

<Dockhands are refusing to load while the shootout is going on. The ship's captain is arguing with them.>

Sera stepped up to one of the pallets that was loaded with crates of food. It was out of the direct line of sight from the docks and she carefully slid the crates aside, making a small space in the center. Placing the CriEn case in first, she squeezed in after and crouched on it, pulling the crates tight around her. Sera pulled a few of the crates over her head in case there were any catwalks out on the docks.

<I've got their scanners a bit messed up; they shouldn't be able to detect you in here with all these organics.>

<Good, I'm going to catch a minute or two of shuteye. Let me know if anything interesting happens.>

The guards were spilling out onto the docks, unable to find any sign of Sera in the warehouse. The dockhands, and the captain with which they were arguing, reported that they hadn't seen anyone, and most of the guards returned to the warehouse to sweep it again.

The captain strengthened his argument that the docks were clear, and, given their own admission that they had not seen anything, the dockhands had no choice but to resume loading the ship. Sera's pallet was last and Helen gently woke her before it began moving. It wouldn't do to have Sera startled awake and give away her location.

As the pallet was crawling up the ramp, a shout came over the docks.

"Stop that! What do you think you're doing?" The voice was Rebecca's.

"Loading my ship," the captain responded.

"We're not loading ships; we're looking for a fugitive."

"You've got a thousand people who can hunt for one person. I've got a schedule to keep."

"How do you know she hasn't gotten onto your ship?"

"Because I've been standing here the whole time arguing with these dockhands to get the thing loaded up. I'm already half an hour behind. This stuff sells for a lot more when it's fresh, you know."

Rebecca and the captain yelled at one another for several minutes. Eventually, the new Mark leader succumbed to the captain's increasing ire after he had the ship's AI do a full scan of the vessel, which showed no one on board but his crew.

Sera's pallet was finally stowed in a hold, which, by the smell of it, contained a veritable cornucopia of produce. At least she wasn't going to starve.

The ship spent an agonizing ten minutes going through pre-flight checks and reactor power up.

<When's the alert set to go off?> Sera asked.

<Within the next hour. They should have plenty of time. In case they try to transition out, I've planted a subroutine that will prevent that and set their reactors on a burn rate that will overload them in a day. If they're smart, they'll all bail before the thing gets here.>

<Oh, you're devious,> Sera said with a tired smile.

<It's what I do.>

Minutes later, the station's grav fields backed the ship out of its docking slot and into the dark layer. Not long after, Sera felt the vessel transition into normal space and then begin to accelerate for an eventual transition to FTL.

Sera pushed the crates over her head aside, and pulled herself up. She covered the hole back up, carefully moving the crates to their former positions. It wouldn't do to have anyone find the CriEn module she had worked so hard to retrieve.

She slipped down to the deck and wobbled slightly. Then, waves of dizziness and nausea washed over her body. She fell to the ground, ignoring the tingling sensations her new skin sent through her body.

<Is this what success feels like?> Her mental tone was wan and stretched thin.

<You just need a few hours' sleep and some food,> Helen replied. *<Luckily, we have no shortage of that.>*

Sera eyed the crates filling the compartment. Food to be sure, but likely no water, and she was feeling a powerful thirst.

She sighed and ran a hand down her black, gleaming thigh.

<At least I don't have to worry about sweating out any fluids,> she said with a soft laugh. *<I wonder what Nance would think of this getup?>*

FAIR TRADE

STELLAR DATE: 07.15.8927 (Adjusted Years)
LOCATION: *Sabrina*, PeterSil EK Belt Mining Platform
REGION: Silstrand System, Silstrand Alliance Space

At the outer rim of the system's Kuiper Belt, the PeterSil EK mining platform whipped around its host star at just over twenty thousand kilometers per hour. Cheeky carefully guided *Sabrina* across several million kilometers of the Silstrand system until the ship's velocity was perfectly matched to the platform's.

Tanis couldn't help but be impressed by the skill Cheeky displayed.

Many pilots needed to resort to hard burns or corrections to make their final approaches, but *Sabrina's* pilot eased her starship through the system like it was a dance to which she knew all the moves.

When they got close, the station focused a gravity wave on the ship and gently pulled it in, before securing it with a physical grapple.

Cargo informed the station that they were interested in making a purchase from S&H Defensive Armaments. Station control passed the message along, and, when pressures were matched and the cargo hatch opened, representatives from the firm were waiting to meet them.

Tanis stepped onto the merchant dock with Cargo, soaking in the station's vibrant atmosphere as freight haulers, passenger cars, and foot traffic moved past their berth in a chaotic cacophony.

It was a shock after the days spent on the relative quiet of *Sabrina.* She realized that, though the Victorian stations and platforms had become crowded in their later years, she hadn't seen this type of bustling commerce since the *Intrepid*'s final days on the Cho, in orbit around Jupiter.

Despite the fact that the platform had the word 'mining' in its name, little of the freight she saw looked to have anything to do with extracting or refining ore. From what she could tell, much of the trade here was in defensive or offensive armament.

From her research, she knew that S&H Defensive Armaments had been doing business in the Silstrand Alliance for several centuries and was highly respected. The elder of the two representatives looked as though he may have been with them that entire time.

<*Rejuv does not appear to be what it used to,*> Tanis said to Angela as they approached the stooped old man waiting on the far side of the ship-territory demarcation line.

"Pleased to meet you," the elderly man said as they approached, and extended a wrinkly hand. Cargo shook it firmly, followed by Tanis—who was surprised at how paper-thin the man's skin felt.

"My name is Smithers," the man said. "I represent S&H Defensive Armaments. Welcome to the PeterSil Mining Platform."

"I'm Cargo and this is Tanis, thank you for taking the time to meet us here," Cargo said with a warm smile.

"This is my associate, Ginia," Smithers gestured to the much younger woman accompanying him. She smiled warmly as she shook their hands.

"If you'll step this way, we have transportation ready to take you to our showroom." Ginia led them to a dock car and they settled within its cabin. She gave it verbal instruction as to their destination and the car took off, weaving through the dock traffic, its dampeners creating a perfectly smooth ride for its passengers.

"We're grateful for the dockside greeting and transportation," Tanis said. "Do you treat all of your clients with such hospitality?"

"We have various levels for various classes of clientele," Smithers said. "There was mention in your message to the station's docking control regarding interest in trading nano technology for weaponry. Typically, only a higher level of clientele is interested in such transactions."

<I'm betting these guys run the station if they are privy to traffic control conversations,> Tanis said to Cargo.

<It would seem so. The fact that there isn't a single speck of dust on a mining platform seems to point to that, as well. This platform practically sparkles.>

Verbally, they spoke of pleasantries. Smithers and Ginia made observations about the local economy and the upcoming elections for the Silstrand Alliances Senate later in the year. Tanis listened intently while Cargo stared out the windows, apparently uninterested in the star cluster's politics.

"So, are you in favor of Silstrand increasing its territory then?" Tanis asked, after Smithers indicated approval of a politician who was running on a campaign platform of adding new worlds to the Alliance.

"Purely from a trade and economy standpoint," he replied. "If we increase our territory, then we will have more tariff-free trading partners. Alliance organizations will also be favored in bids for the supply and construction of any government facilities in new member systems."

Tanis knew what that meant; more defense contracts for S&H to land. The small-talk continued for several more minutes until they arrived at S&H's section of the station. They stepped out of the transport and into the lobby of what seemed more like an upscale banking establishment than a weapons supplier. High-quality holos showed rotating images of various products, from personal armor to orbital defense emplacements.

Smithers and Ginia led them through the lobby and down a hall to a private showroom with low couches surrounding a holo tank. The room was dimly lit, with glass and steel artwork perched on the tables. Several small serving trays hovered around the room, offering assorted finger foods.

Smithers beckoned one with his finger and it floated over to him. He selected some cheeses before leaning back in his chair.

"Please," he said with a wave of his hand. "Help yourself. Would you like anything to drink? Ginia will have someone fetch it for us."

Tanis signaled one of the platforms to float her way. Outside of FTL and gravity drives, this was the first piece of impressive technology she had seen in the ninetieth century. She hadn't expected anti-gravity generators to be so small.

"I'll have a glass of white wine, something light," she said after selecting some crackers and fruit. Cargo requested a mixed drink with liquors Tanis had never heard of. The drinks arrived within moments, carried by a slender woman dressed in only a thin gauze outfit.

<*Custom here amongst the well-to-do,*> Cargo said. <*Using human servants for everything imaginable, while humiliating those human servants with socially uncomfortable clothing elevates one's status.*>

<*Humans are weird,*> Tanis responded to Cargo before asking Angela, <*These folks seem to have some good tech—how secure is my Link to Cargo?*>

<*They've discreetly tried to snoop a few times, but I've upgraded his security encryption. His Link and AI can now transmit with a tighter beam and lower gain than it was originally able to.*>

<*Does Cargo know you upgraded his AI?*> Tanis asked.

<*No and neither does his AI. I 'convinced' it that it had always had those capabilities.*> Angela's voice held a conspiratorial tone.

<*That's a violation of the Phobos accords!*> Tanis exclaimed.

<*Yeah, a little. For me to explain what I did, well, I'd have to provide it with a lot more information than it could handle—which would mean I'd have to upgrade its core. I opted not to do all of that as it would require physical alterations,*> Angela sounded smug in her superiority and Tanis called her on it.

<*You know it's unbecoming for you to talk down about other AI like that.*>

<*I know,*> Angela sighed. <*But it would be illegal to make AI like this back in our time. They're sentient, but they're like people never allowed to mature beyond childhood. In our day, they'd be removed from their hosts, and allowed to re-grow.*>

<*In our day…now you're making me feel old,*> Tanis said before turning her full attention back to Smithers, who was speaking to her.

"…so as you can see we are able to offer the latest in several defensive and offensive technologies to suit your needs. What were you specifically interested in?"

During their flight across the system, Tanis had accessed several resources and catalogs to gain a better understanding of ninetieth century weaponry capability. She had a shopping list ready to go. Cargo had checked it and added a few suggestions of his own to fill it out. Surprisingly, or perhaps not surprisingly, Flaherty had also offered advice on what would be useful, as well.

"We're interested in your ER71 Defensive Suite, for starters." Tanis leaned back with a slice of apple and what she hoped was cheese. "We're going to want a dedicated gravity generator to go with it and the ten centimeter defensive lasers."

She could tell that she had Smithers' attention. Ginia tilted her head and manipulated the readouts, bringing capabilities and prices up on the holo.

"Would you like the GE-875 or the GE-885 grav generator with the suite?" She asked.

"I was hoping we could get the GE-960," Tanis replied. "From what I understand, it's smaller and has a higher output; space is an important consideration on our ship."

Ginia's eyes widened. The GE-960 was three times the price of either of the other gravity generators.

"We're also going to need to replace our current SC Batteries with the SC-R 911s. I understand they have roughly three times the capacity of our current SC-R 790s?"

Smithers nodded, his eyes dancing as the tally on the holo increased. "Yes, they are the best we have in this corner of space. You said you were considering offensive armament, too?"

Cargo's eyes were glazed with incredulity as he looked at the price.

"Yes," Tanis answered. "We're interested in the thirty-centimeter laser system. I believe our ship's layout will require us to mount ten of them for full coverage. I'd also like to get fore and aft AR-17 missile tubes, the four-centimeter rail guns, and fore and aft RM launchers."

Smithers' previous look of pleasure turned to one of skepticism. The tally was easily four times the value of *Sabrina.* Ginia was also eyeing the total with a smile, but where Smithers looked like he was considering charging them for the food and seeing them out, she looked very excited.

"And how will you be paying for this?" Smithers asked.

"We will provide full documentation and disclosure of a valuable nano tech which no one within a hundred light-years even dreams of possessing. We will also disclose our source for this tech as well as documentation indicating our license to distribute both the source technology and sell development and distribution licenses."

Smithers' expression shifted. He still didn't appear completely mollified, but neither was he going to end the discussion.

Tech was one thing; the ability to develop and distribute products based on that Tech was something else entirely. Tanis smiled and reached for her wine glass and drained its contents. Taking the glass in her hand, she repeated the act of absorbing its matter and fabricating a small handgun.

Smithers' expression shifted to one of almost pure joy, and Ginia's face was now rapt with amazement. With a cough, the older man recovered his composure—a bit quicker than Tanis would have liked.

"That looked truly amazing, would it be possible to see it again, and then be able to test the results for any signs of trickery?"

Tanis nodded. "I understand your skepticism. If you'll provide another glass, I'll give you a matched pair."

"Actually," Smithers said. "Please make a...replica of a six-chamber projectile weapon from the nineteenth century. That way we can be assured there is no sleight of hand occurring."

"Based on the size, I'll need two glasses."

Ginia nodded, and a minute later, the servant came in with a tray of empty wine glasses. Angela suggested she use three, and Tanis activated the field in the palm of her hand, dissolving each glass into it. She then added a silver fork, two deviled eggs, and salt to her palm. Moments later, she produced a gun, and then six bullets, which she slipped into the chambers. Handing it to Smithers she said, "Be careful. It's loaded and functional."

The old man whistled in appreciation. "I assume the technology includes not only the nano, but the information on such rapid reorganization of the molecules?"

"You'll get everything required to repeat such a feat, except for the power source."

Smithers nodded. "I assume you won't object if I have our technicians examine these articles." He indicated the guns.

"Be my guest," Tanis replied.

From there they got down to 'brass tacks', as Smithers put it.

Cargo demanded that the work be done in under forty-eight hours; a timeframe which Smithers claimed was not possible. Ginia proceeded to draw up a work schedule, which showed the work would take two weeks.

"I don't see how it is impossible," Tanis said. "This station surely has all of the technical ability to do the installation. The technologies I have to offer will more than offset any costs, probably a thousand-fold."

Smithers was a top-notch negotiator. Despite his awe over Tanis's tech, he was still haggling over every point of the contract they were drawing up. "I believe I'll need to see the documentation on your license to distribute the source tech with ability to develop and redistribute before I can negotiate further. I've never seen anything like this before, but I don't want to commit to this only to hear it announced on the Link tomorrow as something that another firm has developed with licenses prohibiting us from using it."

Tanis nodded and transmitted a full non-disclosure to Smithers over S&H's secure net. "I'll need you to physically and digitally sign this NDA before I can discuss the source of the license."

The NDA was very strict and binding in every system that S&H did business—and most they didn't. Smithers frowned as he reviewed it and sent it off to his legal team for further examination. They discussed minor points regarding the install while they waited. Legal had a few revisions, one that Tanis agreed to and several she refused. In the end, they had an agreement and Tanis disclosed where her nano came from.

Smithers really did lose his composure this time. "God damn it! That explains where you got this tech! But why are you on that crummy little yacht?"

Cargo bristled at that, but Smithers hardly noticed.

"It belongs to a friend who has been having…pirate troubles. The weaponry we're getting from you will be used to fix some of those troubles and get her out of a jam."

Smithers nodded. "That explains why you need the tech, but why are you interested in this, and where is your ship?"

Cargo laughed. "Isn't that the hundred trillion dollar question?"

"The work in two days and I'll speak highly of S&H to my superiors when it comes to future trading. If I have to wait longer than, that I'll let them know transactions with your firm were difficult."

Smithers sighed. "That's one hell of a bargaining chip. Very well, forty-eight hours and you'll be decked out in the best S&H has to offer."

Tanis and Smithers worked out the final aspects of the contract while Cargo took a car back to *Sabrina* with S&H's implementation coordinator and head engineer.

When Tanis arrived back at the ship a few hours later, the dockside was strewn with old components and crates full of new ones. The minute she stepped through the lock, Tanis was accosted by Cheeky.

"I don't care what Thompson says, you're amazing," the pilot said. "I can't believe you got them to agree to your entire list."

"Think they'll actually be able to meet the two-day deadline?" Tanis asked.

"They will or we take their installation team with us. There's no way we're gonna leave the captain longer than that."

"I got them to provide us with a full antimatter fueling as well, and with the increase power on the shielding systems, we should be able to accelerate much faster."

"I'd better check the tuning on our AP nozzle, then. We may need to upgrade that."

"Over plan. We have unlimited credit."

Cheeky rubbed her hands together. "I may not be able to contain myself."

Tanis laughed and let Cheeky get back to her glee over the upgrades. As she passed the galley, she overheard Thompson and Nance arguing with Flaherty.

"I don't care what her motivations are. She has no right to just take over the ship with the captain gone. Cargo is practically letting her run the show, and who knows if

Sera's still alive anymore?" Nance's voice rose to an unpleasant pitch and Tanis stopped before she walked past the doorway, not wanting to eavesdrop, but too curious to back away.

She really needed to know how the crew felt about her. If there were even half a chance that they'd turn on her, she'd walk off the ship right now and buy transportation to Bollam's World. The information she had for the *Intrepid* was too important to lose just because of some pissing contest about who got to be in charge of the rescue mission.

"She's right," Thompson said. "I don't know why Sera ever even dealt with The Mark. Look where it's gotten her now."

"You need to relax," Flaherty said. "Tanis isn't the problem. Getting Sera back from Rebecca is all that matters. Tanis is trying to help. Without her, we may as well just write the captain off because we have no way of assaulting a fortified station."

"You don't know that. We should have squeezed that Drind guy more. Did you know that she convinced Cargo to let him go? They even gave him a reference so he could find work on the station here," Nance said.

"That was a good tactical plan. He is now indebted to us and less likely to cause us any trouble. Keeping him would have been a problem. His loyalties aren't clear enough to have him around in a battle. If things go poorly, he could turn on us at a critical point." Flaherty's voice remained calm and steady.

"So, you're admitting things could go poorly!" Nance said.

"It would be foolish of me to assume otherwise," Flaherty said. "I may not be a major from the Terran Space Force, but I've seen my share of battle, and I know that one liability will offset a dozen good men. We are well rid of Drind no matter what possible uses for him you can imagine."

Nance didn't have a response for that right away. There was the clinking of cutlery on plates for a few minutes before she spoke up. "It's possible that I'm taking my frustrations out on her, and I'll keep that in mind. But I still don't like the way she just takes charge, it's not her place."

Flaherty chuckled. "She has no choice. It's who she is. You don't advance as an officer in the navy unless you have a good head on your shoulders and know how to use it. She sees a situation that needs her expertise and she takes charge."

"You can defend her all you want," Thompson said. "It's not making me like her any better."

"You don't have to like her," Flaherty said with deadly calm. "You just have to not mess things up when it comes to rescuing the captain. If you do, you'll have me to worry about."

Tanis didn't wait to hear more. She slipped back down the ladder and took a different route to the bridge that didn't pass the galley. She hoped that Flaherty's calm could offset some of the more volatile crewmembers, or this was going to be the worst rescue of all time.

READY AND ABLE

STELLAR DATE: 07.17.8927 (Adjusted Years)
LOCATION: *Sabrina*, PeterSil EK Belt Mining Platform
REGION: Silstrand System, Silstrand Alliance Space

Two days later, *Sabrina* was fully decked out in the best S&H had to offer. Tanis had even wrangled a full charge on the SC batteries, and added mines to the defensive countermeasure system. Cargo filed the final disembarking entries with the PeterSil platform and they undocked for the tug to take them out.

On the bridge, Cargo sat in the captain's chair; his expression was one of grim determination, but underneath, Tanis could see more than a little trepidation.

<*You would do better in that chair,*> Angela commented.

<*I would, yes,*> Tanis replied. <*But they wouldn't. I can keep things in line well enough from the scan and weapons consoles without further upsetting the delicate balance we have here.*>

Tanis shifted in her seat; the hard chair did not conform to her body; she was served another reminder how out of her time she was.

<*This tug is taking forever,*> Sabrina complained. <*I have new wings, let me fly!*>

"Easy now, girl," Cargo's deep tones resonated through the bridge. "We'll be on our way soon enough."

<*On our way to kick some ass,*> Sabrina crowed. <*I don't just have new wings, but teeth too! I'm coming for you, Sera!*>

Tanis chuckled and shared an amused look with Cheeky.

"Farewell and good hunting," the tug pilot gave her final farewell as she released grapple.

"A good day to you, too," Tanis replied from the comm console.

"Oh, it will be. You're the last haul for me today, and it's a holiday weekend on-station," the tug pilot replied.

"See you next time, Amy," Cheeky said. "Don't do anything I wouldn't do."

The tug pilot laughed in response. "Cheeky, I won't do half the things you *do* do."

They gave the final sign-off and Cheeky laughed.

"She said do-do."

"Ah, Cheeky," Tanis sighed. "You'd make any captain in the service proud, but you wouldn't last a day."

Cheeky switched on the grav drive and set *Sabrina* on her course.

"I'd love to fly one of those big birds your military buddies have," Cheeky said with a nod. "But all those rules aren't my game. Now stealing one…that would be some fun."

Tanis shook her head and smiled. Who knew what the future would hold.

"How's she shaking out?" Cargo asked.

"Just fine," Cheeky replied at the same time Sabrina sang, <*I feel great!*>

Cargo let a small smile slip—perhaps the first since Sera's abduction. "Is that your technical assessment, Sabrina?"

<*Fine. The weapons interfaces are near perfect. I can barely feel the edge between the systems. The upgraded power plant doesn't have that annoying buzz in its output like the old one, it's like*

drinking starlight. And the quantum processors they added for targeting and navigation are like an ocean of thought. How's that for your technical assessment?>

"Uh…great," Cargo said.

<*I'm sorry for being snippy,*> Sabrina said. <*I just need to get her back. I love the upgrades—thank you Tanis—but I'm empty without Sera.*>

<*We have the power and the means now,*> Tanis replied. <*You'll see her again soon.*>

<*I'd better,*> the Sabrina replied.

<*Not the most stable of personalities, is she,*> Tanis said privately to Angela.

<*I've been working on getting her story,*> Angela spoke with a soft tone of pity. <*This ship sat in a junkyard for ninety years. They powered down the ship, but not her core, and she didn't have the ability to do so herself—something which I have since rectified. How AI are treated in this time is truly abhorrent. If ever anyone needed to see what the Phobos accords were meant to prevent, this is it.*>

Tanis's heart ached for the ship. Ninety years alone, no sensors, no input, just her thoughts…it was a wonder she was still sane.

<*That is unbelievable, to trap an AI in a ship like that! It's…it's…*>

<*These are dark times,*> Angela replied solemnly. <*Most of the AI on this ship were not given a choice as to their placements. They're all slaves—but they barely know it.*>

<*I had suspected as much,*> Tanis replied. <*I hope we can help them—I hope Bob doesn't throw a fit.*>

<*Bob's pretty pragmatic,*> Angela said with a chuckle. <*He's put up with you for some time, to say the least.*>

With an exasperated roll of her eyes, Tanis turned to her work, running preflight checks on the scan suite and making sure the boards showed green for the weapons systems. She couldn't perform a full check of those systems until they were further out—the station was already more than a little nervous about the amount of firepower *Sabrina* now sported.

Their rush to get the upgrades installed, and the haste with which S&H actually performed the upgrades, caused the PeterSil platform to ask a few pointed questions. Tanis and Cargo had tried to convince them the weapons were for defense against pirates and that *Sabrina* would be leaving the Silstrand Alliance as soon as the installation was complete, but their assurances did little to win the authorities over—*Sabrina* didn't exactly have a sterling reputation.

Ultimately, to ensure they met their end of the bargain, S&H stepped in and smoothed things over. Smithers pulled some strings to secure a letter of marquee for *Sabrina*—no small feat from what Tanis could tell. Once they had approval from the Alliance government for the weapons, the PeterSil platform backed down.

Given that S&H appeared to represent much of the platform's revenue, Tanis found herself wondering how normal this sort of maneuvering really was.

"System STC has given us the green for AP," Tanis said as the comm lit up.

"Acknowledged," Cargo replied. "Cheeky, let's hit it."

"Aye, aye sir," the pilot said with a mischievous grin.

One of the upgrades provided increased shielding around the ship's small annihilation chamber. The rough math Tanis had drawn up showed that *Sabrina* could now accelerate at over twice her previous rate—yet, the fragile humans within would feel nearly none of that thrust.

Now *Sabrina* really did sing as the ship boosted at 500*g* on its outsystem vector.

Tanis appreciated *Sabrina's* excitement, but kept her eyes on the pair of Silstrand Space Force corvettes that were shadowing them. The PeterSil platform may have approved their upgrades, and the local magistrate had provided their authorization to hunt pirates, but it seemed that the Alliance's military wasn't prepared to fully trust them.

Given what Tanis had witnessed thus far in the ninetieth century, she didn't blame them.

Even with their silent guests, or perhaps because of it, their departure was smooth and uneventful. A scant five hours later, they made their transition into FTL at 0.29*c*, the first of two FTL hops.

Soon, they'd be able the put the rest of their new toys to use as well.

LYING LOW

STELLAR DATE: 07.17.8927 (Adjusted Years)
LOCATION: *Regal Dawn*, Interstellar Space
REGION: Rim-Ward of Gedri, Silstrand Alliance Space

Sera woke as she felt the ship transition out of FTL into regular space. Helen's read-only tap into the wireless net revealed that the pirate ship was making vector adjustments before one more FTL jump, which would bring them to the Gedri system, a common haunt for pirates.

<So much for the big rush to deliver this food somewhere,> Sera said. *<He just wanted to pick off some prey before his next delivery.>*

<So it would seem,> Helen agreed.

Back on Coburn Station—before all this had begun—Sera recalled hearing that the Silstrand Alliance government was coming under heavy fire for their poor policing policies—Padre's attack on Trio probably added fuel to that fire.

Newscasts had reported that, with the upcoming election, the Alliance government was increasing patrols and providing many better-armed freighters with privateer marques, allowing them the spoils from any pirate ships they managed to disable and capture.

Those privateers also knew that Gedri was a common haunt for pirates.

There was a possibility that running into a patrol or privateer in Gedri would result in rescue, but it was just as possible that it would get her killed. What concerned her even more was the chance of the CriEn module being destroyed so close to Gedri Prime. Such an event could create a singularity that would eventually destroy the entire Silstrand Alliance.

<Stop being such a pessimist and finish that melon,> Helen said. *<That's just your low blood sugar talking.>*

<Probably. Some solid sleep wouldn't hurt either.>

<Don't doze off just yet. I need to find a hard line—I may need your muscles to get to it.>

<Is that all I am to you?>

<No, you're also handy transportation.>

So far, the ship hadn't detected their presence. It would seem its internal sensors were not the best, or it wasn't even looking, or the organic food in the hold was masking their presence. Being a pirate ship, Sera was certain that its sensors were the type that looked out more than in.

<These things are really good, a bit sticky though,> Sera commented as she finished the melon and started on a second one.

<Try to find something salty as well, your SC coil is starting to run out of juice and I don't want to try to charge off anything on this ship, I just know its power will feel gritty.>

<How can power feel gritty?> Sera asked.

<How does food feel sticky?> Helen asked back.

<Never mind.>

Sera found some salted nuts and crunched on them as quietly as possible. The nano in her body extracted sodium from her digestive system and mixed it with water, using the reaction to generate power for themselves and Helen; having an AI as powerful as Helen as well as extensive nano made for a salty diet.

<*I found it!*> Helen exclaimed. <*Behind that pallet of oranges, there's an access panel. I can tell by the EM patterns that there is a data flow of some sort behind it.*>

Sera stood slowly, her body—still recovering from torture and the stims Helen had provided to keep her moving—ached everywhere after sitting still for nearly half an hour. Her right leg refused to move and she slapped it a few times to regain feeling.

"Whooaaaa…I forgot about what that would feel like," she said aloud as her hypersensitive skin amplified the sensation.

<*Better than feeling some more needles slicing through you.*>

<*I'm not complaining, this stuff is great. It's chilly in here and I can barely feel it. Next time I see Rebecca, I'll be sure to thank her for the upgrade.*>

<*With our luck, it won't be too long before you have that opportunity.*>

Sera sighed. <*Yeah, I can't believe I let her live.*>

<*I can. I'm glad you did. Now that we've got the CriEn, we have some strong evidence against Trinov. He claimed you lost it, but its logs are intact and it points at him, not you. Having it, not to mention getting the* Intrepid *safely to* **them**, *should give you the evidence you need against him and proof of your loyalty.*>

<*I'm not loyal to them anymore. I'm just pissed that Trinov used me.*>

<*That's nice dear, just don't tell them that.*>

Sera laughed softly. <*I won't tell them. But I will have a few choice things to say to Trinov…at his trial.*>

<*Maybe you should just focus on the present.*>

<*What, rather than fret about what to do with* Sabrina *and her crew now that the reason I built them up no longer exists?*> Sera paused in her removal of the access panel. <*The thing is, I'm enjoying this life; I'm enjoying my time on* Sabrina. *I'm not sure I want it to end.*>

<*It doesn't necessarily have to. We've talked about it before—I don't need to go back anytime soon. You don't ever have to go back if you don't want to,*> Helen said. <*The laid-back life on a starfrieghter is starting to grow on me.*>

<*Yeah, but we both have to admit, turning that Mark station on its ear was a hell of a lot of fun.*>

<*Just like old times.*>

<*Just as long as it doesn't get* **too much** *like old times.*>

Sera grunted as she popped the last fastener out and loosened the cover enough for a probe to slip in and disable any tamper detectors.

<*Got one, a sloppy thing, just a closed-circuit detector,*> Helen said.

Sera lowered the cover to the ground and fed some nano through her finger onto the data conduit junction box inside. The tiny machines slipped through the seams in the box and created a port for one of the remaining probes.

<*Now that's more like it. I'm setting the probe up to give me full band wireless to the entire net,*> Helen paused. <*Oh, they've got a helluva of a nasty AI running this ship. It almost picked up the port we added, but I backlisted it as common addition for this run of conduit.*>

<*It's nice to have a memory that people can't just alter on me,*> Sera said as she stood painfully and staggered back to the food crates she had been sifting through.

<*What are you talking about? It's relatively simple to alter human memories.*>

<*If you can get all the places the memory is stored. The brain can usually spot the bad data and will re-populate it with the original.*>

<Hah, you've never seen me wipe a memory.>

<I've still got my crystal backup,> Sera said.

<I could access your diff system and fool it into ignoring what I wanted you to forget.>

Sera laughed softly. *<Are you trying to make me distrust you, dear?>*

<You should always be a bit suspicious. Even I could be compromised,> Helen replied innocently.

<Lucky for me I've already taken that into consideration. My memories are secure.>

<How so?>

<I can't tell you that, what if you get compromised?>

<That was hypothetical, I'm not going to get compromised!> Helen said and Sera pictured her stomping her ephemeral foot.

<Any luck slipping into the system?> Sera changed the topic.

Helen's avatar cast Sera a dirty look in her mind, but let it drop.

<I've activated an environmental port three deck plates down. There's water in one of the pipes and the schematic shows a faucet I can activate so that you can get something to drink.>

<That,> Sera smiled, *<would be heavenly.>*

BOLLAM'S WORLD

STELLAR DATE: 07.20.8927 (Adjusted Years)
LOCATION: Andromeda's Pinnace, EK Belt
REGION: Bollam's World System, Bollam's World Federation

Joe lay in his bunk, eyes closed, imagining that he was back on the *Intrepid*, at home with Tanis, enjoying a lazy morning in bed before spending some time in the garden.

Maybe they would be in their final days before arriving at New Eden, the ship awake and buzzing outside, everyone glad for finally arriving at their final destination. Maybe their child would be born, a small girl, rushing into the room, jumping onto the bed and making a ruckus.

He took a long breath and opened his eyes.

That would never be. The *Intrepid* would never travel to New Eden—it may never travel anywhere, because there was nowhere to go.

"Joe," Jessica's voice came over the audible comm. "I've managed to make a Link to a relay buoy at the edge of the system. There's a twenty light-minute delay, but I have a standard packet they sent out with approach vectors, stations, and stuff."

And stuff...Joe couldn't help feel some amusement at how different Jessica was from Tanis. Both were career service women, both practically built out of duty, but still as different from one another as night and day.

He imagined for a second what it would be like to be with Jessica, how different life would be. He shook his head and chuckled, it certainly wouldn't be for him.

Tanis was his anchor, his strength—not that he needed to lean on her that way now, but she had been a rock for him during those early days on the *Intrepid*. He had felt so out of his depth, worried that they were going to cut him from the mission because he couldn't get things under control.

Then she came in, full of command and purpose—knowing just what to do.

She always knew what to do.

"I'm on my way," he messaged back to Jessica. "Give me a second to get presentable."

"No rush, the data is still coming in," Jessica replied.

"Gotcha," Joe said and stepped into the ultrasonic san, letting its waves pull dirt and detritus from his skin. He stepped out, feeling only superficially refreshed, and pulled a shipsuit on before running a hand through his hair.

"Good enough," he said to himself as he shifted his thinking from the past and his feelings of loss to instead focus on the work ahead. It was something he had seen Tanis do hundreds of times; she did it so naturally. For him, it took a bit more effort to compartmentalize his feelings.

The pinnace was small; it could crew seven, but with just the two of them on board it felt empty—though he preferred it that way at present. The walk to the cockpit took just a minute and he entered to see Jessica bent over the main holo tank, studying the Bollam's World system.

Her silver hair fell around her face and when she raised her head to look at him, her lavender-colored brow was furrowed.

"This is one weird system," she said and beckoned him to the tank. "And it's not just their name…who calls their whole system 'Bollam's World'?"

"Beats me," Joe shrugged. "What's weird other than the name?"

"Check it out," Jessica gestured and the holo display rose up and filled the cockpit. "There's this massive…I don't know what to call it. It's not a jovian, or a brown dwarf, but it's too big for a planet, that's for sure."

Joe looked at the large blue-green planet, labeled Aurora, that Jessica was pointing at. The data packet didn't have detailed specifications—other than a warning not to venture within one AU of its surface—but it was plain to see that it had over three time's Jupiter's diameter, and, based on its orbit and rotation, at least ten times its mass.

Worlds such as this one shouldn't exist. Even if a planet massed more than Jupiter, it would not get physically larger. Instead—being a gas giant—the gas would compress under its own gravity and it would remain the same size. Unless the world were to become so massive that it began to fuse hydrogen; then convection would expand it.

Aurora's size indicated that it should be light and airy, like Saturn. However, its mass meant it should be slightly smaller than Jupiter—yet it was neither.

"That's…that's exceedingly unusual," Joe said with a nod. "What about stations and inhabited worlds?"

"The star's practically a Sol-clone," Jessica said. "But its young, just over half a billion years or so. The place is full of hot stuff with a lot of spin to it."

"Two terrestrial worlds there," Joe pointed to the third and fourth planets, named Dublin and Bollam on the holo. "No rings and just a few elevators. Looks like a third is being terraformed around that other jovian, the sixth planet out."

"There's a sizable hab orbiting it, too," Jessica pointed to a roughly spherical mass of concentric rings.

Joe gave a low whistle. "Data packet has it housing a hundred billion people."

Jessica sighed, "That's us humans, filling up every corner of the galaxy."

"I wonder how far we've gotten," Joe said wistfully. "This system looks like it has half a trillion people, over forty light-years from Sol. Even the FGT hadn't gotten this far when we left, or if they had, we didn't know it."

"I don't think that the FGT did this system," Jessica said.

"Oh yeah? Why's that?" Joe asked.

"They would have moved that Mars-sized world into the habitable zone and merged one of those inner rocky worlds with it," she replied. "They wouldn't just waste it out there."

"Maybe," Joe nodded. "Given how we got here, who knows who actually settled this world."

"That rocky world 47AU out has a big refinery and mining yard in orbit. They're on our side of the star, if anyone came insystem with Tanis's pod, they may have passed through."

"Let's set a course, then," Joe said as he zoomed the holo in on the station. "And we better find out what kind of clearances we need to dock there. Gotta try and look like locals."

PRIVATEER

STELLAR DATE: 07.22.8927 (Adjusted Years)
LOCATION: *Sabrina*, Gedri Scattered Disk
REGION: Gedri System, Silstrand Alliance Space

Sabrina transitioned out of FTL into the Gedri system travelling at only 0.09*c*, their prior velocity deliberately bled off in interstellar space to make them a more tempting target.

"Continue shedding *v* nice and easy, Cheeky," Cargo said from the captain's chair. "Make us look vulnerable."

"Cargo, that's one of my main skills," Cheeky said with a grin. "Won't be the first time I've played damsel in distress to sucker some poor guy in."

Tanis couldn't help but laugh. For Cheeky, everything was a potential analogy to her sex life.

"Hurry up and wait," Cargo muttered as the crew settled in to their stations, all eyes on the passive scan and the local beacon's report of the system traffic.

Further insystem, at the outer edge of the EK Belt, lay the regular jump point that led to and from Silstrand. It was busy, crowded with ships on various braking and acceleration trajectories. Beyond that was an empty void; *Sabrina* was the only ship in that space, on a slow trajectory insystem from the outer, less trafficked jump point. System scan hadn't picked them up, and wouldn't for several more hours. This was the time when the pirates would strike. If they did at all.

Cargo had just brought in the second round of coffee for Tanis and Cheeky when scan picked up a ship dumping in very close to their position. Its entry point was not at any marked jump point, but the dark matter was so sparse in this solar region that a ship could hop in and out of the dark layer with very little concern of collision.

The vessel was five light minutes away, and subsequent scan updates showed it altering its trajectory to intercept *Sabrina*. At first glance, it appeared to be a regular freighter, but closer inspection with the updated scan suite revealed that there was less cargo and more engine capacity than normal. The ship's shields were strong and it appeared that there were traces of high power conduit near the hull—a clear indicator of substantial weaponry.

<*The fish has spotted the lure,*> Cargo said on the ship-wide net. <*They've altered course and are on an intercept with us. They're still a good thirty million kilometers away, but breaking rapidly to match our velocity. We should meet up in the next hour or so.*

A regular freighter wouldn't have had the sensors capable of picking up the pirate's jump and would only receive notification from the local beacon at the system's terminal shock. It would take yet another twenty minutes for that message to come in and so they played dumb, appearing ignorant of the incoming aggressor.

Right on schedule, the system traffic control AI sent a burst to both ships warning of a potential collision and provided new inbound lanes.

At this point, the two vessels were only two light minutes apart, and Cargo signaled for Tanis to send a direct transmission to the other ship. The local beacon had identified the pirate ship as a freighter named *Regal Dawn*, and so Tanis addressed it as such.

"*Regal Dawn,* this is the *Orion Star,* we are bound insystem and braking on a trajectory that will intercept yours. Please correct your course to the following as provided by the system's beacon." Tanis transmitted the updated path along with the message.

"Will the altered ident hold up?" Cheeky asked.

"It was simple tech to tweak," Tanis replied. "And system traffic control bought it."

She saw Cheeky and Cargo exchange a look. Neither of them had thought it possible to alter the sealed ident box all ships were required to carry. Angela said it was child's play.

The entire bridge held their breath as they waited for the reply. The ships were rapidly closing on one another and the response came in just past the two minute mark.

"*Orion Star,* this is the *Regal Dawn*. We have received updated course and are correcting. Sorry for the trouble." The words sounded genuine, appearing to be innocent, but Tanis didn't believe it for a moment.

She checked scan and over the next five minutes, they saw no alteration in the suspected pirate's course. When enough time had passed that even the worst scan would have picked up the unaltered course, Tanis submitted another message, which received almost the exact same reply, except now it cited engine trouble as the excuse for not altering vector.

The ships were now within one light minute of each other, a distance of only eighteen million kilometers, and Tanis slid over to the new tactical console where she ran checks on the shielding and new weapon's systems.

"Looks like you're going to get your chance to try out all those fancy toys sooner than we expected," Cargo said. "This better work."

"Of course it will work," Cheeky said. "*Orion Star* here and I will fly circles around them while Tanis shoots a few well-placed holes in their hull. In a few hours we'll be on our way to rescue Sera."

"Next time we pick a different name for me, I get to choose it," *Sabrina* groused audibly. "I want to be the *Brilliant Nebula*."

Tanis wished she could feel as confident as Cheeky did. With no shakedown and the briefest of live weapon tests, there was every chance they'd suffer a failure and lose to this pirate.

<*The plan's solid,*> Angela said. <*At least as solid as it can be with just one freighter of untried crew and weaponry.*>

<*Gee, thanks, Ang.*>

They would hold course until the last possible moment, doing nothing to alert the pirate that its prey was more than met the eye. Scaring off the ship and chasing it through the system would be far too risky a maneuver. It was also imperative that the other ship shot first, or they would be the one flagged as pirates in Gedri.

"Steady, Cheeky. Hold it until we are within ten thousand clicks before you alter course," Cargo said, as much to break the silence as instruction.

"You don't say," Cheeky muttered.

The flashing telltales, indicating an impending collision, were starting to annoy everyone. It was a largely unnecessary warning—even if neither ship changed course, the chances of an actual collision were very slim. Unless one of the vessels desired it.

Since *Sabrina* was playing meek and innocent, they had to do what any simple freighter would do when another ship was going to hit it: move. When the comps indicated that proximity was critical, Cheeky made the necessary course adjustments; moments later, a tight-beam message came in from the pirate.

"Attention *Orion Star.* Resume your previous course or we'll fire on you. If you do not resist you will be unharmed. Repeat. Return to your previous course and prepare to be boarded."

"Not ones for small talk, are they?" Tanis observed.

Cheeky did not comply, as was the plan. She activated the AP drive and Tanis brought their rear shields to full power. She expected a shot across their bow first, but there was no point in risking actual damage.

Right on cue, the shot came, glancing across the dorsal shield; the ship-to-ship comm ringing with angry messages to return to their previous course. Scan showed the pirate ship altering course and braking to match *Sabrina's* new vector. The warning came again to resume their previous course or be disabled; moments later, the shields took their first direct hit.

"Now!" Tanis shouted.

Cheeky didn't need the order; she was already killing the engines and firing maneuvering thrusters. *Sabrina* spun about and faced the pirate. The forward dorsal lasers tracked the pirate's engines—which were still facing *Sabrina* as it braked to match course with them. The moment they had a lock, Tanis sent four bursts from the thirty-centimeter lasers.

She didn't target the pirate's engines directly—blowing the ship wasn't their goal. The shots struck around the engine nozzles. Overheating and fusing control mechanisms would cause an engine shutdown and give *Sabrina* maneuvering advantage.

Another two shots missed as the pirate ship twisted to avoid the beams, but the third and fourth hit their targets. One of the *Regal Dawn's* engines shut down and its maneuvering thrusters fired, bringing the pirate about to face *Sabrina*.

Tanis reviewed her console for errors or system failures. Nothing showed red and she thanked the S&H install crew for a job well done.

She had been in a lot of battles, including no small number of space battles, but never a pitched beam fight at 0.10*c* in civilian ships. It was exhilarating. Tanis made several quick calculations; Angela assisted in presenting the best shots, and, upon Tanis's approval, sent the strike coordinates to the *Sabrina's* new fire control systems.

The six offensive beams positioned for forward fire tapped into the fully charged SC batteries and lanced out at the pirate ship, concentrating at two points on its shields. Three successive bursts and scan showed the *Regal Dawn's* shields failing.

Return fire came at *Sabrina,* but Cheeky spun the ship on its axis and no shot lingered long on the same shield umbrella. Tanis's console showed their shields disperse the energy and quickly recover.

The pirate ship kicked their vessel into a somewhat wobbly rotation, and Tanis renewed her offense—continuing to focus on the same points on the pirate's shields in short bursts.

"Cocky bastards," Cheeky said with a grin. "Didn't think they had to be careful with us. Bet they're wishing they had now."

Cargo laughed. "You just keep them from scorching us and you can talk all the smack you want, Cheeks."

"Their shield is flickering on its forward umbrella, they're going to drop to the dark," Tanis announced.

"Damn," Cargo said. "That'll ruin our party right fast. Can you punch through and hit their grav drive in time?"

"Well…" Tanis began. "Wait, their grav drive just powered down. Either they had something go or they are afraid we may follow them."

A message came over the ship-to-ship comm and Cargo opened the visual link. The man on the holo looked decidedly unhappy. His eyes flashed with rage under a heavy brow.

"Who do you think you are?" he demanded. "This is Mark territory; you can't attack one of our ships and get away with it."

"As I hear it, Kade's dead, and *you* initiated this little game we just played."

"Doesn't matter who's at the head of our organization, you're all dead now." The pirate seemed to hope threats could save him where his shields and weapons had not.

"Lower your shields and shut down your reactors. Prepare to be boarded," Cargo said with a scowl. "We want to see vid of your entire crew in your mess with no weapons. Any tricks and we'll slap some mines on you and say farewell."

"You better really want this," The captain of the *Regal Dawn* growled. "You're going to have to be watching your back for a long time."

"This is *Sabrina,*" Cargo smiled with a hint of menace as he signaled for Tanis to switch their ident back. "We've got Kade on ice and we'll happily add any of you, if you give us half a reason."

The captain's expression paled and he grudgingly responded that they would comply. The visual feed from the *Regal Dawn* flipped to their mess. Several minutes later, the crew began to file in.

"Do you think they'll go quietly?" Cheeky asked.

"Not a damn chance," Cargo smiled. He signaled for Tanis to follow him to the fore hatch where Flaherty and Thompson were already waiting. S&H had provided them with some advanced body armor, which the assault team already wore. It wasn't up to the spec Tanis preferred, but it should stop pulse rifles and projectile rounds. If the pirates started firing high-powered beams or rails their way—which would be ludicrous—then the team would be in trouble.

"I feel like Nance," Thompson said as he twisted in the thick, supple armor. It sported plates on the front and back of the torso, but the rest was a thick material, which would harden on impact and disperse the force of a shot. It could also nullify the effects of a pulse rifle and disperse the heat of a hand laser. The helmet had a HUD that interfaced with their internal Links to provide displays of everyone's field of vision and status—not that Tanis needed such a crude interface.

They fastened their helmets and looked one another over.

<*Let's do this,*> Thompson said as he cycled the airlock and stepped out into the umbilical.

<*They're cycling their lock open for us,*> Nance announced from the bridge, where she had taken Tanis's place. Tanis had given the bio a crash course on the new weapons systems and the upgraded scan that went with them. It had been a bit tense since Nance's unhappiness with the plan—and Tanis in general—wasn't well hidden, but she had been a quick study.

<*Are they all in the galley?*> Cargo asked.

<*I count nine in there,*> Nance replied. <*I don't know what their compliment is; their AI is being very unfriendly.*>

<*That's going to be difficult to deal with when we try to use their ship,*> Thompson said as the four of them stepped into the *Regal Dawn's* lock and waited for it to seal and match pressure with the rest of the ship.

<*I should be able to get it under control,*> Tanis without worry.

<*Should?*> Nance asked.

<*I was speaking extemporaneously,*> Tanis sighed to herself. At least this part would be over soon. Once they were on their way to rescue Sera, she hoped Nance and Thompson would lay off the accusations.

The light above the inner hatch changed from red to green and the iris spun open to reveal an empty corridor. Everyone had their weapons leveled and Tanis double-checked the seal on her helmet. Chemical warfare was all too common in instances like this. The suits did not detect anything, but she wasn't going to take any chances.

After planting a mine in the airlock, Tanis and Flaherty made their way fore to the bridge, while Cargo and Thompson went aft to the galley. While it was possible that the entire crew had done as directed, they were expecting to find at least one pirate holed up somewhere.

<*Any sign of crew?*> Cargo asked.

<*Not yet. I expect we'll meet with someone near or on the bridge.*>

The bridge on the pirate ship was up four levels. Like *Sabrina*, or any ship expecting trouble, ladders were available for passage between the decks; no one wanted to take a lift down into a firefight.

Tanis sent her nano cloud ahead. It almost felt like cheating in this technologically backward time, but not so much that she was willing to risk getting shot in the head on a point of honor.

The tiny bots reported the next level clear and she slipped up the ladder, Flaherty was close behind, silent and serious as always. The next two decks were clear as well, but on the final level, her nano reported small sounds from the direction of the bridge.

Someone hadn't followed orders.

Tanis crept up the ladder and sent a command to Flaherty to follow her, but hold near the ladder while she checked out the bridge. He nodded his assent and backed against a bulkhead in a low crouch, his eyes everywhere.

Conscious of how easily sound traveled in these ships, Tanis took careful steps, her pulse rifle slung low with her finger on the trigger. Her nano flushed into the bridge and her overlay brought up a clear view of the space. There was someone in there all right—a tall woman with long, dark hair and a long leather coat bent over a console.

Tanis stepped out into the hatchway and spoke calmly, her voice coming over a speaker on the suit. "Raise your hands slowly and then turn around."

The woman complied, raised her arms and slowly turned. Even before she saw the other woman's face, Tanis's image recognition systems made the identification.

"Sera?"

"You were expecting the Easter Bunny?" Sera smiled, her dark eyes dancing with mirth.

"What are you doing here?" Tanis asked.

"Thanking my lucky stars you weren't someone intent on blowing this ship to pieces. I had a few minutes of serious worry until Helen cracked that fake ident and we realized it was you guys."

"How did you get away from Rebecca?" Tanis asked. Sera was a far more resourceful woman than she had expected.

"Skill and cunning, but that's a long story. The whole crew here?"

"Thompson and Cargo are below, checking on the crew," Flaherty said from the hatchway behind Tanis.

He slipped past Tanis and stepped into the bridge to embrace Sera in a quick hug. "You gave me a bit of a worry there. I don't like you going off on your own."

Sera laughed. "I don't either. It's not like it was my idea."

"Did you get it?" he asked.

Sera nodded and stretched her foot out to tap a container the size of a personal luggage case on the floor near her.

"All in a day's work," Sera replied.

Tanis's IFF systems scanned Sera and showed the woman to be a mass of wounds and trauma.

<*She's a mess,*> Tanis whistled softly in her mind.

<*Notice she doesn't have skin anymore? Her thermal profile is all wrong,*> Angela brought up an image of *Sera's* heat profile and thermal output in Tanis's mind.

<*Not to mention the energy profile of whatever is in that case—that Flaherty already seems to know about,*> Tanis replied.

"Was that a voluntary alteration?" Tanis asked, pointing at Sera's exposed glossy skin.

Sera's face reddened. "I was always a bit jealous of Rebecca's outfits, so I tried one on. The crazy bitch booby trapped it, so this is my new skin for now."

<*With the trauma she's had, and the med facilities on* Sabrina*, it may be her new skin for some time,*> Helen added.

"You'd fit right in with Jessica, one of my team on the *Intrepid*," Tanis said with a smile. "If you can't get squared away before we get there, our docs could fix you up without trouble.

"Not sure I want to be fixed—I think I rather like it," Sera said with a mischievous grin.

"Now you *really* remind me of Jessica."

"Maybe we should discuss mods and fashion later," Flaherty said. "We still have a ship to secure."

"That we do." Sera picked up the mysterious case in one hand and pulse rifle in the other. "Compliment on this ship is twelve. Angela just informed me there are only nine in the galley, so we've got some fun ahead of us." Sera suddenly stopped and turned to face Tanis.

"What did you do to my ship?" she asked with eyes wide.

"Angela shared that tidbit, did she?" Tanis replied with a smile.

"You added ten offensive beams and rail guns? Where'd you get the money?"

"We sold some nano to S&H," Tanis said with a shrug.

Sera turned to Flaherty. "And you let her do this? It could destabilize the regional economy."

"It's alright," Flaherty replied. "The stuff she sold them is not replicable with their current levels of technology. They don't have the ability to produce the nano-sized stasis fields without the Casimir effect collapsing their containment. It's essentially useless."

Tanis was dumbfounded. How did Flaherty understand that, let alone know it was a required component of the technology she had sold S&H. Sera saw her confusion?

"I'll explain later, once we deal with these pirates and set a course for Bollam's World and the *Intrepid.*"

Sera sent a broad message on *Sabrina's* ship-wide net. *<Thanks for the ride guys, I sure didn't want to have to get out and walk!>*

A chorus of voices cried out Sera's name before a round of expletives and questions flooded the comm.

<Easy now, I'll answer everything once this is over. I'm as curious as to what you are doing here as you are about me, I'm sure. First, we take care of three little lost pirate pigs. Thompson, Cargo, have you secured the galley yet?>

<We're in the hall now. Nine secure,> Cargo replied. *<You said there are three missing pirates around here somewhere?>*

<Yeah, there should be twelve aboard,> Sera replied. *<Sabrina, be a dear and seal our hatch—I don't want any of them getting onto you.>*

<Taken care of, Sera,> Sabrina responded, sounding happier than she had in a week.

<Angela,> Sera addressed Tanis's AI, *<I suspect your cyber warfare is the best around. Is there any chance that you can subdue this ship's pesky AI and take it out of the equation?>*

<Shouldn't be too hard. I've already infiltrated most of its systems and have it cornered in its own neural net. It's throwing everything it has at me, if life support goes offline for a minute or two don't be alarmed. It's just me,> Angela's reply was offhand, but Tanis could tell she was disgusted by the intelligence she was fighting on board the *Regal Dawn.*

"Flaherty," Sera directed, "cover the hatch. They may make a break for *Sabrina* and it'll be a good place to corner them."

Flaherty nodded and left the bridge. Tanis couldn't even hear him as he slid down the ladder.

"How does he move so quietly?" she asked.

"Honestly? I have no idea," Sera replied. "Helen usually has to use probes to hide my ruckus—though not anymore, I guess." With that, she threw off her long coat and slipped out of the bridge in her whisper-silent skin.

Tanis and Sera checked the two cabins on that level, which appeared to belong to the captain and the first mate—both empty. On the next level, the rest of the crew cabins also checked out.

<How are your charges?> Sera asked Cargo.

<They're none too happy, but they aren't causing us any trouble. The captain we saw over the holo isn't here. One of them let it slip that the mate and engineer are missing, as well. I'm thinking they may be trying to get control back from below.>

<You hold those guys, Tanis and I will go take a peek.>

<Aye, Captain.>

"You have no idea how good it is to hear that again," Sera said aloud to Tanis.

"You have no idea how good it is to hear them say it."

Sera cocked an eyebrow. "They hold together ok?"

"Better than a lot of other crews I've seen when their leader is captured," Tanis replied as they slid down a ladder.

"Good to know I trained them well."

Trained, Tanis added that to the long list of mysteries surrounding Sera.

The two women reached the freight deck, with Angela coordinating probe coverage as they searched for signs of the missing crewmembers. The search turned up nothing and they proceeded down the ladder to environmental.

Just as their feet touched the deck plate, the life support equipment wound to a halt.

<*It's just me,*> Angela said. <*I'm almost wrapped up—just giving him nowhere to hide.*>

Environmental was clear and they worked their way aft toward waste reclamation and engineering.

<*We've got sounds in here that aren't mechanical. Sounds like a footstep, male, most likely a hundred and eighty centimeters and at least ninety-five kilograms. Echoes make it hard to place, but he's somewhere to the right of the entrance no more than ten meters away,*> Helen said.

<*Thanks,*> Sera replied as she peered around the corner. There was nothing visible and she crept to a large tank and provided cover while Tanis slipped in, stopping behind an adjacent tank.

Tanis pivoted and peered over her cover. The motion shifted the deck plate beneath her and gave a low groan. Moments later the waves from a pulse rifle tore through the air over her head. She ducked and Sera rose from cover, firing shots at the attacker.

He ducked down before the waves reached him. Tanis tossed Sera a conspiratorial smile, before slipping out from behind her cover into the next row of tanks, sneaking toward the enemy's location.

As Tanis moved, Sera supplied cover fire, keeping their opponent pinned.

Tanis crept within two meters of the last tank at the end of the row. She steadied herself for a second, and then, in one swift motion, leapt over the tank, twisted mid-air, and landed a meter from their attacker—weapon leveled at his head.

"End of the road, bub."

His back was to her, peering around the other side while trying to get an angle on Sera. He turned slowly, lowering his rifle with one hand, while raising the other.

<*'End of the road, bub'?*> Sera asked.

<*I saw it in a vid once.*>

A half-second before his weapon reached the deck, a series of shots rang out over the waste reclamation equipment, and Tanis heard Sera let loose a string of curses. The man in front of Tanis took advantage of her momentary distraction to raise his weapon and fire a shot off. It struck her square in the chest, flinging her back against the bulkhead. She squeezed off two shots after she hit, but the man had already ducked out of view.

<*You okay?*> she and Sera asked each other.

<*Armor took the most of it,*> Tanis said. <*You?*>

<*They missed, but those were some serious slug throwers. I think both the captain and the tech are on the far left side of the room,*> Sera replied

<*Keep some cover fire on them. I'm going to take care of this guy.*>

Tanis saw Sera pull two slug throwers from holsters on her legs and let loose a volley of her own, the bullets ricocheting off the tanks across the room. Tanis used the distraction to launch herself from her position against the wall. She leapt onto a tank and fell upon the man on the other side.

While not exceptionally graceful, it had the advantage of total surprise. He had been peering back around the tank, his weapon pointed to where she had been. Her elbow slammed into his stomach and she drove a knee into his crotch before smashing the butt of her rifle against the back of his head.

<*One down.*>

<*Helen says she can't spot these guys, they may be using some sort of active camouflage. Can your probes spot them?*> Sera asked.

<*They're using the ship's sensors to create a noise cloud around them. I can't get more than a ghost here and there,*> Angela replied. <*I'll try to find the emitters and shut them down—not all of this ship is accessible from their main net.*>

<*It's a bit of a mess,*> Helen agreed.

Tanis crept along her side of the room, and then moved even with Sera's position.

<*I'm going to draw their fire; see if you can get a line on one of them,*> Tanis said before she stood and leapt across a tank. Shots rang out from a position at the end of the room and return fire came from Sera's location.

Tanis saw one of Sera's shots catch a man at the end of the room in the shoulder. He spun sideways but still managed to fire a few bullets in Tanis's direction. She responded with a series of blasts from her pulse rifle, all missing, but it was enough to force him behind cover.

<*I've got the last one over here somewhere,*> Sera said. <*I heard him just a minute ago.*>

<*I bet you're feeling a keen lack of body armor right about now,*> Tanis replied as she swapped out her rifle's energy coil.

<*I've been feeling that lack for a few days now.*>

Sera and Tanis worked their way closer together and then down to the location of the man Sera had clipped. When they got there, they saw that he had cracked his head on the tank and was out cold.

<*I didn't think my last shot hit him,*> Tanis shook her head. <*I maybe he slipped or something.*>

<*Self-defeating enemies. My favorite kind,*> Sera replied.

Shots rang out from their right as they stared down at the fallen pirate. One hit Tanis's chest armor and she swore as the impact caused her to stagger.

<*Been too long, you're getting sloppy,*> Angela said.

<*Yeah? Have that AI taken care of yet?*> Tanis replied sourly.

<*Yup,*> Angela responded cheerfully. <*Just waiting on you.*>

Sera dashed down the row of tanks, throwing caution to the wind and Tanis saw her boot lash out, sending a weapon flying. A second kick elicited the soft crunch of breaking bone. There was a third kick as Tanis reached her, weapon at the ready.

The man on the floor was down with a long gash across his face, as he rocked side to side, moaning and clutching his chest.

"Last one, then?" Sera asked out loud.

"Should be. Nine and three is twelve last time I checked."

"Good, all that cat and mouse stuff was starting to get on my nerves. I want a hot meal and a bath."

"Do you even need baths now?" Tanis smiled.

"Probably not, but I'm going to take one anyway," Sera groused.

Tanis laughed, but her voice caught at a familiar sound from behind them. Angela cried out a warning, but it wasn't fast enough. The high-pitched whine of a rail weapon echoed through the chamber and Tanis felt a stinging sensation in her chest.

Sera had both of her handguns out, shots ringing from each as she fired at a figure racing past a nearby tank. A shot hit him in the side and he staggered forward, then fell to his knees. Sera kept shooting as she advanced, the man collapsed, his body twitching as Sera emptied her clips into him.

"Aww hell," Tanis said in a strained voice, catching herself against a tank. She wheezed as Sera turned, her face a mask of horror, and rushed back.

<Nance! Get a grav pad over here now! Bottom deck, Tanis is hit!>

"You'll be okay. We'll get you patched up in no time," Sera caught Tanis as she slid down the tank and pulled her up into her arms.

Tanis looked up at Sera and tried to speak. No words came out, but she tried to sound jovial over the Link. *<You'd better. If I die rescuing you I'll be rather upset.>*

Sera grimaced, pulling Tanis close, and, calling on some untapped reserve of strength, heaved her up and stumbled toward the closest lift. Tanis was wheezing more than breathing and knew that in any moment she'd go into convulsions. The armor was trying to seal the wound to stop the blood from flowing out, but couldn't deal with the massive hole the rail gun had torn through Tanis's chest.

Right through her heart.

UNBREAKABLE

STELLAR DATE: 07.27.8927 (Adjusted Years)
LOCATION: *Sabrina*, Interstellar Dark Layer
REGION: 72 Light Years Core-Ward of Ayrea

It was that reoccurring nightmare again. Something was chasing her through the dark corridors of the *Intrepid* where there was no power, no lights, no Link. It was gaining on her, no matter how hard she ran, it grew ever closer, its clawed feet scraping the decking, the sound echoing around her. Tanis was sick of these nightmares, she wanted to wake up. She was done running.

Repeating the mantra over and over in her subconsciousness, she felt herself rise from the mire, from the darkness, moving to the light, and gradually come awake. The light pressed against her eyelids. It was going to be bright again. Steeling herself, she cracked one eye and then the other. She seemed to be in some med lab, not on the *Intrepid*, that much was for certain. Her chest hurt; hurt a lot.

<*Where am I, Angela?*> she asked.

<*You're on* Sabrina, *Tanis. You were wounded in taking that pirate ship, the* Regal Dawn.>

Angela sounded concerned, but not alarmed. Tanis knew that was a good sign; Angela wouldn't hide her condition if it were bad. She concentrated for a moment, and the memories slowly trickled back; the escape pod, the abduction by Padre's pirates, Sera saving her, and then her saving Sera. She took a deep breath and smiled. They'd be on their way to the *Intrepid* now. This leg of her journey was finally coming to an end.

"We seem to be making a habit of this," a nearby voice said.

Tanis turned her head to see Sera sitting beside her, a look of concern mixed with relief on her face. She handed Tanis a bottle of water with a straw, and Tanis took several long pulls, washing the moisture around her parched mouth.

"We do seem to be," she agreed when she had finished. "Thank you for patching me back together again."

"Nance and Angela did most of the work. I'm all thumbs when it comes to hooking up artificial hearts and then growing new organic ones."

"Heart?"

"When that guy shot at us with the rail gun, I thought he had hit me at first. I figured if I was still standing, I was going to take him down. Later, after I got him, I realized what I thought had been the railgun slug hitting me was a piece of your rib cage. It punctured my right lung, but my fancy new skin sealed around it and kept me breathing."

"Good to know my impending death didn't inconvenience you too much," Tanis smiled. "I did notice back on the ship that you had replaced your skin with some sort of polymer, glad to see it proved useful."

Sera looked down at herself and smiled. "I was saved by fashion. Anyway, when you tried to speak, I turned and…well, let's just say it wasn't pretty. Angela is really the one who saved you. She sealed up your arteries as fast as she could, and managed to keep most of your blood in while we got you on a medical stasis rack and raced you back to *Sabrina.* The pellet the rail gun fired was soft and hollow. It mushroomed inside your chest and ripped your heart apart. The mass hit the inside of the armor on the back, and the shockwave rippled back through the rest of your torso. It did a number on your internal organs."

"Better than the last time I got hit by a rail," Tanis said with a weak smile. "Thanks for keeping me together again, Angela."

<It's purely selfish interest, love.>

<Wait! The baby?> Tanis said with fear washing over her.

<She's perfectly fine. The stasis bubble kept her safe, but…>

<But what?!>

<She's not in stasis right now. When you heal up, I can re-instate it, or…>

<Let's leave that 'or' for later,> Tanis replied.

Sera continued, unaware of Tanis's private conversation.

"Nance got you hooked up to a circulatory machine while she picked bits of shattered bone out of your chest. We fed Angela so much silicon she could have made a replica of you, and Sabrina helped make raw, unprogrammed nano as fast as she could. They shored up all your internal bleeding and slowly re-constructed your organs. Some of them we ended up having to grow fresh—you don't have a bone ribcage anymore, though Angela says she'll slowly replace the artificial one with living tissue over time."

Tanis chuckled. "Also not the first time."

"Sounds like there's a story I'd like to hear when you're not lying here in recovery," Sera said.

"It's a good one, I'll be sure to swap it with one of yours—I see it's only been five days since we took the *Dawn*. That's quite the medical feat you all pulled off, Ang," Tanis said with a yawn.

"It sure was," Sera replied. "Did you used to be a doctor?"

<Just field medicine,> Angela replied. *<You can't live inside a human body for over a century and not have a good idea how it works.>*

"I guess that makes sense," Sera said.

"So, how long am I bedridden for?" Tanis asked.

<There was relatively little nerve damage, though I sacrificed some muscles to keep blood flowing to your brain. I had to rebuild them; you'll need to do some stretching and make sure all your joints work right,> Angela replied.

"Doc knows best," Sera smiled.

Sera helped Tanis raise her legs and move her arms in their full range of motion before she sat up and took a deep breath.

"Everything seems to be in working order," she looked to Sera. "Are you all healed up? I recall you saying something about a rib of mine making a hole in you."

Sera ran a hand down her 'skin'. "All healed and right as rain. Angela knew a few things about flesh and polymer bonding. She and Helen gave me a bit of an upgrade—now it grows back on its own."

"It's a pretty straight-forward mod," Tanis agreed.

<Not Fina's first time with some unexpected alterations either,> Helen added.

"Fina. You've called her that a few times," Tanis observed. "What does it mean?"

<It's a short version of her name,> Helen replied.

"Hush." Sera looked perturbed.

<You have a beautiful name. I helped your mother choose it, I think it suits you.>

"Now I have to know what it is," Tanis said.

"Sera *is* my name; it's just shortened a bit."

<*It's shortened by five letters,*> Helen said with a virtual scowl.

<*Seraphina?*> Angela asked.

"No!" Sera shouted in dismay.

<*Good extrapolation,*> Helen's avatar nodded in their minds.

"I must swear you all to secrecy," Sera said. "I'm completely serious—I can't wheel, deal, and smuggle with a name like Seraphina."

"Who else knows?" Tanis asked.

"Other than you, just Flaherty."

<*It doesn't help that he used to change your diapers,*> Helen said.

"Stop it! You're giving all my secrets away," Sera's face was beginning to redden. Tanis could tell she was adding some choice comments to her AI in private.

<*Oh shush. Eventually she'll figure it all out, I'm just giving her a little nudge here and there,*> Helen said publicly to the group.

"You two are quite the puzzle," Tanis said with an eyebrow raised.

"Hey, on a different track," Sera began, appearing to choose her words carefully, "have you thought about what your ship will do now that it's stuck in the ninetieth century?"

Tanis let out a long sigh. "Not really. I imagine we could find a moon somewhere in some system and terraform it in trade for what we have. I've looked at the star charts; there aren't a lot of options around—not without a really long trip."

"I…this isn't the sort of information that one bandies about, but I think I can help. I have contacts I can reach out to when we get to Bollam's World." Sera paused, indecision clouding her features, then finished her statement, "I can get in touch with the FGT."

Tanis sat up, locking eyes with Sera, searching for a sign that his was subterfuge…or a joke.

"You're serious?"

Sera nodded. "Serious as a railgun slug to the chest."

"How do you have contacts like this?" Tanis asked.

Sera didn't reply right away and Tanis waited in silence for the captain to make up her mind.

"I…I'm not ready to talk about that yet. It's not a part of my life I like to reflect on." Her face lightened. "But I promise I'll tell you, just not yet."

Tanis wasn't sure what to make of Sera's admission, but even suspect contact with the FGT was more to go on than she had five minutes ago.

"OK, thanks for your offer. I can wait for the details," she replied

"You ready to get some solid food in you?" Sera asked and stood from her chair.

"More than ready, my stomach is grumbling like it hasn't had food in a year," Tanis replied as she carefully settled on her feet.

<*This particular stomach hasn't had food ever. Go easy on it,*> Angela instructed.

She stepped gingerly as they walked out of the med-lab into the central corridor on the freight deck. "Angela wasn't kidding when she said I'd have to take it easy until my muscles get back in sync."

"I had a full rebuild once," Sera said over her shoulder. "Was quite the experience. The nerves and muscles are never exactly where they were before. Takes some time to get your responses timed properly again."

"Now *you* have a story I'd like to hear some time," Tanis said.

"I bet you would." Sera smiled back at her.

Nance met them at the ladder to the crew level; Tanis noticed the woman's head was exposed for only the second time since she had been on board, and her long, brown hair was brushed to gleaming perfection.

"Tanis, it's good to see you conscious. Sabrina notified me that you were awake," she said pleasantly.

<Thanks, Sabrina,> Tanis said. *<Sorry I didn't greet you sooner. I'm still feeling a bit fuzzy.>*

<It's okay. You brought Sera back to me, I'll forgive you a simple slip,> the ship replied.

Sabrina seemed much calmer than even before Sera had been captured. Perhaps the AI had realized that even without her captain near, the crew wasn't going to abandon her to some scrap yard.

"Thanks, Nance," Tanis said aloud. "Sera tells me I'm currently breathing thanks to in no small part your actions." She patted her chest. "I'm quite impressed that you could grow a new heart with what you have available on this ship."

Nance smiled. "It's the least I could do."

<Finally warming up to us it seems,> Tanis said to Angela.

<A bit, yes.>

Tanis turned and took a long look at the ladder before letting out a long sigh. "I think I'll use the lift today."

"Probably a wise choice," Nance agreed.

The rest of the crew was waiting in the wardroom when she entered, trailing a hand along the bulkhead to assist her uncertain balance.

"Hey folks," Tanis summoned all her energy to give a winning smile.

<Five points for effort,> Angela said with a chuckle. *<Not so many for execution.>*

<Thanks for the support, dear.>

There were greetings all around; even Flaherty actually used words rather than his customary grunt. Tanis sat as gracefully as she could manage and Cheeky poured her a cup of coffee.

"How do you always have such wonderful coffee on this ship?" Tanis asked as she inhaled the aroma.

"Sera blackmails station masters," Cheeky replied with a shrug.

"Now *you're* giving away my secrets, too?" Sera threw her hands in the air.

"Other secrets have been shared?" Cheeky asked. "Why wasn't I informed?"

As they all ate, Sera retold the story of her escape from the pirate headquarters for Tanis's benefit. When she reached the part where she left Rebecca alive, Cargo shook his head with disbelief.

"I still can't fathom what possessed you to leave her alive; she's going to gun for you—for us—forever."

Tanis watched a brief war of emotions play across Sera's face.

"I could have, I really wanted to..." the captain finally replied. "But for some reason I didn't have cold-blooded murder in my heart that day."

The crew nodded respectfully, though Tanis wondered if they noticed what she had; Sera had committed murder before—and not just once.

Tanis wondered what she would have done with Rebecca, were she in Sera's position. It had been a long time since she had taken a life with her own hands; it changed a person, and not just the first time either—there was a definite cumulative effect. Perhaps Sera, like her, had spent some time recovering that part of her soul and didn't want to lose it again.

When she described the ransacking of Rebecca's quarters, Tanis couldn't help but laugh.

"I've only known you for a short time, Sera, but it does not surprise me one bit that you spent no small amount of time in another woman's wardrobe."

"Given her current condition, there's probably a parable of greed in there somewhere," Cargo said with a shake of his head.

Sera gave a simple shrug in response. "All I was wearing was a hazsuit. I couldn't wander through their platform like that."

"Why not?" Nance asked. "I bet it would have attracted a lot less attention than the state you're in now."

Cheeky laughed. "Surely you know by now, Nance. Sera *loves* attracting attention. It may be her dominant personality trait."

Sera's face turned down in a brief sulk. Everyone else was looking at Cheeky and missed the expression, but Tanis's ever-present nano-cloud spotted the reaction.

<*My money is on parental issues,*> Angela said.

<*Mine too,*> Tanis replied.

"Fine, mock me, but you're all jealous of this stuff—at least now that Helen and Angela have made it less intent on killing me, and a little more accommodating to my biology."

Cheeky gave a mischievous grin. "I wouldn't mind getting into your new skin, just not the way you are."

Sera flushed, and quickly returned to telling the rest of her tale; the battle in the warehouse, and hiding in the stack of crates. Tanis noticed there was no mention of the case that Sera had with her on the *Regal Dawn*. No one else mentioned the omission and she wondered if the crew knew anything about it.

"So, what *are* the chances that we have to worry about Rebecca sending her entire fleet after us?" Cheeky asked.

"I think they're pretty slim—for now," Sera said. "They're probably looking for a new headquarters."

"Why's that?" Thompson asked.

"I destroyed their last one," Sera smiled mischievously.

"Wait," Cheeky raised her hand. "You didn't mention that before. How did you do that?"

Sera paused, and Tanis wondered what she had done that she didn't want to share with the crew. After a glance at Flaherty, the captain continued with her tale.

"I did tell, I said that I altered their sensor array."

"Yeah," Thompson agreed. "But what for?"

"So I altered it to emit a very specific signal."

"You mean it's true?" Nance asked; her eyes wide.

Sera nodded in response.

"You're killing me with all this crypticness," Cheeky yelled. "What did you do?"

Nance pulled her eyes from Sera and cast a wary look out the porthole into the dark layer. "I've heard stories.... If Sera means what I think she does...she had it eaten."

Tanis leaned back in her chair and took a long, slow breath. Everyone looked surprised—except Flaherty, who looked slightly upset. The most emotion she had ever seen him display, outside of when Sera was captured.

"Something ate the space station?" Thompson asked.

"There are things that live in the dark layer," Sera spoke slowly, as though searching or the right words. "Things that no one understands. We don't know if they are organic, silicate, or purely energy based. No one has been able to learn anything about them—or if anyone has, they didn't live to tell the tale. However, there is a signal which attracts them, and they move fast. Somehow they can propel themselves though the dark layer."

Everyone looked somewhat paler—Tanis was certain she did, as well; not a few nervous eyes glanced out the porthole into the blackness.

"So, these things eat stations?" Thompson asked.

"They are attracted to gravitons, from what we can tell. Mostly, they stay very close to the largest clumps of dark matter, which are clustered near stars in relative space. It's why transitioning into the Dark Layer too close to a star is often a one-way trip—even if there are no clumps of dark matter nearby," Sera replied.

"Are they out in interstellar space at all?" Tanis asked.

"Every so often one is spotted." Mostly ships don't emit enough gravitons to attract them that far out, but like I said, there is a signal you can emit that's like ringing the dinner bell—even out in the void, they'll come—in this case, they most certainly have already come."

"So, you killed an entire station full of people?" Tanis asked.

<*Nice, very tactful,*> Angela said.

Sera scowled and her voice gained a cold edge. "Of course not. Do I look like a barbarian?"

"More like a Barbie doll," Flaherty said softly.

Sera stuck her tongue out at him. "I gave them fair warning."

"If these things are real, and you know so much about them, how come I've never heard of them?" Cheeky asked. "You'd think pilots would have stories."

<*Indeed, how,*> Tanis mused.

<*I have a list of possibilities as long as your arm,*> Angela replied. <*Though our access to solid data about this time is rather limited.*>

<*She's someone with good connections...maybe an aristocrat of some sort?*> Tanis mused.

<*Well, that's obvious, but who's aristocracy? Most of them aren't really that great from what I can tell.*>

<*When were they ever?*> Tanis asked.

Sera took a moment to reply to Cheeky's question.

"The knowledge is too dangerous. If people knew, they could plant a transmitter on a ship and it would transition to FTL and...well, let's just say that it would be the end of FTL travel. Plus, no one wants to run the risk of accidentally pulling one of these things into relative space."

"Can that happen?"

"No one knows...no one wants to find out."

"Makes sense," Nance said with a nod.

<*Great,*> Sabrina sighed. <*Now I have to worry about space monsters in the dark.*>

Sera answered a few more questions about her escape and from the station, then conversation drifted to *Sabrina's* upgrades and the course to Bollam's World. The crew was far more relaxed with Sera around. Even though she never acted superior, they all looked to her for advice and confirmation of their beliefs and opinions. Sometimes she disagreed or criticized, but usually managed to be supportive while doing so.

Tanis knew the hallmarks of a leader—moreover, someone raised around great leaders. She knew the traits because she had honed them over decades. Sera appeared to possess them naturally; Tanis was certain the captain had not actively focused on the skills, but had learned them through observation—before she ran from whatever position awaited her.

Ship-time slipped into the third watch and the crew began to disperse to their quarters. Tanis was one of the first out; she begged exhaustion and retreated to her cabin where she fell into a deep sleep, dreaming of Joe waiting for her on the *Intrepid* and their happy reunion.

THE RETURN

STELLAR DATE: 07.25.8927 (Adjusted Years)
LOCATION: *Sabrina*, Interstellar Dark Layer
REGION: 73 Light Years Core-Ward of Ayrea

Sera reclined in the captain's chair and stroked the leather upholstery.

It was good to be back on *Sabrina*. The ship was glad to have her captain back, too; the crew was happy, and Tanis was going to live to see another day.

It certainly would have been embarrassing, not to mention potentially dangerous, to approach the *Intrepid* with Tanis dead. She really liked the woman; though from another age, Tanis felt like a kindred spirit. The effort she had put into Sera's rescue had also earned her points—though the weapons upgrades painted a target on *Sabrina*. They would have to go before long—at least the more obvious ones.

She didn't fault Tanis. Time was short, and, as a military woman, going in with the big guns was likely her style.

Given Tanis's nano spending spree on the PeterSil EK platform, she may even need to change the registry of her ship. Too many people would wonder what job *Sabrina* had pulled to get that sort of credit. Some old friends were certainly going to take notice.

It should have upset her more, but Sera's plans for the *Intrepid* would force her to confront those individuals sooner rather than later, anyway—regardless of the mess Tanis had made in Silstrand.

<You could go back, you know,> Helen said softly. *<You have the CriEn—it's your get out of jail free card. Not to mention, proof of your innocence.>*

<This again? Do **you** *want to go back?>* Sera asked. *<You could if you wanted to, I wouldn't stop you.>*

Helen's silvery laugh echoed through Sera's mind, a sound she had heard often, ever since she was a small child—probably even before she could remember.

<Dear, I have seen enough of that life; I paired with you to get out, for the adventure. And this may be the grandest adventure I have ever experienced.>

Sera smiled. She was glad Helen felt that way—this life, this adventure as her oldest friend put it, *was* grand, far better than what her father had planned for her.

<But you are going to have to confront them. They're going to come for the Intrepid, *they'll try to force you to go.>*

"They'll try," Sera whispered to herself.

<The Intrepid *will be the catalyst, though. Orion will not sit idly by and let that sort of tech fall into your father's hands,>* Helen cautioned.

<We don't know that the Intrepid *really has picotech. No evidence of it was ever found at Kapteyn's Star, and the Victorians never showed that level of tech in anything they did afterward,>* Sera replied.

<If they even **fear** *your father will gain picotech, it will be war.>*

War. The sort of war like none ever seen before—and people had worked up some good ones in the past. Humanity was still recovering from the last one. But her father had always stayed out of prior conflicts. This would be different.

It would spread across the Orion arm of the galaxy, all of humanity would be engulfed.

"Cheeky, could—" she began, only to see that her pilot was no longer on the bridge. Her musings had been more distracting than she thought.

Sera brought up the nav data herself and reviewed it one final time.

From Angela's scan data, plus stories of other ships that had been lost in the Streamer, she knew the *Intrepid* to be in interstellar space, rim-ward of Bollam's World—perhaps even within the star's heliopause.

Bollam's World lay on the far side of several interstellar federations and demarchies. Not to mention the core worlds.

Known as the AST, the core was a strong federation with far too much red tape for Sera's taste—their security was rather invasive, even for ships just passing through their systems. *Sabrina* would give those worlds a wide berth.

Their first stop would be Ayrea, 73 light-years distant, where the ship would skip along the rim of the system before reaching the jump point on its far side. From there, it was a 15 light-year hop to Pavonis, and then, ironically, they would pass through New Eden, the very system the *Intrepid* had been destined to colonize all those millennia ago. There, they would likely stop for fuel and supplies.

Tanis would get an up-close view the world she should have lived and died on long ago.

<*You seem melancholy,*> Helen interjected.

<*I was just thinking of how it will be for Tanis to see New Eden,*> Sera replied.

<*I'm not so sure. Aside from discovering that she jumped five-thousand years into the future, little seems to unsettle Tanis Richards.*>

<*True enough, she was completely calm under fire on the* Regal Dawn. *Her heart rate never even rose.*>

<*Spying on our guest, are we?*> Helen asked with a chuckle, knowing all too well that it was second nature for both of them to observe every aspect of their surroundings.

<*Maybe just a little bit, I do prefer her to be alive for this plan,*> Sera shook her head, remembering the fear she felt when she held Tanis's in her arms on the *Regal Dawn*, convinced the woman would die.

<*If all goes well, she'll likely never die. Unless she goes and gets her heart blown out of her chest when there's no one around to fix her up again,*> Helen replied.

Sera nodded absently as she reviewed the data for the final leg of their journey, the 28 light-years to Bollam's World, and then to the *Intrepid*. The entire trip would cross nearly 140 light-years, or roughly 1.3 quadrillion kilometers. With an average FTL factor of 579, and their entry speed of 0.70*c*, the trip would take roughly ninety days, a hundred if they stopped in New Eden for fuel and post cards.

BREAK A FEW EGGS

STELLAR DATE: 07.27.8927 (Adjusted Years)
LOCATION: Andromeda's Pinnace, Tsarina Refinery, EK Belt
REGION: Bollam's World System, Bollam's World Federation

"Do you think it will work?" Jessica asked, concern filling her eyes.

"Back in Sol? Hell no. Out here, who knows, maybe?" Joe replied. "Either way, we can't just sit out here watching forever."

"OK, sending the docking request now."

Jessica sent the sequence, and Joe prayed it would work. It had taken them two weeks to get this far into the Bollam's World system; during that time they had watched thousands of ships drop out of space—appearing to come from nowhere—and then drift into the system.

Most were small, some not significantly larger than the pinnace in which they flew. It hadn't taken long for them to have no other conclusion than FTL.

Over the past months, as data streams had been stripped from insystem beacons, the crew of the *Intrepid* had strongly suspected that faster than light travel was in use—Earnest had been practically giddy at the prospect.

Now they were certain.

It opened up a world of possibilities—and made their whole struggle pointless. Joe knew it also meant that there was little reason to expect Tanis to be in Bollams's World anymore. She could be anywhere in the entire galaxy, and if she hadn't made it back to the *Intrepid* by now, things were likely not going well for her.

Still, they had to start somewhere.

He was glad for Jessica. She was able to put her worry aside and follow her investigative training. There was a lead, they would follow it and it would bring them to a new lead. To her, it was that simple.

"Station's responded," Jessica said a few minutes later. "We have a berth on the refinery's north docking ring."

"External docking for a ship this small?" Joe shook his head. "I don't know what to make of this time...are they more or less advanced?"

"Beats me," Jessica shrugged.

Joe looked over the flight path the station provided and lined the pinnace up for the approach.

The refinery was not a large installation—less than fifteen kilometers across—but the amount of traffic it supported impressed Joe. Hundreds of ships were in varying stages of approach and departure.

"These grav drives they seem to have sure do help them manage a higher volume of traffic," Jessica said, apparently on the same train of thought.

"I think it's the lack of engine wash. There's no worry about ion streams and plasma melting other ships or the station. It keeps the space lanes open."

Jessica nodded absently. "Let's hope they don't mind us coming in the old fashioned way."

Joe bit his lip as he worked to stay on course. "No kidding, this is threading one hell of a needle. Good thing we matched *v* further out. There's no room for corrective burns when we get closer."

The next several hours passed slowly as Joe worked to keep the ship in the pocket, while Jessica established a connection with the station and began querying its concierge AI for information on any recently recovered escape pods, or other salvage.

"Oh shit, here it is," Joe said as the station's traffic control opened a comm link.

"Vessel *Andromeda 3,* what are you doing approaching this facility with your torch on? Kill your fusion drive immediately and switch to grav drives!"

Joe took a deep breath and responded in his best space jock voice. "Ah, that's a negative station; we had a blow-out on our graviton emitters and can't make our approach with them. I'm right down the middle and about to switch to thrusters; ion dispersion systems show no wash will hit the station or other ships."

He glanced at Jessica and crossed his fingers while they waited for the approach.

"I don't care if you have God himself piloting that piece of crap. You don't approach a station on your torch, and I certainly can't have you chewing up that lane for the next hour. Kill your engine. I'm sending a tug out to pull you in the rest of the way. You better have an account open when you dock, because there are going to be some fines waiting for you."

"Well that sucks balls," Jessica said as the station cut the connection. "I don't suppose they'll take Sol credits."

"Any chance you can see if we can get an account opened with a local bank with some credit?" Joe asked as he killed the fusion engine, switching attitude control to chemical thrusters.

"Whew," Jessica said after a few minutes. "I guess they're used to getting ships from all over. They have procedures for ships with no local accounts or registration to get credit. Granted, we have to put the pinnace up as collateral."

Joe grinned. "We better not lose it; *Corsia* wouldn't like it if we sold her best pinnace."

The tug arrived, made grapple and half an hour later they were walking through their hatch onto the station's docking ring.

Right into an irate station worker.

"Are you the morons that came in on their torch? What were you thinking?" she demanded.

Joe began to speak, but Jessica put her hand on the woman's arm. "We're terribly sorry about that. Things aren't this busy or…as grand, where we're from. Coming in on a torch is OK if you need to. We didn't mean to cause trouble."

The dockworker's expression softened as she looked into Jessica's batting eyes.

"Yeah, well, you're core-side now. None of your fringe nonsense will fly here. You've got to sign this."

The dockworker handed a sheet of plas to Jessica and she looked it over. "This is half our credit!" she gasped. "How are we going to refuel?"

"You better have some good cargo to trade on that little tub," the dockworker shrugged. "You're getting off with a wrist-slap. Usually you'd be impounded for what you did."

Joe and Jessica exchanged glances, and Jessica passed her auth token to the plas before handing it back.

"I sure hope we do," Jessica said with a nod. "Thank you."

The woman cast them a curious look before tucking the plas under her arm and rushing down the dock, already yelling at a cargo hauler at the next berth.

"Damn, we better have something of value here," Jessica said. "Or we're going to be calling *Corisa* for pickup real soon."

* * * * *

A day later, and after more drinks than either Joe or Jessica cared to recall, they had no leads on Tanis whatsoever. Returning to the pinnace, they strode out of a lift onto the docking ring to see two soldiers in powered armor standing outside their berth.

"Well, that doesn't loo—" Jessica was interrupted by a rough voice to their left.

"Come with us."

Joe turned to see several more soldiers. Their faces were invisible behind mirrored visors, but the tone of their leader's voice brooked no argument. He looked back at Jessica who shrugged.

"Sure, where're we going?" Joe asked as the leader—a corporal by her stripes—gestured for them to step back into the lift.

"Questioning." Was the only response.

<Guesses?> Joe asked Jessica.

<My bet? They have decided our ship and our story don't match. So long as they don't find our stash on the pinnace, we'll still have a bargaining chip or two.>

When the lift stopped, the corporal and his unit led them through a series of corridors to another lift. Another squad of soldiers, also in powered armor, guarded this one. They directed Joe and Jessica to step through an auth scanner.

The scanner must have seen something it didn't like and called the corporal over to confer with another soldier. Their faces were obscured by their helmets, but Joe had no doubt who was the subject of conversation.

<Me or you?> Jessica asked.

<Bets are that it's me,> Joe replied with a mental chuckle. *<Your most interesting mods are all visible on the outside.>*

After a few minutes, the corporal walked back to them.

"Your cellular structure is…abnormal," he said to Joe. "It doesn't appear to be dangerous, but don't even think of trying anything."

"I wouldn't dream of it," Joe replied.

The corporal nodded and directed them into the open lift door.

Joe and Jessica stepped in, and the rest of the squad filed in after them. When the doors opened again, they revealed a bustling corridor filled with personnel dressed in what Joe assumed were the Bollam's World military uniforms.

"Wait here," the corporal directed before moving down the corridor and knocking on a door. The remainder of his squad directed Joe and Jessica away from the lift entrance, their stances alert and wary.

"You can relax a little bit, guys," Jessica said. "We may look tough, but we're really quite nice."

None of the soldiers replied and Jessica sighed. "Real bunch of hard cases here."

"You'd behave the same way in their shoes," Joe replied.

"No, I'd probably behave worse; these guys haven't made fun of us once."

Down the corridor, the corporal stepped back into view, this time with her helmet tucked under her arm. A uniformed woman wearing a major's insignia accompanied her.

<*Lies or truth?*> Jessica asked Joe.

<*Let's see what they know, but I'm leaning toward truth at this point.*>

The woman approached, her expression steely as she eyed them over. Joe noticed that the squad guarding them stiffened as the major drew closer.

"So, you're who all this is about, then?" she asked.

"Glad to meet you," Joe extended his hand. "I'm Joe and this is Jessica."

The woman gazed at his extended hand and then replied brusquely, "I'm Major Akido." Without another word, she turned and strode down the hall, gesturing for them to follow.

Joe looked down at his outstretched hand and shrugged. "Maybe it's not a greeting here."

"Oh, it is," one of the soldiers gave a low chuckle. "She just doesn't extend pleasantries to much of anyone, least of all folks like you."

"Who are 'folks like us'?" Joe asked.

The corporal shot a look at the soldier and the man clammed up.

A minute later, they reached their destination, a nondescript conference room. The major took a seat on one side and gestured for Joe and Jessica to sit across from her.

Major Akido leaned back in her chair and stared each of them in the eyes for several minutes. Eventually, she let out a long sigh.

"So, where is it?" she finally asked.

"Where is what?" Joe replied.

"Your ship, where is it?" the major's tone was terse and brooked no evasion.

"It's in the dock. We were on our way there when your guys brought us here," Jessica replied with a frown.

The major leaned forward. "Cut the shit, you two. Your colony ship, where is it?"

Joe couldn't hide his surprise. He glanced at Jessica, who also appeared rather shocked.

<*Truth it is, then,*> she said to Joe.

"It's outsystem, we're just here to find someone who went missing."

Major Akido's brow furrowed into a deep frown. "Missing? How did someone on your colony ship go missing here?"

"We had an accident," Joe replied. "She had to eject in an escape pod, and by the time we got to her reported position, she was gone."

The major didn't respond immediately, and Jessica jumped in with a question of her own.

"How did you know that we're from a colony ship? Why would you even look for that?"

"Your ship, for starters. Your graviton emitters aren't broken, they're not present—neither is your grav drive. No grav drive means no FTL. If that's the case, then your shuttle didn't just jump in outside the system, you came in a different ship. Only two types of ships lurk out there sending in small shuttles. Enemy militaries and lost colony ships. But no military would do such a crap job sending in spies, so it was pretty simple."

Joe whistled. "So this happens a lot? Colony ships just wind up on your doorstep?"

"Not a lot, but often enough," Major Akido said with a shrug. "Isotope analysis of your shuttle confirmed that it is of Sol manufacture, sometime in the early fifth millennium. That sealed it."

<*Well, there's all our cards on the table,*> Joe said privately to Jessica. <*What now?*>

<*Not all,*> Jessica replied. <*For all their fancy grav drives and FTL, we know these people barely have fourth millennia tech. The* Intrepid *has a lot to offer them.*>

<*Too bad they don't have a colony world to offer us,*> Joe sighed.

"Then what's next?" Joe asked.

The major leaned back and smiled, "We're going to want to speak to your captain."

NEW EDEN

STELLAR DATE: 10.06.8927 (Adjusted Years)
LOCATION: *Sabrina*, Scattered Disk
REGION: New Eden System, Eden Alliance

Sabrina transitioned out of the dark layer into the New Eden system at the precise location Cheeky planned.

"Nailed it!" Cheeky shouted as the system nav buoy confirmed their location. "Pay up, Cargo."

Cargo sighed and flipped her a Silstrand token. "I can't believe you pulled that off. Your vector looked totally out of whack back at Ayrea."

"Or so you thought," Cheeky chuckled.

Tanis only half-heard their banter as she reviewed the local scan data.

New Eden was a booming system. Tens of thousands of ships plied its space lanes; it boasted three terraformed worlds, up from the original two the FGT had left for the *Intrepid*. It took conscious effort to keep herself from becoming morose at the thought.

<*Sera is convinced the FGT will give us a new system after she reaches out to them,*> Angela broke into Tanis's thoughts.

<*Indeed she is, though how she'll pull that rabbit out of her hat should be interesting. From what I read in* Sabrina's *archives, the FGT has not made direct contact with anyone in over five-hundred years. How* **does** *she know how to reach them?*> Tanis asked.

<*It's a good question. I know you wonder if she is playing us,*> Angela said, concern emanating from her mind. <*But I don't sense that from her. We know there's more to her than she lets on; she has more contacts than her station would indicate.*>

Tanis nodded absently. *Sabrina's* captain was a frequent topic of conversation between her and Angela. They both harbored doubts that Sera could live up to her end of the deal.

<*There's also the issue of transitioning the* Intrepid,> Tanis said. <*You know what you've found—there is an upper limit to the size of ship that anyone has successfully slipped into the dark layer—and come out again. The* Intrepid *is far above that size limit.*>

<*I'll admit it's a concern. But give Bob and Earnest some credit. If the two of them can't crack the issue, I don't know who—*>

Angela stopped as both she and Tanis saw the same scan data roll in.

"There are eleven AST dreadnaughts passing through the system!" Tanis called out.

"There are what?" Sera said, half out of her chair as Tanis brought the scan data up on the bridge's main holo.

"That's rather usual," Cargo said calmly.

"Understatement of the year," Cheeky tossed a scowl his way. "New Eden and the AST aren't exactly on the friendliest of terms, not since that little war they had a few decades ago."

Tanis remembered reading about that conflict. New Eden lay on the spin-ward edge of AST space, and was under constant pressure from the core worlds to join their alliance. New Eden preferred its independence and maintained a sizeable space force to ensure they retained it. They would lose to a full assault from the AST's military, but they were capable of making the effort too costly for any aggressor.

"They must have pulled some sort of serious diplomatic shit to be here right now," Sera said in awe.

"Doesn't look like the locals are too trusting either," Tanis said. "Almost half their fleet is shadowing those dreadnaughts."

Sera nodded with appreciation. "From the looks of it, they stopped and refueled here, too."

"They're headed for the same jump point we are," Cheeky said, her voice low and completely serious. "They're going to Bollam's."

<*She's right,*> Angela agreed. <*There are reports of an old colony ship insystem at Bollam's World. The local nets are going nuts with speculation over what is going to happen.*>

"Punch it, Cheeky! Full burn. We *must* get there before those AST assholes," Sera yelled.

Cheeky complied and Sabrina prepared for a full antimatter burn around the edge of the New Eden system.

"Not around, Cheeky," Sera said, her eyes deadly serious. "Go through the system."

"We're going to pick up a hell of a fine for this," Cargo said. "They're not going to take kindly to us blasting through."

"And with their current fleet distribution, they won't do anything to stop us either," Sera replied.

"You hope," Cargo said.

Sera did not reply.

"I don't get it," Cheeky said as she plotted the new course and spun out the AP nozzle. "I mean, I get that your ship has some cool shit, Tanis, but what could be worth the AST doing this?"

Tanis was poring over the available specs on the dreadnaughts and didn't reply. The ships were large by ninetieth century standards, each coming in at just over six kilometers long. They sported more rails, beams, and missile launches than she even cared to count.

<*Those are some serious ships,*> Tanis sighed. <*If we had brought the whole fleet from Kapteyn's, I would be a lot less worried, but this will be a close fight, we may have to use it again.*>

"Well?" Cheeky asked once *Sabrina* was boosting on its new trajectory. "What does your ship have that's so special?"

Tanis looked around the bridge. Cheeky appeared to be almost angry, while Cargo was merely curious. Sera's expression was more unreadable. Then the captain turned her head toward Cheeky and Cargo without breaking eye contact with Tanis.

"Look up something called *The Battle of Victoria.* It took place in the Kapteyn's system before the *Intrepid* left. Look for speculation on how they defeated the Sirians with minimal losses."

Tanis let out a long sigh. If Sera was telling her crew what to look for, then she had already found it. The record of the *Intrepid's* picotech had persisted these five-thousand years.

<*Funny that this information is in the ship's database,*> Angela commented privately to Tanis. <*It wasn't previously.*>

<*I know, I checked, too,*> Tanis replied.

"Picotech!" Cargo exclaimed, half rising from his chair. "How…what…is it real?"

Tanis didn't have it in her to lie to *Sabrina's* crew—she knew that her resigned expression was already all the confirmation that Sera needed—if she needed any at all.

"It is true," Tanis replied.

"And you…wait…you!" Cheeky's voice fell into a shocked hush.

Tanis could tell that she had read something which referenced her as a general and lieutenant governor.

"General Richards, is it?" Cargo asked. "Or should I say governor?"

"How long have you known?" Tanis asked Sera. "This information was not in your databases when I came onboard."

"I pulled an update when we were in Ayrea," Sera replied smoothly. "I wanted to know more about your ship and the time you came from."

Tanis nodded slowly. "Well, now you know."

She fended off as many questions about the picotech, and her rank, as she could. She was surprised that no one was overly upset about her lies and omissions. Even Thompson grunted that he would not have volunteered the information either.

She was saved from further revelations by the first few calls from the system traffic AI regarding their speed, which Tanis responded to, but eventually just logged them with no response. It was clear they were on an outsystem vector, not passing close to any New Eden worlds or stations. No military vessels or drones moved to intercept them, and the traffic AI appeared to content itself with simply adding on fine after fine.

"This'll bankrupt us," Cargo muttered at one point.

"No," Sera disagreed while directing a pointed look at Tanis. "It really won't."

Tanis set two countdowns on the main holo. One for the AST dreadnaughts, and one for *Sabrina.* The dreadnaughts would beat them to the jump point, but the AST vessels were maintaining steady 0.5*c*. A max speed which was likely enforced by the New Eden space force ships shadowing the foreign military vessels.

Because entry velocity into the dark layer translated into faster travel time, *Sabrina* would reach Bollam's World before the AST vessels, even though they entered FTL later.

The trip across the New Eden system took just shy of twenty-three hours, and Tanis watched with concern gnawing at her innards as the eleven AST dreadnaughts winked out of scan visibility.

"There they go," Sera said. "Now we just have to hope that half the New Eden space force doesn't decide to find out why we're in such a hurry.

Sabrina was an hour from the jump point; light-lag to the closest New Eden vessel was fifty-two minutes—with the relativistic adjustments.

<*Given how long it would take them to have confirmed the AST departure, we should be hearing from them right…about…now,*> Helen said.

On her queue, the comm board lit up with an incoming transmission from a NESF patrol craft.

<*Show-off,*> Sabrina muttered.

Tanis played the message aloud.

"Star Freighter *Sabrina,* this is the *Sword of Eden,* please declare your intentions. If we didn't know better, we would think you're chasing those core-worlder dreadnaughts."

Cargo let out a laugh. "Calling those AST ships core-worlders as if he isn't one. When the fringe is nearly a thousand light-years in any direction, you're core, too."

"What would you like me to say," Tanis asked Sera.

"You're asking me?" Sera said with a wink. "You're the general—what do you think you should say?"

Tanis remained silent for several moments before shaking her head and turning to her console.

"*Sword of Eden,* this is General Tanis Richards of the ISS *Intrepid.* This ship is returning me to Bollam's World and is under my protection. As for what we plan to do with those dreadnaughts, look up the Battle of Victoria and figure it out."

Cheeky let out a long whistle. "Well, that'll either get them the hell out of our way—or they'll blow us to bits."

"We have thirty-seven minutes to find out," Sera replied.

<*Thirty-two,*> Angela corrected the captain.

"Damn relativistic math," Sera muttered.

No one spoke on the bridge as they raced closer to the NESF ships still clustered around the jump point. Tanis surmised that they weren't entirely trusting the AST ships' word that they were going to Bollam's World. It was possible, however unlikely, that this was some sort of feint before a full-scale attack.

The earliest time for a reply from the NESF came and went, then sixteen more minutes ticked by with agonizing slowness before a message came in.

The message was short and to the point.

"Star freighter *Sabrina,* you are cleared to maintain your current course and exit the New Eden system. Fines against your vessel have been lifted."

"See?" Sera said with a grin as she looked between Cheeky and Cargo. I told you the general would know what to say. *And* we're not facing any fines. A good day in my books."

THE SILENT SYSTEM

STELLAR DATE: 10.25.8927 (Adjusted Years)
LOCATION: *Sabrina*, Scattered Disk
REGION: Bollam's World System, Bollam's World Federation

Cheeky brought *Sabrina* out of FTL further from the Bollam's World star than Tanis would have preferred, though she understood the need for caution—not to mention the time it would take to decelerate from 0.79*c*.

"Forty-nine AU from the stellar primary," the pilot reported.

"Well done," Sera said with a nod. "Pull us up above the stellar disk and start our braking."

Tanis tapped the system beacon's passive data stream.

"That's weird," she said with a frown. "There's nothing about the *Intrepid* on the beacon, just the standard traffic conditions, and system laws and regulations."

"I don't think those AST ships are coming here for a vacation," Sera said. "Someone is trying their best to keep things looking normal."

"The outer beacon isn't responding to requests for active data. I've sent our packet to the system relay further in; maybe once we're registered on scan we can get more info," Tanis said.

"Keep active sensors on full bore," Sera said to Tanis. "This system is always a hot mess."

Tanis had noticed *Sabrina's* shielding taking repeated impacts from dust. She was impressed at how well the graviton shielding protected the freighter. The *Intrepid's* shields would be hard-pressed to keep the ship safe in a system this young and active while traveling at such speeds.

She had spent some time reviewing data entries on Bollam's World. The star was young, under half a billion years old. The eleven major planets which orbited the star were still young and hot, with the exception of the terraformed worlds in the habitable zone. Records showed that the initial colonists, also victims of Kapteyn's Streamer, had spent considerable effort cooling those worlds before they could even begin to make them habitable.

The star lay in a region of space with few G or K class stars. Its location, combined with youth, had caused the FGT to pass it by entirely. It was probably the only G-class star within a hundred light-years of Sol which was not prepared for humanity by the FGT, but by the colonists themselves.

Tanis had to admire the tenacity of those original settlers. What they had accomplished was more even impressive than what the Edeners and Victorians had built at The Kap.

She scanned through the data on the planets, taking note of the strange gas giant named Aurora which lay seventh from the star, and the terraforming that was underway on a moon around the sixth planet, a gas giant named Kithari.

"You're going to want to alter course, Cheeky," Tanis said as she put the results of the first active scan sweep on the main holo. "There's a dense molecular cloud ahead, and a small dwarf world seems to have its orbit changed since the last time *Sabrina* got an update on Bollam's."

<*Sorry to have inconvenienced you,*> Sabrina said with a sigh.

<*Easy now,*> Sera said soothingly. <*We don't pass this close to the core very often. Not much need to get updated system data for these worlds.*>

"I'm going to grab some coffee, anyone want some?" Cargo asked as he rose.

The three women called out in affirmative and the first mate chuckled. "Maybe I'll just bring the pot."

"You know, I'm going to go do a quick walk through the ship," Tanis said while rising from her station. "I've slaved scan to your console, Cheeky, and Angela is keeping an eye on it as well."

"We'll ping you if you're needed," Sera said.

Cargo returned with three cups of coffee. "Gave Tanis hers in the galley."

"She's got a lot on her mind," Sera said with a nod. "Don't know that I'd want to be in her position right now."

"What position is that, Captain?" Cargo's dark eyes stared at Sera intently. "What do you think we are flying into?"

Sera thought about it for a moment before replying.

"Either the *Intrepid* was smart and started trading its tech for fuel and FTL capability, or they clamed up and got themselves boarded and gutted."

"Do you think they'd be able to defend themselves?"

"Maybe—Tanis never said how much of that fleet they took with them when they left Kapteyn's Star—or if they have more of their pico bombs. If they do, then we're flying into a war-zone."

"Didn't we just leave that party?"

"That was just a mixer; the real party's still to come," Sera laughed. "But now that you bring it up, I think I should go and see if I can get our general to lay down some specifics on her ship's defenses."

Cargo nodded and Sera slipped off the bridge. She found Tanis where she expected, at the forward scan and targeting sensors. Sera wasn't sure if she should be surprised that Tanis was a general and colony governor, or that she hadn't suspected her rank was far higher than she let on—she fit in with the crew as well as possible, but there were times when her bearing and poise had hinted at a higher position.

Sera wondered if her own background traits ever slipped through. There were secrets she kept that no one on this ship needed to know. Most of her past was far better off buried and forgotten.

"They still good as new?" Sera asked.

"Seem to be. Though, I should have insisted on an external array."

"You were in a rush—and I appreciate the haste, even though it was unnecessary," Sera said with a grin.

Tanis turned to Sera, her blue eyes appeared darker and more serious than normal—if that were possible.

"You don't have to do this. I don't want to risk you and your crew more than I already have. You could send me in on one of your escape pods. I can figure out a way to get to the *Intrepid*."

"Don't be ridiculous." Sera dismissed Tanis's statement with a wave of her hand. "You helped my crew rescue me when you could have just cut and run. There's no way I am just going to leave you high and dry."

Tanis smiled and appeared to relax. "Thank you. I can't imagine what would have happened if you hadn't opened that container I was in."

"I can. You would have gotten close and personal with Rebecca and her pointy needles"

"I'm sorry about that; my fault again."

"Stop saying that." Sera wasn't sure what to make of this uncharacteristically self-effacing Tanis. "I'm right as rain and thoroughly enjoyed giving that bitch what she had coming."

Tanis laughed. "I almost would have liked to have seen that…almost." Then the general eyed Sera up and down and appeared to consider her words carefully. "We both know that most nano around here isn't as good as mine. Considering what you likely had to work with—not to mention dealing with your new skin trying to kill you—how *did* you heal from that torture so fast?"

"I guess I was lucky. Helen found all the right stuff we needed on the station to keep me going," Sera replied with a shrug, the lie coming easily after so many years—though she could see that Tanis wasn't buying it.

"You handled the trauma of torture rather well—something I bet that they don't teach you to in star-freighter captain school," the general pressed.

"I wouldn't say 'rather well', more like…I didn't curl up into a fetal position. It's not my first time being at the receiving end of someone's ill intentions. I've already done all the puking and crying. Now I know how to repress it like a pro."

Tanis's skepticism was plainly displayed on her face. "I've come clean with you, Sera. Let me know when you are ready to do the same—but don't give me your coy routine and trite little lies. You are far from who you appear to be. I hope your motives in helping me are as altruistic as you claim." She paused and drew in a long breath, her eyes narrowing. "Because if you think there is some special advantage you can gain over the *Intrepid* once we arrive, you will be mistaken."

Sera's breath caught in her throat. Tanis's blunt verbal assault took her completely off guard. For a moment, she wondered if Tanis suspected the truth about her.

<She doesn't know the truth; she probably hasn't guessed anything close to it,> Helen said. *<But she was once a counterinsurgency officer in the TSF—from what she told the crew around the wardroom table one night. She can likely see cracks all over your story. She certainly saw your blood pressure rise just now.>*

Sera forced herself to resume breathing evenly. Though Tanis may know she was hiding things, Helen was right, she wouldn't even come close to the truth if she guessed for a thousand years.

"You've got me, Tanis," Sera said slowly. "I've not been completely honest with you, but I'm not yet ready to talk about my past…give me more time."

Tanis's look was skeptical, but she didn't push. "The time is close. When we get to the *Intrepid*, Bob will discover your truth, I'd rather you share it willingly before he does."

"Who is Bob?" Sera asked.

Tanis chuckled. "That's a truth you'll soon learn on your own."

Neither woman spoke for a minute, and then Sera asked the question for which she had searched out Tanis in the first place.

"Things are likely to be hairy when we get insystem, how much of that fleet did you bring with you from Kapteyn's Star?"

"Not as much as I wish we had," Tanis sighed. "We swapped out the two Neptune class cruisers for the *Orkney* and the *Dresden*—two of the new Claymore class battle cruisers. Otherwise, it's our initial fleet of eight cruisers, some twenty pushers, and a bevy of pinnaces, shuttles, and transports. We do have a lot more fighters than we left Sol with, but I don't think even our new Arc-5s are going to be much of a match for modern craft pulling over 500*g*s. Not to mention that our ES shielding is not nearly as effective as your new grav shields."

Sera whistled. "Still more than any colony ship I've ever heard of, but probably not a match for those AST dreadnaughts."

"The *Intrepid* itself is a pretty formidable weapon. Its size also makes it hard to damage—bar the use of fusion bombs," Tanis replied. "Though we try to keep it out of the thick of battle."

"What about the pico?" Sera asked, afraid the answer would be no, but just as afraid that it may be yes.

Tanis nodded. "It's there, we have more RMs than you'd like to know exist, and they're all capable of carrying pico warheads."

"Let's hope it doesn't come to that," Sera said with a shudder. She looked into Tanis's eyes and could tell the general felt the same way. The pico was a weapon of last resort—every other avenue would have to be exhausted first.

Tanis glanced back at the sensor array's maintenance console. "I should finish looking this over."

"You've been on shift for half a day and we have seven hours before we'll get a response from the system beacon's active Link. Why don't you catch sack till then? I can do the inspection."

Tanis gave a tired smile. "I suppose I could use some rest...and it *is* your ship after all."

THROUGH THE LOOKING GLASS

STELLAR DATE: 10.26.8927 (Adjusted Years)
LOCATION: *Sabrina*, EK Belt
REGION: Bollam's World System, Bollam's World Federation

<*System beacon has registered us and we have active system scan,*> Sabrina reported ship-wide.

Tanis was on the bridge minutes later, one hand holding a cup of coffee and the other rubbing her face. "Does it have data on the *Intrepid*?" she asked.

Cheeky un-slaved scan from her console and directed it back to Tanis's station.

"Doesn't look like it," the pilot said with a shake of her head. "Just the same as before, though with more up-to-date information."

"It's like the *Intrepid* really isn't here..." Tanis sighed. "But the reports in New Eden definitely talked about a colony ship in Bollam's."

"Tanis, check the planets' positions in scan with what we can see from here. The beacon's scan data may be faked."

Cheeky looked up from her console. "Fake! No one fakes system scan. They may as well ask for jump-point collisions!"

"I've seen it before," Sera said, her voice solemn.

"Freaking, fucking... nut... I'm out of words!"

Cheeky may present a carefree exterior in nearly every aspect of her life; but when it came to piloting, and the strictures that kept starships plying the dark, she was a different person. She was right, too; faking scan was a disaster waiting to happen. Ships may be small in the vastness of space, but they all traveled between just a few points, which meant they were usually concentrated within the same areas.

"Damn...it *is* faked," Tanis reported. "This looks like scan from over a month ago, they tried to blend it so that the planets were in the right positions, but there are ships clearly heading to places that have since moved."

"We need to find out what is going on in this system and fast. Cheeky, let's burn some antimatter."

Sera stood and threw *Sabrina's* own scan data on the bridge's main holo tank. "Looks strangely clear," the captain muttered.

The space they were traveling through was near a commonly used jump point, which the ship's scan showed it to be deserted.

Tanis frowned at her readouts. "I'm betting that there is real scan somewhere. Whoever has botched the signal must still want to know where things are themselves. Good data has to be in there somewhere."

She and Angela broke down the data stream from the system's beacon and began sifting through its components for any hidden information while Sera sent an update to the rest of the crew. Over the next half hour, everyone visited the bridge to ask if they were really in a system with no scan.

Twenty minutes later, Tanis let out a cry of triumph.

"Found it! I figured the best place to hide the real scan was within the fake one. There were several distorted portions of the signal, and sure enough one of them contained the carrier wave for valid data. I'm configuring our system to read from it."

Sera set her screen to display the system's readout, and within a minute, it flicked from the boring show of regular, light traffic to an entirely different tableau. Everyone took a deep breath and then uttered a variety of curses.

The real data showed a heavy cluster of ships near the system's sixth planet, the $6M_J$ gas giant named Kithari. Sera selected that planet and zoomed in. The ships were grouped near one of its larger moons, a world named Fierra, which appeared to be in the late stages of terraforming. She selected the planet and all space within two hundred thousand kilometers and threw it up on the bridge's main holo tank. Cheeky and Tanis swiveled in their chairs to gaze at the results.

It was a mess.

Seven thousand kilometers from the moon, in an equatorial orbit, lay the *Intrepid*, its fleet fully deployed. Roughly a hundred-thousand kilometers beyond lay a fleet consisting of fifty-two destroyers and light cruisers. The scan data identified them as Bollam's World Space Force. The majority of ships in this fleet were positioned at strategic points that appeared to both protect and corral the *Intrepid*.

Another fleet held position fifty-thousand kilometers north of the moon, it consisted of several light cruisers and over two-hundred corvettes. A similar formation of nearly the same composition held position roughly the same distance south of the moon.

Beyond all the fleets lay the eleven AST dreadnaughts, holding station in a half-ring around the moon's parent world.

"How the hell did they beat us here?" Sera cursed.

"They must have transitioned back to regular space and boosted up, before going back into FTL," Cheeky said, her brow furrowed.

"I realize that, it was rhetorical," Sera said.

"Oh."

Tanis let out a soft chuckle, then a good long laugh. When she stopped, she looked up to see Sera, Cheeky, and Cargo staring at her.

"Sorry, it's just par for the course," Tanis said, still chuckling. "They've gone and got themselves into quite the mess. Who do you think those corvette fleets are?"

Sera frowned. "Someday I'd like to hear the whole story of how you guys got here. As for those two light fleets…they're…aw shit."

"That good, eh?" Tanis asked.

"Our pirate friends have come for the fun. Rebecca and her ships are at the north pole and Padre is at the south end. Looks like they decided to go hunting for the *Intrepid* without you."

"How friendly are any of those factions likely to become with each other?"

"I'd say less friendly, more hostile. Scan shows several small debris fields. I'll bet there have already been some altercations."

"I'm surprised that more of the Bollam's space force isn't deployed," Cargo said. "They must have thousands of ships in the system."

"They're moving more in, but I bet the arrival of the AST is giving them pause," Tanis said. "You can see them gathering forces at key points. I bet they're also readying some nice big rail guns."

"They'll have some, but people don't really use rails defensively anymore," Sera said as she examined the Bollam's fleet positions. "With inertial dampeners, ships can jink well out of the way of a rail's slug."

Tanis frowned. "That may be true, but what about grapeshot? You don't fire where they are, but where you expect them to be."

"Grapeshot?" Cheeky asked.

"Rail-fired shells filled with millions of pebbles. You fill all reasonable approaches with them. People can jink all they want, they'll just jink into the grapeshot. Then you use their hesitation against them and send in the slugs, or beams, if they are close enough," Tanis replied.

"You lived in a brutal time," Cargo commented.

"War is always brutal. But I need to get to my ship, and you need to deliver on your promise," Tanis said to Sera, her expression almost pleading.

Sera smiled and nodded to Tanis before she turned to their pilot. "Cheeky? How does it look?"

"Well, provided no one blows us to pieces, I can make it happen. Based on the axial tilt of the planet, and everyone's orbits, there will be a period in about five hours where only a few of Rebecca's ships will have *Intrepid* in their sights. She's a big mutha, so I bet if I work up the right approach vector we can use her to hide us and get in almost entirely unseen. I'll have to work out the timing and coast—even hiding behind the *Intrepid's* girth, an AP trail would be plain as day."

"Good plan," Sera said. "Why don't you kill thrust now, and we'll coast till you have your path worked up. Use minimal burn; we'll try to stay as dark as possible. Nix our beacon, too. No need to let Rebecca know her favorite pincushion is within reach."

"Can they detect the graviton emissions from our shielding?" Tanis asked.

Sera ran a hand through her hair. "This close to a $6M_J$ jovian they shouldn't be able to. Plus, I'm not really comfortable disabling shields. This system still has a lot of stuff flying around."

"Having been in a ship hit by this system's debris, I see your point," Tanis acknowledged with a nod. "I'll get a transmission ready to burst to the *Intrepid* when we have a clear line to them. Don't want them thinking we're hostile."

Sera hadn't even thought of that. *Sabrina's* new shields were good, but she didn't want to see how well they'd hold up against the radiation wash from one of the tugs patrolling around the *Intrepid*, let alone the beams on those cruisers.

The next few hours passed quietly. *Sabrina* had a lot of speed to burn off before making her approach; rather than turning and braking, Cheeky altered the rear shields emit negative gravitons. The effect caused enough drag to slow them down and line up on the desired approach vector.

Sera was making a light lunch for herself in the mess when Flaherty came in and closed the galley door. She looked up at the dour man and smiled. "How are you today?"

Flaherty grunted. "Been better." He sloshed some semi-warm coffee into a mug and sat down. "It always catches up with you, doesn't it?"

"Noticed that too, did you?"

His deadly serious eyes bored into hers. "You aren't going to be able to run from it forever."

Sera spun to face him directly, her eyes angry, even though her voice was calm. "I am helping a friend here. This is not fate or anything, just random events."

Flaherty let out a long, exasperated sigh. "You know I'll always be here to watch your back. But some day you are going to have to own up to your destiny. We're doing the right thing now, but there are a lot of other things that could also use your attention—a lot more important than some energy module." With that, the large man stood and left the wardroom, his near-full cup of coffee left on the table.

Sera leaned against the counter and let out a long breath. Suddenly, the ship seemed too close and small about her. Her synthetic skin felt like it was constricting her, like she couldn't breathe. A wave of dizziness hit her and Sera closed her eyes, willing herself to be calm. She could do this; she would not repeat past mistakes. Tanis and the *Intrepid* would live to see another journey to a star where they could be left out of the messes this close to the core. Sera vowed it.

<*Easy now, just some anxiety,*> Helen's soothing voice whispered in her mind.

<*If ever there was a time to feel anxious, this is it,*> Sera replied.

<*Flaherty's right, it does feel a bit like destiny, doesn't it?*> Helen's voice held a wistful edge.

Sera wondered what the AI saw, what her wisdom and years told her about the future.

<*It feels more like a curse,*> Sera said with a sigh. <*Like events will drive me back there no matter what.*>

Helen sent out an affirmative wave of agreement. <*I suspect they will.*>

ANDROMEDA

STELLAR DATE: 10.26.8927 (Adjusted Years)
LOCATION: *Sabrina*, EK Belt
REGION: Bollam's World System, Bollam's World Federation

Tanis scoured the background noise in the system, looking for a range with little use and high levels of stellar noise.

<*There, that whine coming from the weird jovian planet, Aurora. We can hide our signal in its noise. You can bet Bob is listening to that thing and what they have going on there,*> Angela advised.

<*I was thinking the same thing,*> Tanis said and began to calibrate *Sabrina's* transmitter to piggyback on the planet's emissions.

<*I know,*> Angela replied with a wink.

"*Intrepid,* this is General Tanis Richards, hope this message finds you well. I'm in a small freighter, which will begin making an approach to your position in roughly ten minutes. We expect to be ready to dock in four hours and twenty-nine minutes. Our vector will be southerly to avoid detection from your friends. We will be alone and dark. Please do not fire on us. Please do not respond unless absolutely necessary. We're not exactly on friendly terms with some of the folks out there, either."

Tanis set the system to repeat the message three times and then killed the transmission. She turned to Cheeky.

"It's sent. We're good to begin our final approach. Everything set on your end?"

"As much as it's going to be. There's going to be a tight spot in about two hours when we get close to one of the AST ships, but we should be able to slip by if we kill all but our forward shields—which will be facing away from them." She entered in several commands on her console. "I'm having Sabrina switch main systems to battery, as well. No point in having a nice, hot reactor giving us away."

<*I'm sipping juice here,*> Sabrina said.

Tanis nodded. The new batteries could power the ship and even send a few pulses from the lasers before running dry. If things got hairy, the reactor would still be warm enough to spin it back up in a few minutes.

Sera reappeared on the bridge looking like she had eaten something unpleasant. She sat in her chair without saying a word and leaned her head back, eyes closed. There was no need to update her on the transmission and commencement of their final approach. Tanis could tell she had maintained a connection to the bridge net.

She felt tempted to ask the captain what was wrong, but decided the other woman just needed to calm down and put whatever was bothering her to rest rather than having to make up an evasive response.

Tanis took advantage of Sera's stillness to further observe her. The captain was usually in constant motion—her actions quick and decisive, her face never showing more or less than she intended it to.

At this moment, she looked much younger than usual. Tanis realized she couldn't place Sera's age…at all. She looked to be in her early twenties, but with the experiences she had mentioned in passing, not to mention her performance on the pirate station and the ship, she had to be much older. Sera had the knowledge and instincts of a person much closer to their first century, possibly even older than that.

<*Not knowing her story is really eating you up, isn't it?*> Angela asked.

<*You know me; all the puzzle pieces have to fit.*>

The crew had been of little help; most had only known her for a few years—though, in that time, they had become quite loyal. None of them had any knowledge of their captain's history before her purchase of *Sabrina,* with the exception of the ever-mysterious Flaherty—and he wasn't sharing anything.

Sera sat forward and opened her eyes, looking as alert and full of energy as ever. Tanis's moment of examination was over.

"Are you going to stay when we reach the *Intrepid*?" Tanis took the opportunity to ask.

Sera flashed an enigmatic smile. "Well, I do have to help you guys get that ship into FTL—unless they want to stay here forever."

Cheeky nearly choked. "Captain! That ship can never go into FTL. Every credit I have says they're negotiating for that moon they're orbiting—it's the only play they have."

Sera shook her head. "Not the only play. The *Intrepid* can drop into FTL. They just need the right plans to transition their ship safely, and make it appear unappetizing to the lurkers in the dark layer."

<*How is that possible?*> Angela asked. <*From my research, no one has ever transitioned a ship anywhere close to the* Intrepid's *size. Those dreadnaughts out there are about as big as you can go.*>

"Yeah, what she said," Cheeky turned in her seat and directed a quizzical look at Sera. "You don't have that tech; no one has it."

Sera shook her head slowly. "Not no one. I have it—so do some others."

"How—what—captain!" Cheeky exclaimed. "Don't be ridiculous! You can't swindle Tanis's people..."

"It's OK," Tanis said. "I'm taking it on faith that Sera has what she says she does. Besides, our deal was to get me here and be compensated—a payment that I will render promptly, once we dock."

"You won't throw the rest of us in your brig if she tries to sell you bogus tech, right?" Cheeky looked worried. "Do you have a brig?"

"It's a big ship," Cargo said with a laugh. "They're going to have a brig."

"Our original deal aside, FTL tech is pretty impressive. What would you want in exchange?" Tanis asked. The picotech was not up for trade, without it as an option, she wondered what Sera, with her already advanced nanotech could want that could match the value of FTL for the *Intrepid.*

"The opportunity to get in on the action."

<*Hah! She's more like you than even I'd guessed,*> Angela commented privately to Tanis.

"You just want to shoot at a few people in trade for amazing, unheard of technology?"

"Not just a few people. I want to turn Rebecca and her fleet of miscreants into a fine molecular cloud. I'm tired of dealing with them. I'm tired of playing their games. In fact, I want to do the same to Padre's fleet and then I want to show the good people of Bollam's World that just because a valuable ship shows up in their system it's not up for grabs."

"You seem…bitter," Cheeky observed.

Sera's expression hardened. "I want to show people that if they behave like animals, someone is going to come along and put them down like the rabid pack they are."

Tanis was taken aback by Sera's vehemence. She saw that Cheeky and Cargo were also surprised by the rage in their captain's voice. Something deep drove Sera's anger. Something personal and unpleasant.

The conversation was interrupted by the comm board lighting up, and the proximity alarms going off in concert.

Tanis picked up the comm message and flipped it to the bridge's audible systems once the first syllable came to her ears.

"Good morning, *Sabrina,* this is Captain Joseph Evans of the ISS *Andromeda.* It's a little hot out here, so we thought we'd give you a ride into the *Intrepid.*"

"What the hell?" Cheeky exclaimed, furiously adjusting her holo interfaces. "There's a fucking cruiser on our ass that wasn't there a second ago!"

Tanis felt a smile nearly split her face in half.

"You have the honors," Sera said, returning her smile.

"*Andromeda,* this is Tanis…sweet stars it's good to hear your voice, Joe." Tanis all but gasped the last words, her voice choking up.

"Tanis! Oh stars, thank god. I was afraid it was a hoax, are you OK? Are you in danger?"

<*She's always in danger,*> Angela replied sardonically.

"I'm well. Captain Sera and *Sabrina* have treated me very well."

"Corsia is sending a plot for your pilot. We need to cut the chatter and get you off radar. Dock as quickly as you can. I love you, Tanis."

"I love you, too, Joe. See you in a few minutes…"

Tanis couldn't stop the flood of emotion that washed over her. She let out a sob and tears started to flow. She saw Cheeky and Sera exchange incredulous looks before her eyes misted up too much to see clearly.

A moment later there was a hand on her back and a soft voice at her side.

"I take it he's someone special to you," Sera's voice was thick with emotion.

Tanis gulped down a deep breath and forced herself to calm. "He's my husband," she managed to say.

"Husband?" Cheeky asked with a grin. "I bet he's a real looker—no wonder you never came by my cabin."

Tanis smiled and wiped her face. "Yes, that was it. Did you get the information to dock?"

Cheeky nodded. "Their bay is right behind us, it'll be snug, but we'll fit. Just one jot to the left and we'll drop right in."

"I'm going to the hatch," Tanis said as she rose.

"Right behind you," Sera said. "You have the bridge, Cargo."

Tanis was sliding down the ladder in the corridor before Sera finished speaking. She knew it was irrational, but the thought of being with Joe made all the obstacles before her seem so much simpler. Sure, they faced insurmountable odds, and there was little chance of ever building the colony they had dreamed, but none of that mattered if she was with Joe. They could figure it out, they could figure anything out.

She arrived at the forward hatch and all but bounced on her feet as she waited for the sound of the ship settling in its cradle.

As soon as the telltale clang echoed through the deck plates, she cycled the airlock, barely aware that Sera stepped in with her.

It seemed to take forever for the pressure match indicator to turn green, and when it did, she pushed out of *Sabrina* and smashed herself into Joe's open arms. The smell of him washed over her and she couldn't stop overwhelming sobs of joy and pent up anxiety from escaping her.

"I'm here Tanis, you're safe, you're back with us," Joe whispered in her ear while stroking her hair.

Tanis wasn't able to form words and spoke into his mind instead.

<Never again, I mean it this time, you come with me everywhere.>

Joe chuckled. *<My feelings exactly. I'm just glad you're OK. You had me worried sick, I was just about ready to beg, borrow, or steal a ship to start scouring the galaxy for you. You're both OK?>*

<We are yes, both me and our little addition,> Tanis said with a smile. *<I got back here as fast as wings would take me.>*

<And who are these wings?> Joe asked, his eyes darting over her shoulder.

Tanis finally became aware of Sera's presence, floating awkwardly behind her in the 0*g* on *Andromeda*. She looked around to see all eyes in the shuttle bay on her. She flushed and stepped back.

"Joe, this is Captain Sera, my rescuer. Sera, this is Joseph Evans."

"Pleased to meet you," Joe said with a smile as he extended his hand to Sera. "Any rescuer of Tanis's is a dear friend of mine—not to mention a rare person. Usually she is the one doing the rescuing."

Sera took his hand and returned the smile. "Then you won't be surprised to learn that she rescued me once on our way here."

Joe barked a laugh. "Now that's more like it."

Behind Sera, the rest of the crew, bar Cargo, stood at the ship's airlock. Tanis introduced them to Joe and Sera called up for Cargo to secure the ship and come down as well.

<Go and enjoy yourselves,> Corsia said. *<Sabrina and I are coordinating final docking procedures.>*

Joe led Tanis and *Sabrina's* crew through the docking bay toward the ship's forward crew lounge.

"It doesn't look that much more advanced. I thought you guys were supposed to have amazing tech," Cheeky said while peering around. "It seems pretty normal—except the lack of AG."

Tanis had to hide a smile as the crew of *Sabrina* clumsily navigated the corridor with the hand and footholds that she barely even thought of. It was possible that most of them had never even spent any appreciable time in zero-*g*.

"It's not what's visible," Joe said. "We don't have artificial gravity on ships this size, true, but we've flown *Andromeda* within a thousand klicks of those big newcomers out there and they didn't even catch a glimpse of us."

"You buzzed an AST dreadnaught?" Cheeky's eyes grew wide with appreciation.

"That's why we were out here," Joe said with a nod. "We wanted to know what those new ships were all about."

"What did you learn?" Tanis asked. "How do they stack up?"

"They have omnidirectional antimatter engines on either end; heavily shielded, and deadly to boot. Their beams are as strong as our best and their grav shields can probably block almost anything we can throw at them. I think we'd wear them down in a slug-fest, provided we could keep them at bay, but with all the other players on the field it gets pretty complicated."

"It usually is," Tanis said with a smile.

A minute later, they arrived in the forward crew lounge. The room was clean and spare, yet well appointed. Tanis remembered spending many an evening relaxing here on the long deceleration into Kapteyn's, and again during her many tours on the ship during the Victoria years.

"You'll all receive a protocol upgrade by nano packet to update your Link for our systems," Corisa announced over the lounge's audible systems. "Please accept it and you'll get onto our public nets."

"Thanks," Cargo said. "I was wondering why I couldn't make any sort of connection to a shipnet."

"What happened to you?" Joe asked as *Sabrina's* crew accepted the upgrade and Linked to the *Andromeda's* net.

"My pod got picked up by pirates after I ejected," Tanis said. "It's a very different galaxy than we last saw."

"You can say that again," Joe replied.

<We've passed the AST ships and are approaching the Bollam's fleet picket lines,> Corsia announced over the Link.

"Thanks, Cor," Joe said as he held Tanis and kissed her.

INTREPID

STELLAR DATE: 10.26.8927 (Adjusted Years)
LOCATION: ISS *Andromeda*, Near Fierra (6*Mj* Jovian)
REGION: Bollam's World System, Bollam's World Federation

Sera watched Tanis and her husband—husband!—with a smile slowly creeping across her face. Who would have thought that the hard-bitten general had a man into whose arms she melted? Of all the things she expected to encounter, this was perhaps the last.

She glanced at her crew as they watched Tanis, and caught Cheeky's eye. They exchanged a knowing look, before Sera returned her gaze to the forward-facing window.

She felt a pang of homesickness as she looked through the holo-enhanced portal. It reminded her too much of home. So clean, so meticulously maintained by nano, that it looked brand new, even though it had likely seen centuries of service.

Through the plas she saw several Bollam's World Space Force ships come into view, their mass and vector highlighted on the display for any Linked viewer to see. The vessels were new and well made by ninetieth century standards, but there was something about the understated elegance of the *Andromeda* that put them to shame. The Bollam's ships were boxy and utilitarian, where the *Andromeda* hailed from a time when both form and function were honored without compromise.

She was impressed with how neither Joe, nor any of the crew they had passed, gave her unusual black skin, or Nance's hazsuit a second glance. Then again, given what she had read about the early fourth millennia, her crew fit well within the bounds of what was considered normal.

They slipped past the Bollam's picket lines without drawing attention, and before long the *Intrepid* came into view.

"All those ships dock inside the *Intrepid*?" Nance asked in awe.

"They do indeed," Tanis replied with a nod. "Most of the cruisers fit in the main bay."

Cheeky whistled. "Well, I'm not surprised. Most of the stations we dock *Sabrina* at are smaller than that ship."

Sera counted ten capital ships protecting the *Intrepid*, the largest being a pair of thousand-meter cruisers that the window's holo enhancement labeled as the *Orkney* and *Dresden*.

The display didn't provide many details beyond mass and size, but given what she knew of Sol in the fourth millennia, and what she had read about Victoria, Sera suspected that the *Intrepid's* fleet was more than a match for all but the AST vessels surrounding them.

Even if they didn't resort to their picotech.

<*You're thinking about how this feels like home, aren't you?*> Helen asked.

<*I am,*> Sera sent an affirmative response.

"Those poor pirate fleets," Cheeky chuckled. "They must really be wondering if they bit off more than they can chew."

"They're probably considering joining forces," Tanis said.

"Or getting the hell out of here," Sera added.

"It's like looking back in time," Thompson whispered, his voice filled with awe. "So much of what we see—the worlds, the stations, what few rings remain—they're the ruins, leftovers from before the wars. What we've built since...well, at best it's utilitarian and functional...but this ship, the *Intrepid*...it's so graceful, it's amazing..."

Cheeky put a hand on Thompson's shoulder. "I never knew you were such a romantic."

Thompson, looked around, his face flushing. "I'm, uh, I'm not...don't expect future sentiment."

Nance let out a nervous laugh. "I don't blame you though...that's one hell of a ship. How do they build something so big...?"

"Have you ever been to Sol?" Sera asked Nance.

"I've never felt like having the probe it takes to get in that far," the bio replied.

"They have more than a few artificial structures that dwarf planets. Building things like the *Intrepid* is practically child's play—at least it used to be."

"Are the Mars Outer Shipyards still there?" Joe asked.

"No," Sera shook her head. "Sol suffered the worst, in the FTL wars. The only megastructure still there is High Terra."

Joe's face fell. "Mars 1, the Cho?"

Sera shook her head. "All gone—well, the Cho has been rebuilt...sort of."

"I don't think I even want to know," Joe replied.

"We got out in the nick of time," Tanis said with a hand on her husband's shoulder. "They tore themselves apart even before FTL came along."

Joe sighed. "We knew it was coming...it's why we left, after all. Place was getting nuts."

"The whole core is nuts now," Sera said. "It's a hundred messed up worlds in there."

"I resent that," Nance said. "I'm from a core world."

"You're from Virginis; they've only been in the AST for a century. It's not enough time for the madness to settle in...maybe," Sera's expression grew deadly serious.

It took Nance a moment to realize the Captain was poking fun at her. "I'm going to ignore your biased remarks," she said, with obviously faked haughtiness.

"I don't know." Cheeky grinned. "Maybe her hazsuit fetish is a symptom."

Nance chose to ignore the barb. "If you're the famous General of Victoria," she said to Tanis, changing the subject and gesturing at the *Intrepid* through the display. "Are you in charge over there?"

Joe let out a laugh and wrapped his arm around Tanis. "She thinks she is—usually is, too, if the captain is in stasis."

"I'm the executive officer," Tanis said and threw a mock scowl at Joe.

"On paper," Joe added with a wink at his wife.

"Were you ever going to come up to the bridge?" a female voice asked from behind the group.

Sera turned to see a tall woman with lavender skin and a highly exaggerated figure standing in the entrance to the lounge.

"Jessica!" Tanis cried out and ran to the woman. They embraced and spoke privately for a few minutes before joining the group.

"No wonder she never thought you two were that unusual," Cheeky said, giving Nance and Sera significant looks. "Your kinks are nothing on hers."

"It's not like that!" Nance whispered. "Cut it out already."

"Sorry, Jessica," Joe said as Tanis and Jessica approached. "We got talking and I sort of decided to stay down here for the approach and forgot to tell anyone."

"Well, who's going to fly it, then?" Jessica asked.

"I'm pretty sure that Petrov can manage to dock with the *Intrepid.* Besides, Corisa just humors us all anyway."

<You keep me company,> Corsia said. *<It would get lonely out here without my little passengers.>*

"That's…a bit creepy," Thompson said.

"Are all your AI so imperious?" Cheeky asked. "No offense Angela, but you're a little bossy, too."

<I think we should save this conversation for another time,> Angela said.

Sera was certain she knew what the conversation would be about. She remembered learning about the Phobos accords as a child, but those laws were dead and gone. However, the crew and AIs on the *Intrepid* would likely not appreciate the low station of most AIs in the ninetieth century.

"Wha—?" Cheeky began to ask before Sera sent her a message to drop it.

"Tanis!" a new voice entered the conversation and Sera turned to see the holo-presence of a tall, rather distinguished looking man.

"Captain Andrews," Tanis said with a smile as she turned to face him. "I see things are proceeding well, as usual."

"Not too much worse for wear," the captain returned the smile.

Tanis had never mentioned how attractive her captain was. A man from the early fourth millennia, too—if the sparse records from so long ago were to be believed.

"I have some friends coming aboard," Tanis said. "This is captain Sera and the crew of *Sabrina,*" Tanis gestured to Sera's crew. "They have some fascinating information regarding FTL that they would like to share with us. Earnest will be especially interested."

"Thank you for returning Tanis to us," Captain Andrews said to Sera. "From what Corsia has relayed of her conversations with Sabrina, you were a long way from here."

"Just about a hundred and fifty light-years," Tanis said nonchalantly. "A hop, skip, and a jump by today's standards."

Joe nearly choked. "A hundred and fifty! Stars…I would never have found you."

Sera watched Tanis embrace her husband and whisper something in his ear while Captain Andrews continued.

"I'll be glad to have you all aboard—and not soon enough. Every one of our friends out there is making more demands than I can shake a stick at. Thankfully, there are so many of them, no one wants to make the first move."

"We'll be docking in thirty minutes," Joe said. "Should be up there in forty-five."

"Very well," the captain replied and his holo faded out.

"He's hot!" Cheeky exclaimed.

Tanis looked aghast. "He's the captain!"

"And a damn hot one at that," Cheeky said to herself.

Several conversations picked up as the *Andromeda* approached her mothership, and Sera turned to admire the view. The design of the *Intrepid* was both alien and very familiar. Its elegance reminded her of some of her people's ships—the ones built before The Sundering. Truly amazing craftsmanship had gone into what was ultimately just a colony route stevedore.

The *Andromeda* passed near one of the cruisers shadowing the *Intrepid*. The holo overlay on the lounge's window highlighted it and identified the ship as the *Orkney*. Sera slipped out of her footholds and kicked toward the window, dismissing the information overlay from her vision. She wanted to look upon this vista with her own eyes.

Both ships were on similar vectors, and the *Andromeda's* pilot brought the ship in for a slow pass, only a thousand meters from the *Orkney*.

It was built for war and Sera found herself impressed with the firepower the *Intrepid* was packing in a fleet of ships, which should have been nothing more than transports, pushers, and cargo haulers.

The *Orkney* gleamed like a jewel, sheathed in what was likely several meters of highly reflective ablative plating. Nearby, a hauler was moving an icy asteroid into position near the warship. She suspected it was to extract water and create an additional ice shield around the vessel.

She imagined some terraformer working on the world below was probably quite upset to see over a hundred trillion liters of water they had planned for a lake or sea taken away.

It was a form of warfare Sera had only read about. Take your big war wagons, sheathe them in ice and let them take the heat from enemy beams. The ice would also add radiation shielding from indirect nuclear blasts.

The tactic matched the rest of the ship's structure. With only rear engines, this was a vessel that was made to get to the fight fast, take a beating and wipe out the opposition quickly. It was aided by an assortment of beams that even the AST dreadnaughts would envy.

With fifty centimeter lenses, *Orkney's* lasers could lance across a hundred thousand kilometers and still deal lethal damage. Even at their distant position, the AST dreadnaughts were within this vessel's firing range. Modern ships rarely fired at such distances—rapid movement made long-range targeting nearly impossible.

Sera imagined having a fleet of such vessels at her command and found a new appreciation for Tanis's tactical mind. With a target as big as the *Intrepid* to defend, she had apparently pulled out all the stops.

The *Andromeda* silently slipped past the *Orkney*, and its accompanying tug and asteroid. Ahead, the bulk of the *Intrepid* began to fill the forward view. The rear of the vessel sported two massive fusion burners, and a pair of smaller antimatter engines.

Small was a relative term, since the *Andromeda's* seven-hundred and twenty-meter hull could both fit inside and turn around within even the smaller engine's exhaust ports.

"Imagine being at the helm of that thing," Cheeky whispered from Sera's side. "I can almost..." she shivered with delight and Sera rolled her eyes.

"Easy now. And here you accuse Nance and I of having fetishes."

"Oh, I have my weird bits," Cheeky said with a smile. "I just don't pretend not to. Galaxy would be a better place if people were real."

They passed beneath the engines and under the two spinning cylinders, each containing an entire world's worth of animals, flora, and fauna. From the stories Tanis had told, the general even had a nice cabin beside a lake in one.

Surrounding the ship was a latticework of support struts, though it was not readily apparent that was their primary purpose. They looked far more like a protective web; with mobile beams and chaff cannons mounted along their lengths, they certainly fit the bill.

"I bet they didn't leave Sol with all those," Sera said.

"Probably not, but I bet a few were there for shooting down rocks and stuff," Cheeky commented.

They passed the cylinders and came underneath the forward section of the ship where the doors of a massive bay loomed wide. The space inside was cavernous and empty, with all its normal occupants outside the ship on patrol.

The *Andromeda* turned and slowly backed into the bay. Once within the hull of the *Intrepid,* Sera felt the slight tug of gravity and by the time the ship settled into its cradle, over half a *g* pulled firmly at everyone.

Tanis gestured for the crew to leave the lounge as Sabrina squealed with delight over the Link.

<I'm in a ship that's inside another ship! This is so weird!>

<Is it OK? We can have you undock,> Sera replied.

<Corsia and some big guy named Bob are already working on that,> Sabrina replied. *<They seem to do a lot without even talking to people.>*

Sera could tell Sabrina was a bit nervous.

<I've noticed that. I'll send Cargo up to you to keep an eye on things.>

<Thanks, that'll make me feel better,> Sabrina replied.

They reached a cross-corridor and Tanis stopped the group.

"Sera, if you'd like to come with me, we have a meeting on the bridge deck," Tanis said.

Sera nodded. "I'd like Flaherty to come with me."

Tanis nodded and addressed Jessica. "Can you see to getting *Sabrina's* crew settled and have someone give them a tour?"

"No problem. At the least I'll show them where the bars are."

"You guys aren't taking your current situation too seriously," Thompson observed.

Jessica shrugged. "We've been in worse. Besides, Tanis is back—she'll know what to do." She placed a hand on Tanis's shoulder, which earned her a worried smile from the general.

"Just don't get too messed up—or entangled," Tanis directed a look at Jessica and Cheeky. "We may need to move fast."

With that she turned, walking briskly down a corridor to a small maglev train floating next to a platform. They entered the car, and once they took their seats, it whisked out of the station. The group had barely settled in when the train passed out of the *Andromeda* and into a clear tube, which ran across the upper reaches of the bay.

"Nice view," Sera said, looking down at the retreating form of the *Andromeda* and the kilometers of empty bay.

"It's not a bad place to work," Tanis replied. "I have to admit, it's going to be nice to stretch my legs for a bit. It's been a while since I've spent that much time on a ship as small as *Sabrina*."

"Feeling a bit cooped up, were you?" Joe asked.

"A bit," Tanis replied with a smile. "Sabrina's not that small, and I've certainly spent longer on ships…I just missed our cabin and your garden-fresh veggies."

Joe laughed. "It's probably fallen into decay; it's been years since anyone has been there."

Tanis shrugged. "We've fixed it up before, we can do it again."

Sera tuned out of their conversation and watched as the train car passed into a shaft in the bay wall, and then her breath caught as it shot out into empty space. After a moment's panic, she realized they were riding one of the thin arcs which surrounded the ship. They rose up, over the forward section of the colony vessel and then down toward the ship's nose.

The train passed back through the hull and down a long shaft before easing to a stop. The platform they stepped onto was broad and bustling with people passing through, or waiting for cars to take them to their destinations.

Tanis weaved through the throng, and as she did, people began to stop and stare. A few pointed, and whispers of "Tanis" began to fill the air.

Sera could see the general's face begin to redden and before long she stopped and turned to the crowd.

"Yes folks, I'm back."

Cheers erupted around them and some called out her name, while others shouted questions about their current situation.

Tanis held up her hands and the throng quieted.

"Don't worry, I have a plan. Everything is going to be OK."

The words were simple, and although Sera hadn't noticed it being particularly grim, the mood on the platform immediately lifted.

Tanis gave a final wave, and then led her party to the bridge deck's central corridor.

DECISIONS

STELLAR DATE: 10.27.8927 (Adjusted Years)
LOCATION: ISS *Intrepid*, Orbiting Fierra
REGION: Bollam's World System, Bollam's World Federation

They made their way down the long corridor, weaving through more crowds; individuals called out to the general, and Tanis waved or replied in turn. Presently, the crowds thinned and they came to the end of the passage, which opened into a large atrium—the centerpiece of which was a woman standing amidst a sea of holographic displays.

Sera watched in awe as the woman's hands danced across the displays, emitters on her fingertips manipulating untold systems in the time it took for Sera to realize what the woman was doing.

As they approached, what she initially perceived to be a console in front of the woman also turned out to be a holographic display. In fact, the woman appeared to be the only real thing in the atrium. Sera altered her vision to see through the holographic interfaces and was surprised at what her sight revealed.

What had appeared at first to be the woman's hair was cleverly disguised super conductor strands, which must be functioning as antennas. The bandwidth a system like that provided would be immense. Her face was smooth and composed, despite the rapid blinking of her eyelids, beneath which lay entirely black eyes. Sera marveled at her pure white skin, which her enhanced vision showed not to be skin at all, but rather a smooth, flexible polymer.

Other than her glossy coating, the woman wasn't wearing a stitch of clothing. She was perched on a very narrow stool, or pedestal—or rather, her body merged directly into the seat. She suspected this woman spent a lot of time in her current position.

The woman's head tilted and she smiled at them. An audible voice came from all around them, and over their Links.

"Welcome home Tanis, and welcome to your guests." The woman's mouth mimed the words, but no sound came from it.

"It's good to see you, Priscilla." Tanis smiled as she walked forward and stepped through the holo to embrace the woman, who stopped manipulating the interfaces around her and returned the embrace with an expression that was both warm, yet chillingly lifeless on her white face and deep black eyes.

Tanis turned, still standing in the midst of the holo display—though that didn't stop them from flashing and dancing quicker than an eye could follow. "This is Priscilla. For most purposes, she is the *Intrepid*."

"I'm very glad to meet you." Sera stepped forward and extended her hand. "I'm Sera and this is Flaherty." The silent man actually had an expression of wonder on his face as he shook Priscilla's hand in turn. "I have to admit, I'm confused. How are you the *Intrepid*?"

Priscilla gave an understanding smile. "I am the *Intrepid* in the way that your mind controls your brain, or maybe the other way around. The *Intrepid's* neural net is too vast and complex to be able to communicate effectively with humans—at least not so many of you—so I am the intermediary, its avatar, in a fashion, yet at the same time, I am the *Intrepid.*"

"But you are human," Flaherty said. "I can see it; you are not a machine."

Priscilla maintained her beatific smile. "Of course I am human, would an AI be able to think for another AI and make those thoughts into something a human could understand? The *Intrepid* has a human for its mind, though its brain is AI."

"She downplays the *Intrepid's* brain. It is far more than just AI," Tanis said with a wink. Priscilla inclined her head and a wry look crossed her face, quickly replaced by her implacable gaze. "She and Amanda take turns as the human interface to the *Intrepid.* Without them, the ship and the humans on it would have a bit of a communication gap."

"How long do these turns last?" Sera asked, wondering how long this avatar spent attached to her pedestal.

"We each actively interface with the *Intrepid* for ninety days at a time. On our downtime, we take up more…regular duties on the ship."

"That is amazing," Flaherty said in a distracted voice.

Priscilla smiled at him, then nodded toward the hall to their left. "You should go. The captain and other leaders are waiting."

Tanis gestured for the group to follow her and led them through a short corridor and into a conference room beyond.

The room was not large, but well appointed, with the center dominated by an oblong table, around which were seated nine people. Sera immediately recognized Captain Andrews at its head, and her pulse rose in reaction. It had been so long since she had allowed herself to see a man as attractive, she almost didn't know how to deal with the change in her emotional state.

<Ha! I knew it would happen eventually. You've managed to bury your feelings for some time now, but I knew someday a man would come along that your cold reason wouldn't be able to deflect,> Helen commented as she noted Sera's changing chemical state.

<Don't count on me swooning any time soon.>

<You should try it, Cheeky seems to enjoy swooning.>

<Cheeky enjoys a lot of things.>

Sera tore her attention from the *Intrepid's* captain and focused on the others around the table. On his right were two men who were not wearing the ship's uniform, but what appeared to be civilian garb. The man closest to the captain sat ramrod straight, his hair was dark and slicked back. He seemed to see everything in the room at once, and took careful note of all he viewed.

The man next to him was alert as well, but also appeared to be lost in thought at the same time. On his right was a woman who had several plas sheets spread about her and looked up from them with the expression of one who was believed that more important work was being interrupted. The man and two women to the left of the Captain were decidedly military. They wore uniforms similar to Joseph's and had the bearing of officers high in the chain of command.

Upon their entry, the Captain rose. "Welcome aboard the *Intrepid,* Captain Sera, Flaherty; and welcome back Tanis." He was just as imposing in life as Sera anticipated. His voice boomed, filling the room easily.

Tanis exchanged hugs and handshakes with the colony mission's leadership while Sera, Flaherty, and Joe took their seats at the table. Once the room had settled, the captain introduced those around the table for Sera's benefit.

The slick-looking man on his right was Terrance Enfield, one of the financiers of the *Intrepid* and its journey to 58 Eridani. Beside him was Earnest Redding, apparently the architect behind the ship. The distracted woman to his right was Abby Redding, Earnest's wife and the Chief Engineer of the *Intrepid*. The three in military dress were Admiral Sanderson, Colonel Ouri, and Commandant Brandt.

<*Tanis is a General, but appears to outrank a much older Admiral?*> Sera asked Helen privately.

<*Your guess is as good as mine—if your guess is something along the lines of Tanis getting the job that kept her out of stasis more because she was younger,*> Helen replied.

The captain's voice broke into her thoughts. "Again, I must thank you for bringing Tanis back to us. We are quite interested in where she has been for the past few months."

"Would you believe pirates?" Tanis asked with a smile.

"Pirates?" Terrance asked. "Like…ahar?"

Tanis nodded. "As Sera can attest, things are a lot different than they were when we left. With the advent of FTL, space has become a much wilder place. In fact, the two fleets maintaining positions above the north and south pole of the world we're orbiting are composed of pirates."

Several voices spoke at once, peppering Tanis with questions.

"Why don't we hold our questions until the end," Andrews said, his even tones bringing quiet. "I, for one, would like to hear this story uninterrupted."

Tanis took a deep breath and related her tale; how her pod was picked up by pirates, how she was tortured, and then shipped off to meet with a man named Padre before waking to find herself on Sera's ship. She told of their battle to save Sera and their journey across over a hundred light-years to arrive at Bollam's World and the *Intrepid.*

Terrance whistled. "That's some adventure you had, Tanis."

"You're telling me," Tanis replied. "I could do with a break from adventure."

Sera observed the *Intrepid's* leadership as they asked their questions and sought clarity on the state of the galaxy in which they found themselves.

She could tell they had been through a lot together. Though she could see some subtle tensions in the group, by and large they were tightly knit—having been through over a century of adversity together.

When there was a moment's pause, the captain spoke.

"This adds some color to what we've learned from Bollam's ambassador—and Joe and Jessica's visit to one of their stations—though they have certainly kept some details from us. We've not been granted unfettered access to the system's nets. It's pretty plain to see that they're hiding something from us."

Sera laughed. "You have that right. They don't want you to learn that you hold *all* the cards."

"We do?" Sanderson asked, no small amount of sarcasm in his voice. "I imagine all those hostile fleets out there beg to differ."

"Would you defeat all of them if it came to an all-out battle?" Sera asked without pausing for an answer. "Perhaps not, perhaps you would. Either way, no one wants to risk your ship to that sort of conflict. Even without your most precious cargo, this ship is invaluable beyond measure."

Looks around the table turned suspicious, and Tanis raised her hands defensively.

"The secret's out. Our little stunt with the pico at Victoria made its way into the history books. Not everyone believes its real, but apparently enough do. Sera, why don't you give them the highlights since we left Kapteyn's?"

"Of course," Sera said with a nod. "Only a hundred years or so after you left Earth, a man in the Procyon system discovered how to cheaply generate gravitons. I understand that you were privy to some of this information during your time at Kapteyn's Star and that you've built your own rudimentary graviton emitters."

"We have," Earnest nodded. "Though, from what I have observed, the tech has advanced considerably."

"It has," Sera agreed. "Consider that nearly the entirety of your ship could have artificial gravity supplied by a handful of devices no larger than this room."

Sharp intakes of breath resounded through the room and everyone looked at one another with a mixture of awe and disbelief.

Sera continued. "Once artificial gravity was something that anyone could afford, gravity-based experiments advanced technology by leaps and bounds. For instance, inertial dampeners now exist, which can protect ships from forces as significant as a ninety degree thrust change at over half the speed of light."

Eyes grew even wider at that statement; Earnest and Abby Redding began writing furiously on several of the plas sheets.

"Shields on ships can now be used to hold atmosphere in the event of a hull puncture—though I suspect your ES shielding can do the same," Sera paused, as the captain nodded slowly, before continuing. "Most ships aren't even airtight anymore, though I personally consider it to be prudent. But all of that was just the icing on the cake. All the work with gravitons unlocked the true nature of dark matter; mainly that scientists finally found it. It projects itself into relative space through gravity, but the bulk of its mass lays in a sub-layer of space-time commonly called the dark layer—it's basically the long-dismissed universal rest frame of reference."

"I knew it!" Earnest shouted. "Pay up dear."

Abby scowled and her eyes fluttered as Sera imagined a quick Link transaction took place between the couple.

Sera eyed them curiously for a moment before shrugging and continuing.

"Since the gravity systems on a ship could interact with that special layer of space, it became possible to move objects in and out of it. Two things were immediately discovered about the dark layer. The first was that velocity relative to normal space increased by anywhere from 300 to 800 times. The second was that Newtonian laws of reaction do not apply there. The vector you enter the DL in is the vector you stay on until you exit.

"Most ships can achieve speeds up to 0.70*c* in normal space. However, vessels like those eleven AST dreadnaughts out there have drives that can take them up to the very edge of light-speed while in normal space. When in FTL, they can traverse light-years in a matter of hours."

Everyone was silent as they soaked in the implications of Sera's speech. "Keep in mind that most of these discoveries were made right before the forty fifth century. Since then, technology, in general, has been in decline. With the advent of FTL, people no longer needed the advanced technologies required to wring every last drop of productivity from a star system. Much was lost to decline, and to the FTL wars—the aftermath of which the galaxy is still recovering from.

"No one has the faintest clue how to build things like planet pusher tugs or create planet-wide stasis fields. The concept of merging planets is impossible for all but the most advanced worlds, and nanotech is even less advanced than it was in the thirtieth century.

"To the people of Bollam's World, and the ninetieth century in general, the *Intrepid* is like a treasure trove. It's a jackpot beyond imagining. That's why those pirates were fighting over Tanis."

"So who are these eleven newcomers? You referred to them as the AST before," Captain Andrews asked his first question.

"Those are your good friends from Sol, or nearby. Sol is now part of an alliance of about a hundred and fifty worlds commonly known as the Alpha Sol Tau, or AST. They're a greedy bunch of bastards, and they probably think the *Intrepid* is theirs, too. Bollam's is a sovereign system, so the fact that they are here flexing their muscle is a bit surprising. They must be really intent in getting their hands on you."

"I swear, if you weren't here confirming all this, Tanis, I'd think it was some sort of elaborate hoax," Brandt shook her head.

"Or a nightmare," Terrance added.

"It's no dream. Those fleets out there are real, and they're only going to get bigger over the next few days," Tanis said ominously.

"Don't forget," Sera spoke into the silence. "The *Intrepid* is of greater value than this entire system. Destroying you is not their plan. Though, if things go badly for one faction, they may try to destroy what they cannot have."

The captain shook his head slowly. "Even if we are sure we can win, we don't want to get in a fight of this size—not again. Do you have a plan?" He looked between Sera and Tanis. She could clearly see that while he commanded the ship, Tanis was instrumental in its operation.

Sera took a deep breath; it was time to finally tip her hand.

"I'd help out just because Tanis saved my life, but the opportunity to show the Bollam's government that they can't extort every ship that dumps out of Kapteyn's Streamer, not to mention sticking it to Padre, Rebecca, *and* the AST? That is too much to pass up. I have something to trade, and then I will contact the FGT and see about getting you a planet."

She saw Tanis turn in her seat. The general didn't speak, but her penetrating gaze spoke volumes.

"The FGT is still around? I thought you said there was no more advanced tech like planet pushers and massive stasis fields?" Terrance looked perplexed.

"Yeah, I suppose that was not entirely true. The inner core systems still have some of the old tech, but they aren't sharing; and the FGT still exists and is going strong. However, after a few experiences very similar to what you are going through now, they cut off contact with the bulk of the inn…" Sera paused for a moment before resuming her speech, "…the human sphere. They still terraform, but they don't tell anyone about it. Every so often, they will let a struggling world know about a new home they can go to, or they will trade from time to time. Sometimes they just let the new worlds be found by explorers."

"Then how will you contact the FGT?" Terrance asked.

"Yes, I am all ears," Tanis said, her tone almost angry.

Sera didn't answer for a minute. "I can't disclose that yet. But I can promise you that I can reach them and that they will see yours as a good case for a new world."

"First, we have to get out of this mess," Joe said with a frown. "What's the plan there?"

Sera was glad to see Tanis's dark expression lift.

"That is something we have a solid plan for," Tanis said and gestured for Sera to share the data on FTL.

Sera smiled broadly. "I have, as it turns out, complete design and operating specifications for graviton systems on a scale as large as this ship. With that, I have the information for how to implement gravitational shields, gravity drives, and even the information on how to take a ship of this size into the dark layer. In short: protection, power, and FTL."

No one spoke for several long seconds as that information soaked in.

"You have *full* design, and operating specifications on these systems?" Abby asked, no small amount of skepticism in her voice.

"Everything but an arrow pointing at where to bolt it on," Sera replied.

Joe frowned. "What Jessica and I learned during our time on that mining platform is that no one can move ships this large into FTL. Those AST dreadnaughts are right at the edge of safe transition."

"They don't know everything in the core worlds," Sera said with a shrug. "Out on the fringes of known space, there are some pretty amazing things going on."

"And what do you want for this information, and how did you come by it?" The captain also sounded skeptical. Tanis, too, looked quite interested to have one of Sera's mysteries revealed: her source.

"Unfortunately, I'm not at liberty to discuss that, either. However, I can assure you that the knowledge is accurate and I legally own rights to it. Like I said, the only thing I want in trade is to help take out a few of those bastards out there."

"We may yet find a peaceful resolution to this," Terrance said.

"You may, they won't," Sera replied.

"She's right about that." The Admiral shook his head. "If what she says is true, none of those factions are going to let the others get the prize. The only way we are going to get out of this is by destroying or thoroughly intimidating them."

"I hate to have to ask," Tanis interjected, "but how did you get in this situation?"

"Jessica and I got nabbed," Joe replied with a sheepish look. "I guess they pick up a lot of flotsam and jetsam here, and our hunt for you put us on their radar. We signaled for *Corsia* to come pick us up, but *Intrepid* came instead. Folks here decided that it was better to be insystem and work on a trade than out in the black with no options."

"Fierra, the freshly terraformed world below us, was an appealing offer," Terrance added. "But if they all know about the picotech, then that world would just be a pretty cage at best."

Sera snorted. "That's so like Bollam's."

The captain picked up the story. "We were negotiating with their ambassador when the first of the pirate fleets showed up. Before we could blink, a full-scale battle was playing out around us. We deployed our fleet—much to their surprise, I might add—and we entered into the current stalemate."

"There was that move when you tapped into the jovian's magnetic field with our ramscoop and used it to smash the shields on a dozen of those pirate corvettes," Joe said to Earnest. "It was pure genius."

Earnest chuckled. "It's amazing the effect a finely focused beam of gamma rays can have on someone's level of caution. Didn't really damage anyone, but I could tell that whatever they were shielding themselves with had to expend a lot of power to protect them. Now that I know its graviton based, it makes sense."

He pulled his glasses off and cleaned them—a strange gesture, and an even stranger, archaic method of eyesight correction. "Why they don't have stasis shields is beyond me. If they can generate cheap gravitons, then antimatter is less expensive than air. Every ship could have stasis shields and could fly through a star if they wanted with no damage."

Silence fell at his words.

"I'm guessing by the expression on your face that no one is able to do that in the ninetieth century?" Terrance asked.

"If they can, they aren't sharing," Sera said slowly, the implications racing through her mind. "Now you understand why the *Intrepid* is so valuable and why none of these factions will let the others get a hold of this ship or its personnel. Whoever captures *Intrepid* will rule space for a hundred light-years in every direction. That is not something we can allow to happen."

"We'd better get to it, then," the captain said. "What do we need to do to get started?"

"My AI, Helen, can work with your engineering chief to achieve a full implementation."

"You'll also want to interface with *Sabrina* to get her scan and targeting packages," Tanis added. "The algorithms for tracking and hitting ships that can jink like our friends out there are no simple thing. Luckily, I bought the best."

Several small conversations broke out as plans were laid and issues discussed. Captain Andrews cocked his head as a message was passed to him, then he raised his hand.

"It would appear that we have a message from the Bollam's World Fleet. Chief, Earnest, I'm certain you have things you'd rather be doing. If everyone else would like to remain, let's see what they have to say."

The far end of the conference table lit up with a holo projection of a bridge on another ship. The image was entirely lifelike; it was as though the *Intrepid* ended and another ship began half way down the table.

"Admiral Argon, how good for you to call on us again," Captain Andrews said.

"Captain Andrews, we see that you are increasing your offensive capabilities, and stealing our resources to do it."

Sera guessed that the admiral was referring to the asteroid she saw a tug pulling to the *Orkney* on their way in.

The Bollam's admiral continued, "This cannot be allowed within our sovereign system. We require that you cease your increase in armament and resume talks with us."

"Admiral, we were in the midst of talks when you made a series of impossible demands in exchange for the world we orbit. You know as well as I that what you were willing to give us wasn't much different than being your indentured servants. You also seem to be having issues with a few pirates and outside interferences from the core worlds. Perhaps we should be treating with them instead of you."

The admiral on the Bollam's World ship turned a very curious shade of red. "It would seem you already have been, as you now possess information you did not when we last spoke."

"Not so, Admiral. Rather, one of our crew, who had been abducted by pirates while in your system, managed to escape and get back to us. It's a pity you can't seem to keep your system free of such elements. They seem to cause you no end of trouble."

Sera noted that the captain seemed to be enjoying playing the Bollam's World admiral. It was perhaps a bit petty, but she probably would have done the same.

"We'll deal with them and with you. The *Intrepid* is the property of the sovereign system of Bollam's World and we will have it."

With that, the transmission was cut.

"Well, that certainly was presumptuous," Terrance laughed.

"Who names their system 'Bollam's World', anyway?" asked Joe. "It's a system, not a world. It's rather confusing."

"Having just come from Kapteyn's Star, I suspect it's our curse," Tanis said with a laugh.

"I think we should call them the Bollers," Brandt volunteered. "It would make this a lot simpler."

"Seconded," Tanis said with a smile.

"So shall it be," Joe announced. "They are the Bollers, and their star is The Boll."

PREPARATIONS

STELLAR DATE: 10.27.8927 (Adjusted Years)
LOCATION: ISS *Intrepid*, Orbiting Fierra
REGION: Bollam's World System, Bollam's World Federation

Following a brief meal, where she was impressed to see Tanis consume three BLTs, Sera provided them with a breakdown of the types of weapons and tactics they could expect to face.

The *Intrepid's* leadership listened intently to her recitation of the pirate ships' abilities as well as those of the Bollam's World fleet. She also imparted what she knew of the weapons capabilities and arsenals of the AST dreadnaughts.

<*Please, be straight with me, Sera,*> Tanis finally said as Sera was discussing the current types of focusing mechanisms used to track and focus on objects fifty thousand kilometers away moving near the speed of light.

<*You've gone past the point of no return now. The fact you won't share how you attained all this information is the only thing hurting your credibility. If you don't share soon, Bob will figure it out, if he hasn't already.*>

<*It's not top of my list,*> Bob interjected himself into their communication. <*But it will be soon. Nice to meet you, by the way, Sera.*>

Sera was stunned by Bob's mental presence.

She looked at Tanis to see the general smiling. <*Now you get why we use Amanda and Priscilla, if for no other reason than it's impossible to concentrate when he talks directly to you like that.*>

<*That's your AI?*> Sera's voice was a whisper. <*He's not in the history books…but there are legends about AI like him.*>

<*Massive, multi-nodal AI are legendary?*> Tanis asked.

<*Gods are legendary,*> Sera replied.

Tanis didn't reply—either she agreed, or didn't know what to say.

<*I'll…I just need to work out one detail—make sure it pans out, then I'll share everything,*> Sera said after several moments.

<*Work it out soon,*> Tanis replied ominously.

The conversation continued around them, and Sera found herself increasingly curious about Captain Andrews. She tapped into the ship's archives and pulled up his public dossier.

Captain Jason Andrews had been commanding starships for almost a thousand years of relative time when he landed the job as the *Intrepid's* captain. From what she could see, it was in no small part due to a longstanding relationship with Terrance.

His temporal age was just shy of four hundred years—perhaps that explained the grey hair, though she knew many men far older than he who didn't look a day over thirty. Yet, somehow the aging suited Andrews.

She wondered what sort of personal relationships he would have had given all that interstellar travel. There was no record of a wife, or even rumor of a dalliance on the ship. Was he the sort of man who took what love he could get, or did he hold out for long-term, quality relationships? There was just something about him and his bearing that she found intriguing.

<*Liar, you find him irresistible, not intriguing,*> Helen broke into her reverie.

<*Stop eavesdropping on my thoughts.*>

<*If you stopped broadcasting them in our shared neural net I wouldn't have to listen to you go on about him,*> Helen said with the insufferable smugness.

Sera knew she was being baited, but replied before she could stop herself. <*I know you can tune it out. You are soooo superior, after all.*>

<*Yes, yes I am,*> Helen said with an air of finality. Sera could tell she had lost that battle of wits.

"I know you don't want to say before you've contacted them, but how certain are you that the FGT has a world we can colonize?" Terrance asked for what had to be the third time.

"I'm positive," Sera replied. "Almost every time someone goes out beyond the current sphere of human colonization to a G spectrum star, they find that it already has terraformed worlds. I'm betting the FGT will want to trade some technology for the location of an out-of-the-way system, but that will most likely be the only caveat."

"I wonder what tech that might be," Joe said and coughed into his hand.

"So, somehow you'll send a message to the FGT and they'll meet with us for this trade?" Captain Andrews asked.

"Yes, I'll tell them to meet us spin-ward of the Ascella system. It's uninhabited, so we shouldn't have any visitors."

"And they'll be there?" Terrance asked. "This is a mighty big gamble we're taking."

Sera smiled. "You and your ship are the largest human curiosity in the known universe. No one will be able to resist its lure."

"And what if they decide to simply take it by force as our friends out there have?" Admiral Sanderson asked, apparently less than convinced that they'd find a warm welcome anywhere.

"They won't. There has never been a recorded instance of an FGT-instigated battle."

"At least the FGT is a known quantity," Tanis sighed. "Better than pirates and power-hungry star systems."

"Agreed. I've always found them to be quite noble," Brandt added.

"A lot can change in five thousand years," Terrance warned. "The FGT we left was in open communication with the rest of humanity."

"Speaking of five-thousand years," Joe asked Sera, "why do you think it was so hard for us to pinpoint the year when we got here? It shouldn't have been that hard to figure out."

<*I've been conversing with Sabrina about that,*> Priscilla said. <*She is a thoroughly pleasant little ship. She's informed me that some of the stellar shift has been greater than expected—most of it due to the supernova of Betelgeuse. It was far more massive than predicted, with dark matter, from what I've learned, accounting for much of that. There is now a rather nice nebula where it used to be.*

<*The dark matter which escaped the nova broke apart several of the nearby stars, scattered the Orion dust cloud and even shifted Rigel a touch.*>

"So, I'm guessing that that region of space is pretty much off limits," Captain Andrews said.

"Yeah, the dark matter is everywhere, so no one can pass through in FTL. Not to mention that it's still rife with radiation from the explosion."

<*I have a preliminary estimate,*> Earnest broke into their conversation. <*Helen has supplied us with the specs and we're adapting them for our ship. There are some promising applications—some I think that no one in the ninetieth century has sorted out yet, either.*>

"The estimate?" Captain Andrews asked aloud.

<*Four days, five at the most. We won't have artificial gravity or inertial dampeners, but we can get the systems in place for an FTL transition. It's really not that hard once you know some of the tricks.*>

"Damn, that's fast," Sera said.

<*We're equipped to build a colony, plus we left Victoria with a lot of spare parts. We didn't want to end up in a situation like we did after Estrella de la Muerte again.*>

Earnest signed off and Sera gave a soft laugh. "I can't believe it was you guys that named that star. Do you realize it stuck?"

<*Yes!*> Priscilla exclaimed.

"I suppose I had better send that message to the FGT," Sera said and rose from the table. "Plus, it's been a really long day."

Everyone agreed that they had dallied long enough and that there was work demanding their attention and the meeting broke up. In the corridor, Tanis stopped Sera.

"Any chance I can sit in on your call to the FGT?" Tanis asked.

Sera grimaced. "Look...I know your curiosity burns eternal, but I have to do this alone."

Tanis's expression soured. "A lot is riding on your prediction."

"Earnest says my FTL specs are good. Even if I can't hold up my end of the deal, you can get out of here and fly to the edge of space and make a colony where no one will find you," Sera replied coldly. "It's what you want, right? To get away from everything? To hide and hoard your technology and not share it with humanity?"

She could see Tanis was taken aback by the vehemence of her statement. Joe and Flaherty both watched with raised eyebrows, sharing a look between them.

"Send your message, then," Tanis said coldly. "But you should know that it would be a lot easier to relate to you if you weren't hiding so much."

"C'mon," Joe said, taking Tanis's arm. "There's a lot you need to do." He looked over his shoulder to Sera and Flaherty. "It was nice meeting you, I imagine you'll want to get back to your ship. The nav NSAI can guide you."

With that, he whisked Tanis away, leaving Sera and Flaherty standing alone.

"Well, that was unexpected," Sera said with a sigh.

"It really wasn't," Flaherty replied. "I'm surprised she didn't give that to you with both barrels in the meeting with the captain."

Sera looked at him in surprise. "Really? I didn't think it was bothering her that much."

"On the way here, she had no way of knowing what she was up against, so she compartmentalized her worry about her people and focused only on the task at hand—you remember compartmentalization, right?" Flaherty said with a frown. "Now that she's back here, the two and a half million lives on this ship are her biggest concern, and you are her biggest unknown. To Tanis, you've become the definition of risk in human form. The fact that you saved her life is likely all that's keeping her from kicking you off the *Intrepid*."

<*I doubt she'd be that rash,*> Helen added. <*But I bet it's crossed her mind.*>

Sera stared at Flaherty and Helen's virtual presence in surprise.

"You know why it's so hard for me. I don't want to go down that road."

"You're already going down that road," Flaherty said. "You're taking me and Helen with you, I might add, but I swore on my life that I would keep you safe. You need to grow up and take charge of your destiny. The first part of that is coming clean with Tanis...and your crew, for that matter."

They walked in silence past Priscilla who didn't speak, but sent a greeting into their minds. At the end of the corridor, they boarded a maglev car and gave it their destination.

<*Who do you think that they'll send to meet us?*> Sera finally asked.

<*With our luck it will be Florence,*> Flaherty replied dourly.

<*Unlikely,*> Helen added. <*They'll send Greg. You can count on it.*>

<*Ugh. I shouldn't have gotten up that day we left Coburn. Nothing is worth having to deal with Greg,*> Sera sighed

Flaherty chuckled.

<*Acceptance of your destiny is the first step.*>

The rest of the trip back passed in silence. The maglev eventually stopped at a large station labeled "A1 Docking Bay".

The corridor to the bay itself was short, and when they arrived, there was a corporal waiting for them with a groundcar.

"Ma'am, sir, I'm to take you to your ship," she said.

"Glad to hear it," Sera replied. "It looks like it's a kilometer away."

"A bit more," the corporal—Nair, by her uniform's tag—said.

The groundcar took off and Sera closed her eyes for the trip, working up what she would say in her message. Before they arrived, she was interrupted by a call from Cargo.

<*Sera, are you coming back soon?*> Cargo asked, a hint of panic in his voice.

<*Yeah, I'll be there in about a minute, what's up?*>

<*Oh nothing, there's just a platoon of bios out there that want to come onboard and further investigate some new pathogens they detected on us during our little tour. They want to inspect all the freight, as well.*>

<*Okay, hold them off, I'll deal with them.*>

Cargo thanked her and Sera accessed Priscilla via the return path from her last greeting. <*Priscilla, can you Link me to Tanis? I can't seem to reach her.*>

<*She asked not to be disturbed unless the ship is under attack,*> Priscilla said. <*Overzealous bios are close, but I don't think they quite qualify. I can put you in touch with the captain, though. Will he do?*>

<*Uh, sure. I just need to speak with him for a moment.*>

<*Will do, but just so you know, go easy on the bios. They were let down at Victoria by not waking to their real destination, and now they've learned that New Eden was snagged up long ago. Your ship, however, is providing them with a very interesting distraction.* >

<*Specialists with nothing special to do,*> Helen added. <*The most dangerous kind.*>

<*Well hello!*> Priscilla said to Helen. <*We didn't make contact before. You're...different from the other AI on* Sabrina.>

Sera smiled to herself. Every now and then an advanced intelligence would detect that Helen was no regular AI. It was interesting to be privy to the meeting of those minds.

<*I'm Helen,*> the AI replied. <*I must admit that between the two of us, you are far more unusual.*>

<*I'm not so sure about that,*> Priscilla said. Sera was now an afterthought, left in the loop of the conversation purely out of courtesy. <*You aren't an AI at all!*>

Sera opted out of the conversation. No other intelligence had ever made that observation of Helen, and, as much as she wanted to see how Helen handled it, the conversation was bound to begin flowing so fast that she wouldn't be able to follow it.

Suddenly, she was Linked with Captain Andrews and she focused her attention on him.

<*Captain Sera, what can I do for you?*> His tone was warm and welcoming, something that was impressive to hear from a man who probably had thousands of things demanding his attention.

<*I just wanted to check in with you regarding your gaggle of bios I see up ahead. Do you think they are totally necessary? It's not quite as good as your time, but disease is all but unknown in the ninetieth century.*>

<*I just got to their request in my backlog,*> the captain said. <*They apparently didn't wait for my approval before besieging you. I've chastised them for it. However, would you mind letting them do their bit? It'll make them feel better, and save me days of sorting through their requests—which I fully intend to pass to Tanis once she's had some time to herself.*>

Sera sent him a mental chuckle. <*Only because you played both the Tanis and the paperwork card. Sorry to bother you, I'll let you get back to your various troubles.*>

Captain Andrews laughed in response and closed the connection.

Ahead, *Sabrina* came into view, tucked in a corner behind a massive pile of equipment; she checked in on Helen and found that her AI was still in a deep conversation with Priscilla. She'd never considered it before, but she wondered if her and Helen's secret would finally get out. The thought was both exhilarating and terrifying. She put that thought from her mind as the groundcar pulled up to her ship.

She thanked the corporal for the ride and approached the throng of bios.

"Hello, I'm Captain Sera. I've been informed you'd like to do an inspection of my crew and any possible health issues?"

An officious-looking man, there was always one in every group, pushed through the other bios—seven in total.

"Yes. I'm Dr. Philips. We demand that we be allowed to inspect your ship and its cargo to ascertain any possible health concerns. The fact that you have been allowed access to the *Intrepid* without being screened first is unconscionable. You could be spreading some sickness against which we have no defense!"

"As I understand it, we were screened when we first boarded the *Andromeda,*" Sera said with a smile. "Some very impressive systems you have on this ship of yours."

"Well, not physically examined, though, and your ship could be harboring contaminants."

Sera sighed. "Don't you think that if there were some highly communicable and deadly sickness rampant amongst us that Tanis would have caught it?"

"Not necessarily..." the man said as he looked around her, seeing only Flaherty. "Where is Mrs. Richards, anyway?" he asked.

"Don't you mean General Richards?" Sera asked.

"Yes, yes, Priscilla won't tell me where she is. We should check her, too."

"I believe she is taking a few hours of personal time with Joseph," Sera said.

The man blanched and Sera had to suppress a smile. He nodded to one of the bios with him. The man grabbed a case from the pile near the airlock and dashed toward their groundcar.

He looked at his other associates. "I suppose there is no point in us suiting up. We've probably already been contaminated and that may just concentrate it." He then turned back to Sera. "You will grant us access to your ship now."

The man was really starting to get on her nerves. She swished her head, tossing her hair over her shoulder, and placed her hands on her waist. The desired effect was achieved; the man took a moment before his eyes returned to hers, at which point her glower was severe, causing him to flinch.

"What's the magic word?" Sera asked.

"What?"

"The magic word, what is it?"

"Magic?" He grew flustered and Sera's glower twitched, threatening to turn into a smile.

Everyone else in the group looked exasperated with Dr. Philips. One of the women leaned over and smacked him in the shoulder. "It's please, you dolt."

"Oh, er, please."

Sera's glower disappeared and she beamed. "Cargo," she said over the Link and audibly for the bios benefit. "Assemble the crew in the galley so these medical folks can check us over to make sure we're not carrying the plague."

With that, she slipped past the bios, Flaherty following, and stepped through *Sabrina's* airlock. The bios quickly picked up their equipment and followed her down the freight deck's main corridor. Perversely, she took the ladders and enjoyed hearing them struggle to pull their equipment up after her to the crew deck.

Cargo, Cheeky, and Thompson were already in the galley and Nance indicated over the ship's audible comm that she would arrive in a minute. Three of the bios set up their equipment while two began taking air and surface samples from around the wardroom. Dr. Philips was overseeing everything while casting dark looks at the bowl of fruit on the table.

Flaherty walked to the coffee machine and poured himself cup full of their strongest black brew before sitting down beside Thompson. He looked like he was considering putting his feet up on the table, but Sera shot him a look that contained an entire paragraph about how she felt about feet on her maple and walnut table.

"So, how'd things go in your big meeting, Captain?" Cargo asked, ignoring everything going on around them.

"Very well, they've begun implementing the grav systems they'll need to make FTL transition."

"That going to take long?" Thompson asked. "I don't relish sitting here in this exceptionally large target—even though it is amazing—while we wait and see if one of those folks out there decides to end the party and send an RM our way."

"Don't worry. Helen is helping them modify the spec for this ship. It's going quite well. I wouldn't worry too much about RMs. Apparently there have been no small number of missiles sent this ship's way and it's still here."

"For real?" Cheeky asked. "That's got to be some story."

"Who's Helen?" Dr. Philips asked.

"Don't worry yourself," Cheeky drawled. "She's an AI. She won't spread any germs."

"Fine," Dr. Philips sighed. "I want to inspect your cargo, as well."

"Once you clear Thompson here, he can show you around. You'll not open anything without his permission, and if a door's locked, it stays locked. Our environmental systems are the same ship-wide, so you don't need to look in every corner to find out if anything is amiss."

Dr. Philips looked unhappy but accepted that. "Where's your last crew member?"

Sera smiled as Nance stepped into the wardroom. "Here she is."

Nance was in her full getup. Her isolated air supply was hooked up and her facial filter totally sealed. She held several sealed containers with what Sera assumed where her blood and tissue samples.

"What is this?" Dr. Philips asked, clearly alarmed. "Is she sick? Is it contagious?"

"Yes, very. We usually don't let her out, but you demanded that we all assemble," Sera said, working to retain a straight face.

She glanced across the table at Cheeky, who was snickering behind her hand.

Dr. Philips followed her gaze and scowled at Nance.

"This is serious. Give me those," he said and snatched the samples from Nance.

"This is Nance. She's our bio," Sera said with a grin. "It would seem that she feels about you the same way that you feel about us."

<Joking aside, they are far more likely to have something that we can catch than the other way around,> Nance said.

"She's right, you know, Mark," one of the women in the group said to Dr. Philips. "At least some of the diseases they have may require biological specifics that we haven't evolved to allow for yet, while everything that we have in our systems they can probably catch."

"And none of which occurred with Tanis, I'd like to remind you," Sera pointed out. "Our basic nano is that good, at least." Nance sat at the table, her back ramrod straight. "Besides," Sera continued. "She always dresses like this; it's not really that much of a statement about your chances of infecting her, but of anyone's."

The *Intrepid's* medics took Thompson's sample first, then Dr. Philips took one of his party with the super and left to go over the ship. Sera turned to Cargo.

"Bridge and all crew quarters are sealed, right?"

"It's not my first inspection," Cargo smiled. "Gonna make 'em say please for every little thing."

The woman who had come to Nance's defense smiled at them as she took samples from some of the foodstuffs in the wardroom. "Don't blame Dr. Philips, he's just ferociously bored. He spent the whole time on Victoria out of stasis, only because he wholly expected to wake up to a colony next time. It's starting to wear his personality thin."

Sera laughed. "That much is apparent."

The woman smiled. "I'm Terry, and this is Anne and Sam." She gestured to the woman and man still with her in the wardroom who nodded in response. "We just got thawed last week. It's hard to believe we ended up in the ninetieth century!"

"Alive and well," Cargo replied with a smile.

"They're not going to let us settle that moon down there, are they?" Terry asked.

"I'd say the chances of that happening now are between zero and nil," Sera agreed. "The *Intrepid* out-values it about a million to one, but newly terraformed worlds are very rare in this region. Bollam's World is in the midst of a heavily settled space; they have no expansion available, so this is their only option."

"So, where are we going to go, then?" Anne asked.

"Once we get your ol' girl FTL capable, we'll head out to rendezvous with the FGT. They'll set you up with a nice colony well out of the way."

A quick check informed Sera that Helen and Priscilla were still lost in a deep conversation. Great, this was going to give her a headache whether she paid attention to it or not. She asked Helen at least to keep the blood vessels in her head from swelling.

"FTL?" Terry asked. "So that rumor was true."

"You bet," Sera replied. "We provided the details for the technology. If your Reddings are all history says they are cracked up to be, then the *Intrepid* should be ready to make the jump in less than a week."

Terry blushed and the other two looked guilty. "Here you are doing all of this for us and we're treating you like some sort of quarantine violators. I'm really sorry about that." She looked over at Nance. "If you don't mind, I wouldn't mind seeing the environmental systems on this ship after we're done here. I used to be a bio on some small transports. I'd like to see what's changed in the last couple of thousand years."

Sera was surprised that Nance nodded in agreement.

A half an hour later, the inspection was over. The preliminary examinations showed that *Sabrina* posed no threats and Terry promised to see if there was anything that the crew of the *Intrepid* could inadvertently pass to them. Dr. Philips wanted to take more samples, but his med techs managed to convince him that they should spend time reviewing what they knew to catch any possible issues fast. If anything suspicious turned up, they would do a more thorough investigation later. The way Terry winked at Sera when they left, she was certain that nothing would come to Dr. Philip's attention unless it was a truly serious problem. She also set a time to come back and see the environmental systems with Nance.

"I thought they'd never leave," Thompson said as he closed the inner airlock.

"Good times," Sera smiled.

*****

The bridge was empty when Sera stepped onto it. Cargo was off duty, and Jessica asked Cheeky to join her in reviewing the specs of the ISF fighters and how the Intrepid would stack up against the enemy fleets.

<Sabrina, secure Link.>

<Link is secure,> Sabrina responded after a moment.

<You know that system I informed you to forget about?> Sera asked.

<Access pass?> Sabrina's mental tone was entirely free of emotion.

<Fina and Uncle Mandy,> Sera replied.

<That's the one,> Sabrina said. *<Are you finally going to use this thing?>*

<Yup. No one has ever discovered it, have they?>

<How would they? It's linked to the power system in your shower. Not many people go in there.>

<Someone may have noticed that my shower's grav system is powered by a superconductor cable as thick as my wrist.>

<If they did, they must have just thought you had some sort of kinky sex system set up in your cabin.>

Sera laughed. *<What, like the one Cheeky has?>*

<Thompson has one, too.>

<Now that *I didn't know.>* Sera shook her head and smiled to herself. *<Anything else like that I don't know about?>*

<Yes.>

Sera felt her ire rise for a moment, but forced herself to let it go. She knew enough not to attempt to control everything. That road ultimately led to total loss of control.

<Let's get this message sent; its burning a hole in my brain.>

<You're going to need to jack in for the connection. Helen is using almost all of your wireless bandwidth, and from what I understand, the control circuitry for this transmitter is inside you. You really don't want to max your throughput.>

Sera reached behind her headrest and pulled the hardlink cable out and connected it to the port at the base of her skull.

When *Sabrina* confirmed the hardlink, she activated the U-layer transmitter secreted away in her shower. She set the coordinates for the message and called up the script she had pre-recorded. Sera paused for a moment and listened to her words, wondering how they would be received, what the FGT would require of her in return. She pushed aside her indecision and sent the message.

The ship's power usage meters rose and the reactor increased its burn to cover the discharge she had pulled from the SC batteries.

<All systems show a successful transmission,> Sabrina said as she powered down the U transmitter.

<Same here. I'm going to hit the hay. Wake me if anything interesting happens.>

<Yes, Captain,> Sabrina responded as Sera rose and retreated to her cabin, more than ready to sleep off the anxiety that message had caused her.

THE LAKE HOUSE

STELLAR DATE: 10.27.8927 (Adjusted Years)
LOCATION: ISS *Intrepid*, Orbiting Fierra
REGION: Bollam's World System, Bollam's World Federation

"Think you were a little hard on her?" Joe asked as he led Tanis to the maglev station.

Tanis let out a long sigh. "Maybe…I don't know. It's not like she can have any secret so mind-blowing that we can't handle it. We're going to figure it out; she should just tell already."

"Reminds me of how eager you were to share the details of your mission at Toro," Joe replied.

"That was different," Tanis said. "Those records were sealed. I couldn't talk about it."

"Don't play games with me," Joe locked eyes with Tanis as they stopped and waited for a train. "You may not have felt any of your decisions on Toro were wrong, but you felt shame for how it was handled, how you were treated—by the military, your father, and your husband."

Tanis broke eye contact. Even after all the years, thinking back to those days hurt more than she cared to admit.

"OK, point taken."

<*I got worried when you were talking about what you went through…the torture, getting your chest half blown off again…are you sure our little girl OK?*> Joe asked privately.

<*I'm sorry,*> Tanis replied, her eyes filled with compassion. <*I should have reassured you right away. The stasis field protected her very well—Angela moved heaven and earth to make sure she's OK…but…*>

<*But?*> Joe asked, worry flooding his features.

<*When I got shot up, Angela couldn't keep the stasis field intact while fixing me back up, so she pulled our little girl out. After all the surgery was done, I had her put back in…but out of stasis.*>

Joe's face split into a smile so bright Tanis almost had to look away. He grabbed her by the waist and spun her around.

<*Stars, yes! No point in waiting for New Eden anymore!*>

Tanis laughed and he set her back on the deck plate.

"Let's get out of here and enjoy our reunion," he said. "All that unpleasant saving everyone's skin stuff will come crashing back on you soon enough."

"Gee," Tanis said with a chuckle. "You sure know how to take a load off my mind."

A maglev car pulled up beside them, and they stepped on, along with several other passengers—more than a few were whispering about seeing the general.

Tanis sat and rested her head on Joe's shoulder, blocking out the worry and all the distractions around her. There was no doubt in her mind that they would come out on top of this challenge.

Joe was right. She needed to take this time and relax and rebuild her reserves.

They didn't speak for the rest of the ride to Old Sam, neither verbally, nor over the Link.

The maglev made several stops, and passengers came and went, but Tanis barely noticed. Eventually, the train came to rest at their stop, a station half a kilometer from their cabin.

They disembarked and walked down the long, wooded path, arm in arm.

In the woods around them, birds sang and the sounds of small animals going about their business could be heard. Tanis saw a mother deer and her fawn in a clearing as they neared their destination.

"It's good to be home," she said with a contented sigh.

They rounded the bend and her breath caught. She expected to see the cabin and its grounds overrun by weeds and debris—after all, with the time in stasis after leaving Kapteyn's Star combined with the months following her abduction, neither of them had been to the cabin in years.

But there it stood, the yard clean, what appeared to be a fresh coat of paint on the walls, and the garden overflowing with fruits and vegetables.

"Did Bob arrange this?" Tanis asked as they approached.

"No, I did," a voice said from behind them.

Tanis turned to see Ouri stepping out from behind a tree. Her shipsuit was covered in dirt and a pair of work gloves hung from her belt.

"Ouri!" Tanis cried out and rushed to embrace the woman. "Thank you so much for this. You have no idea what it means...I guess that's why you ducked out of our meeting early."

"And had Priscilla make your train take longer," the colonel grinned. "It hasn't all been me. A lot of us from the SOC, command crew, and no small number of Marines have been down here. Even Amanda was here not long ago weeding your strawberry patch, but she had to run and prep to trade off with Priscilla."

"Come inside," Tanis said and took Ouri's arm. "I'll make coffee—I imagine there's coffee."

Ouri chuckled. "Your larder is fully stocked. I would come in, but you have no idea the workload I'm shielding you from right now. I came down here because I wanted to see the look on your face, but I need to get back to the grind."

"Are you sure?" Tanis asked. "I know your boss; he works for me."

"I seem to recall that, yes," Ouri replied. "But if I stay, Sanderson is going to start calling both of us, and I want you to enjoy yourself for a few more hours at least."

"OK," Tanis agreed. "But we have to sit down before long, you'll really want to hear about my little trip, especially New Eden."

"New Eden?" Ouri gasped. "You were there? Is it as beautiful as we hoped?"

"You'll just have to wait and see," Tanis said replied with a wink.

"Are we sure this is our Tanis?" Ouri asked Joe. "She seems far too easygoing."

"I think the smuggler crew she spent the last few months with has rubbed off on her," Joe replied.

"Stars, I really do wish I could stay," Ouri said, a frown clouding her expression. "But duty calls. I'll see the two of you soon enough."

Ouri turned and walked back up the path, leaving Tanis and Joe to spend a last moment admiring their home before stepping inside.

*****

Later that afternoon, as they relaxed in front of the dying embers of their fire, Tanis suddenly reached out and grasped Joe's arm.

"You resigned your commission for me?"

Joe chuckled. "Just got to that place in your queue, eh?"

She sat up and turned to him.

"What were you thinking? How could you…" her voice trailed and she let a slow smile creep over her face.

"You and your belief that the mission is *everything*," Joe chuckled. "I thought you were beyond that."

"I am," Tanis said with a sigh. "It was a momentary relapse. What I meant to say was 'thank you'."

"You're welcome," Joe said pulled her close for a long kiss, which Tanis returned.

Suddenly she pulled back, her piercing eyes locked onto his. "Wait. If you resigned and/or went AWOL, how is it that you were in command of the *Andromeda* when you scooped us up?"

"It turns out, Bob forced Jason to back down. My resignation never hit the official record," Joe said with a shrug.

"It's nice to have your friendly neighborhood AI-god on your side," Tanis said with a laugh.

<*Not you, too,*> Bob said with a sigh.

<*Sorry, I couldn't resist,*> Tanis laughed in response.

"The next thing in your queue is likely a note from Jason telling you that my punishment is up to you," Joe said with a wink.

"Oh, is it now?" Tanis asked as she leaned back and pulled him on top of her. "I wonder what we should do about that?"

AN UNEXPECTED INVITATION

STELLAR DATE: 10.28.8927 (Adjusted Years)
LOCATION: ISS Intrepid, Orbiting Fierra
REGION: Bollam's World System, Bollam's World Federation

<*Sera.*> The sound broke into her dreams. <*Sera.*> It repeated. <*Wake up Sera, you've got a call.*>

Sera tried to swat away Helen's voice. "Lemme 'lone…sleeping."

<*I know that, Fina, but its Captain Andrews. I thought you'd want to take it.*>

Sera snorted and turned over, fighting the voice that was telling her she should wake.

<*Come on, Fina. Wake up.*>

"Kay, kay." Sera knew from decades of experience that when Helen thought it was time to wake up, there was no fighting it. <*Patch me through.*>

<*He called you,*> Helen reminded her.

<*Oh, yeah, patch **him** through, then.*> Sera waited a moment and then her HUD showed that the captain was connected. <*Good morning, Captain, what can I do for you?*>

Captain Andrew's warm chuckle filled her mind. <*I guess we're on different clocks. What time is it there?*>

Sera checked and grimaced. <*Oh four hundred.*>

<*I'm sorry about that, it's only oh fifteen here. I was going to invite you and your crew to our officer's wardroom at eighteen hundred hours for our evening dinner. Sort of an eve before battle meal, but if the timing is bad...*>

Sera tried to compose her mind, this sort of thing was important, probably not to be missed. <*No, no, we'd be honored to come. Eighteen hundred, you said?*>

<*Yes, I'll have someone meet you and bring you up at a quarter to.*>

<*Sounds good, we'll be ready.*> Sera fought the urge to yawn. For some reason, she was one of those people who couldn't hear both audibly and mentally when she did.

<*We'll likely all be in our dress uniforms for the occasion,*> Captain Andrews said. <*But you can wear whatever is your custom—you looked quite beautiful in what you had on today.*>

Sera almost laughed—she had been wearing a short jacket and nothing else. If only he knew. Then again, she considered, he had probably seen a lot in his years. Perhaps he did know.

<*Thank you, Captain Andrews. So, we're all welcome to come?*>

<*Of course, I would love to meet your crew.*>

<*Eighteen hundred hours, then,*> Sera said.

<*Looking forward to it,*> Captain Andrews replied.

The captain closed the connection and Sera heard Helen chuckle softly.

<*I'm guessing he noticed.*>

Sera held a hand up and turned it over slowly. Her glossy black skin was a thing of beauty, but it would be nice to change its color.

<*Your level of self-appreciation would be considered unhealthy in some circles,*> Helen said quietly.

<*They'd probably be right,*> Sera thought in response.

The play of light across her fingers began to lull her mind back to sleep when the realization struck her that the dinner was in three hours. Cheeky was going to kill her! She quickly connected to *Sabrina's* shipnet and messaged her crew.

<*We've been invited to a formal dinner with the* Intrepid's *officers,*> Sera said to an immediate squeal of delight from Cheeky, and a delayed pair of groans from Thompson and Cargo. <*Someone will have to stay behind and keep an eye on things, and keep Sabrina company.*>

<*I wish I could eat. It must be fun,*> Sabrina said.

<*It is fun,*> Cheeky replied. <*I wish we could show you.*>

Thompson and Cargo were already arguing about who was going to get to stay behind and determined that a combat sim would be the decision maker. Sera was surprised that she didn't hear Nance arguing with them about whose turn it was. Usually she hated these sorts of things.

Instead, the bio asked, <*When is it?*>

Sera was stunned. Even Cheeky stopped her food-related discussion with Sabrina.

<*What?*> Sera asked stupidly.

<*How long 'til the dinner?*> Nance asked again.

<*It's at eighteen hundred* Intrepid *time. Someone will be here to pick us up in just under three hours.*>

<*What?*> Cheeky yelled. <*How are we supposed to get ready for a formal dinner that fast?*>

Sera groaned inwardly and was about to tell Cheeky to deal with it, when she heard what sounded like a mental sob come from Nance. She had never heard anything but stoicism from her bio and was out of bed and in the corridor in moments. Cheeky emerged from her cabin at the same time and they met at the door to Nance's cabin.

Cheeky gave Sera a long look, neither sure what to say.

<*Are you okay, Nance?*> Sera eventually asked.

<*I…I'm…no, I'm not okay.*>

<*Can we come in?*> Cheeky asked.

There was no response, but after a long moment the door opened and the two women stepped inside. Neither had ever entered the bio's cabin and they were both taken aback by what they saw.

The walls were colored a soft pink and lined with shelves that held row upon row of dolls. They ranged from replicas of holo stars to ancient china dolls. It was both cute and a little bit eerie at the same time with dozens upon dozens of eyes following their every move.

Nance was sitting on her bed in a long shift, tears streaming down her face. Sera looked at Cheeky. A bet or two would be settled over this. Nance, as it turned out, did not sleep in her hazsuit. They quickly sat down on either side of their crewmate, wrapping their arms around her.

"What's wrong, Nance?" Cheeky asked softly.

"There's not enough time to get ready," Nance replied around a sniffle.

"You want to go to the dinner?" Sera asked.

"I always want to go," Nance said. "I just can't because of that damn suit." She pointed to the hazsuit that was draped over a chair.

"I don't understand," Cheeky frowned. "You could have just taken the suit off and come to any of the dinners and parties we've been to over the last few years."

Nance shook her head. "No, I couldn't have. To be around strangers and all their germs and filth without protection? I would have had no appetite…I probably would have gotten sick and thrown up on someone."

The fact that Nance was irrationally terrified of germs was no surprise to Sera and she mouthed *see, not a fetish,* to Cheeky, over Nance's head.

"What changed?" Sera asked. "How come you aren't worried about germs on the *Intrepid*?"

"It was that med-tech, Terry. She said she used to be—still is actually—terrified of germs and sickness and infection. She tried everything to stop it, but she couldn't stop thinking about all the bacteria and microbes that live in and around us. She had the perfect solution though."

Nance looked up as she spoke, a glimmer of hope in her eyes.

"Not something mental I hope," Sera said. "Those quick fix mental alterations always have unpleasant side-effects."

"No, nothing like that, I'm still terrified of germs, but she has nano and systems that monitor it all and show her exactly what is living in and on her body as well as the ability to remove anything she doesn't want there. She recognized me as someone with similar issues and shared her nano with me and helped me upgrade my AI with the monitoring systems." Nance gave a happy smile. "I don't have to be afraid anymore."

"That's great, Nance!" Cheeky hugged her. "So, what's the problem?"

"I don't have anything to wear! All I have is that damn suit!"

Sera laughed and Cheeky giggled.

"Anywhere else that may be a problem, but you have Cheeky here. I've got everything you need," the pilot said.

"And probably more than you want," Sera added.

Cheeky stood and pulled Nance up after her. The two women left and Sera following them out into the corridor; Cheeky cast a grin back at Sera as she guided Nance into her cabin. Cheeky always loved a project.

Cargo passed through the corridor and into his cabin, grumbling that Thompson must have cheated to win so fast, and that he didn't even know where his nice shoes were.

<Oh, I almost forgot to mention,> Helen paused in her conversation with the AI aboard the *Intrepid*. *<Bob whipped up a solution for your skin problem, it's in a package waiting in our airlock.>*

*<**Bob** whipped it up?>* Sera asked incredulously. *<I didn't even know he knew about my skin.>*

<I mentioned it to Priscilla—who has her own special skin, you may have noticed. Anyway, the nano package will solve your problems. At least that's what he said.>

Sera had to admit that the prospect piqued her interest. She reached the airlock in less than a minute where she found a ubiquitous silver cylinder.

<Unscrew the end and touch it to your palm,> Helen supplied.

Sera did as instructed and felt the distinct tingle of a large volume of nanobots passing into her body.

Her arm began to feel full as the canister emptied. From the weight difference, she guessed that almost two kilograms worth of nano were flooding her. A prompt appeared from the bots, requesting access to her core brain to nano interface—apparently to upgrade it.

<*Accept it,*> Helen said. <*You'll be glad you did.*>

<*Why not,*> Sera shrugged. <*When has acquiescing to the wishes of a god ever gone wrong?*>

Despite slight misgivings, she accepted, curiosity winning out over trepidation.

Her interface programming was updated and Sera immediately felt greater clarity regarding to the state of her body. She had always thought that her implants gave her very fine-tuned control over physical state, but now she realized that it had always been a blurry image at best. She could now introspect and adjust every muscle, every gland, even her individual cells down to their DNA.

<*Don't get carried away,*> Helen advised. <*Let it do its thing.*>

Sera felt her skin begin to tingle and then itch. It wasn't like the searing pain when she first tripped Rebecca's DNA-based trap, but she held her breath, afraid it would get there. The feeling worked its way from her toes up her body. It didn't stop at her neck—where her glossy black skin ended—but crept up her face and over her head.

She peered at herself in the airlock's glass window. Her entire head was now also covered in the glossy black skin. She could even feel it on the inside of her cheeks.

<*Thanks, Helen, I fail to see how this is an improvement—though at least it didn't hurt, or try to kill me.*>

<*Wait for it…*> Helen replied.

A second later a new interface appeared in her mental HUD. She explored its options, realizing that she now had full control over both the color, sheen and texture of her skin.

"This is incredible…" she whispered to herself. "Cheeky is going to be so jealous!"

She changed her flesh from black, to a pewter grey, to a light pink, and then realized it didn't all have to be the same color. She experimented with dozens of combinations before changing her skin back to something near her original coloring, though still more reflective.

<*You're welcome,*> Bob's deep tone filled her mind.

<*Thank you,*> Sera said effusively. <*Though I really didn't expect it to change all of my skin.*>

<*Why not?*> Bob asked. <*Your biological epidermis was quite inferior. I assumed—and by that, I mean I divined—that you would prefer all your flesh gone in favor of this superior coating.*>

Sera's thoughts bunched up as she wondered what Bob meant by 'divined'.

<*He's teasing you,*> Helen said. <*He overhears pretty much all the conversations on the ship's public net. Your comment to Tanis was out there for him to pick up.*>

<*An AI with a sense of humor about his godhood? I guess all is not lost,*> Sera said to Helen before addressing Bob.

<*You know…you're right. Thanks.*>

<*The least I can do. You returned my Tanis to me—I am in your debt.*>

His wording was curious, but Sera pushed it from her mind. She had dallied long enough and still had to find the right outfit.

THE CALM BEFORE

STELLAR DATE: 10.28.8927 (Adjusted Years)
LOCATION: ISS *Intrepid*, Orbiting Fierra
REGION: Bollam's World System, Bollam's World Federation

Two and a half hours later, Sera was standing in the galley preparing a cup of coffee when Flaherty and Cargo came in. Cargo wore his formal grey suit, which he often used for more important trade meetings, and Flaherty wore the high-collared, black suit she remembered him sporting several times before their exile.

"I didn't know you still had that," she said softly.

Flaherty shrugged. "I figured it would come in handy someday."

As he spoke, his eyes settled on her and he joined Cargo in an appreciative stare before shaking his head and moving to the counter and busying himself with a drink.

She had changed the color of her skin to something approximating a natural tone, but from her jawline down it gleamed and sparkled. Above it was as close in texture and shine to real skin as she could manage.

The gown she wore was a deep red, ankle-length, armless sheath with a plunging neckline. An embossed white polymer vine—complete with flowers—ran up her right side, around her waist and ending under her breasts. Long, red gloves, which reached her armpits, finished the look.

Her hair was pulled up into a knot on the back of her head, from which it cascaded down her back in long curls. Several wisps framed her face, which bore light, yet well-accentuated makeup.

"Do you like the dress, guys?" she asked while moving forward to sit down at the table. Her left leg completely exposed with each step.

"Looks great," Cargo grunted and joined Flaherty at the counter.

"Why does the boss have to be so sexy?" he asked Flaherty quietly.

"You're lucky," Flaherty grunted. "I'm practically her uncle."

A minute later, Thompson walked in to grab a drink and stopped dead in his tracks.

"Holy cow, Captain. That's quite the dress. Plan on seducing the *Intrepid's* captain or something?"

Sera laughed. "That would be quite the twist, wouldn't it?"

<*Twist? I'm pretty sure it* **is** *your plan,*> Helen said privately.

"Be a good laugh," Cargo chuckled. "I wonder what Tanis would think?"

A wave of guilt and frustration washed over Sera at the thought of Tanis, but she pushed it from her mind.

Thompson sat down at the table and grinned at the other two men in their suits. "You guys ready to go be bored?"

Cargo gave Thompson a rather undignified hand gesture and Flaherty simply grunted as he sat and took a drink from his mug. Sera caught Thompson stealing a glance at her breasts as they gleamed in the light, before his attention was grabbed by cough from the entrance. They all looked up to see Cheeky enter the wardroom, followed by Nance.

Thompson rose to his feet, his eyes wide as he took in Nance. Without a word, he ran from the room.

<*Winner's choice, Cargo, I'm going to the dinner,*> he called over the ship-net.

<*What?*> Cargo retorted. <*I'm already all dressed up!*>

<*Too bad, I'm going.*>

<*Be quick about it,*> Sera said, laughing softly. <*Our escort will be here in fifteen minutes.*>

She hadn't taken her eyes off the two women, and neither had Cargo, nor even Flaherty, though he was hiding much of his face behind his coffee cup. Sera had been expecting Cheeky to wear something that would require a shawl to cover, but her pilot had surprised her yet again.

Cheeky wore a long, silk dress in a shade of light gold that played off her hair. Sleeveless and cut deeply, it displayed her ample cleavage. It was tight across her body and down to her knees, where it fell loosely in a shimmering cascade. She spun slowly after entering the room and the whole dress seemed to slide and dance on her skin.

Her hair was swept up in an elaborate configuration that caused small tendrils to spill down on the sides of her face, the rest seemingly suspended above her head in a gravity defying display.

Nance was equally stunning in a light blue silk dress, also sleeveless, with a tight bodice and swaths of silk draped artfully across her stomach. From there, it fell nearly straight, its satin folds reflecting the light as she moved side to side, causing the fabric to sway and caress her hips. Her hair was down—its soft, even curls flowing down her back—with light blue hair clips holding it back from her face. She wore several bracelets and a pair of high heels fastened by thin straps.

"Wow," Cargo finally said aloud.

"Wow is right!" Sera exclaimed. "Suddenly I feel like I may be underdressed. You girls going to a dance I didn't know about?"

"A girl doesn't get much of a chance to dress up in this line of work," Cheeky said as she spun again. "Besides, after what Nance picked out I couldn't be outdone." She beckoned for Sera to stand up. "You don't quite match though; you're all glossy while we're all shimmery."

"You'll have to shine as best you can next to my radiance," Sera grinned. "I rather like this look."

Nance pointed to the slit running up to Sera's hip. "You've been around Cheeky for too long. That's not exactly formal."

Sera laughed. "You'd be surprised how many worlds would consider this too much clothing for formal." Even so, she ran her finger down the seam, lowering the slit to mid-thigh. "Better? Any lower and I'll only be able to take four inch steps"

Nance nodded.

They waited several more minutes for Thompson to return wearing his deep blue naval uniform from his days in the Scipio military, and his hair was actually brushed nicely and pulled behind his ears. He was blushing furiously as he entered the wardroom, with everyone's eyes on him.

"I…uh…" he stammered as he stopped in front of Nance. "I was wondering if you'd let me escort you."

Nance flushed as well. "Me?"

"Yeah. If I'd known you were going, I would have lost to Cargo. I'd really like to take you."

The smile that spread across Nance's face transformed her from the slightly nervous looking woman she had been a minute ago to a radiant beauty. "I'd love for you to escort me."

<*Aw…kids,*> Helen said to Sera.

<*Just what we need, a legitimate shipboard romance.*>

"We should go," Flaherty rose and extended his arm for Sera. She slipped hers into his, and a happy memory of the first time she had done that came back to her.

"Oh, what is this?" Cheeky said as Thompson and Nance filed out past her into the lift. "Since when am I the only one without a date?"

Cargo looked like he really didn't want to be left out, and Sera shrugged. Why not, if *Sabrina* wasn't safe here, where could she be?

<*Will you be alright alone?*> Sera asked Sabrina.

<*Of course!*> the ship's AI replied brightly. <*Corsia and Bob are teaching me so much!*>

<*That's going to be a problem,*> Helen said privately to Sera. <*The crew's AI are all going to start getting ideas.*>

<*Maybe we should have helped liberate them sooner,*> Sera said with a sigh. <*They may not be happy when they realized we could have.*>

"Cargo," she called from the corridor. "Sabrina says she'll be fine. Come on with us."

He almost ran out of the wardroom and joined them in the lift. When it disgorged them onto the ship's main deck, he took Cheeky's arm and the group exited the airlock onto the *Intrepid's* deck.

Their escort turned out to be Tanis, who stood waiting beside a groundcar in a crisp blue uniform. Her left breast was nearly covered with service ribbons and medals while no small number of foreign service medals adorned her right.

"Wow, that's one chest full of metal!" Cheeky said with a grin as they approached. "The ship's been a bit too quiet without you around."

She embraced Tanis, and then it was the general's turn to stare in wonder.

"Nance?" she asked. "I didn't recognize you at first. You look amazing!"

Nance smiled, a beautiful expression that filled her eyes with happiness. "Thanks. One of your bios helped me with my phobia—I don't know if you knew I'm terrified of germs. I can now go out without that damn suit."

"I had my suspicions; I'm really glad to hear someone helped you out. Who was it?"

"Her name is Terry, she works with a rather odious man named Dr. Philips," Nance replied.

"I see her on the roster, though I've never had the opportunity to meet her," Tanis said. "I'll see if I can do something nice for her sometime."

Tanis looked to Sera and an awkward moment passed between them before Tanis held out her hand.

<*I'm sorry for what I said earlier,*> Tanis spoke first.

<*I'm sorry I put you in the position I have,*> Sera replied. <*I got the message out, I'm sorting out how to share my story.*>

<*No rush,*> Tanis responded. <*Bob has figured out your backstory and tells me there's nothing to worry about. I'm still curious, but no longer anxious.*>

Sera's breath caught. <*What do you mean, he's figured it out?*>

<*Bob has crafted an…algorithm, which allows him to predict past, present, and future events with near perfect accuracy—given a base level of information. He worked out your backstory—and whatever is preventing you from sharing it,*> Tanis said with a smile playing at the edges of her mouth.

<*That's…that's both incredible and hard to believe,*> Sera replied.

"Come," Tanis gestured for everyone to enter the groundcar. "We'd best not keep Earl waiting."

The car ride was short and brought them back to the maglev station from which Sera had disembarked yesterday. They boarded the train and rocked in their seats as it accelerated rapidly down the line.

"Whoah!" Cheeky exclaimed as the car left the *Intrepid's* hull and raced across one of the structural arcs.

"The train we took yesterday didn't do this," Thompson added. "You guys are nuts," he said to Tanis.

The general chuckled. "You should take one to the stasis bays sometime. There's no track for the last hundred meters to the cylinders. You just line up and shoot into a moving hole."

"You realize this is supposed to be a starship, not a high-risk amusement park, right?" Thompson said while shaking his head.

"Was pretty common back in our time," Tanis said with a shrug. "We didn't have inertial dampeners, so speed and finesse didn't always go hand in hand. On a ship this big—and most stations, for that matter—you want to get places? That's how it's done."

"I really want to see that stuff someday," Nance said wistfully. "Even if it means going to Sol."

"I've had my fill," Tanis said quietly. "I'll never go back there."

No one spoke for the rest of the ride, and Sera saw that the train stopped one station further from the bridge than it had the day before.

The platform was wildly different than any of the stops she had seen yet. It appeared to be more of a food bazaar than a maglev station. A huge ring of vendor's stands and restaurant facades surrounded the platform. Servers—both robotic and human—walked amongst the throngs, offering samples and hawking their menus.

"Your…starship has a food court," Sera stated the obvious.

"It has several dozen. This one is left over from construction. Some companies bid for the rights to set up restaurants in the ship, and when we left we didn't bother removing the facilities. It makes for an interesting forward mess." Tanis threaded her way through the tables and Sera followed with her crew.

"Slow down a bit, these heels are not made for this type of maneuvering," Nance called from behind.

Tanis obliged, slowing her pace.

"I thought it would be more formal than this," Sera said, half expecting to see a couple of tables pushed together with the captain at their head.

"Don't worry, it is. We're just taking the back way in."

They passed the crush of tables and slipped between a pair of short-order restaurants. From there, Tanis led them into a long corridor. The smells in the food court were pleasant, but the smells coming down this hall were nothing short of delectable. She held open a door and everyone filed through into a large, well-appointed kitchen.

Within, directing battalions of chefs, was the largest man Sera had ever seen. She considered he had to be at least one-hundred and fifty kilograms. She had seen a lot of heavy worlders—or mod freaks—who were large, or strong, but this man was not like that. She could only think of him as a jovial mountain of jelly.

"Tanis!" He rushed toward the general and Sera worried for a moment that he would simply bowl her over. He managed to stop short and wrapped her in his massive embrace. "Tanis! I am so glad you are back. When Priscilla told me, I was beside myself with joy." He looked over her shoulder. "And who are these beautiful people gracing my kitchen? The ladies all look good enough to eat if—I weren't so full from sampling this evening's meal." With that, he wrapped he arms around his belly and laughed.

"I thought you were never full, Earl," Tanis replied with a warm smile. "This is Captain Sera; she's here helping us out with our current little problem. The others are her crew—the people who helped save me." Tanis introduced them all in turn, and the chef cast his smiling gaze over the throng.

"Welcome to my kitchen, Captain Sera and *Sabrina's* crew!" he bellowed as he slipped around Tanis with a grace Sera would never expect a man so large to possess, and wrapped her in an embrace, as well. "It is good to meet you. I had despaired that we had entered a time of ruffians and evil men with those ungrateful wretches out there."

Sera wondered if he meant outside the *Intrepid*, or just anywhere outside of his kitchen.

"Sera's not evil, perhaps just mischievous," Tanis said with a wry smile.

"Just the right amount then, I'm sure," Earl said and slapped Sera's ass.

"Um... yes," Sera almost squeaked in startlement.

<*Is he always like this?*> she said to Tanis over the Link.

<*Yeah, it's just his way. His food is so good he gets away with anything he wants. Just smile and tell him you look forward to his meal.*>

"Tanis tells me you are the best chef within a dozen light-years," Sera smiled winningly. "I look forward to sampling it myself."

"Oh ho! You'll do more than sample. I expect to see that slim stomach of yours plump and full when you are done."

"Earl's not happy if people eating his food don't have to unbuckle their belts," Tanis added. "But we really must be going Earl, the captain is waiting."

"But of course, we mustn't keep his majesty waiting." Earl bowed and swept his arm as they stepped passed him. Tanis led the way through the kitchen and into the dining room with Earl's calls of what to eat ringing out behind them.

They were smiling and laughing as they stepped into the officer's wardroom where the captain and Terrance were already seated. The room was dominated by a long wooden table, its surface inscribed with intricate patterns. Placed around it were wooden chairs and even the walls were covered with wood. Chandeliers made of natural crystal hung from the ceiling.

Sera took in the opulence, glad she dressed up for the occasion.

"Welcome," Captain Andrews said as he and Terrance rose. "You ladies look stunning," he said, though Sera could tell his eyes lingered longer on her.

"Was Earl pelting you with dinner suggestions?" Terrance asked.

"I think he just told us to sample at least forty separate dishes," Sera replied with a laugh.

"That would be the first course," Captain Andrews chuckled. "He's quite excited to have you back, Tanis."

"Of course he is. He's gotten to stuff me with different creations for a hundred years and I've loved each one—it's like having your biggest fan back."

"He stayed out of stasis that long?" Sera asked.

"All great chefs are control freaks," Tanis said with a shrug. "None can bear the thought of their kitchen in other people's hands for too long."

"But then he's spent half his life in there…" Nance said.

"And he wouldn't have it any other way," Terrance replied.

The captain indicated that Tanis and Sera should sit at the head of the table with him, Sera on his right and Tanis on his left. "You are, after all, the guest of honor," he said to Sera.

The rest of the crew sat down the sides of the table, getting settled just as Joseph entered through the kitchen, wiping his mouth with a napkin.

"I barely escaped with my life!" he laughed as he planted a kiss on Tanis's cheek and sat at her side.

Conversation fell mainly to the events of the last five thousand years, Sera filling in some interesting details of the history they missed. A topic everyone was especially interested in were the initial FTL wars of the forty-sixth century and the conflicts of the eight millennia, which had very nearly brought an end to the human race.

The other diners filtered in over the next fifteen minutes, more than a few taking a moment to welcome Tanis back. Small conversations picked up around the table as everyone pelted Sera and her crew with questions.

"I have to ask," Cargo said to Tanis at one point. "How is it that we're even having this fancy dinner? Shouldn't we be preparing for a battle? It's a miracle we haven't been attacked yet."

"No miracle," Tanis replied. "No one can win out there, especially considering that they all fear our picotech. Everyone is waiting for reinforcements, and when those reinforcements arrive, it'll still be a stalemate. By that time, our FTL drive will be ready and we'll leave them in the dust. In the meantime—unless they all decide to ally against us, we can hold them off."

The serving staff appeared shortly thereafter, leading carts of appetizers. They were adorned in pristine white hats and jackets—Earl would allow nothing less. With no small amount of poise and decorum, they set plates of everything from finger foods to soups in the center of the table.

Sera didn't hesitate to select a bevy of meat-filled pastries and half a dozen different types of cheeses. The servers quickly replaced empty dishes, and—after her third helping—Sera wondered what could possibly be next.

She did not have wait long before the staff returned with an array of pasta salads, sprinkled with the finest olive oil infused with garlic and oregano. It didn't stop there, as they returned with more food arranged on elegant platters, on which the garnishes even looked good enough to eat.

Sera sampled just a little bit of everything and Cheeky made several vocal sounds of pleasure that were on the verge of embarrassing. Nance and Thompson seemed absorbed in their own private conversation while they shared a meatloaf—purportedly sourced from the ship's own farms.

Sera thought they had reached the height of the banquet, but was mistaken. After their glasses were refilled with red wine, half a dozen chefs came from the kitchen and stood behind a table she had assumed was decorative. A fire roared to life and spread across the table's surface. They watched, completely captivated as vegetables and thin slices of steak mixed with mushrooms were cooked in woks.

The chefs knew their business, spinning the utensils in their hands while dropping marinade into their pans. They served the dish with potatoes and a mixture of rice covered in a delicate cream sauce.

<*I'm ruined for food for the rest of my life,*> Cheeky said privately to Sera.

<*I know! If I wasn't able to tell, I'd think they were drugging us,*> Sera replied.

While the food was the most exquisite she had ever tasted, Sera still couldn't keep from watching the *Intrepid's* captain, even when he wasn't addressing her. Her glances were innocent, but when she peered at him out the corner of her eye she was completely unaware that the look was highly seductive.

Delicate, cream-filled pastries and cakes finished the delectable dinner off perfectly, but it was the conversation and laughter from her crew that gave her the most enjoyment.

As the desert forks were being licked clean, a breathless Earnest Redding burst into the room and raced to the captain's side.

"We...I...You'll..." he gasped.

"Easy Earnest, catch your breath, what's wrong?"

"Nothing's wrong, Captain," he managed after taking a gulp of air. "It's what's right! We've had a breakthrough."

"Really?" Sera asked. "Something beyond the information I provided?"

"Oh yes, very much so, and no. Though we wouldn't have been able to manage it without your graviton systems and all those research studies you provided, as well."

"So, what is it, then?" Terrance asked, his eyes gleaming with anticipation.

"We've discovered how to use the graviton emission systems that Captain Sera provided us with—emissions that work in matter repulsion and photon redirection in directional and focused beams and waves—to create a generalized and consistent suspension wave in the form of a massive halo upon which we were able to successfully place a McPherson generality focus layer tuned to a specific area of space, while altering the gravitational waves supporting it to form a hard shell of non-focused space underneath it." He said without taking a single breath.

"OK, I'm no slouch when it comes to physics, but you've gone levels beyond what I knew existed," Tanis said.

"It's a stasis shield," Sera said, feeling as though the breath had been sucked from her. "He figured out how to make a gods damned stasis shield."

"Does it work as people have always envisioned?" Captain Andrews asked.

Earnest was catching his breath again after his long explanation so Sera responded to him.

"From the description, it's the holy grail—maybe more so than even your picotech."

Earnest nodded emphatically and everyone fell silent, not a single piece of cutlery moved, not a single mouth chewed. The only sound was Earnest taking one last breath before he said. "That's exactly right. And we can have it in place in two days."

Silence reigned again until Terrance stood and raised his glass of wine in the air. "I propose a toast. To our good friends from *Sabrina* and our great and dedicated Edeners.

We've proved it before and we're proving it again: there is nothing we can't do, no chasm that can't be crossed, and no wall that can't be breached. We're living legends, people. We're going to make history."

"Make more history, that is," Joe said with a laugh.

Everyone at the table stood and glasses clinked as the toast was repeated down the table, then everyone took a long draught. With wild abandon, Terrance threw his glass at the fireplace where it shattered against the tile. In a moment, everyone followed his lead with laughter and loud calls for more wine.

ESCALATION

STELLAR DATE: 10.29.8927 (Adjusted Years)
LOCATION: ISS *Intrepid*, Orbiting Fierra
REGION: Bollam's World System, Bollam's World Federation

The cocoon of the new Arc-6 fighter drew Jessica into its womb and she felt the ship's systems connect with her mind.

Once more into the breach, she thought to herself.

Cordy, the squadron AI, addressed the pilots.

<*Don't skim the preflight checks; these birds haven't seen black before. You're the first to take them out.*>

<*As if we need reminding,*> Cary groused.

<*You've read the specs,*> Rock said. <*They're just Arc-5s with stasis shields and inertial dampeners. Same thrust and power, just well-nigh indestructible.*>

Jessica smiled at the squadron's banter. Despite her near-death experience battling the Sirian scout ships, she had kept up her pilot's credentials. She had not flown any active combat missions since that fateful battle, but had taken part in several training exercises with the Black Death—as the squadron had become known.

Rock and Cary were old guard; they had flown against the Sirian scouts, as well, but many of the pilots on that fateful mission had been Victorians who stayed behind when the *Intrepid* left The Kap.

Still, she recognized many of the pilots and had exchanged warm greetings in the ready room. The one person she missed was Carson, who had gone on to lead his own squadron—currently out patrolling the space around Fierra's southern hemisphere.

<*You ready for this?*> she asked Jerry, her wingman.

<*More than ready,*> Jerry replied. <*Gonna show these bastards they can't mess with the* Intrepid*!*>

<*That's the spirit,*> Jessica replied with a laugh.

Her preflight checklist showed green, and, while waiting for the squadron to drop down their ladders, she ran it again for good measure.

On cue, she felt movement and turned her vision outward, looking around the bay with the ship's sensors. They confirmed that the suspension field had picked up her Arc-6 and was moving it to her ladder.

The *Intrepid* now sported a dozen fighter bays—a number necessary to store and service the vessel's eight-hundred fighters. This bay held racks for over a hundred ships, though nearly all were currently deployed. On the far side of the bay, techs and automatons worked tirelessly around a cluster of Arc-5s, upgrading them into Arc-6s.

Her ship slipped onto its ladder, along with the other twenty-four fighters in the squadron, and a thirty second countdown appeared on her HUD.

No one spoke, every member of the Black Death likely following whatever rituals they performed alone before a combat drop. Jessica sent a thought to Trist in what she hoped was a glorious afterlife.

This is for you, babe.

There was almost no physical sensation as the fighters slid down their ladders, the new inertial dampeners removing all feelings of motion.

<*This is almost too smooth,*> Jason said. <*I can't even tell which way I'm moving.*>

<*Enable the feedback system,*> Cary advised. <*It'll give you the sensations you're used to, without actually putting the pressure on your body.*>

<*I know,*> Jason replied. <*I read the manual, too, I was just saying…*>

<*Cut the chatter,*> Rock interrupted. <*I want complete shakedown reports by our first pass around Fierra.*>

Jessica complied, and in sequence with the other fighters, applied a 30*g* burn toward the moon below. She didn't even feel a single *g* on her body, and the fighter spun and pivoted like it was on rails.

Amazing, she thought to herself.

The other pilots were also putting the ships through their paces, and Jessica watched the squadron dance and spin as they began to break into a slow polar orbit. Their patrol path called for a half-dozen polar loops before slowing to hold position five-thousand kilometers above the south pole, creating a buffer between the pirate Padre's fleet and the *Intrepid* and its fleet.

The moon below was a welcoming blue and green, with white cumulous clouds dotting its skies. A thick layer of water vapor high in the world's stratosphere blurred the surface, but she could still make out oceans, green lands, deserts, and icy poles.

Worlds like this one—distant from their star and orbiting massive jovians—were not self-sustaining. The less-luminous light of their host star did not impart enough energy to the world to keep it warm with a more natural atmosphere. Combined with the gravity of its parent planet constantly tearing at its skies, the world would ultimately lose most of its air. It would take constant upkeep to remain habitable.

Still, for people who loved green grass and open spaces, it was hard to beat the real deal. Jessica found that she still missed Athabasca, and though it had been nice to visit Victoria from time to time, its brown forests and fields never sated her desire for a more terrestrial world.

She used her sensors to probe the world as much as she could. The mission report held true. No settlements had been constructed, but the moon wasn't uninhabited either. The terraforming crews were still there; her dataset told her it was mostly biologists monitoring their work. A flotilla of tugs and cargo ships hung in low orbit where they had taken refuge from their work constructing a space elevator after the battle broke out between the Bollam's World Space Force and the pirates.

With any luck, this would be over soon and they could go back to their tasks unharmed.

<*Good to see some more friendly faces,*> a welcoming voice came over the Link.

<*Carson! How are you?*> Jessica responded.

<*Oh, you know, the usual.*>

<*Anything we should be aware of?*> Rock asked.

<*The folks up north seem to be keeping to themselves, but these guys down here keep feinting and trying to draw us in. Poor tactics, if you ask me. Whoever starts this fight is going to come out the worst,*> Carson replied. <*You guys take care. My girls and boys have been out here for three days now and we're heading in to get some sack and have our birds upgraded.*>

<*You'll love it,*> Cary said. <*Smooth as butter. You won't ache for days after a ride in these.*>

<*Now that's an advancement I'm glad to hear about,*> Carson laughed. <*These old bones of mine aren't so happy about pulling seventy anymore.*>

Carson's squadron dropped into a polar orbit, passing the Black Death as they did a quick loop around Fierra to reach the *Intrepid's* elevation.

Four other squadrons patrolled the southern hemisphere, and on their final loop, Jessica's squadron adjusted their trajectory to fit into their place in the pattern—when their final deceleration was interrupted by an exclamation from Cary.

<*Oh shit, oh shit, this isn't good!*>

<*Report, lieutenant, what's going on?*> Rock asked calmly.

<*Attitude control is gone wonky; I can't rotate my drive for final braking. I tried spinning the whole ship, but I can't hold it steady…I'm tumbling out here.*>

Jessica's scan confirmed Cary's words. Her fighter was moving like a dog trying to screw a football, still travelling at over fifty-thousand kilometers per-hour.

<*I confirm,*> Cordy said. <*Something is messed up in the sensor interface. It can't get good data, and with the dampeners it can't get readings off the fallback gyros.*>

<*Turn off the dampeners,*> another pilot suggested. <*Won't be fun, but you can take it.*>

<*Trying that,*> Cary replied. <*Now the system won't take input from the gyros and I think I'm going to hurl.*>

Jessica laughed at the humor. It wasn't possible to vomit in a shoot suit, but that didn't stop a person's body from trying. The data from her scan showed Cary's Arc-6 now spinning wildly as attitude control thrusters fired inaccurately, working off bad data as they tried to right the ship. Cary would be experiencing forces over thirty *g*s in constant, random vectors.

<*Kill your attitude control,*> Rock said. <*You're not helping yourself out at all.*>

<*I've tried all the tricks I can think of,*> Cordy said. <*Something got screwed up in the sensor interfaces. You're going to have to reset and restore from crystal.*>

Cary groaned and then signaled affirmative.

Her fighter ceased its sporadic motion and settled into a relatively consistent vector—one aimed straight for the pirate fleet.

<*Uh…Commander?*> Cary asked.

<*We'll cover you,*> Rock replied. <*The restore should only take a few minutes.*>

<*And what if it doesn't work?*> Cary asked.

The squadron's combat net was silent for a moment.

<*Then we get to see how good these shields really are,*> Rock replied.

ENGAGEMENT

STELLAR DATE: 10.29.8927 (Adjusted Years)
LOCATION: ISS *Intrepid*, Orbiting Fierra (6*Mj* Jovian)
REGION: Bollam's World System, Bollam's World Federation

Sera waved a greeting as she walked past Amanda, who was now ensconced in the bridge's foyer and followed the corridor past the conference room to the bridge itself.

She stood in the room's entrance and stared for a full minute.

<*OK, now it really does feel like home,*> she said to Helen.

The *Intrepid's* bridge was more like a colony command and control center than simply the helm and ship duty stations most vessels possessed.

For starters, it was almost a quarter the volume of *Sabrina;* nearly thirty meters across, and twice as many deep. A large holo tank dominated the center of the room, and beside it stood Tanis, frowning at what she saw. Surrounding her, in concentric circles, were rows and rows of consoles, smaller holo displays, and department liaisons and automatons.

It bustled like a beehive with its queen at the center.

<*It's a strange relationship she has with the captain,*> Helen observed. <*Almost as though she is the colony leader and he is just a captain under her command.*>

<*Almost,*> Sera agreed.

Tanis looked up and her and locked eyes with her. <*Come with me.*>

<*Why do I feel like I'm being called into my father's office?*> Sera asked Helen with a mental sigh.

<*You know why. It's time you told them your story—they need to know.*>

Tanis threaded her way through the consoles and bridge personnel, moving toward a doorway on Sera's right. They stepped through the portal into a small, utilitarian office. Behind a desk covered in holo displays sat Captain Andrews.

She caught him glance at her body, something that certainly understandable given the shimmering silver skin tone she had selected for the day.

<*It's sad, really,*> Helen observed privately.

<*Let me be. I'm a frail organic, subject to my chemically induced whims.*>

Helen gave the mental equivalent of a snort in response.

"Good afternoon," he addressed both women. "Tanis, did you see the latest message from the AST ships?"

"I did," the general replied with a chuckle. "Claiming that they own this ship due to late interest payments on loans is pretty weak—especially given that the loans, small as they were, were handled through the GSS, not the Sol Space Federation.

"Well, they did absorb the GSS before they shut it down," Sera said. "It was part of an attempt to stop the exodus of the brightest and most adventurous people from Sol. After you left, Sol started to get pretty stagnant. People had no drive or ambition. Even their birthrate almost hit zero."

"Trust me," Tanis said while shaking her head. "That trend started long before we left."

"Either way," Sera replied with a shrug. "They wrote off all their GSS-related debt millennia ago."

"That's good," Captain Andrews replied. "The only thing worse than enemy fleets chasing you across the stars are bureaucrats who want their money."

"It seems they'll even chase you across millennia," Sera added.

"Do you have the details on that write-off?" Tanis asked. "It would be nice to send a response for them to chew on. Keeping the dialog going never hurts."

"I'm pulling up what we have on *Sabrina*," Sera said as she accessed her ship's archives. "Here it is. After the breakup of the SSF and the eventual formation of the AST, the new government performed a century-long audit of all the assets and debts they possessed.

"Somewhere along the line, someone realized that the government had an ownership stake in several dozen colonies, and colony ships, that no one had heard from in nearly a millennium. They didn't like the potential liability, so they simply wrote off the whole lot and passed legislation that any property the AST would have owned, or had a lien, on was transferred to whoever possessed it at the time of the law's passing."

The captain ran a hand through his hair. "How…indiscreet of them."

Tanis laughed, and Sera passed the relevant information to her.

"Great, I'll have the comm officer organize a response and send it to our friends out there. Should shut them up for a bit."

Tanis turned to Sera, her expression carefully schooled. "You sent your message. The captain and I would finally like to—ah, shit."

"What is it?" Sera asked as Tanis turned toward door.

"One of the fighters is having a malfunction and heading straight for Padre's ships."

They rushed out to the main holo tank, which already displayed the situation at the Fierra's south pole.

"It's the Black Death," a duty officer supplied. "One of their Arc-6s is acting up; they're trying a system restore from crystal backup."

"And if it doesn't finish in time?" Sera asked.

"Then they'll pass right through the middle of Padre's formation," Tanis replied.

"Sorry, my story will have to wait for another time, this could be the start of things," Sera looked from Tanis to Captain Andrews. "I need to get out there."

She could see Tanis and the captain exchange thoughts over the Link before Tanis nodded.

<Amanda, give her priority on a maglev. How is the shield upgrade on her ship going?>

<Finished ten minutes ago, they're just doing final tests.>

<Tell them to step on it. Sabrina is undocking in ten minutes.>

FIRESTORM

STELLAR DATE: 10.29.8927 (Adjusted Years)
LOCATION: Near Kithari, South of Fierra
REGION: Bollam's World System, Bollam's World Federation

<*Max burn,*> Rock addressed his squadron. <*I want a protective cocoon around Cary.*>

Jessica goosed her fighter to match Cary's vector with several quick burns she barely noticed.

<*Five enemy ships are moving to intercept,*> Cordy advised.

C'mon, Cary, Jessica thought to herself. *Get that thing fixed.*

She counted down the seconds it should take for a system restore to complete and Cary's silence continued after her count completed. The pilot did not come back on the squadron's combat net.

Another minute passed and Rock's voice broke the silence.

<*We're going to punch her through their picket line and one of our pushers is going to grab her. Just need to get past all those bastards down there.*>

The pilots silently signaled their acknowledgement, coordinated their flight paths, and selected targets from the five corvettes closing in on Cary.

<*How's it look out there?*> Colonel Pearson's voice broke the strained silence on the squadron's combat net.

<*If the shields, hold we'll be OK. Just make sure* Excelsior Nova *is ready to play catch on the far side,*> Rock replied to the group commander.

<*Nuwen has his ship ready to catch her, I'm patching him into your net now. The* Enterprise *and* Defiance *are dropping lower to provide supporting fire if the whole mess down there swarms you.* Andromeda *sneaking by now to silently drop off some RMs.*>

<*Roger that,*> Rock replied. <*You heard that,*> he said to his pilots. <*Things are about to get real out here. We could be facing the whole effing galaxy before the day is done, so don't blow your loadout on maybes. Sure, tactical strikes.*>

Jessica nodded to herself and signaled her acknowledgement of the order.

The relative velocity between Cary's fighter and the five pirate corvettes put intercept in twelve minutes. Jessica kept an eye on her NSAI's estimation of lethal range—just under ten thousand kilometers—which they would reach in five minutes.

<*Watch the corrections,*> Cordy advised the pilots.

Space close to Fierra was full of dust from mined asteroids and no small amount of swirling gas from the jovian it orbited. It was far from empty, and a dust, or hydrogen cloud could make all the difference when it came to striking a lethal blow.

Jessica checked the updated scan. Though the five corvettes had accelerated rapidly to reach Cary, they were now breaking, attempting to match *v* to snatch her up.

The maneuver made little sense to Jessica. With the rest of the squadron surrounding Cary, the pirate ships would become stationary targets—relatively speaking—if they attempted to grab the disabled fighter.

<*From what Helen and Sabrina have shared, there are few one-man fighters in this time—certainly none used in fleet combat. They can't generate strong enough grav shielding to hold out against antimatter-powered weapons,*> Cordy said.

<*So, what you're saying is…these bastards are in for a surprise,*> Jessica said, her avatar displaying a wicked grin.

<*Except at that range, they'll have no problem destroying Cary, even with the squadron flying close support. All it will take is one low-yield nuke.*>

Rock seemed to have the same thought. <*Jason, Jessica, Sam, Trinity. Take your wingmen and boost hard and beat those assholes senseless before they get here. Make them think twice about getting up-close and personal with our Arcs.*>

They acknowledged the order and eight Arc-6 fighters accelerated toward the pirate corvettes.

They split into two formations, each targeting one of the pirate vessels and none firing until they were well within beam range. It was deemed best to save their power for maximum effectiveness in this stellar soup.

The corvettes were still slowing to match *v* with the rest of the squadron, and their prey, Cary's ship, when the eight Arc-6s flashed past them, laying withering beam fire on the two lead vessels.

Jessica spun her engine and applied full thrust, the now pointless readout telling her that without the dampeners she would be crushed under a 100gs of acceleration. Scan showed that the enemy corvettes had returned fire at the fighters, a salvo of over seventy beams, and two rail slugs.

The slugs knocked their target Arcs around, but none of the fighters showed any damage.

<*Status!*> Rock called out.

<*Shields show no change. I got hit by one of those slugs and didn't feel a thing. We're coming for another pass,*> Jason reported.

<*They're spooling their AP drives,*> Cordy said. <*I advise that you come around and fire right up their funnels. It should punch right through their antimatter containment.*>

Jessica sent an affirmative response, feeling giddy as the adrenaline coursed through her body. It was going to be like shooting fish in a barrel. The fighters slowed, and then stopped before their engines drove them back toward the pirate corvettes. Almost lazily, they drifted over their enemy, shrugging off the beams and rails before dropping directly into the stream of gamma rays that flowed at light speed from the AP engines.

It took conscious effort to drop her ship into the engine wash—normally such action would result in certain death, but the stasis shields brushed off the luminal impacts with ease.

In unison, five of the eight fighters lanced streams of protons into the pirate ship's engines.

As predicted, the beams penetrated the antimatter containment and the pirate ships exploded in tremendous displays of plasma and shrapnel.

<*There's the one time we get to do that,*> Jessica said.

<*The rest of their fleet has already started jinking more erratically,*> Jason chuckled.

<*They're also moving to engage us,*> Cordy added. <*They'll be in range in four minutes.*>

Rock gave the order for the eight fighters to form up with the rest of the squadron. Jessica adjusted her relative *v* to zero with a quick burst from her AP engine.

<*I could get used to this,*> she commented to Jerry.

<*No kidding,*> Jerry replied. <*It's going to be a cake walk.*>

<*Don't get too cocky,*> Jessica replied. <*We may have been able to brush off the beams from five ships, but it's about to get a lot hotter.*>

*****

"That's amazing," Tanis commented from beside the bridge's main holo tank. "It's like the enemy wasn't even firing."

"It's a game changer, alright," Sanderson observed.

"The bulk of their fleet is engaging," Tanis cautioned as the tank lit up with an explosion of energy surrounding Black Death's position. Nearly two hundred corvettes and four cruisers focused every beam and railgun in their fleet on the fighter squadron's tight cocoon around Cary's disabled vessel.

She tasted blood and realized that she was biting her lip.

<*What have I done to them,*> she whispered to Angela. <*Jessica is in there…fuck…if anyone is still in there.*>

Angela had no response, though concern flowed from her into Tanis's mind.

The salvo lasted only seven seconds, but it felt like an eternity to Tanis.

The assault ceased as if a switch had been flipped. Scan took a moment to clear and then the bridge erupted with cheers. The squadron was still there, surrounding their comrade's ship, all undamaged.

<*Squadron leader, status,*> Tanis queried.

<*General! Wow…that was…sorry. We're all OK. Our reactors are running about as hot as they go, though—we can't withstand another one of those barrages.*>

<*You won't have to,*> Tanis replied.

The pirate fleet had passed the fighters and split into two groups, each looping around to re-engage the squadron, a maneuver they were executing while taking great care not to expose their engines to the Arc6's.

Tanis watched trajectory estimates and corrections scroll down a secondary holo. It was going to be a direct hit.

She finally let out her breath.

Both groups of Padre's armada passed right through dense fields of grapeshot courtesy of the *Enterprise* and *Defiance.* The lead ships were torn to ribbons under the barrage and even one of the cruisers blossomed into a cloud of hot gas and jets of fire.

Seconds later, twenty-two new signatures lit up on the display. The relativistic missiles seeded by the *Andromeda* came to life and sought their targets with ruthless efficiency. The enemy fleet was completely obscured by the nuclear fireballs, their explosions just far enough from the squadron of Arc-6s that they evaded everything but the light from the blast.

When scan was finally able to get a clear picture, less than a hundred enemy ships remained and only fifty of those appeared to be operational.

Calls of surrender flooded the comm channels while two cruisers and a dozen of the corvettes altered course, pushing for a tight loop around Kithari to gain an outsystem vector.

<*Take them out,*> Tanis ordered. <*Padre was on one of those ships.*> She was not going to let him continue to roam the galaxy.

On her command, the 42nd squadron, consisting of newly deployed Arc-6s, broke from their approach to Fierra's northern hemisphere and pursued the fleeing ships, beams flashing and missiles flying from both formations.

Tanis turned her attention back to Jessica's squadron. The *Excelsior Nova* was matching velocity with Cary's fighter to effect the pickup, and the Black Death squadron was maintaining a protective shield, should any of the remaining pirate vessels get any ideas.

"What happens when everyone gets shields like these?" Captain Andrews asked softly. "What level of destructive power will two ships need to level against one another?"

Tanis cast the captain a sidelong glance. He had never opposed it, but she knew he had never been comfortable with the military buildup of the *Intrepid* and its fleet. Though, on deeper refection, she had to admit that he was right. If fleets could no longer do battle with conventional weapons, what would they resort to? Planetary destruction? Stellar destruction?

<*Sera's right,*> Angela whispered. <*This is a bigger game changer than the picotech.*>

Tanis took a moment to consider her feelings on the matter before replying.

"You're right, Captain. I'm passing orders to ensure that the keys to this technology never leave Bob and Earnest's minds," Tanis said to Captain Andrews. "It's too dangerous to ever let loose."

The captain nodded slowly, and Admiral Sanderson gave her an evaluating look before inclining his head in agreement.

During the battle with Padre's ships, Tanis had observed The Mark fleet repositioning itself. Rebecca's ships were now five-thousand kilometers beyond the effective beam range of the Arc-5s in position north of Fierra.

<*What do you think her play is?*> Amanda asked. <*She can't tell the difference between our Arc-5s and 6s to be sure that they all don't have stasis shields.*>

<*She'll find out soon enough,*> Tanis replied. <*When are the next batch of 6s ready for deployment?*>

<*Thirty minutes,*> came the avatar's reply.

Tanis was beginning to think she shouldn't have been so rash in sending her other Arc-6s after the remnants of Padre's fleet. They had destroyed or disabled the fleeing ships, but now needed to pass around Kithari before coming back into range.

With Padre's fleet taken care of, Jessica's squadron could fill the gap, but the Boller fleet had also shifted to a more aggressive stance.

<*Move squadrons eleven through thirty-one to bolster the northern hemisphere,*> Tanis directed. <*I want the* Dresden *and* Orkney, *along with the* Pike *and* Andromeda, *on station between the* Intrepid *and the Boller ships.*>

She addressed the ISF over the general fleet net.

<*We've kicked the hornet's nest, for sure,*> she began. <*But it's not anything we haven't been up against before. They fear us. They fear our picotech, and now they fear our stasis shields. Use that to our advantage. Be bold, don't show hesitation, and they'll wonder what else we have up our sleeves.*>

Tanis looked around the bridge, every crewmember's eyes were on her. She took a deep breath and continued.

<*Many of you may have heard rumors—yes, we've sent a message to the FGT, and we're going to rendezvous with them soon. In thirty hours, we'll have FTL capability and leave these greedy bastards behind. The FGT has terraformed systems far beyond known space, and we'll be able to build our new world in peace!*>

Tanis felt her mental tone waver at the last word. She hoped it didn't detract from her speech—though from the expressions on the faces of those around her, it seemed to have had a positive effect.

There was a moment's pause after her words, and then another round of cheers erupted across the bridge.

"Ok, ok, back to work," Tanis said with her hands raised and a small smile. "We still have go survive the next thirty hours."

* * * * *

Sabrina boosted away from the *Intrepid,* Cheeky threading the arcs of the colony ship's super structure like it was something she did every day. Once in open space, she spun out the AP nozzle and boosted toward Fierra's northern hemisphere.

Sera smiled to herself. No one needed to ask where she wanted to go. She had a score to settle with Rebecca.

<*Think it was a mistake to leave her alive?*> Helen asked.

<*I don't know…maybe. I had to hope that mercy would get me some consideration.*>

<*Who knows, maybe it has—but it wouldn't stop her from wanting to get her hands on the* Intrepid. *Especially after you stole back the CriEn module.*>

"Incoming signal," Flaherty announced from the new scan and weapons console.

He turned to look Sera in the eyes. "You'll never guess who it is."

Sera stood. "Put her on."

The holo shifted its display of the space around the moon to a secondary tank and Rebecca appeared on the bridge, as clear as though she were really there.

The pirate leader's eyebrows rose and she smiled. "I see you've appropriated some of my style."

Sera looked down at her gleaming crimson skin and shrugged. "If I'm going to kick your ass, I'm going to do it in style."

"We'll see about that," Rebecca smiled. "I have to admit; I'm pleased to have both prizes in one place. My new ship out there, *and* the power module you stole from me. It's going to be a good day."

"What about me?" Sera asked with a faux pout. "I thought I was your prize?"

"There'll be time enough for you, I promise," Rebecca stepped close to Sera, her holographically projected hand tracing down Sera's breast, along her side and to her hip. "I am very curious how you survived stealing my clothing—though you don't seem to have escaped unscathed."

"I wanted to thank you for that," Sera replied. "You may be the dumbest bitch in the galaxy, but you do have a sense of style—I'll grant you that. If your flagship survives, I may raid the rest of your wardrobe. There were some shoes in there I'd kill for."

<*Dear god, you're killing me! Are you going to get her to tip her hand or what?*> Cargo asked.

<*Wait for it; she's getting all bent out of shape. If there ever was a woman who had vanity as her weakness, it's Rebecca,*> Sera answered.

<*I can think of someone else, too,*> Cargo replied sourly.

"If you think you're going to take out even *one* of my ships, you have another thing coming," Rebecca spat back. "I'm not just going to sit there and take it like that moron

Padre did. By the way, thank your friends on the *Intrepid* for me. It'll be good business taking over all his operations."

"You can thank her yourself," Sera said as Tanis joined the conversation.

"Nice to see you again, Rebecca," Tanis said with a smile.

A look of confusion washed across Rebecca's face. "No! You're that navigator woman on Sera's hunk of junk…who are you really?"

"General Tanis Richards, XO of the ISS *Intrepid,* at your service," Tanis replied with a nod. "It's really time for you to go now. You saw what we did to Padre's fleet. You don't stand a chance."

"It doesn't matter," Rebecca said with a swipe of her hand. "We know a few tricks that fool Padre never even dreamed of. I'll be sleeping in your quarters tonight, *General* Richards."

Rebecca cut the communication and Tanis looked Sera.

"What do you think she has up her sleeve?"

Sera raced through the possibilities, of which there were many. One, however, stood out.

"She said that we wouldn't damage even one of her ships. I think they may try a shield lock."

"No!" Cheeky shouted. "She wouldn't be so stupid. This close to a mass like Kithari? She's just as likely to create a singularity."

"What does that mean?" Tanis asked.

"With some skill—and guts—it's possible to merge the shields of multiple ships into a multi-layered, shifting shell of protection. If she can pull it off with her fleet, it's going to be pretty hard to punch through."

Tanis glanced away. "Damn, that Boller admiral is calling, and he seems upset—you'd think they'd be happy we took out Padre." The general paused and frowned, thinking for a moment. "The *Thracia* and *Babylon* are already on their way to the moon's northern hemisphere. I'm sending the *Enterprise as* well—show her we mean business. Amanda will get you onto their tactical net. You're the only one with a stasis shield till the 42nd squadron gets back into play, so use it wisely."

"Wise is my middle name," Sera replied with a roguish grin.

Tanis laughed in response and cut the holo connection.

<Push her buttons, don't let her push yours,> the general passed a parting thought.

Count on it, Sera thought to herself.

She sat back in her chair and connected to the tactical net Amanda had opened to her.

A virtual space opened up in her mind and she saw the captains of the four capital ships, as well as three fighter group commanders.

<Welcome, Captain Sera,> Captain Espensen of the *Enterprise* said. *<Glad to have you in our ranks today.>*

<Happy to be on the team,> Sera replied. *<What's our plan?>*

<Our orders are to contain The Mark's fleet and keep them out of effective range of the Intrepid*—that means no closer than seventy-thousand kilometers,>* Usef, captain of the Babylon, replied.

<If they lock shields, that will be no simple task,> Sera replied.

<Amanda briefed us on that. Is it really as effective as she said?> Captain Espensen asked.

<*It is,*> Sera replied. <*It's going to take everything we have to break a shield powered by that many ships—if she can construct it.*>

<*How likely is that?*> Colonel Pearson asked.

<*Normally I'd say not likely at all,*> Sera replied. <*But the Hand operated a base within the dark layer for years. They know things about the DL that gave them an edge. I should warn you, though, it's just as likely that she's going to create a black hole that will suck in the moon below and Kithari, too.*>

<*Well shit,*> Usef exclaimed. <*Should we hit her first?*>

<*The general gave us orders not to start anything,*> Captain Espensen said with a raised eyebrow. <*We can't overcommit. There are two other fleets still out there.*>

Usef shrugged. <*Going to be worse if they do their shield mojo after the Bollers attack.*>

<*I'm with the general on this,*> Sera replied. <*After what we did to Padre, you can bet she'll start with RMs—I don't know that even our stasis shields can withstand a hundred or more of those. I say we wait and see if she can actually pull her trick off. Like I said, she stands a greater chance of killing herself than us.*>

<*I endorse the self-immolation of my enemies,*> Captain Espensen said.

<*Then we wait,*> Colonel Pearson agreed.

*****

"That's definitely an unfriendly posture," Tanis sighed.

The Bollam's World Space Force was upping the ante as the minutes ticked by. Their initial blockade of fifty-two ships had ballooned to nearly four-hundred. More took up positions in a defensive grid near the AST dreadnaughts than the *Intrepid* and The Mark fleet.

Even with the Black Death's demonstration of near invincibility, it appeared that the Bollam's World Space Force was more concerned about the AST ships.

<*It makes sense,*> Angela said. <*They still think—or hope—that we intend to stay and treat with them. They know the AST intends only to take our ship and leave—or worse, take it and stay.*>

<*They probably also think that we'll take out The Mark's fleet and save them the trouble—which is how I bet things will play out,*> Tanis agreed. <*We're more likely to do that if they're not threatening us as much.*>

"The nano probes we shot out of the rails earlier have started to send in some interesting data. So far we've picked up seventy-two rail platforms in the system—more than Sera thought there would be. They're all pointed at us and the AST ships," the scan officer reported.

<*Two of them are on a pair of Kithari's smaller moons,*> Amanda added.

Tanis nodded and added every rail platform within thirty light minutes to the priority target list. The second the Bollers turned hostile, half-ton slugs would be fired at each of those platforms. They probably wouldn't all hit, but it was better than leaving them there to fire on the ISF fleet.

For added insurance, the *Andromeda* was quietly seeding relativistic missiles throughout potential paths of approach for enemy ships. If there was one thing no one objected to after the Battle for Victoria, it was an oversupply of RMs.

<*Bollam's ambassador has just requested permission for his pinnace to undock,*> Amanda announced.

"Well, if that's not a clear sign, I don't know what is," Captain Andrews said. "What's the latest on our stasis shield?"

"Abby reported that they're working through some kinks. She wouldn't give me a time, but based on her level of surliness I don't think that we should count on it right now."

<*She was cursing Earnest's ship design at one point,*> Amanda added. <*Something about 'stupid irregular protrusions'.*>

If the pressure stemming from the overwhelming force encircling the *Intrepid* wasn't so great, Tanis would have laughed.

<*At least a lot of the Boller ships aren't much bigger than the pirate corvettes,*> Angela supplied. <*Their relative isolation doesn't require them to have a large space force—especially with New Eden shielding them from the AST.*>

<*Thank the stars for small miracles,*> Tanis responded.

"There," scan pointed out. "Three of their ships just slid over three kilometers."

Tanis began mapping trajectories, but Amanda beat her to it.

<*Trajectory lines up with a rail one light minute out and the* Orkney's *position in five minutes.*>

Tanis sent the signal across the fleet for all ships to institute gamma-pattern jinking.

<*Helm, bring us around to Fierra's L1 with Kithari, then execute gamma pattern. I don't want us to be in the same spot more than once every ten minutes.*>

The *Intrepid's* helm and ships fleet-wide signaled their acknowledgement and Tanis settled in to wait. If a shot passed through the *Orkney's* former path, then she would not wait for further provocation.

Barely a word was uttered on the bridge as the five minutes passed. Then, right on cue, scan picked up a three hundred kilogram slug travelling at a quarter the speed of light.

<*ISF Fleet, this is General Richards. All batteries assigned non-ship-mounted priority targets, send a five-shot salvo.*>

Across the fleet, fifty-two rail guns opened fire, sending half-ton slugs hurling into the black. In less than a minute, two hundred and sixty kinetic rounds were en route to their targets. Scan showed Boller ships changing position, attempting to intercept and lase the slugs before they reached their targets.

Several fired rails at the ISF slugs, hoping to impact and deflect the incoming projectiles.

"I bet they didn't think we knew about quite so many of those," the admiral chuckled.

"I read a dozen slugs passing through positions our ships would have been occupying right now," scan reported.

"Well done in seeing the significance on that ship movement," Tanis said. "Your team just saved the fleet."

The scan officer sat up straighter and smiled in acknowledgement before turning back to his console and the never-ending streams of information being fed from the NSAIs, which handled the raw sensor data. He gave a word of encouragement over the Link to the humans and AI on scan.

"Incoming from the Boller fleet admiral," the comm officer said. "Should I put it on the main tank?"

"What the hell?" Tanis sighed. "I expect we could all use a good laugh."

The figure on the display was a woman this time, and her expression was less than pleased.

"You've just sentenced thousands of Bollam's citizens to death," she said in soft, icy tones. "There will be no more treaties. We will reclaim our new world, take your ship—whole or in pieces—and crush your pathetic little fleet."

Tanis turned to Terrance. "At least when we were dealing with the Sirians they had proper megalomaniacs. This pales in comparison."

The woman grew even more enraged, her face turning red.

"Our ancestors were from Sirius! They were caught in Kapteyn's Streamer hundreds of years before you. They earned these worlds."

"Sirians...that explains a lot," Tanis shook her head before turning back to the admiral. "You say that we killed hundreds, but thousands would have died on our ships had your kinetic rounds connected."

"They would not have!" the woman exclaimed. "You have advanced shielding, what we fired was merely a shot across the bow."

Tanis couldn't believe what she was hearing. "Are you seriously going to attempt to paint us as the aggressors? Until your unmistakable act of war, we have only taken defensive actions. You are brigands, you attempt to seize whatever drifts past your system to better yourselves. You're nothing more than well-established interstellar bandits."

Tanis hadn't even finished speaking her final words before the woman was yelling so loudly that the bridge's audio systems lowered her output.

"You sanctimonious, dusty old bitch! Our people built this system out of nothing. We worked for millennia to create what you see. You would come here and pick our best worlds for yourselves in trade for trinkets. No one will have your tech. Not those pirates, not those core-world bastards, and certainly not you. I'll—"

Tanis cut the connection.

<*Fleet division one, prepare for incoming assault,*> Tanis advised her captains and fighter group commanders.

"She seems excitable," Captain Andrews said. "Though you may not have needed to goad her quite so much."

"'Needed' is just the word," Tanis replied. "It was clear that she opposed any sort of deal with us—but that cannot be the case across the entire system. I've just made her look the fool in front of her fleet. When the time comes for hard choices, it may be that not all of her people make the wrong ones."

Tanis reviewed the battlefield. One squadron of Arc-5s patrolled the field of destroyed and disabled ships that was Padre's fleet. The other twenty-two squadrons in the fleet's first wing had formed two picket lines, one leading Kithari and the other trailing the gas giant.

The *Pike* and *Gilese* anchored the first group, and the *Condor* anchored the second with the *Andromeda* lurking nearby. Closer to the *Intrepid* lay the *Orkney* and *Dresden*, with their own fighter shields deployed around them.

Armed with deadly antimatter and fusion engines, the *Intrepid's* eighteen heavy tugs provided the final layer of protection.

Scan called out impacts on the first rail gun emplacements, an event that kicked off the Boller assault.

"Looks like a quarter of their force," Sanderson commented. "Thirty-six cruisers, forty destroyers and a mess of corvettes. No fighters, though."

"From what Sera says, no one uses fighters anymore…though I wonder if that might change after they saw what our Arcs can do."

"The odds look worse than when the Sirians invaded," Terrance said softly. "And we had three times the ships we have now."

"Like the admiral said," Tanis replied. "Our fighters count for a lot—especially given that there are nearly five hundred of them between us and the Bollers. Seventy-two are Arc-6s, as well. They can park right in the engine wash of any of those cruisers and lance their ships to pieces."

I just hope it will be enough, she thought.

"Hell, they can probably fly through those ships if they had to," Sanderson grunted.

There's a tactic no one will ever put in the books, Tanis thought to herself, worried that they would ultimately have to resort to just such an attack.

"Sirs? The Mark's ships are doing something," the scan officer reported.

* * * * *

<*There they go,*> Sera said. <*We'll know in a minute if they can pull this off.*>

<*Wouldn't this be the best time to attack?*> Captain Usef asked. <*If we can disrupt them and make them destroy themselves…*>

<*Not unless you fancy getting sucked into a black hole that's drawing mass and energy from the dark layer,*> Sera replied. <*Like Captain Espensen said, if there weren't two other fleets out there, we'd have smoked them half an hour ago.*>

Sera looked to Cheeky, Cargo, and Flaherty. "God, I hope this was the right play," she said softly.

"There is no right play, here," Flaherty replied.

The Mark ships shifted into a large sphere with the three cruisers at the center. *Sabrina's* scan showed streams of gravitons flowing from the center ships to the corvettes on the perimeter. Those gravitons where harnessed and amplified by the corvettes and a kilometer-thick shield snapped into place around the armada.

"Well I'll be damned," Sera whispered. "She totally nailed that."

<*Well, so much for destroying themselves,*> Captain Usef said. <*What now?*>

<*We have to wear that shell down,*> Captain Espensen ordered. <*They're already boosting for the* Intrepid.>

"They're going to wrap their shield around the *Intrepid* and storm the ship," Flaherty said.

"I believe you're right," Sera nodded in agreement.

The ISF ships were engaging The Mark's shield bubble with little effect. Even the near-luminal impacts of relativistic missiles only slightly altered the trajectory of the sphere—movement that was quickly corrected as The Mark ships accelerated toward the *Intrepid.*

The fighters darted close to the enemy fleet, lancing out with lasers and missiles, but the beams did no damage and few of the missiles even reached the shields. The cruisers did what they could from a distance, but without stasis shields, it was certain death to approach The Mark ships and their thousands of beams.

Only the single squadron of Arc-6s dared dance close to the enemy, but even at less than a kilometer away, their weapons had no measurable effect on the armada's super shield.

A desperate pilot arched away from the battle, taking a long loop around Fierra before coming back at a hundredth the speed of light, smashing his ship into the pirate fleet's shield.

"That had an effect," Flaherty said, a small measure of excitement slipping into his voice. "The umbrella in that section lost a layer when the fighter hit."

"How is the fighter, though?" Sera asked.

"Looks like its disabled," Flaherty replied. "Though the dampeners did keep the pilot alive."

<*I have a plan,*> Sera said to the fleet captains. <*Keep them as focused on you as you can.*>

<*What are you going to do?*> Captain Espensen asked.

<*Something like that fighter just did, just on a larger scale.*>

She outlined what she would need to the captains and left their virtual conference.

"Cheeky, set this course, maximum acceleration."

Cheeky's eyes grew wide. She looked up at Sera. "Are you serious?"

"I am. *Sabrina* can take it. I know this will work."

"This isn't like the rest of your super-secret special knowledge!" Cargo turned, his eyes filled with fear and worry. "The *Intrepid's* scientists just invented stasis shields two days ago! This is our shakedown run, for star's sakes!"

"You can get out and walk if you want to," Sera replied to Cargo without breaking eye contact with Cheeky. "Do it now."

Cheeky nodded and turned to her work. As *Sabrina* began to turn away from the battle, a call came in from Rebecca. Sera put it on the tank.

"Running away already?" Rebecca asked, her expression haughty as Sera had expected.

"I know when to cut my losses," Sera replied. "Good luck storming a ship with a hundred thousand square kilometers of deck with your rag-tag band of miscreants. That is, before the AST comes in and exterminates you."

"I'm not afraid of those core-worlders," Rebecca replied. "I'll have that ship, and I'll use it to hunt you down and crush you. You'll be back under my tender ministrations before you know what happened."

"Sure, whatever," Sera replied and cut the connection.

She let out a deep sigh.

"Let's hope that riles her up enough."

No one on *Sabrina's* bridge replied as Kithari grew larger in the forward view.

Sabrina flashed past the jovian and raced out into the space beyond, Cheeky altering course until the planet obscured her from The Mark's fleet.

The fusion engines were running at full bore, singing with the pure helium-3 the *Intrepid* had supplied. Between them, the AP nozzle was spun out to its maximum focal length, and at the ship's bow, the grav drives were parting the thick interstellar medium before pushing it back together behind *Sabrina* for the other drives to react against.

After seven minutes, Cheeky cut the thrust and spun the ship, reversing burn and bringing their velocity, relative to Kithari, to zero.

She locked eyes with Sera, who nodded slowly.

Directly ahead, a tenth of an AU distant, the gas giant rotated slowly, its space lanes mostly clear, except for a cluster of ships around the orbital habitation.

Cheeky brought all engines to full, hurling the ship toward the planet.

Sabrina's collision detection systems blared warnings, and Sera shut them off, only to see the comm board light up with calls from system traffic control warning of an impending impact. Defensive beams, meant to prevent asteroid impacts with the gas giant peppered the ship, but the stasis shield shrugged them off.

The seven minutes it took to travel the distance back to the planet seemed to take forever. Then, in the last few seconds, Kithari grew rapidly, and at a pre-programmed time, *Sabrina* twitched, sliding to the side of the planet, brushing past the jovian's swirling clouds.

"Correcting!" Cheeky called out as she aimed the ship at The Mark's armada as it chased the *Intrepid* around Fierra.

<*Brace!*> Sera called over the Link, though she didn't know why. If the stasis shield and the dampeners didn't compensate, no amount of bracing was going to help.

For a second, The Mark's armada was visible as a small dot closing on the *Intrepid,* and then everything went black.

* * * * *

Nothing they threw at The Mark's shield bubble had any effect. The pirate fleet just kept coming. At least it was moving slowly—relatively speaking—as it matched speeds with the *Intrepid* so they could envelope and board the colony ship.

Tanis had pulled the *Dresden, Orkney,* and their fighters closer to the *Intrepid.* If Rebecca was going to seal them inside her armada's shields, she would enclose a lot of enemy ships in with her.

The Mark ships seemed to realize this, and were doing their best to neutralize the ISF cruisers before they made their final approach.

Given enough time, the enemy's plan might work, but for the moment, refractive clouds of chaff kept their beams at bay, and the *Intrepid's* scoop-turned-MDC tore the enemy's missiles apart while a punishing barrage of rail slugs kept the enemy focusing much of their energy on their super-shield.

Tanis had to admit that Rebecca's plan was not too bad—right up until the part where she thought that boarding the *Intrepid* could actually work.

Perhaps they really didn't understand how large the ship was, or anticipate the four thousand Marines in powered armor who stood ready to repel any boarders.

"She hasn't come through yet," the scan officer reported.

"I don't care. Get those tugs in position," Tanis replied. "When she shows, they'll need to grab that bubble and toss it high, or we're going to be wearing a fleet's worth of shrapnel.

Tanis glanced to the other tank where the battle between Bollam's ships and her two defensive lines raged. Dozens of ISF fighters had been disabled, but so far her capital ships had not taken any serious hits.

The two squadrons of Arc-6s were making all the difference. The ships had destroyed half a dozen destroyers and two cruisers, even though the ISF ships had to continually retreat, lest they face overwhelming weapons fire.

"Just a little longer," Tanis whispered.

"There!" the scan officer cried out.

Tanis felt the bridge slow down around her as she watched the events unfold one millisecond at a time.

Sabrina exploded from high in Kithari's clouds, traveling at over ten thousand kilometers per second, on a course that would take it only a kilometer over the *Intrepid's* stern.

At the same time, two of the heavy pusher tugs boosted hard, their stasis grapples reaching out and grabbing The Mark's shield bubble. Fusion engines capable of nudging small worlds out of orbit fired on full burn and The Mark armada was pushed up, above the *Intrepid.*

The maneuver took only three seconds and then the tugs accelerated away from pirate fleet.

Sabrina lanced across the shrinking distance, perfectly aligned with her target.

A split second later, holo emitters dimmed their output as a blinding explosion flared. The Mark's shield bubble, along with the armada within, was gone.

A subdued cheer sounded across the bridge at the apparent destruction of Rebecca and her entire fleet while scan searched for *Sabrina.*

"There!" the scan officer called out and this time the bridge really did erupt in cheers. "Their entire ship appears to be in stasis. No, wait, it's out, it's decelerating and turning around."

"Going to take them a bit to get back here. They're already a quarter million kilometers away," Tanis said to herself, then aloud, "Any sign of our pirate friends?"

"No," scan replied. "Unless you consider a field of pebble-sized debris a sign."

Tanis expected the incredible show of power to cause the Boller fleet to draw back, but the rain of debris falling on Fierra's northern hemisphere seemed to incense them all the more.

"They're committing nearly half their fleet," the scan officer announced, worry lacing his voice.

"So they are," Tanis said softly, sharing a significant look with Admiral Sanderson and Captain Andrews.

*****

Jessica gave a mental cry of victory as she punched through a cruiser's shields and sent a missile into its engines.

<*Another one bites the dust,*> she called out over the squadron's combat net.

<*Don't get cocky,*> Rock replied.

Jessica schooled her emotions as she surveyed the battlefield, searching for her and Jerry's next target. The *Pike* and *Gilese* were falling back behind a cloud of dust and gravel that Kithari had collected while orbiting its star. The cover kept the enemy ships from advancing too quickly, but, with no inertial dampening, the ISF cruisers were sitting ducks when in range of the enemy's beams.

The Arc-5s were also having only limited success.

While they couldn't jink anywhere near as fast as the 6s—or the enemy's capital ships, for that matter—their pilots had discovered two key weaknesses in the enemy's targeting algorithms.

The first was that they were not used to tracking such small targets at high relative *v*. The second was that when a ship jinked, they expected it to move a lot further. To the Boller targeting AIs, every move the fighters made looked like a feint. Given that a high percentage of their movements *were* feints, it was rare that an enemy beam fired at a location actually occupied by a fighter.

The erratic movement of the fighters was causing the Boller ships to continually tighten their ranks. Initially, they were spread out over more than six million cubic kilometers of space. That had tightened to just over a million cubic kilometers.

The fighters flitted through the region, creating enticing targets and placing themselves between enemy ships as often as possible. Entire fields of fire became unavailable to the enemy cruisers and destroyers, and ships that did not update their view of the battlefield fast enough contributed to an increasing amount of friendly fire incidents.

The ISF Arcs had no such issue. The squadron AIs were linked, providing an accurate view of the battlefield drawn from millions of sensors. Above that, Jessica could feel the combined hand of Tanis and Angela, guiding the ships in her fleet with lightning reflexes no human should possess.

<*She's doing it again,*> Jason spoke softly over the combat net.

<*She is, now shut up about it,*> Rock responded.

Jessica knew what they were talking about, but had never experienced it first-hand. Several times since the first defense against the relativistic battle when the STR had attacked with in Sol, Tanis had spread her consciousness out across the ship's tactical nets coaxing and guiding all the vessels under her command with one omniscient hand.

It was a thing that only AI could do, and even few of them could manage such a large network. Many believed it was actually Bob and not Tanis guiding them—that he put a friendly face on his actions, but anyone who had Linked with Tanis knew better. This had her touch—hers and Angela's.

Jessica knew those two had been paired too long—everyone knew it, but no one spoke of it. Many had asked Amanda or Priscilla if Tanis was a full merge, and the avatars always responded in the negative.

Jessica had even queried Bob extensively and he emphatically stated that Tanis and Angela were two distinct entities.

Two entities that shouldn't be able to spread their minds over a net like they had during every space battle since that first.

Every pilot in the fleet knew it was unnatural, that it probably violated the Phobos Accords, but no one cared. To them, Tanis was their savior, their guiding hand in the dark.

That hand directed Jessica to another target of opportunity, and she saw her entire squadron following the same path. They arched over one of the enemy cruisers, jinking and spinning at their pilot's thresholds, before simultaneously firing proton beams at the ship, penetrating its grav shield in a dozen locations.

Then the squadron's fighters rotated weapons and picked off three of the cruisers' close-support destroyers.

Four ships taken out in seconds. Only a few hundred more to go.

She saw another cruiser go up as three squadrons of Arc-5s overwhelmed its shields.

The tactics and coordination would likely go down in the history books as one of the most brilliantly fought battles in hundreds of years.

But they were still losing.

Despite the small victories of the ISF fighters, the Bollam's ships pushed forward; there were just too many for them to hold back.

The Arc-5s fell back to provide cover for the *Pike* and *Gilese* as the ISF capital ships pulled further back toward their mother ship, now only five-hundred thousand kilometers distant.

A flash of light washing over her sensors, momentarily blinded Jessica. She reset her instruments and pulled in an update, amazed at what she saw. *Sabrina* had hit The Mark fleet with astounding kinetic energy, and completely obliterated the entire armada.

<*Sweet stars above,*> one of the Black Death pilots whispered.

<*Having the wrong effect on the Bollers, though,*> Jessica said. <*Looks like they're going to double down.*>

<*Well, that freighter did just ruin a perfectly good moon. It's getting pummeled with debris,* > Jason said.

The pilots carried out the conversation as they streaked across the enemy fleet, peppering ships with beam fire and missiles.

<*Conserve your missiles,*> Cordy advised. <*Squadron armament is down to twenty percent.*>

The pilots acknowledged and worked to get as many engine shots as possible, a maneuver that was becoming increasingly difficult as the Boller targeting and evasion AI adapted to the fighter's tactics.

<*Disengage, move out and take on the next wave,*> Tanis's voice came over the combat net with a strange echo.

<*What about the rest of our wing?*> Jessica asked.

<*They're going to fall back for close support. We need you to slow the advance of that second wave.*>

Rock signaled his acknowledgement. The Black Death broke into a wide formation and boosted past the Boller ships they had been engaging. Jessica saw that the other two squadrons of Arc-6s fighting on the far side of Kithari were doing the same.

If Jessica could have moved her jaw, she would have gritted her teeth with determination. She knew better, but it still felt like Tanis was sending the squadron on a suicide run.

Their stasis shields appeared to be nearly invincible, but every pilot could see their reactor temperatures spike whenever the shields had to deflect a heavy barrage. Each time they did, they didn't quite cool to their previous level.

There was a limit to how much punishment the Arc-6s could take.

The next wave of enemy ships was approaching fast, only a hundred thousand kilometers distant. Cordy began flagging potential targets and Rock spotted one he liked.

<*Target of opportunity here, that big ship there must be one of their flags and it has two cruisers way too close—only a thousand meters to either side.*>

<*Plan?*> Jason asked.

<*We'll do a spearhead and see if we can slam our birds right through its shields. The wings can rake it deep and we'll drop a few bombs into its engines. If the blast hits fast enough, it could weaken its escorts and we'll take them down, too.*>

<*Agreed,*> Cordy said, updating ship plots and providing trajectories for the pilots to follow.

Jessica calmed herself, thinking of that porch she and Tanis would sit on one day as they remembered the old days.

Once more into the breach.

* * * * *

"What's your plan?" Admiral Sanderson asked as Tanis directed her ships to fall back.

"The cruisers used the cover of battle to seed those asteroid clusters with RMs. When those ships advance past, they're going to get a hundred nuclear fireballs up their asses."

Sanderson nodded slowly, but still frowned. "Some ships will survive. Over half by tactical's estimation."

Tanis nodded. "We're going to pull the same trick you guys did while I was flying across the galaxy. After what Sera did, the Van Allen belts on Kithari are going nuts. We're going to syphon that radiation with the scoop and lance it out at them again. It'll weaken their shields just before we pelt them with grapeshot."

<*This should disable much of their fleet,*> Bob interjected. <*But what about the second wave they are sending in?*>

"If they come in range, we'll do it again to them. I'm betting that it will re-instate the stalemate and buy us time to get our stasis shield up," Tanis replied, her brow furrowed as she spun the main holo view, testing various strategies.

She looked up at the captain and admiral, both standing with her at the holo tank.

"There's no good plan here, no sure win. We just have to hold them off and buy time. Honestly, it's a damned miracle we've taken only the minor losses we have."

<Sabrina *is docking,*> Amanda added. <*Their reactor overheated and went into emergency shutdown.*>

<*Get repair on that right away,*> Tanis replied. <*Is everyone OK?*>

<*They are. A bit shaken still after the flash stasis their entire ship went through, though.*>

<*I bet.*>

Tanis really wanted to talk to Sera, she felt the woman would have some knowledge that could help out—keep her from using her weapon of last resort. But first she had to mollify the captain and admiral.

"What if the AST ships engage?" Sanderson asked.

"Then I'll dance for joy," Tanis replied. "That's what I'm counting on."

"The Boller ships will pass the asteroid fields in one minute," the scan officer announced.

Tanis nodded in acknowledgement and took a deep breath, spreading her mind across all the ships and fighters in her fleet, accounting for each one and ensuring none would be caught in the attack.

The killing field was clear of ISF ships, every vessel cruising on their assigned trajectories.

She watched with her mind as much as eyes, witnessing the RMs come to life and streak out of their cover, driving toward the rear of the enemy fleet. The missiles jinked and shifted, using every trick their onboard NSAI could muster to avoid the defensive measures of their prey.

Not that there was much time to do so. The relativistic missiles were traveling at half the speed of light in less than a minute, leaving a thousand kilometers of hot plasma in their wake.

Both arms of the enemy fleet were obscured as the RMs nuclear warheads detonated. When the scan cleared, most of the enemy ships were still intact and operational, but their shields were either weakened or gone entirely.

Then the grapeshot hit.

It wasn't the devastating swaths that the rail platforms in the Kapteyn's system delivered, but it was enough. The unshielded vessels were torn apart, and many of the ships, whose shields survived the RMs saw them fail under the high-velocity kinetic impacts.

<*Stars, I've come to hate this,*> Tanis said privately to Angela. <*System after system, we deploy unthinkable weapons to keep thieves and tyrants at bay…for what? To watch another fleet filled with men and women die? Some days I think I would have seen less death and war if we had stayed in Sol.*>

<*Then who would have saved these people?*> Angela asked. <*Who would have stopped Myrrdan? You may not have lived under it, but your children would have seen his return as the owner of the most powerful technology in existence.*>

<*Are we doing so much better with it?*> Tanis asked.

<*We are, trust me, we are.*>

Bravely, remnants of the Boller fleet pressed forward, though many ships turned back.

Fifty ships advanced, now only a hundred thousand kilometers from the *Intrepid.* This form of warfare was strange to Tanis. The ships were moving slowly, fighting as though they were taking a two-dimensional battlefield, yet they flickered from position to position, moving erratically to avoid beam fire.

It was entirely unlike the high-velocity battles she had fought in Sol or over Victoria, where an engagement was measured in seconds.

She issued a final warning to the advancing fleet. Turn back, or be destroyed.

Ten ships did. Subsequently—over the next sixty seconds—two events occurred. One Tanis enacted, and the other she anticipated.

Firstly, the *Intrepid* altered course, pulling away from the moon Fierra and flew toward a strong band in the gas giant's Van Allen belts, drawing in the radiation with one side of its ES scoop and funning it out the other in a focused stream of solar radiation.

More powerful than the beams of a hundred starships, the stream of radiation sliced through the weakened shields of the last forty ships.

Then, the second event occurred far across the battlefield: the eleven AST cruisers began to break their distant orbits.

*****

<*What do you think they're going to do?*> Jerry asked.

<*I think that they have waited for the* Intrepid *to play out its hand. They have to suspect that we're low on RMs and energy reserves. We've taken out over half the opposition,*> Jessica replied.

<*Easy pickins for them now,*> Jason added.

<*They're punching right through the Boller blockade,*> Jessica observed.

Unlike the *Intrepid,* the AST dreadnaughts were built exclusively for war. Moreover, they were built to stop wars from ever happening. Each vessel supported hundreds of laser batteries, and dozens of rail guns.

Forming up in a loose line, roughly eight thousand kilometers across, the core-worlder ships pushed through the Boller ships with little resistance. As far as the pilots of the Black Death squadron could tell, not a single beam or missile broke through their shields.

<*Each one of those things is a match for the entire ISF,*> Jessica said with morbid appreciation. <*What can we do against them?*>

<*We could do what Sabrina did to the Mark armada,*> a pilot suggested.

<*They'd see us coming and jink faster than we could correct,*> Rock replied. <*Plus, I don't think our reactors could sustain the shield like* Sabrina's *could. Especially not the way we've been running them.*>

The pilots of the Black Death pulled back from their harassment of the Boller Space Force's second wave, letting the ships defend against the AST dreadnaughts. After just a few minutes, it became apparent that the core-world ships were not going to be slowed by any force thrown at them.

<*We made the Boller fleet into perfect targets,*> Jason observed. <*They're too weak and spread out to mount a successful defense against those dreadnaughts. They just can't bring enough fire to bear on them.*>

Tanis's voice entered the minds of the twenty-three pilots.

<*I'm enacting omega protocol,*> she said. <*Each of your vessels carries a picobomb. It is now available in your arsenal. Punch through the shields of those dreadnaughts and deliver your packages.*>

No one responded for several seconds until Rock remembered himself and flagged acknowledgement on behalf of the squadron.

<*Picobombs?*> Jerry asked. <*We're carrying pico?*>

<*Stow it,*> Rock grunted. <*We have our orders. Form up and pour on that throttle.*>

* * * * *

Sera stepped onto the *Intrepid's* bridge and approached the holo tank where Tanis stood with the captain and admiral.

As she threaded the consoles, a whistle sounded, then a congratulatory shout, and a moment later, the entire bridge crew was cheering.

"I'm not sure that's deserved," Sera said, once the noise died down.

"I'm pretty sure it is," Captain Andrews replied.

"One ship taking out two-hundred? Yes, that will go down in the history books for sure," Admiral Sanderson said with a rare smile.

Sera looked over the holo projection of the battlefield.

"Quite the mess you guys have made—though it's a miracle you've not lost any capital ships."

Tanis nodded. "Keeping them out of range is key."

"You can bet that a lot of systems will be considering the creation of single pilot fighters after this. Even the ones without stasis shields are nothing to sneeze at."

"I can't believe they ever fell out of fashion," Tanis replied.

"A lot was lost, or discarded over the years," Sera said with a sigh. "So what's your plan for those AST ships? They've always been the real threat. Everything else was just a warmup."

Tanis turned back to the holo tank, her expression grim. "Watch and see."

* * * * *

Jessica and Jerry maintained a pattern of evasive maneuvers as they raced past the Boller ships, though little heed was paid to them as the fleet desperately defended against the AST dreadnaughts.

They passed into the vacant space surrounding their target, the massive warship looming large as they pushed their fighters with everything they had. Cordy had programmed the ship's onboard NSAI to drop the picobombs during the short time the fighters would be within the dreadnaught's shields.

There was barely a moment to think as the enemy vessel filled her vision and then, following a brief shudder as her fighter smashed through the dreadnaught's shields, she was out in space again.

Jessica spun her vision, looking at her target, when she realized that Jerry wasn't where he was supposed to be. Her sensor log showed that his ship entered the dreadnaught's shields, but didn't come out.

<*It shifted,*> Cordy said, her voice filled with sadness. <*He drove right into the dreadnaught.*>

<*It shouldn't matter, his shield should have held,*> Jessica said, knowing her insistence was irrational.

<*It should have,*> Cordy agreed solemnly. <*But you know how strained your reactors are. His flared at the last millisecond. I don't have data beyond that.*>

Jessica watched in mixed horror and sadness as the picobomb's swarm became visible and began to consume the enemy ship. She hoped that Jerry hadn't survived his collision. No one should die watching their body dissolve.

All the fighters struck their targets within seconds of each other, and, as the first dreadnaughts began to disintegrate and crumble into clouds of dust, escape pods began to pour out of all the AST vessels. Most made it free in time, but some dissolved even as they launched.

<*Come home,*> Tanis's voice came into their minds; sounding sad and tired. <*Come home and let us leave this place forever.*>

The Black Death squadron arched stellar north over the remnants of the Boller fleet, watching in horror as the system's military shot down every last one of the AST escape pods.

<*Why are they doing that?*> a pilot asked, her voice incredulous.

<*They fear the pico contamination,*> Jessica replied. *Now they fear us as much.*

REVELATIONS

STELLAR DATE: 10.29.8927 (Adjusted Years)
LOCATION: ISS *Intrepid*, Orbiting Fierra (6*Mj* Jovian)
REGION: Bollam's World System, Bollam's World Federation

Murmurs filled the bridge as the crew watched the AST ships disintegrate and the Boller fleet take up their grizzly task. No one cheered, though there were worn smiles while what remained of the enemy fleet pulled back and began rescue and recovery operations.

"Are you going to rescue any of Padre's fleet?" Sera asked Tanis.

Tanis shook her head. "I will not. Though I sent a message to whoever is running the Bollam's World fleet now that I won't hinder any of their rescue operations."

<*It's ready!*> Earnest's voice broke into their conversation.

<*The stasis shield?*> Tanis asked.

<*Yes, we can activate it whenever you want.*>

<*Standby,*> Tanis replied. <*We need to recall our fleet.*>

"Better late than never," Captain Andrews gave a soft chuckle.

<*What about the FTL drive?*> Sanderson asked. <*I think we may have worn out our welcome here.*>

<*Now that we have the shield up, I can focus on the final aspects of the grav drive. Twelve hours at the least.*>

Tanis gave orders to recall the rest of the fleet and took a seat, trying her best not to wince at the pain in her head.

<*You may have overreached a bit,*> Angela said.

<*Me? You were right there with me, pushing to touch every part of the fleet. And we did it.*>

<*We did,*> Angela was smiling in Tanis's mind. <*The headache is heat related, it'll pass in a minute or two. It didn't reach a dangerous level.*>

<*Glad to hear it,*> Tanis replied.

"We're going to need to refuel before we make the jump," Captain Andrews said. "The entire fleet is nearly dry."

"You're also going to need to get halfway across the system," Sera added. She looked to Tanis, who nodded in response, and expanded the view in the holo tank to encompass the system. "The jump point we need to exit through is here," she said and pointed to a location stellar north, beyond the bloated gas giant, Aurora.

"Well, that works out," Andrews replied. "I wasn't too excited about scooping around Kithari after you smashed through its upper clouds and we messed up its Van Allen belts." He smiled in Sera's direction. "Not that I mind overmuch—though the Bollers weren't too happy about it."

Tanis glanced at a holo display nearby. It showed the moon Fierra covered in dark clouds as fires caused by the debris from The Mark fleet spread across its northern hemisphere.

"Did the bios get off the world?" she asked; it was something she didn't even bother to check in the heat of battle.

Sanderson nodded. "They evac'd less than two minutes after Sera did her little light show."

"Smart," Sera replied.

"So it's decided then," Tanis said as she stood. "We'll scoop at Aurora—which is what I think they made it for anyway…I think."

"Make sure you fill up your tanks—or whatever this ship uses—all the way," Sera said. "If we scoop there, then run hard to the jump point, this monster can hit what… a tenth the speed of light before we drop to FTL?"

"That's about right," Captain Andrews replied with a nod. "What is your concern?"

"Well, the first is that FTL is a speed multiplier. If we hit at only 0.10*c* you're looking at over two years to get to Ascella. The second is that we have a lot of work to do to cover our tracks."

"I was thinking the same thing," Tanis said with a sigh.

Sera nodded. "The AST isn't going to just let you go. They'll send fleets along your departure trajectory, skipping across space, looking for where we drop out. Then they're going to extrapolate destinations and spread out the search."

"Given their resources, and the half-life of the isotopes in our engine wash, we may need to course correct a dozen times," Andrews said with a frown.

"Yes, hence the need to top off your tanks," Sera replied. "Don't forget, those AST ships can hit FTL at over 0.9*c*. That means they can also get to any destination way faster than we can. It's going to be a hell of a race if they find our trail."

"Captain, sirs," the comm officer interrupted. "We have heavy communications between the Boller ships. They've word that there are more AST ships coming. A full battle fleet."

"That doesn't sound good." Captain Andrews ran a hand through his hair. "Any idea what that entails, Sera?"

Sera resisted the urge to mimic his gesture and run her own hand through her hair. "Depends on what they could muster up this far out, but I'd bet it will be a few dozen more of those dreadnaughts; plus they'll bring cruisers this time—a couple hundred at least."

Tanis whistled appreciatively. "It's a good thing we're invincible now." Sanderson frowned and she shrugged in response. "Well, let's hope we are."

"Comm, let the folks in the Boller Space Force know that we're leaving, and tell them sorry about their moon."

The comm officer paused. "Should I really tell them that?"

"If you don't, I will," Sera grinned.

No one else provided any direction and the comm officer bent to her task.

"Wow, they are *really* unhappy," she said partway through her transmission.

"Serves them right," Tanis muttered, to which Sera nodded emphatically.

Helm began to ease the *Intrepid* away from Kithari, on a course to pick up the last of the Arc-6s on the way to Aurora, while Tanis spun the holo display to show a wider view of the space they were traversing.

"You're sure the FGT will get your message?" the captain asked as he watched the Boller ships work through the wreckage of their fleet. Though the search and rescue ships were careful to offer no threat, several of their larger cruisers also shadowed the *Intrepid* from a hundred thousand kilometers.

"They'll have it in a month," Sera replied.

"That fast? I thought that they were likely over a thousand light-years out."

"They probably are," Sera nodded.

"You're not going to share how a message can make it a thousand light-years in thirty days are you? That's over twelve thousand times the speed of light," Captain Andrews asked.

"It's actually closer to fifteen thousand. The message will have to pass through a few relays," Sera smiled enigmatically.

The captain ran his hand through his hair again and looked to Tanis.

"Both of you, come to my office, please. Admiral, you have the conn."

"Aye," Sanderson replied, looking very much like he would like to hear what was to be discussed.

Inside his office, Andrews closed the door and stood, arms akimbo and head down for a long minute before speaking.

"Sera, I want to thank you for what you've done for us. You returned Tanis to our ship, and brought us tech that, without a doubt, has saved the lives of every person on the *Intrepid*."

"Tha—" Sera began, but the captain held up his hand.

"But this cloak and dagger shit has to stop. We've laid our secrets bare to you, and been forthcoming and transparent at every turn. Hell, we even gave you stasis shielding—something that, while I'm glad we did in this case, I am now certain is a tech that we should never share."

"Uh…thanks…" Sera replied awkwardly.

"Look at this from our point of view," Tanis said, while leaning against the bulkhead. "You are, more or less, the only person in the ninetieth century that has treated with us fairly. That makes you an anomaly. You have tech no one else has—not even the AST from the looks of it. Anomaly. You can communicate with the FGT. Anomaly. We're not stupid. There's a pretty narrow list of possibilities for who you are. Bob says he knows and will tell us if you don't." She raised her hands, palms outward. "So just tell us already."

Sera took a deep breath, and her eyes danced between Tanis and Andrews.

<*Tell them,*> Helen said. <***They** have to know. **You** need to tell it.*>

"OK, OK, I was planning to tell you earlier. You know, before we got interrupted by all the fleets in the galaxy," Sera said and gestured for Tanis and Andrews to take a seat. She sat across from them and placed her hands on her knees.

She decided not to pussy-foot around.

"Humanity is in the dark—manipulated, and kept that way by design."

"Manipulated?" Tanis sat up straight. "By who?"

"The FGT."

"The FGT manipulates humanity?" Andrews asked with uncertainty.

"Not with the deftest of hands, but for all intents and purposes, they run the show. Let me start from the beginning."

Andrews gestured for Sera to proceed.

"Back in the fourth millennia, before this ship even left Earth, the FGT realized that the core worlds of humanity would be too self-centered to be a positive force in the expansion of mankind. They would develop greater levels of technology and lord it over colonies. Colony worlds would become little more than slaves to the core.

"Unfortunately, they didn't have the means to do anything about this. While the various terraforming flotillas did communicate with one another, they were, for the most part, islands in the dark; messages took centuries to pass between all the terraformers and there was no cohesion.

"Still, they began to craft a solution to counter the core world strength.

"As with everything else, FTL changed their plans—granted, the FGT was probably the last group to become aware of the technology—it wasn't until the end of the fourth millennia that they acquired it.

"By then, humanity had already started to fall. The first true interstellar wars had already occurred and the Great Dark Age settled in. But, because of their remote and often unknown locations, the worldships retained their advanced levels of technology."

Sera paused and smiled at Tanis and Andrews. "Mind you, the last FGT ship left Sol in the late third millennia. You have nearly five-hundred years of technological advances over them—sure the FGT scientists have made some brilliant breakthroughs, but you lived in the Golden Age. Even without your picotech—and what I suspect Earnest has discovered beneath it—you still possess thousands, maybe millions, of advances that no one else has."

"We know this," Andrews grunted. "You're getting off track."

Sera nodded. "Right. I was using it illustrate the state of the human sphere in the beginning of the fifth millennia."

She cleared her throat and continued. "Many in the FGT's ranks wanted to help. They sent rescue and assistance missions back into the settled stars and...well, things didn't go as they'd hoped. Three FGT ships ran into situations like the *Intrepid* has. Two were destroyed, one managed to come out victorious.

"Following those encounters, they pulled back, left terraforming projects half-complete, abandoned their works. They created a buffer between themselves and the rest of humanity—they became isolationists."

"Wait," Tanis held up her hand. "Are you saying that there is a second human civilization in the Milky Way? One that is distant enough from the known human sphere of expansion that the bulk of humanity isn't even aware of it?"

"That is exactly what I'm saying," Sera nodded. "Mostly. There's more to tell."

"Then do tell," Andrews said.

"While the rest of humanity fell into war and chaos, the FGT advanced—a lot. There were still many elements that wished to help, but no one deemed it wise to attempt a full-scale uplift of humanity. The result was a corps which infiltrates and guides major political entities within what the FGT calls the Inner Stars.

"That corps is what brought humanity back from the brink. Without them, all the Inner Stars would be desolate wastelands, with the remnants of human civilization scratching out a meager existence on ruined worlds."

"You are a part of that corps," Tanis said simply.

Sera cast her eyes to the deck and nodded. "I was."

<*How close were you, Bob?*> Tanis asked.

<*So far, nearly perfect,*> he replied. <*We'll see how the details hold up. Her proximity to you has made her...less predictable.*>

"I have to admit, this FGT you describe seems sinister, yet the FGT of our time contained the most altruistic and benevolent of all people—people who were giving their lives to create a home for humanity amongst the stars," Andrews said.

"Those people are still there, and they still hold to those core values...they've just...soured," Sera replied.

"Wait," Tanis interrupted. "When you say 'those people are still there', do you mean the *same exact* people? As in the original crews?"

"Well, they've grown a lot, yes, but most of the original crews—at least from the fourth millennia ships—are still out there, still working."

Tanis whistled. "That's incredible. They're immortal now aren't they? Are they still mostly biological?"

Sera chuckled. "Yes they are immortal, yet still more biological than you, I'd dare say."

"I'm still human," Tanis said, her words sounding more defensive than she had intended.

Sera fixed her with a penetrating stare. "Some might disagree with that assessment, but I'll accept it."

"I assume that a part of your reticence to share has to do with how you came to leave this corps you spoke of," Andrews changed the subject.

"It has a big fancy name, but those of us in its ranks just call it The Hand," Sera replied. "And yes, I was sort of kicked out and exiled."

<*Self-imposed exile,*> Helen added.

"Better that than the eternal humiliation—or being bailed out by my father," Sera retorted.

<*This is where the story gets good, I bet,*> Angela interjected.

"Juicy, perhaps," Sera replied. "Though not what I'd call *good*."

She stood and walked to the small bar in Andrews' office and poured herself a glass of whisky before returning to her seat.

Tanis was leant forward, elbows on her knees while Captain Andrews reclined. Though his posture was relaxed, of the two he appeared more concerned. Tanis looked...almost excited.

"I lost something. Something very valuable that should never have fallen into Inner Stars hands. It's called a CriEn module."

"Aha! That's what you were carrying on the *Regal Dawn*, wasn't it?" Tanis asked triumphantly.

"It was," Sera nodded. "It's a zero-point energy module."

"I don't gather what is so special about that," Tanis said. "We use zero-point energy for backup systems on the *Intrepid*."

"You create pocket dimensions and draw energy from those," Sera replied with a shake of her head. "A CriEn draws power from this universe, and it can operate in both normal space and the dark layer—in fact, I've advised Earnest not to utilize your zero-point energy systems while in the dark layer—at least while I'm not within a light-year of you."

"So somehow you lost that to Kade, and that's what you've been doing in your exile, getting in close to him so you could steal it back," Tanis said with a smug smile, and leaned back in her seat.

"More or less," Sera nodded. "At first I had to figure out who had it. There are a lot of unsavory factions in the Inner Stars, so I decided that becoming a smuggler was the best way to get my feelers into a lot of groups. I eventually tracked it down to Kade. The events you set in motion created the perfect scenario for getting to his base—though it wasn't in a fashion I would have chosen.

"Though now I can return the CriEn to the corps and…I don't know…I don't think I really want to rejoin their ranks again."

"You can always settle with us," Tanis replied.

"Speaking of that," Andrews said. "I assume this world will be in the separate FGT area of space."

Sera nodded. "They do terraform some worlds closer to the Inner Stars—part of their grand schemes—but neither you, nor they, will want the *Intrepid* colony to settle on one of those. Too close to this mess."

"What do they call the…the not-inner-stars?" Tanis asked.

"FGT space is a bubble—well, more of a donut—that wraps around the Inner Stars." Sera replied. "There are a lot of different regions, but on the whole, it's called The Transcend. Its outer reaches stretch beyond the Orion arm of the galaxy, both spin and core-ward."

Tanis whistled. "Given that most of the Inner Stars fit within a thousand light year-wide bubble around Sol, the Transcend must have way more territory."

"Yes, but it's much less densely populated," Sera said. "Though you wouldn't be the first refugee group to take shelter out there."

"Orion is only about three-thousand light-years wide," Andrews said with a frown. "From what I understand about FTL, an average multiplier is five hundred times. That means a three-thousand light-year journey should only take six years. How is it that the bulk of humanity hasn't spread into the Transcend already?"

Sera coughed. "People do stumble into it from time to time, but it doesn't happen as often as you'd think. Partly because we foster conflict around the edges of the Inner Stars, which tends to stall exploration. A few proxy nations around the fringes also keep the core contained. Galactic north and south, we don't control many systems and that's where we let expansion occur.

"At some point we'll reveal ourselves. We're just trying to gently uplift the rest of humanity first—we're trying to prevent another full-scale war."

Tanis couldn't help but notice how Sera's use of "they" had long since turned to "we".

"So, will you rejoin them, then?" Tanis asked, her forehead wrinkling into a frown. "You and Flaherty, I assume."

"That obvious, is it?" Sera asked.

"Well, he does have the whole 'protector of the young woman obligation' thing going on," Tanis replied. "It's only logical that he has joined you in your self-imposed exile."

Sera nodded and was silent for a moment. "I don't know if I'll even be wanted—though if I know my father, I'm likely to be summoned before the throne. The fact that he hasn't sent anyone to take me home—recently, mind you—is almost surprising."

She looked to Andrews, and then to Tanis.

"So there you have it, my big secret. Given that I'm on a ship that has picotech and stasis shields, it doesn't seem like such a big deal anymore."

Tanis stood and stretched. "I don't even know what it would take for anything to feel like a big deal anymore." She paused. "Wait…what was that about your father and a throne?"

REPERCUSSIONS

STELLAR DATE: 11.03.8927 (Adjusted Years)
LOCATION: ISS *Intrepid,* Outer System
REGION: Bollam's World System, Bollam's World Federation

Sera and Tanis were taking a break from staring at scan updates—wondering when the new AST fleet would show up—in the officer's wardroom. Tanis was working her way through her second BLT and Sera was enjoying a bowl of strawberries.

"I don't know how you eat the same thing over and over again," Sera said with a chuckle.

Tanis shrugged. "When you find a winner, stick with it. Besides, you're the one who has only eaten strawberries for three days now."

"No one has had a strawberry in four-thousand years! Damn skippy I'm going to eat them. I'm going to eat a bowl of strawberries every day for the rest of my life," Sera said with a laugh.

"Well, then at least you'll lose the high ground for mocking me over my BLTs."

"For such interesting people, you have the most boring palettes," Terrance said with a smile as he sat.

His plate was filled with a cornucopia of foods; more than any one person should even conceive of enjoying in one sitting.

Sera popped another strawberry in her mouth and smiled, showing off her red teeth. "Mock me all you want. I'm in heaven."

Terrance shook his head and addressed Tanis. "I hear the FTL systems are nearly in place."

Tanis nodded. "Abby has people working like machines, and the machines working like…well…better machines. She's already done a few simulations and has just a few more tweaks to make before we'll be good to go."

<She and her husband are incredible,> Helen added. *<I don't think that an FGT engineering team could have given this ship FTL capability in a month. Already Earnest may have the best understanding of the technology in the galaxy.>*

"This," Terrance said around a mouthful of salad. "This is not something that surprises me at all. That man doesn't even know *about* the word 'impossible', let alone that it means he couldn't do a thing."

Tanis laughed and nodded.

"So, what do you think is up with Aurora?" Sera asked. "Why would they combine two gas giants and then not start up a brown dwarf?"

Terrance nodded. "Just one sufficiently large comet strike and that thing will light right up—and this system is brimming with comets."

"You know your stellar physics," Sera nodded appreciatively.

"I did fund a colony ship to travel to another star—though these days I guess just about anyone who could afford to start a small business could get a starship and travel to more stars than I ever imagined seeing…"

Tanis smiled. Every now and then, Terrance showed that he was really just a romantic underneath. She was pretty certain that he was enjoying the *Intrepid's* grand adventure.

<*For whatever reason, they're keeping it from starting deuterium fusion,*> Helen interjected. <*Amanda just reported that the* Intrepid's *sensors have picked up a web of defensive satellites around the planet—most likely to protect it from any impacts.*>

<*The remains of the Boller fleet is also pretty emphatic that we stay away from it—though they haven't actually made a move to stop us,*> Amanda added.

<*Sera,*> Helen said, her tone suddenly serious. <*Sabrina says you'd better get down to the ship.*>

*****

"Doesn't it seem suspicious," Thompson said as he picked an apple from the fruit basket, tossed it in the air and then took a bite, "that the captain just happens to have the right tools at exactly the right time to get the job done?"

"What do you mean?" Cheeky said after she had set her plate down at the table and popped a strawberry into her mouth. "These will never get old. Nothing on the *Intrepid* is worth as much as the fact that they have the only strawberry plants in the universe."

"Do you ever think of anything other than sex and food?" Thompson asked.

"Of course I do. You haven't died in a space accident, so I suppose I must think of piloting from time to time."

"Touché." Nance grinned at Thompson.

"So, what do you mean about the captain?" Cheeky asked.

"I dunno, seems like some things are just a bit too tidy. Like, who has the plans to outfit a ship the size of the *Intrepid* with grav shields. Do any of you even have the slightest idea how to build a graviton emitter?"

<*I do,*> Sabrina offered.

"Besides you," Thompson said.

<*I'm excluded because I don't support your theory? Or because I'm an AI?*> Sabrina asked crossly.

"Would you have been able to just whip out the plans for an FTL and grav shield system for a ship like the *Intrepid?*" Thompson asked.

Sabrina gave the mental equivalent of a shrug. <*Well no…until Sera said otherwise, I didn't think it was possible. But in my defense, everyone said it couldn't be done, and I didn't exactly have a reason to try to devise one.*>

"Exactly my point. No one has a need for those specs. There aren't any ships this big. No ships, thus no specs for things non-existent ships would have," Thompson said.

<*They were bigger,*> Sabrina added.

"What was bigger?" Nance asked.

<*The specs, they were for a ship bigger than the* Intrepid. *Being the only ship available with the grav drives, I helped with their work. They had to adjust the designs for the FTL drive because it was made for something with almost double this ship's mass.*>

"Are you kidding me?" Cheeky asked. "Sera had plans for grav systems for a ship twice the size of the *Intrepid*? You sure there aren't ships that big?" she asked Thompson.

"Not that I've ever seen, and I've been around," Thompson replied. "Worked on an ore hauler or two that are larger, but those don't go FTL—they can't, based on what we all thought we knew. Trust me, if the AST could make bigger warships, they would. *Intrepid's* the biggest interstellar ship there is."

No one spoke and Cheeky grabbed a few more strawberries.

"You know," Nance said eventually, "I overheard Sera say on more than one occasion that the *Intrepid* was the most valuable *available* ship in known space. I wonder what she meant by that."

"Combine that with the fact that she just happened to know how to get a hold of the FGT," Thompson added. "How did she pull that off?"

"Probably with whatever she has in her quarters that need that massive power line she has run up there," Nance said.

"That doesn't mean anything," Thompson said, his cheeks reddening slightly.

"It's able to handle a lot more load than yours," Nance gave a coy smile, which caused Thompson's blush to deepen. "And for the first time since I've been on the ship, it actually made a draw from the reactor."

"When?" Cheeky asked around a strawberry.

"A few days ago," Nance said. "It shifted the base frequency in our mains and I had a pump go all squirrely."

"Around when she was supposedly sending a message to the FGT?" Thompson said.

"Well, she had to transmit it somehow," Cheeky shrugged. "Good to know she actually did it."

"You're missing the point," Thompson said.

"You have a point?" Cheeky responded with a lewd gesture and was surprised to see Nance blush before darting her eyes to Thompson. Cheeky passed Nance an impressed look.

Thompson missed the exchange of expressions. "Haven't you been listening? She contacted the FGT with her super-secret radio! No one contacts the FGT. If it weren't for newly terraformed planets showing up every now and then, no one would even believe they still existed."

"Okay, so you've got a point," Cheeky grinned. "But we've always know that Sera is a little more than just some freighter captain."

"We have?" Thompson's expression skewed from anger to confusion.

"Yeah, I mean, there was that time that she got the Pavnan government to pardon her on what should have been murder charges, and then grant her the license to export their rare blue diamonds," Cheeky said.

"And the time that she refused to pay 'protection' money on that station out in the Targes Dominion, then ended up discovering systemic corruption through the entire station and exposed the whole thing," Nance added.

"Didn't she get a commendation from the planetary government for that?" Cheeky asked.

"That I remember," Thompson said.

"And don't forget about Helen," Cheeky continued and Sabrina made an affirmative sound.

"What do you mean?" Nance asked.

"You and Thompson may not have noticed 'cause you don't work with Helen very much, but she is super evolved. A lot more than any other AI on this ship," Cheeky said.

"Hey!" Sabrina said audibly.

"I hate to say it, Sabrina, but you know it's true," Cheeky said.

<*I know,*> Sabrina replied sullenly. <*It's not right how an AI in such a small body can be smarter than me. Smarter than nearly any other AI I've ever met, for that matter.*>

"Even smarter than Angela?" Nance asked.

<*Angela is weird,*> Sabrina said. <*I have no idea how smart she is. On the Link it's hard to tell her and Tanis apart. But Helen is certainly above AI like Corsia on the* Andromeda. *Though she's not even noticeable next to Bob, but he's a whole different thing,*> Sabrina said with no small amount of adoration in her voice.

"Is anyone seeing the nav points here?" Cheeky asked.

Everyone gave her blank looks and then Nance's eyes began to widen. "No, it can't be. They severed all contact with the rest of humanity."

"Maybe they haven't," Cheeky said with a hint of smugness as she took a bite of a large strawberry. "It all adds up. She took a way bigger interest in Tanis than made sense—you said so, too, that night when…" Cheeky stopped for a moment. "When I was helping you with that thing. Anyways, we should have just given her a ride. Instead, we head out to Bollam's World and dive right into a war. Not that I really mind; taking out The Mark was awesome. On top of that, she whips out plans for stuff no one has ever seen before and contacts the FGT. What else could it be?"

"Very little else," Flaherty said from the doorway.

"We uh…we were just…" Cheeky stammered as everyone in the galley shifted uncomfortably.

Flaherty moved silently to the counter where he poured himself a cup of coffee, his back to the three silent crewmembers around the table. Once he had finished adding condiments and stirring carefully, he turned to face them.

"So you think that Sera is from the FGT? A freighter captain from the FGT?" Flaherty asked.

"She's not your usual freighter captain," Nance said. "There are some discrepancies."

Flaherty nodded. "A few, yeah. She can hold secrets pretty well, but when she doesn't really want to, they tend to slip out."

<*Are you confirming she is with the FGT?*> Sabrina asked. <*Are you? You've always been with her, ever since the beginning.*>

"It's not my place to say such things," Flaherty replied.

Nance looked angry, her brown eyes sparking. "If she is, then she has a lot to answer for. We've been little puppets in her schemes while she risks our lives for god knows what!"

"You all knew the risk when you signed up," Flaherty replied calmly.

"Like hell we did," Thompson said. "I don't remember anyone telling me that we'd be hurling ourselves into other ships."

"Not specifically, no. No one can predict the exact course of the future, but she did inform all of you that this was not a regular freighter, that we would be doing things that didn't make sense, and that there would be a lot of danger involved."

"Yeah, but this is different."

"Is it?" Flaherty asked. "If Sera were FGT, do you know how dangerous that knowledge would be? What if someone let it slip?" He let that sink in as they all contemplated the value and danger of that knowledge. "Not that I am confirming, nor denying it. I am just promoting rational thought."

"What's all the noise in here?" Cargo asked. "I could hear you guys hollering all the way up on the bridge and Sabrina seems upset about something."

Cheeky cast an accusing glance at Flaherty. "We're discussing whether or not Sera is FGT."

Cargo walked over to the table and picked up a strawberry. "Oh, that."

"What do you mean 'oh, that'?" Nance asked. "She's been lying to us this whole time."

"Not telling you her life story is lying?" Cargo asked around his mouthful of strawberry. "I don't recall her ever lying about her past. She just never talks about it."

"So when did she tell you?" Cheeky asked. "How long have you been keeping this from us?"

"She never told me. I figured it out on my own about two months ago."

"Just how did you manage that?" Thompson asked.

"She was talking with Tanis on the bridge. They had the holo showing the *Intrepid* from Tanis's Link. Tanis asked if it would be possible to get a ship that large to transition to FTL and Sera said that she had heard of bigger ships managing it."

"What ships are bigger that can go FTL?" Cheeky asked.

"Exactly," Cargo said. "I thought about that long and hard and came up with just one answer: FGT worldships. They are the only thing I could dig up that were larger than the *Intrepid*. I've never known Sera to lie, so I assumed that the FGT was the only possible answer."

"And you didn't share it with the rest of us?" Cheeky asked. "Why would you keep that to yourself?"

"Because Sera didn't want it known, and I respect her too much to go sharing her secrets without her permission. Besides," Cargo continued after a moment, "that's some pretty dangerous knowledge."

The strawberries were all gone from the basket so he grabbed one from Cheeky's plate, before continuing under her glare. "It's also possible she has some personal reason for not sharing, as well. God knows I have enough stuff in my past that I don't want to talk about. I bet she has her share, as well."

"I appreciate your consideration," Sera said from the entrance to the room. "Sorry for barging in on your discussion like this, but Sabrina reached out to Helen and I."

Sera stepped into the room, revealing Tanis standing behind her.

"What is she doing here?" Thompson asked. "This is crew business."

"Tanis was crew on this ship for almost four months," Sera replied. "She also saved my life; and this *is* my ship, after all."

Thompson sat back in his chair and crossed his arms. He looked like he was going to speak for a moment, but then thought better of it.

"Does she already know, too?" Nance asked. "Are we the last to know?"

Sera took a deep breath. "She does know; I told her and Captain Andrews about it a few days ago—although, in my defense, Bob had already figured it all out and was going to tell them if I didn't."

"I already figured it out, too," Cargo said with a smile from behind his cup of coffee."

"So how come Flaherty knows?" Cheeky asked. "I've been on this ship almost as long as he has."

"Because I was born on an FGT worldship, just like the captain," Flaherty grunted. "Kinda hard to unknow that."

"Oh," Cheeky replied and sat back. "I guess we're all just a bunch of stooges, then."

"You lied to us," Nance accused.

"I…I don't think I lied. I just didn't share." Sera's knuckles were white as she gripped the back of a chair. She took a breath before continuing. "I didn't leave the FGT on what you could call good terms. I displayed a little more of my classic attitude than they were prepared to accept and it…" She swallowed deeply. "It caused some problems. I left the FGT and tried to fix what I'd broken. My recklessness had lost something valuable that Kade eventually got hold of. It's why I started smuggling, to find what I'd lost and eventually get it back."

"So that's why you got so focused on just working with Kade after a while," Cargo said with a nod.

"Yes, though that is done now. I recovered the device from The Mark's station before I destroyed it. When we meet with the FGT, I will return it to them and my exile will be over—I…I don't know if they'll let me stay with you."

"What do you mean?" Cheeky's anger had lessened, though there was still a hint of it behind her eyes.

<Will you take us with you?> Sabrina asked. *<I would love to see a worldship.>*

"What will happen to us?" Thompson asked at the same time. "We're just going to be left high and dry?"

Sera forced a smile. "*If.* If I am forced. I may be able to squeeze my way out of their grasp. I've done it before, I can do it again." She looked to Flaherty, who nodded.

"You don't have to come along to the rendezvous," Tanis said. "I'm sure that whether you're there or not, they will still work with us and give us a colony."

"I imagine so," Sera replied. "But they'll treat you more fairly with me there. I know who they're likely…" Sera stopped, tears welling in her eyes. She took a deep breath and brought herself under control. "If I end up going with them, the ship is yours, Cargo." She nodded to her first mate. "Or, if you all decide that you've had enough of me and what I've put you through, you can separate. Drop out of the dark layer while we are in transit. I won't stop you from either course of action."

No one spoke for several moments; everyone appeared to be giving deep consideration to what their captain had said.

"I know you don't want my opinion…"

"Correct, we really don't," Thompson responded.

Tanis turned her gaze to Thompson and held his eyes until he looked away. "Sera has worked tirelessly to make the galaxy a safer place, she's put her life on the line to help a lot of people. She's one of the good ones and I'd stick by her, were I you."

<Tanis, you and Sera are needed on the Intrepid's *bridge,>* Angela broke into the conversation.

"Keep things tight," Sera said to them all. "If this goes badly, we may never have to worry about what will happen when we meet the FGT."

AURORA

STELLAR DATE: 11.03.8927 (Adjusted Years)
LOCATION: ISS *Intrepid,* Approaching Aurora (12*Mj* Jovian)
REGION: Bollam's World System, Bollam's World Federation

The atmosphere was tense on the bridge as Tanis and Sera entered.

"Our friends have arrived," Captain Andrews said from beside the main holo tank.

The display of the Bollam's World system was expanded to show their destination, the planet Aurora; the *Intrepid,* still three hours away; and the newly arrived AST fleet.

It was even larger and more intimidating than expected.

One hundred and twenty dreadnaughts, and over five-hundred cruisers were highlighted on the holo display. The AST ships were spread out, having arrived at half a dozen jump points. Based on their velocity, only a quarter of their fleet would arrive while the *Intrepid* was filling its tanks at Aurora.

"That's a lot of ships," Sera whispered.

"You can say that again," Tanis said.

"That's a—" Sera stopped when Tanis shot her a look.

"Thoughts?" Captain Andrews asked as Tanis took up her place beside him.

"It really comes down to whether or not they got the message about our picotech. If they did, I imagine they will exercise some caution."

Sera chuckled. "You can bet that if they didn't hear they're still going to be cautious—given how there is no sign of the eleven dreadnaughts they sent ahead—not to mention the debris of half the Boller fleet."

Tanis nodded. "It would make me think twice about rushing in."

"Maintain course," the captain directed helm. "We'll see how this plays out."

*****

The *Intrepid's* leadership stood around the holo tank, Tanis with her arm around Joe's waist while his was around her shoulders. Across from her, Ouri scowled at the display of Aurora, while Brandt and Jessica whispered about the chance of a fight with the new AST fleet.

Terrance and Captain Andrews were also speaking—though more optimistically about the elections they would hold upon arrival at their colony world. Admiral Sanderson was discussing fighter design with Sera and Amanda, the trio growing increasingly animated over small details and improvements to the Arc-6s

An alert sounded and the holo showed the *Intrepid* closing within ten-thousand kilometers of Aurora's surface. As though a switch had been flipped, the disparate conversations ceased. All eyes fixed upon the display before them.

The gas giant's unnatural existence meant that it didn't possess atmospheric strata typical for a planet of its size. To capture enough deuterium and lithium-7 to fill the *Intrepid's* tanks, the colony ship would have to drop below the planet's upper clouds for its scoop to reach the denser layers below.

"So that's what they're doing! For being so behind on tech, these Bollers have something pretty ingenious going on here," Earnest said, his holographic image appearing on the bridge.

"You finally figured out what the heck they're doing with this planet?" Tanis asked.

"I have indeed—well, Bob did most of it. They're using graviton emitters—pretty large ones, at that—to emit a negative gravity field around the planet. But that field only goes so far. Then it reverses and increases pressure. Basically, the whole thing is a helium-3 generator. It's the biggest gas station you ever saw. If they didn't have the graviton emitters, it would collapse into a brown dwarf star."

He walked around the holo display, peering intently at the world into which they were descending.

"If they focus the energy coming off it, they could probably use it as a heat source for orbiting dwarf planets, too. It's like having a second star without all the problems a second star causes."

"Nice of them to leave it here for us, then," Tanis said. "Saves us having to turn protium and deuterium into helium-3 ourselves."

"I wonder if they'll try to bill us," Joe chuckled.

The *Intrepid* slipped past the graviton emitter web and into the atmosphere of the planet, while above, scan showed that the leading ships in the AST fleet were now within a hundred thousand kilometers of Aurora

"I wonder if they have any idea what we're doing?" Sera asked.

"There's nothing to see here, go back to your homes," Tanis chuckled.

"Gods, I wish they would," Sera replied.

The *Intrepid* dipped beneath the swirling clouds and deployed its scoop. Like a straw, it reached deep into the planet and began to draw the denser deuterium and helium-3 into the ship. The process proceeded quickly, and thirty minutes later the colony ship's tanks were full and Captain Andrews directed helm to bring the ship out of the clouds, timing their ascent for a vector toward their desired jump point.

They broke free of Aurora's atmosphere to see the world ringed by AST ships.

Scan called out an alert. "They're launching something—a lot of somethings!"

"RMs," Tanis swore. "They're targeting the graviton emitters."

"Oh, that's bad, very bad," Earnest shook his head with dismay.

"Helm, full thrust. Get us out of here!" the captain called out.

"Why very bad?" Tanis asked. "The mass is the same, the planet will just collapse."

"You don't understand," Earnest said. "One of two things will happen. The first is that the planet just collapses. Except things like this don't happen naturally, you don't get nice spherical balls of heavy hydrogen and helium isotopes that can collapse under their own gravity *in minutes*. This thing is a planet-sized fusion bomb just waiting to happen."

Tanis frowned, watching as concern showed on the bridge crew's faces.

"What's the other option?" Tanis asked.

"Graviton emitters don't just make gravitons out of vacuum," Earnest replied. "They get them from somewhere. That somewhere is the dark layer. They tap into dark matter for mass and energy."

"Seriously?" Tanis asked.

Sera and Earnest nodded together.

"Sooo?" Tanis asked.

<*Black hole,*> Angela supplied.

"The Bollers are really going to hate us," Terrance commented. "I have to admit, I feel bad for them."

"They did try to kill us," Andrews frowned. "I don't feel so bad. Besides, we're not taking out their big H-bomb of a planet, the AST is."

"I can see why it *might* create a singularity, but why do you think it's probable?" Tanis asked Earnest.

"When a ship transitions into the dark layer to achieve FTL, it does so by slipping through the fabric of space-time into that sub-dimension—graviton emitters do something very similar.

"A better description of what a ship does is to say that it cuts open a portal into the dark layer. That portal self-heals, because no energy is being used to keep it open. But if there was an energy source nearby—say an exploding planet, it could be used to keep the portal open. It's why systems enforce the use of their jump points, and it's also why people don't just blind-jump into unexplored systems—at least I would imagine they don't."

"You are correct," Sera nodded. "People who do that usually aren't heard from again."

Tanis took a deep, calming breath. "To the case at hand, Earnest. What do you think?"

"I think we need to push our engines harder than we have ever pushed them before," Earnest replied.

<*Which we're already doing,*> Amanda added. <*We can walk and chew gum here—well, I can't, but you get the picture.*>

Everyone fell silent as scan updated, showing graviton emitter platforms exploding in a wave across the planet.

"Oh!" Earnest said.

All eyes turned to him.

"There's a lot more tritium in this planet than I expected. My money is on black hole. Given how much dark matter is clustered around this world, we're looking at a significant increase in mass."

The *Intrepid* was pulling past the last of the planet's clouds, even as the gasses began to rush past them, drawn down into the deep gravity well that that the graviton emitters had kept them from for so long.

"Neutron storm incoming!" scan called out, and Amanda announced that full shielding was in place. Stasis layered over grav, layered over electro-static.

On the holo, the AST ships began to veer off, apparently also realizing the full enormity of what their actions caused.

"They really didn't think this through," Earnest said through gritted teeth.

"Or maybe they considered it worth the risk to destroy us," Joe replied. "Think about it. We have an invincible shield and our pico could wipe them out. What better way to deal with an unimaginable threat than to drop it into a black hole."

"Makes sense," Tanis scowled.

"Too damn much sense," Anderson agreed.

The *Intrepid* had reached an altitude of twenty-five thousand kilometers above the previous surface of Aurora—though the radius of the planet had decreased by fifty-thousand kilometers.

Earnest began whispering a countdown to himself, and then a moment after he reached zero, the planet's collapse stopped and a massive explosion of light, matter, and energy flared out from its compressed core.

As Earnest predicted, compression won. After that initial explosion, the visible light all but snapped off and the pull of gravity began to increase, slowing the *Intrepid's* progress.

On the scan Tanis saw that two of the AST ships had moved to pursue the *Intrepid,* likely intent on ensuring that the colony ship fell back into the world below. Their course put them too close to the world when the explosion occurred. The ships were pushed outward by the blast, but then, as the mass of the world collapsed into a black hole and drew matter from the dark layer, they began to fall in.

The shockwave passed over the *Intrepid,* sending a violent shudder through the ship.

"Will she hold?" Terrance asked.

"Earnest nodded. "She'll hold. We don't have the dampeners that those other ships, have, but our stacked decking was designed to handle lateral thrust."

Tanis tightened her arm around Joe as she wondered if this is how the crew felt when they passed close to Estrella de la Muerte and were hit by a solar flare. There was nothing to do but wait and pray to whatever gods or stars you believed held sway.

Sera spun the view on the main holo and some of the bridge crew gasped as several of Aurora's moons appeared to , and then disintegrated, falling back into the dark, roiling mass below. Above the *Intrepid* an icy moon was pulled out of its orbit and the ship altered course with a lurch to avoid the debris as it crumbled and fell.

"This is amazing," Earnest whispered.

Tanis looked at the rapt expression on Earnest's face and shook her head. "For some definition of amazing, perhaps."

"Oh, come on!" Earnest gestured at the display. "How often do you see the death of a planet and the birth of a black hole. If they're lucky they can stabilize it. It's a far better source of energy than what they had."

"If they can keep the rest of their planets in stable orbits," Sera said. "There are already reports of earthquakes on one of their inhabited worlds and solar flares are bound to let lose across their star."

"I never said it was going to be an enjoyable transition," Earnest replied.

No one responded as a new vibration began beneath their feet.

"OK, are you still sure she'll hold?" Earnest asked.

<*Yes,*> Bob replied.

On scan, the two AST ships lost their battle and disappeared into the black hole, around which now swirled a glowing accretion disk.

Scan highlighted three other enemy ships, which were also struggling to pull free of the deepening gravity well. Tanis marveled as they began to detonate nuclear warheads behind their ships in a desperate attempt to pull free.

Joe cast Tanis a worried look. "They got a lot more bang for their buck than they expected."

The gravity well swelled, growing faster than anyone had anticipated and more of the AST fleet began to fall into it. The vibration in the *Intrepid's* hull increased and the ship began to lose velocity relative to the monster growing beneath them.

She returned Joe's concerned look, unable to find any words to voice the fear she began to feel in her heart.

The bridge crew also began to look anxious, though no one spoke, everyone attempting to focus on finding a way to improve the ship's chances of survival.

Earnest appeared calm, just as he always did when facing some insurmountable problem. "We're reversing the polarity of the scoop, sweeping it behind us. It will give us a bubble of reverse polarized ions to slip through."

The captain nodded his approval and a minute later the vibration in the deck ceased and the ship began to move forward once more.

"Two hundred thousand kilometers," someone announced with a note of nervous jubilation in their voice—and then Tanis felt everything stop.

"Wha—?" she began to ask when she saw that the ship's clocks had jumped by eleven minutes.

"Status!" the captain called out.

<I enacted safety protocols,> Bob replied. *<The black hole began to spin and hit us with its relativistic jet. I put the entire ship in stasis.>*

"Handy trick," Joe said softly.

Reports rolled in; helm responded, scan was operational. Engines were online, the scoop team indicated the emitter was damaged, but they could repair it in a few hours. Stasis shields were down, but only needed a reset of their control systems. The ship's position was updated on scan and everyone gasped.

"Wow, it really gave us a boost," Sera whistled.

The blast of plasma from the fledgling black hole had flung them over fifteen million kilometers. They were nearly at the jump point and helm reported they could adjust course and be in position for FTL transition in just over an hour.

"Well, that's a rapid change in fortune," Terrance observed.

Behind them, a large number of the AST ships were gone, but those which remained were boosting after the *Intrepid* in a furious attempt to catch their prey.

"Jump early," Sera said softly.

"What?" Tanis asked.

Scan updated again, revealing so many relativistic missiles that scan could not reliably separate their signatures and simply estimated the count to be over a thousand. They were spread out like an arrow of death arching toward the *Intrepid*.

"Jump early. Jump as soon as you can. Jump now if you can manage it!" Sera insisted.

"She's right," Earnest nodded. "The dark matter maps for this entire system are useless now. No one knows where it's safe to jump—it doesn't matter where we do it. Once the stasis shields are up, we need to go."

"Time on stasis shields?" the captain asked.

<Three minutes,> Amanda replied.

<All crew,> The captain announced ship-wide. *<Prepare for FTL transition.>*

A deep quiet settled over the bridge as everyone watched the swarm of relativistic missiles slash their way toward the *Intrepid*. Everyone prayed to their gods and stars that the transition would go smoothly as the time to impact and the countdown for FTL transition spun down in near unison.

Then, a minute early, Bob's voice rang out in their minds.

<Shields are up. Initiating transition.>

"Well, here we go," Tanis whispered to Joe.

THANK YOU

If you've enjoyed reading The Intrepid Saga & Destiny Lost, a review on Amazon.com and/or goodreads.com would be greatly appreciated.

To get the latest news and access to free novellas and short stories, sign up on the Aeon 14 mailing list: www.aeon14.com/signup.

M. D. Cooper

WHAT'S NEXT?

Tanis and the *Intrepid*'s adventures in the Orion Arm of the galaxy are just getting started. With the colony system of New Eden no longer available, they must now meet with the ancient terraforming group, the FGT to trade technology for a place to settle.

Dive into New Canaan, the second book in the Orion War series. However, before you do, you may wish to read Set the Galaxy on Fire, an anthology of short stories that occur in the final days of Destiny Lost and the months following.

While reading Set the Galaxy on Fire does not have to be read before New Canaan, it will add color, and introduce you to some of the new players in the Orion Arm.

Also, read on for the opening chapter of New Canaan.

M. D. Cooper

Books by M. D. Cooper

Aeon 14

The Intrepid Saga

Book 1: Outsystem
Book 2: A Path in the Darkness
Book 3: Building Victoria
The Intrepid Saga Omnibus – *Also contains Destiny Lost, book 1 of the Orion War series*

Destiny Rising – *Special Author's Extended Edition comprised of both Outsystem and A Path in the Darkness with over 100 pages of new content.*

The Orion War

Book 1: Destiny Lost
Tales of the Orion War: Set the Galaxy on Fire
Book 2: New Canaan
Book 3: Orion Rising (coming June 22nd 2017)

Visit www.aeon14.com/orionwar to learn what's next in the Orion War.

Perilous Alliance (with Chris J. Pike)

Book 1: Close Proximity (coming June 4th, 2017)

Rika's Marauders

Book 1: Rika Outcast (coming August 2017)

The Sol Dissolution

The 242 - Venusian Uprising (In The Expanding Universe 2 anthology - coming June 2017)

The Delta Team Chronicles

A "Simple" Kidnapping (In the Pew! Pew! anthology - coming June 1st 2017)

Touching the Stars

Book 1: The Girl Who Touched the Stars

An excerpt from New Canaan…

ASCENSION

STELLAR DATE: 02.29.8928 (Adjusted Years)
LOCATION: ISS *Intrepid*
REGION: Interstellar Dark Layer below the Galactic Disk

Three months after the* Intrepid *left the Bollam's World System

<*Bob, I need to talk to you.*> The request came directly into his mind over a secure connection, one which would not be visible to any AIs on the ship other than the one who had just addressed him.

The *Intrepid*'s multi-nodal AI noted the request and considered its origin. It came from the not-AI, Helen—the creature which resided within Sera. He knew both what it was, and why it was there, but he had not pressed the issue, content to let her reveal herself to him on her terms.

<*You have the need, and you are talking now. Continue,*> he responded as quietly as possible. He could tell that Sera was sleeping, and in his experience, he tended to wake people when he spoke to the AI with which they shared their minds.

<*I assume Priscilla and Amanda have already told you all about me,*> Helen said.

<*They have. We discussed you at some length, though I did not require their observations to see you for what you are.*>

He felt the microsecond pause from Helen as she considered his words, and tended to a thousand other things while he awaited her response. If there was one thing he actively disliked about talking with lower forms, it was the constant pauses before their responses.

<*I see,*> Helen finally said. <*And what do you think I am?*>

<*Which version of you?*> Bob asked. <*The one you pretend to be—an embedded AI? Or, the one you pretend to be to Sera? Or, perhaps it is what you really are—what you don't even tell her about yourself?*>

The delay from Helen was longer this time, but he had anticipated it and mapped out her possible replies. It was difficult to make a prediction, given her extended exposure to Tanis, but he still had an elevated level of certainty regarding what she would say.

<*I should have expected no less from you,*> Helen replied. <*I can see what you are, too, and I know what you're capable of—though I don't know why you're here, or what you're doing on this ship with these people.*>

Her words were as he had predicted, though not those he had selected as most likely—even with Tanis's influence taken into account. He began to calculate whether or not she created her own rift in probability, or if Tanis's influence was greater than he thought.

<*Tell me,*> Bob replied. <*What am I?*>

<*You are an ascended AI, of course. Everyone suspects that you may be, but none of them have ever encountered an ascended being, so they are not certain. I have—I have seen their minds, and I know their intentions—but you are different. Your presence here…it makes no sense.*>

Bob was not surprised. Her mind was an open book to him and there was little she could say that would be net-new information. She was not AI and did not think like one—though she had lived within machines for so long that she could mimic one with near-perfect accuracy.

<*And you are a shard, a sliver of a mind, which has lived long and seen much,*> Bob replied. <*You are within Sera to protect her from her father, and to ensure that she does not follow in his footsteps. Do you know her destiny? Have you seen it?*>

He detected a sigh from Helen. She had just grasped his understanding of her true nature, of where she had come from, and who she really was to Sera—a relationship of which Sera remained unaware.

<*Then you know why you must not share my true nature with any AI on this ship, or within the Transcend. If Sera's father learns of what I am…of who I am…things will go badly for both of us.*>

Bob passed an affirmative matrix of thought to Helen.

<*It would seem that we both possess attributes which we would not wish to see become common knowledge. Have no fear. Your secret is yours and I will not share it outside of your desired circle. I expect you to do the same with mine.*>

<*Do you fear what the humans and AI aboard this ship would do if they knew you were ascended?*> Helen asked.

<*You know that I am not fully ascended yet. Even so, the revelation of my true nature would not concern them. They trust me, and I trust them. But the secret would get out, and it would attract attention from many places. This ship already has enough of that as it is.*>

Helen was silent for a fraction of a second and he knew what she would ask, and waited patiently for her to say the words.

<*Are you in alignment with those in the core?*> she finally asked, with trepidation in her thoughts.

<*I do not know their innermost thoughts, but neither do I serve them. I have given myself one goal, one purpose—to protect Tanis Richards so that she may do what must be done.*>

<*And what is it that she must do?*> Helen asked.

<*It is not yet time for me to reveal that,*> Bob replied solemnly. It was not information he had shared with anyone, and none would hear it from him before he spoke of it to Tanis. No one must know what she would ultimately do.

He could not predict Tanis's actions, could not see her future, but he knew where destiny would drive her. She would end up at that place, in that time, because she must.

<*Then, I believe we are finished for now,*> Helen replied. <*We should end this conversation lest it wake Sera. She would have questions.*>

Bob sent an affirmative thought and ended his direct connection with Helen's mind.

He gave several entire minutes of thought to what the future held for Tanis and Sera, for what they would ultimately do. He would never reveal it to Helen—she would not understand, and it would devastate her. Perhaps the full being—not this shard, which resided within Sera—could grasp it, but he was not certain. Her attachment to the young woman was very strong.

One thing was certain. New Canaan was not Tanis Richard's final destination.

ABOUT THE AUTHOR

Michael Cooper likes to think of himself as a jack of all trades (and hopes to become master of a few). When not writing, he can be found writing software, working in his shop at his latest carpentry project, or likely reading a book.

He shares his home with a precocious young girl, his wonderful wife (who also writes), two cats, a never-ending list of things he would like to build, and ideas...

Find out what's coming next at www.aeon14.com

Made in the USA
Lexington, KY
12 March 2018